THE INNISFAIL CYCLE

L.M. RIVIERE

N
W
E
S
March
Ice
Brés
THE
SEA
OF
AENGHUS
DONN BAY
DOWN
IOLÁIR BAY
Croghan
SLIGO A GREENSWARD
Brí L
Aes Sidhé
Roswea
To
Ten Bells
Bethany
Killarney
Éire
SEA
OF
MANANNÁN
Marching
Ice
Kernow
Ives

The Land Of
Innisfail
Marching Ice
Scotia
LOUGH LUMBER
THE NORD SEA
UMBER
Alba
The Wastes
BRITON
WERTHYN
THE SEA OF REEDS
The Briton Fields
Derby
Marching Ice
TAGN SEA
Created by Talesfromfarcliff

The Sons of Mil

The Southernmost Star

The Sons

of Mil

The Innisfail Cycle

Book One

The Hunt

Ben was bored out of his mind. His arse was fast asleep, and he hadn't felt his toes for eons. At this point, he'd be better served drinking himself into a stupor rather than idle here in solitary sobriety. Never mind the blasted weather, which grew increasingly bitter as the sun sank in the west. Twilight crept into the valley. Long shadows stretched between the trees like poured ink. To the east, swift clouds raced through an amethyst sky, awash with rivers of white stars. As evening descended, owls hooted from their hollows, and foxes and voles gave chase in the underbrush.

Prosaic as the scene might have been, comfortable it was not. Ben shrugged his cloak tight, annoyed by its insufficient weight. He would much prefer to watch the seasons change from a nice cozy window, with his hands wrapped firmly around a piping hot tankard of spiced cider. Spending the night high in a tree, in the middle of a damp forest, was *not* his idea of a fine time. Dor Samna batted her lashes at winter, and Ben missed the Ban months more than ever.

What, in the nine hells, was *keeping* them?

Absent the sun, the wind clawing over the Boyne cut deep. Ben blew into his palms. This was absurd. If the temperature dropped much further, he'd be obliged to work on the flask hidden within his vest or risk his extremities to the elements. That would prove a bit counterproductive, considering the reason he was out here in the first place. Alas, a watchman had a duty to remain sober. His job was to guard the Greenmakers' reentry into Eire, and it would be foolish to get whiffing drunk to keep warm. Ben was an accomplished archer, but everyone knew drink and tedium made for poor aim.

Nevertheless, knowing better would not dissuade him for much longer. When his bollocks started to shrink into his torso, wisdom be damned. Perhaps a nip or two now wouldn't hurt anything? He took one, then another, and by the fourth or fifth, decided a lousy shot was better than none.

It was unlike Robin to dally. Ben's mood soured for the interminable waiting. Any Greenmaker worth his salt knew better than to linger over this border. Robin Gramble certainly understood his business as The Quarter's Headman. Hadn't he emphasized the importance of haste this very morning? Ben would be delighted to know what was keeping him. The wilds of Aes Sidhe were not a pleasant place for mortal men to roam, regardless of circumstance. This delay could only mean something was amiss.

Pocketing his flask with a sigh, he scanned the border for the thousandth time. A thick, aberrant mist crowded the river on the opposite shore, impervious to the bracing wind. Ben strained to peer further than the first line of smoking trees that curled toward the embankment. His head throbbed from having been on the lookout all damned day. The mists of Aes Sidhe marked the border between the realm of men and the land of the Immortals to the north. Even from his elevated vantage, visibility was minimal. This effect was by design. The Sidhe did not invite prying eyes into their domain. That pervasive cloud concealed much more than riches or game. Dark things. Horrible things. Most men who dared to trespass never returned. The Greenmakers of Rosweal were likely the only men in the whole of Eire who fully grasped the significance of that warning. Something was wrong. It must be.

They should have been back by now.

Brooding over a host of potential perils that might have delayed his comrades, Ben finally caught a hint of silver and ivory in the distance. Winking in and out of the fog, a pale figure dashed alongside the riverbank, something metallic glinting from a clenched fist. Ben inched forward on his bough, hugging the heavy branch with his knees while he unslung his bow. That was no Greenmaker. Ben's crew did not own such flashy gear, nor were any of them half so tall. That shock of white was a Dannan cuirass. A hunter from Bri Leith, no doubt.

Ben muttered a curse. Struggling to nock with half-frozen fingers, he searched for any sign that his friends were on their way and in one piece. He saw nothing at first save mist, the impression of dark trees, and great pools of swirling gloom. Then, he heard shouting and the undeniable ring of steel against steel. Shimmying further out on his limb, Ben spotted several charcoal silhouettes running through the haze, dragging men and dead animals between them. Robin's booming baritone was unmistakable.

"Get over, lads! Go, go!"

The Dannans blew their horns. The chase was on.

Someone must have done something stupid. That was the only explanation that would warrant such a swift martial response. Robin was usually a stalwart professional on a raid. He demanded nothing less from his men. Whatever had happened surely hadn't been his call. Ben spied his friend a hundred or so yards to the northwest. Robin ran pretty fast for a fellow of middling age. Gerrod and Paul splashed through the mud behind him, hauling a six-point stag with a snow-white pelt over their shoulders. They were covered head to toe in the beast's blood.

Ben's ears grew hot at the sight.

Ah… he thought.

Bloody fools!

What idiocy prompted this madness?

Sylvan stags were sacred to the Sidhe. Venerated as vessels of the god Herne, the famed beast was the sigil of the High King's Clan. No *wonder* the Greenmakers had a score of Dannan warriors in pursuit. Robin damned well knew better! What had possessed him to allow such an obvious, careless misstep on his watch? Growing angrier by the second, Ben drew his longbow crosswise. No damned good was going to come of this; he was certain. Seamus' vivid red head emerged from the curtain of mist after Robin, two sable fox tails swinging from his wide belt. In his haste, Seamus slipped into the detritus littering the forest floor. An ivory-fletched arrow missed his ear by a breath. Another zipped past his thigh, making him stumble again.

"For feck's sake!" he cried. "Robin! Keep goin'! They're everywhere!"

While Seamus scrambled to his knees, a Dannan hunter leapt from the woods on his right, twin larks poised to slice through his middle. Seamus raised a useless hand to ward off the attack. He needn't have bothered. The Sidhe scout was thrown backward by one of Ben's arrows. His blond head cracked off the trunk of a nearby birch. The arrow's plain brown fletching protruded from a painful but non-fatal wound in the crook of his shoulder. Seamus wasted no time skittering away on all fours. Slithering down the embankment on his belly, he was halfway across by the time Robin, Gerrod, and Paul plodded into the current. Ben fumed, watching them heave their heavy prize through the water by its rack. Robin shoved them off and stood sentry in the shallows, his crossbow poised to defend their position.

"Nat! Marty! Get yer arses moving!"

Another hunter emerged from the canopy on Robin's right, raising his larks high. Robin sent a quarrel through his gut, felling him on the spot. Gore spewed from the back of the Sidhe's lovely white cuirass. Robin reloaded and shot the next Dannan through the throat. Ben heard a distinct click. He was out of ammunition.

"Ben, Siora, damn ye! Tell me yer out there!"

Ben whistled back in mimic of a common marsh swallow. Signal received with a curt nod; Robin drew his daggers.

"Marty," he roared with new urgency as three more Sidhe hunters darted into his line of sight. "Nat! Where are ye?"

Dropping to a lower limb, Ben nocked and fired twice more. The first target took an arrow to the thigh; the second through the ribs. Neither shot was fatal. Ben made sure. He would not kill a Dannan warrior unless he had no choice. A third hunter tore out of the trees and threw himself at Robin with a snarl. They splashed into the river in a rolling tangle of limbs and steel. Ben didn't have a clear shot.

Robin would have to sort himself.

Instead, Ben focused on a burst of activity in the distance. Red-faced, Marty dragged Nat's flaccid frame by one shoulder. An ivory shaft bloomed from the center of Nat's chest. A thick line of blood dribbled down his dirty green jerkin.

"Ben!" squealed Marty. "They're comin'!"

More Dannan hunters tracked them to the riverbank. Two were mounted on dappled grey horses. Ben was too far removed to nail either one from his vantage.

"Robin!" his voice carried over the river. He slung his bow over his shoulder to descend. "They're not going to make it!"

Aware that he'd given away his position, Ben clambered to the ground like his feet were on fire. The Sidhe were the finest marksmen in Innisfail. He would pay for one wrong move with his life. Sure enough, an arrow sailed into the trunk where his head had been a moment before. Another tore a hunk out of his cheek. Dodging a third missile, his boots bore into the mud below his rowan. Ben returned fire. His arrow struck something solid, but he was already running from another volley by the time he was ready to draw again.

Robin dumped his attacker's corpse face-down in the Little Boyne. The slain Dannan's pale hair churned in the frothing red current. Clutching at a fresh wound in his side and with one dagger remaining, Robin bellowed, "Where are they?"

An arrow ripped through one of Ben's sleeves, very near his ribcage. "Damn it! I'm a little busy here! On your right!"

Robin waded downriver toward his two injured men. Marty attempted to run to him but wobbled forward onto his knees. Robin screamed a warning too late. A razor-thin lark slammed into Marty's back, shoving bits of his heart through the front of his tunic. The Dannan withdrew his blade with a wary green eye on Robin. Marty slumped face-first into the river. There was nothing to be done for him now. Nat, on the other hand, bobbed just shy of Robin's reaching fingers. Waist deep and ducking arrows, Robin snatched at the unconscious lad's cowl, desperate to drag him over. If they could make it across, they might be safe. The Sidhe never trekked into Eire unless expressly ordered to do so. Though, there would hardly be a need if the last two poachers died in an attempted escape. Robin would never make it out alive if Ben didn't start shooting with real intent. He had no desire to kill anyone for this day's idiocy, but he wouldn't let Robin die in front of him either.

At the waterline, Ben dropped to a knee in the sand. Gerrod and Paul heaved the stag's carcass up the beach toward the ridge. Ben had no doubt that hauling it through the river was no small task. The stag must have weighed at least four hundred pounds and was easily six feet or more in length. With a resolute sneer, he refused to acknowledge either poacher while they ran for cover.

Ignorant bastards, Ben mused. If their stupidity got Robin killed, Ben would personally string both of them up by their innards. Meanwhile, Robin side-stroked for shore, dragging Nat by his hair. Ben drew and fired twice, sending more Sidhe hunters to the ground. He had a third arrow nocked and waiting for a decent shot when a Dannan Captain strolled out of the mist, his superior ash and yew longbow trained on Ben. He was taller than the others, his status evident by the six gold chains dangling from his left ear. He wore an immaculate sealskin cloak trimmed in arctic ermine, with a massive silver torc fixed at the collar. His long flaxen hair was unbound, save for a pair of braids at his temples. The leaping stag on his cuirass was crowned by three gold stars. Here was a member of the Ard Ri's personal guard. Ben dropped his elbow a fraction. *Fionn?* The Dannan Captain mirrored Ben's motion. His mint-green eyes narrowed in mutual recognition. Ben noted the disbelieving derision on Fionn's face, the surprise, and silent condemnation. Ben stared, riveted by the cruel irony of the situation.

Of course, it must be Fionn. Ben had shite luck.

"What in the hells are ye doin'?" cried Robin, struggling for the shallows on the Eirean side of the river. The Dannans lined the far shore, their numbers replenished, bows drawn. Ben knew they wouldn't fire for the same reason he could not. Fionn's handsome upper lip curled in disgust. With a sigh, Ben released his bowstring. Robin was nearly over. Gerrod waded in to help him out. Nat trailed in the river behind them, his skin as grey as a winter sky. Ben didn't see them. He stood motionless, staring across the river. The echoes of a former life traced clammy fingers up and down his spine.

"Feckin' snap out of it, will ye?" Robin followed Ben's gaze to the knot of Sidhe hunters gathered at the river's edge. The look between Ben and the Sidhe Captain was not lost on him. "Damn ye, Maeden! Shoot him!"

Fionn shook himself at Robin's voice. Nostrils flaring, he raised his bow.

Ben threw out a hand as if that would stop him. "No! Don't!"

An elegant, ashen shaft hammered through Nat's prone body, straight through the heart. With little time to respond, Robin and Gerrod were obliged to dive underwater to avoid the following volley. When they came up for air, Nat had turned over in the current.

His body bowed under the weight of a dozen or more arrows.

Unable to prevent the lad from washing downstream, Robin snarled abuse at Ben, the Sidhe, and the world at large. Gerrod managed to pull him out of the river, despite the older man's girth and flailing limbs. Robin's screams shook the leaves overhead with heart-rending vehemence. Unperturbed by the drama unfolding before him, Fionn waved at Ben— a flippant gesture dripping with contempt. Shaking his head on a wry laugh, Fionn handed his bow to an aide and climbed into his saddle. He didn't spare Ben a second glance.

Wordless as the wind, the Dannans melted into the trees after him, carrying their dead in silent procession. Ben didn't call out to Fionn as he faded from view. How could he? Slinging his bow back over his shoulder, he tucked his shaking hands into his pockets, where they wouldn't be seen.

Out of nowhere, Robin's fist crashed into his right cheekbone. Ben staggered a bit. Paul and Seamus clawed at Robin's arms to halt a second attack. The veins in his scarred forehead bulged. He spat, red-faced, "What in the hells was that about? Why didn't ye do somethin'?"

Swatting Gerrod's helping hand away, Ben got to his feet under his own steam. "Whose clever plan was it to shoot the stag, Robin? Which of you was arrogant enough to kill one of the High King's deer?"

Robin fought so hard to free himself from Paul's grip that his lips purpled. Saliva trickled over his bleeding chin. "I'll kill ye for this. I'll do it. I swear to Siora. How dare ye attempt to scold anyone? Nat and Marty died today!"

"Nat was dead long before Marty dragged him into the river, Robin."

"It's true, boss," cut in Gerrod, in Ben's defense. "I saw it. One o'them took him right in front o'me. Marty, rest him, shot the stag. I tried to tell him, Ben. I did."

Paul waved his red right hand. That was his way. Insolent and blockheaded. "The hide's worth at least a thousand fainne. Rack, near five thousand, I'd say. The fox-tails on Seamus' belt, maybe two hunnerd'? Three? Who cares about a dead deer?"

"You don't kill white stags, simpleton. They're charmed beasts. You're lucky every Dannan for twenty miles didn't answer the call!" Ben shoved him hard. He couldn't help himself. Someone had to answer for this mess. Why shouldn't it be Paul, who didn't have the sense the Gods gave a goat?

Paul raised his hands in mock surrender. "Tryin' to see the good here, Maeden. That's all."

"The good? Are you mad?"

"That's why ye let Nat die?" seethed Robin. "Because Marty shot a deer? We're bloody Greenmakers, ain't we? It's what we do. Tell me ye didn't take their side, Ben. Tell me yer bollocks don't swing so low."

"Three of you are alive at this very moment *because* of me. If I'd killed him as you asked, we would all be toasting each other in Tech Duinn right now. You know it as well as I do."

Robin towed Seamus and Paul at least three feet in his urgency to get at Ben. Ben threw down his bow and unbuckled his swordbelt, letting his weapons thump into the sand at his feet.

"Let him go!"

Robin barreled into him with a guttural grunt, but it was no use. Ben was twice his size and outweighed him by at least fifty pounds. Ben let him take one or two swipes before he hooked an arm under Robin's shoulder and spun him around. With one blow from his right hand, Robin's arse struck the earth with a solid thud. Dazed, Robin gaped up at him with unfocused malice. Ben leaned in, ready to strike again if he must.

"You deserved that, Robin. Stay down."

"Aye," said Robin, spitting out part of a tooth. "We're done, Ben Maeden. Yer no Greenmaker. We don't choose the Sidhe over one o'our own, do we? Don't think I didn't see ye."

"Have it your way," agreed Ben. "You're too old to learn common sense, aren't you?" He retrieved his weapons, shoved Paul again for good measure, and turned on his heel. He refused to look at the stag where it lay broken against the riverbank; its perfect white coat speckled red and black from the wound in its ribs.

Sacrilege of the first order.

He spared Robin one last withering glare.

"I quit."

Gerrod ran to catch up with him. "Wait, Ben. He don't mean it! We're sorry 'bout the stag, all right? Marty got desperate. Ye weren't over there. Ye don't know what it was like."

Robin threw out a spiteful laugh. "He ain't ever over there, is he? Stays on our side o'the river like a bleedin' coward, he does. Tell us, ye faerie bastard… how many kills have ye made to keep our folk fed and clothed? How many times have ye given over the last coins in your precious purse to help one o'ours? None. Yer a selfish sack of shite, ye are."

Ben ignored him. It wasn't easy. Robin Gramble had been his friend for almost fifteen years. Gerrod's anxious expression bordered on despair. "We'll meet up at Barb's later, yeah? C'mon. Ye can't leave it like this. We'll sort it all out."

Ben paused, for Gerrod's sake if no one else. "Later then."

"Ye'll meet us there?"

Ben blew out a protracted breath. His oldest friend had gone to stand by the water's edge, hiding a face full of tears. Nat was his kin, his sister's son. Ben could understand his irrational rage, even if it was unfairly directed. "I'll go and look for the bodies first. They can't have gone far."

"Thank ye, Ben."

Ben faced east. "Don't thank me, Gerry. Robin isn't right… but that doesn't make him wrong." He didn't give Gerrod a chance to process his statement. Ben yanked his hood low over his eyes. He faded into the Greensward like the Sidhe, only minutes before.

⚲ ⚲

THE DEAD WERE LAID OUT SIDE-BY-SIDE. Tallow candles flickered from lanterns tucked into cobweb-laden corners. Though the roof was well-tended, water trickled from one of two boarded windows. Ideally situated between the infamous *Hart and Hare* and Rosweal's high northern wall, The Greenmakers' Guild used this dilapidated stable as a waypoint for their nefarious gains. Long-abandoned stalls overflowed with crates and barrels stuffed with pilfered goods: bows, arrows, daggers, pelts, and the odd cask of peat-rich uishge. In the center aisle, Nat and Marty were stretched out on a broad oak table. Rose took the time to close their vacant eyes while she and Violet washed and prepared their bodies. Usually, the families would bear such a responsibility, but Marty's wife passed three winters before, and Nat's widow had two small children to manage. The task had to be performed in-house, as it were.

Rose met Ben's muted expression over Nat's gaping chest wound. She gave him a weak smile. He looked away. He'd done his part, as he said he would. Bringing both bodies back in one piece hadn't been a simple errand. He owed none of them a bloody thing now. Confident that tonight would be his last here in Rosweal, he saw no point in getting Rose's hopes up. Besides, a clean break was always the least painful sort.

The stag's white pelt dangled from the rafters in the farthest stall. A stinking pile of discarded organs, fat, and bone was all that remained of the magnificent beast. Ben's stomach roiled. Its glorious rack had been taken to the salt-shed outside to dry. To think of it made his skin crawl. That such a holy creature could come to this end was more than he could stomach. Seamus and Paul had no idea what evil they'd invited into their lives. Ben stared at the exit, eager to leave. He didn't have to wait long. From the raucous tavern next door, Colm stepped into the stable, a grim cast to his painfully thin face.

"Apologies for the delay."

"Not coming then, eh?"

Colm rolled a bony shoulder. "Grief's a bitter dose, Ben. He's not hisself right now."

"You know I didn't do what he's accusing me of?"

"Course I do." Colm strode over to stare at his fallen comrades, tugging a bone flask out of his jerkin. He toasted the pair, then took a long pull. "Bad business all around, and for what?"

Ben tugged a thumb behind him. "For that."

Colm shuddered at the sight. "Bloody bad luck, that."

"I said so."

"Barb'll murder the lot when she finds out that thing was here. Anyway," heaving a sigh, Colm jerked a hefty purse from his belt. "All the wages yer due, minus today's mess. Plus, severance."

Ben took it without complaint. "What else?"

"You already know. I'm sorry for it, Ben. This here weren't yer fault, but with Barb away, Robin's word is law. Best to stay clear o'town for a while, yeah? He wants ye gone by mornin.'"

Rose's lip quivered. "Ye can't be serious?"

"Outta my hands, missy."

"But—"

"It's fine, Rose," said Ben, tucking his earnings away. "A dreadful line was crossed today. It's time."

Rose came around the table, reaching for his fingers. Violet made a grab for her but missed. "Barb will sort this out when she gets back. You don't have to leave!"

Ben pried her hands from around his neck. "Some things are best left unsaid." He felt terrible for the hurt in her eyes, but that wouldn't change the outcome of this failed raid, would it? Robin's mind was made up. Staying would only invite more trouble. Ben would sooner avoid another row for everyone's sake.

"Don't go, Ben, please!"

Ignoring her took some effort. He paused in the open door. "Colm?"

"Yeah?"

"Make sure Gerry doesn't touch a spare copper of that stag's take."

"Aye," Colm agreed. There was an appropriate dose of fear in his voice. "It won't be easy to convince any o'them. Fools have gold on the brain."

"Then, I wish them luck. They're going to need it."

"Wait!" Rose cried out, wrenching herself free of Violet's staying hand. "What about Gerry? Seamus? Don't ye want to say goodbye?"

"Tell them for me, won't you? I wish you health and fortune, Rosie," Ben smiled. Without another word, he swept outside.

The night swallowed him whole.

The Kelpie

A five-hundred-ton galley bobbed alongside the jetty, awaiting passengers, goods, and crew. Una was so close now that she could taste linseed and tar at the back of her throat. She'd been wringing her hands in the queue since first light, eager to get on with it. *The Kelpie* wasn't what she would consider an impressive vessel in her limited reckoning of such things. Years of bad weather in the Straits of Mannanan had taken their toll on the old girl. The ship's rigging sagged from three puny masts. Patched sails were hastily strapped to her creaking crossbeams; bits of frayed rope and sailcloth streamed from the mast like stockings on a clothesline. *The Kelpie's* starboard side was pocked with poorly tarred holes, some perilously near the waterline.

Una didn't have the luxury of worrying whether the ship was comfortably seaworthy. *The Kelpie* was the only available boat for the next few weeks. As winter tiptoed into Innisfail, the shallow straits between Eire and Cymru would clog with ice. Shipping and transport would dwindle to a trickle for the next month, then halt altogether by the following. Only heavy ice-crushers and barges would dare the Straits of Mannanan in winter. Most of those were unfit for human cargo. This galley was Una's last chance for a clean escape from Eire. If she didn't board now, she would be forced to travel south to the Port at Bethany or west to Ten Bells to book passage at a later date. Neither option was an attractive one. The first would bring her well within her greatest enemies' reach. The latter would require many travel days, costly accommodations, and weeks of potential waiting. Both avenues were too dangerous to incite enthusiasm. She had to leave now, today, before it was too late.

So far, so good.

From here at the Port of Drogheda, the Boyne slogged five miles east to the Straits. The distance was not too great to taste the salt in the air nor smell the decaying seaweed dumped into the river's mouth at each high tide. Unused to the gastric stench of brackish water and vegetative river mud, she covered her mouth and nose with a gloved hand. Dockhands hauled crates and barrels overflowing with salted mackerel, whiting, turnips, cabbages, and leeks up *The Kelpie's* gangplank. The cacophony of competing odors intensified a hundred-fold as her queue wound up the ramp. She could get used to the smell. She might even learn to love it.

She would endure whatever she must to be free.

The crush of people waiting to board was another matter; three score stood on the wharf, herself included. Most of these folks were small-time Merchers, workers, or Agrean Migrants. Una didn't see how this many people could fit inside a ship this small, never-mind comfortably. Few passengers carried much in the way of luggage, but some did have children or small animals in tow. A grizzled, middle-aged man in front of her held a goat leashed to one hand and a wire cage bearing two hens in the other. Beside her, a young mother clung to two unruly children. The boy eyed Una with frank, unblinking curiosity. She wiggled her fingers at him. The child grinned around the drool-slathered fist he'd crammed into his mouth. In the distance, the Citadel loomed stern and oppressive. The Cloister of the Eternal Flame rose from the center of that menacing fortress. Its seamless granite edifice glinted red in the sun. Una shivered at the sight. If she never had to set foot there again, it would be too soon.

A commotion at the inner gate caught her attention. The harbormaster made a beeline for the waiting passengers, holding a wadded document in one meaty hand. He didn't look happy, nor was he alone. The black and gold cuirasses of the Citadel guard dogged his heels. Gasping, Una whipped her head around. There were four of them, she noted with rising panic. They shoved through passengers at the rear line, irrespective of age or disposition. An elderly woman cried out as she was knocked to her knees on the dock. The crowd parted for the guards like a stream diverted by a large stone. Una kept to her place at the rear of the queue, her head down. Willing herself as small and insignificant as possible, she tugged her cowl low over her forehead. The harbormaster stomped past.

Relax, she commanded herself.

If you appear anxious, they will wonder why.

She sent a surge of Spark into her blood to calm her nerves. She wasn't going to panic. Not now. She'd made it this far, hadn't she? Just a bit further… and she would be out of reach. Gone. Free. Safe.

Breathe, she chanted inwardly.

Everything is fine.

They have no reason to suspect you if you stay calm.

Upon first glance, she was just another Agrean migrant worker awaiting transport to the Colonies. Her papers were in order. Gan had seen to them, along with the coins bulging from the purse strapped to her thigh. An official Union Seal was stamped into her patent of labor. Her boarding pass read 'Kea Folna.' Kea was an average girl from the Midlands, shipping out to seek work in Swansea, like so many others on the wharf this morning. She would make it. She had to. If only *The Kelpie* would start boarding.

One of the guardsmen grabbed a girl at the front of the line. She was forced to remove her cap and tatty cloak. Una's heart skipped a beat. A cold knot of fear hardened in her belly. She watched the girl comply; her face streaked with tears. Her parents were held at arm's length while the forward guardsman searched her. He was not gentle. His gauntleted fists rent the girl's sleeves to the elbows. When nothing but her sun-kissed brown skin was revealed, he shunted her away and reached for another.

The harbormaster paced alongside the crowd. Fat beads of sweat slid down Una's nose. He held up a bit of vellum with its bright red seal: The Red Wyrm of the Union of Commons. Nema's seal. Una would know it anywhere. For a moment, all she could do was stare at the scarlet wax, her pulse louder than any drum.

"This here," he bellowed over their heads. "Be a warrant for the arrest of one 'Una Moura.' We'll thank ye lasses for cooperating with our search by rollin' up yer sleeves before ye make yer way up the ramp. If ye resist in any way, one o'these men will arrest ye. Raise yer hands if ye heard me, please."

A host of dirty, shaking fingers floated upward.

Una took a step back. *No, no, no…* she was too close! Gan assured her that no one would come looking for her until her journey was well underway. How did these guards have a warrant already? Why did it bear Nema's seal? Every second that passed made Una's nerves sing with renewed anxiety. Had Gan betrayed her? He must have… but why? Had Aoife discovered their plan and informed Nema? That was entirely possible, likely even. Aoife was a loyal snake: clever and ruthless. Ahead, *The Kelpie's* sails were rolled down. The ship would sail soon, with or without its passengers. Una might have known. Things had been going too smoothly.

"What's she done then?" asked the matron beside her, hefting her son high on her hip. Her antsy daughter wriggled around her knees. "This girl yer searchin' for?" As she spoke, another woman was jerked from the line and forced to partially strip. A second guardsman moved in from the opposite side, yanking hoods and hats off every female head he approached. It wouldn't be long before it was Una's turn.

She closed her eyes in silent prayer.

So much for her easy escape.

"Raise yer hand please, missus, so I know who's speakin'," boomed the harbormaster, holding the warrant over his eyes to block the sun.

"I've little'uns here, master," the matron snarked. "I've no free hands to spare. Answer the bleedin' question. What's this dread girl done, requires the manhandlin' o'respectable women like us, hey?"

A murmur of 'ayes' rumbled through the crowd. Women did not expect such treatment in Tairngare. Her neighbor stared straight at Una, her interest plain. Una took a step backward.

"She's a Prima of the Cloister, missus. Them women don't deign to tell us men nothin.' They want her. That's all I know," he replied, signaling the nearest guardsman to follow her voice. Una shot the matron one pleading glance. To her surprise, she winked. The next thing Una knew, she was holding the woman's sticky, squirming son. The little boy blew wet bubbles into her ear while his mother made a grand show of rolling up her sleeves on a dramatic, put-upon sigh.

The guardsman neared. Una was bustled further down the line.

The matron raised her arms, making a grand show of her bare wrists. "When he comes, hand my son back and go, milady," she said over her shoulder. "I'll keep him busy long as I can."

"How did you know?" Una was dumbfounded.

"Yers isn't a face I'd forget."

"Aye," said a nearby man. "Me neither. He's close, milady. Pass the boy, then get behind me. I'll cover for ye."

Una didn't have an opportunity to thank either of them, for as soon as the guardsman approached, the woman wrenched her son out of Una's arms and placed herself firmly between them. The man who'd offered his help swung Una into the mob by the waist, then dove headfirst into the soldier's chest. Her defenders tumbled to the dock with the guardsman, a tangle of curses and fumbling limbs. Una didn't waste a moment of the reprieve they'd bought her. She clawed through the rear of the crowd toward the Drough Gate. A shout went up at her back.

"Long live the Moura! Long live the Queen!" cheered the matron. Some took up her chant; others booed or jeered her for it.

Una was near the arch when the harbormaster singled her out. "The Gate! She's headed for the Market!" Heavy footsteps pounded down the wharf after her. She dumped all the Spark she could spare into her legs and sped on, ignoring the dumbstruck faces in her way. Hands reached out to halt her. She dodged, kicked, or slapped anything in her path. Under the arch, she took a sharp left toward the Market, then another leading her back to the city. She had no choice now but to run for the Ward Gate. The Navan High Road would lead her west to Ten Bells – her next best option. As long as she remained in Eire, anything could happen.

"Stop her! Stop that woman!" barked one of her pursuers. Una barreled through the Market, driving through people and bounding over impediments in her way. A quarter mile up, she cut a second corner at Oisin, then another at Pennyroyal. Thankfully, there weren't many people out this early, save workers and vendors loading their shops and stalls. The streets were mostly clear. Rounding the intersection at Balmoral, she veered left into a narrow alley. Her lungs burned like lamp oil, but she could not stop. The men chasing her had much longer legs, unfortunately. On Aine, a large stone wall abruptly halted her progress toward the Ward Gate. Too late to stop, she ran into the wall, nose first. Her rump struck the cobbles with an uncomfortable crack. Stars swirled before her eyes like multifaceted gems. She groaned and rolled onto her side, tasting blood. Newly cut stones were stacked under the scaffolding above her head. How could she have known they were working on this end of the Citadel? This was the first time she'd set foot outside of the Cloister in years. Groaning, she held a hand under her streaming nostrils.

"There ye are!"

Her ears rang. Shaking her head to clear it, she pushed herself to her feet. Una glared up at two Citadel guards. One of them unwound a bit of rope from his forearm and slunk toward her with an oily grin. He was an odd-looking fellow, with spindly limbs but portly round the middle, like a spider.

"Careful," his companion huffed from the corner. "She'll kill ye if she gets a hand on ye. Don't rush."

Una tilted her head. That wasn't a Tairnganese accent, was it? Come to think of it; these men didn't even look the part. Neither were exceptionally fit, and the Citadel did not tolerate sloth of any variety. The pair wheezed like they hadn't run in a decade or more.

"Who are you?" She wiped her face against her sleeve and slowly removed her gloves. The larger man watched her do it, his expression wary.

"Conor, like that time in Innisport, yeah, but easy. She's got fight in her. I can see it."

"No worries, boss," said the spider. "So do I."

Una leered at him. "Your friend was right, Conor. If you touch me, I'm going to kill you."

Another man thudded around the corner behind them. This one was probably the bulkiest person she'd ever seen. Instinctively, she jumped back a pace.

"Boss!" he rasped, holding his quaking ribs. "Guards're comin.'"

"Hold there, Fergus," sighed the balding man. "We got her now. Just make sure they don't come this way."

"Boss," Fergus droned, sparing Una the briefest disinterested glance. He ambled off like a sleepy bear. She heard his heavy, rhythmic steps for quite a while after he'd gone. Conor gave her a sloppy grin. He slung a makeshift lasso toward her. She stepped out of its testing path with a hiss.

"Careful, Conor. I mean it! The Duch don't want her harmed."

Steaming heat filled her cheeks. "The Duch?"

"That's right, missy," the leader told her. "Yer Da wants ye home. Where were ye gonna go in that rickety little dinghy, eh? The Colonies?" He blew a wet stream of air over his lower lip. "Don't think a fine lady like ye would like Swansea much. Everywhere ye go stinks o'shite, and the flies come at ye in clouds. Bethany's a sight better, I can tell ye."

"A damn sight better," Conor chuckled. "Bloody buggers'd gobble all that soft skin o'yers, right up. What a shame that would be, eh?"

"Conor, mind yer manners now," warned his boss. "That there's a princess. She's worth a hunnerd o'any one o'us."

"Patriarchal drivel," Una spat. "That's 'Prima Moura,' to you scum."

The leader pulled a face. "A thousand pardons, milady. Conor, grab her, will ye? We need to get gone."

As he advanced, she kept her eyes on Conor, withdrawing a dagger from her belt. Conor laughed. "I think I like her, Rawly. She's awful cute."

"Yer not gonna think so when she melts the skin from yer bones."

Conor shrugged as if to say, 'sorry, can't play anymore.' He lashed out at her face with his rope. She swerved, then dipped forward to plunge her blade into Conor's reaching hand. She would have connected, too, had she been quicker. He side-swept her clumsy blow, then smashed his elbow into her gut. The breath burst out of her lungs in a rush… but she dug her fingers into the cloth at his elbow anyway. He couldn't shake her off in time.

"Burn," she whispered. Instantly, the fabric sparked and caught fire. Conor spun aside on a howl, slapping at the smoking wool with his free hand.

Rawly, their leader, threw up his hands. "What in the hells did I say, ye bleedin' idiot?"

Una kicked Conor while he was down, in her hurry to leap past him. Grunting in pain, he snatched at her heel. She tripped over him with a cry. Rawly was on her before she could roll aside. He tamped down on her fingers with a booted heel. She heard two distinct snaps and screamed.

Rawly's left hand grasped her hair while Conor twisted her ankle about ninety degrees the wrong way. "Sorry, missy, but orders are orders." Rawly smashed her face into the dirty cobbles, hard. It wasn't stars that crossed her vision this time. Waves rolled out of the dark crevices of her mind like ripples over a silent lakeshore. A tiny, dilapidated galley sailed into that obsidian curtain, its tattered sails billowing over an empty deck. As it passed, all hope of liberation faded to black.

⚲ ⚲

Ben found himself at a seedier tavern on the outskirts of town. He had no idea what time it was nor how long he'd been there and couldn't care less. No one would come looking for him. That was the important bit. On this side of the city, no breeze could penetrate the miasma of human filth, refuse, and unwashed flesh that loomed over the slums. The South-End was a hive of ramshackle huts, rotten buildings, and mud-slick streets: the perfect place to hide. This nameless tavern, for example, was one of many unlicensed and unregulated establishments that catered to Rosweal's poor. Northers referred to this sort of hole in the wall as a 'dive.' A reference to a vat of spirits perched on the edge of a dusty wooden bar, laced with dregs from emptied tankards and the odd scrap of meat or bread. Less flush patrons would pay two coppers to take a 'dive' with the dipper chained to its rim. The very meanest among them would wait all night for the vat to be dumped into the muddy sewer.

In the taproom, there were rats and fleas in the rushes. Birds and bats roosted in the rafters. Feral cats lurked in the shadows hunting omnipresent vermin. Several customers were asleep (or perhaps dead) on the pine-strewn floor. Some lay in the damp outside, snoring bubbles into greasy mud. Whores plied their trade in full view of patrons without shame. The sounds of rutting, drunken argument, and fevered gambling rang throughout the structure. The stench alone could drop a boar at ten paces... and the liquor. If one had to guess what might be killing patrons, they wouldn't have to search very hard for the culprit. Ben had had a very good run at a game of Porter for a while but soon became too inebriated to maintain his lead without cheating. He hated to cheat at cards but couldn't very well let these ingrates outwit the last copper from his pocket, either. At one point, he'd considered curling up on the floor with one of the girls. He thought better of that brilliant idea when he realized the floor was *squirming* beneath a reeking layer of urine-stained straw.

In disgrace, as he was, he'd likely be sleeping outdoors. More's the pity. The air outside felt about as soft as a slab of granite. He did have another flop on the other side of town, but realistically, Rosweal was not a large place. His rooms above *The Hart* might as well have been on the moon for all the good they'd do him tonight. Ben was adrift on a lonely, friendless sea for the first time in over a decade. He'd forgotten how miserable solitude could be. He would miss *The Hart*: Rosie, Gerrod, Seamus, and Colm. Hells, he'd even miss Barb, and she was a badger on her best day. Robin, too… though part of Ben wanted to bash in the old codger's brains for his idiocy.

Ben took a long pull from his tankard, all but immune to the sharp bitterness of the raw liquor within. It wasn't the worst he'd ever had. What unaged spirits lacked in flavor, they made up for in efficacy. He couldn't feel his tongue anymore. That was just fine. The more he drank, the less bothered he could be about anything, least of all the life he left behind. Deprived of one's illusions, the mind made spears of the most mundane details. He was going to miss Rosweal, warts and all.

With a sigh, Ben laid his hand down. Four cups and two nails. A concert of groans circled his table. Several inferior hands were tossed into the center in disgust. An opponent dropped two coppers into the pile and got up. The others glared spitefully at Ben over their mugs.

"Another?" the nearest inquired.

Ben rolled a shoulder. "Why not? Who wants to deal?"

"Not ye, ye pretty peacock," snapped a rough fellow on his right.

Ben handed him the deck with a smirk. He wasn't sure which perturbed these men more: that he was winning or that none of them could catch him cheating. He took another sip, accepting his newest hand without comment. One of the girls, emboldened by his winning streak, worked up beside him. She smelled of smoke, onions, and cheap perfume. She did have expert fingers, however. As she worked them into his shoulders, he decided he didn't care what she smelled like. The next hand finished much the same as the last, with Ben emerging the victor, three gems over three bushels, this time. With his masseuse nibbling at his ear, Ben grinned. Two more men got up to leave, their faces red as his dulcet lady's hair. An insistent rapping on the tabletop dragged his attention upward.

The poacher seated across the table, whose name he couldn't recall – Padraig, was it? – flashed a short knife at him.

"That's yer last hand tonight, Ben Maeden. If I were ye, I'd place me fainne on the table and duff outta here afore I gut ye like the cheatin' swine ye are."

Ben blinked slowly, willing his brain to order. He gave Padraig his best if sloppiest, grin. "Relax. I think I've lost as many hands as you have."

He hadn't, of course.

Cursing, Padraig nodded to other unamused players at the table. If Ben were sober, he might find the situation humorous… ousted from two establishments in less than a day. He was on a roll.

"For some reason, that stack o' coins on yer side hasn't lost a shred o' weight. I call that suspicious. Don't ye agree, boys?"

A murmur of general acquiescence rumbled around the table.

Ben spread his hands. His reputation preceded him. "You wouldn't be threatening me, would you, Padraig?"

"Ye might be a dandy with that elven sticker at yer side, but there's more o' us than ye can handle, Ben. Do it now, slow like."

Ben thumbed his pommel. Pointless comfort. He had no desire to waste the effort on weaklings like these. What purpose would it serve? It wouldn't repair his wounded pride nor improve his situation in the least.

"If you say so." He couldn't halt the blatant mockery in his tone. "No need for such bother. I'll be off." He stood up, pleased he didn't waver on his feet as much as he expected to. Leaning over the table, Ben scraped his winnings into the pouch he made of his tunic.

Padraig slid his chair back; knuckles stark against the tabletop. "I said, leave yer coins on the table."

Deliberately, Ben drew his purse-string taut and looped it through his belt. "I believe I left enough to go around. Plenty for you lot. Night, gentlemen," he snickered. Dipping a derisive bow, he shuffled to the door. He'd barely made it two steps before he felt the prick of a blade against his neck. The stink of onions and unwashed skin enveloped him. His lady of the evening also took a shine to his newly fattened purse. Figured. If he hadn't felt overly sorry for himself and hadn't gotten sloshing drunk in this stinking shithole in the first place, he would never have allowed her anywhere near him. For that matter, he wouldn't have sat in on a game of porter with poachers of Padraig's ilk either. If he hadn't cheated (though he had… just a bit), he still wouldn't have walked out unmolested.

Straight Ben would have known better.

Straight Ben was a much wiser man.

"Sorry, lover," said the woman in his ear. Her breath stung. "I have little un's to feed, meself. Why not hand Padraig yer purse there, and we'll let ye off with no more trouble?"

"Of course, milady," said Ben. "Why don't you reach around my chest and undo the strap? I'd do it for you, but I find I don't fancy a shave just now."

"Yer sweet," she purred, pressing close as directed. Her humor dissolved into shock when Ben pulled her across his chest and flung her bodily onto the table. Coins, cards, and tankards flew in every direction at once. In a lunge for Ben's throat, Padraig launched over the screaming bawd. Ben ducked and kicked Padraig's leg out at the knee; audibly, the bone crunched inward. Keening like a girl, Padraig crumpled to the rushes below. In the meantime, Ben wasn't about to let the others have a go. He grabbed the nearest table and heaved it into at least three charging torsos. Two men fell backward. The third tripped over Padraig's thrashing body and crashed into the rushes face-first. Ben didn't linger.

He was out the door and darting through the alley before the proprietor could shout for help. Unfortunately, this nameless juke also had a back door. Five men, including Padraig's two cronies, were fast on his heels.

Ben was usually quite fleet of foot, but he was also drunk as a satyr and severely outnumbered. Looking up as he splashed through the alley, he realized the buildings on either side were too high to scale without a boost. No doubt, the racket his pursuers made would summon the profligate constabulary sooner rather than later. He had two options: get out before he was cornered, or turn and fight. Neither was appealing nor likely in these narrow, malodorous lanes. Slipping and sliding through the slums and back alleys, he made slow progress. After his second dousing stumble, he skidded around a sharp corner on his right. A sheer wall lay ahead: no windows, railings, or bricks to climb. Ben caught his breath on a curse. He heard whistles and shouting from whence he came.

He was out of alternatives. The last thing he needed was to be dragged to gaol in the East End. He would likely be beaten, robbed, and promptly murdered there, not necessarily in that order. Rosweal's gaols were less a punishment for deserving offenders than a venue for blackmail and homicide. That was not an outcome he longed to experience for himself.

Offering a prayer of apology to Danu, he begrudgingly drew his sword. The hum of pure, sylvan steel sang into the night. The first thug tore around the corner with a crude cudgel in his right hand. Before the fellow could register the weapon waiting ahead, the cudgel and the hand that held it followed his head to the cobbles below. Two more pursuers, one carrying a lamp, were not far behind. When they splashed into view, Ben was ready for them. Howling in rage, the largest of the two hurled himself at Ben with his long dagger raised. His head rolled to a stop under an oxcart. His companion with the lamp backpedaled. Ben held his bloodied sword aloft and steady in his right hand. All traces of intoxication faded. His arm did not shake. His eyes, which once seemed a dull blue-grey, flashed silver in the lamplight.

"You have one chance," he said.

The poacher gaped, surrendering every inch that Ben advanced. All color drained from the fellow's ruddy face as he dropped his lantern, throwing spirals of sizzling lamp oil into the muck at Ben's feet. Sucking in a gulping breath, the poacher screamed at the top of his considerable lungs. "Help! We're under attack! There're High Elves here!"

Ben's sword took him through the middle, cutting his exhortation short. The blade had barely exited the fellow's guts when the next round of lamps came bobbing up the alley. Ben belted for the next lane and fumbled at his collar for something missing. He cursed to a new and spectacular degree. The whore's knife must have severed the cord, or perhaps he'd dropped it at the dead end. Without that ogham stone, he wouldn't be able to conceal himself any longer. He had to get out of Rosweal post-haste. He ran with no direction in mind except out. Finally emerging from the web of alleyways, he, at last, came to the Navan Gate. The Gate was closed, but no matter. He could scale the wall here easily enough. Ben was just cresting the top as a cadre of armed men with lanterns emerged from the labyrinthine alleyway. The lamps' glow hit him full in the face for a brief moment.

Thankfully, he was over the wall and deep within the Greensward when the real screaming began.

Sojourner

n.e. 508
15, Dor Samna
The Greensward

Dawn arrived before he knew it. Slow to wake, Ben squinted at a sky the color of ash. A thick layer of hoarfrost crunched in the underbrush as he worked himself upright. Winter was nigh, and no mistake. What few animals he spied were as sluggish and maudlin as he. Squirrels, rabbits, and deer hardly flinched at his intrusion of their domain. They slagged off into the Greensward, more interested in foraging for food than a wandering drunkard. Even the birds knew better than to loiter outside their nests on such a wretched morning. His hangover didn't help, of course. Whatever had been in the uishge last night must have been equal parts sugar and lamp oil. His head throbbed so hard that his teeth rattled in their casings. Added to this was dazzling fatigue, a mouth full of long sour ale, a belly full of cheap meat pie, and crushing regret. All told, it was the beginning of a rubbish day.

Ben was, by far, the sorriest sad sack in Innisfail. This wouldn't be his first winter outdoors, but the prospect was infinitely less attractive now than ever. A decade of relative warmth and comfort had seen to that. Ben knew he had no one to blame but himself. He should have led the Greenmakers farther west, into largely vacant territory. He was aware that Fionn kept close to the border in Dor Samna. Hells, he'd done so himself when he boasted command of *An Fiach Fian*, hadn't he? The Wild Hunt's purpose was to safeguard the border between Aes Sidhe and Eire. Not only to defend those who dwelled within the Sidhe realm but also to protect the Milesians in Eire from many of those same inhabitants. Rosweal was the nearest Milesian town to the border. Therefore, her citizens were well advised of the peril such proximity afforded.

Nevertheless, fear of starvation often outweighed common sense. Raiders braved the border every autumn with limited recourse and little reward. Most raids were fruitless and often spent more lives than they benefited. Many Eirean men and women died to bring Aes Sidhe's natural treasures home to their impoverished communities.

When his sojourn in Eire began, Ben had derided the ballsy stupidity of poachers who dared to cross for meat or pelt. Since he'd witnessed firsthand the toll winter could take on whole families in the Greensward. Having watched folk bury their nearest and dearest each year, he could no longer fault them for their audacity. Ben could attest that unfounded bigotry rarely survived the nuance of experience. Coming to Rosweal had taught him the meaning of desperation, a lesson well learned. He could not, however, forgive rampant greed. To kill a sylvan stag was crude iconoclasm. Pure barbarism. Even had he been invited to stay in Rosweal, he wasn't sure he would have. He was disgusted with the Greenmakers, who should have known better. More so himself. Ben sighed.

Dwelling on it wouldn't change anything, would it? In the uishge-addled depths of his overtaxed brain, he couldn't forget the shock on Fionn's face when their eyes met across the Boyne. They'd never had any great love for one another, but the disgust and ire writ in Fionn's eyes had wounded Ben more deeply than any arrow ever could.

How the mighty had fallen…

Of course, Robin had been right about Ben. So what? No one living in the Greensward was whom they wished to be. Some were there to flout the rules of the 'civilized' Southers in Ten Bells or Bethany. Some fled the rigid theocracy in Tairngare. Some sought adventure. Most simply had nowhere else to go.

Rosweal was not an illustrious destination, by any reckoning. Its few charms appealed to a tiny fraction of the population. Despite this (or perhaps because of it), Rosweal had become a second home for Ben somewhere along the way. He shook himself. Hadn't he vowed not to brood?

Feeling lost, he shuffled through a deep gulley choked with thorns and dead leaves. Over a jut of stone encircled by rotting vegetation, the forest fell behind him, opening a vista into the bog at *Bru na Boinne* below. He groaned. Why in the nine hells had he come this way? Did he have some internal inclination to compound his torture? Taking stock of his surroundings, he leaned on his Milesian longbow and scowled down at the river valley. There, just beyond the bog, was an ancient meander in the Boyne's path. The trees were too dense to see much across the border, but he smelled the watchfires burning at *Si an Bhru.* A deep pang squeezed something soft within his chest. Rather than prolong his homesickness, he turned away. Ben's people once called this place *Bron Por,* though the Milesians did not honor that tradition. To them, it was nothing more than a massive, malodorous swamp named Bally Lough. The bog spanned a circumference of no more than three miles, but it was treacherous all the same. It might have been bottomless in some places, for all the hope one had of escaping some of its well-hidden pools.

Opting to maintain a healthy respect for the unfathomable, Ben carefully backtracked uphill toward the Greensward. A nest of twigs snapped beside him. He froze. Never in his long life had he been distracted enough to allow a Milesian to sneak up on him… and in the Greensward no less? He half wished the intruder would just shoot him to alleviate his acute shame.

He heard a familiar giggle, then let out a bit of the breath he'd been holding. "That you, Gerry?"

"Robin, don't keep me on for me looks."

Ben couldn't help but chuckle. Not much in a tussle was Gerrod, but woe to any quarry he meant to track. The fact would chafe if Ben were in a position to be proud. "Planning to shoot me in the back?"

"Nah. Robin would box me ears if I did— angry though he is. Ye really cut his teeth this time, Ben. Three more decent fellas is lyin' dead in town. You coulda picked a better time for it. Summer maybe? When folks ain't like to starve, 'cause we can't provide."

"They tried to rob me."

"We figured. Padraig's a right twat, but he works hard. Robin's got him tucked safely away in gaol now. For disturbin' the peace and all. Only audience there are rats and half-dead drunks."

That was interesting. Robin must not intend to broadcast Ben's identity. Why not? "How many men know?"

"About ye bein' Sidhe?"

"What else?"

Gerrod blew air over his lower lip. "No one with any smarts. Don't worry. Robin sent me ahead to warn ye. We had to make a show of it, at least. Folk wouldn't like it if we let a murderer duff away unscathed, would they? Any reason I shouldn't shoot ye somewhere painful for bein' a dishonest prat?" What he meant was, did Ben have anything to bribe him with? Ben cursed at Gerrod's cheek but wasn't about to kill the lad for a pittance. He was rather fond of Robin's apprentice. Growling, he tossed Gerrod his smaller sack of coins. The lad hefted it with a grin. "So," Gerrod resumed with his usual humor, "an Elf then, eh? Robin's actin' like he ain't the least surprised, but ye could blow me down with a whistle right now. Were ye always so bloody tall?"

Gnashing his teeth at the common racial slur, Ben stuck his hands up and faced him. Gerrod sucked in a sharp breath.

"Yes, Gerry," said Ben. "I have always been this tall."

"*Siora's tits*! Seamus owes me twelve quid for this," hooted Gerrod. "What's yer real name then?"

"I… don't think you want to know."

"Oh, come on! I'm the last fella in the Greensward ye have to worry about right now." Gerrod flung his homely little bow to the ground to prove his point. He waggled his fingers in the air. "See? Now yer name is all I'm askin' for." Gerrod's spotty smirk nearly ground the words from Ben's mouth. Thankfully, before he could answer, voices and popping twigs alerted them of approaching company.

Gerrod glanced furtively over his shoulder. "We don't have much time. A lot o'the boys don't know it was ye in that juke, and they certainly won't know who ye truly are. Robin's keepin' that close to his chest," he said, cracking his bow over his knee and mussing the leaves and foliage below. "Ye'll have to hit me. Come on then. Be quick," he tugged his bare chin in Ben's direction. The distant footsteps moved closer. "Go on then. We're mates, ain't we? Ye'd do it for me." His eyes were full of innocent confidence.

Ben shoved a surge of raw guilt down his gullet. He probably would not do the same for Gerrod, and that thought brought him fresh shame. A figure materialized from the trees on his left.

"I owe you," said Ben, clouting the boy across the temple with the butt of his longbow. Gerrod crumpled. An arrow whizzed past, taking a lock of Ben's pale hair with it. He had no choice but to run and leap over the rise, straight into Bron Por.

⚰ ⚱

HOURS LATER, BEN STOPPED TO rest below the eaves of a great rowan, some miles past the infuriating bog. Every inch of his body felt heavy, sore, and bruised. His once fine boots were sopping wet with mud and algae. His tunic, vest, and trousers weighed an additional forty pounds for all the sulphuric water they'd absorbed. He'd mislaid his cloak, longbow, and two of his daggers somewhere. Doubtless, they'd sunk to the bottom of one of the bog's mercurial pools. When afternoon had melted into evening, Ben struggled to discern the sparse patches of dry ground from deceptively shallow pools of noxious green water. Twice he'd gone under, submerging his head and shoulders in a murky, foul-smelling mire. Both times, he'd managed to claw himself out, but he was lucky. Many who strayed into Bron Por often never made it out again. It took ages to cross in one piece. He was thankful not to have lost his sword or purse. He wasn't sure which deity he owed for that minor miracle but vowed to honor them all in turn, regardless.

Ben's pursuers gave up after the first quarter mile, as expected. Even gutsy Northers like Robin and his Greenmakers knew better than to chase through Bally Lough at dusk. They'd have to travel around for miles and miles to try and reach him from the other side. Since the wind was cold as a tomb in the Riverlands, Ben was sure sane men would prefer the warmth of their beds to drowning or frostbite.

Danu knew *he* would rather be hugging a tankard of ale in a nice fire-lit room right about then. Instead, he dug mud, grass, and reeds out of his ruined boots. An impatient hangover roared like a caged bear in his skull. All the running, tumbling, and dousing had worn him down to the nub. He was cold and starved and right about then, would have paid any amount to return to his rooms in Rosweal whence a warm meal and his soft bed beckoned. His stomach snarled at the thought of something other than rotgut uishge roiling within its hollow, trembling cavity. It would be dark soon. If he didn't find something to eat swift enough, he could be in real trouble. Ben wondered if he would be the first Sidhe to starve to death in the history of his race.

How mortifying…

He might as well have been naked for all the use he'd get from his ruined gear. His sword stuck fast in her scabbard, encased in nearly a foot of cloying bog mud. Without a bow to bring down game, he had no idea how he would feed himself tonight. Perhaps he could build a trap or snare, but that would take too bloody long. Ben jerked a small silver flask from inside his spoilt vest. At least he had more uishge… thank Herne for small favors. He might be buggered about nine different ways, but at least he didn't have to greet his next pathetic dawn sober.

To busy his hands, he cleaned out his scabbard, then his boots, and scrubbed drying filth from his sword with a soggy shirt sleeve. Samn was high in the sky when he realized his hair had frozen stiff to the trunk behind him. Reciting a retraction of formerly grateful prayers, he pried himself loose, donating a patch of scalp in the process. Just as he considered cradling a log in his arms and heaving himself back into the por, the most wonderful, mouth-watering aroma wafted toward him on the breeze. Ben's mouth flooded with saliva at the scent. Though, as quickly as it came, it evaporated. Skittering around the little copse of trees with his nose in the air like a dog, he searched for the source.

Liquor and fatigue barked through his veins, urging him toward a small game trail that led back toward the river. Here, the scent was more pungent. It seemed someone else shared Ben's sojourn… someone with food. An olfactory parade of smoked salmon, charred potato cakes, and roasted venison conquered his thoughts. Whoever they were, they weren't exactly roughing it, were they? Wait… was that ale he smelled? Ben would trade all his silvers for a cup of ale and a quarter-hank of their venison. He rambled down the game trail, intent to buy, beg, or steal anything these fellows might spare. Whatever they might be doing in the woods, in this weather, at such an hour, didn't make the slightest difference to him.

The uishge burning in his gut demanded company, *now*.

It didn't occur to him to consider his appearance, nor what a shock he was bound to give the chef. What decent man camped in the borderlands at night when there were two towns nearby with warm beds? This was a question he might have pondered had he been sober. Instead, he marched downhill with nary a second thought.

⚜

SHANE RAWLY WAS TOO OLD for nonsense such as this. Thirty-odd years of smuggling and head-cracking in Duch Donahugh's name had worn his bones brittle. Yet, he was again, in a godforsaken wood along the border, doing the old bastard's dirty work. And for what? For a bit of property in the garden district for his wife and five children. For a lump of coin that wouldn't last a year if the winter went hard. For the privilege of being the fellow Patrick called upon when he needed something reprehensible done right. The things a body must do to climb upward in life: morally defunct and *illegal* things. Rawly knew a man not born to comfort had less choice than experience.

He squinted at the waxing moon and spat out his second wad of bitterroot in under an hour; his nerves jumbled taut. He scratched at his grizzled cheek and glanced sidelong at his young son Gabriel, who was meant to be on watch. The lad struggled to keep both eyes trained on the package they were to deliver to the Duch. With a full belly and a mite too much uishge, Gabriel's chin had already dipped toward his collarbone several times. He was such a scrawny boy, both slight of stature and bearing. Rawly could remember a time not so long ago when it took only one of his burly arms to hoist him high. The lad was nearing seventeen winters now.

By Bethonair law, Gabriel was of age to inherit his father's chosen craft. Wasn't it a shame that Rawly's profession would never earn the respect of their peers? Ah, but such was his lot. The Duch paid better than any lord in the South. His lordship often looked after Rawly's kin when all others would have let them starve in the street. To put a fine point on the matter, Rawly owed the Duch his life, livelihood, and anything else the man might ask of him. Such was the debt he owed for a lifetime in servitude. Rawly was a valuable tool for better men. Though, because of this, he was also an utter failure as a father.

Gabriel looked up for a moment, his blue eyes sparkling. His lopsided grin showed the uneven tooth his sisters constantly teased him about. Thought it was all a merry jig, Gabriel did. This awful business the Duch demanded… the lad had no idea what he was doing. Rawly was his father! No matter what he owed the Duch, a father knew better than to ruin his child to stave off a creditor. Duch Patrick had commanded Rawly to teach the boy his trade. Not having a choice didn't make Rawly feel one whit better about it. This quandary reminded him of his long-suffering mother. She'd been a Kneeler from Cymru in the East and had spent a great deal of effort trying to cure him of his delinquency. It did no good, of course. Rawly's fate had been fairly sealed as soon as he realized it was easier to pick a pocket than earn a coin. Now that he was older and a parent, he recalled her lessons with a twinge of conscience. What was it she had said most often?

The sins of the father…

"Boss?" Fergus's rumbling voice interrupted his musings. Rawly looked up. Fergus was a beast of a man, at least six and a half feet tall and weighing nearly three-hundred pounds. He might have been terrifying were it not for his obvious case of idiocy. Fergus blinked in that slow, stupid way, which made Rawly want to bash his monstrous head in with a rock.

"Fergie, I told ye to keep yer gob shut until we left the river behind," Rawly sneered, contemplating slitting the buffoon's throat before they made it to Ten Bells. He'd always threatened to but never had, despite an ever-present urge. The truth was the lumbering oaf was a handy man to have around. A drooling fool he might be, but easily worth three in a fight.

Fergus' shaggy, straw-colored hair glowed white in the rising moonlight. "I know that boss, I 'member. It's just I think I hear somethin' out there."

Rawly rolled his eyes and stretched to his full height— considerable at six feet but not outstanding when placed beside the likes of Fergus. The way the giant shrank from his approach, Rawly might have been eight feet or more. "Keep yer bloody voice down! We're close enough to Aes Sidhe now; the smallest fart might bring one o'their hunters across the border to slaughter us all where we stand."

An empty threat.

No Sidhe warriors crossed into Eire unless they were on a march. Nevertheless, the warning achieved its desired effect. Fergus's beady eyes widened to their maximum capacity. Perhaps it was cruel to torture a grown man with a mind trapped in childhood? Rawly didn't do so without purpose. Fergus' voice carried very far. Any number of unwelcome visitors might follow its boom into their little camp. Like the Tairnganeah, for instance, on a mission to reclaim the thing Rawly and his fellows had successfully stolen from Drogheda yesterday morn.

"I don't like elves," Fergus pouted. His mountainous shoulders quivered in irrational fear. Rawly adjusted his sword belt with a groan.

"No shite, ye sweet lass. Keep yer bloody comments to yerself until we clear the bog." Gabriel laughed once, then covered his mouth to prevent a further outburst. Rawly set a searing eye on his son. "That means ye too, boyo!" Still grinning, Gabriel turned back to his task.

Their fourth companion stomped through the trees just ahead of them, making Fergus yelp and stumble back several feet. Gabriel giggled into his hand, careful to avoid his father's glare.

"What's all this about then?" wheezed Conor. His trousers were filthy with muck and grime, and he stank of mold so strong, Rawly sneezed. Conor was the exact opposite of Fergus in temperament and appearance. Outwardly, he looked more like a harmless moneylender than a brutish ruffian. Rawly had never known a man more ruthless— save for Duch Patrick. Conor was Rawly's right hand. He was cunning but loyal. On the other hand, Fergus was mere mindless muscle: his purpose was to dissuade fights before they began. His bulk was effective, so long as he didn't speak.

Rawly shook his head. "Nothin' of note. This large girl here has a fear o'elves swoopin' down on him in the night." His expression imparted that he meant to keep the impression solidly in place.

Conor nodded. Message received. "Oh, aye. Terrible close to Elf Land now, ain't we? Ye ever hear about Dumnain Fergie? Them longhaired devils hung each o'the villagers in the square by their entrails. Their leader was the bloody Kneeler's Devil hisself. I was there, ye know? A great white-haired brute he was, with eyes cold as knives…." Conor's rotted teeth looked a bit like fangs in the night.

Fergus deflated. "I don't like that story."

Sensing weakness, Conor's favorite, he leaned closer. "Lasses and babes with their guts strung over clotheslines. The stink was somethin' like Butcher Lane in summer, only worse. Ye ever smell decayin' people, Fergie? Not much difference 'tween us and rottin' meat."

Fergus went green.

Rawly heard his stomach shift. "That's enough now, Conor. What did ye find?"

"Not much but Eire's longest, widest, most vexin' swamp a mile west. We can't cross her in the night, Shane. Some of them ponds are deeper than a man is tall and damned near invisible in the dark. I know ye don't want to hear it, but we should wait till dawn."

Rawly glanced back at his son's expectant, trusting face. "We hafta get movin'. Them witches in Tairngare got outriders fast on our trail by now. I'm not waitin' here with me stones in me hand." He scowled into the forest behind them. If the Tairnganeah caught up with them now, they'd have no choice but to drop their prize and escape into Bally Lough anyway. They'd packed light for the trip to Tairngare and back, and by his reckoning, they still had a week to reach Ten Bells. The Duch would have his head if Rawly failed him… or worse. "We're gettin' through that bog tonight. Make no mistake."

"Not gonna happen, Shane. Ye'll get us all killed and lose the Duch's prize anyway. I like to gamble, but not with me life," said Conor.

"Bogs are bad places, me mam told me," Fergus declared. "Pooka play in them at night, waitin' for folk to wander in," he crossed himself.

"Me own mam told me I was the handsomest dandy in the world. What's yer point?"

Ignoring them, Rawly scratched at his stubble, eyeing the loose branches and boughs littering their clearing. They could make a raft if they had to, using the longer branches as measures.

"I know what yer thinkin', but it won't do no good if we can't see where we're walkin.' Not even if ye marched us single file, tied to the same log, would our footing be sound enough to carry her over all that uneven ground. Yer outta yer bloody mind."

Growling in frustration, Rawly gazed at Gabriel for a long while. No. He wouldn't risk his son in Bally Lough at night any more than he would risk him to Tairngare's city guard. Damn, damn, damn! The Duch wouldn't have hired him if he'd thought this task would be easy. Rawly was sorely disappointed to discover how bloody difficult it was turning out to be.

⚜

BEN CONCEALED HIMSELF IN A dense thicket, quickly realizing he'd bitten off a mite more than he wanted to chew. How he'd ever imagined these men might have been out here for pleasure or sport was lost on him. Probably, he shouldn't have downed the rest of that uishge on an empty stomach. There were four men in this camp. All were armed to the bloody teeth. Ben didn't fancy losing a hand for a meal. He should find somewhere to sleep it off, then head down to Navan in the morning for a flea-ridden bed and a hot bowl of porridge. Of course, that was what he *should* do… but no matter how insistent the thought, his legs would not obey. Uishge whispered courage in his ear. The pickled part of his brain was highly susceptible. He had no doubt he could take them.

Although, Ben knew the difference between common thieves and professional smugglers. From the look of things, these fellows were expecting to be laid upon at any moment. The shivering girl they'd tied to a tree on the opposite side of the fire was the reason they were so well armed and jumpy. Poor thing. She was blindfolded and gagged, wearing only a fine linen tunic and thin woolen trousers. A filthy burlap sack barely covered part of one leg. Likely, she was freezing. Ben's lip curled. *Kidnappers…*

He was so inebriated he'd practically strolled right up to them with his hands out for scraps. Worse, these men were *Souther* mercenaries from Bethany, if he wasn't mistaken. Their costly serrated sabres plainly bore the truth of that. Northers preferred slimmer, more practical weaponry. He figured these men must have been sent here for the girl. Drunk he might be, but Ben knew which end of his arse was up. No Souther mercenary would venture so far into the inhospitable North without the promise of a hefty purse awaiting his return. There were far easier pickings in the South. Ben didn't have to work hard to determine where she must have come from. There were only two wealthy cities in the North, and from the tattoos he spied roaming her exposed clavicle, he could guess which it was. She was Tairnganese. Noble too.

Worth quite a lot of fainne to this lot.

19

Ben watched the bald man very closely. Clearly, their leader, his steady eye roved the makeshift camp with wary regularity. Of course, shrewd and vigilant as he might be, he was no Sidhe. Ben smirked. If this intelligent man only knew what lurked in the shadows, he might fear the 'elves' across the border as much as his oafish friend Fergus did. The largest of the gang snored in his bedroll, utterly oblivious to the world around him. He was a gentle, simple creature in an overlarge package, nothing more. Ben felt he wouldn't be much trouble. The reptilian creature Conor, however, would be slightly more challenging. He lay prone as if asleep, though his right hand fingered a vicious dagger at his hip. There was another strapped beneath his left leg and a smaller one in his right sleeve. Ben marked him well. He would have to kill Conor quickly. No one who found a need for so many knives loathed their uses.

Beyond him, the youngest of the band perched nearest the fire. He made a grand show of pretending to be awake, but his breathing gave him away. This was the leader's son. Ben would've inferred that at a glance had the boy not already called the man 'Da.' He was a gangly, underfed lad of scant years. What did his father mean by bringing him along on such a job? Ben would have to incapacitate the boy first, to keep him from underfoot while he killed his father… that is if he felt up to getting involved here. They were all nearly in the same profession, weren't they? Ben was hardly an innocent. He'd done many things he wasn't proud of in the past few years for a profit. He didn't know this girl nor particularly care where she came from. Her family must be rather important in the Red City for brutes like these to go to such lengths. Either that or someone in Bethany paid good money to make her his leman. Ben wrinkled his nose.

What did he care?

She was nobody to him.

Yet… his feet refused to budge. Did it matter where she came from? If he walked away now, whatever might happen to her would weigh on his conscience. Ben was in a position to do something to help her, and as much as he knew he should, he couldn't bring himself to leave. He was still his father's son, beneath the years of poverty, anonymity, and self-inflicted degradation.

Ben Maeden might be a degenerate criminal, but inside, his father's lessons held firm.

Not like this.

She *was* a tiny little thing, and there *was* quite a lot of meat drying over the fire. Besides, he was too hungry to walk to Navan in the cold and too drunk to bother.

He looked up. The night had matured. The uishge in his ear assured him that his intrusion wasn't merely the right thing to do; it was the best thing to do. Why should these Southers get to keep all that food, all that uishge, and make it out of the Greensward without paying a toll? Besides, he hated the cunts in Bethany. This was the North, and Southermen hadn't been welcome here for almost fifty years. To taunt him with meat and good strong ale… by Herne, he could kill them for the brass alone. With a gurgling gut, Ben waited for his moment. The fact that the scene blurred before his eyes and his head spun a little every time he moved meant less than nothing in the face of such sport.

Heart of Darkness

n.e. ſ08
Iſ, Dor Samna
eire

Rawly's eyes snapped open. He'd no idea how he'd managed to fall asleep. At some point, he dreamt a silver wolf stalked him through an impenetrable mist. Just before waking, a feeling of imminent peril dug into his semiconscious brain like a tick. Odd. He rarely dreamt at all. Shifting himself into an upright position, he took stock of his companions. First, he looked to Gabriel to be sure the lad was doing his duty. He wasn't, of course. Gabriel was fast asleep, with his dark head tucked into the crook of his arm. Fergus, too, snored beside the fire's dwindling embers. Conor had stopped thumbing his daggers, which never happened unless he had drifted off. Rawly knew he must rouse these fools before the sun broke. They should be well past Bally Lough by afternoon. It wouldn't be long before the Siorai girl's pursuers discovered their little campsite.

Having rested for half the night had already sawed into Rawly's tight schedule. He got up, did his business against a tree, and glanced over his shoulder at the Duch's prodigal daughter. Either the girl had grown weary of struggling or was blissfully insensate. He didn't much care, either way. It wasn't Rawly's place to question the Duch's orders. If Patrick demanded she be hauled back to Bethany in burlap… so be it. She'd put up a good fight, in any case. Everyone knew the Siorai had strange powers. He'd been duly warned not to touch Lady Donahugh casually. Lord Bishop had been implicit on that score when Rawly was hired. Even so, Rawly hadn't expected her to be such a bloody handful. He'd love to see what the girl could do if the numbers had been in her favor.

To subdue her, they'd been forced to strike her; quite a few times, he was sorry to say. She'd set fire to Conor's sleeve, broken three of Fergus' teeth, burned two heavy ropes, and tried to bite off one of Gabriel's ears. Rawly discovered that the Duch's errant daughter was easiest to handle when sound asleep. They'd divested her of her boots because she'd kicked two of them in the face and burned her cloak to ash in her last attempt to escape her bonds. She was exhausting. 'Twas a pity. She was such a tiny thing, despite her gifts. Rawly could never command such indignities to be inflicted upon one of his daughters. He pitied any man that might ever try. Though, he and his lord were different men. Duch Patrick would sacrifice a hundred daughters to achieve the throne of Eire. That was hardly a secret. Lady Una was merely a means to an end for her ambitious father. Rawly didn't much like Patrick, but he was hardly in a place to give his opinion to a man of Donahugh's stature. Better to serve and serve well, for there were few rewards in innocence or integrity.

After retying his stays, Rawly bent to secure the blade at his ankle, which had worked itself partway from his boot. He heard a faint sound— almost a sigh— from the woods behind him. The dagger was in his palm before his eyes came up. Straining his senses, the only sounds he heard were breathing men and the clamor of his own heart. Focusing his gaze on the trees, he scanned the area for a complete turn. Nothing but black forest all around. He couldn't smell anything but evergreen, moss, dried leaves, and smoldering wood. Did he imagine things? Some trick of an overtaxed mind? After a while, he felt a bit foolish. It was probably a bird or other night creature swooping down on its prey. His nerves were coiled so tight that he counted phantoms.

Rawly shook his head and bent to dissemble the campsite. Time was running out. They needed to get on the road.

Bᴇɴ ʜᴀᴅ sᴛᴏᴏᴅ sᴄᴀɴᴛ ɪɴᴄʜᴇs from Rawly for quite a while and hadn't been spied. A thrill coursed through Ben's veins at the revelation. Perhaps he was sobering up? He bloody well hoped so because as the night wore on, he began to realize what a terrible idea this was. He had only his broadsword and a pair of daggers. Usually, when one attempted to rob a gang of criminals, they had help, or at the very least, better weapons. If he didn't get a move on soon, he'd sober up and talk himself out of this altogether. He was too damned hungry to nitpick the details. Also, he was reasonably sure yon girl would prefer not to be tied to a tree any longer.

He slunk closer, eyes raking the camp for something he could *use*. He grinned when they alighted on a worn yew longbow lying atop one of the mercenaries' packs. See? He knew Herne listened when he prayed! Wraith-like, he slid around the campsite toward the heap of piled packs, careful not to disturb so much as a blade of grass. He might have been a leaf blown about on the wind or a shadow flitting from tree to tree. He was the very soul of stealth. The heart of darkness… nay, its master. The girl snorted from behind her gag. She stared directly at him; her brows knitted together in disdain. Ben froze, fingertips inches from the bow's haft. What witchery had she employed to spy him in the dark, silent as a shade?

"Now, this has got to be the queerest thing I ever did see—" Rawly's voice broke in from just beside him. The blood pounded in Ben's ears. Rawly chuckled. "Never heard o'anyone sneakin' up on a Sidhe before. I'd ask if ye was sober, but from the smell, I'd say I have me answer."

Ben straightened, swaying only slightly. The girl made a rude sound in her throat. He frowned at her. The bloody cow could have warned him! Her answering glare was incredulous as if to say, '*How would I do that, you idiot?*'

"If this is a rescue attempt, it's the worst one I ever heard of." Rawly's laugh inspired another from behind him. Conor, too, was awake.

Fantastic, Ben thought. *Next time sleep it off, hero.*

"Or didya come to rob me, maybe?" Rawly asked, his tone taking the hint of an edge. Rawly's sabre rested inches from Ben's throat. It would take but a single thrust to force it through flesh. Conor struggled to his feet over his bedroll but remained several paces away. Ben thought he might dodge past Rawly and smash in his nose… but then, both the boy and the big man stirred. *Damn*. Whatever he was going to do, he'd have to be quick.

"What's tha— holy Chrissakes!" cried Fergus, rocking up to his knees. "Boss! Ye brung him down on us!" He crossed himself.

Rawly muttered something unintelligible. "This one's not a fine elf-lord out for yer blood, Fergie. Not even sure this fella's a Sidhe a'tall. Fathom a guess; I'd say he came here to steal food and supplies from us. Am I right?"

Ben realized he'd been asked a question a tad late. He was too busy doing sums in his head. Four paces to the woods behind him, nine to that fellow Conor with the sharp daggers. Two to the girl, five to the big man who ogled him in abject fear.

"Think what you like," he said, recounting.

"Well, ye could blow me down with a whistle. I've half a mind to let ye take what ye were aimin' for, poor, sad bugger that ye are."

Ben's nostrils flared. Even in Rosweal, which sprouted men like Rawly by the dozen, he was treated with cool, respectful disdain. Men simply did not speak to him this way. *Not ever.* He met Rawly's eye with a caustic scowl.

"Appearances can deceive, don't you agree?"

Conor swore from Rawly's far end. "Shane, be careful there. That big fella… can't say as how, but I know I've seen him before."

Rawly took Ben's measure. "Doubt it."

Gabriel stirred near the girl. "What's happenin,' Da?"

"Nuthin' to worry over, boyo. Ye stay back there."

"But, Da—"

"I said, stay back!" hollered Rawly, taking a firmer grip on his sabre.

Ben knew what was coming. Though he'd made a hilarious botch of his entrance, there would be no talking his way out of the situation now. These men would have to kill him, even if they didn't want to. He'd seen them with the girl. That suited Ben just fine. He came here to pick a fight.

"Conor—" Rawly began, but Ben ducked under his arm, too fast to follow. He rolled for the longbow he spied earlier. Mercifully, its quiver rested just beneath. It wasn't full, but four arrows would be plenty. Rawly lunged forward as expected, sabre raised for a high slash over Ben's shoulders. Ben twisted himself nearly double to avoid it. Shifting his weight onto his heels, he rocked back, using the longbow's butt as a lance. It shot out, taking Rawly first on the chin, which sent him skittering backward, then hard in the center of his chest. Rawly yelped as his spine crunched into hard-packed earth. About five paces from the girl, Ben nocked and knelt low. The bow was taller than his kneeling form and took some extra effort to draw. He flipped it crosswise to level it with his shoulder span. Arrows had a greater impact that way. "Don't move an inch further."

Rawly went still as a stone. Ben crab-walked the last few feet to the girl, keeping his bowstring taut. From the corner of his eye, he watched Conor slide around the fire, his hands hovering near his belt. Fergus, on the other hand, squeaked like a frightened rabbit. Rawly's boy faded into the trees on Ben's left; hands raised high. No matter, Ben must only worry about their leader for now.

"'Spose I should apologize for mockin' ye?" acknowledged Rawly dryly. A thick trickle of blood ran down his chin. Ben didn't answer. "If the girl is yer concern, she's not worth the trouble. She stole some o'the master's silver. Takin' her home for a whippin.'"

"Let's pretend that you and I are both intelligent men. I'll give you one chance to clear out of here. The girl stays."

Conor set his feet; both hands crept toward partially concealed blades. As for Fergus, the look on his face broadcast that he hadn't yet decided if he should run or stand and fight. A good thing too. Fergus was twice as wide as Ben. If he weren't an obvious simpleton, he would be a serious challenge, all by himself.

"There are four of us. Yer alone. That's a sure bet, I'll warrant," said Rawly. The timbre of his voice hinted at a secreted fear. Not only had he not expected something like this to happen, but he was also unprepared for its outcome. "I'll let ye keep that bow and even a few coins if ye walk away now."

"Part like old mates?"

"Why not? Stranger things have happened."

"Not in my experience, Southerman." As soon as Ben lowered his bow, that scrawny arachnoid behind Rawly would send one of those thin blades sailing into his throat. That is if Rawly failed to cut him in half with his sabre first.

"Well then," sighed Rawly. "Can't say I didn't try."

Two things happened at once. Rawly shouted an alert to the group, and Conor jerked aside to throw a dagger. Ben snaked his upper body out of its path and twisted around, firing his first arrow into Conor's dominant hand. The spider shrieked like a diving bird. Ben nocked and fired the second arrow into his thigh, right into the knee joint. Yowling, Conor went down beside the firepit. In the meantime, Fergus sprang at Conor as if to shield him. Instead, he tripped over his bedroll. His chin slammed into the ground, hard. Fresh piss clouded the air around him as he whimpered into the dirt.

With an enraged howl, Rawly pitched himself at Ben. Ben side-stepped his first thrust and bent at the waist to tug his nose away from the next slash. Snarling, Rawly hefted his sabre for another wild swing. Too fast for Rawly to track, Ben, reached out and struck him in the face with the butt of his bow. Dark blood spurted from Rawly's busted nose. Grunting, he slashed blindly to keep Ben at a distance while he struggled to wipe his streaming eyes. Rawly's face was a horrible mask of blood and wrath, but he lacked the strength and speed to maintain a proper defense. Ben's third arrow burst through Rawly's skull, directly between the eyes. The arrow's point exploded from the back of his head; bits of brain and bone splashed to the ground beneath him. Rawly's last sight was of the earth rushing toward his face as he fell.

A rustling near the fire spun Ben back around. With a roar, Fergus bounded over on all fours like a lumbering bear. His massive hands stretched up to yank Ben down by his calves, dragging deep runnels in the earth. Knowing he was done for if the big fellow got his arms around him, Ben struck out with the broad haft of the bow, putting everything he had into the stroke. Thankfully, Fergus' windpipe cracked like a reed. He careened backward, eyes darting around like a frightened rodent. His cheeks went purple from lack of oxygen. He choked to death on his own blood.

Ben felt something whistle past his ear. Several strands of silver hair departed with it. Without looking up, he fired his last arrow into Conor's chest. Twitching, Conor dropped the blade he'd intended to throw next. It splashed uselessly into the dirt. Ben strode over and jerked the arrow from his ribcage. A widening pool of gore spread beneath the man's knees. There was a lascivious cruelty in Conor's eyes that Ben did not care for. Who knew how many innocents Ben might have saved by putting an end to him tonight? A hissing breath rattled out of Conor's closing throat. Ben dug the remaining daggers out of the mercenary's cloak. There were many.

"I suppose you're wondering why I didn't put this arrow between your eyes as I did your boss?"

Speechless, Conor glared defiantly up at his murderer.

"I've seen eyes like yours a thousand times before." Ben spared the girl a glance. Her jaw set, hard. The bruises around her eyes and mouth said it all. "Your boss didn't strike me as the sort to do that to a woman. That's your handiwork, is it not?"

With the hatred on Conor's face— the sadistic tilt to his mouth, the empty vacuum of his eyes; Ben had his answer. Without ado, Ben took the daggers he'd collected and jammed them one by one into Conor's guts. The spider died without much fuss. Before Ben had time to sigh in relief, he heard a shuffling sound behind him. The boy. He turned.

Gabriel trembled, not ten paces away. Strong, cold moonlight shone through the thinning canopy overhead. The lad's features were pale and soft-cheeked. He stared vacantly at his father's remains as if his mind couldn't register any other sight in the world. "Da…"

Something dark rustled in the depths of Ben's limited conscience. This fate was more or less what Rawly would have received at the hands of Tairnganeah or any other pursuant force. Yet, the heartbreak on the lad's face shifted something at Ben's center. Sobbing, Gabriel ran a hand over his tousled hair. He reached into his belt for his dagger. Ben tensed. The arrow he'd reclaimed from Conor's corpse was nocked and waiting.

"Don't, boy," he pleaded. "Your father deserved what he got. Don't add your death to his litany of failures. What was wrought here today was the only end he would ever carve out for himself. Do you understand?"

"Dunno about that. Ol' Paddy ordered me Da to get her. He don't leave much choice, ye know," said Gabriel. A bead of sweat slithered down Ben's collarbone. The bodies were already beginning to attract flies from the bog.

"There is always a choice, lad. I know of what I speak."

"Yer awful preachy, for a murderer," he said. "I went to school, ye know? Learned all about you Dannans and yer Fir Bolg cousins. All that gold in yer ear means yer a noble, don't it?"

Smart kid.

"Doesn't matter who I am."

The strange smile again. "Why do ye look like that if yer a noble?"

Too clever by half.

"Go home. Take whatever you need to get there but go. I beg you." The tension in the atmosphere swelled to bursting. Gabriel pulled himself as tall and straight as his meager height would allow. Grasping his dagger, he bared his teeth at Ben.

"Ye should have walked on, ye know?"

Ben's hand moved on the bow of its own accord. "Gabriel, stop. Please, don't make me shoot you."

"Ye know, it's funny. Always wanted to meet one o'yer kind," Gabriel sobbed. "It just… ain't fair." With an adolescent scream that Ben would hear in his sleep for years to come, possibly forever, Gabriel charged.

Ben had no choice but to let fly. The force of the impact sent the boy sailing into the oak behind him. His back hit the trunk with such force that Ben heard something snap inside his chest. He sputtered for a moment but lay still, silent too soon. Ben lowered his bow, unsure of the emotions roiling through him. He'd never killed someone so young before. He tried to tell himself that it was probably for the best. Gabriel's father had been a mercenary with skewed morals. The boy had undoubtedly been headed into the same societal breach. Ben told himself this, though deep down, he believed that each man might choose his destiny. The boy could have made a different choice had their paths not crossed this night. Gabriel's vacant eyes stared up into the moonlit sky, his mouth agape as if in wonder. Ben pried the arrow from his ribcage with a resigned sigh.

He'd done what he must.

For a while, he almost believed himself too.

Having exhausted his last ounce of strength, Ben fell upon the remnants of the mercenaries' meal like a starving wolf. There wasn't much left but thank the Gods; it was still warm. Heedless of the blood and filth coating his fingers, he tore into the charred meat with relish. He didn't even bother to chew. Cramming mouthfuls of muscle, gristle, and tendon down his throat at breakneck speed, he barely noticed the girl grunting at him from her tree. Still swaddled to her waist in burlap, she thrashed about, her eyes, two accusatory white beads.

Ah, he thought.

I nearly forgot about you.

Looking around, he spotted the waterskin across the firepit. Tearing another hank of mouth-watering venison from the bone, he shuffled over to pick it up, still chewing. She kicked out at him as he approached and muttered something unflattering around her gag. He unstoppered the vessel and tossed a fair amount into his overfull mouth with a sigh. Licking his fingers, he leaned over to remove her gag. She drew in a deep breath as if she meant to give him a piece of her mind, but he jammed the waterskin's beak into her mouth instead. Sputtering, she coughed up a good portion before basic human need took over.

When he felt satisfied she'd drunk her fill, he removed the skin from her mouth and replaced its stopper. Again, she sucked in a lungful of air to protest, but he swiftly replaced her gag. She thrashed, bucked, and screeched behind the soiled cloth like a newborn eaglet.

"Wait right there, mistress," he said, swallowing another enormous mouthful of meat. Dodging dead men and their puddles of oozing fluids, he gathered arrows, pocketed daggers, coins, and any other supplies he could stuff into his vest. All the while, the girl vowed bloody murder from behind her gag. Rummaging through what he assumed was Rawly's pack, he threw a glorious oiled sealskin cloak over his shoulders with a relieved sigh. The expensive garment boasted a wool-lined interior and a deep, comfortable cowl. It didn't smell very nice, but then again, neither did he. For the girl, a second, smaller cloak from Gabriel's pack and a quilted blanket to tug up beneath it. From skinny, diminutive Conor's feet, he prized a workable pair of boots. They would serve.

When he dropped his findings at her feet, she muttered invectives that he could scarcely comprehend. She must have realized by now he wasn't interested in anything she meant to shout at him, surely?

Kneeling, he wrenched the bag off her lower body. He took a seat on her legs to hold them down. She grimaced dramatically when he tugged each boot over her bare feet. They were a bit big and reeked of dead mercenary, but they were warm, and warm meant she would keep her toes. Next, he tossed the small, fur-lined woolen cloak over her shaking shoulders and tucked the blanket around her legs. She uttered so many foul things behind the obstruction that spittle ran down her chin. He stomped to the fire and stuffed a few more handfuls of meat into his mouth and several more into his pockets. When he returned, he laid two greasy piles on her lap. She gave him a look that should have boiled his guts to broth. Disinterested, he reached behind her to saw at the rope binding her to the elm. Only the topmost layers, mind. She must take responsibility for the latter bit. He slid the handle of one of Conor's daggers into her grasping fist. He pressed her fingers around its grip and laid the waterskin across her knees. She stared up at him in silent accusation.

"Don't look at me like that, mistress," he said, shaking his head. "Shouldn't take you more than an hour to saw through that rope if you get busy." Giving her a mock salute, he moved off. She thrashed around, attempting to shout over her gag. Ignoring her, he discovered one item in his path that he'd nearly overlooked. He whispered a prayer of thanks to every God he knew, as he bent to retrieve the small stone jug of uishge, he spied near the fire. He was grinning again. The girl's mumbled protests faded to a hum behind him.

The Siorai Girl

Ben awoke to the forest creaking around him. *Again.* He pulled a face. A blustery wind whistled through the treetops, dispassionate as a scythe through wheat. Not a single bird sang overhead, nor did anything rustle nearby. The animals in this thicket had better sense than he. Perhaps the numb ringing in his ears finally stirred him, or was it the weight of the ice coating his cloak and collar? If neither, then maybe it was the prickling, lumpy bracken he slept upon— who could say? All he knew for sure was how bloody uncomfortable his accommodations were. His back was stiff as a ship's prow. Every move he made was agony. Gods, even the feeble, waxy bit of light peeking through yon heavy silver clouds made his eyes sting. If his gut weren't churning like the sea in a storm, it would be for the noxious fumes seeping from his clothing, hair, skin, and mouth.

Great Herne.

He was a rising corpse. Without a fire, the little lean-to he'd hastily constructed in the night was hardly protection from the weather's searching fingers. Shaking ice chips from his new sealskin cloak, Ben ran a hand over his grimy face. Just how much had he drunk last night?

Gods… *all day?*

"Rough night?" a piercing voice inquired, penetrating his skull like a hammered nail. He spun round to face the speaker, who perched on a nearby rock staring down her grubby nose at him. Head swimming, stomach sloshing, he tripped over his own clumsy feet into the frozen grass below. There she sat, with his dagger dangling nonchalantly from her right hand. The Tairnganese girl had an intense, judgmental sort of disapproval on her face. Ben frowned. What in the hells was *she* doing here? Hadn't he left her tied to a tree some miles in the opposite direction?

"How'd you get here?" he gagged down a greasy surge of bile. Just opening his mouth to speak was risky.

"Walked. Same as you."

"I didn't realize they taught woodcraft in the Cloister?"

"A child could have followed your trail last night," she snorted, rolling her eyes. "You made enough noise to rouse half of Eire. I don't know how far you planned to go, but we're less than half a mile from where you left me."

He watched her tap the flat of the blade against her knee. The scowl on her dirty little mouth would unsettle a troll.

"I see. Come to kill me, then?"

"Thought about it for a bit. You snore, you know? Like a bloody boar. I suppose you dispelled many of my notions concerning the Sidhe last night."

A direct hit.

"Sorry to disillusion you, mistress. Now, is there anything else I can do for you before you slog off?" He would throttle her if she didn't stop tapping that bloody dagger soon. The repetitive racket made his gums throb. All this talking was murder. His voice made the pressure in his head feel like someone was attempting to squeeze his brains through a vice. In no mood for company, he figured now was as good a time as any to get going.

She cocked her head at him. "Don't you want to know whom you killed last night? Who I am?"

"No," Ben grimaced. "Not my bloody business. You should save your breath. I have places to be, so—" he waved her away with his right hand and struggled to his feet. Bones creaked, and joints popped all the way up. Why did he feel like he'd aged a thousand years in a single night?

The girl didn't budge. Her eyes were steady: calculating, estimating.

"What, damn you? I have nothing to share. No food, no drink," he swallowed, his throat dry as vellum, "and no interest in your problems. I did you a favor last night because I was drunk, and it seemed like a good idea at the time. The way I see things, we're square."

She considered him for several tense moments while he limped about his little makeshift camp, gathering what few items he had left. "I can pay you."

"You don't know how to get home?" He raised a silver brow at her, pleased to watch her flush. Tairnganese women were notorious for their independence. In fact, their entire society was built on the absurd notion that females were the superior sex. Bollocks and nonsense, of course, but no concern of his. He made it a habit to keep as far away from the Red City as he could manage. He was sure 'Ben Maeden' had a hefty bounty awaiting him there. Danu only knew what the Cohort might do to him if they saw him as he was now. Without his ogham charm, no city along the border would likely roll out the red carpet for him. His best bet was to make it to Ten Bells as fast as possible and buy one from the Sidhe Consulate. Aside from lurking in the Greensward for the foreseeable future, he didn't have many attractive options. Though, there was a man he'd known many years ago who might be able to help him.

Arthur Guinness didn't live far. Ben intended to make for his farmstead first. Failing that, he'd have no choice but to trek down to Ten Bells. As unattractive as the prospect was, he would commit himself to it if necessary. What he was not prepared to do, however, was babysit a Tairnganese brat who should be thankful to be alive. Ungrateful wretch. He didn't appreciate her haughty stare in the least.

"In theory, *yes*," she enunciated. "But I don't know what to expect between here and there. It'd be safer if we traveled together. For both of us, I expect."

"Not interested." He spared her a curt nod. "Pleasant journey, then." He waggled his fingers at her as he ambled onto the path and away from his camp.

"I can pay you your weight in fainne!"

He paused, turning back. "Do you have any of that gold on you now?"

She stammered, gulping air like a goldfish. "Of course, I don't! But—"

"That's too bad." He pointed. "Tairngare is that way, milady. Brida's luck upon you!" Plugging his ears against the litany of curses she spewed behind him, Ben marched toward his purpose with nary a backward glance.

⚲ ⚲

In Navan Village, torrents of freezing Dor Samna rain rushed through the muddy lanes at his feet. Ben waited for dusk before entering the town; his cowl pulled low over his face and hair. He was thankful for Rawly's big, shapeless cloak. It would serve so long as no one bothered to peer too deeply into the hood. When the sun disappeared over the Western Hills, he could safely stroll into the inn across the street.

Two days out in the wind and cold were plenty. The sign over the entrance bore two arrows crossed at their hafts, points skyward. *Bowman's Cross*, the sign read: a typically Norther title. Navan wasn't as rough as Rosweal but didn't lack for ne'er-do-wells or questionable characters intent on their privacy. Folk shouldn't be quick to ask questions in a dive like this. He hoped, anyway. He'd had his fill of waking up covered in ice and filth and could do with a dry bed and a hot meal. When thick shadows stretched between buildings, he shrugged his cloak close and splashed into the downpour. He could only pray the *Cross* had more to offer than porridge or gruel. A hearty stew would warm his bones better than a nice dram of uishge. Well, almost. Just as his boot struck the tavern's jamb, a host of fully armored Tairnganeah marched down the opposite intersection. Fat raindrops pattered against their black and gold armor. He watched them trudge past until they disappeared around a far corner. His hand frozen against the door handle, he let out a breath he hadn't realized he'd been holding.

That was somewhat unexpected. Tairngare's martial corps didn't often patrol this far west and rarely within town limits. In Rosweal, soldiers didn't dare march beyond the Navan Gate— the Guild would pick them off from the rooftops like grouse. Rosweal rejected governance of any stripe. Woe to anyone who meant to prove otherwise. Navan might not reside under the Greenmakers' protection, but even so, she was a long way from the Red City. He wondered what Tairnganeah were doing in this insignificant little village on the rim of the Greensward anyway. The only explanation he could surmise was that they searched for that blasted girl. As he thought, she must be some important noblewoman's spawn to warrant such concern. He wished them luck but kept well out of sight.

Pulling his cowl low as it would go, he discovered a renewed appreciation for Navan's poorly lit lanes. There weren't many who could afford tallow candles in Navan, far fewer proper oil lamps. The streets were almost always dark, wet, and treacherous. Most lanes lacked cobbles or even wooden planking to break up the sluicing drainage that plagued each intersection in a downpour. Residents here made do with one-quarter of the luxury Roswellians were accustomed to, which wasn't saying much.

For example, the *Bowman's Cross* didn't boast *The Hart*'s fine glass windows or even a fraction of her light fixtures. There might have been five scrapped candles burning within the whole of the windowless, dank little structure.

Shoving the door open, a blast of poorly ventilated peat smoke, body odor, rotted cabbage, and flat moldering ale rushed into Ben's face. Eyes watering, he coughed his way to the bar, which was essentially four un-sanded boards propped over two rotting ale barrels. As he suspected, the taproom was silent as a kirkyard. Various patrons were scattered around a few rickety tables gathered before the hearth. No one looked up as he entered; all were seemingly as desirous of anonymity as he was, their hands wrapped around wooden tankards, hoods pulled deep, eyes resolutely forward. This was just the sort of establishment he'd hoped for. The innkeeper didn't look up when Ben took a seat and set two coppers down on the bar. He was a large fellow; his pocked cheeks sagged into a grizzled, graying beard, and he had a frown that could cleave stone.

"Ale," Ben said, his tone casual. The silent innkeeper slid the coin into his palm, then turned to fill a clean tankard. The right sort of place for Ben, indeed. Sliding his mug over, Ben placed two more coppers on the bar. "Came to ask where I can buy a horse and supplies? Maybe a room for the night, if ye have vacancy?"

Again, the innkeeper scraped the coins into his palm without investigating their donor. He had the attitude of a man who was used to answering, rather than asking, questions.

"Have a room at the rear o'the buildin', top o'the stairs. Nuthin' fancy. A bed and dry beddin.' Not the cleanest, nor the biggest spread. Six coppers, and it's yers."

Ben reached into his vest for more coin. "A meal, if ye have that as well?"

"Two more coppers," said the innkeeper. "For a silver, ye'll have yer choice of nag from me own stables out back there and two bowls o'porridge with bread and cheese. Ye want more ale or uishge? Pay as ye go. Fair?"

"Fair indeed. Thanks." Ben's stomach grumbled at the promise of hot food and warm ale. He didn't mind that it was bound to be tasteless mash. Anything would do. The proprietor tossed down the cloth he'd been wiping mugs with, then disappeared through a small doorway toward his dimly lit kitchen. Ben sank into his shadowy corner, keeping his back against a mildewed wall.

When the innkeeper returned, he carried a steaming bowl of grey shapeless mush, topped with a massive crust of hard bread and a half-wheel of greenish cheese. He set a wooden spoon beside the bowl, no knives for the bread. In the North, folk ate bread and cheese with their fingers. If meat needed cutting to chew, it was expected that one produce their own cutlery.

Ben laid into this bounty with a blissful sigh. The porridge was surprisingly palatable despite its underwhelming appearance. Bringing out a second helping, the innkeeper was visibly pleased someone appreciated his cooking. Ben was confident he could win a third bowl for a few colorful compliments.

Behind him, at a small table beside the hearth, he overheard two men having a rather heated political debate. One had the look of a constable, or perhaps a lamplighter, even though there weren't many lamps to light in Navan. He was some sort of town official, from the emblem sewn into his coarse woolen coat.

"Ain't what I heard," he was saying. "I heard ole Drem and that Nema woman have come to blows in Parliament over this."

"Nah, we was at market three days ago, and I'm tellin' ye, the Doma's forcin' a bill through. Nema's not got the clout in the Cloister that she do in the Commons. It'll pass," said the other fellow, puffing on a hornpipe.

The town official pursed his lips, blowing air out of his nostrils. "Aye, that's nepotism, that is. Parliament won't stand for it. Lady Nema is second in the Cloister and holds more power with the folk than them grand Mouras in the Citadel. The Merchers will vote it into oblivion."

"Olly, ye know how these things work. Parliament 'tis naught but a dog and pony show for the mob. Drem Moura's been Doma for near a half-century. She didn't bother about the law twenty years ago, and I'm sure she ain't worried 'bout it now."

"Has it been two decades already?"

"More. Closer to thirty years, by me reckonin.'"

Olly, the official, took a long pull from his tankard, a dubious expression on his wind-lined face. "I don't think as ye should count Ole Nema out, Dan. She's been fightin' for us wee folk for as long as I can recall. None o' us want any more religious twiddle-twaddle crammed down our throats. If Parliament can't stop the Doma, the Commons will revolt. I'm sure o' it."

"I think yer underestimatin' how much power the Cloister holds in the Red City. There's been a Moura Doma all me life… nigh a full century, if ye trace it back to my Grandda's time. Ye don't gather such power and just let it go, now do ye? Drem's done it before, and I'm tellin' ye, she'll do it again."

Olly swore a host of foul-mouthed oaths into his tankard. "Just ain't right. Me mam was Siorai, and so is me wife. It ain't that I don't believe, I just don't see as them Moura should run things as they used to. We're an open-minded sort o'folk, ye know? Laws should give all o'us a chance at a better life… not just them ole hags in the Cloister and them toity bitches in Parliament. But what do I know, eh? I'm just a bloody *male*."

"If that ain't the truth," Dan toasted with a self-depreciative smirk. "Still, don't see as it'll affect us much out here in the townships. They can make whichever Moura cunt they want a queen, and it won't make a lick o'difference here, will it? Life don't change for those o'us actually works for a bloody livin'—"

Ben tuned out. He wouldn't trade a tinker's fart for Eirean politics. He didn't care which self-important ass sat in whatever symbolic chair; it was all smoke in the breeze to him. Milesian governments were cyclical and predictable as the tides. When one ruling class rose, another fell, and on it would go, so long as people walked the earth. Power was viciously fought for, imperiously wielded, and jealously guarded. A merry farce, which Ben eschewed at all costs. He preferred to keep well out of the cities so he wouldn't be subjected to this opera of short-sighted, rhetorical fallacy.

There was only one true king in Innisfail. Midhir did not concern himself with the political pantomime in Milesian Eire. These fools may argue over this or that city's social constructs and governing classes until their bones crumbled to ash. Midhir had been Ard Ri for almost a thousand years and would be High King long after their grandchildren's grandchildren faded from memory.

Ben finished his second bowl of porridge, then withdrew his belt knife to work on the bread and cheese. When the innkeeper came to collect his discarded crockery, Ben tossed two more coppers his way.

"More ale, and I'll have a snort o'that uishge ye mentioned before."

"Aye, sir." He warmed to Ben's coin, if not Ben himself. While he poured, Ben leaned closer. "I was wonderin' if ye might know a man used to live round these parts some years back?"

"I 'spose I know most folk who do. What's his name then?"

Ben realized he was breaking his moratorium against asking questions, but he didn't want to waste a day's ride if he didn't have to. "Man, by the name of Guinness. A doctor or was. He's an old friend. Ain't been in these parts for some time and wondered if I should drop by for a visit?"

"Aye, I know him. Ole feller, with that faerie woman," he spat into the rushes. "Friend o'yers, ye say?"

Ben cleared his throat. He was thankful his hood hid most of his features from view. Northers didn't care for half-breeds like Arthur's wife. Faeries were Sidhe half-breeds, and often, the blood mixture wasn't ideal. They tended to be off-putting physically or overly weak or aggressive, sometimes mad as a rabid dog. Come to think of it, they weren't well-regarded anywhere in Innisfail but especially not in the North, where they were most common. Poor buggers. They were hardly at fault for the misconceptions of others. Ben curbed the rebuke coiling on his tongue. Without an ogham stone, he would receive no better treatment in a backwater like Navan.

"That's the one," Ben said, taking care to keep his tone light. "Made a tonic for me missus that soothed her nasty cough for a time. I thought to drop in for a second dram. He still got a stall in town?"

The innkeeper relaxed. "Ah, well, no. Keeps to himself o'late. Me Martha thought he was likely ailin' hisself… what with that woman's passin,' some while ago. Still sells potions and other cures from home, though, last I heard. Ye remember how to get there, then?"

"Aye," Ben passed him another copper for his trouble. Innish tradition. "I do, and thank ye. Two more snorts o'that uishge, if ye please, and I'll head up to sleep. Top o'the stairs to the right, ye said?"

"Yep," the barkeep answered, happily supplying Ben with generously poured libations. He probably wasn't used to patrons who didn't haggle over fair prices and was pleased to return the favor. "I'll have me boy set ye up with our best nag in the morn. A goodnight to ye, sir."

Ben polished off his two shots. He gathered his cheese and his tankard in hand. "Many thanks for the food and hospitality." He tipped the edge of his cowl at the grinning innkeeper and made his way upstairs.

⚜

Ben rose before the sun, well-rested and eager to be on his way. He didn't want to risk being seen in full daylight without the benefit of his ogham charm. Guinness' farmstead was only ten miles or so southwest of Navan. It would take him a couple of hours to get there, no matter which way he went. No need to hurry. He could only hope that Aednat left some of her charms in Arthur's keeping when she passed.

He was sad to hear of it. He hadn't known many faeries before or after his time in Eire began. Aednat was the first of a small few. He was ashamed to acknowledge that both sides of the border suffered from the same cruel preconceptions where half-breeds were concerned. Aednat was a sweet girl, gentle and quick with a smile. She was also one of the most beautiful women he'd ever had the fortune to meet. She'd quite stopped him in his tracks the first time he'd laid eyes upon her. Despite her twisted arm and slightly malformed fingers, she had pure, sky-blue eyes, pale cornsilk hair, and a lovely neck. If Arthur, assigned to one of Ben's units all those years ago, hadn't commanded every corner of her heart, Ben might have stolen her away. She was a good woman. He'd never heard her utter an unkind word to anyone, even when they deserved it.

The air outside held a bite that could leave a mark. Ben jerked his cloak tight over his chest, tucking his ears deep into his wool-lined cowl. Bloody weather. Perhaps once he had a new charm, he'd winter in Ten Bells after all? Ben Maeden could find work anywhere. There were Guilds aplenty in the city. Might he exchange his loathing of cosmopolitan life for fine ale, more refined dining, and warm, properly insulated apartments? He would be free to decide soon enough. Maybe it was time to move past the Greensward for a few years? He wondered why the very idea felt so wrong.

A person he assumed was the proprietor's son stomped into the stable, carrying two large hay bales over each shoulder. He spied Ben waiting by the door.

"Ah, hello, sir. Got yer mount ready for ye here." He led Ben to the second to last stall. A decent middle-aged mare stood inside, awaiting her breakfast with a sloe-eyed glare. The burly, red-cheeked lad set some hay in her trough, then moved along her flanks to check her saddle straps. "This here's Vixen. She's a smart, loyal lass, she is. She don't run so fast no more on account o'her age and all, but she'll get ye where yer headed sure and steady. Just... if ye don't mind me sayin' so, take it easy on her? I'd be much obliged. She were me mam's favorite."

"I will, lad. Ye have me word." Ben meant it; he didn't love many things in this world, but he did hold a soft spot for animals. That was his mother's doing, right enough. Ben stuck out a palm, allowing her to snuffle his fingers.

"See! She likes ye. Well, that's good enough for me, then. She's a picky lass. Me Da chose her for ye cause she's our tallest nag. He did say ye was a big fella, so—" The lad handed Ben a bundle with another hunk of bread and a generous slice of cheese. "That's from me Da, too. He says to thank ye for yer patronage and to come back whenever yer in these parts. He'll give ye half rates at yer next visit."

"Most generous. Thank him for me, will ye boy?"

Nodding, the stable lad patted Vixen's flank. "Will there be anythin' else, sir?"

"Actually," said Ben. "Is there a haberdashery in town or some other shop that sells tack and the like?"

The boy pointed him toward a building two lanes over. Ben thanked him, hitched his pack to Vixen's saddle, and took his leave.

⚹ ⚹

He spent maybe ten minutes in the haberdashery. He bought a second-hand tunic of heavy rough-spun wool, a fur-lined vest, and a new linen undershirt, which he tucked into a pair of thick, sealskin trousers. A good deal warmer than he had been when he entered the shop, he left sporting a newish pair of high, boiled leather riding boots. He also purchased arrows for his empty quiver, a pot and kettle, two pouches of strong black tea, and two heavy blankets— one for himself and one for Vixen, who wasn't used to roughing it outdoors. All told, it was a successful venture. Like the Bowman's Cross proprietor, the shopkeeper was only too pleased for the polite patronage.

Well, Ben did enjoy being appreciated.

This was one thing Navan had over Rosweal. If it weren't for the women, the porter, the uishge, and the company… he could very well mark Navan higher in his esteem. The shopkeeper had seemed so happy to be making a sale of this size that he didn't mind waking at dawn to open his doors. Like most folks Ben encountered in Navan, he did not ask impertinent questions. If Ten Bells weren't his next destination, maybe Navan would be a good place to hang his proverbial hat.

Ben was pleased with himself when he rode out of town. After five miles on the Navan High Road, he would turn south at the tiny village of Keller, then ride on for a further five. The road to Ferndale, where Arthur lived, was narrow and much less traversed. He'd feel more comfortable in broad daylight once he was off the High Road. About two miles outside of Navan, he noticed a peculiar amount of activity through the trees around the next bend. He tugged on Vixen's reins. There were mounted men up ahead, at least six of them. From the color of their cuirasses, there could be no mistaking their identity. Another Tairnganeah patrol. Corsairs, to be precise: Special Light Cavalry. Ben's brows knit together. What now? He moved Vixen into the woods on the North side as quietly as he could manage.

Dismounting, he crept forward on foot, taking care to muffle his steps. Whatever they were doing here, he doubted they'd be pleased to discover a fully armed Sidhe archer on the road. Assured that he couldn't be seen or heard, he crept closer to get a better look. The Corsairs advanced upon a small, unarmed quarry. Their spears at the ready, they backed the figure into the trees. She held a single dagger in a shaking, bleeding fist. Ben cursed long and low under his breath. Of course, it was that bloody, troublesome girl! With her clenched teeth flashing white against the mud crusting her face, she slashed wildly at anything that came near. Ben shook his head, intending to head in the opposite direction, but made the mistake of taking a last glance over his shoulder. He stopped cold. The first rider, most likely the commander, barked a curt order. Two of his men lobbed long spears at the Tairnganese girl as if she were a boar they hunted for sport. She dodged the first. The second sliced through her side on its way past. She cried out, tearing back into the trees. As if she could outrun four mounted Corsairs.

They pursued.

She did not get far.

THE RED CITY

Aoife grew bored of this sycophantic display: the bowing, the scraping, the affectation of reverence. The endless fog of heady incense turned her stomach. Its cloying stench singed the back of her throat from dawn to dusk each day. Worse, the silence within the microcosmic hive they called the Cloister of the Eternal Flame was smothering. A person could wander its halls for twenty-four hours without hearing a single voice, save for those inside their head. As if the heat, stench, and cavernous silence weren't enough— there was little reprieve from one's thoughts. No escape. No respite. This fortress was a prison, despite the wealth and prestige of its prisoners. No one of her rank and position was free to come and go as they pleased. She must remain behind the Citadel's stifling walls lest she lose the standing she'd striven for.

As a Prima, Aoife could move from the bottom near the Initiates' spartan cells to the sumptuous Eighth floor at will— but no further. She could not depart the Cloister without express permission from on high. Thus, the city piling around the Citadel might have been a thousand miles away for all the distraction it afforded her. To gain the privilege to come and go as Aoife pleased, she must climb literally and figuratively. Only an Alta Prima had total agency over her own body. Therefore, sponsorship from higher castes was the simplest way to rise in the Cloister. Women who passed the Eighth Ordeal could ascend higher than the Primas' Eighth Floor, but one must prove her worth to do so. Most would fail and return to their families as very wealthy women. Some would rise to the level of Prima, but no higher. Many would never step foot outside the Cloister again. Like the Unknowable Tenth Law, the Tenth Floor was forbidden to all but the Doma herself.

Aoife was fortunate to hold the sponsorship of the great Vanna Nema. Nema was second only to the Doma in power. Differing from most Altas on the Council, she was favored by the people, being the sole representative for Parliament in the Cloister. Aoife was Nema's right hand with all accordant honors, such as they were. Unlike most girls who entered the Cloister at age five or six, Aoife didn't submit to the First Ordeal until she was already an adult. As a result, many in the Cloister viewed her with equal parts suspicious jealousy and respectful fear. Siorai twice her rank, believed she held a singular gift. Because of this, she must always guard her back. The Cloister of the Eternal Flame was not a welcoming place for those with natural talent, especially those who lacked the proper family names.

Nema was herself an outsider to the Tairnganese aristocracy. Her origins were reputed to be common, and her name new to the Citadel's Registry. Nema was an enigma, one that challenged convention at every turn. Despite this, or perhaps because of it, Nema's star was ascendant in the Cloister, whilst the Doma's had been waning for decades. Her influence with the Commons had much to do with this upset to the natural order. Without the support of the masses, the Doma's hold on the reins of power waned by the day.

The government was designed to operate as a theocratic democracy, but that was also changing. Parliament ran the day-to-day affairs of the City, its colonies, and its citizenry via its two warring houses: the Libella and the Union of Commons. The Libella featured only scions of Tairnganese nobility. None without a Patent of Maternas could gain entry into this esteemed collective of noblewomen. On the other hand, the Union was for educated people of the Merchanta and Agrean classes, into which any class was welcomed. Above these, but without direct access to the people, was the Cloister of the Eternal Flame and its Council of Nine. Parliament wrote and decided whichever laws could be presented to the Holy Order in the Cloister but had limited power to gainsay directives from on High. Nema currently strove to repeal another of Drem's high-handed directives.

Drem intended to put her granddaughter forth as a second puppet Queen. Nema had spent decades stoking foment against the Moura for heretical tyranny since Drem's first attempt at regal dynasty. With the support of the people, Nema was winning her argument too. The merchants, farmers, guildsmen, artisans, and laborers: all adored Vanna Nema. The nobles, however, were a different story.

On her way to the Grand Arcade, where Parliament was about to convene, Aoife dodged courtiers, clerical Secundas, Cloister stewards, servitors, Academians, and Citadel Cohorts in their black and gold breastplates. The halls were stuffed to bursting with people, a far cry from the quiet isolation upstairs in the Cloister. She often had to press herself into the walls to avoid collisions. A multitude of hands reached out to stall her, and voices were raised with incessant and impertinent questions.

One fellow, an overweight Agrean Exciseman, jogged to keep up with her.

"My Lady Sona," he said, his breath short. "When can we expect Alta Nema's address?"

"In due course, Master Birna." She brushed past him. But he was barely shoved aside before another pest took his place. This one, a self-important Judge's clerk dipped in the colors of House Tenma. Aoife wrinkled her nose. The Tenmas were almost as bad as the bloody Mouras.

"My lady! Will she order a purge of the Cohort? Judge San will want to know!" Aoife swerved and turned the next corner, striding swiftly past the gilded floor-to-ceiling windows. An oiled steward with many fat gems winking on each stubby finger caught at her sleeve.

"Do tell Lady Nema that we are expecting an answer to our—"

Aoife shrugged her arm free and continued forward at twice the speed. People oozed from corners, doorways, and alcoves, frantic to impede her progress. So far, every Judge's effort to assuage public outcry was met with raucous jeering from the mob gathering outside. Noblewomen generally did not go missing in the Red City. The fact that both victims in the past quarter century were Dominas of the Moura clan was not lost on anyone. Primas did not wander from the Citadel on their own, and they certainly did not attempt to flee, scions of the powerful Moura family, especially. The whole affair smacked of treason at worst, or at best, rank incompetence.

Prima Moura had been missing for three days. Already, violence had erupted in the markets and gathering places. Several hunting parties were dispatched to find her, but therein lay the crux of the problem. Many factions in Tairngare believed the Moura girl to be a heretic and her grandmother a charlatan and fraud. No one could be certain if she'd been kidnapped and manipulated by unknown agents or if she'd fled growing political instability in the Cloister. Either way, the event spelled trouble for the Moura Clan. Vocal members of the Union of Commons seized upon the opportunity to further their cause: the unequivocal surrender of Drem Moura and the installation of Vanna Nema as the new Doma. Others sought to hamper the Union's cause by accusing its venerated members of collusion and treason. Despite growing unrest in the city and the Citadel, Nema had been expertly feinting all claimants away. She would not take a side.

Not publicly, anyway.

Aoife found it all quite amusing.

She pushed open the heavy iron door leading into the Grand Arcade. Heat and smoke licked at her eyes. Her ears rang for the noise. Commoners shouted from behind a golden gate and could not be silenced. Their volume was tame compared with the aristocracy. Ladies of the Libella screeched down at the panel of Judges on the dais. Their male relatives squawked from the balcony above. Seated below them in the Arcade, Union members howled scorn up at their social betters, some with spittle dappling their livid cheeks. Judges beat their gavels to splinters, to no avail. It was absolute chaos. Smirking, Aoife slid a scrap of parchment from her robe, crept onto the dais from the rear, and tucked it into Vanna Nema's open palm. As always, Nema sat dead center on the dais. Her shrewd green eyes blazed emerald against the crimson of her Alta robes. On her either side sat eight Parliamentary Judges who'd gone hoarse from trying to bring the Arcade to order. Nema appeared nearly fifty or so years old. Though, she would never admit to whatever age she truly was. Her bearing, beautifully braided grey-black hair, and the regal tilt of her head were hard to ignore, regardless. Nema raised a single elegant eyebrow at Aoife's note but did not reply. Aoife kept her head down as she backed away from the dais. Taking her place beside the door, she kept her eyes held sharp on the Arcade.

"This treachery can have no other author!" bellowed a frequent speaker from his seat in the auditorium's center. Mel Carra, former Master of the Academy, now Union Minority Steward. He shook a meaty fist at the Panel on the dais, his face purple. "Who else would dare to infiltrate the Citadel to reclaim her?"

An ear-splitting chorus of protests and base name-calling exploded over the chamber like gunpowder. A woman from the Libellan Balcony smacked her hands on the banister.

"Lies! You slander our greatest ally in Eire! A good, noble man who has always been true to his word!" Pors Yma shrieked. Her fine silk robes were dyed a brilliant vermillion, the color of her House.

Mel Carra snorted theatrically. "We are all aware that House Yma has its interests in Bethany, madam. We are equally cognizant of the importance you place upon nobility."

"How *dare* you? Your family was scrubbing dockside latrines for coppers while mine paid to build your precious Academy! Upstarts like you are nothing without us, Carra. You forget this at your peril."

Carra bowed. "You are quite right, my lady. What would we Merchers do without the nobles? Tell me, how many years' taxes did anyone in your clan pay, before or since your most generous donation?"

Pors' lips nearly puckered into her spine. "I will have you beaten from the Citadel… whipped through streets like the mongrel you are."

"Ladies and gentlemen, please!" cried two of the Judges at once, each banging their gavels with furious futility.

Eva Alvra stood up next. She was a respectable noblewoman whose second husband brought her family great wealth from his vineyards in Cymru. She once aspired to the title of Alta Prima herself, though she'd failed the Ninth Ordeal. Having retired honorably from the Cloister, she was now the Domina of her House. Her ochre skin and amber eyes were the envy of every woman present save Aoife, who couldn't care less. The Alvras were related by blood to the Mouras. If Aoife had her facts straight, Eva was the Doma's favored niece. This would explain why she tended to take the Doma's side in every Parliamentary meeting.

"I disagree with Lady Yma. One does not require an astronomer to see facts when they are right before their eyes. Of course, Donahugh planned this. Who else benefits more than he? What a coup for him. He's thought of little else since Lady Arrin died!"

The crowd burst into so many banal quarrels that Aoife was obliged to plug her aching ears. Judge Isa Ganon's gavel broke in half. The mob behind the gate all the while called for Drem's word, Siora's Mercy, and justice. Heaving a heavy sigh, Vanna Nema vaulted to her feet. Her red robes painted a blazing exclamation point against her fellow Judges' somber black silk. All eyes gravitated toward her.

Nema fixed the assemblage with a grim smile. "You dishonor yourselves and this Institution with your behavior. Sit down, all of you." Her tone was soft but carried the length and breadth of the chamber. The citizens in the Gallery obeyed first. Most sank to their knees. Aoife rolled her eyes. Nema was second to Drem in the Cloister, but for many of the easily led sheep in the Gallery, she was the most beloved Siorai in Tairngare. "Each of you is the leader of your respective House, Guild, or Establishment. Do you think," her eyes were sharp, "that this infighting and finger-pointing will bring the Doma's grandchild back? Do you suppose petty accusations will allay the people's fear?" She gestured to the myriad faces squeezed into the gate.

Aoife was pleased to watch Pors Yma and Mel Carra resume their seats. Lady Alvra also sat down, her back ramrod straight.

"Now," Nema went on." The Cloister holds this affair as its foremost priority. The Doma commands that you submit to Siora's Word and heed the Judges' decision in this matter."

A murmur passed through the assemblage. A man stood up; he had the look of a merchant from a middling Agrean family. "Begging yer pardon, Lady Nema, but many o'us here have another subject to put before Parliament today."

The silence deepened. Aoife would swear she heard everyone swallow. Alta Nema smiled coldly at the erstwhile speaker. "I know what you would say, Master Hollin. I assure you we will not be discussing such things today."

An outcry issued from behind the gate.

Nema bit her lip, rather than smile, Aoife knew.

"But my Lady!" objected Hollin. "When shall we discuss it, if not now? The people demand to be heard! The Doma reaches too far, and we've—"

Another woman in the Arcade bounced upright. "That is blasphemy!"

Supporters jeered. The women and men in Hollin's camp bawled back.

Hollin finished his statement by raising his voice as many octaves as he could: *"We've had enough o'Moura rule*! This is a democracy, madam! We do not require another puppet Moura Queen! 'Tis sacrilege!"

"Sit down, you!" Mel Carra roared. "Or I will *cut* you down!"

"We'll not be cowed by corrupt nobles nor lickspittle Merchers, what have been in the Moura's pocket for eons. 'Tis time to vote them out. The Doma means to make herself an empress, at OUR expense!" A dozen lawmakers rallied around Hollin for his brave words. Many people tussled on the other side of the gate: Nema's supporters versus the Doma's loyalists. The Libellan nobles in the Arcade threw shoes, papers, and whatever they could find to mark their outrage.

"I SAID BE SEATED!" Alta Nema shouted at the top of her considerable lungs— but it was no use. The mob would not be laid to order. Disgusted, she pulled the red robes of her office tight over her bony shoulders and stormed from the dais. Many gaping, floundering faces surged forward to stop her from leaving. Aoife grinned as she shut the iron door on the lot.

⚓

"You're sure this information is correct?" asked Vanna Nema when they entered her lavish apartments on the Ninth Floor. Long latticed windows, shuttered by white Cmyrian double doors, were gorgeously appointed with five panels of thick mottled glass edged in gold flake. The walls were polished pink granite, as the Cloister was carved from a single slab of rose-hued stone. The city glowed a warm, brilliant red in the light of dawn or sunset. Many referred to Tairngare as the 'Red City' for this phenomenon. In Vanna Nema's chamber on the Ninth Floor, she dressed her share of these walls with many stark tapestries, various paintings and collected artworks, here and there, the odd animal hide. Indeed, the flagstones at their feet were at least four layers deep in gorgeous ornamental carpeting. Her bedchamber was draped everywhere with furs, curtains, and heaped woolen blankets. Vanna Nema did not care for the cold. That was one thing this drafty old fortress had in abundance.

Without knocking, Fawa Gan bowed his way through the door. Aoife hated this little toad more than she hated most everyone else. Holding far too high an opinion of himself, he was rude, snobbish, and greedy. Moreover, Aoife felt sure he'd been skimming Nema's books for years. Not that Nema would mind. There were few people the old witch cared for more than her precious Gan. Aoife had tried many times to get rid of the oily little prick. Each time, Aoife had been the one to suffer for the accusation. Honestly, she had no idea what Nema saw in him. Only women sacred to Siora might ascend higher than Secunda in the Cloister. In Gan's case, males might offer their lifelong service and loyalty to Primas or the Dominas of powerful families. This was the only way a man could rise any higher than the Fifth Floor and therefore install themselves near the fount of power swirling around the Doma. Fawa Gan might expect a seat in Parliament one day for his service.

That is if Aoife couldn't get rid of him first.

"Your Excellency, the Doma has requested your presence at your earliest convenience," Gan whined, in his horrid, nasally drawl. His family had been quite influential in the Libella once upon a time, but they hadn't presented a girl born with any Spark for decades. Therefore, they were underrepresented in the Cloister. The lack of a female heir could have doomed the Gans to exile in the Colonies. Fawa had been their last hope. He was born with just enough Spark to make him appealing to the Novitiate but not enough to propel him to the coveted rank of Secunda. Lucky for them, having hitched himself to Nema almost thirty years before, Gan had risen with her through the ranks. He was an officious, soft-bellied snob, but he got things done. Most of the time, Aoife wanted to spoon his eyeballs out with a spade.

Vanna gave him a long searching look. "She asked that nicely, Gan?"

"Of course not, your Excellency. Her request was peppered with language I shall not repeat, but you gather the gist."

"I do indeed. If you would be so kind, please alert her steward that I will be there before fourth hour is called."

"Yes, your Excellency," he genuflected. "What should I report is the reason for your delay?"

"Do you think 'rampant disinterest' will play well?"

"Sadly, I do not."

Nema rolled a shoulder as if to say, 'well then.' Gan saw himself out without waiting for dismissal. He knew his task better than most. Nema strolled to her banquette and poured herself a tall glass of her favorite Bretagn vintage: a crisp, bubbling white wine that only the Bretagns could produce. Aoife concluded it must be something to do with the soil across the Bretagn Sea. They *did* tend to get more sun and less rain. Nema took a dainty sip of her wine. "You never answered my question. How old is this news?"

"Hours. Less than half a day, at most."

"That damned girl. She has the luck of the Sidhe, I vow," Nema said and popped a dried grape into her mouth. "Do we think she can survive out there alone?"

"She never appeared very resourceful to me. More concerning is who helped her and why."

"The area is rife with poachers and low-born scum of every stripe," sniffed Nema, pouring herself a second glass. "One can only hope this individual is clever enough to sell her back to our agents in Tara or contact us through the usual channels."

Aoife looked away, knowing she would pay dearly for her opinion later. "I wouldn't be sure of that, my lady. Whoever killed the Duch's men did so viciously. My informant vows the scene was a bloodbath— grisly but meticulous."

"A random act of violence, perhaps? Someone who happened upon the scene and decided to intervene for the girl?"

"If so, why not take her? I'm told the larger set of footprints were hours older than hers. This individual seems to have come for Rawly and his men, specifically. Killed each of them, rummaged through their supplies, then departed – leaving Prima Moura to free herself. None of it makes an ounce of sense to me."

"Give me your best guess."

Aoife blew a strong breath over pursed lips. "Robbery, maybe? Perhaps Rawly had a fifth companion he didn't report to us? Perhaps they argued, and the fifth man killed them all in a rage? Who knows?"

"I don't appreciate your glib tone, child."

Aoife flushed. "Forgive me, my lady."

"This matter is quite serious, is it not?"

"Of course."

"I would advise you to recall to whom you are speaking."

"I beg your pardon."

"Una Moura should be collecting worms at the bottom of Bally Loch by now. Though, if this interloper abandoned her after the slaughter as your man believes, we may yet have hope." Nema rustled papers on her desk. "Is everything arranged downstairs?"

"It is. Commander Hamma is quite worried that his involvement should be discovered before Parliament can force the vote through."

"As am I," said Nema. "Too much hinges upon this. I will take personal exception to discover the girl has been reclaimed by Donahugh, after all." She pressed a finger to a sensitive spot at her temple. "Perhaps we've been betrayed?"

Aoife felt the skin at the back of her neck crawl. She'd guessed the old hag would somehow attempt to blame her for this. The stripes on her back from last month's displeasure had yet to heal. "From the description of the scene and the random nature of the violence displayed there, I believe this person is an outside agent. My source is a talented tracker. He was as perplexed as we are now."

"Who is this male?"

"Tav. Third Equestrian Corsair, my lady. Head of scouts."

"Hm," Nema sighed. "How long has he been in our service?"

"A year. His family hails from the south side, near the pleasure district. Solid Mercher class. They loathe the Libella more than we do. He has no reason to lie."

"If I discover differently, it will go very badly for you, Aoife. Surely you realize this?" Aoife swallowed. She did. Oh, she did.

"Of course, my lady. I will happily end him should any sign of disloyalty arise."

"I'm afraid I cannot afford to risk this reaching new ears."

Aoife kept her face blank as parchment. "As you command, Excellency. I shall see to it immediately."

"No need," Nema waved her comment away. "It's been managed. I expect you to handle these affairs before I am apprised of them from now on. Understood?" Her stare bore a hole straight through Aoife's ribcage. Of course, Nema knew who her contact had been. She likely knew what Aoife had for breakfast this morning and every expression she wore on her face each hour of the day. Nema trusted no one. How could she? Serving as her right hand held as many perils as benefits. Aoife did not feel anything resembling sympathy for Tav; he was only a male, but he had been a useful tool she would now have to replace.

It took months, sometimes years, to develop reliable sources. Nema, in her usual imperious habit, discarded those hard-won relationships at the slightest provocation. Inwardly, Aoife longed to rip the old woman's throat out for wasting so much of her time, yet again. "You are quite right. I will seek a suitable replacement."

"Well," laughed Nema dryly. "This is disappointing, at any rate. We're too far along to let that blasted girl get in the way. I want it finished, Aoife. Whatever method you must employ, by whatever means you deem necessary. I cannot afford to have that Moura creature back in the Cloister. The people are close now. I can feel it."

Aoife dipped her head. "Yes, Excellency. I have Corsairs loyal to us, searching the roads in all four directions. Surely, if she is out there and alone, she will run straight to them for help?"

"I want you out there. You will handle this personally, am I clear?" Nema gave her a long, meaningful glare. As much as Aoife's heart surged at the prospect of even a few hours' freedom outside these oppressive walls, she also knew that any failure to achieve Nema's commands would be on her head. Nema wouldn't kill her. She'd demonstrated that principle many, many times. It would be worse than that.

It always was.

Aoife bowed low, heart racing. "As you wish, Excellency." She backed out of the room. The faster Nema's goals were achieved, the swifter Aoife's freedom gained. If one spoiled girl had to die to accomplish that… so be it.

It took a few hours to pass beyond the Citadel without being noticed. Primas simply did not have the liberty to come and go as they pleased. It might be the beating heart of political power on the Continent, but the Cloister was still a cage, however gilded. Aoife would have been remanded to the Censors at ground level if she'd been discovered attempting to leave. Thankfully, she had a few tricks up her sleeve that most Siorai would never dream possible. She was through the Citadel's portcullis, past the Ward Gate, and onto the Navan Road before sunset. As she walked, the fetters of despotic Cloister life slipped from her shoulders like a discarded cloak. She intended to stroll through the night and enjoy the crisp autumn air— the smell of damp fallen leaves, the bite of the Dor Samna breeze— for as long as she could. Nothing was as sweet as freedom, however temporary. She would locate her quarry before long, she knew. Aoife was drawn by the flash of Una's power. A faint vibration pulsated along the strands of Aoife's Spark like a fly caught in a silken web. A genuine smile tugged her lips upward. She marched forward, content to be asked to do something she would enjoy for once.

The High Road

N.E. 508
16, Dor Samna
Eire

Ben couldn't believe his eyes. Breathing hard and bleeding, the young girl he'd encountered twice already clattered through the trees like a hare pursued by hounds. She clutched the dagger he'd left her in a white-knuckled grip. Of the six Corsairs present, four gave chase. They spurred well-trained palfreys into the woods after her, heedless of the uneven terrain. With a piercing cry, she slipped into the leaf-strewn duff and tumbled to a sobbing heap at the base of a slight rise. The nearest horseman charged down the escarpment, his fellows close behind. In a flash, the girl was surrounded on four sides by fully armored men. These were no mercenaries like Rawly and his gang of miscreants from Bethany. No. These were proper soldiers: Tairngare's finest, by all accounts. Ben hadn't seen Corsairs at work for a long time, but he remembered their predecessors well enough. Ben's brow furrowed. She struggled to her feet; his dagger held out before her— like she had any chance of warding off the swords these men drew with such a small blade. What could she possibly have done to prompt this attack? Ben felt a tiny pang of guilt. If he hadn't left her to fend for herself, this might not be happening to her now.

Sidling away from Vixen's flank, he crept closer to get a better view of the scene. Three soldiers dismounted. A fourth remained in his saddle, holding the knot of communal reins. Another hung back, just in case the girl attempted to bolt. While the nearest trio circled her, Ben factored distance and velocity in his head. He had plenty of arrows now, didn't he? Ruthlessly, the Corsairs struck. They took turns working her over with fists, shins, and boots. The iron-sweet tang of fresh blood tainted the air. She managed to land quite a few cracking blows, but his dagger did not. It pinged uselessly from a tree trunk near her head. Ben uttered a foul *Ealig* curse low in his throat.

These pig-fucking sons of whores.

He was many things, but a woman-beating sack of shite, he was *not*. Whatever their excuse for this, he didn't care to hear it. These were dead men.

In the next few moments, as she gasped for air, Ben readied his feet. He no longer worried if they caught sight of him first. He rather hoped they did.

"Stop… please," she choked into the forest floor. "I don't want to h—"

One of them leaned down to wrench her up by the hair. His companion shouted. "Careful there! Don't let her get a hand on your bare skin!"

Ben plucked an arrow from his quiver, counting paces from these men to those waiting on the road above.

Her captor grasped one of her breasts above her tunic. "A shame, that. If she weren't a Siorai witch—"

"Well, she is, and you can be certain you won't live through it," remarked his accomplice. Snarling, he cuffed her hard with one gauntleted fist. A thick line of blood ran down her chin. Her left eye swelled up like a gourd. Gritting his teeth, Ben drew his bowstring taut.

"You 'don't want to' what, heretic slut?"

Moaning, she sagged into the soldier behind her. Ben took that for a cue. His first arrow dove through the bastard's right eye. Before the would-be rapist's back struck the earth, Ben was already nocked and drawn for a second shot. Distracted by the arrow that had killed his friend, the speaker's eyes bulged elsewhere— a fatal mistake. The girl leaned forward. She slammed her palm flat over his unguarded cheek.

"*Reorder*," she hissed. Beneath her fingers, the leader's cheekbones smashed into one another, spurting his eyeballs from their sockets like pressed grapes. He was permitted one loud pitiful shriek. His jaw met his forehead with a sickening crunch. In the split second it took for this horror to manifest, the girl had moved deftly to her left and snatched at the third Corsair's cuirass with one hand. With the other, she swiped a finger across the bridge of his nose. "*Boil*," she whispered. The soldier fell backward. Growling, she tottered with him to the ground. This one's eyes dissolved like cream from a hot spoon. Dark fluids gushed from his open mouth, steaming like a geyser in full vent. He lay there twitching, his throat melting as if he'd swallowed acid.

She struggled to her knees beside his body. Gulping air, she watched the mounted soldier unwind a rope from his saddle. "I said, I don't want to hurt any of you!"

In shock, Ben dropped his elbow. His newest arrow sailed into the bracken, useless. He'd never seen anything like this in all his life. Siorai were forbidden to kill, weren't they? Or so he'd been told once, many years ago. A girl with this one's ability was clearly something special. Ben sincerely regretted not taking the time to learn her name. As his mind raced along a host of interesting possibilities, the fourth horseman slung his rope around her throat. With a single twist of a gauntleted wrist, he jerked her from her feet. Ben heard her wheeze and watched the rider wind the rope around his saddle horn drawing it tighter and tighter. Ben slunk after them, bow drawn. Oblivious to the threat, the Corsair dragged the girl over the ridge behind his horse, shouting an alert to his comrades on the road above.

⚔

Before her captor returned to the road, five arrows sailed out of the woods on his right; two burst through his throat, shoving him arse over ankles from his mount. Rope gone slack, the girl, tumbled face-down into the dirt. Ben's next arrow took a second horseman through a gap in his armor between the armpit and ribcage; another propelled him bodily into the nearest trunk. Rearing, his horse thundered off without him. Ben's final arrow pinned the last Corsair's un-gauntleted hand to his thigh where he'd been reaching for a vicious throwing knife. His screams grew shrill when Ben emerged from the trees. Reaching over to grasp the dagger the fool had been trying to draw, Ben plunged it to the hilt into his clavicle. The whole affair was over in moments. Taking stock, Ben sighed.

What a damned mess.

At least this lot had died for a better reason than meat or uishge. With a scowl, he approached the girl gingerly, lest he accidentally touch her. After what he'd seen her do, he wasn't fool enough to try her now. Her eyes spun white as she lay there, scarcely conscious. She had a terrible, oozing gash above her left eye. Blood poured freely from her mouth and nose. The wound on her head was already a fierce blue-black and engorged with fluid. One more strike might have killed her. Crossing his arms, Ben stared down at her.

He didn't have time for this, did he?

He had matters of his own to attend to. If Guinness was no longer alive or unable to help him, he'd many miles to go before he could rest. He desperately needed a new ogham stone. Without one, he'd be cursed to live in this wilderness alone for the next two decades. He wouldn't go back now. He could not. Arthur was a physician or had been, once upon a time. Who better to help the girl than a doctor? Perhaps Ben could kill two birds with one stone? Realizing the direction of his thoughts, he swore aloud.

Gods damn it.

He was obligated now, and he bloody well knew it. If he didn't help her this time, his conscience would nag him to the ends of the earth. Ben was no hero. He didn't suffer romantic delusions of grandeur nor fancy himself a champion for bothersome females astray in the Greensward. Truthfully, if he didn't already feel bad about leaving her tied to that tree the other night, he would probably be long gone.

Not today, the annoying voice in his head assured him. He could be a rotten bastard for the rest of his life, but… *not today, damn you*. Despite his inclination toward self-preservation, he couldn't leave her again. He would never forgive himself for something so foul. Ben unwound the cloak from the nearest dead horseman, tearing strips to bind first her head, then her scraped, bleeding hands.

Just in case, he thought, while he wrapped the remaining bulk of the fabric around her small, limp body. Hefting her over his shoulder, he tracked back through the trees toward Vixen.

⚜

APPROACHING THE LITTLE FARMSTEAD, BEN stopped to catch his breath. A weather-beaten chimney blew little tufts of silver smoke above the treetops. He recalled Arthur being quite proud of this place when it was newly built. After so many years of service in the militia, Arthur had been happy to have such a fine home to call his own. Seeing the place now, Ben was struck by how small and isolated it was. Arthur was a friendly man. It didn't suit his tastes to live so... alone. Aednat had undoubtedly been the reason for this solitude.

Ben had only visited once when the foundations were freshly laid. The charming couple had received him graciously, as they were able. Until this moment, it had never occurred to him that they might not have been given a choice but to retreat to this backwater. He understood that some folk were bound to be unaccepting of Aednat, particularly in the cities. By the time Ben had made his acquaintance, Arthur had planned to leave his family's small medical practice in Ten Bells to start a life with his new bride. Ben only realized the extent of that decision as he looked over this homely little farm. How preposterous and unfair? Aednat would have been the toast of Ten Bells society were her heritage not an issue for the locals. Well, it had been almost three decades. Who knew what plights the Guinness' had encountered since? The fields suffered from a lack of tending and the outbuildings for want of nails. Perhaps Arthur had gotten too long in the tooth to manage on his own?

The hedges were trimmed, if poorly. A few skinny sheep bleated in a small meadow. A hoary dairy cow chewed cud at Ben as he neared, sparing him a haughty glare. "And to you, missus," he huffed back. The heifer snuffled a curt reply.

He tied Vixen to a short wooden gate near the house and tugged the girl into his arms. She didn't utter a sound, which was a bad sign. Ben stopped shy of a faded yellow door to tuck his cowl tight over his ears. He could attempt a glamour, but without his ogham stone, he wouldn't hold one for very long. He must make do. Besides, if this trip proved fruitless, he'd need his strength for the journey ahead.

The door cracked just as he raised his fist to knock. A lovely, vaguely familiar face materialized at the gap, a cautious look in her cornflower blue eyes. Aednat? But... it couldn't be? This girl was far too young. Even if faeries did not age as Milesians did, Aednat had been well into her third decade when he'd met her. She would have been nearly seventy if his maths served. Ben was sorely disappointed to learn the Innkeeper must have been right about her passing.

"I saw you coming through the trees there," she pointed at the hills behind him. "Is she alive?"

Ben had about a gallon of blood dried into the back of his cloak, so he wasn't laying any odds just yet. "I think so, but I'm not sure how."

Aednat's doppelgänger leaned in to check his ward's pulse. Ben gently intercepted, pushing her hand away. "I wouldn't do that," he warned. "It could be dangerous."

A little crease formed between her delicate blonde brows. Now that he was really looking, she wasn't quite as lovely as Aednat. Her cheeks were too thin, her complexion slightly sallow, and her pinched brow smacked more of shrewishness than beauty.

"How can I treat her if I can't touch her?"

Ben blinked. "Treat her? You? Where's Arthur? It's been a long while, but I was sure this was his home."

She ran a hand through the hair at the nape of her too white, too long, too thin neck. "My father died last autumn, sir. Influenza."

"Aednat?"

43

She reddened at his impertinence. "Gone more than a decade. Who are you?"

Ben fidgeted. This was Arthur and Aednat's daughter? Both parents gone? He honestly didn't know how to respond. He was disappointed, to say the least. Arthur and Aednat were the only two people in Eire that knew who he was and wouldn't find it a detriment. In the second place, he desperately needed another ogham stone. He'd hoped to avoid having to risk the city to get one. Aside from these concerns... he'd liked Arthur a great deal. There was this blasted Siorai girl to deal with, as well.

"I'm very sorry for your loss, lass. He was a decent sort, your Da." He dipped his head with respect.

"You knew my parents?"

"Once upon a time. Not to be indelicate, but would you perhaps know of another physician in the general area? I do think this damn— er, this *girl*— might be in danger if she isn't treated."

Her eyes narrowed to blue slits. "I did say I was capable but since you're after being rude, by all means... take her that way," she gestured up the path, "about fifty miles, and you shall find a proper barber. Good day." Without ado, she shut the door in his face. The hinge came into hard contact with the boot he shoved into the jamb. Grunting, he jerked it open again with his heel. The door bumped her on the shoulder, knocking her into the wall. "Ow!" she cried, rubbing her offended arm. "How *dare*—"

"You did not say. You implied. Since you're so sensitive about your skills, consider yourself hired." He barged past her. An easy feat, considering he was thrice her size and outweighed her by at least a million pounds. "Where do you want her?"

Irritation rumbled in her throat, but she didn't answer him. Instead, she hobbled past a tiny kitchen toward a small door to the left of a stone hearth. Her right foot, twisted about forty degrees the wrong way, impeded her progress. Ben refrained from comment, knowing how she came by it without asking. Many faeries were marked in such ways. She didn't appear embarrassed by its obvious deformity, but he knew better than to open his mouth. He had some manners, thank you. Sourly, she gestured for him to proceed her.

This chamber was much larger than its stunted doorframe portended. He bent almost double to get through the door. On the other side, the ceiling was a good four feet higher than in the foyer: an addition, no doubt. White scrubbed walls were lined with shelves, overstuffed with books of every variety. Arthur hailed from a moderately wealthy Mercher family and had a particular enthusiasm for the written word. There were hundreds of tomes to choose from, most of which was likely more valuable than any of the animals outside. Ben raised a brow. Arthur's girl clearly knew what a treasure she possessed in this little study. What care was lacking outdoors was doubly applied here.

On a wall opposite the library, pine shelves were stacked high with jars, vials, and vessels in various shapes and sizes. Everything was lovingly labeled and arranged according to the Common alphabet. Medicinal tools were laid out in neat rows on a metallic cart: a handsome pair of copper scissors, various pincers, and grips, all honed to a high gleam. Beneath a south-facing window on his left stood an ornately carved desk with snarling hounds for feet. Upon it sat a small painted globe, clearly ancient, as evidenced by the place names the world had not seen for a half millennium or more. The Guinness girl moved some books and scraps of loose paper from a second rolling table. Many were open anatomical volumes, with hasty notes scribbled in their margins. She motioned for him to lay his burden down, so she might make a cursory examination. Noting the seeping lump that had once been her patient's eye, her lip curled.

"*Siora*," she pulled a face. "Did you do this to her?"

"If I had, would I have brought her here?"

"Good point. I'll need your help, then. We have to ascertain whether or not she's bleeding internally. Will you hand me those scissors behind you?"

Ben threw up his hands. "Oh no. I have business of my own to get to. I'll be leaving her in your care."

Her fingers froze over the girl's abdomen. "You what? You're just going to leave her here?"

"Well—"

"No," she said, setting her tools back down.

"What? But—"

"No," she repeated more firmly. "You may as well throw her back over your shoulder and duff off. I'm not taking responsibility for your mess."

Beneath his hood, Ben squinted. This was Aednat's daughter? It couldn't be… Aednat had been the sweetest woman alive. She could no more ignore a sick bird in the grass than leave a possibly dying human being right before her eyes. Perhaps some horrible, Otherworld creature had devoured Aednat and went about wearing her face?

"You would refuse to treat an injured woman? Your father never denied a patient, no matter the circumstances."

"Sir, my father was a good honest man. I buried him in burlap. I am not my father, and this is no charity."

"Ah," said Ben, digging around in his cloak for his purse, the very one made heavy by cheating others at porter. "I've coin aplenty if that's your problem. You may have an entire royal fainne. What I lack is time, mistress." He set the heavy gold coin on the injured girl's open, insensate palm. "Do we have an accord?" He watched color bloom in the faerie's thin cheeks and heard her swallow as she gazed down at the gleaming yellow metal. A single gold royal was nearly triple the amount a prolific farmer might hope to earn in two full years. For an orphan living in the middle of nowhere, miles from any reasonably sized town, full of Milesians hostile to her for her heritage… maybe four times the average?

"No," she breathed.

"I got a good look at those scrawny animals on my way in. I know you need the money. With your father gone, I'll wager you don't get many folks ambling up your walk with coin to spend, do you?"

"I decline. Take her and go."

Ben ground his molars over the injustice of his luck. He reached again into his purse to produce another sparkling fainne. His last, as it happened. Its glitter reflected from her large, glassy eyes. This would leave him a mere handful of silver stags and three coppers. If he must pay for the materials he needed to make his ogham stone, he'd be obliged to sit in on another game of porter to earn more coin. Hells, he might resort to base robbery at this rate. He'd almost be better served heading back to Rosweal to search for his own missing stone. That wouldn't be any more troublesome than what awaited him in Ten Bells, the way things were going. When had a bout of conscience ever benefited him in the least?

"Two then, but mark me, it's my final offer."

"Again, no," she said, looking like she might be sick. Two royals were a fortune for a girl like her. She could pack up this dusty old farmstead and head off to a proper life in Tairngare, Ten Bells, or hells, warm Bethany in the South. She could buy herself a shop to run, maybe even find a husband. The possibilities were limitless.

Ben was tempted to snap her delicate little neck. "You're joking? Two fainne are more than you could hope to earn in years out here by yourself with your erm, malady."

Her cheeks burned a brilliant scarlet. She elbowed past him, rummaged about in her tiny kitchen, and stomped back with a fresh rag and a bowl overflowing with strong herbal tea. He moved to let her through the door rather than suffer a second jab to the ribs. Resuming her place at the girl's side, she held up a warning hand when he opened his mouth to speak. Lightly, she dabbed mud, blood, and muck away from the unconscious girl's outstretched arm. The skin beneath all that grime emerged a smooth, golden brown. Emblazoned in blue woad coiled dozens of whirling, entwined serpents. No, not serpents… dragons. Everywhere she moved her cloth, beautifully appointed wyrms were revealed. Ben had no idea what these markings meant, but the solemn expression on the Guinness girl's face did not bode well.

"Do you know who she is?"

"No idea. Do those markings mean something to you?"

"Anyone who's ever spent time in the Red City knows which family flies the Blue Wyrm. Only the women of the Moura Clan are permitted to wear them as decoration. Tattoos of this sort… do you follow?"

Ben sat heavily on the edge of the hound-footed desk. He didn't like where this was headed at all. "I figured her for a noble or an escapee from the Cloister. These markings make her someone from an important clan, I suppose?"

"You could say that. She would have to be Doma Drem herself to be marked like this, or her heir apparent."

He went still. A terrible foreboding slithered into his veins. He couldn't stifle the groan that escaped his throat.

"You're telling me this girl is the Domina of the Moura Clan?" She'd offered her name to him, hadn't she? That morning when she found him in the woods, sleeping on the frozen ground— she'd asked him if he wanted to know who she was. *Damn. Damn. Damn.* He'd stuck his foot in it this time.

Beyond the shock of her identity were the incessant questions her situation posed. Why would a noblewoman of her stature, the future leader of the most powerful family in Eire, be attacked by her own Citadel Corsairs? Furthermore, how was anyone able to infiltrate the deepest sanctum in the Cloister of the Eternal Flame— the most heavily guarded structure in Innisfail— and manage to remove her without bringing an entire Cohort of Tairnganeah down around their ears? The thought of common Souther ruffians from Bethany accomplishing this herculean task unaided was about as likely as the sun rising in the west. Someone must want this little lady out of the way very badly. Someone with enough power and influence to smuggle her out of the Citadel and seduce many Citadel cavalry officers to their cause. Just what in the hells was happening in Tairngare? Ben had spent so long hiding out in Rosweal and other border hovels that he had no idea what went on in greater Eire besides whoring, drinking, and the next card game.

The thought brought a small pang for his loss.

"I'll do my best to help her," Mistress Guinness said, breaking into his reverie, her expression stone serious. "Both royals will be fair payment. Though, you'll take her elsewhere when I'm done. Whoever had the stones to do this to *her* wouldn't think twice about silencing someone like me. What good is gold to me if I'm dead?"

⚷⚷

AOIFE GREW BORED OF WALKING a few hours outside Tairngare. She'd bought a pony in Fennick, but riding was just as tedious. By the time evening set in around Slane, she'd been on the go since dawn. There were dozens of Cohort patrols moving up and down the road, stopping to question suspicious individuals or otherwise hassling travelers for the missing Moura Domina. Aoife's disguise dissuaded any interest directed her way. The little stone at her throat guaranteed very few second glances. To fellow merchants, tinkers, and farmers on the High Road, she was merely another old woman, ambling along at her own pace. Once or twice, she spotted Corsairs roving through towns or farmsteads. Some she recognized immediately as loyal servants of Alta Nema. If they found the girl first, they had orders to destroy her on sight. Aoife didn't bother to hail them or alert them to her presence.

Their numbers were a sign that the search was not going well for either interested party. If they'd found Prima Moura, they would have already ridden back to the Citadel to deliver the news. Loyalist Cohorts and Tairnganeah Infantry outnumbered Nema's Corsairs two-to-one. Aoife was not encouraged by the sight. These soldiers were out in their hordes to do the Doma's bidding and bring the Domina home by any means necessary. There was no guarantee that Nema's forces would find her first. If the loyalists managed to drag Una home in one piece, Aoife's mission would end in failure and punishment. She refused to worry just yet. There could be only one reason the girl had yet to be found. Aoife stared straight into it. Vivid autumnal trees thickened beside the road, obscuring the sky overhead. The Greensward stretched hundreds of miles to the west and still further north, into Aes Sidhe. An unwary person who dared step off the road might be lost forever in this teeming ocean of trees. Soldiers could search for months and never find Una, should she choose to hide.

Well, Aoife would see about that, wouldn't she?

When the road curved toward Slane, she dismounted and led her pony through the woods on her left. Trekking southwest, she kept the road on her right but well out of view. Here the forest marched on for days, crowding hills and dells in every visible direction. If Aoife wandered too far, she could quickly lose her bearings. Without the sun to pierce the net of shadows creeping between the trees, one copse looked like another. Best not to linger.

She stopped at a slight rise less than a mile from the road, stripping her right hand free of its warm leather glove. Aoife drew a tiny dagger out of her vest and, without ceremony, drew it across the breadth of her palm. Clenching her fist around the wound with a hiss, she held her arm out in front of her. Bright blood dripped into the black mud at her feet.

"*Come,*" she called, tapping deep into her Spark. A sharp wind ripped through the boughs around her, threatening to snap them at their joints. The earth trembled and quaked, and great chasms rent the ground, from which it seemed the very soul of darkness spewed forth. Two sets of glowing eyes slinked into view, growing wide on a pair of monstrous black heads. The world smudged wherever these beasts moved, two pinholes of absolute night. Aoife grinned at her pets as they slunk forward, hungry. "*Go and play,*" she commanded and laughed as they eagerly bounded away.

Aednat's Child

Leave, Ben thought to himself, for the hundredth time in an hour. *This is not your problem. You owe them nothing.* He wasn't sure why he hadn't laid the girl on the front stoop with a couple silver stags, and then fled back into the Greensward. He wasn't noble or chivalrous. Who were either of these women to him— Milesian women at that? He had troubles of his own. He couldn't continue to wander around undisguised like this. If Ben didn't do something about his appearance soon, it could cost him more than precious anonymity. His was not a face Milesians in Eire would be apt to appreciate. If he couldn't mockup a new ogham charm, he would have to hide again. He was bloody tired of hiding. Ben didn't thrive in solitude, he could admit without shame. He knew he should go, *must* go. Why risk exposure for a girl he didn't have the least connection with?

You should have freed her from the start, you miserable shite, said the other voice. The one from his gut. The one he liked least. *You involved yourself. You are obliged.*

"Bah," Ben grumbled aloud, well into his third dram of Arthur's finest uishge. He was bored of the argument raging inside his head. Having made it as far as the rear stoop of the Guinness cottage, he eyed the looming Greensward with longing. How did he manage to get himself into these things? If only he'd led the Greenmakers further west last week, none of this would be happening. He'd still be in Rosweal, snug in his own bed with Rose, or drinking at *The Hart* with mates. His mournful sigh was bone-deep. Busy wallowing in self-pity, he didn't hear Arthur's daughter limp out onto the stoop until the hem of her skirt brushed his boot.

Drying her freshly scrubbed fingers on a rough linen towel, she reeked of camphor and other medicinal odors.

"Well, she'll live," she exhaled hard, sounding easily as old as his father. "I'm fairly certain she's concussed. I'll have to dose her with a stimulant to prevent her from slipping into a coma. All that aside, most of her wounds look much nastier than they are." She moved closer. "May I have some of that?"

"It *is* yours," he pointed out, passing it up to her. The grimace she pulled after the barest sip earned her a chuckle. She handed it back.

"Siora, that's bloody awful. Tastes like burnt grass and lamp oil." She took a seat beside him, not bothering to wait for an invitation. "I'm surprised you're still here." His shrug was half-hearted.

"Who says I mean to stay?" She watched him sidelong for a moment. Finally, he gave up, and snorted, "When she wakes, we'll decide the safest place to take her, then I'll be on my way. Fair?" He didn't care for the measuring expression on her face. "Gods, what now?"

"Nothing…" her voice trailed off.

For Brida's sake. "Out with it."

"Well, I left that fainne on the table."

"You wish me to take it back?"

"I suppose I'm surprised you haven't tried."

His head swiveled around like an owl; eyes narrowed to slivers. "Ouch."

Demurely folding her hands in her lap, she stared straight ahead as if the trees were suddenly fascinating. "I thought you had something important to get to?"

"Are you giving my money back?"

"Not a chance."

"Shut up, then. We made a deal. Despite your rather unsubtle implications, I never break my word once I give it. Satisfied?" Inwardly, he fumed. He took another sip to keep his head cool. "How long before she can be moved?"

"Two days? A week? Who knows? That blow to her head could have killed her. Half her face is swollen black. Not to mention the bruising around her throat or the hemorrhaging around her ribs and kidneys. She needs to rest."

Ben blew a long breath through his nose, cursing whatever unfortunate star he'd been born under. He shifted his attention to the farm around them: the pasture, the hills, and the forest that pressed in from all sides. The Guinness farmstead was remote. He doubted that Arthur and Aednat's young daughter here got around much. There was a good chance anyone searching for the Moura girl would miss the place entirely. If he set some rudimentary wards, he might ensure no one would ever find the place unless they were explicitly determined to do so.

"Look," he began cautiously, "there is something I must see to before I can take her anywhere else. I was on my way when I witnessed her attack."

The second encounter, at any rate.

He didn't feel a need to share the first.

" For an ogham charm, I suppose?" she smirked at Ben's startled expression. "Don't look at me like that. You said you knew my father. It stands to reason you also knew my mother and how she supplemented my father's earnings. My mother's mother came from Aes Sidhe, same as you."

"Right—" Had Arthur been as infuriatingly direct? Ben couldn't remember. Aednat definitely hadn't. He struggled to equate the sweet, biddable mother with the observant, slightly shrewish daughter.

"I knew the second you crossed my mother's wards in the forest, just there." She tugged a thumb toward the front of the house. "Only a trueborn Sidhe could stomp right through them without even noticing they were there. My mother called it her 'peasant magic.' At any rate, they keep the house safe from unwanted visitors. This is the Greensward. The locals here don't much care for my family."

Setting down his bottle, Ben half-promised himself never to pick up another. "*Right...*" he repeated. This week just got better and better.

"You can take off that hood now," she said. "Doesn't fit, anyway. Stole it, I gather?"

A hard-blown sigh was his answer.

"Figured. As it happens, you passed my test. You may both stay until she's well enough to leave. But I warn you; if you get any ideas about breaking our deal, you won't like the consequences." He could tell she resisted the urge to wag a finger at him. She laced her fingers instead. "Can you reinforce my mother's wards? I'm afraid I never learned how."

Ben pursed his lips. "Might. It'll take a bit, though."

"Good. Because it isn't common knowledge that my father passed recently. Many townsfolk will recall he was the only qualified physician in the area, though he stopped practicing a few years ago. They will eventually be directed here if anyone comes looking for her."

Damn, Ben mused. The thought hadn't occurred. It wouldn't take an overly clever tracker to work out that the Moura girl might be injured after that tussle on the Navan Road. He hadn't bothered to hide the bodies, either. He'd stripped their horses and packs of anything useful and dragged them from the road. If anyone clever investigated that scene, they would infer that at least three of the dead Corsairs bore arrow wounds. That someone had come to the girl's rescue should be obvious. Ben swore under his breath.

"I didn't think that far ahead," he removed his hood. "I can't do anything for anyone in Eire like this. I was on my way to remedy this situation when I found her."

She paled. "Where are you from? Connaught? Donegal? The Isles?"

He had no idea which lie she would believe. Therefore, omission was the safer bet. He didn't reply.

"Fine. If you don't want to talk about it, that's all right. I know you came here partly to look for my mother, for obvious reasons. I wouldn't worry too much about it. She taught me how to make charms. Thought it might help me cope with my… erm, peculiarity."

Hope soared anew in his breast. If this was indeed the case, perhaps coming here wasn't such a waste of his precious time after all.

"Please don't say this if you're unsure about your ability."

"It could never be as strong a charm as what I'm sure you're accustomed to, but I've made one before. An old woman on the road alone is less a target than a half-breed. It won't be perfect, but it'll be better than nothing."

Ben had been preparing himself for another, even more, dangerous journey than the one he'd been on for the past few days. Could his luck have changed so suddenly? Why, if she could do what she said, he would be free to roam where and when he willed. Tara maybe, or perhaps Man? The Peninsula was neutral territory, wasn't it, not quite an exclusive Sidhe domain? Hells, if Ben could convince Robin of what an enormous braying ass he'd been for casting him out, perhaps he might return? He could be back in Rosweal in his flat above the Boyne in no time, drinking, dicing, and whoring himself into oblivion. The point being that the stone gave him options he currently lacked. By Herne, maybe he wasn't so unlucky as he thought?

"Aside from that girl, this is what you were hoping to find, yes? For two fainne, new wards, and some light help around this farm while she convalesces. I'll consider this a fair deal. Is this acceptable to you, erm, what's your name?"

"Ben," he said firmly, ignoring her dubious frown. "The name's Ben Maeden. Mistress–?"

"Rian."

Ben stuck his hand out. "Rian, we have an accord, and you— my thanks."

⚜

IN THE MORNING, RIAN GUINNESS roughly nudged him awake with the toe of her boot. Ben lay on the back stoop, curled around the empty uishge bottle as if it were a woman. His collar stuck to the wooden slats beneath his head, and a thick coating of frost crept over his cloak and right cheek. A second prodding jerked him upright. He rubbed at his sore, chapped jaw. *Again?* So much for abstaining from spirits. One would find it difficult to be certain, but it appeared to be midday. The clouds overhead were thick enough to cut with a knife and dark, save for the barest milky smudge in the center. Groaning, Ben ran a frozen hand over his aching eyes. Rian's pinched expression hovered over him.

"You smell like a vagrant." There was a reason why most of Innisfail had outlawed uishge, even if the law was all but ignored. His brain sloshed inside his vibrating skull. *Gods,* Ben thought. *You need to quit drinking, sir.* Rian wrinkled her thin little nose at him. A worn but clean tunic struck him in the face. He refrained from comment.

"There's a stream behind the barn. My father dug out a small pond for the geese, but they've long gone. I think you'll find it's about chest deep. It won't be anywhere near warm, but," she sniffed.

"Wonderful," he grumbled, momentarily praying she'd fall down the steps and break her neck. He couldn't believe she was Aednat's child. "Is there no tub indoors? A pitcher? Hells, a bloody kettle?"

"You're not to set another foot inside this house until you get it over with. I'd get to it if I were you. There's a horse brush and a brick of lye soap there for your… erm, clothing. Here's some lavender soap for the rest of you." A small, fragrant missile thumped from chest like a rock. Ignoring his wince, she said, "It took almost four hours this morning to scrub the mud and muck from my floors. Anyway, I have to head to Ferndale for supplies. I go every week on the same day, so if I fail to show today, it will look suspicious. There's food – just some bread and cheese, mind you, on the block in the kitchen. I've nothing fancier to spare. You're welcome to it when you're as clean and respectable as you can manage. Any questions before I go?"

"No," he croaked, wishing he'd managed to drink himself dead last night.

"Good," she hobbled down the steps but turned when she made it halfway around the porch and marched back. "One last thing, which I'm sure you're smart enough to figure out on your own. Keep an eye on her. Her fever broke last night, but she could dislodge her bandages or hurt herself if she tries to get up too soon. There's a pot of tea loaded with willow bark on the larder in the kitchen. If I'm not back by nightfall, be sure to make her swallow half a cup at dusk."

"How am I supposed to do that?"

"Are you an idiot?'

Ben scowled back.

"Then, figure it out," she spared him a flippant wave over her shoulder and took her leave.

⚔

Ben had to break a great deal of thick ice to get into that 'pool' behind the barn. Although he didn't feel the cold as sharply as a Milesian might, jumping into a bowl of ice water, bare-assed, on a frigid day in the Greensward, was far from pleasant. After ripping nearly every hair from his head and grating off swaths of skin with the sandpaper Rian Guinness claimed was soap, he was thankful he wasn't bleeding from head to toe. Once clean, he donned a pair of Arthur's old trousers and a moth-eaten linen tunic. Both were too small for him, but the trousers at least fit into the tops of his boots. Arthur had been quite tall for a Milesian, though Ben had still towered over him at close to seven feet.

He finally ambled back to the house over an hour later, with his wet clothing over one arm. His lips had taken on something of a bluish tinge. All the way up to the house from the barn, he recited the foulest curses he could conjure. He couldn't believe how ridiculous his life had become. Coming through the back door into the cottage, he felt the hearth's intense blast of warmth straight to his toes. Steam curled from his exposed skin like fog. Beside the larder lay the promised trencher of bread and cheese. Rian, bless her contrary soul, had left a cup of homemade mead beside it. Maybe he had been a bit dramatic when he labeled this the worst week of his life. Why, things were looking up already, weren't they? While his fingertips stung and thawed, he laid his wet clothes on the flagstones by the hearth... and froze. There, beside the mantel, stood the Moura girl. She clutched the back of a chair as if it were a lone buoy in a storm, huffing, shaking, and furious. Ben gave her a weak smile. Gods, he really must cease making things worse for himself by entertaining optimistic thoughts.

"*You!*" she hissed, her eyes blazing. "*You bastard.*"

The chair-back she gripped for support cracked. So much for the faint hope that her head wound would take care of her memory. Ben raised his palms, feigning surrender.

"You should be abed, mistress. You've been through somewhat of an ordeal, and I—"

"*Left me.*" Wood splintered under her nails. "You left me there to *die!*" Her one good eye glowed molten amber, bright as any coal in the hearth. A nasty seeping cut over her eyebrow strained against its stitches. Her left eye was a red and blue bubble. Her throat, neck, and collarbone, where she'd been roped and dragged behind that Corsair's horse, were torn to the tissue beneath.

Ben swallowed hard. "Now, that's rather harsh. You're only standing here because I came back for you." A half-truth, but she didn't need to know that. He'd be damned if he'd admit to spending a relaxing evening in Navan Village while she most likely spent a sleepless night in the wilderness. Worse – that he'd been spending coins lifted from her captors while she was chased down the High Road by her city guard. No way in nine hells would he tell her any of that now!

She stood up a bit straighter. It did not improve her height. The top of her head would barely crest his ribcage if she stood on her toes.

"You came back for me?" Her voice was as harsh as the sandpaper soap he'd been forced to use. He supposed she meant to sound dubious.

"Of course, I did."

She attempted to snort, but the fluid in her nose prevented anything but the weakest whistle from escaping her nostrils.

"Never-mind. You needn't bother to lie. For whatever reason, you *did* come back," she gnashed her teeth, "so, I suppose I must be grateful for your interfering when you did. I would bow and say the words, but you'll pardon me if I refrain this once, won't you?" Halting like a fawn, she moved around the chair and slowly inched herself onto its seat. Ben resisted the urge to help, instead tucking his hands under his arms. His head still thrummed; his gut roiled with oily, queasy emptiness. A reminder that neither of them was enjoying themselves overmuch in this little cottage, deep in the Eastern Greensward. Though he must concede, listening to her try to breathe, it was obvious which of them was worse for wear. "Would you mind, terribly," she inquired, in a frog's impersonation of a clipped Tairnganese accent, "bringing me something to drink?"

He didn't mind if that meant he wouldn't have to face her for a few moments. Gods, but they'd made a mess of her! Guilty and searching for a means to make amends, he rummaged through Rian's small kitchen like the useless clod he was. There wasn't much to the place save two small cabinets, one wooden countertop, and a stone tub with a hole drilled into its base for drainage. He returned with the tea Rian mentioned before and waited nervously while she tried to tip the cup against her ruined lower lip. She wrinkled the good side of her nose.

"Ugh. Laudanum and willow-bark? Isn't there anything else?"

"No," he lied again. He could go and fetch her water, but she needed to sleep, and, as it happened, so did he. If she was up and about this soon, there was a good chance he wouldn't have to stay here much longer. Gods be merciful. If Rian hurried with that stone, he might be able to… well, he'd worry about that later. Despite her aversion, the Moura girl drained the cup dry. He poured her another cup. That too, she slowly choked down. Afterward, she settled into the cushions with a pained sigh. He poured himself the next dram, filling it almost to the brim.

She raised her right brow at him. "Someone beat the shite out of you too?"

"You could say so." He tossed the noxious liquid back, then poured himself another. "That, and we're out of uishge. You really should sleep. That shrill girl will scold me for letting you out of bed."

"Who is she? And where is this?"

Ben wiped his mouth on his too-short sleeve. "An old friend's farmstead. He was a doctor. The girl seems to think she is too. Not that I'm complaining, mind." He indicated her state of semi-upright mobility.

Mute, she frowned at him for several pregnant minutes. When next she spoke, her voice was a little less grating. The opiate had gone to work in her bloodstream. "What happened to those men? The Corsairs?"

"Dead."

"All of them?"

"Yes."

"Siora," her voice bore genuine regret.

"They were trying to kill you, you know? Don't waste your sympathy."

She didn't answer. Ben didn't understand what she could possibly have to feel guilty about. Those Corsairs were scum of the lowest stripe. They'd nearly beaten her to death right in front of him. While he puzzled over her empathy, he noted the way her hands shook in her lap, the tremors that quivered through her shoulders.

A sudden explanation for her behavior dawned.

She's never killed anyone before.

All that terrible power, and she'd never used it on another human being— at least, not as he'd seen her do. She must have walked right up to them, looking for aid. If true, what a horrible shock all of this must be to her.

Ben squirmed. He was a rare shite, indeed.

"You did what you had to do," he meant to reassure her, best he was able. "I did the rest. Do you understand?"

"They were… you're right," she said. He wasn't witness to her internal conflict for long. She drooped like a dying weed. Eager to avoid further questions, he waited for her to fully succumb to Rian's brew. His brains had finally stopped pounding against his skull, so there was that to be thankful for too. "Wait," she struggled against the drug. "Where are we again?"

"Safe."

"There… is no such place." Three heartbeats later, she was gone, leaving him blessedly alone. He watched her sleep for a while, his thoughts all the more confused by this new, burdensome knowledge. If she were an innocent, which his instincts assured him she was, how had this happened to her?

Better yet, why?

Later, Ben crammed a few bites of bread into his mouth, then stretched out on the floor beside the hearth. His head a riot, he'd wrapped the girl in one of Rian's old, patched cloaks by the door before laying her on the small couch that divided the tiny room. Making sure she got some rest was the very least he could do for her, given everything that had happened in the past three days. He felt increasingly remorseful for his own part in her situation. If only he hadn't seen her shed genuine tears for men who didn't deserve it, he could continue to convince himself that this was all a horrid inconvenience and not a tragedy. How'd she come to this pass?

None of it made any sense. Ben didn't want to consider anyone else's circumstances, needs, or feelings. That way lay trouble, complications he didn't need. He didn't know anything about this girl. The Moura family had been in power for at least six decades that he could recall. He also knew that they could be a little heavy-handed with their policies. That debacle with the 'attempted' queen… what was her name? What a tone-deaf, political fiasco that had been. He didn't know all the particulars but understood that Tairngare's citizens were bound to be displeased about the Doma's daughter being elevated to autocrat overnight. What was worse, Drem claimed the girl— thereby the family— was fated to absolute rule by prophecy. If Ben remembered correctly, this very foolish move had prompted the Duch of Bethany to instigate the war in '84. If Drem Moura hadn't tipped her hand in her quest for power, the North wouldn't yet bear the scars of that ugly conflict.

Ben shook his head at the ceiling, conflicted by unpleasant memories. If this girl was the next Domina of the Moura Clan, it stood to reason that Drem was grooming her for her own position. If such was the case, perhaps there were new players on the board in the Red City who sought to oust the Moura from the Cloister? This may explain why some of the Citadel's Corsairs would label her a 'heretic' (as one of them had called her) and attempt to hunt her down. She couldn't become the next Doma if she were dead, could she?

It was a sound theory if a bit underdeveloped. For one thing, it didn't explain Bethany's involvement. If this were a plot from within the Cloister, why didn't they simply kill her inside the walls? Why pass her off to agents from a hostile city to the south, then send soldiers out to finish her off? One thing of which he was sure— if he hadn't killed Rawly and his mercenaries, someone would have. Ben would wager that whoever planned all of this never had any intention of letting this girl out of the North alive. Which begged the question— why? Why go to so much trouble just to undo it all again?

Ben told himself that he didn't wish to know. He didn't want to be involved. He didn't care about this girl, her problems, or the intrigues that threw them together. This wasn't his business. She was not his business! He had his own life, such as it was, and his own plans. If Rian could make the stone he needed, he should leave. Still… the sight of her fragile shoulders quaking in silent, personal horror tugged at him. She seemed a decent enough person. He was sorry she was caught up in the middle of this, whatever it was. Maybe he could take her as far as Tara or Ten Bells? Leave her silver to book passage to Cymru, Scotia, or even Bretagne? There were plenty of Siorai retreats in the Colonies. One of them would surely give her sanctuary until all of this blew over. Honestly, what else could he do for her? He was nothing. A nobody. He lived at the edge of the Milesian world, in the wilds of the Greensward. He was in no *position* to help someone like her.

Was he?

Tall Tales

Martin reclined in the Great Hall, enjoying a well-deserved ale when Cunningham's corpsmen marched in. Cunningham's close-clipped red hair, brilliant blue cuirass, and greaves were liberally caked with reeking black mud. His men rushed to tables situated below the dais. They tore into the bread, ale, and porridge laid out for the guards' luncheon like wolves. The Duch was absent. Martin happened to know Patrick was locked in his chambers with the doctor, who was busy trying to coax the Duch's old bowels into relative usefulness. As he'd been at it for about twelve hours, one could safely assume it was not going so well.

Martin set his tankard down as Cunningham approached – the scowl on the captain's face could have been carved in. "That bad, huh?" asked Martin dryly, needing no response. Before this group of outriders even made it south of Ten Bells, he'd known that their trip had proven fruitless. Patrick's daughter was not among them. Cunningham glared. The Duch's absence could only mean he'd have to accept Martin's assessment of this failure— an inconvenient fact which rankled. Martin felt just a pinch of sympathy. Serving the whims of wealthy men was not always a pleasant occupation. "Report."

"I need to see His Grace. What I have to say is for his ears only."

Martin's grey brows shot upward. "That's a bloody shame for you, Wallace because it's my ears you've got." He took a large, sloppy bite out of an apple. "Either make your excuses here, or you can scream them from the dungeons later. Up to you."

Cunningham's unshaven cheekbones went stark white under all the road grime. It rained bloody sheets outside, and the Corps had ridden through it for almost two days at full clip. Martin knew because he paid to know. In due course, nothing came or went along the Shannon Road that he was not apprised of. He knew the hour Cunningham and his men emerged from the Greensward and precisely when they'd entered Ten Bells to lay over. Martin was also apprised of the meals Cunningham had had each day (dried tack, bread, and hard-boiled eggs), what he whispered to his closest companions, and how many times he took himself in hand every night (twice, which was a bit worrisome for a man of Cunningham's age). Martin probably knew more about him than Cunningham's own mother. What Martin did not know was how such a carefully plotted task could have been bungled to such a degree. Only Cunningham had the answers he required. Martin would have them, one way or another.

"May we retire to someplace more…."

"We may not. Say what you must, Wallace. For your sake, I hope it's worthwhile. The Duch is furious. I think you know how dire that is for you and your men," prompted Martin, chewing. Plenty of men and women dangling from cages over the ramparts outside could attest to the Duch's temperament.

"He will not want this information bandied about."

Oh? Well, that *did* sound intriguing. Martin spat out a seed and waved a hand at the men seated around him. Nearly as one, they rose, carrying their trenchers and ale to tables set against the far wall. The Great Hall was much warmer than most of the castle, with its four imposing fireplaces and tapestry-laden walls. At the end of each table, a bronze brazier radiated slow-releasing heat throughout the communal space. The chamber was vented by narrow rectangular windows set high into the slate walls, just below the dramatically arched timbers overhead. Four massive iron chandeliers hung from the ceiling, providing warm tallow light for at least ten hours a day. Each of the eight tables in the room was hewn from whole-split oak and could seat up to twenty men apiece on long benches at either end. Martin sat highest, just below the dais. That was his place, after all, as Commander at Arms. He was the highest-ranking knight in the Duch's service. Aside from Lord Bishop, of course, who was the Duch's nephew. Martin gingerly patted the bench beside him, encouraging Cunningham to get on with his tale. The Captain of the Steel Corps seated himself somewhat farther away than expected, stiff as a board. Martin chuckled.

"Now you have me all to yourself, Wallace."

Cunningham's expression bordered on dread, propped up by baseless bravado. Well, he had cause to worry. Martin had orders to nail his bollocks to a post in the courtyard if he did not like what the captain had to say.

"Sir—"

"That's 'Commander O'Rearden' or 'milord' to you, Captain. I haven't been a 'Sir' since you were swinging from your mam's tits. Get it right, or I'll drag you outside myself." The Steel Corps liked to imagine themselves apart from the hierarchy of the regular army; they were not. Martin enjoyed knocking them down a few pegs whenever he had the opportunity. Especially Wallace Cunningham and his lot. They were fine warriors, true – the finest if he were being honest. That didn't grant them the privilege to flout their superiors. Martin's family had been Merchers. The Cunninghams were gentry… such was the way of the world. Nevertheless, Martin didn't make third in command by being an insufferable lickspittle. Nor would he let cunts like Wallace forget it. Not *ever*.

Cunningham's Adam's apple bobbed. "They were not at the appointed meeting place, milord— I'm sure you expected to hear that. So, we waited a full day more. Bally Lough claims victims daily. We thought perhaps they were forced into the bog before Navan."

"Go on."

"They were nowhere. We searched the bog, the outlying moors, the woods leading into the Greensward, the roads…."

"To the point, Wallace."

"We found them on the third day, at dawn. Dead, to the last man."

"How?"

"I don't know. At first glance, you'd assume it was a raid by poachers or some other ragtag group of ruffians."

"You don't believe that?"

"I don't. The violence was random but efficient."

"Tairnganeah?"

Cunningham squinted. "Possibly. They could have sent one or two men in to do the job and make it look like a raid. I don't think so. In fact, from the sparsity of tracks in the area – I'd say this was one man, maybe two. We didn't find any trace of a large unit of soldiers at the site. We would have to. Citadel Cohort travel shoulder-to-shoulder in groups of six to nine. You know how they work."

Martin dropped his core into the rushes. "I've known Shane Rawly a long time, you know. I fought with him at Dumnain and countless battles besides. There is no bloody way one man could take him and that cunning bastard Conor alone."

"I'm telling you, *milord*." There wasn't an ounce of levity in his tone. "I can read a scene. The tracks don't lie."

"You're saying one fella marches out of the woods, takes Rawly and his men out, then marches back into the trees with our girl? Bollocks."

"Not at all. I'm saying one man wanders out of the Greensward sometime in the night, kills Rawly and his companions, rummages through their supplies, and leaves the bloody girl where he found her."

Now he had Martin's full attention. Cunningham was many things, but a jester, he was not. Martin doubted the man had ever made a joke in his life. Cunningham had risen through the ranks of the Steel

Corps very fast for a man as young as he was, mainly because he didn't have much of a sense of humor. He did what he said and said what he did—a proper soldier.

"And?"

"She was tied to a tree. From the look of things, whoever he was did his deed, fed her, then left her a knife. There was blood on the ropes where her hands would have rested. His tracks say he knelt in front of her for a moment, then slagged off. Took a few coins and some food then disappeared. I think she followed him sometime later when she'd finally managed to free herself. Two sets of tracks lead a mile or so away to another campsite. Only those two. There, they diverge. It's as if he wandered into Rawly's campsite to beg or buy food, was rebuffed, and things went south from there. I think she may have followed him to ask for help, and he refused. It's the damnedest thing I've ever seen, Commander."

"Huh," said Martin, supremely confused by this news. "Some vagabond wanders into their camp to beg for food and just happens to get the best of some of the most vicious men I've ever met. A poacher or other Greensward tough?"

"Doubt it."

"You struggle with the point, don't you?"

Cunningham exhaled sharply. "A trained individual, sir... erm, milord. Someone good. Damned good. Better than anyone in that armpit of the world should be. He'd have to be."

"A former soldier then? A deserter, down on his luck?"

"I don't think so. Mostly used a longbow – the lad's, I expect. Only shot four bloody arrows. I only know of one group of fighters that bloody good with a bow."

Martin slapped his hand against his knee and grinned over at Cunningham. "You're tellin' me this fellow is a *High Elf?* Bollocks! What a bloody pillar of shite."

The look on Cunningham's face said he didn't share the Commander's humor. That's precisely what he thought, though he didn't bother to defend his opinion. He crossed his arms over his cuirass; his mailed vambraces scraped against the steel plate embedded in the leather.

"Do what you want with me, O'Rearden. That's my observation. I know I'm right."

Martin stopped laughing, though the smile remained fixed over his mouth. "That's certainly the most inventive story I've heard in ages. You're serious, I take it?"

"Perfectly."

"You want me to tell the Duch that a rogue Sidhe wandered over the border for some unknown reason, killed Rawly and his fellows, robbed their corpses, and left the bloody Princess of Bethany tied to a tree? You must know how this sounds, Wallace?"

"I did say it was the damnedest sight I've ever seen."

"Doesn't explain where she got to after that, does it? Or why you haven't found her already."

"I left men up there, sir. Disguised as tinkers or other backwoods trash. If she walks into any town East of Navan, I will hear of it. But... there's another problem."

"Of course, there is," Martin waved him on.

"Tairnganeah are everywhere now, and not just foot soldiers. There are Citadel Corsairs lurking at every crossroad. I don't think they're working together, either."

"Well, they wouldn't. Half the city has sided with Vanna Nema against the Cloister, last I heard— including the Corsairs. It's in Nema's best interest, Lady Una never be found." Martin didn't like where this information was headed. "The Duch will be incensed to hear this, regardless."

"I thought the Duch made arrangements?" Irony.

Martin had argued that the old hag could never be trusted from the start. "No one but His Grace believed that, honestly," Martin issued a long-suffering sigh. "Is there anything else, Captain?"

Cunningham straightened. "I take full responsibility for our failure to bring Lady Una back. My men are not to blame."

Martin stood, rubbing his palms together. "Ah, well, that's the thing, Wallace. That part was never up to me. I was only granted the final say about you personally," he nodded to men at a nearby table. Six of them, wearing the white and grey cuirasses of the City Guard, dragged the five Steel Corpsmen to their feet, some midbite. Others spilled tankards, hunks of meat, or bread. Their heavy pewter plates clattered to the flagstones.

"O'Rearden, please! They did their duty!"

"Captain Cunningham." Martin injected every ounce of authority he could muster into his voice. Wallace's men were led away, protesting. "By order of Duch Patrick Donahugh, your men are remanded to the stocks for failing to heed their Duch's commands. He loves his Corpsmen so well that he will spare their lives. Are you protesting the justice of the Duch's command?"

"No. I… no."

"Good. Bully for you, Wallace— I don't think you deserve to die today. You are docked a half-year's wages and will be given ten lashes for your incompetence. Do you object?"

Cunningham drew himself to his full height. "No, Commander. I do not."

"I thought not. Remand yourself to barracks."

Cunningham saluted relief (commingled with abject loathing) apparent in his eyes. "*Sir!*" he spat and stalked from the Hall; his spine as rigid as a marble column. Martin didn't bother to correct him again. The lad might be an arrogant peacock, but he was no liar. Martin watched him go, only allowing himself the luxury of distaste for the situation when he was no longer observed. It did not please him to punish good soldiers for events that were not of their own making. Martin may not care for Cunningham or half his corpsmen, but that didn't mean he blamed them for their inability to foresee the unknowable. They were fine soldiers, and things happened. He'd done the best he could for them. Heaving a bone-weary sigh, he took another long pull from his tankard. He must report what he'd learned to the Duch. Patrick would be incensed. Martin could only hope Lord Bishop would receive the news better and intervene on the men's behalf.

DAMEK PACED BACK AND FORTH in the Duch's privy chamber, squeezing a lavender-scented handkerchief over his nose in revulsion. Martin stood just outside the chamber door with his eyes averted. Thankfully, Damek had caught Martin in the stairwell on the way up to the Duch's apartments. Otherwise, he might have missed the exchange, as the Duch would no doubt prefer. As Bethany's Lord Marshal, Damek kept his own spies and likely knew what Martin knew long before he learned it. In fact, Damek had been dancing attendance upon the Duch for the last two days, waiting for the chance to ambush the old prick with something he didn't already know. This argument between them was long overdue. Damek only wished the Duch had the bloody decency to ask for him after his arse vacated his privy.

"Uncle," Damek said, prying the shutters back to let in some fresh air. He didn't wait for permission to continue. "You should have let me go in the first place. This wouldn't have happened if you had, and Una would be home by now."

Duch Patrick Donahugh, his doughy face gone red round the edges, looked up at Damek with an irritated groan. His jowls were wet with perspiration. One hand gripped the hem of his nightshirt while the other clutched the rim of the privy dock. His gut hung well over his privates, blocking anything untoward from view except his knobby knees and overly thin legs.

"Who is Duch here, boy?" His tone lost some of its bite for the strain.

"You are, Uncle— but that hardly invalidates my point. If I don't go and handle this as it needs to be handled, we could lose your daughter before she's of any use to you."

Patrick wiped his damp brow with the back of a greasy hand. "Humph. Do I look like a bloody fool to you, Damek?"

"I'm not sure I take your meaning, My Lord. Please, tell me how stalling me here has helped in any way?"

"It's done wonders for my peace of mind, not handing my greedy, ungrateful nephew the means to supplant me – that's bloody how."

"The Barons won't sponsor me for Duch unless you do, Uncle. I am not so great a fool as you'd paint me."

Patrick's eyes hardened. "No, they won't, boy. Best not forget it. Some might like your look now, but we'll see what they think of you when you've kidnapped and made a whore of my daughter."

"Marrying her is hardly making a whore of her."

"Tell her that," chortling, Patrick tipped his head at Martin, then raised a brow at his nephew. "You are too young to recall my late wife, boy… that Siorai witch. I lost half an ear and a quarter of my tongue getting that worthless girl on her. If you think my Barons will stand by while you attempt the same on a Donahugh, you're dreaming."

"I won't lay a hand on Una until she asks me to."

"Is that what you think? That you'll make an ally of her?" Patrick's laughter boomed throughout the chamber, drawing Damek's molars into one another like a press. "You know what they teach them, don't you? In that red mortuary, they call a Cloister?"

"Yes. Better than you do, Uncle."

"Humph. I'll bet that's what the Bolgish slut would have you believe, but you'd be wrong. They teach them that men like you and me are irrelevant, boy. She'll never give you what you want. I daresay, especially not you. Remind me, Martin – how old was Una when this young jackass attempted to bed her?"

"Thirteen, your grace," Martin spared Damek an uncomfortable frown. Damek bit the inside of his cheek hard enough to make it bleed.

Patrick shook his head. "*Thirteen*. You hope to make her another offer now? You're lucky she didn't kill you. Hells, that I didn't kill you."

"I was young. I loved her, and she loved me."

"Well, she bloody well might have before you forced yourself upon her. You blithering nonce! Do you realize the trouble I've gone to to undo your idiocy?"

"I did *not* rape her, damn you. You'll never comprehend what's between us. I'd die for her."

"You'd die for her inheritance, more like. Boy, who do you think I am?"

"Believe what you like, Uncle. I'm still the best choice for her, and you know it. Who else could match her but me?"

"Reason save me from ambitious gallants," Patrick pinched the bridge of his nose. "It's been years, Damek. To her mind, she doesn't need any man, least of all some snot-nosed upstart who's presumed too much already!"

"It was a misunderstanding! She fled because she believed I betrayed her to *you*, not because I took her without consent. This has always been your doing, old man." Blood filled Damek's face. "I would *never—*"

"That's enough," Patrick waved his defense away. "I don't care that you lust after my daughter, Damek. Nor do I care that you long for the throne. If you didn't want it, I'd have little use for you. What I do care about is that damned girl returning home in one piece, where she can be put to good use. If you continue to please me and make no attempts to thwart my plans, you may get what you want… one day. Until then, obey."

"May. Soon. One day. *Never*. I've heard all this so often, I wonder if your imagination is drying up? What are you so afraid of, Uncle? If I have an heir, it is your heir. A Donahugh heir, through and through. What else did you bother to raise me for, if not this?"

"My point, dear nephew, is that you reach too far, too fast. Every step you take in your effort to force this issue only brings you closer to a very dark precipice, my boy. You will obey me, or I will teach you the lesson you so richly deserve."

Damek wouldn't bother to argue that he didn't seek the throne. He was the only male left in Donahugh's line. That he was the bastard son of Patrick's long-lamented sister made no never-mind to most. By rights, he was the heir apparent. Let none mistake it. The only thing that could make him a more viable Duch than Patrick himself was a Donahugh bride. If he could get Una with child, there'd be no dispute. The people tired of Patrick. He was ruthless, callous, thin-skinned, and despotic. His Barons respected his rule, but the people most certainly did not. They longed for a more sophisticated ruler, someone with respect for the arts, and an eye to improve trade and foreign relations. They wanted Lord Bishop, and Patrick certainly understood this better than anyone. The only thing Damek lacked was legitimacy: all he needed was Una. Patrick kept him from marching North for that very reason. His power waned in Eire. Soon it would be time to pass the torch to the next generation.

No benevolent god saw fit to make Patrick Donahugh immortal. He had no intention to take his fist from the reins of power until his cold dead hands unfurled of their own accord. He had a legacy he meant to carve out first, a grand design that would cement his name above all his ancestors. Una was the key to the North. Patrick wouldn't give her to Damek right away. Likely, not for some years. He would use her to gain supporters in the Midlands, thus attracting more able men to his cause here in the South. Only after she'd brought him what he required would Patrick consent to give her to his nephew. However long that took. Damek had no bloody intention of waiting. He'd had a bellyful of that already.

"You have my word, Uncle—"

"Oh, shut your mouth! Go and charm your fawners and bum boys with these meaningless platitudes. I know precisely what you will do if you manage to find her. But I'm telling you that if by some miracle I let you go – a rather large *if*, mind – you'd better resist the urge, or it will be the death of you. I vow it."

Damek glanced at Martin, who tactfully averted his gaze. Patrick could play it off, deny the obvious, speak banalities until he was blue in the face. Hells, it was what he had been doing the past few years in general and the past two days in particular. Look where that tactic got him.

"Fine. Cards on the table?"

"It had better be worth hearing," Patrick cautioned.

"I do intend to disobey you. I will suffer her to belong to no one else— not now, not ever. What harm will it do? I am your heir! You raised me, you taught me, and you certainly intend that it should be me who rules after you. Give her to me. Not later. Now. I can be of greater use to you if you legitimize me."

"You are not the anointed heir, Damek. If you continue to test these waters, you'll drown in them. I will give her to whomever I deem worthy... as many men as it takes until my investment bears fruit. Then, and only then, will I consider giving you what you want."

"The Barons will not allow—"

"My Barons will do whatever I tell them to do!" Patrick blasted spittle down the front of his tunic. He waved a cowering girl over from the corner of the wood-paneled chamber. She dipped her sponge in lemon water, then went to work behind him, her expression impassive. When she'd finished, and Damek thought he might vomit, she patted the Duch's arse with a dry wad of linen. The sponge and bowl she removed. Patrick readjusted his clothing. "As will you, boy. As will you." Chuckling, he strode into his bedchamber. Damek and Martin followed, both mute. "So, those witches in Tairngare mean to outwit me, do they? I would dearly like to know what old Nema thought she would accomplish by betraying me in such a way?" He lit a gilded pipe and marched toward the fireplace on hoary bare feet. "Any ideas, Martin?"

"Your grace, I don't presume to know what goes through any woman's head, especially not one of the conniving witches in the Red City."

"Fair. However, the question demands an answer."

"I would think there's likely a disconnect between our source and Nema herself. Perhaps each hand works a separate thread? Who knows? All I can say for sure is someone knew what we planned and set up a counter-maneuver. Until we glean who that may be, we shouldn't depend upon our original source for information."

Damek, wisely, kept his mouth shut.

"Agreed," growled Patrick. He shook his head at Damek. "That doesn't mean I want them to know we're suspicious of them. Boy, I want you to keep your meetings with that woman. Bring every scrap of information back to me. No detail is to be omitted, or I shall know of it. Do you hear?"

"Of course, Uncle," said Damek, rolling his eyes. "I wasn't born yesterday. Besides, I enjoy our meetings enough that it would pain me to halt them over this unfortunate turn of events."

"I bet you do, lad. Would that I still had your stamina. Nema's pet is quite the piece. Isn't that right, Martin?" Patrick's hoarse laughter grated the very limit of Damek's endurance. Martin found something new to ogle, far above his head. "All right then, Martin, take troops north. As many as need be– I leave it to you."

"But, My Lord!" protested Damek.

Duch Patrick shook his fist at his nephew. "You heard me, boy! Do consider yourself duly warned. Disobey me this time, and it won't go well for you. Not at all… do you hear me? Not at all!"

⚜

"My lord," sighed Martin. "I'd be remiss if I didn't advise against this tomfool plan. Your uncle has expressly forbidden—"

"I don't give a tenth of a shite what that sodding old tyrant has to say about anything. I'm going, and that's all there is to it," Damek assured him, adjusting the saddle straps personally. An aging guardsman rounded the corner of the stable, where O'Rearden's men gathered to leave.

"Lord Bishop!" the guardsman huffed, out of breath. "The Duch commands your presence in the—"

Damek grabbed the fellow by his collar and flung him onto his arse. "Do you wish to lose your pension, your home? Have your children sold off to work the mines in Cymru?"

"N-no, milord."

"Then you'd best pretend you never saw me to relay that command. Who do you think will rule here when the Duch finally ceases plaguing us all with his presence?"

The guardsman flushed, his head low. "Very good, milord. S-sorry, milord." He scrambled out of the courtyard so swiftly that the colors of his doublet were but a smear.

"Perhaps that wasn't the wisest course? He will surely rush back to your uncle with news that you've disobeyed him."

"So, what? Let him."

"My Lord—"

"Patrick will fart and wheeze a bit, no doubt. Wax poetic about the myriad ways he'll have my corpse displayed," Damek shrugged. "All meaningless twaddle. He's been vowing to murder me my entire life."

"Damek," Martin used his given name on purpose, "how many times do you think he'll allow you to call his bluff? Publicly or otherwise? My family has served this clan for almost two hundred years. My father once imparted a piece of advice I will now pass on to you: 'never embarrass your betters.' It's saved my life more times than I care to count."

"That dithering old snake is hardly my better."

"At the moment, he is. What's more, his Barons and landsmen believe he is. The Merchers in Ten Bells know he is. As long as they *know* this, they'll never finance another. Least of all, a half-breed lordling, with more bollocks than brains."

Damek's hand paused on his straps. "They sold her out, Martin, and they betrayed us. I must go. I'm all she's got."

"If Patrick disinherits you while you're gone?"

"Don't you realize by now? He can't do a damn thing about it! All he has are threats! If he could have stamped me out by now, don't you think he would have done it? The people love me. The Barons might be loyal to him, but I have the love of literally everyone else. I am the only presence keeping him in power. He needs me now, far more than I need him."

"That may be true, but this wouldn't be the first time Patrick acted against his own interests in a rage. I advise you to be cautious. A defanged bear still has claws," Martin said.

"You know what he will do to her, Martin. He leaves me little recourse. I can't allow him to get his hands on her first. I will not."

"As you say, Lord Bishop. I merely work here. What do I know?"

"Don't be like that, old friend. Your concern is appreciated, as always. But I thought you liked our little princess?"

Martin went quiet. Target struck. He loved every hair on her head as if she were his. Far be it for him to say as much, however. "I do, of course."

"Then don't you think she'd be better off with me than placed on the auctioning block?"

"Yes, I do— but I know your uncle, Damek. He'll find a way to hurt you for this. Hurt you both. I merely caution, not condemn you for your intent."

"I'm going to bring her back. I vow it. Once she's home and safe, I will deal with the treacherous dogs who've betrayed us."

"*All* of them?" Martin's stare was direct.

Damek had the grace to look down. "Most of them, anyway."

"If you will not listen to me about your uncle, Damek, you'd best heed me about that woman. Aoife is the last person you should put your faith in. Has it occurred to you yet, I wonder? For selfish reasons, she might be vested in removing Una from your orbit?"

"It has."

"Well, what do you mean to do about it? She betrayed you. My lady might even now be dead or dying for it."

"I will deal with Aoife, and her mistress, in my own time," Damek said. "For now, let's go find my cousin, shall we? If anyone in Tairngare has harmed her, I'll raze that city to the ground."

Martin's nod managed to appear more like a flinch. "As you say, My Lord. Please consider my council. It's well meant. Caution is always wise, lad. Patrick's rage may be less engulfing than it once was, but it still burns, all the same. He will pay you back for this disloyalty. Never forget it."

"Fair enough," winked Damek, throwing his leg up and over his saddle. Once seated, he shrugged his heavy wolf-skin cloak tight over his shoulders. "I'm sure you're right, Martin. If he lives so long."

From Darkest Dreams

At full dark, a blunt object connected with Ben's bruised shoulder. Half-awake, he tried to shove the offensive appendage away. It wouldn't budge. Grumbling into the dusty floorboards, he cracked an eye open. Rian's moon-pale face stared down at him with unspoken urgency.

"Ugh. What? You are a terrible host, you realize?" he said, attempting to roll over and face the opposite wall.

She nudged him again.

"Keep it up, and I'm going to break that foot. What will you do then, hm? Hop?" He jerked his pilfered blanket over his head to ignore her. The laudanum in her tea wasn't strong enough to render someone of his size completely unconscious, but neither did it make him eager to rise. He was snoring again when her toe plowed into him with renewed force. "Ow! Damn it. Didn't I tell you to slog off?"

"*Be quiet.*" Kneeling beside him, she clapped a shaking hand over his mouth. He was ready to fling her across the small room when he absorbed her expression. Though the fire had long since burned out, he could see the stark whites of her eyes and the bloodless pallor of her cheeks. She was terrified.

He sat up, wrenching her fingers from his face. "Tell me," he said, blinking himself to full cognitive speed. He might not be able to recite a sonnet, but he could at least string coherent thoughts and words together. That was a start.

"Did you try to reset the wards outside?"

He winced.

"You idiot!"

"What's happening?"

She pointed to the back door. "They're out there…."

"How many men?" he asked, getting to his knees.

"Not men. Something… else."

"What is that supposed to mean?"

Having just been kicked awake after a nice drug-induced nap, it wasn't entirely his fault he wasn't quick-witted enough to immediately grasp her cryptic answer.

"Whatever they are, they're not human."

He looked at her like she'd been at her own tea. Then, suddenly, he heard the barest hint of a scrape: a sharp object dragged faintly over stone. Rian opened her mouth to say more, but his palm mashed over the lower portion of her face. Concentrating hard, he tapped into the deep well of Sidhe gifts he'd been born with but found so little use for of late. Now, he could hear *everything*—the two women breathing, one erratically. Rian's heart thudded cavernously against her ribs. The Moura girl's thumped slowly, evenly, in a happily sedated rhythm. Her breathing, however, was not as reassuring. Sucking thin streams of air through her bruised windpipe, she exhaled in rasps.

Narrowing his focus, he marked the more frantic heartbeats of nearby animals: mice in the cupboards, behind the walls, and beneath the floorboards. Birds nested in the eaves, and voles and rabbits dug burrows below the house. Spiders tapped along their webs in the rafters, jingling strands like silken bells. He reached further, listened harder, and cast a wider net. The cow snored in her stall inside the barn. Cud still clung to her broad, flat teeth. Sheep and chickens, snug in their hay, were oblivious to the owls and other nightbirds calling from the trees beyond the barn. Vixen, however, was not so restful. Whickering, she stamped the earth in her unlocked stall. She was upset about something, though he couldn't immediately sense it himself. Cocking his head, he listened while the old mare reared and pounded out of the barn as if something chased her.

He stood up.

"What?"

Ben held out a hand to halt Rian's questions. Leaves rustled in a mild but insistent breeze. Water trickled in the brook, disrupted only by crackling ice and encroaching frost. A half-mile or so distant, a doe scraped her teeth against a birch.

Too far.

Again, he shifted focus. Reeds and long grasses sighed over the pond; a loose gate creaked to and fro in the wind; a latch rattled against the paddock; a magpie chittered from the front of the house.

Nothing.

"What do you think you saw?"

Rian fumbled closer, her clothes sodden from the rain freezing in the meadow. It seemed she'd been caught out in it. Touching her finger to her lower lip, she gestured to the back door, begging him for silence. *That* was when he heard it again. Not the wind nor the flutter of nighttime wings: a shuffle and thump. Bird sounds ceased. The doe halted mid-scrape, ears no doubt twitching toward the farmstead. She leapt into the forest for safety. Her hoofbeats faded into the night, as had Vixen's. The animals in the barn jolted awake. The cow dropped her cud. Sheep bleated in instinctual alarm. A heavy but nimble body stalked through the grass. Vixen, whose ears were sharpest, sensed the danger early enough to escape. A predator drew near. A bump against the back door.

Ben's head whipped around.

"How many?" he mouthed at her.

She held up two shaking fingers. Ben took a step back. His heel unsettled a loose board. He might have shouted a challenge. An unearthly whine… then a snuffling at the keyhole. The back stoop groaned under the thing's substantial weight. Rian squeaked. The creature let out a trill, such as Ben hadn't heard for a very long time. This wasn't a sound one could forget. "Siora!" Rian whimpered.

"Ghasts—" the blood drained from Ben's face. That was why Rian couldn't describe what she saw. They weren't always visible to the naked eye and were certainly *unlike* any animal she would occasion to see in Eire. "Dor Sidhe…" His voice hadn't been any louder than hers, but the thing outside heard him anyway. It screamed, grating as a knife drawn over glass, and hurled itself at the structure. The cottage shuddered beneath its weight. Rian covered her ears and dashed for the corner at the opposite side of the hearth. Ben spread his feet for balance. The door took another timber-splitting blow.

⚶ ⚶

Una's eyes popped open. A thunderous roar shook the house from top to bottom. Something substantial hammered into the back wall like a battering ram. Glass shattered. Crockery burst from their cupboards. Books, utensils, and other bric-a-brac clattered to the floor. She struggled to rise from her couch, only to hear the unseen assailant howl.

A terrible, hair-raising bellow that propelled her heart into her throat. *What was that?* She'd never heard anything like it, nor could conceive of such a sound in her worst nightmares. She sucked in a slow breath, making her one good eye water from the pain. The beast outside shrieked, heaving its bulk repeatedly into the door. Iron hinges bent inward, birthing a deep crack in the lintel above. Una's hand flew to her swollen throat.

"Siora," she croaked, carefully slipping to the floor and moving toward the smoldering hearth on skinned knees. "What is that?" The moment the words left her mouth, she found cause to regret them. A second creature bayed from the front yard. This one flung itself against the house hard enough to bow the heavy oak door inward. The presumed pair took turns barreling into opposite ends of the dwelling with murderous urgency.

She had no idea what was going on. A girl she couldn't quite place cowered in a corner beside the fireplace. In front of her, lowering himself into a defensive crouch, was the enigmatic Sidhe who'd twice saved Una's life. She didn't even know his name. He skimmed her as she approached, his face inscrutable. She didn't know what to make of him. He seemed two different men entirely, depending upon his mood. One, a heartless ruffian with little regard for anything, save his own comfort; the other, someone willing to risk his own life to save a woman he'd previously abandoned. She couldn't puzzle him out. Every one of his actions was contradictory. Her instinct might be to dismiss him as a shiftless scoundrel down on his luck, yet… *nine gold chains* swung from his right ear. Una had the education to wonder: why would a high Sidhe lord prowl the wilds of Eire dressed like a beggar and kill for crumbs? Though she longed to ask, she wasn't afforded the time.

A blood-curdling howl shook the cottage to its foundations. The ceiling's main support timbers shuddered, showering them all with curtains of dust and splinters. Una crept toward them.

"What in the nine hells is *that*?"

Her erstwhile savior's silver eyes flicked her way, then back to the fractured lintel over the rear door. "They're ghasts."

"What?"

"*Ghasts*… Hounds of the Dor Sidhe. They hail from the deepest reaches of the Oiche Ar Fad. Full of insatiable hunger and bloodlust– sound familiar?"

Una's brow furrowed. "You're saying these things come from the Otherworld? Why? How did they get here?"

"Been asking myself the same question," he drawled with pointed cynicism. The creatures circled the dwelling, each searching for any weakness in the structure– a way in. One sword-length claw jabbed through the broken south window, but the opening was too small to garner any purchase. Every wall was reinforced at the casings to prevent buckling. Having been built of weathered Innish oak, it would take some effort to pry loose. Even so, the beast wasn't given much opportunity to try. Some invisible element singed the meat of its obsidian paw, leaving a foul-smelling trace of black smoke in its wake. It yelped in frustrated pain and backed off. Its companion responded in kindred fury. The pair circled twice, then thrice more, growling, snarling, and snapping. On the fourth circuit, they abruptly bounded away. Soon after, a chorus of splintering timbers and baying animals rent the night outside.

The girl in the corner crumpled into herself, sobbing, "*No!* Oh, no... no!"

The vagabond Sidhe laid a hand on the girl's shoulder. "I'm sorry, Rian. Your mother's wards don't extend to the barn."

The girl, Rian, flinched at every pitiful cry.

"Can they get in here?" Each hopeless wail trailed cold fingers down Una's spine.

"I hope not."

"If you're unsure, we have to get out while they're distracted."

"You won't get far."

"*We* won't get far? What about you?"

"I very much doubt they're here for me."

"What's that supposed to mean?"

"I'm sure it will come to you."

She returned his accusatory regard with alacrity. "I've never even heard of such creatures, *My Lord*. They hail from your homeland, not mine."

His head swiveled slowly around. "The name's *Ben*."

"Is it? Nice chains, by the way. You steal those too?"

"Funny." His tone wouldn't melt cream.

"Of the three of us, only one is hunted by her people. Why is that, I wonder?"

"Shut up, both of you!" Rian cut in, with gobs of snot running down her chin. "Who cares why they're here? My animals are out there dying, and we're trapped. What are we going to do about it?"

"We should go," Una repeated, "before they come back."

"That's quite a plan. They'll be on you in seconds, no matter which way you run."

"What else are we supposed to do? Sit here and wait?"

"My mother's wards are only good so long as the house stands," Rian said.

"Can you set more?" Una watched the crack in the lintel widen before her eyes. That wall wouldn't take many more strikes. Of that, she was sure.

"My mother spent years on them. Ben, can you?"

"Bit late to try," he said.

Una kicked out at him with her right foot. "If all you're going to do is sit there and make a sarcastic arse of yourself, then get her out of here, and I'll–"

"Do what? Nag them to death?"

"I'm stronger than I look."

Ben grimaced, remembering. "True, but that sort of thing won't work on Dor Sidhe. You'll be dead long before you can get a hand on one of them."

"Fine. I'll lure them away. Take her somewhere safe, at least," she sneered, raising her chin to conceal her shame. *You insufferable bastard.* "I'll buy time."

Whatever sharp retort he'd been saving died on his tongue. He stared at her as if he couldn't decide what sort of specimen she might be. "Don't be stupid, girl. They'll kill you."

"My name's Una, not *girl*. And, you don't know that."

"Yes, *Una*. I do."

"What else are we supposed to do?"

"Not that," he sucked his teeth at her.

"You're annoying. You know that?"

Rian swiped at her nose. "We're wasting time."

The noise outside grew less ghoulish by the second. Una was tired of arguing with him. "Rian, help me up, will you?"

"Only if we're leaving. I'm a healer, not a sadist."

"Just–"

"Stop!" Ben drew himself up to his full, considerable height, cutting her statement short. "Save your breath. *I'm* going. If you run, it would merely sweeten the chase." He had a very petulant tilt to his jaw that Una wanted to clobber with a brick.

"I can help. If we work together—"

"You'll just get in my way."

Fuming, she watched him stomp to the back door. He paused to retrieve a beat-up Souther longbow Una happened to know he'd stolen from Rawly's camp and a heavy broadsword with a leaping silver stag for a pommel. He slung the bow over one shoulder, and its plain leather quiver over the other, cursing in Ealig all the while. Sliding his sword free of its scabbard, he heaved an annoyed sigh. Shooting her one last indignant glower, he kicked open the door. It dangled queerly from its warped hinges.

"Stay inside!"

Ben didn't have time to fletch more arrows, nor were there any conveniently lying about that he could steal. The few he lifted from the Tairnganeah he'd slain allotted him a whopping three to work with. He must make them count.

Of all the idiotic, pointless things he could have gotten himself into… this was by far the prize.

You just couldn't leave her to die, could you? You see where conscience gets you? You bloody daft lummox. Still mumbling invectives, he slammed Nemain point-first into the ground at his feet. Her hilt vibrated from the impact. Some fifteen feet from the battered cottage, sickening sounds of shredding meat and crunching bone wafted from the barn. Ben was no vegetarian like most of his people, but the horrors he heard and smelt from within that structure might change his mind. The whole farmstead reeked of blood, piss, and putrefying flesh. Wet, smacking mastication accosted his ears. Eyes watering in revulsion, he groaned. The feasting paused. An atonal rumble filled the pasture. The small hairs at his nape stood on end.

Too late to change your mind now…

Two pairs of glowing yellow eyes, set in massive misshapen faces, skulked from either end of the dilapidated barn. Each of their grinning maws poured steaming gobs of gore onto the grass below. Multiple rows of razor-sharp teeth rotated mechanically in their hideous, malformed jaws. Spear-point claws carved great furrows in the soil as they loped forward. Ben's nose twitched at the ozone that crackled along his skin. Everywhere they moved, traces of miasmic void lingered like a charcoal smudge. Like most Dor Sidhe, Ghasts were notoriously rapacious, gluttonous, and difficult to control. Left alone, they would slaughter and feed for weeks. They were insatiable. Whoever summoned these was stark raving mad. One didn't send a lion to hunt a mouse.

He knew of no Sidhe that might have cause to hunt *him* at the moment. Therefore, there was only one person these beasts could be after. He cracked his knuckles, aggravated by the imposition. He'd never heard of Siorai's ability to tap into the Otherworld. Who exactly wanted her dead? Someone with power— serious power. There was more to that blasted girl inside than met the eye. He intended to have it out with her as soon as he finished here. He'd had enough surprises for one week, thank you.

Ri Tuiathe, one of the beasts, snickered, fangs snapping in delight. The second grinned back; a macabre rictus split its garish mouth wide.

Ard Tiarne… it agreed, advancing.

Nocking two arrows at once, Ben droned, "Yeah, yeah. I'm excited to see you too." He widened his stance and worked out the maths. Distance, wind speed, arc, velocity…

Both ghasts stalked around him, cackling. These were creatures crafted from mortal man's darkest dreams. Their bodies were lithe, though ungainly, having the hindquarters of wolves and the grasping forepaws of mountain cats. Their fur was a burning onyx, dark as the gaps between stars, on a moonless night. Sniggering to each other, they were most pleased with the unexpected prey that stood before them. He was the very last Daoine Sidhe they likely imagined they would get the chance to eat. The stench of their fetid breath was so overwhelming that he could taste it. They drew near, taunting, jubilant.

Ard Tiarne! the first chortled with glee.

Ben was unmoved by their elation. "Come and get it then. I'm bloody bored of standing here," he said, taking aim. With twin howls, the ghasts swerved in for the kill. Ben let fly. Two arrows sailed into the nearest beast's open maw. It struck the earth face-first. Its gaping mouth plugged with dirt and rubble. It had scarcely breathed its last before its partner bellowed in rage, a racket to shake the very hills.

Una wasn't one to heed orders, even when they were wise. She hobbled to the open doorway to see what was happening in the yard outside. Clutching a rather useless kitchen knife in one shaking hand, she hefted herself up the ruined doorjamb with the other. Despite her best efforts, it took several painful minutes to crawl so far. Now, she *knew* she wouldn't have been the slightest use against these creatures. Breathing hard, she hoped she was not about to witness their reluctant ally being torn in half. What she saw instead, she could scarcely comprehend. A host of armored men would fear to approach monsters like these, even should there be a dozen or more in their company. Ben, however, marched right up to them with only a sword and three arrows left in his quiver. To add weight to the matter, he did so totally *alone*. Watching him work, the swift deaths of seven well-armed men no longer shocked her. Her jaw slack, Una could only stare.

Ben drew and slew the first beast without stopping to watch his arrows land. Two missiles sailed its open craw mid-leap. It slammed to the ground and died long before its body slid to a halt. Ben jumped out of its way; his attention already fixed upon its partner. Enraged by the death of its mate, the creature beat the ground with a mammoth forepaw. His arm drawn back over his last arrow; Ben casually shifted left as a three-foot claw gouged into the earth near his feet. Just as the thing paused to retract its paw for another swing, he released his bowstring. His last arrow plunged through the beast's right eye. Its baleful roar rattled the teeth in Una's gums. The ghast reared, its head taller than the massive oaks towering over the roof. She'd never seen such a horrific sight in all her life.

Ri Tuiathe, it thundered down at Ben, manic with pain. His quiver empty, Ben flung it aside and rolled for his sword. He moved so fast that Una had trouble tracking him in the shadows. She lived in the most heavily guarded fortress in the world. The Citadel was infested with fine preening soldiers– presumed to be the best in Innisfail. None of them had ever moved as lithely or with such sure-footed grace. She was astounded.

"*Siora…*" she breathed in morbid fascination.

Swinging his sword into a high, arcing guard over his left shoulder, Ben waited for the creature's next lunge. As its claws lanced downward, he charged– so unbelievably quick, all she could discern were the metallic flashes of his sword in the moonlight. A slash here, and the beast stumbled. A brilliant streak there and its flailing claws obliterated one-half of the now empty barn. Again and again, his blade whirled around its torso like lightning crackling through a swirling fog. A strike to its rear hamstring and it backpedaled, uprooting two trees in the process. Another, and it came down with a forceful thud, driving a wall of dust and debris toward the house.

Una coughed as the cloud rushed through the open door. She couldn't make out much beyond the bulk of its spasming body for a moment. Its partially decapitated head leaked mellifluous black fluids into the dry, frigid soil. Dying, it glared at Ben with impotent fear as he approached, sword in hand.

Ard Tiarne… Mo Flaith… it whined as if begging for mercy. She strained to hear. Ben spat on the ground near its twitching claws and hefted his longsword for the final stroke.

"You talk too much." He brought the heavy edge down, cleaving its head in a final stroke.

⚚

AOIFE **W**ATCHED **THE** **S**PECTACLE from the trees, amazed, her fists balled at her sides. This unwelcome complication boded ill for her carefully laid plans. How was this possible? *How?* The girl should be a gory stain in the grass, her severed head an offering laid at Aoife's feet. What could Aoife do? Myriad scenarios played out in her head, each ending very poorly for her, indeed.

I must report this, she thought.

Her agitation bordered on desperation. Her hands shook with the urge to march into that pasture and slay the interloper where he stood so proudly… so *alive*, poised over his kill with perfect authoritative arrogance.

Why is he *here?*

This was such a ludicrous coincidence; she had no idea how she would explain it. A dead man stood between Aoife and her prey, wiping her pet's inky blood from his blade with a bored, disgusted pout. If she hadn't just watched him slay her beasts as easily as he would rub his nose, she might imagine he'd done something inane or perfunctory. Aoife burned to destroy him, once and for all. Without a backward glance, he stomped toward the house, mumbling. Much, which rested on this day's effort, now lay in tatters. The Moura Domina was there, a few paltry paces away, just waiting for the justice she so richly deserved. Not today, Aoife surmised with gritted teeth. Now, she had bigger problems. The one person she'd never expected to see again had materialized out of thin air, like smoke. Worse, he was *defending* the bloody girl! This defied all logic. Aoife had to blink a few times to assure herself she was seeing things correctly.

That unmistakable silver hair, the sword with the prancing stag at the pommel, the merciless skill required to wield it— there was no mistake.

Her ghasts, sacred Dor Sidhe hounds bought with blood sacrifice and tremendous energy, were dead. All because one bloody Dannan lordling didn't have the sense or grace to stay dead as he should have.

How are you alive, you Dannan bastard?

Aoife stumbled away in shock. Now was not the time. This was far too inexplicable a coincidence to be believed. Nema would know what to do if Aoife could convince her not to destroy her for her failure. If *he* was here and involved with the heretic… there was a good chance he wasn't alone. Maybe the Ard Ri sent him here for this very purpose? She pursed her lips. Perhaps not? All she knew for sure was that Nema would not take this news well. Aoife could lose more than her standing in the Red City. She could be marching to her doom.

How would she have had the faintest inkling that such a curious, tricky snag would appear at just this moment? Aoife took her time and planned each word she meant to use, each expression, every gesture. Nema would seize upon any hesitation in her description of the night's events to punish her mercilessly. Aoife had only one chance to convince Nema of the truth. Aoife had no friends, no family to protect her. She had only her word and Nema's dubious mercy.

How can this be?

She raged at the night sky, the wind tearing through the trees, the hardening loam beneath her feet, and the very air she breathed. The walk back to Tairngare was sure to be a long one. She made sure to take it slow.

The Prisoner

Patrick shuffled along the corridor, hands tucked under his arms to avoid touching the moldering walls by accident. There were very few torches lining the way. He found that no matter how many times he underwent this journey, it was best to watch where he stepped. He'd never liked coming down here. The dungeon was endlessly murky, consistently damp– and reeked of piss, vomit, and stale flesh. His father used to bring him here twice a week when he was a child. Duch Michael insisted that to be a strong ruler, one must harden oneself to the pain of others. From a very young age, Patrick was forced to watch as men were interrogated and tortured. His father had been a notorious sadist. He enjoyed the screams, the pleading, the sight and scent of blood. Nothing delighted the old bastard more, in fact. Michael would often take his supper here as if the suffering of men who'd displeased him was mere spectacle for his entertainment.

The first time his father made him watch a man having his teeth scooped out with a speculum, Patrick was ill. Michael had him whipped for that weakness. Patrick was only six. The second event was made grislier by the Duch's express order. A house steward– one who'd practically raised Patrick– had his tongue ripped from his mouth and the skin peeled from the soles of his feet. His father had never given a reason, but Patrick knew it had been a personal punishment, designed to harden him against his squeamishness. He'd learned to swallow his sympathy, strangle any inclination toward empathy, to guard the slightest hint of emotion.

Watching men whipped, bludgeoned, scourged, branded, and flayed before his young eyes, Patrick vowed never to flinch again… and to date, never had. He had very few fond memories of his father. Though, he'd been told his grandfather, Duch Kevin, had been the greatest ruler Eire had seen in a thousand years. Kevin was brave, wise, merciful to the deserving, and exacting when required. Either every tale spun of that great and noble man was false, or Patrick's father had come by his cruelty from some other source.

Sighing at his unpleasant memories, Patrick rounded the next corner. He plodded down the last set of stairs into the dungeon's bleakest bowels. Each of the twenty-six cells on this level was built into the main support arches for the floors above. Every one was a windowless chasm of oblivion– save the farthest alcove, on the right. A flicker of pale sunlight shone from an arrow slit high in the rear wall. Patrick strode toward it with purpose. On his way past each cell, men moaned from somewhere in the deep wet dark they stewed in. None called out to him. Most knew better than to beg the Duch for mercy. Before the rusting iron bars, he snapped his fingers. One of the three guardsmen worked a pronged key through a series of triple locks, then slid the grate wide for his Duch.

"Leave us," Patrick ordered, taking the torch in his right hand. "But remain near." The guards moved a mere six paces from the open door. Patrick hooked his torch into a creaky sconce on the wall inside. It took a moment for his eyes to adjust. Perched on a cot with his back against the seeping wall sat the prisoner he sought. The figure blinked wildly, holding one gnarled hand over his eyes to shield himself from the invasive flame and clutching a bit of chalk in the other. He'd been using it to decorate the walls of his cell with verse. Patrick frowned at the sight. From floor to ceiling were thousands upon thousands of white-etched words and phrases.

A single line was repeated several hundred times: *He knows what lies in the darkness…*

"You know," Patrick's voice carried an added boom in this hollow stone chamber. "I can have these walls scrubbed clean again." Even the ceiling bore evidence of the man's ravings.

The prisoner's blackened fingertips were bundled with bits of filthy cloth. His scrawny arms and legs were bone-white and bare. Nervous, he inched forward until he knelt before Patrick on his cot. The poor bugger reeked of urine and excrement, body odor, and decay. His shaggy grey hair and beard were wild about his face.

"I will only rewrite them." His voice was dry with disuse.

"If I take your chalk away again, what will you do?"

The prisoner held up the dried, bloodied nubs of two bandaged fingers. "One less won't kill me, I'm sure."

"You've gone mad, Brother," said Patrick. He snapped his own arthritic fingers a second time. A guard brought in a tray laden with fresh bread and broth. Patrick gestured for it to be set down upon a moldy carpet.

The starving man, all awkward limbs and animal hunger, leapt upon the tray like a slavering dog. Patrick covered his mouth and nose. The sounds the man-made turned his stomach. The prisoner looked up, mouth wide open, mashing food into his rotting gums.

"If I am, you saw to it yourself."

"You've held the key to your release for years, Henry. Renounce this lunacy, and I shall be lenient."

Henry sat back on his haunches and sucked the last bits of broth from his bread. Despite his obvious cataracts, his eyes hadn't lost their defiant gleam. It pained Patrick to see him like this. Henry had once been a handsome man, far grander to look at than Patrick ever was– that was sure. In their youth, Henry wooed ladies by the dozen. They used to joke that half the Pleasure District was set by just to house Henry of Bethany's mistresses. Now… here sat a scabbed old beggar, decaying from the inside out. He was older than Patrick by some five or so years, but having been bastard-born, he'd spent his life in service to his younger brother. That is until Henry decided *he* should rule in Bethany, despite his illegitimacy.

After Patrick's failure at Dumnain, Henry took it upon himself to rouse the South against him. If Patrick's loyal Barons hadn't betrayed him, their roles today might have been reversed. Escaping his failed coup and Patrick's subsequent wroth, Henry fled to the Outlands of Cymru, a place where folk outside the Colonial Law lived hardscrabble, often brutally short lives at the rim of the Briton Wastes, the soil there too thin and too stony to yield but the weakest crops. The air in the Wastes was noxious with methane vented from beneath the remnants of the Ancients' faded civilization. Only those with no alternative would dare attempt a life there.

When Patrick finally caught word of his brother a decade after his rebellion, he discovered that the once brutal, bastard son of Michael Donahugh had become something of a self-appointed cleric for the Kneelers who subsisted there. Henry would rail long and hard against the injustices of the Eirean city-states and their sacrilegious, immoral peoples. He'd whipped up such fervor among the uncouth frontiersmen– Patrick believed it another of Henry's ploys.

He didn't expect his elder brother to believe the drivel he preached. When arrested, Henry's newfound zeal burned from his eyes like kindling. Henry longed to martyr himself; he craved it like a drowning man craves the press of dry sand. Thus, Patrick had been obliged to toss him into a dank cell: unseen, unheard, and all but forgotten by those above. What satisfaction could be gained from killing a man who lusted for it as Henry did? None that Patrick could stomach.

"Kill me, Brother," goaded Henry, gumming his crust, "and you can keep your walls how you like them."

"If I ever design to have you executed, I will simply have you strangled down here in the dark and your body tossed out with the rubbish. No one will ever hear what became of you."

That wiped the manic smirk from Henry's toothless face. "Then what have you come here for, little brother? To glower at me? Please yourself by my state? Well, look all you like. You will atone for it in the end." Smirking, he crossed himself.

Patrick rolled his eyes. He shifted against the bars and rubbed a clean hand over his balding scalp. "I don't know which is more pathetic, Henry. Your spectacular fall from grace, or this pathetic nugget of theosophical drivel you cling to? Where is this god you claim sees all, hm? It seems he left you here in hell, cloaked in your own filth. I'm the one who will release you… one way or the other, Brother. No one else."

"As you released your lady wife, Patrick? She whom you stole from her people, imprisoned, drugged, and abused? Didn't she drown in the Shannon outside your summer palace?" Bits of moistened bread dribbled into his ragged beard. "So sad that the Duchess had been given no guards that day, don't you agree? The only time you ever permitted her to wander the grounds, absent a half-dozen armed men."

This was not a subject Patrick wished to discuss with Henry FitzDonahugh. "What purpose would it have served to kill Arrin before she bore me the son I needed? You go too far."

"Forcing another's suicide still amounts to murder. Why, just ask Alis about that—"

"I had *nothing* to do with Alis's death, damn you! I loved that girl as much as you!" shouted Patrick, heat rushing into his cheeks. Here it was again: the very same accusation Henry had lobbed at him before the citizens all those years ago. Irrelevant as it was untrue, it had been the bone of contention between them for the past thirty years. Henry blamed Patrick for Alis' death; tragic twist of fate, it was. She went with them to Council in Aes Sidhe before the war. After disappearing from the feast one night, neither brother saw her again. That is, until she reappeared some months later, heavy with child and mad as a tanner. She died shortly after giving birth to Damek.

Patrick gave the boy their mother's surname. The Bishop family were all but extinct from the annals of Bethonair nobility, saving one useless old uncle. It would never make Damek trueborn, but it did help to alleviate some of the stigma associated with his bastardy— a notion Henry should have appreciated more than anyone else. Alis had stopped nursing Damek a week after his birth. For weeks afterward, she haunted the rooftop, 'waiting for her fine 'Sidhe Lord' to take her back. Alis believed he would simply reach down from the sky, like some avenging god, and scoop her into his arms. Patrick would not chain his sister like a dog to stave her madness. Perhaps because of that lapse of judgment, she fell to her death. He didn't have a thing to do with it, but Henry would never forgive him for her loss, all the same.

Henry never let him forget, either.

"I didn't come here to rehash the past, Henry. What you accuse me of, I did not do. You know I didn't. We fought a war against the immortal tyrant who stole our sister, if you recall. A war we very nearly won, if I may be so bold? Now, it's a matter of family I've come here to discuss with you, Brother. Will you listen, or shall I leave you to your ramblings?"

Henry gave him what he assumed was his most condescending stare, stretching his bony back as straight as it would go. "You come to *me* for counsel? That's just… sad, little brother. Run through everyone loyal, have you?"

Patrick refused to take that bait. He turned to the door. "Guard," he said, allowing himself a tinge of pleasure while Henry scrambled backward like a frightened rat. "A chair, if you please? Perhaps a stool, for Lord FitzDonahugh?" When the guard came and went, Patrick seated himself. Henry eyed his brother and the waiting stool with commingled fear and mistrust. Deprived of dignity, men were little more than whipped dogs. Patrick held out a hand. "Please, Henry. Let's have a civilized discussion for once, shall we?"

Henry worried a single black tooth against his swollen lower lip. "It's a trick. You'll have that ape beat me if I try."

"I'll have him beat you if you don't. Stop this. I am not our father." Like a skittish fawn testing thin ice over a streambed, Henry lowered himself to the mildewed carpet, then crept slowly toward the stool. His eyes shifted wildly, as if the guard would burst into the cell with a cudgel at any moment. When no one came after several moments, awkwardly, he lowered his angular rump to its seat. He looked uncomfortable, disused to sitting upright like a human being. That was as well for Patrick. He preferred him disquieted. "I would ask your help with the boy, Henry."

"What boy?"

"Alis', of course. The only Donahugh male left in my family."

"What of him? He's a bastard. I thought you'd have him locked in with me by now?"

"I have no sons, Henry. I'm too old to try for more. After twenty-six years, I have only daughters to carry my line. The eldest of these is an ungrateful Siorai witch, like her mother."

"And? Why are you bringing this to me? The Barons will never support a bastard for Duch. Trust me, I know. You'll have to marry him to your girl and pray Wickert or Sibley don't take it into their heads to oust the Donahughs altogether. Recall what happened with Herbert O'Rearden."

"I do," Patrick squeezed through his teeth.

"What then? If you mean him to rule after you, marry him off, legitimize him. I hope the Barons don't interfere. What's the problem?"

"He's too eager for rule. He takes power before it's granted, defies my orders at every turn, and if I can't bring him to heel... the Barons will have his head on a pike. My line will end. Our grandfather's legacy, all of it... gone."

"What does this have to do with me, Patrick?" At last, a trace of the old cunning flickered to life in Henry's eyes. Patrick felt a thrill course through him at the prospect. The game was never any fun without Henry. He'd ever been his only worthy opponent. "I don't give a damn about your legacy," Henry assured him.

"Ah, but you *do* give a damn about your own, don't you?" Acute silence was his answer. Patrick detected a note of resentment in the air. *Good.* "You have an opportunity here," he went on, sensing blood in the proverbial water, "to cement your own."

"I have no legacy to speak of."

"You have two sons, Brother. Born to a Cymrian woman you wedded outside the Briton Wastes. I've taken the liberty to bring them here, to Bethany."

If possible, Henry went even whiter beneath all that hair and grime. "You wouldn't dare."

"'Tis already done. They reside within these walls, where they receive regular meals, etiquette lessons, and basic schooling. Really Henry, why would you wish to leave them in that shithole? They were half-wild, all but illiterate, and crawling with parasites when we found them."

"I wanted them kept safe... from *you*."

"You should have known you can't keep anything from me. As soon as you decided to appoint yourself some nomadic religious leader, they were as good as mine. Your wife is dead, by the way. What was her name?"

Henry heaved a sudden sob, a pathetic, mewling sound that part of Patrick enjoyed very much. He might not be his father, but he did inherit a bit of his sadism. "Bledydd."

"Lucky for you, we found them, Brother. They would have starved or perished from the same wasting sickness that killed her. Most of your flock are dead from famine, and many of the survivors have formed ragtag bands who roam the settlements, raping and pillaging. I've been told there have been atrocities such as the world has not seen for hundreds of years. You should thank me."

Henry swallowed. He was defeated, and they both knew it. His self-inflicted martyrdom deflated before Patrick's eyes. "What do you want from me?"

Patrick leaned back in his chair, folding his hands together. "I would have you back, Henry. Fully endowed. Your lands, your titles... all."

Dumfounded, Henry shook his head voraciously. "You've never forgiven a single offense in your life, Patrick. Least of all, mine."

"Whom should I pardon if not my blood?"

"You mean to use my boys against me."

"Well, I won't allow you access to them until you've proven yourself to me. These boys are Donahughs. Properly born too— if to a tribesman's daughter. No matter, we can concoct a grander origin for her. They belong here. I want them at my side, towing the family line, same as you." Henry was mute for a long while. His mind ticked through the potential benefits and pitfalls of accepting Patrick's offer. Henry was no fool, despite his irritating newfound philosophy. Patrick needed him. He knew he could never be fully trusted again, but if he could maintain proper leverage, Henry could be invaluable to him— in more ways than one.

"Why now?" asked Henry softly. Patrick forced himself not to smile.

"Checks and balances, Brother. Checks and balances. More Donahughs to stand between my Barons and the throne. Simply put, I aim to remind them who rules here in the South. Given your history with Wickert and his ilk, I should think you'd be eager to upset their plans. Besides, with two more Donahugh boys in the line of succession… Alis' son must try much harder to earn the throne he aspires to."

"Ah," said Henry with a wry, grotesque grin. "The point emerges. You mean to remind him that he needs *you*. Threatened by a rising star, Patrick? I see. If he fails as a potential heir, you gain two spares. I can accept that, so long as my boys are kept from the resulting drama. I'll kill you if either of them comes to harm for your ambition."

"You're hardly in a position to make threats, Henry."

"All the same, you have my vow. Micah, for one, will only heed you at my behest. I expect you already knew as much before you bothered to come down here, didn't you? Isaac will follow Micah's example, as always. They have no reason to trust the man who imprisoned their father these past ten years."

"I do not wish to harm them, Henry. I wish to make men of them— Donahugh men. Even if Damek takes the throne, he will have no support from the aristocracy. Our House will have none. Don't you see? Your sons will be lords of Bethany. Proper Southers, no matter how the succession plays out. The Barons will fall all over themselves to support their rise."

Henry *did* see. He *was* easy to read. "You'll protect them."

"I will."

"From our nephew, chiefly."

"Of course."

"You'll take no revenge on my sons for my failures. Not ever, Patrick. Or I will strike at you in any capacity I have left."

"Yes," Patrick growled. "You've said. Again, my plans will be better served with your assistance but do not depend upon it. Remember this while you're making your threats, Henry. I'm offering you the only olive branch you'll ever get. Accept it or die here. It's up to you."

Henry was silent for a long while, absorbing the magnitude of Patrick's uncharacteristic proposal. Patrick felt no fear that he might refuse. Simply put, what choice did he have? Henry would never be the martyr he desired to be if he died in this god-forsaken hole in the ground. Furthermore, that part of him that longed to see his sons grow tall and strong would never be satisfied. He had only this one chance. Despite the duplicity of the source, any opportunity was better than none, wasn't it?

"I accept."

"Excellent." Patrick rose without aplomb. "On your feet. We must make you nominally presentable before you return to Court. I've stricken the 'Fitz' from your boys' surnames in my records. As far as any need be concerned, they were born to a noble Cymrian lady. It's enough to legitimize them."

Henry cursed. "So simply done."

Patrick paused at the door. "Of course. I'm Duch, Brother. I urge you to remember that I didn't make you a bastard nor drag you to your present circumstances. As long as you serve our house and this family well, I will elevate your sons higher than they should ever hope to rise."

"You want me in your debt."

"You *are* in my debt." Patrick took one last look at the crazed scribbling Henry etched all over his cell. The one phrase which repeated itself over and over dragged a curious scowl over his face: *He knows what lies in the darkness…* perhaps Henry was truly mad? Maybe Patrick had waited too long to redeem him? Only time would tell. Damek had to be collared before he ruined everything Patrick had spent the last three decades striving for. Reappointing his brother to Court was no subtle move. He refused to suffer only one reckless choice for heir. His Barons could rail all they liked. Patrick would be damned if he'd be forced from his throne before his life's work was complete. The boy would learn or be replaced. Patrick exited the way he came, leaving the guards to whisk his brother out of the dark and into the land of the living once more.

WHEN THE NEWS CAUGHT THEM up from Bethany, Damek and his outriders had just arrived at The Ferryman, within the limits of Ten Bells proper. The ride was almost twelve hours for a single horseman and nearly twenty-seven hours for an armored force. Lord Bishop and his men had made the journey in a tidy sixteen hours. Damek never traveled anywhere without fresh mounts at the rear of his line. He prided himself for the speed his priceless Bretagn thoroughbreds could muster. As always, he kept a steady network of spies and messengers at his back, guaranteeing he never lacked pertinent information on a march. It so happened that the latest message beat him and his impressive speed record by half a day. The ranger who'd brought this news had ridden all the way from Bethany in under eleven hours. He'd half-killed his horse to manage it too.

The ranger, Blane, knelt in the rushes beside Damek's booth, clearly done in. Damek ordered the man a chair, but the ranger refused it.

Blane reported, "Milord, there's no fancy way to put it, so I'll just give it straight. The Duch has released Henry of Bethany, Lord FitzDonahugh, from his long internment."

Damek's spoon paused midway between his mouth and a steaming bowl of rabbit stew. Violet eyes flashed below his coal-black brows. "Say again, Ranger?"

"Lord FitzDonahugh has been freed, milord. He's been granted rooms within the interior Keep and the use of Duch Patrick's personal surgeon. He's ailing, it seems, but is expected to recover in due course."

Martin scratched at his beard, eyes going to the ceiling with a rueful smirk. Damek and his guard weren't alone in *The Ferryman's* dining room. Dozens of wealthy travelers gathered nearby, eating meat pie and tarts or tugging at their tankards. None were likely to have missed Lord Bishop's colorful reaction, but few dared to eyeball a man accompanied by so many swords. Damek and his officers were seated at the rear-right corner in a well-appointed part of the Inn reserved for gentry and wealthy Merchers. Six high booths were set into the private dining area, divided from common patronage by a slim paneled wall. A stately fireplace dominated the center of their alcove, which blasted comforting warmth between each row. Only Damek's officers were afforded a fine meal with the Lord of Clare. His rear-guard and uniformed regulars occupied rooms in the dormitory next door. There they would take their meals and sleep on cots in the hall. Lord Bishop himself would claim the lavish suite on *The Ferryman's* top floor—leaving his officers to bunk at the lower levels. As for this ranger, his reward would be a hot bowl of gruel in the stables outside. Such was the messenger's lot in life.

"You're sure of this?" Damek let his bread splash into his broth, rubbing his fingers together to dislodge any crumbs. He gave Martin a long look. Martin smiled without mirth.

"I am, milord. I came as soon as I learned of it. By now, the whole of Bethany must know," Blane replied. He kept his head low, as was proper in such exalted company. Damek had used this man before, he vaguely recalled, looking into his face. The ranger was one of his best riders, and a grand tracker, too, if he wasn't mistaken. Though he was vastly irritated by the news Blane carried, Damek was impressed with the speed by which it arrived.

"Understood. Consider yourself promoted. Speak to my steward at the eleventh bell. He'll register your new rank and pay. First Ranger sounds about right for smashing my speed record. Also, inform him that I wish you to have a proper meal and a bunk downstairs for the night."

Blane couldn't conceal his genuine surprise. Rangers were rarely promoted, remembered even less, and never granted such fine accommodations. His grimy cheeks glowed with renewed admiration for his lord. Damek was well-loved for a reason. That this affection was carefully calculated made no never-mind to men on the receiving end of his generosity.

"Th-thank you, milord."

Damek waved him away. "If that's all?"

"Well, ah…"

Martin stood up, knuckles white against the table. "Speak damn you, boy. What else have you ridden so hard to say?"

The Ranger bowed low again. "The FitzDonahugh, that is, Lord Henry… he has two sons, milord. The Duch announced them to the Court this morning." He withered under Martin's glower. "His grace named them true-born sons of the Donahugh Clan, milord, and he, ah, had their names added to the line of succession."

Martin resumed his seat, mouth twisted. "I suppose he had the exchequer sign and read the document before every courtier in Bethany?"

"Yes, milord," Blane answered with a guilty frown.

"Is there anything *else*?" Damek's tone blew as cold as the wind over a distant mountaintop.

Blane cowered. "No, milord."

"Then go. Do as instructed."

Blane backed out as fast as he could manage.

"Well," Martin said when he'd gone. "The old bear still has claws. I think I said as much. He can still take you out of the running altogether."

"Did you know about these boys, Martin?" Damek inquired, around a mouthful of stew. His typical, slightly bored mask was fixed again upon his face.

"He kept that little tidbit close to his chest. It seems I must have fallen out of favor, somehow. Can't imagine why?"

"Martin, I doubt even *he* knew what he was going to do with them until an opportunity presented itself. He makes much of being some grand strategist, but in truth, he's merely an opportunist with a cruel streak. He never does a damned thing that isn't meant to hurt someone else and waits for these moments with singular pleasure. If I know my uncle, he hung on to the truth of these boys just to spite Henry, personally. If I hadn't displeased him by daring to inspire meager confidence in his Barons, he'd probably have squatted over the knowledge until he died, or Henry dared to before Patrick was done humiliating him."

"Henry rebelled, My Lord. That was quite public."

"Doesn't matter. He locked the man in a stinking cell for almost ten years. There can be only two reasons he didn't have him killed. One, he was waiting for the day Henry might be useful to him again. Two, there's no sport Patrick enjoys more than pitting family against one another. He'll juggle us all like pins. Any who dare falter in rotation will lie where they fall. In truth, I feel for those poor boys. They have no idea what hell they've just been inducted into."

"Aren't you alarmed?"

"Of course I am," Damek said, tearing into his bread with a faraway look in his eyes. "It's Una who will suffer for all of this, you know? If I don't bring her back, he'll supplant me but won't kill me. No. He'll grant me the Henry treatment until I'm needed again. If I bring her home, he means to dangle her in front of all the men in the family– a carrot before the cart."

"Whatever your uncle's intent, I doubt his Barons will support those boys. They had no love for Henry after Dumnain and have even less for him now. You're the obvious choice, no matter how your uncle spins things," said Martin, toying with his tankard. "What will you do?"

"What I set out to do. He's only prompted to act because he fears I'll succeed with Una. We all know his health is failing. It's the worst-kept secret in Innisfail. At best, he has a few years left. Meanwhile, I am young, capable, and best placed to take power. The knowledge must gnaw at his guts every night."

"Here's to the success of our mission then, My Lord. Though I caution you, and you must hear me on this score— Henry of Bethany... now there's a man you must be wary of. Just as Patrick is cunning and manipulative, Henry is cautious and clever. He's trouble, I vow it. He once held the love of the people, much as you do now. Never forget it."

Damek's smile did not reach his eyes. "Never fear, Martin. The Duch isn't the only one who knows how to plan a decent intrigue. The difference between us is our approach. He sees only the rules of the game as he makes it."

"And you, what do you see?"

"There are no rules, Martin," Damek's teeth flashed very white, wolfish. "And I stopped playing his game a long time ago."

Prima Moura

"**Y**ou!" Ben dragged the Siorai noblewoman from the doorway and dropped her heavily onto the couch. Rian lurched to her side, but Ben stalled her with an imperious wag of the finger. His gleaming eyes promised he'd do worse to Rian if she interfered. "Stay," he warned and fixed his attention upon his intended target. "Explain this now while I'm asking politely."

"Explain what?" Una's expression teetered between nausea and shock.

"Don't play with me, girl. Why are they after you?"

"I'm... not sure."

Crossing his arms, he pushed his face into hers, eyes narrow. "Oh, *really*?" Rian made a fumble for his elbow. Shrugging her off, he growled at Una. "You're going to tell me what in the hells is going on, or, by Herne, I'll wring what's left of your neck." Ben had never maltreated a woman in his life, but just then, he seriously considered altering that policy. He was owed answers. If he must shake them out of her, so be it. Una met his glare with a deep reservoir of calm. Something slid behind her face— an unseen energy coiled there beneath her skin. Without realizing it, her fingertips came bare centimeters from his jaw. He backed away so fast that he nearly tripped over his own feet. That indefinable sound he'd heard when she touched the first Corsair hovered in the air between them like an afterimage. His skin crawled.

She gave him a slow, smug smile. "Touch me again. I dare you."

"You wouldn't."

"Why don't you try it and find out?"

Bluff called; his nostrils flared. Instead, he scowled down at her with all the masculine derision he could muster. "Three times, I've been obliged to kill to help you."

"Twice, I think you mean? You helped yourself to a hank of venison the first time and left me tied to a bloody tree."

He shrugged. "Still counts."

"You *can't* be serious?" scoffed Una, incredulous.

"You're alive, aren't you? Now, answer the question."

"You're one to talk, *tuaithe*. Why is a Dannan lordling traipsing around the Greensward, dressed as a stinking vagrant and murdering for uishge? Hm? You tell me that– and I'll tell you whatever you want to know."

Ben bared his teeth. "Ladies first."

They stared each other down for quite a while. Having grown uncomfortable at the tension between them, Rian resumed her seat by the hearth. Ben didn't budge. Una looked away first.

"Fine... but I'm not sure where to start."

"Try the beginning."

"All right then. Ah, you might have heard there's been some trouble between the Cloister and Parliament?"

Ben's brows cinched up. "What does that have to do with—"

"Prima Moura, isn't it?" Rian cut in.

"How'd you know?"

She pointed. "Your tattoos."

Una glanced down at her exposed arms. "Oh. *Right.*"

"You're the Domina, aren't you?"

"Not by choice."

"I see."

"*I* don't," rumbled Ben. "Why were you taken from the Cloister, only to be hunted down by your men after? It doesn't make sense to me."

"I wasn't taken. I left of my own accord."

Ben went quiet for a moment. That hadn't occurred to him at all. "Then, how did you end up with Rawly and his lot?"

"I trusted the wrong person," she said. "Rawly caught me on the docks at Drogheda. My escape was foiled, you see?"

"In Brida's name, why were you trying to leave?"

"I meant to start over in Scotia, or perhaps Bretagne. It hardly matters now, does it?"

"All right... let me get this straight. You made arrangements to leave the Cloister but were set upon by mercenaries from Bethany. I'm assuming this person you shouldn't have trusted arranged to have both you and your abductors assassinated on the road. Again, why? Why would someone want you dead?"

"Do you have linen between your ears? I *just told you.* I'm the Moura Domina. Doma Drem is my grandmother."

"That means nothing to me."

"My mother was Arrin, the eldest...." Una said, nodding slowly as if teaching a child how to speak.

Ben ignored her condescending tone. He knew that name but couldn't quite remember why it was important. Something to do with the Doma, and... he'd had a bit too much of Rian's tea tonight.

"This means what, exactly?" Both girls looked at him like he'd asked why water was wet. He bristled, spreading his hands. "Am I not speaking the common tongue? Explain it to me."

"Do you live under a rock? Everyone knows who Arrin Moura was, you fool," said Rian.

Una rolled her eyes at his blank face. "My mother was Queen of Tairngare, inasmuch as anyone can actually rule in the Red City. Nothing more than a figurehead, really. Do you get it now?"

Ah. That Arrin... great gods... you are a fool.

Slowly, a deep crease formed between Ben's brows. Drem Moura used Arrin to reach for more power in Tairngare, and it had cost the girl her life. That's what he recalled anyway. Supposedly, the Doma had something new up her sleeve that everyone was incensed over. He'd heard a few snippets of gossip swirling through the North about this more recently but couldn't have cared less if he tried. Milesian politics were as pointless and impermanent as a cloud tracing over the sun. He could never keep the details straight.

"I'm sorry about your mother, but why does this matter? She died years ago, I think."

"My grandmother is determined to repeat her previous mistake by holding me up to Parliament as the next Queen. I assume she believes that by forcing me into this, she can instill a Moura Dynasty. The Commons are unamused, and frankly, so am I."

More silly Tairnganese politics. "Mercenaries from Bethany kidnaped you because your grandmother declared you Queen... and Corsairs from the Citadel want to eliminate you for this reason?"

"Isn't it obvious?" Rian broke in with a huff. She held out a hand to the girl on the couch. "This is Una Moura, daughter of Arrin Moura, granddaughter of Drem Moura... and that makes her father Duch Patrick Donahugh, you dolt. Honestly, you *have* been living under a rock, haven't you? Lady Moura here is the heir apparent to the two greatest cities in Eire."

A sudden, irreversible heat clawed its way into Ben's throat. The room vibrated at the edges of his vision as if every nerve in his body decided to stand up all at once.

"*What?*"

Una Moura *Donahugh* stared back at him, visibly surprised by the venom in his tone. "Patrick tried to use my mother to take Tairngare before I was born. I'm sure you've heard of that, at least. Not long after, your High King was forced to wrestle the North from him." She looked anywhere but at him. His silent glare must have unnerved her. "Anyway, he took her against her will and held her captive until I was born. I fled Bethany when I was thirteen. In the South, I am his property, you see? He means to reclaim me."

I have soiled my hands for a fucking Donahugh?

Clenching and unclenching his fists, he cleared his throat. He couldn't believe his rotten luck.

"What were you thinking just now?"

"You don't want to know."

"Fair enough."

He should have left her in the woods… he should have dropped her on this doorstop and walked away… he should have… he grew more incensed by the breath.

"Who helped you escape the Cloister?" He should have walked to Navan that night and drank himself to death in the *Bowman's Cross*. Or walked to Slane, maybe? Hells, he could have gone *anywhere* else. If only he hadn't been drunk, hungry, and curious, he would have avoided this mess from the start. Better yet, if he hadn't pretended to hold some moral superiority over her Souther captors, they might all be alive, and Patrick fucking Donahugh's daughter would have met whatever fate she deserved by association.

He was furious with her. Livid with himself. Positively irate with the Gods. This was a sick, cosmic joke.

It *must* be.

"They're irrelevant—the point: they work at Vanna Nema's behest. Nema offered me a way out. I was desperate and stupid enough to take her at her word. All of this is my fault. My irresponsible cowardice. I'm sorry." Her apparent sincerity didn't assuage Ben's anger in the least.

"What will you do now, my lady?" asked Rian, flinching from Ben's thunderous, disapproving face. He couldn't help it. There wasn't a name in all of Innisfail that he loathed more.

The daughter of Patrick Donahugh, he derided himself. *You've saved your worst enemy's child.*

"I don't know. I haven't exactly had time to think it over," said Una, absently touching the wound at her temple. Her eyes popped at Ben. "Will you please stop glaring at me like that? You're making me nervous."

"Sorry," Ben lied.

"Look, I know how your people feel about the Duch. Just so you know, he's not my favorite person, either. I didn't ask for any of this, and I can't help who my family is."

She was right, but that didn't make him feel any better. Patrick Donahugh was the author of his present circumstances. There wasn't a man on earth Ben loathed more. He let out a long hard breath.

Calm down.

"Well," interrupted Rian, throwing up her hands. "Let's get you back to bed. We can figure out what to do later–"

"No," Ben refused. "We can't stay here."

Rian turned on him. "What? Why not? She should be abed. We might not get the door fixed tonight, but we can at least close it off…."

"No," he repeated. "Whoever sent those beasts is bound to know they've been destroyed. They're unlikely to stop now if they've gone to this much trouble."

"Wait, just a moment–" Una began.

Ben held up a hand, cutting her rebuttal short. "Do I need to spell it out for you? It's not safe here for you, for me, or for anyone around you. We have to go as soon as possible."

"We?"

"*I* can't leave… are you daft? This doesn't have the first thing to do with me. It's you two who should go!" Rian protested, hands on hips.

Ben prayed to Danu for patience. "If you want to wait for Corsairs to follow these beasts, by all means. Do as you like, Mistress. I thought you were smarter than that." He scrubbed a hand over his face. Of all the random encounters in the world, Una just had to be a Donahugh. This was going to get messy. Bound to become a bloody political carnival, no doubt. The thought incensed him. What did he care for Milesian politics? Which temporary body occupied whichever impermanent throne was all the same to him! All he wanted was an ogham stone, to return to his life in the border towns, to drink, dice, and fornicate his miserable way through his remaining time in Eire. Ben wanted to be no one. He'd no wish to involve himself in these pathetic Milesian power struggles. He should leave the girls here to fend for themselves. Hadn't he spilled enough blood already? Yet… something else nibbled at the corners of his mind—something he hadn't considered until now.

"Where will we go, hm?" Rian asked. "Where *can* she go, where she would be safe? The colonies? Bretagne? To the High King?" She paused when the color drained from Ben's cheeks. His eyes flew wide as if she'd just imparted the secret to life itself. "Siora," she said. "I was being sarcastic, you know. The High King doesn't involve himself in Eirean politics. Unless someone is marching on the border, why should he care?"

"I'm sorry I got you into this, Mistress… Rian, is it?" Una offered, despite Ben's comments. Rian waved her away. Instead, she watched Ben closely. He said nothing, but he might as well have been shouting.

"You can't be serious? You might cross that border without repercussions, but her? You're deluding yourself. You'll have to apply for a permit at the Sidhe Consulate in Ten Bells and wait for your case to be reviewed. It'll take months to be considered. By then, she could be dead."

"He can't cross on his own either," Una said.

Ben rounded on her. "What do you know about anything?"

"Stop assuming everyone you meet is a fool, *tuaithe*."

"What do you mean he can't cross? The stone? Is that why–" both parties ignored Rian's questions while they glared at one another.

This time, Ben broke eye contact first. The damned girl had far too much sand for her own good. "I must think this over. Get packed. Only the essentials, mind. I'm not a bloody mule! When I return, be ready to leave."

Rian stammered, "Wait just a minute! You can't order me to leave my own home!"

"If you want to live and possibly make something out of this situation, you'll do what I say," he cleared his throat, ignoring Una's suspicious glare. "I'll be back." He needed to get away, outdoors, where the cold air waited. His thoughts were a riotous jumble only the night wind could untangle.

❦

SIMPLE. OBVIOUS. WHY HADN'T HE pieced it together from the first? Ben truly was a blithering dolt. All this time, he'd been trying to avoid involving himself in Milesian troubles… and the answer to *his* had just dropped into his unsuspecting, ungrateful lap.

You're a spectacular fool!

Donahugh's child– indeed. His heart hammered against his ribs. His palms were clammy. Why had it taken him so long to realize the advantage here? He was so determined to avoid any inconveniences that he'd almost wholly missed the glaring point.

Una was a Moura, but she was also a *Donahugh*!

As much as he loathed her father and the Southers in general, the fact that she happened to be Patrick's daughter made her extremely useful to him. Who would most benefit if he removed her from the playing field altogether? If the Moura faced internal conflicts in the Red City, Tairngare's government would be unstable– weakened to advance from the South. This was a flaw Patrick must be salivating to exploit. Whoever sent those Corsairs to 'clean up' after Rawly and his men knew what the Duch would do next.

The girl was fodder for the ambitions of others.

Unless she could escape to the High King's Court… Midhir would want to know about this. He would want to eliminate any claim Duch Donahugh could manipulate to rule over a unified Eire. The Ard Ri did not want another war. He would be happy to intercede in this matter, Ben knew. If only someone could hand the High King complete control over the situation before it came to that. Someone with no inconvenient ties to either faction in Eire. Someone with nothing left to lose… someone like Ben.

The knowledge brought a fresh current of electric anticipation with it. Pacing around the front of the battered cottage toward the North road, his nerves felt like they might burst into flame over his skin. He took a deep breath to still himself. He could go home! Not to Rosweal. Not to Navan. No more border hovels and backwaters. Home. To his own life– his position, his family, his name. The girl was a free pass back to Aes Sidhe. This was *beautiful*. He mustn't embellish a single detail. He'd saved her life three times without having the first clue who she was or why anyone wished her harm. Better yet, she could readily testify to that. By bringing her to the Bri Leith, he'd prevent another bloody conflict in Eire and stall any future invasions of Aes Sidhe from the South. Ben might be welcomed back into the Ard Ri's court with open arms!

Ben felt like he'd just discovered a pot of gold under a thorn bush. There were, however, a few minor details that needed seeing to before he could make this thrilling new prospect a reality. Item one: he was forbidden to cross the border upon pain of death. A trifle this was *not*. He would either have to take the girl to the Consulate in Ten Bells to await a permit to cross or brave the border alone. If the first, he would likely be turned away at the gate or be forced to wait months for a temporary pardon. Worse, the Ambassador could simply seize the girl and negotiate with Tairngare or Bethany for her release. Odds were, if he took her to the Consulate, Midhir would never hear a word about Una… or of Ben's involvement. That would not do. Not in the least. What was the point to any of this if it didn't benefit him too?

The latter option was far riskier.

Far deadlier.

He'd need help… someone who could get word to Bri Leith and negotiate a temporary reprieve for himself before he attempted to cross with an Eirean fugitive. There was just one individual in Innisfail he knew of that could help him manage this. The only person that might help him, regardless of his current standing in Bri Leith. He had to get word to his uncle, Diarmid. Moreover, Ben needed a place to lie low until he could get in touch with him. Since the girl was bound to be pursued through every town, hamlet, and village in the North, there was only one logical place Ben could go.

He winced at this further complication.

He must return to Rosweal.

※ ※

"I WONDERED HOW LONG IT would take you to figure out how this could work in your favor," mocked Una as he boosted her onto Vixen's back. He shot her a look that should have made her blush. Instead, she blew an exaggerated breath through her pursed lips. "What a shame. I haven't any gold or uishge to pay you with, either."

Shoving her foot viciously into the stirrup, he waited for her answering hiss of pain before he jabbed a finger at her. "Let's get this straight. You simply appeared in my life. I didn't leap into yours, causing trouble and mucking up your plans. Did I?"

Her lip curled. "I suppose not."

"Then shut your mouth, hm? If it's occurred to me that this situation might— just might— have a decent ending for me, then so be it. You'll just have to make peace with that, or I'll slog off, and you can figure out the rest on your own. Ten Bells is that way," he tugged his thumb behind him.

Rian hobbled up to the gate where Vixen was tethered, already huffing from the weight of the pack at her back. Ben had ranged over two miles to find the old nag, and it took him quite a while to calm her down enough to follow him back. Vixen nervously pawed the ground beneath her hooves. She didn't care for the foul stench of the two deceased beasts nearby nor the hostility of the people holding her reins. Rian patted her flank as she walked by.

"What are you two arguing about now?"

"Nothing of import," Ben replied, with a narrow eye on Una. "Only that we should stick to the game trails, far from the roads."

"Surely we can't just stroll across the border," said Rian, crossing her arms. "I'm not taking another step until you explain yourself."

"He's exiled," Una suggested helpfully. He chewed the inside of his cheek at her, but she ignored him. "Seems an important one too. What? I told you I wasn't stupid, *Ard Tiarne*."

"I liked you better when you couldn't talk," he said.

"Ard Tiarne?" Rian choked back a laugh. "Do you know what that means, Lady Moura?"

"Given the amount of gold in that right ear, it seems we should be honored," Una made a rude sound. "Means he used to be a big someone in Aes Sidhe, doesn't it? In the past tense, of course."

Ben shouldered his small pack and readjusted his weapons without comment. If he lingered too near her, he might reach up and jerk her into the mud, the ungrateful, waspish, little wench. Maybe he should leave her and be on his way after all? It would cost him his first solid chance to go home in almost three decades, but he just might finish the job the Corsairs started at this rate.

"That makes us quite a pair then, doesn't it? 'Queen Donahugh.'" He watched her grin fade with intense pleasure. "We don't have time to discuss pedigree at the moment, do we?" He gestured up the muddy lane toward the west. "Shall we?"

"Which is it?" Rian prodded. "O'Ruiadh, Bres, O'Donnell… come on, there's only six High Lords in Aes Sidhe. What do they call you–"

"Ben," he said with finality. He grabbed Vixen's bridle and turned up the road, cursing long and loud in his own tongue. Una shifted uncomfortably in the saddle. Rian was forced to stumble up the lane behind them. "My name's Ben Maeden, and that's as good as you're going to get."

Misery, In Company

Ben, Una, and Rian spent the better part of two days wandering the Greensward southeast of the Boyne and avoiding the roads. As expected, the weather was dreadful. After an evening, squalls had stripped the leaves from nearly every tree. A stark wasteland spread before their eyes– full of drab browns, dull greys, and mournful blacks. The only sounds were spattering raindrops, creaking limbs, and the steady chattering of their teeth. Omnipresent mud ruled all. It seeped into their boots, dragged at their cloaks, and wormed its clammy way into their stores to mingle with their swiftly dwindling supplies.

The girls bore up better than he thought they would. Other than a few questions pertaining to direction or to clarify a plan, he didn't hear a single word of complaint from either of them. He was both surprised by their steely-eyed determination and irritated by it. It was rather embarrassing that they should feel less daunted by the abysmal climate than he. What sort of Sidhe loathed the wilderness? The shame he felt at that thought amplified his general insouciance.

Ben would lean into the wind a bit and dream of distant taprooms. It was easy enough to resist temptation for the first day or so. When they came too close to a town, the flash of steel winked at them through the trees. Everywhere they went, Tairnganeah patrolled in force. Rather than risk being seen, they would press on. In short, order, playing it safe lost its appeal. By late afternoon of the second day, the persistent fog they'd been muddling through graduated to a torrential downpour. They spent a sleepless night under a canopy of hardy pine trees that offered little protection against the elements. Most of the next grim day was spent hacking and sniffling into their soaking wet cowls.

As their third night in the Greensward loomed, they were all sodden, shivering, and despondent. Ben conceded defeat. They must find somewhere to dry out, a place to sleep, and something warm to eat. With few trustworthy options nearby, Ben had to make a decision fast. Navan might be the safest place outside of Rosweal to spend a night. Warmth. Food. Sleep. *Uishge*— siren songs, all, lured them through the trees like a match in a cave. At dusk on the third day, they hesitated outside Navan Village, wretched and desperate. Rian sidled up to him, holding her already soaked hood up against the rain. Her thin face was as blue as her eyes.

"W-will we… be safe in there?"

Ben patted the little river stone resting below the neckline of his tunic to ensure it was snug and secure. He'd strung it through two strips of leather this time, just in case. Rian's arcane skills were no match for the craftsman who'd carved his previous ogham charm, but they would do. He didn't look quite so much like Ben Maeden as he had before. Maybe he was a little too tall, his bones a little too fine, or perhaps his eyes were a mite too bright? No matter. Only those who knew him well would be given real pause. He was satisfied that he could walk around without drawing attention to himself.

"I don't see we have much choice," he said, meeting Una's wary expression over Rian's head. She, too, drowned upright in Vixen's saddle. Una made a reflexive gesture, proposing he make the call. If Ben chose wrong, they might be forced to fight their way out. He was too bloody tired to fight. Too hungry, too wet, too cold… and far too sober, all told. He needed to dry off, eat, and drink himself to sleep– in that order. "Rian, I'll need you to loan me one of those fainne."

"Not blo… ody likely," she argued, her lips purple.

"Do you fancy freezing to death?" She didn't answer immediately, but Ben knew what her response would be. The longer they waited, the colder it would get.

She dug into her pocket with a stern scowl. "Jus…t so you know, I'm keeping tally."

He shifted the coin to his belt. "Course you are. Look, I've been here before. If we pay the innkeeper well, he'll overlook the oddity of our circumstances and say nothing about us to anyone. I'll wager on it." he nodded up at Una. "Cover your face, and whatever you do, don't say a word. That haughty Tairnganese trill is a dead giveaway."

She muttered something unkind under her breath, but he ignored her. Taking Vixen by the bit, he led them downhill. The old mare nickered, excited by the scent of home and the prospect of her cozy stall, no doubt. He felt a genuine pang of pity for the poor creature, being treated as she had been for the last few days. Maybe it would be best to trade her for a more spirited animal? He didn't have time to consider the matter too carefully as they rounded the muddy intersection near the *Bowman's Cross*. Turning down a dark side-alley toward the stable, he was grateful for the poorly lit streets all over again. Tonight, the lamps were lower than they had been upon his first visit, and far less light shone through firmly fastened shutters in the tavern proper.

As they neared the stable, the proprietor's lad looked up from the tack he was polishing. He was so happy to see Vixen that he scarcely glanced at either girl. Ben knew he liked this place. It wasn't Rosweal, but in a pinch, it served. The stables were largely devoid of horses, which suited their purposes quite well. Most folks had better sense than to travel through a Dor Samna deluge. Ben could only pray that any advancing Tairnganeah would eschew humble little Navan altogether. There were undoubtedly much finer inns and more illustrious company, a short march back east. Ben handed the boy an extra two coppers for his tact and care. The proprietor's son slid the coins into his vest and led them inside with nary a word. Enveloped in a blast of heat and smoke, both girls sighed. Ben slid off his gloves and placed his florid fingers on the bar to thaw.

The innkeeper took one look at Ben's sealskin cowl and gave him a gap-toothed grin. "Good to see ye again, Master. What'll it be?"

"A single room? For me n'me sisters?"

The proprietor hardly glanced at the girls, but a slight twitch to his lower lip said he was far from stupid. "Very good, sir. The same room is available. I'll have me boy bring ye a cot and some peat for yer hearth. Will ye have hot water and a tub brought up? A rack for yer wet things, perhaps?"

As polite as he was, Ben repressed a groan at the cost this would likely incur. "Aye," he said, sliding Rian's royal fainne across the bar. "I trust ye'll have the means to make change for this?"

Gold sparkled from the innkeeper's dilated pupils. He licked his lips. "Indeed, sir!" he scooped the heavy coin into his palm and shoved it deep in his apron before any wandering eye might catch its gleam. "I'll get that ready for ye, directly. Ye shall have extra blankets, pillows, and all the ale ye wish for on the house. Also, I have some ladies' things set by from me own dear wife. I'll have me lad bring those up as well, shall I?"

"Just the thing. If ye will, the lasses will take their porridge upstairs."

Grinning happily, the proprietor poured Ben a towering tankard of spiced ale and a full pint of uishge to match. Ben plopped down, eying this bounty with a fat lump in his throat.

"If ye'll follow me, ladies," said the innkeeper, coming around the bar with a heavy set of swinging keys. "We'll get ye sorted."

"Wait," stalled Rian, reaching around Ben to grab both his tankard and the glass of uishge. He moved to stop her, but she batted his hands away. Una attempted a hideous wink as they were herded upward.

BEN FELT SOMETHING BRUSH HIS elbow. He'd fallen asleep at the bar; arms wrapped tightly around his tankard. The innkeeper, for once, wasn't wiping anything. He leaned over the bar, arms splayed, palms down.

"And to ye, good sirs." His voice carried a bit further than it should have. "What will ye have?" Ben shook himself. Someone stood near the rear exit, on his right. Several someones, in fact, escorted by the stable lad, with a poorly concealed panic evident on his face. Ben sat up, suddenly alert as a hare. Three men, wearing the black and gold emblazoned cuirasses of the Citadel Corsairs, waited impatiently for service at the opposite end of the bar. Ben dipped his nose into his pint, feigning drunken disinterest. Each bore the typical Citadel-issued rapier sheathed in their belts, and their silver spurs were slung low over their ankles— cavalry officers, no less. Their heavy grey cloaks dripped lakes into the rushes beneath their boots, and due to the warmth from the peat-fed hearth, tendrils of steam curled over their shoulders. Ben took a long pull from his lukewarm ale and observed them from the corner of his eye. One of them spared Ben a cursory sneer. His companions seemed more interested in the innkeeper and his wares.

The tallest of the three, marked out by his golden torc as a captain, dropped a fistful of coppers onto the bar. "For our mounts," he demanded in his nasally Tairnganese drawl. "There's more where that came from if I find they're brushed and clean come morning."

The innkeeper cleared his throat. "O'course, sir. How many beds will ye need? We have only two rooms left, but I can have me lad set cots in the loft, above the stables–"

"That won't be necessary. We'll split the two rooms. There are five of us. Two beds to a room, I hope?"

"Beggin' yer pardon, sir, but no. I have cots aplenty if that will do?"

"I suppose it must, though my men won't thank you for it," the captain said sourly. "We're accustomed to better service."

"Porridge and ale, on the house, sir. Boy, get upstairs and see to them rooms." He handed over his heavy ring of keys. On his way, the lad sent Ben a non-verbal warning. Message received. Ben set his empty tankard down as quietly as he could and relinquished his stool.

With a pointed interest in Ben, the Corsair stepped in front of him as he neared the stairs. "You," he sized Ben up. "You're rather tall."

"So I've been told." Ben tried to step around him. The smaller, stockier soldier pressed a gauntleted fist into Ben's chest. Ben froze.

The look on the proprietor's face was mild, but the tension in his jaw belied his neutrality. He seemed well aware of the danger.

"You a… what're they called?" the Corsair's nose cinched up. "A 'faerie'? That why you look like that? Yana, what do you think?"

The third soldier shrugged; he was more interested in the tankard of ale the innkeeper hastily placed in front of him. "Don't care. Ask him if he's seen our fugitive."

"I hear you're all deformed," laughed the man with his hand on Ben's sternum. "Born without cocks or brains. You have a cock, faerie?"

Ben took a deep, stilling breath. If he killed this man, he'd have to fight all of them at once, alone. He was damned good in an open field, but close quarters like these were nowhere near as promising. Ben held his tongue while the two soldiers laughed at his expense.

Their captain wasn't as amused. He commandeered Ben's discarded stool. "That's enough. You may follow him upstairs for a peep and tickle if that's what you're after, Dara?"

Dara's hand slid away, and his smile faded. "We're looking for a girl. She's about five-and-a-half feet tall, amber eyes, curvy. Loads of tattoos. You see a girl like that, faerie?"

"No," replied Ben, straight-faced.

"If you had a cock, you'd remember her. Warm, brown skin. Sweet, full mouth. Sure you haven't seen her?"

"Sergeant," warned the captain, sipping at his tankard. He twisted to focus on Ben, his face stiff as a stone. The captain was tall for a Milesian and broad through the shoulder. He had an unmistakable, aristocratic tilt to his jaw. The Corsairs of the Citadel— which defended both Parliament and the city gates— were most often selected from the grandest houses in Tairngare. To achieve the rank of captain so young, he must belong to a relatively important family. He wore his hair in traditional, foppish Tairnganese fashion: long braids bedecked with golden beads and unpolished gems. "What's your name?" he asked, his tone casual.

"Ben."

"Just Ben?"

"Maeden."

The captain held his tankard in front of him. "That a Souther name, Ben?"

"No. My folk're from the West, near Fenn."

"Ah, I see," he took another sip while Dara moved around Ben in a slow, calculating circle. Yana attacked a plate of bread the innkeeper placed on the bar, heedless of the interrogation. "Tell me, how'd you come by that fine cloak? Last I checked, there aren't many seals in Fenn, being landlocked and all."

"Bought it off a tinker's cart in Ten Bells. Seemed a good investment at the time. Proved handy this week, sure."

"What brings a half-breed from Fenn to the Greensward?"

"He's got a nice bit of steel in his belt there, Captain. Sidhe make if I'm not mistaken. Real longsword." Dara whistled appreciably.

"Answer the question, Master Maeden," the captain persisted.

"I'm a trader."

Dara slid around Ben to kick open the front door. "Everyone but the two of you," he pointed from the proprietor back to Ben. "Out. Now."

There weren't many patrons, but the few there were rushed from their seats, abandoning tankards, card games, and the odd pipe.

The innkeeper backed away from the bar, raising his palms. "I don't want no trouble, Sirs. I run a respectable establishment."

"Shut it, you," ordered Yana, over a mouthful of bread and cheese. His right hand patted the rapier at his hip. Dara stalked to the stable door, his eyes on Ben. If he called for the men outside, things would get ugly in here, fast.

Ben risked a glance at the innkeeper. "Just came for a bed and some ale, fellas. No need for all this."

"I'll decide that," said the captain. "A villager saw a very large man with two females pass over the High Road some miles back. Told me he paid attention because he found it odd that they would head into the woods rather than make use of the road. The weather being foul as it is…."

Dara moved to push open the back door. *Think, damn you, think!* Just as Ben's fingers flexed over his pommel, a high-pitched voice wafted down the rough wooden stairs. Her hair damp from a bath and wearing an overlarge, misshapen dress that had seen more years than she had, Rian stepped down beside the stable lad, her blue eyes wide.

"Brother, I left ye some bath water. Will ye order me an ale and… oh, what's all this?"

The Corsairs' heads swiveled toward her simultaneously. The captain launched to his feet, still holding his tankard. "You there, come down here!" Rian obeyed, looking every inch the frightened country girl.

"Oh my," she gasped, strolling into the taproom with exaggerated timidity. "What has me brother done, sir?"

Blinking at her pretty face, the captain frowned. "This man is your brother?"

Rian edged around Sergeant Dara to stand at Ben's side. "He is. What's this all about?"

"I'll ask the questions, mistress. Dara?"

"Aye," he drew his dirk and jabbed it at the stable boy. "To her room, now." Watching them head upward, Rian slid her fingers over Ben's forearm, applying light but reassuring pressure.

"Where is she?" the captain's attention honed on Rian.

"Where is who?"

Ben didn't have the first bloody clue what was happening. Rian dug her nails into his wrist, and he took the hint. He allowed her arm to wind through his as if she sought protection from these vicious armed men.

The captain exhaled through his nose. "The other girl. You were seen, mistress. 'A larger than average man, leading two women away from the road.' If you don't tell me where she is, it will go worse for you. Stay right where you are, old man." He didn't turn to watch the innkeeper place his hands back on the bar.

"There's only the two of us, sir," deflected Rian with perfect innocence. Clearly, the innkeeper had sent his son up to warn the girls. Ben found that very interesting and entirely unexpected. Why would someone who balked at Rian's family go out of his way for two supposed 'half-breeds' now and endanger his boy like this? Ben hoped he'd get the chance to ask him.

Dara stomped back downstairs, shaking his head at his captain. "Nothing. Unless this one—" he pointed at Ben— "hid her somewhere outside. She isn't here. I searched every room, every window, every cupboard."

"Girl," the captain crossed his arms. "Where are you from?"

Damn it.

"Fenn, sir. Round the Shannon. Why? What's me brother done? Are we in some kind o'trouble?"

"Could be if you don't start telling the truth."

At last, Ben found his voice. "My sister doesn't lie. We're on're way home from a rather successful trip to Tara."

"What is the nature of your business?"

Ben opened his mouth to reply, but Rian beat him to it.

"I'm a midwife, sir. A healer, if ye like. I tend to the ailin,' and me brother sells me remedies at market."

"What remedies?"

"Herbs, tinctures, and the like. For burns, scrapes, head pains… ye see?"

Dara sheathed his dirk. "Got a hitch in her step. Like I said, all faeries are disfigured somehow," he spat into the rushes near her hem. She pulled a genuine face in revulsion.

"You gonna ask her if she has a cock next?" Yana giggled into his tankard. Dara opened his mouth to retort, but the captain cut him off.

"Quiet, both of you! All right, mistress. What would you recommend, for a toothache, say?"

"Willow bark, four times a day with tea. But if there's an infection at the root, ye may want to pull the tooth and apply a poultice of nettle and honey for a week after."

"How about a cough?"

"First ye have to determine a cause. Many agents can lead to infection or irritation in the lungs. Do ye suffer from either? I can examine ye to prescribe an appropriate dosage. For a small fee, I can mix ye—"

"That won't be necessary. You may go." With a bored grunt, the captain turned back to the bar. The innkeeper leapt to pour him another round. Dara and Yana sniggered as two more soggy soldiers came through the stable entrance. They gave Ben and Rian a hard once-over but moved to the bar without comment.

Ben understood a cue when he saw one. He grasped Rian's elbow and steered her toward the stairs like a recalcitrant child. The stable lad led them upward with a weak smile.

"Let me get some fresh hot water for ye, sir. I fear the tub has run cold." The look in his eyes was loaded.

Ben patted him on the shoulder. "Thank ye, lad. I could use a soak."

"Just so we're clear," the captain's voice followed them upward. "I expect you'll let us know if you see a girl fitting the description you were given. I think you'll find there are a great many of us searching for her. You might say hundreds. I imagine you'll see us every step of your way home."

"Of course, sir," said Ben, half-shoving Rian before him. "We'll be sure to report anything we happen to see. Ye have me word on that."

ONCE THE DOOR CLOSED, RIAN leapt to action. She and the stable lad darted to the wall beside the window to remove a large piece of heavy paneling. Una poured out, coughing, and covered in cobwebs. Rian helped her to her feet.

"We have to go!"

Una spat out a mouthful of dust.

"How many?"

"Five," Ben scowled. He moved to the window to glance down at the streets below. It was still pouring out but windless, which allowed a thick fog to creep in from the north. All to the good, if they could get out without incident. "Presumably more on the way."

"Siora," Una shook her head. Ben noticed she'd eschewed the homespun gowns that poured out from an untidy trunk before the hearth. The proprietor's wife had been at least four inches taller than either girl and twice as wide if Rian's dress were any guide. Una opted for a clean nightdress and woolen leggings, which she'd belted together with a wide blue sash. Remnants of another gown lay over the single bed, presumably the source of her new belt.

It seemed that the girls had been busy while he was downstairs enjoying himself at Rian's expense. A wooden tub sat before the hearth. Their attire—boots, cloaks, scarves, and gloves— dried on a rack before the fire. Too bad these newly clean items were destined once more for the tempestuous elements outside. Rian scurried about like a frantic mouse, whipping on her cloak and gloves and helping to shove Una's feet into her boots. The lad twiddled his thumbs at the door, ear pressed against the wood. Ben opened the window and stuck out his head. Ten feet to the ground, maybe less. The wall was too steep to climb, but he was over six and a half feet tall. He could drop to the street without much effort. The girls, on the other hand, might break a bloody leg. He turned.

"I'll have to go first. Rian, hand me your packs."

She passed hers, then Una's. The lad clutched the door handle. "Ah, if ye'll excuse me? Them soldiers have their mounts and hounds stalled with Vixen. I should go tend to them, or it'll look suspicious."

Ben nodded, pulling Una toward the window first. "We'll leave her in your care then, young man. Where we're going, it'll be too dangerous anyway."

The boy was visibly relieved. He reached into his vest for a small leather pouch, which he tossed to Ben. The purse was heavy with coin. Ben gave him an odd look.

"What's this?"

"Yer change. Da charged ye a lil' extra for the trouble, but ye'll find yer remainin' stags and a handful o'coppers in there." Ben didn't need to open the purse to know he'd massively underpaid. There had to be at least seven silver stags in there and another twenty coppers besides. A small fortune. The innkeeper would have been justified to keep the entire royal fainne. Ben was nonplussed.

Una shrugged on her damp cloak, sporting a dubious brow. "Well, isn't that generous?"

"Why would your father do this, boy? He owes us nothing."

The boy blushed under his scrutiny. "Da said ye'd ask. Tole me to tell ye he was at Dumnain." The blood drained from Ben's head. "Said to thank ye for what ye done, yer Lordship. Never forgets a face, ye see— even one done up, as yers is now." His red-chapped fingers closed over the doorknob. "We'll keep 'em busy long as we can."

"Wait," asked Una. "How did you know they were looking for me?"

"We didn't, until the Corsairs startin' askin' questions. Ye two girls, and them patrols," he shrugged. "Made sense."

"Thank you," Una said, awed. "Sincerely."

Before the boy slid through a crack in the door, Ben called out. "I will remember this, lad. Tell your father."

"He said ye'd say that too," the boy grinned, taking his leave as quietly as he could. Ben stared at the closed door; his mouth pressed into a firm line. This was… unexpected. He wasn't accustomed to anyone sticking their neck out for him—especially those who remembered him as he used to be.

"What was that all about?" Rian bolted the door behind him. Ben hurried toward the open window. "No time now. Let's get going."

※ ※

Struggling through the mud about three miles outside of town, they paused when they heard the first howls. Una's breath puffed silver, and Rian clutched at her chest; her eyes were two large white pearls in the dark.

"Wolves?" Rian was a long way from her comfortable, warm cottage now. Ben scanned the eerie fog-shrouded forest to the East. He saw nothing but a silver and black smear on the horizon. The howling came again, closer.

He shook his head. "Hounds. They must have realized we've escaped. We must get to the river." Cursing, he drew Nemain with one hand and scooped Una under his arm with the other. She yelped as his rough handling jarred her ribs. Too bad. She'd only slow them down if he didn't carry her.

He handed Rian a dagger. She stared at it like it might burn her. "What am I supposed to do with this?"

"Swing it at anything that tries to bite you." He shifted Una onto his back and passed her his pack. He tossed hers, which contained most of their muddied food, into the trees. One last scent for the beasts to track. "Put that on. It'll be better protection than nothing if they get behind us."

The howling inched nearer. Owing to the heavy rain and sluicing mud, the sound held a tin can quality, a haunting, mercurial echo. Distantly, Ben caught the unmistakable jingle of a bridle and the clink of spurs. Horsemen waited on the road to the South. Ben tilted his head in the opposite direction, listening to the telltale rush of the river on his right. Rian tied her skirt over her knees and hugged her pack close. She was terrified, he could tell. The prospect of being torn apart by dogs was not a pleasant one.

"*Run*. Don't stop until you hit the river. Go!"

With a whimper, she shot off as fast as her twisted foot would carry her. Ben followed, keeping her ahead of him. The going was tough. They slipped down steep gullies and struggled up every slick rise. Ben could smell the river and heard its rapid overflow about fifty paces ahead. A snarl on his right-hand side made Rian cry out in fear. She stumbled down the next slope, slashing wildly at a snapping set of jaws. The hound, an ugly, ungainly beast with grizzled fur and wide-set clipped ears, launched to its feet before Rian could regain hers. Ben slid down to her on his knees. Nemain's point sliced through its neck before it could latch its teeth around her ankle. As it died, another burst through the trees, yellow eyes wild, mandibles dripping. Snarling, it sunk its fangs into Ben's right arm. Grunting in pain, he dropped Nemain into the muck and used his free fist to pound at the animal's ears. Terriers did not respond to much else; their eyes and ears were their softest spots. A third hound joined the fray. It tucked into a crouch near Rian's flailing body. She gripped his dagger in a trembling fist when a fourth beast edged around the top of the rise to guard against potential escape.

※ ※

Una dropped from Ben's back. He was too busy punching the animal biting his arm off to pay much attention. It shook its head back and forth, trying to snap his forearm like a hambone. He kicked out at its ribs with his left heel but lost his footing and went down hard on his right knee. The dog took advantage, using its bulging chest muscles to roll him over onto his side. Ben heard a telltale creak, the herald of an oncoming break. Then, the searing pressure abruptly ceased. The hound whined pitifully as Una's hand came away from its rump. Its spine concaved, nearly folding the animal in half from the wrong direction. Kicking its mangled corpse into the flooded gulley, Una held a hand out to Ben. He took it with a grateful groan. Pulling Nemain out of the mud, he ignored the boiling pain in his right arm.

Rian screamed as the beast she faced sprang at her for a second time. She slashed wildly at its eyes, as instructed, but barely grazed its ear. Ben turned his attention to the one just ahead of him, which growled low in its throat in anticipation. He reached into his belt to pass Una his last dagger.

"Can you help her?" Una took the blade without bothering to answer. "Good," he said. "Kill it, then get to the river."

She hurried to Rian's side. The fourth dog snarled, waiting for Ben to give him an opening. He anticipated it would lunge in whichever direction he moved. As it leapt, he spun right, severing its head. The torn nerves in Ben's arm shrieked in agony. By necessity, he shifted his sword to his left hand. Newborn howls reverberated through the rain-soaked forest to the south. The beast that circled the girls below seemed to derive courage from the imminent support. It snapped at Rian's front left ankle. Una struck out at its nose to distract it. Summoning all the courage she had, Rian jumped forward with a bellow and plunged her dagger through its right eye. She fell backward, gasping. Una helped her up.

"Well done, Rian."

"Can you run?" Ben asked, keeping his eyes on the trees. Una shoved Rian up the rise with renewed urgency. He followed, impressed by the speed they could summon between them, considering one dragged a crippled foot behind her and the other sported a dozen wounds that would keep a man twice her size abed for months. He was not used to being surprised. People tended to irritate rather than astound him. He caught a growl on his right. He lashed out with Nemain from his left, gratified by the beast's answering shriek. "Keep going!" he shouted.

They cleared the last copse of trees. Una's breath rattled from her chest as she pounded through the thin ice on the riverbank. With gritted teeth, Una dragged Rian upstream. Ben pointed north-west.

"Keep to the river! When you get to the second bend, there'll be a cliff with heavy overhanging trees and a wide beach. Wait for me there!"

Una looked back; lips already blue. "Where are you going?"

He wiped Nemain's blade clean with his cloak and faced the wailing forest behind him. "To pay our new friends a visit."

Ard Tiarne

Dara rubbed his hands together and blew into them, hoping to still the prickling numbness that leeched warmth from each digit. His thin leather gloves were all but useless out here. Excited as he was for the hunt, he couldn't get over the cold. As if this stinking, primitive strip of Innisfail needed any help being less pleasant or inviting. He couldn't wait to get back inside that warm publican. He was going to plant himself beside the hearth and sip warm liquids until he set down roots. While he mused, the howling muted in the distance. Relief struck like a dart.

"Bloody finally! My bollocks are crawling into my chest."

Yana snorted, taking yet another pull from his flask. "It's cold as Siora's tits out here. When we get back to the Citadel, I'll be lucky if I have any bollocks left."

"What I hear, you never had much, to begin with."

"Your wife begs to differ, Dara."

"If I had one. Your wife, on the other hand, never stops raving about mine."

Yana sniggered. "Everyone knows it's the tackle that counts."

"Quiet," the captain snapped, leaning low over his saddle. "I don't hear the hounds anymore." He nudged his charger forward with his knees, reaching into his cloak for a small silver whistle. After blowing into it several times, without answering yips or barks in response, he frowned. "I don't like this."

The captain didn't like anything in Dara's experience. He was another Tenma by-blow, and because he had the right name, he'd practically been handed his commission in the Corsairs. Dara's mother was an Agrean administrator, long retired. Any wealth his family might have had evaporated the minute she bore a son rather than a coveted daughter. Dara's family scraped together enough for him to enter the Citadel guard. He worked his way up without sponsorship or recommendation. It didn't bother him that most of the elite guardsmen in the Corsairs earned their way via intimidation and bribery, but he would be damned if he would take any shite from those that did.

"Perhaps they're out of range?" He offered, not caring a whit for the captain's bloody terriers. He'd like to see the heretic Moura bitch get what was coming to her as much as anyone, but preferably *after* it stopped fucking raining.

"Their ears can detect sounds some miles distant," said Yana.

Dara rolled his eyes, but that wouldn't stop Yana from reciting meaningless facts, as usual.

"Did you know they can discern the nuances in a human sigh? No, they can. They're smart."

"There's a lifelong mystery solved."

Yana gave a mock salute. "That bastard did have a fairly savage longsword. You don't think?"

"Impossible," Dara blew a puff of air over his lower lip. "Eight vicious coursers against one man with a sword, him with two girls clinging to his trousers? Not bloody likely. Those mutts probably can't track through this Siora cursed downpour. It's a bloody swamp out there."

"I said, quiet!" the captain shouted, shifting uncomfortably in his saddle. His charger's ears twitched sideways. Dara's mount nickered, prancing nervously from one leg to the other. The rain came down in a steady drizzle, blighting all but stark shadows between the trees. Something made the horses nervous. The captain drew his rapier. Instinctively, Yana and Dara followed suit. A slight rustling ahead; faint splashes on their right. Raindrops or footsteps? The captain struggled to urge his charger forward, but the beast fought his lead.

"Sir," urged Dara. "We should regroup."

The captain growled. "Dara, I bloody well told you—" his head suddenly tilted forward at an unnatural angle, down his collarbone, chest… then over his knees. With horrific finality, it bounced from his horse's flank and rolled into the mud under Yana's stirrups. Dara's eyes bulged. The captain's horse reared, dislodging his headless body, in its hurry to gallop away. Yana shouted a belated alarm and swung his mount around to guard against an unseen assailant. His arm came down with a grunt; steel met steel. Dara couldn't get there fast enough. Yana suddenly spewed blood as the business end of a sylvan longsword sprouted from the middle of his chest like a pillar. Yana gurgled; his expression peppered with shock. His mouth opened as if he were about to ask Dara a useless question, but the blade retracted, and his body drooped sideways. Yana's horse trampled him in its rush to chase the captain's up the road.

Dara turned in his saddle, rapier high in his right hand, his long dirk clenched tight in his left. The tall half-breed from the tavern stood less than six paces away, watching him. He held his vicious longsword in an impossible arc over his right shoulder. That bloody sword must have weighed thirty pounds or more. Furiously blinking rainwater from his eyes, Dara sputtered, "There are more of us coming up the road. Two more, at least."

"No, there aren't." The specter tossed two bloodied daggers atop Yana's steaming corpse. "I prefer to be thorough."

"You… but how did you get there so fast? In this?" Dara waved his dagger, indicating the atrocious weather. "On foot, no less?"

"Let's just say, you boys are out of your depth."

Dara couldn't argue that. "All the same. I'm going to kill you, you pretty bastard," he snarled, stilling his jittery mount with his spurs.

The tall stranger chuckled, unfazed by Dara's bravado. "You'll try."

Dara dug his heels into his charger's ribs. The horse bolted forward, pounding through the mud toward his assailant. Dara's rapier was poised to take the leering bastard through the eye, but the figure jerked aside too quickly to track. Something hard connected with his right leg. Unseated, he toppled backward over his horse's rump. His spine slammed into the mud below, sucking the wind from his lungs. The half-breed kicked his rapier from his twitching fingers and knelt over his left hand, grinding his wrist under one knee.

Dara gasped for air. White-hot flashes of searing pain burst behind his eyes. He couldn't feel his toes anymore. He couldn't feel his foot… why couldn't he feel anything below the fire in his thigh?

Where is it?

"Now," his tormentor said. "In these last few minutes you have, there are some things I would like to ask you. Every time you refuse to answer, I will hurt you. Do you understand?" Dara shuddered beneath him. "What?"

In the dim mist-ridden light, the figure's teeth gleamed white as a Prima's robes. "Ready?"

⚚

Una and Rian huddled under Rian's heavier cloak on a small beach choked with fallen boughs and heavy stones. When they emerged from the river at the place Ben described, they found a wide cut bank tucked into a low limestone cliff. Its chalky face was overgrown with moss and bracken and partially obscured by an impressive ancient oak. The tree's mammoth boughs stretched far over the river, cutting rolling rapids through its overflowing current. Nearer the cliff, they discovered a little copse tucked into a nest of low-lying limbs, dried shrubs, and furrowed trunk. At the rear hid a small, barely discernible cavity. Rian moved some branches and fallen twigs away to get a better look. The depression seemed to be a small tunnel that widened as it went on, shielded from the elements by the weight of the mighty roots twisting overhead. They wasted little time crawling into that hollow with mutual cries of relief. The air within held a stale, musty flavor. There were odd shapes ahead, and her breath echoed queerly in her ears. Una inhaled sharply. This had to be a cave! She scrabbled to the end, heedless of the sharp roots that tore at her face and hair. When she stopped, Rian came up beside her, squinting.

"W-what is all th... is?"

"Sh-shelter, I think." Scant, murky moonlight filtered in from the entrance and trickled through myriad holes below the root wall. After a few moments of intense concentration, details emerged from the dark. The cave was much larger than it should be— wide enough to accommodate a half-dozen people lying side by side. They no longer needed to crouch as the tangled roof hovered four or five handspans overhead. Rian tripped over a pile of long-dried sticks bundled in a slight depression at the center.

Una knelt to run her stiff fingers over a hand-dug pit. Firewood was stacked neatly in the middle as if waiting for their arrival. "S-someone lived here." Frowning, she took in the indistinguishable lumps scattered all over. Feeling her way around, Una brushed against a low shelf containing dozens of dusty items she couldn't identify without a lamp. A cot stood against the rear wall with two moldy blankets piled on top and a few things stacked beside it that she thought felt like armor or something similar. Her eyes had trouble adjusting to the dark.

"There's kindling in h-here already," shivered Rian. "Prima, erm?"

"It's Una, please."

"Right." Una could barely make out Rian's narrow shoulders while she hunched beside the pit. "C-can you reach into m-my pack there? There should be a leather pouch toward the bottom."

Una retrieved the pouch, then fumbled back to Rian, taking care not to trip. Rian set to work straightaway, layering the little stone circle with flammable fodder and stacking twigs upright over the top.

"Break up the bigger pieces first. Good. L-like that. Can you find any more?"

Una found quite a few, actually. Rian struck the flint she'd removed from her little bag, and a fire sprang to life within the pit after a few minutes. Una felt like crying. She held her shaking hands over the little blaze while Rian stacked larger twigs around the rim. Now lit, the chamber's mysteries fleshed out. One intriguing fact that leaped out at them was the obvious sign of tool marks carved into the soft limestone of the far wall. This cave was probably formed by roots pressing mercilessly into the pliable stone, but it took a human hand to expand the depth of this chamber to such a degree. There were two homely little tables, the larger shelf Una discovered earlier, and several oddments scattered over each. A few parchments, grown yellow and green with age; a silver box, etched with intricate curling vines; a few gleaming bits of gold— jewelry perhaps; a carefully folded, if slightly mildewed white tunic; gloves of soft kid; and a dagger with a silver hilt, which was covered in cobwebs and a thick patina of grime. Opposite the shelf, what she guessed correctly to be armor, leaned against the wall; a cuirass of once brilliant white leather embossed with metallic shapes too dusty to read. An impressive, unstrung longbow arched over one shoulder, half-covered in a filthy bit of tarpaulin.

Pursing her lips, Una looked over the cot with its long-forgotten blankets, the parchments stuffed below one of the homemade tables, and the pewter candle holder with a burnt nub protruding from its taper. Her brows drew together over the scene. Clearly, this was no mistake. The rushing river outside, and the tangle of roots, tree limbs, and boughs provided the perfect cover. The beach could only be accessed from the river, and the limestone cliff-face would prevent any but the most determined climber from attempting a descent.

How much time had Ben spent here?

He'd gone to considerable trouble to make it somewhat comfortable, hadn't he? Why? She didn't have the chance to seriously ponder what she was seeing before Rian jerked her upward by the elbow.

"All right, get these things off. There are blankets in that crate there." She pointed with her right hand and unbuttoned her own vest with the other. "A fever would end our little adventure on the lowest possible note."

Una rifled through the crate. Eschewing the topmost coverlet for its abhorrent layer of black mildew, she dug for better fare. She discovered one partially clean woolen mantle, another heavy tarpaulin, and a moth-eaten, fur-lined cloak in some fabric that felt very much like velvet. She wasted no time stripping off her sodden clothing to her thin, wet underthings. Handing Rian the warmer blanket, she threw the cloak over her puckered skin inside-out. Its soft fur tore a heavy sigh from somewhere deep inside her chest. She dragged the tarpaulin over to their little fire and spread it over the flattest portion she could find.

Meanwhile, Rian busied herself by hauling soiled textiles from the cot and cramming them into the roots over the entrance: a makeshift door to block the elements searching through the gap. In moments, the small space filled with reassuring warmth. Una buried her face in the smelly cloak.

"Siora, but this is wonderful."

Rian adjusted herself beneath her blanket, tucking in her bare toes. "I've never been so cold in my life."

"You said that yesterday," said Una, her voice muffled by fur. Her extremities stung as they thawed. A more welcome pain, she couldn't fathom.

"Consider this the new standard," laughed Rian, reaching out to teepee two more branches over the fire. She looked around, her smile fading slightly. "Where are we?"

"His hiding place, I expect." Una snuggled further into the cloak. "He spent some time here too, I'd say."

"You know who he is?"

"I'm pretty sure I do now."

"What tipped you off?"

Una nodded at the shelf. "That cuirass. It's filthy but take a good look at it. I suspected before, with the garish amount of gold swinging from his ears."

Rian got up and bunched the blanket around her knees to squat before it. With her bare hand, she wiped the dust away in a single brown-grey crease. The white leather under her palm bore heavy silver embossing: a leaping silver stag adorned by three gold stars. Rian sucked in a breath.

"*An Fiach Fian*! This is the standard of the High King's elite guard."

"That's the one."

Brow furrowed, Rian reached for the covered bow and removed its protective covering. The most beautiful, intricately carved longbow Una had ever seen emerged into the firelight. The bow was easily seven feet long, hewn from a single piece of gorgeous white yew, and tipped at each end with heavy silver plating. Its staggering beauty and exquisite craftsmanship drew appropriate sighs of admiration from each girl. Such a thing was unheard of in Eire. It would be so costly that none but the wealthiest Lord could afford it. The artistry was superb. A stag, a boar, a fox, a raven, and a bear chased each other around its haft. Rian ran her fingers lightly over some Ealig wording carved into the underside of the arch.

"*Sinnair*," she read in apparent awe.

"What does that mean?" Una spoke only Eirean and Bretagn. Ealig was not highly prioritized in the Red City since only council members had ever been invited into Aes Sidhe.

"'King killer.'"

"You're joking?"

Rian shook her head, folding her hands beneath her blanket. "That's what the inscription reads."

"Confirmation then?"

"Certainly makes a strong argument. If this is the weapon I've read about, this bow is quite famous. It was made especially for—"

"Someone unworthy of it," said Ben from the entrance.

Rian nearly jumped out of her skin. "Don't bleedin' do that! You almost gave me a heart attack!"

Unlike the two girls, he'd had to crawl through on all fours. Soaking wet and scowling, he dragged himself through Rian's homemade doorway.

"My apologies, Mistress." He gave no warning before divesting himself of his sodden outer garments and depositing them in an unceremonious heap by the door.

"Are you all right?" Una winced at the state he was in.

Ben wasn't as clean as they were, so he must not have come via the river. He must have climbed down. His tunic was shredded, and his boots were spattered with something darker and thicker than mud. He spared her a dismissive smirk.

"I'll live." He unlaced his sopping jerkin with his left hand; his right was a tad worse for wear, though he'd wrapped it with a torn shred of cloth, which was a suspicious black with gold threading. Una recognized it instantly. She opened her mouth to ask him about it, but he turned away. Without a shred of modesty, he peeled off his inner vest, tunic, shirt, and boots. Una flushed as a broad expanse of scarred flesh was revealed. Her eyes drifted to the roots curling above their heads. She struggled to affect an intense fascination with the smoke curling upward from their fire.

Rian was not as shy. "How'd that happen to you?" she gestured to the swirling mounds of scar-tissue tracing over his pectoral muscles. They were long healed but ragged and must have been debilitating when inflicted.

He grabbed the mildewed blanket Una discarded from the knotty floor. "A mistake, long forgotten."

Once he was appropriately covered, Una cleared her throat. She wasn't a prude, mind. She'd just never seen someone like him before. Come to think of it; he might be the very first Sidhe she'd ever met.

"Will they follow?"

"No." He met her eyes firmly.

"I see." She couldn't say she wasn't grateful to be alive nor that he'd gone to such obvious trouble to ensure their safety… but the ease with which he took life unnerved her.

"You'd mourn these men too, I gather."

"No," she lied. "I'm not accustomed to so much death. All right?"

"Some ruler you'd make."

"I don't want to 'rule,' damn you. Besides, why shouldn't I despise killing? Civilized people do."

He rolled his eyes. "Don't delude yourself, princess. Those men meant to kill all three of us. How civil were they?"

"I didn't say you were wrong, only that it's such a simple matter for you. Life and death. I'll kill if I must, but I will never find your ease with it."

"It's lucky for you that I am the more efficient killer, don't you think?"

"You *enjoy* it."

"You have an odd way of showing thanks."

"*Listen—*"

"Where's your stone then?" Rian interjected. She was eager to prevent yet another pointless spat between her companions. They'd had dozens in the past two days already. Una just couldn't stop herself from rising to the occasion every time. Rian seemed to handle him better, though Una couldn't imagine why. He was insufferable.

Ben raised a silver-blond brow. "In my pocket. Don't worry."

"Why bother to take it off?"

"Didn't want to lose it on the way here."

"Well," she sniffed. "So long as you have it."

"Was the river too cold for you?" Una quipped, half-angry, half-relieved. He settled beside her, sparing her a rue twist of his upper lip.

"Obviously, it wouldn't be prudent to come from the same direction."

Una glared at him in silence for some time. He pretended to ignore her.

Rian bustled around, retrieving things from her pack, then taking a seat on his opposite side. "Arm, please?"

"Why?" Ben jerked away, suspicious.

"I need to wrap it, you infant. We're in a bloody cave. Now give it."

While their heads bowed together over his wound, Una couldn't help but be struck by their fair beauty. They were quite something, the two of them. Both had the same luminescent skin... like sunlight glinting over a pearl. Though, in Ben's case, the effect was startling. He seemed to carry that light inside as if a candle burned within. His eyes, a true silver, flashed her way more than once in suspicion. She pretended her heart didn't skip the tiniest bit each time. He was too lovely to be male, yet there could never be a doubt of his gender. She knew dozens of warriors in both Tairngare and Bethany who would gnash their teeth in envy at Ben's physique. It seemed a shame he was so... disagreeable. Her mind wandered for quite a while until she was forced to bite the inside of her swollen lip hard enough to make her eyes water. Why was she thinking about such useless drivel now?

"What?" he asked, brimming with ready irritation.

"Nothing." Una sat up a bit straighter.

She pulled the cloak closer to hide her burning face. She'd sooner be raked over hot coals than admit to her train of thoughts. Instead, she chewed the interior of her good cheek. Rian poked at Ben's arm while he glared down at Una. The soiled, stolen scrap he'd haphazardly wound around the wound, Rian threw into the fire. Flames hissed and popped around the sopping wad of black fabric. His flesh was torn wide near the wrist in a couple of places, but he didn't seem to bleed as badly as Una expected he should. Rian cut away the free-swinging pieces of skin with a tiny pair of scissors, then slathered it liberally with a healthy dollop of the honey and nettle mixture she'd used on Una's face.

Once properly bound, she folded her tools back inside her pack. "There." She handed his arm back.

He mumbled something incoherent, which Una assumed were thanks.

Rian blew her drying hair out of her eyes and settled again into her blanket. "You killed them then? The dogs?"

He considered Una pointedly. "Yes. All of them."

Rian blew out a deep breath. "Good." She slid a somewhat guilty look Una's way.

Una wouldn't argue that the death wrought tonight wasn't necessary. She just wished it wasn't. Siora, she was tired. Tired of running, tired of being in pain, and tired of being afraid. That aside, Ben had killed more people in a handful of days than anyone she'd ever heard of. He made her nervous. His lack of empathy, his disdain for life— all of it. Could she ever call someone like him an ally? Did she want to?

He leaned in. "You truly believe I enjoy this?"

"I'm trying to figure that out."

Ben grunted. "Don't bother. Whatever you think of me, I don't kill for pleasure. I won't shed tears over any of those men, and neither should you. Get some rest. No one will find us here." He motioned to Rian, whose chin had already dipped toward her collarbone. The day's events seemed to have caught up to her all at once. Chuckling, he gently nudged her onto her side so that she wouldn't tumble headfirst into the fire. "To be clear, I didn't ask for any of this, but I'm making do."

Una acknowledged the justice of that statement with a cold smile. "Fine. That's fair. I didn't mean to imply that you're a base murderer. I'm struck by how easy it is for you to take life."

"Let me put it this way: I kill when I have to. The men hunting you kill because they're ordered to, and they obey those commands because they choose to. You've taken life recently, haven't you?"

Target struck. She flinched. "I suppose I lack your comfort with it."

"You should start getting comfortable, my lady. In my experience, it is better to be sorry than dead."

Kicking him wouldn't make him less right. "I haven't known many soldiers, personally. Far fewer with your, erm... talent for it. I have only one basis for comparison."

Ben sneered. "I am nothing like your father, girl."

He wasn't. Patrick wouldn't bother to feign offense; he was proud to be a megalomaniacal beast. On the other hand, Ben didn't seem overly pleased by any of this, but neither did he hesitate. It unnerved her. He struck her as the sort to avoid conflict not because he feared its outcome but because he knew how events would play out if forced to act. Given what she suspected of him, it made sense. He *would* wish to avoid trouble for one reason alone. Her eye slid to the cuirass against the wall. He saw.

"Go ahead and ask."

"Are you… really…?" She was embarrassed by the wonder in her tone.

"I used to be." The fire cast shadows over his profile, enhancing the sharp planes of his face. "Makes how we met all the more absurd, doesn't it?"

She swallowed. She was coming to understand why Eirean women tended to disappear over the border fairly regularly.

"Who else knows?"

"Does she know?" He jerked a thumb at Rian.

"I'm not asleep." Rian pulled her blanket over her head. "And yes, I do."

He held up two fingers. "There you have it."

Una wasn't sure what to say. She'd wandered into a bedtime story and become entangled with one of its most iconic characters. "What, ah, should I call you then?"

"Ben. It suits me fine."

She didn't believe that for a moment. "What happened?"

"It's irrelevant. We have more pressing matters to discuss."

He leaned backward to tug his rumpled, soggy cloak from the entrance. Reaching inside an interior pocket, he lobbed her a sheaf of damp papers tied with a red leather strap. A warrant from the Citadel, she knew without having to unravel the wad. She'd seen them before, hadn't she?

"Someone named Alta Nema has ordered your arrest on the grounds of heresy and usury."

"I know, and it isn't legal. Nema holds no such power in Parliament."

"Most common folk won't know that, will they? The Corsair I questioned said Parliament voted to rescind your status as Domina of the Moura Clan three days ago. Some claim you're the victim of attempted regicide. Others, namely this Nema's supporters in the Commons, label you a heretic and escaped criminal."

"Nema, and her cronies in Parliament, arranged all this in the first place. She's manipulating the Commons against my family."

"I'm sure, but it hardly makes a difference if half the city is howling for your blood, does it?"

She stared down at the wet bundle as if it were a nest of spiders she'd accidentally set her hand in. She threw them onto the fire. "If that's the case, then perhaps I should return to Tairngare as soon as possible."

"You won't make it five miles down the Navan High Road before a patrol picks you up, or worse, drags you into the Greensward to finish the job the first batch started. Use your head."

"But… how can I trust you to help me when you aren't permitted over the border yourself?" She felt a bit bad watching him wince, but the question was warranted, nonetheless. "Look, I know this was thrust upon you, and you hope I can help you get home, but how do you propose that's going to happen? There's no guarantee the High King will even see me."

"He'll see you," Ben smiled, melting her ready retort like butter from her tongue. "Trust me. Midhir is the finest king in this or any land. He won't allow either faction to harm you. I vow it."

"Easy to say," she let out a long breath. She would get a hold of herself, *by Siora*, one way or another. "But will he see *you*? I don't fancy fleeing across the river, only to run straight into a Sidhe arrow for the gall. Nor do I love the idea of being carted to Bri Leith in chains."

"I'm asking you to trust me. You can, or you can't. It's that simple."

Did she trust him? Could she? She didn't know. She was unused to depending upon others, and Ben didn't make anything easy. Still… he'd saved her life many times— whether he found this inconvenient or not, it didn't cheapen his effort. He was offering to help. True, he hoped to benefit from the arrangement, but that didn't mean she couldn't or shouldn't trust him. He was a sour, sarcastic drunkard with a talent for death and an acute disdain for people… but he was also brave. He was also capable. Simply put, what choice did she have?

None.

Absolutely none.

"I do trust you."

He seemed as shocked by her acquiescence as she, more, perhaps.

"Don't tell me you were expecting me to say something else?"

"I was," he admitted freely, without sarcasm.

She rolled a shoulder under her stinky moth-eaten covering. "I suppose we're stuck with each other, for now. So, let's do this the right way, shall we?" she unwound her arm and extended her hand. "I'm Una. Pleased to make your acquaintance… Ben."

Hesitantly, he wrapped her fingers in his own massive, clammy hand. "And I, yours… Una."

"There now. Friends?" Ben said nothing. He expected he would have to prove his case and was somewhat off-guard now that he did not. It was written all over his face.

"If you like?"

"'The true mystery of the world is the visible, not the invisible,'" she mumbled, tucking her cloak carefully around her knees with a sigh.

"What was that?"

"Oh, just something I read once. I never understood the quote until now." He stared back, silent and inscrutable. "I'm glad you found me, Ben… and thank you for everything." With that, she took Rian's cue and hunkered before the fire to get some sleep. She could feel his eyes boring holes into her back for quite a while until slumber finally hushed the hammer of her pulse.

Ethics of Cruelty

Aoife wept silent, bitter tears. Her ears and nose bled. Her fingers scratched uselessly against the heavy, cold granite, tearing out several nails. She gasped for air, helpless against the monstrous pressure that smashed her in place. Her robes were torn open at the back, and the skin there was corrugated like a plowed field. Her arms and legs were twisted at awkward angles. Mortifying pain flashed behind her eyes each time she tried to move. Aoife would do anything to make it stop, but she was far past begging. All she could do was struggle to breathe and pray.

"She's bleeding all over your favorite rug, Excellency," Fawa Gan said from somewhere below Aoife's navel.

"Then you'll buy me a new one," Vanna Nema replied from further away. She was at her desk, signing papers and shuffling parchments— scratching away with a knife-slashing quill that made Aoife twitch.

Gan whined, "This rug dates from before the Transition, Excellency. There *isn't* another to be found." Aoife could practically see the pernicious little toad setting doughy fists on his wide girlish hips. She might spit on him if her mouth weren't smashed into a wide crack on the ceiling.

"Fawa, do you fancy a place beside her?"

"If you want to start braiding your own hair and mixing your own tea, by all means. I'd adore a lie-down, thanks."

Nema's quill paused long enough to glare over her desk at him. Aoife had seen the same false threat a thousand times before. Truth be told, Gan got away with bloody murder. Aoife hated him for it. In Nema's eyes, Gan was irreplaceable. He had a talent for ingratiating self-promotion that Aoife could never lower herself to match. As much as she longed to watch him drown in a pool of his own fluids, replacing him would be a nightmare. Who else could keep the old hag happy? Run her errands, keep her books, and order her appointments? He was too damned good at his job. This was the only thing that kept Aoife from shoving him off the Citadel's highest parapet. *She* certainly had no desire to take his place. Head bootlicker was not a position to which Aoife aspired.

"You're here for a reason, I presume?"

"I am Excellency. Did you happen to hear that racket outside?" He referred to the mob gathered before the Citadel's gates. Thousands of angry, riotous citizens descended upon the Grand Arcade. They pounded on the walls, gates, and windows, desperate to lure lawmakers into the streets to face the mob's justice. The outcry began before Aoife had returned from the Greensward three days before, and the violence grew worse by the hour.

Riots broke out in the Spice District, the Docks, and the Merchanta Ward. Homes and shops in residential areas were looted and burned. Merchants and civil servants were attacked and bloodied in the streets. The mayhem grew to such a fevered pitch that the Council was forced to summon troops from the Academy to clear the city thoroughfares. Citadel Corsairs trampled at least a dozen people during midday prayers, and by sunset the previous day, the city had been placed under strict martial law. Guards stood four men deep at every gate. Commerce in the Red City ground to a screeching halt. Brothels in the Pleasure District emptied, taverns and publicans ceased pouring libations, and markets shuttered. Even Parliament refused to convene, though the people cried out for deliberation. Judges and Libellan representatives preferred to cower behind scores of armed Tairnganeah rather than face the wroth of the Commons. In one week, Tairngare's government had been pushed to the brink of collapse. Vanna Nema certainly wasn't displeased by the violence and fury outside. She was its architect, after all.

"I have." Aoife heard Nema's lips slide over her gums in an audible grin. "How calamitous. I do hope the matter is cleared up soon. Every day this unrest persists is another the Citadel loses revenue. It's most perplexing."

"Oh, of course, Excellency. Most dreadful, indeed. However, I've just been informed that Judge Zelda San has proposed you undergo the Tenth Ordeal."

The scratching stopped altogether. "Already?"

"Seems so. As you said, the longer this goes on the more coin hemorrhages from the Citadel's treasury. I was informed you're summoned to a private interview with the Judge's Panel in chambers, Excellency."

"When?"

"Tomorrow, or the day after. Perhaps sooner, if the guards are forced to shoot any more citizens from the Ward Gate."

Aoife heard Nema's chair creak. "I should have had that girl dragged from the Citadel years ago." She gave an uncharacteristic giggle. "Wonderful news. Please extend my humble apologies to Judge San's staff. Of course, I am but a servant in the Cloister of the Eternal Flame. These are ecclesiastical matters that must be decided in Council."

"You mean to refuse again?"

"Absolutely." Aoife could picture Nema moving to the windows to admire her handiwork, though Aoife would have to skin her nose to see it for herself. Nema laughed. "Caesar refused the title of Imperator before the public three times, did he not? I will continue to decline until the people tear the gates down around Parliament's ears. Now is not the time for haste, Gan dear. We must be patient."

"You've been patient, Excellency. Folks are ready to burn us out of here as it is. Don't you think it would be wise to give them what they want before we're all out there, begging in the street?"

"Not at all. I won't accept half a victory. There must be such a clamor in the air that those who oppose me fear to speak out. No change can be permanent unless it is unanimously craved. My detractors must see me reject power as often as it takes."

"Until when?"

Aoife heard her tap a long nail against the glass. "Come to think of it; I should probably request Parliament to convene on the issue. Publicly decry this rebellion. Show the people how reluctant I am to seize power."

"Ah, I see," Gan chuckled. "A grand gesture. If only they knew how many years you've waited for this."

"Coups are fallible, my dear. They ignite, consume, then burn out just like that." She snapped her fingers. "I mean to remake this city from the ground up. To do that, the people must be willing to bleed for it."

"Oh, I think they're bleeding well enough. I urge you to remember what happened to your Caesar, Excellency, but I concede the point. When should I send your summons?"

"Tonight, but we won't convene until the day after tomorrow. Let them stew in their failure for a while."

"Very good. And the girl?"

"I have fresh warrants signed and sealed. I want them nailed to every wall in town." Nema moved back toward her desk, shuffling papers into piles. "Here, have these copied and distributed quickly. I can't allow that creature to stir false hope in any Libellan breasts."

"No, not that girl. That one." He looked up at Aoife. Aoife whimpered in mortified loathing.

"Ignore her. Better you serve those amended warrants as soon as possible. I want it clear that we mean to get to the bottom of this debacle as swiftly as possible. Was the girl abducted, or did she escape? This is the question I want on every citizen's mind for the next few days."

"What if the opposition apprehends her?"

"Then she'll be treated to a very nasty, public trial," Nema said. "I'd prefer she didn't return at all… but I'll make sure we take the win, regardless."

"As you command, Excellency." Aoife heard Gan's joints creak under one of his flamboyant bows. "Still, I wonder that you don't need her," he was referring to Aoife again. "She does have her talents, doesn't she?"

"Come now, Gan. You loathe one another. Don't tell me you're speaking up for her after all this time. She failed me."

Gan ignored her barb. "Did she? I'd say the information she bore tends to exonerate her. If she's right, perhaps she may still be of use?" Nema went silent for a while. Aoife fumed that such a slimy little creature as Fawa Gan would dare to contradict Alta Vanna Nema on her account. This was so completely out of character for him; his ploy couldn't be more vivid. He hoped to gain leverage over Aoife. That was the only reason he'd speak on her behalf. Aoife wouldn't trust Gan to agree that water was wet.

"Perhaps you're right," Nema sighed. At once, the immense pressure at Aoife's back subsided. She cried out as her torn belly flopped onto the hard floor. "Tell me again, girl," Nema ordered, strolling back to the window to observe the crowd.

Aoife sucked in as much air as she could and rolled slowly, painfully, to her side. Her ribs were broken. One jabbed into her left lung, which made each breath burn like inhaled vinegar. "I swear… was… h… him."

"Preposterous. That man is dead. Condemned by the Ard Ri, himself."

Aoife tried to shake her head. Her brain sloshed queerly against her skull, and she gagged. Gan sat beside her to dab a silken cloth soaked with wine against her parched lips. Mistrustful, she tried to turn away, but he persisted until her body's needs betrayed her. The first few drops seared her throat like molten iron.

"Leave her."

Gan dipped the handkerchief into the pitcher at his knee, defiant as only he could be. "If she can't speak, how can she tell you anything?"

After a few minutes, Aoife pushed his hand away and struggled up to her elbows. She met Nema's imperious glare with trembling sincerity.

"I s-saw him with my own eyes, Excellency. He has the girl in hand."

"I don't believe it. How? How could the most infamous Dannan in Innisfail simply appear in Eire, twenty-odd years after his death? And at such a time—?"

"It was him; I swear it."

Nema threw up her hands and resumed her pacing. "All those Dannan pigs look much the same: big, blond, and thick as a lump of stones. He was probably a half-breed. There are hundreds of these crazed, disfigured creatures in the Greensward. You're making excuses to save your skin."

Aoife leaned forward. Blood streamed down her jaw. "He was Kaer Yin Adair. N-no faerie wears nine gold chains in his right ear, n-nor carries a Dannan broadsword. I'm not a fool."

Nema clenched her fist. Aoife was lifted into the air again. This time, she crashed into the wall nearest the blazing hearth. She spat up something darker than blood. Nema loomed, the green in her eyes predatory.

"You dare to speak to me in that manner? I made you, Aoife Sona. I will unmake you as easily."

"Your Excellency!" cried Gan, trying to intervene. Nema extended a single finger, and he was flung to the carpet himself. He squealed like a girl half his age. Nema leaned close to Aoife's breathless face. She smelled of ink, woodsmoke, and crisp linen— and power, always that.

Aoife could only glare back, vulnerable in her defiance. "I s-speak true, Excellency. He was the Adair."

"How can you be sure?"

"He used a Dannan longsword with a silver stag for a pommel."

Nema cursed. Aoife suddenly crumpled to the floor in a choking, boneless heap.

"Impossible! Why now? Why here?" Nema clawed at the edge of her desk. "Did you confront him?"

Aoife paled. "Of course not! He would have killed me."

"If you're telling the truth, this is an infuriating complication."

"Why?" Gan struggled to his feet. "Who is he?"

Nema sneered at him. "He is a Sidhe lord, Gan. Not some garden gnome. You would do well to forget that common racial slur."

"Who?"

"He's someone who shouldn't be alive. That's who he is." Aoife wiped the blood from her nose. "Someone that doesn't belong in Eire, and even less, in our way. Your Excellency, he must be dealt with."

"Distribute those warrants as ordered. Also, I want to triple the Corsairs on the High Road."

"But—"

"Do it!" With the put-upon grace only he could manage, Gan bowed his way out of the chamber with the stack of leather-bound documents in hand.

When he was gone, Nema whirled on Aoife. "Tell me everything. Leave nothing… not a single detail out."

"I have, my lady."

Nema shook her head. "Oh, not yet you haven't. How did he seem? I want to know what he looked like, down to the buttons on his vest. Every action, every mannerism. Most of all, I want to know if he was truly *alone*…."

⚵

Fawa did not hurry. As a rule, he never rushed anywhere, even when he had cause. As the great Vanna Nema's personal steward, he must always reflect a serene mask of control. Rumors, he found, often started with the servants.

He held his sheaf of warrants tight against his chest and sauntered down the South Hall. He held his head high, despite its not being overly handsome or of any great height. He was calm, composed, and well-dressed as usual. He wore a tunic of Bretagn silk in Nema's brilliant scarlet, belted by a bright vermillion sash, interwoven with solid gold threading. His slippers were the finest kidskin, dyed a regal red. Gan thought himself rather dashing today. How others saw him was a matter of perspective. Those in the Cloister viewed him with grudging respect. In the Citadel, Union members treated him with a shade of the fear they felt for his mistress. Nobles in the Libella, however, would sooner see him dead than pass by him in the hall. Gan didn't care what they thought of him.

Today, even less than usual.

He came to the last turn at the far end of the Hall and veered left, down the long Southern windows, then up a half-flight of stairs toward the Eastern Wing. Here, he cut right through a door set into the wainscoting on the other side. The next chamber was supported by a long row of arches, lit only by oil sconces mounted on either stone wall. He sailed past these, conscious of the subtle footsteps behind him. He smiled to himself. What fools. He'd been dodging spies in this fortress for almost forty years. He wasn't about to let one catch him now.

After a complicated network of turns and descents, he shut the last door softly behind him. In a painfully dark antechamber, straddled between two rear halls, Gan pressed his ear against the moldering oak door and withdrew a delicate little dagger from his golden sash. The spy was light on her feet. Very carefully, he tiptoed to the far entry. When it opened, he held a finger to his plump lips. His expected guest froze. Gan slid back to the door he came through. The door swung inward after several breaths. Gan reached out quick as a serpent and yanked the little spy inside. She was only a Nova, perhaps no more than twelve. She squealed when Gan's hand clamped over the lower half of her face. His guest, robed entirely in black, waited into the darkest corner, silent as death.

"There you are, you little shite. How long have you been following me?"

The girl shook her head, frantic, her dark eyes pleading.

"She must die," said his contact in a low, muffled tone.

Gan didn't like it, but there was too much at stake. "Tell me who sent you, girl? Tenma, Carra, Nema? Who?"

The spy squeaked and kicked her slippered feet, while clawing at his hand.

"Do it."

Gan wasn't to blame for this girl, was he? Whoever had forced her to spy for them held that honor. He turned, so he wouldn't have to watch the life leave her eyes and twisted as hard as he could. A sickening crunch reverberated around the small, windowless chamber. He let her little body flutter to the dusty stone floor. "You owe me for that."

"I owe you nothing. You're lucky I haven't killed you already."

Gan trembled. "I risk *everything* for you!"

"You risk everything for *coin*. Don't confuse things."

Gan wiped his mouth with his guilty right hand. "I have new information."

"How much are you asking this time, Gan? I can't come down here every time Vanna Nema kills an underling or writes a speech she never gives."

"This information is worth more than anything I've ever given you. The Doma will want to know— to plan. I mean it. This changes everything."

The figure considered him in silence for a long while.

"Fine. Tell me."

"Oh no! Not this time." Gan fidgeted a bit. He'd just murdered a child, and his nerves were already catching fire in his body. "I want what you promised. Now. *Today*. After this, you and I are done."

"Very well," the figure replied and turned to exit through the far door. Gan slapped his palms flat against the jamb.

"No! We had a deal! My freedom for Vanna. You promised me."

A strong hand shot out from beneath the cloak and wrapped itself around Gan's throat. Gurgling, he stumbled backward. "I do not take orders from traitors, you delusional insect." The hand squeezed. "Maybe I will kill you after all? Or let slip to Nema, whom you really work for? Wouldn't that be fun?"

Gan wheezed. "She'll kill me," his chins quivered.

"As will I if you continue to waste my time. You know? I'll never understand how you managed to elude the Judges all this while. Perhaps you hold more Spark than the average male? Is that it? Is that how you've fooled Nema for over thirty years?"

"I… serve her well. She needs me."

"I'm sure she'll be delighted to know that her trusted steward is a thief and a liar. Does she know about your little harem on the Third Floor? What you've made her party to?"

Gan's eyes bulged a bit. "Please… you promised."

"A vow given to a pimp is hardly worth the effort used to speak."

"He… is… alive…" he choked.

"*Who* is alive?"

"Kaer Yin A-Adair."

The figure released him. He crumpled down the door, landing heavily on his rump. "… You lie."

He held his stinging throat with a free hand. It would probably be bruised now, and he'd have to invent some story to explain it. Nema would notice. Nema noticed just about everything. Well, perhaps not everything.

"No. I'm not. The Sona girl recognized him. Said he has gold chains in his ear and uses a sword with some kind of prancing deer. I remember that part very clearly."

"It can't be. After Dumnain—"

"Aoife is Fir Bolg or at least half-breed. I told you this a long time ago. She would know. They hate him almost as much as they loathe Duch Donahugh."

"If I find out you're lying—"

"I'm not. And that's not all. *He* has your girl."

"*What?*"

"Siora's Truth. He killed two creatures Aoife summoned to finish her. Ghasts, I think she said? He's protecting her."

"Is that all?"

"What do you mean, is that all? I've just given you the juiciest gossip in Innisfail, not to mention the Moura Domina's whereabouts. That's quite enough, I'd say. Now, you promised me an escape. I have done everything you've ever asked of me."

"For which, you have been paid a fortune."

"All the same!"

"The Doma will consider it. It's out of my hands."

Gan fumbled to his feet. "You swore! You SWORE you'd help me!"

"If you remain useful, the Doma will honor her word. You are in no position to make demands of anyone."

Gan swallowed the lump in his throat. It wouldn't be long before his myriad deceptions unraveled around his ears. Nema would forgive him many offenses, but not this. By allowing the Mouras to gain leverage over him, he'd forfeited his safety long ago. The only hope he had now was escape. The figure tossed him a small purse as if that would assuage his terror.

"Go back to Nema. I will triple this amount if you can discover what she plans to do with this information. I must verify all of this. I'll contact you in the usual way in a matter of days. Do not ignore my summons if you value your life." The cloak fluttered as the figure spun to leave.

"Wait!" Gan pleaded. "What should I do with her?" He was referring to the young girl stashed in the corner.

"Leave her. No one will notice."

⚓ ⚓

WHEN NIGHT DREW DEEP OVER Tairngare, three women climbed the highest set of stairs in the Cloister. The youngest of them held a thick black cloak over her right arm. Straight-backed, she led the way up the tenth and final flight of steps. At the top, she nodded to the guards with their heavy black shields. She led the others through an opulent hall, hewn of pure polished obsidian; its peerless black surface showed no veins, no tool marks, nor crevices of any kind. At the end of this oblique tunnel, past two wide doors, waited a room decorated entirely in burnished gold and gems. The women strolled into this lavish space with scarcely an upward glance. The ceiling here was easily twenty feet high. Gold panels bedecked with fistfuls of amber adorned each of the four interior walls. An opulent hearth, molded from one gigantic amber core, yawned cavernously beneath a diamond-studded mosaic; its polished curves cast sensuous light, like warm honey, over the walls. A lapis lazuli dragon with amber chips for eyes dominated the ceiling, dripping expensive beeswax candles from each of its four-inch talons.

The eldest woman paused to sneer at this pretentious display, as always. The scene never failed to vex her, no matter how many times she'd glimpsed it. However, the women weren't there to admire the craftsmanship of an unknown architect. The youngest craned her neck to peer within two smaller chambers set at either end of the towering northern wall. Candlelight winked from a garnet room on the left, but she saw no one inside. Moonlight gleamed through the window in the Doma's office on the right, which Drem referred to as her 'silver box' for evident reasons. It, like the parlor, was done entirely in leaf, only this, in unalloyed silver. A shadow passed before the window. The women walked toward it.

Within, a small, slightly rotund old woman stared down at the burning city below. She was wrapped in a white sealskin coverlet, her arms folded over her ample bosom, her rich brown skin still taut and fresh despite her age. Wild silver curls sprang around her face like an angry cloud. Doma Drem Moura slid an almond-shaped, honey-brown eye over each of her visitors.

"What took you so long?"

"She's asking you, Eva." The eldest crossed her bony arms.

"I believe she's asking all of us, Mother," sighed the middle-aged lady.

Drem glared at the eldest of them with thin lips. They were old rivals, she and the Dowager Domina. "I don't like your tone, Basa."

"Since when have I given the slightest shite about what you like or don't, Drem?" retorted Basa, as her porcelain denture clacked awkwardly in her weak jaw. "You made me climb up here. Now I expect you to get to the bloody point."

"Mother, please?"

"Enough, the pair of you," Eva — the youngest — chided, shaking her head. "I'm sorry, Auntie Drem. My nona isn't used to answering summons so late at night. Mother and I apologize on her behalf."

"Humph." Basa took a seat without asking.

"You're not old enough to pretend senility, Basa. Just because we share blood doesn't mean that I won't fuse your arse to that chair," Drem warned with a curl in her lip.

"Humph," Basa repeated.

Drem considered the trio in silence for several moments. "Ana, do you share your mother's reluctance?"

"No," Ana replied. She flushed under that imperious glare. "I'm ready to do my duty to the Ancestor, my lady. As are we all."

Drem stared at Basa pointedly.

The older woman threw up a hand. "Would I bloody be here if I wasn't? Tell her what you learned, girl."

Eva cleared her throat. "I had to ascertain a few facts before I felt my information was sound."

"Oh?" Drem's velveteen voice betrayed no emotion whatsoever. "Was Nema's little pet telling the truth?"

"I'm not sure. I don't believe he could invent such a fiction alone. He's not very bright nor brave enough to lie to me. My talents are insufficient here. Too much noise for me to 'hear' properly."

"That isn't good enough."

"I know, and I'm sorry, Auntie."

Drem exhaled through her nose. "I want to know where my granddaughter is, and I want to know why she'd be traveling with a rogue Sidhe lord. I never believed he was dead, you know?" she scoffed, "… Always did find it hard to believe that Midhir would execute him, despite his crime."

Ana nodded. "I struggled with that too. Truth be told, If I'd been in the Adair's position that day at Dumnain, I'd like to think I'd have done the same. Many think him a hero."

"Most think him a monster," snorted Basa.

Ana patted her mother's shoulder. "Perhaps, but I'll contend that if he is alive and takes Una under his protection, there's hardly a safer place she could be. He'll surely take her to Bri Leith if he can."

Drem pursed her lips, thinking hard. "If this person is *the* Adair, he wouldn't be in Eire unless he had no choice, would he? I don't believe he can cross that border unaided. No matter how I picture the encounter that supposedly brought him and Una together, I can't figure he'd be wandering the Greensward looking for damsels to rescue."

"Likely not," Basa conceded.

"Must have been pure coincidence or Siora's love for my girl."

"Must have," Ana laid her hand over her heart.

"Midhir's a just ruler, but his punishments are cruel poetry. If he's not dead, he's been exiled. I'll wager my title on it."

"How do you suppose?" asked Basa.

"Knowing the Grand Marshal as I did once, banishment here would be the worst sort of hell for him. He always was arrogant as the day is long." Drem said. "If it *is* him, you may take his protecting her as confirmation of my granddaughter's worth. Ana's right. He'll take her to Midhir. The trouble with that will be either smuggling Una into Aes Sidhe without getting shot or procuring a special warrant to cross with her, legally. I'm betting he plans on the former."

"And Nema?" Ana cut in before her mother could argue.

Drem traced the iron latticework on the windowpane. "She's done her work well. I'll say that for her."

"She'll ensnare herself in her own net," said Eva.

"It pleases me that you are such an optimist, child, but I fear we're caught in that net, just the same."

Ana folded her long brown fingers together. She always did have such beautiful hands. She'd been quite the lutist when Drem had chosen her for her only son. But that was many years ago, and her Kaya long dead. Ana never remarried, and Drem loved her for it.

"The Corsairs may be loyal to Nema, my lady, but they alone cannot hope to hold the city against Souther forces. Nor, dare I speak it, forces from Aes Sidhe. Nema's coup can never be a success so long as Arrin's daughter lives. She knows it as well as we do."

"I don't believe she intends to hold this city against any army, my dear."

That was something Eva hadn't expected to hear. "How so?"

Drem shot her a wan smile. "You're too young to have witnessed Nema's ascent through the Cloister, but we did." Every woman present, save Eva, could attest. "No one is that gifted from birth. It takes training, as you well know, but also blood. Our great families were made great by breeding. Selectivity is the key to power. *Genes.* Manipulation is a discipline founded on genetic inheritance. It's not a calling."

"Perhaps Nema is an exception to that rule?"

"And her follower— that creature Aoife?"

"I could accept Nema as a genetic fluke but not her little helper too. Genetic variances resulting in Manipulative Ability are so rare that they might as well be pebbles on a lakeshore. Aptitude is a by-product of selective breeding, Eva. I don't believe in lucky coincidences."

Basa grunted. "That's the red truth. No Patent of Maternas. No family. No children. Nema appeared out of thin air." She twisted her nose. "Though I hate to admit it, however she came by her gifts, they're *formidable.* We must acknowledge her power, Drem. I could almost respect her for her brass if she weren't trying to eradicate the Libella."

Eva leaned in. "Auntie, do you believe she somehow stole her powers from another? Broke the Ninth Law?"

"No, I'm saying she isn't who she says she is," answered Drem. Eva digested this statement with a perplexed frown. "I know it, though I've never been able to procure any evidence of this. Believe me, I've tried. There was something else about her. Something… *more.* It's been in her eyes for almost four decades. I suppose I've been expecting her little coup for years."

Basa said, "I told you to kill her long ago, Drem. You disobeyed my order. Now look what your sympathy bought." Drem made a face. Forty years before, Drem had won the right to the Tenth Ordeal before her cousin Basa, who'd once been her superior on the Council of Nine. When Drem donned the Doma's robes and ascended to the Tenth Floor, Basa vowed never to forgive her. All water under a dusty bridge now, but the embers of that old enmity still smoldered in Basa's eyes.

"Our only hope is to raise an army in Swansea and pray the High King will heed my request for aid. The rabble in the street will pull the Cloister down, brick by brick, unless we stop them. Without Una… without a sure, stable future— Nema will have her way. Is everything prepared?"

Ana, the senior Alvra Judge, bobbed her head once.

"Good. We have very little time to waste, it would seem. I expect that mob outside to have the gate down in days, maybe less. Have you made your arrangements?"

"House Alvra will not be in residence when this debacle gets heated, of course," said Basa sternly. "I don't like you, Cousin, but I'd fain see my family suffer for your abysmal mishandling of this office."

"I'm so pleased for your support," Drem growled.

"You should be. Our House is only doing this for the Ancestor's Heir. Nema is your mess. Now she's grown too tall to hack down, hasn't she?" the older woman chuckled. "Consider yourself fortunate we like your granddaughter better than you."

"My mother means," Ana smiled nervously, "that we are eager to help. Isn't that right, Mother? For Siora's sake."

"Humph," granted Basa.

"All right then. Eva, my dear, how many have sided with us?"

"All, save Houses Yma, Hamma, and Ganon."

"None of which bear surprise."

"Jumped up Merchers, the lot," added Basa. "As bad as Hollin and his band of lowborn lickspittles."

"Nema wants war with the Libella, so we shall oblige her. She may have the people's love now, but let's see how much they adore her when the markets dry up. They'll run out of food in a month— less if Siora is merciful."

"I like my estate in Bretagne this time of year," Basa noted. "Lord Gaelin is a particular favorite of mine. He'll be pleased to see me."

"Let's hope he'll be even more enamored of our terms," Drem said dryly. For Ana, she softened her regard. "Kernow is not quite as civilized nor pleasant this time of year, I'm afraid."

"I enjoy the sea air, Eminence."

"Excellent." Drem turned to Eva. "How fast can you get to the Sidhe Consulate in Ten Bells?"

Eva's smile flashed white in the dimly lit chamber. "I'm bringing Mel Carra. I have yet to see him lose an inch to bad weather. If Una is in Eire, we will find her. I swear it."

Drem tucked herself deep into her sealskin mantle. "And I shall await you all in Swansea, around Imbolg. May the Ancestor hold us in her wisdom."

"*In Her Eyes, In Her Heart, In Her Spine,*" they chanted in unison.

As her visitors bowed to leave, Drem turned back to the window to watch the rain patter against the panes. At the very least, the weather would slow the burning and chaos in the streets for a while.

"Let's see how you win a rebellion without fainne, Nema. Let's see how the people love you when their children are starving."

ROSWEAL

"**I** don't see why *I* must be dragged all the way to Rosweal. I could as soon walk to Tara or even Ten Bells. They're not looking for me," Rian grumbled from behind Ben. Her twisted foot wasn't helping her move any faster, and having to evade the roads at all costs took its toll. Ben was heartily sick of the woods. He wanted to drink himself to sleep in Barb's bathhouse, wake up to one of Rose's famous massages, and dive headfirst into one of Colm's salmon stews. Above all, he longed for a warm mug full of honey-gold uishge.

Gods…

Just imagining any one of these luxuries was its own relief.

They were arriving a bit later in the evening than he would have preferred, but they'd made it. That was something. Each of them was exhausted. Several miserable days in the Greensward would do that to anyone. Even Ben, usually a light sleeper, didn't crack an eye until last evening, and only then to stuff his mouth with dried tack. They'd spent most of the previous day camping and consuming the remainder of Rian's stores. Finally departing at first light this morning, they were hungry, despondent, and reeked of mildew. Illness and fever would inevitably follow. After another full day trudging through abominable terrain, Ben caught the familiar scent of civilization on the air. At last, emerging from a high thicket of elms, they looked down on a large, wooded valley. Three gently sloping hills intersected at a bend in the rapidly flowing Blackwater. Nestled into this natural bowl sat a large walled hamlet he was avidly familiar with. How many days had it been? Ten? A hundred? He couldn't tell.

Rosweal looked just the same: little squares and warbled rectangles, mashed together in a stinking, impersonal jumble. Twisting lanes wound their muddy way in every direction. Hundreds of chimneys puffed greenish peat-smoke into a coral and grey sky. Rooftops were dusted white with sparkling frost. All around the shale exterior walls, the Greensward pressed in. Even fallow fields to the south were threatened by hungry trees. From their vantage, they could clearly see the smoking mists that curled over the river. Rosweal was the last Milesian settlement of any size along the border, the wildest, most lawless region in Innisfail. Ben couldn't think of a better place to hide. He glared at Rian.

"We've been over this."

Una huffed in his ear, and he readjusted his grip on her knees so she could breathe easier. She'd walked most of the way on her own, but her broken ribs eventually caught her out. Without Vixen to share her weight, Ben had been obliged to carry her himself. *Reduced to a bloody pack mule, indeed.*

Rian pulled up short, noting the scowl on his face— a look she definitely deserved.

"What? I'm just saying there's a good chance we will have to head south anyway. What if your brilliant plan doesn't work, huh? It's not like you've told us how you're going to—"

"Rian," interrupted Una. "If you go home, you could be arrested or worse. You heard what those soldiers said. There are possibly hundreds of them on the road, searching for us."

"For *you*," sulked Rian.

"Say you head south? They've been to your farm, and into town looking for its owner. I guarantee it. The townsfolk will surely tell them all about the unwelcome faerie girl living in Arthur Guinness' house," added Ben, dryly. "They're looking for you as well. Believe it. Whoever sent those creatures for Una knows you were there. You're safer with us."

Rian swore under her breath. Something about 'trouble' and 'fault;' Ben ignored her. Una gripped his shoulder with silent pressure.

"I'm sorry you were dragged into this, Rian. I vow, I'll repay you one way or the other, and so will he. Won't you, Ben?"

He sucked his teeth and tilted his head, so she could see the likelihood of *that* happening. Bloody women and their need for useless platitudes. How in the hells was he supposed to know what was going to happen? He was making this up as he went along. He needed a drink, is what he needed.

He hadn't been sober so long in *decades*.

"But," argued Rian. "I can't eat promises, can I?"

"Then go. Take your chances, what do I care?"

"Ben…" Una warned.

"None of us is happy about any of this. We're coping, best we can. Life isn't fair, Rian. You'd better get used to that."

Rian wiped at her damp eyes with the back of a filthy hand and pretended to ignore him. He understood that she just wanted to go home, but what could he do? Staying alive was the priority, not comfort.

Una shook her head at him. "You're an ass, you know."

"So I've been told," Ben said. "Look Rian, I know this isn't a holiday but for better or worse, we're alive, and none of us are alone. All right? Let's try to make the best of this."

After a while, Rian bobbed her head. "Fine."

"Necessity provides all the faith one needs, right?"

She marked his point with a clenched jaw.

Good. A silent fury would suit his taxed nerves much better. Gazing down on the city, he thumbed the crude ogham charm below the hem of his tunic. Most folks he'd spent any amount of time with wouldn't immediately notice the difference between this Ben Maeden and the one they remembered, but he had to admit a select few most certainly would. His reflection that morning in the river was very similar to the one he'd worn for over a decade… though not quite. Rian, being only one-quarter Sidhe, couldn't hope to produce the same strong glamour his previous stone held. He and the old Ben Maeden shared the same height, weight, and build. His hair was Ben's— shaggy and yellow. He wore the same rough patches on his hands and stubble on his chin. However, the similarities stopped there. Rian's stone couldn't alter the translucent sheen of his skin, nor obscure the shape or depth of his silver-blue irises. He *was* Ben Maeden again… and distinctly, not. At least Gerrod and Robin already knew. He only hoped he'd be given a chance to explain himself before Robin had him shot in the street like a dog.

Well, he thought to himself.

No point worrying over it now.

He'd figure something out. He always did.

"Listen," he cleared his throat. "Rosweal's not a pleasant place. Everything you've heard about it is true. There are very many bad, desperate people behind those unkempt walls."

Rian leaned against a birch to catch her breath. "Can't you get in touch with whoever you need to somewhere *safer*?"

"Rosweal's the last place in Eire that anyone would think to look for Prima Moura. No one from the Red City will wander in here on a hunch."

"You'd better be right," Rian said. "Because if we're murdered down there, I will curse you to the blackest depths of the lowest hell in Tech Duinn, *tuiathe*."

Ben thought about pitching her over the hill. Una's blasted fingernails were going to give Ben a rash at this rate. He tried to slap them away.

"Damn it, woman, stop that!"

"We're in this together, like Ben said," Una sighed. "Can we move past this now? We can claw each other's eyes out when we're dry."

"Siora, help us," Rian pined. "At this point, I'd hand over every coin in my purse for a bath and a warm meal."

"Gods, *uisghe*," moaned Ben.

Una, for once, agreed. "Or the tallest mug of spiced cider in Innisfail."

"Uishge *in* the mug of spiced cider."

"Don't tease me. They do that here?"

"Hells yes, they do," Ben assured her. "I intend to drown myself in a cask at the first opportunity."

Rian wrinkled her nose. "Don't look at me when you're both puking your guts out."

"It'll be nice to have *something* in there to throw up," Una said.

"I'd better get something grand out of this. A house, a new farm, or better yet, my own peerage. *Lady Rian Guinness* has a nice ring, don't you think?"

⚜

THEY APPROACHED THE NAVAN GATE from the riverside. The sky had faded to a dull charcoal overhead. Ben pointed to a small, homely gap in the low city wall overgrown with weeds and piled high with discarded refuse.

"Best to avoid the gate, for now. We'll head through there." Both girls gaped at his proposed entrance with mirrored horror. The 'wall' was constructed of crudely stacked shale without a hint of mortar. This was the old Innish way to build, unchanged from the dawn of time. Perhaps it wasn't beautiful, but it would stand for centuries, so long as no one bothered to knock it down. Ben would tell them this if he thought either would hold the slightest interest.

Behind the section they crept toward stood hundreds of dilapidated huts, crammed one on top of the other. Weak lamplight flickered from flooded rivulets carved into each lane by heavy wagon wheels and overburdened horse carts. Dor Samna rains had left their ugly brown mark everywhere the eye rested. Rosweal often took the brunt of any storm, as it was perched at the crux of three steep hills. Here in the low east-end of town, where the poorest souls made their homes, folk trudged through ankle-deep filth just to get to their front doors. After so long spent in the relatively fresh air in the Greensward, the stench was overpowering.

"Dear, sweet, Siora," Rian gagged.

Una buried her face in her tunic.

Ben smirked. "Welcome to Rosweal, ladies."

"We're not staying *here*, I hope?" pleaded Una, her face scrunched up like she'd swallowed a lemon whole.

"We'll take the alley past the Hunter's Quarter to the other side of town. Those buildings on the hill, facing the river. See them?"

He felt her nod at his back. Rian hitched her skirts as high as she could and still managed to keep hold of her walking stick. It wouldn't help. Even with the boards hammered into the middle of each lane, there was no escaping the sludge below. They would likely have to burn their garments when all was said and done. Ben didn't frequent this end of town. He did have standards… well, he once had them, anyway. He shifted Una forward a bit so he could step carefully onto one of these semi-useful boards.

"I have a place overlooking the river. It's not much, but I doubt anyone will be expecting me."

"You sure?" inquired Rian, with a suspicious scowl.

"… We'll worry about that later."

"Oh, great," said Una. "I suppose you owe someone money?"

"No need to be rude."

Rian squeaked when a dead rat floated over her boot. "Who'd want to live here?"

"Not everyone's father was a successful physician," said Ben.

"How magnanimous of you, your lordship," jeered Una.

Ben bristled. "I've lived here for years, *princess*. Be careful not to stare too long into the light you're attempting to shine upon me."

"I'm *not* a princess. How about you? Did you grow up on a farm like Rian, I wonder?"

"No, but I've been here longer than both of you are old. So, shut up."

"Siora!" Rian snapped. "Will you two *please* stop bickering?"

"We're not bickering," Una sniffed. "We're merely—"

"Didn't you just get on my case about arguing with him?"

That did the trick. Una's mouth clapped shut over her retort.

"A plan, Ben. Do we have one or not?" Rian demanded, forced to grab onto the back of his tunic to keep her footing on the way uphill.

"I'm working on it."

She grumbled several unflattering things beneath her breath. "Right. Why plan ahead? It's more fun this way, isn't it?"

"Do you fancy a bath and clean clothes, or not?" He was slightly mollified by the intense, hopeful longing that chased her sarcastic expression away. "Well, they're this way. You can come along or make your own plans. Got it?"

Una patted him like he was a faithful pony. Because, clearly, she knew it irritated him. Grumbling, he led them through the complicated patchwork of lanes through the slums and the hilltop perched above.

⚎

THEY PASSED EVERY SORT OF low establishment imaginable. What Rosweal lacked in size and grandeur, it made up for in squalid, belching, screeching, raucous humanity. People everywhere were hanging from doorways, shouting drunkenly at their neighbors, or shuffling aimlessly down mellifluous lanes. Women cackled, spat, scolded, and catcalled from various misshapen windows and rickety awnings. The rain didn't dissuade any of Rosweal's citizens from wandering outdoors to seek their various entertainments. Men gathered outside run-down shops and taverns, smoking, arguing, fighting, or generally carousing. Ragged, half-starved sticks Una assumed were children ran hither and thither through foul streets, dodging grasping hands, abandoned carts, and the odd animal carcass. As Ben and company ambled up a narrow lane crushed between two leaning wooden tenements, an overhead shutter slammed open. Without a word of warning, a bucket full of human waste splashed downward in a reeking brown cascade. Rian shrieked, almost knocking all three of them into the muck to avoid it. Ben hauled her upright by the collar.

"Don't draw attention to yourself."

"I don't think we could if we tried," said Una with a dismayed glare.

"Oh, you *can*. I mean it, don't make eye contact and keep your voice down." His eyes darted around. "You don't want to appeal to anyone here."

From the shanty town, with its flooded streets and violent surging mortality, they ascended a steep hill, which leveled out around a much more stoic neighborhood. Everything seemed quieter here, less cluttered and congested. The air was a bit cleaner too, but not by much. Una turned to marvel at the bobbing lights and ramshackle roofs whence they came.

"How many people live down there?"

"Hundreds, maybe more. Who cares?"

"Awful," said Rian. "Did you see those poor children?"

Ben shrugged. "Half of those kids likely have no relatives left to depend upon. People starve out here in the wilds come winter. The smart ones will live. The rest… well. As you can see."

"Their parents and guardians could make their lives better if they wanted to," she argued. "Besides, what does a nobleman like you know about poverty, *tuiathe*?"

"I know who I am, Rian, but I also know them," he paused to jerk his chin downhill. "This *is* a rough place, but I'm telling you, these people make do. While I might not always understand them, I know how hard these folks work to survive, and I'll not fault them for their efforts."

"Then why don't you live down there with them?"

"I said I respect them, not that I envy them. We each must make our way, heedless of circumstance or consequence."

"That's rather poignant for a debauch like yourself."

Una said nothing for a moment. It surprised her that Ben found some measure of camaraderie with the outcasts in Rosweal. Everything she'd ever been told about him suddenly seemed somewhat biased. Perhaps he didn't despise 'Milesians' as much as everyone believed he did? Or maybe he'd been here long enough to develop an appreciation for those he once considered inferior? One thing she knew for sure: solitude courted strange bedfellows. She probably knew this better than most. The Cloister of the Eternal Flame was not a place of communal harmony. To dwell within that sumptuous prison, one must accept that they are well and truly alone. She wondered if Ben might have been brought up to feel the same way. She folded that kernel away for later examination.

"I think if more people knew of the suffering here, they might seek to lend a hand," she said.

He craned his neck to give her a dubious glare. "Some things are easier said than done, princess."

"I won't forget those children if I ever make it home."

"You may want to remember the ones in Tairngare first," Ben chuckled. "Poverty is not a novelty anywhere in your Milesian societies. As soon as people figured out it was easier to exploit others than work for themselves, it's been much the same throughout your history. Be careful not to applaud yourself for your condescension."

Rian stumbled up the rise. "No child deserves a life like that. Besides, grand lords and ladies, like yourselves, should ask what can be done. Don't you think?"

Una decided just then that she liked Rian Guinness very much. She smiled over at her. "Well said."

Rolling his eyes, Ben led them through two more alleys connected with the first, then up a crudely carved set of stairs to a semi-cobbled lane. Again, the streets got cleaner the higher they climbed; the air more tolerable. Ben took them below an arch down the wide main street, then cut right into another alley. This row was easily the best of the lot. The buildings here had sturdy stone foundations and high stucco walls painted in various cheerful shades. Almost every window had two sets of shutters: some even fine latticed glass. Almost every cross-street featured tall lantern poles, which poured muted lamplight onto the cobbles. There were more people out on this side of town than there had been in the last two neighborhoods— though nowhere near as many as the mob in the slums. There were one or two publicans with heavy creaking signs. Random knots of nominally well-dressed individuals gathered in front of each. Ben paused at the sight and gently tried to steer the girls into the next lane. One fellow leaned out, waving.

"Ho there! Ben Maeden? Is that ye? Well, I'll be blustered. Ole Gerry said ye left town. Where ye headed?"

Ben cursed as the caller trotted down the street toward them, two others close on his heels. Ben shoved Rian against a dark wall, prodding Una to slide down to her feet.

The short, dark-haired fellow who'd called out to them slowed about five paces away. "Oh. Who's that ye got there, huh?"

"Looks like girls, to me," remarked one of his more brilliant friends.

"Don't look like any'o Matt's goods. Maybe Barb's got some new stock?"

"Oh, aye. One's quite fair, ye ask me. The other looks like she's been done for. Who beat the shite outta ye, lovey?"

The first's easy smile faded when he saw Ben's fingers close over his sword pommel. He slid his hands up. "Whoa, Ben. Just came to greet ye. No need for that."

"You've never greeted me in your life, Vincent. What do you want?" The erstwhile Vincent backed up a step. His mates were still arguing about what establishment Una and Rian might have been prized from. Una ground her teeth. She was not used to treatment like this *at all*.

"It's just Vick, Ben. Sayin' hallo, s'all." Despite his harmless grin, Vick kept his hands up, but he wasn't leaving. Ben's reaction made Una nervous. These lads didn't look dangerous, and their clothes weren't fine by anyone's standards— but they were cleaner and better tailored than anything they wore, saving Ben's stolen sealskin cloak. Rian seemed to anticipate the trouble they might be in. She clasped Una's fingers in hers to propel them both backward along the wall.

"You've said it, now slag off."

Vick didn't stop smiling his affable smile. "Yer on the wrong side o'town, ain't ye, Ben? Ole Lon, at the *Juke*, said ye roughed up some o'his customers few nights back. Been mighty noisy 'bout it too."

"Guess how much he'll pay for yer corpse," sniggered the taller of Vick's companions. "Offerin' a full stag, what I hear. Said he'd pay Matt double, jus' for signin' off."

Ben gave them a cold smile. "Crossing me didn't work out so well for them, did it?"

Vick's smirk flickered. "Them were friends o'mine, Ben Maeden."

"*Were*, being the operative word."

The three louts didn't appear eager to leave. Ben slid back until his right heel connected with the toe of Una's boot. "Three up, one over. Understand?"

"What?"

"Will ye listen to that voice? Gave me a chill, that did," said the tall one.

"Long as ye don't have to look at her face!" laughed his friend.

"*I* do." Rian drew the little dagger Ben gave her from her belt. She yanked Una away from the wall. From then on, Una couldn't say what happened because all she could hear was shouting, shuffling, and steel striking steel. She and Rian ran until Una's broken ribs felt like they might pierce her lungs. When Rian jerked her around the corner three lanes up, they discovered a sad little park of sorts. The space was set into a wide cul-de-sac down the end, overgrown with weeds and littered with debris— not much to look at, save for a low stone bench and the remnants of a fountain. A playful howl echoed from the buildings around them. The taller youth swaggered into the slanted moonlight, his face a ghoulish leer.

"There ye are. Thought there'd be a bit more chase in ye's."

Rian raised her dagger. "Oh, there is."

He clapped his hands together like a giddy child. "Good! I hate it when there's no dash in me ladies, ye know? Dull, that way."

Una inched forward, but Rian stopped her. "No. You'll just hurt yourself worse."

"But—"

Without warning, the boy sprang at Rian with a skeletal grin. Rian moved left to slash at him with her right, but he was faster. He grabbed her around the waist and swung her to the ground, yowling with excitement. Rian thrashed, but he struck her once, hard. She went limp for a split-second too long, and he took advantage. Wrenching her forward by her vest, he climbed up her torso to snatch at the front of her dress.

The dagger skittered away, out of reach. With a snarl, Una lunged at him. He tumbled backward, smacking the base of his skull against jagged paving stones. Grunting, he grabbed a fistful of the hair at Una's nape and tugged her head back. White stars traced across her eyes at the pain. One meaty fist smashed into the right side of her face, from her ears to her chin. Una blinked and clenched her jaw against the chorus of bells in her ears. Blood ran down her cheek from her already swollen eye. She shoved her knee into his solar plexus to keep the boy from dislodging her and brought her elbow into his nose. He screamed as the cartilage gave way to the bone. She hit him again, and several of his front teeth cracked and splintered. Una wasn't given time to enjoy the sounds. He drove both fists into her face, then bucked her aside with his legs.

He got to his knees. "I'm gonna cut yer tits off!"

Una spat out a mouthful of blood. "Thought you liked a woman with fight?" He caught her ankle, intending to drag her within reach, but wasn't watching Rian.

Wiping the blood from her nose, Rian gripped Ben's dagger in a white-knuckled fist. Before the boy could speak or make another move, Rian drove the dagger hilt-deep into his neck. He gurgled in surprise and crumpled forward. His eyes bulged when he hit the ground.

"So happy we could oblige you. You piece of shite." She didn't wait to watch him die as he deserved. She pulled Una to her feet. "Siora, I think he broke your cheekbone. Can you walk?"

"Quick, before he's gone. I need to…."

"What are you talking about?"

"Just take me to him!"

Visibly confused, Rian lowered Una beside their scrawny, would-be rapist's dying body. Una didn't have time to explain. He was moments from death. She could not waste him. She shot Rian an apologetic glance and placed her right hand over his gore-slick face. He choked as her palm covered what was left of his mouth. Una took a deep, stilling breath. She let her Spark reach for him… *into* him. Life flowed back into her body, streams, and streams of pure raw energy. She tapped, molded, and sent it where it was most needed. Her heart beat clearer and stronger. She felt her lungs expand; her air passages widen. The blood replenished itself in her veins, cells divided with the speed of a rushing river. Her ribs and throat burned. The bones in her face glowed hot as coals under her skin. Una shuddered when those same molten bones fused; fractures mended on each breath.

Then it was done.

Incomplete. Her Spark retreated, stilted and unsatisfied. Una collapsed on her haunches, gasping. Her burning palms slid over her partially mended ribs.

Rian gaped at her like Una had just helped herself to the man's brains. "What in the *nine hells*… did you just do?"

"He intended to use us. I used him instead."

"Hallowed *Siora*. I've never seen anything like that before."

"Nor will you. It's forbidden."

"I can bloody see why!"

"Rian, I'm sorry. Truly. But I didn't have the time to explain myself. My injuries were going to get me killed. Can we leave it for later?"

"… You tried to save my life just now."

"And you certainly saved mine."

After a while, Rian exhaled. "Give us some warning next time, is all I ask."

Una smiled. She held out a hand to be helped up. When they were face to face, she patted Rian on the shoulder. "Deal."

A scrape behind them, and they both turned, alarmed.

This time, it was only Ben. He stood at the edge of the cul-de-sac, taking in the shriveled dead man and the bloodied girls standing over him. Ben didn't seem the worse for wear himself if slightly winded… the bastard.

"What in blazes happened here?"

Rian wiped her hands on her skirt. "You know, more *fun*."

He crept toward them, eyes wide. "We should go. Right now. This isn't Guild territory, and we've killed *two* men."

"Is that supposed to mean anything to us?"

"We're on the wrong side of town."

"Does that imply there's a right side?" Rian asked Una, who shrugged.

"Doubt it."

"I've lost Vick but killed his mouthy friend. They'll be looking for us. Let's go, please. *Now.*"

Una sidestepped the corpse toward Ben. Rian stooped to retrieve her dagger, making a disgusted snort while she scrubbed the blade clean on the dead boy's tunic.

Ben's fingers caught Una's elbow before she could walk past him. He stared. "What happened to your face?"

"Fast healer, remember?"

"Right," he frowned.

"Won't they just follow us to your preferred end of Rosweal?" Rian asked, coming to stand beside them.

Ben couldn't seem to stop scowling at Una's face. Una purposefully ignored him. He gestured for them to follow him to the north end of the park, where another alley twisted along the wall, then angled westward.

"Not at all. They know better than to enter the Greenmakers' Quarter."

"Oh, so we'll be safe there?"

"Well, in a manner of speaking," said Ben, still staring at Una in morbid fascination.

"Wonderful," she breathed. She wasn't sure why, but the prospect of danger didn't seem to frighten her as badly as it might have a few days before. Either she was getting used to this chaos, or she was beginning to trust her new comrades. For Una, this was uncharted territory. She'd spent the past ten years in her apartments, reading, writing, and honing her Manipulation. Monthly training sessions with Mel Carra in her private courtyard on the Ninth Floor had been her sole means of physical exercise. That Una seemed so far away from her now, they might have been staring across a vast ocean at each other. It had been less than two weeks since she'd been taken from Drogheda, but already, she felt like a completely different person. Though she hated killing, she was learning the value of her life. She wasn't afraid of herself any longer. Her revelation felt surreal— odd.

Optimistic was too solid and preposterous a word for the situation. Wasn't it? *Foolhardy* seemed a far more appropriate term.

Twelve Steps

Damek left the wooden gate swinging free in the strong, northerly breeze. He circled the partially destroyed cottage with a wary eye on its damaged façade. Frowning, he traced a gloved finger over the huge claw marks that bisected the north wall. Deep, gaping slashes cut through the siding and mortar to the stone beneath. Several shingles had pried themselves loose on the roof, exposing the roof's supporting timbers to the elements. After a few days of steady rain, huge sagging holes already coalesced there. The roof would eventually cave in without someone to shore up the damage. Damek tread around the rear corner and raised his eyebrows at the damage done to the back of the house. The doorway leaned haphazardly sideways, its lintel having fallen and smashed against the stoop. He took a few steps back to admire the scale of the destruction. One more heavy rain and the house might crumble like stacked kindling. Holding his breath, he faced the mutilated barn. There were shredded piles of livestock rotting all over the place. Flies choked the air in dense, buzzing clouds. A ribcage discarded like so much dross lay over the splintered remnants of what once must have been the door; bones glinted white in the morning sun.

A thick coating of frost did little to hide the carnage he cataloged in that yard. The barn's roof had been smashed to splinters. What animals made it out before the collapse were ripped in half and only partially consumed as if they were killed merely for sport. Whatever did this must not have been able to do the same to the house. Otherwise, it might have been Una he found lying here, half-eaten, in the mud and frost. Perhaps there was some rule associated with Otherworld creatures like these? Could they not enter a person's home without invitation? The owner was rumored to be a faerie girl. Did she know some charm that could have prevented these beasts from leaving her home in the same state as the barn? He had no idea. He'd never encountered anything like this before. Damek drifted toward Martin, and his men, careful not to step in any of the gory remains littering the pasture. His knights were gathered around the monsters' carcasses, jabbing sabres and spear shafts at the still-smoking hides. From the state of things, all of this must have happened days before— yet the creatures in question did not desiccate. Why? Who would send beasts like these after Una? Who could?

Damek had only one suspect in mind.

Martin, he noted, arrived at the same conclusion. Their eyes met over a steaming foreleg. Damek knew Una had escaped the smugglers he'd hired, and he'd heard there were six dead Corsairs back east, rotting in a wooded dell beside the High Road. He was certain Una had also survived that encounter because two men bore sure signs of her handiwork. One man's brains had been boiled out of his open orifices, and the other's face had been crushed from inside his skull. He knew of no one, save Una, with the macabre ability to mangle flesh and bone from within. What had happened to her after was less certain. Why did Corsairs hunt her in the first place? Were they not armored knights from Tairngare's Citadel? Hadn't Damek paid a small fortune to smuggle her from the city in one piece? His connection assured him that nothing would serve their purposes better than to have the Moura Domina out of the way. Apparently not. Either the Citadel Corsairs were engaged in a coup, or Damek's contact had lied about her intentions through her pretty white teeth.

Damek did not believe in coincidence or bad luck. He'd been betrayed, likely from the very first. It seemed his blasted uncle had a point, after all. Their contact in the Cloister was a double agent. There could be little doubt now. Damek wasn't sure which angered him more: that someone he held a modicum of affection for was a traitor or that Patrick had been right about Aoife from the start? She was not the only complication plaguing his overtaxed mind, however. He'd already paid a visit to the campsite a mile north of Bally Lough, where Rawly and his men had been viciously slain. It took almost three days to backtrack from their appointed rendezvous to the site. Everything was precisely as Cunningham had said it would be. Though badly decomposed in the harsh elements, the evidence was plain; Rawly's crew had been slain by someone exceptionally skilled with bow and blade. Damek doubted that archery was a prized subject of study in the Cloister. Therefore, this ruled out Una having taken matters into her own hands.

According to the rumor about the six Corsairs who were found beside the High Road, they'd been observed chasing a small woman about twenty miles west of the village of Slane. Witnesses didn't see what happened to the woman in question. They could only point to the place the Corsairs' corpses had been found. Again, all were slain by an experienced hand.

It seemed Una *had* found herself a reluctant protector.

While Damek was relieved to learn that Una wasn't out here alone, he was annoyed that some unknown agent had intervened. Furthermore, he was incredibly apprehensive of this mysterious individual's intentions. First, Una should be in Bethany now and safe in her father's house. None of this incessant backtracking should have been necessary in the least. If Rawly had made their rendezvous, she would have passed into Damek's company in Ten Bells, grumpy, no doubt, but otherwise, none the worse for wear. Secondly, whoever interfered to save her was taking her farther west rather than back to Tairngare to presumed safety. That could only mean the rumor about the Corsairs chasing a woman into the Greensward bore truth, and Damek must infer that someone had pursued Una from the Citadel. He was having a hard time denying the obvious. Nema had no intention of honoring her arrangement with Bethany. Clearly, she and Aoife played a side game that didn't include him. Well, he would just see about that, wouldn't he?

He knelt beside a decapitated head larger than his torso.

"Martin. Call for Cunningham."

"Aye, My Lord." Martin barked orders to the men behind him. It took a few minutes to wrangle Cunningham from the back of the line, bound to his horse as he had been. The disgraced Captain of the Steel Corps scowled down at his liege lord, infuriated by his inhospitable treatment. Damek couldn't blame him, but he had to be sure of the man's absolute loyalty.

Damek nodded at the Corps Lieutenant. "Hisk. His bonds, if you please?" Cunningham's eyes burned with mistrust. Martin's fingers curled over his pommel in response. Hisk unlocked his manacles, and Cunningham shoved him backward, hard. "Now now, Captain. Behave yourself."

"Fuck you, O'Rearden."

Damek laughed. "Charming, don't you think, Martin?"

"I wonder how adorable he'll be without a tongue?"

Cunningham stood as straight as he was able. "I've taken all the shite I mean to for telling the truth."

"You got a complaint you'd like to lodge now? Formally?" Martin's steel sang a bit as it slid partway from its sheath. Cunningham swallowed audibly.

"No, *Commander*."

"Very good, Captain." Martin's blade snapped home with a sharp click. "Now, you may address your lord. Respectfully, remember."

"Why was any of this necessary?"

"You're not a stupid man, Wallace. I've been fed one line of horseshite after another. I wanted to be sure of you. As you can plainly see," Damek gestured to the general nightmarish absurdity of the scene, "we're in uncharted waters here. It doesn't appear that my fair cousin has merely been abducted, does it?"

"No," Cunningham agreed with a semi-shrug. "Forgive my tone, but I believe I said so in my initial report?"

"Watch yourself," Martin droned.

Cunningham raked a frustrated hand over his scalp. "Lieutenant Hisk can attest to my observational ability, My Lord. I'll swear to it again if that's what you want. She was taken by your man and his crew, as ordered. Someone in the Citadel must have observed their leaving or knew their general escape route, for they were soon chased into Bally Lough by scores of Corsairs and Tairnganeah Regulars. There, they were slain to a man by someone who came from the *wrong* end of the woods. Someone too good to be considered incidental, yet, all the physical evidence left at the scene would argue the contrary. I can't put it any plainer than that."

Damek shot Martin a twisted lower lip. "A High Elf, I believe you said?"

Cunningham absorbed the laughter that echoed around him with a rigid spine. "That is my assessment. I have no reason to invent such an odd tale, nor do I enjoy a fable. I stand by my report."

"Very well." Damek waved Hisk and his men back. They took Cunningham's manacles with them. Cunningham looked around, guarded and uncertain. "Your ability is quite clear, Major. You've exceeded my expectations. Now, would you be so kind as to examine this scene and report your conclusions?"

Cunningham gawped from Damek to Martin and back, his mouth opening and closing. "M-My Lord?"

"I asked you to examine these beasts, *Major* Cunningham— and tell me if it is your opinion that the same hand which slew Rawly and his men also did this. Was that clear enough? I do hate to repeat myself. You could as easily be retied to your horse. Your choice."

Cunningham flushed crimson to the roots of his red hair while he fumbled a salute. "Right away, sir, erm, My Lord!"

Damek winked at Martin, who shook his head. He veered away from the bestial corpses and headed back toward the house. Martin followed.

"Well," he said, clasping his hands behind his back as they walked. "I doubt a field commission is what young Wallace Cunningham expected back there."

"The man earned it. He was right."

"You agree with his assessment then?" Damek saw the lesions on the larger beast's carcass. Arrowheads, he was certain, though said arrows were long absent. Any self-respecting archer would do his utmost to preserve his supply, so Damek was not surprised to find them gone. He didn't need them to confirm the sheer artistry of each wound. They were too clean to be hurried and loosed from too far away to be directed on the fly. Given the scene, each shot should have been practically impossible. Distance, velocity, angle, inertia: all of these were imperatives in a bowman's arsenal. What was evident here was a haphazard disregard for basic calculations. The hand that drew down on these creatures did so too quickly to guarantee aim yet hit each target without a second glance.

How did Damek know this? The tracks.

The beasts' prints were everywhere, hard to miss for their size and irregular gait. Of the archer, there were only two well-defined sets. This person had walked, rather than ran, in a straight line from the cottage; the tracks there were too narrow and shallow for a dash. There was a slight impression upon the right heel at the end of the line, which indicated the bowman had tilted back to draw, but that was all. He didn't hurry. Damek wasn't as skilled a tracker as Cunningham, but he saw the wounds on each creature's bodies. The archer took a couple of shots from this position, which dropped the first beast with little ado. From there, the second beast seemed to rise on its hind legs. The fellow had emptied his meager quiver, then took up a sword or axe to finish the job. Damek followed the mess of tracks in the earth around the headless beast's body.

Whoever this person was, he had slain both of these unnatural beasts in about twelve steps. The whole affair had probably lasted less than five minutes. If Damek didn't already have Cunningham's previous testimony, he wouldn't have needed it to make an educated guess. "I concur with the Major. No one is this good. We can't be sure who he is, but I'd wager my arse against his heritage."

"You rather *are* making that bet."

Damek made a face. "I suppose I am, aren't I?"

"At least one mystery has been solved."

"Yes," Damek's expression darkened.

"I suppose your girl had other plans, then, eh?"

"I'll be damned if I know why." Damek ducked under the leaning doorjamb, careful not to touch it. The last thing he needed was to trap himself inside a crumbling building. He motioned for Martin to wait shy of the jamb. Martin was almost twice as wide as Damek and therefore couldn't hope to squeeze through that gap unmolested.

Martin crossed his corded arms. "You'll forgive me for saying so; I daresay she's been leading you by the nose."

Damek laughed without mirth and picked his way through the largely undamaged interior. Whoever built this little cottage had known what he was about. Aside from puddles collecting beneath holes in the roof and the imminent threat of collapse, the foundations were strong. If the outer walls could be repaired in time, perhaps the roof could be mended. Though, what did it matter? The owner was long gone. Damek stepped over to a little couch beside a homely fireplace to retrieve a bloodied shawl draped over its arm. This was one of the few items strewn about the cottage which wasn't soaking wet with moldering rainwater. He held it briefly beneath his nose. Whatever alchemical mixture of components caused human scents to leave an indelible scar upon one's memory assured him that Una had been wrapped in this garment. The scent was faint and hampered by the coppery sick sweetness of drying blood, but present, nonetheless. A carefully concealed fury surged through his veins. She was injured—badly, it would seem. Was that Aoife's doing, or Nema's, working independently of her right hand? To *whom* should he direct his rage?

"I've known Aoife for most of my life, Martin. This entire plan was her idea, to begin with."

"My point exactly."

Damek looked up. "I won't argue her treachery or complicity. No point to that now. I simply can't help but wonder what she thought she'd gain. Why spend a decade planning this, only to betray me before I could see it to fruition?"

"Why indeed, your lordship?" Martin toed a loose clod of earth with his boot. "Perhaps something went wrong on her end? We have reports that Tairngare is in chaos. Rioting, and the like. Maybe, she worried that Lady Donahugh would return to Tairngare and ally with the opposition? We know how much the Alta Prima loves the Mouras."

Oh, Damek knew. He knew better than Martin, that was sure. But this was not information he intended to share with anyone, even his most trusted friend.

"It's possible." Damek tossed the soiled garment back on the couch. "There's a deeper game here that I'm not seeing."

"If you'll pardon me? I, for one, am not in the least surprised by this double-cross. I think you've been played for a fool here, and the Duch with you from the very first."

"It suits Nema's interests to have Una out of the way, and it suits mine to take her to wife before Patrick can get his hooks into her. They were to cede Tara and Malahide to me, and I would use them to hold the Midlands against the Duch until the Barons fell in line. This was a win-win."

Martin gave him a smile that told Damek he knew more than he let on but was willing to keep his peace. "I know how you like to second-guess your conclusions, My Lord. I think you arrived at the answer long before I did, and I doubt it shocked you any more than it does me. In no scenario can I figure does Una being married to a powerful Souther lord bode well for Nema's new government. You must realize, as much as your piece might please you, that her loyalty has always lain with her mistress. With Una out of the way, Nema can cry foul and retract her support for Patrick's siege."

"This will only goad Patrick to hostility, and without me to intervene, how does she propose to block him?"

"I gather she *wants* Patrick to attack. Unrest in the Red City, Una's abduction, enemies marching through the North— sounds like she's makin' her bid for the Tenth Floor. All this," Martin waggled three fingers at Damek, "helps her cause, don't you think? If her main argument is that the Mouras are unfit for leadership, everything that's happening now can only encourage the people to see things her way. Honestly? What does she need you for, begging your pardon, My Lord— other than to serve as a distraction?"

That gave Damek pause.

He must assume any additional promises made to him on a more personal level were equally nullified. It didn't seem likely that Nema would attempt to set Damek on such a wild goose chase unless… she intended to divide him from the bulk of Bethany's forces in the first place. Nema wouldn't have to concern herself over invading nobles from Ten Bells, Tara, or Malahide if Damek was busily revenging himself upon them for Una's loss. Wasn't this fascinating? Either Nema believed Damek could still be manipulated after showing her hand so baldly this way, or she had no further use for him at all. If she didn't fear reprisals from any Souther lord, what else had she been keeping from him for so many years? Nema was not one to act in a hurry. Plans within plans, Nema had— like a fat spider at the center of a web.

It seemed everyone in Innisfail had a mind to use Damek to achieve their own ends and discard him after. He'd be pleased to disappoint them all, wouldn't he? Before now, he could never hope to hold onto the Northern cities without backing from the Souther Barons. He knew it, and Nema had surely counted on it. She perhaps hadn't realized before she stuck the knife into his back that she was handing Damek an invaluable gift: *cause*. The Barons would fall all over themselves to accommodate him now. The Cloister had not only kept their future Duchess from her true home in Bethany all these years, but now they'd attempted to murder her too. The irony was beautiful. Perhaps if Nema had managed to kill Una as planned, she might have pulled off her little coup without a hitch. Damek *would* have burned the North to cinders in a fury for his lost chance at legitimacy, and Patrick *would* have had him killed or imprisoned for his failure to hold it. But… Una had defied the old bitch and her shoddy plans, hadn't she? She was alive. All Damek had to do was find her, and his chips would fall into place on their own.

Perhaps he should write Nema a 'thank you' note? She could remove it from Aoife's conniving mouth after Damek strangled her and sent her body back to Tairngare in burlap. Musing over how he'd make the women in his life pay for underestimating him, he ducked into a parlor with books strewn about the floor. A handsome desk held several broken jars of herbs, foul-smelling fluids, and pungent powders. On a table along the right wall lay a bowl and cloth stained with dried blood, all of which alluded to Una's state when she'd arrived. She was alive, but for how long? He had no time to waste. Damek strode outside to find Martin sitting on the stoop, cleaning his nails with the tip of his dagger.

"Anything of note?"

"Una was here. She's injured. If I may hazard a guess, I'd say our strong fellow carried her here to see the good doctor Guinness before they were attacked by these Otherworld… things."

"Townsfolk in Ferndale say the doctor died some while back. Must mean his daughter has some skill with the needle herself?"

"Must do," agreed Damek. "I found no trace of human remains in that barn or anywhere nearby. The owner left with them or fled elsewhere."

"I would have if those beasts came to blow down my house and eat up all my pets. Wouldn't you?"

"Hm," Damek marched past his forward guard as they set up cookfires for mid-morning luncheon. The majority of his forces waited in town, about five miles south. His officers saluted him as he strolled past. He approached the larger of the two dead beasts, where Cunningham knelt. All Damek needed now was confirmation of his assertions before deciding what to do next. "Martin?"

"My Lord," said O'Rearden from behind him. As faithful a shadow as there ever had been.

"You've fought them before, the Daoine Sidhe?" This was more a statement of fact than a question, as everyone knew very well what a hero Martin O'Rearden had been at Dumnain. Bethany may have lost that battle and ultimately the war against Aes Sidhe, but Martin had famously made them pay for every inch the Sidhe gained. No one in the South would ever forget it. "Do they fight with such weapons? Broadswords, I mean?"

"Not generally. They prefer the lark—a long slender blade made from an alloy we've never been able to duplicate. Most of their foot soldiers carry two of these larks; built for speed, not bone-cleaving strength."

"What do you make of this, then?"

"Could be Sidhe, sure. Though I haven't seen many elves use a weapon heavier than the lark outside of pitched battle. Don't need anything heavier, you ask me. Bastards are bloody quick and strong enough without the added weight."

"Cunningham?"

"My Lord?"

"What's your verdict?"

Cunningham looked flabbergasted. "It's the same blade, or I'm daft."

"You're sure?"

"I am. Damned strong steel, if I'm any judge. Two-hander, likely twenty-five to thirty pounds, as the Commander said. And another thing." Cunningham gestured to the earth around each corpse. "He's very, very good. I saw the same at Rawly's campsite."

Damek scowled to hear his own opinions restated. "You're positive this is a Sidhe warrior?"

Cunningham didn't bat an eye. "I would count on it."

Absolutely fucking wonderful.

If Aes Sidhe knew what was afoot in Eire, Damek might already be too late. "All right then. It's unlikely that we're all misreading this scene."

"The Duch will gnash his teeth over this." Martin scratched at his scar.

"So too, will Nema," said Damek with a quirk to his lower lip. "But I'm sure her agents arrived at our conclusions days ago… *and* they have a head-start. As for the Duch, I don't give a damn about him right now. We have to find Una fast. I can't spare any men to keep him apprised."

"You know I love you, lad, but be careful now. You know what Patrick will think of that."

"What d'you think he'll make of his daughter being spirited over the border while I waste time penning messages and waiting for orders?"

"I empathize, My Lord. But you need him as much as he needs you. Don't make a mistake that could cost you everything later."

Damek cursed. He hated that Martin was always bloody right. "Reason, damn it. Fine. *Hisk!*"

The lieutenant saluted again. "My Lord?"

"Find someone willing to go home and face my uncle's wroth for me. One horse only, do you hear?"

"Aye, My Lord."

"Lord Bishop…" Martin attempted.

Damek ignored him. "I need every available man on the hunt. Send outriders to every town, village, and way-house for twenty miles. Una's injured, on the run… and in the company of at least two others. One, it seems, is likely a Sidhe agent. He'll be taller than the average man, likely fair of skin, and armed with a thirty-pound longsword. They cannot be far if they haven't crossed the border already."

Martin said, "We don't know all the details yet. He could be some nobody who happened by. Let's not leap to judgment."

"What self-respecting Sidhe have you ever heard of that would willingly loiter around this shithole, Martin?"

"I can't say, but you never know. Wallace here said himself. He thought the individual that killed Rawly and his band wandered in from nowhere. Wasn't that what you told me?" He glanced at Cunningham.

"I did. My Lord, it was as if this person drifted into Rawly's camp to steal supplies. I don't think he set out to capture the girl at all. He left her tied to a tree that first eve."

Damek wanted to hit something. "Then how do you explain the rest of it? The dead Corsairs? *This* horror? If you're telling me he's some kind of Sidhe sneakthief and murderer, why didn't he leave her to die when he encountered her next? It doesn't add up."

Cunningham lifted a shoulder. "Maybe he realized who she was and decided she was worth the effort, or maybe he carried her away for himself? Who knows?"

Damek ground his molars with no small amount of personal bitterness. "Even injured, I doubt she'd let him touch her unless she had reason to trust him. He's offering her something. I can feel it in my marrow. The only thing I can imagine is sanctuary."

"Whatever the reason," interrupted Martin, sensing the circular nature of this debate. "I agree. We'd better find her. The longer she's out here, the less likely she'll make it home in one piece."

Annoyed, Damek nodded. "Major Cunningham, alert the men as instructed. If they find her, they're not to approach. Observe and report. Understood?"

"Aye, Lord Marshal."

Damek clapped Martin on the back. "Let's go, old friend."

"Where to?"

Damek tugged his gloves on, while his squire held his mount steady. "West, Martin. And wherever that leads."

Martin paled. "That leads to Rosweal."

Damek drew himself up into his saddle and took the reins. "If they're still in Eire, there are few options left to them. If I were in this bastard's place, it's what I would do. Where else would he hope to hide her from me and Corsairs from Tairngare?"

"But… Rosweal's a stinking charnel house for fur trappers and poachers."

"Exactly," Damek said, kicking his mount to motion.

Tenement Blues

Una was surprised to learn Ben's tenement had a bathhouse at its lowest level. She didn't expect such luxury could exist in rugged, unpretentious Rosweal. Ben explained that the foundations dated to a time before the Transition when many buildings in the area had similar accommodations. The ancient Eireans had placed this structure directly over a natural spring that funneled mineral-rich water from deep underground. When the most recent owner purchased the building, she'd had the baths renovated. Stone stoves were carved into the outer walls from which copper and clay pipes ran between two large, tiled pools. For a price, the stoves could be loaded with slow-burning peat and peppered with dried lumber to retain heat. These step-down pools were separated by a low stone wall, one for either sex.

The baths were tended by a stern-faced old matron, who spoke very little and pretended to observe even less. She had two little boys waiting to bring in towels, harsh soaps, and oil of lavender upon request. Ben warned Una and Rian not to help themselves to everything in these baskets, but as usual, both girls ignored him. Eschewing Ben's miserly advice, Una and Rian took the longest, most satisfying soak of their lives. The women's chamber was some ten feet wide and eight feet long, covered from floor to ceiling in white rectangular tiles, saving those in the pool, which were blue faience. The polished glass felt wonderful against Una's bare, blistered toes. Their cerulean pool was deep enough to completely immerse oneself when sitting over the drain at the bottom. Seats carved into the edges kept the midsection warm while one washed their hair or reclined in a soak. Rian floated on her back in the middle with a satiated sigh.

"Dear Siora, I never want to step outside this room again."

"Agreed," said Una, scrubbing the mud and muck from her tangled curls with a wad of honey soap. Ben's edict be damned; she was going to use every drop of oil, every cream, and every salve in that bloody basket. "Who'd believe such a place was possible in a town like this?"

Rian submerged herself and popped back up. She hugged her knees underwater. "The Greenmakers are quite famous, you know? It may not look it, but a lot of coin gets shuffled from hand to hand 'round here. The tavern next door is infamous throughout Innisfail."

"How so?"

Rian's pale hair floated around her head in a slippery flaxen cloud. "You've never heard of *The Hart and Hare*?"

"Should I have?"

"It's only the most notorious brothel in the North," Rian laughed.

Una made a face. "Oh."

"You don't have brothels in Tairngare?"

Una cursed. She tried and failed to untangle a particularly fastidious knot. "Of course, we do, but they're different. Clients are selected and must apply to the Voluptatus to ascertain health, wealth, and temperament before their patronage can be approved."

"That's rather complex, given the clientele."

"It's meant to be. Siora forbids sexual predation."

"Then who may… erm, imbibe?"

"There are various sects in the Voluptatus, but the law is designed to protect the women whom they most affect. For example, every Red House pays a yearly stipend— a pension of sorts— for women who retire, have children, or are unable to work due to illness or infirmity. Men are welcome to patronize any of these establishments, but they must adhere to the law to do so. They learn to regret it if they abuse any of these women."

"And this works? Men don't try to get around the law?"

"Sometimes, but they pay dearly for the error."

"They're fined?"

"Castrated," said Una, matter-of-factly. "We don't suffer brutes in Tairngare. Unlike Bethany, or other less civilized points beyond." Una didn't care for most external policies regarding women, especially among the lower classes. Often, a girl was taken while extremely young and roughly used until her youth and desirability waned. Eventually, she would be cast out, forced to try to sell herself for scraps. Sex workers of this sort were beaten, diseased, reviled, and ignored. Such was the fate of thousands of women living outside Siora's grace. The Ancestor herself had been such a woman. The Cloister of the Eternal Flame was founded by souls she'd liberated from sexual bondage, after all.

In Her Heart, In Her Blood, In Her Spine, Una thought to herself. If it weren't for Siora, what a terrible place the world would still be. Rian waded over to borrow Una's soap. "Well, prepare yourself. Rosweal is *not* known for its fair treatment of women, least of all its 'entertainers.' I don't think you will like this place much, My Lady."

"Rian, please. I gathered as much, despite this gorgeous bathing chamber. It's a shame, really." Indeed, when Ben led them through the complicated twists and turns of Wanderer's Alley, she became aware of that fact rather swiftly. This neighborhood wasn't as refined as the one they'd passed on the Hilltop, nor as clean— but it did boast randomly placed street lanterns and sturdy brick buildings, though none were in good repair. The Greemakers' Quarter, as Ben called it, was cut into a large wedge by two wide lanes, which led to opposing corners against a high stone wall. This wall was easily twenty feet higher than the low-shale barriers that encircled the town on three sides. Evidently, the wall had once been the parapet of some long-forgotten fortress facing the border.

Outside the Western Gate, a wide stone jetty sliced rudely into the river's rapid flow. Many wooden boats and nets were moored to its covered docks; even at night, the boatyard teemed with people. Some were loading or unloading merchandise to be shipped downriver past the confluence. Some directed wagons and carts laden with lumber, dry goods, and furs, no doubt intended for markets in Tara, Slane, or Ten Bells. Una hadn't realized Rosweal was capable of such bustling trade. She'd stared a bit until Ben scolded her. He reminded her that Rosweal's citizens didn't care for prying eyes, then none-too-gently nudged her toward the building where they were now accommodated. Before she followed him into the darkened rear entrance, Una had spied several haggard women poised beneath sparse streetlights catcalling workers as they shuffled past. Una averted her eyes, having noted one or two of those girls being used quite casually, in full view of anyone who happened by.

It turned her stomach.

Ben tried to explain that in Rosweal, most 'respectable' women wouldn't brave the harsh Greensward winters to live such paltry, complicated lives. The men of Rosweal weren't grand tradesmen, farmers, or fishermen. They scraped together a meager living through smuggling, poaching, and scavenging. This was not a lifestyle most women would prefer for their children, excluding those with no choice. Ben seemed acutely embarrassed by her questions on the subject but spared her no answers. He elaborated that many of the brothel girls were bought from finer establishments down south and worked until the debt was repaid or until they were banished to the streets— whichever came first.

It made Una's blood boil to think of their suffering. That any woman should be forced to sell herself to eat was abhorrent to her. In Tairngare, the Voluptatus refused girls that made the choice under duress. Girls of that sort were remanded to the Agrea, where they'd be housed, fed, and clothed. There, they were taught various agricultural skills and given a base living upon which to build. Education at the Libellum was offered freely to every class, and every woman had the opportunity to improve themselves if they so desired. No one should be forced to debase themselves to survive. Tairngare had many flaws, as any society must, but in this matter, she was superior to every city in the world. Una wondered how different this horrible little town would look if it adhered to the Cloister's laws.

Done scrubbing her monstrously neglected hair, Una sank into the deep warm tub to her eyeballs. Rian dunked herself once more and stepped from the pool to dry off. Her skin was as red as an apple.

"You know," she said, wrapping herself in a long towel. "I think the housekeeper launders clothing too."

"Such extravagance," Una chuckled, wincing when it jogged one of her ribs. She still had plenty of wounds to contend with, even if they were far less painful or visible than the day before. Rian hadn't said anything concerning this since Una had used her Spark on that street thug, but Una caught her stealing glances at times, and they weren't always flattering.

"I think Ben is waiting for us in the next chamber. He said he didn't want us walking around alone in here. Said it was dangerous for us even to use these baths."

"Hang Ben," Una said. "This was *his* bloody idea. Besides, he told me he has another hiding place he means to take us to tomorrow."

"I don't know why he's being so bloody secretive. It's not like we don't realize he's playing all of this by ear," Rian frowned, observing her soiled clothing. "I'm not putting any of that back on."

Meanwhile, Una dug through the perfumed basket, pleased to find a pair of linen robes at the bottom. "We'll use these. Siora, this is bloody fantastic service."

"Yeah, but it costs. Ben said—"

"Since when do you care what Ben says?"

Rian thought about that for a moment. "I don't. I just don't want him to whine about the spent coin later."

"It's your coin, Rian."

"I can hear everything you two are saying, you realize?" growled Ben from behind the wall. A thin grate in the ceiling allowed light in from the window on the men's side. The girls heard a splash and a curse. "Don't spend all your money on linens and oil, Rian."

"You shut your mouth," she called, defiantly ringing a small bell beside the door. Almost immediately, a little redhead popped into the crack.

"Missus?"

She handed him the pile of discarded clothing. "Take this to your Mistress for laundering, if you please?"

"O'course, Missus. Will ye be needin' anythin' else, some food? Mam told me to tell ye we have salmon stews, black bread, and boiled turnips. Will ye have some?"

"No!" Ben roared from his side of the wall.

"*Shut up!*" Una shouted back.

Rian tucked some coppers into the boy's little palm, smiling as his face brightened. "We'd love some supper… breakfast in the morning, too. If available?"

"'Tis, Missus!"

Ben's curses grew in volume.

"Excellent," Rian patted the boy's unkempt curls. "You know where to bring everything?"

"I do, Missus. Ben Maeden's room, right?"

"That's right," smiled Rian, while Ben thumped around in the next chamber. "Run along now, and don't forget to bring Ben the bill."

THAT NIGHT, LONG AFTER RIAN had gone to sleep in Ben's Spartan apartment, Una was still wide awake, tucked into a (thankfully, clean) woolen blanket she found in Ben's solitary wardrobe. Inside, she was pleased to discover a few tunics, some worn leggings, and several pairs of woolen socks. She helped herself, of course. Since it was clearly Ben's intention to dump the two of them here while he went out to do, Siora knew what, she was going to make herself as comfortable as possible. Ben didn't have much in the way of amenities, but a thick pair of warm, dry socks could be luxurious when one has spent days in a frigid, wet wilderness.

There had been moments in the Greensward when she'd almost wished someone would put her out of her misery. Una craved long summer days with a high cheerful sun dancing overhead, and long warm nights with the sweet scent of flowers and herbs on the air. She was told Bretagne boasted an entire third month of summer. Watching frost creep across the mottled glass in Ben's window, she rather hoped she'd have a chance to experience it for herself one day soon. Una was exasperated with the cold and the damp, and it wasn't even Dor Oras yet. Sighing, she snuggled deep into her pilfered blanket and gazed outside. She could just make out the river snaking through those dark, foreboding hills. The north side, as always, was obscured by a dense, obfuscating mist. To the far northern horizon, Aes Sidhe was shielded from mortal eyes.

Una wondered why Northers accepted the presence of the Sidhe so readily yet never bothered to complain of their exclusion from Sidhe society. Indeed, Una couldn't recall ever having met one before Ben. They didn't mingle much with Eireans nor Cymrians, as far as she'd gleaned from her studies. They kept their own company and never involved themselves in Eirean affairs unless any upstart 'Milesians' dared to breach their firm Natural Law.

The High King allowed each city and province to self-govern but forbade them to mine, divert rivers, or otherwise tamper with the lay of the land. The Southers, for one, chafed under Aes Sidhe's detached edicts and made no secret of their contention at every Five-Year Council. Bethany, for example, believed this heavy-handed ruling prevented them from achieving true economic prosperity. Hence, the enmity between Bethany and her neighbors over colonial resources and the many failed revolts instigated by the Donahugh Clan to throw off the High King's yoke. Tairngare, on the other hand, was not hampered economically by the Law. Thus, they had less need to be offended by it. Shipping and trade with the wealthy colonies lined the Red City's treasury with fainne, and her thriving Mercher class kept the economic wheels turning.

Bethany was hardly land-locked, but it lacked the lumber to build ships or the Cymrian mining rights to purchase them. In many ways, Bethany was at the mercy of both Aes Sidhe and Tairngare due to basic geography and the lack of a meticulous central government. At its core, Bethany was a feudal patriarchy, dependent upon fiefdom and the eternal servitude of the poor. There, the common folk existed simply to prop up the landowners… and women had it worst. They could neither own property nor inherit their wealth. In many ways, Bethany was not all that dissimilar from Rosweal. It seemed to Una that Tairngare possessed the only thriving society in Innisfail, given its wealth, influence, and social privilege. Perhaps if Bethany empowered their women and working classes, might they not share in some of Tairngare's success?

Thinking of the Sidhe, she wondered how they treated their women. One did not hear much about them if anything at all. Were matrons autonomous, like the women in Tairngare? Or were they subservient, like those in Bethany? Even in the Colonies, women could own property and have a hand in their own governance. Cymrian women oversaw the rearing and education of their children and administered their individual unions. Was it the same in Aes Sidhe? Una honestly had no idea, and her lack of knowledge on that score vexed her. Civic Law had been a favorite subject of hers, after all. Why did she know almost nothing about the Sidhe? She determined she would ask Ben when they had time. For instance, why did they not allow Eireans into Aes Sidhe, as a rule? Why did the Sidhe refer to her people as 'Milesian' when that ancient tribal king, Mil, had little to do with modern Eire?

She had so many questions that she scarcely knew where to begin. Not that she expected Ben would be forthcoming on this topic. Far from it. An irritated smile crept over her mouth at the thought. Secretly, she found she didn't mind his dry wit as much as she had from the start. She supposed he was growing on her. If she was honest with herself, his bravery and frank practicality might have softened her regard. Though she would rather be raked over a bed of hot coals than admit it out loud to anyone, least of all Ben… he wasn't very hard to look at, either. Perhaps it was just the novelty of his height or his fine Sidhe bones that struck her? The sharpness of his smooth brow, maybe the angle of his sculpted jaw? She couldn't say for sure.

Una did not lack a solid foundation for comparison. Tairngare was filled with bronzed, dark-haired, bright-eyed specimens of every stripe— but Ben was something else altogether. If his manners weren't atrocious, Una might be forced to concede that he was the most beautiful person she'd ever met, male or female. She shook herself. Perhaps this was the reason the Sidhe kept to themselves? She could only imagine the chaos that having such unspeakable creatures underfoot would reap through the female population of Eire. If Ben was so, Siora only knew what the women were like. She bit back a chuckle so as not to disturb Rian, who snored lightly into the mattress behind her.

As if summoned by her train of thought, a thump against the short iron balcony outside the window made her jump. Ben cursed through the glass and fumbled unsubtly for the latch. Shaking her head, Una got up and pried it open herself. He tumbled inside, almost taking her with him on his way to the floor.

"Herne!" he giggled into the floorboards. Una fanned the air around her face and shut the window behind him. He reeked of uishge, witchroot smoke, and cheap perfume. Maybe he *wasn't* attractive, after all?

"Where've you been?" she whispered, covering her nose. "You stink to the nine hells."

"Had to clear up some things," he bellowed. Rian groaned and buried her head, mumbling something colorful into the mattress.

Una nudged him with a toe. "Keep your voice down. What things? What're you on about?"

"Robin's not here. Thank Lug."

He was still too bloody loud. She nudged him again. He caught her foot in one absurdly large hand and held it with a satisfied smirk. She couldn't dislodge it nor use it to prod him again. "Means we have a tentative run of the place, so long as we keep a low profile."

"How does getting stinking drunk, scaling balconies, and raising your voice in the middle of the night even approach a 'low profile?' Let go."

He grinned at her. "No one saw me," he at least attempted to whisper.

"Fine. Let go of my leg, please."

"Nope. Gonna keep it." He grinned like an idiot for several uncomfortable moments while she tried to tug herself free. The moon finally broke through the cloudbank, which flooded their corner of the room with light. His steady stare made her nervous.

Una vowed she would not blush. Not today.

Not ever.

"Should I kick you with the other foot?"

"I'd say I hold the advantage in a wrestling match, but you're welcome to try. I'll go easy on you."

Una fixed a glower on him that should have singed his hair. "You're drunk, and I'm going to hurt you if you don't stop messing about."

Ben didn't let go. Neither did he cease giving her that churlish smirk. "You know," he whisper-shouted. "You're looking a lot better. Were you always so… you know?"

Her eyes narrowed until they were barely wide enough to see his flushed cheeks. "I am not some tavern wench, you clumsy sot." She brought her free heel down hard into his midsection.

His breath came out in a rush. Her foot came free. "Ouch! Damn it, woman. I'm trying to compliment you."

"I don't need your bloody compliments."

"I was only going to tell you how the moon—"

Una rolled her eyes hard enough to crack her brow. "*Insufferable!* Did you learn anything of value on this excursion, or was it merely to have one off that you bothered at all?"

Blinking himself semi-straight, he cleared his throat. "I did need to find out if Robin was in town because that could be a problem."

"Who in the hells is Robin?"

Pursing his lips, he waved her query away. "No one, no one. Nothing to worry about. I thought I'd pop 'round *Solomon's*, to be sure. All is clear, for now, it seems."

"Did you discover how you will get us across the river at the bottom of your tankard, your lordship?" Una's mouth wouldn't melt butter. Ben sank onto his elbows. His irritatingly long legs stretched out before him while he ogled her. His vest was unbuttoned, and his tunic unlaced. Noting the direction of her attention, he grinned wider. She averted her eyes, cheeks flaming. She took back every positive thought about him in the last hour.

"I did. I figured I'd please myself with a good strong drink while it was available. Did you wait up for me?"

She chewed the interior of her cheek. "*No.* What have you decided?"

"Later," he hiccuped. "I'd rather talk about you. For example, I didn't realize you were so… under all that grime. It's distracting, you know. You're quite—"

She muttered a vicious oath that had something to do with melting eyeballs and disintegrating tongues. "I'm going to sleep. You're obviously in no fit shape for an adult conversation."

"Please, Siora!" roared Rian from her tunnel of pillows.

Una darted past Ben's legs to leap into the bed beside her. Una wound herself in her woolen blanket, even though she was warm already from her pilfered socks. Like a worm, Ben wriggled up to the side of the bed. Una clenched a fist.

"What now?"

"That's my bed, you know?"

"*And?*"

He propped himself up on his elbow and fidgeted with the mattress' exposed threading. "It's pretty cold down here."

"Ben?"

He beamed. "Yes, Una?"

"Does this boorish, suggestive attitude ever actually work with women?"

"What do you think?" He gave her a wolfish, white grin.

"Go to sleep, or I'll punch you in the throat."

With an exaggerated groan, he flopped to the floor. "You're quite right. 'Tis the cold boards for me, missus. I've only saved both of your bloody lives a thousand times so far. Only carried you on my back for twenty-odd miles. Only brought you to my home, given you my bed and all my bloody pillows. I *adore* the floor. Really. A gentleman does not complain."

"When I see one, I'll ask him if you're right," Una snarled and folded herself into the fetal position below her warm blanket. After several minutes of listening to the blood rush through her ears, she cracked an eye to find he was still watching her, with the oddest expression on his face. He had his hands folded behind his head, with only the rough rag-woven rug beneath him and his sealskin cloak for a blanket. He looked almost… pathetic. With a long breath, she struck him full in the face with her pillow.

"Ow! What in the hells did you do that for?"

She pulled her blanket up over her ears. "You're welcome?"

He rattled off some very unflattering curses, but Una ignored him. She drifted off to sleep with a smile, despite the thumping, cursing fool on the floor.

The Waterhorse

Ben was in a terrible state. He woke before dawn with a splitting headache and an oily stomach. His right arm was numb, and his back was a network of shooting pains. Unwinding himself from the cocoon he'd made of his cloak, he glared over at the two happily sleeping traitors tucked into his bed. Una, having pilfered one of his tunics, lay belly-down on the mattress, the blanket scrunched up around her shoulders. Like darkest honey, a riot of sable curls floated around her face and back. Ben caught himself staring again and scrubbed at his eyes with a groan. He didn't have time to be distracted by ridiculous notions. When he finished his task for the day, he'd apologize to her for his behavior last night and make himself scarce for the next. Mollified by this solution, he scraped himself from the floor as quietly as he could manage. He wasn't overly enthused about his plans for the day, but after a night's drinking and ruminating over the matter, he couldn't argue it was the swiftest possible course. Ben didn't remember removing his swordbelt and boots. While he fumbled to put them back on, he caught one of Una's large uishge colored eyes on him. She yawned into the back of a tattooed hand.

"Morning, Ben dearest," her voice was husky with sleep, her tone teasing. "How fares your head?"

He looked away. "Ah… I must apologize for uh, well, you know." He focused on his boots. "I was drunk, and—"

"No need." After stretching like a cat, she propped herself up on her elbow. "You aren't the first man I've met, you know." Her laughter irritated him. He didn't know why. "Where're you going?"

He wasn't sure how to answer. "I'll fill you in later." Daring a second glance at her, he wished he hadn't. His cursed tunic, much too large for her, displayed a swath of unnecessary skin from the deep 'V' at her neckline. He struggled not to gawp at the corded brown column of her throat or the hollow above her intricately tattooed clavicle. Unselfconsciously, she gathered up her floating cloud of soft springing curls and piled them high atop her head. Ben's throat dried up. What was *wrong* with him? He buttoned his vest as fast as possible. Escape was his only course.

"Listen." He was proud of the even timbre of his voice. "You should be careful of the people in this building. There could be trouble if my return is advertised. Keep to the room, for now. All right? And don't open that door for anyone except me."

"The boy will be bringing us food later."

"Fine but be sure it's him before you open the door. If the Housekeeper herself comes up, don't answer any question she asks. She'll take everything she hears to Barb."

Una gestured for him to keep his voice down. "Who's Barb?" The only evidence Rian even existed was the spill of cornsilk hair dipping over the opposite side of the mattress.

"Barb is the proprietor. She owns the entire block. The brewery two doors down, the livery across the street, the haberdashery, the mill at the north corner, and *The Hart and Hare* next door. She's the Boss around here."

Una's pert nose wrinkled. "Oh, the madam."

Ben looked anywhere but at her while he adjusted his swordbelt. "You have brothels in Tairngare, remember."

She sniffed. "Hardly the same thing."

"Barb's not such a bad sort if you don't have something she wants or try to take what's hers. I think you'd find her girls are better cared for than most in the North… erm, but that's beside the point. I'd very much like to avoid her, if possible."

"How long?"

"What?" He stalked to the windowpane. It'd be safest to come and go from the balcony, so long as it wasn't too late or too early for most residents to notice a tall figure scaling the wall. He'd rather not get hung up at the door downstairs.

"How long will you be?"

"I've no idea, but don't expect me." He had no intention of returning until he could make more comfortable arrangements. This situation was going to get him into trouble. "We can't go to the other place I told you about until I've ascertained the consequences from Vick or his boss."

Una paled a bit. "The boy we killed?"

"I killed one of them too, so try not to punish yourself overmuch. Matt is bound to be livid. The Hilltop isn't in Greenmaker territory. So, I'd prefer to be sure of the consequences before I make a move."

She wasn't satisfied with this excuse in the least. That was obvious. Still, there was little he could do about it now, was there? Though they hadn't had much choice at the time, two more dead men in Rosweal were sure to cause problems. He could only deal with one crisis at a time. The girls would just have to make do until he found the help he needed. Opening the window allowed a much-needed blast of frosty air into the over-warm room. He paused, daring a look over his shoulder.

"Just in case I'm not back until tomorrow, will you do me a favor?"

"What's that?"

"Put on your own clothes. That," he pointed, "doesn't fit." He shut the window on her bemused expression and swung himself into the alley below.

⚜

BEN BROODED OVER HIS CIRCUMSTANCES as he walked out of town. He was beginning to wish he'd spent more time thinking things through. If this plan didn't work out, he'd be forced to try the border through the mountains to the west—a far more dangerous and unpleasant path, by far. Conditions were already becoming needlessly complex. Necessity, combined with proximity, made a muddle of relationships. Hells, he was even viewing Rian with a begrudging sort of affection, and he'd encountered badgers with better temperaments. Ben didn't want to form close ties with anyone, whether it be a civil acquaintance with Rian Guinness… or whatever nonsense burgeoned in his blood for Una. He had no idea what God he'd offended, but they were having a good laugh at his expense right now.

Ben should never have taken her hand in that cave. When she said she trusted him, he'd been relieved. Worse, he realized he *cared* what she thought of him. That wouldn't do. Not at all. As soon as her tiny fingers wrapped around his, he knew… she was trouble he didn't need. Not now. Not *ever*. Una Moura Donahugh was a means to an end, nothing more. He would deposit her safely in Midhir's court, then return to his own life. Anything else was pointless.

Ben sighed as he pushed through reeds and half-frozen cattails on the riverbank. He supposed he could charm Rosie into taking him in for a few days. She wouldn't ask many questions. She never had. Her shift ended an hour past midnight. Maybe he would finish up here, have a few drinks at *Solomon's*, and head back to look for her? She'd be happy to see him, though part of him would feel bad about imposing upon her hospitality; worse, considering he did so merely to avoid another woman. What else could he do?

Ben had already made a fool of himself once… damned if it should happen again. He did have a larger place absolutely no one knew about on the Hilltop. Unfortunately, the encounter with Vick meant they'd run afoul of the only non-Greenmaker of real consequence in Rosweal. The Hilltop was Matt's territory, and though he and the Greenmakers held a long-standing truce, that didn't mean Gilcannon would appreciate more of his subordinates lying dead in the street. He'd be even less pleased to learn it was Robin's right-hand man he could thank for both transgressions.

Matt considered himself something of a tosh, with the enormous profits reaped from his illegal distillery in Rosweal. Owing to Gilcannon's bootlegging operation, Rosweal had access to Cymrian wine, silks from Bretagne, lamp oil from Scotia, and produce from Ten Bells. The Greenmakers, who traded only in poached fur, timber, meat, and female flesh, owed many of their connections to Matt. However, that wasn't to say he was well-liked in the Quarter. Barb Dormer, the Guildmistress herself, probably despised him more than anyone alive. She'd been searching for a means to get rid of him longer than Ben had been in Robin's employ.

As yet, unsuccessfully.

Matt was a bad enemy to make, but Ben knew it wasn't Gilcannon he should worry about. Robin Gramble would be his greatest challenge. Barb Dormer might be the queen of Taverner's Alley, but Robin ran the men. If Ben intended to get over the border with the most significant bounty in Innisfail, he needed to patch things with Robin soon. Without the Greenmakers' backing, Ben was a marked man, and neither girl would be safe in Rosweal.

So much was plaguing his mind that he was having trouble focusing on the task at hand. Beneath the sparse autumnal umbrella of a sheltering oak, he stopped just shy of the waterline. In reality, the Blackwater posed no great challenge for those who wished to cross. The river was not especially wide nor deep. What was in it, however… Ben drew his shoulders back and took a deep, thoughtful breath.

Well, you made up your mind.

Get it over with.

Looking around to be sure he had no witnesses; Ben unlaced his boots and placed them in a dry spot beneath the oak. Next went his vest, trousers, stockings, and tunic. Once clad only in his woolen leggings, he took care to tuck Rian's ogham stone beneath a loose blanket of moss for safekeeping. Unarmed and undisguised, Ben waded in. He hadn't done this in a *very* long time. Come to think of it, the last attempt hadn't worked out so well for him, either; two very deep scars ran down his left arm, and another curled over his chest— ever-present reminders of his former hubris.

At first, nothing happened. River mud squeezed between his toes, and ribbons of slimy river grass snaked around his torso. When the water reached his collarbone, the riverbed shuddered. The current shifted around him, flowing in reverse. A heavy fog crept toward him from the far bank like milk poured over mottled glass. He dug his heels in and waited. Silent as silk, a large misshapen head slid from the water. Its black eyes burned with ravenous hunger. Ben repressed a shudder. Amorphous and changeable as the river, its features rippled through simultaneous aspects. First, a smallish humanlike skull with gleaming liquid eyes. Then, the shape of a monstrous stallion. Streaming rivulets of dark water articulated its impressive mane and thick muscular neck.

Ard Tiarne… it gave him the barest hint of a nod, its tone amused but dry. *You are forbidden, as you well know…*

"I'm aware."

It considered him intently. *Do you tempt fate again?*

"No," Ben said, keeping his voice flat. There weren't many creatures Ben feared, but he'd developed a healthy respect for the pooka over the years. Should it wish to try, it might feasibly drag Ben into the darkest depths of the Oiche Ar Fad, never to be seen or heard from again. It wasn't often that the pooka could snare higher Sidhe like himself, but given the slightest opportunity, it wouldn't hesitate. Ben's immortal body— his bones, skin, hair, and blood— the pooka craved above all other prizes. Such a rare feast would be a victory of untold proportions to this prince of the Dor Sidhe. The pooka were formless monsters from an endless, fluid void. One mistake while bargaining with such a creature could prove fatal. Ben knew from experience how troublesome an opponent one could be. This one, in fact. If Ben held his birthright, title, and name, the pooka would never dare to cast aspersions on his person. Exiled as he was from Aes Sidhe, and absent the Ard Ri's good graces, however… *best not to overthink*. Ben willed his clanging heart still. "I have a request to make of you."

A queer gurgling sent tiny waves of greenish brown water into Ben's chin. He ground his teeth. He'd give this thing something to crow over soon enough. "You find that humorous, *isesaeligh*?"

The pooka stopped laughing; the mud between Ben's toes vibrated with its ire. *Insults now? You are very foolish or very brave.*

Ben didn't blink. "You watch your filthy mouth. I am still a high lord, you realize?"

The pooka sniggered. *You were Daoine Sidhe… once. Now, you reek of spirits, mortal stink, and fear. How sad you seem, tuiathe. How feeble.*

Ben ignored that as if he wasn't the least intimidated. He was going to bluff his way through this. To do so, he must play his part well. A pooka would exploit any weakness he dared reveal. Ben lifted an eyebrow as haughtily as he could.

"This isn't a social call. I said I've a request to make of you." Water flowed over the stallion's head until Ben stared into an odd three-dimensional reflection of his own face. Minus the ill-fitting, elongated fangs protruding from the mouth, it was a fair mimic. With a sour taste on his tongue, Ben feigned disinterest. "Handsome enough, I suppose."

The figure's grotesque grin turned his stomach. *It will be an honor to peel the skin from your skull, Ard Tiarne. I shall wear it with pride.*

"You would try, pooka."

Hm, so I might, it cackled.

"Enough of this. Your rudeness may deprive you of the gift I meant to offer in exchange for your aid."

You've tried to trick me before. I do not forget.

"That was ages ago when I was desperate to regain my status. Now, I merely wish to protect those I care for."

The pooka considered him. *You* are *much reduced… Ard Tiarne. A shame. You were a challenge… before.*

"If you persist with these invectives, I'll find another to put my request to and keep her for myself."

As expected, the pooka's mercurial fangs lengthened, catching the sunlight in a horrifying leer. *Her?*

The lecherous old bastard.

"Of course," said Ben, rubbing his chin. "I *should* keep her, after all. She is still so young. Far too sweet to part with so casually. Perhaps I'll ask another—"

Wait. The pooka inched closer; its solidifying teeth snapped in its watery, Ben-shaped jaws. *Tell me more of this sssweet young girl.*

So bloody easy, Ben scoffed inwardly. He turned away as if to abandon his purpose. "I shouldn't have mentioned her. Forget what I said. She's too precious to part with, considering her heritage… I must find another way…"

Now, the creature was almost upon him. The current swirled. As it grew, gallons of brown water sucked up and into the pooka's body. The river barely crested Ben's thighs as the beast towered over him; tiny fish, clumping mud, and reeds swam through its massive, translucent torso.

Nooo! it cried, suddenly eager to hear what Ben wished to say. Nothing tempted a pooka more than the promise of a young, beautiful plaything. Never mind that nearly every girl one snatched drowned in the first few minutes or expired from sheer fright. On Samhain, when the pooka took corporeal form, many unwary females were dragged to the bottom of wells or lured into bogs and ponds. Once captured, they'd be ruthlessly ravaged, broken, then savagely devoured. Never satisfied by the flimsy human flesh the pooka hunted most often, they wanted more, something they could not break easily. They craved women of Sidhe blood, perhaps more than they longed for Sidhe bones to shuck.

Is she not mortal? salivated the pooka.

Ben feigned abashed shame. "Well, her father was."

A gurgle of pure excitement.

She is Ban Sidhe?

"Half, but I haven't agreed that you should have her… yet. You would abuse her horribly, no doubt. I couldn't allow that. She is precious to me."

No, no, no! I would never, it lied. The riverbed thrummed with its shameless glee. *All sweet girls are safe with meee. I would treasssure herrr.*

"I don't believe you." Ben crossed his arms.

What mussst I do, Ard Tiarne?

"I need you to deliver a message for me." Ben looked up into his own maniacal face and repressed a shudder. "To Diarmid Adair."

The pooka recoiled with a hiss. *Fiachra Ri? You trick me! He will desstroy meee!* It shrank down to Ben's size, its fingers lengthening into monstrous claws and its fangs growing long as walrus tusks. Though opaque, its eyes took on a serpentine shape, even more terrible than the enormous teeth protruding from its impression of Ben's face.

Thisss iss your purpossse? You mean to lure me out of the way, ssso you may crosss into Aess Ssidhee! One of its dagger-like claws stretched out. It stopped mere centimeters from Ben's nose.

Ben did not flinch. "No. I mean to speak to my uncle before Samhain, and if I do not, I will lose a legitimate chance to cross. I mean to make a deal with you because, frankly, I have no choice. Aes Sidhe is threatened by the South, again. I do not trust the Consulate in Ten Bells, and Fiachra Ri may be my only hope. I am Daoine Sidhe. It is my responsibility to try."

The pooka thought this over for some time. When it spoke, it seemed to have collected itself. *You do not lie, Ard Tiarne. I would taste it, did you dare. Perhaps, we can come to an arrangement… but it will cossst you more than the girl if you deccceive me.* Ben could hear the rank covetousness in its voice. It would do anything he asked for such a prize. A Sidhe girl, even a faerie, was worth twenty mortal women to a degenerate pooka. Herne only knew what it would do to her. Ben forced himself not to overthink it.

"Well," he asked, lining his tone with regal impatience. "Do we have a deal, or not?"

Iss sshe beautifulll?

"Hair like winter wheat, skin like milk, eyes of bluest sky."

Squealing in delight, the pooka leapt below the surface with a hearty splash that doused Ben to the roots of his hair. When its head popped up, it was Ben's features it wore, free of animalistic embellishments. It smiled.

We have an accord, Ard Tiarne.

I shall tell the Fiachra Ri, you wish to meet by Samhain. But by the Hallowed Hour, you shall bring my prize to me? Yess?

"Of course," Ben agreed. "But if he fails to show, you get nothing. Remember that."

As you wish, tuiathe, as you wish… If you fail to bring the girl to me, I shall find you on Samhain. The pooka's predatory grin seemed almost harmless by comparison to the horrors it had exhibited previously. *And it shall be your bones I embrace her with.*

⚷

HAVING SURVIVED THE FIRST ORDEAL of his three-stage plan, Ben decided to soothe his nerves with the drink he'd promised himself that morning. Hells, perhaps he'd have five after that nightmare on the riverbank? Pulling his hood down close, he sauntered back through the West Gate and down the far end of the Greenmakers' Quarter without looking up. Until he found the time and the means to speak to Robin personally, he'd rather not press his luck.

Solomon's was a sliver of a building, crammed between two larger stone structures: one, a three-story warehouse that had once been a factory of sorts; the other, a long-vacated tenement, which was only safe at its lowest level. Solomon used it to store his ill-gotten gains and often loaned it out to Greenmakers seeking a layover from points beyond. Both buildings were boarded and crumbling. There were gaping holes in their roofs which sometimes poured sheets of mellifluous rainwater down descending floors. The warehouse's few remaining tenants were either of the avian or rodent variety.

Consequently, Solomon's relatively tidy two-story brick edifice crawled with unwanted pests. The patrons didn't seem to mind, as Ben certainly would not. Sol had the best ale in town, with or without the rats, bats, and beetles— or perhaps because of them, who could say for sure?

Solomon made each batch of spiced ale per an old family recipe and, by Herne, if it was not the finest in Eire. Barb herself had been after Sol for years to hand it over, but the old codger would not be swayed by threat or by coin. He paid his tithes to remain in the Guild and always kept ragged men on hand to aid in whichever Greenmaker venture had need. Sol remained free to operate as he saw fit, so long as he didn't venture into any more lucrative avenues reserved for the Guild's upper echelons, namely courtesans, furs, and uishge. Still, women of a certain stripe often congregated outside the brewery, seeking to throw themselves on the mercy of any stray coppers that might come their way.

Those that couldn't cut *The Hart* were too squeamish for life at *The Corset* or unable to procure a personal patron, made do in the streets. That was the law. Rosweal had a way of chewing the good out of everyone and spitting the remnants into the dirt. Several haggard girls, trying their best to look appealing, pawed at Ben on his way inside. Without provocation, he recalled Una's comments to Rian on the subject. The sudden thought made him squirm—gods damn that bloody meddling woman and her sanctimonious morals. Looking around now, he couldn't get her disdain out of his head. He wasn't about to apologize to Una for every man in the North, damn it. These women had choices, no matter what Lady Moura believed. They chose to take their chances out here in rough Rosweal, and there wasn't a thing he could do about it.

Was there?

Scowling at his newfound guilt, he tossed a few extra coppers their way. He supposed they needed it more than he ever would. One of them, a woman he remembered from *The Hart* a few seasons back— Daisy, was it?— gave him a weak, embarrassed smile. Feeling like the worst shite in the world thanks to Una and her big mouth, Ben slipped a few extra into her open palm without saying a word.

"Thank ye, love. I can—"

He waved her away as he opened the door. "No need, Daisy." He paused as real tears formed at the corner of her green eyes. "What's your given name?"

She straightened, despite the underfed sag in her shoulders. From her expression, he was ashamed to realize no one had ever asked her for her name before. "Sara. Sara Crover."

"Well, Sara, a pleasure. Buy something warm. It's cold out here."

Her fingers dragged at his sleeve. "*Wait.* Vick and his lot was here, lookin' for ye. Ye should know. Sol told 'em ye'd been here."

Of course, he did. Bloody opportunistic coward. "Thank you, Sara." He reached deeper into his vest with a wary eye on the six other faces gleaming with open hunger and handed her something heavier. "Appreciated, love." Ben went inside. He wouldn't worry about Sara Crover. Assuming she was under his protection, the others would leave her well alone. Ben had his own reputation in Rosweal. Folks knew better than to cross someone he favored. Maybe he would talk to Barb's housekeeper? See if she needed an extra pair of hands in the laundry. Sara would likely reject such an offer, but he could try, all the same. She'd always been a nice enough girl. Mind wandering again to Una; he clenched his teeth. This was bloody *intolerable*. He did NOT crave her approval, gods damn it. Her opinion meant absolutely nothing to him. Less than nothing. He bit the inside of his cheek to keep from muttering to himself like a lunatic.

Sol gave him an exaggerated, gap-toothed grin when he took a seat in the far corner. As always, Ben preferred to face the door. He noticed the tap was nigh empty, save for two harmless-looking fellows at the back, half-asleep in their ale. That was good. Ben shoved a free hand into his unbuttoned vest. Sol came over with his pint, a steaming mile-high horn filled to overflowing with the spiced Roswellian favorite. Solomon managed to be portly in a town full of half-starved sticks. Ben had always suspected he fermented his ale with animal fat. Sol set the horn down, and Ben slid it over. He looked up slowly, watching the smile flicker from Sol's dimpled brown face.

"What's it then, Ben?"

"You know."

The old man laughed. "Sure, I don't?"

"Really?" Ben picked up his horn with his left hand, leaving his right below his vest, near his belt. He flexed his fingers with exaggerated sloth.

Solomon didn't miss it. He dropped his rag and backed up. "Now Ben, ye know I ain't got the clout to argue with Vick. Gramble ain't here, and I ain't on Barb's shortlist neither. They asked if ye was here. That's all. I swear."

"I don't care, Sol. They're not Greenmakers, and they don't belong in the Quarter. Do you think Robin would approve? I'll give you a hint— that was rhetorical."

"Robin Gramble ain't me boss, Ben. Nor are ye, last I checked. Get out."

"No."

"What was that?"

"You heard me."

Without ado, Solomon tried to dart through the curtain behind the bar, which led through his kitchen to the rooms above. Ben was faster. He leaned forward, grasped Sol by the collar, and slammed his face down onto the bar. Ben's horn spun over the rail, slinging ale every which way. Solomon briefly attempted to struggle, but he was no match for Ben. He threw his hands wide.

"All right, Ben! All right. Ye don't have to make such a fuss."

"Don't I?"

"No!"

Ben pressed his elbow down. "I want to know everything you told them, Sol. If your answers are satisfactory, I won't kill you. How's that sound?"

"But Ben. I didn't—"

"Furthermore, I want to know what they told you, who they've spoken with, and what you told Barb about my visit here last night. If these answers satisfy me, I won't tell Robin that you've been stuffing your pockets with Hilltop crumbs. How's that for fair?"

"I didn't... I don't... I mean—"

Ben nudged him with the butt of his dagger. "Start talking, Sol." Solomon stared over at the two men near the fire with pleading eyes. They turned away, content to sip their pints unmolested. Ben Maeden had never been bested in a fight. Everyone in Rosweal knew that. Besides, hadn't he killed two men for calling him a cheat some weeks back? Ben wasn't worried anyone would intervene to help a rat like Solomon Trant.

"Fine, let me up."

"I think I like you as an armrest, Sol. Very soft."

"I'm not tough like ye! They come 'round, askin' questions, and to get them to leave me alone, I'll tell 'em what they wanna hear from time to time. We all have to live here, Ben. Matt's a scary fellow."

"And Robin's not? What do you think he'd do to you if he heard any of this? I'm not going to ask you again." Ben pressed the flat of his blade against the old brewer's fleshy cheek.

"Ye won't... kill me?"

"Who knows? I've had a rough time of late."

Sol swallowed so hard that his Adam's apple thumped against the bar. "Matt's ordered ye be brung to him. Says ye owe him. Vick is 'sposed to come in tonight, then nab ye."

"And?"

"They was gonna cut me half on my next six barrels of uishge and get me ale to Matt's suppliers in Ten Bells. That's all, I swear. They didn't tell me anythin' else. Why would they?"

That was a fair point, but Ben wasn't swayed. He tugged Solomon up by the back of his tunic and pressed his dagger's tip deep into Solomon's quivering chins. The blade drew a tiny trickle of blood.

"I can respect self-preservation, Sol, but here's what you forget— Matt Gilcannon might have a fellow slit your throat in your sleep. I'll happily do it here, right now. Perhaps in the street? The market? In full view of anyone. There won't be a single person who can stop me, either. Have I made myself clear?"

"Y… yes. I'm sorry, Ben. Please don't."

Ben put his dagger away, and Solomon sagged against the bar. Heady beads of sweat slid down his nose. "No harm done, then." He patted the brewer's shoulder. "How about a pint then, hey? Then we'll sit and wait for Vick together, like the old pals we are."

Ben resumed his seat while Solomon shuffled sluggishly around his taps. Hands shaking, he dropped the first two mugs he groped for. Ben chuckled to watch the old crook try to gather the remnants of his dignity. When Solomon turned around to set a new pint in front of him, he froze. Ben slid a silver stag across the bar, allowing its gleam to hold the dim lantern light overhead.

"Now. Let's make a new arrangement, shall we? One that I think will suit us both much better…."

Domina

Una stared through the window, deep in reverie. *Can you trust him?* Despite her every effort, the longer she spent locked within these four walls, the more anxiously her thoughts churned. She resumed her pacing. She'd been at it for hours already, and still no Ben. When he left that morning, she'd assumed he'd be back before dark to take them to that place he'd mentioned— a house or another apartment he knew of somewhere in the middle of the city. Surely, they'd be much safer far from prying eyes? That is if they weren't to cross into Aes Sidhe tomorrow, the following day, or even within the week? She didn't have the first bloody clue what Ben was up to. Aside from a muttered 'soon' or 'I'm working on it,' he'd yet to be forthcoming. How could they trust him if he refused to share his plans? He was out doing Siora knew what, while they languished here, out of sight and out of his hair? The nerve of the bastard!

Just where in the bloody, stinking nine hells *was he*?

"Will you stop that? You're driving me mad," hissed Rian from behind her book. A dusty little number, one of a whopping two stacked on Ben's nightstand: *A History of Eire* by Jonathon Grathin and *Seasons of Transition: Climate and Culture in Pre-Transition Innisfail* by Dominic Callaghan. Rian held the latter of the two, which Una had read during her first year as a Secunda in the Cloister. *Seasons of Transition* was probably the most boring book she'd ever been forced to endure but loaded with fascinating details if one could bear the droning, monotonous text. "He's not going to come back any faster just because you're wearing grooves into his floorboards." Rian held the book under her nose, pretending to read, though she'd scarcely turned two pages. The book was in Old Angleish. Una doubted Rian understood a single word.

Una ran a hand through her hopelessly tangled hair. Today, Rian was trying very hard to be contrary and sullen. Una wasn't surprised. The girl seemed to struggle with her emotions quite often. Una recalled that the very term 'faerie' in old Innish meant '*fey-touched*': literally, 'doomed.' Faeries rarely, if ever, led happy lives. Whether that ascribed to Rian's case or not remained to be seen. At the moment, Una couldn't tell if she was '*fey-touched*' or just a genuinely disagreeable person. She had a rotten temper. That much was plain. Still, if she hadn't risked so much by opening her door to them, Una would likely be dead. As if sensing the temperature of Una's thoughts, Rian's expression darkened.

"I don't like it any more than you do, you know?" She tossed the offensive Callaghan across the room, where it bounced off the wardrobe and slipped under the bed in a flurry of ruffling pages. She rubbed at her temples. "We could still go south. We don't need his permission, Una."

"We wait."

"Siora's mercy, why?"

"Because he's right. The safest place for any of us is over that border."

"… Never mind that he's playing for time with our lives in the balance?" Rian sat up, tucking her bare feet beneath her. "I'm not saying he hasn't proved himself a strong ally, and I'm not forgetting that he's saved both of our lives more than once. All I'm saying is, if we try to cross with an exiled lord, we might be killed anyway. Have you considered that? You know who he really is, Una."

"I don't believe what he was accused of. Nor, I believe, do you."

Rian mulled that over for a moment. "All right. I'm not as sure as you sound, but if he was guilty, I don't think he would have been merely exiled for the crime."

"Exactly."

"Just don't forget that he was banished here. He might not have done as much as they say, but he's guilty of *something*."

"I'm not daft, Rian. I'm not arguing that he's a Kneeler's saint. Only that I think there's more to him than we know. Give him a chance."

Rian's eyes slivered. "'*Give him a chance?*' Ugh. You fancy him, don't you?"

"Why on *earth* would you say such a thing?"

"All that nonsense last night." Rian made a face. "You sounded like a pair of rare idiots."

Una cleared her throat. "I *do not* fancy him. You're after being clever and forget that we're all in a heap of trouble. We need each other. All of us. All right?"

"I don't trust that great lummox, even if you *do* fancy him," Rian said. "He'll let you down. They all do that."

Now there was a statement that resonated. Intrigued, Una cocked her head. "All of whom?"

"He's Sidhe. Trust me, I know."

Ah.

"Is that what happened? With your grandmother, I mean. Is that why—"

"Oh, forget it. Just remember what I said, okay? You're Milesian. *Impermanent.* Keep him distant."

Una affected a weak smile. "Well, we gave him our word, Rian. In return, he has given his. We have to trust each other." Una might have hoped to convince herself, perhaps more than Rian. In this case, actions spoke louder than words. Ben might be many things— a criminal, a thief, a vagabond— but a liar, she knew to her bones, he was not. If he said he would get them across, she chose to believe him. "It's not just crossing the border he worries over. It's getting us all safely to Bri Leith under the High King's protection. That is a far trickier task than simply wading across a river."

"Right. How long have we been here, and what's he doing while we rot in this room? I could appreciate his efforts more if he bothered to share them with us."

Una took a seat on the edge of the bed. "Maybe he's scouting the border? Could be connecting with associates? Gambling, whoring— who knows? We told him we'd wait, so we wait."

"I heard you tell him you left Tairngare on your own before you were taken. Is that true?"

"It is."

"Why?"

"If you heard me tell him, then you already know."

"You told him what you wanted him to hear. I want to know the truth. Why would you leave Tairngare while your grandmother worked so hard to make you a queen? Where were you planning to go?"

Una blew air over her lower lip. "What does it matter? I won't get there with so many people out to kill or use me, will I?"

"I don't trust Ben, Una, but I *may* trust you," Rian paused to emphasize her point. "If you give me an honest answer."

That was fair. She thought quietly for several minutes, avoiding Rian's eyes until she could bear her unblinking judgment no longer. "I wished to take a ship to Swansea and, from there, travel to Alba. There is a place there, beyond the Wastes, I want to go. After that, I thought I might sail to Bretagne."

"Why Alba?" spat Rian, incredulous. "It's dead for hundreds of miles. Hills stripped of every tree, nothing green to see to the horizon. Just hills, rocks, and stale water."

"You know this for sure how?"

"Everyone knows it. It's common knowledge. 'After the Flood, the land was stained by salt and fire.' Why would you go there?"

Una shrugged. "Siora came from there, didn't she? Anyway, I told you it wasn't important. Not now. I won't be going anywhere without the High King's leave. If I try to backtrack to Ten Bells now, I'll probably run into agents from Bethany, if Corsairs don't kill me on the road. Ben's plan is the only one that makes an ounce of sense."

What she wouldn't say burned on her tongue like acid. Some things Una would keep to herself… indefinitely. For instance, how many times had she broken the Ninth Law in the past month? Too many to pretend devotion to Siora's strictures. She was a heretic, and Vanna Nema knew it. So too did Una's grandmother. Una squeezed her jaws tight, hoping Rian wouldn't press her any further on the topic.

After a few tense moments, Rian shrugged. "All right. I believe you. You're not telling me the whole truth, but you're not lying either. I can accept that for a while."

"Thanks?"

"Still, I do find it very interesting."

"What?"

"Your face *has* healed remarkably well."

"What of it?"

"It's monstrous."

Una deserved that, though it didn't hurt her any less to hear it. "That's why it's forbidden." She chewed her lip. "I need my strength, and that scum deserved his fate."

"I'm not judging you. I've just never seen anything like it before. It is rather incredible." Rian set her chin against her knuckles. "How are the ribs? Improved since yesterday?"

"A bit. I've always marveled that the healing should hurt worse than the actual wound. Siorai are taught to control their bodies before any other skill. A girl who can't focus her Spark this way never makes it past Nova in the Cloister."

"Is it so dangerous? The Cloister, I mean?"

"I often wonder if it isn't the most dangerous place in the world," said Una. A shadow crossed her brow. Even in this shoddy room, in this ramshackle hovel at the edge of civilization, Una was freer than she'd been nearly all her life. She should never have trusted Fawa Gan. Had she used better judgment, she might even now be strolling off the dock at Swansea. Anonymous. Unimportant. No one. She refused to dwell on it.

"I admit, I'm impressed. You don't spend your whole life brewing remedies and setting bones without developing at least a mild interest in your subject," Rian said. "I've never met a girl above the Grey before. Can you tell me about it?"

Una lay back against the mattress, letting her arms flop heavily to either side. Siora, but she was tired of this room. She didn't feel up to sharing her experiences with Rian, but what else would they talk about? Ben?

Not bloody likely.

"I was born in Bethany, I'm sure you know? It's a long story, how I left. No, I don't want to discuss that before you ask." Una squinted up at the ceiling. "Let's see, my mother was made an Alta Prima at age twenty, but not because my grandmother shoved her through the Cloister ranks. Far from it. A girl without the Spark to progress through each level would never survive each Ordeal."

"What's an Ordeal? Like a test?"

"If that test was potentially lethal and the worst torture imaginable."

"How so?"

Una raised her hands over her face. She felt the sure crackle of an invisible energy lurking just below the skin. "The Spark isn't passive energy. We're each born with the aptitude to tame it, mold it— as it were, but only a select few can *force* the change. Every person reacts to the particles around them according to their arrangement; wood is solid, water is wet… and so on. Siorai are born with a gene… an, erm… inheritable trait that gives the particles in their bodies a sort of gravitas; a pull. We do so from within when we wish to alter an object's particles. It's not just asking your cells to obey you. You're commanding them to remake themselves according to your design."

"I don't understand."

Una closed her fist, and the air around it popped and fizzed as if she were stoking a small fire. "We're altering the chemical composition of our own cells to attract or repel particles around us. We call this

Manipulation. Essentially, we rearrange those particles at the sub-atomic level, using energy from inside our cells."

Rian puffed out her cheeks. "How?"

"Everything in this world is composed of a set number of particles. The arrangement changes according to its... how do I say this? Its *program*? Siorai study these particles and learn how to harness and rejoin them as we see fit."

"Magic, you mean?"

"No." Una wiggled her fingers, and the energy dissipated. "Not really. Vibration and electric impulse cause particles to either attract or repel one another. We like to think of ourselves— our bodies— as conduits for these forces. Frequency and pitch are what we study most. For example, would it change shape if you were to take one of those pillows and smash it between your hands as hard as you can?"

Rian looked down. "Yes?"

"Manipulation is the same, only at the most fundamental level. Our Spark gives us the ability to push and pull on these particles. To use our life energy as an anchor. The level to which a girl may do so determines her value in the Cloister. Does that make any sense?"

"Not really. Sorry."

Una considered how she might better explain the process. "Okay. How'd you do it when you made that ogham stone for Ben?"

"I carved the correct symbol into a bit of river quartz and repeated the words my mother taught me to say."

"There you have it. You *Manipulated* the stone's particles, using energy from your own body to do so. Spark."

"If that's true, how did it know what form to take if I have no idea how that works? Sidhe magic is different. It's memorizing words, knowing which items can be brought together to... *oh*."

Una tilted her head back to grin at her. "Exactly. I daresay you've achieved more with one little stone than you believe. You could likely wear the Grey yourself if you'd a mind to."

"Would I pass the Ordeal, do you think?"

Una's smile wavered. "Well, perhaps. Perhaps not. There's no way to know until one has tried. The First Ordeal is about focus."

"How many Ordeals are there?"

"Ten."

"How many have you passed?"

"Eight." Una repressed a shudder.

"Humph." Rian smashed her pillow with all her might, and Una laughed. "There. I'll take my pension now, My Lady."

Una opened her mouth to answer, but a scrape outside the door clapped it shut. She sat up. Rian's eyes flew wide. The handle was tried first, followed by a thump, a shuffle, and a muffled curse from the hallway. A heavy scuffing, like a boot sliding back. Una flung her hand out to Rian just as the door burst inward on its hinges. Bits of splintered wood and flaking green paint blasted into the room. Screeching, Rian darted from the bed to the corner. Una froze. She perched near the headboard on all fours. A very large man stood in the ruined doorway, with hands like anvils. He blinked at the two unarmed women inside and stepped back, a slow, childlike wonder in his beady eyes. A heavy-set, middle-aged woman stepped from the hallway behind him. She must have been attractive once, with her high clear brow, auburn hair, and delicately arched brows. Those days, however, were long gone. She wore so much rouge; her bulbous cheeks were twin bullseyes in a sagging sea of white talcum. Two dangling jowls swung free of a square jaw as she swatted at the giant's shoulder. The blow held all the ferocity of a kitten batting at a feather, but he flinched like she'd struck him with a stave.

"Damn it, Dabney! I bleedin' told ye to watch yer strength! I said a slight nudge— a nudge, damn ye. Not a feckin' jackhammer."

"Sorry, Barb. I din' mean to."

"Ye never do! For feck's sake! Ye better believe that bloody door's comin' outta yer pay." Stepping past him, she started to discover the room occupied. Una glared back at her from the bed. "What's this then? I told that no good, lecherous dog there be NO bleedin' talent on this side o'the buildin'! I've bloody respectable tenants in here!"

Una's nostrils flared. "*I beg your pardon?*"

Barb wagged an imperious manicured finger at her. "Oh no. I'll have no sass from the likes o'ye, girlie," she gave Una the once over. "Yer one o'Matt's girls then? Feckin' savage, lets his gents do as they please, don't he? Too bad. Ye'd be pretty enough, wit'out all that," she waved a hand at Una's healing bruises. "I'll never understand why ye girls let his boys do that to ye."

Rian held up her bookend like a shield. "Una, is she—?"

"*Yes,*" Una hissed.

Barb ignored them both. "Dabney!"

"Missus?"

She jerked her thumb at them. "Get these two gashes outta here."

"Missus," he said, stepping into the room.

Una flounced from the bed and parked herself in front of Rian. "I wouldn't do that if I were you."

Barb was already moving around the room, presumably taking inventory. "Ye tell that good for naught Ben Maeden, that this ain't no bleedin' toy box to keep his trash in. Owes me half a stag for the room this month, and that don't count what he's racked up this week, neither. Booze and girls cost money in this joint. For now, I'll be takin' everythin' in here."

Dabney moved to grab Una's arm. She swatted his hand away. "Madam, I assure you, you're mistaken."

"What's he got in here then, hey?" Barb disregarded her. "Haven't seen the bastard in nigh two weeks, and he has the brass to come back here lookin' for a flop? I won't have it, I tell ye." She dug around in the wardrobe, sucking her teeth at its poor selection of items: a few tunics, an extra pair of boots, and two pairs of moth-eaten leggings. There were no coins, no weapons, and no valuables of any kind. The girls' packs, they'd stashed under the bed. Una didn't doubt it would take the madam long to find them at this rate. The last of Rian's coin and all her medicines were in those packs. They couldn't afford to lose them now.

"We're not, erm, working girls, Mistress," said Rian, keeping a wary eye on the big man's reaching sausage fingers.

Una slapped them away again.

His lip jutted out like a pouting toddler. "Ow."

Barb laughed. "None o'us ever are, dearie. Hurry it up, Dabney! I wanna surprise that sack o'shite when he deigns to show up. Bleedin' show pony has coin to bathe and take meals in here like I run a bloody hotel for degenerate gamblers and thieves. Bringin' girls in off the streets when he ain't paid his tab next door in months!"

Una seethed.

She'd never been spoken to like this before.

Not ever.

Dabney leaned forward to hook her around the shoulder. Grabbing the bedpost for support, she kicked out with both legs. He staggered, bleating like an injured lamb. He looked back at her with a trembling chin.

"Why'd ye hit me?"

"I don't think he's right in the head, Una," opined Rian.

"I don't care. You try to grab me again, Dabney, and I'll put you down. That's all the warning you're going to get."

He fidgeted while Barb made a tidy pile of useless junk at the far end of the bed. "Missus? She hit me."

Barb stopped, exasperated. "So, hit her back, ye bleedin' bairn! Honestly, what should I do with ye, hm? Lettin' a little slut like that push ye about. Yer three times her size! Get on with it."

"We are *not* sluts, you *ham-fisted cunt*," Una growled.

Dabney covered his mouth in shock. Una watched Barb's head come up. "What did'ye just say?"

Undeterred, Una glared back. "Oh, I think you heard me. We're not prostitutes, and Ben's debts have nothing to do with us. Now *get out before I put you out*. Was that clear enough?"

Barb drew herself up to her full height. "Second thought, Dabs. I want ye to knock that gash's teeth out. Now."

The giant lunged, but Una was faster. Like a shot, she leapt up. Her hand slipped over Dabney's eyes, her fingers digging into his brow bone.

"*Down*," she rasped. He hit the floor so hard that his head pounded through the floorboards. The impact rattled the window and sent a spray of splinters into the air around his prostrate body.

"Siora!" Rian squished herself into the corner as far as she could go.

All color but the overdone rouge leached from Barb's face. Mouth agape, she stared at Una— who hid her sudden exhaustion— as if seeing her for the first time. Barb's eyes now marked the exposed tattoos at Una's collarbone, her hands, and along her arms. She let out a slight wheeze.

"Of course, ye aren't, *milady*. Forgive me poor manners." Barb traced the ghost of a clumsy curtsy.

Una didn't reply.

Tossing Ben's things back into the wardrobe in an inelegant pile, Barb was at a sudden loss for words.

"He'll be fine in a while," Una told her as she observed Dabney snoring into the dusty underfloor. "I did warn him."

"Well, he ain't the brightest gem in the box, ye know?" Barb patted her dyed hair with a shaking hand.

"Now then, perhaps I shoulda led with this, but would ye two *ladies* care for a stiff drink? Siora knows I could use one meself about now."

⚝

BEN TWISTED THE DAGGER, AND on cue, Vick screamed behind his palm. The boy muttered something nonsensical, but Ben didn't care to hear it. He stiffened his forearm, then smashed the back of Vick's skull into the wall. Solomon hovered nearby, alternating between handwringing and complaining of the mess. Astride Vick's knees, Ben leaned in close.

"I warned you not to come into the Quarter, Vincent." Ben removed his hand. Vick stole the opportunity to suck down as much air as possible. His brown eyes boiled with hate and pain. "I hope it was worth it?"

Vick spat at him, but Ben dodged the bloody mess. Cursing, he set his knee down hard over Vick's bleeding thigh. Vick cried out, uselessly trying to shove him off. Ben outweighed him by at least fifty pounds and was twice as tall. Vick didn't have the slightest hope in a wrestling match. Solomon stepped gingerly over Vick's unconscious friend, mindful not to slip in the gathering pool of blood.

"Is that necessary?"

Ben ignored him. "I asked you a question, Vincent. I expect an answer."

"Feck yerself, Ben Maeden. When Matt's done, ye won't be able to piss upright. I promise."

Ben gave him the kind of smile that made the younger man swallow. "I'm sure he'd like you to believe that, but without boys like you to do his dirty work for him, he's just a bootlegger with a paunch. Your boss is a coward."

"Whatta I care?" Vick snorted wetly, "I just work for the man. He says he wants to see ye, so I come to get ye. Simple."

"Funny, isn't it? That he waits for Robin to leave before making a move like this?"

"I dunno what yer talkin' about."

"Sure, you do. Matt heard Robin and I were on the outs, so maybe he figured he'd intimidate me into taking his side, using your two dead pals as leverage. Or maybe this is all about Robin? For Matt's brother, all those years ago. Both, maybe?" Ben jerked the dagger out of his leg. Vick yelped, mumbling nonsense under his breath. Bloody spittle ran down his collar. Ben jabbed the blade point first into the floorboards

143

between them. He watched Vick pretend not to consider trying for it. "Go ahead, if you think you can get to it before I shove it into your eye socket."

"Feck ye."

"I heard you the first time." Ben shifted onto his haunches. "I have to say I'm flattered, but Matt overvalues me. I have neither the influence nor interest to assist in his coup. But you knew I'd say that, didn't you? You brought all this extra steel in vain."

Vick coughed. "Why ask me? Ye've killed friends o'mine, Ben Maeden. I won't forget that, no matter what Matt says. I was hopin' ye'd refuse him, and ye did."

"How's that working out for you?"

"Just kill me. If it keeps that poncey mouth o'yers from waggin', I'm ready."

"Matt surely couldn't have pinned all his hopes on me. He doesn't have the numbers. What else does he have planned, Vincent?"

"Stop callin' me that! Me own mam don't call me that! It's Vick!"

"Cute nickname."

The boy groaned. "Sol, can ye please hand over somethin' to cut me own throat with? This is like arguin' with me bloody grandda."

Shaking his head, Solomon went back to polishing the horn mugs he'd already polished half a dozen times in twenty minutes. No help there.

"You know, I don't make a habit of killing men unless they make the mistake of drawing down first," Ben pointed at him. "The other night, too, was on you. Both events were in self-defense. End of tale."

Vick had to think it over for a while, but his tone was less acerbic when he answered. "Don't change the fact that they was friends o'mine."

"You ever hear that you should choose your battles with care?" Vick chewed the inside of his cheek but refrained from comment. "That end of Wanderer's Alley is almost Greenmaker territory. You shouldn't have been there anyway. What *were* you doing there?"

"You'll have to ask Matt yerself. We done here? If yer not gonna kill me, there's lots o'things I'd rather be doin' than bleedin' all over Sol's floors and listenin' to ye prattle on."

"I'm not going to kill you, Vincent."

Vick couldn't repress a gory grin.

"I'm going to take you to *The Hart* and let Barb sort you out." Ben was amused by the speed at which that arrogant grin vanished. Vick shifted. He tried like hell to buck Ben and get to the waiting dagger, wildly lashing out at Ben's face and hands with everything he had. Ben grabbed one slim wrist, then twisted until he heard a definite crack. Vick didn't scream this time, only sniveled like a beat dog. "I can hurt you all night, or you can plead your case to Barb. Your choice."

"She'll kill me!"

"I doubt it. She's a bit less bloodthirsty than Robin or Colm. She'll probably trade you for something she wants."

Vick blew air and bloody sputum over his lower lip. "Good luck with that. Matt don't make trades, and he don't bargain, neither. Ye may as well kill me."

"If Matt's so ruthless, why do you support him?" Plainly, no one had ever asked Vick that question before. He seemed, finally, at a loss for words. Ben stood up. "Stay. If you flutter an eyelid, I'll break that leg. Clear?"

Vick dipped his head at the ogling, traitorous brewer. "Ye know Matt will make ye pay for this, don't ye?" Sol dropped the mug he'd been working on with a startled look on his face. "Whatever this lout promised ye, don't matter. Yer a dead man."

Ben administered a swift kick to Vick's lower ribs. "I thought I told you to shut up. Sol, you can disregard that threat. Matt won't do any such thing."

"I don't like this, Ben," whimpered Solomon.

Vick threw his head back and attempted to laugh. "He'll send more knives when I don't come back. Yer a fool to trust Robin's errand boy here!"

"Ignore him, Sol," Ben sighed.

"How's that? Ye think Barb is gonna trouble herself to protect me? Ye should strangle this whelp and dump his carcass in the river."

"That won't stop him, old man," Vick said. "None o' ye can stop him. He's got means, ye know? And time. Robin's days is numbered, and everybody knows it."

Ben took a long pull from a half-empty mug of ale and set the vessel on a nearby table. Any patrons had cleared out as soon as the fighting broke out. Ben sniffed, using one of Sol's rags to wipe the blood from his hands.

"It'll be rather hard for him to threaten anyone if he's dead. Don't you agree?"

Vick snorted. "Yer sure enough now. It'd be war."

"That's where we'll have to disagree, Vincent. I doubt a single person on the Hilltop would mind in the least. You know why?"

"Yer mad, or stupid. Can't tell which."

"No one will mind because Matt Gilcannon isn't the only boss in town. Barb runs a tighter ship, and no Greenmaker is ever knifed in the dark for aging out. I daresay that removing Matt from the equation solves everybody's problems."

"Yer gonna kill Gilcannon?" Solomon asked dubiously.

"After I drop this cretin in Barb's cellar, yes."

"Yer a crazy bastard, Ben Maeden! He'll kill ye… he'll kill all o'ye…" screeched Vick in frustrated disbelief.

Solomon shook his head at the boy and turned back to Ben. "Ye'll let Barb know I helped ye, won't ye? Do that, and ye can keep yer coins. If she's willin,' all I want is a share."

He filled two mugs, then passed one to Ben. Ben raised his. "I'll go one better and tell her the whole thing was your idea, Sol."

"I'll drink to that," Solomon tapped his mug against Ben's while Vick sputtered vitriol from the floor.

"*…and yer mother's… and all ye cunts….*"

Solomon frowned. "Ye sure ye need him alive?"

"Barb will want him."

"Can ye do it?"

Ben gave him a lazy smile. "What do you think?"

"*…feckin' tear yer throats out with me bare hands… I'll feck yer corpses… ye feckin' dogs… bugger ye with my knife… I'll…*"

"I think ye'd better get to work."

"Keep the stag, Sol. For the mess. I'll see you soon."

Ben set his mug down, grabbed Vick by his collar, and dragged him to the door. Vick kicked and howled like a rat in a boiling pot, but Ben had no trouble hauling him to his feet. He clamped a free hand over the lad's mouth to keep the noise down. Sol took stock of the bodies on the floor.

"Wait! Yer dagger. And what do I do with all o'them?"

"Leave them," called Ben over his shoulder. "I'd send a message to Matt. Tell him I attacked you and the boys in your bar. Do it within the hour before someone beats you to it."

"You want me to betray you?"

"Why do you think you're still alive, Sol?" Ben kicked the door open, smashing Vick's temple into the jam. The boy deflated slightly, making it easier to keep hold of him. "I trust you to tell him everything in *detail*."

Sol sputtered, "But I—"

"Word for word. I'd rather Matt knew I was coming for him."

"Siora, *why*?"

"It's more fun that way, isn't it?"

The Madam

Barb excused herself from the parlor. The Siorai girl watched her leave, though her companion was too engaged in chatter with Rose to notice. Barb didn't have to worry about her girls. No one was immune to innocent, polite flattery… especially when it came from one's social inferiors. Barb's girls would simper, flatter, and charm their way into the Moura Prima's ease. That was precisely what Barb paid them for, wasn't it?

Gently closing the door behind her, she bustled down the hall to the staircase overlooking the taproom. *The Hart and Hare* never officially closed for the day, but there was a distinct deficit of patrons until after sunset every evening. Only one or two stragglers warmed themselves beside her two infamous hearths. Barb ran her hand along the polished birch balustrade on her way to the top landing. She tapped her nails on the railing. Downstairs, a thin man with a face full of scars stopped wiping tables to blanch up at her excitable posture.

"Colm! I need the fellas," she whisper-shouted at him, bosom heaving. "Gerry, Rich, Seamus, and Paul. Anyone ye can find. Have 'em wait down here. I want Paul standin' guard at the back door."

Colm's triangular chin pulled downward. "What for?"

"Don't ask me what for. Just bloody do it!"

Colm tossed his rag onto a partially clean round-top and stomped toward the kitchen door, grumbling the whole way. Barb whirled on one of her guards, who was busy chewing on an apple core from his chair on the first landing. He was there to prevent patrons from wandering upstairs without paying for the privilege and often to keep her girls from ducking out of a shift. He was easily twice Colm's size but possessed half of his acumen. He reminded her of a fatted calf chewing cud. She twisted her nose at him.

"Which are ye?"

Apple-tainted spittle clung to his sparse, unruly beard. "Dean, Missus."

"Dean, I don't keep men that chew with their mouths open."

He forced himself to swallow. "Sorry, Missus."

"*Siora's mercy,*" she prayed, brows skyward. "Dean, when Colm gets back, I want ye to send two men to the walkway. Gerry should guard that door there."

"What door, Missus?"

"The one I just bloody came out of."

"Oh right." His brow scrunched up. "But if yer in there, why d'ye want it guarded? I can see it from here."

Barb pinched the bridge of her nose. "Dean?"

"Missus?"

"If ye wanna keep yer job, don't talk back. *Ever.* Understood? Just do what I tell ye."

She watched him struggle to respond until she felt her brain might leak from her ears if she stared too long. Colm came through the kitchen door with two filthy men of similarly lean statures. She inclined further over the balustrade.

"Where's Gerry and Paul?"

"Sleepin'. They only got back from a raid this mornin'. Robin says let 'em be," Colm sighed with a put-upon air. He'd been around so long hthat e didn't worry much over Barb's temper.

She swore under her breath. She'd fix him soon enough, the insolent worm. She shoved past Dean on her way to the landing, her lips pressed into a grim line.

"Colm, get yer *bony* arse up here. And ye two," she pointed to Seamus and Rich. "I want one o'ye guardin' the walkway and the other the alley. Don't ye dare look to Skinny! I pay yer feckin wages, don't I?"

"Yes'm," both mumbled and slouched off to do her bidding. Seamus slid by her, careful not to bump into her elbow, which jutted from her hip at a ninety-degree angle. She didn't budge to accommodate him; he was forced to squeeze himself along the banister on his way up. She didn't waste much attention on him. Her ire was reserved for the man who surely knew better than to back-talk her in front of subordinates.

Colm, none too eager for the boxing he was about to receive, inched up each step sideways, a sullen mope tugging at his cheeks. "Barb?" he squirmed under her scrutiny.

"Ye wanna head back out with Robin to earn yer bread, Colm? Because that can be arranged."

He went a shade paler than his typical fish-belly white. "No, Barb."

"Then ye'd better start mindin' yer mouth, don't ye think? Ye work for me, not the other way 'round. Ye could be back over that river in a flash, dodgin' Sidhe arrows, and fey beasties. Am I clear?"

"Yeah."

"*And?*"

"Sorry, Barb."

"Now then," she gestured behind her. "I've got the shock o'me life waitin' in that office up there, and I need to be sure it don't stroll outta here unfettered. I daresay, Robin needs to be apprised o'this."

"I thought ye was interviewin' new girls?"

Barb grinned. "In a manner o'speakin'… one o' them is more'n a common crofter's daughter, that's for sure."

"How's that? Where'd they come from anyway? I saw 'em stroll into yer office, but they didn't come through here."

She almost giggled; she was so pleased with her good fortune. "From the rents next door. A gift from bloody Ben Maeden hisself, can ye believe it? Me an' Dabs were bowled to find them in his room." Her smile flickered. "Now I mention it. Someone might wanna check on the poor lamb. He was out cold, last I saw him."

"Wait, what? What about Ben? Why would Dabs need helpin'? Yer pardon, Barb, but yer makin' as much sense as a cloud does to a fish."

She took a breath, then patted her thudding heart. "Listen, I don't have time to explain. The girl's not stupid, and she's got power. *Loads*, I reckon. We'll have to overwhelm and be quick about it."

"Who? What power're ye talkin' about?"

"She's got to know I put nightshade in her tea with the uishge. I don't expect it'll be long afore—"

"Barb! Slow down! *Who?*"

Barb blinked back. "The Moura girl! She's upstairs in me office."

"What the feck is a 'Moura'?"

"Yer havin' me on, Colm? The fecking Mouras… the richest family in Tairngare? Hells, likely the whole bloody continent. *That Moura.*"

"Oh," said Colm, as it sunk in. Then his eyes bulged. "OH! It can't be, can it? What would a girl like that be doin' here?"

"I bloody well grew up in Tairngare, didn't I?" Barb sniffed, "I think I'd know a fecking Moura when I see her. She's covered in blue dragons, ye dolt."

"Dragons?" Colm threw up his hands. "I ain't ever been to Tairngare, Barb. I don't know what that means."

"Siora, preserve me." She squeezed his shoulder. "Just go get Robin and tell him what I told ye. Got it? I don't have time for all this. She'll be gettin' antsy." She paused on her way back upstairs, worrying her nails. "One last thing. Make sure ye tell Robin that it was Ben brung her here. That's very important."

"Why? They're still hot at each other, ain't they?"

"Just do it, Colm," Barb snapped. "Make sure ye keep an eye out for that lanky, blond bastard too. We don't want him buttin' his nose in, do we?"

Colm blew a gust of air out of his gut. "Whatever ye say, Barb, but I'm tellin' ye, Robin ain't gonna be happy. He's knackered."

"Oh, I dunno about that, Colm. I think he'll be plenty happy once ye tell him 'bout our guest."

⚔ ⚔

For once, Ben was marginally pleased with himself. He'd managed to catch his first clean break in weeks. He'd stashed Vick in the cellar of an abandoned tenement two lanes east of *The Hart*, where he could be certain no one would find him. Ben should send Matt a gift for attempting to interfere in Greenmaker business just when Ben needed him to. With Matt's bid to oust Robin from the Guild, Ben had a genuine opportunity not only to earn Robin's trust once again but his gratitude as well. Yes, things were looking up, thank Herne. Finally, he could relax a bit. Maybe let the girls out? Take a few pints with folks he generally mixed with? Why not? By sunset tomorrow, he'd be a hero to half the Quarter and likely, achieve a proper escort over the border for the girls if all else failed. Ben was in a good mood. The first, after so many days on the run, bleeding, fighting, chasing, and hiding. All he needed now was for Diarmid to respond to his message. If his uncle agreed to help him, Ben might not require the Greenmakers' help at all.

Gods be kind.

Diarmid Adair possessed the authority and power to break Ben's geis without a proper hearing at Court or an impossible personal trial. As the Ard Rí's Brehon, Diarmid was allotted powers no other individual in Innisfail could boast of. *Fiachra Rí*, the Sidhe, called him: Raven King. Though Ben had no doubt the pooka would deliver his message as promised, there was no guarantee Diarmid would respond. Ben hadn't seen his uncle in years, and quite possibly, the old bastard had no further interest in involving himself in his problems. Diarmid had spoken up for Ben once before, which hadn't worked out in the Raven King's favor; Ben had heard Diarmid was anathema at Court to this day. If he did show up, he would probably demand some absurd payment for his aid, no matter how limited his involvement. Ben was prepared for all of this, just in case.

Thanks to Una, there was a real need for an audience with Midhir. Diarmid was no fool. He would understand how important this was. At the very least, he could carry the news Ben bore to Bri Leith and let the Ard Rí himself make the decision Ben knew he would. There was no way Midhir would allow Bethany to conquer Tairngare, not while he drew breath. Ben wasn't prepared to depend on Diarmid alone, however. That would be foolish. Diarmid Adair was a great lord but also mercurial, duplicitous, and irresponsible. He was hardly the most charitable or honest fellow in Aes Sidhe. Diarmid ruled over many but dwelt with none. He was rarely invited to festivals or encouraged in Council, nor did he often feast in any rath. The Raven King was unpredictable and intemperate as lightning. Ben prayed for Diarmid's help but would make alternate plans regardless. Ben, too, was no fool. Thanks to Vick and his boss, things might just work out.

Drawing his cowl up, Ben rounded the corner at the rear of his tenement. Leaping to the second-floor balcony without much effort, he was barely halfway through the window when the sight of his room brought him up short. The door wasn't simply ajar; it had been smashed inward and dangled precariously from its splintered jamb. The armoire lay on its side, with its drawers crushed beneath it. The floorboards at the foot of the bed were bashed in, gaping cavernously at the ceiling above. Neither girl was anywhere to be seen.

148

Panic traced a slow burn from Ben's gut to his throat. What in the *nine hells* had happened in here? Where were they? He darted around the scene to glean clues until he caught a muted gag from the hall. Quick as an adder, Ben ducked through the ruined doorway. He discovered Dabney, Barb's boulder of a bodyguard, crawling toward the walkway on his hands and knees. There was a foul-smelling trail of sick marking his glacial progress. The big tough blubbered the whole way like a whipped child. Ben turned him over with his left foot, sword drawn.

"What in the name of Herne is going on, Dabs?"

Dabney's face was streaked with tears, bloody snot, and rubbed in vomit. He put his hands up in a pathetic, defensive posture. "Don't hurt me no more, Ben! I didn't do nothin' to her, I swear!"

Ben backed up as a fresh puddle of gelatinous fluid burst from the fellow's swollen nose. "*What's* that, Dabs?"

"The girl! She was so lil'… but she hurt me!"

Una. Only one tiny woman he knew of could make a grown man of this size cry like a baby. Ben slid Nemain back into her sheath and eyed the walkway with a furrowed brow.

"Where is she then?"

"I dunno." Dabney wiped at his streaming eyeballs with the back of his knuckles. "She broke me, and I woke up here. She's scary, Ben."

"Dabs, you have *no* idea. You came here with Barb, I presume?"

"Uh-huh."

Damn it. "What happened before she hurt you?"

Dabs blubbered. "Barb told me to grab them two girls and throw 'em out. The scary one called Barb a bad name, so Barb told me to hit her. I wasn't gonna. She was so lil'. Then she… she… that's all I 'member, Ben. Swear."

"Danu's tits! These bloody girls are going to get me killed!" Ben roared in frustration. Cursing, he inched around Dabs' sniveling bulk to get a good look at the walkway. Thankfully, he didn't see anyone at the other end, but that could quickly change. If Barb had Una and Rian, it wouldn't be long before she'd send someone out to inquire about a missing Siorai Prima. Everyone knew Barb had more than one or two bones to pick with the Cloister in Tairngare. If he didn't get to them soon, all the trouble he'd gone to today might amount to nothing.

"You won't tell Barb I was cryin,' will ye, Ben?"

"No, Dabs. I won't tell her."

The oaf gave him a relieved, toothless grin. Ben drew up his cowl and cut around the corner toward *The Hart and Hare.* This was not how he was hoping to end his day. He prayed that both girls were unharmed because he wanted the pleasure of listening to their neckbones snap when he throttled the life from them both.

⚜

"THERE'S SOMETHING IN THE TEA," Rian whispered behind her hand. Una took a dainty sip, a false smile mortared to her mouth. Barb's girls worked very hard to maintain a pleasant, harmless façade. Rose was dark-haired with smooth dark skin; Violet was fair and pale as soft cream. Rose was clearly Tairnganese, with her coloring and high cheekbones. Violet must hail from the South, or perhaps she was a Cymrian or Kernese transplant? One did not come by such fair skin in the North unless they were from some far-flung backwater. Only faeries and trueborn Sidhe, like Ben, had the bones to pull off 'wan'— but perhaps Una was biased? There weren't many fair-skinned girls in Tairngare.

She supposed the girl was pretty enough, in her way.

Una might even feel bad for having such catty thoughts about her if the pasty-faced trollop weren't trying to poison them. "I know," she murmured back. "Work your throat when you pretend to swallow."

Barb's girls prattled on about Tairnganese fashions and bombarded Una with inane questions about this or that city custom. They were so animated that it would have been hard for the unwary to detect the authentic current of nerves bubbling just below the surface of each expression. Una refused to feel sorry for them, Madam's orders or no. Rose seemed wiser and more watchful than her pastoral accomplice. Her gorgeous black eyes were careful not to linger on Una too long. She knew to which house Una belonged, there was no doubt. The lowest girl in Tairngare would never mistake Una for anyone else, with such a wealth of blue-limned skin exposed. Una took another tiny sip of her drugged refreshment. Of course, the Madam knew. She was Tairnganese, too, if from an Agrean or Merchantan household. Una detected the barest smidge of Spark in Barb, as she did with many women who had the misfortune to be rejected by the Cloister. Barb did not possess nearly enough to challenge Una directly, however. She felt sure the old madam was downstairs at this moment, preparing her guards.

Una knew she didn't have much time to decide on a course of action. Rose leaned in to pour more tea into Una's half-finished cup. If she was confused by the fact that the tea didn't seem to have the slightest effect on her, she was careful to conceal it. Rose smelled like mint and something sweeter. Her fingers were long, thin, and elegantly tapered. Her hair was ironed flat, though, at her temples, many natural curls refused to be tamed. Una could admit to a slight pang of envy there. Her own wild hair wouldn't take the iron, no matter how many attempts were made.

"My Lady," Rose simpered, her voice sweet and deep. "Ye have the most beautiful skin (horseshite, if Una had ever heard any before). How d'ye care for it? Oil, balms? Many girls would weep for yer secret." Her accent was softer than anyone she'd met outside of Tairngare, saving Rian. Una returned Rose's ingratiating smile but didn't seem to have a firm grip on her cup. A hot line of black tea laced with nightshade dribbled down the front of her tunic. "Oh no!" cried Rose, hastily setting the pot back on the larder.

She wadded up her shawl to pat Una's lap dry.

Una flushed. "I'm sorry. How clumsy of me."

Clucking, Rose shook her head with reassuring denial. "The fault was mine, My Lady. There's nothin' to forgive."

Una's fingers wound over Rose's own.

"Not for that. *For this.*"

A sound like rushing bees filled the parlor.

On cue, Rian launched herself at Violet, who didn't have time to cry out as the taller girl's hand clamped over her lower jaw. "Don't kill her!" Rian hissed, using her body weight to hold Violet down. "You don't have to."

Rose whimpered in a half-faint.

Una frowned. "We have to get out of here."

"Fat chance of that. That woman went to get help."

"Make her drink that tea."

Violet's struggles gained intensity, but Rian knocked the back of her head against the floor, and she went limp. Rian's resilience floored Una. Just a smattering of days before, hadn't the faerie girl seemed to be the weakest member of their trio? Now, Una wasn't sure if Rian wasn't the strongest... Ben included. Her ability to adapt to circumstances, however unpleasant, was impressive. Rian retrieved her cup, then tilted the girl's head back to pour the substance down her throat. Violet sputtered, but enough trickled down that Una was satisfied she'd present no further trouble. Una tucked Rose into her own abandoned chair. Rian watched the door with wary eyes.

"Now what?"

"Get behind me." Una jumped over the fallen teapot to lace her fingers through Violet's. The sound came again.

Rian covered her ears. "Why're you doing that? They're already incapacitated."

Una closed her eyes as her Spark surged inside her. Putting that hulk of a man down had cost her heaps of energy. She'd already expended so much in the past few days. She needed what little she could muster to heal and keep moving. A slow burn could potentially get them both out of this mess in one piece.

Consequently, if she hadn't depleted herself, she'd never have allowed that abhorrent woman to lure them into this situation in the first place. Una's strength had to be replenished— that was all there was to it. They must get out of here before that old whore sold her to the first group that came looking. Siora only knew what she would do to Rian. Una knelt and slid her palms along either side of Rose's face. Rose blinked languidly as if fighting sleep.

"Is there another way out of here?"

"Just the walkway or the door downstairs."

"I don't believe that for a second."

"The truth."

"Siora. Guess it's back the way we came, Rian."

"Then what?" Rian fidgeted, looking around for anything she could use as a weapon. "Where will we go?"

Una shook Rose hard. "Which way? Where can we run?"

"She'll have me flogged."

"*I'll* do much worse if you don't help us. I can make it look like you tried to stop us, or I can break every bone in your pretty face with a thought. Your choice."

"The alley, just behind the laundry. Second stair after the walkway, on yer right." She reached out and clutched Una's arm, her pupils dilated. "Don't stop for anyone. She'll sell ye if she catches ye. If ye see Ben, warn him Robin's back."

Una chewed her lip to conceal her surprise. "I don't know what that means."

"Just tell him, please? I think ye'll have to strike me."

"No need." Una pressed her thumb into the girl's forehead. Rose's chin sagged until she bent nearly double. Una scowled down at her for a moment, confused by her sudden concern. Then, her attention snagged on a scrape in the hall. Someone was coming. She grabbed Rian by the elbow. "Ready?"

"No," snarked Rian, wielding a pewter candlestick like a club. Una opened the door on Barb's surprised face. Without a word, she ducked low and rammed her shoulder into the older woman's gut.

Barb's breath burst out in a gush on her way to the floor. "What— *oof!*" she exclaimed.

Una didn't wait around for Barb's next shout. Two men were racing up the stairs on one end, and another peeking around the corner from where they needed to go.

"Go, Rian! Don't stop!"

They ran. Barb screeched orders, but that didn't deter either girl. Thudding steps behind them made Rian turn only long enough to chuck her candlestick into a pursuer's knees. He crashed into the floor with a yelp, taking one of his companions down with him like pins in a bowler's game. As Una and Rian rounded the corner, they came to the darkened hallway they'd been brought through earlier. Faint, sickly light shone through the sole window in the walkway. The scrape of a booted foot in the passage made Una's blood burn with determined rage. A tall shadow emerged from the light. With an animalistic grunt, she heaved herself at the figure, hoping to offset his balance with her weight as she'd done to Barb.

She might have been a feather for all the effect she managed. Bouncing off a broad chest, her arse thumped soundly into the floorboards. She barely had time to curse her bad luck before a pair of large hands clamped over her shoulders and hauled her upright. He slammed her into the wall one-handed while fending off Rian's feeble blows with the other. Una's ribs still cracked, making their displeasure known.

She gnashed her teeth. "Rian! Go for his legs!"

The figure let go.

"Una? What in the *hells* are you doing?" Ben dragged her into the walkway, tugging Rian behind him by the back of her neck. She slapped at him until he released her. He pressed Una against the windowsill. Breathing hard, she frowned at his bemused expression.

"They're coming!" huffed Rian. "We have to go!"

Una had quite a lot she wanted to say to this bastard, but it would have to wait. "Get us out of here!"

Ben's mouth twisted. "Told you to stay put, didn't I?"

She bared her teeth at him like a badger. "Oh, we're going to have a long talk, you and I. Very soon."

"Can we please get out of here first?" urged Rian.

Ben shoved both girls ahead of him into the walkway as several stomping feet thundered up the hall behind them. From beneath the alcove came Barb, followed by a new tough Ben had never seen before. Seamus and Colm brought up the rear. Barb clutched at her side, her bosom heaving. She set a hand against the wall under the last red lamplight. Her graying hair was wild about her ruddy face.

"Wasted a full bottle o'me best uishge, and this is the thanks I'm due?"

"Bad manners, that," came a familiar voice from the opposite end of the walkway. Ben shut his eyes with a silent curse. He turned. Robin walked into the light, followed by Paul and Gerrod, effectively blocking their exit. Dabney slumped in a corner and tried not to look at anyone. Gerrod flashed Ben a warning with his eyes, but Ben didn't need it. He already knew what Robin was going to say. His scarred mouth set a grim line. "Ben. I thought I told ye, ye weren't welcome in Rosweal?"

"What? Ye didn't tell *me* anythin' like that," interjected Barb.

"Wasn't yer business, Barb," Robin boomed, never taking his eyes from Ben's face. "It's *ours*. Ain't that right, Ben?"

Barb sputtered. "That's some brass ye got, Robin Gramble. Tellin' me, what pays ye lot, what I oughtta know or not."

"This is men's business."

Barb's chin said she'd make him pay for that comment sooner or later. Ben knew them both very well.

Una's fingers tightened on Ben's shoulder. "Who is he?"

"Robin," Ben nodded, ignoring her. "I came to see you, for the record."

Robin cocked his head. "Is that right?"

"I have a proposition for you— for both of you," Ben tugged his chin at Barb. Rian's belly squeezed into the window casing while she searched for the latch. Ben found himself moving out front to block the girls from view. "Something you both want."

"Don't bet on it." Robin drew his sabre.

With a groan, Ben mirrored him. "I'm serious, Robin."

"Love, I dunno what ye two are on about, and I don't care," Barb pointed. "But them two girls're worth a bloody fortune. I want 'em back. Unharmed."

Rian sucked in a sudden breath. Scratching at the glass, she jerked Una around to help. Ben set Nemain's point against the floorboards. "Will you listen to me? We have to talk!"

"I don't care to hear anythin' ye'd say, Ben."

"There's much you don't know, Robin. It's not all black and white."

"Yeah, it bloody well is. Ye lied to me for years, Ben. Nothin' ye could say to me now would change that."

"This is boring the shite outta me." Barb snapped her fingers, "Dean, Seamus. Bring those girls back to me office. Don't scratch 'em up neither! They're worth more than any o'ye."

Parties advanced warily from both sides for fear of Ben's vicious two-handed longsword. Ben reached for the nearest lantern on the wall.

"Una," he said. "Get ready to run right through them."

Rian pushed the window open, letting in a gust of damp, chill air. Without ado, she climbed over the sill. Ben didn't have time to process her intent because Dean lunged clumsily from his left, and Robin took a testing jab from his right. Ben parried Robin's blow and knocked him into Gerrod, who broke Robin's fall with a shaky right arm. Then Ben whirled, grabbed Dean by the back of the neck, and smashed the bulky fellow's nose into his knee. Dean went down, howling. Before Robin could rush back in from Ben's right side, Ben tossed the lantern onto the floor. It shattered into a million glittering pieces. Barb shouted something unintelligible and ducked behind Dabney. Ben had the brief satisfaction of watching every opponent scramble for cover as burning oil splashed throughout the hall, flinging spurting lines of flame over the ancient wooden floorboards. Ben caught only the briefest glimpse of Robin's furious face before Una pulled hard at his elbow. They tipped through the open window together. Smoke and curses filled the void they left behind.

No Quarter

They didn't fall far enough. Two bolts struck the canvas nearest Ben's head. Rian managed to drop them into the alley between the two buildings, where Barb's housekeeper ran *The Hart and Hare*'s profitable laundry. There were dozens of carts and crates piled high with dirty sheets, tunics, linen, and hose. Lines between each brick wall were crowded with drying bedding, gowns, and curtains. Rian clawed her way out of a crate of soiled linens and limped over to help Una and Ben out of theirs. The drop wasn't more than eight feet, which made the landing relatively soft— if unsanitary. Eight feet wasn't quite far enough to escape the hail of quarrels that followed. Ben dodged another missile and another. The air filled with smoke. He got to his feet and dragged Una upright beside him.

Rian led them around a flimsy wall of drying sheets. "Which way?"

Barb trilled orders from the burning walkway. Ben knew they had seconds before Paul, Seamus, and Gerrod dogged their heels. "To the docks! Follow me!"

They fled as fast as their feet would carry them, over slick cobbles and down partially flooded lanes. At the end of an alley, Ben took a sharp left. On a dime, he stopped and kicked down the door to a short, squat warehouse. The girls moved to enter, but he drove them toward the docks instead. Rian, with her bad foot, had trouble keeping up. Ben was obliged to hook an arm under hers and half-carry, half-drag her along with him. Despite this, they made swift progress toward the West Gate. Here he turned again, circling abruptly back around to the east. Ben kicked open another door, shoved both girls inside, and slammed it shut after them. They stood in the unkempt back garden of a small, vacant house. Rosweal had plenty of abandoned spaces for the nefarious to utilize, thank Herne. He pressed his ear against the rotting garden door, waiting for the tell-tale splash of footsteps to come pounding up the alley.

"We're not going to the docks?" huffed Una, near his ear.

"They'll expect us to, won't they?" Rian held her ribs. Ben met her eyes over Una's head. He had to admit that Arthur's daughter had sharp wits and keen instincts. Once again, if not for her quick thinking, their situation could have been much worse.

"Right," he peeked over the retaining wall. No one followed. Yet. "We have to get to the Hilltop. If it hadn't been for Vick and his little helpers, I would have taken you there from the first."

"How far is that?" Rian asked as if doing sums in her head.

"Not far. But we'll have to be quick and quiet. Robin's a keen hunter, and with Barb's promised payday," he pointed at Una, "he'll be getting serious about now. What happened back there?"

Una shrugged. "The madam was a Novitiate in the Cloister."

"How'd you know that?" Rian gestured for both of them to whisper. "She didn't look very refined."

"Not all of them are. I'll wager she came from an Agrean household. Folks often try to improve their lot by offering a girl in service to one of the great houses. Happens all the time. Most of these girls don't make it past the First Ordeal. Anyway, she knows who I am."

"Damn it," Ben groused. "I told you not to open the door to anyone."

"We didn't," snorted Rian. "They kicked it in, looking for you, you ingrate. Apparently, you owe the madam a good deal of money. She took us for courtesans and tried to maltreat us. Una put a stop to that. Then she invited us to tea and promptly tried to drug us. You weren't there."

"I assume she's already made plans to sell me. Tairnganeah patrol the Navan High Road. It won't take long for them to get here."

Ben kept his eyes on the alley behind them. Maybe they were searching the warehouse or the docks? He still smelled smoke. Possibly the Greenmakers got caught up putting out the fire? No matter what was happening, it was better luck than he expected. He had more weapons stashed at his house. They just needed to get there. He ducked away from the door, pulling the girls further into the garden. Behind a hedge, he shook his head at Una,

"No. She wouldn't."

"What do you mean, 'no?' She was going to sell me— both of us."

"I know her. She wouldn't sell you to the first patrol that came looking. Not Barb. She'd send people to find out if there were any other interested parties and how great any rewards might be. Then she'd auction you off to the highest bidder. Very clever and patient is Barb."

"*Wonderful*," Rian grumbled. "Me, I assume, she'd simply put to work?"

"No. She'd sell you to Matt Gilcannon," Ben said. "But that's neither here nor there. We need to get moving. The sooner you two are safe, the quicker I can get back to work and get us out of here."

"Where to?"

"There's a house up the hill, nine lanes up and two over. That's our destination. Move when I move, where I move, and how I move. Whatever you do, keep quiet. Understood?"

"I thought it was too dangerous to go there?" Una looked around with a dubious cast to her amber eyes.

"It is, but after tomorrow that won't matter. We must get moving. Remember what I said?"

Both girls nodded.

"Good. Let's go."

⚚

IT TOOK EONS TO SLINK around each corner, turn, and rise, strafing from shadow to shadow through gardens, empty alleyways, and across busy thoroughfares. On one residential street, they passed dirty children playing with sticks and balls while matrons eyed them suspiciously from open windows and front stoops. Trying to appear as nonchalant as possible, they crept over garden walls, through yards littered with rusted tools, and lots choked with weeds. Up and up, they climbed, passing shuttered shops, empty taverns, and crumbling tenements. The sun was long gone by the time they rounded the last turn at the hill's apex. The houses here weren't caked black and brown with soot, nor were the lanes six inches deep in stinking, malodorous mud.

This was Gilcannon's territory, and the difference was stark. The Greenmakers might have more money, men, and connections than Matt, but they weren't as concerned with appearances as he was. The underlying rot and social debauchery on the Hilltop far exceeded the vices approved in the Quarter. Ben should know; he was technically a resident of both districts. He'd won this property in a game of porter many years ago but kept it to himself. At one time, he considered taking up regular residence. All things considered, he found he preferred the noise and up-front chicanery in the Quarter.

Since Gilcannon had bought the distillery on the North End, Ben could count the number of times he'd visited the neighborhood on one hand. The characters that flocked to Matt's standard weren't Ben's preferred sort of scum. He took a few switch-back turns from Fulcrum Lane to Goddard, then down Heritage, until he approached an iron gate tucked into a stately brick wall. The back of the house was dark and silent, as always. Ben couldn't recall if he'd ever used the front door.

The lack of street lanterns here certainly held sweetened its appeal. He didn't have the gate key on hand, and there was no time to delay. Looking around to be sure no one was watching, he leapt up to straddle the wall, then stretched a hand down to hoist each girl up. He pulled Rian over first because she looked like she might drop dead at any moment from exhaustion. Of the three, Rian was the most disused to running and the least likely to ask for help. Una came up almost entirely on her own. She just needed a hand back down due to her diminutive stature. He raised an eyebrow at her, but she looked away before he could catch her out. Whatever Siorai tricks she'd been using, they worked all too well. Una had a definite spring in her step that hadn't been there the day before, and the more he looked at her face, the more obvious was her blooming health. He could only guess what she'd done to accelerate the healing process, but it would keep, for now.

They had bigger problems.

Rian flopped onto a stone bench, strangled by creeping vines. Chewing her lower lip, Una stared over the gate on her tiptoes. No one seemed to be following them. Ben wasn't so sure. They were either very lucky, or something must have distracted Robin. He'd been known to hunt a single stag for three days at a stretch. He'd never let them get away so easily. Maybe the fire got out of hand, or Ben lost him back in the warehouses? Whatever happened, it wasn't over. They must lie low until Ben could regroup. He dug around in his dead flower beds for the wide, flat bit of shale he'd stashed his key under. Finally finding what he sought, he fumbled with the lock until he heard a withered metallic click; the door swung inward on its rusty hinges. He waited for the girls to head inside, then shut it behind them all as quietly as he could manage so as not to alert the neighbors to their presence. In the silent musty darkness of a small but effectively appointed kitchen, the trio let out a collective sigh of relief.

"*Siora*," breathed Una. "Let's not do that again."

"Agreed," Rian said. "Ben, do you think anyone followed us here?" Looking through a greasy window facing the back gate, Ben opened his mouth to say no, but a scrape and flash further inside whipped his head around.

Robin Gramble set a lit match to his pipe bowl. Its dim glow illuminated his crooked grin. "No need. We knew where ye was goin' the whole time." He gave Ben a mock salute.

Una tucked into Ben's side. Rian didn't move. "Took ye long enough too. Almost forgot which house was yers."

"Of course, you knew about this place. What was I thinking?" laughed Ben.

"Dunno, but ye was never as clever as ye thought."

Rian inched toward the exit. She jumped when Robin glanced directly at her. "I wouldn't do that, missy," he dropped a heavy crossbow on the table. Its clattering bulk made her squeak. "I'd hate to have to shoot ye in yer good leg. That's right, hands way up there. That's good."

Ben cursed long and colorfully. "You wouldn't happen to be alone, would you, old friend?"

"Am I ever?" A nervous cough issued from the front room. Gerrod emerged from the shadows, taking his place behind Robin's chair. He wouldn't meet Ben's eyes.

"How many more did you bring?"

"Enough."

"I doubt it," smirked Ben.

With a chuckle, Robin shifted his crossbow a half-inch to the right— directly at Una's heart. Ben froze, as Robin knew he would.

"Oh, I dunno about that, Ben. I'd say I brung plenty. Ladies? If ye'd be so kind, would ye take a seat in yon parlor there? Where I can see ye if ye please? Ye'll find me friend Seamus by the door. He'll be happy to build ye's a fire."

Una shot Ben a long, wary frown. "Go ahead," he told her. He was unsure which angered him most: that Robin had outfoxed him or that he had the brass to order him about in his own house?

"Seamus won't hurt either o' ye. Lad wouldn't know what to do with one o'ye if he tried. Paul and Dean, on the other hand, aren't as nice. Best stick with Seamus. Go on now."

With an uncomfortable pout, Gerrod moved aside to make room for them. He was Robin's man, through and through. Ben couldn't fault the lad for his loyalty, though he wished he wasn't involved.

When the fighting broke out, he'd rather not have to hurt him for Robin's stubbornness. Una stepped near. Gerrod crushed himself against the wall to let her pass. Robin's smug grin faded slightly when she got close.

"Siora, Ben, did ye do that to her face?"

Una answered for him. "No. He saved my life and hers," she waved a hand at Rian. "More than once."

"Bah," Robin scoffed. "I know him. He ain't no bloody hero."

Una didn't respond. Instead, she lifted her chin and bristled as if to sweep between them into the parlor. Suddenly, she stumbled, the toe of her boot having snagged upon some unseen impediment. Gerrod's hands instinctively darted out to catch her around her waist. She beamed up at him. He only had a heartbeat to wonder at her curious expression when a sound Ben had only heard twice before surged through the room. Perhaps it was less a sound than a feeling, like the vibration of a thousand bees buzzing through a hive or the flapping of wings against a pane of glass.

Rian cried out. "No!" but it was no use.

Una's left hand clapped over Gerrod's bare wrist. "*Down*," she said. Down is where he went.

⚲ ⚲

ALL HELL BROKE LOOSE AT once. Gasping for air, Una toppled with Gerrod into the rushes. The lad's head lolled against the wall as she dived chin first into his chest. Robin flew out of his chair. He reached to snatch Una off Gerrod by her hair. Ben got there first. His fist cracked into Robin's nose, forcing him to stumble backward into the corner of the fireplace. Seamus cried out with a cracking voice and flung himself into Ben. They tumbled to the floor.

Meanwhile, Paul dashed from the parlor into the kitchen. He grasped for Rian with an excitable leer. Screaming as he wrenched her into his arms, she kicked, bit, and scratched like a demon. Rian pummeled him with her knees, heels, forearms— anything that she could. Paul was wiry, but he had a strong grip. He trundled her against the counter and pressed his fingers around her slender throat. Ben smashed Seamus' head against the floor, once, twice… until his eyes rolled back in his head, and his legs stopped twitching.

"Rian!" Ben shouted, trying to scramble to her side.

Robin bashed him over the head with his crossbow. "I think you broke me feckin' nose!" Ben ducked under his arm, using Robin's own body mass as ballast. He came at him from the opposite side, then struck a hard blow with his left fist. Robin spat blood, but he didn't fall. Instead, he drew a dagger, and opened a wet line across Ben's chest. Ben backpedaled into the front parlor, careening into the covered furniture. Meanwhile, Una got to her hands and knees over Gerrod's prone body.

"Una! Rian!" Ben tried to point, but Robin slapped his hand away. Nodding, Una crawled toward Paul and Rian.

Robin wiped a trickle of blood from his nose with the back of his hand. "Where're ye lookin' then?"

With a grimace, Ben skimmed a hand over his seeping ribs. "Leave the women out of it, Robin!"

"Yer the fool who brung 'em here," said Robin, swapping his blade from hand to hand. "If Gerry don't get back up again soon, I'll string that Siorai cunt from the Navan Gate by her guts." Robin jerked right but flipped his dagger to his left hand to drag its point over Ben's thigh. Ben grunted, then hammered his elbow into Robin's reaching arm at the joint. Something hard crunched within. Robin hissed in pain. His dagger clattered to the floor. Ben kicked it away and shoved him back so he could draw his sword. Robin watched the light play over Ben's sylvan blade with a bloody grin. Pushing himself back up, he drew his Souther sabre. "It's to be that sort o'business, eh? Good. Was startin' to think ye'd gone soft."

Ben couldn't see what was happening in the kitchen. He heard Rian screaming and… something else, but it was lower this time, subtler. Una's power seemed to hold a different pitch now, like the sigh of a wave over a sandy shore.

"Una!" Ben called. No one answered.

Robin's blade thrust forward, testing. "That big Sidhe bitch of a blade just for show then, or d'ye aim to use it?"

"If I wanted to kill you, Robin, you'd be dead."

"Prove it." Robin sprang forward just as the back door flew inward. Dean, Barb's newest meat, rushed into the kitchen with his cudgel raised high. Ben didn't have time to react. Robin's attack was swift and brutal. Ben parried with a twist of his wrist. Then Robin's fist cracked into Ben's jaw like a cannon shot. "Ye'd better start takin' this seriously, shouldn't ye?"

Robin struck out again, and again, and again. His head thrumming, his ears ringing— Ben had no choice but to slide his right foot behind him. He hefted Nemain over his shoulder in a high *Neithana* guard. Blood poured from his abdomen, his thighs, and his mouth.

Robin bared his teeth. "That's more like it, ye Dannan bastard. *Come on.*"

❦ ❦

WHILE BEN AND ROBIN WERE making each other bleed in the front parlor, Paul bent Rian over the counter by her throat and tugged her skirts up with his free hand. Her bloodied hands flailed around. She snatched at anything she could to turn herself out of his grip. Various domestic items clanged together or clattered to the floor. Finally, she managed to grasp a small black pot. Backhanded, she landed a glancing blow to his temple. He staggered a bit, then came back, bleeding and furious. Paul struck her twice. She withered, and he held her down while he fumbled with his laces. Ben shouted Una's name. Rian kicked and thrashed with all her might.

Una dragged herself upward. Red-faced, Paul fought to hold Rian still so he could wrench her underskirt out of his way. Una gritted her teeth on a ragged breath and hauled herself forward on her hands and knees.

"Hold still, ye faerie bitch!" Paul barked down at Rian while he tried to jerk himself forward. Una's fingers slid under the loose leg of his threadbare breeches. She dug her nails into his calf muscle. Surprised, he let go of Rian, who fell into a rasping heap on the floor. His beady eyes bulged. "What?"

"*Splinter,*" Una snarled. The bones below her hand burst to pieces within his flesh. His forehead banged off the dusty iron stove on the way down.

Screeching like an owl, he scratched at his leg like it was on fire. "You *witch*! What did ye do to me?"

Una clawed herself up his prone body while he tried to shove her off. Grinding a knee into his naked groin, her hand latched over his face, ramming it into the floorboards with audible force.

"I'm going to eat you, little man. Every last drop."

He whimpered in confused, impotent pain. Una drew down deep. She gave her Spark liberty to dip its thousand greedy fingers into every one of his cells, to sap every morsel of energy his thin, repulsive body contained. She shuddered against him. Any remaining wounds she bore stitched themselves together in moments. Her bones realigned and snapped into place; nerves and joints popped, stretched, and fused. The energy drained from Paul reinvigorated her blood like a pitcher beneath a tap. She pulled and pulled until his skin sagged inward and his tongue dried up in his gaping jaws. Paul's heart shriveled like a prune in his desiccated chest. Crackling with a new and electric vitality, Una finally felt something like herself again.

Completely whole for the first time in nearly two weeks, she stood over Paul's mummified corpse and spat. Una wound her arms around her choking, shaking friend. "It's all right now, Rian. He's dead. He can't hurt you anymore."

Suddenly, the back door blew inward on its hinges. The dark-haired guard from *The Hart* stepped in, bearing a mean-looking cudgel in his grubby fists. Rian gave a short hoarse scream as he took in the scene. Paul's corpse did not escape his notice. His wide eyes traveled from Paul's remains to the fight in the parlor, and back toward the girls. His cheeks went a bit green at the edges. Someone else stepped in behind him. This one was smaller and skinny as a rail.

"What in the hells happened in here?"

Una put herself between them and Rian. The larger man, Dean, she thought she'd heard Barb call him, pointed his cudgel at her.

"Did *ye* do this?"

"Your friend liked to touch ladies without permission."

"Dean..." his friend eyed Una warily.

Dean shrugged him off. "I'm gonna tear yer head off yer shoulders, ye fecking witch!"

"Kill them, Una!" Rian raged, adjusting her clothing. Una shrugged her shirt over her head, leaving only a thin chemise above great swaths of exposed skin. The swirling blue dragons emblazoned on her arms and chest seemed to glow silver in the moonlight.

"By all means, boys, who wants to touch me first?"

⚜

BEN WAS LOSING. DEFENSIVE TACTICS were all but useless in such close quarters. If he couldn't reason with Robin, he would have no choice but to engage him seriously. He parried another blow, which drove Robin's sabre into the wooden paneling in the upstairs hallway. Robin jerked his arm forward to dislodge it with a tired grunt, but Ben's fist hammered into his chin.

Robin backpedaled into the alcove. Deprived of his sabre, he slipped two more daggers from his belt. Sweating, Ben leaned on his sword for a breath. Nemain was too heavy for such a claustrophobic space, but she still held the advantage over Robin's thin daggers. Both men were aware of this fact, though only Ben seemed reluctant to exploit it.

"Come on then," Robin croaked. A nasty bruise welled over his right eye and another over his jaw. His nose gushed blood from both nostrils. Ben wasn't in much better shape, truth be told. The cut to his ribs burned like a brand. So much blood was in his boots that his toes squished against their soles. Robin might not be able to beat him if Ben were serious, but neither was he a slouch. Every moment Ben wasted trying not to harm Robin further wore him down. This had to stop.

"Robin, I didn't come here for this," Ben panted. He held his left palm out. "I need your help."

Robin couldn't have looked more surprised if Ben had jammed Nemain through his heart. "Yer havin' me on? *My help*? What in the *nine hells* made ye think I'd help ye?"

"Because we've been mates for almost fifteen bloody years." Ben wavered a bit on his feet. "Do you think I'd be here if I didn't know I could trust you?"

"Ye have the bollocks to ask me for favors? After Nat? Are ye out of yer feckin' skull?" Robin launched himself at Ben, whirling high and low. Each blade came a hair's breadth from vital areas. Ben retreated, unable to get his sword up in time to deflect. He took a deep slash to his battered forearm, which cost him the half-second Robin needed to kick his sword out of the way. Next, the butt of Robin's dagger caught him in his temple. Ben crashed through the bedroom door and tumbled head over arse into the far wall. With a shriek, Robin hefted his blade to slam it to the hilt into Ben's shoulder. Ben jerked his knee up just in time— catching Robin solidly in the pelvic bone. Robin sucked in a sharp breath and doubled over, retching. Face gone chartreuse; his daggers clattered to the floor beside him.

Ben's fingers closed over the gash in his side. He was losing an alarming amount of blood. Robin sank to the floor on his rump. Ben winced.

"You didn't leave me much choice."

Speechless, Robin glared silent murder at him.

Ben hauled himself partway up the wall. Now was as good a time as he was likely to get.

"Robin, I'm serious. I need your help. It isn't just Ben Maeden asking, either. Put aside your anger for just a moment." Ben swallowed, trying to find the right words. "That Siorai girl downstairs? She was smuggled out of Tairngare by a gang of thugs from Bethany. Robin… she's Patrick Donahugh's daughter."

Finally, able to breathe, Robin's eyes narrowed. "Ye lie, as usual. Why in the bloody hells would the Duch kidnap his own girl?"

"Because he means to march on Tairngare— the North, obviously. Overplaying her hand, the Doma set Una forth as some kind of prophesied ruler. Don't look at me like that. I'm dead serious. There's been some sort of coup in Parliament over this."

"What's that have to do with the bloody Duch?"

"With the turmoil in the Red City, Drem's just granted Patrick a viable excuse to annex Tairngare beneath his own rule."

"No," laughed Robin. "The High King would stop him. Hells, the whole o' the bloody North would stop him. He tried that tack before, remember? Our naughty Crown Prince put an end to all that at Dumnain."

Robin spat out part of a tooth and cradled his sore crotch like a basket of eggs. "Besides, Drem would never allow that Souther cunt access to her prize fortress. It would take—"

"… a faction of people inside the Cloister, who believe by allying themselves with the Duch, he'll support the Union's rise to power in Parliament. But that's just one layer. Someone paid a rogue faction of Citadel Corsairs to eliminate her before she could be exchanged."

"Yer barkin'."

"I saw it with my own eyes, Robin. If I hadn't intervened, they'd have beaten Una to death right in front of me. What's more, they're patrolling every road from here to Tairngare in hopes of finishing the job."

Robin fell silent.

"It's only a matter of time before Donahugh discovers he's been betrayed if he hasn't already. What do you think is going to happen then?"

"War… but the High King—"

"He *doesn't know*, Robin. There hasn't been a High Council in almost five years. From what I hear, Midhir didn't even attend the last one. Only one Sidhe consulate operates in Eire, and I doubt they're apprised of the situation. The Sidhe are too absorbed with defending their borders to notice what's brewing behind closed doors down here. Tairngare has been a historically reliable and capable ally. No one expected Drem to make such a huge blunder, nor did anyone suspect Patrick might have the resources for another campaign. Now is the *perfect* time to strike."

Robin wiped his nose on his sleeve. "So, what? Ye expect me to help ye avoid another war? How'm I to do that then, eh? Rosweal ain't no fortress. We'd be better off sellin' the girl to whoever will pay the most for her."

"You do that, and Patrick will own the North, one way or the other. Even with half the standing army he had twenty-plus years ago, he still has thrice the soldiers and siege weapons Tairngare has. They're too busy bickering in Parliament over the ruling class to withstand a protracted siege. Their only hope is to kill Una before Patrick can get his hands on her. If they fail, he will line the North with Souther troops."

"If all that's true…."

"*It is.*"

"If so, what d'ye expect me to do about it?"

Ben held his eye. "I must get her over the border, Robin. Midhir must intervene before it's too late."

Robin threw back his head. He laughed until gobs of snot mingled with the blood on his chin. "Oh, that's *rich*, that is! Ye want *me* to organize a raid for ye? That's a golden apple that is!"

"Robin." Ben got to his feet. It wasn't easy; every inch of him was cut or bruised. "I'm forbidden to cross the border. I didn't let Nat die… I *couldn't* save him. You'll have to forgive me for that."

Robin reached for one of his daggers, drawing it point first along the floorboards. His eyes sparked like two burning coals. "'Forbidden' ye say? Why's that then? Why'd me nephew die, Ben? Tell me."

Una appeared in the doorway. The determination on her face dissolved in shock at each man's state. "What—?"

Ben threw up a hand. "Stay there!"

"But—" He spared her a glare, too preoccupied to notice the sudden health she wore.

She scowled. "If you don't want to kill him, *I* will."

"Lovely lass," Robin spat.

"Your friend Paul thought so. Now he's dead," said Una with a ghoulish smirk.

"Una!" warned Ben. "Stay out of this. I'm begging you."

Robin gave her a long side-eye. "Hurt one o'ye?"

"Tried to."

"Siora sorts 'em," he shrugged. "Bit of a blockheaded cunt he was, ye ask me. No great loss."

She opened and closed her mouth. She clearly expected her news would have a greater impact. She crossed her arms. "Well, yeah."

"Now, ye'd better start talkin' Ben, or I'm gonna jam this to the hilt through yer bloody eye."

Ben was unarmed. That hardly mattered now. Deep down, he had to trust that Robin was the man Ben thought he was.

Now or never.

"The river isn't just a border for me. It's a curse. A *geis*."

"Horseshite!"

Ben shook his head. "It's not. I swear it, by Danu."

"Ben, just show him," Una attempted.

"*Shut up!*" they shouted back.

She threw up her hands.

Ben clutched the charm at his throat, feeling more exposed than he'd ever felt. Robin waited impatiently, a furious sort of curiosity in his expression.

"You were at Dumnain, Robin."

"Everyone knows I was. What's yer point?"

"What I'm about to show you… don't make me regret it."

"I'm makin' ye no promises, ye—"

Ben tugged the strap from his throat.

Robin's insult puffed into the air like smoke.

Hierophant

Henry limped through brilliantly tapestried halls on his way through the Duch's throne room. He was fully cognizant of the whispers he earned as he passed. Not that he wished to mingle with this crowd. He lacked the words to describe the withering contempt he held for every familiar face he encountered in Patrick's Court. Time and age may have dulled his recollection of events, but certainly not his memory of their many betrayals. Hadn't Lord Corrigan sworn Henry absolute fealty after the disaster at Dumnain? Corrigan was fatter now and missing several of his front teeth, but Henry remembered his bulbous, upturned nose. Wasn't it Lord Murphy who vowed to cut Patrick in half if he marched against them at Bantry? Murphy looked much the same as he had all those years ago: thin, overdressed, and boss-eyed. Henry's worthless uncle, Lord Thomas Bishop, had railed loudest against Patrick at their clandestine meetings. Bishop had been the first to swear fealty to Henry. His dedication to Henry's rebellion had been the fiercest. Now, Bishop was an ancient white-haired puppet in piss-stained robes, begging Henry's pardon with insincere, liver-spotted lips.

Twenty-six years had slithered by. Henry might have spent a decade in the dark but did not forget a single name. These men were responsible for his disgrace, capture, and subsequent imprisonment. He marked every simpering, duplicitous face. Now that Patrick had set him free, these treacherous dogs fell all over themselves to curry Henry's friendship. The great Henry FitzDonahugh was home at last! This false exuberance did little to disguise their collective condescension.

Behind their hands, the courtiers scorned his eccentric appearance. They mocked his life in Cymru— his deceased wife, religion, missionary work, and bumpkin children. They spread tales of madness, uncontrolled self-abuse, and the myriad inhuman habits Henry supposedly enjoyed in his cell. Simultaneously, he was a figure of fun and pity. Henry stared past their smug, self-serving smiles to the raw fear lurking beneath. The veneer wouldn't bear scrutiny.

Truth be told, they were *terrified* of him. Henry had nearly overthrown Patrick— his own brother. By all accounts, Henry should be a sack of bones rotting in a pauper's grave. The nobles turned themselves inside out to fathom Patrick's intent. Why would the most powerful lord in Eire publicly forgive a traitor such as Henry? Why now, after nearly thirty years? Seeing the creature Henry had become was perhaps even more shocking than his abrupt return to the Duchal Court. Henry wasn't the same man they'd betrayed. He retained enough pride to own his reduction in stature. Henry FitzDonahugh had once been a tall, barrel-chested youth with a handsome face and a wealth of curls: the envy of every man in the South. Now, Henry was a half-starved phantom with bleeding gums and carrion breath. His spine was bent from years of deprivation and enforced isolation. What hair he had left must be shorn, for the bare patches of greying scalp were far too numerous to ignore. The wooden teeth in his sunken cheeks did little to recall the boisterous, endearing grin his former followers recalled. It seemed the best parts of him had been melted away from the knobbed wick below.

Henry FitzDonahugh was a grotesque shadow of his former self. Though, perversely, he enjoyed the Court's disdain. He was happy to revile them, these perfumed, overfed whores. He understood what they did not. Patrick never did anything without a thousand-fold purpose, and pardoning Henry wasn't an exception to this rule. Foremost, Henry was a reminder. Behold, this once towering warrior! See him now.

Look how low the Duch's retribution had laid him. If Patrick could destroy his only brother… imagine what might become of them? Henry did not care what nonsense the nobles cooked up to explain his presence, nor for their feeble attempts to mollify him. He had no use for any of them. Useless, feckless, faithless dogs, the lot. Soon. Very soon, Henry would prove their folly. They should never have betrayed him. Patrick may have inherited their grandsire's scheming mind, but Henry had their father's patience, his hard stomach, and his single-minded determination. In every way that mattered, Henry was more Donahugh than his foppish little brother had ever dared dream. Patrick had his reasons, but Henry had his purpose. All he must do now was wait.

His boys were *here*, within reach.

Henry would never get such a chance again.

Patrick's oily steward attempted to head Henry off at the second-floor library, but Henry ducked through the Chamberlain's Hall to the rear staircase and the armory on the first floor. Patrick's Court was far from a Spartan affair. The Donahugh Clan conquered, scavenged, thieved, cajoled, and bribed their way to half the Continent's treasures for centuries. If it gleamed or glittered, their forefather would drown whole villages to possess it.

Vibrant tapestries hung from every scrubbed wall. Rich carpets, dyed a thousand different shades, covered polished slate floors. Huge, gilded frames bearing priceless works of art lined every hall. Above the Grand Stair, hundreds of portraits were arranged in descending rank, beginning with the first Duch Donahugh Mather, who died in battle after the Transition. Henry's likeness had resumed its former place way down the line. Henry was immune to such overreaching egoism. He was insulated from it all, safe in the might and wealth of the soul. He would be damned if he would allow this riot of color and wealth to seduce him again. He would keep his innocent sons clear of corrosive idolatry and extricate his family from this nest of devils, even if it killed him. Henry knew God would protect his innocent sons.

Dipping through a door to the right of the Great Hall, he sped below an arch that reeked of linseed. The unlit armory was quiet this time of day. Its cavernous length stretched through far-flung shadows like a mountain tunnel. Micah saw him first. He darted from behind a cask with a muffled cry, dropping his torch against the flagstones. Henry embraced his son for the first time in nearly twelve years. His heart overflowed with joy. When had the lad gotten so tall? His shoulders so broad? Why the last time Henry saw his eldest son, he'd been whittling wooden horses for him. Trembling, Micah clung to him like a buoy. "There now, lad." Henry could hardly trust his voice. "No need for all this. Let's have a look at you."

Micah wouldn't be set off so easily. "I missed ye, Da."

Henry was obliged to pry Micah's too-large hands from his shoulders. The size of him! He was nearly of a height with Henry now. Had so much time truly passed? Henry swallowed a burning lump of ash in his throat.

"Tis pronounced, 'you,' Micah. You must maintain your diction."

Micah's sun-kissed cheeks screwed up in a half-smile. "I ain't seen ye in near on twelve-year, Da. And yer fussin' bout me accent?"

Henry patted his son's golden head with a scarred hand. "Aye, so I shall every time we meet. Remember where you are now, lad. These vipers will make you suffer for every mistake you make. Don't forget that for an instant."

Micah crushed himself into Henry's far leaner chest once more. "Now yer free, can we go home?"

Henry sighed into his son's meaty shoulder, vowing he would not weep. Weeping would not keep Micah safe. Henry would invite no weakness now. "God knows, I wish we could, my boy. Alas, He's brought us here for His purpose, and we'd do well to honor His command. Don't you agree?"

Micah swiped at his runny nose and stepped back a pace. "I 'spose so. Uncle won't allow Isaac and me to speak o'Him. We may pray only in private. When Isaac forgets, Master Holden swipes his knuckles with a stick."

"Never mind that now. I don't know how much time I have with you, and we have much to discuss. How does Isaac fare?"

"Well as a boy o'thirteen can, I 'spose. He went from learnin' how to mind Aunt Tilda's fields to bein' the nephew o'a fancy Dutch in a matter o'weeks. We're bushed and boggled, sir. If I'm honest."

"I am sorry for it, son. I did not think Patrick would ever reach so far for any of us. And it's pronounced 'Duch,' lad. Are they not tutoring you properly?"

Micah flushed. "Yes… *Father*, they are. I just thought ye know."

"Well, *you* thought wrong. I want you to master this, and I want you to do so with all the dedication you brought to your Bible studies. I mean it, Micah. You mustn't give anyone the least advantage over you. Do you understand me?"

"Yes, Father."

"You will need to help your brother too. You are allies now. The only ones you will have here. Do not be fooled by their sweet words, sumptuous clothes, or false smiles— these people are the Devil's own. Do not be swayed."

Henry didn't like the way his son's eye darted discreetly sideways. "I won't, Father. Ye… *you* have my word."

"Much depends upon you now, lad."

"That is what I don't understand, Father. Why do ye… *you* wish me to play the lord if ye despise all these folks? Why can't we just leave? If they're evil, shouldn't we go?"

"Not all of them are evil, son. Some are lost. Some are hopeless. Some have simply been deprived of His grace for far too long. We can change that, Micah. *You* can change that. You *will*."

"How? Uncle says we are important to him. He treats us well enough, but I gather he don't mean it. Looks at us like wild goats he pulled outta pasture."

Henry placed both hands on Micah's shoulders. Micah was uncomfortable, Henry could tell. Henry was also not the same healthy, happy bear of a man he'd been for his son either. He allowed himself one long pang for all his sons had lost on Patrick's account.

"Micah, how old are you now?"

The boy straightened. "I'll be twenty-one, Father."

Perhaps two pangs then? For all Henry had lost too.

"That's old enough to be wise. Why do you think your uncle brought you here? Why go to so much trouble to have you primped and educated as a lord?"

"He said he don't have a son o'his own to pass the title to."

Henry nodded slowly. "'Tis true he lacks a male heir. We must be ready."

"Ready how? We're nobodies, Father. We've only spoken with a handful of folks since we've been here. Who'd support us against a great lord like him?"

"I will, for one. If I know my brother, so will he… if you prove worthy. The key to all of this is Una. Win her, and you win the throne."

"They say she's a witch. I don't wanna marry a witch, Father."

Henry glared at him. "You'll do what you must to keep your brother safe, won't you? I don't care if she's the Devil's mistress… you'll marry the slut and get her with child as soon as possible. I'll brook no refusal."

"What about my cousin? Everyone says he's a right unholy enemy."

"You were enemies the moment Patrick set you up in his household. No matter what you do now, Damek will seek the first opportunity to destroy you and your brother. He means to be Duch, and no son of mine or anyone else will set him off that goal. You'd better start taking this seriously, son. You're both in this race now, whether you want to be or not."

Visibly shaken, Micah hugged himself. Henry was sorry for these tidings. Sorrier than he'd ever been about anything in his life. However, Henry was desperate for this second chance God was granting him.

His sons might be at risk, but they were also being given a gift. If only Henry could make Micah see it in time.

"What do I, Da?"

"Soon, Damek will return with your intended bride. I want you ready long before they arrive."

"My uncle says they should be here within the month! How will I be ready to fight my cousin in time?"

"You're not going to fight him with fists or blade. You, my sweet son, could not hope to defeat an experienced soldier like him with martial might. No. Instead, you'll beat him by being *better* at everything else. You will outshine him in every way. You're a legitimate Donahugh heir. You're handsome, kind, soft-spoken, and intelligent. Those qualities should be enough to tempt your uncle and certainly his daughter. For what you don't know is that Una despises Damek. Can't bear the sight of him, from what I've learned. Show your uncle, his Barons, and his people that you are the better candidate for her hand. Can you do this, Micah? For your family?"

"Won't this only make my cousin hate us more?"

Henry pulled his son in for one more embrace. "It won't matter. I have a way to deal with him. The only requirements are that you study diligently, speak as your tutor instructs you, and stay within your uncle's good graces for the love of God. Can you do this?"

"I think so."

"You're a good boy, Micah. God loves a dutiful child."

"By His Word, Father. I swear to work my hardest. What if she don't... *doesn't* care for me? What if our uncle—"

"Micah, focus on your studies. Spend as much time with your uncle as possible, and don't shame yourself by speaking as a savage. You must hold your head high at table, watch your manners, and smile only faintly. You'll answer no questions and ask none of anyone... and *never* let slip that you intend to succeed your uncle to the throne. Watch my brother and learn from him, but don't try to ingratiate yourself to him. Simply be the empty vessel he requires you to be. Show him you are forthright, clever, and eager to learn. That is all you must do, my son. Be silent and learn."

"But Da... *Father*, these people, they aren't godly folk. D'ye... *you* mean me to break His Commandments?"

Henry's answering smile was calculating. "We must render unto Caesar, my son. Sometimes, the shepherd must brave the lion's den to secure his flock...."

⚔

"So," Patrick's voice interrupted Henry's prayers. Henry dropped his wooden cross in surprise. He hadn't heard his brother enter because the door was still firmly latched. As if he'd been caught stealing, Henry shot upward. Patrick leaned against the window casing, wrapped head-to-toe in white bear fur, looking as diminished as his haggard brother. "How did you find my nephew this afternoon, Henry?"

Eyes narrowing, Henry lowered himself to his fur-lined cot. His knees popped mechanically along the way. He might have known Patrick would never place him in a room with any true privacy. He scanned the room again yet found no hint of a hidden door.

"Where did you come from, Patrick?"

The Duch chuckled. "This chamber is just beneath my own. Quite convenient, really. The better for us to reacquaint ourselves, don't you find?" The better to spy on Henry, he meant.

"Of course," his response rang hollow. "What do you want?"

"I want to know what it was like to see your son again, Henry."

"Your steward disclosed my whereabouts?"

"The chambermaid. You needn't bother about the glow of murder I see in your eyes. I'll simply replace her before you can harm her. Honestly. You used to be so much better at this."

It didn't matter where Patrick put her; Henry would find her. Patrick knew that too. "I suppose I'm long out of practice. I wished to hold my son. If you were any kind of father, you might understand that need."

Patrick blew a stream of air over his chapped bottom lip. "My daughter would as soon spear me as embrace me. But that's hardly important. She'll bend to my will, regardless. Just as your sons shall, Henry."

"They're good boys. I daresay, you've seen as much yourself?"

"Spare me the false sycophancy. You needn't pull the lad from his studies to warn him to mind himself. I have it all in hand."

That was precisely what kept Henry awake at night. So much hinged on this pathetic man's fickle attentions. "I have a care for my son, little brother. I wish him not to shame himself before this nest of vultures. They'll tear him apart for the smallest breach of decorum. It's unfair to throw him to the wolves so unprepared."

"I am preparing him, Henry. Or didn't he tell you?"

"He said you've been most kind. I thank you for that."

"I don't require your thanks."

"You have them, all the same."

With a snort, Patrick rubbed his balding pate. "By Reason, you are so fucking boring now. *Are* you actually in there, I wonder?"

"Do you wish me to caper for you? I warned Micah to behave himself. Now, how will you punish me for it?"

"I'm not going to punish you, Henry. I don't need to ask what you discussed either. The lad willingly shared everything with me, as a good boy will," Patrick grinned.

Again, Henry ignored the barb. "Micah knows the Lord loathes a liar."

Patrick's smile disintegrated. He got up and poured himself a glass of wine from a decanter on the larder. The fire in the hearth hissed a greeting as Patrick moved near, drink in hand.

"Enough of this. Micah impresses me, Henry, as I'm sure you longed to hear, but it won't be enough. Damek is more than thrice the Micahs of this world. If your son has a prayer of remaining impressive to me, he must defeat that dragon first."

"Didn't you cart them over here to bring Damek to heel?"

Henry didn't like Patrick's answering smirk. "*Perhaps*. Perhaps, I merely enjoy having more boys from which to choose? Damek does grow a bit large for his boots. He could do with the competition; a bit of sport to sharpen the teeth, don't you agree?"

Henry laughed. "Patrick, you must think I'm a fool. You'd never have brought my sons here unless you intended to make one of them Duch. Let's not pretend you truly support Alis' son for your heir. He's a bloody half-breed and a bastard to boot. What sort of legacy do you mean to lay by with an heir named 'Bishop,' hm?

What's more, your Barons won't have him without Una's consent, and I hear she won't have him, either way. You *need* Micah. We both know it. It must irk you to no end that one of my sons will follow you to the throne. It must gnaw your guts to splinters, to have no choice."

With a growl, Patrick dashed his wine into the hearth. A steaming, fragrant puff of smoke billowed upward. "If you imagine your son is so much better than the outstanding soldier and statesman I raised, you are worse than a fool, Henry. Your sons are here to remind my nephew to behave himself. Nothing more. If Damek should fail me, Micah may serve as a suitable replacement. One day. *That* is why they are here."

He was lying. Henry could always tell. Even when he was little, Patrick had had a spoiled little tilt to the tip of his nose that always gave him away. What's more, he was afraid. Henry could smell it, like wine seeping from his pores. Wisely, Henry kept this knowledge to himself.

"So you say, Brother. I don't think Micah, sweet soul that he is would care for the job anyway. Still, I would appreciate it if you would keep your precious nephew from cutting into either of my boys the moment he arrives. Both of my boys will do credit to the Donahugh name if you allow them to."

"Damek won't lay a hand on them. They're under my protection." Another lie. *Interesting*. Henry understood now. Patrick was afraid of their sister's son. That's why they were all here now. He was losing control.

Very interesting, indeed.

"I pray that you're right, Patrick."

Patrick sniffed and shrugged his heavy fur closer to his shivering chest. "Anyway, this isn't what I came down here to discuss with you. I have changed my mind, you see." Henry felt a flash of cold dread. He could not— would not return to that dungeon. He would chew out his tongue. Claw out his own throat. Stab out his own eyes… "I don't mind so much anymore. About your absurd religion, that is."

For the second time, Patrick had managed to shock Henry to numb silence. Patrick scoffed. "You look like a fish, with your mouth agape that way."

"I may wear my cross openly?"

"For now, yes. I'd hate to deprive you of your comforts, Brother. So long as you vow to remain apart from these boys, I will grant you free use of the small chapel in the North Wing. I'll have Carne bring you whatever Kneeler's tomes our grandsire kept in the library. Of course, you'll need a servant or two to help you clear the place of dust and vermin. We don't hold enthusiasm for such things in the South."

Henry's heart hammered in his chest. There was a deeper game here that he could sense but was far too elated to see with any clarity. Patrick would never give this to him, never. "You mean to let me worship publicly?"

"I'll go one better. I mean to let you use the chapel as you see fit. You may preach empty words to empty pews to your heart's content. I care not. So long as you keep out of the affairs of the succession, I may relent further and let you seek followers one day. If you are tactful about it, of course, and behave as a Donahugh— with dignity."

"All this, for the price of two sons?"

Patrick gave him a smug, confident grin. "Perhaps; when you've proven your devotion to our family's legacy when Micah proves himself a successor, worthy of the Donahugh name. When Isaac is safely fostered in Lord Corrigan's household, learning to squire. When Una is safely home and ready to do her duty, perhaps, when all of these things are as I desire them… perhaps then you may have your family *and* your faith too. Peace. 'Tis the last hand I'll extend your way."

"… This is another ploy."

"Of course it is! I'm no fool, Henry. I won't suffer a second betrayal. This will be the last offer you will ever receive from me. You'll give me those boys and stand apart from their education. Devote yourself to your god and keep out of my way. Do anything else, and I'll hang the three of you from the North tower by your innards. By Reason, I'll smile as they slit you open like a fatted sow. I'll place your sons' heads on pikes beside your rotting corpse and leave their bones for the crows. Do you doubt me in the slightest?"

Henry said nothing. He knew better.

"What is your answer?"

For God… and for *Duch Micah Donahugh*, Henry answered in the only way open to him. "I accept, Brother."

Patrick opened the inner door in the far corner. Within, two knights stood at the ready, decked in full mail. Henry had no idea he went to sleep every night with that passage waiting just beyond an old moth-eaten tapestry.

"Very well. Should you attempt to grow bold, just remember, there is not a man or woman in this city who would hide you from me. Your sons will be Donahugh men, Brother— not bare-footed zealots. You don't have to thank me. You'll come around to it, eventually."

With that, the passage swallowed Henry's brother with nary a sound. Once alone, Henry seethed, cried for joy, and wept for misery all at once. He didn't notice when the hearth burned out nor the depth of the moonless night beyond his windowpanes. Darkness wrapped itself around him, as it always had. Patient. Sympathetic. Vengeful.

He knows what lies in the darkness…

Tonight, it was Henry himself.

He would wait.

When the time was right, he would be ready.

Enemy of My Enemy

Vick staggered down the alley, with Ben shoving him from behind. Bound and reeking of stale effluence, Vick muttered to himself the while. Robin walked slightly ahead, which left Ben to suffer close proximity. Their motley group moved through Taverner's Alley toward *The Hart and Hare*, silent and unsure of one another. Una and Rian shot nervous glances around each corner as if they might be set upon at any moment. Seamus half-dragged, half-carried Gerrod, who was still too woozy to walk under his own steam. Following at a sedate pace, Dean twitched like a hare every time Una so much as breathed. Colm had yet to meet her eye even once. Rightly so, if Ben were any judge.

He saw what was left of Paul before Seamus dragged his corpse into the back garden. So far, each Greenmaker seemed eager to grant her a wide berth.

Ben hadn't had time to ask her what had happened in that kitchen, but from the bald hostility she displayed whenever anyone had the stones to look at her... he could guess.

To make matters worse, she'd somehow managed to heal herself at Paul's expense. The effects were obvious… and disturbing. Ben was far from an expert in the New Religion, but he felt sure he'd never heard of such horrific marvels. To grant her the benefit of the doubt, Ben didn't believe she'd do such a thing unless she felt she had no choice. Although, the fact that she *could* unnerved him. Busy explaining himself to Robin for most of the night, Ben hadn't had much chance to pull her aside. She'd been keeping this information from him; he wanted to know why. What else hadn't she told him? Rian didn't seem surprised by her appearance, which told Ben Una had trusted *her*.

Why not him?

Una's ability to sap another person of life was a rather large piece of information she should have imparted to him. Wasn't it? He shot her a glance over his shoulder. She wouldn't even look at him. Perhaps that was just as well? Her beauty was both startling... and macabre. He wasn't sure if he was angry with her or hurt.

Either thought cast a pall over his morning.

At dawn, Robin had insisted everyone regroup at *The Hart*. He had a point. With all the activity at Ben's Hilltop residence, there was no way Gilcannon's boys hadn't learned of their whereabouts. Robin didn't believe any of them were up for a serious fight outside of their territory just then, and Ben could hardly argue. On the way, they'd made only one stop. Vick didn't bother to struggle. After a full day in a hot empty warehouse alone, he seemed eager to get on with it.

"Are you sure about this, Ben?"

This was only the fourth or fifth time Una had asked. Should he be upset that she'd kept such a secret from him? He hadn't told her about... well, many things. He ground his molars. He didn't share his plans for her own good! She didn't need to know everything.

Neither do you, remarked the irritating voice from his gut.

How do you think she will react when she learns the truth of your geis, Ard Tiarne?

Ben shoved Vick out of pure frustration. The lad took one look at his stony face and bit his tongue.

"Ye gonna ask every five minutes then?" sighed Robin.

"I might," Una retorted, her eyes thin as razors.

"Well, forgive *me*, milady."

Ben took a measured breath. With his ogham stone safely around his neck once more, none of the others were any wiser about what was really going on. All save Una, of course, and she was not entirely satisfied with his decision to trust Robin Gramble again. Ben's revelation had been for Robin's eyes only. As yet, no one else need be informed. He could count on Robin to keep it quiet, but the dynamic had shifted between them. The cessation of hostilities between them must appear to depend upon the information Ben possessed against Gilcannon. Hence, the need for Vick to back up Ben's story. If everyone knew what Robin did— things would get complicated fairly quickly. "Una, we don't have a choice," Ben begged her for patience with his eyes.

She sucked her teeth at him. "You can't honestly believe that old whore will bargain with you for one skinny wimp?"

Robin poked Vick. "That's ye, I expect, Vincent."

"Name's not bloody Vincent! It's Vick!"

"Oh aye, 'cept ye was Vincent to us, afore ye went off and changed teams. How's Matt's pay? What's the goin' rate for a back-alley stabbin' nowadays?"

"Feck yerself. Matt feeds us year-round. That's a damned sight better than the pittance ye shitty Greenmakers offer." Vick squared his bony shoulders.

"We do just fine without earnin' our bread on the backs o'little girls," Seamus spat. "Ye chose the wrong side, ye puny gobshite."

"What's he talking about?" asked Una.

Seamus wouldn't look directly at her. "Gilcannon runs girls, erm... missus. Not like Barb's girls neither, what have a say in it."

"He means they're slaves, Una." Rian's voice was rough as sandpaper.

"To my mind, all sex work is a form of slavery," sniffed Una disdainfully. "Brothel-keepers, male or female, turn profits from the hopeless and desperate— even in Tairngare, where the industry is regulated with an iron fist. Your Barb isn't a lick better."

Robin said, "Oh, but she is, milady. I'll thank ye to keep yer personal feelings outta things ye don't understand."

"She tried to sell us only yesterday!"

"I didn't say she were a Kneeler's saint, nor one o'the Ancestor's Faithful, but Barb don't sell lil' girls an' boys. She don't chain 'em, nor force 'em to serve at the expense o'their families neither."

"Gilcannon sells... *children?*"

"Oh, aye. Worse than that, believe me. Barb's been lookin' for any means to oust Matt from Rosweal for years. So far, the bastard has kept it too civil to make a justifiable move. All our businesses depend upon one another, ye see? He has contacts and supporters who could ruin some folk here if Barb moved against him without good reason."

"The children aren't reason enough?" scowled Rian.

"The world's a dark place, missus."

The alley widened a bit, and a row of familiar buildings rose ahead. *The Hart and Hare*'s sign creaked back in forth in the early morning breeze. Taverner's Alley was mostly deserted, save a few determined streetwalkers who scattered at first sight of them. The odd inebriate snored into the muddy cobbles.

"To answer yer charge," said Robin to Una, nodding at the sign. "Barb wants Gilcannon more than she wants ye or the missy there. Ben's bringin' her a means. She'll be pleased as a kitten in cream, I vow."

"And you?"

"What of me?"

"You were set to kill Ben... and both of us," she gestured to Rian, "only hours ago. How can we trust you?"

Robin sized Ben up out of the corner of his eye. Ben said nothing. "Far as I'm concerned, we're square as we're gonna get."

"Well," growled Barb, leaning against the bar. Her pudgy elbows peeked from the excessively voluminous sleeves of a fluffy pink dressing gown. Her graying auburn braid dangled over one shoulder, and her unpainted lips were pulled low in an unamused pout. To Una's mind, she looked much younger than her first estimate suggested— barely middle-aged. Without the overdone cosmetics, Barb might even be called handsome. This observation didn't improve Una's opinion of her, but it did serve to humanize her a bit. She could almost imagine the bright young pupil Barb must have been in the Cloister before life sunk its fangs into her. Almost. "Ye got me outta bed at this disgraceful hour. Someone better start talkin'."

Ben cleared his throat. Barb's finger caught his statement cold. "Not ye, ye fancy twat. Someone who don't owe me a bleedin' mountain of fainne."

Ben shut his mouth again, tight.

Robin crooned, "Barb, love...."

"There'll be none o'that neither. Ye were 'sposed to bring me that girl," Barb jabbed a red nail at Una, then Ben, "and see this lanky vagrant made good his debts to me. Can ye imagine my surprise at yer sittin' together, all companionable again?" Her hazel eyes fell on Vick, who sat stuffed between the corners of the bar and Dean's oppressive bulk.

"What's he doin' here then?"

"If ye'd shut yer trap, I'd be happy to tell ye," Robin grumbled.

Ben took a breath, but Barb cut him off. "I told ye, not a word! If ye've any idea how much rebuildin' that walkway's gonna cost me, ye'd better keep quiet, Maeden. Robin, me sweet darlin' man. Go on... but I warn ye, make it fast. I'm peppered enough to throttle the pair o'ye, together."

Robin tapped the bar with a bloodied fist. Barb threw up a hand when Dabney moved to respond. The hulk's nose was wrapped tight in linen bandages, and the hollows of his eyes were nearly black with bruises.

"No pints, no food, no nothin', if ye don't explain yerself this instant."

Robin, his own nose stuffed with bloodied bits of shredded rags, threw his arms up. "The short? Matt was tryin' to bribe Ben to have me killed!"

"He's been tryin' to kill ye for fifteen years, Robin. What else is new?"

"Aye, but this time, he made his move *after* he bought a bunch of our accounts in Ten Bells and Tara. Our contracts won't be renewed as long as Matt's running uishge outta that stinking distillery. It's not me he's after. Long as he can claim to have no hand in it, that was a grudge between old friends like Ben and me... he's free to strip the legs right outta the Greenmakers' operation."

"That all? We've been playin' this game with him since ye retired from the Cohort. He takes territory. We take it back. Matt's an upstart— hasn't got the clout to replace our contracts with the Guilds."

"He does now." Ben ignored her sharp stare. "I had it from Sol himself. Matt offered them better terms than they'll ever get with the Greenmakers, Barb. Those Matt can't turn for shares in his distillery, he threatens or removes. They've all but issued him his own bloody charter. No, it's true. With Robin and me out of the picture, preferably dead at each other's hands— you'd be all alone. He doesn't just want *The Hart*, Barb. He wants Rosweal."

"I 'spose yer fallin' out gave him the opportunity?"

"The cleanest he could manage. According to Vincent there, he's been skimming from the bottom of your earnings for years, and now that his uishge has started filling *The Butterfly*'s cellars in Bethany, he's got the means to bump you out altogether. He waited for a good clean shot before aiming at you personally."

Barb got up, poured herself a tall pint, and sat back down. "Right," she said after a long drink. "Ye found all o'this out in just two days, Ben?"

"Vincent let some things slip on my way back into town," Ben grinned at the filthy little rat-faced urchin, who attempted to shrink into his corner. "I followed my nose to the rest. There'd be no reason for Matt to attempt to abduct me unless he meant to use me. Until now, his business has depended upon the Greenmakers' contacts in larger cities. It didn't take long to figure out he's long outbid you."

"If Ben hadn't come back, Gilcannon woulda bided a bit longer to make his move against us. I'm sure he figured what few holdouts we had wouldn't pose much trouble if he took advantage of our internal strife," Robin said. "Bastard's got finesse. I'll say that for him."

"I take it ye two made nice again when Ben told ye what he learned? That's just dandy, that is. How's that help me? If what ye say is true, it's a matter of finance, and Matt's holdin' a monopoly on that score. We can sell home scratch as well as any honest bootlegger, but he's got the market fair cornered for properly distilled spirits. We can't compete with him. He's out-earnin' us!" she raised a brow at Una. "Sale o'this piece here might square us up, though.

"Got half o'the Citadel's Corsairs out there lookin' for her. What's more, two full cavalry units from Bethany, led by one Lord Damek Bishop hisself, are movin' up the Taran High Road for her as we speak. Oh," she laughed when Una stiffened. "Ye didn't know? Well, one o'them sorts'd pay a king's ransom for ye. I'm bettin' on the latter, meself. Seems most keen to have ye back if what I'm told holds water."

"Barb," interrupted Robin.

"What?"

"We're not sellin' the girl to the Duch, and we're not handin' her over to the Corsairs neither."

"Oh, we're *not*, are we?" The temperature dropped by a few thousand degrees. Una couldn't repress a shiver.

"No, we're not." Robin's jaw clenched.

"Barb," Ben leaned in diplomatically. "She's worth more to you, to all of us, as an ally. I'm asking you for your help."

Barb threw back her head and laughed so long, she was quite out of breath when she finally settled down. "Yer outta yer mind if ye think I'm gonna help anyone for nothin', Ben Maeden. Ye owe me plenty already. What possible help could I be to someone like her anyway? I've got bloody problems o'me own, as we've all just learned. The competition is edgin' me outta me own bloody business... and I promise ye, it's occurred to her hunters where they might look next."

"I'm aware," Ben shot Una a meaningful look. "I'm not asking you to do anything for free. I'm offering you an exchange."

"Oh, this should be rich," Barb waved him on.

"Una, and that girl's safety," he gestured to Rian, "and your discretion, in exchange for what you want most in all the world."

"What's that then?"

"I'll give you Rosweal. Matt's distillery included."

She considered Ben silently for a long while. "Ye can't just kill him, ye know? Never leaves that gaudy pink mansion o'his, from what I hear. Has a bloody army of knife-wieldin' imps at his beck and call too. It ain't just a matter of beheadin' the dragon, as it were. I need his contacts, his signatories, and his recipes. He ain't likely to hand those over, neither."

Ben winked at Vick, who shriveled under his attention. "I know where he keeps those documents. I know when his guards rotate shifts, and I even know where he sleeps. If you give me your word, Barb— your utmost, to the bloody letter *vow*— to keep faith with me... everything Matt has is yours. His contacts and the names of those who've turned coat."

"Yer serious? Ye think ye can do this?"

"He can," Robin answered for him with surprising confidence. "He won't be goin' alone anyway. I, for one, think ye'd be a fool to refuse."

"No one bloody asked ye, love." Barb took another drink, then toyed with her tankard. Her eyes slid from Robin to Una, Rian, Colm and finally rested again on Ben. He didn't look away. "I just wanna know one thing before I give ye my answer. Why go to so much trouble for her, Ben? What do ye get outta any o'this? Ye in love with her? The other one, maybe? *Both*? What can she offer ye but trouble, deposed and pursued as she is?"

Ben swallowed. "I can't tell you now, Barb."

"That's not gonna work, dearie. I'll send bits o'that girl to that fine Souther lord what marches this way and dispatch Matt in me own good time with the proceeds. Ye tell me what I want to know, or ye have my word she'll suffer for it."

Una bobbed her head at him.

He cursed. "Fine, but not here. The four of us will talk about this upstairs. *Privately.*"

"No, ye'll give it to me now, as I—"

"*Barb,*" Robin interjected, getting to his feet. His face was solemn as a Merchanta exchequer. "It's for the best."

The feeling that she was being ganged up on won out. She stomped around the bar to the stairs, snarling, "So help me, if this's a waste o'time, or yer stallin'—" Barb's grumbles lost volume as she made her way upward. Una patted Ben's shoulder as she passed. He followed like a man marching to his execution.

In a way, he was.

⚜

"SIORA'S TITS!" BARB CAREENED BACKWARD into her chair. Ben slipped his charm back over his head, and the startling effect vanished. Barb's left hand flew to her heart while the other rummaged through her desk for a silver flask. After several sips, she sat up straighter and folded her shaking hands together. "All right. What's this mean then?"

Robin pulled a chair over. "What d'ye think it means, love?"

Una sank into the only other seat in the room. She rubbed at her healing face with the heel of a dirty palm. The hollows of her eyes looked etched in. Ben sent her a long, sympathetic frown from where he leaned casually against the closed door. He, too, was covered in seeping scratches and bruises. Robin looked worse than the pair of them together.

"That... yer," Barb flushed, "not Ben, then?"

"I'm the same man you've known all this time, just somewhat more than he appeared."

"Oh, for feck's sake. Yer... one *o'them.*"

"Yes."

She wagged a finger at Robin. "Ye said he was a faerie, didn't ye? Some Sidhe lord's by-blow, like the piece downstairs."

"Not quite," Robin laughed mirthlessly.

A sudden thought occurred to her. "Is the faerie down there—?"

Ben made a face. "*No.* Gods, what a misfortune that would be. I did know her father, all the same. He served under my banner during the war."

"*Under yer banner,* ye say?" She took another drink from her flask. Her hand shook. "Right. Can only be one war, ye mention. Who are ye then, Ben? Which o'the Ard Ri's servants are ye?"

"Barb, we don't have much time," Robin attempted to help. The look on Barb's face shut him up. Ben shifted from one foot to the other like a recalcitrant child caught stealing from the larder.

"Ye didn't ask him this question, Robin?"

"Not exactly..."

"I told him," Ben held Una's encouraging stare. "Because I owed it to him, same as I owe it to you. Ask your question, Barb."

"*Who are ye?*"

To speak the name for the second time in less than twenty-four hours wouldn't make its recitation any easier than the first. Ben had become used to concealing himself, grown comfortable in anonymity. It wouldn't do any longer. There was no point in hiding anymore. Ben needed them. Without the Greenmakers, there was no way to guarantee he could get Una safely over the border if he should fail to break his geis. What's more, they were, for all intents and purposes, his friends. They deserved to know.

Ben lifted his charm and dangled the stone, with its crudely carved little figure, before his nose. He smiled ruefully.

"If the Gods had been kind, I'd never have needed a stone like this. I'd be in my proper place, serving my people, as I was born to. It's funny that one's gifts should be so entangled with failings. Why make a man brave if he can't resist arrogance? Why make him a great leader if he can't command with compassion? Why grant him lands, titles, honors, and nobility— if he can't appreciate them until they're taken away?" He let the little stone thump against his tunic. "I think you know who I am, Barb. You're too quick by half."

"But," she stammered, searching for the right words. "*He's dead*. He died after Dumnain. Everyone said so. Robin, ye were there! Ye said they held a funeral for him and all! Didn't they?"

"Aye," Robin admitted. "On the hill, overlookin' the valley. The Sidhe under-commander… that red-haired fellow—"

"Tam Lin O'Ruiadh, Prince of Connaught," Ben nodded.

"Aye, that one. He lit the pyre hisself. Said some words, then we was all sent home. Those that could walk that is."

"Tam Lin's my cousin. His father is Bov Dearg, the Red King of Connaught. Son of Crom Dagda, brother to the Ard Ri of the Tuatha De Dannan. The Adair are my tribe, you might say."

"*Your tribe…*" Barb breathed.

Ben shrugged. "It wasn't a funeral, but a ceremony. The Ard Ri, mortified by my actions at Dumnain, ordered a geis be placed upon me. I'm not to cross into Aes Sidhe, under pain of death, for a period lasting no less than fifty years. In a way, to your kind— I suppose it *was* a funeral, after all. By the time the geis runs its course, most everyone who knew their Crown Prince, or fought under him, would be long dead."

Barb covered her mouth with quivering, pudgy fingers. "That's rather cruel."

"I deserved it."

"No, ye didn't," Robin crossed his arms. "A great many innocents lost their lives that day, Ben. Lots more didn't that would have. I speak from experience. We was pinned down in the bog, surrounded and outmatched. Souther spearmen and archers were pickin' us off from higher ground. If the horns hadn't blown from Dumnain Village, every man o'us would be dead. I might add that there were half a thousand men— good Norther men— who lived 'cause ye did what needed doing."

"I made war on non-combatants, Robin. Women and children died."

"Aye, innocents die in every war that's ever besmirched the face of the bloody world. By takin' on the garrison, ye freed the town from Souther troops. Ye ended the bloody war that day, no matter what the scribes in Ten Bells say about it. Sure, the chronicles claim that yer countryman, Fionn or other, did it by avengin' the death o'that dark elf prince."

"Falan."

"Aye, Falan. Son o'the king o'Ulster, right? Got killed by a green lad, so they say. Cuz o that, the Sidhe rallied and took the field."

"That did happen, yes. But I wasn't there. I spent the day in chains."

"I was." Robin got up and took the flask from Barb. Ben had never heard Robin speak of his time in the war. "It weren't a proper battle o'any sort. The Southers didn't have much left after what ye did to 'em at Dumnain. That fine lord Fionn chased mere stragglers and a handful o' light infantry across the valley. 'Twas over 'fore it even started— didn't draw me bow once. That 'great battle' lasted a mere fifteen minutes, by my count. Why? Because the bloody Crown Prince o'Innisfail slaughtered half the Souther troops in one vicious night, that's why," Robin took a long sip and passed the flask to Ben. "Maybe in fancy Aes Sidhe, or down south among perfumed Souther lordlings, ye might seem a bit of a bastard. Who knows? I can say, in the North, yer a bloody hero. Whatever yer folk believe won't change that neither. Mark me."

Ben was speechless.

No one had said as much to him before. He'd spent the last two decades avoiding his name for fear it would see him hunted across Eire like a dog. That anyone might consider his sin a blessing was a thought he could scarcely comprehend. Una cleared her throat, helpfully pulling the tension toward her. Ben appreciated her effort.

"Mistress Dormer. This isn't about any erm, feelings between Ben and me. Nor personal reward for my bounty, for that matter. Ben is taking me to the High King to prevent another war, a war that my father has been eager to make since long before my birth. He considers it a family legacy. Patrick won't stop until all of you are kneeling to him as King. With my inheritance in hand, given the unrest in Tairngare... he's got his chance. Don't you see?"

"Aye," croaked Barb. "I do. But if yer, erm what d'ye call it?"

"*Geis*," Ben offered.

"Right. If it don't end for another twenty-four years, how can ye hope to get her over the border yerself? Ye have a proxy, or someone ye mean to pass her off to?"

"I mean to break the geis myself, as is my right— on Samhain. This is the swiftest possible way. If I don't take her to my father personally, I can't vouch for her safety. So much rests upon this; I have no choice but to try."

Una's face tightened in distrust. "You didn't mention *anything* about Samhain."

"I am *now*. It's a long story. One I didn't have time to explain. You'll just have to trust me."

"Humph," she sat back, eyes narrow. "More blind faith?"

"I'm not the only one keeping secrets, am I?"

Point taken, she frowned into the hearth fire.

Barb stood up. She reached into a cupboard behind her desk, which held row after row of raw hooch. As soon as she opened the cabinet the sweet, starchy smell nearly overpowered the room. Una held a hand over her nose. Barb popped a jug and sat back down, grasping a small clay cup at the corner of the desk. She filled then emptied the cup twice before she managed to look up at Ben without a quiver to her lips.

"Not Ben Maeden after all, are ye?"

His mouth twitched. "Sorry for it, Barb."

"Bleedin' sneaky bastard, ye are. All this feckin' time, and the Ard Ri's brat in this bloody house drinkin' me swill, and swithin' me girls. Ye owe me a king's ransom for all that too," she guffawed and poured another cup. "What should we call ye then? Yer highness? Yer royal... arseness?"

"Ben will do."

"Oh aye, 'spose ye'd not want the rest o'the lads to know, would ye?"

"Not yet."

"Right," she made a face after a particularly long gulp. "Ye don't know this, but me Da fought at Dumnain with Robin."

Ben's head snapped around to meet his friend's scarred face. "Oh?"

"He lived, cuz o'ye. Same as me man there," she pointed at Robin. "Look, ye don't owe me nothin'... yer highness. I'll sort Gilcannon. I'll not have a prince dirty his hands on our account."

"Barb—" Robin tried to cut in.

She splayed her fingers. "What would ye have me do, love? He's not a bleedin' assassin, is he? He's the Crown feckin' Prince!"

Ben knew the sprout of an argument when he heard one. "No, Barb. I'll keep my word. It'll be trouble if you suddenly agreed to help me without any profit. I'll do this, and gladly. I've been waiting for an opportunity to gut that malicious pederast for years."

"But—"

"No 'buts.'" Leaning over her desk, he gave her one of Ben Maeden's most persuasive grins. "Besides, it's still me in here, Barb. Don't tell me you'd treat me differently just because you found out my Da is rich?"

Her answering grin was slow but dramatic. "All right then… Ben. Do yer worst. I'll keep yer girls safe until you get back… if ye come back, that is."

"That's more like it." Ben jerked his chin at Robin, "Shall we? I'd hate to think Matt's feeling safe and secure in that gauche pink fortress of his."

Una got to her feet, aiming to follow them to the door.

Ben held up a hand. "*No*. You stay here."

She bristled. Her lovely cheeks burned a dusky rose. "If you think you're leaving me behind, you're a fool." The top of her head barely grazed his sternum, but the look in her eyes might have made her ten feet tall or more.

Ben forced himself to look away. "You'll get in the way."

"I'm worth ten of your Greenmakers, and you know it."

"Hey now!" Robin wagged a finger at her. "That's rude."

"Nonetheless, true."

Ben shoved him through the door into the hall before he could return sally. Noting Una's furious glare, Ben paused in the narrow opening.

"Una… just this once, please don't be a pain in the arse."

She drew in a breath to berate him, but his fingers caught at a loose coil of her dark golden hair, halting her argument in its tracks. Her hair was dark at the root, like rich molasses, but golden at the ends, like burnished gold. When contrasted with her dark skin and bright eyes, she was so beautiful that it made his teeth ache. Ben repressed a groan.

"Get some sleep while I'm gone. A bath, some food, and a drink, maybe? You look… like shite." He shot her a wink before shutting the door on her furious retort.

Ben followed Robin downstairs and into the tap below, chuckling to himself.

The Hart and Hare

They'd been gone a long time. Una struggled to hide her concern, to little avail. Rian was far too astute to miss her evident disquiet over the matter. Una had nothing new to reassure the girl with, save her word, and that had worn thin hours ago. After another restless, sleepless evening in Ben's old apartment, Una strode through the charred walkway at first light to seek news. She found *The Hart* deserted but for the skeletal Colm wiping tankards behind the bar and a smattering of workers who darted about with brooms or rags.

Colm scowled at her approach. "Bit early for ale, missus." He sucked a browning tooth at her. Una flexed her fingers with exaggerated effort. He jerked into the shelves behind the bar. Tankards and bottles clanked together ominously.

Batting her lashes, she said, "I'm looking for Barb, not ale."

Colm's Adam's apple bobbed. "She don't usually come down afore noon. We keep late hours round here."

Una failed to curb a sneer. "Undoubtedly. Where might I find her then?"

"Oh, missus. Ye don't wanna poke that bear."

"Do you imagine I'm afraid of your boss?"

"If ye was smart, ye would be. Anyway, I imagine ye mean to ask her about yer man, Robin, and Gerry?"

"He's *not* my man. Mister ah—"

"Colm."

"Right. How do you know what I meant to ask?"

He rolled a bony shoulder, then carefully placed another glass on the shelf. "I run this place, don't I? The day-to-day that is. Ain't much goes down in here that I don't know about. To answer ye, before Barb graces us all with her presence— no, there ain't been word."

"Do you know where they've gone?"

"Aye, but I'm the only one down here that does, and I'd keep it to yerself, I was ye. Barb don't want it bandied about."

"I should say not." Una sank onto a stool with a groan. She watched as kitchen hands scrubbed the flagstones in both mammoth stone hearths. Looking around, Una must admit that *The Hart and Hare* was the best-appointed tavern she'd ever been in. Not that she'd had occasion to visit many, given her seclusion within the Cloister. She supposed vice had a way with profit that reputable ventures might envy. "How long have you worked here?"

He squinted. "Used to scrub pots and pans when I was a mite. Me Mam came up with Barb, ye know. A bit older'n her, but she were one o'Barb's Da's best girls."

"Your mother was a… erm."

"Oh aye, she were a right smart businesswoman in her day. Set by enough for me to have a bit o'letterin' and pay me dues to the Guild. We lived better'n most, I must say."

"You're proud of her?"

He gave her an odd look. "Why *not*? Thanks to her, I had schoolin', food in me belly, a roof over me head, and a job set up. Me mam was a fine woman."

"But she had to... don't you think that's a terrible fate?"

Colm leaned close, his expression inscrutable. "Cuz yer a lady who comes from a far fancier set of folks than us, I'm inclined to let that insult pass."

"I didn't mean—"

"I know what ye meant. Maybe in the Red City, lasses have better odds and more choices? In Rosweal, they make do. Though, I daresay they have it easier than them poor Souther ladies. At least here, they have a choice."

"I assume you're equating respectable matrons with women desperate enough to sell themselves for food. I don't buy that."

"Them that marry for position, wealth, or title— how is that so different?"

"I can't speak to Souther ethics, but in Tairngare, women are not required to sell themselves to men for any reason. They're edified, encouraged, and empowered to decide their paths. Survival shouldn't cost one's dignity."

"Aye, in bloody grand Tairngare where the Parliament is so corrupt, a Union Charter may only be purchased by sacrificing one's daughters to the Cloister. How is that different from a father sellin' his girls to a brothel?"

"That is a gross misrepresentation. Novas are given to the Cloister to be educated. To learn to hone their Spark, to study the mysteries."

"No," Colm held up a finger. "They're *sold* to the Cloister to serve the uppity womenfolk what run the city from behind those heavy walls, all so the family can sit back fancy on her stipend. Why don't ye ask Barb about that, love? Her mam's family sold her for that purpose. Later, she was tossed out on her ear for mentionin' the unfairness of the arrangement. Girls what don't have the right name languish in service so their families can use their earnin's to climb the ranks. If that ain't prostitution, I don't know what is."

Una's cheeks burned hot. "That's not a fair comparison *in the least*."

"Name me one common girl, ever made the rank o'Prima, wasn't sponsored by one of the great families?"

Una couldn't, as he knew she couldn't. He took a peek at her stymied expression and poured her a tall tankard of cider. "No disrespect intended, missus. Just see ye judge fair. Society o'any sort makes whores of us *all*."

It took Una quite a while to find her voice again. "I apologize if I gave your mother insult, Colm."

"None needed, milady. There's more'n one sort o'education, I spose."

Una hadn't come down here intending to offend anyone, yet she had. Almost immediately at that. Wasn't she above classist drivel? Apparently not. She sipped at her cider in silent shame. Colm went about his work as if the stool she sat upon remained unoccupied. She'd never been upbraided like that before. The fact that she'd earned it only made her embarrassment more acute. While she mulled over her ideological arrogance, a few shadows passed before the mottled windows. The heavy oak door rattled under the weight of several fists.

"Siora's cunny!" Colm slammed his rag down on the counter. "Feck off! We're bloody closed!"

"Who'd come out at this hour?"

"No one that means to let me get on with me work," Colm scowled at her. Una flushed anew, knowing she deserved that comment too.

Something heavier than a fist struck the door from outside. Colm's expression darkened. "Mickey!" he called, reaching below the bar for a vicious wired cudgel. "Get Dean and Dabs, and someone better wake Barb. Don't take yer time, neither!"

"What's happening?"

"Ye should get upstairs, missus."

Una watched the custodians scramble into the kitchens with real panic on their faces. "Does this sort of thing happen often?"

"Nope. Must've been waitin' for the all-clear."

"Gilcannon?"

"Aye." An object rammed into the glass full force, and they both jumped. "I bleedin' *told* Barb we needed more men down here today."

"They were waiting for Robin to leave?"

"Takin' third o'our forces with him too, yeah. I told Barb as much last night. If I were Matt, it's what I'd do, sure."

"How can I help?"

He gave her a long, appraising look. "Ye ain't gonna run?"

"And leave you here alone? No. I can handle myself."

The door bent inward on its hinges. A large crack split the main window down its center. Colm nodded at her. "Aye, I'll say that much for ye, at least. Come 'round here. There's a sticker in me boot."

Una hopped over the bar as the door splintered. A bevy of laughter shook the window casings. There must have been dozens of them out there. Una knelt behind the bar to retrieve Colm's dagger, then slipped behind him, ready. The window took a second impact and the door another.

"I dunno what ye did to Paul, but I hope ye got more o'that in ye."

The window crashed inward before Una could formulate a reply.

⚒

LYING FLAT ON THE ROOFTOP, Robin passed his glass back to Ben. "There's somethin' happenin' down there. Somethin' wrong. Have a look."

Ben took a drink from his water skin, then replaced the stopper with a grunt. His back was to the wall, beside the gap. He waved the glass away. "No need. They know we're here."

"Feckin' Hilltop cunts. Why'd we spend all that time sneakin' round them sewers, anyway?"

"So they wouldn't know *where* we are, at least." Ben snuck a glance through the crevice. Matt's house gleamed a vivid pink in the early morning sunlight. No one was about, which was highly irregular. Gilcannon might as well have hung a sign on the front door with 'TRAP' written in bold red script.

"I don't like it, Ben. There's no tellin' how many fellas he's got down there."

"Doesn't matter."

"Yer sure enough now?" snorted Robin.

"See that row of windows on the second floor?"

"Aye, so?"

"That's Matt's office."

"How d'ye know?"

"Even if Vincent hadn't filled me in, it's obvious. It's the only room in the house with open shutters. I might add that candles in the window were a fairly desperate touch."

"He wants us to attack from the front?"

"Doubt he cares either way, so long as we believe that's where he's held up."

"So, what's yer plan then?"

"I think surprise has lost its luster," Ben sighed. "Call Gerry back. We'll have to come at this another way."

Robin signaled to Seamus on the opposite end of the rooftop, who whistled back in a perfect imitation of a marsh swallow, common as grass in this part of Eire. One whistle in return meant that Gerrod understood. Two that he was moving shop.

179

"Wait." Ben paused. He caught the barest hint of something in the courtyard: a dark flash, which was out of place against Matt's vivid color selection. Ben jerked the glass from Robin. In the courtyard, a bit of fabric flapped in the wind— black on gold. The cloth was tucked tight against the rear of the building. The wearer tried very hard to remain out of sight. Ben had only managed to detect it by focusing hard on the outer edges of the house. He cursed long and low in his mother tongue.

"What's that mean then?"

"Something fucking uncouth." Ben took a second peek through the glass. All of a sudden, it was gone. Ben handed Robin's spyglass back. "Call Gerry to our side of the street. We need to regroup. Now."

"Why? What'd ye see?"

"*Tairnganeah*. Gilcannon invited the Corsairs to Rosweal."

UNA WAS A BIT RUSTY at this. She might have been somewhat proficient with a rapier or even moderately adequate with a crossbow once upon a time—long before she submitted to the Eighth Ordeal at age twenty. For the past six years, she'd been getting fairly soft in the library while she crammed for the Ninth Ordeal. To say she was out of practice was an understatement. Long daggers were never her forte. Colm's was easily the entire length of her forearm. She leapt over the prone bodies of the two boys Colm put down, then swung around to intercept a knife reaching for his kidney.

There were too many of them.

Una and Colm were squeezed back-to-back to ward off a boiling tide of elbows, knees, and sharp objects. Youths clambered behind the bar with whatever weapons they could muster. Some ran for the stairs and met with considerable resistance from above. Dabney's roar filled the tavern to the rafters. He swung left and right with his cudgel, sending men flying from their feet and over the railing. Dean protected Dabney's flanks with a pair of daggers, just like Una was attempting to do for Colm. A blow to her midsection sent her scraping backward. A line of blood opened up at her collarbone. Una grunted and ducked low. She brought the flat of her blade up into the crook of one boy's knee. He went down with a screech. Almost simultaneously, someone grabbed her by her nape and dragged her from Colm's side.

With her head jerked back, her attacker was able to hook an arm around her throat. The youth smashed her into the bar, and the air whooshed out of her in a rush. Her dagger skittered away. As his humid, stale breath assaulted her face, her attacker's hands fumbled at the collar of her tunic. Una dug her fingertips into his forehead.

"*Boil*," she hissed. Going limp, he crashed to the rushes in a wailing fit. She didn't wait to watch the fluids burst from his nose and eye sockets. Another set of hands reached for her. Una smacked them into the wooden bar with both palms. "*Break*," she commanded. Every one of this lad's finger bones snapped beneath his skin, bending each digit at an unnatural angle. He bolted from the tavern, screaming. When the next boy hacked at her with a short cleaver, Una jumped onto the bar to avoid its path. She grabbed her assailant from behind, crammed her nails into the fellow's neck, and crushed his face against the bar with her left hand. Taking a deep breath, she reached out with her Spark, drawing deep into the boy's core. A river of stolen vitality flowed into her blood, which she put to immediate use.

Una's right palm slid over the bar, heedless of the shriveling creature she held captive against it. Anyone that had been thinking about making a grab for her took a wary step back. The wood below her hand warped and rippled— as if billeted by an unseen wind. The lacquered surface became a puddle at first, then a roiling stream into which various hands and feet sank. Panic set in. Those who could not get away fast enough called out to their comrades for aid. Instantly, the fight fizzled out of half a dozen young men. They looked on in horror as their companions descended into the oak surface: two to their elbows, one to his thigh. The last, having been knocked onto the bar by Colm's cudgel, plunged in face first. Una removed her hand, and the bar smoothed over, solid once more… except for the various figures trapped within the wood. Those that could, bellowed frantically at the top of their lungs. As suddenly as the fight started, it stopped. Every combatant in *The Hart* paused to gawp at this terrible marvel, as if their eyes somehow deceived them.

"Witch!" cried one of Gilcannon's boys. A leader of sorts, he held out an arm to keep any of his foolhardier companions from rushing at her. Colm threw another unconscious boy to the floor. For a wiry fellow, Colm didn't lack strength. The speaker's cheeks purpled. "Ye feckin' witch! *What did ye do?*"

"What I'll do to all of you, if you don't leave," she promised, wiping at the seeping wound on her collarbone. She was sick of being cut, struck, shoved, pulled, or otherwise manhandled. The Greenmakers, having rallied on the second floor, had dumped most of their foes over the balustrade. *The Hart's* Hilltop assailants had lost their advantage. Eyes agog, Colm crept around the bar, careful not to disturb the bodies trapped within its glossy oak facade. As for the victim stuck to the thigh, his snivels degenerated into full shrieks. With a sardonic smirk, Una tapped her nails near his left elbow. His remaining comrades didn't wait around to witness further horrors visited upon one of their own. They darted for the busted door as if their trousers were on fire. "Do you want out, boy?" asked Una.

Her victim's nostrils flared. Chest heaving, he looked around for anyone at all who might help him. No one moved a muscle, save Dabney, who moaned his way back up to the second landing. He was petrified of Una, and that fear was catching. *The Hart's* defenders stared at her like men possessed.

"Ple... ase," the boy cried. Gobs of snot bubbled down his chin. His friend beside him wept openly; his arms were quick to the biceps in unyielding wood. Another dangled awkwardly from his fists, in a stone-dead faint. The last, who'd fallen in to the shoulder, would never move again.

None of them had seen a day over sixteen winters.

"I want you to tell me why you're here, lad. You should hurry before I lose the remainder of my patience. I may decide you should drown in that bar, like your friend there."

Barb shoved her way through the line of Greenmakers into the taproom. "What in the *bloody hells* is all this then? *Siora,*" her eyes bugged out of her skull. "Milady... what in the name of the sweet Ancestor have ye *done?*"

The boy blubbered. Ignoring everyone, Una focused on him with a purposefully cruel grin. "Tell me what I want to know, this instant, and I'll let you go."

"M-Matt sent us."

"Why?"

"To distract ye."

"From?"

"Them soldiers needed time to... missus, please! *It hurts*! Hurts so bad!"

Barb stepped over the corpse of the first assailant Una put down; the gases and fluids in his skull still burbled into the rushes. Barb paid him no mind. "What soldiers? Where?"

"You'd better answer her question lad." Una flexed her fingers by his jaw. He jerked, battling desperately to get out of the wood as a rabbit fights a snare. After only a few moments, he gave up. All the blood drained from his cheeks.

Barb slapped him awake. "Answer the feckin' question, boy! What bloody soldiers?"

"Tairnganeah, missus," said the other, who was probably younger than his compatriot. Fat tears rolled clean streaks down his otherwise grimy jowls. He set fearful, hateful green eyes on Una. "They came for the witch."

⚔

No bloody wonder, Ben thought, tracking the train of Hilltop thugs and Tairnganese soldiers through the Quarter.

This was a clever trap.

181

As it turned out, Matt wasn't in residence at all. If Ben hadn't caught that hint of fabric flapping on the breeze, they'd have walked right into a nest of fully armed Corsairs. *Very clever, indeed.* Slinking along rooftops on their way back to Taverner's Alley, the full scope of the Greenmakers' near-miss dawned. There were easily one hundred soldiers winding toward *The Hart*, spears aloft, rapiers and crossbows strapped to their wide gold belts. Gerrod signaled from the row of roofs on his left, and Ben whistled a response. Robin, who breathed hard from the effort required to descend over slick shingles and rain-soaked gutters, looked up at Ben with a heavy frown.

"I see him, just there," Robin pointed. "Not at the front exactly, but close enough. Yellow cloak, the bloody dandy. Ye see him?"

"Yes," Ben growled. He handed the glass back to Robin. "There's Sol Trant, sitting beside him."

"I hope ye didn't expect that he'd honor any deal ye mighta made? That weasel would sell his mam if he thought there'd be profit for hisself in it."

Ben rather liked Sol. A shame the old man wouldn't live to see nightfall. "No matter. Obviously, Matt took a deal of his information from Sol, but I doubt he's the only turncoat we need to manage today."

"Oh, aye." Robin squinted into the eyepiece. "Sam's there too, with his Souther sabre. Ye can count on him followin' his brother's lead. Two Trants means the brewery must be hurtin' for profits."

"I imagine Barb will love having a distillery *and* the best brewery in the North."

"Yer daft. We're outnumbered over three to one."

Ben slid forward on his belly, then shimmied down a tin gutter to get a peek out the drainage hole. In a long line, soldiers were wedged in the alleyways below, perhaps three abreast.

"We've got vantage and arrows aplenty. Tairnganese crossbows aren't worth shite, and their spears are too long to avail them much use. Seems they've just made it easier for us."

"Wonderful. Gonna take the thirty o'us against that lot of professional murderers down there?"

"Don't tell me you'd rather there were more?"

"Course I do," Robin scoffed. "I worry for my reputation, ye know? We'll take many of 'em from up top, but not all."

"Well, it wouldn't be any fun if we could, would it?"

Robin pulled an arrow out of its quiver, jerking his longbow over his head. "'Spose not. Singles or doubles?"

Ben drew down. He counted the nearest dozen men as they milled between tightly packed buildings. "Doubles."

Robin gave the signal with a dramatic roll of eyes. "Had to make it more interestin?'"

"Nah, just cheap. Why waste ammunition when they've made it this easy for us?"

⚜

"SEND THE HERETIC OUT," THE voice outside boomed, *"and we won't press our advantage."* Una thought the speaker looked slightly familiar, with his long braids and handsome dark eyes. Then again, she'd seen most of these men before, hadn't she? A Tairnganeah Cohort with gold cuirasses and long hazel spears gathered behind mounted Corsairs. The Regulars were lined up in neat little rows, awaiting orders. There must have been at least thirty Corsairs out there, all told. She couldn't even begin to count the Cohort. Sixty, maybe? More? Rian clutched at Una's arm, seemingly frightened. Una knew better. She was attempting to steady her.

"Siora," Rian mused. "How'd they get this many in here so fast?"

"Thanks to that pompous lecher standin' below a sign what reads '*Solomon's*,' down the lane there," Barb jeered from the bar. She carefully sidestepped a greasy puddle of blood where one of Matt's boys had met a grisly end to pour herself a healthy portion of cider. She didn't bother looking through the broken windowpanes as Dabs and Dean were busy piling tables, chairs, and anything else they could find into the gap. "See him?"

Rian peeked through the barricaded door. "Bright yellow cloak, a bit of a paunch?"

"That's the one," Barb nodded into her pint. "As I said, yer men out there weren't makin' it no secret they was searchin' for ye. Out in bloody force for it too, ye ask me. Matt's an opportunist, same as the rest o' us."

Una scowled over her shoulder. "Well, here's your big chance. See what terms you can make for me."

Rian squeezed her bicep somewhat hard. "No, Una. They'll kill you."

"They'll kill all of *you* if I don't." Una unwound Rian's fingers from her bruised flesh. "Barb knows it as well as I do."

"Can ye do to them what ye did to this lot here?" Barb gestured to the pile of mangled bodies stacked by the stairs. Una had released her victims from the bar, but what remained of their limbs was a corrugated mess of shredded skin and torn muscles. The lad who'd been stuck fast to the thigh would surely lose the leg now— if he ever woke up again, that is.

"Not all of them. I could probably take any that laid hands on me, but en masse, they'd have the better of me, and they know it."

"Then, we wait for the boys. We ain't exactly defenseless in here, are we?" More Greenmakers filtered through the upstairs walkway. Some had been sent out on the rooftop to tuck themselves against the shingles, short bows drawn. Others gathered at the windows or guarded the walls shy of the door, waiting for anyone to try the barricade. They had perhaps fifteen men downstairs and ten more upstairs, guarding the walkway and alley. Barb sent Colm up on the roof with the archers, which rounded the bulk of their forces to twenty-two. Spread over two large rooftops, the archers were the single best line of defense they had.

"We're outnumbered," Una said flatly. She stepped away from the crack in the window so the Greenmakers could finish their rudimentary barricade. Dean moved aside for her with an ugly scowl on his face. He didn't speak to or look at her, and she sensed a deep hostility within him. Well, that was to be expected. Aside from the day's events, she'd drained his friend and would-be rapist dry as toast— as Paul had deserved. Nonetheless, she understood the unfairness of the situation for everyone else. This wasn't their fight. The tense, tight-lipped malice she detected on scores of faces didn't escape her notice either. Una realized they were afraid of her. She'd seen and done things these simple folks would barely comprehend, not all of it good. Una was well aware of the disparity between them. Why should they suffer for her? A Siorai priestess? A disgraced noblewoman from a corrupt, power-hungry family? She couldn't blame them for their distaste, nor for their reaction to the situation she'd brought down upon them.

"There is no point to this. I will go out."

"Do that, and they'll burn this place down anyway." Rian's fair cheeks flamed scarlet. "You're not a fool, so don't pretend to be one."

"You don't know that, Rian."

"Yes, I do! *You* didn't cause the problem here. You're merely a convenient scapegoat. That fat man at the end of the lane there is using these soldiers to settle a personal grudge. She knows it too!" Rian waved at Barb but didn't stop there. Folding her thin arms over her chest, she narrowed her cornflower eyes at the gathering. "You *all* know it. If Una steps outside that door, you're dead. That Gilcannon character will have beaten you. Is that what you want?"

"They won't get us all," Dean argued in his rich baritone. "Seems to me, with *her* outta the way, our archers up top'll keep 'em honest."

A half-hearted round of 'ayes' followed this statement.

Rose, sans cosmetics and looking much older than she'd first appeared, sighed from her seat on the stairs. She wore a simple brown homespun tunic. Her unironed hair floated about her shoulders in a lustrous black cloud. "No offense, little miss, but we ain't all fighters in here. Some o' us have little-uns or elderly folks to look after. We can't afford to take the chance."

"*… or face the might of the Citadel Corsairs,*" the voice outside continued. "*The Heretic, one Una Moura Donahugh, has been judged by the Common Collective Alliance in Parliament, and by the people of Tairngare, as an imperialist fraud and treasonous defiler of Siora's Sacred Laws. For these offenses, she is condemned to….*"

"I have a little daughter," added Violet from beside Rose. "She'll starve without me."

"Aye," said another girl from the balcony. "We all have someone."

"*… immediately, or we will be forced to burn this establishment to the ground and execute any who attempt to flee….*"

"I don't mean to die for ye today, or any day, missus," Dean curled his lip at Una. "Even if ye was the Queen of bloody Innisfail, as yer bloody grandmam vows, I'd still not die for ye. Yer naught but trouble, I say. Maeden shoulda never brung ye here."

"Now, now." Barb set her pint down. "Watch yer manners, me lad. Trouble or no, the faerie girl has the right o'things. Matt's done this, not this lass. I don't like her neither, but that's not the point. No offense, girl."

"Feeling's mutual," Una shrugged.

"She's just an excuse for Matt to snatch *The Hart*. To have done with the Greenmakers, all at once. If I wasn't so bleedin' furious at his brass, I'd be impressed by the neat little stack he's made o'things here."

Dean held out a hand to the tangle of fearful, angry expressions. "We coulda handled Matt if this gash hadn't brought the Red City's troubles into Rosweal."

"If you call me that again," Una drifted close, "you won't live long enough to finish your rant."

Dean went three shades lighter and dropped his hand. Rose was made of more potent stuff. She stood up; her fingers wound tightly through Violet's.

"I have nothin' against ye, milady, please believe that, but I have to think on my family. We all do."

Una's smile was rueful. "I'm very sorry for the trouble I've caused you. All of you. I will do whatever is necessary to keep anything worse from happening. I vow it."

Rian growled into her hands. "*No.* You're all missing the point. They don't care whether you send her out or not. They can't march in here unscathed just yet, and they know it. They don't know how many people are in here or that you have archers on the roof. If you send her out, they'll throw torches through the cracks in the windows. They'll burn the entire block, just to be sure. They could set fire to the place now, but that wouldn't guarantee they'd killed the one they were after. Do any of you follow?"

Barb folded her hands. "Aye, I believe yer makin' a case for keepin' them windows shuttered and waitin' till they march them foot soldiers in here."

"Yes," Rian agreed. "Have your archers shoot the Corsairs from their saddles. Funnel the remnants through the walkway. You could pick them off like rats."

Dean gave a harsh, biting laugh. "Why should we bother? We could sooner run out thatta way, ourselves."

"Because, ye bloody half-wit," Barb balked, "they'll burn me livelihood to the ground. Matt feckin' Gilcannon will be yer new boss, by default. Next time Dean opens his mouth, Dabs, knock his feckin' teeth down his throat."

Sloe-eyed, Dabney nodded. "Missus."

"*… not comply in a reasonable order, we will….*"

Rian pressed her advantage. "I know this is hard; believe me, I empathize. If you give her up, they'd have no reason to leave your Quarter intact. If you give her to them, they'll burn you out for spite, or because that Gilcannon character has paid them handsomely to do so. Either way, our only chance is to let them know they have no choice but to fight for her."

"Maran?" said Barb.

"Missus?" a kitchen hand called back.

"Head up and tell Colm to kill that loudmouth on the grey first." Barb dumped her empty tankard into the stone sink behind the bar. "And I want Missy, Ronald, and Beal up along that walkway."

"Aye," said the lad. He squeezed past the girls on his way upstairs.

"*… respond? If not, we will….*"

"Dean, ye gonna fight, or do ye want me to send ye out to offer yerself to Matt now?"

Dean sent Una a nasty look, which she roundly ignored. "But, Missus—"

"Choose now." Dabney stepped closer to Dean; his bulky fists prepared to deliver the blow Barb ordered. "I'll not have a half-hearted sissy in my employ. Yer either a Greenmaker, or yer buggered."

He stretched to his full height. "I'm a Greenmaker, Barb. I swear it."

"Good. Ye'll stand at the windows with Dabs, Ned, and Hal. Anythin' tries to get through, I want it to lose a limb. Ye hear me?"

"Yeah."

Stalking around the bar, she waved at Una and Rian. "Ye two, upstairs with the girls and me. Whatever tables we have left, I want 'em stacked up at the second landin'. One thing we got plenty of is arrows. Yancy, George? I want ye to gather up every bow, crossbow, arrow, and cudgel ye can pull up from the cellar— and be quick about it."

"They'll throw torches in the windows, eventually," Una said. "Once they start losing men, they'll fall back on the dependable."

"Well." Barb patted her shoulder almost affectionately. "Let's hope we kill enough o'em that it don't happen too fast, eh?"

Best Laid Plans

The Greenmakers took their time advancing along the Tairnganeah's rear line. Careful to make as little noise as possible, Ben and company inched from rooftop to rooftop on the balls of their feet, hiding behind chimneys, trestles, and windbreakers. Gerrod's group claimed the first victims on the south side of the alley. Foot soldiers at the back with little protection from overhead attacks pitched soundlessly to the muddy cobbles, unbeknownst to their comrades in the forward line.

Stealth and speed were the Greenmakers' allies. For a while, anyway. Fifteen men fell under their arrows at the first flash, then eighteen, twenty, and nearly twenty-two. The Greenmakers' luck was not to last, however. A dead soldier rolled into the group ahead, where the alley spilled downhill into the Quarter. One of Robin's arrows protruded from his right eye. In a panic, soldiers jostled for cover. They stumbled into one another like pins in a bowler's game. Commands were shouted, and easily thirty-five pairs of eyes marked the two groups of archers taking aim from above. Gold shields came up, and crossbows were hastily loaded. Despite the ensuing crush in the narrow lane below, several bolts hammered into the wall near Ben's head. He threw his arm around a weathervane to keep himself from incidentally tumbling down the drain.

"Shite!" Wincing, he jammed a boot into a jagged crevice to take some of gravity's punishment. "Robin, I might have underestimated those crossbows a bit."

"Ye think?" Robin took a glancing blow along the crown of his shoulder. The man behind him took one through the throat. With a curse, Robin retrieved the fellow's quiver before the body tumbled into the alley. Ben dodged one quarrel, then another. "Suppose our presence has been noted. A shame because I was rather enjoying myself for a bit there."

Seamus' chin hit the tin roof with a loud bang as he dipped beneath the next volley. "Feckin' tits! Tell me one o'ye had a backup plan?"

"I don't appreciate yer tone, whelp." Robin struggled to nock his short bow. "O'course, we got a plan. Erm, don't we, Ben?"

Having scooted to the edge of the wall, Ben lobbed fallen bricks, tiles, pots... whatever he could summon to hand. "We'll have to backtrack. Cross over to the south side with Gerry and the others."

Seamus muttered something rude into the soot-stained puddle beneath his chin. A torch fizzled past the lip in the wall, and they watched it turn over in the air. It skidded to a sputtering stop by Robin's knee. "Feckin' idiots. Don't they know it's too bloody damp for that? They should toss them inside. What sort of soldier don't know that?"

Seamus dragged the hissing missile toward him. "Grab any o'them ye can before they fizzle out."

As he spoke, a second torch sailed over the wall. Ben shimmied toward it on his backside and kicked it over with the toe of his boot. "You got an idea?"

"Might do." Seamus ducked under the next volley of quarrels and wormed a little brown leather pouch out of his waistband.

Robin raised his brows sky-high at the sight. "Feckin' hell! Ye've been keeping bloody *gunpowder* in yer trousers?"

"Got plenty of saltpeter left after slaughterin' that bull last month. Figured 'twas a shame to waste the leavins. Hand me that torch, Ben, thanks."

"How long you been carryin' that around?"

"For a bit. Me and Colm thought to give it a go for winter. We had the peter, and a stock o'sulfur we nicked from that tinker last spring. This here's a test batch. Didn't think 'bout it till now."

"Yer a mad bastard, Seamus." Robin shook his head. A bolt passed through his sleeve. He snatched his arm back from the wall. "Whatever ye aim to do, make it quick, will ye? I don't fancy bein' shot or blown to the nine hells."

Seamus accepted the flask of rotgut spirits Donell passed over to him. Next, he tore a shred from his tunic, soaked it in raw uishge, and dropped a tiny pile of powder into the rag.

"Ye'll wanna back off, just in case I muck this up."

Everyone squeezed as far away from him as gravity or ammunition would allow. When the next volley launched over the wall, Seamus stood up. Quick as an adder, he slapped the wad into the hissing flame, and dropped the torch before the rag made contact. "Get down!"

The resulting boom wasn't overly dramatic, but the answering cries from the unfortunate soldiers below were. A cheer went up from the opposite rooftop. Ben grinned from ear to half-deafened ear. Robin threw back his head and laughed. "Don't think they were expectin' that!"

Seamus shredded two more strips from his shirt. "Hand me that second torch…"

⚔

Despite the Tairnganeah's impressive turnout, there wasn't much wiggle room through Rosweal's winding, illogical alleyways. Matt figured as much when he opened the Navan Gate for the Corsairs only yesterday. These mounted dandies cut fine figures, with their gleaming armor embossed with coiling blue dragons. Quite handsome, indeed. All were rather large men, well-muscled, and scrupulously clean. No simple feat for fellas who'd been in the saddle for the better part of a month, hunting an escaped heretic. Matt supposed he might have been temporarily dazzled by their initial presentation. The second sons of aristocratic families were often wealthy enough for the smartest kits. Too fine, however, by half. In Matt's experience, *real* soldiers didn't make a habit of style. Once upon a time, Corsairs from the Red City did not prance and preen. There was no need. They were worthy of the fear that the blue dragons inspired. Times had changed. This new batch dressed the part, but that was all they had on offer.

Matt was seated at a short round table under a wide awning outside Solomon's, and sipping the finest ale in the North, Matt had a front-row seat to a miserable show. Rosweal was a tricky beast to tame. He understood this better than most. Though, the Tairnganeah he recalled from his youth were a far cry from the foppish showmen who were failing him now. Matt folded hoary hands over his well-fed belly. His mouth curled up slightly at the left corner, twisting his manicured mustache into a semicolon. This was hardly worth watching at all, was it?

Sol, who hovered like an agitated bee, wiped nervous hands up and down his spotless apron for the dozenth time in the last thirty minutes. The Tairnganeah had broken *The Hart's* windows. That was good. Then, the Corsairs' captain made his demands. That was good too… but not long after, the situation soured. Sol wasn't taking the spectacle as impassively as Matt. Sol's fat brother Sam was preoccupied with stuffing his swollen jowls with cold ham. Sol's fidgeting seemed to target Matt exclusively.

"Matt?"

"Don't ask again, Sol."

The meek little brewer wasn't as eager a convert as Matt wished him to be, and the fact rankled Matt's already taxed nerves. Sol crossed his skinny arms as if to buoy himself in the gale of Matt's glare.

"What if—?"

"We'll burn 'em out ourselves, won't we?" Sam offered pork smacking odiously over his brown teeth. He tugged a greasy thumb at Matt. "He's got it all worked out, Sol. These shites will soften 'em up for us, and we'll take it to the finish after. Easy."

Sol wasn't convinced. He claimed to have heard several loud booms when he'd made his rounds through the brewery an hour earlier. Matt hadn't heard any such thing for the racket outside *The Hart and Hare*. Sam had only stopped stuffing his face long enough to drop into a periodical upright doze. Of the Hilltop Boys that hadn't fled back to the slums for fear of the Siorai witch inside, only a few answered his summons. Matt had been told what had transpired inside was a horrific scene, the likes of which he'd only read about. Still, he noted the ones who stayed. He would reward them with extra rations once this ugly business was properly sorted. These few remaining boys stalked the alley, forward and aft, providing a bit of useful human fodder between himself and any stray arrows which managed to make it this far down the lane.

"All I'm sayin' is, shouldn't we prepare for things to turn the other way? Ye don't know Ben Maeden as I do, Matt. Ye can't hang yer cap on the hope that ye've outwitted him. He's a canny bastard, and I daresay, a better fighter than this lot." Sol gestured toward the dead Corsairs lying face-down in the mud outside *The Hart* spotted with arrows, glass, wood shards, and anything else the Greenmakers could call to hand. Their archers started shooting before the final demands left the fine young captain's mouth, then immediately went to work on any fellow not wise enough to dismount and flee or ride up to higher ground.

Matt lit his prized ivory pipe with a sneer. "What *is* this horseshite anyway? Ye can't steal a ribbon in any town along the border without hearin' tales o'what the Tairnganeah do to thieves and traders what don't pay their respects to the Merchanta." He spat into the muddy cobbles. "What a load of tripe! Look at these bleedin' pansies. There can't be more than forty men and women inside or up top. The way they're chargin' straight forward with them useless spears, ye'd think there was five hunnerd."

Blessedly done gnawing on ripe hunks of meat, Sam Trant let out a long odiferous belch. "Aye, they do turn out rather bad, don't they? Spears're only good for open ground. Why'd they bring 'em here, where ye can leap from one door to another without getting yer feet wet, I'd be buggered to know?"

Matt couldn't believe what he was seeing. He remembered an entirely different sort of soldiery, some twenty years past. He'd been in the fight for Eirean freedom on the fields at Dumnain. He recalled the discipline, the hip-to-shoulder lines the Tairnganeah made, marching down the lists. His youthful admiration of the Tairnganese infantry had impressed upon him for most of his life. Either Matt had simply been enchanted by the vibrant colors snapping in the breeze or the flash of gold on their cuirasses because *these* were not the same glorious warriors he'd imagined all those years before.

"Please. Ye don't know. I heard—" Sol buzzed in his ear.

Matt and Sam ignored him.

"Ye know." Sam sat up straighter, pushing the table out with his girth. Matt was hardly slim any more than Sam was, but he at least was conscious of himself. He took pride in his presentation and bearing. Sam Trant was a butcher and cheesemaker of little repute— when he wasn't financing cutpurses from the slums to harry Merchers on the road, that is. Sam had been a disgusting slob as long as Matt had known him, but a clever one, all the same. "I don't think this lot has seen a fight in near thirty years, so I reckon. Not that that's a bad bit, but it don't serve to make 'em shine in a scuffle." He shook his meaty head.

Matt sniffed. "I think it's more to do with politics. The Libella's losing control— power like that just don't last. The upper classes are so wealthy that they've gone soft. I hear a rich family on the climb can purchase commissions in the Citadel for a song now that Drem's star has waned over the past ten years. That new Alta Prima, Nema, I think... she's been in control o'the office o'the Union Registry all that time and been sellin' Patents of Maternas cheap to families that would never've dared to try and ascend to the nobles' ranks. Ye got wine merchants from Cymru, sons o'tanners, and Agrean small landowners. Most o'these boys never held a sword 'fore their parents bought their commissions, I'll wager. Ain't the same anymore, I 'spose."

"Bad business, all 'round."

"Whole place is bound for the midden, ye ask me. Just look at 'em." Matt waved a bejeweled hand at the soldiers that scampered away from *The Hart*. "They shoulda trained them up from nappies like I do.

Get 'em young, and show 'em how to handle themselves properly. This just shows that money doesn't make the man… or the family, it seems."

Sol removed Matt's empty tankard with a furtive, trembling insecurity on his heavily lined face. "Matt, please…"

Matt's fist struck the tabletop, rattling the crockery. The boys around them fidgeted. They were well acquainted with Matt's infamous temper. Two large black holes peered up at Sol from below Matt's browbone.

"Solomon, *I heard ye.* We should all be scairt o'this Ben bloody Maeden. Well, I've done for him, ye can rest assured. Him and that scum-slug Gramble, both. Now, quit yer keenin.' Bring me another red ale. Any o'that stew ye have left over from last night, too. Sharpish." He waved his empty tankard back and forth for emphasis. Sol struggled with it; Matt could tell plain as his nose. But like any weasel, Sol was quick to retreat when an easy victory wasn't in the offing. With one last pleading glance at his indifferent elder brother, Solomon slunk back into the taproom to do Matt's bidding. Frowning, Matt watched him go. He cut his eyes sideways at Sam. "Ye think he'd be happier with the arrangement. Was half his bloody idea."

Sam blew his nose on a woolen sleeve. "Aye? Not even me own mam could make him happy, lo she did try. Poor lass. Died in a Tairnganese lock-up for plyin' her trade in the streets rather than pay homage to the Voluptatus. Worked herself ragged to feed and clothe us best she was able. That one—" Sam tilted an ear at the tavern door. "Never did care for what he had. Always thought hisself a bit better'n the fatherless whelp he was." His deep-throated chuckle shook the table braced against his gut.

"Always, ye say?"

Sam gulped his warm tankard and fixed a cool glare on Matt. "I can hear the cogs whirlin' in that pretty head o'yers, Matt. Don't fish around in mine for an excuse to increase yer shares."

Matt feigned perfect outrage. "I would never—"

"Ye needn't bother to lie, neither. Know this, ye make a move against Sol, after what he just done for ye, I'll shove yer own cock up yer arsehole."

"*Now see here….*"

Sam leaned over, taking most of the table with him. Matt sat back on an expelled breath. The butcher reeked of onions, sour ale, and decaying meat. "Oh, I do see, Gilcannon. We're sittin' here with ye outta necessity, not loyalty. Ye'd do best to remember that. The second I suspect ye mean to double-cross one o'us, yer a dead man. Ye think on that the next time ye plan to open that perfumed mouth o'yers."

He turned back to the petering skirmish down the lane, guffawing at the scrambling Tairnganeah. The folk inside *The Hart* gave a merry little cheer as the soldiers fled. Matt seethed in silence. The thud of his heart bore the only indication that he still breathed. Sam was not as easy as his brother. If he said he'd have Matt killed, he certainly believed he could do it. All evidence implied that he had a point. The pair of strongmen standing guard at Sam's right hand weren't known for their cultured opinions. Altxhough, Matt was hardly the man to be put in his place by the lord of pickpockets and sham men. Matt could buy and sell Samuel Trant four times over. How *dare* this jumped-up thug speak to *him* that way? Behind Matt, one of his boys tapped a fingernail against the pommel of his dagger. Matt held up a hand to still his impatient fingers.

"I'll forget ye made that threat, Sam. Today. Our work isn't finished just yet, and there's no sense to be makin' enemies o'ourselves. I have not, nor would I harm sweet Sol for bein' cautious." He'd be sure to stuff Sol's bollocks into his brother's gaping craw as soon as this was all over… but he didn't bother to broach that topic just yet. "Seems our brave soldiers've had enough."

An unhorsed Corsair dashed down the lane toward them, followed closely by three attendants. The lieutenant, a young man with dark hair twisted into the typical Tairnganese nest of complicated braids, came to a huffing halt three paces from Matt's guards. The angry, frustrated pride on the man's handsome face tickled something high in Matt's throat.

"Let me pass!" the lieutenant growled, a bloody hand on his rapier for emphasis. Matt's boys didn't blink. Some were half the size of this fellow, but their bearing made them nine feet taller, to all impressions. You can always spot a killer. A *true* killer, those who possess real menace— from the smallest street rat to the most hardened veteran. It is something in their eyes, a surety. As if they measure each individual they encounter by the effort they might spend to bring him down. Matt's boys were barely adults, but they had what this poor fancy sod did not.

What's more, the Corsair knew it instantly, like a rabbit scenting a fox. Matt observed the immediate change in the lieutenant's demeanor. He stepped back a pace and licked his lips. Fabian, a lad of thirteen, glared back with amused malice.

"Master Gilcannon, you swore to give us your aid!"

Matt splayed his hands. "What the sweet feck do ye call this, then? I opened the bloody gates for ye lot, didn't I? Gave ye shelter, ale, food, and women for the night. All but rolled out the purple feckin' carpet for ye."

"They have trained fighters in there!" protested the lieutenant, "Our men weren't prepared for this sort of pitched engagement."

Sam laughed so hard that the little wads of ham stuck to his teeth sprayed all over his tunic, the tankard, and the table. Repulsed, Matt twitched back. "What did ye say? Weren't yer men 'prepared' for a fight? Yer trained feckin' soldiers, are ye not?"

The lieutenant shifted from one foot to the other. "Yes, but on open ground. Not crammed into tight, filthy corridors… like these."

"I see," Matt nodded. Sam turned a queer shade of magenta, he laughed so hard at their expense. "This isn't the sort o'civilized engagement yer used to, is it? All that bluster on the provin' grounds and not much to back it up."

The Corsair held out a bloody torn arm to keep the men behind him in place. As if their bravado could scare Matt now.

"These people are savages. They fight like beasts, dirty like vermin. They burned two of my men alive, and what they can't catch inside, they shoot from above, like cowards."

"Well, that was yer first mistake, lad." Sam wiped his eyes. "Ye came to bloody Rosweal expectin' a fair fight. Only a fool would make that sort o'blunder, I reckon."

"I believe I sent my boys in first if ye recall?" Matt reminded him. "That witch did unspeakable things to four or more. Here, we thought ye'd have done better?" Sam laughed again, earning him a withering glare full of aristocratic loathing.

"We're leaving. As far as I'm concerned, this city has earned the blaze our army will set upon our return."

"Send in yer reserves. Ye left enough men uphill. I doubt ye'd have much trouble overwhelmin' 'em with—"

The lieutenant blanched. "*What men?* Before they killed him, my captain summoned the reserves stationed several streets away. Many more were sent to circle the tavern, to staunch escape. They're all gone."

Sam's smile flickered, then faded. "What was that?"

The lieutenant tossed him a soot-smeared spear-shaft. Sam fumbled the object a bit before dropping it on the table under his gut. It was broken and burnt black at the butt as if someone had used it to stoke a stubborn brazier.

"Of the fifty men we left in your odious slum a mile or so back, only ten managed to flee whence they came. The rest are piled up at the end of the alley."

Matt shot to his feet. "You lie. That ain't bloody possible."

"Isn't it? I wouldn't put it past scum like you to lure us in here for an ambush. Though, given the state of the area around my dead comrades, I'd say you lost quite a bit on this gamble yourself."

Another soldier approached from the rear. He held his shield above his head for safety while he brought the remaining officer his mount. The lieutenant slid his hands inside his gloves, spat, and spun on his heel.

"Wait! What do ye mean, 'the state o'the area?'"

"Can't you smell the smoke? The natives set fire to their hovels, it seems."

They were upwind. The Hilltop was at their back, to the east. Matt could see nothing in that direction save eaves and close-pitched roofs. "*Fabian.*"

"Aye, boss." Fabian sheathed his dagger for the run south toward the slums. From there, he would double-back and head up the Hill to the east. That was the fastest route.

The lieutenant smiled without mirth. "My family name is Hamma, Gilcannon. You'll be hearing it again soon." He pulled himself artfully into his saddle, then kicked his mount forward.

Matt was forced to stumble out of his way, almost into Sam's overflowing lap. "Wait! Ye can't just leave. The heretic is still in there, ain't she?"

"If she manages to survive the animals in this pen, she'll spend the rest of her days a hunted traitor with no people. I wish you all joy of her." Lieutenant Hamma waved a rude gesture over his shoulder. He and his train of spiteful soldiers filed southward down the alley.

Perplexed, Matt watched them go. Of course, he'd meant to double-cross them, but not until he'd exhausted them to extinction on *The Hart*. The girl wasn't what Matt was after, but her bounty wouldn't hurt his coffers either. He'd arranged things just so, and now… suddenly, the street felt far too quiet. Matt's boys chattered amongst themselves. They were all hardened souls, to be sure, but if the Hilltop was aflame, the slums might be next. The families they worked so hard for were in danger. Matt couldn't smell any smoke. Couldn't hear any crackling timber. Only laughter, whistles, and jeers from *The Hart*, as the Greenmakers watched the Tairnganeah march away in defeat.

Sam used the window casing to help himself upright. He had a strange tilt to his mouth that alarmed Matt more than the retreating Tairnganeah or their lieutenant's cryptic warning.

"What?"

Sam waddled toward the open black chasm of a doorway. The day was bright, despite the periodic rainclouds that raced overhead like silver cannonballs. It had drizzled off and on all afternoon, broken by intermittent sunshine. Just now, the sky gave them a bit of both.

"Sol! Where ye got to, then? Ye hear what's goin' on out here?"

Nothing. Not even a whisper in return.

Sam shot Matt a startled round eye. "Solomon? Quit feckin' about!" Silence. The open door took on the appearance of something much more sinister than a simple tavern entrance. Matt shoved two or three of his boys in front of him. Strong light made for long shadows in tight spaces. That yawning black maw beckoned ominously. Hadn't it only been a doorway mere moments ago? No sound rustled within save the 'drip, drip, drip' of a poorly shuttered tap. Matt's palm wound over the small, stiff muscles of Lance Shoren's shoulder. The boy didn't wince, though Matt's fingertips ground into bone. Sam drew the Bethonair sabre he kept strapped to his side. His stone-faced guards flanked the beckoning entrance. "Solomon Trant! If yer not dead or dyin' in there, ye'd better bloody well speak up now!"

Not a peep at first, then… as if barreling through a mountain tunnel into the cold light of day, something small and silver rolled over the slate paving stones at the stoop, clinking as it sped toward Sam's feet. It was a coin: a whole silver stag. The coin sank into the muck near Sam's right toe. Sam didn't bend down to examine it (as if he could, the pig). He exhaled a rattling breath. Three more coins rolled into the street from the fathomless darkness within. Matt paled. These were the very coins he'd given Sol to betray the Greenmakers Guild, a small fortune in this sad, desperate part of the Continent.

The last silver to find a home at Sam's feet was stained red— presumably with its owner's blood. Sam gave a wheezing sort of half-scream, half-roar. Matt propelled himself backward into the lane, safe behind his boys' bony, startled backs.

"Greetings," sang an elegant, slightly accented voice from inside. It sent shivers down Matt's spine and tore a guttural curse from Sam Trant's chest. "Sol won't be needing this wealth where he's off to. Please, help yourselves."

One of Sam's men took a step toward the door. A thin arrow-shaft burst from the back of his skull. His companion dodged left to avoid the next shot, though Sam was far too bulky to move as quickly. He took one through the quadriceps, near his groin. His answering scream rattled every awning for a mile in each direction. Matt didn't wait around to see more. He shoved two of his boys toward Sam, desperate to escape the brewery. He looked back only once. A tall blond figure emerged from Solomon's taproom. He wore at least a quart of blood and a maniacal grin. The fair-haired fellow whirled about with a two-handed broadsword, painting the stoop a garish red. Matt didn't dawdle. He'd only seen fighting like that once before at Dumnain and wasn't about to hang around in awe.

Those of his boys who didn't stay behind to fight Ben Maeden, Gramble, and others who entered the alley from the darkened tavern, fled south toward Haymaker's Lane with Matt. Some outpaced him, though he'd had quite a head start. Nothing could halt the sounds that traveled up to them: the laughter, Sam's bleating cries, the hacking, pleading, metallurgic sounds of slaughter. Matt rounded the first bend, past old Barnaby's shut-up haberdashery. An arrow thwacked into the brick façade just shy of his kidney. Whimpering, he ran on. That same voice came again, higher and louder, dogging Matt's slip-shod progress over mud-slick cobbles.

"See you soon, Gilcannon!"

Matt could hear the mocking superiority in the speaker's tone, could *feel* the triumph. Terrified, he rounded the next corner, which faced south by east. The air here was thick with smoke. It stung his eyes, burned his sinuses, and seared his throat. The further south he sprinted, the more overpowering it became. Despite the weather, half of the bloody city must have been on fire. Wet rooftops meant squat if interior walls, floors, and joists were dry.

Only minutes ago, he'd been sure of his victory. The Greenmakers were beaten. The Tairnganeah had left of their own accord. It would have been a simple matter to have both Sam and Sol knifed on their way home. In a flash, this day warped into something else: something unforeseen. The Greenmakers hadn't fallen into his trap. Matt had barreled into one of theirs.

That was all right… he would live.

He had another plan.

Hot smoke singed his lungs, but Matt ran until he thought his aging heart would implode. At the crest of the Hilltop, he followed his boys right toward the slums. The Taran Gate loomed ahead. His next chance waited five miles to the south. He could make it. He had to. The low-end of the Hilltop was ablaze, but it was too damp to hold for long. Surely only the low-end near the quarter would have been damaged when he returned tomorrow? Whichever way it played out didn't matter. He only needed to get out alive. He would come back and take what was rightfully his.

He put everything he had into his two feeble legs, pleased to note that despite years of relative comfort, they could still perform their first occupation. Matt Gilcannon fled as if a lad of ten once more, shirking the justice he so richly deserved.

Quid Pro Quo

Rian was exhausted hours before the Tairnganeah stopped lobbing flaming darts through their barricades or throwing men with ridiculously long spears at the cracks in the door. When a chill afternoon rain put out the soldiers' torches and diminished their chances of burning *The Hart* down with everyone inside, the worst of the fighting petered out. At the close, over two-score dead Tairnganese soldiers piled up in Taverner's Alley. Rian was bone tired. Fatigue sapped every ounce of energy she had to spare by the time the remaining Corsairs called for a retreat.

The fight had been nearly comical in its seeming one-sided advantage. The Tairnganeah had the numbers. They had the weapons: expensive spears, crossbows, and shields. They had mounted commanders, vantage, supplies, and an organized line. Yet, nothing worked out the way anyone (save perhaps Barb) had expected. If one were to judge by the smug humor on the madam's face, she'd never had a single doubt about the Corsairs' ability to bungle a skirmish. Rian, however, knew nothing about battle. Until recently, she'd never even been in a fight. Hostility, mistrust, and veiled accusations, yes. She'd experienced plenty of that. But an actual physical altercation? Never.

In Ferndale, she was treated with restrained tolerance. The townsfolk preferred to pretend she didn't exist, even when forced to interact with her. They would lower their eyes when she approached or squeeze their mouths together in a solemn line. Few had any kind words for Rian, less the thanks she deserved for treating so many of their women and children for whatever pittance they could muster. Rian understood subtle enmity, sarcasm, bigotry, and disgust— but real violence? No. Not until Ben dragged Una to her door had Rian witnessed barbarity like this. She'd read about such things. She wasn't a fool. The histories her father lined his treasured shelves with detailed the horrific depths of human depravity. To witness it firsthand, however… Rian was at a loss. Each day away from home was a new trial. Her quiet life had not prepared her for the horrors she'd seen since. The Greenmakers stacked dozens of bodies beneath *The Hart*'s shattered windows. Colm swept glass, wood splinters, and puddles of quarrels from red-stained floors. He scowled over the mess, covered head-to-toe in welts, scrapes, and seeping cuts.

"Bleedin' savages. Just feckin' mopped, didn't I?"

Rian was running out of room and supplies. In her little makeshift clinic at the top of the stairs, she did not lack for patients: men and boys with cuts, broken bones, severed digits, or limbs. She treated dislodged teeth, burns, countless contusions, and colorful abrasions. Almost since the fighting broke out, she'd been on her knees in these halls, tending to casualties. So many, in fact, *The Hart* ran out of bed linens by sunset. Rian sent several of Barb's girls running back and forth from the laundry, hauling clean linens, skirts, chemises, and curtains back to the hall. The girls foraged for anything that could be torn or shredded to meet the ever-increasing demand for bandages. Some scoured both buildings for whatever needles, thread, and small blades they could scavenge. Others hauled bucketloads of sulphuric water from the baths below the tenement. The girls scrubbed floors, walls, or human skin on demand.

Rian wasn't even sure how she came to treat the first few injuries. The fighting commenced, and there she was: staunching, wrapping, sewing, and soothing. Not every fighter's wounds were shallow, either—many required sedatives… or worse. At a critical point, someone had handed her a tincture of belladonna. It wasn't until much later that Rian realized the donor had been Rose. It turned out that Rose had been beside her the whole time, her sleeves rolled up and her forearms wet to the elbows in blood. Unbeknownst to Rian, they moved in concert through each new emergency. Rian mended those that could be mended, and Rose helped make comfortable those who couldn't. Six men died. They lay in the hall, with scraps of linen covering their blank, staring eyes. Two more would likely not recover. Of these, the big man, Dean, took a quarrel through the gut. His cries were weakening but meaningful all the same. Rian could do nothing for him but pour a dollop of belladonna into a uishge decanter and send him off to sleep forever. Such wounds were terrible, degenerative, and far beyond her ability to heal. Dean's last hours would have stretched on in agony. She spared him that, at least.

Thankfully, most fighters bore superficial wounds: a broken finger, a gash on the arm, a blow to the head, a cracked rib, or a cut that simply needed stitching. These would return to action before Rose could tie off their bandages. Some would take a second or third wound, then return to the landing, impatiently awaiting their next treatment so they could return to the barricades. The noise had been deafening: metal clanging, manic laughter, screams, shouts, curses, cries, and moans. Barb's taproom was a riot of foul odors, raucous sounds, and chaotic activity. The smell was overpowering, too: smoke on damp wood, rain against the mud outside, the sickly stench of blood and vomit, an acidic tang of urine, sweat, and stale ale from broken taps.

Several times the Tairnganeah broke through the Greenmakers' line at the front of the tavern but were beaten back with a relish that would surely shame the survivors for years to come. Not a man made it through that wasn't immediately put down, forcibly ejected over the heads of their fellows, or tossed face down into the muck outside. For every Greenmaker felled by Tairnganese bolt or slash, three Tairnganeah either left their guts in the effluent stew that used to serve as common rushes or were shoved back into the street from whence they came. If Rian hadn't been so preoccupied, she might have paid more attention to Barb, who stood framed against the balustrade shouting orders and laughing like a harpy. With her best remaining archers on the roof shooting anything in black and gold with abandon, Barb might have had reason to find humor in all of this. Rian was up to her elbows in blood and excrement and did not share the sentiment. What joy could one derive from such senseless bloodletting?

When the noise died down and the horde of patients thinned along the landing, Rian felt a gentle touch on her shoulder. She was busy stitching a jagged cut over another nameless lad's forearm. He blubbered and teared up as if *she'd* been the one slashing at him with a rapier rather than attempting to staunch a slippery wound he most certainly earned.

"Wait your turn, please." She didn't look up. The needle was too small for this sort of work, a lace needle, no doubt. She struggled to keep it between her thumb and forefinger through each pass.

"Here now, lass," cooed Barb's voice. Rian made a face. The needle sailed through its last damp layer of flesh. She held her left index finger over the exit while she made her loop.

"Ye should take a break," the madam persisted. "It's well and over."

Rian noted four or five boys waiting near the stairs to be seen. Each wore varying stages of triumph or wounded pride on their filthy features. "When I'm done, I'll stop."

"I respect that, I *do*— but yer done, nonetheless. Let Rose take over. She knows how to tie a tourniquet and sew a scratch back together."

Done with the fidgety lad, Rian spared Barb an annoyed glance. She waved the next one over. "I'd rather not have to check someone else's work later when I can do it right the first time."

An elderly gentleman who smelled of uishge and rank cabbages took the lad's place by the wall. He pulled his shirt up with a sheepish, toothless smile for Barb. He had a mean gash down his skeletal ribcage. It wasn't life-threatening but would cost him several weeks of healing, regardless. Rian frowned.

"Violet?"

"Missus?"

"I need more of that nettle stew you brought me before. Mix in at least two cups of the strongest spirits you can find. We're going to need more bandages." She didn't look up to watch Violet rush down the hall.

Instead, she patted the old man's hand encouragingly. "I'm going to see those others over there for a bit, but when Violet returns with my supplies, we'll take care of this. All right?"

"Yer a saint, missus," he cackled back.

A Kneeler. Rian hadn't met one in some time. She gave him a reassuring smile and waved the next one over, ignoring Barb and her crossed arms. This fellow had a nasty burn. His eye was swollen shut and seeping pus. She'd need a salve and a thin, scrupulously clean blade to—

"Are ye bloody well deaf, girl? Yer wavin' where ye kneel. Dabs!"

Rian opened her mouth to argue, but a giant meat hook looped around her waist. Dabney hoisted her aloft without much effort. Rian's teeth clacked together over her trite retort. Indeed, she was too tired to squeal. Instead, she settled for silent but sanctimonious reproach. Barb snorted.

"No use givin' me that face, missy. I've seen a great deal more'n ye to be frightened of today. Bring her into me office, Dabs but be careful with her. Rose!" Barb hollered, still glaring down at Rian. "Ye know what to do with this lot?"

"Yeah," Rose droned, easily as tired as Rian. "His eye needs lancin', and that burn needs greasin'. When Violet gets back with the brew, the old man's ribs need disinfectin' and a handy stitchin.' Am I right, missus?"

She was asking Rian, who was impressed, despite being held under the crook of Dabney's arm with her backside high in the air. Rian sniffed. "Yes. Do you—?"

"Oh, fer feck's sake! She'll bloody manage. Siora, but ye'd think none o'us ever coddled a man afore. On the couch with ye. Get some broth and cheese down that scrawny gullet."

Rian was carted into Barb's well-appointed office. There, upon the settee, lay Una… wounded yet again. Una did her level best to pretend such things barely affected her. Sweating, she held a damp cloth against her temple. The rag was tainted a rusty crimson from the purpling laceration Rian saw winding its way along her upper ear. Rian wriggled out of Dabney's grasp and was by her side in a flash. She slapped her defensive fingers away.

"I swear! Do you *know* how to duck? It looks worse than it is, but I'll need to—"

"Rian, it's all right." Una gently shoved Rian into the seat beside her. "Your hands are trembling. Are you hurt?"

"No," Barb barked from the doorway. "But she's been in the thick o'it the whole bloody time. Needs to get some food into her."

"Una," Rian growled. "That could fester if I don't see to it."

"It'll heal."

"But—"

"*It will heal*, Rian," Una's tone was firm, but her eyes were soft. Rian rolled her bottom lip and looked away. Una nodded at the table, which was set with tea, bread, broth, and cheese. Rian couldn't begin to guess how someone managed to get into the kitchens to unearth such treasure. The tavern was a disaster, from the broken windows to the smashed-in doors. Rian fell on the food like a starving rat.

"There now, poor mite. Get somethin' hot into ye." Barb had Dabney pour the tea. He was black and blue as everyone else, save for his dripping hair and clean fingers. Barb noticed Rian's attention. "Keeps everyone in high morale if a fella as large as Dabs here looks no worse for wear. If ye saw what he looked like afore…" She gave a mock shudder and helped herself to some tea. "Anyway, I want ye to know, what ye did for me lads out there, girl— I'll not be forgettin' anytime soon. I mean that."

"S'aright," Rian squeezed out, behind a hunk of muenster cheese with a bit of browning apple. Una, she couldn't fail to see, was having none. She watched Rian silently, with the most peculiar look on her face. A momentary panic crept up the veins of Rian's neck. She looked down at the food, suspicious.

"Oh, not this time, lass. Ye needn't fear," laughed Barb.

"Then… why are you being so nice to me? To us?"

"Pish and posh, girl. All water under a dusty bridge that is." Rian didn't like Barb's smile. It reminded her of the way a hawk eyes small prey. "I owe ye that much, at least." Barb reached inside her vest and pulled out a small bone flask, which she upended into her own spot of tea. "Now, that's not to say we don't have somewhat to discuss before the menfolk return, to pretend they have a say in anything.'"

"Ah," said Rian, as if she had the first clue what the old bat was hinting at.

Barb dragged her chair over. She offered her flask to Una, who, for once, needed no prompting. She dumped a fair amount down her throat and handed it back with a grateful sigh. "I'm not gonna forget how you fought down there, milady. Ye took that wound for Colm, who'd be dead now thrice over if ye hadn't stuck at his back. That's more'n bravery. As the boys say, that took *bollocks*."

"I owed him. Those bastards would never have come here if—"

"If Matt fucking Gilcannon hadn't found out about ye. Don't bother to blame yerself. If it wasn't ye, it'd be somethin' else. I'm not gonna claim to like ye overmuch, but I can lay all this 'pon ye, neither. Yer an opportunity for Matt, same as ye are for those lads to the South, and that old prune what leads the Union o'Commons in Parliament. Bad luck for ye, all around, I 'spose."

"Right. Now, where're you going with this?"

Barb's smile held even less warmth than the previous one. "To the point then? Dabs, close the door behind ye," she said, pouring them a round of tea each and making sure to dollop healthy doses of uishge in each cup. She settled herself against a worn magenta cushion and winced when one of her sleeves brushed against her burned forearm. She'd applied some sweet-smelling salve, which Rian believed to be honey and mint.

"I've got news I feel sure yer not gonna care for, but I'm bound to tell ye anyway." Without the cosmetics, the bluster, or the hordes of male hangers-on, Barb looked almost normal and harmless. What might her life have been like if she hadn't been called to sell herself and others for profit? Rian had little experience with the world. Therefore, she couldn't begin to comprehend the motivation or self-effacement required to make such a decision. Una thought Barb's choices displayed a weakness of character. Rian suspected something different altogether. Only the very strong had the grit to survive at any cost to their dignity. Rian knew this as surely as she knew the length of her nose. Why? Because she understood such strength was not one of her gifts. Rian could *never* do it. The weight of that choice.... the cost would be far more than she could bear. To not only endure but *thrive*, as Barb had— said something for her. She wasn't sure that something was flattering, but it intimated a particular strength of character, regardless.

Rian was less tainted by the Siorai faith than Una. She could see what Una could not. Barb wasn't evil, cruel, or wanton; she was a survivor. She was also someone in a position to help others survive. What's more, she was good enough at both to keep herself and her tiny ignoble corner of the world in relative comfort. Una could barely look at the woman without a curl to her upper lip, but that was her rearing. Rian hadn't been raised to believe herself superior to anyone else. As kind as Una was, Rian believed she had no idea she held such bias. This revelation wasn't something that could be taught, however. Una would come round to it on her own, or not at all.

Una set her compress down. "Bethonair Knights? When you mentioned them before, I gathered they were closer than I'd like them to be."

"Too bleedin' right, ye are. Less than ten miles, last report. Probably much closer than that even. They're setting up a supply camp in Vale, just down the Taran High Road."

Rian gasped. "That's just seven miles away."

"Wonderful." Una pinched the bridge of her nose with blackened fingers. "I suppose he'll send his demands soon enough?"

"No need. We all know what he wants. Them Tairnganese wimps beatin' a hasty retreat from the city walls would've made it obvious to the Southers yer here." Barb eyed her speculatively. "Ye know what I'm getting at here, doncha?"

"Yes."

"I don't." Rian wanted to hear Barb say it aloud. She pushed the bread and cheese away. "Why does it matter?"

"She's asking me to leave, Rian."

"Politely too, I might add." Barb didn't look thrilled about it, nor did she seem sorry. "I've had it from Seamus, who got back about an hour ago— Ben and Robin have split their men into two forces. One to pursue Matt, who's fled through the Taran Gate with whatever Hilltop Boys remain loyal. Another to raid his home and warehouses. I don't expect 'em back for ages. Now, I'll ask ye missy... please don't make me break me word to... Ben. If ye left of yer own accord, ye'd be sparin' these folks more pain on yer account."

Rian inhaled. "You gave your word to Ben, didn't you? To keep her safe while he went out to do your dirty work for you."

Barb gave her a tight-lipped smile. "I bloody well have, haven't I? She's still breathin'. Moreover, there are good folks in the hall who ain't. What just happened ain't nothin' to what the Southers can muster. Yer too young to realize this, girl, but them Corsairs ain't like Bethonair Knights. Them are *real* soldiers. They've plate armor, mail, and siege weapons— keepin' her here is like wavin' a red flag under a bull's nose. If they coulda been kept in the dark about it, that woulda been one thing, but Matt's fled straight to 'em. He'll be hopin' to bribe yer cousin with yer whereabouts. Rosweal be damned." Rian watched Barb's hand shake a bit against her teacup, a barely discernible tic she was likely unaware of.

She was afraid.

Really afraid.

Rian sat back.

"Ye've never seen a city sacked before, have ye?"

"No, but I'm no dolt. I can guess what happens."

"No," Una interrupted. "What *will* happen. I understand, Mistress Dormer. I do. I'll not ask any of you— any more of you— to endure that on my account. I'll go."

Barb breathed a sigh of relief. "Thank ye, milady. There's a good deal spoken in yer favor. I'll say that. But there's hundreds o'families in this town, despite appearances. They do the best they can. No matter what his lordship asks o'me, I owe me first duty to them."

"His *lordship* will be furious about this." Rian snarled. "Una, we're in this together, remember? What about the promise you made him? The one you keep reminding *me* of. You can't go."

"He made a bargain with Barb too, which she must honor because she has no choice. Whereas I have made no such bargain with Barb. Damek will raze this town to the ground if she tries to keep me from him."

"You can't run off on your own without a word. What was the point of all this if you do? Besides, they'll catch you if you run south or east. There's nothing in the west but miles of empty Greensward and barren hills beyond. There's nowhere else *to* go."

Una's answering sigh was half a groan. "I'm aware."

"Then what in the hells are you agreeing to here? Wait for Ben, Una."

"Look," interjected Barb. "I'm not askin' ye to hanker off into the wilderness with naught but yer skin and good intentions to keep ye warm. I ain't so cruel as all that. I know a place ye can go, and I'll send fellas with ye— good fellas I trust. They'll keep ye fed and safe, till yer able to cross with... Ben. Or at least until this first emergency is sorted. I just can't have ye here when they ride in. Ye know I can't. They'll take our protectin' ye as an act o'war. If I can prove ye've been and gone that's another matter. That might buy us a reprieve."

"Una, you can't trust her. She'll have one of her men knife you the minute you're out of town. Worse, she'll tell Ben you left on your own, and hand you over to your cousin for the reward money. Don't do it."

Barb slammed her cup into its saucer, chipping the delicate white porcelain. "I don't appreciate the picture yer attemptin' to paint of me, little lady. I may be an old swindler, but I give me word only rarely, for a reason. If I say she'll come to no harm, she bloody well won't."

"That doesn't mean you can't subtly subvert that word. Work around it in some way as you're doing now, with the promise you made to Ben." Rian laughed dryly. "I know that Una's family is a problem for everyone. Believe me. I've lost both my house and my livelihood to help her."

Fresh guilt flickered over Una's brow. "I'm sorry for it."

"I know you are! It's infuriating, really. I'm here with you because you saved my life, Una. Both of you. I'm here because I understand what's happening is larger than me, you, or Ben. It's bigger than Rosweal, Bethany, or even Tairngare. I'm here because we're all caught up in this together. Bethany will make its war, with or without you. It's just easier with you. Tairngare will have its revolution, with or without you. It's just more convenient if you're a suitable scapegoat. Don't you see? *This isn't about you*! It isn't because of you. *It just is*. If you run away now, that won't stop anyone from dying. You won't guarantee that this city or any other will survive intact. It's war, Una. The more cities the Duch burns, the stronger his message will be in Bri Leith. That's what this is all about. What it's always been about. You're just a pawn and have been since you were born."

Una absorbed every word, silent as a stone well.

Barb cleared her throat. "I won't argue ye don't have a point, missy. Ye do, but yer fergettin' some things in that fine speech. These're folks' lives we're talkin' about here. *Folks I know*. Folks I'm responsible for. Ye may say we have no control over what these fine lords have in store for us, but I'll be damned if I sit back while he slaughters folks I care for to get at her— never mind if it's her fault or not. Now, I could sell her and avoid a fight altogether. I could profit for havin' her in my keepin'. I could do that, and no soldier's boot will cross the Taran Gate again. It's not as if the Tairnganeah have siege weapons at their disposal. I'll wager they learned their lesson here today." Her chuckle was mirthless. "I could sell her, and it will save lives, time, effort, and supplies, for what promises to be a rough starvin' season. By rights, it's what I bloody well *should* do. I'm offerin' ye a compromise. I think, given the state o'me livelihood downstairs, ye'd best accept."

"Una," Rian protested. "Wait for Ben…"

Barb scoffed. "For what? If he was standin' here now, I'd give 'em both the boot without an afterthought. Ben's no fool. Once he realizes what's squatting down the High Road like a fat vulture waitin' to spring, he'll come to the same conclusion."

"Why not wait for him, and put the question to him too? We'll leave together, and you'd still get what you want." Rian narrowed her eyes to blue slits. Barb said nothing. "I notice you don't leap to respond. Let me help you. You can't wait because you know he'll have another plan. It'll be something that you won't like, and you'll be forced to accept it. He's the Crown Prince, isn't he? That makes this *his* land, and you *his* vassal. You don't like that, do you? Exiled or not, he's our liege-lord. You'd like to retain command of this situation for as long as you're able. Isn't that right?"

"Rian, calm down." Una swatted her leg.

"I won't! This isn't about Rosweal, or Barb, or you, or anyone else! This is about Bethany, and Aes Sidhe. The only hope any of us have to stop this war before it gets started is to get you to Ben's father. Stick to the plan, Una."

"Now see here, ye mouthy little—" Barb hissed, but Una launched to her feet.

"That's enough! *Siora*. I know what's at stake here. Thank you both very much for your opinions on the matter." She chewed her lower lip. "You're both right, but in the end, neither of you knows my cousin as I do. Damek's not going to bargain with anyone. While it may be true that this war isn't my fault, any more than it is either of yours… it will be me he uses as an excuse to sow the seeds of my father's war. If I'm here, he'll take me if he can, and burn you all out for spite. If I'm not here, and you make it seem as if I escaped from your clutches before I could be traded… it'll go better for all involved. Barb, I accept your terms. May I caution you to take your plans a step further?"

Clearly not expecting Una to acquiesce so easily, Barb stared up at her, mouth slightly agape. "How so?"

"You'll have to tell him where I've gone. You'll have to point him in a reasonable direction, and you'll have to be honest about it. Rian, you don't know him!" She held out a hand to stay the rebuttal burning on Rian's tongue. "He'll do worse than burn this place down if he smells a lie, and I warn you, *he will*. He has a nose for deception."

"If I do that, I'd be breakin' me word to Ben. Ye may not realize this, either o'ye... but we Northers fear the Ard Ri far more'n we dread a Souther army. There's a reason yer Da's family ain't ever won against the Sidhe."

"I've seen Ben fight. I know what you mean, but it's beside the point. He can't fault you for this if it was my idea."

"Una!" Rian smacked her palm against the table.

Barb cocked her head. "Ye'd do that? For us?"

"Damek can't kill me. I can't say the same for any of you. I just need a head start, and hopefully enough distance."

"Oh, it has that. In the hills to the west. A high valley hedged on all sides by the bloody Greensward. He'll waste a day're more searchin' for ye. Even with directions. Used to be my Da's village, afore the war. It's completely overgrown and well hidden. Odds are, Ben finds ye long afore he does."

Rian spread her arms. "Lord Bishop is supposed to believe that you didn't send her there? *Come on*! Una, you have to see how stupid this is."

"It's the only place one could reasonably go from here. I'll tell him... I dunno how many men ye have with ye, nor how long a start ye have. The Greensward grows thick and tall there. In some places, there's not a foot between the trees. I'll send Ben after ye as soon as I'm able, and with luck, ye'll be over that border before the Marshal gets a mile after ye."

"I'll leave immediately. Thank you."

"Wait! Una—"

"Thanks?" Barb's brows knit together. "That's just—"

"Aside from Rian and Ben, that's the most anyone's bothered to offer me these last few weeks. What's more, it's fair. I'll get out of your hair, Mistress Dormer. Remember, give Damek whatever he asks for, within mortal reasoning. If I'm ever set right again," Una paused, a sad acceptance of the immutable in her expression, "I'll see Tairngare grants you whatever contracts you require. I swear it, by the blood of the Ancestor."

Barb held out her hand. Una took it. "It's Barb to ye, milady."

"Una. Please."

Barb clasped Una's hand between both of hers. "I'll tell ye somewhat else. Maybe I do like ye just a bit, after all."

The Everyman

The road behind gaped dark and silent as an open tomb. A marching bitterness kissed the earth from above, spinning whirlpools of silver mist through stark trees and searing exposed flesh like acid. It would soon snow. The night air was nearly electric with ozone— a warning all warm-blooded creatures must heed. Drifts could drive upwards of three feet in an hour this far north. No one wanted to be caught in a whiteout without the appropriate gear: fur, gloves, and sealskin boots. A numbing gust burst through the northwest trees and straight into Ben's face. He bit back a sharp curse. Whistling, Robin squinted at the treetops, snapping overhead.

"Don't bode well for us, Ben."

Ben pulled his cloak tight. "Dor Oras is impatient to arrive, it seems."

Gerrod wore a deal less than either of them: only a quilted vest over a long-sleeved woolen tunic, and damp woolen trousers. Ben heard his teeth clacking together, even when he'd stood far down the line.

"Fellas, I hate Matt more'n the rest o'ye combined for what he done to me mam all them years ago… but he ain't worth freezin' to death over." His dark eyes were owlish against his saffron cheeks. "Besides, what're we 'sposed to do about *that*?"

He referred to the Bethonair occupation of Vale, about a mile south. A queer orange halo hovered over the village in stark contrast with the snow-bright sky above. Ben, having commandeered Robin's spyglass, counted some three dozen fires just shy of the low town wall. There were so many tents, they might have been whitecaps on a rolling sea. Ben lost count after he reached sixty. Robin nudged his shoulder.

"How many then?"

"Four hundred, give or take. Who knows how many more are hidden in town, or camped at the southern end of the High Road?"

"Siora," shivered Gerrod with a distinct note of dread.

Robin said, "I think we mighta bitten off a bit more'n we can swallow here, Ben."

"Aye," Gerrod agreed, "a *damn sight* more! The Greenmakers don't have a quarter that number in all o'Rosweal. Matt's done for us all, I say."

"Don't be so bloody dramatic, Gerry. Even if he rode back home on the back of this Souther cunt's saddle... one o'us will do for him. If he don't know it, he will soon enough."

"We don't stand a chance against that, boss."

"Gerry, you're right," said Ben. He compressed the spyglass, then handed it back to Robin. They exchanged a knowing look. "I wouldn't dream of raiding that camp in the night. When they'd least expect it. Just before the first snowstorm of the season."

"I'm not hearin' this. It's bloody *mad*."

"It's an opportunity..."

"Them're mounted knights! They've armor, sabres, and pikes half as long as a man. Ye know who their commander is?"

Robin took a speculative peek through the remaining foliage. "They ain't on them horses now, are they?"

Gerrod closed his eyes, as if in prayer. "Oh, that's *brilliant*. Say we make it out alive, then what? They'll just say, 'ah well, bad luck, fellas', and go home? Yer barkin', both o'ye. This lord," he jerked his chin toward Vale, "is the most lauded commander in the South. Ye hear the things they say about him?"

Ben shrugged. "He's a boy. Overeager, arrogant, and, if I'm not mistaken, disobeying orders to march on the North, prematurely."

"Quite a lot of men to capture one girl," Robin added.

"*Indeed.* My guess? Lord Bishop is betting everything he has on this. Donahugh's sole claim to Tairngare runs through Una— paltry though that may be. If Bishop can collect her now, he's in a position to make demands of his uncle."

"That's Heir-Apparent Bishop, to likes o'us."

"He has to take her first." Ben's sneer carved deep.

Gerrod waved his hands over his head. "Makes no bloody difference why he's here. He's *here*. He's got more men, more horses, and better weapons than any o'us."

Ben tapped Nemain's pommel. "Speak for yourself, lad."

"If ye pick a fight with him tonight, he's gonna know why, and where ye came from. Me sisters're only four and six. Remember what men like that do to folks like us."

That gave Ben pause.

Robin shook his head. "Gerry, all the bloody towns along the border are ripe for the pluckin.' Ye see? If we can cut some weight outta his purse, he'll have less to spend on any o'us."

"If I'm right, and he's not sanctioned by the Duch in this matter, then this..." Ben gestured toward the multitudinous campfires, "is likely all he could muster. We break his supply line, and his men will lose enthusiasm."

"Ben, that's *four hunnerd men*. Cavalry. Armor. We're less'n *twenty*, all told. No boots, furs, nothin'. Can't ye see what the sky promises for tomorrow? We ain't been home in near three days."

"Don't ye worry 'bout Barb and the boys, Gerry. They beat 'em back fair."

"Ye don't know that for sure, boss. Even if the Tairnganeah retreated, don't mean *The Hart* is in good shape. We coulda lost heaps of folks in there! Don't ye care?"

Robin's smile faded. "Course I care, but we vowed to bring Matt back to Barb. That's what we're bloody well tryin' to do."

Frustrated, Gerrod tried a different tack. "Ben, yer lady is in there. What if she's been hurt? Siora's sake, what if she's been killed? Or Barb?" He turned back to Robin. "Or anyone else? Don't ye think they need us?"

Ben coughed. "She's not *my* lady. Besides, you've seen what she can do, Gerry. If ever there was a woman that could take care of herself, it's her."

"I won't say she ain't tough... and well, scary— but she ain't immune to steel, is she? Can happen to anyone, no matter how tough they are. Even you." Ben mulled that over. The boy had a point. There was a good chance that they were needed at *The Hart*. They'd been too focused on the task at hand to consider it. A full day's scouting, a second fighting Tairnganeah in the streets, and another in pursuit; they were stretched as thin as they could be. There were no rations left in any of their packs, save the odd flask of uishge. The weather was turning savage, as only Innish weather could. Soon, fatigue would spread through their ranks like the pox. The Greenmakers were hungry, tired, cold, and concerned for their families back home.

Ben could hardly blame them for wanting to leave. Yet if they stayed... they could put a solid brake on Damek Bishop's expeditionary force. A host of this size required a constant stream of wagons loaded with grain, ale, meat, and women. Without them, the Southers would be forced to scavenge for meals and entertainment. While that might be bad for the towns and farmsteads nearby, it would also finish them faster than plague. Soldiers who aren't fed, won't fight. Discipline depended upon order; without a steady supply of food and drink, there could be none.

"Lad's not wrong, Ben," Robin said.

"Not everyone needs to stay."

"That ain't gonna happen."

"Look, it isn't about Gilcannon anymore, is it? I won't ask everyone to stay. Gerry's right about *The Hart*. I didn't get a good look at the place from *Sol's*, but I could tell they'd been through it."

"It ain't a good idea to split our men up. Don't be daft."

"Robin, we may not get another chance."

"O'course we will," he chuckled. "Rosweal's uphill. With the weather, I'd say they might be good and buggered anyway."

Ben cursed. Bishop was so close. Gilcannon too. He didn't like that he was near enough to smell the meat roasting over their fires but lacked the men to relieve them of their comforts. Perhaps if he went alone— slipped past their sentries, and snuck into town from the western rim? Could he not guess which building Bishop had appropriated by the number of guards? Ben knew his own strength. He had no fear of these men. Milesian soldiers, Souther or no, were no match for him in close combat. He'd cut through them like curd.

"I know what yer thinkin,' Ben. So you're aware, *over me own bloated corpse,*" Robin growled. "We stay or leave together. Seein' as I'm the boss round here, yer bound to obey me."

Ben's eyes slivered. "Is that an order?"

"Why shouldn't it be? Ye work for me, *Ben Maeden.*"

Ben thought about knocking the grin off Robin's face. "Robin—"

"Home then, shall we?" Robin ignored him. "Me bollocks have crawled into my arsehole. It's so bloody cold out here. I agree that it should be done, but *not tonight.* We need more men. That's all there is to it. Truth be told, I could do with a hot meal and a bed. So could ye."

"But—"

Robin gripped his shoulder, hard. "Another thing to consider. Barb knows this lot are out here by now. I'll wager she knew afore we did. I love the ole girl more'n me own life, but she do have a way of bendin' her word to suit an occasion, don't she?"

It took a moment, but Ben drew himself up to his full height. "She wouldn't *dare*. Not now."

"Rosweal means more to her than any one o'us, Ben. She'll do whatever she thinks she has to."

⚜

SNOWFLAKES DUSTED HER EYELASHES AS Una's small retinue shuffled into the hills beyond the city. A fellow named Keeley took the lead. He was a man of few words. His heavily lined face and gruff demeanor hardly endeared him to either girl. His companion, a boy a few years younger than Rian, guided them along the riverbank, then uphill. The boy had the same hard-eyed focus as his leader. Una supposed the pair might be related but was unable to entice them to confirm or deny the notion. In fact, both males ignored her as much as possible, and deigned to acknowledge her only when she stepped outside the imaginary line they kept in the underbrush. After the riverside, where sluggish currents churned swollen brown headwaters, the group hooked left into the forest. From there they climbed up, up, and up. Weighed down by a pack she insisted on bringing, Rian huffed behind Una, her cornflower eyes forward, watchful. Una didn't like Rian being here. What Una felt sure was about to happen would only be another trial for the girl to needlessly endure. Though, the look on Rian's face said she didn't need to be told what was afoot. Una vowed: she'd repay the girl for her unwavering loyalty if it was the last thing she did.

The moment she'd clasped hands with Barb, Una knew the truth. There was no deserted village in the hills. Merely a ring of shacks, some ten miles out of town; a hovel in which Una was to be kept until the Bethonair threat passed. She imagined, once they arrived at their destination, the boy would be sent back to ascertain the state of things in town. If all went well, Una could expect him to lead her cousin right to her for the reward money. If it went badly, he would return with more men… to kill her. If she'd refused Barb, as Rian advised (wisdom, under different circumstances), Una wouldn't have survived the night. She saw Barb's intentions in her Spark, clear as day. It wasn't out of malice or spite that Barb intended her violence, either. Barb felt she had no choice.

When she'd taken Una's hand, Barb held a clear memory of the North after Dumnain in her mind's eye— on purpose, no doubt. Una smelt the smoke, watched the bodies piled high along the roadside. She heard Barb's keening for her younger sisters. Spite hadn't encouraged this betrayal. Barb was *afraid* of Una, and through her, the war brewing outside her gates. The lives she might be forced to waste in her defense. Una was angry (who wouldn't be?) but that didn't mean she couldn't understand the old bawd's motivation. Whether that made the pill more or less bitter to swallow, Una couldn't say. Barb was responsible for hundreds of people. She wouldn't risk her friends and neighbors for one girl, no matter who she was. The moment Ben left them in *The Hart*, Barb had laid her plans. She would doubtless concoct some story about Una taking it upon herself to flee into the wild, as Rian predicted. That would prove a very convenient lie when Bethonair cavalry followed Barb's breadcrumbs in the snow. Better still if Una was never heard from again. Barb was a shrewd woman, and no mistake.

While Una climbed, she felt eyes on her from the trees. How many men had Barb sent to ensure the girls couldn't escape? Una had no idea. It didn't matter. She would fight them if she had to. She'd be damned if she was going to let Rian die out here, in the middle of nowhere. The prickling, eerie sensation of being watched from an unknown vantage was only trumped by the urgent holes Rian bored into her back. She had something to tell Una, but they couldn't stop to converse and let their captors know they were on to them. Nor could Una be sure they could fight off a number of professional woodsmen, so exposed. She was waiting for the right moment. A hairpin turn, perhaps? An escarpment or perilous drop? She'd seize the first opportunity she could muster. She feared for Rian, but perhaps selfishly, was glad for the extra pair of hands. They needed each other now if they were to get out of this in one piece.

Over her shoulder, she sent the younger girl the briefest of apologetic smiles. Rian returned something more. Something important. Una shook her head. *Not now*, she signaled with her eyes. *Soon.* They wound up, rise after rise. Trees grew thick and dense here, leaving spare room between their twisting roots to navigate. Rian stumbled more than once. Their rigid guides showed little interest in slowing down to accommodate her, either. Una decided if she was only able to kill two of their captors, it would be those two— for their cruelty.

Their guides plowed ahead, never stopping, never slowing. Aside from the occasional turn to check the girls' positions, neither man showed any concern for Una or Rian at all. Several times, Una thought about feigning an injury of some sort, just to see what they'd do. If they made her angry enough, she might do it for the sheer pleasure it would give her to make them acknowledge one of them for two bloody seconds. *Bastards.*

Finally, the invisible trail they were on curved into the mountain, which placed a sheer granite wall on their left and a deep ravine on their right. All but the tips of the mightiest conifers were hidden from view in the fog. Ahead, the wall ascended a few hundred feet, then cut around the cliff face in a sharp bow. Whoever was following them would have to take a higher path toward the summit or risk exposure. Una had a pretty good idea they'd been dogging their steps from the south side of the Greensward, which would place the bulk of the hill between them. Once this ugly business was over, she and Rian could make it back to the river in under an hour. With luck, their pursuers might have gone too far out of the way to catch them up. Praying to Siora to lend her strength, she decided this was as good a place as any.

They neared the dome, and wet granite scraped at Una's boots. She risked another glance over her shoulder to find Rian's tiny white fist wrapped around the hilt of a dagger. Una took a deep breath and cracked her fingers. The boy was nearest. His hand traced the cliff face for support while his feet danced up the trail as if by thought alone. He'd been here before. That could mean Ben had too... in case they failed to escape now. Una shook herself. She'd got them into this mess. She would get them out, one way or the other.

The trail thinned, and the cliff face loomed overhead. Una and Rian mimicked their guides, sliding along with their backs against the wet stone. This was challenging, when one considered the drop twelve inches to their north. Rian made a startled sound when the toe of her bad foot slid too near the ledge.

Una tugged her into the wall by her tunic. The boy glanced at them, dispassionately as ever. Una ground her teeth. If either girl fell, it would likely save their guides the trouble of killing one or both of them later. With renewed determination, she pulled herself along the wall, and seethed. The boy's fingertips splayed against the face for balance. All Una had to do was reach. She stretched out her arm until the tip of her nail scraped against his knuckle. Just a bit further… and she would have him. All of a sudden, he came to an abrupt stop. Una faltered, and almost lost her footing. Rian cried out, and clawed Una upright by her cloak. Both gasping, Una and Rian clung to the cliff face for dear life, arms akimbo.

The boy bore a blade in his own hand by the time the girls righted themselves, but he wasn't looking at them. A few paces up the trail, Keeley stared down a dark-hooded figure who'd simply appeared around the next bend. Una couldn't get a good look at him from her vantage, but neither of their guides were pleased. The figure raised his hand, as if in harmless greeting. Keeley growled a curt response.

"What's happening?" Rian whispered into her back.

"Dunno. There's someone ahead of us."

"*Up here?* This isn't even a trail," Rian swallowed, her breathing ragged. "Maybe it's one of the others, come 'round the opposite side?"

"I don't think they know him. They've got their daggers out."

"Who then?"

Una couldn't say, for the man had materialized out of the clouds. One minute there'd been nothing ahead but rock, moss, and treetops… next, he was there. Keeley shouted something unintelligible. The figure didn't budge. Though the newcomer's face was largely concealed within his cowl, Una could just make out a glint of white when he smiled. Her heart leapt into her throat on a brief, piercing hope. That smile reminded her of Ben, however unlikely that might be. As soon as that hope arose, she shoved it down deep. Ben wasn't here. Whoever this was, he wasn't here to help them. She and Rian were on their own. Slowly, so as not to rouse the boy's notice, she nudged Rian backward. "Una, I have to tell you—"

"Later."

Rian's hand squeezed hers. "I left word. Ben will come."

Not soon enough.

"That's good, Rian. Stay here."

"Don't. You don't have to."

"You know I do."

Rian slid the dagger into Una's nearest hand. "Be careful."

Una slunk cautiously into position behind the boy. "What's the hold-up?" she asked him. He jumped to find her so close. Keeley's skinny back straightened as he ordered the figure out of their way. The mysterious stranger held both hands aloft, as if to say, 'look how harmless I am, friend.'

"Some wild man, or other," the boy grunted. "Don't worry, milady. Keeley can handle him."

Una rested her hand casually over his. He scarcely had time to suck in a surprised breath. "Oh, I'm not worried a bit." She unfurled her Spark like a net. The boy gave a soft helpless sort of squeak. His dagger scraped against stone as he slid nose-first down the wall. Una tried to catch him, and the noise snapped Keeley's head around like a top.

"Breccan!" Keeley's grey-brown eyes burned with fear. "What have ye done to Breccan, ye feckin' *witch*?"

"Rian, get back!" Una steadied herself against the rock. Keeley didn't even stop to examine the boy. He leapt over Breccan's prone form to slash at her from higher ground. Backpedaling with caution, Una managed to put a wide boulder between them. Cursing, he climbed over the impediment with the ease of a mountain goat. His next swing opened a four-inch seam along her exposed forearm. Hissing, she dropped onto her backside. Her other arm dangled over the infinite. Vertigo struck with sickening urgency.

"Una!" Rian cried, from further down.

"Rian, get away!" Una called as Keeley hunched over her, his dagger high. Kicking out at his legs, she braced herself against the boulder. He came at her twice as quick as the last time. He was certainly more experienced with the slim Eirean dagger than she was. She parried one blow, then another, but jerked to a halt when her heel clipped the edge. If she got up now, she'd fall. He was on her again, shoving his dagger into hers until it scraped the underside of her chin. With bared teeth, she pushed up with all her might. For a sack of bones and loose skin, Keeley was stronger than she'd hoped he'd be. If her arm gave out, he'd drive his knife straight through her clavicle. His hot, fetid breath moistened her cheeks.

"I'll kill ye, ye Siorai bitch!"

Gagging, she rammed her free heel into his spine. Her attack accomplished nothing. Sharp metal dipped through the first two layers of her skin, and she cried out. Summoning every ounce of Spark she could spare, she sent a current of electricity down the shaft of her dagger where it connected with his. The resulting jolt caused him to drop his blade in howling pain. He rolled aside to clasp at his arm. Una's boot slammed into his knee. Keeley's pathetic scream availed him nothing. He tumbled over the side of the mountain, into the ravine. Out of breath and bleeding, Una bit her lip, and pulled herself up the wall. Rian stood a mere four or five feet down the trail, her face ashen, her eyes large white bulbs.

"Una, look out!"

Una hadn't heard him approach over the moss-ridden shale. Like a puff of smoke, the hooded figure was suddenly there, standing beside her with a curious tilt to his head. Rearing back, she reached for a dagger which wasn't there. The toe of her boot ground against its pommel, where it lay uselessly against the ledge. She cursed.

"Stay back!" She couldn't fight fairly this time. The newcomer was tall. Taller than any man she'd ever laid eyes on before, save Ben. Though his clothing was shapeless, rumpled, and clearly worn, she could tell he was a bit broader through the shoulder too. Without a weapon, Una could only hope he made the mistake of laying hands on her bare skin. Otherwise, he could snap her wrists like kindling, and toss her from this precipice like a ragdoll.

"No need to be afraid, little one." Unbidden, his voice summoned all sorts of irrational, unrelated images to her mind: the far-away rumble of thunder in the rush of an oncoming summer storm; waves lapping at her favorite childhood beach in Bethany; her mother's quiet laughter; the bells chiming in her grandmother's chapel; her first kiss— and the wind billowing over the silk curtains in Una's bedchamber. The small hairs on Una's arms and nape stood on end. Why did she recall such things at a time like this? He inched closer. Had she ever seen teeth so white? So neat? "I mean you no harm. I vow it."

Rian was only half a step behind her now. She clutched at Una's wrist. "*Get back!*" she spat. "You're not welcome here."

Una allowed herself to be handled. She puzzled over the power in the figure's voice. Why did it summon the most comforting images she could conceive of? She felt she could wear that voice like a cloak— bundle up in it, as if it were the safest, warmest, most beloved garment she owned…

"Am I not?" he asked, pushing his cowl back. A middle-aged man, with a broad plain face, smiled back. He was so ordinary, so positively *average*, without a single memorable feature to focus on. Una blinked, and the spell evaporated in an instant. "I only meant to see if ye two were all right," his voice now bland as unsalted butter.

Had she imagined it? Blood loss, maybe? Her arm *was* bleeding rather badly. Rian forced herself ahead of Una, using her lithe form as a bony shield.

"What do you want?"

Una shook herself.

"Rian, there's no need."

"*Shut up, Una!*"

The man frowned, with a face like a whipped puppy. "I came to help ye. That's all."

"I don't believe you!"

"Rian, what is the matter with you?" She'd never seen Rian so disturbed before, and they'd almost been eaten twice in one week. The man seemed unperturbed, if slightly crestfallen. He was just a woodsman. Even the bow slung across his back proclaimed his ineffectual normalcy. He must have been as stunned by the outrageous scene he'd wandered into as Keeley had been to discover him around that bend. After a lengthy pause, the newcomer laughed. This time, a ghost of Una's first impression shone through his ever-so-ordinary veneer. Una grabbed Rian's arm, without thinking.

His smile unwavering, he tilted his head at something above them, as if tracking sounds neither of them could hear. Dull brown eyes fell upon them with a sardonic gleam.

"Very well." That voice again! Una shuddered against the onslaught of images that raced through her mind. "Seems we've no time for games, fun though they might have been." His laughter was like the trickle of water in a fountain or the chill of snow on the tip of her tongue. With a gasp, she sent a short burst of Spark into her blood to purge these illogical thoughts.

How was he doing this?

"I *am* here to help. I don't require your belief, or permission. You've many enemies up there," he gestured to the ridge above. "They've heard Keeley's shouts. Even if you make it back to the river, they will follow."

"Why would you want to help us?"

"Because my nephew would want me to."

Una opened her mouth to speak, but Rian's elbow jabbed into her ribs. Una's jaws snapped shut over an 'oof.'

"You won't make it to safety before they're upon you," he added. "I think you are aware what they mean to do with you both? Why kill that knobby old man, otherwise?"

Rian said something in a language Una would only recognize as *Ealig* much later. Its musical quality was simultaneously soothing and alarming. The tall stranger answered in kind, and Una felt the muscles in Rian's back relax slightly under her hand. The scuffing along the upper portion of the trail grew louder.

"Well?" he asked, adjusting a dusty, moth-eaten sleeve as if it were the most delicate lace. "Are you satisfied, or will I have to take you out of harm's way by force?"

Una looked from one to the other, completely befuddled. Rocks slid down the trail from on high. Rian shook her once, hard. "Una!"

"*Yes?*"

All at once, the world rushed by her ears, as if drained through a funnel centered in the core of her brain. Falling upward, racing down, spinning through... all these feelings occurred to her at once. She felt her spine lengthen and shorten; her skin stretched taut to tearing, then clenched tight again, as if rolled into a wad. Her bones disconnected, scrambled, then rearranged themselves of their own accord. She heard Rian scream from a great distance, its timbre as deafening as it was difficult to discern. Then... the vortex abruptly abated. Una skidded over a grooved wooden floor. Her head struck a wall with a hard crack. The smell of pine was ubiquitous, like the sawdust rushes swept into her open mouth. With a groan, Una choked the offensive offal out of her throat. Rian lay on her back beside her, huffing up at the bare timbers on the ceiling. Una tried to still her roiling guts when the stranger's bland face bent down to grin at them.

"There now! All better, yes?"

Una hacked up another mouthful of dirt, as he stood framed in the open door of this seemingly abandoned cabin. "Who are you?"

His grin was swift and dull as dry toast. "Give it time. I'm sure it'll come to you."

Turncoat

Damek leaned against the slanted window box, his arms crossed over his chest. Outside, snow fell in a steady rhythm. He'd taken to wearing his cloak at all hours of the day. If it didn't warm up come morning, he'd also start sleeping in it. He had many reasons to dislike the North, but her early, ruthless winters were perhaps his foremost complaint. Frowning, he watched millions of swirling specks dance on the wind. If this got any worse, he would be forced to march on Rosweal a day earlier than planned. Damek had business in Rosweal. Weather be damned.

Martin caught his eye over their informant's bowed head. Gilcannon blubbered nonsensically. Dawes' expert fists had left huge red welts on the planes of his formerly pleasant face. Damek had very little use for men of this sort, especially one as arrogant as this preening little prick. The bootlegger had tried to make demands of *him* as if the Lord of Clare was some lice-ridden street creature awaiting orders. Martin begged permission to kill the fool for his arrogance hours ago, but Damek thought better of it. The man may be a jumped-up pimp looking to profit at their expense, but he knew things they needed to know. Gilcannon wheezed, and a blood bubble ballooned from one of his nostrils. Damek watched his reflection twitch in the windowpane.

"This would be much simpler if you'd tell me what I wish to know."

Gilcannon flinched from Damek's clipped voice. A thick trickle of pink spittle swung from his trembling chin. "I told ye everything already, yer lordship."

Martin reclined beside him with his legs thrown over a nearby chair. He prodded the bound informant with the toe of his boot. "The world hates a liar, Master Gilcannon."

Dawes delivered another swift open-handed cuff that snapped Gilcannon's head sideways. He sniveled like a whipped girl. Damek waved Dawes away.

"You expect me to believe that you've known this man for over ten years, and you can't properly describe him? That's rather remarkable, I think."

Gilcannon sucked a long stream of air through his open, seeping mouth. "I ain't never met him afore today. Just know of him, don't I? He's Gramble's boy. I told ye what I saw," he shuddered. "What more do ye want from me?"

"You watch your mouth," growled Martin. "Your life's worth less than a wet fart to us, Gilcannon. You'd do well to remember to whom you are speaking."

"I swear it on me mam's teats. I only saw him for a moment. He *killed* me friends, I think. *All o'em.*"

Damek faced the scene again, arms still crossed. "Did you notice anything about him that struck you as strange— aside from this 'bloodthirsty leer,' you went on about at length? You said he was tall? How tall? You said he was fair-haired? Brown, blond? Give us something to go on."

"He's t... taller than most men by a mile, I'd say. Taller than ye, milord."

"And me?" Martin, the bloody tower, pointed a thumb at his own throat. "He's taller than me?"

"Aye, sir. A bit."

Damek circled Gilcannon's chair. "Is his hair a blond so pale, it looks like spun spider-silk, or merely yellow, like hay?"

"Milord, some water, *please.*"

"Answer the question."

"Seemed common to me, sir."

Damek paused, mid-circuit. The floor was smeared red with blood and piss. He was careful to avoid the effluent stream. "That doesn't fit the picture Wallace has painted."

"No, My Lord," agreed Martin. "But as I said before, these faeries can be quite formidable. Perhaps he is half-breed after all?"

Ignoring that, Damek focused on Gilcannon's quivering face. "You said he had a sword. What did it look like?"

"Water..."

Damek waved Dawes over with the dipper. When the slurping and racking coughs ceased, Damek leaned in close. "Now, tell me about the sword."

"It were a big bastard, milord. Not like the ones ye all carry nor what we had in the war— beggin' yer pardon. 'Twas a broadsword, I think, but it were different like..." he struggled to find the right words. "Thinner and curved a bit at the point. Sidhe-make, maybe. Never seen one quite like it afore."

"Different how?"

"Well, it were a fine piece, but... it looked old. Worn and beaten, like. 'Cept for the pommel."

"What do you mean? A gem or device of some sort?"

He shook his head. "An animal. A deer, I think. I weren't close enough to get a good look afore I ran. Solid silver too, I 'member that. All the way down the handle, to the guards."

"Could it have been a stag?" Damek held his breath.

"Aye, it coulda been that, yeah."

Martin slid his feet under him, bracing his elbows against his knees. "My Lord, that doesn't mean anything. He could have stolen the sword or bought it. A number of explanations are possible."

"Too much is adding up to the same conclusion, Martin. Our man is a Dannan lord." Damek pinched the bridge of his nose to still the headache brewing behind his eyes.

"You don't know that."

Damek snorted, "A silver stag for a pommel?"

"He could be a thief, a collector, or a wealthy faerie. There are many possibilities. You heard the pimp's description. You're jumping to conclusions again."

"We all saw what he did to those beasts."

"I'll not argue that he has training. Doesn't make him Sidhe, and certainly doesn't make him a lord."

"He's Sidhe, Martin. *I can feel it*. Our men are some of the best-trained soldiers in the world, but I doubt an entire contingent could have killed one of those creatures as easily as Una's mysterious savior killed *two*. Three arrows and twelve steps— that's all it took. He's carrying a Dannan longsword with an Adair device at the pommel."

"My Lord, don't you think we should—"

"Martin, follow me." Damek didn't wait for Martin to get up. He strode into the hall and waited at the upstairs landing. Scowling, he observed his officers in the Greatroom below. Busy drinking, eating, and carousing— they'd demolished Vale's winter stores in only three days. Twice now, Damek had sent raiding parties into neighboring villages to replenish their dwindling supplies, an order he would likely have to repeat tomorrow. Armies were never self-contained for long. Men signed up to plunder. They may soldier for whichever lord swore to feed and house them, but without swift reward, that lord was often hostage to their whims.

Point in fact: the sight Damek beheld downstairs. Here was one act of disobedience that spelled trouble; however he reacted to it. Once boredom set in, insubordination was never far behind. What few prostitutes the farming hamlet boasted were here now, entertaining his officers against his express command. Worse, not all of the women he saw here tonight were professionals. One of them was the Headman's daughter. Damek's jaw set when he heard Martin's step behind him.

"Who allowed them to take these girls out of confinement?"

He heard the air whistle through Martin's nose. "I did, My Lord. They were making trouble in the farms again. Two families done to death for ale and women. I had to string up four good men, including two officers."

"Why wasn't this information relayed to me immediately?"

"You have many concerns to trouble you just now, My Lord. It's my duty as Commander to manage the troops. I made sure only women who volunteered were taken."

"And the ale?"

"That too."

"I don't like it, Martin."

"I knew you wouldn't, but it's this, or I hang more of them tomorrow. They're bored. No damned good ever came from armed men who're idle."

Damek gripped the railing. "That one there," he nodded at the girl in the corner with Killian and his friends. She was pushed, pulled, and prodded from nearly every direction. Damek could see the tears on her cheeks from here. "She's the Headman's get. She can't be more than fifteen. I want her out of here, Martin. Now."

"The Headman's dead, My Lord. Not to put too fine a point on it, but you're the one fucking his widow in their marriage bed every night." Martin clapped a hand on his shoulder. "The girl was given ten silver stags, which she accepted eagerly. That's more coin than she might earn in three years otherwise. Perhaps when we leave, they'll have a new Headwoman?"

"I'm not laughing, Martin."

"The lads may be loyal to you, Damek, but they didn't ride north to sit in camp and make love to their fists. They came to raid. They know the Duch hasn't sanctioned this. No reinforcements will be marching up from Ten Bells, either. These boys are all you have. Let them have their fun, or I swear they'll take it, with or without your permission."

Damek considered the scene before him with a curl in his lip. "We need to get on with it. Every rape and every farm they burn for coppers reflects upon me, Martin. No more paying local girls to whore for them either. I mean it. Tonight's concession is the last I'll make. They'll save it for Rosweal or hang by the roadside, *sans cocks*. Their choice."

"As you will, Lord Bishop," Martin sighed. "Better a drunken fumble than a bloody struggle, I always say. It's a long, cold slog back home, isn't it? Just remember, keepin' these boys happy is your responsibility."

Damek cursed. Bloody savages, the lot. He'd lost more decent fighters to mischief on campaign than flux or combat combined. "Is it true that Sidhe armies don't raid or rape?"

"I hear they raid each other's *raths* in Aes Sidhe twice a year for a laugh. On a march, however, they don't rape or pillage, and they never kill unless ordered. Bastards have steel in their blood, you ask me."

"No finer fighters in the world, I'm told."

Martin raised his brows high. "Aye. If our men had half their patience and skill, we'd give His Majesty real cause for concern."

"Alas, we do not," Damek gestured to the scene below. "If only I knew their secret."

"Immortality, My Lord. I assume patience of that nature can only be earned. Neithana, for example, is the pursuit of many lifetimes."

"I know. The Adair is a master."

"*Was*," Martin corrected.

"It's him, Martin. I know it's him."

"No, you don't."

"I've seen that sword before. It's emblazoned in the glass over my uncle's dais. An elven longsword: four feet long, curved at the tip, and crowned with a leaping silver stag. The man wielding it was nearly seven feet tall. He was said to cut through men as the wind cleaves waves."

"He wasn't the only Dannan with a sword like that. I've seen others. His red-haired cousin, for one, and their champion Fionn. That pretty bastard carried one almost six feet long."

"You're making my point for me. It's a Dannan sword— an *Adair* sword. The Bolg don't carry them, and Northers could never afford one."

"My Lord, we don't know—"

"A *silver stag* for a pommel, Martin."

"It could have been stolen. It could have been made to mimic the others. Don't shake your head. You know it's possible."

"Stolen from an Adair lord? Not likely. Purchased? A forgery? *No.* I don't believe any of that. You saw for yourself. There's no way someone just happens to discover a talent for swinging around a thirty-pound longsword. He's the Adair, or I'm buggered. I grew up listening to nothing but tales of his sack of Bethany. Of what he did to my grand-uncle Kevin and the defeats he dealt his predecessors. I've always wanted to see him fight. The man's a legend."

"All right then, My Lord. For whatever unholy reason, if Kaer Yin Adair is alive and seeks to help your cousin across the river to his father, why? That's the last question I'll ask you. Why would he fake his own death, hide in Northern Eire as a lowly woodsman, and creep around rescuing damsels by accident?"

"You said it yourself: 'by accident.' I don't think he planned any of this. As Cunningham said, Una wasn't his objective from the first. The Crown Prince did some very naughty things at Dumnain, didn't he? I'll bet he means to use her to barter his return. He must have taken her to Rosweal to buy himself time to procure a warrant."

"There's still a chance it isn't him."

Damek didn't belabor the point. They would discover the truth in due course. He said, "Anyway, we've gathered all the intelligence we're going to. Rosweal's just ejected a host of Tairnganeah from their walls," he returned Martin's barking laugh, "and I'm sure they're preparing for us next."

"A fat lot of good it'll do them. Our men are so pent-up that they could chew their way through the walls. When do we march?"

"Dawn. We'll discuss tactics in the morning, but I want it finished by sunrise the following day. We've been here too long, as it is."

"Very good, My Lord. What do you want me to do with the bootlegger?"

"You can make him a nice home somewhere along the baggage train. If Rosweal decides to negotiate for Una, we may need him. I'll be in my quarters. Any man who disturbs me will regret it."

"Aye, My Lord," Martin smirked. "Understood."

The Headman's wife was far too young for the mealy old miser Damek had cut down days before. It took his men less than a half-hour to sack the village, all told. By the end of the day, the majority of Vale's men were either dead or imprisoned, and the women were confined to the Millhouse under guard. The Headman's wife proved most eager to cooperate with him. He was hardly one to deny an attractive woman the occasional parlay. Damek was pleased to note she didn't bemoan her newfound widowhood, either. With his hands full of her rich brown hair, he lay back against the headboard while she went to work against his pelvic bone. Her tongue slipped out to test his length, and he sighed. Things were just getting interesting when a delicate cough broke his concentration. His eyes flew open. A dark cowled figure stood in the shadows of the farthest corner of the room. In the dim lantern light, Aoife's pale bronze skin gleamed copper. Her eyes, however, glowed a murderous violet.

Sitting up with a start, he shoved the widow from the bed. She tumbled to the wooden floor, a screeching tangle of sheets and flailing limbs.

"Get out," he snapped. "Tell no one what you've seen, or I'll kill you. Do you understand?"

She bobbed her head and scrambled from the room with the ghost of her dignity held before her ashen face. Damek swiftly drew the coverlet over his nudity. With a sneer, Aoife pulled her hood back.

"I should've let you finish, Lord Bishop. I would've liked to see that girl's blood mingle with your fluids."

"Too late for you to feign jealousy now, cousin."

Aoife manufactured a pretty pout and ran her fingers along the furs at the edge of his mattress. "Are you still angry about your little heretic?"

"I need her more than I need you."

"That so?" She unbuttoned her cloak, revealing the simple white robes she wore beneath. Her hair, a midnight mass of glossy black waves, had been clumsily shorn to the tips of her delicate ears. Damek hated seeing her in this Siorai getup, could never get used to it. Forcing a starling to waddle with chickens was cruel. Though, he refused to be swayed by her distracting beauty. She sat at the end of the bed and folded her hands demurely in her lap. "Who'll make you King of Eire if not me?"

"You betrayed me. I should kill you."

Her laugh was like a brush of velvet over his chest. "I didn't betray you, Damek. Vanna Nema gave an order, and I had no choice but to obey. You know that. She holds my geis, as she will one day hold yours."

"*Never*. I'll never swear to that manipulative old hag."

Aoife pursed her lips. "You speak so of your grandmother?"

"I'm not her puppet, nor her plaything. If she desires the house of Donahugh under Armagh's rule, she will cease dangling legitimacy before my nose like a carrot. Una is *mine*. An attempt upon her life is an affront to me."

"That girl is worthless, Damek. She's the heretic spawn of a spent lineage. Her own family has given her up for dead. The Duch's barons didn't love her mother enough to stop Patrick from killing her, and they won't lift a finger to see her daughter crowned Duchess. You don't need her. Our grandmother has striven all your life to ensure that Tairngare is divided and weak. The time to strike is nigh. Be patient, my love."

He leaned toward her, drawing his legs up under the coverlet. "You don't understand a gods-damned thing, do you? The barons may not love her, but they'll fight for her because she holds the right bloody *name*. You might get half of Tairngare to consume itself against the Moura, but the other half— indeed, the whole fucking North— will back Drem if it comes to civil war. You may take the city, but you'll lose Tara, Ten Bells, and all the towns east of the Shannon. If by some miracle I'm wrong… you'll never hold them. Names have meaning. The old alliances have meaning. Una has the name Aoife. Both names. Patrick didn't marry her mother for her cooking."

"*Might* has meaning. How do you imagine these grand names of yours ever managed to craft those alliances in the first place? Not by standing in a field, with only their banners to declare their intentions." She tucked her head in the crook of her arm to watch him. "They took their alliances at the point of a sword. Forged those names through blood and cunning."

"You've been peddling this old chestnut for so long; the tree should be twenty feet tall by now." He rolled his eyes.

"The Bolg will come, Damek. You're Falan Mac Nemed's son."

"I don't need them. I'll have Una Donahugh." He made sure she couldn't miss the deadly sincerity in his eyes. "Next time one of you makes an attempt on her life, I'll take it personally. I don't intend to conquer here for Liadan's pleasure. I mean to rule, and rule well."

Aoife flounced onto her back. "You just want to fuck her."

"That's not your business."

"Isn't it? I would make a much better queen than that dwarf. Have you seen her once in all these years? She's not as beautiful as everyone says she is. She's too masculine, too introverted, and too short. Besides, she isn't Fir Bolg. Our lowest serving women outshine her in every way. Wouldn't you rather have a Bolg queen, Your Grace?"

Damek gave her a knowing smile. He slid down the coverlet on his elbows until his face hovered over hers and drew her full red mouth close. "You'd make a beautiful queen, cousin. Though, you're not free to entice me. Nor do I think I'd enjoy having my throat cut in my sleep."

"Wait for me. I won't belong to Nema forever, Damek."

"I believe it," he smiled and crushed his mouth to hers. Her fingers wound into the hair at his nape. He forgot how angry he was with her for some time. Moaning into his mouth, she rolled atop him. Any further thoughts he might have had departed like vapor. Lifting the hem of her robe, he pressed himself upward. Her skin felt like heated silk against his. He was partway inside of her when she broke off with a gasp. "What?" he blinked.

"I almost forgot to tell you what I came to say!"

His fingers splayed over her bare round hips. The damp hollow between her thighs beckoned. "It can wait."

"No, it can't. Something… odd has happened. Your precious princess has got herself a very interesting ally. I'm not sure how, exactly."

Damek's mood clouded. He bucked her off his lap.

"You already know she isn't alone?"

"Who is he?"

"Someone who should be dead."

"Stop playing games, Aoife."

She snickered. "You can't imagine. I saw him myself. Sudden as thunder, there he was: silver hair swirling in the wind. To think of it gives me shivers!"

"So, it is him— the Adair?"

She smacked his arm playfully. "You did know! How clever of you."

"Don't patronize me, Aoife. I thought he was dead."

"After what he did to those villagers, we all thought Bov Dearg slew him upon the tor. They even burned his effigy," she shook her head. "He shouldn't be alive, but he is. I saw him, plain as I'm seeing you now. Gods, what a sight. He's so beautiful. It's almost terrible. Well, I suppose all the bloody Dannans are beautiful if you've a taste for bloodless ferocity."

"He protected Una?"

"What is it about that girl, Damek? She's some kind of trophy, always waiting for the next hand to hold her. It's pathetic."

"You're trying to kill her. In a way, I owe him a debt."

"This is worse for you, Damek dear. If Midhir's son means to keep her, all of our plans will have to be amended. No King of Eire can exist so long as the Prince of Innisfail lives. Surely you know that?"

He did. Only too well. "I have them cornered in Rosweal. I don't think he can cross without a warrant for her. I believe he's playing for time."

"No. I know what he's planning to do. If he's not dead, he can't cross the border."

"A geis?"

She shrugged. "Why else would he stay in this impoverished wasteland? A prince of the Tuatha De Dannan? He's been exiled. I can feel it."

"He must have an ogham charm." Damek toyed with the cool sliver of rubbed quartz at his own throat. "Our captive said he was abnormally tall but unremarkable, with hay blond hair and rough features."

"Not when I saw him, *trust me*."

Damek ignored this paltry attempt to induce him to jealousy. "He's going by the name 'Ben Maeden,' according to Gilcannon."

"Who's this?"

"A base flesh peddler who incited a trade war between the guilds in Rosweal. Thought he could use me to further his own ends."

"More fool he."

"Do you think he means to pass her off at the border? He could be waiting for someone. A messenger from Bri Leith, or a proxy perhaps?"

"No. What good is a trophy if you can't carry it home yourself? I believe he means to break his geis. All Sidhe have the right to challenge their fates, but some challenges are unequal, even to our gifts."

"What does that mean?"

Aoife propped her head on her elbow, squeezing her warmth into his side. Her eyes were luminous. "There are dread creatures between this plane and the Oiche Ar Fad, Damek. You know that well enough. One guards the gates of Aes Sidhe and rules the waterways between realms."

Damek's breath hitched. "Pooka? Gods… they can't be killed." He repressed a shudder. Pooka were shape-shifting monsters from the darkest tales. They assumed the guise of whatever the victim most longed for or feared.

"They can, but only once a year, when the veil thins between realms." She traced little circles on the flesh of his stomach with her fingernail.

"On Samhain, you mean? That's less than three days from now. That doesn't give me much time. If he kills that thing, he'll spirit Una over the border." His stomach knotted in anxious fear… *never to be seen again.*

"Don't be so sure. There is a good chance the pooka will destroy him. Kaer Yin must be desperate for an opportunity to return to his father's good graces. Whoever has the girl holds Eire— as you said. Midhir will reward his errant son for risking so much to avoid another war. That must be his motivation."

Damek scrubbed his face with his open palms and groaned through his fingers. "That *must* not happen."

"Relax," her lips brushed his ribs. "I'm here to help you."

He stared at the top of her head; eyes narrowed to slits. He didn't need to guess that this was part of some grander scheme to eliminate Una before she made it to Aes Sidhe. The destruction of an old enemy before he could return to power was surely an added perk. Damek wasn't a child. He couldn't trust Aoife, and he certainly couldn't trust Vanna Nema. Nema would use him for as long as he served a purpose. When she could find no longer find one, she would eliminate him. This had been the fate of uncounted illegitimate children descended from her rapacious bloodline: pawns, all. He and Aoife were no exception. Though, of the two of them, Damek was the only one who understood this, deep down. Aoife believed in Nema. One day, it would be the death of her.

"Stop. I am no longer in the mood."

Her mouth closed over him, and he gritted his teeth. She smiled on her way back up. "You lie. You must be disappointed I scared off your little conquest."

His smile was cold. "*Not at all.* I'll save it for my wedding night."

She raked her sharp nails over his thigh on her way off the bed, bringing a triumphant chuckle to his throat. "You've become a bore, Damek. I wonder if you realize?"

"I don't care." He stood up and padded to the Headman's wardrobe which held his clothing and boots. On the chair beside it lay his cuirass, mail, and fox-lined cloak. He tugged on his leggings and trousers first, so there could be no confusing his intentions. "I have much to do, Aoife. Unless you have something useful to offer, I suggest you leave before Martin sees you. He's never killed a woman before. In your case, I imagine he'd make an exception."

"I'm not your servant, Damek," she purred. "I came to warn you about the Crown Prince, not to help you trap your little Milesian cousin into matrimony. The prince must be destroyed. I'll do it myself, if I must."

Damek gave her a crooked grin. "Will it be so simple?"

"You may make your jokes, but he is the most celebrated swordsman in Innisfail. He's not a foe to take lightly."

He knew that too. For Damek, who was covetous of the title, Aoife's barb had the opposite effect from the one she desired. A wide grin tugged both of his ears up high. "I can't wait to meet him."

Lesser Evil

As soon as the Greenmakers crossed the Taran Gate, they were called upon to alert every person in the slums of the approaching army. The south-facing neighborhood was low-slung, crowded, and terminally flammable. If one shack caught flame, so would all the others. With Lord Bishop's troops dragging a massive trebuchet behind their lines, Ben doubted this end of town would remain upright through the first shot. Thus, Ben and company roamed from dwelling to dwelling, shoving men, women, and children from their beds. Gerrod and Jimmy took charge of directing the excitable citizenry to the northern end of the city, where every structure was built from solid stone with roofs of tin or tile. It would take quite a bit of effort to raze that end of town, catapult or none.

Bearing tidings of a larger incoming force did not buy the Greenmakers copious affection. After all, Rosweal had just fought off one onslaught, hadn't they? These were the poorest folk in Eire and were acutely cognizant that they didn't have many places to flee. Indeed, many would sleep outside in the Greensward until the threat passed or be forced to beg in the streets of some neighboring village. With more bad weather coming on and a decided lack of supplies to travel with, many would die from exposure long before they starved. In light of these realities, most preferred to remain behind their useless city walls rather than brave the elements for a conflict they had no hand in starting. Ben couldn't blame them. Wasn't he the one who brought this reckoning upon them? If he hadn't returned to Rosweal, would either group of soldiers have bothered to march this far northwest? He didn't need to hear the answer. All of this was on his conscience and his alone.

Rather than wallow in pointless guilt, Ben opted to save as many people and homes as possible. The Greenmakers worked through the night, carting people and belongings up and downhill to the Quarter. At some point, he managed to cram something halfway edible into his mouth but couldn't recall when or what it was. The snow stopped sometime after dawn. Ben took a break to watch the sunrise. The next thing he knew, Gerrod's toe prodded his heel. Startled, Ben lurched to his feet, hand flying to his sword-pommel. Gerrod's palms shot out.

"Whoa! Whoa. I been lookin' everywhere for ye."

Shaking himself awake, Ben leaned against a rickety timber post for support. He hadn't slept in days and must have collapsed after clearing the area. "What's happening?"

Gerrod looked uncomfortable. "Well, I'm not sure how to tell ye this, so I'll just say it. Robin was right about Barb's intentions. Says the girl left Rosweal of her own accord, but—"

Ben scrubbed filthy fingers over his aching eyes. "Gods *damn* that scheming bawd! When? *How long have I been here, Gerry?*"

"Ye've been here an hour or so, all told. Colm says she was long gone afore we got back. I know yer sore about it, but Ben, please try to see it from her side. None o'the folk here asked for this trouble. We lost good men yesterday. She did what anyone in her position would."

Ben glared a hole through Gerrod's flushing face. "I know that, Gerry. I'm not planning to gut her. Well, likely not, anyway. I need to know where Una is before this gets any worse."

Gerrod visibly relaxed. He chewed his chapped lower lip. "Them ole loggers' huts, in the hills some miles west. Barb only said as much 'cos Robin ordered her to. I expect he'll be around shortly to give ye the news hisself. I just thought rather than waste more time… ye'd like to know, quick as possible." He shuffled his feet. "I know ye didn't mean for this to happen, and it's hardly yer fault that yer lady's hunted, but Rosweal can't bear the brunt for her— beggin' yer pardon. Four hunnerd men takes piss right outta us."

Ben adjusted his sword belt and slapped himself, alert. "I know you all believe that, but I'm afraid you'll have to accept that one way or the other, Rosweal would have been drawn in. Both sides mean to make war, Gerry. Una's just a convenient excuse."

"I do feel bad for her. Ye can't choose yer parents, believe me, I know."

Ben gently pushed past Gerrod. About six steps ahead, he stopped. "When did Barb send her message to Lord Bishop?"

Gerrod's cheeks burned scarlet; he didn't want to be the one to tell Ben about it. "Dawn, I expect. I don't know more than that, Ben. I'm sorry."

Ben nodded once. "Right. Where's Robin then?"

"At *The Hart*, helpin' with the cleanup. It's a right mess. We lost six fellas to them Corsairs. Lots more took bad wounds— dozens, really. We couldn't stand a fight now, even if we wanted to."

Ben exhaled through his nose. "Gerry, here's a free lesson for you— a fight is never fair. The powerful don't make deals with those they consider insignificant. Whether or not you could marshal a defense against this Souther commander makes no difference to him. Bishop's men came here to support him, inasmuch as they are allowed to sack and pillage at will. All Barb has managed to do is buy time."

"But—"

"They didn't come here to make peace! The sooner you realize this, the better prepared you'll be for what follows," Ben pointed to the buildings around them. "Una or no Una, they'll take what they want and burn the leavings. You know why? Because they *can*. Pray to your Siora that I get to her before Bishop does. This is only the beginning. The Sidhe are the North's only hope now." Ben didn't wait for a reply.

Gerrod's voice called after him. "Ye can't mean to try and fight alone? He has hunnerds o'men. Ye'll get yerself killed!"

Ben held up a hand as he stalked away. "He won't send hundreds of men onto uneven ground, Gerry. He'll leave them here with orders to launch an assault come nightfall. He'll take a handful of experienced trackers into the hills for Una."

"How do ye know that?"

Ben raised a shoulder. "That's what I would do."

🦌🦌

BEN'S RIGHT FOOT BARRELED INTO the heavy oak door, blasting it inward on its hinges. He ignored the sharp tremor that sang along his shin, his eyes ablaze. With a shriek, Barb leaped out of her chair. Robin had been leaning against her desk with his arms crossed over his chest, no doubt berating her for her impetuous meddling. Robin's hand instinctively twitched toward his belt. Behind Ben, Dabney melted into the darkened hallway like a frightened child.

"*You!*" Ben strode into Barb's office with murderous ferocity.

Slipping between them, Robin placed a firm hand against Ben's heaving chest. His feet slid back a few centimeters. Ben was nearly twice Robin's size.

"Now, Ben," Robin grunted with the effort to hold him in place. "Let's not be rash."

"*Rash*? What in the *bloody nine hells* do you think is happening here?"

Barb craned her neck in defiance. "I did what I had to, Ben! She tole me to give the bastard everythin' he asked for! I swear it!"

Ben shouldered Robin aside. "Oh, she *did*, did she? Tell me, did you happen to mention the reward money you asked for?"

"Well, no, but—"

"You're not this stupid, Barb. Bishop will never pay the likes of you for anything. His men will mutiny if they aren't free to raid. *Why did you do this?*"

Barb licked her lips. She looked to Robin to save her from Ben's wroth. Robin wasn't fool enough to speak for her now.

"His man gave his word! These are my people, Ben. This is my home. Our home. I won't risk the lives o'so many for a spoiled Moura bitch. They're welcome to her, as far as I'm concerned."

"You broke your word, Barb. You took my hand, looked me square in the eyes, and *lied*. If you think that was wise, perhaps you are not as smart as I thought." Ben kicked her chair away from her. She fled toward the windows. Robin leaned nearly horizontal with the floor, trying to drag Ben away. Without another word, Ben reached up and yanked the ogham charm from his throat. His glamour fluttered, then faded. Several answering gasps from the busted doorway only fanned his temper the more. "*Just whom do you think you've betrayed?*"

"Ben, I don't think now's the time to—" Robin attempted.

Ben's silver hair swung wild over his shoulders. "The name isn't Ben, is it?"

Robin cleared his throat. "No, milord. It isn't."

Barb paled. "Ben, please! Ye have to see—"

"My *name* is Kaer Yin Mac Midhir Adair, Mistress Dormer. *Ard Tiarne* of Aes Sidhe, Lord Marshal of *An Fiach Fian*, High Commander of the Doaine Sidhe, and Champion of the Tuatha De Dannan. I am Lord of Meath, Dowth, Knowth, Muenster, and Man. I am the Crown Prince of Innisfail, and this is my land. Everything you own, the earth you live on, the very air you breathe— *belongs to me*. You and everyone you know owe allegiance to me, not to the Lord of Clare, the Duch, or the Citadel. Rosweal isn't yours to bargain with, Barb. Rosweal is *mine*."

Murmurs escalated to raucous volume behind Ben's back. He didn't care. He was done cowering behind a meaningless face and a worthless name. Hiding had brought him to this pass. Because he'd been too cowardly, too ashamed to confront his past, Aes Sidhe was now closer to war than it had been for nearly three decades. As long as he'd been trying to remain anonymous, events in Eire had been on a slow crawl to ruin.

No longer.

Ben was done with secrets and done with shame. Rosweal owed fealty to his father. They owed allegiance to *him*. He would not allow Barb Dormer to drag them all into war for her pigheadedness.

"I am your liege lord, Mistress. You broke faith with the wrong man."

Fat tears rolled down Barb's livid cheekbones. "Ben, it woulda been a war. Don't you see?"

"It will be war *because of what you have done!*" His bellicose shout rang throughout the building. "What do you think Bishop means to do with her, hm? Head to Bethany and live quietly as a private citizen?" he snorted. "Una means nothing to these people, save for a legal means to march on the North! How could you honestly believe handing her over would be better for all involved? Unless…" His silver eyes thinned over a new, unpleasant thought. Barb sank to her knees, head low. "You didn't mean to exchange her at all, *did you?*"

"Ben, please…"

A rage he couldn't quantify surged through Ben's gut. Watching her grovel, he willed his lungs to pump clean, level oxygen into his blood. "You will use my title from this day forth, Mistress. I assure you, if your plan has any success— *in either direction*— you will pay for it with your life. Do you understand me?"

"Y… yes, Be… milord. *Your Highness*," she blubbered. A consummate actress to the end. Her tears didn't move him an inch. Ben shot Robin a scowl, then whirled on the watchers gathered on the other side of the door. He felt slightly bad about misleading so many of those shocked, familiar faces. Though, he couldn't alter the past any more than he could inflict his will on the present. A choice had to be made, and he'd made it. There was no going back.

"I don't have time to explain this to any of you, and I'm sorry for that. Truly. Given what is marching up the Taran Road as we stand here arguing amongst ourselves, events will soon spin out of our control entirely. I'll be happy to answer questions as soon as this matter is settled. Agreed?" The stunned, noncommittal response he received would have to do for now. He pointed to Gerrod's wide-eyed face. "We don't have much time to prepare. I assume the Southers will arrive by nightfall. You'll need to get all the women and children who remain in town over the river as soon as possible."

Rose gasped. "Ye can't be serious, Ben… I mean, milord." She shook her head at the unfamiliar phrase. "We can't cross into Sidhe territory!"

Ben tossed her his ogham stone. She caught it instinctively, rolling the crudely cut quartzite over her long fingers. "Most things won't touch you if you hold that close. When the Sidhe come, plead sanctuary. Tell them who sent you and what's happening here. You'll surely be detained, but it's the best I can do for now. Can you manage?"

It took some time. Conflicting emotions chased over her features. Rose dipped her head and wiped a stray tear from her cheek. "Aye. I can, milord."

Ben gave her an apologetic smile. He owed her a much longer apology, but she'd have to wait for it. He couldn't spare the time as much as it pained him.

"Good. Running to Navan or Slane won't do. Your best bet is to cross and brave the consequences. A marauding Souther army trumps the Law. I vow it. Leave no women here for the Southers to find."

He waited for her awkward curtsy before turning to Colm, Seamus, and Dabney.

"You lot. Gather up any valuables that won't rush downstream immediately and sink them just shy of the docks."

"Now, wait just a minute!" Barb launched to her feet.

Ben wagged a warning finger at her. She bit her lip hard enough to make it bleed. He swung back to the gathered audience.

"Did I stammer? Do it!"

Hesitantly, those to whom he'd given orders floundered off in separate directions, appropriately stunned. "As for the rest of you, I wouldn't bother trying to defend the city from within. You'd do better to harry them from Greensward once they've burned and looted to their hearts' content. You stand no chance against fully armed, heavy infantry— not head-on, at any rate. Those that can't fight or track send over the river with the women. Those that can move east through the pines, then head south. The Souther's supply trains are a wonderful place to start. You all know how to raid. I won't explain your business to you. It's more important that none of you are here waiting for the axe to fall. Are we agreed?"

Mouths agape, they looked to Robin. Clearing his throat, he clapped his hands hard.

"Ye heard yer prince! Go, go, go!"

Gerrod didn't move a muscle even as Robin rushed past him, chasing men downstairs like a demon sent to harry them from the Otherworld. The lad spared Ben a small, sarcastic smile.

"What will ye have me do, erm, milord?

"I've sent word ahead to Aes Sidhe. I'm not sure how long it'll be before a response is mustered, but it's coming, I assure you. It may take a few days, maybe a month, but I expect Dannan troops will cross the Blackwater soon. If any of these fools hoped to rampage through Eire unsullied, they'll be sorely disappointed."

Barb sucked in a sharp breath. "Why didn't ye tell me that to begin with!"

"Because I clearly couldn't trust *you* with the information!" Ben roared back. Her teary-eyed pretense melted into something far less feminine.

"Well, that's just bloody perfect, ain't it! We'll exchange one occupyin' force for another!"

"For your sake, Barb," Ben said evenly. "You'd better hope it's sooner rather than later. After I retrieve Una from the snare you've placed her in, I expect the Southers will be none too pleased to leave empty-handed."

By midday, Ben's orders had been carried out with a fierce dedication he might find humbling if he were inclined to believe any of it was out of respect. He couldn't afford to be shy about his identity now. Whether he liked it or not, he'd made a decision he must live with. Perhaps stripping away his glamour in a temper wasn't the wisest course, but it was too late to change his mind. The deed was done. It felt odd to walk around such a familiar haunt as Rosweal in his own skin. He'd spent so long pretending to be one of them that he'd forgotten how to be at ease with himself. He felt vulnerable, exposed.

The stares he received as he sauntered toward the docks burned hotter than any brand. Not only had many of these people never seen a full-blooded Sidhe so close before, but many of them were also visibly disturbed to have shared pints, the odd game of porter, and countless skins of uishge preceding various raids into his *own father's lands*. The Roswellians' shock and mistrust prickled along his spine like a thousand needles. Ben had effectively given it up by casting off his disguise in a fit of justifiable anger. Many of these folks had been his friends. His comrades. His rivals. Gone were the days when he could share a companionable meal, or pint of ale, with any of them. They would not invite him to share their fires nor slap his shoulder in mirth or maudlin. It would never be the same again.

Deep down, Ben realized this is what he'd been waiting for these twenty-six years— to reclaim his heritage, his place in the world… his home. He couldn't allow himself to mourn a disguise any more than he could lament being born a Dannan prince. These things simply *were*. No matter how many layers of sediment piled atop that fact, the truth, as the adage declared, will out. He wasn't sorry to leave Ben the Poacher behind in Barb's office. Instead, he would miss the camaraderie he found amongst the rough men and women of Rosweal.

Decades ago, this little backwater had been the last possible place he'd ever expected to spend so much time in the years since he'd come to admire the people here more than he could say. He ignored the frightened glances, the whispers, and glares and made his way toward the Greenmakers on the dock. Ben kept his back straight and squared his shoulders. He was not ashamed. Seamus saw Ben first. Choking on his own saliva he threw a fist into Robin's shoulder. Robin stopped barking orders at the men threading counterweights over heavy chests of non-perishable goods and rounded on him with a snarl.

"Ye bleedin' nonce! I've got a wound in me arm there, ye know!" Robin noticed Ben striding up the gangplank. "What in the *hells* are ye wearin,' then?"

Ben concealed a relieved smile. Well, maybe he hadn't lost everyone after all. He crossed his arms over his white cuirass. Its sigil was a leaping silver stag crowned by three golden stars. Above that, he wore a white and silver sealskin cloak clasped at the throat with a massive silver torc, capped with a gold pin bearing an emerald as large as an eye. A peerlessly crafted longbow of white ash and blond yew was slung around his shoulders, expertly traced everywhere with cavorting woodland creatures. This bow was a masterpiece. Every experienced archer's eyes glittered in awe.

Ben's scabbard drew an appreciable glare from Robin, who swore into his open palm. Whittled from one long piece of bone, the knotwork and etchings along its face were the product of a hundred years of loving toil. Such an object was unheard of in humble Rosweal. The blade beneath shone brilliantly through the knots, like the sea after a storm. The leaping stag on its pommel took on new meaning for those glimpsing it in its proper context for the first time. Ben drew the sword and leaned against its newly polished blade.

"Nemain," he explained. He flicked it broadside. "Named for the goddess of the springs and rivers. She, who spilled her blood to poison the enemies of Lug." Ben slid the dread, infamous blade back into her magnificent sheath. "Only the bones of her beloved, Bronn, can assuage her thirst for retribution."

Seamus shook his head, astounded. "I've seen that bloody sword half a hunnerd times. Who could believe this?"

"And that," Gerrod pointed to the longbow on his back, "is—"

Ben nodded. He'd tied his hair back from his face, allowing the gold chains in his ears to chime free as he moved.

"*Sinnair*. 'King-killer,' in our tongue."

"Yer tellin' me, that's the bow what slew ole Kevin Donahugh? Can I hold it, Ben… erm, milord?" Gerrod breathed. Seamus punched him next, for good measure.

"It's the bow that unhorsed him, yes, but Nemain took his life." He tapped a forefinger against the sword's pommel. "The sword was given to me as a boy long ago."

Everyone in Innisfail knew that tale, whether they believed it or not. The silence stretched between them as the Greenmakers gawped in bewildered silence. Robin broke the spell. Coughing, he shoved Gerrod toward the ropes.

"Yes, yes. His Royal Arseness is a fine, shiny new fellow. Stop moonin' already." Sighing, he sidled up to Ben. "Well then. I'm pleased to see ye had time to go and fancy yerself up while we've been here, sacrificin' all our gold and uishge to yer goddess."

Ben shrugged. "I do like to make an entrance."

"Just where do ye think yer off to then, all done up like a princess?"

"Had to make certain everything still fit, didn't I?"

Robin sucked his teeth. "I think it's a tad snug 'round the middle."

"Nothing soft over here but your head, Robin."

"The girls'll scratch yer eyes out for that pin."

"Lasses are free to fight over my jewels any time."

"Answer the feckin' question."

"Got some work to do out west."

Robin retrieved his pipe from a hidden pocket in his tunic. He struck one of Seamus' well-made matches against a post to light it.

"Ben, if ye think I'm lettin' ye hie off into the wild on yer own, yer out o'yer gourd."

"Robin, dearest," Ben grinned. "That's not my name, and I don't recall asking your permission."

Robin blew a wad of smoke in Ben's face. "Don't be ridiculous. Ye'll get one or two 'milords' outta me now and then, but ye'll always be Ben bloody Maeden to me. Boys, what do ye say to that?"

"I think ye owe me twelve fainne, milord. I'm adding loads o'interest," said Seamus, whom Ben had once carried over his shoulders for over two miles to escape a team of competing bandits. Colm waved him away like an overgrown child. Gerrod made a crude noise.

"See? Yer a feckin' Greenmaker, same as the rest o'us. Ye mighta been born a poncey lord, sneerin' down at folk like us all yer long life, but yer a bit more'n that now, ain't ye?" said Robin.

Ben had no idea what to say. He'd merely come down here to make his goodbyes and wish them well. He hadn't expected this at all.

"Robin, you *can't* come with me."

"It's adorable ye think ye can stop me. Ye don't get to go off on yer own and have all the fun."

"I appreciate the sentiment... beyond words, but you must help your people to safety."

"Buggers'll be bloody fine. They got Barb and this skinny ole codger to help them," Robin jerked a thumb at Colm. "I don't know if it's occurred to ye yet, but this cunt Bishop probably wants ye to come out on yer own. We may be lots o'things in Rosweal, but we're loyalists to a man. No Souther lord is gonna raid the North unimpeded, by Herne. Not today, not ever."

Ben said nothing.

Robin groaned. "Colm?"

"What?" Colm snarled. He was busy helping Gerrod and four others lower the next basket laden with goods into the river's sluggish current. These containers held nearly all the gold, silver, brass, or glass in Rosweal, four baskets full of uishge pilfered from Matt's stores, trunks containing heavy pewter plates, antique silver utensils, and dry casks stuffed to bursting with costly furs, imported textiles, and fine linen. The Greenmakers would leave nothing to the Southers— not even a pair of dusty curtains. Dragging the haul back up again would be a chore of no mean size, but Ben doubted he'd be around to witness it, either way.

"I want ye to lead the raids on their supply train. I want that blasted catapult in ashes before it can be dragged in range o'the walls. I want ye to kill every man o'them ye can manage without makin' yer presence known till it's too late to stop ye. Can ye do all that?"

Colm snorted, then went back to work.

"See? Everyone knows what to do."

"Robin, you don't understand. It's almost Samhain," Ben lowered his voice to a whisper. "There's going to be more in those woods than a handful of Bethonair troopers. Worse, in fact. *Much*, much worse."

"Aye, I heard ye the first time. Here's the thing, milord. Lord Bishop gets the girl and his war if you die on us. None o'us will stand for that. I vowed to help ye, and that's what I'll do. If ye can't get her over the border, we'll damned sure try in yer stead. Besides," Robin spat, "if ye do cock it up and die, I've called dibs on that shiny bow on yer back."

⚶

Ben found Rose by the river, helping little girls and old women into small boats shored along the eastern cutbank. She flinched a little when she saw him approach. She was lovely in the low afternoon light. The long dark column of her throat was cast copper in the fading sunlight. She looked away from him, embarrassed. He caught one of her hands, threading her slender fingers through his. How many times had those fingers held his? Ben couldn't feasibly count. Despite all, Rose had been special to him for quite a long time. He would even go so far as to say he cared for her in his way.

"Rosie, you don't have to be afraid of me."

He could feel the pulse ticking furiously in her palm, like a highly wound clock. "I'm not afraid of ye, Ben… yer highness. I'm afraid of myself. What ye must think of me…."

He pulled her close and brushed her full lips with his. She whimpered, her eyes downcast. "I think highly of you, Rose. Never forget it." He pressed something heavy and metallic into her hand before releasing her fingers from his grip. She looked down at the object with a gasp. "What's this?"

"My father's ring. I want you to keep it safe, along with the stone I gave you. Do you have it?"

She touched the cord slung around her neck. "I do. I remember what ye told me. I won't fail ye if I can help it."

"There's more I would tell you, so listen closely." He nudged her chin up with his knuckle so she couldn't look away. "Don't stay near the river— not for any reason. This is very important, Rose. Any girl that strays could be lost to more than the current. There's a road a half-mile or so from the water's edge. Stay on it, and take it northeast, only northeast. Don't wander. No matter what you hear or what you might see. Do you understand?"

She nodded.

"Good. There'll be a small stone structure astride the road. It won't be far, but don't hurry to find it. The roads in Aes Sidhe sometimes have a mind of their own. When you get there, get everyone inside, and answer the door for no one. A creature that begs entrance to that place is not welcome by nature. Any trueborn Sidhe may enter of their own will. When one does, you give them that ring and tell them what I told you. You tell them their Ard Tiarne has sent you over for your safety. Do you need me to repeat any of this?"

"No, Be… milord," she smiled sadly. "It'll be as you say. I swear."

He brought the top of her head in for a kiss. "Take care, Rosie. I wish you well in the future."

Brushing her fingers along his jaw, she jerked his head down to hers for one last, lingering kiss. Ben could taste a hint of salt on her lips. When she pulled away, her eyes were wet.

"No goodbyes, Ben. Ye do what ye must. Maybe I won't be as jealous o'her as I thought?"

Despite his perplexed frown, she turned away. She grabbed Violet's child and settled her over her hip while she waited her turn to board. She didn't look back. Barb, he noticed, sat sulking in the prow of the next boat, avidly avoiding his eyes. That was as well. Ben wouldn't soon forget what she'd done, and Barb wouldn't forgive him for chastising her publicly, as she so richly deserved. Nonetheless, that wasn't to say he wouldn't miss her, just a bit. Ben cupped his palm around his mouth as they shoved off and called out to her.

"Oi, Barb!"

She looked up; her lips pinched in anger. "I'm not speakin' to ye, yer *high royal arse*!"

"You think you'll still run girls, now that you're the Governess of Rosweal?" he asked.

She blinked at him like an owl for several pregnant moments until she threw back her head and howled with laughter. Leaning over the side, she spared him an obscene gesture.

"Hells yes, I'll run girls! The finest, juiciest, randiest whores in all Innisfail! Ye just wait and see."

Surfeit of Will

Una twisted her wild hair into an inelegant knot. Most days, she quite liked her spongy golden-brown curls. Today, however, she could yank every strand from her scalp without a second thought. She was sweating, sore, and exhausted. Her damp tunic and leggings chafed her already abraded skin. She was pretty sure one of her molars was loose, and her right wrist was probably sprained. On her second trip down, she'd jarred something in her hip that made her right knee ache to an infernal degree. To make matters worse, the gash Keeley cut into her forearm had gone a suspiciously puckered purple. Una didn't need Rian to tell her it was likely infected. Bent double and huffing into the floorboards, she reached her limit.

Rian scoffed from her place beside the window. "You're wearing yourself down for nothing."

Una shot her a withering glare. Wordless, she got to her feet, rolled up her sleeves, and dashed once more for the open doorway. The trees outside were so close that she should have launched herself smack into the nearest trunk. She smelled soggy pine needles in the duff on the hillside, fresh ozone, and verdant moss. She tasted an incoming rainstorm and heard the trickle of water as the season's first snowfall melted into the earth.

Her heel sunk into the dissipating slush outside the door, and she grinned triumphantly. That hadn't happened before! Maybe this time she had it? Slipping her left foot past her right, Una prayed gravity would propel her forward and move her out. It did not. Like the first time, she incurred the same gut-wrenching feeling of falling upward, of being sucked through a too-small container, then poured out again at breakneck speed. She screamed. The floor inside the cottage rushed up to meet her face again. Groaning in exhaustion, Una turned herself over onto her aching back. Her arms flopped to either side. She'd sell one of her limbs for a bit of that cool water she heard running down the hill outside.

"Una, stop thinking about it," Rian said. "And stop looking at it."

Una couldn't help it. On a table beneath the far window sat a beautiful silver tray embossed with elegant filigree. It hadn't been there during her second attempt to escape, but just as her exertions prompted thirst, this bounty materialized to taunt her. Two crystalline glasses full of sweet, lemon-scented water beckoned mercilessly. Both tumblers were dusted with condensation from the ice chiming within— ice that retained its shape and size, regardless of time or temperature.

One fat teardrop slithered down the nearest glass, fashioning a shiny little pool on the tray below. Una licked her cracked lips. An overflowing water pitcher sat beside them, accompanied by three plump apple slices and a hunk of creamy white cheese. The more she stared, the greater her longing.

"I said, stop thinking about it." Rian removed the stopper from her water skin and shoved it none-too-gently in Una's face. She drained as much of the stale, unappealing liquid as she dared. They only had this one skin. If the day's events were any indication of what was to come, they'd need to make it last. Hugging her knees, Rian gave Una a tired look. "If you'd stop trying to muscle your way out of this, you wouldn't be so thirsty."

Una wiped her mouth. "I have to try."

"You've tried. It's not working." Rian passed half a stale biscuit over. "Eat that. Slowly. The longer you savor it, the harder your brain will work to convince itself you're satisfied."

The ice clinked together. Una stifled a moan. "How can you be sure he means to poison us? You can't know that the food and drink are bad."

"Don't you know anything about the Otherworld? If you drink or eat anything in the Oiche Ar Fad, you'll be trapped here indefinitely. They don't teach anything about the birth of magic in the Cloister?"

"You don't know that's where we are. It could be… well, it could be—"

"Una, we're in the Otherworld. I guarantee you. Don't you realize who that character was?"

"He said he was Ben's uncle," Una frowned.

"*Yes*. That leaves two individuals, doesn't it? One wouldn't bother, and the other is infamous for toying with mortals. Which one do you imagine he could be?"

"He helped us, didn't he? Without his intervention, I doubt we'd have made it down that hill." *Although*, Una stole a glance at the tempting delights displayed on that silver tray. She wondered why they appeared only when she seemed most desperate for them. Perhaps, whatever enchantment that held this place together was designed to meet the basic needs of those it confined? It wouldn't serve Una's argument, but she must concede that one glaring detail favored Rian's assertion over hers…. *we cannot leave*. No matter how many times she tried to run, the result was always the same. If he meant them no harm, why trap them in this place? This was a question she couldn't logically ignore.

"Okay then. We'll suppose you're right."

"I *am* right."

"*Fine*. It would be wise to assume that you are even if you aren't. I'll accept that. What are we going to do about it?"

"I don't know."

"How much food did you bring in that satchel? A day's worth?"

"Probably less. I was in a hurry when I packed. I hoped we'd be well south by now, at least as far as Vale. I hadn't realized Barb would send so many men to, erm, escort us." That point was moot. Of course, Barb had sent several men. She'd seen what Una was capable of firsthand. Barb wouldn't send her favorite or most trusted lugs, but she'd be sure to send plenty. Una had been actively trying to forget the double-crossing old whore for hours.

"Wonderful. We have about half a day's worth of water, too." She squinted at the sunlit scene outside. "We look to be in the same hills we were in yesterday."

"We probably are. The enchantment could be restricted to this structure only. Maybe a pocket or a sliver in time. Do you understand what I mean?"

"Not really."

Rian padded to the open doorway. The wind howled eerily over the hilltop, but not a single hair on her head stirred in sympathy. She held her palms out to press them through the opening. Una watched her arms quiver under an invisible strain. With a curse, Rian snatched her hands back, rubbing them furiously against her thighs.

"That's awful."

"Tell me about it."

"We can figure this out. There's always a way. We just have to keep trying."

"How do you figure that?"

"Everyone knows. It's the way of things."

"I hope you're right." Una set the precious water skin against the wall. "Because I can't promise not to help myself to whatever refreshments are offered when this skin runs dry. I don't think my throat has ever been so raw."

"That's by design. All that running around surely made it worse."

"Point taken, Rian!" Una snapped. Shivering, she rolled into a ball. "I'm sorry. I'm out of my depth in here."

Rian didn't respond. She took a second turn around the cabin, then a third. By the fifth pass, she stopped short. Her hand flew to her heart. An overlarge shadow flitted across the glass. Then another. Rian backpedaled. Someone squished their nose into the pane from the outside.

A man they had seen before at *The Hart* screwed his eyes up to peer inside. He seemed to stare straight at them. Neither girl so much as breathed. Una's fingers clenched Rian's so hard that Rian winced.

The figure in the window shook his head and retreated. He mumbled something to a companion, who took his turn at the window. The girls heard only muffled, discordant grunts or the odd scrape and rustle as heavy boots disturbed the foliage under the casings. Askance, Una stared at Rian. Couldn't they see them? The girls should have been spotted from the first. Perhaps they *were* in the Otherworld?

If these were Barb's men, then Rian's instinct might have been on the mark. Una dragged herself up the wall, and Rian squeezed as far into her side as she could. One of the woodsmen loitered in the doorway for quite a while, considering the shadows in each corner. Without ado, he stomped inside, sopping boots leaving muddy imprints wherever he walked. For a moment, his nose passed so close to Una's that she could have planted a kiss directly on his cheek. Burly brows knit together, he glared at the wall as if something mocked him from within. One of Rian's long blond hairs brushed against his shoulder, and *still,* he did not see them. Fascinated, Una held her fingers just shy of his face. She meant to trace the ridge of his grizzled brow.

She never got the chance to test her physicality. With a disgruntled sigh, the intruder slid his dagger back into its sheath and exited the cabin. Una released the breath she'd been holding in a torrent. Rian found her feet and raced to the window. Her cheeks were white as the snow outside.

"Una, come look! The farther away they move, the slower they go."

Of course, Una wasted no time trying to follow them out the door. She prayed that whatever magic held them here had faded from the woodsman's intrusion. Again, it did not. The next time she struck the floor, she smacked her nose hard enough to make it bleed.

"Owwww!" Her eyes welled with tears.

"What'd you do that for?" Rian mashed a torn bit of her dress against Una's face. "If they couldn't see us, then we're not really in here. Don't you get it?"

Una kept her stinging rebuttal to herself. "Seemed like a good time to try again," she said, batting Rian's fingers away. "Rian, what are we going to do?"

"Our captor could come back and deliver his terms. Maybe he'll hand us over to Ben, wherever he may be?" She blew her hair out of her eyes. "Or we could succumb to thirst and hunger and be stuck here forever."

"I thought you said there's always a way out of situations like these?"

"There is, but the heroine doesn't always see the key until it's too late. Sometimes, these tales are told to warn their listener to beware the Sidhe. To keep well out of their way."

"Don't tell me that *now*! I don't want to hear anything but how we will get out of here."

"All right, all right. We're going to get out of here, Una."

"How?"

"I'm not sure, but we'd better think of something soon. Time moves differently here."

"I swear, you live to give me bad news."

"I'm serious," Rian said. "Running out of food will be the least of our problems if we fail."

⚼ ⚼

THE SOUTHERS HAD ALREADY STRETCHED their forces between the Navan and Taran Gates at Rosweal when the last boat carrying the women and children reached Aes Sidhe's shore. Colm and his group of twenty reasonably fit raiders were the first to exit through the Ward Gate, intent to track around the Southers' left flank. Colm knew his business. As soon as the forward troops advanced, he'd do everything he could to cripple Bishop's rear line. With his supplies and reserves under attack, the Lord of Clare's assault on the city wouldn't last long.

An hour or so after the Greenmakers split up to manage their various tasks, Ben immediately tried to ditch his retinue. He did not get far; as usual, Robin outfoxed him. He caught up with him just beyond the Ward Gate. Heaving an annoyed sigh, Ben didn't bother to protest a second time. No one told Robin Gramble where he might go, not even a prince— defamed, exiled, and unloved as Ben was.

Gerrod and Seamus, it seemed, shared Robin's pigheaded determination. Thus, the four of them headed into the wild, moving up the trail at a steady clip. These hills weren't especially high, though they were deceptively steep. No simple task, to establish one's footing over moss-slick granite and crumbling shale. A wide variety of trees crowded close: strong Innish pine, squat rowans, slender birches, and oaks as wide as houses. Hordes of roots dove in and out of the stony earth, like sea serpents undulating through dark green waves. Their path was the swiftest to their destination but also the most difficult. After they'd slogged two miles into the teeming Greensward, Ben caught a slight rustle on the wind: the rattle of spurs or the jingle of a harness.

He stopped dead in his tracks. Trying to pinpoint the source of the sound, he leaned into the wind to detect it again. Gerrod, who had pretty good ears for a Milesian, had heard it too. Absentmindedly, he tugged Robin's spyglass out of his pack without permission. Snatching it back, Robin spared the sheepish lad a filthy glare, then set it against his eye. Ben pointed, and he trained the glass on the southeastern terrain. There, the land rolled a bit more than it did at this height. A team of horses would never make it up such a mess of tumble-down rocks and claustrophobic flora. Riders would be obliged to utilize the thin remnant of a pre-Transition road, a mile or so to the south.

"How many?" Ben whispered. Sound tended to travel in these barren hills, bouncing from rock to rock like an amphitheater.

Robin handed him the spyglass with a snort. "Lemme put it this way. If it comes to a fight, we're properly buggered."

It took a moment to place the flashes of blue and grey through the trees. As soon as he did, Ben wished he hadn't. He beheld quite a line of soldiers, winding slowly upward. Many Southers walked their stalwart mounts rather than punish the beasts with this climb. They'd cover twice the ground when the road leveled out higher up. Ben lowered the glass.

"Shite."

"What? How many?" Seamus whispered.

"Fifty, maybe less. Can't be sure."

"*Fifty*?" Gerrod exclaimed.

Seamus held a finger to his lips with one hand and socked Gerrod in the side with the other. "Keep yer voice down, idiot."

"Sorry… but fifty?" Gerrod rubbed his ribs. "Why'd they bring so many into these mad hills?"

"The fucker's got plenty to spare, don't he?" Robin said. "Best we beat 'em there, ain't it?"

Ben didn't like this at all. Armed men climbed the road below, two missing girls ahead, and behind… something *worse* would come calling from the river's murky depths.

"You should go back," Ben said, clutching Robin's arm so he couldn't look away. "I'll have none of your deaths on my conscience. I mean it, Robin. Once they burn through the slums, which they will, and soon, Colm will need your help to divide their forces. You must go."

Robin drew his craggy brows up. "Tellin' me what to do again, are ye? We sunk anythin' o'value in town. Girls and old folks're all gone off to get arrested by yer kin. No booze left anywhere in sight. Far as I'm concerned, they're welcome to burn that shitehole down. Make room for a proper market town once yer daddy rewards us for bein' such loyal pals to his poncey son."

"*Robin*—"

"We're wastin' time jabberin', ain't we? I'll make ye a deal. Ye kill yer beastie when it comes for ye, and we'll get yer girls clear. Fair? I promise I won't lift a fingernail to help ye." Robin covered his heart in mock oath.

"Gods damn you, Gramble," Ben grumbled, getting to his feet. Glowering, he readjusted his weapons. "If you die, I'll visit you in Tech Duinn twice a week to remind you what a useless, bullheaded moron you are."

Robin shoved him forward with a grin. "Can't wait. Now let's see how fast ye fancy Sidhe bastards can really move."

⚹ ⚹

RIAN'S WATERSKIN BELCHED ITS LAST drop shortly after their visit from Barb's henchman. Neither girl could ascertain how much time had passed, but they felt its effects all the same. The environment beyond the cabin offered few clues. Nothing moved as it should. Rain clouds that Una watched gather in the west days before had yet to crest the summit of their nearest snow-dappled peak. The sun inched across the sky on such a slow track that it scarcely seemed to move. The wind moaned over the roof like the lowest note in a wood flute: eerie, discordant, and monotonous. When twilight finally deigned to descend upon their valley, sluggish shadows oozed between the trees like tar.

Rian believed a day inside took just under three-quarters of an hour outside. She'd spent indeterminable spans watching the sunlight trace over the floorboards and marking measurements in the dust beneath the window. Una couldn't gainsay her— she didn't have the education nor strength to argue with Rian's observations. Whatever the truth, both of them were miserable. They were parched, starved, and afraid. The unbearable scent of cool water on the tray by the window was exquisite torture. Though they ignored it as much as possible, their throats burned with need by the end of Rian's reckoned third day. Una imagined a desert with hot blowing sands and a merciless sun blazing overhead. Searing winds stripped the parchment of her flesh to insubstantial bone. Her tongue leaden, blood boiling, she wandered alone, burning and desolate.

She couldn't shake herself free of this waking nightmare. Every breath she took, the ice within those glasses would clink together, and chill droplets would slide down the pitcher like a drumbeat. The scent of apples and warm summer cheese twisted her guts to frayed chords. Una tasted nothing save the barren, brittle acid of her sunken cheeks. Her lips were rough as raisins. Each blink pierced her eyes with a hundred needles. The ice would clang. The pitcher would *drip, drip, drip…* until she thought she might run mad. Rian gripped her fingers, and Una would find the strength to resist for a while longer. Then again… and again… and again: *drip, drip, drip…*

Una might weep, but she had nothing wet left in her eyes. Only salt, only burning, only despair. In their wretched state, the girls' surroundings lost meaning. Time and its importance became less vital from breath to haggard breath. When they still needed to relieve themselves, they'd move toward a pair of buckets that appeared in the corner as needed. When they slept, they unrolled mats and fluffed pillows that would disappear as soon as they woke. When they were at their lowest possible humor, a chorus of sighing bells would echo in the rafters, only to fade as they raised their eyes to mark them. They were haunted, supervised by unseen magic, or otherwise ignored.

Once, Una thought about the copper tub in her apartment on the Eighth Floor. She closed her stinging eyes and dreamed of immersing herself in that sumptuous, splendid warmth how she would idle there for hours on end, reading or dozing. She heard Rian gasp; sure enough, this very tub appeared in the corner, steam rising from its fragrant, oil-scented interior. Una cried out, and the vision melted away, same as the rest.

It seemed they could only enjoy these luxuries if they accepted them without question. If either girl spent too long in consideration or spoke of them aloud, these visions would evaporate like smoke. All save the tray and its siren song… that bit of perfidy was as steady as the floor beneath them. Nourishment had a sound. Satiation had a melody. Relief, a chant. It went *drip, clink, drip.* The sun went down. Five full days had passed, by Rian's whispered estimation. They couldn't speak much anymore for lack of lubricant in their throats and could hardly move for the empty void within their bellies. Una and Rian lay side-by-side, fingers woven together and trembled with hunger and dehydration.

Una must have fallen asleep. In her dream, a great *nothing* hunted her through the spaces between lucidity and wakefulness. The thing cackled in her mind, bearing a formless menace as insubstantial as vapor, yet painfully near. It clawed at the fringes of her subconscious. A louder, stronger burst of wind thundered into their valley. On its heels came the glacially slow patter of rain on the shingled roof. Una felt every drop slither down the exterior walls with a lust that made her gums ache. The simmering storm provided somber background music to this torment. Una's nightmares merged. A sinuous creature folded the girls within its ravenous embrace. It whispered things through the rain… horrible things; greedy, wanton things. The pitcher toppled, pouring reeking fluids into a deep black well. This fathomless pool contained a substance fouler and thicker than water.

The *drip, clink, drip…* now talons climbed out of that abyss, up sweating walls slick with blood, ether, spittle, and death.

She felt Rian shudder as if she shared her fear. Una's eyes snapped open. A surge of adrenaline jolted through her heart. She could swallow. There was moisture in her mouth. She was still hungry but no longer starving. Her blood flowed through her veins at regular speed. Her eyes were no longer crusted over with dried salt. Una licked her lips, feeling the weight of her own wet tongue. With a cry, she released Rian's cold fingers like they'd scalded her. Sobbing, Una scrambled to her knees. She pulled Rian into her lap by the shoulders. Her flesh felt waxen, hollow. Her bones were light and fragile as a bundle of twigs. Una pressed her thumb to the hollow of Rian's throat. She was barely able to see Rian's face, for the stolen tears flooding her eyes. Rian had a pulse, but it was very weak— erratic as the wingbeats of a dying hummingbird.

Una screamed at the top of her taxed lungs. In her sleep, her Spark roused itself, searching for the sustenance it needed to keep her alive. Una might have *killed* her friend! She buried her face in her hands: guilt, shame, and rage filtered through her every fiber.

She'd done it again— unwittingly harmed another human being— broken the Ninth Law. Her Spark had a mind of its own. It had prioritized her survival over basic human decency. Revolting. Horrible. *Vampiric.* A hot stream of bile bubbled below her collarbone, promising to surge upward if she dared to breathe. *Drip, clink, drip,* called the tray; ice tinkled its cheerful taunt; wind and rain buffeted the roof with exaggerated stealth. Una held Rian close, willing whatever mechanism that enabled her to leech life away to reverse itself through Rian's skin. The spectral image from her nightmare resurfaced in the depths of her conscience. *Una* was that abhorrent aberration, wasn't she? Crippling self-loathing, fear, and guilt must have leaked into her dreams as ink soaks into a sponge.

What could she do? How could she undo the damage she'd done? Letting Rian's head slip gently to the floor, she resumed her pacing. It was time to *solve* this puzzle. Rian was already so weak and malnourished… if Una failed, she might die. Chewing at her jagged cuticles, Una prowled the confines of their wooden prison like a caged animal. She could figure this out; she *must.* The room attempted to appease her frustration by tapping into her desires. Random thoughts she had flashed briefly in the various corners of the room. An axe appeared and disappeared. A saw, a spear— then a torch, a hammer… she gritted her teeth, willing herself to focus. *Drip, clink, drip,* chanted the tray, and she wailed into her palm… *drip, clink, scrape…*

Her feet skidded to a halt.

Drip, drip, drip, went the pitcher. *Clink, clink…* went the ice. Drumming raindrops struck the roof, and Una shuddered at their lethargic downward progression. *Scrape…* went another sound from the north wall. She whirled. A huge yellow eye bulged at her from the window. Its pupil was a sword-slash vertical slit, which contracted at her answering gasp. On recoil, Una's spine slammed into the back wall.

The eye quivered as the thing laughed. "*There, there, little birdssss….*" Its voice was sweet and corrosive as acid. Una felt every word pound into her eardrums like a bodhran drum. She covered her ears. The thing cackled, an oily, lascivious sound that turned her stomach. The creature slid around to the open door. A formless black shape shifted through a dozen figures at once: a bear, an ox, a raven… then a man. It settled on a perverse, alien amalgamation of Ben's handsome face. Mammoth obsidian talons caressed the barrier between them, curling Ben's hands into unnaturally large, gnarled hooks. Huge tusks sprouted from its mouth as it peered in at Una with unadulterated hunger. "*You're sssso, sssso thirsssty, aren't you, little one? Do not fear. Where I will take you, you'll never thirssst again….*"

The Veil

As night descended, Ben felt a change in the atmosphere. A subtle tremor rumbled through his bones, raising gooseflesh over his arms. His nostrils twitched at the faint alchemical shift in his environs. Serpentine mists seeped from the earth, soft and seductive as satin. Ben paused to take stock. He rolled that indescribable *something* over his tongue, like bittersweet toffee. Did the rain smell a bit sweeter than usual, the soil a bit richer? Disjointed whispers rose and fell with each gust of wind. Boughs creaked and groaned in mournful chorus through the valley below. Water trickled from somewhere higher up. Did Ben spy faces moving through each hollow— eyes of various luminance, glittering from the deep dark spaces within? Samhain was at hand. Soon, the veil between the corporeal world and the Oiche Ar Fad would vanish. Many things that should remain forever apart from this realm would seep through like blood through silk.

Ephemeral spirits always came first: phantom wisps and vapors, bearing little intellect or self-awareness. They were as lanterns over still waters, flitting here and there with no purpose save to be. Ben caught a few ghostly flickers on the hillside, winking in and out of sight among the trees. Lu Sidhe would come next: sylphs, undines, piskies, gnomes, and mad faeries. Some delighted in mischief. Some merely wished to troop through this strange literal world that most perceived only once a year. They would band together: a parade of prancing tricksters, pests, and pantomimes. Though… it wasn't the inconsequential Lu Sidhe who were responsible for the cold dread coursing through Ben's heart.

Dor Sidhe would follow their lesser counterparts— malignant, bloodthirsty monsters of man's blackest dreams. They were manhunters, all: avartagh, ghasts, dullahan, bogarts, wraiths, kelpies, goblins… and pooka. Unleashed from the Oiche Ar Fad only on Samhain, Dor Sidhe craved flesh as a starving man craves bread. Ranging far afield, these unnatural beasts stalked human prey in every corner of Innisfail, from deep mountain lakes to the deceptive comfort of one's own home. On Samhain, whence Dor Sidhe roamed, mortals dared not tread. However, once the underworld gates swung wide, these horrid creatures were merely its penultimate terror.

The last of Samhain's gifts was by far its worst. Dor Sidhe were harbingers of the dead. The Sluagh were tortured souls, released from Tech Duinn in search of lost loved ones… or the heat of living blood. Sluagh could not comprehend that they no longer belonged to this plane. In ancient times, many thousands of years before the Transition, Milesian tribes held ritual sacrifices the length and breadth of Eire. Druids burned massive wicker effigies stuffed with willing human sacrifices to appease Donn, the god of death. To honor Samn, goddess of the moon, those sacrificed remains were scattered over fallow fields to guard against pestilence and famine for the following year.

On Samhain, countless fires once dotted the Eirean landscape. Dancers in masks adorned with blood and ash would sketch a living wall between burning men and the dead. The Sluagh were ever near. Empty eyes watched from silent shadows, waiting for a break in that bright mortal line. In modern times, people refrained from burning their neighbors alive, but lamplighters still worked overtime to ensure each town remained lit through the night. Perhaps, if men saw the world as Ben did, they might revive the old ways in a hurry.

An hour after sunset, heavy rainclouds blew in from the west. Hard rain brought their upward mobility to a veritable crawl. Mossy stones, slick with sluicing rainwater, carved treacherous little canyons beneath their unsteady boots. Between the bracing wind and the wet, the Greenmakers might have been attempting to scale a waterfall. Hours passed while they struggled to maintain their footing up the melting tor. The evening was already fully mature before they emerged from the wooded slope. Halfway to the summit, they discovered a rocky outcrop jutting from the hillside, like the keel of an overturned boat. Ben eyed the path that curved along its face. Just shy of the ledge, a copse of bare treetops were snapped as if something substantial dove into them from higher up the trail. Ben crouched near the precipice, dripping brows drawn together. Squat bushes that traced the slope were crushed or uprooted, indicating whatever had gone over had fought hard to remain upright.

"Shrubbery over here's been bothered with," Robin shouted over the wind. Ben got up to see for himself. Robin gestured to his left. "Body was laid up here, ye ask me. A bit of a struggle over that pile o'big stones ahead."

"There are broken branches over the ridge there," Ben pointed. A crack of lightning illuminated the frown on his face. "Someone was thrown off."

"Couldn't be either lass," Gerrod added, his voice holding a note of hopeful urgency. Ben might find that intriguing later on. "Neither o'em weighs more than a bushel o'apples. Whoever it was, wasn't slight."

"There's blood on the rocks here," Ben dipped a gloved finger and inhaled. "Una's, I think."

Robin scratched his wet pate. "What I know o'her, Ben, she got the better o'em. My fainne's on Keeley. He and his grandson are the only two trackers Barb sent. Not enough prints to suggest t'others were on this trail. Too narrow."

"You think they took the high pass?"

"Not enough room for many more than four up here." Seamus ran a hand along a scratch in the granite face. "I think Robin's got the right o'things. The trail tapers ahead. Too many feet would increase the chances o'dislodgin' the dirt holdin' the path against these stones. My guess? Breccan and Keeley were down here with 'em, and I gather Keeley went over. Breccan's just a mite and no fighter."

Ben nodded. "That's as it may be, but the prints end just ahead here." He hoisted himself over the last set of stones in the trail. No fauna was disturbed, and the scent of blood dissipated. Perplexed, Ben ranged ahead several paces, detecting no evidence of either girl's footprints. Robin and Seamus combed the cliff edge, looking for signs that perhaps they'd gone over too, while Gerrod tracked downhill to ascertain if he'd missed a sign of them retreating from whence they came. No such thing, he announced with a confused shrug. He indicated that there were only two sets of tracks: the four they'd followed to this point and their own. The girls might have floated away on the wind.

"Ye don't think they'd have climbed down *that*," Gerrod grimaced into the gorge, with its plump, deceptively gradient slope. One might believe the decline relatively gentle if not for the impressive oaks and elms peeking over the rim. "I'd be buggered to try that bitch, myself."

Robin mashed his lips together. "Mhm, no way. We'd have some sign o'em amblin' near them rocks and bushes. Siora, this is odd. If they didn't slide down, fall, or retreat... where in the hells did they go?"

Ben picked his way back to the spot stained with Una's blood. He flung his senses outward. Concentrating on the immediate vicinity, he marked wet earth, fallen leaves, soaked bark, saturated minerals, and crackling ozone from the storm above. He sensed the clod of hooves and the chime of bridles on the opposite side of the hill— though these were too far away to warrant immediate concern. Ben did find those amorphous shapes and flashing pulses that he'd noted before had increased in frequency. Bright eyes were seemingly everywhere, dipping in and out of sight like fireflies in a summer's gloaming. Tittering chatter, murmurs, and tinkling laughter trilled through the Greensward, buzzing like angry bees. Of the Greenmakers' quarry, there was no sign.

Frustrated, Ben groaned, "I have no idea."

Gerrod jerked, hand on his dagger. "Did ye hear that?"

"Aye," Seamus clutched the sprig of mistletoe dangling from his neck. The Lu Sidhe did not care for mistletoe, all Eireans knew. One could reasonably hope that the sacred plant would guard them against harm. Ben did not have the heart to tell Seamus that on this night of all nights, peasant charms were useless out here in the dark. "Tis Samhain, ain't it? Bloody Greensward'll be filled with randy beasties tonight."

"Superstitious sot," said Robin, tugging his chin at Ben. "We got us our own good luck, don't we? None o'the Folk would dare step wrong with him."

Ben ignored them. Removing his glove, he ran his fingers over Una's fading blood stain. The faintest trace of indelible energy brushed against his skin. There was something else here: less a scent or a sound than a feeling. Crouching in the scree, he held his palm out as if to absorb that something through his skin. A trace of power— dark power— lingered in the damp, like an afterimage. Ben hadn't felt anything like it in a very long time.

"What is it?" Robin knelt beside him.

"Something *took* them from here."

"What, and leaped over the cliff?" Seamus snorted.

"No," Ben struggled to find the right words. "The erm…veil. The fabric between worlds is thinnest on Samhain. We all know that, but here—" He rubbed his hands together to offset their discomfort. "Here, it was cut."

"What's that mean then?"

"Dor Sidhe, or something else. I can't be sure, but I can feel it." Ben scrubbed his hands against his soaked trousers as if to remove a taint. "Una and Rian didn't fall over. They were taken… somewhere *else*…."

"Ben, ye know we don't speak that gibberish. What in the hells is a 'doo-er shee'?" asked Gerrod, slapping Seamus' hand from the weed at his throat.

Seamus glowered back. "Dor Sidhe, ye nonce. Randy beasties, what eat little girls, and skinny lads like ye."

"Shut yer hole, Seamus, or I'll bash yer good teeth in too."

"Both of ye shut up!" Robin barked. "Ben, if something already had at yer girls, what can we do about it?"

"I don't think this was violence. This feels more like a clinical slice than a tear. All magic leaves a trace. Even this." Ben stared up the trail. "Two girls, both mortal. He can't have taken them far. Not before midnight tonight, anyway. It'd be exhausting to try."

"He?"

"I misspoke," Ben said. He focused on a faint glimmer, guiding his steps ahead. "This isn't Dor Sidhe magic at all."

"What do you mean?"

"It's worse— one of *my* kind. We must go."

Ben heaved himself up the next level of mud-slick rocks without another word. He didn't bother to wait and see if the men behind him could keep up.

⚔

Damek almost regretted the decision to lead this expeditionary force himself. The weather made every inch an agony. Their progress couldn't have been slower if they had forged ahead on their knees. Mud sluiced downward at breakneck speed, making an arduous chore of each step. After three miles, Damek and his men were forced to walk their mounts. The following rise led to the base of another punishing slope. Damek repressed a groan. These hills were hardly high, yet they might have been sky-scraping mountains for their tortuous, slick gradients. The Headwoman's lackey hadn't given him a precise distance, but Damek felt sure this hell had to end sooner rather than later. They'd been trudging up this bloody road for hours already. If Una wasn't trussed and waiting for him at the end of this journey, Damek would gleefully order every house in Rosweal burned, every stone smashed to powder, and every man, woman, and child piled in the ashes. He'd endured about all of the North he could stomach, thank you.

Having left Martin and the bulk of his forces behind to guard the city, Damek's impatience crouched in his gut like lead. If that Sidhe bastard managed to spirit Una over the border… Damek wouldn't merely condone a slaughter; he'd *initiate* one with relish. Every moment that passed in this godsforsaken wilderness at the edge of the civilized world only served to quicken his ire. So much depended upon Una, he doubted even she knew the extent of her worth. Marrying her meant he'd be his own man— exercise his own power. He'd be owed allegiances rather than beggar them. With a Donahugh bride, he was half a flight of steps nearer his ultimate goal. Without… well… he wasn't going to entertain that notion. Damek would not fail. He must not fail. No one would get in his way now: not the High King, not his bastard son, not Vanna Nema, not the Doma Drem— not even Una herself. He would lock her away for the rest of her life if need be.

Ages ago, he'd pitied her. She'd always been a forlorn and solitary creature, forever hostage to her name. Once, he'd even imagined that he might become her protector. No longer. Now, she was merely a rather palpable means to an end. Damek's determination, however, did little to take the edge off Martin's intense distrust of this little adventure. Indeed, Martin had vehemently argued that the risk should fall upon his shoulders. Damek wouldn't hear of it. One did not send underlings to claim a queen.

This wasn't to say that he was a fool. Escorted by sixty battle-hardened knights and infantrymen, Damek was the best-guarded man in Innisfail. The weather, however, remained unimpressed by his numbers or the martial might at his back. It wasn't raining hard, but by Reason, the deluge was *relentless*. They were forced to stop and slide wooden planks into the mud every few hundred yards to lead their mounts and wagons upward. Each impediment cost him precious time he did not have. To make matters worse, many of Damek's soldiers were reprimanded for spooking their comrades with tales of eyes following them from the trees. He ordered a pikeman clipped soundly across the jaw for making such an outrageous claim when yet another roadblock halted their progress ahead.

Gritting his teeth, Damek leaned into his saddlehorn. "What now? Just shove the limb over the slope and be done with it! We don't have time for this!"

One of his scouts jogged back to the forward line, eyes huge in the lantern light. "Milord! Beggin' yer pardon, but there's men on the road ahead. They're… they're…"

"Out with it, man!" snarled Cunningham from his dappled charger. "Or you'll dine on your teeth."

The scout wrung his sopping hands. "They're in pieces, milord. In pieces! *Reason…* I ain't ever seen anythin' like it."

Killian and Hamish strode over first. The men at their rear reached for their weapons.

"In pieces?" Damek craned his neck to peer over the fellow's head. There wasn't much to see save a downed tree limb and scattered foliage billeted by the occasional violent gust of wind. Damek dismounted. "Show me."

The scout's face bleached white as a whale's underbelly. "No, milord! No! You *shouldn't* go that way. We should turn around. They're not… they're not—"

"Killian, restrain that man." The scout's answering yelp caused Damek to raise a hand. "No, don't hurt him. Hamish, you're with me."

"Milord," the scout cried as they dragged him to the rear of the line. "They're not dead!"

Hamish drew his sabre; his left hand gripped his dagger's hilt. Damek slogged up the road to the downed limb. He couldn't make much out at first except mud, rocks, thinning trees on his right— and the deep black chasm on his left. Damek heard them before he saw them. The scout's lantern lay smashed beside one of their heads, its candle long extinguished by dauntless rain. The smell struck him next. Damek lurched sideways, smashing his hand over his mouth and nose. Hamish made a weak, mewling sound.

"Major! Lieutenant Killian! *We need more men up here!*"

One of the poor souls in the road attempted to crawl toward Damek, his mangled fingers grasping pitiably as if toward a parent. "C... cold...", he moaned, towing his half-eaten torso behind him like toppled rigging. "So... cold."

Damek had to blink a few thousand times to be sure he was seeing what he thought he was. The dead man's skin was blue and grey, but what spilled from his center was black, putrid, and oily as pitch. Though, this wasn't even the most horrifying part of the scene. The boy behind him stared ut the sky, no doubt heaving his final wasted breaths. He had quite a hole in his guts, and his arms had been gnawed to the bone. Meanwhile, the crawling corpse's mouth spilled open over each pathetic whine, pouring gobs of fresh gore down its half-eaten jaw. One eye hung from its socket, asif pecked out by carrion. Chewed fingertips grazed the top of Damek's boot. He recoiled.

Hamish wasted no time. His sabre sang out, severing the thing's head from the root. The head spun over the drop and disappeared into the night. The body sank soundlessly into the mud. Cunningham loped to their side, holding a fresh lantern aloft.

"Dear Reason... *what* in the hells is happening?"

Damek righted himself as best he was able. "He... it... *ate* the other fellow," he gestured to the young man dying against the downed limb. The victim gurgled helplessly. His fingers twitched from a shredded forearm. That appendage resembled a desiccated chicken wing, neatly stripped of every ounce of flesh save the stubborn bits clinging to the cartilage beneath. Damek was careful not to step in his steaming viscera. Lips trembling, the lad tried to speak. Damek had to get close to hear. "What's your name, boy?"

Hamish knelt astride the limb and gently lifted the boy's head. The victim couldn't have been more than seventeen years old, if that. "Bre... ccan."

"What happened to you, Breccan?"

"C... old. I'm so..." The blue-white flesh around Breccan's mouth split wide as if in a maniacal grin. Damek saw what was happening too late to stop it. Breccan's mandibles clamped over the meat at Hamish's wrist; his fleshless arms lashed out, drawing Hamish close with supernatural speed. Breccan's teeth tore into the muscle and tendons below the skin. Scrambling to shove the boy away, Hamish howled in shocked pain.

It took Damek, Cunningham, and Killian all pulling at once to separate them. Snapping like a dog, Breccan flopped onto his side. He tried to snare anything his teeth could connect with. Damek kicked him hard in the chin, breaking the boy's jaw with a sickening crunch.

Unfazed by such a severe wound, Breccan gnawed at the ground with his top incisors. His gray tongue lapped at the spill of his own blood. Cunningham stepped onto his back, driving him into the mud with his boot. With a furious cry, he shoved his sabre through the rear of Breccan's skull— its point protruded from the boy's gaping, grisly mouth. His eyes rolled back to the pearls. Cunningham retracted his blade but brimmediately brought itown from the broadside to sever Breccan's head.

Hamish's shrieks pierced the night around them, despite every effort to keep him calm. His wrist looked like it had been caught in a grinder; blood spurted from the artery, which had all but been scraped away by the lad's ragged teeth. Damek could spy flashes of ivory bone peeking through the mash. Hamish fell on his rump, face stricken. His lips turned blue. He looked up at Damek with eyes full of fear.

"*He bit me...* I can't... can you believe it?" A line of spittle dribbled onto Hamish's stained cuirass. "I don't feel so good..."

Damek sighed, eying Cunningham in silent appeal. Wallace shook his head. Damek's fingertips brushed his pommel. "We'll get you fixed up, Hamish."

Hamish's head bobbed around like a top. "It's just a bite, right? Could you help me to my horse, Wally? I have a blanket in my saddlebag. It's... freezing all of a sudden, isn't it?"

An alarming shudder ran through the large knight that Damek had known all his life. Hamish's cheeks waxed ashen.

"It's... I'm... *cold*..." the whites of his eyes spun toward Damek, same as Breccan's had as if drawn to the warmth radiating from his lord's body. Damek swallowed the solid lump in his throat and brought his sabre down, just as Cunnigham shoved Hamish forward. Headless, the knight's body slumped sideways. Neither Damek nor Cunningham said a word. They merely watched the rain patter over Hamish's breastplate for some time. Only then did Damek notice the sounds coming from the trees around them: plodding footfalls, moans, and muttering from the dark. Damek slid his sabre back into its sheath with a curse.

Cunningham was visibly alarmed beside him. "We should turn back, My Lord. There're more of those… things…out there."

"Every man with a lantern or a torch, get them lit, right now!" Damek bellowed to his horrified troops. "We've enough pitch to last three nights! Let me see no man without a light on his person! Answer if you understand!"

He waited for the appropriate bevy of hesitant but dutiful 'ayes.'

Cunningham gripped his shoulder. "My Lord, if those things come for us—"

"They won't. They crave warmth… but the warmth of flesh and blood, Wallace— the life spark inside the living. Fire, on the other hand, they fear. They won't come into the light. I promise you."

"How can you be sure?"

"Don't you know what today is, Major?"

"But… that's ridiculous, lord. Peasant talk. It's just a day for festivals and the like."

Damek gestured to the moaning treeline. "Tell that to *them*. It's Samhain. In the North, we'd best heed that 'peasant talk' to the letter." He stalked back to his horse, taking the hissing torch Killian handed over when he remounted.

"Lord Bishop, ought we not to wait for daylight then?"

Damek waited for his infantrymen, armed with fresh torches and lanterns, to shove the tree limb out of his path. He nudged his horse forward, sparing Cunningham a determined glare.

"You'd leave Lady Una Donahugh to Hamish's fate, Major?"

Cunningham snarled, "Hells no."

"Then get on your fucking horse, Wallace. Pray we get there first."

⚼ ⚼

SHAMBLING SOULS, LURED BY THE spray of blood in the road, shied from her approach. Shielding cavernous eyes and horrid rictus grins behind rotting fingers, they moaned in fright. Aoife pitied these creatures half as much as she reviled them. Careful to conceal her disgust, she pushed her hood back. Her amethyst ogham charm swung from her fist by a thin gold rope. She whispered a small incantation, etching an illuminating circle of dry air around the crown of her obsidian hair. Her violet eyes blazed through the misted gloom. Suddenly, as entranced as they were afraid, the dead scrambled away from their kill— weeping in pathetic awe of her might.

The wind rustled through the four silver chains in her right ear, making a music that was at once soothing and terrible, for the dead did not belong in this realm. Only those of high Sidhe blood like Aoife could release them from the torment of their cravings. She could send them back to the peace of Tech Duinn. However, some did not wish to return. These souls hissed at her approach. They were resentful of her power to thwart their revenge upon the living. She smiled back at them. They'd do.

"Don't be afraid." Easily beguiled, they crept forward, dragging bits of themselves behind them. She reached inside her grey cloak and removed a tiny brass bell from an inner pocket. "It is warmth you crave? I shall give it to you."

Movement from her peripherals made her smile the wider. An army of Sluagh ambled toward the shining beacon she presented. All helplessly drawn toward the cool, radiant light in her blood. She tipped the little bell in her fingers once, twice, each stroke eliciting a convulsive response from her growing audience. Like a putrid wave, they swarmed the road from every conceivable direction, macabre features rapt.

"Come," she sang, shaking her bell. "I've all the warmth you can hold… just ahead. Follow me."

234

THE THING OUTSIDE

Ben might have been flying up that craggy hillside. His boots danced over the stone and scree beneath their soles. The rain had let up a bit. The sky overhead bloomed deepest cobalt in the reach of cloud-swept stars. Clear, silver moonlight illuminated their path: a metaphor painted on the evening air. Ben and company dashed upward as fast as they could until the trail banked sluggishly left at the summit. Soon, they arrived in a high valley billeted by bare oaks and fully resplendent conifers. Focusing on the outer rim, Ben discerned a small group of huts and cabins gathered at the opposite end. He pointed at a cabin perched at a distance from the others, which faced the northern slope.

"There," he said. "That's where they are. I can see the traces, but—" He squinted at a peculiar smudge that lurked around its perimeter. Panic struck a resonant chord within his mind.

Robin noted his sudden silence. "What?"

Ben dragged his frown sideways. "You know."

"Already?"

A curt nod was the best Ben could muster.

"Right. Don't 'spose there's any way to kill it from a distance, like?"

"*You* shouldn't get anywhere near it. I mean it, Gramble. That thing will rip through each of you like parchment. Keep to the east of the cabin, on the low trail there. Downwind. I'll draw it off."

"What then?"

"If I can distract it and move it upwind, get the girls down that trail as fast as you can." Ben hacked off a lock of his hair and handed it to Gerrod. "Take that. It won't stop them all, but it'll be better than nothing."

A sharp laugh issued from the cauldron of pines on their right. Ben's head whipped around. An average-sized man with a wan, flat face materialized from the dark. He was eating an apple... ripe and red as no fruit to be found in all of Eire.

"Grand plan you've got there."

Each man went for their nearest weapon, save Ben, who growled deep in his chest. "What are you doing here?"

The mysterious woodsman smirked while he chewed. "You invited me, remember? Or, as I recall, begged me for aid. So here I am." He waved a hand like a shabby magician showing off a dubious trick.

"Ben... is that...?" Robin bristled.

The figure cocked his head. "Do I *look* like a pooka to you?"

"Never seen one, but I'd say yer ugly enough."

Seamus, by far the most superstitious of the lot, turned away. He squeezed his sprig of mistletoe until his fingertips went white.

The newcomer took another bite out of his apple. "That won't work on me, boy."

"What does?"

Their visitor shrugged. "Not a damned thing."

Ben moved between them. "If you've bothered to come all the way up here and interfere, please tell me you've done as I asked?"

Sighing, the newcomer tossed his apple core behind him as if bored already. "Perhaps I have, perhaps I haven't. I am not yours to command, Kaer Yin."

"I wonder then, Uncle, why you bothered to come at all... if my request for aid was so far beneath your regard?"

"Uncle?" Robin's face screwed up. "I heard yer Uncle Bov was a fine lord. Red-headed, like Seamus here."

Seamus drew Gerrod against him like a shield. "Not that uncle, Robin. *The other one...*"

"Yer tellin' me this is the Lord of Tech Duinn? Bah, I have more impressive boots."

"You shouldn't insult him." Seamus looked like he might faint.

"That's the 'King of Tech Duinn' to you, friend," the fellow sneered. "But in this guise, you may call me Faris. It's a wonder you don't remember Faris, Robin Gramble. You've met him many times."

"Can't say I do. Ben, if he ain't here to help, let's go. We've a date with yon beastie, don't we?"

Faris shot Ben a sidelong glare. "Kaer Yin, your friend is extremely rude." The air around him shimmered with tangible malice. Robin did back up a pace then. Seamus prayed aloud to Siora, and Gerrod stared at Ben with his hand on his dagger.

Ben didn't have time for this. "It's why we get along. Answer the question or get out of the way."

"As tedious as ever, I swear. Fine." Faris gave Ben's shoulder a condescending pat. "I gave word days ago."

"To whom?"

"I wonder..."

"Diarmid—"

"Don't you want to know what I've done with your lovely princess and her clever friend?"

Ben went still as a stone. "Maybe I'll just kill you?"

"I'd love to watch you try, Nephew."

Ben tapped Nemain's pommel. "Don't count on it."

"Now, now, gents," Robin interjected. "Surely we can work this out afore that thing down there gets its supper?"

"*Kaer Yin Adair*," a wholly different voice emerged from Faris' lips. Ben cursed under his breath. "I offer you a choice."

"I refuse. This is neither the time nor place, Uncle."

"Then, I will take both girls home with me. Surely a far preferable fate to the one you've set upon them. No?"

Ben winced. He deserved that. Robin spared him a raised brow, which he roundly ignored. "You don't have the right to challenge me."

"I couldn't allow such a delicate flower to be consumed by Dor Sidhe scum simply because you offered it bait. Could I?"

"I forbid—"

"You don't have a thing to say about it, Ard Tiarne. It's done. Those girls would be dead twice over if I hadn't interceded." Faris crossed his arms over his chest. "Wouldn't my keeping Una achieve the very same you strive for? Presumably, her removal from Eirean politics, for the cessation of hostilities in Eire. Your father will be pleased with you, either way. You'll be lauded in Bri Leith as a hero and be back to preening in your silver spurs in no time. Why should it matter how this end is achieved, hm?"

A slow grin spread over Faris' irritating face. "Unless... but it *couldn't be*, could it? A Milesian woman, Yin?"

Ben fumed in silence. He neither wished to confirm nor deny a Herne-damned thing. Behind him, Seamus muttered a curse and slapped a pair of coppers into Gerrod's open palm. Robin, too, begrudgingly passed the lad his coins. Smirking, Gerrod found something very interesting on the ground to stare at.

"Gods damn you, Diarmid..." glared Ben.

Faris chuckled, "You may take them back before the third hour past midnight. To do so, you must give up your scheme to break your geis. I'll personally send the beast back whence it came, and neither girl shall know how close they came to the most horrid of fates."

"Or?"

"Or, my dear nephew, you may cross into Aes Sidhe this very night. A free man. You shall have your name, titles, and all that you were born to possess… but the girl will go with me. Choose wisely."

Ben launched himself forward. His fist caught nothing but air. When Faris reappeared, some distance away, he laughed at his nephew's pathetic display.

"If you lay a hand on her—"

"Tsk, tsk, Yin," Faris mocked and faded. "Time's running out." With a giggle, he vanished altogether.

Gerrod leaned close to Ben's ear. "What happens in," he looked up at the moon to mark its movement, "three-quarters of an hour?"

"The veil will diminish entirely. The pooka will be freed."

"Ye gonna accept his offer, then?" Robin eyed him closely.

Ben scoffed. "He was stalling."

"For what?"

"He's trying to keep me from getting there too soon and spoiling his fun."

"What does he want with them?"

Ben sighed. "You've seen what Una can do?"

"Aye, so?"

"I imagine he has, too."

⚹ ⚹

Una felt each impact against the cabin in her molars. The creature leered at her from every opening it could squeeze its eyes into. Cackling, it scraped the walls with claws easily as long as Una was tall. It whispered horrible things into the cracks, promising violence she'd never imagined possible. It yearned to shred her insides with its teeth, slather its tongue over the soft core of her still-beating heart, and shuck her bones to the marrow. It vowed to treasure her screams above any prize. It pleaded undying love and devotion. It swore to wear Ben's face for her if she came willingly How it longed to hear both girls weep, to taste their skin, their blood! Perhaps it would be gentle? If they came out sooner, it promised to kill Una long before it ate her. If only she'd allow it to embrace her first. Maybe, let it chew on her a bit before it stopped her heart in its teeth? She would like that, wouldn't she? Wouldn't that be better than fading into Tech Duinn with the Sluagh?

Drip, drip, drip, taunted the water from the tray. Una mashed her hands against her ears to keep either racket from burrowing into her skull. She begged the creature to stop, but that only excited it more. She heard its rows of teeth gnashing all around her. Its lewd suggestions turned her stomach in gleefully described detail. The more excited the thing became— the higher its keening howls.

Water sang *drip, drip, drip,* down the pitcher. Rian's uneven breathing grew weaker by the moment. The ice clinked together in the glass. The wind tore over the roof in an unending cadence. *Drip* went the water. *Clink* went the ice.

I will peel your skin back with my fangs, promised the voice outside. *How you will writhe beneath me.*

Una could bear it no longer. She buried her face in her hands, folding into herself like a child. She screamed until her shrill voice drowned out every other sound. There was no tray of enchanted refreshments. No hollow spaces between worlds to be trapped within. No beasts from deepest abysses vowing to maul, rape, and eat her. There was no wind outside. No time. No battles raging in Rosweal. Nothing. There was *nothing.* Just her own harsh vocal cords, and the beat of blood in her ears. She wailed until she thought her lungs might explode. For a moment, as she drew in her next breath, she heard nothing save the thud of her own heart in her palms. Then, the litany began again…

Drip, drip, drip…

Clink, chime.

…your skin… your bones…

She stumbled into the wall, weeping. Beside her, the silver tray beckoned. Tantalizing beads of cool sweat ran down each glass. The fruit perfumed the air with luscious, irresistible sweetness. She turned her face away on a sob. Her body wracked with fatigue, hunger, thirst, and fear, she pressed her hot cheek to the clapboards, wishing for someone, *anyone,* to make it stop.

A hand slid down the wall, covering her own with reassuring warmth. She cracked a stinging eye to follow that hand to its owner. Tapered fingers bearing simple silver rings engraved with unreadable symbols; an arm wrapped in a linen sleeve, dyed a flat black; silver-white hair brushing the curve of a large shoulder; sympathetic eyes in a green so vibrant she could almost smell the river-slick moss within them.

Ben! She mouthed his name, desperate for comfort, for reprieve. Those inexplicably green eyes held hers long enough to stop her breath.

No… she was wrong.

The planes of this fellow's face were similar but decidedly sharper— symmetrical to the point of perfection. His lips bordered on the feminine. His arched brows were a shade too dark for his impossibly fair hair. They wound together over those beautiful green eyes. Ben's eyes were silver. Una jerked away from the wall, but her visitor did not release her hand.

"Don't be afraid," he said. It was the same voice that had brought her to this pass in the first place. That voice brushed over her arms like velvet, raising gooseflesh along her spine. He was taller than Ben, and there was something else to him, something indefinable that made him feel taller than the pines outside. If she were not terrorized, starving, and dying of thirst, she'd have been staggered by the excruciating beauty of his face. A light, like a candle flame, seemed secreted within his skin. This light illuminated the small cabin to an almost blinding degree. Ten gold chains swung from the arch of his perfect right ear. "I won't harm you, Una."

The sound of her name from his lips sent a shudder thrice as disturbing as anything the lascivious creature outside suggested through her. She wrenched her fingers free and rubbed them against her filthy trousers like he'd stolen their warmth.

"*Who are you?*" she croaked, placing herself between him and Rian, who was still unconscious on the wooden floor. Una realized she couldn't hear the creature anymore nor see its eyes squeezing against the glass to look in on them. Where was it? Had it gone? Were they free? Her visitor took another step toward her as if approaching an unbroken mare. She cleared her blistered throat. "Why have you done this to us?"

"I've saved you, as I said I would." He tugged a sculpted chin toward the serving vessels. "Why haven't you eaten anything I provided? Have you taken one sip of water? You poor things! Had I known, I—"

"*Shut up!* You're a lying bastard!" The effort required to shout was gargantuan. She slipped to the floor, huffing. "Does that… thing out there belong to you too?"

"No. The pooka has come for your friend here. I'm sorry to say." Slowly, keeping his hands visible all the while, he pressed two fingers to Rian's jaw. "She's alive, but barely. How did this happen?"

Una ignored the greasy feeling in her gut. "You first."

"Una, you both must take refreshment. Only a little will do for now."

"Don't you dare call me by my name!"

"Ben pledged to get you to safety in Aes Sidhe, did he not? Well, here I am," he said, splaying his beautiful fingers— a lutist's fingers… or a weaver's, maybe?

She recalled how lovely her father's bard's fingers had been. How fast they flew over the strings. How deft and skillful they were. Admiring him, as only a child of six might do, she wanted nothing more than to possess the same beauty and skill in her own hands one day. She felt herself smiling. Her eyes flew wide.

"Stop that!"

Her visitor knelt beside her. "Your hands *are* beautiful, Una. Will you share what the markings mean?" He ran the tip of an index finger along one long blue whorl. "Especially this bit. I can hear it singing to me from beneath your skin. How does it do that? Will you teach me?"

She snatched her hands back, then shoved them beneath her arms. "Don't touch me. Don't touch Rian either. *Get out!*"

Here, his smile lost some of its charm. "If I leave, Yin's pet comes in."

"What do you mean, *his* pet?"

"Why, you're bait. I thought you'd have put this together by now. More appropriately, she's the bait," he pointed to Rian. "I'm sure the pooka is more than pleased to take the pair of you, though, in exchange for summoning me."

Una opened her mouth for a sharp retort, but despite the cruel delivery, she detected no lie in his words. If what he said was true… no. She wouldn't think of it now. There'd be plenty of time to kill Ben later. "You said, before, he was your nephew? That makes you—"

"Fiachra Ri, at your service, My Lady." His smile was warm as honey again. "Take some refreshment, Una. We'll leave this place, the three of us. I shall give you sanctuary. There'd be no war, death, or struggle— no one to use you for their gain. I know you crave peace above all else. Who'd dare to challenge the King of Tech Duinn to reclaim you?"

"In exchange for what?" Una avoided the magnetism in the swirling emerald depths of his eyes. He was too near. He smelled like pine needles in a rain-swollen meadow or the white lilies that bloomed over her mother's fountain in Bethany. She could almost feel that cool water beneath her searching fingers; hear her mother's throaty laughter. She gasped, "Stop!"

"I'm not doing anything, Una. These are your thoughts and feelings, not mine. Everyone responds to my voice differently, but that doesn't mean the images you see are harmful to you. They simply are." He reached out, holding a perfect white lily in his palm. She recoiled. She could hear her mother's voice, almost see her reflected in the translucent pearl of each petal. "What else do you see?"

Una had that strange sensation of falling upward again, but this time through chill clear water choked with lilies. Her bare toes scraped against the bottom of her mother's fountain. Pushing herself upward, she emerged dripping into warm summer sunlight. Una wore a gown of purest white as if it had been made from the petals she waded through. The air was sweet with their scent and dusky with sun-soaked earth. Her wet hair clung to her back, already curling from the heat baking into her skin. She pulled herself over the stone rim, wringing her hair out behind her. A pleasant, half-dreamy smile pulled her cheeks wide. Someone approached her from behind and pressed something smooth and dry against her damp skin. His arms wrapped around her waist. She snuggled into him with a contented sigh. A lock of his silver hair coiled over her shoulder as he bent to whisper against her nape.

Distantly, shock infused the joy in the scene. The image was a feeling… a desire she wasn't aware she had: those warm hands, the familiar, comfortable weight of that body against hers. Her dream self laughed at something he said. She spun in his arms to press her mouth to his. Then Una fell again, back into her body: cold, starved, and afraid. Her cheeks burned with morbid embarrassment. This was something she hadn't known she wanted. She'd been forced to share its realization, with *him*. She squeezed her eyes shut. Her breath caught in her throat. *Ben*, her heart wept for stunted need. No… *Kaer Yin*. The ache was worse for the numbing lucidity the name inspired. It could never be. Hidden longing made a fool of her. He was the future Ard Ri. She'd age and die in mere decades, while he would live on, safe and powerful, in the might of his immortal Sidhe blood.

The King of the Underworld's voice was silk and sinew, spice and balm. "I cannot give you the man, but I can give you everything else." He prodded her chin up with his knuckle. "I know your fears, your pain, and your joys. I sympathize. In Tech Duinn, you'll never age, yearn, or feel pain again. You've had a hard life, Una. Very hard. Born to be a pawn for all who claim you as kin. I can take all of that away.

Midhir will only use you in his own game— another endless, painful play for power. As will they all. I will not. Won't you let me give you that fountain, that endless summer's day? Perhaps, even in time…"

"*No*." Una swiped at her eyes with her wrist. "It wouldn't be real. What you're offering isn't real. What's more, you mean to use me, too."

He watched her for some time in silence. When next he spoke, his voice rang clear. It was only a voice, and he was just a man. His features cut a harder edge, as if he grew more corporeal by the instant.

"I'm in earnest, nonetheless. I'll give you what I know you want most, Una. Solitude. A world without ambition, without war. No one to abuse you for your gifts. A place to hone your skills, to study, to learn. Isn't that what you want? More than anything?"

Somehow, his tone was more seductive without the enchantment. Her Spark flared bright in her blood. A warning. No, more than that. Encouragement. Self-assurance. *Clarity*. This man, this *thing*, whatever he truly was or had been many thousands of years ago was trying to manipulate her— expertly too, there was no point denying. He was the most beautiful creature she'd ever set eyes upon and somehow, fouler than the beast waiting outside to devour her. This wasn't about Una at all. Hidden within his voice, she caught a different note: discordant, patient, and *ambitious*. He didn't want to save her from the world. He wished to mold her, sap her of will and agency, remake her for himself. There was no mercy or peace. The King of Tech Duinn would take her power and use it toward his own ends. All he needed was her consent. There were rules in the Oiche Ar Fad, weren't there? Rules by which even he must abide. Her silence must have impressed upon him some faltering weakness. He snapped a finger. One of the glasses from the tray appeared in his hand. He held it out to her, features pulled into the most perfect mask of tender concern she'd ever seen.

"Take my hand, Una. Free yourself."

Una's fingers wound through Rian's of their own accord. Rian grew colder, her breathing more irregular. Staring into the gratifying liquid tempting her from the glass, Una reached inside herself to a place she hadn't known she possessed. Her Spark flared at the touch. It purred like a cat ready to spring.

Yes, it sang along her nerves, be free. She took the glass, her hand steady. *Be free*! Without a word, she poured its contents down her throat. Her tormentor's smile lit up the whole world. He took the empty glass from her, then tossed it into a darkened corner. It never connected with the ground. The water sloshed around inside her empty belly. She concentrated for only a few seconds; her brows knit together as if she was grateful for the relief the cordial proffered. His hand slithered over hers.

"You've made the right choice, my dear."

She squeezed his fingers back. "*Oh, I know*." Without mercy, she unfurled her Spark from that secret place at her center. His eyes bulged in surprise. She clamped down hard, wrenching him forward. His power funneled from his body into hers, like a burst dam. Relentless, she pulled until she thought she might overflow. Teeth flashing, he fought to free his fingers from the ever-increasing strength in her grip. "It's called Manipulation, My Lord. I'm only sorry it didn't occur to me sooner… I'm *better* at it than you."

"Let go, you *witch*!"

The walls of the cabin hardened in her vision. The storm finally kept time with their prison inside. The beast's claws penetrated real wood. Her stomach churned a bit at the glee in its poisonous chants. She must be ready for that wall to come down. It wouldn't be long now. The cornices creaked under the pooka's solidifying weight.

"Let me go!" the King of Tech Duinn cried in horror. Such strength he had! Una had never felt anything like it before. It couldn't be all that dissimilar from sucking down the wind at the center of a gale, or swallowing lightning from thin air. She felt the depths of his power boiling straight through the mountain's core, the river snaking through the valley below, and the impenetrable mists of the border beyond. The Veil was apparent to her now— a gossamer thread separating each realm, ready to snap free at any moment.

She sensed riders coursing up the road on the far side of the summit. Their horses were lathered, their eyes bright with lantern light and quaking fear. Next was the dull static of the dead, clambering after them by their hordes. The impression they left upon her psyche made her gasp. She shivered in empathetic alarm. There was more.

Living beings. *Thousands* of them. Some diaphanous as cobwebs, others filled with low cunning, mischief, or unabashed abandon. In this pulsing haze, she discovered men on this side of the hill: four of them. Men she *knew*.

In her relief, she let go. Una positively thrummed with Diarmid Adair's stolen power. He gave her one last withering glare, folded in on himself, and blasted through the rear wall like a cannon shot. Shrieking in anticipation, the pooka rushed toward the opening. Grabbing Rian by the arm, Una dragged her to her side. Una's hand shot out: her best defense. The creature slithered into view… teeth snapping, claws tapping together in delight.

"*Kaer Yin!*" she screamed into the night, just as it launched itself inside.

The Raven King

N.E. 508
31, Dor Samna
Samhain

Save for the prowling, amorphous creature outside, the rundown cabin appeared empty. No light glinted from either dirty window, nor could Ben hear anyone moving inside. If it weren't for the pooka's frantic attentions, one could reasonably assume the girls were long gone… but Ben knew better. His intuition told him both girls were trapped within, and they were not alone. The dwelling hummed with Diarmid's dark influence. Ben might have known his uncle would pull something like this.

Inwardly, he kicked himself for his lack of foresight.

Una possessed a deep well of unfathomable gifts, which a Brehon of Diarmid's talent would find irresistible. The knowledge stuck in Ben's throat like a burr. If he'd had the time to ask someone else, *anyone* else, for aid, they wouldn't be in this bloody mess in the first place. Diarmid was a much-beloved family member. Equally, he was the least trustworthy man Ben knew. Beggars, as they say, cannot be choosers.

Whatever was happening inside those walls, there wasn't a damned thing Ben could do about it now. He had to trust Una and Rian to resist whatever his manipulative uncle threw at them for a while longer. Due to the wailing westerly wind and the racket the pooka made trying to rip its way through Diarmid's enchantment, Ben and company were all but invisible, creeping along the hillside. They tucked in among a thicket of tangled alders to take stock. Robin patted Ben's shoulder.

"Well, what're we doin'?"

"What we came here to do."

Each of them ogled Ben, brows raised.

"What?" he scoffed. "None of you *believed* that tripe, did you?"

"He said he'd let that thing eat 'em, Ben," said Gerrod. "Ye don't think he meant it? Or what he said about—"

"Gerry, here's a free lesson in Sidhe wisdom… *never* trust the King of Tech Duinn. Of course we're not going to let him do either thing he bloody well promised to do. Diarmid can shove his demands up his arrogant arse."

"We're going to get them out?"

"Same plan, same goal."

Slapping Seamus' bicep, Gerrod held out his hand. Grumbling, Seamus dug another coin out of his tunic and slammed it indelicately into Gerrod's waiting palm.

"Bleedin' me dry, ye half-grown weed."

Ben glared. "You boys have something you'd like to ask me?"

Robin cleared his throat, "Just a bit o'nonsense, that. Anyway, I don't think yer, erm, uncle meant to put ye off at all. Seems to me he was testin' yer intent."

"How so?"

"Sounded almost fatherly, ye ask me. 'Son, ye can keep that pup ye brought home, but ye'll have to give up somewhat to keep it.' Like that."

"… Ridiculous."

"What I took from it."

"He's hoping to take advantage."

"Maybe, that too. Point is, I think he was needlin' ye to see how serious ye were about goin' home… and the girls, o'course. One in particular." Robin tactfully avoided Ben's burning gaze.

"It *isn't* bloody like that."

"Sure it ain't." Robin's mouth twitched. Seamus tapped his shoulder before Ben could articulate an appropriate insult. He pointed to the bushes ahead. Something large and misshapen passed before them. "Remember what he said about the time? If we can see that…thing, does that mean the girls're where it can get to 'em?"

Ben peered hard into the small clearing. As the pooka gained strength and substance, it shifted through shapes with rapacious enthusiasm: here, a great black stallion, there a bird of prey, searching for weak spots in the roof. The damage it inflicted increased by the moment. The Veil was fading. While they watched this monstrous display, a small light flickered to life in the nearest window. Ben could see the top of Una's golden head. A dark-clothed figure with fair hair bent over her. Ben was on his feet before he realized his intent. His uncle smiled smugly, his hand over Una's. Ben watched her drink something Diarmid offered. Then, his uncle drew her into his arms.

"Una!" Ben bellowed, heedless of discovery. "Don't!"

"Ben!" Robin shouted. "Watch yerself!"

The pooka loped around the window, momentarily impeding Ben's view. Dragging massive claws along the outer wall, it sought to obliterate all remaining impediments to its feast. Ben ducked, but he needn't have bothered. The beast was so concerned with demolishing the cabin that it didn't even glance up at Ben's shout. On a frustrated growl, it melted into a shape halfway between man and winged serpent. Skittering onto the roof, its claws began to gain purchase.

Ben made a beeline for the window.

Inside the cabin, the atmosphere had changed. All of a sudden, Diarmid cried out and fell to his knees. Una held his hand in a death grip, her nails scraping bloody lines over his bare knuckles. Ben was near to the cabin wall when she let Diarmid go. She staggered to the floor beside Rian. His uncle tore through the back wall, smashing it outward in a blast of splinters, dust, and limping magic. Ben barely had time to absorb what had happened when the wall came crashing into the dirt behind the cabin, bits and pieces scattered over the hillside.

Shrieking in delight, the pooka oozed toward the opening. In the wreckage, Una pulled Rian close. She held out a hand, as if that could slow the creature down.

"*Kaer Yin!*" she screamed as the beast lurched through the breach.

"Robin, now!" Ben shouted. Sword drawn, he dove head-first through the open window.

⚹

BEN'S BLADE SLID UNDER THE pooka's foremost claw just as the beast attempted to plunge it through Una's chest. Rolling upright, he wrenched the talon painfully aside with the broad side of his blade. Shunting forward with all his body weight, he forced the beast back half a pace.

Its answering hiss blew the hair out of Ben's eyes. The chains in his ear chimed in the malodorous cloud.

"*Ard Tiarne… you betray meeee?*"

"Your fault for being such a gullible, greedy piece of shite." Clutching at its wounded claw, it wriggled outside. It flashed through an assortment of shapes in a clicking, keening rage.

While it vented its anger on nearby trees and buildings, Una's trembling fingers dug into Ben's forearm. "Kaer Yin, *how* did you get here?"

He flinched to hear her speak his name. Without warning, he jerked her into an embrace. "Are you all right?"

"I think so. That *thing*—"

"I know. I don't have time to explain. Rian?"

"She will be, I think. It's my fault, I—"

"Una… it doesn't matter. It's going to come back." Pressing her close for a moment, he lightly brushed the top of her head with his lips. Ignoring her indrawn breath, he shoved her toward the far exit. To know she and Rian were alive was enough for now. "Get out of here quick as you can. Robin is waiting."

"Why did that sound like 'goodbye?'" Her voice quivered.

"In case it is," he stared through the hole in the wall, keeping his back to her. "I'm no good at this… Una. I want you to know, *I* don't care what your name is. My uncle was right, this is purely selfish. I think it has been, all the while."

"What? I… don't understand."

"Yes, you do," he gave her a last, lingering look, wishing he had more time to explain. She blinked at him in befuddled embarrassment. If he lived through this, he wondered how she'd react. Ben didn't stick around to make sure she made it out. Head high, he stepped through the back wall. The pooka found another form it liked better than the stallion, the bird, or the lizard. It wore Ben's relative features again, only taller, broader. "Come on then." Ben swung Nemain into a high guard. "Come and see how *reduced* I am now, *isesaeligh*."

With an ear-splitting roar, the pooka charged him, talons unfurling like hooks. Vaulting in from below, it took a testing jab which Ben easily slashed away. Melting left on the next breath, it came at Ben's kidneys from the rear. Ben dipped under its reach, then drove Nemain's tip behind him, slicing a chunk out of its left arm. Howling, the pooka charged again. It hacked wildly from both sides at once. Ben swiveled through each thrust, inching toward its center of gravity. It tried to shove him against the cabin, but he rotated his blade high into a forward guard. Using his own momentum, he whirled Nemain's edge around him in cyclonic fashion. The pooka's talons could find no gaps in his defenses. Orbiting the creature in a dizzying, infuriatingly complex series of dips and turns, Ben got near its core three times before his sword finally bit into its flank. Shrieking, the pooka flailed on the ground like a frightened goat. Ben wasn't even winded.

Smiling, he hefted Nemain over his shoulder.

"That all you got?"

"*LIAR! DECIEVER! I WILL WEAR YOUR BONESS LIKE ARMOR! I WILL RAPE YOUR WOMEN CLOAKED IN YOUR OWN HIDE!*" Into the earth below its morphing body seeped something oily and malodorous. Grasping at the new hole in its side, the pooka's yowling rage shook the hillside like thunder. Now in the form of a great black bear, it took a swipe at Ben's head. On a backslash, Ben cut a deep vertical slit into its unsteady foreleg. A small victory. Before he could get out of the way again, it swatted him into a pine with a gigantic forepaw. His spine struck the trunk with a bone-cracking snap. Also grievously injured, the pooka collapsed against the crumbling cabin, hissing, snapping, and snarling.

Momentarily disoriented, Ben didn't see it melt into the shape of something much smaller, with the head and hindquarters of a boar. Sluggish, Ben reached for his fallen sword. One of his ribs was broken, and his breathing wasn't what it had been moments before. Using Nemain for balance, he struggled to his feet. He hadn't quite made it fully upright when Una screamed his name from somewhere nearby. Ramming into Ben headfirst, the pooka drove one of its tusks straight through his ribcage, piercing his lung. Ben's knees buckled. Grunting, they rolled together through the damp leaves along the slope. He managed to throw a hand out, catching the ledge just in time to stop himself from careening over the first drop. The pooka took advantage. Its claw burrowed deep into his chest cavity, ironically, the very place he'd been wounded the last time he'd tangled with this beast. Ben might find it funny, if the wound wasn't sure to kill him.

With every ounce of strength he had left, Ben heaved the pooka up with his knees and hammered Nemain through its middle to the hilt. Viscous black fluid filled his eyes and mouth. Ben turned his face away.

"Son of Midhir... I cursssseee youu... you shall never..." Its reeking heart's blood poured down Ben's sword arm. He spat out a wad of the putrid malfeasance, reached into his tunic, and rammed his dagger into the pooka's brain from the ear. Whatever it meant to utter next died on its slackening tongue.

"I'll hear no more of your curses, *isesaeligh*." Ben drove it off his sword and over the precipice. After hacking up everything in his throat, he dragged himself part way uphill, using his sword as an awkward lever. He was sorry to admit that he left a fair amount of his own blood on that slope. Reaching the woods on more level ground, he flopped onto his back to wheeze at the sky. An unhealthy gurgling caught more blood than air in his throat. Footsteps pounded through the foliage close by, but... someone *else* stood closer, breathing almost as harshly as he did. Diarmid met his eyes from the trees beside him. Ben tried to smile as if to say, '*you too, huh?*'

Diarmid crawled to him, his face as pale as milk. With the skeletal smudges beneath his eyes, Diarmid looked easily a thousand years old.

"Yin... no." He laid a shaking hand over the gaping wound in Ben's chest. Ben wanted to sneer at him, but only blood gurgled from his mouth. This was half the old bastard's fault for being such an opportunistic arse. Though, Ben wasn't really angry with him. There wasn't any point now, was there? It figured Ben's plan would end in such a disappointing defeat— that had been the story of Ben's life, hadn't it? Each defeat bore a lesson, and every victory its fair share of shame. No bloody *wonder* he had to cheat at cards.

Then, Una was there. She pulled his head into her lap.

"Kaer Yin!" Her beautiful, filthy cheeks were flooded with tears. He reached up to touch one. How strange. A *Milesian* woman should mourn him, after everything he'd done? He was amazed. She twisted a glare at Diarmid. "Do something!"

Diarmid flinched from her voice. What had Una done to his mighty uncle to make him fear her so? Ben could only guess. In all likelihood, Ben would never find out.

"What can I do? He took a terrible wound."

Una swiped at her eyes with shaking hands. Furious, she said, "I know you can do something! I know it! He's your nephew, isn't he?"

"Una..." Ben wanted to tell her it was going to be all right, that he was happy it wasn't for nothing, but she cut him off.

"Shut your idiot mouth! *You're not going to die.* I won't allow it." She turned back to his uncle. "I'll give you whatever you want in return. I swear it. Save him!"

Diarmid stared at her and those gathered in mutual shock, with wide green eyes. "Yin, do you see what's happening here?"

Ben couldn't answer. His vision clouded over. A dry humming echoed in his ears. He was dying. It didn't hurt much, which surprised him more than the doing. Una squeezed his hand.

"Yin, these are human voices begging for your life."

Ben was just as mystified as his uncle.

"I'll do as you ask, lady... not because you bargain for it, but because I believe he broke his *true* geis long before tonight. Do you hear me Kaer Yin?"

He did, but had absolutely no idea what Diarmid was talking about.

"I can't heal him." Diarmid's weight shifted over his chest. "But I can save his life. When it's done, get indoors as fast as you can. Light fires in every window. I won't be here to stop them."

"Stop who?" Robin's voice sounded odd, weak.

"Sluagh," answered Seamus from farther off. "It's Samhain."

"You'll owe me for this, little princeling," Diarmid whispered into his ear. Next thing Ben knew, the worst pain he'd ever experienced filled his ribs with molten steel. Scorching white flames licked over his eyes. When had Ben swallowed all nine hells? His back bowed. His arms and legs thrashed in the duff. Diarmid screamed with him. For a while, he couldn't discern his own voice from his uncle's... until, suddenly, Diarmid was gone. Searing pain blew the world and all its newfound oddities out of his mind—like a candle smothered in the dark.

⚜

Una gathered her wits first. Anxious, she tugged Ben's inert torso up by the shoulders.

"Quick! You heard his uncle! We have to get inside!" As if shaken out of a daze, Robin leaned down to grab Ben by the ankles, while Seamus helped Una lift his top half. As for Gerrod, he tossed Rian's wilted frame over one shoulder, making sure to leave his dagger hand free. With what she'd stolen from the Raven King thrumming through her veins, Una could feel those thousands of frigid empty vessels moving in from every direction. The dead were coming, and they were not alone. Sylphs, sprites, and phantoms zipped from bough to bough overhead. Mad faeries unblessed with Rian's Ban Sidhe blood wandered the wilderness, laughing or aimlessly chattering to themselves. These were Lu Sidhe… *lesser Sidhe*. They were no threat, so long as they were ignored. Marveling at the breadth and depth of her newfound strength, Una reached further still. In the distance, she caught traces of greater creatures in search of sport and slaughter: Dor Sidhe, like the pooka. Some were worse than that lascivious, revolting beast— so much *worse*… she nearly tripped over her own feet at their discovery.

"Ye all right?" Robin regarded her with a concerned eye.

Blood drained from her cheeks. "There are so many… so… *many*."

Robin clearly had no idea what she was babbling about. "Milady, if ye need to rest, set him down, and I'll—"

Her head snapped around at a sudden hum from the east road. "Quiet," she said, tilting her head toward the sound. "Do you hear that?"

Robin frowned. Una could guess what she looked like to him. Her unkempt hair was in wild knots that she would likely have to shear. Dark bruises pooled beneath both of her eyes, and her cheeks were sunken around bones too sharp for her bloodless flesh. She was covered head to toe in grime; days spent in a dusty cabin in the middle of nowhere without food and water had taken their toll. Her tunic and leggings were caked with a dozen species of stain.

Hearing things on the wind no mortal could ever hope to detect must not have helped her case.

"Lady I think…" he began, lowering his voice to as gentle a croon as he could manage. Several snaps from the woods snagged his attention before he could complete his thought. He squinted into the dark; the wind made it even harder to peer through the blowing, waving fauna. A flash of lighting cracked overhead, and in that brief moment of illumination… Robin's eyes widened to the pearls. "Siora's tits!"

He pulled Ben's heels up so high, the motion almost knocked Una off her feet again. "Move, move, *move*! Get inside! *Get inside!*"

Another crackle of light, and Una saw them too: faces…*hundreds* of faces… shambled up the road. There were so many of them, in varying stages of decrepitude, they might have sprung from the earth like weeds. With renewed urgency, Una and Robin managed to half-pull, half-drag everyone toward the abandoned cottages. The dead were so close, Una could smell them. That sweet, rank scent of overturned earth and corrupted flesh. She gagged, nearly dropping Ben in the process. Why was he so blasted heavy?

Seamus whizzed past her, kicking in the nearest door. He yanked something sour smelling from a chord round his throat. Nodding to him, Gerrod laid Rian down just shy of the open doorway, then helped Seamus break off all the shingles and dried bits of wood the cabin could spare. Kneeling on the stoop, they used whatever they could pilfer to start a small fire. Mere paces away, the dead flinched from this tiny, burgeoning light. Seamus wasted no time. He handed burning shingles to Robin and Gerrod to toss into the nearest cabins, setting their long vacant interiors alight. With each new fire that bloomed before them, the dead slunk back, shielding what remained of their eyes. Una labored to drag Ben through the door, while the Greenmakers went to work starting as many fires as they could manage.

246

Rian, now somewhat sensate, reached out in an attempt to help Una heave Ben's torso through the opening.

"What happened to him?" she whispered sluggishly, as if fighting upward through a drugged haze.

Her little white face seemed needle-thin to Una's guilty eyes. "Long story, can you help me get his feet inside?"

"Where?" Rian yawned, still half-heartedly trying to pull at Ben's bloody shirt. Una moved her hands back into her lap.

"Never mind, love. Why don't you rest there? Set your head against the wall. That's good. Ben's going to use your knee as a pillow, is that all right?" A single snore was her answer.

Out of kindling, Robin paused to help force Ben's boots inside. Gritting her teeth, Una tugged until the crown of his head rested against Rian, where she slumped against a crumbling wall. Even with both of them pushing and pulling, the big Sidhe bastard weighed too bloody much. Una had to think up a new plan. They didn't have time for this. Sweating, she scowled down the ridiculous length of Ben's inert legs. "Go, Robin. Burn everything that will catch, then get back here."

"What about ye?"

The dead corralled themselves further down the north-facing slope to come at them from the shadows on the opposite side. The second road cut through the trees on her left, a broad avenue filled with rotting corpses. Unseen by Una's companions, Lu Sidhe clapped encouragement from the sidelines, gloriously entertained. She swallowed, then leaned against the side of the cabin for support. Taking a deep breath, Una drew power out of her belly and into her mouth. She wasn't sure how she knew which words to use, only what she intended. Her voice filled with an incomprehensible charge. Under her fingers, the wall burst into flame so bright and pure that it shone like a star in the darkness. The blaze licked around her hand: spreading, searching, reaching— until the whole building was wreathed in brilliant orange flames.

"They'll burn!"

Una caught Robin's arm before he could dart inside.

"*No*, they won't."

Under protest, she held his hand over the fire. She knew the wood beneath his fingers would be cool as spring water to the touch. Beguiled, Robin unhooked his arm from hers.

"How'd ye do that?"

"I have *no* idea. Go get the others. These cottages are too wet to burn long, and more are coming."

"How many more?"

Una stared off into space. She heard a seductive, corrupt chiming in the distance. There were so many dead souls in the woods, they seemed a wave crashing up the hillside. Whoever the bell-ringer was, they were not alone. Dozens of soldiers preceded that cruel siren's song.

"Many." Una held onto Robin's sleeve, her eyes too far away to notice his instinctive recoil. "Riders too. Damek is coming, with an entire corps of soldiers."

"Feckin' figures! How many?"

That bell rang over and over again, seemingly filling the valley. She heard a voice calling over that beautiful, melodious charm.

Follow, follow, follow… it sang over the wind *…all the warmth you crave is just ahead.*

They were everywhere. All around. She gasped with the incredible, overwhelming power in that bell… the hungry, pathetic emptiness enticed by its peal.

"Get inside!" she screamed over the wind. "ALL OF YOU! Get inside now!"

Robin did not argue. Snagging Gerrod by the collar, he hauled him toward the house.

"Seamus! Get yer bony arse away from that—"

As Seamus turned to look at him, a crawling thing caught his ankles from a black gap between the houses. He gave a sharp cry and dropped his makeshift torch into the sucking mud. Una had only a single breath to witness the startled, petrified look in his eyes before the thing bit deep into the back of his thigh. Screeching, Seamus scrambled to regain his footing. Ceaselessly, he punched, kicked, or cut at the dead man's bare skull. Undeterred, it buried its decayed face in his blood. Helpless, his friends watched in white-knuckled horror as Seamus' assailant tore great hunks of flesh out of his leg.

"Help me!" he wept, grasping for purchase anywhere he could find it.

Gerrod tried to lurch to his side, but Robin locked his arm around the lad's thrashing arms. The fire Seamus had lit already sputtered out. There were far too many wet holes in that sagging roof.

The fresh scent of blood emboldened the dead.

"SEAMUS!" Gerrod roared over and over. Whimpering, Seamus was drawn into the grass beside the cottage. A second pair of hands snatched at Seamus' writhing arms, then a third, and a fourth. His shrieks were dulled by wet, smacking, gnawing sounds. Bones were wrenched open by greedy fingers; flesh and organs spilled into the moaning maws of several nightmarish creatures. In mere moments, Seamus' cries ceased. All that was left of him was the revolting feast.

Una shoved Robin and Gerrod through the doorway. Bleary-eyed, Robin held Gerrod's weeping body in a vice grip.

"Get inside! Do it!" she sobbed.

They'd only partly obeyed her when the nearest hoofbeats sounded behind her. Mounted soldiers galloped up the road. Three men rode abreast, holding torches aloft in each free fist. Damek reined his mount between them. His horse spun to a stop before her and he gaped as if he was surprised to find her so easily.

"Una?" his voice was much deeper than she remembered.

Before he could get another word out, she launched herself at his saddle. Squeezing his reins, her eyes were wild with fear.

"Damek! The dead! They're everywhere!"

His Adam's apple bobbed. He didn't appear surprised by this insane news in the least. Glancing around, he took in the burning building (occupied somehow by still breathing faces), the blood on Una's clothes, the dark smear against the grass, and the things creeping along the ridge. Without warning, he kicked her over. She fell on her rump, just shy of the door. Robin jerked her back by the waist. Tossing his torch down, Damek drew his sword.

"Shield wall! Torches at the front!"

His men moved with practiced efficiency. They formed a tight semicircle in the road between Una's enchanted flames and the dead. Rotted fingers sought every nook and cranny below the light, desperate to get at the warm, living blood on display. A single misplaced step, or an opening in an otherwise solid line was an invitation waiting to be exploited.

Queen of the Night

Damek's men fanned out, locking shields on either side of the road. Pikemen jabbed torches into the gaps while the shieldmen pressed the flats of their curved sabres point-first overtop. The dead encircled their phalanx in an oozing throng so tight that torches were as nothing before the horde. Una slipped out of Robin's grip and ran into the road. There, Damek and his officers belched orders over the ever-widening circle of steel and torches.

"Damek!" she shouted at the top of her lungs. "The flames won't be enough!" Either he didn't hear, or he ignored her altogether.

A wooden-faced redhead spurred his mount between them, his sabre slapping time against his charger's flank. He spared Una a single, authoritative glare.

"Get back, My Lady. The Lord Marshal has it well in hand."

Her lip curled. "I'm telling you—" The bell chimed from somewhere beyond the trees opposite. Singsong chanting rose and fell with it, like the gentle lapping of waves on a wide sandy shore. The rider heard it too. He cocked his head, his brows weaving together like twin caterpillars mating. She pointed toward the sound. "There! Can't you hear it? The dead are *lured* here."

Disinterested, he kicked his mount down the line and away from her exclamations. Una tried to wade through the men guarding their makeshift perimeter, only to be shoved back by another firm hand. Then another, and another— until she walked in circles, babbling to no one. The soldiers were preoccupied with the slinking things creeping toward them from the woods. They didn't have time to entertain the notions of a bedraggled, half-starved madwoman. Rationally, Una understood this, but she knew what she knew. She held the King of Tech Duinn's power in her belly— a tumultuous cauldron, which threatened to burst from her mouth and over the hillside like a river in flood. As her bones rattled with the overflow, a sudden thought occurred to her. She raced back to the burning house. Damek barked a command, and his men went to work, slashing and burning as a unit. At the door, Una stumbled over Ben's gangly legs. Robin's eyes met hers with apparent concern.

"I don't think they're listenin' to ye, missus."

"*Hang them*! You have to get out of here." She hauled Ben up by his collar. No simple task— he outweighed her by a ton, at least. "One way or the other, Damek's men won't leave anything alive on this hillside," she huffed. Ben's wound was no longer seeping, nor was it half so deep as it had been, but his gore-spattered cuirass sported a new hole about four-inches wide. She wiped the drying blood from his mouth and cheeks with a tattered sleeve. To observe his beautiful, infuriating face so marred struck some deep chord in her heart that she had no wish to contemplate.

"We can't just leave," Gerrod sniffled, still teary-eyed from witnessing Seamus' grotesque end. "Them things're everywhere. This is cause o'the High King's stag, Robin! It's me fault! Seamus, he'd never have killed a white stag if I hadn't..."

"Quiet, boy." Robin trained a wary eye on the door. "There's somethin' happenin' out there now. D'ye hear that bell?"

Shivering, Una gulped down the surge of molten iron in her throat. "I do. Listen, I can't get you home, but *he* can. The dead won't dare touch him. The Lu Sidhe will go out of their way to avoid him."

"The *what?*"

"Never mind. Damek's men don't know what I do. The dead were lured here by that bell. Someone powerful and cunning is behind this. I think… I'm the only one who can stop them."

"Slow down, missus." Robin placed a warm hand on her shoulder. "What're ye gonna do?"

She let out a long breath. "I'm going to break her enchantment. You'll know it when it happens. Get out that rear window and up over the ridge when I do. Do you hear me?"

"Aye, but it'll be hard to clamber down the slope luggin' this big bastard over me shoulder while Gerry's occupied with yer skinny friend there."

Una took Ben's head in her hands. "You're not going to drag him anywhere. I'm going to give him back to you." Again, she didn't know how she could do such a thing, only that she *could*. She could taste a static, a thunderstorm on the root of her tongue— could feel it laying heavy in the pit of her womb. There was so much of it… too much for one person to carry alone… yet, she could. Una had no idea how any of this was possible. "When he wakes up, tell him I'm sorry. I never meant for any of this to happen, not to any of you. Tell him I said 'thank you,' and I did what I could to make it right. Whatever that's worth. Tell him… I'm glad it was him."

"Yer comin' with us," Robin growled. "I won't leave ye behind."

"You must," she smiled sadly. "If I don't stay, none of you will leave here alive." The bell intensified in volume, and screaming followed in earnest. The valley rang with shouts, horses shrieking in terror, and the sickening crunch of steel hacking into meat and bone. Above all, a woman's sonorous voice lilted in a wicked, melodious chant.

… take your warmth… it is within your grasp.

Una closed her eyes and concentrated on the simmering furnace at her core. She shut out every sound, save the magic rushing through her veins like a bottled inferno. Una drew Ben's mouth to hers. Cupping either side of his face, she poured her altered Spark into him with tender violence. In moments, his body convulsed. Renewed vitality coursed through his limbs as a newborn flame rushes through kindling. Each breath brought quickening light and color into his skin. His eyes snapped open just as she broke contact. He stared up at her, bewildered. Una's heart beat a mournful tattoo. It could never be. Brows drawn together, she pressed her lips to his one last time. Her cheek came away wet. Too late, Ben reached for her, his twitching fingers catching nothing but air. On her feet, Una gave him a sad smile.

"Goodbye, Kaer Yin. Thank you for everything."

He slumped sideways in the entrance while she slipped outside. "U… Una!" he croaked. She didn't look back. Her shoulders squared, she disappeared into the chaos beyond the glowing doorway. He couldn't heal fast enough to stop her.

THE CHANTING GREW LOUDER WITH every step Una took. The soldiers were busy slashing, gouging, and burning through the dead. Even so, she was surprised they could not hear it. The bell was *deafening*, a melodic, hammering thrum that shook the earth beneath her feet. The semi-circle of shields and spears shrank back to the middle of the road, making it difficult for Damek's cavalrymen to ride up and down their line. His men worked hard. Torchmen pushed fire through every gap from shoulder to eye level. Shieldmen held the line in a tight phalanx while pikemen jabbed at anything wriggling on the ground.

Despite the practiced effort, the Southers were hardly winning. The dead were too numerous to fend off with might alone. Rotting fingers and gnashing teeth exploited every undefended chink in their steel wall. Some men were dragged below their shields to meet violent ends in a mess of shredded meat and exposed viscera. Others would take bites then were unceremoniously slain by their companions.

Noting the rapid loss of at least a dozen men, Damek bayed a command. The Corps changed tactics. The second tier of infantrymen threw their smaller shields over the heavier ones at the bottom. A third tier moved in to stab through the low gaps with pikes. This heightened bulwark of steel, wood, sword, and sabre braced itself against the tide of dead faces. Decomposing limbs and snapping jaws scraped against that wall as it moved forward, inch by brutal inch. A breach opened up after one soldier's wrist was caught. He was dragged over his shield. The men behind him closed ranks over his body, swiftly stabbing downward to silence his frantic cries. The skeletal thing that had been consuming him alive was ground to dust beneath their shields.

The gap, however, wasn't easily sealed. Too many arms, teeth, and weapons clashed on either side. Una raised a hand crackling with power. It kept the shields apart long enough for her to glide through. Several soldiers tried to top her, but she ignored them. One mounted officer called a panicked halt as she moved past. She had no fear of the Sluagh. Soon, the Southers saw why. Bearing the King of Tech Duinn's power in her core like boiling quicksilver, the dead shied away from Una as if she were a walking bonfire. She walked straight through their center, unmolested. The afflicted scattered at her approach; her every footfall quaked through their ranks like thunder.

Behind her, Damek bellowed, "Una! What the devil do you think you're doing out there? Get back here!"

Disregarding him, Una scanned the wooded slope, feeling anguish and hunger for life all around her. So many tragedies. The Sluagh fled from her with pleading eyes or covered frightened faces with shaking desiccated hands. Their stories swirled in the air around her: a mother stolen from her children by a fever, a son caught in the river during a flash flood, a daughter murdered by a jealous lover, a father who'd fallen under the plow while striving to feed his family… on and on it went. The Sluagh didn't know they were dead; those lives over. They could only feel the bottomless cold beneath their feet as if the earth were an open maw waiting to swallow them whole. Longing for heat and comfort, they sought to hold living warmth inside their mouths, cradle and nurture it within their vacant bellies. Anything to feel alive once more. In their midst, the unseen enchantress' spell wound around them like a coiling chain. The bell pealed steadily.

… feed, take your warmth.

Una felt the pull of that bell, anchored somewhere in the distance. Her hands balled into fists. Focusing hard on the trilling music, she sensed the spellcaster on the ridge above.

There you are.

"UNA! What are you doing?" Damek screamed. "Someone get her back!"

… come… the feast is near…

"No," Una breathed. Unfurling her magnified Spark, she didn't so much sever that chord as set it ablaze in the caster's hand. She heard a gasp; felt her opponent stagger in the dark. Una smiled. *Got you, bitch.* Without the bell to urge them forward, the dead hesitated— lulled by the vibrant pillar of Una's presence. Damek's men breathed a communal sigh of relief as the Sluagh ambled away, moaning in desperate longing. Una drew them close. Without fear, she smoothed withered cheeks, patted shrunken heads, and caressed withered fingers, humming a simple tune she couldn't say she'd ever heard. They crowded around, enraptured by the light raging within her.

Kneeling, she cleared away a smattering of dead leaves to place her bare hand against raw earth and stone. Here, Una unleashed the unbridled power grinding through her bones. A torrent of wild energy roared through her palms, channeling the Sluagh's need through her own body and into the ground where it belonged.

Here is the warmth you seek… the peace you crave.

Hunger no longer.

A thin network of glowing blue lines traced over the hillside like a spider's web. The dead sighed. A gentle burst of wind blew their mangled, unnatural figures to dust. Hundreds of wandering souls vanished beneath the soil at once. Una's spell shimmered in the air for a heartbeat before fading below her web.

She gasped for air, astonished at the ease with which it was accomplished. Her might felt herculean, her power infinite. Though, once the floodgates were opened, they were difficult to shutter. The soil softened under her knees, melted, and merged, intending to drink her down like rain. A splintering shock of cold flowed up her arm and into her head, bleaching the hair at her temple white as a cloud. Her right eye burned as if pierced by a sliver of ice. Una snatched her hand back with a cry to avoid being sucked in. Scrabbling backward, she clutched her hand to her chest to stymie the searing cold singing through her nerves. The world went a queer, milky sort of gray. She fell into that fog with a relieved sigh.

⚜

AOIFE SPAT BLOOD INTO THE moss at her feet. She reeled as if skewered by lightning. She fell. Her listless body drifted toward the trail's edge and the waiting chasm below. Throwing an arm out, she caught herself against a granite boulder just shy of the precipice. She tore out most of her fingernails in the process. Writhing with the unimaginable pain in her chest, she crawled up the slope on her belly, gulping air like a drowning man. Aoife fumbled at her bosom, searching for a wound that should have split her in half. There wasn't anything to find. Nothing marred her formerly pristine tunic but mud and sweat. The damage was internal as if the hand of Donn had shot out of the night and ripped out her heart. Vibrant hate coursed through her veins, bright and lethal as mercury.

Una. Una did this to you…

Aoife could smell the Moura bitch in the ether— feel her presence at the back of her throat like a budding sore. Whatever Una had done, it was built to last. Dark energy pulsed in the rocks and soil, the wind buffeting the hillside, and the river snaking through the valley like a silver snake in the moonlight. Ubiquitous. Unalterable. Unfathomable. How Una did such an inconceivable thing was as enigmatic as it was infuriating. Even Vanna Nema could not strike her enemies from the heavens.

Full of bottomless pain and quivering outrage, Aoife summoned every particle of Spark she had left to locate the source of her ills. It took a while for her limping magic to snag upon the object of her ire. She found Una amidst the smattering of fearful men and horses. They beat a hasty retreat on the far side of the tor. Her heart beat sluggishly in Damek's proximity— unconscious but very much alive. Aoife gnashed her teeth. No mortal woman should have been able to harness a god's power and live. That damned pest had more lives than a lynx! Well, Aoife would just see about that, wouldn't she? Straining with the effort, she propped herself against a large rock out of the wind. Una had managed to chase away the Sluagh and a handful of sneaking Lu Sidhe. So, what? More than a few terrors were running wild on Samhain, weren't there? The Oiche Ar Fad was wide open. Pookas were not the only Dor Sidhe stalking the night in search of mortal prey.

Aoife smiled.

She recast her net toward one such pack of beasts that lurked along the eastern riverbank. The leader lifted its head. Its opalescent eyes narrowed as if it could see her smirking down on it from above. With the last of her strength, Aoife dangled a thread… to show it the way.

Come… she called, weaving images of a hillside road dotted with terrified men on horseback. Men who bore a morsel more delicious than anything they'd ever tasted.

Come… come and feast.

The creature reared its misshapen head, baring its fangs in a macabre grin. The hunt was on.

⚜

THE SOUTHERS WERE LEAVING. FROM above, Ben watched the infantrymen hastily gather their undamaged supplies and toss them into one of the two wagons they'd brought along for this excursion. One wagon held pikes, ropes, bloodied sabres, piles of unlit lanterns, and flasks stinking of paraffin. The second was burdened with textiles: tents, tent poles, stakes, and the like. Lord Bishop's men came prepared.

252

Ben would say that for them, at least.

The second wagon must be his target. At the rate the drivers were moving, they'd scarcely notice the added weight. Ben slunk carefully along the last roof, closest to the back road. Lord Bishop and his officers were already well down the slope by now, outpacing his supply train by a full five minutes. Ben had ground his molars when the Souther lord rode past. Tucked into the crook of his arm and swaddled in Bishop's own cloak, Una looked small and frail, despite the incredible magic she'd performed for all and sundry. That such a tiny vessel could hold such terrible power seemed improbable as a fire kindled under the sea. Walking through a wall of ravening dead unscathed was feat enough— drawing them back into the earth with a touch was quite another. Ben caught the shock of white at Una's temple as they passed by, and worried she may have done serious damage to herself in the process. If she had, he vowed to slay every one of these Southers to a man. He swore it, by the Horns of Herne.

Robin perched behind him on the rooftop, carefully avoiding the burned or sopping bits that would surely dump them into the cottage below. He'd ordered Gerrod to stay safe within the flaming cabin until dawn. The boy didn't protest. This night had already robbed him of his closest friend, and poor Rian was scarcely cognizant. There was no reason for either of them to suffer any further on Ben's account. With Una's enchantment wreathing the place in a protective light, they would both be safe.

Ben tried to make Robin stay with them, but Robin threatened to cram his dagger into Ben's arsehole if he uttered another word about it… and Ben tactfully dropped the subject. Now, the two of them waited for an opportunity to creep into the supply wagon before it lurched down the road. Ben wasn't as quick as he had been at the start of the evening, but he would be damned if he'd hand Una to that Souther fop. Not while he had two working legs, two functional arms, and a semi-operational torso.

Ben wasn't exactly sure what happened after he slid into catalepsy on the slope, but he recalled every moment inside that burning cabin. Una had pressed her lips, her hope, and her Spark into his mouth like a prayer. He could still taste her tears. She'd thought she was going to die. Nevertheless, she'd stood apart to face it alone. For them. For *him*.

The kiss lasted all of a moment, but its effect was permanent. Had he ever met anyone so infuriating, nonsensical, condescending, or rash? No. Then again, he'd never known anyone as brave, passionate, or full of raw *hope* either. Una was a whole new world for Kaer Yin Adair. She'd dragged a selfish, useless scoundrel from the wild, and shook him out of his own self-imposed exile. Ben could never have imagined a woman like her.

The Grand Marshal of the Wild Hunt… that fading fantasy of yesteryear could never deserve her. Ben Maeden might breathe his last here tonight, but Kaer Yin Adair could be reborn. He wanted to be the man he saw reflected in Una's eyes at that moment. Maybe then, he'd be worthy of her?

Robin patted his shoulder. A silent understanding passed between them. "We'll get her back."

"If I must burn them all down."

Robin chuckled low in his throat. "Very good, yer Arseness. Ready?"

Ben stood, pulling his cowl over the golden chains chiming in his ear. "Eager, you might say. How about you?"

"I'm always ready," Robin assured him, drawing his daggers.

"Prove it." Kaer Yin Adair leapt from the roof into the wagon, swift and silent as death itself.

THE ARMAMENTS WAGON HAD A loose wheel, which impeded the speed of the Southers' exit. The driver was forced to stop, climb out, and kick the hub back into its axle every few yards. The stops were so frequent that most of the skittish rear-guardsmen left the driver behind to deal with the hindrance alone. No man wanted to remain on that haunted hillside a moment longer than necessary. They'd left over thirty of their own in the dirt already. What was one or two more? Marching doggedly forward, most survivors were so traumatized by all they'd seen that they hardly spoke to one another.

The only sounds were the creaking of the wagon wheel, the driver's frustrated rants, and the trudge of their boots through the ankle-deep mud.

This was all to the benefit of the men hidden beneath a thick tarpaulin in the wagon bed. Robin leaned over the side to pop out another rivet with the tip of his dagger, then ducked under the tarp at the front. The expected clang tore another aggravated growl out of the driver's mouth. Stilling the horses, he dropped into the mud for the fourth time. He bent to kick the hub back into place, cursing like a Bretagn sailor. This time, the soldiers kept their eyes on the road. They preferred to ignore the angry little man and his problems when so much already weighed upon their overtaxed sensibilities.

The driver had been guarding his wagon whilst they'd been burning, dismembering, and decapitating their friends. His bellyaching only made them march faster toward the textile wagon a few paces ahead. That driver, at least, kept his thoughts and complaints to himself. Therefore, no one noticed when the driver's grousing suddenly ceased. They didn't turn around to hear him pop his axle into place, nor to mark how long it took for his whip to crack, or his horses to plod forward. They didn't glance backward to note that he'd somehow grown nearly two feet taller or several handspans wider, either. Therefore, they didn't hear a thing as Robin cut the nearest guards' throats. The bulk were too far ahead to detect the clatter of armor clanging off the rocks, as their comrades' corpses were flung over the side. In fact, they didn't turn around once until the horses were breathing down their necks. Ben cracked the whip and lashed the reins with ruthless determination, steering the horses and their weighty burden down the road at a breakneck pace. Men were trampled or violently shoved into the valley below.

Having hauled himself into the driver's seat, Robin took the reins from Ben with a maniacal grin. Clapping him on the back, Ben leapt onto the lead horse's back and severed its tether with a quick swipe of his sword. In a panic, men corralled into each other to avoid being flattened, knocked off the hillside, or cut in half by the massive sword they saw swinging right and left with abandon. That sword decapitated the driver of the lead wagon in one go, then gutted a handful of guards all scrambling to escape. Kicking the headless driver out of his seat, Ben cracked the reins like a madman, setting the forward wagon on a frantic downward course.

By the time Damek's officers looked back to see what all the commotion was about, the wagon and its spooked horses had already trampled or dislodged a dozen or more men. A surprised corpsman squeaked a belated warning to Damek's lead group. Just then, one of the stampeding horses stumbled under its own hooves. It went down with a terrible shriek, bowling into its fellows. The wagon flipped end over end, tossing sharp spears, arrows, and paraffin into the air. At gravity's mercy, Lord Bishop's men had nowhere left to run.

The Prince

Damek's head whipped around just in time to avoid the spear-tip that came sailing toward him from higher up the road. His honor guard rounded the last high corner when the artillery wagon upended, slinging metal, wood, iron nails, lanterns, and other heavy supplies into his men. Soldiers screamed as they were tossed over the ledge, impaled, bludgeoned, or crushed beneath the runaway wagon.

For the third time that night, the sickly-sweet scent of blood choked the air. Driving right as far as he could without tipping himself over the last incline, Damek spurred his charger's flank hard. Banking into the final turn in the path, he shouted for his men to follow suit to level ground. He reached the bottom first. Cunningham and Sergeant Douglas wedged their mounts between him and the soldiers rushing to escape calamity.

Shifting Una's dead weight to his left arm, Damek drew his sword with his right.

"Cavalry, to me!" His eyes widened at the bloodbath behind them. There were another fifteen men down, at least. He couldn't get a fix on the rear wagon, but the remains of his artillery were scattered all over the hillside, smearing human and animal gore in their wake. Those few who managed to dodge the catastrophe were running or riding down the last slope as if the dead still snapped at their heels. Many flung their weapons aside in haste to evade the tangle of limbs, steel, and splintering wood tearing toward them. Damek absorbed all of this with a caustic frown. At this point, nothing could shock him. Watching dead men drag their own corpses after the living... he might be permanently impervious to surprise.

He'd missed no detail of the horrors to which he and his men had been subjected since they ascended this cursed hill, yet his emotions were weaker, duller. Damek felt as if he'd been hovering outside of his own body, an impassive observer in all that had transpired. Not even the weight of the prize he'd fought so hard to gain, resting safe in the cradle of his arms, could move him. Perhaps, this was shock, some reflexive dampening of emotion as a result of all he'd been forced into on Una's account. Thus, when he noticed an odd silver shape speeding toward him like a vicious steel-tipped wind, he mustered only an impatient aggravation. *What now?*

As the figure neared, Damek got a good look at a face full of inhuman concentration and impartial disdain. He'd seen it before, glowering from a stained-glass window over his uncle's throne— the very relief that commemorated the murder of his great-grandfather. Heat rose up Damek's throat at the sight. *You!*— he wanted to scream over his men. He *knew* this man, even if he'd only seen him immortalized in glass or imagined him falling under his sword in childhood fancies. He didn't need to witness the disciplined precision of each measured sword-stroke to know that he was facing the greatest swordsman in Innisfail. This bastard *was* the infamous Crown Prince, Kaer Yin Adair. There he was, the very man Damek had longed to meet his entire life, cutting through his men like chaff. The how and why no longer mattered. Cunningham belched the command to form a vanguard before Damek's mount. Douglas stiffened beside him; meaty fingers gripped his sword until the knuckles bled.

"Reason," he breathed. "That's—"

"Never-mind him now," Major Cunningham sneered. "He'll come no further. Lances up!"

The vanguard of mounted men and shields deflected their panicked infantry like a massive plow. Damek didn't mind their breach of discipline. All he could see was that whirling sword barreling through man and beast alike. When it reached the bottom of the hill, it dipped and came up red again and again. Hardened spearmen and heavy infantrymen carrying spears and pikes shoved against Damek's line of horseflesh, desperate to escape that vengeful maelstrom.

"Company, drop shields!" Cunningham barked. Damek's honor guard slammed their steel-capped shields into the earth before the warhorses, resting their lances and swords over the top lip. Damek's surviving infantrymen dashed behind their makeshift wall. The prince halted some feet away, his bloody sword arced over his shoulder in a high guard.

"Archers, get your shite together back there!" Douglas bellowed. A handful of yeomen unslung their longbows from their backs, then dropped into firing positions. Damek was aware of all this, if impassively. He couldn't tear his attention from the blood-streaked figure who stood astride an unbroken line of corpses at the bottom of the rise. The prince didn't appear winded. Despite the simmering rage in his gut, Damek could only smile. So, *this* was what a legend looked like. He couldn't say he was disappointed.

"Nock!" called Douglas, while Cunningham shouted abuse at the vanguard.

Kaer Yin Adair didn't move a muscle. His piercing silver eyes met Damek's without an ounce of fear. He knew a few shields and arrows weren't enough to stop him. Damek knew it too. He couldn't help the tingle of excitement that trickled down his spine at the thought.

"Damek Bishop." The prince's voice managed to resonate without rising. "Let Una go, and you'll leave here alive. I give you my word."

"Is he mad?" guffawed Douglas, incredulous. Cunningham said nothing, merely kept an eye trained on the speaker, his fist poised to give the next command. Damek threw back his head and laughed. He couldn't help it. Perhaps the prince's comment was funny because Damek understood it was no idle boast? If any one man could take down a dozen mounted knights with a single sword, Damek believed the Kaer Yin Adair he'd read so much about certainly could. Hadn't he just cut through as many men on his way down? More? Damek couldn't stop laughing. After quite a while, he was forced to cram a knuckle into his mouth to still the fit.

Cunningham spared him a worried glance. "My Lord?"

Damek shook himself, pulling Una close. "She's not your property, Dannan! She's my blood, you know. If you think I'd leave her behind in this place, you're sorely mistaken."

Kaer Yin didn't blink. "Nor is she your plaything. Considering that she's spent near a month fleeing from you and your men, I'd say her preference is plain. Hand her over. I won't ask again."

Douglas raised an arm to order the archers to fire, but Damek caught his wrist. "Don't. He'll be over our makeshift wall and through your arrows before they ever hit the ground. We won't beat him that way."

"But My Lord—"

"Don't you know who that man is, Gilbert?"

Douglas didn't, but Cunningham nodded. "*I* do."

"Good," said Damek, looping his reins around his forearm. His horse danced impatiently beneath him. "I want you to take Una to Martin, Wallace. Ride like the wind. Let nothing stop you, no matter what comes out of those trees at you."

"Respectfully, Lord Bishop… no," spat Cunningham.

"*What* did you say?"

"Beggin' your pardon, but you're wasting time arguing with me."

"Wallace, I'll suffer no man in my regiment to fight my battles for me," Damek said. This was a fight he'd longed for since childhood. He'd be damned if the glory he craved would be snatched away so easily. How many chances would he get to slay the Crown Prince of Innisfail in single combat?

"You *will* go. That's an order."

Cunningham's brow furrowed. "Get her home safely, My Lord. That's what our men died for, isn't it?"

Damek covered his shame with gritted teeth.

There was an argument he couldn't foil. His men would take the night's slaughter as a selfish whim if he tried. They were here for Una. He had no rebuttal. "*Damn you—*"

"Then get the hells out of here." Cunningham didn't wait for Damek's reply as he turned to the men. "Nothing gets past this line! D'ye hear? Douglas, escort his Lordship to the city!"

"Aye, Major," Douglas replied with audible relief. Cunningham lowered his fist, and a cascade of arrows converged at the center of the road. The prince wasn't there to receive them. He dashed forward and leapt over Cunningham's wall of shields. His longsword dealt death from every conceivable direction. Damek had time to suck in a breath at the unimaginable feat of speed just as Douglas' sabre slapped into his mount's haunches. Mouth agape, Damek was forced to grip Una tight as the scene shrank behind him. His last glimpse of Wallace was of his sabre catching the prince's longsword mid-stroke.

He launched into a valiant counterattack. Cunningham was a crack swordsman, one of the best in Bethany. He wouldn't make it easy for the Adair, no matter how unnaturally gifted the big blond bastard was. Even so, Damek knew the match was unequal. He'd never seen anyone move like him before, as if the wind obeyed him, and gravity was merely another servant at the prince's beck and call. Damek didn't feel concern for his friend, nor pride in the courage and skill of one of his best warriors.

He felt… *envy.*

As Wallace's sabre slid down that monstrous silver longsword; as the prince ducked under his next thrust; as Wallace grunted, stepping sideways to bring his sabre around for another strike, and another, and another— all of which the prince batted away as easily as he might a child's sparring stick— Damek seethed, his regret keener than any blade.

One day, he vowed silently.

One day, my *sword will be there.* He and Una were soon at full gallop, and Damek could no longer see them. He faced forward, his heart heavy. *One day soon, you'll meet your match, Kaer Yin Adair. Once Una is safe, I'll be back for you…*

⚜

THE SOUTHER WAS GOOD. VERY GOOD. Ben had it within himself to give credit, when due. The major hadn't mastered the high guard and lacked the footwork necessary to maintain a steady rhythm, but he didn't want for strength. Wild as his thrusts were, and defensive his parries, he kept Ben on his back foot more than he was eager to admit. A few loyal pikemen remained to cover their lord's escape. They hovered near, waiting to strike at Ben wherever there was an opening. Without ado, Ben killed two and hamstrung a third, whose screams rent the pre-dawn air with chilling intensity. Ben met the Souther's next barrage with several glancing thrusts, before he leaned in with a closed fist and cracked his opponent in the face. The major staggered; his nose had imploded like a smashed melon. Ben switched Nemain to his left hand, intent to ram it through the Souther's kidney, but the fellow rolled out of Ben's grip to the ground. His serrated sabre bit deep into Ben's shin. Hissing in surprised pain, Ben fell onto his rump, his sword skittering into the trees at the edge of the road. Wasting no time, the major clawed himself up Ben's legs like a limb over deep water, attempting to drive his dagger through Ben's heart.

Ben caught his arm and held him aloft, though the effort cost him dearly. The wound in his chest hadn't fully healed. Fresh blood seeped through the gaping hole in his once snow-white cuirass. Grunting, the major pressed down with the total weight of his body while jabbing his gauntleted elbow repeatedly into the wound. Livid stars flashed behind Ben's eyes, but he held on. Summoning every ounce of strength he had left, he twisted sideways. The motion displaced the Souther's weight far enough to draw his blade into his shoulder. Ben gasped as the tip dragged against bone. Sucking in a deep breath, Ben pounded his forehead into his assailant's broken nose. Dazed, the major splashed into the mud on his back. Ben rolled with him, wrenched the dagger from his own flesh, and shoved it to the hilt through the major's eye. The Souther's body jerked; limbs twitched, then stilled forever. He'd been a tough bastard. Ben was impressed, if angry.

Breathing hard, he got to his feet, stumbling just a bit. The remaining pikemen circled, eying him like a wounded boar. He spat blood beside the major's corpse, brandishing his hard-won blade.

"Come on then," he goaded.

With a cry, the first jumped forward, his pike aimed at Ben's gut. Ben grasped the pikeman's forearm, then stepped in close enough to carve out the fellow's Adam's apple. The next took a slice out of Ben's thigh, but he barely felt the blade sink into the meat above his knee. Instead, he spun the spear he'd stolen over his shoulder, and cast it through the eager fool's midsection. The pikeman slumped forward, impaling himself further as he sank down its shaft. Ben retrieved Nemain from the roadside and used her length to keep himself upright. He was huffing now, and furious. Despite the blood spattered over his face and armor, his eyes were hard with determined ire. Rather than meet his comrades' fate, the last pikeman threw down his spear and ran.

Ben's eyes drifted to a small cadre of battered archers a few paces up the road. One got off a single shot. Directed from a shaking arm, it went wide, bouncing harmlessly off a tree trunk and landing somewhere in the leaves. Ben was on the archer before his finger left the string. His head followed his misfired arrow into the woods. Ben killed another contender with a backward slash that nearly cleaved his victim's shoulders from his body, and the next, he nearly cut in half at the pelvis. Pulling Nemain free for anyone else impatient to die, Ben heard Robin's voice from somewhere behind him.

"Ben! Watch yer arse!"

An arrow caught him in the side. Its tip sailed between the ribs under his arm. His back struck a tree trunk with a solid thwack. Groaning, Ben pried the missile free and searched for its source. The archer dropped his bow and held his hands up as if he hadn't meant to release his string. Reaching for the major's dagger, Ben flipped it up by the tip, and threw it straight into the archer's open mouth. When Robin arrived on the scene, the remaining archers took a last look at their murderous target and fled. Robin caught Ben under the arm before he fell. With a curse, he heaved him upright by the waist. Pausing to marvel at the river of corpses lining the road, Robin's eyes stretched wide.

"*Siora*. Ben... remind me to never get on yer bad side again. There must be... I can't even count 'em all."

Ben tore a wad of cloth from his tunic, then undid his belt to strap it in place over the wound on his leg.

"Bishop can't be far ahead. The mud's too deep. I need a horse, and every blade you have on you."

Robin gaped, mesmerized by the carnage all around them. "How did ye even manage all this? Great Ancestor, but yer a monster..."

"There's no time," Ben pointed at the horses wandering the road ahead, deprived of their riders. "It's not over yet. I need your help."

"Ye can't mean to go after him now? Yer bleedin' all over yerself as it is."

"Robin!"

Throwing up his hands, Robin picked his way over the dead toward the abandoned mounts.

"All right, all right! If any o'these bastards stands up and takes a bite outta me, I'll haunt ye for eternity, singin' every song ye loathe until ye hack yer ears off at the root."

⚜

"So much for our swift retreat," Douglas grumbled beside Damek. From his saddle, he kicked out at the infantrymen working to shore up the mud. "Put your backs into it, damn you! Or do you want to die in this bloody wood with the rest of your mates?"

Damek paid no attention. He stared behind them. He'd marched up that hill with *sixty* men. Now, fewer than a dozen remained to guard him and his prize. Una rested motionless in his arms, her cheek pressed into his breastplate. She was more beautiful than he remembered, by far. Her golden-brown skin, the curls he knew would gleam when they were clean and coiffed once more, and that generous mouth that drove him to distraction in their youth, lush with ripening maturity. She was worth every dead man. He wouldn't deny it. If he had to do this all over again, he would doubtless make the same choice.

Yet… *he loathed her for it too.*

He hadn't realized it was possible to hate and love with equal intensity. Damn her eyes. He hadn't expected her to leap into his arms with glee, but this… he'd lost over fifty men for her. Good men. Loyal men. Men that fought for her honor with as much zeal as him. Yet, he knew it wouldn't matter to her in the least.

Damek swallowed as a burst of hatred flared in his gut. Those men lost their lives to save her, but she wouldn't see it that way. He despised her for it. To her, *they* were the enemy— her own people. Her father's bannermen. She'd spent over forty lives for her pride. Damek thought he might choke the life out of her for such cruel treachery, such undeserved disdain. What had happened to the girl he knew all those years ago? The absolute kindness she showed to all creatures, great or small? The love that shone from her soft brown eyes when she'd looked at him? The warmth of her tender embrace?

Una made a small sound in her throat. A thin trickle of blood slid down his breastplate from her nose. Snapped alert, he realized he'd been crushing her. Hands shaking, he wiped the red smear away with a conflicted tenderness that only made him angrier. He wasn't sure he'd ever forgive her for the horrors of this night. Perhaps Aoife was right? Maybe she *would* serve him better dead? He thought about it. He was tempted to wrap his fingers around her throat. He could declare that she'd been afflicted by the dead, as so many of their fellows had been. No one would gainsay his word. He could suffocate her right now, and no one would stop him. In her sleep, her dark brows knit together in unconscious pain. Her full mauve lips trembled. Before he knew it, his fingers wound through her hair and smoothed her cheeks. He cursed himself for his weakness—his pathetic attachment to the past.

She deserved to die for what she'd wrought this night. If only he had the strength to do it!

If only he didn't need her.

If only he did not *love* her.

A sharp, ululating shriek pierced the riotous haze of his thoughts. Another answered. Dozens more followed. The roadside came alive with ear-splitting, guttural, animalistic cries. Douglas spurred his mount around to guard Damek's back. His eyes weren't on the trees or the road ahead. He pointed behind them with the tip of his sabre.

"My Lord!" Douglas shouted in alarm. The men had no idea which way was safest to turn. They crowded around Damek's charger like the last bit of wood floating up from a wreck. "That elf lord is a devil!"

Damek's brows rose in surprise... and not the least amount of competitive elation. "He's neither. He's Kaer Yin Adair, Douglas. I imagine we each seek the same goal."

The prince's stolen horse wound through the trees opposite like a half-mad dervish. Damek had but a moment to grin. The prince wasn't alone in the wood. Hundreds of twisted shapes dropped from the highest boughs, surging toward every moving thing within reach. Damek's men broke ranks. They clattered up the road as fast as their armored legs could carry them.

"*Reason*, what now?" Douglas groaned as the yelping horde descended upon their battered cavalcade.

Damek said, "Goblins. Drawn by the slaughter, no doubt."

"I fucking *hate* the North," declared Douglas, as the pool of snarling imps swirled around them. His mount reared when a humanoid shape barreled into its chest, rotting teeth snapping in delighted bloodlust. Douglas severed its misshapen head from its sleek grey body. "Company, hold your bloody line!"

Damek hacked left and right of his saddle, slashing at anything brave enough to reach for Una. He lost sight of the prince, who must have been swept into this undulating wave of reeking, grasping, goblins, same as everyone. They swarmed the road like wasps. There was little he could do but fight. In mere moments, a wire-thin arm coiled around Damek's waist, while another dug its claws into his arm to pry Una loose. A goblin with carrion breath leaned in to chew her throat out, but Damek's sabre exploded through its hideous skull, spilling its gnarled yellow teeth over the ground like coins.

"Douglas! Get the shieldmen down here!" he bellowed, but to no avail. His sergeant was as imperiled as he.

A sudden glancing blow to the back of his head disoriented Damek long enough for a pair of sharp grey claws to rip Una from his grip.

"No!" he raged. Knowing he'd never catch them on horseback, Damek dismounted and pounded through the mud after them. Something had already taken a bite of her upper arm, leaving a brilliant trail of bright red blood through the woods on his right. He carved a wide path through milling grey flesh in his haste to retrieve her. One squirming thing jumped onto his back, sinking its razor teeth deep into the meat at his shoulder blade. With a sharp cry, he reached behind to tear it off by its jagged jaws. While it spat and scratched, he smashed its skull in with his boot heel. Una, still unconscious, was dragged away again. Damek couldn't get there as swiftly as he needed to. They were everywhere. "Una!" He yelled at the top of his lungs and redoubled his efforts with every atom he had to spare. They swarmed him, clawing and biting.

He would never reach her in time.

All at once, a tremor ran through each writhing beast. The goblins raised their warped heads, sniffing the air like frightened rabbits. He saw Kaer Yin then, striding from the forest like a wraith. Damek's guts roiled with hatred and frustrated longing. He was so close! The victory he'd longed for all of his life was at hand. Though, it wasn't his sword that cut through these beasts like water through a sieve.

It wasn't *Damek* who the Dor Sidhe rats took one look at and covered their slimy faces in fear. It wasn't *Damek*'s hands that plucked Una from the ground, nor held her in his arms like some priceless artifact. Damek ground his molars in envious loathing. The prince was wounded too, but everywhere his eyes drifted, goblins shrank back.

Ard Tiarne! they wailed, fleeing as if in despair of his very presence. Damek's men recovered themselves as best they were able with their numbers reduced to ten.

Douglas had managed to keep his mount and his sabre, despite the scratches covering his face. "My Lord! They're leaving. Let's get out of here!"

Damek didn't hear him. He was already moving for the prince. He clutched his sabre in a quaking fist. Goblins fled into the woods with abandon, yipping in retreat. The prince didn't see him coming, for the mass of grey bodies shoving past him. Damek's shoulder caught him square in the spine. He tipped forward, dumping Una like a sack of kindling at his feet. Kaer Yin Adair reeled; his leg and ribs bled freely over his once pretty armor. Damek didn't spare him a moment to recover. He kicked Kaer Yin in the face on his way past, jerking Una upright by the elbow. Douglas waited at the corpse-strewn roadside, ready with a fresh mount and a reaching hand. Damek flung Una face-down over Douglas' saddle.

"Get her to Martin! Go!" He slapped the sergeant's charger on the rump. Ducking low in the saddle, Douglas spurred his steed to a gallop.

Damek watched until Una was well out of sight. Drawing a deep breath, he turned to catch the prince's first thrust with a backhanded parry. Kaer Yin skidded sideways from the impact, but the blow didn't bow him in the least. He righted himself, then came again. Soon enough, Damek broke out in a sweat. It took everything he had to dodge each lightning quick attack. Up, around, up, down came his blade. Damek would backpedal, and the prince would slide his foot forward. Without pause, he used his own body weight as a fulcrum for the unending vertical and horizontal pendulums his blade etched between them. Its edge forged a wall that was nigh impenetrable. Damek knew he wasn't going to beat him in a fair fight. Never. Not like this. After five minutes of losing ground, he limped into the road, gasping. He wasn't good enough to beat the Adair. Not yet. Furious with himself, Damek spat a long low curse. Following, the prince swung his sword back up into his high guard. *Neithana*, Damek knew. The Dannan Art, which took lifetimes to master.

Kaer Yin Adair was *unbeatable*. He was so far above Damek's current level, his former hubris seemed laughable.

Very well, Damek thought. *Any victory is better than none.*

Just as he reached toward his saddle for his crossbow, something bright sailed out of the trees from the east. The arrow plowed straight into his hand— pinning it to his own chest. His howl of pain startled the prince enough to look behind him for its source. While he was distracted, Damek took the cue. Using his uninjured hand, he launched himself up into his saddle. Noting the unmistakable swish of several fired arrows, he tucked himself low over the reins to escape the next volley. His groom, and any other waiting soldiers, fell into the mud, arrows sunk into each of their skulls with perfect accuracy.

Damek didn't need to hear the horns blowing throughout the clearing to know he must get out of there fast. These were not Eirean horns. Not Tairnganese. Not Taran. These were Dannan horns. *Daoine Sidhe* horns. The prince's own people had come for him. Damek peeked over his shoulder before he made it out of range. White and red flags swirled into view. A host of scarlet-tipped arrows soared into the brightening sky. Damek smashed himself tight over his charger's sweating neck. He hung on for dear life as he kicked the beast into a slavering gallop. He didn't look back again. He might not have killed the one man he wanted to above all others, and he may have lost his first match with the deadliest swordsman in Innisfail… but he'd beat him, all the same. Damek had won this round. He got what he came for, no matter the cost.

I beat you, princeling. He allowed himself to smirk through the pain. *I beat you, nonetheless.* Una was his, and the North with her.

⚐ ⚑

AOIFE TUMBLED INTO THE RAVINE, the last of her magic spent. An empty, feeble husk, she crawled forward on her knees, groping for somewhere dry to hide. Her body sang with pain. Every nerve, every vein, every muscle— was a stinging, burning wreck. She had *failed*. She'd failed Vanna Nema… *twice more.* All the pain she felt now would pale in comparison to the symphony of morbid delights that awaited her in Tairngare. Aoife longed to dig herself a hole and bury herself deep within it, never to emerge again. She wished she had the power of Transmutation. Then, she might transform herself into a salmon, a fox, an insect— it didn't matter. She would do *anything* to escape the fate she knew she'd earned by failing to kill one simpering, Milesian girl.

Aoife knew there was no safe harbor anywhere. If she became a salmon, Nema would become the bear that ate her whole. If she became a fox, Nema would become the wolf that dragged her from her den. If she became an insect, Nema would become the fish that leapt from the river to swallow her in one gulp. Everywhere, anywhere, any way she ran, Nema would follow and exact her vengeance. Nema did not tolerate failure in her disciples… even less, in her own grandchildren. There was no hope. Aoife could feel the pull of the geis in her blood, even now. Nema would exact her due.

Aoife dozed for a time. She cowered beneath a knoll, shivering in the chill Samhain air. When she awoke, the sun beckoned from the east— a spotlight, searching for Aoife in the dark. Helpless against it, she dragged herself toward that beacon. She might crawl all the way to Tairngare, just to be torn apart for her own miserable failure.

Forgive me grandmother, she pleaded with that immutable sunlight. *The girl lives. The prince is yet free… and your grandson has the means to make himself a king at your expense.* The sun held no warmth in its cold brilliance. No sympathy. Neither would Nema, Aoife knew only too well.

THE SOUTHERNMOST STAR

Patrick sneezed his way down the corridor, wrapped head to toe in white bearskin. With each day dawning colder than the last, his old bones ached for warmth he doubted he'd ever feel again. His physicians had passed through his chambers so many times in the past week that his imminent expiration may as well be painted on his forehead.

Consumption, they told him.

Six months past, they'd warned of a growth blooming in his gut like a weed, its tendrils slithering deep into his blood, sapping the remnants of his strength. Now, this. The malignancy had spread to his lungs, throat, liver… and soon, his heart. Patrick's physicians declared he would likely be dead long before that happened. The lungs would do the job much faster than the stomach, throat, or liver. *Months,* they'd told him. *Less,* if he didn't take to his bed now.

Dying was a bothersome business. Untidy. Inconvenient. He couldn't afford to sit back and let the sharks circle his corpse for the final feast— not yet. He had things to see to: a country to run, a kingdom to forge, a daughter to marry off, a war to plan, and an heir to crown. Patrick was too damned busy to play invalid. There was much left to do! His legacy was on the line. He was the last Eirean lord who could trace his bloodline to Eber Finn, the first Milesian High King: the hero who cut the hand from King Nuada of the Tuatha De Dannan. The very man that sent the Sidhe scurrying into the Otherworld in the first place. In Patrick's blood walked giants: Fionn Mac Cumhail, Cu Chulainn, and Brian Boru. His ancestors *were* Eire. Men who faced the Sidhe time and again and emerged victorious.

Patrick had far too much to live up to, to die now.

His grandfather's chapel lay at the southernmost tip of the fortress, facing a roaring Dor Oras sea. Duch Kevin had it built more to honor Innish heritage than as a place for prayer and contemplation. The old ways had died out well before Kevin's time. New gods sprang from the soil after the Transition, taking root the breadth and length of Innisfail. The cult of the Ancestor in Tairngare, with its alchemical Mother Goddess Siora, was undoubtedly the strongest faith remaining in Eire.

Above the eastern arch, *Siora* was represented by a winged dragon bearing the sun in her talons. Astride the Southern lintel with its tall glass doors, two converged circles signified *Reason*: the only God of any importance in Bethany. Striding into the knave, he stepped over the beautifully rendered symbols on the floor—*the Cross, the Scimitar*, the ancient Hebrew character for law— *Elohim*.

Behind him, over the northern lintel, The World Tree reached toward three shining stars that winked with diamonds the size of eggs. On the West wall, the fulcrum and anvil— *Innovation*. Entering this chapel, one was meant to stride over the old gods and be swept into the future, toward the True South: *Reason*.

The point was to be awed by the might of human potential. A smug bit of architectural theater on his grandfather's part, but effective, all the same. One *could* imagine the scope of human existence as a romp through myth and superstition. Patrick never much cared for the lesson. He found the chapel crass, its symbols meaningless, and its uses impractical as they were pompous. To his mind, humanity *was* its history, no matter how punitive, servile, self-aggrandizing, or absurd. Men could no more sever ties with the stories that sculpted them than they could move about without skin.

The most human trait that Patrick could conceive of was the ability to learn from one's failings. Humans could imagine worlds far outside of their collective experience, strive toward goals most creatures could scarcely conceive. No other animal on earth could boast of a human being's potential. The Sidhe, by comparison, suffered for their stability. They were too long-lived, detached, and selective. In the bosom of immortality, there was little change and less urgency. Mortals thrived because they knew *want*… they could endeavor to greater heights because they understood *fear* and *need*. That was why Patrick couldn't allow himself to die, not with his final victory so near. He was going to teach the immortals why humans had held the biological advantage for thousands of years. Lost in his musings, Patrick shambled past the last row of dusty pews and hobbled up the steps toward the southern promenade. He was well-armed against any impertinence his caller meant to throw at him tonight. Her immortality be damned.

To Patrick's mind, his very humanity made *him* superior.

His guest may pontificate all she liked.

Outside, the ocean roiled. Crashing waves sent frigid spray dozens of feet over the cliffs below. He pried open a latticed door coated with salt, tasting the ether of a storm on the air.

His visitor approached from the far balustrade, mindful of the ice coating the paving stones. She sniffed, tucking her hands deep within her ermine-lined muffler.

"About time. Your thoughts are as loud as that racket down there. I despise the sea, you realize. It stinks of dead things."

He leaned against the open door, huffing, "You'll have to forgive me, madam. I'm dying, apparently."

Liadan turned, her violet and green eyes narrowed in the ochre perfection of her skin. "Do you suppose I find that a reasonable excuse? My time is more valuable than you can possibly comprehend."

"Yet… here you are. I wonder, Lady MacNemed, that you'd bother to come so far south, if my message was a mere inconvenience?"

"Perhaps I wished to hear the explanation from your own wormy lips?"

He let the insult slide. "My daughter is coming home, no thanks to you."

"Is that all you meant to say? I wish you joy of her."

"You've tried to kill her at least three times in the last two months, or so I'm told. Odd, considering that you went well out of your way to ensure her birth, education, and rise through the Cloister's ranks." Patrick crossed his arms with some effort. "As I recall, it was *you* who arranged for Arrin's capture those many years ago… begged me to take her, if I'm not mistaken?"

"You *are*. I never beg."

"You might say, you planned every step of Una's life from birth on. I'm merely curious why you'd wish to undo all of that hard work, those years of careful plotting, just as she became useful to me?"

She gave him a cold smile. "I needn't explain myself to you, mortal. Long before your cursed forebears set foot in this land, my people ruled here. The Children of Danu were our enemies thousands of years before you or your infuriating offspring were conceived."

"All utterly irrelevant. Do you think that hive of self-important women and soft boys in Tairngare stands a chance against my army?" He made a rude sound. "When we're done with the Red City, I think we'll march on Armagh next. The High King will keep, for now."

"You wouldn't *dare*."

"I absolutely would, dear lady. We had a deal, and you've broken it. I want to know why, before I decide what revenge suits me best."

"I suspect you decided days ago, Patrick. Let's not pretend either of us is a fool." She pulled her heavy fur cloak tight around her shoulders.

"Make no further attempts on my daughter's life."

"She could undo everything we've worked to achieve."

"… *ah*. You fear her? That *is* interesting."

"I'm wary of anything I cannot control, as you can attest. She is… unnerving. Dangerous. Her gifts are unnatural, and entirely without precedent. I fear you'll never be able to take her to heel."

"That is for Damek to decide."

Her eyes flashed. "You shan't wed that abomination to a son of Falan Mac Nemed!"

"I'll do whatever I damned well please, Liadan."

Patrick possessed a standing army some five-thousand strong in the South alone, not to mention the troops scattered throughout the midlands. He held forts bursting with soldiers in Swansea, Kernow, and the isles ringing Bretagne. With a word, he could muster a force of twenty thousand. While Liadan Mac Nemed, the Dowager Queen of Armagh, boasted her own impressive Fir Bolg combatants, she had half his numbers, and they both knew it.

"My sister's son will be King of Eire and my daughter will reign beside him as queen, or I *will* destroy you. Living or dead, I vow it. If you wish to crown your son Ard Ri, back off. This is my last warning. Please assure yourself of my profound sincerity."

She was quiet for a time, observing him from beneath lowered lashes. As beautiful as she still was, he found the weight of her ancient eyes unbearable. She'd been a woman of middle years when she'd led her people up the hill at Tara to partake of the Dagda's brew. Time stopped for her then, eons before Patrick was born. He imagined, to her, mortals like himself were fleeting as grass in winter. Though they were allied against a common enemy, he could never trust her; nor she, him. No matter. Patrick had his own reasons for this tremulous alliance, didn't he? Plans within plans, the pair of them. A pity he wouldn't live to see her suffer the loss she so richly deserved.

"If Falan is to take and hold the throne, he needs my nephew to prop it up for him. Never forget that, Liadan. Perhaps once the Dannans have been pushed into the West from whence they came, you'll have your chance to purge Innisfail of Mil's bloodline. Who knows? *Who cares?* Without my men, my daughter, and my nephew, Falan Mac Nemed will be king of the wind, and nothing more."

She exhaled, slowly. "Very well. I'll allow your spawn to live, so long as she devotes herself to my great-grandson, and remains out of sight. In return, I demand that you formally declare Damek your heir. No more grandstanding with your zealotous brother or his inferior children."

Patrick chuckled. *If only she knew.* He let no trace of his triumph reveal itself on his face. "Done. Your hand on it, My Lady?"

She wrinkled her nose, unamused. "I hope you realize, any agreement forged between us is valid only so long as you draw breath. I can smell the taint in your blood, Patrick. You aren't long for this realm."

"For your sake, it had better be a long time coming. I shudder to imagine what will become of Armagh if my people are able to imagine a world without the Sidhe. How far did your people ever come, Liadan? What marvels have you wrought, frontiers have you explored, mysteries have you solved? Have you ever set a foot anywhere else?" he laughed. "You believe you have some divine right to rule over men, simply because you cannot die. I say that is your greatest weakness and, in the end, it will be your undoing."

She spun on her heel. Her scarlet robes swirled beneath her cloak like blood. "Yours is unfailing arrogance. Your impermanence and short-sighted greed are laughable. We, as always, will *outlast* you."

Patrick shrugged. "Perhaps. Perhaps not. Have a safe trip back to the Cloister, madam Nema. I doubt we'll meet again."

"Die well, Donahugh." Liadan stalked from the chapel, her back straight as a prow. Patrick at last allowed himself to cough, wiping the blood it produced against his sleeve. He couldn't stop smiling. He was in a fine mood. For that vaunted old schemer to travel so far in the midst of an engineered revolt against the Cloister, meant only one thing— she came because she was *afraid*. Without Patrick, she was running thin on reliable Eirean allies. Damek was no pawn. Liadan would learn that fact, very soon. *Nine hells*, he'd raised that boy to be a bloody pain in the arse, hadn't he?

Patrick almost pitied the whole Mac Nemed Clan, for they had no idea what they were in for. Though he longed to watch Damek cast the arrogant Sidhe from their self-appointed throne, Patrick could go to his rest confident the best was still to come. He'd unleashed a final weapon: one with the potential to burn through the Sidhe like a forest fire. The very same insidious force that banished them to the Otherworld before the Transition. That which had wiped them from living memory for a time, like a half-remembered nightmare. This weapon was *faith*. Its arbiter, the most charming, focused, and singularly arrogant man he'd ever encountered— Henry Fitz Donahugh. Patrick's laughter rang throughout the chapel as he took his leave. His attendant closed the heavy iron doors behind him. The torches in the hall cast an ever-thinning stream of light over the symbols on the floor, until it winked out altogether, shrouding their majesty and mystery in a patient, protective darkness.

KAER YIN RESTED AGAINST A ROWAN with his tunic open to the waist, while Rian cursed over his bleeding torso. The sun was out and shining over the river. Its incandescent rays spread reassuring warmth over his closed eyelids. He felt its heat all the way to his toes. Now that Dor Oras had arrived, this brief glimpse of sunlight might be the last in Innisfail until Imbolc. He sighed. Six months of dark and cold to come, yet he didn't mind so much, now. Something larger and more pressing took up every inch of free space in his mind. Rian snorted, and he cracked an eye. Her face was tear-streaked, filthy, and much thinner than he remembered. She was angry too. Her cheeks had gone red as an autumn apple. Shredding scraps of linen out of whatever anyone could scavenge for her, she refused to look him in the eye.

Well, at least he knew where her ire was directed.

"Pull him up, if you please?" Shar Lianor hovered close, as if waiting to do her bidding. His pristine white cuirass creaked as he moved.

Kaer Yin was jerked upright by a pair of too large, too strong hands. He yelped. "That hurts, damn it!"

Shar dipped his fair head, silver chains jingling in his ears. "Forgive me, *Mo Flaith*. The lady must see to your wounds." The ghost of a smirk tugged at the corners of Shar's mouth, though his eyes were tactfully trained on his feet.

Rian wrapped torn bits of fabric around Kaer Yin's torso. She tied several makeshift bandages in place over his chest, shoulder, and ribs. Whatever she'd doused his wounds with smelled strongly of peat, ground nettles, and something fouler, which he fervently refused to investigate.

"If her *ladyship* would be kind enough not to break my ribs in the process, I'd appreciate it."

Her nostrils flared. "I'm sorry, does this hurt?" She knew it did.

He glared back at her.

"Now, now, lass," cooed Robin from his right side. He passed Kaer Yin his bone flask full of miraculous uishge. "We know he's a charmer, but ye needn't bother to kill him to mark yer snit. He's half-killed hisself for ye as it is."

That shut her mouth with an audible snap. She bent back to her work, silently fuming. Shar set Kaer Yin against the tree trunk when she was done. He visibly fought the urge to grin. Kaer Yin was happy to see him, even if he couldn't show it. He hurt too damned much to crack a smile for the young Sidhe's benefit. Rian stole a veiled upward glance at Kaer Yin's face.

"What now? Am I breathing too hard?" he scowled.

She flushed. "No. I… ah, that is… thank you, Ben."

His head swiveled toward her. "Forgive me, *what was that?*"

"You heard me."

"One more time?"

"Fine, fine. Thank you for saving my life," she mumbled.

Well. How about that? "Thank Una, Rian. Not me."

"Don't tell me you're discovering humility now? How… annoying."

"You're welcome, Rian."

"You don't deserve her, you realize?"

"Trust me, *I know.*"

Nearby stood a tall figure in white and crimson. The eight gold chains dangling from his ears chimed when he shook his head at one of his scouts. He waved the fellow away, then turned. He had familiar violet eyes and flaming red hair shot with silver blond streaks which he kept tied back at the temples, as all Dannan nobles wore it.

"Yin," he said, his tone bland. "They're already marching South. They left the city burning behind them."

Kaer Yin exchanged a long look with Robin. "Get me a horse."

"Now wait a minute, Ben," Robin objected.

"Absolutely *not!*" interrupted Rian.

"*Mo flaith*, I don't think," began Shar.

"We could take the game trails, and—" Gerrod piped in.

The redhead's answering sneer trumped each response. "Why? So you can beat him to death with your one good leg? Should I have this girl saw it off for you so you might wield it as a club?"

Kaer Yin growled, "I am your Ard Tiarne! You'll do it or—"

"You going to hop along after me too? Quick, protect me, Shar. I *quake* with fear for my life."

"You know these scratches won't stop me. I *demand* a horse, Tam Lin. I have places to be, and no time to—"

The redhead crammed a finger in his ear. "Bah. I'm your cousin, not your slave. The only place you're headed is the nearest bed. You there," he ignored Kaer Yin and rounded sharply on Robin. "You're from Rosweal; I take it?"

"Aye?"

"My men hold many of your fellow citizens at the crossroads outside Donaghmore. Are you their Headman? This Gramble character?"

"I am." Robin crossed his arms.

"Unfortunately, your little town is the nearest with reasonable shelter. My men have already put out the blaze. I'm sorry to say, you lost quite a lot of real estate at the South End."

"Figured. Wasn't the best neighborhood anyway."

Tam Lin had no idea what to say to that. "*Quite.* Well, we'll have to beg your hospitality for a few days, if that would suit you fair?"

"Why not take him straight to his father, at Bri Leith?" Rian asked, wiping her hands dry on the underside of her homespun skirts.

Tam Lin's eyes cut sideways at her, as if he couldn't imagine why such a lowly creature should have the nerve to address him without invitation. "For reasons you needn't worry your pretty head over, sweetheart."

Gerrod sucked in a breath. He grasped her shoulder to keep her from launching upward, but it was a near thing. She stilled when Kaer Yin's hand caught hers.

"I know he's an arrogant bastard, Rian... but he *is* the Prince of Connaught. You can't kill him for cheek."

She settled back onto her haunches, her expression dripping ice. "No, but I can slap his face, and will, if he ever speaks to me like that again."

Tam Lin wandered closer to get a better look at her. Gerrod positioned himself between them, embarrassed but standing firm. There was no telling what Rian might do, if Gerrod let him pass. The Sidhe lord quirked a brow at the lad's bravado. Tam Lin not only towered over Gerrod by at least four handspans, he was also half-again as wide.

"What charming company you keep, Yin. Are all Milesian women in Eire like this one? Brash?"

"Only the good ones," Kaer Yin said.

Tam Lin batted Gerrod away as if parting a flimsy curtain. "What's your name then, girl?"

She chewed at the inside of her cheek. "Drop dead."

Tam Lin's men laughed with him. "Rather mouthy, aren't you?"

"Lin," Kaer Yin warned. "You're being a bore."

"Am I?"

"Yeah, ye are," answered Robin, tapping his dagger.

Shar dispelled the tension by retrieving a skin from his saddle. "More water, *Mo Flaith*? This is from the spring at Aislin Bres."

Kaer Yin shook Robin's flask. "Got something better."

Tam Lin pried his gaze from Rian's burning face. "Yin, I know your geis is broken, but that doesn't mean all is forgiven in Bri Leith. I meant to spare you until you were well again."

"I know."

"If you wish to go home first, I'll gladly escort you. Though, I can't promise you'll be pleased by your reception."

"I know that too, Lin," sighed Kaer Yin.

Tam Lin crouched beside him, grinning. "My father has no quarrel with you. Come to Connaught for a time! We'll hunt the hills of Sligo, as we did in our youth, and climb the pass at Donegal. There'll be wine and feasting *for years* in honor of your return. Surely my uncle's anger will wane in time and you'll take your proper place soon enough?"

If only he'd made such an offer a year ago, hells, four weeks ago, Kaer Yin would have leapt at the chance to return to Aes Sidhe. No longer an outsider. No longer forbidden the wilds of his homeland, or the hearths of his kin. Still, the homecoming would be bittersweet at best. He'd be unwelcomed in his family's *tuath* until Midhir deemed him worthy by edict. Kaer Yin might've slain the beast that jailed him but that had been a technical victory, at best. As far as Midhir was concerned, Kaer Yin remained an exile. A month before, he might not have minded. He might've leapt at Tam Lin's offered hospitality and considered it his due. Not so now. He knew *better*. Midhir hadn't banished him to Eire merely to be rid of a disobedient, dishonorable son. Finally, Kaer Yin comprehended his father's compassionate mind.

His father had exiled him to find Una.

Kaer Yin Adair, the ruthless Crown Prince of Innisfail, son of the Ard Ri, Midhir Mac Nuada— once loathed the Sons of Mil with every fiber in his being. He'd disdained them as *lesser* creatures: the unhappy children of a downtrodden god. Kaer Yin dealt with them when ordered to, meted justice where it was warranted. Otherwise, he held nothing but contempt for their meager lives. Their woes, joys, and loves were once alien and inscrutable, as the cold blackness between the stars. They were insignificant as autumn leaves; impermanent as a passing cloud. Despite these sentiments, Kaer Yin had meant to rule over them one day. His would have been a reign of condescension, cruelty, and inequality.

Midhir sent his only son to Eire to alter his perspective. Kaer Yin was meant to walk amongst the Sons of Mil: to fear, hunger, thirst, rage, laugh, cry, and strive alongside them. Midhir wished for his heir to know mortals, to feel the power and purpose in their lives. He intended that Kaer Yin share their hearths and friendships; for him to respect them, as Midhir respected them… to love them, as he loved them— as any noble king should. Midhir wanted to make him *their* king. A real king. A *great* king. Kaer Yin understood everything now, as if he could read his father's intentions on the wind. He wondered how he'd ever believed himself anything but a fool. Nearly a thousand years of life… and Kaer Yin had never actually felt *alive* before this moment.

"I thank you for your offer, cousin," Kaer Yin smiled. "But I'm afraid I must decline."

Tam Lin blanched. "Why on earth would you *want* to stay?"

"I have my reasons."

Tam Lin gawped at him, as if unsure what sort of lunatic he was looking at. "Girl. Give him something to clear his head. He's raving."

"May I slap him now, Ben?" inquired Rian, sweetly.

"Surely they know your name, Yin," Tam Lin ignored her comment. Again. "Why won't they use it?"

"Go ahead Rian, but he'll enjoy it," sighed Kaer Yin, patting her hand. He should keep his cousin away from the faerie for a while, for Tam Lin's own safety. "He loves a challenge. Best to pretend he's an overlarge tree, and skirt around him."

Her nose wrinkled. "Ugh. Duly noted."

Robin doffed his cap to scratch his head. "Ben, ye should go home while ye can. Isn't that what you want? What ye've wanted all this while?"

"… It was."

Robin ogled Kaer Yin for several breaths. All of a sudden, he tossed back his head on a hoot of laughter.

"Oh, aye? 'Not like that', then eh?"

"Hang yourself, Robin."

"What in the hells are all of you on about?" demanded Tam Lin. "Shar? Do you have any idea what this nonsense pertains to?"

Shar spread his hands. No help there.

"Tam Lin O'Ruiadh," Kaer Yin said.

"*Ard Tiarne*," Tam Lin mocked, in return.

"I ask that you and your Blood Eagles escort me South to Bethany, as soon as my wounds allow."

"… You've gone daft," scoffed Tam Lin.

"Donahugh's nephew took something from me. I want it back. Will you help me or not?"

On the spot and at a disadvantage for explanation, Tam Lin paced a bit. "Tell me, what could be so bloody important?"

"A woman," Rian answered for Kaer Yin, failing to hide a knowing smirk. "One *far* too good for him."

Kaer Yin squirmed. "Afraid she's right, Lin. Now, are you going to give me the men, or would you rather go home and hunt the same boar you always hunt? Raid the same boring *raths* you always raid? Hm?"

"*A woman?*" Tam Lin's voice cracked. His men all found something very interesting to observe in the trees around them. "You *have* gone mad."

"If I told you she was a princess and her father is Patrick Donahugh himself, would that change your mind?"

"Yin, you're barking."

"Better yet," Kaer Yin said, holding up a finger. "Her grandmother is the Doma of Tairngare, and in the Red City, she's wanted for a heretic by Parliament. Any interest yet?"

"Did she cast a spell on you? Bash in your brains with something heavy?"

"All right," Kaer Yin chuckled. "What if I told you she's the future Princess of Innisfail? How would that hold you?"

"The… *what?*"

"Think the boy's in love, ye dolt," Robin guffawed; his craggy cheeks shook with mirth. "Ye want me to spell it?"

Rian made a face. "She'd be mad to take you."

"Aye, she would at that," agreed Robin. Kaer Yin rolled a bandaged shoulder.

"What are you two on about? I'm a bloody prize." He gave a hacking cough and spat. "I'll keep asking. As many times as it takes."

Rian shook her head. "Poor Una."

"What am I listening to right now? Yin, have your brains melted inside your skull?" Tam Lin held his hands up.

Robin patted Kaer Yin's good arm with an exaggerated wink. "I'll try to talk ye up, but I'm afraid I can't make ye smarter or more dashin'. She'll have to be satisfied that yer daddy is rich."

Kaer Yin shot Robin a doleful glare, while Tam Lin sputtered. "Take your time, Lin. I can see you need it. Rian, would you be overly put out if I asked you to help me to the river?"

She blinked a stray tear away, wiping her nose on her sleeve. "You'll wet your bandages, and I'll kill you."

Kaer Yin crossed his heart. "My solemn vow only to wade."

"Fine," she sniffed. "Gerry, would you mind giving me a hand? And, oh—" Without ado, Shar Lianor hooked an arm under Kaer Yin's opposite shoulder while Gerrod helped Rian bear up his left side. She gave the Dannan soldier the briefest smile. "Erm, thank you. I might ask you both to help me drown him if he splashes that bandage on his thigh."

"I'm not going to!" protested Kaer Yin as they shuffled past Tam Lin's thunderstruck expression. Robin sidled up to him as the argument moved to the river's edge. "You gods-damned nag! I only want to wade, all right?" continued Kaer Yin. "I haven't been allowed in this cursed river for nearly—"

"You're already knee-deep! Take your boots off! I *swear to Siora…*"

"Rian, we can always wrap 'em again. I'll do it meself," placated Gerrod. He winked at Kaer Yin. "Swear."

"Stay out of this, Gerry!" Rian said.

"*The Princess of Innisfail?*" Tam Lin mumbled, his cheeks wan, "A *Milesian woman?*"

Robin took a long pull from his flask and handed it to the Prince of Connaught. Tam Lin stared at it like it might be a bubbling cauldron full of poison. Perhaps, in a way, it was; the best kind.

"Ye look like ye need this more'n me, yer highness."

Tam Lin grimaced as the warm amber liquid sailed down his gullet. "*A Milesian woman?*" he repeated, dumbfounded.

"Aye, and a bloody terrifying one, ye ask me," Robin's laughter rasped in his throat, "but a finer one, I've never seen. Brave. Smart. Good for him, I think."

Tam Lin took another drink. "*The Duch*'s daughter?"

"Well, nobody's perfect, I expect, but that ain't what matters. I've known Ben a long time, and I must admit, she's the makin' of him. None o'us would be here now if not for her."

"My uncle won't approve of her. None of my people will." Tam Lin watched his cousin argue with Rian while she helped him out of his boots. Shar held him up so he might stroll into the current. Once there, the erstwhile Crown Prince closed his eyes and raised his chin to the setting sun— a free man at last. Encouraged, Kaer Yin waded too far toward the center, splashing his bandaged thigh to the skin. Rian's infuriated screech shattered the idyllic scene. Gerrod moved to intercept her lunge for Kaer Yin's ear, nearly dousing her in his haste to prevent her from murdering her patient.

"I said I was sorry, you harridan!" Kaer Yin used Shar as a massive, affable shield.

Rian was livid. "You *will* be when I start stitching!"

"I wouldn't be too sure of that, milord," said Robin to Tam Lin, gesturing to the fracas. Gerrod lost his footing and dragged Rian bodily into the icy, slogging current. He came up first, shying away as she rose from the riverbed like a vengeful sea goddess. Laughing, every man fled her boiling wrath. "Seems to me this mighta been what his majesty intended, all along."

Tam Lin blew air over his lower lip. "Don't be absurd. Have you ever been outside of Eire? These wilds? What does a woodsman like yourself know about anything?"

"Well, when ye put it like that, not much, I 'spose," Robin conceded. "But some things I can see, plain as me own nose. For one, I probably know Ben better than ye do."

"Is that so?"

"It is." Robin clapped him on the back, hard as he would any man in his acquaintance. Tam Lin was too surprised to conceal his flinch. "Come on. I'll show ye where we stashed the rest o'our uishge and tell ye all about it over a few drams."

The Prince of Connaught held up the bone flask. "Is it as good as this?"

"Better," Robin promised, leading the way.

Eva

Navan Village was a smoking scar in a wasteland of skinny charred sticks. The air was heavy with smoke and the sharp tang of blood. Eva heard the wailing long before she passed through the Slanic Gate from the east end of the High Road. There weren't many people around, save those keening outside the ruins of their homes and businesses. She did not stop to ask what had happened. No need. They'd passed the Corsairs on the road. Their faces were smudged with blood and soot as they limped back to Tairngare, their few remaining mounts burdened by ill-gotten gains. Mel recognized one of their officers, Lieutenant Camur Hamma, from the Citadel Guard. The Corsairs had been in quite the fight from the looks of them, and Hamma must have taken command from a fallen captain. He didn't appear pleased by his new rank in the least. He wouldn't be, would he? Knowing very well, he was marching home to announce his failure to Alta Nema. Eva and company passed them, disguised and unnoticed. Opening her Spark like a tap, she listened to their hearts' anger, hatred, fear, and despair. She pitied them, despite the crimes they'd committed in their rage.

The Corsairs lost the Moura Domina in Rosweal.

Along with nearly seventy men.

Eva suppressed the relief that surged through her at the news. These men, frustrated by their defeat in Rosweal, took revenge on every town they passed in retreat. Navan ahead had taken the brunt of that rage. Eva stymied her disgust at the disturbing images she prized from each of their depraved minds. Punishment was not her purpose, as much as she longed to mete the justice they so richly deserved. Knowing what awaited them in Tairngare, Eva had to be satisfied. Most of them would hang from the outer walls by nightfall tomorrow, including fine Lieutenant Hamma. That was not to say that she didn't leave each of them a special gift to mull over for the remainder of their march. Like a rotting tooth, the specter of their bodies swinging from a chain thirty feet from the ground gnawed its way into their subconscious like a persistent rat. She'd utter no prayers for their loss.

In Navan, the devastation was so much worse than she imagined it would be. Using all the Spark she could muster, she soothed the survivors as much as she was able. Their minds were a dark jumble of pain, shock, and anguish. Through their memories, she watched the Corsairs ride into town from the Rose Gate in the west, battered, impotent, and furious. The soldiers sought an easy target: someone to blame, someone to still the quaking fear in their souls.

They did to Navan what they could not do to Rosweal. The villagers in this small, inoffensive hamlet paid the price for the Corsairs' ineffectual cowardice. Women were savaged and slaughtered before their children. Husbands, fathers, and brothers were dragged through muddied lanes behind the Corsairs' horses. Some were slashed, bludgeoned, or cut down for attempting to protect their wives, mothers, and daughters. Some fled in time. Many died in their burning homes. Most lay broken in the streets, unseeing eyes filling with rainwater as they gasped their last. Mel, for one, hadn't seen horrors like this since the previous war. It was unconscionable: treacherous and unnecessary. He was unashamed to weep openly before his men. That fellow soldiers from their own city could do something like this made it unbearable. None of them were prepared. *Tairnganese* men did this. Men from the grand, *enlightened* city they loved enough to die for. Eva shoved a fist into her mouth to stall a bubbling scream. She did not have the right to mourn with these people, did she? Navan reeked of death and despair. She doubted that a single soul in this town would ever again trust anyone from the Red City.

Eva's heart broke a little more with every step she took.

They stopped under the charred awning of a tavern to rest—an illegible sign with the barest hint of two crossed arrows crumpled to charcoal beneath her booted foot. The structure was a husk of blackened beams and smoking timbers. Tugging at her Spark to search for survivors, Eva was led down the alley on her right, toward its stables. Mel Carra ordered his men to wait as he followed at a sedate, respectful pace.

This stable withstood most of the flames, owing in no small part to its heavy stone walls. Only half of the roof was burned away, which left the northernmost end largely intact. She followed her Spark through to the rear. A filthy boy covered in poorly tied bandages lay beside a dying mare in the hay. He whispered meaningless words of comfort as he stroked her mane with all the love he could muster. Softly, Eva approached. Mel waited just shy of the entrance, covering the lower half of his face with a large, strong hand. Mel Carra had five children of his own at home. This was too much for him. The mare had a broken spear shaft embedded in her lovely brown throat. She fought the fluid that filled her lungs with a valiant effort, but it wouldn't be long now.

The boy's father was dead. He had no one now to care for him. Eva crouched, reaching into him with her Spark. She saw the night's events through his eyes; saw Hamma and his men rush through his father's door. Saw them cut the old man's throat for a cask of ale. She watched them chase the lad into the stables; watched the mare, *Vixen*, charge the soldiers to protect him. The violence was… she couldn't look any longer. She forced her Spark down deep. Her fingers sought the curve of one narrow shoulder.

"There now, lad. She's gone," Eva crooned. Wet tears slid down her cheeks. He looked up, his face a swollen mass of welts and purpling bruises.

"Who're ye?"

She pushed back her black hood. "A friend."

He clutched at the silent muscles of Vixen's throat. "She tried to save me."

"I know. She was a brave girl, wasn't she?"

"She were me mam's."

Eva gently pulled him upward, tucking the top of his head into the crook of her arm. "Hush now. She's with Siora in the Land of the Undying— the wind in her mane, a blue sky stretching forever over her proud head. I vow it."

The boy's body shook with hacking sobs. His mind lay open to her like a bubbling fountain. There, in his recent memories, she caught a glimpse of a face she longed to see. *Una*. Una had been here. This boy's father had risked his own life and livelihood to help her and her companions. Eva took a deep breath. The knowledge would keep for now. The boy had too many wounds inside. He didn't have long. If she had her queen's gift, she might have been able to stitch him back together with her Spark. Fuse veins, join bones and cartilage, perhaps even shore the seeping organs around his pancreas. Alas, Eva's gifts were different. She could only hold him and direct his mind to all the fantastic, beautiful places he imagined. She heard him gasp with delight and felt him relax in her hands.

"I… I see Vixen! Ye were right! She's there, waitin' for me…"

Eva wiped her face with the back of a shaking hand. "What adventures you'll have together, but not yet. Your father is waiting in the hall with your supper. Do you see him? He's just there, waving."

"Da," his voice trailed off. "I fought so hard. Ye'd be so proud o'me—"

Eva sat in silence for what felt like hours. She wrapped the boy in a discarded tarpaulin and tucked him in beside his beloved friend. A slow simmering rage swallowed the consumptive sadness in her blood. She couldn't break down now. She had work to do.

"How long 'till Rosweal?"

"A day and a night if we keep to the road. Four, maybe, if we don't," Mel answered, absently stroking the daggers concealed beneath his Mercher's cloak. The disguise would not bear intense scrutiny, but it had served them well enough for the last few days. "The roads should be largely empty now this lot has burned their way through every town."

"Don't worry. They won't live through the week."

"Aye," he swiped at his own tear-stained face. "It'll have to do."

"I know where Una is. This boy and his father helped her. She travels with two companions. A man and a girl."

"That's good, by Siora. I'd rather the queen not be on her own out here."

"Me too," Eva sighed. "She's in Rosweal, Mel— as you suspected. Though, I'm not sure if they've moved on already."

"Well, there's only one way to know for sure."

THE SOUTHERNMOST STAR

THE INNISFAIL CYCLE:
BOOK TWO

SOUTH

Una wished she was dead. Every breath was a losing battle. Any air she managed to squeeze into her lungs burned through her airways like acid. The pounding in her head might have been a thousand-pound bell, pealing back and forth for hours. The furs she lay beneath were as heavy as a two-ton stone. Something rattled within her chest, as if one of her ribs had come loose and was attempting to work itself into her gut. Is this what suffocating felt like? She couldn't be sure, but if this went on much longer… death would be a blessing. Every inch of her hurt, from the tips of her bruised toes to the bleeding hollows of her shrinking gums. She was an aching husk of herself: a parchment stretched taut over disintegrating bones.

"What's wrong with her?" asked a gruff voice from far off.

"Spark drag, I'll wager." *That* voice, she knew. She'd have gone cold at the sound if she had any blood to spare. "She's used too much."

The unknown speaker whistled. "Reason. Too bloody right there. If I hadn't seen what she did with my own eyes, I'd never believed any of this was possible. Is she dying?"

As another tremor galloped along her nerves, bowing her swollen spine, Una also wanted to know the answer to that question. She heard the scrape of a boot near her ear. The air drew close as a hulking figure bent over her. Why couldn't she open her eyes? If her last living act on earth was to spit in his face, she would count her stars. She tried to move her head, but the effort sent spears of lightning down her throat. She might have choked if she had the strength. Instead, she sucked tiny ribbons of air into her taxed lungs and trembled with the urge to weep. The familiar voice cursed. "Not if I can help it. *No*! Don't touch her."

A flurry of movement. "I meant to—"

"If you touch her now, she'll likely kill you without meaning to. Siorai of her skill level are forbidden to fuel themselves this way, but it can happen."

"I see," said the heavier voice, clear revulsion in his tone.

Gloved fingers probed her face from brow to jaw. Only Damek Bishop would have the gall to lay hands on her so boldly. Pity, she was unwell, for she would have loved to drain the arrogant bastard dry.

"No help for it, I'm afraid," Damek sighed, smoothing back her hair. She hoped he'd be stupid enough to remove his glove. "Bring me one of our prisoners. Someone healthy, but not over-strong. Martin, *discreetly*, please. The men are already terrified of her."

"Yes, My Lord." Now she recognized that deep, oak-rich voice. Martin O'Rearden, her father's Commander at Arms. Though she hated the circumstances, she was glad of his presence all the same. She had nothing but fond memories of the old soldier and prayed she wouldn't have to harm him to escape. Distracted by distant memories and unbearable pain, she hadn't quite heard Damek's order. What had happened? How had she come to be here? She couldn't glean the details, simply snippets: flashes of brilliant orange flame, men and horses screaming, a cottage consumed by oppressive emerald eyes, Rian's small body limp against a filthy wooden floor, a black beast with an appetite as bottomless as the sea— Kaer Yin, the erstwhile Ben Maeden, silver eyes half-lidded, pale hair laying limp over his collar, lips still and cold as wax— and the dead, so many cold creatures she could never count them all.

How long had she lain here? Frustration nearly outpaced her pain.

Where was Kaer Yin? Was he alive?

Had Rian survived what Una had done to her? How had Damek gotten hold of her?

"Una," Damek whispered. "Can you hear me?"

Yes! She wanted to scream. *Tell me what happened! Where are my friends? Where is Kaer Yin? What did you DO, Damek? What did I do?*

"I'm sorry for this, but neither of us has a choice." His breath dusted her cheek.

Was that genuine regret she detected in his tone? Why? Not the Lord of Clare, surely?

Her mind wandered. A flower bloomed in bright spring sunlight. A garden filled with birdsong, damp green things, and warm male laughter. She knew this place, didn't she? The first brush of infatuated longing, small pleasures, fleeting as the sun in winter. Then, she felt the cold stone at her back, the sharp sting of betrayal. A mouth full of teeth and animal hunger chewed through blood and sinew to her thundering heart. Slow-simmering rage chased this vision away, cloaking her girlhood fancy in blackest hate.

Oh, Damek, come closer. Press your lips to mine, I beg you.

"My lord," Martin reappeared, bearing unhappy resignation in his voice. Someone new whimpered beside him. "This one killed a man trying to escape. Best I could find."

"Good," said Damek. "Bring her over."

The whimpering melded into panicked gasps.

Una's broken body flooded with dread.

Oh no... no, no, no, NO!

A silent scream bubbled within Una's chest, raising icebergs in her already frozen blood.

Siora! Forgive me!

⚓ ⚓

HOURS OR DAYS LATER, SHE couldn't say which, Una woke from a doze to find herself tied to a creaking saddle. Disoriented, she shook herself to clear her head, though it did little to help her gain her bearings. From beneath the rim of a heavy cowl, she spied the hard-worn road below her horse's hooves. Steady rain bounced back up to her knees from deep puddles on either side, and a host of stripped trees fell away from a broad river snaking past on her right. *The Shannon*, she knew at a glance. Those blue hills she spied over the horizon told her all she needed to know. This was the Taran High Road, and soon they would hug the river at Dumnain and then trek South-by-South-west to Bethany. She was headed home. Damek was taking her to her father. They were leaving her life, friends, and freedom behind in the North. When they crossed at Ten Bells, she would be her father's subject once more.

Princess of Bethany.

The words soured like spoiled milk in her throat.

Patrick Donahugh's kingdom.

The one place in all the world she'd rather die than spend a day. She gnashed her teeth in silent loathing. Una held one power there, one worth. Her value was measured by the potential fruits of her body and whatever price might fetch for the most ambitious man in Innisfail. There was no worse fate she could imagine for a liberated Tairnganese woman, autonomous in her own right, than the one that awaited her in Bethany.

The Duch would marry her off as soon as he was able. Should she dare use her gifts against any would-be suitors, innocents would suffer in her place. That had ever been the way between Una and her father. She hardly believed anything would have changed, saving maybe the brutality of his vengeance. She'd defied him for fourteen years already.

He didn't care about her, who she was as a person, who her mother had been, whom she loved, what she believed, nor what was best for her. Patrick cared about *Tairngare*. He lusted for an Eire unified under

276

his rule. His interest in her terminated with the claim she held in the North and the viability of the meat between her legs.

Patrick Donahugh wanted to be a king.

He would sell her a thousand times over to achieve that goal.

Una must escape before it became impossible. She was not chattel to be bought and sold for anyone's gain, least of all Patrick's. Setting her jaw at a determined angle, she slid her eyes forward and aft. She was surrounded by Souther knights, but none paid close attention to her. Walking their horses at a gentle clip, many were engaged in hushed conversation or leaned over their horse's necks, sound asleep. A knight beside her held her reins loosely, gnawing at a browning apple with a haunted, faraway mien.

Everywhere her eyes came to rest, she saw men worse for wear. Some were missing digits from appendages swaddled in unsanitary bandages. Many sported cuts and bruises that no one had bothered to tend. All wore expressions loaded with disbelief, pain, or numb horror. Una felt little sympathy for them; they were murderers, all. Led North by lust and greed, these men were no less guilty than her duplicitous cousin in his quest for power.

Maybe one of them would lean down to grab her if she slipped quietly from her saddle? No, too public. Perhaps she should demand a nature break, and when led away, she could…

"I can hear the cogs turning in your head from here, cousin," Damek laughed from behind her.

She didn't bother to crane her neck to look at him. Why waste the effort on such a useless view? "Mmm," she hummed. "Afraid yet?"

He kicked his mount forward and drew up beside her. She looked away, fuming. "Not really. Though, seeing you now after all these years, I wonder how I never noticed that *you* are. Always have been, too, I gather. How charming."

She ground her molars together.

The only words with the power to sting bore truth.

You are not cowed, she told herself.

He will make a mistake eventually, and you'll be free again, one way or the other. She squared her shoulders and raised her chin as high as it would go. "Perhaps all these armored men frighten me. Will you hold me?"

He rewarded her with a throaty chuckle that was much deeper than the one she remembered. She stole a glance at him from the corner of her eye and wished she hadn't. His smirk made her want to rip his jugular out with her teeth. "Not yet, *Lady Donahugh*. I won't presume until you ask me seriously, of course."

"I'd rather drink crushed glass, Lord Bishop."

His smile bordered on the lascivious. The years had been kind to her cousin. He was taller, broader through the chest and shoulders, and the flesh of his cheeks had settled into the sharp bones of his face. Arching black brows swept over his violet and green eyes.

He was very handsome. She hated him the more for it.

"Oh, I don't know about that. One day I may grow on you, my Lady Donahugh."

"My *name* is Una Moura. I am Prima of the Cloister of the Eternal Flame and a free citizen of Tairngare. You have no right to hold me against my will."

He shook his head with that annoying, affable grin. "Reason, but you're beautiful in a temper. Even covered in filth and scrapes… hm," he hummed a sound that made Una burn with rage.

Don't get angry. That's what he wants.

"What do you think, Martin? Is she not the loveliest woman you've ever set eyes upon?"

Don't get angry. Don't get angry. Don't.

"My lord," Martin cleared his throat. "Perhaps not?"

Damek was having the time of his life at her expense. Her nostrils flared. "I am not some tavern-wench, Damek. I am the Doma's granddaughter and heir."

"For all your education, your sense of direction is rather pathetic, isn't it?"

His men, save Martin, chuckled around her.

"When my grandmother hears of this—"

As if he'd been waiting for this threat, he pulled a rolled bit of vellum out of his tunic and wagged it under her nose. She looked away, taking deep breaths. Recognizing Nema's seal at a glance, she could guess what it read. "Should I read it for you?"

"No." She knew where this must be headed.

"Oh, what a shame," he said, waving the scroll back and forth. "It's such a fun yarn. Old Grandmama has been deposed. It seems the Red City is under new management, and this," he paused to read the name, "Vanna Nema is now Doma. Want to know what the new Doma thinks of you and your family, my love?"

"Fuck yourself."

"Whatever My Lady advises, of course."

"You've made your point!"

"Have I?"

"Yes!" she hissed, fighting tears. Her grandmother… her family. She didn't know how they'd come to this pass so quickly but had no doubt who had orchestrated the coup. Nema had tried to kill Una three times already, and only Siora knew what she'd been doing in Tairngare since. Though Una had been oblivious to the trouble brewing within the Cloister while she remained within its walls, now that she was out in the world, she'd been disabused of that ignorance rather quickly. The Red City had chafed under Drem's rule for some years. Hells, half the North cried out for Moura blood. Forty years of heavy-handed doctrine and policy had stripped the poorest in Innisfail of taxes they could ill afford and resources they could hardly spare.

Furthermore, Una bore her share of responsibility on that score. Her untimely disappearance revealed a chasm of weakness within the Cloister that had surely fanned these flames. The people sought new leadership, justly or no.

It seemed the scales had finally tipped in Nema's favor.

Una didn't want to know anymore.

Her heart couldn't process so many tragedies at once.

Damek threw the scroll at her. She let it bounce off her wounded arm and roll into the mud from her horse's flank. "Unless I march up there and force the issue, your mother's name means nothing now. Your inheritance, your power, and your titles: *nothing*. That missive declares you a heretic and traitor, Una, anathema. Your beloved city would have you burn. The way I see it, I've saved your life. When you're done playing the selfish child, you might see sense one day." He watched her closely while she swallowed wave after wave of misery. She averted her gaze, blinking back the hot tears boiling in her eyes. The men around her, making no bones about their disapproval of her, curled their lips and shook their heads.

How many of their number were now dead because of her?

"Lost your tongue?" he pressed on.

While the blame couldn't wholly be lain at Una's feet, neither could she deny she'd played her part. If she hadn't trusted Nema's creature, Gan. If she hadn't tried to run away… before that, if she hadn't buried herself in her studies and shirked her duty to her family, perhaps none of this would have happened. If she'd stayed in Tairngare, would things have been different? Could Nema have been thwarted, or the Moura Clan have presented a unified front?

Who knew?

There was an equal chance that Una would have been murdered in her bed, and the same result achieved, regardless. She might never know, but that wouldn't dispel her guilt, in either case. She was an outcast now. *Anathema*, precisely as Damek had said.

"Una," his tone softened. "Did you really think that old miser in Aes Sidhe would help you? The Sidhe couldn't spare a tinker's fart for any of us. So long as we pay our taxes, keep off their lands, and steer well clear of their kind, they don't care what we do to each other here in Eire. We're all you have, cousin. I hope you come to see that before it is too late." Rather than allow her to spoil his speech with a rebuttal, he kicked his mount into the forward line.

He didn't look back—an old trick, this, but effective.

Una was left alone in a sea of creaking leather and hostile glares.

Friendless, unmoored, and insolvent, she bit her lower lip until it bled and suffered in silence.

⚑ ⚑

As THEY LED THEIR MOUNTS close to the river two days later, Una's chances to escape thinned by the mile. Damek had thought of everything, of course. She was bound day and night. No one spoke to her unless directed. No one touched her or came near her without a thick pair of gloves. No one even looked her way except to feed her, cart her to the privy, or tie her to her cot every night. The first time she attempted to talk to someone, Damek had the poor fellow digging latrines that evening. When she tried to wander deeper into the woods to relieve herself, Damek had her escort replaced with prisoners, each given a lash for every yard she had dared stray.

Una was fed with wooden spoons and drank from wooden dippers. If she drifted too far when they stopped, struggled with her handlers, or made any moves that appeared suspicious in the least, Damek punished the innocent to spite her. After a few days of this, Una had retreated within herself. She moved when and where she was told, kept her eyes resolutely forward, and never opened her mouth but to accept food or water. She might have been a doll for all the trouble she caused. If he wanted her docile, so be it. She would wait, watch, and plan.

Damek made none of the mistakes she'd hoped he would. He didn't converse with her except to impart orders or inquire about her wellbeing. He spent little to no time in her immediate vicinity and scarcely looked at her save when necessary. So much for thinking she could tempt him to lower his guard. She knew escape wouldn't be easy, but Damek was going out of his way to make it impossible.

When the gulls called from the bay and the smoke from Ten Bells rose in the distance, Una swore she wouldn't be trounced. She would get out of this, even if it killed her.

Kaer Yin, she thought.

Please be alive. Please be safe.

I will come back for you.

⚑ ⚑

A GIBBOUS MOON WAS HIGH IN the late autumn sky when Damek's men wound their way through Ten Bells' twisting lanes. Una was in the lead group, strapped to her saddle as usual, and Damek himself held her reins. Another hope dashed. She had thought of creating a ruckus in the street and praying the towns-folk would intercede long enough for her to get away—no such luck. If the Lord of Clare held her leash, no one would dare challenge him for his prisoner. They were in the South now; Damek's influence held far more weight here than hers. Not many of these folks would even know who she was on sight. Tairn-gare was a faithful trading partner here, but few Siorai ever made the trip. Merchers and students of the Libellum were the few Tairnganese faces she spied. Her people tended to congregate around the university in the West Moorings, while here in the North End, there were primarily local farmers' stalls, taverns, and stately inns astride the Taran High Road. She imagined they'd cross the Limerick Bridge at first light tomorrow and from there travel due south along the Mallow High Road to Bethany.

It wouldn't be long now. She had but a few days left to get away. Once she was in her father's Keep, she might be chained to a wall for the rest of her days.

Her mind worked so furiously to uncover a solution to her situation that she barely noticed they'd stopped until Damek pulled her into his well-covered arms. Without ado, he set her down, grasped

279

her shoulders, and wheeled her toward an impressive three-story building. *The Ferryman*, its beautifully painted sign read, was easily one of the most well-appointed inns she'd ever clapped eyes upon. This was no surprise. Ten Bells had fainne to spare. Though it wasn't as large a city as Tairngare or Bethany, 'twas likely richer than both. Ten Bells was a thriving commercial hub overflowing with more rich trade guilds, labor unions, and banks than anywhere else in Innisfail. Ten Bells' Mercantile Union traded as far away as balmy Francia in old Europa, and its banks held a fair monopoly over the bustling Tairnganese colony in Cymru. If she wasn't mistaken, the Cymrian Winemakers Guild's Home Office wasn't far from their present position. Just over the Limerick and down the docks, or so she recalled from her studies. Ten Bells owed much of its success to that Guild's founding charter.

Additionally, the city was neutral. It took no sides in any conflict continent-wide. Since almost every other town in Innisfail depended upon it for crucial trade, there was very little danger of that changing anytime soon. When someone makes you rich, you tend to leave them to their business. Sure, men had made the mistake of sacking the city in the past— her grandfather, for one— but when the fainne ran dry, and those men couldn't replicate the Guild's results, Ten Bells' Charter was returned, and their Merchers left well alone.

Only madmen and zealots bite the hand that feeds.

Damek led her over swept cobbles in perfect repair toward the expansive covered veranda yawning from the Inn's northwestern façade. A lamplighter on stilts tapped his way down the street, brandishing his matches like a well-trained magician. A snap, twist, and flare, and another glass bauble would cast ambient light over this charming thoroughfare. Though the rooftops climbed too high to view properly from her angle, every structure's architecture was pre-Transition. Stone rowhouses lined each side of the street with corniced windows and exquisite gabling. *The Ferryman* took up the majority of the southernmost corner.

They were met at the door by a fussy majordomo who led them through a series of candlelit alcoves to a private dining area beneath a sweeping grand staircase. Damek nodded to Martin, whose job it would be to sort the men and see to their accommodations for the evening. The majordomo bent almost double in obeisance to the Lord of Clare before Damek waved him away. A few wealthy patrons were seated inside the dining room. These diners tucked themselves deep within their booths to avoid the attention of so many armed men.

On the opposite side of the vast double-hearth lay a larger taproom occupied by the general public. If the fire wasn't so hot, Una could almost squeak through to the other side and out the front door before anyone could stop her. Her cousin noted the direction of her gaze and wagged his finger, 'no.' Soon, she was unceremoniously shoved into a tall wooden booth near the rear wall. Damek took the seat beside her. Chewing her cheek raw, she faced the polished window to observe the lamplighter's progress; she didn't turn when others squeezed into their booth. Upon his return, Martin, as always, took the seat on his lord's opposite side. Damek's hand found Una's shoulder, his pressure firm.

"Keep your hood up. Speak to no one and try not to let anyone see your face."

She shrugged his hand away.

"Martin," he said aside. "Have you ordered?"

"Yes, My Lord. Whatever was best for our officers in here—soup and bread for the boys outside. Room and board are sorted, too. Fellas will head to the waystation next door, brass upstairs two to a room. You are to have the suite on the top floor as soon as its tenant is vacated. I had them send out for, erm, ladies' things, as well."

"Excellent. What's for supper then?"

Martin shrugged. "Didn't ask. I could eat a bloody horse."

Damek leaned over Una. "Are you thirsty?"

She didn't look at him. A serving girl carried over a heavy tray laden with bread, salted butter, and five tankards of ale. The men leaped at the tray like starved hogs. Damek slapped one fellow's hand and set his tankard in front of Una. "Wait your turn, Ridley. Ladies first."

Una rolled her eyes but didn't waste her breath to argue. She *was* parched. Living in patriarchy was Ridley's bloody problem. Even with her hands bound, she managed to lift and pour half of the heavy vessel's contents down her throat in two gulps. The spiced ale warmed her from her throat to her toes. She hadn't had a decent meal in days; though she was becoming somewhat accustomed to roughing it outdoors, she could hardly refuse one when offered. Amused, Damek slid his trencher of bread and butter toward her. It, too, did not last long. She stopped chewing long enough to take a sip of her ale before returning to work. Damek passed her a second helping, then his own tankard.

She didn't complain.

Siora bless the Brewer's Guild in Ten Bells.

Only *The Hart* in Rosweal had had better ale, and she was working very hard not to think about that at all. Damek wore an odd smile on his face while he watched her cheeks puff out like a chipmunk. Chuckling, Martin also slid her his bread and the hunk of cheese he'd pilfered from another table.

Bless Martin O'Rearden, too, she thought.

"How'd you meet him?" Damek asked, pressing his chin against his knuckles.

"Meef hoo?" she managed around a mouthful of cheese.

"Kaer Yin Adair, of course."

She would not rise to Damek's bait. Not now. She kept her eyes on her food. Torturing herself wouldn't help anyone. Swallowing, her bread went down her throat like a lump of coal. "Does it matter?"

"Yes, damn you. He killed over two-dozen men trying to take you back—one of my best lieutenants, a man of no mean skill. I've never seen someone move like him," Damek frowned at the air as if conjuring Kaer Yin's face. "His reputation was understated, you ask me."

Una said nothing, her heart racing.

He'd come for her? Tried to save her?

After that… *thing* tore a hole in his chest the size of Lough Neagh, he'd come to take her back? She couldn't believe it, not Ben— er— Kaer Yin. He wasn't the type. Yet, Damek had no reason to lie. It certainly didn't make him look the grander for having said anything, did it? She hesitated. "Did— I mean, was he killed in the attempt?"

Damek's smile was cruel. "You first."

The serving girl brought another round of tankards. Damek claimed two more without breaking eye contact. Una reached for hers, but he held it shy of her fingers. She groaned. "If you're asking why he wanted to help me, I don't have an answer for you. He happened by when I was dragged behind a horse and almost beaten to death, and this after I'd managed to escape Rawly and his men."

"You're lying about Rawly. He and his boys were killed by the same man that killed those two beasts in Ferndale and a cadre of armed Corsairs on the road. Come on, cousin. Try showing me at least a fraction of the respect I deserve."

"I don't know what you want me to say. He saved my life, and we traveled together. That's all there is. He thought he might help me over the border, and I intended to help him reclaim his title. We met in the middle."

Damek took a sip of his ale and snorted into his tankard. "You're in love with him."

Una went still as a stone. She didn't respond for quite some time, but when she did, her tone aimed to kill. "*What of it?*"

Damek's hand paused over his trencher, eyes glowing cold murder. "Oh, good. I hoped I'd have the pleasure of watching your heart break."

"My lord—" Martin attempted from his left elbow.

"What do you mean?" Una asked, trying in vain to keep the fear from her voice.

Damek's grin was a knife-slash in the firelight. He toasted her. "The Crown Prince is dead, Una. I watched him fall myself. You're on your own now, love. I hope you're ready for what follows."

Siora's Mercy

Vanna Nema's brilliant golden robes snapped in a bracing northerly wind. She could address the people en masse from her newly constructed pulpit above the Grand Arcade. They came in their thousands, an ocean of faces breaking against the Citadel in unending waves. Nema's smile was like the sun after a storm. She held out her hands to hush her audience, her black miter flashing onyx in the sun. On either side stood Nema's favorites, the Cloister's newest Alta Primas, Pors Yma, and Kalen Hamma. Each wore the blazing scarlet of an office neither had earned nor deserved. They were here for the same reason everyone else on the terrace was today: Nema was now Doma, and they each had played their parts. Further back, a line of newly minted Primas in their bone-white robes and a smattering of grey-cloaked Secundas knelt with their heads bowed in prayer. Parliamentary Judges and representatives of the Union of Commons occupied the dais once reserved for members of the Libella, most of whom stood below Nema's pulpit, nude and covered in filth.

So many people were gathered within and around the Grand Arcade, yet none spoke a word. The only sounds were collective breathing, the gulls crying over the Citadel's high walls, and the occasional whimper from Nema's aristocratic prisoners in the Gallery. Among them, Aoife narrowed her eyes at the Tenma Judge in the next row. Twisting her bruised and bleeding mouth into the darkest sneer she could manage, Aoife shot the sniveling woman a withering glare.

Have some dignity, you milksop bitch.

Feeling Nema's imperious gaze upon her shorn and seeping scalp, Aoife faced forward and raised her chin. Naked as a newborn child, with oozing slashes tearing over her back, buttocks, and arms, she shivered in the chill morning air. Her spine was as straight as she could make it. Although beaten, burned, cut, and humiliated, she would not give her ruthless grandmother the satisfaction of seeing her cowed.

Let the soft-bellied whores around her make a fuss; Nema would get no such pleasure from Aoife.

Did Nema's mouth quirk a bit at the corner? *Good.*

If the old witch wanted a show... by Balor, she would get one.

Aoife's one consolation stood three rows back, reams of snot dribbling down his fleshy chins. Quivering like gelatin, Fawa Gan was too weak to stand beneath Nema's judgment. Rather, he knelt in a weeping, pitiable mass of torn flesh. Aoife didn't have to look at him to know he'd pissed himself recently. She could smell it from her place at the front, in the very terminus of Nema's vengeance.

If Aoife was going to die today, she could but pray she got to watch that fat pederast meet his maker first. How he came to cower among the condemned had everything to do with the woman in the center of their company. Basa Alvra, easily the oldest amongst them and by far the most powerful, had fingered him as Drem's erstwhile informant. Basa was the former Doma's cousin and was once the most influential politician in Tairngare. Aoife had to hand it to the ancient hag; she had a pair of bollocks that would shame any man in Innisfail.

Basa hadn't been whipped or scourged as Aoife, and so many others had been— she was far too old. Instead, she'd been stripped of her clothing and forced to carry her daughter's severed hand around her neck like a trophy. Basa and Ana had been caught on the docks at Drogheda, attempting to flee to the colonies for aid. Ana had died under interrogation, and Basa had been present for the occasion. Even with

"

her daughter's rotting flesh resting against her sagging collarbone, she did not bend. She stood tall and as straight as she could make herself at seventy-four years of age, her wild white curls blowing around her head like a stormcloud. Basa revealed nothing but condescending contempt for these proceedings, the new government, and especially the new Doma. Nema ignored her, but Aoife knew... deep down, she seethed. For Basa's arrogance, Nema would kill every Alvra supporter in this crowd before she granted her adversary the mercy of death.

"Good people of Tairngare," Nema's voice carried far and wide without embellishment. This was more than simple acoustics, as presence had ever been one of Nema's foremost gifts. "We stand here at the birth of a new era. Too long have we suffered the whims and rages of an elite caste with little regard for the lives of those they were ordained to serve. In Siora's name, we abjure them. In Siora's name, we strike their works from the Register. In Siora's name, we seek justice."

Aoife gritted her teeth.

Get on with it. I'm ready.

The people outside murmured the appropriate prayers, though she could tell their hearts weren't committed. Until recently, Tairngare had been one of the world's safest, most privileged cities. Since the coup Aoife had herself helped foment, every possible change was occurring much too fast for many to keep up. Last month, they'd had a thriving elite class and a Doma who rarely interfered in the commoners' lives. Now, everything was different. Nema's reformist government was made possible for the love she inspired among the merchants, guilds, and the poor... but many of them had no idea how far she'd planned to go. In just a few weeks, the nobles had been ousted from the Libella, and The Union of Commons had taken over Parliament. What few nobles remained in the Red City were gathered here, condemned by the new Doma and her cronies in the Commons. When news of Drem Moura's escape from the Cloister swept through the city, the rioting and mayhem had reached such a fevered pitch that it had taken the Cohort nearly a week to put down the mob and douse the fires. A week after, people were dragged from their homes and imprisoned by the fledgling government, not all of them loyalists, either. Indeed, the general public appeared to be reeling from the violence and disarray that trailed in Nema's wake. Her rise to power had been a painfully swift but bloody affair. Aoife didn't doubt many folks who supported the new Doma a half-month before had discovered they'd bitten off far more than they could chew.

Nema had been waiting for this for almost fifty years.

She had no intention of leaving any dissenters alive to challenge her later. As for Aoife, well... she had failed Nema for the last time. Allowing the Moura Domina to escape was the final nail in Aoife's coffin.

She's dragging this out to spite me.

"If any among you wish to speak for the condemned, please step forward." Nema gestured to the knot of nude flesh on display. "Without their fine clothes and dazzling jewels, they no longer seem so untouchable, do they? These slavers— these base, corrupting idolaters— see them *as they are*. They are not beautiful, powerful, strong, or superior. They are weak, simpering mortals with more flesh than honor. Who among you pities these sad creatures? Which of you bears compassion for those who spare none?"

Here it comes, Aoife thought with an irritable smirk.

Basa Alvra threw back her head and laughed. Her audience scarcely moved a muscle save to gawp at the old Alta's manic outburst. Aoife hadn't expected this, and from the expression on Nema's pinched face, neither had she.

"Well? No one has anything to say, hm?" taunted Basa.

Nema folded her hands. "Of course, the accused has the right to a last word in my court. Though I warn you, old schemer, you'll find few sympathetic ears here."

Basa looked around. "Oh, I dunno. It seems to me plenty stand behind me."

To Nema's intense ire, Aoife knew, that statement earned several chuckles from many places in the Grand Gallery, even from among Nema's supporters. Basa, massive sagging teats swinging in the breeze, spat for the Commons' benefit. "That scrawny bitch up there would have you idiots believe she has your interests at heart. Tell me, short of the few corrupt witches that supported her rise to power, how much richer are any of you that have laid us low? Hm? Do you feel safer, more respected, and better protected? I hope so since the streets are filled day and night with her foot soldiers."

"Basa Alvra, you stand accused—"

"You said your piece, you withered old cunt. You have us standing out here in the cold in naught but our skins, waiting to die. Where is the *justice*? Without evidence, trials, or representation, you have declared us guilty. The wealthier our families, the greater our guilt." Basa tugged her chin at the horrified Merchers gathered far below the dais. "She'll be after you all next, mark me. History's full of over-reaching despots like your new Doma. Her 'reformist' smell will sour, and you'll all realize what a terrible mistake you've made today."

"*Basa Alvra, this is—*"

"Executing anyone with the power to challenge her on her coronation day?" Basa sucked her teeth over a wry grin. "Best of luck, you bloody gorgeous fools."

"Captain, if you please?" Nema gestured, and a Cohort officer reached over and punched the old woman in the gut. She staggered to one liver-spotted knee. Before she could gasp out another blistering reproach of the new Doma, the Captain wrenched her head back while a second officer pried her mouth open. Amidst her gurgles and grunts, they dug into the open cavity with a pair of iron tongs, stretched her tongue out as far as it would go— and severed the offensive muscle as if carving mutton for luncheon.

Aoife stood very still, watching the spectacle without passion, even as those around her moaned and fidgeted in fear. She, for one, had seen worse… had *done* worse.

This was merely a prelude.

When a lump of hot coal was shoved against the bloodied stump between her teeth, Basa fainted in a pool of her own blood and piss. Aoife looked up to meet her grandmother's eye. Nema was smiling. "Alta Alvra is such a brave woman, despite her many failings. This Court believes that she would best serve Siora as a living but silent reminder of idolatry's folly. Take her below," she purred.

The Captain and his assistants hauled Basa up and carted her somewhere within the Citadel's black bowels. Aoife imagined she would likely be trotted out at every gathering and paraded before the masses. If Basa had kept her mouth shut, she might have escaped such a macabre fate. Surely, it would have been better to watch her friends put to the Spark than rot in the public eye.

"Now," said Nema, beaming at Aoife. "I think we've had enough entertainment for one day, don't you? Pors?"

Pors Yma stepped forward on the dais. She raised a fist, and suddenly, Aoife and everyone in her company crumpled to the ground, twitching and writhing in unimaginable pain. The veins in Aoife's neck seized, and the blood halted mid-course. She felt her eyes and nose drain of fluid— of oxygen. No air would enter or leave her lungs, frozen in place as she was, a spider in a jar.

"As Siora's representative on earth and Doma of The Cloister of the Eternal Flame, I condemn you all to die by emulation. We are not so crude as to draw out your suffering for our amusement. Kalen?"

The Hamma Alta Prima sidled up beside Pors, whose brow was damp with perspiration. Manipulation was hard work, especially for women who had no business pretending to have truly mastered it. Kalen mumbled under her breath. A slow serpent of flame undulated beneath Aoife's flesh. First, it uncoiled itself from her core, then slithered beneath her ribs. Inside her chest, she knew her ribs blackened. She exhaled smoke as her eyes filled with blood. Choking on cinders, she gurgled uselessly, unable to move far enough to claw out her own throat. From the inside, she burned. Though she couldn't see beyond the thickening red haze nor hear anything save for the fat popping in her ears, Aoife was aware that those behind her had already succumbed to Hamma's Spark. Moaning, they collapsed as charred smoldering sticks against the flagstones.

The pain was exquisite, but Aoife did not die.

Her skin popped open at every joint, releasing torrents of steam and hissing fluids. What was left of her hair caught next. The kiss of these flames seemed almost a relief in contrast with the raging inferno within. She heard the crowd whisper, and felt their eyes on her, disbelieving and petrified. Then, as suddenly as the assault began, it stopped. Cold, clean air hit the wreckage of her lungs with startling clarity. At last, the cauldron in her airway subsided, and she coughed up bits of black she knew had once been lung tissue.

Doubled over, Aoife could squeeze out the barest wail.

Nema's laughter rang throughout the open-air chamber.

Aoife titled her working ear toward the sound. One of her eyes had burst from its socket, but the other merely swam with blood and soot. She could see the sky above her grandmother's saffron robes. It seemed to have snowed in the Grand Arcade that morning. Great ribbons of ash swirled overhead. She turned her face away. Her nearest neighbor disintegrated beside her. This formerly important someone was a whirl of dust flirting with the wind. Aoife croaked a half-scorched scream. Everywhere she looked, human beings were reduced to piles of ash; even their bones were no match for Hamma's flames.

Dazed, Aoife pushed herself up to her elbows. Behind her, she heard a familiar wheeze. Summoning her last ounce of strength, she took a peek beneath her blistered forearm. Gan, singed and bloodied from the crown of his steaming scalp to the soles of his formerly corpulent feet, looked back at her in shock. His eyes, too, had been spared the worst.

The better to see, my dear, Aoife knew.

Every condemned prisoner but she and Gan floated on the morning air; whether to Gods or grace, she didn't care to know. The nobles of Tairngare might drift toward the heavens, but they would never gain entry. Their every thought and feeling, their very lives, were fodder for storms. She was reminded of an ancient quote: '*But the devils cannot interfere with the stars*' and wanted to howl with laughter.

If only she could. The ruin of her throat had other ideas, alas.

Unto dust thou wilt return.

Aoife admired the perversity of Nema's justice. The crone might have been a Kneeler for the poetic brutality of this moment.

The horror of this scene was not lost on the witnesses above, either. Aoife was beyond caring how the complicit bastards in the Gallery covered their mouths or fainted away in revulsion. She wasn't moved by their cries of protest or the chorus of weeping that chased the desecrated into the atmosphere. She wasn't even afraid. After a while, she could focus on Nema's triumphant leer. Pors and Kalen had crumpled and were now being carted away to enjoy their imminent—and, Aoife hoped, fatal—Spark drag. Their task done, Nema had no further use of either. Such a vulgar display of power might very well cost Hamma her life. Nema wouldn't mind, of course. She certainly hadn't chosen Hamma because she cared a whit for the odious lickspittle's wellbeing. She'd selected her for this purpose alone.

Aoife's hatred burrowed deeper and burned hotter than any part of her that an inferior Milesian had Manipulated. Why *had* Nema spared her and Gan? She didn't have much time to ponder her dubious luck when her forehead struck the slate beneath her with a hollow thud.

Before the night claimed her, she was granted a final thought.

What a joy it is to be Grandmama's favorite.

THE ART OF NECESSITY

Rian took several deep breaths at the door. She had no time for this. With half a dozen critical patients downstairs awaiting her attention and a total deficit of sleep, she'd rather have left Kaer Yin's cronies for later. Though, as always, she was not asked for her opinion. She groaned, resting her forehead against the painted jamb. What she wouldn't give for a hot cup of tea, a bit of bread, and a week-long nap. The blond oak tree standing behind her cleared his throat. Rian spared him a bit of curled lip. Niall was this one's name, or so she thought she'd heard him called. Honestly, she didn't care. These Dannan brutes looked much the same. Scowling, Niall pushed the door open and none-too-gently nudged her forward. She immediately nosedived into someone else, who grunted and knocked her into yet another oversized Sidhe. Clawing herself upright in the crush of towering males crammed into the shrinking room, Rian growled and dug her nails into the next fool who tried to step on her.

The big bastard flinched as if a favorite kitten had scratched him.

She'd had about enough of this, truth be told.

"There she is," remarked a rich, deep voice. Rian tried not to sneer. "Let her through."

Beneath an exaggerated portrait of a stout but curvaceous woman of middling years was the subject herself. With her greying auburn hair coiled over one round shoulder and her bandaged fingers clutching her favorite bone-handled pipe, Barb Dormer leaned against her massive fox-footed desk with a pinched expression. Beside her sat Robin, shirt open to the waist, while Rose fretted over the seeping wound around his midsection. He was working on a dwindling bottle of Gilcannon's best uishge while the Prince of Connaught held him fast to his chair with a firm hand. The faintest irascible frown marred the cold perfection of Tam Lin O'Ruiadh's face. Robin's stitches had come undone.

In true Innish fashion, he'd sooner drink himself into a stupor than admit he was in pain.

Rian blew a lock of hair out of her eyes. "Wonderful. Who let him get like this?"

Barb took a long pull from her pipe. "No one *lets* Robin Gramble do anythin', love."

Robin burst into song on cue, tone-deaf as a toad in a bucket.

"Wonderful," Rian repeated with a sigh. "Well, hold him down."

Tam Lin waggled his fingers. Three blond mountains shuffled over with persistent irritation. The largest of them, Tam Lin's lieutenant Shar Lianor, slunk behind Robin's chair while Rian rolled up her sleeves. A dangerous gleam flashed in Robin's eyes, and upon the next breath, he had his dagger up and swinging about.

Barb artfully dodged away when the knot of Dannan males descended upon her stammering mate. She shook her head. "Ye'll have to brain him, ye know? He'll fight till he's minced."

Robin's grunts and thrashing limbs did little to advance their cause. Through the muddle of elbows, knees, and shouts, Rian could see the gash in his side seeping anew. "Easy, Siora, damn you! He's bleeding all over the floor."

Tam Lin shot her an unkind glare with his face having gone as red as his hair. "We have your permission then, Mistress Dormer?"

Barb shrugged. Robin's dagger drew a scarlet line down Niall's forearm, and he guffawed in unintelligible victory. "Don't see as ye have a choice."

Tam Lin wasted no more time; drawing himself up to his full height, he brought his fist into Robin's clenched jaw. Robin slumped a bit, but the blow did not finish him. Sluggish as a newborn colt, he turned to grin at his attacker, a thin line of bloody spittle dangling from his swollen lower lip. "*Herne!*" Tam Lin barked and struck again. This time, Robin crumpled to the floorboards. Shaking his aching fist, the Prince of Connaught laughed. "Great Gods, that's one Milesian I'd rather not tangle with in the dark."

Everyone laughed at his astonishing wit… save Rian, of course. "If you've broken his jaw to boot, I'll have you know, you're going to be the one feeding him through a tube. I have enough to do, thank you."

His smile flickered as he blinked back at her, his long golden lashes sweeping against his impossibly high cheekbones. He was beautiful, as all Sidhe were— outwardly, anyway. His build, height, and lovely violet eyes did not impress her in the least. Rian despised her blood enough not to value its benefit in others. Her mother had always warned her that *a serpent is most colorful when venomous.* "Mistress… ah, I'm sorry. What was your name again?"

Rian was too tired to project any outward emotion, even irritation, though he'd been told her name half a thousand times already. She'd been running back and forth for days, stitching cuts, mending bones, and treating myriad burns since they'd all returned from the Greensward more than a week before. Indeed, if she didn't return to it soon, she'd probably faint. "Rian Guinness," she said, her voice bland as her mental acuity at the moment. "You summoned me, remember?"

He snapped a finger as if in sudden recollection. "Of course. Master Gramble here needs fresh stitching, I find. I fear Mistress Dormer here is unequal to the task. She asked for you, not I. You know one another, I take it?" His eyes slid between them like a child seeking to instigate a brawl.

"We've met," offered Barb helpfully. "Wasn't under the best circumstances, ye might say."

"A shame," he remarked without a shred of warmth. "Now would be a perfect opportunity to mend impressions, moving forward. Don't you agree? Now, Mistress… ah, damn it. What was your name again, girl?"

Rian bit her tongue. "Guinness."

"Right. Master Gramble and I have many matters to discuss and prepare for. That will prove impossible if he falls feverish. Also, though she has refused, I'd like it very much if you would also see to our hostess' hands."

"What happened?" asked Rian dispassionately.

Barb pursed her lips. "Struck a wall when I saw what them Souther cunts did to my *Hart.* Bout a temper, nothin' more."

"Hm," Rian sniffed. "That finger looks broken. Needs a splint."

Barb took one look at Rian's face and snickered. "I don't need nursin', thanks very much. 'Sides, ye'd sooner bleed me than mend me. Wouldn't ye, girlie?"

Rian raised a brow at her. "I don't let my dislike of someone affect my practice, Barb. Lucky for you."

"I don't need charity, little miss."

"Suit yourself. Now, if you will set Master Gramble upright in that window seat, I'll see what I can do about these seeping wounds." She gestured to Robin's snoring carcass on the floor. She'd already stitched him together twice. She silently swore this would be the last bloody time. Whoever kept giving him uishge could tend to him themselves from here on out. She reached into her bag for a clean needle, thread, and what few bandages Rose had managed to scrounge from the laundry a few hours before.

Tam Lin's brow darkened. "I'm asking to be polite. Would you prefer an order?"

"This is not Aes Sidhe, and I am not your subject. Now," she held up her fingers to tick off items one by one. "I'll need boiling water, oil of lavender, and more clean linens. There should be some left hanging on the line in the alley; if not, petticoats will do. We may have run through most passable material at this point already. Let's see. I'll need more thread… I left some on the bar downstairs… uishge, though not for bloody drinking, mind. He's had plenty. Also, for Siora's sake, a pot of tea if your men can manage it?"

If she didn't get some into her soon, she might fall down dead.

Tam Lin just stared. Barb laughed herself purple. Rian couldn't see what was so funny. There was a bleeding man on the floor who might now be wholly concussed. What was so funny about that? Tam Lin's men shuffled their feet, searching for anything else to fix their attention upon. The prince sighed. "Anything else, *Mistress* Guinness?"

Rian thought about it for a moment but ultimately shook her head. "The tea first, if you please? I haven't slept in some time."

Barb wiped at her eyes. "*Siora*, girl. Ye, I like fine."

Tam Lin didn't turn. He glared at Rian for an indeterminable length as if she were a peculiar sort of insect he could not identify. "Shar?"

"*Mo Flaith?*"

"See to Mistress Rian's requests."

Ah, so he did know her given name after all. *Bastard.*

Shar dipped his blond head and strode through the door, wearing a poorly concealed grin. He, at least, Rian found moderately tolerable. Tam Lin crossed his arms while Rian confiscated Robin's discarded bottle of uishge. Niall and Derck hauled Gramble from the floor and worked him into the worn cushions of Barb's window seat. Rian made a face when she got a closer look. His bandages were filthy, and he'd lost half a dozen stitches at first glance. She was beginning to wonder why she bothered sewing these fools back together if they were just going to get drunk and destroy all of her hard work.

She had a mind to go to bed for the next week and let them all sort themselves.

"How fares my cousin this morning?" Tam Lin asked jovially.

She prodded Robin's wound and frowned. "He, too, will live. Though I daresay, I'm not sure how with that hole in his chest."

"That would be Diarmid's handiwork. I'm amazed the old codger bothered. I suppose the question of favorite nephew has been summarily answered." Rian had no idea what he was on about, but she assumed he meant that Diarmid— whom she'd met as Faris, the man who'd trapped her and Una in the Otherworld on Samhain— had used some sort of dark magic to heal the majority of Kaer Yin's wounds. She couldn't be sure what a spell of that sort would cost— and all magic costs, she understood— but she'd be willing to bet the Dannan sorcerer was equally as wounded as Kaer Yin. "Anyway," Tam Lin continued," I suppose I'm asking if he'll be worth a shite in the foreseeable future?"

She pried a pair of tiny scissors from of her hem and squinted over Robin's bare ribs. "Was he ever? I'm not sure what you'd like me to say."

Tam Lin threw back his head and laughed. "Fair enough, Mistress! I need to know if I should plan an extended stay in this, erm, charming hamlet?"

She rolled a shoulder. "Ben's in a terrible temper since you ask, but I have at least a hundred patients gathered beneath this roof that shares his mood. He's alive. Best I can tell you."

⚜

Later, after having sewn Robin's cuts back together and begrudgingly changing the bandages on Barb's hands, Rian scarcely looked up when Tam Lin gently steered her into Kaer Yin's room by the elbow. She was too tired to complain of his touching her and far too emotionally drained to argue. She had a heap of tasks to see to after this, and her lack of sleep was taking a heavy toll. If Tam Lin noticed her reticence, he refrained from comment. In the doorway, a slight sound from within the chamber snapped Rian's head up. The sight she beheld there sent a fresh surge of furious vitality straight to her brain. Kaer Yin lay on his back, overtaking the small bed and its homely flower-patterned coverlet. Rose, who'd been charged with caring for Rian's remaining patients for the day while Rian was busy tending to their betters upstairs, had tucked herself against him, feeding him spoonfuls of raw, stinking uishge.

"Ben!" Rian barked, spilling her fifth cup of tea down the remnants of her once presentable homespun skirt. Her head pounding, she slammed her empty cup down on the larder so hard that it cracked. "*You*," she pointed to Rose, who bloody well knew better. "Out. *Now.*"

Rose simpered beautifully; she'd had years of practice. Too bad Rian was a woman and not over-fond of anyone much, least of all a hard-worn prostitute of Rose's ilk. "I came to see if Ben… I mean, His Highness, needed anything while ye were occupied. It's a wee bit of uishge, Rian. Nothin' to get upset over."

Tam Lin leaned against the doorjamb, watching Rian intently. "I think you've poked the bear here, cousin. Not enamored of drink, this one."

Kaer Yin, the bloody stupid Crown Prince of Innisfail, squirmed under Rian's murderous gaze. "Ah, right. Rosie, love?"

"Hm?" Rose breathed, unable to tear her eyes away from his moronic face.

Rian narrowed her eyes to slits.

"They need you downstairs. Would you mind leaving the bottle?" He asked, fidgeting.

Rian stamped her foot. "No bloody uishge, damn you. Take that bottle with you and bring no more in here, or I swear to Siora, you'll regret it, Rose."

Rose winced from the venom in Rian's tone.

Kaer Yin patted Rose's knee. "Best do as she says, Rosie."

She pouted, but you don't become a favorite in a place like *The Hart* by arguing with your patrons. She got up with exaggerated sloth, leaning appreciably forward here or suggestively flouncing there. By the time she made it out of the damned door, both males in attendance had long forgotten Rian. With a vicious jerk, she pulled Kaer Yin forward by his collar to mash another pillow behind his head. Not for comfort, mind; she needed to change his dressings. "Ouch!" he cried, reaching out to curb her manhandling.

Rian slapped his hands away as she would a child of five and set a stare on him that would boil water. "Sit still, or I swear, I will make this hurt."

Tam Lin hovered behind her. She ignored him and went about unraveling yesterday's bandages. Being comprised of laundered burlap and scraps of linen hose, the dressing was far from ideal, but given what they'd all been through in the past two weeks, they might have been spun of gold and rainbows. There wasn't much left in *The Hart* but splinters and broken glass these days. Ben winced under her fingers. "*Créatúr fíochmhar, an ceann sin.*" Tam Lin remarked dryly.

"*Olc, go fírinneach,*" answered Kaer Yin.

"*Ní haon ionadh nach bhfuil fear céile ann.*"

"*Aye, bheadh sí marbh air.*"

More laughter. Rian's cheeks burned.

Tam Lin cocked his head. "*Fós, tá sí thara bheith álainn le haghaidh faerie.*" [1]

That did it.

"*Gabhaim buíochas leataraon le cuimne a thabhairt go bhfuilim sa seaomra, agus níl aon rud cearr le mo chluasa.*" [2]

She spat in rapid, fluent Ealig.

Tam Lin's mouth snapped shut. Ben gave her a knowing smirk. He'd never asked her if she spoke his language, but the discovery didn't seem to surprise him in the least. He didn't mind Tam Lin's obvious embarrassment either. "Fine." He tactfully looked away from Tam Lin's lowered brows. If the Prince of

---

[1] Tam Lin: 'Fierce creature, that.'
Kaer Yin: 'Evil, truly.'
Tam Lin: 'No wonder she doesn't have a husband.'
Kaer Yin: 'She would have killed him.'
Tam Lin: 'Still, she's quite lovely for a faerie.'
[2] Rian: 'I'll thank you both to recall that I am in the room, and there's nothing wrong with my ears.'

Connaught didn't already know that his cousin was a bit of an ass already, he certainly did now. That would teach him to talk over others as if they didn't exist, wouldn't it? "To business then. What's your diagnosis, Rian?"

"Well," she took a breath. "You've two broken ribs, a cracked breastplate, damage to your collarbone— I pulled teeth out of that, thank you for the nightmares— a fracture in your left forearm, three broken fingers, and of course, a massive hole in your chest that should have killed you. Aside from that, millions of scratches, several concerning cuts and contusions… and that's just your torso. Not to worry, though, as fast as you purebloods heal, I'll have to rebreak whatever doesn't heal properly and reset it for you."

Kaer Yin grimaced. "Saying what, exactly?"

"You're lucky to be alive right now. Why push things any further, you blithering idiot?"

"Now now, Mistress," cooed Tam Lin. "Don't fall in love with him. He's a scoundrel, you know. The very worst sort."

Roundly ignoring Tam Lin, she inspected the nearly fatal wound in Kaer Yin's chest. The skin was puckered pink and red, but it looked and smelled better than it had the day before. He *did* heal remarkably fast, thank Siora. She knew what he was waiting to hear, and maybe, just maybe, she had better news today. She sighed. "Two months, at best."

"No bloody way am I going to lay here that long."

"You don't have a choice. What good will you be to her riddled with holes?"

A muscle kept time in his jaw. "I can't wait that long, damn you!"

Tam Lin took a seat on Kaer Yin's right, cleaning his nails with a jeweled dagger. "Is this about that bloody woman again? I've told you repeatedly, it will come to no avail. Your father will never—"

"*Clúdaigh do bhéal*, Tam Lin."[3]

Tam Lin pointed the dagger at him. "You wouldn't be so pissy about it if I wasn't right. Forget her. She's but a Milesian sweetmeat anyway. When we go home, you can have your pick of far more suitable women."

Kaer Yin slapped the dagger out of Tam Lin's hand, his eyes gone a terrible silver. "Say that again, *ceathrar*, and I'll cut your tongue out with your own blade."

Rian, sensing another pointless brawl on the horizon, moved between them. Her mother always told her the Sidhe burned hot as a brushfire then cold as the wind through a cairn. She never believed such extremes were possible until she witnessed so many together at once. There were fights nearly every night; almost all resulted in bloodshed, and few were ever started over something worthwhile. Oddly, despite the heat of every disagreement, no friendships ever suffered from the violence. Indeed, as if the roughhousing and discord brought them closer together. Rian struggled to equate her calm, sweet mother with this gang of overgrown brutes. "Will you two *please* be better behaved than your men downstairs? I swear. I've seen wee bairns with better temperaments."

Tam Lin rolled his eyes. "It's our way, little one. Yours too, if you aren't too lofty for self-reflection?"

She opened and closed her mouth like a goldfish.

Kaer Yin guffawed and tried not to hiss when the movement jostled his ribs. "He's got you there, Rian."

She flushed. "*Tá tú an dá leathcheanns.*"[4]

A round of chuckles did little to cool the heat in her cheeks. Clearing her throat, she patted Kaer Yin's wound with the nettle and honey salve she'd brought from home all those weeks ago. He was a mute patient for a while. A faraway look settled in his storm-bright eyes. She pursed her lips. "She's alive, Ben. That's what matters. They need her too much to harm her."

"For now," he said, swallowing hard.

"You did everything you could. You can't blame yourself."

---

[3] Kaer Yin: 'Shut your mouth, Tam Lin.'
[4] Rian: 'You're both idiots.'

"I don't. I blame Bishop, and when I see him again, I'll make him pay for it."

"No woman is worth so much trouble, Yin. I beg you to let this go," argued Tam Lin, more cautiously this time. "You're finally free to return home after all these years. Let's leave the Milesians to themselves."

"I am the Crown Prince of Innisfail, Tam Lin. The Milesians are my people too. Bishop broke the Ard Ri's law to take Una back. Even if I didn't care for her, it would nevertheless be my responsibility to ensure my father's justice is done. I don't understand why you're fighting me so hard on this."

Tam Lin sheathed his dagger with a sullen shrug. "The last time you went South, I didn't see you for nearly thirty years. I don't want to lose my cousin again over some Milesian girl," he paused, tugging his chin at Rian. "What's your opinion of this lunacy, then? Surely you don't think it's wise to march on Bethany with a handful of Sidhe, especially for such an absurd reason? What do *you* think?"

Rian blew a lock of hair out of her eye. "Well, you don't know, Una, Your Highness."

"What does that have to do with my extremely rational argument?"

"None of us would be alive now if it weren't for her. Everyone in Rosweal owes her. Me and Ben, especially."

"So, you support his cockamamie plan, then?"

She gave Kaer Yin a long look. "Yes, I do."

"For *Herne*'s sake, why?"

She twisted her lip sideways at him. "Because I love her too."

⚹

"Is she sleeping?" Barb asked from the crack in the doorway.

"Yes, finally." Kaer Yin replied, motioning her and Dabs forward. "Though, I'd hide that teapot somewhere she'll never find it. If she realizes you've drugged her again, I'll never hear the end of it."

Barb giggled. "Poor mite. She'll work herself to death one day, won't she?"

"Probably."

Barb patted Rian's flaxen head where it lay against Kaer Yin's mattress.

Tam Lin had no clue what to make of all this. "Why not go and rest?"

"Och," Barb blew smoke at him. "Rosweal don't have a proper doctor, ye know. After them Southers came and went, we have lots o'folks needin' care. This tiny slip o'a girl takes it all upon herself. Won't hear o'rest until all have been seen to. She's a bleedin' Kneeler's angel, ye ask me, no matter how sharp her tongue. There ye are, Dabs, be careful with her now! Make sure ye give her Tansy's quilt. She wanted her to have it."

Even with the fair-haired Dannans clogging the room like hulking tolls, Dabney's bulk was impressive. Gentle as a giant with a tiny bird, he plucked Rian into his arms and carefully laid her over his shoulder. Her long thin fingers trailed down his back as he ducked through the open doorway and into the hall with her, passing several curious Dannan faces along the way.

Tam Lin stared after them for a while, as if the mystery of her character would materialize in the darkened alcove like smoke. "What a strange girl."

"Lin, you have *no* idea," Kaer Yin chuckled while slowly resettling himself against his mound of pillows. He was ash-pale and weak, but there was a glimmer in his silver eyes that Tam Lin was happy to see returned. Maybe the girl did know what she was doing.

"How did you meet her again, cousin?"

"Oh, well, it's a *very* long story...."

"Never mind all that now," Barb interjected, lighting another wad of witchroot in her pipe. "We have matters to discuss. Robin, bless his larcenous heart, won't be fit for much for a few days. Has almost as many marks on him as ye do, Ben."

"I know. I gave him most of them," Kaer Yin snickered.

"Well, that's as may be, but my sweet man don't have yer constitution, Yer Arseness," she blew another cloud of smoke and pointed. "It's Robin ye need to see all this through, ye know?"

"I do. He's my best friend, no matter how many times he's tried to kill me in recent weeks. We're of the same mind on this issue."

"Good. Now, can we count on ye lot?"

She was asking Tam Lin directly. He held up his hands. "Under protest."

Kaer Yin groaned. "Let it bloody go, already!"

Barb tapped her teeth. "Does that mean yer in or out?"

Tam Lin folded his arms and exhaled heavily. "In. My men too, as promised."

Her smile was macabre in the poorly lit chamber. "Well then, gather close, and I'll tell ye everythin' ye want to know about the Machine City, starting with her brothels…."

My Brother's Keeper

Henry caught his son in a bear hug, once more amazed by the breadth of the lad's shoulders. Had he grown again so soon? It had been less than two months since they'd met in the cellars below the Great Hall, yet it might have been years. Henry patted Micah's broadening back with an appreciative smile. Was he taller too? By the Lord! Micah's brilliant golden curls hung low over his beaming face. He wore the cobalt and scarlet of Donahugh's house, and Henry was proud to see they suited his handsome son quite well. Henry stepped back a pace. What was Patrick feeding his sons to effect such a marked change? He forced the expected knot of bitterness that always rustled when he was allowed to speak to his own children, deep down. There would be time enough for all of that later.

For now, he must not show Micah one ounce of doubt or fear. God had plans for Henry's boys… for them all.

"There now, let's have a look at you, lad! You've grown a mile since last I saw you. Where are all these bloody muscles coming from?"

Micah gave him a sheepish grin. "I've been training with Carrigan and Grimley, father. Six hours a day. The few reprieves I'm allowed are on Feast Days and at table in the evenings."

His diction was much improved as well. Henry's heart swelled with pride. "That is wonderful news, my son. Isaac? Is he training also?"

"Not yet. Uncle says he must learn his letters and table manners before he'll be allowed the tiltyard. He's doing quite well, though he can't wait to swing a sword of his own. You should see him, father. He's already Uncle's height."

The second knot of bitterness was more difficult to swallow than the first.

"Is he? Well, that's as God would have things. Please send him my love and tell him we'll be reunited again before long."

Micah ruffled his hair, clearly anxious that he'd inadvertently wounded his father. "He misses you too, Da. Old Grimshaw speaks of your many victories all the time. Isaac lives for them."

Henry waved this placation away and steered his son toward the stairs, which spilled out of the dungeons above and into the river below their feet. In the dark, the River Lee slapped lazily against the castle's stone moorings. This cavern was an underground port designed to ensure deliveries of goods and services were private and out of the way. For Henry's purposes, it served as his sole means of transport in or out of the Keep. That Micah could visit with him here was an artfully engineered prospect that had cost Henry several hundred fainne to procure.

Though, this was neither here nor there.

"No matter, no matter, my boy. Now, let us sit here together and have a chat. Hm?"

Micah's smile faded but allowed himself to be led. No doubt, he was already acutely aware of what his father wished to discuss, as anyone within a hundred leagues of the city knew Una Moura Donahugh was on her way home. Micah gulped. "Father, I know what you would say, and I would like to remind you that—"

"Micah, if you mention Damek again, I shall strike you. You are not some defenseless weakling, are you? Or is your uncle training you for nothing?"

"No, father."

"Well then, what is there to remind me of?"

"I should like to be friends with my cousin. I don't wish to be enemies. I would like to serve at his side, as you did, with my uncle. Why is that wrong? Doesn't the Lord wish for families to support one another?"

Micah had been practicing this speech.

Henry tried not to chuckle. How innocent were the young? "Micah, I've told you already. Damek Bishop will not allow any man, especially not a legitimized Donahugh man, to share his dais for long. You were enemies the moment my brother discovered you and will be so until one of you is dead. Don't forget this again. It is not just your life and safety you must protect. Isaac will be Damek's prey after he's sunk his talons into you."

"I don't see why things should be so. She's a godless wanton, from what I hear. They say the Siorai in Tairngare f-fornicate with the inferior males of their order during their rituals. Jasper told me that my cousin was even with child once, but she sacrificed the infant to her goddess for power."

Henry chewed the interior of his lip. He could not tell Micah that Una and Damek had been twice married and divorced by her father in pursuit of other wealthy lords, willing to exchange armaments for her dowry. "The customs in Tairngare are not your concern, Micah. Nor hers anymore, by the by. She's a Donahugh. I don't care if she has a hairlip and walks with a limp; you're going to marry her and sire an heir of your own. This is your duty, and you *will* accept it or die. You can't go back."

"It's not—"

"No one said life was fair, Micah."

Micah groaned. Henry prayed for the strength not to abuse his son physically.

"Look, boy. She's rumored to be beautiful. Hells, my nephew, has been obsessed with her all of his life. From what I hear, she's kind, intelligent, and honest. What more do you want? She's the most desirable woman in Innisfail, and you're whingeing because she isn't a virgin."

"Father, God forbids us to f-fornicate before marriage."

"Aye, so? She's not of our faith. It will be your responsibility to teach her how about our God and his mighty works. Can't you see what an opportunity this is?"

Micah hadn't thought about Una converting to their faith. Again, Henry could tell what he was thinking. He really must do something about the boy's face. Every thought Micah had was visible as the sun in a clear blue sky. "I suppose when you put it that way… but what about Damek? He's handsome, they tell me. Rich in his own right. Powerful. The people love him. How do I steal any woman from someone like him?"

Henry couldn't help but snort. "Don't you worry about Damek, son. She hates him. All you need do is be kind to her. Speak to her. Treat her with respect and admiration, and she'll be yours in short order." He did not say that she had been so mistreated by her father, by Damek, and every man in either's service that she'd cling to any act of kindness like a lone buoy in a roiling sea. "Be her friend, Micah. Her confidant. Trust me, Damek could never be either."

Micah was quiet for a moment. "He hurt her, didn't he? Before?"

Henry turned around to look at him. "If she's a witch, what do you care?"

"God won't like it, but I can use it if it's true. Can't I?"

By God.

There might be some Donahugh in the lad, after all.

⚒

SHANLEY, PATRICK'S NEWEST STEWARD, SET the scroll in Patrick's open palm. The sheaf was heavier than Patrick expected. Unwinding its leather stays, he frowned as a wad of crudely inked vellum sprang free from the binding. He didn't need to read any of these pages to know what writ upon the heading of each leaf was.

He Knows What Lies In The Darkness…

Patrick tossed the papers aside with a snort. "What nonsense is this?"

The fellow's yellow eyes bulged from his pinhead. "These were confiscated in the Mercantile district only yesterday. Someone has been proselytizing treason to the poor, it seems."

Patrick snapped his fingers with an impatient sigh he did not feel. His groom returned to his throat with a cautious razor. "Many men and women attempt to convert Bethonair citizens every year. It never holds. Southers have no patience for dogma. We're guided by Reason and the True South, remember? We require no creed."

"Yes, My Lord," said Shanley, attempting to moderate his tone. He would have to work on that, or Patrick would see him swinging from the Mahon Gate one of these days. "But these were not crafted by an outsider. My source insists they were written by your brother and distributed by Lord Warrick and his retinue."

Warrick, eh? Now that *was* a surprise to Patrick. Sure, he'd had Warrick's Colonial Commission revoked a few years back, but he'd never have expected such a stalwart man to fall under Henry's thrall. How interesting. "Nonsense. Warrick wouldn't dare cross me in public. Like all rodents, he will always seek the path of least resistance. You sure it wasn't Hamley, Knockburn, or Morton who've been abetting this drivel?"

"No, My Lord. This morning, Lord Warrick's squire was caught with the documents in his valise. The lad has confessed all, without torture."

"How convenient," Patrick quipped while his groom grinned up at him. "No doubt his master will prove equal to the lad's cowardice. See to it that he and his family are stricken from the registry. I'll give his lands to Lord Bander, and Warrick's coffers will help finance my eager nephew's latest campaign North. Well, is that all?" Shanley squirmed. Patrick growled. "I asked, is that all?"

"No, My Lord…"

"Reason, one would think I were a patient man."

"More documents have been procured in Lord FitzDonahugh's apartments. They are… well, they're of an incendiary nature, My Lord. In his own words, he condemns the Barony, women's freedom to buy and own property, trade with the colonies and the 'unholy' Sidhe, the lavish lifestyles of those at Court, and your own indolence and erm, 'depravity,' My Lord. He's taken issue with everyone in Bethany, it seems. What's worse, he's garnered quite a loyal following among the poor working class and an alarming number of stolid sorts from among your courtiers. He's dangerous, My Lord. My servants have heard him praised as a martyr to your ambition."

The razor's course stopped mid-swipe. Patrick's groom flushed and backed away. Patrick sat up. "Where is Henry now?"

"In his quarters, My Lord. Confined there, under my orders."

Patrick made a face. "Release him."

Shanley blanched. "Forgive me, My Lord, but he has committed treason."

"Shanley, do you know how martyrs are made?"

"N-no, My Lord. I believe they must be persecuted and scourged by their rulers?"

"Exactly so. What do you suppose will happen if I imprison my brother again?"

"I take your point." Shanley genuflected but persisted, chalk-white cheeks ablaze. "We can hardly allow him to sow discord in the city with his vitriol, can we?"

"No, we cannot. I want his followers arrested and their property and funds confiscated. I will make an example of every one of them. As for my brother, I believe we'll honor him with lands and a bevy of titles, which previously belonged to his flock."

"You'd reward him?"

"Hardly," Patrick smirked. "I'll make a hypocrite of him. His sons are fine boys who will one day be peers of the South. I'll lavish them with gifts, accolades, and feasts while Henry's followers are ground into obscurity beneath the Barony's yoke. Hard to believe in a man who embodies the opposite of his professed ideals."

"I… see, My Lord." He didn't, but Patrick wouldn't bait him further. Maybe he should have Shanley here replaced? The fellow was thick as butter.

"What else, Shanley?"

"Well, My Lord," he cleared his throat. "While investigating this business with the letters, your housekeeper had some rather disturbing things to report."

"Meaning?"

"Several reports of manhandling and molestation upon the serving girls in the East Wing. The housekeeper has applied for a general ban on female servitors in that part of the castle."

Patrick cursed. "How many girls have been tampered with?"

Shanley fidgeted. "Three, My Lord. One was so badly beaten that her family filed a formal complaint. They mean to apply to you personally, in full view of the Court."

"That absolutely cannot happen. Pay them off and move them to Clare or Kerry as quietly as possible. The others?"

"One is with child. The other has been reassigned to the North Wing."

Patrick covered his half-damp face with one hand. "Reason. Grant the housekeeper's request. I want no women below the age of sixty servicing the East Wing. My brother will have to make do with boys and old women for sport. Is that all?"

"Ah, well… no."

Patrick stomped to the fireplace and leaned against the mantle. His groom handed him a flagon of wine, though his stomach had turned far too sour to drink anything. "What?"

Shanley wrung his hands, stealing a nervous sideways glance at Patrick's impassive groom. "Two girls are missing, My Lord."

"From the East Wing? Why didn't you say as much before?"

"Not from the East Wing. From the Central Keep. They didn't report to their chambers after the Feasts last week."

"Gods damn that pig-fucking pederast!" Patrick threw his flagon against the wall over Shanley's quivering scalp. Dark red Cymrian spattered the drapes and carpet near the steward's feet. The poor steward blubbered. "I want him watched at every feast. He's to have two bodyguards dogging his heels at all times. Fuck's sake! Why wasn't this brought to my attention when the first girl complained?"

"Lord Fitz Donahugh vows he has never laid a hand on any of them, My Lord. None of the girls' families wished their names dragged through the muck in opposition to a peer, the Duch's own brother. They're all terrified of him. Respectfully, My Lord, I restate myself: your brother is dangerous. I represent all of your household staff when I urge you to reconsider his liberties. Please, Your Grace. This could easily spin out of our control."

Patrick was silent for a while, mulling it all over. He'd known there would be trouble when he'd released Henry but perhaps not this much, so soon? How that gnarled old predator managed to get it up high enough to force himself upon his maids, one could hazard a guess. Perhaps, the violence did the trick for him? Patrick couldn't say it didn't hold a certain appeal, but he'd never been aroused by a screeching female before. He liked his women soft and pliant, excluding his late wife, of course. That bitch had earned her stripes in the best way possible.

"All right. Restrict his access to all but the East Wing and the Keep, though I want him followed as I said, and there are to be guards in his hall day and night. See that the staff are alerted to steer clear of him, and even the housekeeper is to remand her duties to a male servitor for the time being. I want him lavished in food, furs, gifts, and books in the meantime. If allowed, he'll pretend to this preposterous notion of martyrdom at every opportunity. I want him kept clean, well-fed, his sons admired and coddled, and his coffers growing. This is imperative, despite his less-public urges."

"As you wish, My Lord, but, well…."

Patrick's nostrils flared. "For your sake, I would suggest you spill every ounce of information at the start from now on. Speak, damn you!"

"He, ah, has been meeting with the young Lord Donahugh, as well. They met this very afternoon in the Moorings."

Patrick's right eye twitched to a painful degree. "Have I not commanded that I am to be informed immediately should the lad be unaccounted for at any point during the day?"

Shanley backed up a pace. "Yes, My Lord. We were—"

"Your excuses mean less than nothing to me, Shanley. Today, you will take ten lashes for this failure. On the next occasion, it will be your head. Do you understand me?"

Shanley knelt, weeping openly. Patrick's former steward currently dangled from the North Tower, a sack of bones plucked white by crows. That fool had failed to prevent Damek's rebellious march North and elected to run rather than inform Patrick of his nephew's perfidy. Patrick had executed a fair share of stewards in his time. Motioning for the guards to remove Shanley to the courtyard, he took a seat at his desk and sighed. His groom waited patiently by the fireplace, Patrick's towel dangling from his forearm.

"I swear," Patrick grumbled, scribbling furiously over a fresh sheaf of vellum. "It is *so* hard to find good help these days."

Having no tongue with which to comment, Patrick's groom nodded vacantly.

⚕ ⚕

NOTING THE GUARDS WAITING BEFORE HIS chamber door, Henry slowed his pace slightly. He might have known Patrick would have been told already. He chuckled under his breath. Much that the old fool could do about it. Henry wouldn't be cowed. Holding his head high as it would go with a bent spine, he strolled past his brother's stolid guards to discover the Duch of Bethany rummaging through his personal effects. It didn't matter. He was welcome to look. Henry waved at his brother as he shrugged out of his heavy outdoor cloak. With an eyebrow raised toward his balding pate as he read through the notes in his left hand, Patrick scarcely looked up.

"Evening, brother," said Henry, noisily taking a seat to remove his shoes.

Patrick chortled through his nose, tossing the wad of papers into the fireplace. "'Licentious tyrant,' am I? Dear me, Henry, but you've lost your talent for wordplay."

"I'm out of practice. Don't worry, I'll find my rhythm again."

Patrick took a seat, tucking the tankard in his right hand against his chest. He fixed Henry with a cool glare. "Oh, I've no doubt. If you'd half the talent for sermons as you do for rape and violence, I say you'll corner the market in no time."

Henry wasn't cowed. "Ah, a servant has been telling tales, I see? They're nonsense."

"Are they? It's funny. I'd have figured you were impotent, given the general state of your health." He tsked. "Ironic, considering that you're soon to be a father again."

"The girl lies. Ask your housekeeper. A few weeks ago, she was found with one of the grooms in the stables. She means to fleece me for a living. As you know, I am in no state to inspire scandals."

"Huh. That is quite a tale. And the others? I suppose they're all lying too."

Henry flashed his wooden teeth. "Of course they are. You've given me quite an allowance, and a title always attracts this sort of chicanery. As I recall, you fended off dozens of these accusations in your youth?"

"In my case, none were true."

"Suppose this is where you'll warn me to hold my tongue about that girl's heritage, then?"

Patrick went very still. Henry had seen that same iron-edged glare many times in his life, and when he'd been a younger, more cautious man, it would have concerned him. "Is that why you're forcing yourself on my staff? To threaten or insult me?"

Henry shrugged and leaned back on his knobby elbows. "If I had done any of the horrible things they say I've done, I imagine it would be a compulsion outside of my control and very little to do with you. Yet, you'll concoct your theories, regardless."

"Una is *my* daughter, Henry."

"If you say so, little brother."

"I know so." The blood rushing to Patrick's cheeks blazed violet. "And if you ever—"

"No need. I intend to marry my eldest son to your peerless daughter, don't I? Why would I ruin that perfect Donahugh union with ancient rumor, hm? Besides, it's not as if she would wish to know that her impotent father kidnapped and raped her mother under the advice of a Fir Bolg witch, only to fail in her conception time and again. I imagine she might feel rather put out when she learns I was the one who—"

"That's enough. You are not her father, Henry, and you are not Duch, despite your imagination. You have no power over her or your son. Let me be clear."

"It *is* a sin to tup one's siblings, but in our family, that line's always been a bit murky. Hasn't it, Patrick?"

"I said that's *enough*, damn you!" Patrick had gone a rare shade of puce at this point. Henry didn't bother to conceal his smirk. "Shall I have your tongue torn from your head? Perhaps your hands, from the wrist down?"

"Why not pitch me over the Mahon Tower, like our beautiful Alis? It must have been quite infuriating to see her belly swollen with another man's child, though you never seemed to mind with Arrin, did you?" Henry's tone was acerbic with an ancient enmity. "Ah, I vowed I'd pay you back for our sweet sister one of these days, Patrick."

Patrick leaned forward. "So, you'd have me believe you're a reformed man but would happily condone an incestual union between two of your children? Pah. Arrin was kept in seclusion and well away from Court when Una was conceived. You were not even there, but truly— a fair attempt, brother."

Henry gave a mock bow. "God will forgive me for wedding my children together if it purges this city of your filth."

"You're insane, you know?"

"Does it keep you awake at night?"

"Your lunacy?"

"No, Alis' son?"

Patrick didn't answer, as Henry knew he wouldn't. Instead, he got up and stalked around Henry's bed to the windows. "Yes. I lie awake at night, but not for the reason you suspect. I worry he will make me kill him."

Now seated on his bed, Henry tucked his hands behind his head and settled against his mountain of pillows. The finery in his chamber increased by the day. Since Patrick saw fit to reinstate him to the peerage, he had coin to spare. After a decade in a dank, dark cell, he didn't mind the added comfort.

"You should have adopted him when you had the chance. Now, he's your greatest liability. Not that I care overmuch. I'll be happy when Micah sits on my father's throne, and the Damek Bishops of the world are gone."

"I thought you had a care for Alis' son, brother?"

"He's a half-breed, Patrick. Brilliant he may be, but you know his kind run to madness more often than not. Or do you suppose he will march in here with his prize and allow you to pretend to power for much longer? The fate of your kingdom hinges upon the decisions you make when he returns. You're wrong if you truly believe he'll make a grand ruler."

Patrick took a long pull from his tankard and belched. "Why not? His being in your way does not lessen his worth in my eyes. Forgive me if I don't take succession advice from a man convicted of high treason." He paused with a heavy sigh. "Never mind all that. I'm not here to discuss Damek, Henry. I want your word that you'll cease interfering with my staff."

"I've already given it."

"Have you?" Patrick turned. "Do you know what awaits me in the cellars at this very moment? Two girls had gone missing from the Central Keep last week. Both were fished out of the river this afternoon. The things done to those girls turns even my stomach, Henry."

Henry's brow furrowed together. This was news. "Where were they found?"

"A dozen yards shy of the bay. Swept downstream on the outgoing tide. My surgeon believes they were killed at the same time and dumped into the Lee from the Moorings. The very same spot you've been taking meetings for the past month, including with Micah, whom you've sworn to avoid upon penalty of death. Is the image I'm painting for you vivid enough, or do you require further illumination?"

"I did and do take meetings there, yes. To sermonize, which you've allowed me to do at my discretion. As for Micah, to encourage him not to shy from his duty to you and this House. I will not be shamed by my sons, no matter what Damek might conjure for them. Otherwise, I have kept to my word, Patrick. I know nothing of any girls."

"Right. Just as the complaints from my staff here must be lies, let me tell you what's going to happen now, brother dear. You will be under guard from the moment you wake until you close your eyes at night. You will never take another meeting that isn't officially approved in full view of the Court, and you will never be given the opportunity to harm any of my staff again. Starting today, only men and old women shall serve in this tower, and you are restricted from any feast that I am not attending. I want no more of this. Am I clear?"

"As glass, brother. Though I'm afraid, you are censuring the wrong man. One of the maids, yes. I— how did you put it? — 'interfered' with. God will forgive me for that weakness. The others are bald liars, especially that slut from the Narrows. Her child is her own business. Now, as far as these slain girls are concerned, there's simply no way it *could* have been me, Patrick. I am not as deft a sneak as I once was. I am already guarded at every feast, led to and from the Hall, with no exceptions. To accuse me of this, you're assuming I'm capable of walking over a half-mile, going up and down four flights of stairs, passing through several brightly lit halls and hordes of workers… at night, in the dark, with these knees." He tugged his robe up so Patrick couldn't mistake the gout, which bloomed green and purple over his knee joint. "Walking, standing, lying down, or sitting on my bed… there's no relief."

Patrick visibly turned off his ale, set it down on the larder. "Yet, you're still able to maltreat a girl half your age. No matter what you say, brother, no one else in this castle has your history. Those girls were gutted."

Henry covered his knees with his long black robe. "I *am* a reformed man. Beyond that, I've never done such things to a woman. I've taken from them, sure, but murder? One throttled thief a lifetime ago does not make me a butcher. Besides, I struggle to hold my bread knife these days." He held up his gnarled, arthritic hands. "I'll take your point on the one serving girl and accept my punishment without further argument, but I don't know the first thing about the others. That is God's truth."

Patrick didn't believe him. Well, Henry expected that. "Una returns in a week or less. If you attempt to fill her ears with any of your nonsense, I'll kill one of your sons. I vow it."

Henry clenched what was left of his teeth. "So you've said, and I have consented. Visiting Micah was a necessity you may thank me for later. The boy is smart but needs prodding to do his duty. What use would he be if he didn't provide a rational alternative to our brash young nephew?"

"Then we are agreed. Please don't make me restate this for a third time, Henry. Mind yourself. Whatever machinations you think you're hatching in secrecy, remember, you can conceal nothing from me for long. Two young men are relying upon you to keep them alive."

Patrick shrugged his cloak tight. Having said his peace, he moved toward the hidden staircase in the east wall. Henry's voice caught him short at the bottom step. "How were they done?"

Patrick paused. "What?"

"The murdered girls. How were they found?"

Patrick looked very small in the torchlit passage. "Throttled, beaten, and slashed."

Henry felt a chill creep down his spine. "Raped?"

"No."

"Virgins?"

"No. It is the opinion of the coroner that the killer might be impotent."

Ah. "You suspected me, naturally?"

"Until you admitted to raping one of my servants, yes."

"I hope he is found quickly."

"I've no doubt of it, Henry." The passage closed behind him, leaving Henry to sweat in the dark, alone.

Lady Donahugh

Una chewed hard-tack and pretended not to see any of the men riding around her. She wasn't shaking anymore, which was a vast improvement. Though she'd long since given up hope of escape, she did keep an eye roving for any potential scenarios she might utilize to regain *some* agency over her person. Being strapped to a horse all day and tied to her cot every night, she was running out of ideas. A day's ride south of Ten Bells, the single change to her situation was the view. Having left the river valley behind, they were now marching through reconstituted forest, which led through the bogs at Skiberdeen, then over the low hills of Blane. Not long now. The snow-kissed forests and knolls of the North had given way to the rolling greens and browns of the Southern plains. She could taste the sea on the western wind and smell the peat burning in the city, a few miles away. The road yawned up at her, muddy, malodorous, and merciless. Her mount's hooves beat her doom into the earth.

Every step brought her that much closer to a fate worse than death.

Here sits the property of Duch Patrick Donahugh and any male he might have a mind to share her with.

She spat, not caring if she hit anyone in the process. Served these bastards right, believing a woman should surrender her fate to the males in her family. As far as Una could reckon, the only thing men managed to be better at was violence, and some were *infinitely* more skilled than others. She ignored the sharp pain in her gut. She wouldn't think of him now. She must not. Damek would love nothing more than to berate and belittle her for her feelings, so, she would display none. She kept her face as impassive as marble while her insides bled.

"What did you study, My Lady? In the Cloister, I mean?" Martin leaned in from her right side. His affable, grizzled cheeks did give her a tiny pang of guilt for her generalizations. Some men were kind, too. Though, in her experience, Martin O'Rearden was one of a very select few. Martin didn't have a cruel bone in his body, though he served the worst of men. That he was so loyal, despite this, softened her regard. She would speak with no one else.

Damek, blissfully, ignored her.

She stole a peek now and then to make sure he remained well outside her vicinity and had yet to see his head turn, nor his shoulders uncoil. That was fine by her. He *should* stay well away. If he got close enough, she'd relish the opportunity to feed him his teeth. She spat out another seed. This time, a nearby soldier swiped the offensive missile from his cheek with an irritable grunt.

Ha! she thought. *I'll take what I can get.*

"Particle theory and practicum."

Martin chuckled. "Peapods and pigpens? There's a smile! Haven't seen that in an age."

Una tucked her lip back into place. "Well, don't get used to it."

"Ah, now. Try not to be like that, My Lady. I know how you feel about your Da, but I vow it won't be as bad as you believe." He tugged his chin at Damek's rigid back. "He'll never let any harm come to you. Nor will I."

Una felt a bit like a fly under glass. "Martin, I would appreciate it if you wouldn't peddle my cousin's wares to me. We are enemies. That's all there is to it."

"Hogswaddle."

"Excuse me?"

"You heard me, missy. That lad's loved you since the day you were born."

"That is not my problem."

"You're right. It's your privilege."

Something burst behind Una's eyes. "Say that again, one more time. I dare you, Commander. Tell me how lucky I am that a man I want nothing to do with believes he has the right to hunt and take me captive against my will." She held up her bound wrists. "Is this your definition of a lucky woman?"

Martin didn't flinch. "These fetters you earned by running away from your own family. Tell me, in your grand matriarchal city, how often were you free to do as you pleased? Did your grandmama allow you outside of the Cloister to exercise your 'free will' very often, ever? In the decade or more that it's been since I last saw you, how many trips did you take to the surrounding towns? The markets? Hells, the opposite end of the Citadel? No need to answer, for I already know, Una. None. That old hag kept you under lock and key, day and night."

"I wanted to be where I was. You don't understand the Cloister, Martin. Freedom is a relative term."

Martin shrugged, scratching his scarred chin. "Once you were free, did you run home?"

She flushed to the roots of her hair. "That is none of *your* business."

"Kaer Yin Adair, no less." He shook his head. "When we first began to suspect that your protector might be Sidhe, we immediately assumed the tale a ruse to foil your father's plans by spiriting you across the border. I was loudest among that set. When we discovered his identity... well, the shock hardly dispelled that notion. We believed he meant to use you to earn his father's forgiveness."

She would not cry. She *would* not. "He did. All of that is true."

Martin gave her a long look. His eyes held a modicum of pity. "I heard how he fought for you, lass. We all did. That man will have my respect till the day I die, no matter which side we stand on. I'm sorry it came to this pass. Truly, I am."

She hadn't expected his sympathy. "Why are you saying this to me?"

"He's gone now, My Lady. Make do."

She saw Damek's head swivel slightly in her direction. "I will never have him, Martin."

"You loved him once. He fights for you, though you're too self-absorbed to see it now. Many good men died to bring you home. Don't give me that face. Listen, imagine this from our perspective. You are heir to our kingdom and greatly beloved by the people, no matter how you revile them. Your grandmother has kept you locked in a tower for over ten years, and once you were freed, we believed you were kidnapped by a rogue Sidhe agent, then hunted and scourged by your chosen people. We set out to save you, and what do we find? Murderers and cutthroats on your trail, a hive of villains, resolved to sell you for profit, otherworld beasts and nightmares seeking your flesh... and through it all, a man who should have been dead ages ago, seeking to use you for his own gain."

He paused to let the words sink in, deep.

"How are we the villains in your mind? As far as Damek is concerned, he saved your life and your dignity and did so at great personal cost. Your father is frothing at the mouth to disinherit him for disobeying a direct order to march to your rescue, young lady. He has a fight ahead of him you cannot be bothered to conceive of, all because he refused to let you die in the wilderness or be swept over the border, never to return. You have as much to account for as Damek in this, and you know it."

She fell silent for a long while, fuming. She wanted to rail at these accusations, to berate O'Rearden as a ruthless patriarch with little understanding of the world or her situation, but she couldn't. Though lobbed without much insight, his statement rang with more than one note of truth. She stared at the trees around their limping band, her jaw burning. "I never asked any of you to come, and I certainly never wanted anyone to die in pursuit of me. I am no victim, but neither are any of you. Damek knew before he marched that I would reject his help. I didn't want him there, and I don't want to be here now. You don't chain someone you value, do you?"

Here Martin squinted a bit. "You do have a point there, My Lady. However, sometimes to save someone, you must drag them out of harm's way by the hair. In this case, you are right that you never asked for our help, but we determined you owed it all the same. You didn't wish us to intervene on your behalf, but you are alive because Damek fought for you. You might have wished to remain by this Sidhe lordling's side, but you were almost killed many times for that desire. To protect you, we were forced to drag your nearly lifeless body from a horror no Souther has ever seen. I am not saying you should find all of this fair, but you should accept that we have your best interests at heart. We *are not* your enemies, and though you have a right to be angry at Damek for his impulsive youth, you do not have the right to punish him for his affection for you. Reject him as you please, but don't avoid your share of this mess."

"You know why I ran away, damn you."

"Aye, and I never blamed you for it either. Given the events of the last few months and all the unrest in your Grandmother's city, it's time to come home, Una. You have responsibilities that other women, even the nobles in the Cloister, can never match. Your father isn't as evil as you'd paint him, and the future of our kingdom rests with you. If you truly mean to improve the world, how about you start where it would matter most, hm?"

Her ears burned. Upbraided *again*.

She watched the trees slip past her in nondescript uniformity and willed her retort back down her throat. She wouldn't win this debate, and she knew it. He was brushing over many essential details, but neither was he wrong. Damek sent her one searching glance over his shoulder, and she glared back until his neck twisted forward again. He always did have the ears of a bat, damn him. Martin had a point about the men and their sacrifices to save her against her will, but she would be Siora damned if she'd buy any of Martin's drivel about love.

Damek didn't love her. He needed her.

He wanted what she represented more than anything in the world. She knew this better than anyone. Una would never allow him to manipulate her again. Whatever her father had planned, Damek could be certain: she'd never accept him.

"Fine. When my father dies, and I'm Duchess… I wonder how I'll repay your Lord Bishop for his kindness?"

"Una, don't be like that," Martin sighed. "One kind word from you would mend all breaches. If you'd let him, he will be your greatest ally in the trials to come."

She opened her mouth for a stinging rebuke, but Damek's fist popped up, and the company halted to a man. From the thicket on Damek's right side, Una thought she caught the flash of something bright. Martin saw it too. His sabre sang as he slid it from his scabbard. The men, as a unit, followed suit.

"Double cover," said Damek, walking his horse backward to place himself between the woods and Una's mare. His knights drew their shields around her in a semi-circle. Martin's own blade deflected the first arrow. "Killian, Dawes! Bowmen to right rear flank!"

The archers rushed behind Una's knot of protective swords and shields while pikemen hammered their halberds into the earth before them. "What's happening?" She hadn't realized she asked aloud. Damek grasped her mount by the reins.

"Bandits, no doubt. They'll have been informed that a woman matching Una Donahugh's description is among our party," he whispered back, eyes moving furiously. "Our numbers are depleted enough that we appear vulnerable. Your ransom would be their goal."

She groaned. "Damek, untie me."

He glanced sideways at her. "Not a bloody chance, Una."

Motion through the shrubbery ahead was the least of their concerns; they were likely surrounded, as Damek surely knew. The brigands would attack all at once, from all sides. To make a move this bold, there must be dozens of them.

"Untie me! I can help, you arrogant idiot."

He made a face but slipped his dagger out of his vest all the same. "Dawes, if Lady Donahugh attempts to run, you have my permission to break one of her legs."

"My lord." Dawes saluted.

"Lord Bishop," a voice cried from somewhere unseen while Damek sawed into Una's bonds with a meaningful glare. She was unamused. "Surrender the lady, and yer men may leave in peace. Refuse, and every one of ye will die here today."

Damek waved the dagger at her. "I mean it. No tricks."

She took the dagger from him by the blade. "I heard you the first time."

With a wry smirk, Damek cupped his free hand over his mouth. "Come and get her, you lowborn dog!"

Una didn't see what he had to smile about

Then every hell broke loose at once.

⚔ ⚔

DAMEK HAD NEVER BEEN HAPPIER to have someone to kill than he was at that moment. Weeks of frustration bottled up inside him burst forth in bright red spray. Every look, every gesture, every ounce of Una's derision came pouring out of him in a hacking, slicing, gouging surge. Gods, how he hated her. If there had ever been a more selfish cunt in all the world, Damek would never believe her worse than his sweet cousin. A fellow leapt upon his horse from an overhanging tree bough. Damek nearly cut the fool in half. The warm spatter of blood was a soothing bath. Martin roared from the road ahead, taking on three poorly armed bandits at once. Damek spun, slashed, ducked, and sidestepped so many rusty weapons he might believe every peasant in the South had the gall to try for the Duch's daughter.

Well, come one, come all.

He very much needed the distraction. Somewhere further down their line, Una was hard at work defending her honor. He could tell from the resulting horrified screams. Dawes remained close by to hold her back up, but from what Damek saw, she hardly needed his help. Indeed, they'd be in serious trouble if she decided to use her abilities on any of his men. When did she gain such power? Once, Dawes was distracted by multiple assailants, and Damek thought he would guard her back himself. He needn't have been concerned. Wielding his dagger expertly in one hand, she set the other against any flesh that reached for her with divine retribution. He watched two men melt from the inside out before realizing he must stop. What had her grandmother made her? Surely, she was no longer human… what human woman held such a cursed gift? With that shock of white at her temple and the golden gleam in her eyes— she looked like an avenging goddess from the Age of Heroes: the Morrigan herself, lady of death, astride a mountain of corpses.

The longing that kindled in his gut at the sight made his arm work harder. More death. More pain. More vengeance.

More, more, more.

He wasn't sure when he'd run out of things to cut through until Martin found him gasping against a tree, where he ground a bandit's guts to sausage with the point of his sabre. "Reason, Damek! Leave off!" Damek didn't object to being shoved away from his kill. Martin's eyes were round as saucers. "You think he's dead?"

Winded, Damek squinted. "Report?"

"All dead or fled. Most took one look at our lady and sped away screaming. Damek," Martin struggled to articulate his thoughts. "She's…"

"I know."

"Now you're hurting my feelings, Martin." Una stepped over Damek's piled victims, wiping her hands on her soiled skirts. She didn't appear the least winded. Damek almost flinched from her newfound glowing health. Had there ever been a woman this beautiful? Her dark skin, bronze in the dappled sunlight; her wild silken curls, full mauve mouth, and high cheekbones... he longed for more things to kill. "I thought you wanted to know what I studied in the Cloister, Commander?"

Dawes, Damek noted, maintained a respectful distance. None of his men seemed over-eager to approach her again, for that matter. While Martin searched for something to say, Damek cleared his throat. "Dawes, her bonds, please."

Those golden eyes flashed at him, and Damek's blood rushed into his ears. "If he touches me, he will regret it." Dawes shrank away. Damek cursed. Slamming his sabre into the earth, he marched over to retrieve her manacles from his cowardly aide-de-camp. She said nothing as he dragged her to him by the elbow. Brow raised, he lashed her hands together and clicked the irons shut over her wrists. She rolled her eyes at him. "You're welcome?"

Next, he moved to clip one end of her chain to the manacle around her ankle. "Don't be cute, Una. It doesn't suit you."

"I didn't run, did I? This is hardly necessary."

Once her bonds were fixed, Damek tied the other end of her chain to his belt with a vicious jerk. "I will not have you believe that I'm going to forgive you so soon. Fenley, Bors— our mounts, if you please. The rest of you, back in line."

"Forgive *me*? Did you hit your head? What in the *Nine Hells* do you think I owe you, Damek?"

He ignored her, dragging her behind him while he stomped around his bustling men. Martin followed at a sedate, tactful pace. Damek's pulse beat so loudly that he thought Martin probably heard it from a yard away. "Your life, for one."

"As I recall, all of you would be dead now if it weren't for me. The Sluagh would have taken you a man at a time. We're even now, as far as I'm concerned. Untie me already."

She wasn't wrong, but that didn't make him feel better. He wanted to snap her wrists like kindling. He wanted to wring the column of her throat in both hands. He wanted to crush her against him and never let go. He had never hated anyone so much in all his life, not even her father. "Let's get something straight. You are not in control of this situation. I am. You will be given no privileges, and I will hear none of your whimpering."

"Whimpering? You blockheaded son of a whore—"

She planted her feet, which yanked him backward. In a trice, she used her meager bodyweight to fling him to the dirt, arse-first. The next thing he knew, she was on top of him, digging the heels of her hands into the exposed flesh at his chest. Teeth clenched, she held on tight though he should have bucked her easily. His men pooled around them with their weapons drawn, though they clearly struggled between fear and uncertain duty. To which did they truly owe fealty? Even Martin wrestled with this conundrum as Damek and Una rolled around in the dirt like two hissing cats. Una got the upper hand once and nearly dragged Damek's dagger out of his belt, but he pulled her leg from beneath her and crushed her into the soil. Her hand shot out, quick as a snake, and struck him hard enough to make his nose bleed. He swiped the red line against his sleeve and ground his elbow into her chest. Her breath came out in a rush, but her right knee pounded into his kidney.

Throwing his head back on a bellow, he tried to stand, but her temple smashed into his chin, and he howled, "Gods damn it, you little witch! Stop!" He turned aside to hold her down with his flank while he tightened the iron at her wrist. Kicking like a mule, she hooked both arms over his neck and dragged him backward by her manacles. Choking, Damek rammed his head as hard as he could into her nose. Slightly dazed, her grip slipped, and Damek was free to hoist her up and slam her into a nearby trunk.

"Lord Bishop, that's enough!" cried Martin, though he might have been a gust of wind. All Damek could see through the red haze of his vision was Una.

"You're pretty brave with an unarmed, bound woman, Damek," she mocked, straining against her iron bracelets. "Take them off, and then we'll see how you do."

"Fine," Damek decided with sudden inspiration. Nose streaming, he maintained eye contact while removing her restraints. They bounced off his knee and into the dirt with little fanfare. With his free hand, he loosened his collar for her. "Go ahead. I'll give you the first shot."

"Damek, you bloody fool!" growled Martin.

Grinding her canine teeth together, she dug her nails deep into the flesh at his throat. Damek didn't move a muscle. "I'll kill you, you know?"

"I doubt it," Damek smiled. "Go ahead and try, you spoilt, selfish cow. *Do it.*"

Her nostrils flared, but she removed her hand long enough to shove her fist into his eye. Her knee came up, missing his bollocks by an inch as he staggered away, swearing. "No need. Patrick will do it for me, you blithering braggart."

Damek marched toward her with murder blazing from both eyes like a lantern, but Martin's heavier shoulder caught him midstride. "That's plenty, that is. The two of you."

"I will wear no more restraints from today on, Commander O'Rearden," said Una, spitting out a wad of blood. "I will return to Bethany with you, as ordered, so there is no further need for these theatrics. If that strutting peacock comes near me again," she pointed at Damek, who grumbled low in his throat. "You'll have yourselves to blame for his death."

Spine straight as it would go, Una took her reins from Fenley without another word. She remounted and waited at the fork in the road while Damek collected the remnants of his dignity. His men looked anywhere but at him, and he couldn't blame them a whit. Martin watched him reseat himself with a concerned eye. "What in the Kneeler's Hell do you have to grin about, boy?"

"She still loves me."

Martin covered his face with both hands. "Reason help me… why would you imagine such nonsense?"

Dawes passed Damek's sword up to him with an uncomfortable grimace. Damek flashed his teeth as he snapped his blade home. "I gave her the chance, and she didn't take it."

"She didn't kill you, so she has to care for you. Are you mad?"

"She didn't take my life when she had the chance, and after what I've done… not wanting me to die is the same as a confession to me, Martin. Una is as fatalistic as I am and always has been. I'm so bloody relieved right now, the next town we stop at, all the ale and women any of you wants is on me."

The round of cheers he expected did not come to pass. The woods reeked of bloating corpses, but if one were to judge the situation by Damek's grin, they would have reason to be utterly confused.

⚹

FOR THE FIRST TIME IN weeks, Una was allowed the comfort of a bed without restraints. Having bathed and washed her matted hair, she lay down in a clean tunic, a bit sore but blissfully free of roots, damp soil, and the snores of sleeping men. The fire blazed, and her belly was, for once, full of something more substantial than hard-tack and cold tea. Despite these comforts, she could not sleep. Part of her wanted to run downstairs to Damek's quarters and pop his head off like a top, while the other longed to weep herself into oblivion. Perhaps she'd made the wrong decision? Maybe she should take the feeble trust she'd earned by not killing the idiot Lord of Clare and climb out that window to her freedom, after all? It would take some time, but she could make it back to Rosweal before the heavy Dor Cromna snows. Once the roads became impassable, she'd have to wait until spring to find out whether or not Damek's claim held any truth. She couldn't imagine Kaer Yin dying so easily after all that they had been through together, all that she'd seen him survive.

He couldn't be dead. He *couldn't* be.

Why would Siora open her heart this way, only to rip it from her chest so soon? Surely the Ancestor could never be so cruel?

Now that she was alone, she couldn't stem the flow of her tears. Great racking sobs had soaked her bedding clean through by the time she collapsed atop them, spent. Hours later, her mind offered no ease, and she still could not sleep. Rian? What had happened to her? Did she linger in Rosweal, alone and afraid in a strange, hostile place? Would that horrid old bawd try to sell her again, now that Una and Kaer Yin were no longer there to keep her safe? What happened to the townsfolk after Samhain? How had they come down the mountain in one piece?

Not knowing was the most onerous burden to bear.

Kaer Yin's face flashed in her mind, in repose, blood spattering his fair cheeks. She could never forget the look in his eyes as her lips came away from his that terrible night as if she'd told him a secret he'd never imagined possible before. She would hold that image in her heart and pray every day that he made it home to mend ties with his father. He would live inside her now, if nowhere else.

He must. She owed him that much, at least.

A thud against her door forced her upright. Damek, battered from the fight earlier but otherwise clean, entered with a lantern and a small tray of something hot and peaty poised atop it. He did not smile, nor did he sneer. His features might have been carved of stone. He took a seat between her and the fire without asking. She wiped her nose and looked away.

"Why are you crying?"

"None of your business."

She heard his plodding, indrawn breath. "For Kaer Yin Adair?"

"For many things lost to me now."

He was silent for quite a while. She heard his Adam's apple bob in his throat, his hard exhale. "It will get easier, Una."

"I don't want to hear that from you."

"Why not? It's true."

She turned, unable to blink fast enough. "Why are you here? To gloat? To fight? I am in the mood for neither."

"To tell you that I'm sorry. For everything."

She almost forgot to breathe. "How *dare* you?"

He did not flinch from the fury in her eyes. "Again, it's the truth."

"You unbelievable bastard," she laughed. The sound held very little mirth. "Did you think this would make me forgive you, huh? Meaningless words? Or perhaps you thought you'd come up here and I'd welcome you into this bed? You're dreaming either way."

He leaned forward so she couldn't escape the cold sincerity in his gaze. "You came to me of your own accord, and I made love to you, my *wife*."

"*Get out.*"

"Not until you listen to sense. I'm the greatest ally you're going to have, Una. Wield me as you see fit. I will make no complaint. I owe you that."

"I'm going to kill you if you don't leave."

"No, you won't."

Her head swiveled round. "Are you daring me?"

His eyes were huge and liquid dark in the firelight. "Begging you. If you can't forgive me, then use me. I mean it. Do you know what he has planned?"

"Of course, I do. I'll be a first-rate prize for the highest bidder… or three."

His fists clenched and unclenched. He licked his lips. "He's discovered our uncle had two boys. They are, even now, awaiting our return. He will use you as a lure for rich war enthusiasts while he pits our newfound cousins and me against one another. This will be purely for his amusement, and you will never have a say in it."

"And you can stop him?"

"I can stop them all. If you'll trust me?"

She tucked herself into bed again, facing the window and away from him. "I've heard you. Now, leave."

He fought to get to his feet without retort. Una could tell from his breathing. She refused to look at him again. "Una… what… happened to our daughter?"

She felt like her insides were suddenly screaming. She tried and failed to keep the waver out of her voice. "Damek, if you don't leave this room right now, I *will* kill you."

She didn't notice when the door shut behind him, for the burning hole in her chest.

THICKER THAN BLOOD

How long d'you think it's been, Aoife?" Gan's breathy trill issued from somewhere in the dark. Aoife could just make out the hint of his prone form, where he lay in the farthest corner of their spartan cell. He was wrapped head-to-toe in stained linens and reeked of spoiled medicinal salve. He'd never be whole again, considering most of the flesh and fat had been melted from his bones, but he might heal someday. He'd be even more revolting to look at than he had been before, but he would live, which annoyed Aoife more than her aching scabs.

"Stop asking, damn you," she spat. "Why Nema didn't see fit to remove *your* tongue instead of Alvra's, I'll never understand."

He issued a rasping cough that might have been a laugh. "She spared both of us. That's something."

Aoife stopped scratching at her throat long enough to snort in his general direction. Her wounds were terrible, to be sure, but she would heal, given time and effort. Being half-Bolg sometimes had its benefits. However, the maddening itch she'd developed in the meantime was its own hell. "Gan, you nonce, she *did not* spare us. Only a spoilt, selfish, simpleton like yourself could even dream such a stupid thing."

He was blissfully quiet for some time, pondering the leaking ceiling over his cot as he was wont to do for most of each day. Aoife mostly filled the cacophonous silence with scratching. "She'll kill us eventually, then?"

"Of course. Once we've served whatever purpose she intends for us, yeah." Gnashing her teeth, she strained for a particularly hard-to-reach spot. "You'll go long before me, I'm afraid. She'll wait until you've debased yourself by every conceivable standard, then save your death for the moment you believe its possibility has long passed. I've seen it happen many times."

He didn't respond immediately, but when he next spoke, his voice lacked any trace of the old fear. "Good, then it will be the sweeter to disappoint her on that score. Aoife? You want to kill me, don't you?"

That gave her pause. Her leg shackles rattled as she sat up. "I'm not going to steal Nema's prey, Gan. Though, I admit, I've often longed to."

"How old are you?"

She couldn't recall anyone ever having asked her such a question before. She stammered a response, "O-one hundred and sixty, or thereabouts."

"For how many of those years have you served Vanna Nema?"

This line of inquiry was getting a bit intolerable. "That's—"

"None of my business, right? Do you know how long I've served her?"

"Forty years, give or take?"

"Yes. Nearly the whole of my life. You've quadrupled my record if you're one hundred and sixty years old. Is that not fair to say?"

She stared at his dim white outline. "Yes, it is."

"We've both become terrible in her service. Haven't we? I, a degenerate popinjay, and you, a vicious henchwoman who loathes the wide world, perhaps only slightly less than you loathe yourself."

A hot tear ran down her cracked cheek. "*Shut up.*"

"Aren't you tired, Aoife? I know I am. I won't live near as long as you might, yet forty years in blind obeisance to that beast is quite long enough. You won't have to do it yourself. You might hand me that broken bit of grating dangling from the window there, and I'll—"

"*No.* Stop sniveling."

Again, the silence stretched long in their dank hole in the Citadel's deepest bowels. One would expect to hear the ravings of fellow prisoners, guards' gruff admonishments, or at least footsteps and clanking metal. Here, however, it seemed Nema had tossed her former favorites in an oubliette so far removed from every living thing a whale might have swallowed them. Aoife knew this sojourn couldn't last. Nema had a purpose for them that was sure to be far from pleasant. Her grandmother might have spared their lives, but they were hardly forgiven.

"Don't you want to be free?"

Of course, she did. She'd never wanted anything so much in all of her life. To have her *geis* broken was her tiny black heart's fondest, deepest wish. There'd been a moment when she'd lain on the cold flagstones outside when she thought it was finally over. Aoife wasn't sure what she hated Nema for most: holding her *geis* and forcing her to poison, manipulate, corrupt, and kill in her name; or that Nema hadn't let her die when she'd had the chance? Aoife had been ready to die for most of her miserable life. Not that she'd share such information with a traitorous pervert like Gan. Be that as it may, as much as she loathed him, he did look tiny and pathetic in his cot.

Surely, he hadn't always been an opportunistic ferret, any more than she'd always been a hateful, murderous minion? They were each as circumstance has made them: useful, bitter, and cruel.

"If you would hold my head down, I think I could swallow my tongue," Gan wept.

Aoife exhaled slowly. She didn't want to feel sorry for Fawa Gan. He didn't deserve anyone's sympathy any more than she did. "If I did, Nema will take her revenge through any or all of your remaining family. You know this, Fawa," her tone was softer than she'd expected. "She won't be deprived of her toys. Why did you betray her in the first place? I know you loved her. No point denying that now."

"Eva Alvra discovered my… arrangements with the Third Floor stewardess and reported me to the Doma. If I hadn't informed on our mistress, Drem would have fed my family's Patent of Maternas to the fire and had them all shipped to the Colonies. After she had my bollocks sewn into my mouth, of course."

"Point's moot now, isn't it?" scoffed Aoife. Gan's family had been decimated in the Reformist Purge. Now his mother and two sisters yet lived, and both were bound for indenture in Swansea. They would live short, terribly hard lives gathering Sulphur in the Wastes. "You should have told Nema what you were up to years ago. You might have escaped with a reprimand. Now, look at you."

"You're not in much better straits, yourself."

"No, but I'll heal. Well, eventually, anyway. She counted on that, I'm sure."

"I'm sorry, Aoife."

She flinched as if he'd struck her. "*What?*"

"I wonder what sort of girl you were before she dug her teeth into you?"

Aoife would *not* weep. Not in front of Fawa fucking Gan. "I've always been this way. Your problem, Fawa, is that you can't help assigning desires to each person you meet. This one wants something forbidden that one craves the success of others, and on and on you run. Me? I want one thing alone, and it isn't something you can rub your greasy palms together and profit from. In this, you are powerless as I am. I'm compelled to serve, so I serve. That is all. You'd be better off seducing the wall to your side."

"She'll burn Innisfail to bedrock, Aoife. She means to kill every man, woman, and child in Eire."

"I know."

"Faeries, too."

"I *know.*"

"How can you accept that?"

"Because I have no choice. Free will is a luxury, Fawa."

"I could never face this with your calm. How you can consent to such a terrible fate."

Aoife leaned her head against the damp wall, watching a tiny sliver of light creep across the roughhewn ceiling. "Because nothing truly lasts forever."

⚷

Fawa was removed in the night. Where to, Aoife had no idea. His screams pealed through the labyrinthine halls for hours, it seemed. Sometime later, when Aoife's heart had stopped pounding enough for her to get some sleep, they came for her as well. Unlike Gan, Aoife wasn't afraid. If Nema had meant to kill her, she would have let her burn. Now it would merely be a matter of punishment, and frankly, Nema grew less enthusiastic for torture with time. Aoife could bear whatever Nema threw at her.

She'd had lifetimes of practice, after all.

She was led through narrow, close passages by either arm. Limp as a wet leaf; she didn't bother to struggle—no bloody point. Aoife refused to fear. She wouldn't give the ancient bitch the satisfaction. Once you've been roasted from the inside out, nothing much could compare. Up endless flights of stairs, through myriad nondescript halls, and over countless thresholds lit by dusty, flickering sconces, she was dragged into a room constructed of nothing but pure, uncut onyx and flung against the slick, polished floor. Aoife knew where she was, even if she'd never set eyes on Drem's throne room. She scrabbled upward, ignoring the pain. Any move she made opened a partially healed sore. The Doma's throne was a magnificent architectural marvel. Every square inch gleamed with dark magnetism, unadorned and opaque as a starless night. She felt consumed by its dark grandeur. She supposed the woman in yellow at the far end of that ocean of ink was meant to appear as if she were suspended in the pupil of some cosmic beast.

Siora's Eye, indeed, Aoife thought.

Nema reclined in the center of that seamless hunk of obsidian, plucking at the edges of an open map and smiling at her. Off to the side, dwarfed by the mammoth throne, sat a younger woman cloaked in the unassuming grey robes of a newly minted Secunda.

Grainne.

Aoife had almost missed her. She wrinkled what was left of her nose.

If that bitch is here, something is happening.

Grainne dipped her head to the slightest possible degree. "Aoife Mac Sionnovar."

Aoife sketched a mocking bow. "*Bhean Tiarne.*"

Grainne made a rude sound and tossed her lustrous braid, her violet eyes dismissive. "Pleasant as always, *isasdeligh.*"

"I'm sure you can see it's been a rough fortnight, cousin."

Grainne *did* see. She failed to limit the horror in her expression. "Balor, *seanmatháir*, what did she do to deserve this?"

"She let Drem's little abomination escape to the South, unscathed," answered Nema dryly.

"Perhaps 'unscathed' is too mild a term for kidnap and unlawful incarceration? There's a future rape in there somewhere too, let's not forget," replied Aoife, without a shred of irony.

"Those blessings are owed to my grandson's efforts, stupid girl. Not your own," Nema snapped, folding the map and passing it back to Grainne. "She'll be ready. She doesn't need to be beautiful to be useful."

Grainne frowned at Aoife as if she were a prized mare suddenly afflicted with mange. "I don't know that I agree, *seanmatháir*. *Deartháir* has given me this task in the strictest confidence. I must not fail him on account of one mad faerie."

"Now, now. We're blood-related, princess. Let's not be rude." Aoife brandished her perfect teeth. Hoping the effect earned the discomfort she was aiming for. When Grainne shivered, Aoife chuckled and turned her eye on Nema. "Your Eminence, why am I here? For what dread purpose did you spare my life?"

311

Nema was wise enough to know that Aoife had been pushed as far as she would allow. They had a long, long history together, hadn't they? "I mean for you to aid your cousin in the Midlands."

"In what capacity?"

"Whatever I bloody well require, you insolent bitch!" snapped Grainne.

Nema raised a hand, and she stilled. In all the Mac Nemed Clan, only Aoife had the bollocks or license to speak out of turn to Nema. What else could Nema do to her that hadn't already been done? Soft, *precious* Grainne would never know. Would she? "Child, you are my best soldier. I want to grant you the opportunity to prove yourself worthy of my service again."

Aoife's opinion of that was plain. "Who am I to kill for you now, old woman?"

Grainne sucked down a breath, but Nema clenched her fingers, and her voice evaporated. Nema's eyes glittered a fierce emerald. "I'll allow your acerbic attitude, Aoife… though you know I won't forget it. Now, don't you have anything else to say?"

Aoife attempted a mock curtsy. "Congratulations on your new office, My Lady."

Nema frowned at Aoife's disrespectful tone and clapped her hands. A handful of Fir Bolg Warhammers entered the chamber from a hidden door concealed along a glossy black wall. However, they weren't wearing the typical black cuirasses stamped with the Red Bull of Armagh. They wore the white and silver cuirasses of An Fiach Fian: The Wild Hunt of the Tuatha De Dannan. They were dressed as the Ard Ri's guards.

Ah, mused Aoife with a grim smile.

So that's to be the game this time, is it?

"You'd better not let me down again, girl. You are sorely mistaken if you've convinced yourself that nothing worse could happen to you."

Aoife knew better.

There was very little left that the Dowager Queen of Armagh could threaten her with now. Every pain, every fear, every loss, every ounce of despair; Aoife had lived through them, time and again. A queer sort of furious hope kindled anew in her duplicitous breast. She would beat Nema yet. She would simply outlast her.

"As you command, Eminence," said Aoife, pressing her fist into her blistered chest with perfectly feigned obedience.

The Erstwhile Prince

"You're rushing this." Tam Lin shook his head at his cousin through the glass. Shar was busy helping Kaer Yin shove his feet into his boots, and neither flinched at Tam Lin's complaint. They'd both heard it more than once today already. "I received my father's orders only yesterday, I might add. I'm in no great hurry to disobey him. It wouldn't be the first time he's banished me to the Oiche Ar Fad for listening to one of your rash schemes."

Kaer Yin finally glanced up; his face nearly healed save for a few yellow bruises. "They were always *your* rash schemes, Tam Lin, and your father never minded when you behaved like a boorish fool. You two are one of a kind. No, it is *my* father you're referring to and *my* frequent banishment for not discouraging you from being yourself."

Tam Lin pursed his lips. "That's not how I remember it at all."

"*Pft.* As you say. Anyway, how many men is he sending to Rosweal?"

"Two hundred."

"So few?"

Tam Lin shrugged. "I think they're meant to keep you here until the Ard Ri decides what to do with you, and of course, Diarmid will have filled his ears with your tomfool plan to raid the South. I'm telling you, this is a terrible idea. There are better ways to handle this."

Upright and fully dressed for once, Kaer Yin *did* look a lot better, but that hardly meant the idiot was fully healed and ready to march on the Souther capital. "I'm all ears when you come up with one, cousin. Hand me my swordbelt, will you?"

Tam Lin passed *Nemain* over with an intense frown. "No woman is worth dying for, you horse's ass. I don't care if her teats leak honey and she can crack a man's spine with her thighs. She's Donahugh's own daughter. Let it go."

Kaer Yin said nothing but clapped him on the shoulder on his way past. Shar shrugged, and Tam Lin rolled his eyes as he followed him downstairs. The semi-renovated *Hart and Hare* was filled top to tail with exhausted, worn-down Roswellians and their elegant Sidhe counterparts in their white and silver cuirasses. The madam leaned over the bar, nursing a dram of skinny Colm's newest batch of uishge. Tam Lin's mouth watered at the sight. There had been a decided deficit of spirits in the last week since Robin ordered Gilcannon's remaining stores cellared. Tam Lin doubted this batch would live up to the standard, but he wouldn't mind the effort in the least. Ale and cider simply wouldn't do any longer.

Robin caught Tam Lin's grim expression over Kaer Yin's head and sniggered. He, too, rolled his shoulder as if to say, 'Well, I told ye.' Why did it seem that only Robin and Mistress Dormer had any bloody sense? This stupid Souther girl was going to get his cousin killed, and for what? Love? Fat load of twaddle, that. "Thousands of gorgeous Sidhe women await your triumphant return to Bri Leith, Yin. Did she cast a spell on you? What?"

Kaer Yin shook hands with a few well-wishers and pulled Gerrod in for a brief embrace. The lad winced at Tam Lin's scowl. "Och. What's that all about then?" Gerrod asked Kaer Yin.

"Wants to know for the thousandth time: why Una?"

"Oh," said Gerrod. "Well, me and Robin think it's cuz she scares him."

"That is not even funny," groaned Tam Lin. "She'd better be the most beautiful woman in the world, who lays golden eggs, and whose tears heal the bloody sick."

Gerrod couldn't stave a laugh. Vince, who was busy wiping tables nearby, shivered in agreement. "Well, I dunno about 'most' beautiful, but she's the prettiest I've ever seen, 'cept for one, that is." Gerrod flushed around his freckles. "I 'spose I don't have much basis for comparin'."

"No, you do not. In Aes Sidhe, there are women so beautiful; a single glance could freeze a man in place for a whole year."

"That sounds nice."

Tam Lin pulled him close, giving Kaer Yin a pointed look. "Know the worst part of that? They're all in love with this ungrateful wretch. When he was banished, hundreds cut their hair in mourning."

"Did they, Ben?" Gerrod's eyes were very round.

"How would I know?" He answered, stepping aside for Rian to hobble by. As she passed, she gave Gerrod a small pat, and Tam Lin instantly recognized who Gerrod's 'one' had to be.

Ah, young fools, he thought.

"Have you eaten?" Kaer Yin asked Rian with a sigh. She held up an apple and sank onto the stool Dabney held for her. Kaer Yin grumbled something about 'real food' and 'idiot waifs.'

Tam Lin squinted at her. "Let's hear it from a woman then. *Oi*, Mistress Nursemaid. What makes this Una person worth so much trouble?"

She didn't turn around. "Ask your cousin."

"I did. Now I'm asking you."

"I imagine someone like you will never understand the answer to that question."

"What's that supposed to mean, then?"

Kaer Yin replied, "I think she's intimating that you have the emotional depth of a gnat, dearest cousin."

Gerrod's answering giggle earned him one of Tam Lin O'Ruiadh's finest scowls. The lad shrank into Rian's side. She sliced her apple into quarters with her belt knife and handed the scrawny boy half of them. Tam Lin couldn't halt a scowl. Kaer Yin noticed. He gave Tam Lin a smile that annoyed him very much. "Well, perhaps not? Anyway, Barb, my love, are we ready?"

"As ever, Ben."

"Good. Help us over to that stool, will ya, Dabs?"

Dabney's outrageous girth shook the glass behind the bar with every step. Tam Lin leaned against the corner of the bar with Robin, taking sips of a moderately decent first batch and glaring at the back of Rian's flaxen head. The cheeky wench. Never had a kind word for him. Not one. If Tam Lin had a mind to, he could make her life miserable. Perhaps, he should take her back to Croghan and force her to serve as his stewardess? He highly doubted she could maintain such priggishness when forced to help him bathe and dress daily.

It would serve her right.

Tam Lin dragged his eyes away from her hunched frame to watch Kaer Yin limp to his fate. He managed to stumble onto a chair before the fireplace, thanks to Dabney and his massive arms. Kaer Yin slapped his shoulder, but Tam Lin doubted the lug even felt it.

"Hello there, everyone. Thanks for coming."

Tam Lin's eyes rolled back so hard that he feared he might bruise his brain. A sea of dirty faces stared up at the Prince of Innisfail with mild disinterest and not a little humor. Already, tiny beads of sweat formed over Kaer Yin's brow, though he put a good grin on it. Tam Lin hoped this fiasco ended quickly; the moron had no business being out of bed so fast. Tam Lin swung his glare back to the bar, hoping this irritating faerie girl would acknowledge her lack of foresight, but her head lay against her arms, her fair hair pooled around her like a shawl. Mistress Dormer gave him a saucy wink, patted the girl's slender arm, and returned to her pipe and uishge. Gerrod hadn't seen a thing. He was too busy giggling with that stringy Vincent character. Tam Lin wasn't sure why the damned girl had to be drugged to sleep at night.

There were more capable adults in Rosweal, weren't there? Why should she fantasize that the wide world needed her particular attention, every moment of every day?

There was something wrong with her. *That* was plain.

"Well," said Kaer Yin with a stupid smile. "Guess you've figured out my name isn't Ben Maeden?"

"Ye don't say, ye sneaky cunt!" shouted Barb, raising her tankard for the crowd's praise.

Kaer Yin took his jeers with an affable grin. "I suppose it takes one to know one, Barb."

Barb sketched a courtly bow, and the crowd roared.

Milesians, Tam Lin thought, shaking his head.

At least Kaer Yin understood them because he didn't.

"My name," boomed Kaer Yin. "Is Kaer Yin Mac Midhir Adair. First Prince of the Tuatha De Dannan; Lord Marshal of the Wild Hunt, High Commander of the Daoine Sidhe, and Champion of Bri Leith. I am Lord of Meath, Dowth, Knowth, Munster, and Mann, Crown Prince of Innisfail, and heir to the Ard Ri's throne. Any questions before we move on?"

Tam Lin scanned the suddenly silent room waiting for the outcry, or at the very least, a well-earned round of boos for that atrocious introduction. Nothing. It went so quiet; Tam Lin could hear the heartbeat of the fellow nearest him. After an uncomfortable eternity, a young man stepped away from the windows. "Does tha' mean the future High King owes me twenty coppers for booze and four hands o'stacked porter?"

The Hart filled with a deafening bevy of 'oohs.' Kaer Yin, casual as a tinker, scratched the scalp above his ear with a sky-high brow. "I think you'll find I cleared the debt with your wife, Dan."

The laughter shook the rafters overhead. Kaer Yin, mimicking Barb, raised his glass and shared a bow with the erstwhile Dan. Tam Lin couldn't believe what he was seeing.

Kaer Yin was one of them.

Rosweal, a town of poachers, thieves, cutthroats, and whores of every stripe, had claimed the Crown Prince of Innisfail as one of their own. What's more, they bloody well loved him, too. Who could have guessed such a thing was possible after Dumnain? Then… most of these men and women weren't old enough to recall the events of that day, were they?

"All right!" shouted Kaer Yin over the din. "Now that's all cleared up, does anyone have anything they want to get off their chest?"

"Nah," said a faceless voice in the crowd. "Me mam's got stew on. Wrap it up, ye ponce."

"He's too bloody pretty to fight now. Be like breakin' fine porcelain," agreed an old woman at the back.

"In that case, so much for the fine speech, I didn't have. Anyway, who wants to come kill some more of the Duch's men with me…?"

⚜

THAT NIGHT, WHILE THE BOYS and Barb pored over maps and strong uishge, Rian appeared at Tam Lin's elbow, yawning but alert. Tam Lin couldn't be sure, but she seemed to be building a particular tolerance for Barb's sleeping draughts. From the perplexed scowl he glimpsed on Barb's face, the old bawd seemed to think so, too. Tearing his attention away from the map he and Robin were perusing, Tam Lin scowled at her. "No."

The hollows under Rian's eyes made her look like a half-starved owl. "I haven't even said anything yet."

"I know what you would ask, and I'm telling you: don't waste your breath."

She bristled; a high-burnished rose bloomed on each cheek. "I'm *not* asking, though if I were, it wouldn't be your permission I'd be interested in," she retorted, sweet as pie.

Across the table, Kaer Yin looked up from a worn bit of parchment. "What's this, then?"

Rian raised her chin. "I'm going with you."

Kaer Yin laughed in her face. "Not a chance."

Her nostrils flared. Tam Lin thought he'd seen a similar look on a cat once or twice before. "Oh no? You owe me, Ben Maeden."

"That's not—" Shar attempted, but the glare she set on him stopped his statement cold.

"I prefer Ben, thank you very much."

Kaer Yin sighed and leaned back in his chair. "Why would you *want* to come, Rian? We're going to fight, not make pleasantries."

She tilted her chin at him. Tam Lin stifled a chuckle. "We just went through a fight, remember? You can barely climb the stairs alone, Ben. You're going to need me. Besides, I owe her my life, same as you lot."

Kaer Yin struggled with a response. After a few tense moments below her glare, he squirmed in his seat. "We can't take you with us. You'd be a liability. I'm sorry."

Twisting her mouth, her attention snapped back to Shar. Shar, always weak around women and horses, sat up straighter. "May I borrow your dagger?" With a moon-calf grin on his stupid face, Shar passed her his long dirk. Tam Lin made sure there could be no mistaking the intensity of his scowl. Shar shifted in his seat.

A headstrong, impertinent faerie wench was this Rian Guinness.

Tucking the blade into the sash at her waistband, Rian smiled. "There, now I'm armed. Feel better?"

"Do ye even know how to use that thing?" asked Robin, whose legs were stretched across the chair in front of her.

She speared him with a bit of side-eye. "Funny, you didn't ask me that when I used one to cauterize wounds, remove splinters, or dig arrow tips out of dozens of your men. Did you?"

Robin sputtered, "No, I… Ben, yer gonna lose this one."

Kaer Yin groaned. "I'm aware. Fine. Have it your way, Rian."

Tam Lin's head swiveled around. "You can't be serious. She's a— well…." He didn't like to insult her, but a limping, sarcastic, lightweight female wasn't going to march into Bethany and take the Doma's heir back, and she wasn't going to swing a sword in anyone's defense either. The road south was undoubtedly not going to be a leisurely affair. They couldn't afford to worry about how it would affect her. Rian shook her head as if she expected his comment.

"What do you think is going to happen to your neat little plan if His Highness here," she jerked her thumb at Yin, "falls face-first into the dirt as soon as someone bumps into him, hm? I'm the least of your concerns right now." She turned back to Kaer Yin. "You shouldn't even be out of bed. You go, I go."

Tam Lin wagged a finger at her. "I warned you not to fall in love with him, didn't I? He's fine, woman. Leave him be."

She shot Tam Lin a withering stare that would have made him flush were he a weaker man. Instead, he found himself decidedly uncomfortable in his own seat. "Listen, Ben's my patient, and since I'm the single healer available to treat him— and since he's the Crown Prince of Innisfail— someone ought to be keeping him alive, don't you think?"

"'*He*' has already agreed to let you come," Kaer Yin added for posterity. "Truce, you two. You're giving me a bloody headache."

"Not sure why ye have so many fierce lasses circlin' round ye, Ben, but I can't say as I envy ye." Robin shivered. Barb reached over and slapped his boot.

She cackled. "Mind yer mouth. I like this one just fine."

"You would," Robin chuckled.

Tam Lin ignored them. He decided he liked this sharp-eyed faerie less and less. What Milesian woman in her right mind would *dare* to speak to him the way she often did? None, damn it all. He found himself grinding his molars to dust. "My idiot cousin will live, Mistress. He'll heal faster than your average patient, I think. I cannot spare the men to keep you safe, and I refuse to claim responsibility for you."

"*Responsibility for me?*" The air in the room chilled by half-a-thousand degrees. Without ado, Rian leaned over and lightly punched Kaer Yin in the chest. His face bleached white as herringbone and his head dropped onto the table with a resounding 'thwack.' His whimpering, pathetic attempts to suck air into his lungs made Tam Lin's fists clench. "I rest my case, *Your Highness.*" She kicked Robin's feet out of the way and leaned over Kaer Yin with a gooey pellet of something that stank of willow bark and nettles. Kaer Yin gasped when she shoved the offensive little missile down his gullet.

His eyes burned with betrayal most foul.

Tam Lin cursed aloud.

You were outdone by this slip of a girl, again.

"Fine! You'll haul your own gear, ask no questions, and remain well out of my sight, Mistress Guinness. I'll not risk a single man for your comfort."

She patted Kaer Yin on the back. "I'm Eirean, remember? I don't need to beg your leave to travel where I will."

"I am the—"

"You've said. Welcome to Eire, Your Highness. I don't think you're going to like it much."

Barb eyed Rian with a new appreciation. Robin visibly repressed a guffaw, and Shar found something fascinating to ogle on the ceiling. Barb pushed a chair toward Rian with an ear-splitting grin. "That was well done, girl."

"I beg your pardon?" Tam Lin hissed from his defeated corner of the table. For the first time in his life, he felt there were too many bloody females in his presence. Barb shot him a bit of a sneer. He *did not* like Eire in the least now that he thought about it. A shame, for he was growing inordinately fond of Eirean uishge, if not her women.

"Take a seat and help me explain to these fools that Bethany ain't some backwater. The Prince o'Connaught and his two companions here haven't set eyes on the South for eons." Barb said around her pipe.

Rian took the proffered seat, mindful of the murderous glow rapidly coloring Kaer Yin's face. Sniffing, she tactfully folded her hands over her knees. "I've only been once or twice, but I'll never forget it. It's not as large as Tairngare, but it's better built. Every building is made of stone and laid out in a grid, not smashed together around the palace, like the markets around the Citadel. Streets are paved with cobbles or flagstones, and even the stables have tiled rooftops. Tairngare might be grander to look at from a distance, but Bethany is cleaner and more orderly. I remember the guards on the walls. Hundreds of armed knights walked back and forth, day and night. I don't think you'll be able to march in."

"I thought Tairngare was the best-guarded city in Eire?" Asked Shar, who flushed for his question. "One never hears of Bethany boasting better fortifications."

"That isn't strictly true," wheezed Kaer Yin, rubbing his chest. "Tairngare is larger and more impressive for its wealth and population density, but if we compare the two based strictly upon their defenses, Bethany has always had the upper hand. Tairngare is huge but jumbled; buildings stacked one on top of the other to accommodate its populace. It's hard to say if the South boasts more soldiers or stone."

"Wonderful," grumbled Tam Lin to himself.

"Bethany's well-built and well-guarded, that's true," offered Robin. "But that ain't to say she don't have her soft spots. Getting in won't be the trouble; it'll be getting out."

Tam Lin raised his brows at Kaer Yin. "I told you. Two hundred Blood Eagles aren't going to fight their way in and out of a stone fortress, Kaer Yin. Meanwhile, Aes Sidhe will remain unguarded for far too long with the bulk of us down south. We should go home. I said I would help and will, but we need reinforcements."

Kaer Yin straightened. "No."

"Yin—"

"She's only in this position because of me. She traded herself for me, for all of us. I refuse to let her suffer for that choice."

"Perhaps, it's best if we wait it out, Ben? A shame about the girl, but I don't see what good a handful of men would be against the Duch's twenty-thousand retainers. D'ye?" said Robin.

"Who said anything about a fight?" Barb tsked at Robin and stole his map. "Here," she pointed at a cluster of boxes labeled the 'Pleasure District.' "Tunnels from the Lee lead straight into the sewers, and from there the cellars of several skin-shops down the posh end o'the city. My Da made his coin smugglin' spirits and furs 'neath Duch Michael's long nose."

"They might have closed up them tunnels, love." Robin scratched his chin.

She shook her head. "Nah. Got Gilcannon's contracts now, don't I? He had a special relationship with *The Butterfly*'s proprietor. Now seems as good a time as any to let them know they've got a new supplier."

"You're sure of this? I'd hate to get overly enthused about this plan just to have a Corpsman's spear shoved up my arse for the trouble." Kaer Yin said, visibly intrigued.

"Funny ye should mention it, but that's the sort o'play one might seek at *The Butterfly*. When I was a grand dame, once upon a time, they kept very the rarest sorts o'entertainment in Bethany. So rare, none but the gentry could afford them." Barb cleared her throat suggestively, tapping another block of scribbles a half-inch to her right. "Gentry never want anyone to know what they get up to at night. In Michael's time, there was a passage leadin' from the Northern Gatehouse to a stairwell below the Pleasure District. Since I'm no fool, I'd argue things ain't likely changed much. Ye've been runnin' our ale back and forth to Ten Bells all these years, Robin. Ye've never smuggled the odd cask into the Machine City?"

"Sure, but never dealt with any o'the bastards at *The Butterfly*."

"Why's that?" asked Rian.

Robin squirmed under her narrow eye. "Well, ah… same reason we didn't deal with Gilcannon's *Black Corset*. Don't approve of 'em, as it were."

Her nose wrinkled. "I see."

Tam Lin didn't. "What's this mean, then?"

His cousin let out a long sigh. "*The Butterfly* caters to pederasts."

"*Tá morghanna beithigh…*"[5] hissed Tam Lin.

"Indeed," agreed Kaer Yin. "Many are."

For the first time, Rian didn't look at him like his breath soured the air. He ignored her. "Are you implying we're to creep in and out of the city through this *Butterfly*'s cellars?"

"Smartest plan I can conceive. Lots o' nobles and wealthy merchers in there, keepin' their heads down. I daresay, if ye grease the proprietor's palm well enough, no one will bat an eye at any o'ye if yer careful."

"Anyone have a better plan?" Kaer Yin looked at each of them in turn.

"Aside from abandoning this scheme altogether," snarked Tam Lin, "no."

Kaer Yin spared him a warning glare. "All right then. Barb's plan seems the best we've come up with so far. Now, for the hard part. Provided we can smuggle ourselves into the city, how do we get inside the castle and get Una out again?"

"Disguises, definitely," noted Robin. Might scare up some Corpsmen's tunics or somethin' like that?"

Rian leaned forward. "Why disguise yourselves at all?"

Scowling, Tam Lin disregarded her entirely. They all did. "Well, sneaking in through sewers and cramped cellars will be one thing. Leaving the brothel as noblemen and sneaking into the keep will be another. I assume your girl will be locked up tight or under heavy guard. As Robin said, getting in won't be the problem."

"Aye, we need someone on the inside to—"

"I *asked*, why would you disguise yourselves at all?" Rian raised her voice.

"What are you on about now?" Tam Lin growled.

---

[5] 'Mortals are beasts.'

She inhaled. "Seems to me the Duch is going to wave Una under the nose of every Eirean lord he can in hopes of attracting men and fainne to his banner. I imagine he'll advertise a contest or some ridiculous patriarchal ritual for her hand. The Princess of Bethany *and* the Domina of the Moura Clan will be a handsome prospect for any ambitious nobles with fainne and influence."

Kaer Yin's smile was slow but beatific. "Rian, you're a bloody genius."

"Aye," grinned Barb. "She is that."

Tam Lin coughed. "Yin, I know you're not stupid enough to believe you can play suitor to the great-granddaughter of Kevin Donahugh, a man you're infamous for murdering. They'll shoot you on sight and declare war on Aes Sidhe for your gall."

Kaer Yin's grin got on Tam Lin's nerves. "You're right. *I'm* not that stupid."

"Oh," Robin threw back his head and laughed. "That's bloody brilliant, that is!"

"If you're not going to play the suitor, who should?"

"Ben's not the only Dannan noble in the room, is he?" said Rian.

It took a minute, but Tam Lin's neck flared hot. "*No.* No bloody *way* will I agree to this. It's daft."

"Think about it. Donahugh hasn't advertised that he means to go to war with Aes Sidhe. We are the only ones who know what he's got stuck up his sleeve. A tourney or series of feasts to promote his newly returned daughter's hand will surely attract a horde of suitors from all over Eire and points beyond. Why *wouldn't* a Sidhe noble answer that call? You're our liege lords, aren't you? No matter Patrick's true intentions, he'd be mad to reject your suit outright."

Every pair of eyes in the room rested on Tam Lin with renewed vigor. He didn't like it one bit. "No. You're all barking."

"It's a great idea," prodded Kaer Yin. "We'll be granted rooms within the interior keep, and you'll be feasted and fêted upon Donahugh's dais. He'll have no choice. Your father is a king. It'll gnaw his guts to splinters, but he wouldn't need Una if he were ready to declare war outright. Admit it, Lin. It's the perfect plan."

After several moments of fruitless, silent pleading, Tam Lin crossed his arms over his chest. "Fine. But since I'm to woo your girl publicly, you'll have yourself to blame when she decides she prefers me."

Kaer Yin gave a short bark of laughter. "Good luck with that."

Robin's laughter grated the last of Tam Lin's patience. "Oh aye, I wouldn't, were I you."

Rian, he noticed, smirked into her ale. "Hope you brought *lots* of fainne with you, Your Highness. Because a prince of the Tuatha De Dannan should court a princess in style, don't you agree?"

Bethany

Una slid from her saddle into Damek's waiting, if covered, arms. His cool mask of indifference was once more firmly in place. He might have been a block of wood to her at that point, so little difference his presence made. So many days on horseback, with meager rations, terrible weather, and the constant ache of the Spark drag of a lifetime, had all taken their toll. If he meant to embrace her in full view of everyone in her father's Court, she was too bloody exhausted to mind. If his arms tightened the slightest touch too close or his breath dusted too near the damp hair at the crown of her head, no matter. She needed a bath, food, and weeks of sleep to approach anything resembling her former self again. More's the pity, these luxuries were not to be. Once she crossed the threshold into her father's Great Hall… she wouldn't be free to do anything she wished for the foreseeable future. Damek must have sensed the futility of her thoughts. Without asking, he tucked his arms beneath her knees to carry her through the portcullis. Vaguely, Una was aware that they received several shocked and curious stares as they passed. Martin followed behind, giving her a sympathetic but altogether helpless smile.

That was as well.

Nothing he could do would help her, either.

Damek carried her past the iron Gatehouse towards the Inner Bailey. As they approached the Keep and its yawning arch, his boots made hard, wet smacking sounds over the sodden flagstones. Una realized she was entering the heart of the spider's web now, no mistake. Greasy torches sputtered in the late autumn mist, lighting their way through the courtyard and up to Duch Kevin's four-hundred-foot Keep. Somber and silent, the massive granite edifice stared her down. Her grandfather had seen to it that every surface was as smooth as polished glass; only the hundreds of murder holes placed at every third level betrayed a hint of a handhold. On the opposite side, facing the sea, the Keep dominated a monstrous cliff face that plunged to a precipitous drop of nearly nine hundred feet into the churning Sea of Manannan. She could hear the relentless surf beating its ceaseless, eternal rhythm against the crags. She'd found the sound comforting when she lived here long ago.

Now, that steady tattoo might well have been her death knell.

As Damek brought her through the foyer and into the Great Hall, a blast of warm air sent pins and needles over her frozen skin. Goosebumps raised up and down her arms, and her cheeks caught flame. People poured out of every nook and cranny to ogle the Duch's prodigal daughter and her handsome, disobedient cousin. Damek ignored them with a clenched jaw. Courtiers, servants, and clerks dashed every which way, eager for a peek. Their whispers might have been trumpet calls.

"Ignore them," Damek said into her hair. "They're merely curious. You owe them nothing."

Marching toward the stairs, Damek tugged a chin at Martin to intercept, should any of their onlookers dare to impede his progress. Taking a turn beneath the stairs, he strode through a narrow series of corridors that led to a hidden staircase past the kitchens. This passage tunneled directly to the Duch's private apartments. Una had played on these steps as a child. However, Damek didn't seem in a hurry to whisk her upward; he took his time. The stairs wound upward, lined with fine glass windows overlooking the vast grey sea. Una's stomach churned with those waves. She wasn't sure she wanted to face what came next. It seemed too cruel a fate after all she'd accomplished in Tairngare. Damek pulled her nearer still, as he used to when she was young.

It wasn't a lascivious move, and for once, she didn't mind.

He'd been her dearest friend once upon a time. She hated his guts and always would, but he knew better than any what she faced here. "I won't let him use you, Una. No matter what he threatens… I won't allow it. Do you believe me?" his voice wasn't even strained, despite four floors of winding steps. How he wasn't as exhausted as she, she failed to guess.

"No. Don't pretend to be my ally now, Damek. It's too late for that." She wanted to cry, but she was a Moura. Moura women did *not* weep like weaklings. She would endure. She must.

His answering laugh was far too warm for her taste. "I'm the last ally you have, Una. Accept it. Accept me." He paused on the landing. She saw Martin hesitate a few steps down to give his lord room. Ahead of them, the fourth floor's sconces illuminated the cold, isolated stairwell. A gloved finger slid below her chin. "You know he can't harm you. You're too valuable, and his ambition is too great. Stop fighting. You'd do better to play his game and win."

"I will not be his broodmare, Damek. I'll kill any man who tries. *Every* man. He knows I'd rather die, and so do you."

"Any man? Una, think it over. Why let him choose for you?"

She stared up at him, her ears growing hotter by the second. "I mean it, Damek. *Any* man."

He groaned. "You misunderstand. You've always misunderstood me." His tone lacked any trace of sarcasm. "He means to use you, but he's an old man, and like or not, you're his sole direct heir. He has no sons. You are all he has. Why hasn't this occurred to you?"

Damek wanted to be Duch. That's what 'occurred' to Una… no different from before. This time, she wouldn't have free reign of the castle to escape him and his incessant plotting. "Damek, you don't have to use my womb to launch yourself into his position. Go ahead and take his throne. You have my full and free support. I couldn't care less."

Something crossed his face, then— disappointment, hurt, maybe? Indifference numbed her. She was fairly sure Damek Bishop didn't have feelings to dampen, nor would any stop her from speaking her mind, either way. "You have no idea what I want, Una. Don't presume to know me, and don't you dare equate me with the simpering, sycophantic effeminates in Tairngare, either."

She wished more than anything that she had use of her own damned legs. "Whatever you say, Lord Bishop."

"As you like, *Lady Donahugh*," he mocked through his nose and hefted her higher to resume his climb. "But remember this, if you honestly believe I'd let another man touch you or attempt to take my birthright from me, I won't settle with the man alone. I'll kill everyone in his sphere… women, children, parents. It won't matter to me in the slightest. Unless you wish for dozens of deaths on your conscience, I suggest you find a way to implore the Duch to be done with the whole business and choose me. Am I making myself clear?"

"Why sweet cousin, you make me blush. Why not seal your lovely proposal with a kiss?"

He didn't flinch away as she expected. Instead, he gave her an odd smile. An alarm rang somewhere deep within her gut. The air tingled with unspoken malice— and confidence.

What?

Damek's soft but insistent mouth locked over hers.

You arrogant son of a bitch!

In her blood, the remnants of her Spark surged to life. Spent though she was, she sent every bit of it into the crush of his heated skin.

Nothing happened.

The last of her strength fizzled out, useless. Her Spark retreated in hissing, unsatisfied hunger. She was merely a woman, lighter and smaller than him. His free hand pressed the back of her head, forcing her against him. She made a frustrated, furious mewling sound in her throat, and Damek took advantage. His tongue slipped between her lips with a heady, masculine groan. She did the only thing she had the strength left to do. She bit down hard on his lower lip. He came up bleeding but smiling, a triumphant sparkle in his hazel eyes.

"I think you'll find, dearest cousin," he licked the blood from the corner of his mouth. "As things change, the more they remain the same."

⚶

HER SPARK HAD FAILED HER.

How was that even possible?

It had never failed her before. Not *ever*.

The serving girls who bathed, dried, clothed, and braided her hair wore gloves and long, thick sleeves. As if she would harm any of them… yet, they had reason to fear. Didn't they? Why didn't Damek? How had he managed to foil her Spark in such a way? It didn't make an ounce of sense. Had she wholly depleted her reservoir? No. It couldn't be. Beneath her flesh, she could feel the definite current in her blood. She was far from bereft. Why hadn't it latched onto Damek and drained him dry as toast? It must be a random occurrence! Damek's mother wasn't Tairnganese, so there wasn't any way he'd been born with the Spark… right? How else could he manage such resistance? The triumph and sheer, perverse pleasure in his eyes when he deposited her here, in her new prison, was unmistakable. Somehow, he'd developed the ability to defy Siora's Grace. Whether by talent or potion, she couldn't say for sure. Perhaps he possessed some charm or other, which bolstered his resistance? She *must* discover the truth. If he were resistant… *no*, she wouldn't give that gloating beast the satisfaction of her.

"You've grown," rumbled a deep, distinct voice from somewhere behind her. She jumped. Distracted, she hadn't heard anyone enter her chamber. The maids bowed so low; their foreheads nearly brushed their knees as they backed away. Duch Patrick Donahugh stood in the doorway, arms tucked behind his back. His balding pate and stone-grey eyes gleamed in the well-lit antechamber. Her quarters were largely windowless, save for a single rectangular slit facing the wild sea on the far-right wall. Beneath the glass was a stone seat overflowing with vibrant cushions. Patrick was slightly shorter than he had been. Portly now, too. His midsection swelled beneath a loosely belted tunic. Perhaps her perception was skewed by years of trying to forget his malevolent presence.

He wasn't smiling.

Good.

She'd take imperious over smug. "I despise those witch-marks, you know. I'll have to summon a skin healer from Bretagne." His nose wrinkled at her tattoos.

She exhaled long and hard. "Sure you don't want to check my teeth first?"

He chuckled, moving to her bedside, and leaning against the massive chestnut bedpost. "Ah. It's to be bravado, then? Fine, daughter. We can pretend your opinion of these circumstances make the ghost of an appeal to me." He looked around appreciably. "Anyhow, I hope you earn this room. There are others that you would enjoy far less— so you're aware."

"I'm ready to move whenever it suits you."

"Defiance now? Capital! I'll doff pretense altogether and simply chain you to the wall. Failing that, certain men enjoy a bound and helpless woman, you know?"

Bile rose in her throat.

Fucking bastard!

"You malodorous piece of shite! I'll kill *any* and *all* comers. Don't doubt it for a second. Send in two dozen, and I'll drain them dry. Mark my words."

"Two dozen? Who do you take me for? In Bethany alone, I hold twenty thousand troops. You're sure you want to play this game?"

She felt the blood drain from her face.

"Oh yes," he went on. "You might be a witch, little queen, but you're still a woman, and we both know your strength isn't boundless. Perhaps you'll kill the first three? Maybe it'll be the fourth or the fifth… maybe the fifteenth… who'll sample your wares? What do I care? Maybe we'll make sport of the affair. Yes! That's it! The first rider to remain mounted wins!" His laugh was dry, cruel, and utterly humorless. There wasn't an ounce of levity in his expression. Not a bit. Could he watch a group of men attempt to gang-rape his own daughter?

She would never be sure.

Her bones felt hollow and empty as air.

That despair she'd been battling coiled deep in her heart; he saw it. "Now," he said finally, smug as a cat. "Will we be making a spectacle of our familial drama, or shall we retain our dignity? Hm? I mean to have my way, Una, whether you care for the details or not."

She watched him in silent fear for a long while. He never blinked once. Finally, she declared, "I'll kill myself. I will not breed more thuggish males for your line, Patrick. I am a Moura—"

"You are a *Donahugh*!" he bellowed, though his face betrayed no emotion whatsoever, not even anger. "Your Tairnganese witch-whoring family no longer exists. I am the last of your family. If I say you're going to fuck the chamber-boy to give me heirs, I bloody well mean every word. Decide now, here, how you will perform your duty. Shall it be your way or mine?"

Una's temper flared hot and ready, chasing all traces of fear from her blood. "Go to the Hells, old man. I *dare* you to feed me fifteen, twenty… *a thousand* men to drain. How sad and impotent their little corpses will look. Why should I fear? They're only males."

She expected another outburst, but he surprised her again. He threw back his head and guffawed until he had to grasp his sides to halt his fit. When he finished, his eyes were wet. He wiped at them with both thumbs. "Oh, how I've missed you, Sprout. You've a pair of bollocks on you that would shame any man."

Coloring, she clenched and unclenched her fists. "Whatever pleases you, My Lord Duch. My mind won't change."

He held up his palms in a placating manner. "Truce. If I thought for a moment you'd allow any man to take you against your will, I'd slit your throat myself. That fire is the spit of my grandfather, I tell you. He would burn with pride."

She sighed. "No need for the sales pitch. Get to the threats. They're more convincing."

He shook his head. "No threats. You're my daughter and my heir. You'll wed and produce a Donahugh child that I will designate the next ruler of Eire. It's that simple."

"I'll choose no one. I don't accept you, your title, or your imperialist fantasies. I'm a Moura Prima. My grandmother is the rightful Doma of the most powerful city-state in Innisfail."

"Aside from Aes Sidhe, of course. Our benevolent overlords…."

"Apart from Aes Sidhe, yes. I don't need you. Find yourself another 'kingmaker.'" She paused, watching him beam back at her as if she were describing the weather. "What do you even need me for? You have Damek. He'd be more than happy to take up the family standard."

She didn't like the grin that he gave her. A chill traced down her back. "Eventually, I intend to, little girl, but not yet. The boy reaches too far, too fast. That's always been his failing, as your arrogance is yours." She understood. He knew, then, whatever Damek could do to resist her Spark. Perhaps even engineered the marvel? *No.* That would undercut his power, and Patrick would *never*. It must be something Damek had managed on his own. "For the immediate future, you will entertain my barons. I don't expect you to mate with them. Never fear. Merely allow them to believe you might desire them. I expect these men to linger here and lavish you with coins and gifts, and I expect you to be a gracious, indecisive hostess. At the close, we'll perform a small drama in which the fair princess despairs of her impossible choice; then you'll choose Damek."

"I will *not*—"

"— You're to use these greedy fools for their bride price, then deprive them of both a bride and their gifts. Do you understand?"

"You'd abuse your men this way?"

He sat down with a chuckle. "Of course. You're a princess, my dear, and your father's the most powerful man in Eire. They'll fall all over themselves for the opportunity to win Bethany. I expect the gifts to be lavish, indeed."

"That's rather disingenuous of their liege lord, isn't it?"

"Bah. Men love competition."

"You expect me to flirt and play courtier? Are you out of your mind?"

"No. Is that what I said? Forgive me. I expect you to do this and show me respect as your father."

"What a dreamer you are."

"I think not. I know how you feel about the girls in this city, Una." He marked each servant trying to squeeze themselves through the walls to avoid his eye. "I can leave one in your bed with you each night. Try me—a new death for every act of insolence. You *will* come to heel if I must keep you in chains like a mongrel. Do you doubt my resolve? Don't take too long to answer. I need only snap my fingers, and you'll be sleeping with fresh corpses within the hour."

Una felt ill. "No."

"'No,' what?" he tucked two fingers behind his ear. "I don't hear you."

"I don't doubt you."

Good," he said, slapping a palm against his knee on his way off her bed. Stopping an inch shy of the doorway, he turned back. "Oh, one last thing. I expect an heir rather soon, and I think you know well whom I expect to father it. Perhaps you'll take the time to appreciate his affection for you before I give you to someone else for spite? The faster you warm to the idea, the better. I could always arrange a less attractive prospect. Might teach you both a bit of respect, no?"

He shut the door quietly behind him, but its gentle click might have been a cannon shot for its effect on her already taxed nerves.

⚵

"I REFUSE," DAMEK SPAT, STALKING the length of Patrick's throne room with sheer pent-up rage. "The first hand that reaches out to touch her will be severed from its body. I'll have none of this ridiculous scheme!" He'd worked himself into quite a lather. Sweat dampened the dark hair at his brow, and his eyes flashed a particular shade of green wrath.

Martin, stalwart as always, stood between them. The gathered were aware there'd be little choice but to cut Damek down should his temper get the best of him. "Lord Bishop," he warned in a whisper. "Your best behavior now, as promised."

Most of Patrick's Court squirmed in discomfort in mute observance of this absurd family squabble. This wouldn't be the first time the Duch and his nephew had quarreled in a public venue, but it was the first time any worried it might come to blows. Damek was incensed. Dressed in his road-weary trousers and mud-stained boots, his black brows drew deep runnels in the muck on his face. The Lord of Clare had no doubt expected a warmer reception than this. Having returned less than an hour ago with the Duch's precious captive in hand, many of them visibly sympathized with his plight. Furious as he was, Damek marked them all. This was important information for later examination. Now, however, the foremost priority was his thrice-damned uncle and his absurdist schemes.

Patrick, never enamored of his ostentatious stone throne— brutal on his old bones, he would often remark— sat on the top step, rifling through Damek's hastily scratched reports with a raised brow. The tale they told was vivid as any fable and unlikely as a fire kindled beneath the sea. He should know. He'd lived through each one.

"Damek, you're behaving like a spoilt child. It's a harmless bit of competition, hardly an execution. It might be if you don't move your hand away from your pommel."

Nostrils flaring, Damek relented. Martin heaved an audible sigh of relief, and Patrick's guards backed up a step. The Court, too, relaxed. Damek cleared his throat of burning bile. The rage in his gut threatened to burst from him in flood. "I require no competition, Uncle. Una is mine by right and Reason."

Eyes roving a sloppy bit of vellum, Patrick blew a hearty scoff. "Indeed? I think you'll find Una is *mine*, boy. My child, my burden, and heir to *my* throne. Any claim you've ever imagined you have over her comes through me. What did you think you'd accomplish here? That you'd flout my express orders and return to make demands of me? You've been a malign boil on my arse, nephew. This is the price you pay."

Damek sent his eyes around the room. None of Patrick's courtiers seemed eager to meet his gaze. That was telling.

Interesting.

Patrick lost face today, though Damek was sure the pompous old rat was scarcely aware of it. Damek had marched North with only a few hundred men to save a woman each regarded as the rightful heir to Duch Kevin's legacy. They respected him for it, as he hoped they would. *Quite interesting, indeed.* He squared his shoulders. All he must do to prove himself the better man was keep his temper firmly in check. "Did I not bring her home to you? For over ten years, the Doma and her flock have kept our Lady Donahugh under lock and key in that zealous mortuary in Tairngare. How can you punish me for being the one man here whom you could count upon?"

Ignoring this rather poignant statement, Patrick set his scroll down and reached for another. He shook his head with a wry grin. "I will say, this is quite the yarn. If soldiery fails you, you might turn a pretty coin penning tinker's tales for simpletons. Dead men on the road. Betrayal and calamity. Murderous monsters and treacherous cutthroats." He smacked his lips. "Did you meet Finn Mac Cumhail on your travels, too?"

The Court gave a nervous, rumbling titter in response.

Damek's ears burned. "It's bloody true. Every *word*."

"If you say so, it must be true, mustn't it?"

Again, his courtiers laughed. Damek turned to give Martin a long, searching look. "Aye, Your Grace," Martin sighed. "Lord Bishop speaks true. Our men *were* ambushed by dead… things in the Greensward. Soon after, a host of stinking goblins descended upon them from the trees. I've interviewed each survivor at length. Not one uttered a single disparity. Besides, what few of our casualties we could reclaim were in a state I despair of describing."

Patrick nodded slowly. "Martin, you know I trust your word over any man here— but you were not there, were you? To escape my wroth, I mustn't put it past Damek's loyal honor guard to back this story."

"Uncle, ask Una. She was there. Many more would have died if it weren't for her and her… abilities."

"I intend to, in due course," droned Patrick. "For now, whatever might have befallen over forty of your troops does not mitigate your profound disobedience to me. I ought to have you scourged for such blatant disregard for my commands."

Careful, Damek thought.

Three of his barons are watching. "I stood in your company, Your Grace, and told you I had no intention of leaving my cousin in the barbarous North to die. I made a decision for which we are all better served, Una most of all. Forgive me, but what choice did you leave me?"

Patrick absorbed that performance with a tight, knowing smile. So the Duch did realize the game they played?

No matter.

He is too old to win, and he knows it.

Lord Wender, Damek noticed, smirked as he waited for Patrick's response. Patrick wasn't well-loved; he had never been. Men served him because he left them little choice, not for undo loyalty.

Damek counted on that.

"Very well. So, you've saved my ungrateful get from Otherworld beasties, walking dead men, and randy Sidhe lords risen from the dead. You have my thanks *and* my edict."

Damek laughed through an open mouth. "You can't be serious? Farm boys from Reason knows where— in competition with *me* for the throne?"

"Oh, I'm very serious, Damek. Better get used to it."

This time, it wasn't just Lord Wender who visibly soured on the Duch. "Fine. If my long-entombed uncle's sons mean to challenge me for Una's hand, by all means, let them meet me in the courtyard now."

"You'll leave them be, or I'll hang you from the walls by your bollocks."

Damek's filthy cloak swirled muck over his uncle's mosaic floor as he turned with a wry leer. "I don't believe you. Name a better soldier, aside from Martin here. A better statesman? Someone with a greater love for his home or its people? You can't, for that man does not exist. I refuse to compete with a pair of feral rabbits who can barely read or write their names."

Patrick stood up, crossing his arms behind his back. "I'm sorry if I gave you the impression that you'd be competing with Henry's sons— alone. Any man of means and property is free to present his suit for her dowry. Why so pale, nephew? Surely you didn't imagine you were the only worthy man in Eire?"

Damek's jaw flexed. He was suddenly even more acutely aware of how many powerful men were watching this exchange. "You would not *dare* to dangle *my wife —*"

"— Again, the union was annulled."

Martin's fingers dug into Damek's chest. Stout Lord Wender grabbed hold of his right elbow. Damek nearly dragged the pair forward in his urge to throttle his pernicious old uncle. Patrick, to his credit, did not flinch. "We were wed beneath the light of the Southernmost Star, Your Grace! By Reason, our union was *consummated*. She is not yours to give or take as you please!" If the other lords and nobles had any sympathy for the justice of this statement, Damek was beyond caring.

This age-old grievance boiled like venom from his pores.

Martin leaned in close to his ear. "If you press him any further, he'll be forced to make an example of you. You are wiser than this, lad. Let it go."

Patrick patted his belly, his grey eyes hard. "If this was meant to soften my stance, I daresay you've done better, Lord Bishop. By all means, dig your grave here today," he waved a hand. "We could do with a bit more entertainment."

Martin's firm hand moved to his opposite shoulder, squeezing hard, his expression pleading. After several calming breaths, Damek balled his fists and choked back his pride. He stepped back from Martin and shrugged his arm out of Lord Wender's grasp. He adjusted his blood-stained cuirass, his cheeks thin. "How long will your feasts and tourneys last, uncle?"

Patrick was never one to resist a smug smile, especially when he'd won an unfair argument. Taking a glass of wine from his terrorized steward, he resumed his seat on the steps. "Weeks, I expect. Maybe months, should it please me. So, what will you do? Shall you acknowledge your cousins' right to contend or be removed from Court altogether?"

Not having a choice didn't make Damek feel better about his obvious advantage. If he'd been paying attention, he'd have noticed the mutual look of revulsion each of the present Barons shared between them. Insulted and livid as he was, he must admit, deep down, Patrick's purpose was sound. He needed fainne, lumber, food, and troops to march on the North. How better to gain the men, promises, and supplies he needed than to charm it out of wealthy men and Merchers eager to woo a great heiress? Indeed, the added bitterness between them would spice the broth. Time was Damek's real punishment here. He must accept it if he wished to remain in the game a bit longer. With his grandmother's coup in Tairngare having pushed him so much further from her orbit, he had little recourse. "As you will it, your Grace," he said, his tongue sour in his mouth. "If it is your wish that I formally throw my cap in the race, so be it."

"It is."

"However, allow me to say this once and very clearly: *any* man with the gall to lay hands on my wife— including the sons of Henry FitzDonahugh— will taste my steel."

Patrick sipped his wine with a deep chuckle. "Well, there wouldn't be any sport without a strong contender, now would there?"

Thither, Bound

All necessary preparations having been made, Kaer Yin and his troupe of thirty-five men— Green-makers and Sidhe alike— readied themselves to depart at first light. They'd gathered all the extra weapons, furs, uishge, and supplies Rosweal and its demolished environs could muster for the trip. Tam Lin had taken to sulking around the city, avoiding Kaer Yin and his retinue until the last excusable moment. That was as well for Kaer Yin. He'd had enough of his cousin and his ceaseless nagging for a while. Everyone was ready to move on, whether eager to return home over the border or trek into the inhospitable South with Kaer Yin. The Sidhe, Kaer Yin remembered, grew restless very easily. Though reserved and unfailingly polite in mixed company, they could be boisterous and quarrelsome in large groups. Already, the Roswellians shied away from the horde of towering, bored, blond giants. Several semi-serious fights broke out in Wanderer's Alley due to a copious amount of unaged uishge and general carousing. The Sidhe did not drink much uishge in Croghan or Bri Leith, a fact Kaer Yin grew more thankful for by the day.

As for Kaer Yin himself, he'd divested himself of his bandages and escaped Barb's stuffy office as soon as Rian's back was turned. Free of his swaddling, at last, he accepted Barb's invitation to take a turn around the walls. The sky threatened rain, but the weather wouldn't deter him. He wouldn't get back into that bloody bed, not for all the uishge in Barb's cellar. If he didn't move as swiftly or smoothly as usual, no one had the nerve to say so aloud. Shar, for one, followed him and Barb at a respectful distance, his mouth twisted in the slightest of half-smiles. The lad knew better than to gainsay his Crown Prince. Pent-up as Kaer Yin was, he could drag himself around the city with his teeth.

At a wide tumble-down gap in the South Wall, Barb pointed. "That there is what I'm talkin' about, Ben. The whole bloody wall might as well be made of snot and thistle."

Feeling the wound in his chest more than he'd like, Kaer Yin pretended not to sweat. "These walls were built long before the Transition. I'm amazed they've stood so long."

"It's a problem." She pursed her painted lips. "Ye and Robin are the only two fools who honestly believe we've seen the last o'Gilcannon."

"Matt's not coming back, Barb. You beat him fair and square."

She made a face, taking his arm to lead him onward. "Ain't no such thing, love. Ye'd bloody well know that too if yer head weren't crammed up that Siorai girl's—"

"Barb."

"Right. Well, aside from the Matts o'the world, if we aim to repel another invasion, we won't manage it with a farmer's pen for walls."

A chill breeze rustled the gold in Kaer Yin's right ear. Rian had done her level best to entomb him in shirts, jumpers, and scarves, but he felt the wind in his blood, regardless. Rian had been vehemently opposed to his walking around like this, but he would be damned if he'd heed her. It was well past time he was up on his own two feet. Fresh air was what he needed now, not the irritable prodding of a mean-spirited faerie. Gerrod, bless him, intercepted Rian in the tap so Kaer Yin and Barb could duck out the back. Gerrod seemed too happy to help. Kaer Yin wished the lad all the luck in the world.

He would need it.

Realizing Barb waited for a response, Kaer Yin sighed. "Not you too, Barb?"

"Course, me too! They're bound to return and bury Rosweal for good once you get that blasted… erm, yer *lovely* lass back. I was in the bloody room when you heard about Navan, wasn't I?"

Target struck.

Kaer Yin flinched. He was sorrier for Navan than he could say. The Tairnganeah, thwarted in their attempt to drag Una back to the Citadel in chains, had left quaint, pleasant Navan a smoking ruin. The Innkeeper of the unassuming *Bowman's Cross* and his son were killed in the onslaught. Kaer Yin had sent Niall and Ferdam to verify the Greenmakers' report. The village had been razed to the ground, and all that was left of the *Bowman's Cross* were two blackened walls and the charred remains of its former occupants. Kaer Yin might not be alive now were it not for the Innkeeper and his lad. He would never forget their kindness, and as soon as he set things straight with Bethany, he'd be back to deal with the Corsairs and their new mistress. He was certain Barb had poked that raw wound on purpose. "Tairnganeah were to blame for Navan, Barb. Not Una."

"Aye, all the same. They woulda done the same to us if we'd let 'em. Them Southers, a sight worse, yet. What d'ye believe is gonna happen, Ben? Ye'll have a grand caper, stealin' the Duch's get from under his nose… and no one will try to stop ye for your brass?"

"My father's troops—"

"Ain't here yet, and them that are, yer dividin' again to march South. Ye know Vanna Nema's taken the Doma's hat. Yer girl's family has fled or been imprisoned for heresy. Smartest place for the Domina now is her father's hall in Bethany."

Kaer Yin sucked at his gums while he considered her impertinent observations. A light rain began to fall as they walked. Though he felt stronger with each step, tripping over any tumbledown stones in their way would end this little foray on the lowest possible note. "What would you have me do? I cannot allow her to suffer for me."

"What about the rest o'us? We should be made to suffer for *her*. Don't be ridiculous, love. Her dear ole da won't live forever, ye know? Girl's his bloody heir, ain't she? She can wait him out. Meanwhile, we can get on with rebuildin' our lives under the protection of our restored Crown Prince. Ye belong here, guardin' the North, milord. We got plenty troubles o'our own."

He stopped midstride, drawing her up short. "Are you implying that I'm shirking my duty now?" He scoffed. "You realize that I'm technically still an exile, and none of you would have been the wiser about me if not for Una?"

"Would it make ye feel better if we pretended to be happy to know?"

Ben recoiled slightly. "Ouch, Barb…"

"Ben, I love ye, same as I do Robin, Gerry, and Dabs— I swear it. But the North can't bear the brunt for yer romance. Leave her be to make it up with her da. I'm beggin' ye."

Kaer Yin snuck a glance over his shoulder at Shar. Tam Lin's lieutenant affected the ghost of a smile. Kaer Yin's heart sank a bit to see it. No one seemed to know what they were up against, did they? Only those who'd been in the Greensward on Samhain had the first bloody clue of what they'd faced and lived to discuss due to the Duch's prodigal daughter. How could he make someone as self-centered as Barb understand? "You weren't there on Samhain. No, don't make that face. You've no idea what we survived that night or how much worse it could have been. Una put her life on the line for us. In so doing, she sacrificed the one thing she wanted above anything else: her freedom. This is not a romantic whim. We owe her a large debt. You may say she'll learn to live in Bethany and accept her fate. You may say she'd be better off, that we might all be better off. I beg to differ. Her father and his thuggish Barons mean to make war through her. You seem eager to ignore that fact. That war will come to Rosweal, whether you like it or not. For my part, I will not leave Una *anywhere*, ever again, unless I hear the demand from her lips."

"Ben, see reason—"

"No. As a friend, I appreciate your counsel," he said, gently gripping her elbow. "As your liege lord and the Crown Prince of Innisfail, I do not require it."

Barb trudged along in silence for a while, chewing at her cheek. Her sulk was fine by him. He didn't need her blessing or her permission. As long as Patrick Donahugh had Una in his custody, Bri Leith could never truly be safe. To Barb's—and perhaps most of Rosweal's— isolationist way of thinking, Una might serve the realm better dead. Kaer Yin did not share the sentiment. He'd scour the blackest depths of Tech Duinn for her if he must.

"Politics aside, she deserves a choice, Barb."

"So do we, damn ye."

"War will come, with Una or without. Wouldn't you rather serve your Ard Ri in this matter rather than hinder him?"

"Yer assumin' we'll have the option. If there's to be a war no matter what we do, why bother to conflate it by raidin' the lion's den? Ben, ye must see sense here. I know yer cousin has said as much many times, but one girl won't change the course o'things. Our Crown Prince and his Wild Hunt, now, might."

There was a thick ring of fairness to that statement.

Nonetheless…

"I won't abandon her, any more than I would Robin or Tam Lin. She saved my life, and I owe her. Robin, Rian, and Gerry owe her. *Rosweal* owes her. I'll have it from her what she wants to do and where she'd like to be, questions no one has ever bothered to ask her. Rosweal will not go undefended, Barb. I vow it."

"Between 'em, Tairngare and Bethany have the whole of Eire divided into opposin' camps. Sure as the sun sets in the west, we'll be someone's target. We need ye here to keep the peace, Yer Arseness, not off chasin' a skirt into enemy territory."

Kaer Yin rounded on her for a stinging retort, but Gerrod jogged up to them from the ramshackle Taran Gate. "Ben," he panted, jerking a thumb behind him. "A woman is askin' for ye."

Both Barb and Kaer Yin blinked back at Gerrod. "A woman?" asked Barb.

Gerrod fidgeted to a profound degree. "Yeah, um, Ben… she's—"

"A bloody *Moura*," Barb spat, peering around his scrawny back.

The woman in question calmly stepped past Shar without fear. Behind her, a small retinue of Tairnganese Merchers loitered beneath the Gate. She was tall and lean, with lustrous dark skin and bright, uishge-colored eyes. She spared Barb the slightest twitch of her nose.

"*Alvra*, actually. Eva is my name. My lord prince Kaer Yin, I've come to offer you my service."

⚹

EVA ÄLVRA WAS PERHAPS THE most imposing woman anyone, save the Sidhe, had ever seen. Her fine, honey-dark skin, and bright amber eyes, caught and held the light in fascinating ways. Added to the stark beauty of her face, there was something *present* about her bearing that made her all the more substantial, despite her thin frame. The Greenmakers had no idea how to look at her, much less speak to her. Kaer Yin invited her and her man-at-arms to converse with him in the privacy of Barb's once-private office. Mel Carra struck an equally impressive figure, being nearly as broad through the shoulders as he was tall. Refusing a seat, he stood at Eva's right elbow, watchful and silent as a stone lion.

"Your Highness," said Eva, her voice rich as a wind flute. "My aunt, the true Doma of Tairngare, has sent me to bring her granddaughter home."

Barb sat beside the window, her brow cross as she could make it. "To execution? Yer families're outta power now, ain't they? The bloody girl *is* home. Ask anyone with a brain."

Eva's gaze raked Barb without mercy. Kaer Yin saw the hardened bawd flinch for the first time, ever. "Do you know to whom you speak, *novitiate*?"

"Y-yeah."

"Then I would mind that mouth, were I you."

The threat was enough to force Barb into a chair facing the hearth, her cheeks livid. Robin and Kaer Yin shared a look over Eva's head.

"Well," said Kaer Yin. "I'm pleased to make your acquaintance, My Lady. Though I don't wholly agree with Mistress Dormer, I do have to restate the obvious. Tairngare is hostile territory now. Surely you knew that before you approached me?"

"I do know it," she frowned. "My aunt has fled to Cymru, though I fear she'll find no harbor there. In the meantime, my mother has been executed, and my grandmother scourged and imprisoned. Thank you, my followers and I are well aware of the dilemma."

Sitting beside Kaer Yin, Rian covered her mouth, her brows drawn down hard. Tam Lin and Shar touched two fingers to their temple, then their hearts: Dannan mourning.

Barb scowled into the flames, sullen and unsympathetic.

"Siora," breathed Robin with a grimace. "I am so sorry, milady. Terrible luck that, but I'm not sure how we can help ye?"

"On the contrary, it is *we* who aim to help you. Your Highness, you mean to liberate my niece from Bethany, correct?"

"Yes," Kaer Yin answered, ignoring the tightened lips of two people in his company. "But I do not intend to return her to the Red City. It's my opinion, and my father would concur, that she'd be safest in Bri Leith. I intend to offer her the choice. I will respect her decision if she wishes to remain in Bethany." The intensity of Eva's stare made Kaer Yin slightly uncomfortable, but he would not bend. Not for anyone. "Forgive me, but the Doma's wishes are none of my concern."

Eva studied him so long that he struggled not to squirm. After an eternity, her mouth quirked. "I see your intent quite clearly, Your Highness. I approve."

He did squirm a bit then. Was that this one's power? To read the hearts of men. *Wonderful,* he thought. "Not everyone shares your sentiment."

She scanned the dissenters with a raised brow. *So, she* does *know a person's innermost thoughts? Herne, Una. Your family is terrifying.* "They fear for you, Your Highness, and for their homes. They have reason to. Many terrible things are happening in Eire."

"Exactly," grumbled Barb to the fireplace. Robin patted her leg.

"None of this is Una's fault," Rian said, crossing her arms at Barb's back. "How often do we have to explain it before it sinks in?"

Barb ignored her. Tam Lin's expression remained flat and disinterested as he could make it, but Kaer Yin knew he was dying to speak his piece. "Then we are after the same thing, Your Highness," smirked Eva. "My aunt wishes for Una's safety, above all considerations. You have my full and free support if this is your goal."

Tam Lin butted in, "What support can you offer for this absurd quest? A lone woman and a handful of barely armed men?"

Eva folded her hands. "I hear the fear of the unknown in your voice, Prince O'Ruiadh. Thus, I will forgive your insult."

"No slight intended, but honestly— I don't understand why we need another woman on this march. We've already got one, and she'll be about as useful as tits on a bull."

Rian's head swiveled around to Kaer Yin. "I can slap him *now*?"

Kaer Yin pinched the bridge of his nose. "My Lady Alvra, what my cousin means to say is—"

"He can speak for himself, *Ard Tiarne*," Tam Lin interjected. "We're leaving in the morning, counter to every argument. I fail to see why we require another damned woman to defend along the way. It's not as if we're headed to Ten Bells for a bloody fête, now is it? I'll not have—"

Tam Lin broke off as suddenly as he started. His eyes went slightly slack at the corners as Eva leaned forward to tug up the hem of her robe. Sinking to his knees with a mooncalf expression, Tam Lin pressed his lips against the toe of her boot. When he looked up, all adoration and innocence, Eva patted his cheek. The spell was broken. "Doubt any males in your company could do anything like *that*, could they, Your Highness?"

Acutely embarrassed, Tam Lin lurched to his feet and scrambled away from her as fast as he could. "You... *witch*!"

Rian threw back her head, laughing until her cheeks went scarlet.

Gerrod, Shar, and Niall backed as far into the wall as they could.

Kaer Yin wrenched Robin's flask out of his hand and took a long gulp.

Barb didn't move a muscle.

Mel Carra coughed into his fist while Eva grinned at the Prince of Connaught. "Domina Alvra is the finest practitioner of Mentis Imperium in Tairngare. She had many acolytes in the Cloister before she retired."

"I can see that," Kaer Yin set a steadying hand on Tam Lin's shoulder. "Ah. Forgive my cousin. He never met Una, you understand?"

"Of course." She dipped her head.

"Yin, you mean to say the girl you're after can... I knew it! I knew she must have cursed you in some way!"

"My niece's gifts differ greatly from mine, Your Highness. She does not practice Mentis Imperium at all. Rather, Corpus Imperium— a discipline so advanced that there are no precedents. In a thousand years, only Una was born with the aptitude for it."

"And that means... what?"

"'*Corpus*' means 'body,'" said Rian behind her hand, cutting her eyes at him. "Thousands of years to live and no time to read. How did your kind conquer Innisfail?"

Tam Lin curled his lip but refused to take her bait. "You're telling me this idiot's paramour can control a man's body? Why am I not surprised?"

Kaer Yin shoved him into the mantle with a dismissive snort. "She's not my paramour, erm, or whatever. And that isn't what Lady Alvra said, is it? Una can... well, maybe we should discuss that later?" A mutual chill ran through several of the gathered occupants.

They'd each seen what Corpus Imperium meant firsthand.

"I appreciate your offer, Lady Alvra, but I warn you, it may come to a terrible end. I'm taking those who fully grasp the danger. I can't promise you or anyone else will return unscathed."

"Oh," Eva winked at Mel Carra, who chuckled in return. "No need to worry about us, Your Highness. I ventured here for my niece. If I'd doubt you or your ability to retrieve her, no conversation would have been necessary between us."

Kaer Yin shivered. He didn't doubt it. "Right."

"We're with you, Prince Kaer Yin. Who knows? You may find your men are on their best behavior all the while."

⚵ ⚶

THE BOAT, SLAPPED BY INCESSANT, frigid green waves, slid onto the pebbled shore. In the hard rain, the crewmen who dragged her up the beach could scarcely see the end of their noses. Between these eight half-frozen bodies sat a tiny woman huddled within the vessel. Despite a layer of furs capped by the finest sealskin cloak fainne could buy, Drem shuddered for the unrelenting cold. Almost a month of ceaseless travel in abysmal Dor Oras weather had taken its toll on her. She was disused to the outdoors, to put things mildly. Nearing her seventh decade on earth, she'd spent most of her life in the safety and warmth of the Cloister of the Eternal Flame, where she belonged. To her mind, she had no bloody business traipsing around the Continent like some crazed bard-seeking patrons.

Yet, what choice did she have? Her great enemy's long reach had all but chased her to the edge of the world. With most of her allies dead or imprisoned, Drem had grown desperate for more.

Driven from her rightful seat in the Cloister, she went first to Cymru to garner the aid of Merchers loyal to the Moura Clan. Nema's heretics had gotten there first. The Ruma Clan, who had been granted oversight of the Tairnganese Consulate in Swansea, had been wiped out to a woman, and one of Pors Yma's toadying relatives installed as Governess. Loyal Siorai were rounded up and defrocked en masse. Those who disavowed the Mouras and the Libella were granted lands, titles, and honors in the new Doma's name.

Drem had barely escaped the Swansea cesspit of Unionist vipers when she came upon another well-plotted coup in Kernow. Before reaching the Siorai rectory to gain her bearings, a mob descended upon her retinue, killing several handmaidens and a dozen of her loyal Cohort. This second escape proved more harrowing than the first. Sometime later, while she lay sick upon the freezing Sea of Mannanan, her chief of staff informed her that her niece Ana had been captured on the dock, then executed in Tairngare's dungeon a week after. Drem hadn't had time to mourn or lament her cousin Basa's lengthy internment.

Nothing much she could do about it now, was there? When Lord Gaelin fled his Hall in Bretagne, rather than meet with her, Drem realized there was one place left to sail.

Aes Sidhe.

The only Sidhe harbor friendly to Eirean transports was located on the peninsula of Man. Once she landed in Lomond, she was forced to hire ponies for the long trek around the Bay of Man, over the hills at Dalriada, then through the Argyll forest to Dale. The going had been quite hard on her old bones. From ice-choked waterways to long muddied roads snaking through impenetrable forests below snow-capped peaks, the wilds of Scotia were not for the faint of heart.

She had caught a cold in Dale and rested at an inn reserved for Merchers and visiting dignitaries for several days. Mortal men and women were not much welcome in Aes Sidhe, and her reception in each port and town had been as frosty as the weather. That was as well; she was too tired and ill to mind. Once her cold subsided enough to travel, she booked transport to Skye with the last of her ready funds. If Lord and Lady Bres would not have her, she had no one else to whom she might turn. She knew this was the end of the line for the once mighty Drem Moura.

Vanna Nema had done her work well.

So well, Drem despaired that things might never be set right again.

On the beach, some fifty paces ahead sat three silent figures atop smoke-grey mounts: Duskendales, Drem recalled from her studies, thoroughbreds of unequaled breeding, for which the Port of Dale was named. If the Sidhe felt the cold in their marrows as Drem did, they didn't show it. Motionless as statues, they waited while she was ushered from the inundated boat by two burly Eirean sailors and carried to dry sand. Her ladies followed, the hem of their robes dragging behind them in the surf. The middle rider— a female, Drem noted— nudged her mare forward. Huffing, shivering, and miserable, Drem held out a hand to keep the boatmen from leaving should this meeting fail. The rider had the white-blond locks of her Dannan ancestors. Her skin was pale and smooth as spun moonlight, and her full pink mouth drew into a sharp line as she neared. Her beauty was staggering. Drem flushed to the roots of her grey hair. She dreaded to know what she must look like to such an ethereal creature.

The pale lady circled Drem twice before spinning her mount to a halt. Silver eyes flashed. "Doma Drem Moura. What brings you to Skye?"

Finding her voice with some difficulty, Drem croaked, "I've come to beg the hospitality of the Lord and Lady Bres. I hope our near-forty years of friendship and fidelity will not be forsaken."

The lady considered her for some time, rain falling in sheets around her. "The new Doma has you on the run, it seems? Yet you come here last. Why is that, your eminence?"

"Had I known I'd be welcome, it should have been the first. Let's not pretend the Sidhe hold any great affection for my race."

The lady's mouth twitched. "True. Though I wonder that you'd venture here instead of Bri Leith or Croghan. The Ard Ri and his brother hold far more influence in Eire than the Lord and Lady of Skye. What did you hope to gain from Lord Jan Fir?"

Drem chuckled. She was not a fool; the lady's torc marked her out as no crier could have. "I didn't come to treat with Lord Jan Fir. I came to see Lady Eri, specifically. I have news that is sure to interest her personally."

"Oh," the lady's brow quirked. "What might you wish of the Ard Ri's daughter?"

"That her brother has emerged from his exile, and if I'm not mistaken, means to take my granddaughter to your father's court."

Eri Ap Midhir Bres, the Lady of Skye and Queen of Scotia, stared down at Drem as if she'd told her the sun was filled with cheese. "Kaer Yin would *never*...."

"He would. He *has*. You and I have much to discuss, it seems... Your Highness. If we might—" But here, Drem faltered. The world spun a bit on its axis. The heavy grey sky overhead swirled and frothed, riotous as the sea behind her. The Queen of Scotia had but a moment to stare at her in confused horror when the stony beach rushed into Drem's face.

Poisoned Well

Aoife hated Grainne more than she'd ever hated anyone in her life. She thought she'd already accumulated quite an impressive list of people she'd love to murder in a lovingly articulated order. Those at the bottom, she thought to kill in an offhand, incidental sort of way: casually, caustically. Those at the top, however, inspired half-a-thousand scenarios in which she'd exact revenge for every ounce of pain, humiliation, or derision they'd ever spared her. Vanna Nema, of course, had squatted at the very top for ages. Now, Grainne Mac Nemed dueled the imperious Nema for first place. Grainne was the new standard by which Aoife would gauge her deepest loathing. The woman was officious, vain, posturing, and indiscriminately cruel.

The Mac Nemed Clan were the most arrogant creatures to plague the Gods' green earth in Aoife's vaunted experience— but that was not to say some weren't worse than others. Much, much worse, in Grainne's case. The spoilt, selfish grandchild of Falan Mac Eochaid, the Elder; Grainne had been born to imagine herself superior to every living thing, including her relatives. Unlike their cousins among the Tuatha De Dannan, the Fir Bolg left their rule almost strictly to their women. Thus, she'd been the great Liadan Mac Nemed's only true heir for centuries. Insignificant half-breeds like Aoife were nothing to the immortal descendants of the Fomorian King, Balor.

Aoife forgot that for any length of time at her peril.

Having descended upon a nameless village twenty miles from Tara, Grainne's troupe of 'Dannan' warriors looted, pillaged, and burned at her command. Aoife, partially healed of her wounds, had watched the flames stretch high into the predawn sky while chained to the rear wagon. Two days later, their disguised Warhammers struck a pair of towns ten miles nearer the city.

None were left alive.

The broken bodies of women and children were strung from trees or displayed before their burning farms. Aoife, manacled and humbled before her compatriots, was tasked with many of the macabre decorations herself. On the fourth night, the Bolg rested. Ignored, starved, and humiliated, Aoife spent that eve and many after bound and gagged among the supply train. It took days for someone to remember to feed her and longer for Grainne to find a reason to strike her from her iron bracelets. Ten days into their clandestine mission, Aoife was ordered to take a branch of their force into Tara itself to sow discord, foster fears, and murder with impunity. Aoife was whipped again at Grainne's pleasure before she allowed her to roam unfettered. The purpose of this cruelty, Grainne told her over a glass of Cymrian wine, was to reaffirm Aoife's newfound humility.

If the unwitting citizens of Tara had any idea why their Dannan overlords were slaughtering Eireans in increasingly ingenious ways, they had Grainne Mac Nemed to thank for their terror. Aoife had thrown herself into her work with malicious fervor. Each child she had strangled in the dark, every man they gutted or woman they garroted, bore Grainne's mocking face. Each further whetted her appetite to add parricide to her list of sins. Aoife vowed to kill her cousin first. Even Vanna Nema, her oldest and most persistent torturer, could wait. When all of Eire was conquered for the Bolg, at least Grainne wouldn't live to see it.

Mighty Balor, Aoife prayed.

Bless this child of your bones with your patience, power, and vengeance. When the blood of your enemies soaks the soil of your forebears, I will ravage your bloodline, purge the Clan of Eochaid's filth... hear me, Balor. Grant me your blessing.

Bearing an ogham charm and the false silver hair of their greatest foes, Aoife and her kin crept through slums and back-alleys, spreading death and discord like a plague.

⚴

Gan wasn't sure why he was still alive. The slightest twitch sent hot waves of roiling pain throughout his body, yet he lived. How could one feel the anguish of a thousand wounds and not die? Each breath was agony. He could scarcely speak above a whisper for the raw ruin of his throat. What was left of his stomach grew thinner each day for lack of stable nourishment. He could not eat or drink save from a tube that was mercilessly shoved down his blistered gullet three times a day. He couldn't urinate on his own, either. Another tiny cylinder had to be inserted into the scarred remnants of his phallus, an organ that had been burned clear of skin and fat, leaving behind a nerveless muscle devoid of purpose. Nearly all of the skin on his body was cracked and sloughing off like charred pork. For days and days, tormented by hunger and terrible thirst, the smell of his cooked flesh had almost driven him mad. He might have wept had he any tear ducts left to cool his eyes. A few weeks ago, Fawa Gan had been a plump, well-dressed figure of some importance in the Cloister of the Eternal Flame. Now, he was a hairless, skinless monster from his own worst nightmares, a pitiful wretch, too odious to kill.

Fawa Gan would never know mercy again.

Nema would have it no other way.

After being dragged away from Aoife, however many days, weeks, or months ago— he had no idea how long— he was shut up in a minor ward on the Second Floor. The Secundas' medical wing, he knew instinctively. At least this new cell was not so dark as it had been underground, nor as filthy or endlessly damp. He had a dry cot to lay upon, a small window to wail through, and a steady stream of silent Secundas to care for him, bearing various implements of well-intended torture. Some brought soap and water. Some brought stinking medicinals. Others brought sharp things: needles, slim knives to cut away his dead flesh, or silver rollers to test his reflexology. Most, he could not feel enough to mind. The nerve endings that snaked through most parts of his body were dead. There were a few, however, which tore at his sanity to touch... and touch them, Nema's servants did. The pain was unreal, unimaginable, *mythic*.

A worse hell he could never dream possible.

Relentlessly, the Secundas came. They poked, prodded, abraded, squeezed, popped, tore, shredded, pounded, and cut at him like handmaidens of the Kneeler's Devil. Throughout, he was offered no sedatives, no pain relievers, and no sympathy. The Secundas Nema selected to treat him were chosen for their lack of squeamishness and, likely, their lack of empathy. As it wore on, Gan found himself rather used to the pain. Their needle-pricks didn't sting as they had at first, their tiny blades did not bite so deep, and their salves and unguents did not sear his exposed tissues like acid. The longer he lay there, he grew less and less interested in how much he hurt; and oh, he hurt.

His was an absolute symphony of suffering.

Though, it was also true that he minded *less*. He feared *less*. Hope had dwindled to the smallest particle in his heart. Its imminent loss pained him *less* every hour. In its place, a rich, beguiling apathy took hold. Nema had something more planned for him. A spectacular terror should have gnawed at what remained of his guts. He should have lain awake nights, feverish (if he could sweat, that is) with fear and dark anticipation. He did not. Indeed, he struggled to care at all. The pain became familiar, almost welcome. It might be all that he would ever feel again. Internally, his spirit was cold, flat, and heavy as lead.

At some point in the haze of silent grey days, Nema's head bootlicker came to inspect him. Pors Yma, reinstated to the Cloister and appointed to Alta Prima without undergoing the Ninth Ordeal, squinted

335

down at him for quite some time. He turned his face away from the commingled horror and sadistic pleasure in her dark eyes. "How long before he'll be fit to move, Secundus?"

One of his stoic nurses dipped her head. "He might be moved now, My Lady. Though I doubt he'll walk on his own. His muscles are intact, though the outer flesh has been largely damaged beyond repair."

"I don't care that he's in pain. I care that he's able to attend the Doma. When will that be?"

"His fingers lost most of their nerve-endings, My Lady. I cannot say when—"

"You there," she addressed Gan directly. He ignored her. "The Doma has spared your worthless life for a reason, ingrate. I'm going to hand you this stylus," he almost felt a cold object pressing against his partially healed right hand. "You'd better grasp it, you pathetic, mewling worm."

He did not. To the Hells with them all.

He was a hollow, quivering tragedy of a man. What urge he'd ever had to please any of these arrogant, ungrateful witches had peeled off with his skin. He was a new man, ready and eager to die. Gan chose a dark spot beneath the windowpane to focus upon. Pors struck him. Blissfully, he didn't feel that either. She shouted unintelligible invectives into his ear, but he did not care. Instead, he imagined the stain was a tiny rabbit hopping through spotty bracken. Shapes emerged and coalesced all over that filthy rear wall. By the time Pors left in a huff, quite a menagerie of harmless woodland critters frolicked before his milky eyes. He slept for a time then, and when he woke, he immediately tumbled into a dreamless slumber.

Hours passed. Days, perhaps. He had no way to tell.

In one of these wakeful dazes, they came for him again. Rough arms hauled him upward. Burly hands hefted him from his cot. His rabbit hopped along the wall, unable to stall the inevitable. Dragged down the hall and up many flights of stairs, Gan wondered how Nema would do it. Would she have him gutted before her? Thrown from the Crown of the Citadel? Beaten to death, perhaps? Impaled, poisoned, or hacked to bits? He was unmoved. She'd already burned him alive; what else could she do to him that would hurt near as much?

In an unfamiliar room, with a particular rug that he'd purchased for her from Lady Devaschelle in Bretagne twenty years before, Gan was tossed to the floor. The pain was a bright sword in his mind, but that hardly mattered to anyone, least of all himself. Nema sat in her high-backed chair, smirking at him from her vanity mirror. "Ah," she said, her tone light and teasing. "There you are, my dear boy. We have important guests today, so I expect you'll have your work cut out for you."

He blinked back at her in dumbfounded silence.

She raised a brow. "Is his hearing affected?"

"No," said one of his manhandlers. "Secunda Marta was clear, he retains his faculties, if not the full range of motion."

A vivid green eye held Gan captive in its cold depths. "Gan, I will have the Cyrmian knot today, I think."

Wait… she *could not* mean…?

"Get him up."

He was jerked upright and held to his feet from either side. One of his captors shoved a comb and stylus into his hand, viciously closing his mauled fingers around each implement. Gan wavered in their arms, unsteady as a reed in the wind. His fingers shook. "What are you waiting for?" she asked, watching him through the glass. "I expect your best work, of course."

Gan dropped the tools and spat, thin spittle trailing down his peeling chin. His guards struck him until his breath came in thin whistles, though they did not allow him to crumple to the floor. They held him up and shoved the tools into his hands once more. He wheezed while Nema grinned from her chair. "Now, now, Gan. We mustn't be rude. If you'd rather, perhaps your sister Hela would take your place for you? Your mother, Nina, maybe? They are both here, of course. I'm surprised you did not see them in the dungeons on your way past?"

Another kind of pain gripped Gan's heart then, digging its sharp talons in.

"Shall I send for one of them?"

A guard shoved Gan forward, keeping a forearm against his spine to steady him on his feet. A helpless gurgle escaped his chest. He could feel the stylus in his hand but struggled to grasp it. Had he imagined there was no worse pain? What a fool he was. He had always been such a pompous, greedy fool. Hadn't he?

"I give you no leave to exit my service, Fawa Gan. Where once you held the honor and privilege of being my most trusted steward, you are now my dog. Where I walk, so shall you crawl. Where I sit, you shall kneel. This is the *geis* I place upon you, treacherous Gan. I curse you to shadow my every move in perfect adoration for the rest of your miserable life. A simpering, loathsome toad you shall be. A disgusting wreck of mangled flesh and putrid obeisance. *That* is your punishment, my love. Is it not perfect? Are you not grateful?"

One of her guards punched him in the middle, hard. He doubled over but was not allowed to fall. He glared at Nema with all the defiance he could muster. She observed the display with dispassionate humor. He took a second blow to the belly, then dangled queerly from his captors' arms.

"Each time you flash me an independent eye, your family will bear the brunt. Every wound you have shall be replicated in your mother's hide. Your sister, I will pass through the Cohort's Hall for *any* disobedience. Do you understand?"

Inside, Gan bled. His heart's blood boiled anew.

He *did* understand.

He and Aoife shared the same fate, the same curse.

He didn't answer. Nema smiled. "Excellent. I hope I won't need to explain myself again for their sake. Now, pick up that comb, and come here."

🦌

THE CORPSE SWUNG, PURPLE AND bloated, from the clothesline, small face distended, head twisted at an unnatural angle. Beside him, his mother wailed, kicked, and thrashed at any who meant to pry her away from him. The child couldn't have been more than ten when he'd died. His neck had been broken. His scrawny little body posed like a scarecrow at the end of a line of sheets and petticoats. Dumbfounded and infuriated by the discovery, the citizens who should have been preparing for the day's market stopped to gape and rail at their neighbors. The outrage was palpable but not quite *perfect*.

Not yet.

The victim was too old. That had to be it. A wizened street urchin was hardly the picture of youthful purity.

Oh well, Aoife would catch a younger one next time.

Nothing motivated a mob quite so much as innocent blood.

A filthy farmer in high-patched coveralls careened around the corner, accompanied by half a dozen men. His roar rattled her teeth in their casings. From her place at the rear of the crowd, Aoife was careful not to smile.

Now we're getting somewhere.

The farmer threw himself at the woman as she cradled her murdered child: the father, no doubt. In slavering disbelief, the farmer's heartbreaking, pathetic cries echoed about the market. "*Who?* Who would do this to my Denn?" he bellowed, drooling into his sobbing wife's hair. "He were a good lad! A good lad!"

Aoife smothered a cough. She had caught the little bugger with his hand in her pocket. He'd picked the wrong person to rob, as it turned out. From the fading lash marks she spied peeking out of the neckline of his tunic; this wasn't the first time he'd been called to account, either. These two carried on like he'd been a Kneeler's saint. The way his mother's tits sagged out of her garish bodice told Aoife all she needed to know about the family. Should she weep for the lice-ridden child of an uneducated ruffian and an obvious whore?

Hardly. Who cared about one more dead pickpocket, anyway?

Yes, yes. Grab your pitchforks, Milesian scum, and be quick about it already. I'm starving.

A constable arrived on the scene to control the crowd and get to the bottom of this terrible affair. On his heels jogged an overweight lamplighter and two more officials, each bearing the appropriate bands over their upper arms. The lamplighter, perhaps the most important of these unimpressive personages, mounted the communal drying platform with slackened jaws and grey cheeks. He gawped at the dead boy and his hysterical parents as if he'd never seen such a thing. Aoife resisted the urge to scoff. Tara had been sacked by Bethany and retaken by Tairngare more times than she could count.

The loss of one boy would hardly tip the scale.

The lamplighter set a calming hand on the howling father's shoulder and whispered soothing, nonsensical gibberish to the mother. This was taking entirely too bloody long. Aoife cupped a hand over her mouth. "What's he got in his hand there, master?"

The lamplighter glanced at the crowd to locate the speaker, but Aoife had already moved along the far wall, near the exit. After several more minutes of shouting and carrying on, he finally knelt to pry open the boy's blue fingers.

Took you long enough, fool, she thought with palpable relief.

She was bored of Tara and more than ready to move on. Despite the noise, she heard his high gasp well over everyone's heads. In apparent disbelief, he mumbled over his discovery for an undue span. Aoife rolled her eyes. Just how thick were these people? Gods! He showed the wad in his palm, first to the boy's parents, who shook their bleary heads in confusion, then to his two companions in town governance. They scratched their heads and argued amongst themselves to an infernal degree.

The crowd grew more curious by the second but not fast enough for Aoife's taste. "Ain't those *Sidhe* colors?" she called, moving further away. The gasp that rippled through the onlookers was precisely what she wanted to hear.

"I was at Dumnain, Master Lilken! Them are Sidhe colors— the High King's guard!" bayed one fellow. "Leapin' stag, three stars. All done up white."

"Why would the Sidhe murder a young boy in Tara?" disagreed a matron behind him. "Yer barkin'."

"How would a lad like Denn have such a thing if it ain't true?"

"I seen them colors too. At Palsneath, two days ago. They found a pair o'girls dead by the riverside there. One o'em, lovely lass by all accounts, facedown over the white arrow what done her in," said another.

A bevy of 'nays' answered that accusation.

"What's he doin' with that sort of tunic in his hand then, eh?" asked someone else.

"Well," said a neighbor. "Denn *were* a bit fleet of finger, ye ask me. Maybe he—"

"… heard there's been loads o'these sorts o'attacks, younguns, mostly. Up and down the—"

"… Aye, they all say the High King's ailin'. Ain't left his hall in near on twenty years. Maybe he's losin' control o'his—"

"… Ain't the same no more since the Crown Prince died. I hear—"

Mission accomplished.

Aoife whirled away from the gathering. Creahal and Carn waited for her in the woods, a mile outside of town. They were twins. Aoife had known them since she was a girl. Their presence was the sole kindness Grainne thought to provide for her on this most odious of quests. They'd been her father Sionnavar's thrains and, technically, part of her inheritance. Blood-bonded men were hard to come by and equally challenging to keep from their masters. They could not serve her within the Cloister, but they were ever ready to ride to her aid. Once Grainne grew bored of punishing her, she'd given Aoife leave to choose her accomplices.

No choice could have been simpler.

She wouldn't call the brutal pair 'friends': Aoife did not understand what that word even meant, but she disliked them least. Besides, they came in handy. Usually, she was left to perform Nema's impossible tasks on her own. Creahal passed her a bone flask once she was properly seated on her mount.

"Any word from Her Whorish Majesty?" she asked.

Carn grinned at his brother. Their skin gleamed bronze in the cold morning sunlight. "Aye, Lady Sionnavar. She bid us tell you we're meant to march south this time, closer to Bethany."

"Whatever. Where will she be while we're doing all the work?"

The brothers were well used to Aoife's vitriol. If her grandmother couldn't break her of the habit, two low-born Bolgish warriors would be hard-pressed to try. "In Tairngare, lady. The Dowager is holding a banquet for visiting dignitaries."

Aoife whistled, tugging on her reins. Behind them, Tara's bells chimed furiously, and farmers trickled through the gates like their crops were after them. They would lock those gates now and stand watch on the walls while their officials sent messages to neighboring townships. A murdering band of Sidhe warriors was on the prowl. She expected the news would be all over Eire in a few days. "So soon? Well, she is in a hurry, isn't she?"

Creahal concurred, "Our time approaches."

Aoife half-laughed. "We'll see if it's an improvement. She can't repudiate Midhir this quickly. She must have some other game in mind."

"She intends to feast the lords and ladies of the Cymrian Merchers Guild, her most recent converts, and allow them to air their grievances over the High King. The Dowager is quite clever, Lady Sionnavar. You take after her," said Carn.

"I'll forgive you for that, once."

Carn ducked his head. "No offense intended."

She made a face. "While she and my worthless cousin Grainne are busily stuffing their holes with pie, we have work to do."

"Yes, My Lady," they said in unison.

Unrolling a worn map from the breast pocket of her tunic, she traced a forefinger around the mound of Tara to the South. "I suppose Malahide and its satellite townships are ripe for a raid? Let's hit the villages first, then round up in the city, as we've done here."

"Very good, My Lady."

Ahead, under the shade of crackling, winter-stripped trees, waited twenty well-armed Bolgish Warhammers. Each wore a lovely white Dannan cuirass, stained with blood and darker things. Giving them a slight nod, she reined in below the far-reaching boughs of an ancient oak. "We're headed south. Keep your ogham charms close, boys. We don't want these simpering Eireans to have the first idea what's coming for them, now do we?"

This Gilded Cage

Una watched snowflakes gather and swirl outside her tiny window and longed for the courage to squeeze through and leap. If the seven-story fall didn't kill her, and the cold idn't finish her, perhaps she'd swim to safety on the far shore? Donahugh's Bay was not especially deep at its northern side. The muddy, dark Lee wound inland through spotty reeds and shallow tidal pools. Here, below Kevin's Keep, the dark green sea writhed and churned along its engineered cliff. Many centuries ago, before the waters receded and ice reclaimed the northernmost reaches of the continent, the ocean had nearly gobbled up all of the southeastern shoreline.

In a furious bid to salvage their coastland and protect their farms and homes from inundation, the ancient Eireans had hastily constructed huge cofferdams filled with limestone and shale from the Eirean interior. Massive granite girders and artificial cliffs of cultivated earth and stone were stacked one on top of the other until the Southeastern shore bore as many crags and cliffs as the Ring of Kerry in the west. None could ever deny that Bethany's builders had been a remarkable group of engineers.

Her ancestor, Duch Thomas Donahugh, had been more enamored of the Bethonair legacy than anyone before him. He spent decades adding to the founders' achievements. Substantial stone walls were stacked atop cliffs he'd heightened by another twenty feet. The old roads, leading through to the ancient city of Cork a few miles upriver, were repaved to stretch to the coast, where the foundations of his new fortress were laid. Naturally, the citizens followed the workers. A new city sprang up around his rudimentary Keep. By the time her grandfather Kevin had become Duch, Bethany was already a bustling seaside port, with some four hundred thousand families thriving under Donahugh rule. Duch Kevin was himself an avid builder. He spent twenty years rebuilding Thomas' fortress to its present might and grandeur. Hence, it now bore his name. For Una, the engineering marvels that produced such an imposing seaside citadel were equally infuriating. A sheer drop over steep cliffs into frigid waters choked with ice and sharp stones muddled any escape plan she might have— as Patrick had known it would. If she survived the fall, she'd be sucked out to sea by the current long before she made it to the shallows on the opposite side of the bay.

She was well and trapped.

Short of condoning the murder of her maids, she had little choice but to wait for a better opportunity. She couldn't fly, could she? What else was she supposed to do? Sighing, she watched the snow billet against the glass pane and buried her longing down deep. Moaning over her fate would do her no bloody good. She had time to *plan* if nothing else. That must be how she approached things from here on. Defying Patrick's wishes and remaining cooped up in her chambers for weeks might have satisfied some inner need to humiliate her father, but it did nothing to further her cause.

Indeed, the one person suffering from her sulk was herself.

Perhaps, Patrick's greatest weapon was boredom.

"Planning to leap into the wind, my dear?" inquired the man himself from the open door. His voice made her jump.

She hadn't seen him for some days. Chuckling, he turned to wave his guardsmen in. Each bore a heavy trunk, which they heaved onto the bearskin rug and took their leave. Una groaned. "What in the Hells is this?"

"Clothes, jewels, pretty things I expect you to wear. What else?" he said, patting his shrinking gut with a knowing smile. "Come, Una, a lovely frock is hardly torture."

She wrinkled her nose and turned away. "Leave them and go."

He looked around. "It's dull as a library in here, girl. Get up. We're going for a walk."

"*No*, thank you."

"You can walk on your own two feet or be dragged through the halls by my Corpsmen. Don't test me, Una. There are people I want you to meet."

Patrick crossed his arms. They glared at each other in silence for a long while. In the end, Una's acute boredom won out. What was a little humiliation to weeks of self-imposed solitary confinement? Sucking her teeth with exaggerated malice, she stood up and smoothed her gown, a cream and gold-colored bit of frippery that looked well with the pearls winding through her hair. "Fine. Where shall I pretend to be a simpering maiden first, father?"

Patrick cocked his head. "I believe that's the first time you've called me 'father' in years. I'm overcome with paternal pride, child."

Una smiled. "Finding a fact odious doesn't make it less true."

It was his turn to snort. He stuck out an arm, and Una took it without further comment. Steering her out into the hall, Patrick grinned from ear to ear. The walls had been recently washed and rehung with thick, colorful tapestries, Una noted as she was led toward the winding stair. When she'd been carted up here so many days before, there had been dirty rushes scattered everywhere, soot-stained walls, and endless leaves had blown in from a broken window. Now, the glass was refitted and sparkling, the walls were clean and brightly decorated, and the candles illuminating their path were scented beeswax. It seemed the servants had been quite busy while she'd been incarcerated in her mother's former apartments. She tried not to look too impressed.

"So," he said as they reached the third-floor hall. Workers rushed about, hanging textiles, cleaning, and making minor repairs. Undoubtedly, Patrick intended Kevin's Keep would be gleaming for the coming festivities. She chewed her cheek in silence. "Tell me of yourself. What do you enjoy most?"

They passed through an arch, then down the second flight of stairs to the Grand Hall. She caught sight of Martin O'Rearden barking orders at a group of Corpsmen in the far alcove. Raising his head, he grinned when he saw her. The ghost of a smile flickered over her face as they strolled by. "Freedom," she answered.

Patrick patted her forearm, where it wound through his. She chewed her cheek in irritation. Courtiers crushed themselves into the rich wooden paneling before his throne room to make room for the Duch and his scowling daughter. "You are free, Una. Realize it before you ruin yourself... or someone else."

"What is *that* supposed to mean?" she hissed, trying to keep her voice down. There were far too many curious faces in here for her comfort. Every one of them stared, some with their mouths wide open. She felt like an insect under glass. "I am not here by choice if you recall?"

He led her past the throne and the huge stained-glass mosaic that depicted her great-grandfather's demise. She forced herself not to look up into Kaer Yin's face, emblazoned there in brilliant, multifaceted relief. She refused to weep in front of anyone. Patrick snapped his fingers. His guards opened the door to his private apartments, then shut them again on the whispering crowd. Inside her father's rustic office, two boys that had been seated leaped to their feet. Well, one was a boy— twelve or thirteen, at most. The other was taller and broader through the shoulder, blond, handsome, and nervous. He was perhaps twenty years old or less. Both squirmed when they saw her. The younger sulked while the elder's face flushed a vivid scarlet. Una raised her brows.

Patrick nudged her forward, ever so slightly. "Una Alis Donahugh, future Duchess of Bethany and heir to my throne, meet your cousins, Micah and Isaac Donahugh."

The boys ducked into the most awkward bows Una had ever seen. She bit her lip.

"Well, daughter. Say hello," urged Patrick, shuffling off to the fireplace and his armchair. His steward, Shanley, had a full tankard of spiced cider already waiting. Una fidgeted a little. This wasn't what she'd expected at all. She thought the old bastard wanted to parade her through his court and humiliate her to the nth degree. Meeting two twitchy boys who appeared to be as nervous and out of place as she was far from that.

"Ah, hello. Prima Una *Moura*, sirs. Pleased to make your acquaintance." She dipped into a half-remembered curtsy, ignoring the sharp flash of her father's eyes.

"It's your turn to say something, Micah," the Duch prodded.

Micah had a hard time glancing up from his shoes. "Ah, we… ah. That is… we're pleased to make yer… I mean *your* acquaintance too, milady." He elbowed his brother.

With his wild, dark eyes, Little Isaac glowered back at her. "Yeah, whatever."

Una failed to repress a smile. "Erm, thank you."

Patrick patted the chair in front of him. She tucked herself into the seat without complaint and accepted a tankard from Shanley. The boys took chairs opposite, backs ramrod straight. Micah turned an even brighter red. "Now, Una, Isaac here is going to be a knight. He's quite fierce. Try not to be frightened."

Isaac, she noticed, perked up at that.

"Oh, indeed?" she asked him. "Will it be quests and noble deeds, or will you be the bravest knight in the tourney?"

"Battles, o'course." His narrow chest puffed out. "I'll be more famous n'me da, one day. He were the best knight around. Everyone says so."

Una had yet to meet her wayward uncle and was somewhat surprised not to find him here with his sons. She tucked that tidbit away for further examination. She took a sip from her tankard, politely waiting for Micah to cease swallowing before she addressed him.

Not so good with girls, this one.

"I see. And you, Micah? To which discipline do you aspire?"

"Uh… s-statecraft, milady."

"Is that so?"

"Yeah… er, *yes.*"

"Una is quite studious herself, Micah," interrupted Patrick. "For twelve years, she studied Civic Law in Tairngare. Is that not so, daughter?"

How did he know that? "Yes."

Micah blinked at her. "Ye did? But yer so… so…."

"Una's mother hailed from the Red City. In Tairngare, noblewomen are expected to be highly educated. I think you'll find the two of you have many interests in common."

Una's head swiveled toward her father.

Pimping me out already, old man?

"The Duch is right. I studied Civic and Ecclesiastical Law, Particle Theory, Economics, History, and Bretagn. You?" The way Micah flushed anew told her all she needed to know. Poor boy. He, too, was another of Patrick's pawns, in way over his head.

"Law and History, milady. S'all."

"So far," amended Patrick. "Master one subject at a time or understand none, I always say. Now, in a little while, I'll be holding Court. I'd like it if the two elder children were there. What better way to learn? Isaac, my brave lad. You'll be sent to practice with Master Gremel." Isaac beamed. No politician would that one be. "After the proceedings, I think we should have supper in here. Doesn't that sound nice?"

Una shifted in her seat.

Micah echoed her sentiments. Neither answered.

"Excellent! Let's chat a bit longer, then—"

The door burst inward. Damek stalked inside, his expression thunderous. Martin followed as always, with his furrowed brow and apologetic demeanor. "What is the meaning of this?" Damek demanded, raking his eyes over those gathered. When he came to Una— her tankard paused midway between her lap and lip— he feigned a simper. "Having a family meeting without me, uncle? That's hardly sporting."

Patrick groaned, "Don't be so dramatic, Damek. The boys wanted to meet their cousin now that she's home, as is proper."

"*Did they?*" Even Isaac shrank beneath Damek's murderous glare.

Una twisted her lip at him. Unperturbed, he kicked over a chair and took a seat beside her. "In that case, let's *do* get to know one another. Shall we?"

Patrick struggled between laughter and rage. Una could tell. "Boys, this is Damek Bishop, Lord of Clare, Marshal of my Souther Legions, and High Commander of my Steel Corps. Damek, this is Micah and Isaac *Donahugh*."

Una nearly winced at the venom in that last dig. She watched a muscle tick low in Damek's cheek and hid her grin behind her tankard. Her uncle Henry's boys murmured scarcely decipherable greetings. Without warning or excuse, Damek snatched Una's tankard and glared at them over its rim. Patrick snapped his fingers again, and another was hastily placed in her hand. "Charming as ever, aren't you?"

Damek didn't turn. Wherever he'd been, he was filthy and reeked of sour ale. His raven hair was unkempt, his collar askew, and if she weren't mistaken, he bore a fair slathering of rouge at his neckline. Disgusted, she leaned away. Observing her from the corner of his eye, he shrugged. "You can pretend you don't like it, and I'll pretend to be duly chastened."

"You're *nauseating*, you—"

"Was there a bloody point to this embarrassing interruption?" growled Patrick. Martin had the grace to flinch and back up toward the door.

Damek rolled a shoulder. "Part of the family, aren't I? Maybe I wanted to meet them, too? Besides, now they've seen *her*, *my* face should be the image burned into their eyelids forever afterward. That, my dear cousins, is the point of my being here." He took a long sip and made a face. "Reason. Don't we have anything better than this swill?"

Patrick's steward dashed off to find more robust fare. Patrick chuckled. "You burn through all the uishge you brought south?"

"Unfortunately. I'll say this for that cesspit of trees and backward fools, they know how to make a drink."

Micah sent Una a sympathetic half-smile. She was surprised. Was it so obvious how she felt about her brutish cousin? "F-forgive me, milord. What is 'wis-key'?"

Damek raised a brow. "You're kidding, right?"

Una answered for him. "A spirit made from smoke and peat. The old Eireans used to call it 'the water of life.' Currently, it's illegal, but that hardly stops it being made."

"Can I go to practice now, Uncle? This is borin'," whinged Isaac, as a young lad would. Una, again, couldn't conceal her amusement.

Patrick waved a hand, and a guardsman escorted Isaac from the room. He didn't spare any of them the slightest interest, including his older brother. When he'd gone, Micah cleared his throat. "Apologies for my brother. He's young yet, and ah… as ye see."

"Quite all right. It does wax stuffy in here," laughed Patrick. "Now then. Damek, Micah is a great admirer of your career."

"Oh?"

Patrick opened his mouth to make further pleasantries when Micah finally found his voice. He sat up a bit straighter, his attention fixed. "Yes! I've wanted to meet ye, long as we been here, milord. They say yer the best swordsman in the South. How many battles have ye fought? I heard about the time ye were ambushed by that Bretagn Lord Gaelin and how ye—"

"Micah," Patrick chided.

Faced with such guileless flattery, Damek's ire deflated. "Ah, well, that's all right. Perhaps I'll give you a demonstration—"

"Damek!" Una snapped.

"As My Lady commands." He saluted her with his stolen tankard.

She turned to Patrick with an irritated huff. "I think that's enough for today, don't you? This idiot is dawdling here to mark territory that is neither his nor wants to be. I'd rather spend the day pondering the leap from my window if it's all the same to you?"

"I suppose you have a point, my dear," Patrick agreed. "Micah, would you care to escort your cousin to her rooms? My old knees, you understand. The climb is not so simple as it once was."

Una could hear the air whistle through Damek's nostrils.

"Of c-course, uncle." Micah blushed, getting to his feet.

Damek gripped Una's elbow first. She clawed at his arm, but he wouldn't be detached. "Nonsense. I'll see her back—"

"Lay a hand on me again, and I will make you eat your tongue," she warned, shoving him off. Before he could collect himself and lunge again, she strolled behind Patrick's chair. "Father, I'd prefer it if Lord Bishop were kept apart from me."

Damek snickered. "Oh, well *done,* Una."

"Martin?" Patrick called.

"My lord?" he replied.

"See that the Lord of Clare is scrubbed, chastened, and *sober* when next he's in my presence. If he refuses, remind him he may be denied the privilege of the Keep altogether. What a shame that would be, eh? With so many fine lords on the way?"

Una watched that muscle flex again in Damek's clenched jaw. "Una. Don't forget what I said. I'm all you have." He gave her a long, accusatory look, spun on his heel, and marched out as suddenly as he appeared. Una's fingers unfurled.

"Is he always like that, uncle?" asked Micah, with an anxious sag to his shoulders.

"Lad, you haven't seen anything yet," Patrick sighed.

⚐⚑

IN THE FOLLOWING DAYS, UNA opted to sit with her father and Micah at Court. As long as Damek was disinvited, she had nothing better to do. After a few tankards of cider, she could even imagine she was having a good time. Her cousin Micah, it turned out, was a sweet, biddable young man with an inquisitive mind and wholesome manners. He was a bit rough around the edges, having been raised in the less cosmopolitan Cymrian lowlands, but to Una's mind, his flaws were part of his charm. He sat beside her, asking questions and answering those directed his way. Despite herself, Una quite liked him. Their family squabble aside, she was glad to have at least one relative in the South she didn't despise. Two, actually. She couldn't help but enjoy savage little Isaac as well. Since their introduction, Patrick had a sideways smirk on his infuriating cheeks that she didn't care for at all. She endeavored to ignore him unless he spoke to either of them directly.

Thankfully, she and Micah sat upon the dais, slightly behind the throne. Patrick's courtiers buzzed like bees over their convivial appearance, but neither paid the least attention. Una felt she might have made her first friend in Bethany. After all, they were both hostages here, weren't they?

Why shouldn't they find some common ground?

The proceedings passed with uneventful adjudications and quiet conversation until a farmer stomped up to the dais with an armful of bloodied rags, which Una assumed had once been a girl's gown.

Bleary-eyed, he tossed the wad at the Duch's feet.

Patrick stiffened. "What's the meaning of this?"

His guards tugged the farmer upright by his grubby collar. "My girl," he sputtered. "Found her at the mouth o'the Lee, not a fortnight past. Ye've done nothin'!"

"Watch your tongue, peasant," the Duch spat. "We are doing everything—"

"No, yer not! *Three* so far, last I heard, been pulled from the river in bits and ye sit there protectin' that foul brother o'yers, what done this!"

Lord Wender put his hand on his sabre. "You'll be whipped for that!"

Perplexed, Micah got to his feet. Una stood with him. "You can't be speakin' o'my da? He can barely walk by himself!"

Struggling against the guards who held him, the farmer shook his daughter's bloodied clothing at him. "Ye don't know him, do ye? Many o'us are old enough to remember— oof!" The guard nearest the dais rammed his gauntleted fist into the farmer's hollow midsection. The farmer shrank in their grip, but his burning eyes met Micah's nonetheless. "Why don't ye ask him, eh? Ask anyone who don't fear the truth."

"That's enough," Patrick rumbled, slapping a hand against his knee. "The crimes you're alluding to were solved. My father strung the perpetrator from a crow's cage. Now, the Court mourns your loss but lobbing accusations at a man confined to quarters for his health most days will not bring your girl back. Sir Gaffigan? Please ensure this man is given a warm meal and enough coin to see him and his family through the winter." Patrick waved a hand, and the farmer was dragged out, spewing denial and curses. The blood-stained rags remained on the floor before the throne.

"Uncle?" asked Micah uncertainly.

Patrick smeared his palm over both eyes with a heavy sigh. "Court is convened for the day. Leave us."

Courtiers filed out, their footsteps against the flagstones half as loud as their whispers. Una absorbed every shocked, suspicious glare, every nervous giggle, or mocking comment. She watched the Duch shrivel in his chair. It seemed the notorious Henry of Bethany was not the only tired old man in residence.

"Uncle?" Micah repeated.

"You too, lad. Both of you, return to your quarters."

Micah flinched away. His expression proved a war between uncertainty and indignation. Dutiful lad he was, he bowed and awkwardly extended his arm to lead Una away. She shook her head. "I will stay a while."

He retracted his hand with a brief nod. "As you will, milady."

Patrick leaned back against his ancient, mahogany throne with a dry laugh. "Now she wants to stay behind. Surrender, is it?"

"Hardly. Tell me about these girls."

He attempted a caustic shrug. "The corpses of three servants were found near the river in the last month."

She sucked in a breath and took a seat on the stairs. Patrick gestured for his guards and servants to back away from the dais. "How were they found?"

"All done the same way: beaten, strangled, then stabbed."

"*Siora*," she whispered. "Were they… interfered with?"

"You mean raped?"

She flushed. "Yes."

"No. Killed merely for the sport of it, it seems."

Una was silent for a time. "Why would anyone believe your brother did this?"

He gave her a cruel sort of smile. "Why the sudden interest? Aren't we Donahughs all murderous brutes? I know I am… as are you, so I'm told." The blood rushed into Una's throat. Above her head, Kaer Yin glared down at her from the stained-glass window. She didn't look up, as if his eyes might bore a hole straight through her skull. Patrick noted her discomfiture. He pointed. "Some say your great-grandsire's murderer rescued you. Damek is drinking himself half to death, believing you cared for the Sidhe bastard. Is it true?"

"No," she lied through clenched teeth. "You're changing the subject."

Patrick fiddled with one of his rings. His father's, Una recalled, set with a great round emerald the size of her pinky nail. "Once upon a time, my brother was the most handsome man in Eire. He was a brave and brilliant knight, charming, intelligent, and well-loved by everyone, despite his bastardy. Much as Damek is now," he said, staring up at the mosaic she refused to acknowledge. "Then our father died, and I was crowned Duch. Henry considered himself better than me at everything, and I suppose he was. His temper grew worse by the day. My men often found him in the Pleasure District, drunk as a satyr. He vented his bitterness on the commoners, most. Women, especially.

"I wasn't forced to intervene until a few of their families made formal complaints. To expedite this tale, I will tell you Henry was sent away for a time, and when he returned, he'd found the Old Religion. He behaved himself for a great long time after, and I heard no more of any molested girls. That is, until our sister went missing from the High King's Council," Patrick's voice went cold as the sea outside. "We declared war to reclaim her. We lost. That pretty Sidhe princeling you purportedly admire smashed Henry's vanguard to bits on the first day of battle, then crept into the village where Henry's officers were encamped and murdered them to a man. Henry, himself, escaped the same fate because he and his honor guard had gone to spy on the Tairnganeah's camp, some five miles east. Without our officers, the troops were leaderless and divided. The next day, Fionn O'More, the High King's next champion, rode over our footsoldiers like insects in the road.

"Henry did not take defeat or the loss of Alis well. When he returned home, beaten and conflicted, many more girls were abused. So many, I was forced to confine him to chambers. He didn't like that one bit. Still raw at me for our losses up North and for the death of our sister (no doubt, for the air I breathed), he attempted to overthrow me. Again, he was defeated. He fled to Cymru, got those two boys on some washerwoman in the Wastes, and styled himself a wandering priest. When we found him years later, he and his followers were making a name for themselves as crusader bandits. They burned half a dozen small villages to convert the Ancestor's worshippers. I had him brought home in chains and thrown into the dungeon for a decade."

Una's brow wrinkled after this recitation. "Why would you release such a monster?"

"Henry has a part to play in my plans, Una. A critical one, at that. He's a sickly specter of a man now, but he has his uses."

"He's a rapist and a murderer."

"Rapist, yes. I won't argue that, but none were ever killed. I'm told that one died in childbirth, but otherwise, his victims lived. Cruelly used and discarded, yes. Never murdered."

"Then why?"

"Did that farmer lob the accusation? He was distraught, and Henry had lost his favor among the common folk long ago. His circle is limited to dithering old bigots and dry old women seeking validation from his backward religion."

Una mulled that over for a while. "That doesn't mean his… tastes have changed. Why would you assume that he isn't responsible this time?"

"Do you genuinely take an interest in this case?" he tested, tenting his fingers. "These are Souther girls, after all. Why would you care?"

He had her there. Her cheeks blazed. "Whatever we think of each other, and however much I despise this place, I take a *keen* interest in the suffering of my sex."

"Very well." With a curt nod, he reached into his doublet to retrieve a folded sheaf of vellum and handed it over. Una sifted through the hastily scratched report on each page, perplexed. "Coroner's reports."

Una skimmed through as quickly as she could. In the end, she gasped. "None?"

"None," he agreed and leaned forward to tap the conclusion on the last page. "Henry assaulted one of my serving girls this past month. I had to pay her off and move her family from the city. The girl is carrying my wizened elder brother's fifth illegitimate child."

"This is not conclusive evidence."

"The killer is impotent."

Una tsked. "You can't know that for sure. I'd say your brother is a very likely candidate. Some men are not, erm, always able to—"

"Look at the dates."

She did. The final entry was dated two days before. "What does this prove?"

"I confined Henry to his quarters a week ago. He's had neither the time nor the opportunity. It can't be him."

She set the sheaf down on the top step. "That means?"

"… Someone else is doing the killing."

Bone of Contention

Damek watched her from the southern parapet, drinking from a horn flask and grinding his molars to powder. A familiar dragging step behind him brought an even deeper scowl to his face. "For an ailing man, you do get around. What do you want?"

Wearing his prized white-bear cloak, Patrick slid beside his nephew and looked down. He made a sort of chuckle that heated Damek's blood to boiling. It had stopped snowing, but in true Innish fashion, a frigid rain dappled the white earth brown in the courtyard below. Una and Micah strolled together, arm in arm, guards following at a respectful distance. Their two golden heads dipped in mutual mirth.

"She is a beauty, I'll say, so much more than her mother ever was. Arrin quite stole my breath the first time I beheld her. A shame about all those ugly tattoos, though," Patrick mused. "Nevertheless, she'll be a formidable Duchess."

"You haven't answered my question."

Patrick ran his gloved fingers along the stone wall, clearing it of ice. "You'll never woo her this way, you know? Watching her from afar, goading her to fight each time you see her, or drinking yourself unconscious in the bloody *Butterfly* every night. She is angry with you, and you're making it worse."

"I ask again, whose fault is that? You played the game of matrimony with us to tease wealthy lords to jealousy. You ripped us apart."

"You broke into her chambers and assaulted her after the annulment."

Damek thought about pitching him over the wall. Patrick's guards—silent, ever-present sentinels—gripped their sabres at his expression. "I've had more than enough of that baseless accusation. She's furious with me because I told you of our child. That's the truth. Because of my mistake, you incarcerated her to keep it a secret from your Gods-damned barons. If you try that tack with me again, your guards will never stop me in time, *uncle*."

"Fine," Patrick conceded with a tight-lipped smirk. "I'm to blame for your unhappiness. I tried to save my daughter from an unseemly union."

Damek took another long pull from his flask, his guts stewing. "You stole her from me for amusement and spite. With an heir, female or no, *I* would have been too powerful for you to control. Our child might have pushed you from the throne. You couldn't have that. Could you?"

"No, I could not," Patrick admitted with a sidelong glance. "Had I known what a miscalculation that would have been in the end, I might have merely had you murdered. Nevertheless, the failings of yesteryear grow rotten on the vine. Here we are now, all this while later, and we must make do."

Damek's fists clenched and unclenched. "That's the first time I've heard you admit to folly, uncle. I hope you choke on it."

"I'm dying, Damek."

Everything stopped: the rain, the starved gulls circling overhead, the crash of relentless green waves beneath, and the hammer of his pulse. "*What?*"

"Weeks, maybe more. That's what I have left."

Damek drew a long stream of air through flaring nostrils. "Why tell *me?*"

Patrick quirked a lip. "You're my child, same as she. I raised you and need you now, as you need me."

Utterly floored, Damek took a step back. "I—"

"Don't bother. I require no sympathy or honeyed words. Instead, there are many things we must discuss. Obviously, I desire my daughter on the throne."

"Of… course."

"I've had papers drawn up. You *will* sign them or be expelled from my service. You'll be beholden to my barons, as I am, and make no premature bids for the throne. I will have your vow or your head."

"Are you… passing me the crown?"

Patrick made a face. "Of course not, you idiot boy. I'm passing *her* the bloody crown." He swiped a hand at where Una and Micah made for the Hall once more. "If you want her, you'll have to convince her yourself. I won't force her a second time."

"I could kill you now and take them both."

"You could. I've no doubt you'd best my guards, but for Una's sake, you won't. Why are you up here brooding, hm? You make so much noise about being the only man worthy of her, don't you? Here's your chance to prove it. I'm legitimizing you, Damek. You no longer need Una to achieve your goals. Hells, I imagine right now she'd even abdicate in your favor if you'd turn her loose, but I'm hoping she'll stay and rule of her own accord. My barons won't approve you as Duch unless she wills it. So, what will you do now? Is it Una you want or my throne? I believe you could have one without the other right now."

Ears buzzing and head gone hot, Damek crouched against the wall. He could be Duch. *In weeks*, if he wished. All he had to do was ask, and she would give it freely. Happily, even. He could be Duch and, eventually, King of Eire. He could do it.

He *would* do it.

This was the only thing Damek had ever wanted. The crown was in his grasp, at last! He could let her go; she was just another woman. He had dozens of women, heiresses, and whores, alike.

What did he need Una for, if not the throne?

Patrick saw the ambition clouding Damek's face. "If the crown is all that matters to you, set my daughter free when I pass. Keep Henry's boys busy but unharmed. It will be *that* simple for you. I'm giving you everything you've ever wanted, as you deserve."

Una laughed in the distance.

The sound whipped through Damek's middle like a scythe.

Patrick saw that too. "Remember, this offer is valid so long as my daughter is unharmed and happy. My barons will revolt the minute you press your luck and be warned, there's a reason why the High King has never tried to sack the South a second time."

Damek expelled a long breath. "Why the sudden concern for her happiness? It's never troubled you before now."

"It doesn't matter why. If you mean to be King of Eire, despite that old hag you call 'grandmama,' you will obey me. Let her go and be all that you ever wished to be."

He could do it. Live without her.

She hates you, anyway.

His mind raced.

"However, if you wish for both, you'll have to earn them on your own, boy. My tourney will provide all the wealth, troops, and suitor-gifts I require for my barons to reclaim Tara and the Midlands. My final wish as Duch Donahugh is a country of our own. I would very much like to imagine my daughter and her children will follow me as queens and kings of Eire… but I will not force her, and by Reason, neither shall you. I won't stand in your way if you can woo her during the fête. However, that is all the time you'll be given to decide."

A black grease spot settled in Damek's gut at the thought of another man taking his place. He'd already calculated the myriad ways he planned to murder his cousin Micah for his brass. Additional suitors were sure to drive him mad.

Forget her. You don't need her.

Look what he's offering you. Finally!

He stood up. Decision made. Una meant nothing to him.

Nothing. She could take herself back to Tairngare or the Kneeler's Hell for all he cared. He would be Duch. "I value the crown over a woman's whims, even hers."

Patrick observed him from under lowered lashes. "Good. Then you won't mind that the Prince of Connaught has bid for her hand and is on his way here with a 'mountain of gold and silks' for his prospective Milesian bride?"

"*What?*" he repeated darkly.

"I did warn you. She's the catch of the Continent, nephew. Lord Gaelin and his sons are travelling here to hail her, as well as Ladies Wendelin and Penwyth of Kernow and their broods. Let's see, there's Baron Grim, Lord Talbot, Earl Jasper of Cymru, Lady Rhiannon, and all our Courtiers here, of course. Why do you look so green? I hear the Prince of Connaught loves a challenge and is wealthy and stupid enough to venture here to bid for her hand. Must be pretty dull in unchanging Aes Sidhe, no?"

"The Prince of Connaught? Uncle, you can't be serious? That's *his* cousin! He's surely coming here to—"

"So what? If you aim to be Duch and rule over all of Eire one day, Una will have to go somewhere, won't she? I won't take that remiss if she taints the Adair Clan with my bloodline. You'll hear me laughing from Tech Duinn."

"I will *never*—"

"You're not Duch yet, boy. I repeat, if you'd have *both*, you must earn them. Now, I've said my piece. I'll give you two weeks to decide. If you eschew my offer and attempt to wait me out, I must warn you, you'll be wasting your time. I've had two wills drafted. One shall be fed to the flames the minute air ceases to pump through my lungs. One names you my heir and the other Una's enemy. My barons already have my instructions. Some are very eager to remove you altogether." With that, he patted Damek's shoulder and shuffled away.

Damek's voice caught him at the bottom step. "What of Henry, uncle? Why let him go if this was going to be your decision?"

A dark smirk crossed Patrick's mouth. "Why don't you think on it a while? It'll come to you."

❦

Henry was escorted into the Hall for supper. With a tight smile, he took in the shining tableau, his resplendent family, and their accouterment upon the dais. Patrick sat in the center, in state, their father's slim, iron coronet upon his balding head. He looked up at Henry's announcement and waved his brother over. Ignoring the knights and commoners gawping at him from the lower tables, Henry glided by. The Hall positively glittered as it hadn't in Henry's memory. Their father certainly hadn't prioritized a tidy Keep nor a grand reception space in which to feast. Patrick must have been keen to impress the incoming gentry. Behind the throne swung two massive banners emblazoned with the Southernmost Star, and the Donahugh colors flashed from every dust-free corner and bench throughout the room.

To Patrick's either side sat his heretic daughter and Henry's own son. Supper was a small, light meal of stew and bread for the courtiers seated below the nobles. Finer fare—pheasant and roasted boar— awaited him upon the dais. Micah beamed down at Henry, his blond curls gleaming in the candlelight. Henry nodded, careful not to display too much pride, or else his brother would seize the chance to humiliate him further. The girl appeared even less enthused about her surroundings than Henry. She was pretty enough, he supposed, for a witch. She had that lovely Tairnganese complexion many Souther girls had envied in his youth. Her mother, Arrin, had been a gorgeous, refined lady. This one seemed a touch savage for the cutting amber gleam in her eyes. He could sense her disdain like a brand.

Wasn't that interesting? Patrick must have been telling tales. He stopped at the bottom stair while Patrick sucked at a chicken wing.

"Brother."

"Bilford? Get Sir Henry a chair, if you please, and a setting."

So, he was to be included in a 'family' meal?

Bilford dragged over a stool and situated him at the foot of the table, directly below Patrick's eye. Inclusive but unequal. He didn't mind, did he? He'd been through far worse indignities than this. While the soldiers and Courtiers tittered from the room's rear, he mocked them in his heart: *Laugh now, for I'm up here… and you're all down there.*

As if he'd been invited to take Patrick's seat, Henry folded his rough linen napkin like delicate lace and clutched his wooden utensils like the finest silver. They'd really get a show when he removed his dentures to gnaw at his meat. For now, he stuck to the potatoes and softest fare. "To what do I owe this rare honor? I hadn't thought I was meant to dine with other human beings in a civilized manner."

Patrick chuckled. "Stop whingeing, Henry. Our guests will be arriving for the fête next week. I'd like everyone in the family to know what is expected of them, yourself included." Patrick paused, dropping his bones onto his plate. He looked around. "Matter of fact, where is my irritating nephew? Hisk?"

"My lord?" said the Corpsman, rising from his place at the back. The local lords and ladies were gathered on cushioned benches arranged below the dais in four rows, though many seats were empty in expectation of incoming guests. Their tables were nearly as decked out as the Duch's, with roasted boar and geese awaiting carving at the center and many gleaming goblets of ale and mead held aloft in bejeweled hands. Beyond this collection of wealth and privilege lay the less-ostentatious tables and benches reserved for Damek's officers and elite Corpsmen. Of these, Martin, Douglas, Ridley, and Hisk sat nearest the front.

"Where is Damek? He'd better not be at that infernal tavern again, or I'll have someone's fingers. I vow it."

"I'm here, uncle," said Damek, revealing himself near the windows.

Henry nearly gasped at the sight. Aside from his Bolgish height and coloring, Damek was Alis' spit, through and through. Same narrow nose, wide mouth, and winged brows. The lad turned, tankard in hand, with a sardonic smile. He wore a cobalt doublet over a dusky scarlet tunic, the colors of Donahugh's house.

A bit on the nose, wasn't it?

Henry had to admit, though, that the boy did turn out. Damek's gaze skipped everyone in the room to rest directly on Henry's wild niece.

Bold too, Henry thought, slurping his ale.

"Lady Wendelin's troupe have begun to arrive. I can see her colors on the hill," said Damek.

"Excellent. Shanley, run out to the stables and make sure all is prepared for our guests. I don't imagine they'll be joining us until tomorrow morning," barked Patrick.

"My Lord." Shanley bowed awkwardly and dashed off.

Damek strolled over with surefooted grace and sank into a chair beside his favored cousin. Una stiffened slightly but made no comment. She kept her eyes firmly on her plate. "Her sons might join the men later for ale and songs. I assume Lord Gaelin will be here the day after tomorrow?" Damek inquired of his uncle, though he grinned at Una.

"Last report, yes. Micah," said Patrick, leaning over. "Lord Gaelin's youngest, Castor, is also quite studious of Civics, as you and Una are."

"Is that so, uncle?" Micah hummed. "Perhaps we shall be friends?"

Damek coughed behind his tankard. Una shot him a very dry glare. He spread his palms. "Let's not forget, we're all here to compete for my fair lady's hand. Gaelin's sons are great burly beasts, more interested in horseflesh than women. But do go on. I love a good fable."

Una set her fork down. "I wish to be excused."

"You may not. Eat your potatoes. You're too scrawny by half," Patrick chewed at her but pointed a greasy bone at his nephew. "Mind yourself, remember?"

Damek dipped his head. "Of course, uncle. I merely meant to encourage my cousin to direct his affability at more… appropriate targets."

Henry dipped his head at that. "Bravo, boy. One might urge a man in your position to heed his own advice, Lord *Bishop*."

Damek's teeth flashed white. "You're quite right. Una, my dear. Shall I take you riding tomorrow?"

"Drop dead."

He spread his hands dramatically, and the Hall burst into laughter. "I'd make a poor groom, I see. I'd best stick to what I'm good at, eh? Hisk? Would you care to remind everyone what that is?"

Hisk resumed his feet with a half-drunken leer. "Lord of Clare and the Isles, Lord Marshal of the Bethonair Legions, Commander of the Steel Corps, Victor of the Siege at Guernsey, Hero of the Kernian Campaign, nephew to the greatest lord of this or any other land… and finest swordsman in the South! Hail!" Hisk raised his pewter tankard, and the Steel Corps officers pounded their table with their fists, howling approval. Hisk curtsied like a dancing girl. Damek toasted him.

"Perhaps, it's not *all* in the name, is it, uncle?"

Down the table, Micah sat back, defeated.

Henry crossed his arms. "You lost *how* many men on your failed raid North, nephew?"

"Many," Damek didn't flinch. "My cousin's life was worth every man."

Una pushed her plate forward, visibly put off her meal. "My lord father, I respectfully request—"

"Oh, stop!" Patrick cooed jovially. "This is a celebration. Lady Una is home! I'll have no more of these backbiting jabs. Eat, everyone, and be merry!" When the observant crowd bent back to their conversations and ale, he spared Damek a stern glare. "I thought I bloody well warned you?"

"I *am* behaving myself, uncle. If the boy can't bear a bit of light-hearted ribbing without his father leaping to his rescue, perhaps he should take his supper with the children?"

Ignoring the jibe, Henry's smile deepened, despite his son's obvious embarrassment. "Lady Una. You have the look of your mother."

That sent Patrick back into his seat with a low grumble.

"You knew her?"

"I did. Quite lovely, as you are now."

Patrick struggled not to fidget. Damek drank quietly from his tankard, brows raised.

"Then, I assume you know how she died?" she asked dryly.

Henry delighted in his brother's discomfort. "Slipped in the Lee and drowned. The cliffs around high tide are never very stable. Especially in spring. All the rain, you see?"

"Hm," she answered, mirroring his pose. "That's odd. I heard she was thrown off."

"Now," Patrick cleared his throat. "Let us return to more pleasant topics. I would hate to have you dragged from the Hall in chains."

"You surround yourself with hostages and wonder why none love you?" She exhaled through her nose.

Henry held his cup up for more ale. "Well said. Though some could argue you've fashioned those chains. Disobedience is a sin, My Lady."

Damek interjected, "You would know, wouldn't you, My Lord Fitz-Donahugh?"

Una held out a hand, her spine very straight. "I can answer my own challenges, thank you. Disobedience, to *whom*?"

"Your father," Henry spat. "Your family, your people, and your honor. Had to be dragged home in burlap, last I heard. Covered everywhere in those vile witch marks. Aren't you ashamed of yourself?"

Someone behind them gasped.

Damek drummed his fingers against the tablecloth.

Patrick had to wave his guards off. Several Corpsmen had gotten to their feet.

"Funny you should mention 'shame,' uncle. I've been introduced to your exploits only recently, but I must say, you might reflect upon your deeds before mine."

"Da," begged Micah. "Please?"

Henry's attention clapped back to his mortified son. His tone softened. "I meant that your father mourned your loss for many years. *Honor thy father and thy mother*, child."

"Henry, if you speak to my daughter that way again, you'll be taking your meals in the kennels with the dogs. I've had enough of this." Patrick clapped his hands so the lutists in the music box above would dispel the tension. "We've all got our measure, eh? Planted our flags and taken the piss? Good. Bore me again at your peril."

Micah, good lad that he was broke in: "I've been told you've read Callaghan's '*Seasons of Transition,*' My Lady?"

Una severed eye contact with Henry and leaned over. "I have, cousin. You're reading it now?"

"I am! I'm a bit muddy with the language he uses; otherwise, it's an intriguing tale. Who could believe such a civilization once lined these shores?"

Henry had never been prouder of his son and gummed his bread rather than disturb Micah's excellent showing. Una's demeanor wasn't affected in the least.

Very good, boy! Very good. Henry smirked behind his bread.

"Some find it a dull read, but the details are fascinating. Did you know our forebears were said to have flown through the clouds on steel wings? I find that tidbit the most outlandish."

"Callaghan was a staunch literalist," Patrick added. "I doubt the old fart ever made a joke in his life. However, one need only visit the hill at Dubh-lin to see proof of his claims."

"In Drogheda, the remains of several iron-bellied ships were discovered below the marshes. My grandmother displayed them in the Citadel for a time before they were removed to the Libellum in Ten Bells."

"Did you see them?" Micah breathed.

"I did! They were in pieces, so some reassembly had been necessary, but as sights go, I've yet to see their equal. Judging from a single prow, one could put them at nearly two hundred feet in length."

Patrick grunted his approval. "Bloody brilliant, the old Eireans were. Great ships, carriages, and entire cities were built from steel. No substance ever aided man more, save maybe fire."

"I disagree," dissented Henry. "Nothing ever inspired a man more than faith."

Damek snorted into his cup. "How many cities did faith build?"

"Many. *All.*"

"I believe stone and steel hold the monopoly there, old man."

"I'm not speaking of base materials, son. The purpose… the *intention* for humans to gather has always been to ward off invaders and congregate in mutual worship. Most ancient cities were built to house soldiers or temples."

"Tairngare was not. Siora's Mysteries were scarcely contemplated when the markets sprang up in Drogheda. You're leaving basic geography out of your observation," remarked Una with a slim smile. "I see where you're directing this conversation, uncle. Far be it for me, a lowly woman, to argue."

Henry gripped his tankard. "Yes, there is something to be said for the Old Ways. Women have a place in God's Plan, but it isn't seated in dominion over men. Tairnganese men must be mad, allowing you females to dictate to them. An educated woman is an affront to God."

Damek's stare blew as cold as the North in winter. "My Lord Duch, I believe it is well past my uncle's bedtime. Don't you agree?"

Pinching the bridge of his nose, Patrick opened his mouth to speak, but Una beat him to it. "Which 'Old Ways' are you referring to? The more recent, in which men and their arrogant greed nearly drove our species to extinction, or the distant past, in which a woman could be bought and sold for the price of a goat? Enlighten me, *sir*. To which misguided past should I aspire?"

"You should respect your elders, especially the men in your family. If I were your father, you'd be allowed no opportunity to wag your heretic tongue until you were properly wed and under control."

"Henry," Patrick rumbled.

Una pushed her chair back. "I imagine a base rapist and murderer like yourself would have fairly strong feelings about a 'woman's place,' uncle. As always, *beneath* you. Let me tell you what we do to your kind in Tairngare since you're curious about our audacity." She rocked forward on her knuckles. "Men who dare to abuse and violate women, as you have and do, are dragged through the Drough Market and castrated before a howling crowd. You see, men and women in more civilized parts of the world find malicious worms like you unworthy of manhood."

Henry launched upright, his blood boiling.

"Do it, old man, and I'll take your arm," Damek warned.

Patrick gesticulated wildly to his guards, but not before Una's hand clasped down hard over Henry's, where it lay flat against the table. Shocked, he tried to lurch away, but she was stronger than he, and her nails made little half-moons in the skin of his wrist. "I do not require a man's advice nor his protection. You sad, hoary little beast."

Patrick struggled to wrench her behind him, but she shrugged him off. Micah watched the guards inch close, horrified and embarrassed. "Gods damn it, Una. Leave him!" Patrick cried.

The Hall erupted into whispers and outright arguments. Damek's Corpsmen got up, mouths full of meat and mead. Meanwhile, Henry strained to pull his hand back, but Una's strength was quite unequal to her size. What devilry could make a woman so absurdly strong? Her teeth were very white against her dark skin. "Perhaps you think I am cowed because I'm here against my will? That I must be susceptible because I'm simply a humiliated female? Well, you'd be wrong."

"Una, don't...." Damek protested halfheartedly.

"You're a *witch*," raged Henry. "You'll never be—"

"*Down*!" Una said, and the world spun white at the edges.

Henry's last glimpse of the Hall that eve was his niece's face leering down at him in vivid triumph.

⚹

Patrick's hand shook as he handed Martin a drink. His elbow propped against the mantle in his wood-paneled office, Patrick sucked down his own like a drowning man gulps air. Damek and Martin eyed each other from opposite ends of the room. "*Reason*, it's all true, isn't it?"

"We told you so," grumbled Damek from the stacks while he thumbed through a dusty old tome from the Reference section. "Still think you can parade her before the Lords of Innisfail like a prized heifer?"

"I... suppose not. Though, it's too late to disinvite anyone. Lady Wendelin is already here, and Gaelin is sharp on her heels. I can't exactly keep Una locked in her chambers until they leave, either."

"Don't bother," said Damek, tossing the book back on the shelf. "Saves me from murdering half a dozen overeager fools."

"My lord," ventured Martin. "Wouldn't you rather she was capable of defending herself?"

"Of course, but... *Reason*." Patrick drank. "Poor Micah is terrified of her now."

"Good," observed Damek. "To be fair, that boy flinches from his own shadow. I told you this wasn't going to go how you planned. If what we discussed on the parapet this morning holds, you must realize there's not a man in this world who'd want her now but me?"

Patrick turned a stern eye on his nephew. "You'd prod me again? Now? Why aren't *you* afraid of her, Damek? What protection do you imagine you have from power like hers?"

"She won't harm me."

"You don't know that."

"I supplied her with many chances. She never took one."

That gave Patrick serious pause. He shuffled to his desk and sat down on the polished wood. "Is this true, Martin?"

"It is, My Lord," said O'Rearden. "The lad dared her many times."

"Interesting. I knew she wielded some dread gift, but I'd no idea she could utterly drain one of life at a touch. My physician fears Henry's heart isn't strong enough to pull him through this coma. He scarcely breathes."

"He'll wake, though he might wish he hadn't when I'm through with him," Damek assured him. "Regardless, I'd urge you to take this as a lesson, uncle. Don't push her, or she'll push back."

"How did she learn of Henry's reputation?" asked Martin.

"I told her," Patrick bemoaned. "She was in Court with me when a farmer levied a formal complaint. His child was one of the murdered girls."

"What 'murdered girls?'" Damek asked, oblivious.

Patrick gave Martin a sour look. "A handful of servants have gone missing from this castle, only to turn up bloodied and broken in the Lee."

Damek laughed sourly. "No bloody wonder! What were you thinking?"

Patrick shrugged. "My daughter and I were having a conversation for the first time in nearly fifteen years. I didn't think she'd try to kill him."

"Oh, if she meant for him to die, he would have. Horribly."

Patrick noted Martin's silent agreement with a deep sigh. "So, what do I do now? I can't punish her, or it will cheapen her before My Lords. I can't allow her free reign, either."

"For one, Henry of Bethany should be kept well out of sight. If I see that poisonous old bastard once before this bloody tourney of yours is over, I'll gut him, I vow it. Secondly, Una should be given gloves to wear in public. Make it a suggestion for her dignity, not admonishment for an action that odious zealot richly deserved. Lastly, give her a purpose other than the role of 'rich demoiselle.' Now you know how much she values women's rights. Make use of that."

"How do you mean?"

Damek pursed his lips. "Show her the women of Bethany could benefit from such an educated lady's perspective. She hates this city for its 'patriarchy,' right? So, introduce her to the other half. Give her a reason to love the people here, one gender at a time."

Patrick pondered this for a while, stroking his beard. "Hm, you're on to something there, boy."

Damek's smile was dark and full of hidden wheels. "Of course I am, uncle. I'm sure I understand your daughter better than anyone else in the world."

❧ ❦

THAT NIGHT, TWO MORE BODIES were dragged from the reeds beneath the cliffs. This time, each woman had been brutally violated... by a blade.

The Damage Done

"*A mountain of gold and silks?*" asked Kaer Yin, incredulous. Looking around their homely little camp, he turned back to Tam Lin with a snort. "Bit of an overstatement, you think?" Kaer Yin did his best to ignore Rian's 'I told you so' glare.

Digging into the stew Gerrod ladled into his bowl, Tam Lin's lip twitched. "Do you think I oversold it?"

There were less than fifty of them, all told. The Sidhe, realizing the mortals in their company would fare poorly on the Shadow Path, opted to take Eva's suggestion and travel as common Merchers on their way to Market at Ten Bells. Once there, Tam Lin proposed an idea to use his father's credit at the Sidhe Consulate for appropriate gear and supplies. To woo a princess, a man was expected to arrive in style. Their current state, however, decried any notion of such an outlandish claim.

Gerrod busied himself, drying several pairs of holey socks over the fire. Having dressed the night's supper, Robin and Shar were occupied with stretching a buckskin over a broad branch. Niall and several other Croghenian warriors were engaged in a fierce archery competition: shooting at a target one-hundred yards away. Jeering onlookers pummeled those who failed to split the previous contender's arrow. The game grew steadily more serious, the drunker each contestant became. Horrified, Eva and her Tairnganese retinue remained close by Kaer Yin's side. He supposed they'd be even more appalled when he and Tam Lin joined the game after supper. As for Rian, she sat close to the fire, mending holes in a tattered homespun skirt. Her cheeks were filthy, her fingers soot-stained, but she didn't seem to mind.

Kaer Yin smirked to himself. At this point, she was nearly better suited for the wilds than some of his countrymen. What a difference a few months could make. "I think your name might have been advertisement enough. Not every day, a prince of the Sidhe rides south to hail the Duch in his own fortress."

"This was her brilliant plan." Tam Lin jerked a thumb at Rian.

Kaer Yin chuckled around his spoon. "You could be the prince of farmers, maybe."

"Whose fault is that? I told you we should wait for more men and supplies, but *no.*"

"My family holds an account with the Libellan Bank on Freal," said Eva. "I'm happy to contribute whatever is required. She is my niece, after all."

"Your offer is appreciated, Lady Alvra. We're owed obeisance (of sorts) from the Consulate. Their coffers essentially belong to my father." Kaer Yin gave an embarrassed cough.

Robin's knife paused over his strip of buckhide and wagged at Kaer Yin. "What the Hells are we doin' out here like a pack o'brigands, then? I could use a nice feather bed, me. A fire and a hot bath, too. Remind me why we're roughin' it?"

"It's safest to travel in disguise, Master Gramble," answered Eva. "Wealth is not something one wishes to advertise along the High Roads these days."

"We could have traveled through the Oiche Ar Fad, but you tender humans would be far too delicious a lure," said Tam Lin.

Kaer Yin pulled a face. "Again? I'm tired of arguing about this. We'll draw less attention traveling this way, either here or on the Shadow Path. Stop griping, Tam Lin. You'd be drinking yourself blind through border *raths* and taverns in Aes Sidhe right now and be bored to death. Don't tell me you aren't enjoying yourself, at least a bit."

Tam Lin humphed and dug a bone flask out of his cloak. The amber ogham charm around his neck jangled on its silver chain. Every Dannan was obligated to wear one. While Kaer Yin's shaggy blond hair and less brilliant eyes were recognizable to the Greenmakers who'd known him as 'Ben Maeden,' the rest took some getting used to.

Tam Lin's once fiery red and gold hair was now a dull, flat auburn. His teeth were too broad for his mouth, and his eyes, which burned a glittering violet, were transformed into a ruddy brown. Shar went from a barrel-chested youth with fern-green eyes and a fair complexion to a lanky young man with a cowlick and coarse brown hair. Niall, much the same. Even Eva, who lacked the talent for Sidhe glamor, managed to tame her dark, radiant beauty to an impressive degree. Her skin no longer held its luminescent sheen, and her hair had been painted white at the temples. She'd made herself look a great deal older and feebler.

In Rian's case, she had neither the need nor desire to humble herself further. As far as Kaer Yin could tell, she'd never owned a proper gown in her life. Like the Greenmakers, she was right at home on the road. Being in such 'illustrious' company hardly bothered her, either. Outwardly, she was the frailest person one could conceivably meet, but with regard to her personality, he'd met decorated generals with less grit. A ways away, Niall missed his mark and submitted to his lashing with a grinning grunt. "Do any of you know how to enjoy yourselves without making each other bleed?" sniffed Rian.

"I can think of *many* things I enjoy more," commented Tam Lin, with a pointed stare.

Sucking at her cheek, she elaborated, "Long as you idiots live, you'd think you'd have developed some class."

"Rian," Kaer Yin sighed. "What did we talk about?"

"I remember," she relented grumpily.

"I'm going to ignore your misguided judgment, Mistress Guinness," Tam Lin said. "Games with consequences are training. The Tuatha De Dannan are the finest warriors in Innisfail for a reason."

"If you say so," she dismissed him, holding her skirt up to the light to check her handiwork. "Ben, when we get to Ten Bells, you owe me two Royals. Don't think I forgot. I need a new dress, among other things."

"I am well aware, Rian. We have many things to buy, apparently." He spared Tam Lin a sour look.

Tam Lin pursed his lower lip, unaffected by his cousin's ire. "Who's the Ambassador these days, anyway? I've honestly no idea."

"Sioarse Cathal, last I heard."

Tam Lin's nose wrinkled. "That Bolg woman? Sionnavar's sibling? Gods. That's going to be loads of fun."

"Why?" Rian asked. "What does that matter?"

"Bri Leith and Armagh might be allies, but they're far from friendly. The Cathal Clan serves the Black Bull— the ruling family. They're descended from Eochaid Mac Nemed, the last Fir Bolg Ard Ri."

"But that was *ages* ago."

"In Aes Sidhe, bad blood festers with time. A commodity we have in abundance," explained Kaer Yin. "They can't move directly against my father, but that doesn't mean they don't try to be a thorn in his clan's arse whenever an opportunity arises."

"Wonderful," she cut her eyes away and dug another roll of thread from her bag. "I gather they're going to hand over any funds and weapons you need without a word of complaint?"

"Well…"

"Whatever. I hope you have a backup plan for your 'mountains of gold and silk,' then? We won't get more than one shot at this."

Robin patted his chest. "That's where we come in. Greenmakers are connected down in Ten Bells. Ye'd be surprised what we'll come up with."

"I want my Royals, damn it," repeated Rian more sternly. Her expression promised an intolerable amount of nagging. Kaer Yin scrubbed a palm over his eyes. He was going to throttle her one day. He was sure of it.

Heath and Dorcan both missed their marks, and the beating each earned sounded worse than Niall's. Eva's lip curled. Mel patted her shoulder on his way over to watch. Gerrod went too, after the briefest guilty smile at Rian. "All right," announced Tam Lin, tossing his bowl in the midden. "Time to show these ingrates how it's done. Yin, you're not invited."

Robin hooted with laughter.

Eva craned her head, askance. "Why not?"

"Ye ever seen His Arseness shoot?"

Kaer Yin stood up anyway, skirting around Tam Lin's groan. "He's just bitter because I *always* win. Look at it this way, Rian, you might get one Royal back tonight after I'm done embarrassing our fine Prince O'Ruiadh here."

⚔

COLD FLAMES LICKED THROUGH A cavernous doorway crowded by the dead. In the distance, a high bell peeled above a windblown hillside. Wet pine and ether thickened the air. It was Samhain, and he was dying. Then… she was there. Her amber eyes loomed large and bright in the filthy perfection of her face. Though brief, the weight of her in his arms left his palms quaking with need. Una's soft mouth poured warmth into his.

He gasped.

Kaer Yin came awake with a start.

The salt of her tears lingered on his tongue like heartbreak. He sat up, gripping his head. She was far away now and alone.

Soon, he vowed to the night sky.

Wait for me, Una.

The fire dwindled to embers outside his tent. Beside him, Tam Lin turned over in his bedroll. In the second tent, Rian and Eva slumbered fitfully. Kaer Yin could hear the young faerie whimpering in her sleep again. Eva's presence helped— her abilities being such as they were— but she could not cure all. Now, Rian called Una's name in fearful wonder.

So, he and Rian shared nightmares this eve?

The bell in his dream chimed from the corners of his mind.

Perhaps that terrible night would haunt them all the rest of their days? For Kaer Yin, Samhain had been both a terrible curse and a blessing. He'd gained and lost the only thing he'd ever cared for in the sweep of a single hour. Frowning, he rubbed at his sore temple.

I won't fail you again.

I swear it.

With a defeated sigh, he got up. Dawn would break soon; they should get back on the road. The horses were tethered together beside a mound of sleeping men and Sidhe, cradling packs and each other for added warmth. Robin had argued that a sea of Sidhe tents and furs would've drawn undue attention. Kaer Yin had attempted to eschew one altogether until Rian swore to gut him in his sleep if he dared try. He clutched his itchy but swiftly-healing chest wound and strolled from camp to relieve himself against a frozen tree. He was beyond nursing now, wasn't he? Cursing when the frost-ridden breeze bit into his bared flesh, he hurried through his natural duty. Then, replacing his stays with godlike speed, he jumped to discover Eva standing a few feet away, watching him with her eerie, Una-colored eyes. He fidgeted.

"Ah, good morning?"

"Not quite, Your Highness."

"Right, not for some while, I suppose. What can I do for you?" Nervously smoothing his tunic down and shrugging his cloak tight, he made to brush past her.

Slender fingers caught at his sleeve. Her eyes gleamed like polished jewels in the snow-bright darkness. "I know what you dreamed, Your Highness."

Kaer Yin was proud not to flush. "I can't say I love that about you, My Lady."

"I hear it too."

He cocked his head, confused. "What?"

"The bell," she said, gesturing. "Listen."

He heard nothing but icy leaves rattling together in the wind and the deep silence of newly fallen snow. "I don't—" but then he *did* hear something. Faint, crunching footsteps along the road and the jingle of a distant bell. No, not a bell... a bridle. His eyes flew wide. "Bandits?"

"They'll overwhelm you."

Kaer Yin muttered something foul in his mother's tongue. "Can you keep Rian safe?"

"Not for long. They're coming from the river. There are twenty in the first rush. Twelve more are waiting ahead. They're hungry, and—" she craned her neck as if listening to a voice he couldn't hear. "Many are wounded. It seems they ran afoul of your Lord Bishop earlier this month."

Kaer Yin's heart thumped to life in his chest. "Una?"

She smiled. "Unharmed."

Thank you, Brida. "Good."

Shar slid from the pre-dawn shadows, his expression alert and wary. "*Ard Tiarne*, you have heard them?"

"Yes. Go wake Tam Lin and Robin."

"No need," assured Tam Lin from his left side. He wasn't smiling. "Get the women to safety, Shar. Be quick."

Shar saluted both princes and melted into the trees. Kaer Yin signaled to Tam Lin and Eva and marched into camp to find Robin passing daggers and bows to his men. Of course, Gramble was already awake. He never could sleep after so much uishge. He and Robin shared a smile over Eva's head. Gods, but this had been a dull month. "Singles or doubles?"

Robin affected an offended snort, pulling his sabre. "I've a reputation, you know?"

Tam Lin warned, "By Herne, take any from me and regret it."

Kaer Yin tripped Tam Lin on his way past. "Then you'll have to catch up!"

⚜

BENEATH THE RISING SUN, THE Greenmakers and their escort descended upon their would-be attackers like starved locusts. The Sidhe were used to hunting poachers like the Greenmakers this time of year and had taken to their Souther-bound mission with a collective groan. Days of drinking, riding and sedentary camping had made for poor sport. Sure, it would get exciting enough once they passed Ten Bells, but for now, they couldn't have been more excited for the distraction. The bandits had no clue what they were in for. That was pretty obvious from the outset. "No arrows!" Kaer Yin mouthed from his perch among the lower boughs of a fir tree. Shar slid his bow around to grasp his larks. Tam Lin grumbled something unintelligible but drew his dagger anyway. He preferred to shoot than engage hand-to-hand, though Kaer Yin knew he was aware of their predicament. Any arrows they left behind would prove a complication for the utter secrecy of their purpose.

Having lost their quarry nearly as quickly as they'd been spotted, the bandits crept around their abandoned camp, faces smeared with equal parts mud and frustration. Several passed very close to Rian

359

and Eva's hiding spot but didn't so much as glance in their direction. That was interesting. Kaer Yin reminded himself to ask what else she could do.

High above the invaders in the canopy, the Sidhe waited. Not one to permit Kaer Yin a lead in any aspect, Robin had sent Gerrod and the boys to track the group around the river, then shimmied up with the Dannans. Reclining at height like any Sidhe, Robin impatiently flipped his daggers and pointed at the ground. A road-weary young man shuffled through the underbrush beneath Kaer Yin's tree. Tam Lin gestured to do something about him.

Lip curled, Kaer Yin shook his head.

"*Not enough*," he mimed.

Tam Lin shot him a mocking glare.

Three more bandits squirmed up behind the lad. With a wink for his cousin, Kaer Yin dropped from his perch, flashing a mouth full of white teeth. The landing hurt more than he'd like, but that hardly deterred him. He rolled upright, taking the first bandit through the middle with a quick, one-handed swipe. Before the lad could cry out, Kaer Yin slit his throat with the lark in his left hand. The boy crumpled to the ground in gurgling surprise. Kaer Yin didn't stop to watch him die. His lark sailed through the air ahead, pinning his next opponent through the ear to a tree. The loud 'thump' whipped several larcenous heads around to face him. Holding up two fingers for Robin to sneer at, he launched himself into the knot of thieves like a cannon shot. Whirling left and right with vicious accuracy, Kaer Yin dealt death with gleeful abandon. He scarcely noticed if the bandits he slaughtered brandished weapons little better than spades and cudgels.

If most of them seemed barely old enough to shave, he couldn't have cared less. Weeks of pent-up aggravation and stunted urgency took precedence over the gnawing ache in his chest and midsection. By his sixth victim, he leaned against a tree to catch his breath. His wounds were no longer urgent, but they were present, nonetheless.

He muttered a curse when Tam Lin vaunted past him, chasing one of the quicker bandits down. "Eight." Tam Lin blew both Robin and his cousin a kiss.

From behind him, Kaer Yin heard Robin growl, "No one invited ye to play, ye pretty bastard!"

The element of surprise was long gone. Realizing their mistake, the bandits dashed for the road with all the speed they could muster. Most were slain fairly quickly. A few pounded down the muddy thoroughfare as if the Kneeler's Devil snapped at their heels. From the southern edge near the river, a handful of Greenmakers burst from the hedges with ear-splitting grins. The whole affair was over in moments. Those bandits who didn't try to run for the frigid riverbank dropped their weapons and threw up their filthy hands. Colm kicked one fellow over, stripping him of a rusty sabre and a pair of daggers.

Sheathing his sword, Tam Lin waited for Niall to tie up the remaining prisoners. Kaer Yin and Robin arrived last, both scowling. "How many?" Kaer Yin asked him.

"Four," Robin sighed.

"Damn Tam Lin to the Hells."

The redhead shot him a raised brow. "Sore loser."

Grinding his molars, Kaer Yin nudged the nearest prisoner with his boot. "Well, look who chose their victims poorly. Which one's the leader?"

The fellow— a youth, really— glared back. "I don't have to tell ye nuthin.'"

"You're right. Niall? Cut his throat."

The boy squealed when Niall's gorgeous silver-handled dagger hefted his chin. Not even fourteen, if Kaer Yin were any judge. "Wait!" the boy begged. "We was hungry, sir. I swear it. Saw yer fire and thought ye'd have food and maybe better weapons."

"Horseshite," said Robin. "A gaggle o'girls like ye ain't out here lookin' for mutton. I know raiders when I see 'em."

"You might say he's a bit of an expert," Kaer Yin whispered behind his hand.

The boy squirmed. "The road's our meal ticket, sir. I swear it."

"That's as may be, but ye answer to someone, doncha?" Robin prodded.

Kaer Yin knelt, refusing to wince at the pain in his aching thigh. "Do you know who this is, boy? I bet you've heard of Robin Gramble, haven't you?"

The boy had. He paled by five shades. "I don't… I mean… we can't… *Siora*."

"Where do you hole up?" Robin pressed him.

"Cairnream, twenty miles southeast."

"Whole town, or just ye scamps in on it?"

"Not much of a town, sir. Was once, afore I was born maybe. Now, it's our camp."

"Young fella like ye could hardly be the leader. Who d'ye pay tribute to, boyo?"

The boy hung his head. "Wencel, sir. He's raisin' funds for some toff from the North. Bootlegger, I hear, though I never met him."

Kaer Yin perked up. "*Bootlegger?*"

Robin scooped the lad up by the collar. "What's this toff's name, then?"

Under Robin's fist, the boy shrugged as best as he could. "Dunno, sir. Never met him, like I said."

Robin dropped him to scratch at his grizzled cheek. "Who would know?"

The boy sent a nervous glance sideways, fat beads of sweat dribbling down his muddy cheeks. Another boy, some ways back, flashed his teeth. Shar hauled him up by his neck. "Matt, sirs. That's all any o'us knows."

"Shut yer gob, Ian!" another hissed.

"I din't come out with ye's to be murdered, Lance! Ye prats can die for him if ye like?"

Shar shook him silent. Robin advanced, eyes sparking like twin coals. "Matt *Gilcannon*, is that right?"

The boy shrugged as best as he was able, considering he fairly dangled from Shar's overlarge fist. "Gil-somewhat sounds about right. Yeah."

"He's gonna have yer tiny balls in a jar, Ian!" swore the first.

"*Shut up!*" answered four voices in unison, including Kaer Yin's.

"Well," Robin intoned, giving him a long look. "Do we have time for a slight detour, then?"

Kaer Yin shook his head. "I wish we did. I promised that fat pederast his comeuppance, didn't I?"

"Aye. No more than I or any Greenmaker, Ben."

Irritably, Tam Lin folded his arms. "Who's this now?"

"A nasty sort who deserves what's coming to him," Kaer Yin scowled. "We don't have time for him right now, Robin. You know we don't. When we get Una back safe, he'll have my full attention. I swear it."

"It ain't me yer gonna have to reassure. Once Gerrod hears about this, he'll—"

"I'll what?" asked Gerrod and the lads, emerging onto the road from a thorny knot of brambles toward the riverbank. They were all wet to the knees and none worse for wear than Gerrod himself. He had a bloody nose and a longish gash on his left cheek but seemed otherwise as hale and amiable as always.

Robin scratched at his scarred chin, silently pleading with Kaer Yin to change his mind. "Ah, well, ye see boyo… the thing is—"

"I don't see why some shiftless bootlegger would warrant the attention. Yin, we have more pressing issues at hand, yes? Let's strip these lads of anything useful and get a move on," interrupted Tam Lin irascibly. "This Matt character can't be more important than your girl?"

Robin threw his hands up in the air.

"*Dénann déithe dochar do bhéal mór, Tam Lin O'Ruiadh!*[6] Kaer Yin barked. Tam Lin opened his mouth to retort, but Kaer Yin shouldered him out of the way to face Gerrod, whose face puckered nearly purple. "Now, Gerrod, we have to—"

Gerrod's ordinarily warm brown eyes darkened. "Aye? Were gonna keep it from me then? Why's that?"

"Well, lad. Ye know we want to finish the job we started all them weeks ago, same as ye but the lass—"

---

[6] 'Gods damn your big mouth, Tam Lin O'Ruiadh!'

"Not me problem. Matt, on t'other hand, *is*."

"Gerry, you know I want his head as much as you do, but I have a promise to fulfill," Kaer Yin said, attempting to pat his arm. Gerrod jerked away.

"Ye made a promise to me and to Robin too. And to Barb, Colm, Dabs, and half of Rosweal, while ye was at it. Matt's *our* top priority, *milord*. Or does pretty quinny take top billin' over yer mates?"

"Gerrod!" Rian screeched from the side of the road. She and Eva had come down the track from the opposite end. Her face was livid with confused shock. "What would make you say such a thing? Una saved all of our lives. You know that!"

Moderately cowed by the outrage in Rian's blue eyes, he turned away. "Nothin' against her, Mistress Guinness. Just sayin,' if Matt's around, I got somewhere else to be."

"That's lovely, that is," Robin told him. "Gonna haul off on yer own and get yer fool self killed. For what?"

"Who's gonna stop me?"

"I bloody well will, Gerry," Kaer Yin rumbled, making sure Gerrod couldn't mistake the deadly-serious tone. Despite his bravado, Gerrod backed up a pace. Perplexed, Tam Lin spoke to Shar in rapid but inaudible *Ealig*. Shar zipped back into the trees. Meanwhile, Gerrod squared his shoulders under Kaer Yin's glare.

"If yer not gonna help me, ye don't have the right to stop me neither."

"Who in the Hells do you imagine you're speaking to?"

"Someone I thought was my friend."

Kaer Yin flinched like he'd been bitten.

Tam Lin made a rude sound at the back of his throat. "I don't understand what the fuss is about. Apologize to your Lord while I'm asking nicely."

"Gerrod has his reasons, Prince O'Ruiadh," Robin spat over his shoulder. "Best stay out of it."

"Gerry," Kaer Yin held up his palms as if to soothe a wild colt. "Matt'll keep. I promise we'll see him soon. You have my word. I wouldn't give it if I didn't mean it."

Despising being the center of attention, Gerrod muttered a curse. A sharp glance at Robin told all. "Ye too then?"

"Aye. Ben's the boss here, Gerry. Not me. Besides, he's right."

Gerrod shrugged. "Fine. Let's go and save Ben's piece. Nevermind what Matt's done to Rosweal, or me family, Hells, to *loads* o'families in the North. That's not nearly as urgent as the weight of Ben's bollocks, is it?"

"Gerrod! What is the matter with you?" Rian cried, aghast. She'd never seen this side of the lad before. Ignoring her, Gerrod sheathed his dagger and spun on his heel. Kaer Yin moved to follow, but Robin's hand caught at his shoulder.

"Nah. Let him go. He'll have a stew for a bit and give us sass the next couple o' days, but he'll be right as rain in no time. Matt does it to him. Gnaws his guts we had to let that bastard go when we might have had him."

"Why does he hate Gilcannon?" Rian wondered aloud. "I mean, so much more than the rest of you?"

It was Eva who answered. "No hatred burns as bright as a son's for an abusive father." She paused to see her expression. "What? You didn't know?" Rian's owlish silence spoke the truth of that. Eva chuckled mirthlessly. "He seeks vengeance for his mother and two sisters."

"His *father*?" Tam Lin inhaled hard. "You're a dark bunch down here. You know that?"

"This isn't funny, Lin." Kaer Yin elbowed past him. "Gather these lads' weapons and anything useful. We should get back on the road as soon as possible."

"What do we do with this rabble?" Shar tipped his blade at one whimpering bandit.

"Set them loose. Matt won't have them again after failing him. Leave them for the winter roads."

"Ben, he didn't mean what he said. Ye know that," said Robin.

Kaer Yin lacked the oxygen to formulate a grand defense. "Of course he did, Robin. What's more, he might be right."

⚸

LATER, WHEN THEY'D PUT A safe distance between themselves and their previous camp, a lone rider kicked his mount onto the High Road, veering East. That this rider seemed to possess little knowledge of the animal he'd stolen was lost to the wind, the dispassionate gleam of a sky full of brilliant white stars, and the plodding of the mare's hooves against a frost-bitten road.

Common Cause

Una threw down her wad of vellum and sat up, scrubbing her eyes. She'd been at it for hours already. The library was as cold as a windswept moor, and she was pretty confident every chair in the room doubled as a torture device. Yawning, she stood up to crack her aching back. If only one could relieve a bruised tailbone as easily. From his seat in the opposite chair, Micah glanced at her from beneath his unruly blond fringe. What he lacked in age and couth he made up for in scholastic enthusiasm. She admired that about him. For one so intelligent to be reared in such an intellectually desolate environment as the Briton Wastes, he took to his newfound resources with a relish that nearly shamed her. How dreadful to be born inquisitive in a world of privation and drudgery! For all the injustices she might have suffered in her brief life, a lack of education and rearing was not among them. After Rosweal, she must accept that her understanding and empathy for the less-fortunate parts of the world was decidedly lacking.

Knowing an inequality exists from an intellectual perspective is not quite the same as bearing its experience. She was ashamed to admit that, on this subject, her education far exceeded her grasp.

Micah's bright eyes clinched in a warm smile. "Uncomfortable, milady?"

"'My Lady,' and yes," she sneezed, tugging her cloak tight. "It's too bloody cold by half in here. I forgot how drafty this old pile of rocks was."

The library was a grand but largely neglected space on the top floor of the Keep's west side. Una's great-grandfather had been a voracious reader and intellectual, but the rest of his family did not seem to share his enthusiasm for learning. Each of the library's four long, slate walls was draped with floor-to-ceiling mahogany bookshelves that had once graced the ancient library at Trinity in old Dubh-lin. While many of the college's once impressive books and scrolls had long since disintegrated, Duch Kevin had managed to salvage what treasures he could and add to the collection throughout his life. The result was this beautiful, stately room with its grand fireplace beneath the delicate glass and lattice windows on the western wall, crowded everywhere by books of every shade and binding. Tall ladders climbed stacks that were now dusty with disuse but somehow managed to emit the faintest hint of linseed and Bretagn lemon oils. Una was reminded to ask Shanley about a proper housekeeper for the library's precious contents. She could manage that much, she hoped.

Micah set his book aside with a flush. He was a rather attractive young man. She hoped he wouldn't be ruined by the political machine in her father's head. "What was it like, erm, *My Lady*? Growin' up here, I mean?"

"Tiresome as it is now, cousin. Though, in those days, I had free run of the place," she smirked at the impassive guards. "Not so much, now."

"How did you... you know?" whispered Micah conciliatorily.

"What do you mean?"

"How did you escape? Can't have been easy."

"It wasn't." Smile flickering, she turned to warm her numb fingers by the fire. Though he blissfully did not share his father's rigid adherence to Kneeler superstitions and Scripture, she doubted Micah was keen to learn more about her... talents. "Perhaps we'll discuss it some other time? For now, have you found anything?"

Micah groaned over his abandoned book. "Nothin'. Haven't seen Da's name in any of these court records so far. Ye?"

"No. Patrick did say he had the majority of the records expunged, but that doesn't mean the incident reports would be concealed as well. Maybe we're looking in the wrong place?"

"How so?"

"Well, if the Duch wanted to conceal the crimes, I thought he'd have them brought here with Duch Michael's accounts. We've been through these stacks eight times. They're not here."

"Do ye think they've been destroyed?"

She pursed her lips. "No. Blackmail is much more effective with ample documentation. I imagine he held onto them in case he need bribe or intimidate those involved."

"Would they be in his chambers, d'ye think?"

"Too obvious."

Micah's groan mirrored her mood perfectly. "Beggin' yer pardon, milady. I know Da's a rough touch, but he ain't no murderer. Maybe we should ask someone who was there? Why d'we need to dig up his old, erm, 'incidents?'"

She turned around with her arms crossed. "Because I'm not inclined to take Patrick's word. Once you learn how theatrically devious he is, you'll feel the same. If Henry is innocent, the records will add credence to his defense. If not..." she cleared her throat and gave the lad a long look. "You don't have to do this, Micah."

He squared his shoulders. "I swore to help ye."

"Well then, I can think of one other place they might be. Though, we'll have to be careful. I'm forbidden from that wing of the castle."

"Why? Surely you don't mean to run away again, do you?"

She flinched. She couldn't do anything but blink back at his perplexed expression for several moments. Did she not? Honestly, she hadn't thought about it in a while. After everything that had transpired in Rosweal, what good *would* it do to escape now? Hadn't she inflicted enough harm upon innocent (well, relatively, anyway) people already? How many lives were lost throughout the North in her attempt to shirk her responsibilities? Having nothing but time to think these past weeks, she realized many unpleasant truths about herself. While no amount of introspection could repair her relationship with her father, she had to admit there was much she could do for Bethany.

As Queen of Tairngare, she might have held power to effect change the Continent over— including the belabored and long-suffering women of the South. She could have bridged the gap between both cultures have encouraged something of a social coup by example. Now, however, the likelihood of any of that happening was as feeble as a feather in a storm. All she'd ever wanted was to be free. To make that dream a reality, she had purposefully trod over that potential future on her way out of the Citadel. She'd been beaten, hunted, terrorized, and abjured by her people ever since. It seemed the only place she had left was the last place she'd ever wanted to be.

Bethany was not an ideal destination for her by any stretch of the imagination. She loathed every slab of stone in this castle, point in fact. However, no one in the South had plans to burn her for a heretic, did they? What little news she could wring from any of her guards or her father's courtiers about Tairngare was dire. Her grandmother had fled to Siora-knew-where. Her aunts, Ana and Basa, were dead or imprisoned. Commoners burned the Moura sigil in the streets and dragged any loyalist nobles or Merchers before the mob for censure or execution. Many lives had been lost, most undeserving. Una's grief over the affair had been a daily trial to conceal. That so many were suffering on her account, intentional or otherwise, was more than she could bear. At least, here in the South, she had a purpose. If she so chose, perhaps power enough to march North one day, herself? Returning to Tairngare for the foreseeable future would be foolish with her family in public disgrace. Resuming her plans to travel east into Alba seemed equally redundant... and Kaer Yin was gone.

She had nowhere else to go.

Her father was right, loathe as she was to admit it. She had a place here: a *purpose.* Her life needn't be spent fleeing from one fate to another. Bethany was a terrible place for women. Did it have to be? What might she achieve as Duchess for the women here and everywhere? Fresh guilt burbled in her throat at the thought but clung all the same.

Free yourself, Patrick had said.

Clenching her fist at the memory, she felt her power thrumming through her veins. Hadn't Diarmid Adair said the same?

Whatever she decided, her fate must be her own. "My plans are irrelevant. Girls are being slaughtered on our doorstep. I want to know why and by whom."

"My uncle said—"

"Again, irrelevant. Patrick is ill, Micah. I doubt he has the stomach for this, with the tourney and Cromnasa Feasts to oversee. This wolf requires a snare."

Micah's flush teetered between pretty and petulant. She frowned. He should learn to mind his expressions if he wished to survive the South. Though the political atmosphere here was far less labyrinthine than in Tairngare, it was perilous, nonetheless.

One should never broadcast one's thoughts.

Unaware of her scrutiny, he ruffled his hair. "Forgive me, cousin, but yer a lady, and I'm a nobody. Neither o'us is an expert in crime-solvin'."

She picked up his ledger and held it under his nose. "Here's your first lesson in statecraft, My Lord. Murder victims make terrible supper guests. If you mean to save your father from further accusation, help me find the court records which prove he's never slain a victim. Otherwise, any number of my father's Barons might ask for his head, and Patrick will have no choice but to imprison or execute him. Do you understand?"

He stared up at her for a moment, face white. "He wouldn't lock him up again?"

"He'll have no choice if more girls turn up dead."

"But why would ye want to help me Da? Ye didn't get on, last I saw," he understated.

"I don't," Una replied without hesitation. "I'm ruling him out."

Micah chewed his lower lip in silent debate with himself for a long while. Eventually, he took the tome back with a wry smile. "All right then."

Leaning against the arm of his chair, Una smiled. "Good."

⚷ ⚷

AN AGING LIBERTINE WITH A penchant for wine and cheese— that was what his uncle had said of Lord Gaelin. Damek was amused to find the statement comically accurate. Though he'd defeated him in battle once, he'd never actually met the man before. He was tall and thin through the back and shoulders, with an overlarge paunch and greasy fat fingers. His heavily tanned face bore sagging jowls, deep lines, and a plump lower lip. Damek supposed he must have been handsome once upon a time on account of the many tales he'd been told of the Marquis' many conquests. Now, the Duch's description rang all too true. A bejeweled hand patted the thinning brown hair at his crown as the Marquis Gaelin affected an effeminate bow. Damek inclined his head slightly; he was not in the habit of genuflection. Gaelin narrowed his dark eyes but made no comment. Martin saluted after Damek, and the Steel Corpsmen in the ranks hammered their breastplates.

"I see your men have manners, Lord Bishop," observed Gaelin.

Damek slung his leg over his saddlehorn to lean closer. His smirk was mirthless, as intended. "They know how to treat their betters in Bethany, My Lord Marquis."

Gaelin muttered something foul behind a strained smirk. His horse, a lovely white mare, pranced nervously beneath him. "Shall I grovel for you then, boy? Would that appease your arrogance?"

"Not at all, My Lord. Your sons will do it for you."

Gaelin's nostrils flared, but he did not rise to the bait. Damek had superior numbers, better mounts, and the right to stamp Gaelin and his brood into the mud if he so chose. By right of conquest, Damek now owned thirty-five percent of Gaelin's modest kingdom. The price of betrayal was steep in Bethany. All the same, Gaelin waved two riders forward. One was fatter than his father, with the same complexion and bearing. Vexos, no doubt: fond of the axe, a fight, and not much else, Damek had been told. The younger, on the other hand, was a good deal finer of frame. He sat his palfrey like a man born in the saddle. His eyes were blue and quite direct. Damek had heard of this one too. Castor Gaelin: a man with two mistresses—both male. Castor's interest in Damek was plain. Damek shared a long look with Martin.

"My sons, Lord Bishop. Vexos is my champion but of course. No finer man with a blade in all of Bretagne. The skinny spare is my youngest, Castor. He prefers books and poems to a skirmish, but the Gods made him clever at least. One of these two lumps should serve as a good bridegroom for your cousin, no?"

Damek filled his mouth with teeth. Every lord in the South knew Una was technically Damek's wife. He let the insult pass with a caustic shrug he did not feel. He'd better get used to the treatment, for not a single incoming noble would let him forget it. In Gaelin's sons' case, however, he was less worried than annoyed. "I'm sure she'll be charmed. We're here to escort you to the castle. Any men in your train who aren't in your immediate retinue should follow at a sedate pace. My uncle's steward has prepared the barracks in the West End for all incoming soldiers."

Without waiting for a reply, Damek spurred his mount around to march toward the city. Gaelin's mare settled in beside him. "So?"

"What?"

"Tell us of her! Is she as beautiful as they say? Dark, soft skin? Luscious tits? Vexos likes a woman with curves, as did I, when I was younger," he leered.

"She is the most beautiful woman in Innisfail, My Lord," responded Damek without flair.

Vexos' nasally giggle hardly matched his oxen frame. Gaelin said something else in Bretagn, but Damek refused to let on that he understood. The eldest and his father threw their heads back in a shared laugh. "Wonderful news! Tell me, since you're the expert, is she a screamer or a prude?"

"If you'd met her, I think you'd regret that comment."

"Oh, *oui*. We've heard of her powers. It's disappointing, no? That the women in Tairngare are bred to witchery? Some would be quite charming did they accept their place. Basa Alvra, for one. When we were young, I greatly enjoyed her wit. Her and that mouthy piece your uncle took to wife," Gaelin made a face. "Don't think Vexos will tolerate that. Will you, my boy?"

"*Non*," droned the ox. "I'd knock her teeth out if she tried, *mon père*."

Castor spoke up in a bored, flat tone. "I heard Lady Donahugh once melted a man's flesh from his bones for the attempt."

Vexos picked at his nose. "Then I'll keep her trussed like a sow. She doesn't need to be conscious to breed. Does she?"

"*Père, tu devrais lui mettre une laisse. Nous sommes des invités ici.*"[7]

"No need. I'm sure Lord Bishop has heard it all before," chuckled Gaelin.

"Indeed," Damek allowed, with his eyes on the woods ahead. "I have. Nevertheless, you've come to woo her anyway, haven't you? She will rule a kingdom ten times the size of your modest holdfast, My Lord."

"So grand, the lot of you. Bretagne was once the mightiest kingdom in all Europa, boy. You might recall that, were you not so arrogant."

"Once, perhaps. Now it is an overgrown string of rocks with soil suited for naught but grapes, where men are forced to pirate and raid to sustain their families. Any power you might have had fled with your black soil."

---

[7] Father, you should put a leash on him. We're guests here.

Gaelin bristled. "Bethany is not much better. You're hostage to a gaggle of elves and women simply for lack of timber. Timber *we* have in abundance. The few mighty Innish ships our sailors spy in the Straits of Manannan are Tairnganese or Cymrian. Bethany's sole boons are steel, tin, and cattle. Not much to brag about."

"Oh, I dunno about that. Seems our soldiers more than make up for our lack of ships, wouldn't you agree, Marquis?"

"Humph," said Gaelin.

"If I'd been of age, you'd have died on the field that day, and *mon père* would be Lord of Clare, no? Yes," sniggered Vexos. "I'd have been fucking your wife from her first bleed, and she'd never have learned anything but the length of my cock."

"Lucky for me, you were yet a pimple-spotted lass, humping dead animals in your father's stables," Damek said. "I've heard of you too, as it happens."

"Once I win your woman, perhaps I'll fuck her over your corpse, *joli garçon?*"[8]

"Vexos!" susurrated Gaelin. "*Garde ta langue!*"[9]

Damek met Martin's eyes over Vexos' head. He held up three gloved fingers. Behind him, Ridley fell back a few horse lengths. Weak, mottled sunlight glinted from their armor. Gaelin's men seemed ill-equipped by comparison, being that they wore ancient, poorly oiled leather cuirasses and held spears and swords that bore touches of rust and wear. The woods inched closer, with them, yet more shade for an already frigid morning. "Perhaps."

Vexos glared back. "She threw you over, did she not, *mon ami?* I think I'll offer her your finger bones on a chain. What I hear, that'd make her wet as the *Aber.*"

He turned to his father, whose face had gone an ugly shade of green. "*Pourquoi ce subterfuge? Nous devrions le tuer et prendre le château! Nos hommes sont prêts, mon père.*"[10]

Bare treetops creaked overhead. Martin gnashed his teeth at Damek, who straightened in his saddle. "You'd allow your heir to insult your liege lord, Gaelin?"

Gaelin fidgeted at the stern faces gathered around him. "Ah, he is young, My Lord. Eager to meet your cousin, that is all."

"Do you believe threatening to murder My Lord and rape My Lady was a wise way to introduce yourself to the Duch's men?" demanded Martin, with a tick in his jaw.

While Gaelin fumbled for excuses, Vexos engaged his fellow Bretagn soldiers in an animated conversation in Bretagn, replete with vulgar gestures. None of his cavalry appeared comfortable in their seats. Several nervous sets of eyes shifted around for obvious offense. Given the Steel Corp's general readiness and reputation, the Bretagns would be the obvious underdogs in a tussle.

Castor's upper lip curled at his brother. "*Mon Père, est-ce que tu vois? Quelle bête stupide, il est.*"[11]

"*D'accord,*" answered Damek, earning two very surprised glares. "*Mais bien sûr, il n'aura jamais l'occasion.* Martin?"[12]

O'Rearden waved a mailed fist, and Damek allowed himself the satisfaction of watching Gaelin's face crumple. A cloud of arrows sailed out of the trees on their right. Fourteen Gauls fell under the first volley. Vexos' stallion reared, hurling him from his saddle. Hearing a nasty crunch as Vexos clutched his mangled shoulder, Damek smiled to watch the oaf roll around in the grass, keening like a whipped girl. Still seated, Gaelin went for his sword, but Damek got there first. Beneath the whistling arc of a second volley, his hand lashed out, ripping Gaelin's weapon away from him— a useless piece, really— too thin, too light, and too ornamental to be lethal. He scarcely had time to gasp before Damek's dagger plunged into the hollow beneath his clavicle. Surprised, Gaelin stared back at his murderer in silent contempt. A

---

[8] pretty boy?
[9] Watch your tongue!
[10] Why the subterfuge, father? We should kill him, then take the castle! Our men are ready.
[11] You see? What a stupid beast, he is.
[12] Agreed. But of course, he will never have the occasion.

thin ribbon of bloody spittle dangled from his over plump lips. He cut his knuckles attempting to wrench the blade from his chest to no avail. Damek jerked it out again with a malicious grin. On the ground, Vexos' wail reached a particular pitch. With Gauls dying on either side of him, while countless hooves and booted feet threatened to trample him at any moment, he cried out, *"Père! Castor, sauve-le!"*[13]

But Castor was nowhere near the fracas. He and a handful of comparably well-attired retainers arranged themselves at the opposite end of the road. None made the slightest move forward, swords stuck fast in their scabbards, quivers pregnant with arrows. Vexos lurched to his feet, clutching his wounded shoulder.

"Espèce de salope! Je vais vous arracher les tripes pour ça."[14]

The loyalist Gauls around Vexos attempted to surround him with their heavy oaken shields, to no avail. Damek's archers were better. Vexos' defenders fell nearly one-by-one into the muck at his feet. Through it all and dying slowly, Gaelin watched from his saddle, eyes furiously raking the tableau ahead. He grunted something unintelligible at his youngest, who merely shrugged.

"Nous sommes comme vous nous l'avez fait, mon cher père,"[15] Castor replied, with a venom that chilled even Damek's lukewarm blood. Taking one last look at his beloved eldest child, Gaelin slumped from his saddle into the mud. In its desperation to flee the scene, his charger smashed his brains in on its way out of the wood. Damek tossed a cheap, wood-handled dagger atop the Marquis' corpse.

Raising a fist, the arrows stopped. Roaring in rage, Vexos faced him. With his good arm, he ripped off his cloak and tunic, showing a swath of swirling red tattoos over his well-muscled chest and abdomen. A thin but vicious-looking sword sprang to hand. "I will kill you, half-breed."

Damek pursed his lips. "I'd be disappointed if you didn't try."

"Be careful, *mon ami*. He's not a noble fighter," advised Castor.

"Neither am I," Damek assured him, dismounting. He tossed his cloak to Hisk. His Corpsmen gathered close. The Gauls had been slain to a man, save for the several dozen pooled behind Castor.

Vexos didn't see them. He couldn't pry his eyes away from Damek. "You're a fool to trust a man who'd murder his father."

Striding over, Damek unsheathed his sabre. "Who said anything about trust?"

Vexos aimed the point of his blade at his indifferent brother. "When I'm done with this faerie scum, you're next, *mon frère*."

Castor said nothing.

Damek flipped his pommel into a low guard, his arms and feet perpendicular with his shoulders, back slightly hunched.

Vexos hefted his cumbersome two-hander with a wheeze. "What's this? You look like a frog."

Damek dashed forward rather than bandy words. Coming in too low for Vexos to block in time, he swung into his middle with two testing blows that rocked the Gaul back on his heels.

Vexos parried but clumsily, gritting his teeth. Damek spun around him, keeping his sabre level with the ground. Vexos took an audible slash to his rear-right knee and a second to his left calf. Grunting, he stumbled, forced to lean against one of his broadswords for support. *"Espèce de bâtard infidèle."*

"I thought you'd be more of a challenge, mighty Vexos?" mocked Damek, reclaiming his ugly but efficient low guard. "A large man with a long arm, indeed."

With a hearty bellow, Vexos hacked wildly at him. The air whooshed in Damek's ears with each wild swing, though he effortlessly danced out of their way. Bloodied and breathing hard, Vexos staggered against a tree trunk. He faced the amused onlookers with an increasingly heavy brow. That Damek made sport of him was not lost on anyone— least of all, Vexos. The realization of an imminent and ignoble death dawned all at once. He threw down his sword and drew a dagger with his injured left hand. "Where did you learn to prance around like that? *Merde*, your father's people taught you, *n'est pas?*"

"Something like that."

---

[13] Father! Save him, Castor!

[14] You bitch! I'm going to rip out your balls for this.

[15] We are as you've made us, dearest father.

Vexos glared over his head at his brother. "You think our ships and timber will be enough for him, *mon frère? Non.* When he's done with you, your bones will rot in the midden, same as mine and *papa's.* To slay an ally under a flag of truce?" He shook his head once. "I'll await you in Tech Duinn, Castor after the High King finishes you both."

Damek cocked his head. "Which High King?"

"What?" Vexos blinked.

Too sluggish to parry, Vexos could not prevent Damek's next charge. His dagger skittered away from him as Damek's sabre sank deep into his midsection. The blade was finally halted by the girth of the oak behind him. Vexos' fingers flexed uselessly, dropping his broadsword. Damek backed up a pace to enjoy the fading light in his eyes, but Vexos, bloody spittle dribbling down his chin, reached out with the last of his strength and smashed his forehead into his. Damek backpedaled, cursing. Vivid stars flashed behind his eyes, his nostrils streaming. Vexos' grin was a macabre rictus as he died. "Not so pretty now, are you?"

Martin handed Damek a torn bit of tunic to hold below his nose. In the meantime, Hisk accepted his lord's sabre for cleaning. "Gods *damn* it," groaned Damek, tilting his head back to staunch the bleeding. "That whoreson had a massive blockhead."

"Not much of a fighter, though," noted Martin with a shrug.

Castor waved a hand. "Brute strength has its uses in a melée, not much in close combat with a swift opponent, *non?*"

"I suppose," Martin conceded, his steely grey eyes unabashedly suspicious. "No feelings for your departed family, then?"

"I knew them better than you, My Lord."

Damek tossed his bloodied rag into the muck, accepting Martin's waterskin. He spat out several mouthfuls of blood before turning to his newest ally. "I don't care about any of you. A swift death will not factor into your fate if you fail me. Am I clear, Marquis Gaelin?"

"*Oui,*" Castor agreed with a half-bow. "As a mountain spring, My Lord. My men are ready for what comes next."

"Excellent." Damek allowed Hisk to refasten his cloak, then remounted his destrier with renewed purpose. "The bruise should help, don't you think, Martin?"

"Oh, aye," said Martin with a wince. "You're going to be beautiful for a day or two, I'd say."

Damek spared him a wink and bloody grin. "Maybe My Lady will kiss it better?"

"For the love of Reason, don't ask her to," sighed Martin.

Damek waved at his Corpsmen. "Remember, you're in pursuit. You know what to do. Wait for my summons."

Two dozen men saluted and kicked their mounts to a gallop, heading west.

Castor pulled up beside him, his expression impassive. Damek winked at him. "This should be fun."

In their wake, the sky opened up. Rain pattered against the steel-capped cuirasses of nearly fifty dead Gauls, left to rot where they lay.

Unmoored

The dark was stale and close, wet and sour as a whale's tongue. Swirling below, the Lee waited, frigid, black, and greedy. She shivered at the thought. The river lapped over a stack of tumbledown stones that held up a small dock at the end of this semi-cavernous chamber. Its walls were slick with moss and damp from unseen water trickling from within the bedrock. Above, huge stone arches were cut or engineered to bolster the castle from beneath. Bats and other chattering vermin tittered from the deepest shadows on the dripping, recessed ceiling. The floor was made up of enormous slate paving stones her grandfather had laid, which were warped from the years and slanted perilously steep toward the edge of the cliff. Una made sure to place her booted feet carefully, lest she slip. Gulls shrieked from the cavern opening at the bottom, though very little fresh marsh air made it inside the crack. A few wooden boats clacked together at the end of the manufactured jetty. Spying the one she sought, Una made her way to the dock, clutching her hissing torch like a shield.

According to Shanley's report, this is where both girls had been found. She crept up a short set of grimy wooden steps that had surely seen more years than she had and onto a creaking, dilapidated dock. Ancient wood groaned beneath her heels, and she sucked in a breath. She'd never thought to worry about plunging to her death in an icy river fraught with hidden currents, but the possibility increased with each halting step. This place had been used for decades, but she couldn't imagine how or why. This was hardly the safest or most cleanly space in Bethany to conduct trade. Though this cavern had been cut into the cliff for the safe and swift delivery of goods and men, any use nowadays must be clandestine or nefarious.

Why else would anyone seek out this moldy, dank little Hellscape?

A fat river rat squeaked across her toe. Una bit down on her tongue rather than cry out.

Disgusting.

She'd bet that if the river were drained, one would discover an entire city's worth of the nasty, gnawing beasts. She did not care for *that* thought either. A light sweat broke over her brow, thinking of each victim's wounds. While they'd been strangled and bludgeoned, the report she'd pilfered claimed neither had been raped nor 'cut' while living. Shanley's nervous, quivering penmanship seemed to show that he'd scribbled the following words out as fast as he could— *'extreme distress to the soft tissues of the throat, eyes, nose, and mouth. Wrists, ears, palms, and the under soles of their feet chewed away. We did not cut into the distension of each belly, for both girls were infested with rats and other vermin.'*

Meaning that rats went for the softest pieces they could get to, then crawled inside to help themselves to the girls' innards. Thank Siora, the girls were long dead before they went into the river— or so the report read. The bodies were so badly mutilated that no one could be sure of the order of events.

A sharp gust of wind found its way through the crack and into her face. Eyes watering, she gritted her teeth and knelt near a mainly discolored spot near the end of the dock. Reaching out with a gloved hand, she ran her finger over the stain. Dried blood. She was certain of it. Quite a lot of it, too. She waved her torch over the area. About a foot wide, and three feet long, was the ruddy black mark where one or both of the victims had met their end. The spot was now dried to a rusty void, but she felt wide nicks in the wood, where the murderer's weapon must have slammed into it.

There were dozens.

The assailant must have struck as hard as he could several times to make such indentions. Pity and anger commingled in her throat. What sort of creature did such things? How crazed did an individual need to be to beat and choke a woman to death, then leave her body for the rats? Having done the deed twice that she knew of, how long before he struck again? She got to her feet, raising her torch higher. The curious and insistent squeaking grew louder the longer she remained. She wrinkled her nose—little bastards. The killer's disease-ridden accomplices were likely eager for another meal.

Not today, you monsters.

As soon as I catch your horrible friend, I'll burn the lot of you together.

Someone really *did* need to do something about the Lee. It had never been the cleanest waterway in the South, nor did she imagine the loveliest— but the rats, flies, and refuse seemed to have worsened in her absence. Due, in no small part, to the Duch's obsessive war efforts, no doubt. Most of the fainne he collected from the populace had bought the Corpsmen's shiny cobalt armor, their brilliant, razor-edged sabres, and the obscenely expensive Bretagn warhorses they rode into battle… and battle they did. Whatever coin wasn't demanded from the populace was earned at the tip of Damek Bishop's blade. She sniffed. Bethany boasted the finest army in Innisfail, aside from the mythic Sidhe armies of the North, that most had never seen. Every inch of Bethany suffered for it too. Unclean waterways were choked with rubbish and vermin. Rundown streets were filthy and poorly lit— an invitation for larceny of every stripe. On her daily walks, Una could see many of these crumbling lanes from the northern parapet. Even Duch Kevin's once mighty fortress had fallen into a bit of disrepair. The bulk of the castle reeked of neglect, except for the halls that Patrick had scrubbed to impress their incoming guests. Her father had more lofty pursuits on his mind than the health and wellbeing of his citizens. He'd spent so much time and fainne building an army worthy of challenging the High King that he didn't have much left for anything else.

Una knew very well that was where she came in.

With a potential dowry of millions to look forward to, Patrick expected this year's *Cromnasa* to refill his much-beleaguered coffers. Of course, that her would-be suitor was sure to be fleeced of every coin, and she remarried to her oafish cousin, in the end, made no difference to the Duch. What was one more battle in pursuit of a crown? Well, the Duch may make his plans.

She'd be happy to disappoint the old meddler in the end.

Her eyes flicked to the hardiest of the little boats slapping time against its moorings. She could disappoint him *now* if she chose to. She stood, staring, for quite some time; she wasn't strictly sure why she didn't.

No one was here to stop her.

She could be well away, long before the watch was ever raised. She had enough ridiculous jewels draped around her neck to buy a team of horses, guards, and even weapons if she wanted them. So, why didn't she? The little curragh bobbed up and down at her.

Her feet wouldn't budge.

Why?

You have nowhere else to go, Damek's voice rang in her ears.

She looked away. The hatred that crept into her heart at the memory would not lessen its truth. He was right. Her father, too, damn his eyes, was equally succinct. She had no refuge to escape to. No Tairngare to return to. No silly adventure quests to look forward to.

Una was home now, for better or worse.

If she wished it to be the former, she resolved to do what she must. Someone had to see to the people; why shouldn't it be her? These murdered girls were the first of many wrongs she intended to right. They'd died in service to her family, such as they were. By rights— she would fight for *them*. No more women would be brutalized in her father's house if she had anything to say about it.

If she couldn't live the life she wanted to, then by Siora, she would make something of the one she had.

Sighing, she got to her feet. Wherever the murderer had gone, she was positive he'd return to this spot. Her father's questionably brilliant steward had assumed he'd merely dumped each body into the Lee from here, but the stain and nicks in the dock begged to differ. The river entrance was the darkest, least likely place for interruption in the Keep. Plenty of loose rocks, nails, dock chains, and other detritus with which to bash in a girl's brains… and a vast, obsidian pool with built-in disposal at the end of the dock. Hidden currents would rip anything not nailed to the cliff through the crevice in the wall and eventually out into the harbor. That is if they weren't caught in a fisherman's net as these two girls had been… or eaten by rats first.

There were no records of women having been found mutilated in the river until this year. While that didn't wholly rule out a practiced villain, it did lend credence to the argument against one. She'd wager Henry of Bethany was a lot fleeter of foot than he let on. He made much of being a knock-kneed cripple, but she'd spied him climbing the garden steps alone as late as the day before. He was stronger than he appeared at first glance. She remembered the way the table shook under his fists the night she'd taunted him, the fury and cold hatred in his eyes, notwithstanding. Her uncle was fully capable of such violence against a woman, no matter what her sweet, foolish cousin might have to say. Indeed, she aimed to prove it and rid the city of the fiend as soon as possible.

Be careful that you don't fix your conclusions before you've ascertained the facts. Una frowned again, sick of other people's voices fleshing out her conscience. She was quite capable of rationalizing on her bloody own, thank you. Having seen what she came to, she carefully retraced her steps up the rickety steps to the shale level. A heap of fallen stones blocked a good portion of the path, so she had to duck around them toward the wall. A good thing. Someone appeared at the top of the far stair, his face obscured by a deep hood. She shrank back with a hiss, allowing her torch to tumble into the Lee. When her eyes adjusted, she stole a peek at her visitor from around her stack of stones. If he hadn't seen her, he *had* spied the light from her torch, hadn't he? Straining to be as quiet as possible, she leaned over a tad farther. The figure stared into the shadows that concealed her, lifting his torch high. Her heart leaped into her nose. He said nothing. Pulse pounding, Una flattened herself against her stone. Had he seen her, or was he merely being cautious?

You don't even know if this is the killer.

He could be a custodian or a servant meeting someone for a tryst.

But the figure grew more menacing by the moment in his perfect silence. If he weren't the individual in question… wouldn't he call out or announce himself somehow? Holding her breath, Una traced around the stone to the far edge to get a look from the other side. The figure was no longer there; only his torch remained, stuck fast against the rotted iron railing. The air caught in her chest. She backed away, tucking her body into the darkest crevice she could. Now in near-total darkness, she waited. Sure enough, a vague shape limped by. His footfalls were clumsy but largely silent. *So, it is you,* she thought with a rueful grin. *And how very sneaky you are, my dear.* Had he followed her down here, perhaps? Maybe raced her steps through the armory and then below the dungeons?

She took off her gloves with a tight smile.

Come closer, friend.

Her ears pricked at a small skittering of pebbles on her right. Una lunged at the sound and was immediately slammed into the wet, hard stones below. He caught her wrists in one hand, dropping a sharp elbow into her temple. Her body slackened, and he struck her in the eye. Ears ringing, she felt something warm trickle down her jaw from both nostrils. The noise had been a ruse to draw her out, obviously. She might have kicked herself if she could manage the task before he killed her. Only an overeager fool with something to prove would have shown her hand so quickly.

Rats squeaked excitedly near her head, and her stomach swam.

His breathing labored; he leaned over her, gloved fingers pawing at her breasts and abdomen. She didn't have long to experience the intense revulsion that surged through her blood at the action. The figure soon groaned in frustration and struck her anywhere he could with balled fists. Una gathered every ounce of sense she had left and kicked out with her left heel. Her boot mercilessly plowed into his groin. With a mewling whimper, he crumpled to the slate floor. Knowing she had bare seconds to escape before he smashed her skull like an egg, she doused her blood with every dollop of Spark she could and scrabbled to her knees. The killer roared in a fury, snatching at her cloak. She stumbled before she could make it much farther than the dock. Desperate fingers dug into her ankle with bone-breaking force, dragging her backward. Thankfully, her Spark revived her enough to get moving. Again, she struck out with her heel, connecting with his unseen jaw.

Once his grip loosened, she slithered for the dock on her belly.

Una slipped into the freezing, malodorous Lee with scarcely a splash. She heard his furious bellow, despite the rushing whir of the current tugging her down, down… then out through the crack toward the sea.

⚑ ⚐

SHANLEY, RED-FACED AND HUFFING, dashed from one corner of the Duch's antechamber to the other. Patrick was in a lather. His cup spewed wine in every conceivable direction while he cursed and ranted at his nephew. Shanley was beside himself as he attempted to keep the vessel full. Sweating and bleary-eyed, Patrick threw a sheaf of half-written warrants at his mud-spattered nephew. Lord Bishop took the abuse with an irritable sigh.

"Uncle, I have men combing the forests and hills as we speak. They'll ride halfway to the Kneeler's Hell to get to the bottom of this, I assure you."

"Who would *dare* lift a hand against one of *my* guests but you, boy?" screeched Patrick, with vein-bursting volume.

Damek spread his hands wide. "Don't be absurd. Ask the Bretagns yourself, damn you. They were all there."

Rumbling, Patrick speared Martin with a glare. "Explain, Commander. *Not you, boy*! I've heard all I mean to from you. Sit down and shut your bloody mouth before I fill it with iron. I want to hear Martin's version." Damek refused the chair. Instead, he bowed and took up space beside the larder. Shanley raced to fill his cup too. The poor fellow looked no less harried than a whipped dog.

Martin cleared his throat. "It is as My Lord says, Your Grace. We discovered the party on the road. They were already engaged. Honorless shits couldn't resist the lure of so many wagons in Lord Gaelin's train, no doubt. We saved who and what we could, but much was lost, I'm afraid."

"And Gaelin?"

Martin shook his head. "Died in the first rush, or so his surviving son, Castor, tells us. Bandits were waiting for them in the Brough Trace, Your Grace. Not a large wood, but deep enough to hide a decent-sized force. A clever trap."

"Mm," jeered Patrick, narrowing his eyes at Damek. "Practiced this together, did you?"

"Your Grace, we did no such thing. You have my—"

Patrick waved him away. "That's enough! I don't know why either of you thought I'd be foolish enough to believe this tripe. I'm ill, not mad. Shanley, for the love of bloody Reason… why is this cup empty?" Shanley did his duty with a shaking arm. Once finished, Patrick shoved him to the door. "Don't show your face in here again until you've retrieved the whole barrel!" When his nervous steward had gone, Patrick sank into a high-backed chair beside the window. It was snowing again, though this time heavy enough that it might stick. Damek sipped his wine, thinking of all those dead faces buried in fresh white snow. He broke off a laugh. "Dismiss them all, now," said the Duch, his haggard face pinched in visible suspicion. Martin bobbed his head in answer. His officers saluted before filing out and closing the door behind them. Only Damek, Martin, and the Duch of Bethany were privy to any further conversation. "Tell me the truth."

"We have, Your Grace." Martin didn't blink. "It happened just as we said. We were attacked ourselves a few weeks ago. The bandits are getting bolder, with so many visiting nobles on the roads for Cromnasa. It happens every year, but not on such a scale."

"Damek?"

He turned his face a mask of perfect indignance. "I've said repeatedly that Cairnream should be purged once a season, Uncle. You never want to waste the arrows; now, look what they've done."

Patrick blew air over his lower lip. "Oh, *very* good, nephew. You've got the Donahugh bollocks. I'll give you that. Very well, 'murdered by bandits for his gold' will play before my more foolish Barons, but not all. I suppose you and this Castor have struck some sort of arrangement, no? It had better be worth it for the trouble this will rouse between the remaining nobles at feast."

"Uncle—" protested Damek again.

Patrick enunciated: "Not another word. I warned you not to press your luck, didn't I?"

The threat crackled in the air between them. "You did," relented Damek. "Anything I do benefits this family. On *that,* you may depend."

Patrick's lips puckered around the rim of his cup. "It had better, or I will live long enough to ensure you regret the lie."

Martin opened his mouth to say more, but a sharp and frenzied pounding preceded Shanley's tumbling inside. Apoplectic, he shook himself to his full height. "Y-Your Grace! I bear grave news!"

Patrick rolled his eyes. "Haven't we already discussed 'getting to the point,' Shanley?"

Shanley flushed puce. "Y-yes, My Lord. T-the Lady Una. She's not in the Keep, Your Grace!"

Damek's head whipped around at that. "*What?*"

Shanley shriveled under the attention. "She was in her chambers for breakfast but hasn't been seen since, Your Honors. One of the armory attendants saw her in the Low Hall sometime before noon."

Patrick buried his face in his hands. "She's escaped again! I *knew* I shouldn't have trusted her to honor her word any more than yours, idiot nephew of mine."

"You don't know that, Uncle. There may be more to this than you realize."

"How so?"

Damek pointed at Shanley, who flinched. "This fool has been very irresponsible with his reports, it seems."

Ignoring Shanley's sputtered amazement, Patrick scratched at his chin. "Indeed?"

"My man found four hastily penned missives in her valise two days ago. Taken from your desk, I would imagine, Uncle."

"The murdered girls?"

Damek rubbed his temple. "The Low Hall leads to only two places."

Patrick visibly brightened, then noticing his nephew's smug smirk, immediately darkened. "How do you know what she's been reading and where she stole it from, boy?"

With an odd smile for Martin, Damek said, "We are as you've made us, Uncle."

"D'you think she would take it upon herself to escape once down there? It wouldn't be hard. There are almost always boats waiting at the dock. She could be halfway to Kinsale by now!"

"Send riders out in both directions, My Lord," said Martin, in his sure, deep voice. "Just to be sure. No matter how hard she rows, she'll never outpace my Corpsmen."

"I'll head to the Moorings, myself. Martin, when you send outriders, have men comb the riverbank from here to the Bay," Damek agreed. "Even if she hasn't taken it into her head to run, I doubt she's gone far."

"No need for such a fuss," replied a weak voice from the far door. Una, soaked and dripping blood from at least three points on her face, had come in through the hidden door from Patrick's bedroom. One of her maids and two pageboys held her upright by the elbows. She looked half-drowned at best, nearly frozen at worst, aside from the marks on her face and neck. "I'm too damned cold to run anywhere right now."

Martin recovered himself first. He ripped off his cloak and threw it around her shoulders before tucking her into a chair beside the fireplace. Shanley was fast on his heels with a tall goblet of wine. Damek stared like a man possessed. "What in the *Hells* happened to you?"

Martin handed her a kerchief with which to wipe her blackened nose. "Someone tried to murder me."

"*Who would dare?*" repeated the Duch, with thrice the venom. He came around his desk, eyes full of brimstone. "Please tell me today's events are not some hair-brained scheme hatched between the two of you to vex me?"

Una glanced up at Damek. "You nearly get beaten to death, too?"

"Something like that."

She tugged a shoulder up. "No, father. I ran afoul of our mysterious villain, I'm afraid. As I suspected, he's been murdering his victims in the caverns, then dumping them in the river. Rats do the rest."

"You went after him? Are you mad?" thundered the Duch. "Shanley, get the remainder of her maids down here, *now*, and I want every available guard in this hall for the night, d'you hear?"

Una snuggled deeper into Martin's cloak while her maid dabbed a cloth at her seeping temple. Though he kept his expression mild as a summer breeze, inside, Damek's rage boiled hot as any tempest. He couldn't stop staring, as if the bruises and gashes on her cheek were happening before his eyes.

"Who did this?" he managed to ask evenly.

"The man who's been murdering our serving girls. I assume he followed me downstairs hoping to catch finer fare, as it were."

"Did you get a look at him?" asked Martin softly.

She tried to shake her head and winced. "No. I went down to have a look at the site. I didn't expect him to turn up so soon or brazenly. He must know I'm looking for him."

"What? How could he know you're looking for him?" her father piped in, taking the opposite seat.

"He knows about me. About my, erm, gifts. He went for my hands first. Everything else, after."

"Everything else?" Damek's voice finally found its edge.

She waved a hand at her father. "You were right. He can't… perform. I think the murders are a form of vengeance for his lack of ability. Almost an afterthought."

Patrick paled by four shades. Martin looked as if he couldn't decide if he wanted to embrace or throttle her. Damek went cold as a mountain peak. "That is to say, he tried and failed?"

She ignored him. "Anyway, he'll find somewhere new to take his victims now. We have to catch him before he strikes again."

"Una." Patrick patted her hand. She swiftly concealed her disgust. Damek saw. "You're remanded to quarters until further notice. No more walks on the parapet, no more trips to the library, and no more bloody detective work from you! Stupid girl. You could've been killed!"

"If I were anyone but me, I daresay I would have been," she scowled at the fireplace. "My Spark, as usual, saved my life. He's quite quick despite that limp and very clever."

"A limp, you say?" Patrick asked.

"Yes." Her eyes came up hard. "Like a certain someone we both know and revile. I told you, father. It's him."

"It can't be. You've said so, yourself. He tried and failed."

"Perhaps the serving girl you sent away *did* lie, after all? Even you can be wrong from time to time."

"Excuse me," interrupted Damek in his flattest, most dispassionate voice. "You're bleeding all over your father's rug, and the two of you are arguing over facile details? Tessa? Will you please escort the lady into her father's bedchamber for the evening? See that her wounds receive the attention they require and allow no one but myself or the Duch entry into these apartments. Am I clear?"

Tessa nodded, flushing.

"Issuing orders already, are we?" chided Patrick.

"This blackguard isn't likely to let her escape without a peep, is he? With all the incoming guests, as I've said, this place is an open invitation for villainy of every stripe. Or, if you'd prefer, I'll take her to my chambers?"

"Not on your life, you cur," Patrick got through his teeth. "I will sleep in the next apartment. Shanley will see to the arrangements," he frowned. "What'll we do about your face, my dear?"

"It will heal," Una said sourly. "We won't disappoint your guests, Duch Patrick."

Patrick bristled for a fight, but Martin quickly handed him a goblet and steered him toward his chair. In the meantime, Una sagged a bit in hers. She caught Damek's stare with a tight-lipped smile. "Go ahead. I know you're dying to scold me to the moors and back."

"I'm not. What you did was attempt to help someone else. Who am I to scold you for that?"

She seemed surprised to hear him say so; that probably hurt him worse than the deep welts in her skin. "This man must be found, Damek. He's not going to stop."

"I know, and you're right. We will find him."

She was quiet until Tessa came to help her to her feet. Una stumbled against the girl. Damek gently shoved the maid away and hoisted his cousin into his arms. Una didn't protest, for once. Her skin was hot to the touch, which he knew firsthand meant she was healing already. Most people with so many head injuries should be kept awake at all costs, but in Una's case, her Spark worked best with rest. She would sleep for a day or two and be right as rain in no time.

Patrick eyed the two of them with something nearly akin to human sadness in his steel grey eyes. "Una, do you think you'll know this man if you see him again?"

"She's already asleep, Uncle." Damek carried her to Patrick's bedchamber door but paused a breath shy of the eave. "I'll stay with her tonight."

"Not likely, boy. I will sit with her and Shanley after me. *You'll* hie off and entertain our guests in my absence. I'm interested in how your intrigue with the new Marquis of Bretagne will play out."

"Uncle, I've told you—"

"Pish and posh, Damek. Worth less than nothing to an old schemer like me. Just be sure to play the bystander to the hilt, or it'll be war with men you had better not cross yet. Am I understood?"

"Perfectly."

"Good. Now, you may set my daughter down and get to work. Martin, while my nephew sees to the guests, I want you to raise every able-bodied man in my guard to the castle grounds. This murderous ruffian will have to hunt for victims elsewhere until he is found and eliminated."

"Yes, Your Grace," saluted Martin.

"Also, I want my brother removed to the lower cells in the East Tower. He'll have no ink, vellum, books, or company until I am sure my daughter is wrong about his guilt."

"Forgive me, Your Grace, but I doubt she is. I never liked your brother much, even before he found this odious religion."

Patrick's expression was inscrutable. "We'll know, sooner rather than later, I expect."

Damek tuned them out on his way through Patrick's spacious but spartan chamber. He shook with an unquantifiable fury as he lay Una on his Uncle's bed. She looked so tiny, like a drowned songbird. His lips touched hers before he could stop himself, and he heard Tessa gasp from the doorway.

"My lord, ye mustn't! She's got an ailment, ye see, and—"

"Get her out of these wet things, immediately," he cut her off and stomped past without a backward glance.

Cairnream

Kaer Yin hadn't felt the urge to limp in days. That was something. Even though Rian made a lot of noise about 'overeager idiots' every chance she got, he no longer gasped when walking, and the hole in his chest had nearly healed. Perhaps he wouldn't win any races for a while yet, but at last, he was no longer an invalid. That he had the opportunity to be simultaneously elated at his newfound strength and livid over the actions of a trusted member of his inner circle was equally of note. The climb up to this promontory cost him less than the gnawing anger in his gut for the scene below. There, in the distance, was a tiny Gerrod stripped to the waist and dangling from a crow's cage. In the five days since he'd seen the lad, Gerrod seemed to have lost ten pounds he could scarcely afford. His ribs jutted from his flesh like the carcass of a gutted fish. He was left to dangle from a sturdy tree some distance from the rudimentary walls of tiny, insignificant Cairnream.

If Kaer Yin weren't currently gulping brimstone at Matt Gilcannon's gall, he might be impressed by the genuine cruelty of the scene. He passed Robin's glass back.

Robin spat witchroot into the dirt, shaking his head. He'd looked long before Kaer Yin and refused to do so again. "I say we kill that piece of shite today, Ben. Be done with it."

"After I'm done stripping Gerrod's hide to ribbons for the trouble, of course."

"Think his dear ol' da's already done for him."

Kaer Yin's mouth tasted of metal and bile. "Shar?"

"*Mo Flaith?*"

"I want you and Niall to track up that ridge there. I want to know exactly how many people are in there, where they sit, where they sleep, and most importantly, where Matt fucking Gilcannon stains the earth with his arse."

Shar gave a nervous sort of chuckle. "Erm, we don't… I mean."

Robin stuck his chin out at him. "He means where the bastard lives and works. I swear, ye lot are meant to have spawned our bloody language, and none of ye seems to speak it."

Shar saluted and sped away with an odd grin. Robin watched him go, scratching at his scar. "Strange one, ain't he? Finds everything funny."

"Not everything, just Yin," offered Tam Lin from down the trail a pace. He wasn't even slightly winded. Kaer Yin decided they should have a fistfight at the first opportunity. He was tired of Tam Lin's pretty, bored face. "What are we waiting for, *Ard Tiarne*? My Blood Eagles could sweep that pathetic compound in minutes."

Marking Kaer Yin's scowl, Robin answered for him. "He's a slippery one, Gilcannon is. The last time we rushed in, he got off scot-free. Won't be happenin' again, ye ask me. I owe that cunt the closest shave he'll ever get."

"Fine, fine," sighed Tam Lin. "Have your fun, then. I'll dawdle here, and someone can wake me when this nonsense is finished."

"Tam Lin," said Kaer Yin through his teeth. "You're being a boor, again."

Tam Lin threw up his hands. "What do you expect, cousin? None of us came here to chase after headstrong teenagers, nor 'rescue' questionable damsels from their own father's house! We *should* be on our way home to Croghan for Cromnasa, not traipsing through the South dressed like flea-ridden Merchers on the stupidest mission in history!"

"Is that *all* you'd like to say, Lin?"

Tam Lin gestured to Gerrod's cage, downhill. "That young man is hanging from a tree right now, Yin. Let's get the boy and get out of here. Or aren't you worried for your lady any longer?"

"Of course, I'm worried about her!"

"Well, she's fifty miles in the opposite bloody direction. I swear. This is ridiculous, and you know it."

"Everything is ridiculous to you, Tam Lin. Unless it's got teats, a horn of ale, or a *rath* to rob, you're never interested, are you?"

"What was that?" Tam Lin crossed his arms.

"You heard me. I'm calling you boorish, predictable, and dull. Do something about it."

"That's fine talk from a mooncalf cripple."

"Why don't you step up here and see how crippled I am, Lin." Kaer Yin had already dropped his bow and was busy unstrapping his belt. He shrugged Robin off as easily as swatting a fly. He was near twice the woodsman's size, after all.

Tam Lin tossed his daggers into the dirt, removing his cloak. "Love to. Your stupid face is looking far too lovely these days." He pulled his arm back to swipe at his cousin, but Rian got in between them. Tam Lin staggered a bit. "Brida's teeth, woman! That could have been your head."

"No one has time for you two idiots to dry hump each other into the dirt right now. Knock it off, or I swear to Siora, I'll poison the pair of you." Her fists balled at either hip. "I believe Gerrod is more important than either of your gripes at the moment."

Tam Lin reared back as if she'd slapped him. "*You dare—*"

"She's right," added Eva. "The boy hasn't had water for two days. He needs to come out of there."

Instantly sobered, Kaer Yin cursed. "Gods damn it. His own son."

"Now ye see why that perfumed pederast has to go? He's a real gem, he is," reminded Robin. "We let him leave again, who's to say he don't have more half-starved brats waitin' on the road home? Not to mention them lot what serve him. Know what he's doin' to them?"

"I do," Eva assured them. "He's… abominable."

Kaer Yin turned to her with renewed interest. "Can you see him?"

"After a fashion, yes. He's in the second-largest building, on the right there. Do you see it?"

He did. Rian came up beside him, squinting. "I don't."

"Red paint on the shutters."

"Oh," she said, wrinkling her nose. "Hideous."

"That's Matt for ye," tsked Robin. "Gauche till the end."

Kaer Yin studied Eva's fine-boned features, again dismissing the pang summoned by the resemblance to her niece. How was Una now? What was she doing? Was she being mistreated or locked away? He shoved those thoughts down deep, lest they plague him to distraction. Gerrod first, Gilcannon next, then Una. One thing at a time, like he constantly preached. "Can you tell if he's in there at all times?"

She peered into the distance, craning her neck a bit. "No. There are so many voices down there that it's hard to drown them all out. I can hear the echo of his thoughts but not the full litany. I'm sorry."

"Not at all. If you were down there, could you do it?"

"Yes."

"Looks like you're about to get your wish, Robin."

Tam Lin made a rude sound. "If I end up bleeding by the end of the day, Yin, I'm breaking your nose."

"If you don't stop whingeing, Tam Lin, I'll be happy to test that vow."

379

The Greenmakers, including Kaer Yin, approached the crude hamlet from the South, while the Sidhe crept in from the Northeast, effectively blocking any mass exit. The town was situated on a broad plain tucked between two youngish woods, and it would appear to anyone on lookout that their group had materialized out of thin air. The walk toward the roughly hewn gate wasn't a long one. Kaer Yin didn't feel the familiar and irritating catch in his side, which made this predicament far less annoying than it should have been— he was thankful for the Sidhe blood in his veins.

A horned owl screeched from the opposite end of the field, behind Gerrod's cage: Shar, checking in. Kaer Yin nodded. Bru called back. Shar and Niall would free Gerrod before Kaer Yin and Robin scaled the squat southern wall. Rushing through frozen, waist-high weeds and bracken, they made the dash in under a minute. Robin set his hand to his mouth and whistled into it: a marsh swallow… common as nettles in the Midlands. They waited for half a dozen heartbeats, then heard back. The deed was done. Gerrod had been removed from the scene; now, all that remained was vengeance.

Tam Lin had volunteered to accompany Kaer Yin's party if only to catch a scratch that would earn him the right to take it out of his cousin's hide later.

They really did need to have that fight, never mind what the bloody women had to say about it. Animosity would fester so long as the wound wasn't properly lanced. Tam Lin was raw at Kaer Yin for many things, but chiefly for choosing the company of Milesians over the notion of traveling home to Aes Sidhe. He couldn't understand it yet, and that bitterness seeped further into him each day.

Well, it would have to wait. Gilcannon was the priority.

An ugly, pitch-stained inner gate had been hastily erected at the center of the village, where mismatched logs of varying heights and girths had been driven into the hardening soil at all angles—several youngish men filtered in and out of the haphazard structure. One or two reclined on top as if the need for guards were perfunctory rather than necessity. Kaer Yin's mouth quirked a bit at the corner. If only they knew what was about to happen to them. The tallest guard noticed Kaer Yin first as if he'd materialized from thin air. Matt's hideouts and outbuildings lay beyond the rusty length of this boy's spear. Eyes agog, the lad yipped a curt command, "Ye! Stop right there."

Kaer Yin raised his hands as Robin came up beside him. Tam Lin, Bru, and Carn Gor hung back a pace. Kaer Yin gave the guard his most affable grin. "Well met there, friend."

The other teenage guards stumbled together in an awkward, ill-practiced knot. "Who the feck are ye, and where'd ye come from?" demanded the first lad. The others were so shocked by Kaer Yin's sudden appearance they couldn't seem to move fast enough.

"Oh," hummed Kaer Yin, craning his neck around to see through the gap to the house beyond. "An old friend of Matt's. I wonder if you'd mind announcing us?"

One of the junior guards got a good look at the sword strapped at Kaer Yin's waist. "Shoot 'em, Billy. He's trouble." Billy was the lone archer. He struggled to nock his poorly strung bow.

Kaer Yin kept his face impassive. "How about you do as I asked, and we'll leave you well out of it? If not…" He raised a hand, and a silver-fletched arrow kicked the bow out of Billy's fumbling hands. Billy skittered backward with a cry. The first guard gripped his spear with renewed menace. The others filtered behind him as if he were taller than the wall around them. Bedraggled people in the courtyard stopped in their tracks to see what all the fuss was about. Robin gave them his best wink and a wave. Someone dropped the water pail they were hauling and trudged up to the big house in a hurry. Another belted an alert to anyone within earshot. Much good it would do them. Kaer Yin set his hand on his pommel. "For your own sake, boys, get out of the way. Matt's not worth one drop of your blood. This, I promise you."

Alarmed bellows rang within the inner courtyard, causing ruckus inside the house. A single shutter was thrown open, and a familiar head popped out and back in again with lightning speed. Robin glanced his way. "Ben?"

"Saw him," said Kaer Yin. He gestured to Bru, who cupped a hand over his mouth for yet another birdcall, a loon, this time. "Get ready. They're going to rush us. It's all they can do. Try not to kill them."

Robin made a rude sound. "If any o'em gets too close, their own damned fault."

"Try, all the same. It isn't hard to manipulate the desperate."

"Bloody do-gooder," Robin groaned.

The first rush was comical at best. The lead guardsman tilted forward with his half-broken spear, only to trip over the heel of Kaer Yin's boot. Face-first in the mud, the boy, sputtered and lashed about beneath the weight of his heel. Kaer Yin drew his sword and let the rest of the ragtag get a good look at the length of Nemain's pure, sylvan steel. "Now, I did ask nicely the first time. Won't happen again."

Despite his obvious lack of skill with a bow, Billy had a pair of daggers on him that might make Robin proud. He rolled past Kaer Yin's reach toward Bru, brandishing his little blades with a sloppy but deadly serious fury. Bru had no choice but to draw his blade in defense. Meanwhile, the others spilled from the gate like oversized ants fleeing a hill. That none of them carried a weapon better than an old farmer's spade didn't lessen their ferocity a whit.

Robin grabbed the next boy who attempted to rush him by the scruff and tossed him aside to fend off another. "Ben," he said, sweating already. "Move yer arse before I change me mind."

Kaer Yin ducked under a wide spear thrust, grasped the wielder by the shoulder, and cracked his forearm in half. The young man screeched like a hungry eaglet and collapsed into the muck beside his fallen friend. Kaer Yin leapt over both inert figures and into the thickening crowd without pause. Bodies flew this way and that as he spun into the courtyard proper. Many went down with nasty wounds, though he was proud to say most would bear a painful lesson rather than a fatal mistake.

Two boys darted for him from the first outbuilding. One swung a wide cudgel with a howl. Flipping his blade upside down, Kaer Yin hammered the lad with the flat, forcing all the air from the boy's lungs and breaking several ribs. This youth didn't have the wind to wail as his fellows did. The other attempted to wedge a spade under Kaer Yin's sword arm, but he pulled the fool in by his elbow and smashed his forehead into his nose. This one squealed like a ten-year-old girl. Six more questionably able individuals attempted to stay Kaer Yin from the side door of Matt's buzzing household to no avail. Each was merely a minor impediment for Robin to step over as he followed a half-pace behind. Kaer Yin grabbed one boy by the scruff and threw him head-over-arse into the wide door. It shattered inward in a spray of garish red splinters. The house's interior didn't appear to be finished, with its low ceilings, bare timber stairs, and plain wooden walls. It also seemed quite empty save for a plush violet couch, a lovely pin-back walnut table and chairs, and the odd Bretagn silk cushion. Kaer Yin frowned, eyes tracing upstairs.

"Matt, love. I suggest you come down before I come up."

His answer was silence, save for the weeping of an unknown child.

"He's hidin'," scoffed Robin, tracking around the stairs. The kitchen was unfinished, and the back door remained locked from the inside.

The one place Matt might have gone was up.

Tam Lin, who had yet to lift a finger to help in this endeavor, crossed his arms. "Well, after you, cousin."

Kaer Yin glared back for a moment, then took the steps two at a time. He was obliged to leap aside on the landing as a heavy oak bureau came clattering down the stairs. Hearing Robin's colorful curse, he imagined his friend had taken the brunt for him. Next, a pair of boys, no older than seven years each, took turns whacking Kaer Yin's shins with broken broom handles. Grunting, he shunted one away with his knee and the other with his stick. Growling for his smarting shins, he turned to find Matt Gilcannon at the window. His former paunch was a shadow of its old girth. His once fine, if greasy, black hair had withered from his freckled scalp like ink from a pitcher. He held up one scarred but bejeweled hand.

"Ben Maeden, Robin? What're ye doin' here?"

Kaer Yin's grin was easily a thousand watts. "Matt! Delighted to see you." A third small boy dashed for his ankles as he strode forward, but a swift kick sent the kid rolling. "I'm sorry we missed each other last time."

Matt backed himself into the newly painted window frame, his cheeks white as spoiled milk. He was clean-shaven and smartly dressed, though the scars around his neck and collarbone were telling. Had he been tortured by Lord Bishop's men before or after he betrayed Rosweal? Did it matter, either way? How many people had died for this man's greed? Matt wagged a finger with a weak, terrified smirk. "Too right! We should've been introduced properly. There're so many opportunities we might yet—"

Robin cut him off with a snarl. "Shut yer mouth. Thought ye could hide from me, did ye?"

Matt gulped loud enough for the whole room to hear. Whatever defense his thugs could manage seemed to be waning. The piercing shouts and metallic clatter had stopped almost as abruptly as they'd begun. "A man has a right to rebuild when his life's work has been destroyed, no?"

"Whose fault was that I wonder? Whom was it invited that Tenma by-blow and his soldiers into Rosweal? Whose plotting with Souther mercenaries brought that Bishop cunt to our door? Hm?"

Kaer Yin filled the space on Matt's left side, leaning over his sword. "Who strung his *own son* from a cage like a common criminal? After a lifetime of rape, larceny, and murder?"

"Gentlemen, please. Be reasonable," begged Matt, shrinking into the wall. "He came to kill me. No one did him any harm."

Tam Lin grunted, "My men tell me he'll lose two fingers to frostbite. Is that not harm?"

Confused, Matt's black eyes flicked around at all the new faces. "Who're ye, sir?"

Tam Lin ignored Kaer Yin's warning glare. "Tam Lin O'Ruaidh, at your service." He bowed an unimposing figure in his disguise. "Peer of the realm, as it happens."

Matt gave a nervous laugh. No one else moved a muscle. After several rapid breaths, he giggled, "I too love a good jape, now and again."

Tam Lin scratched at his newfound stubble. "Not particularly fond of jokes, myself. Yin, kill him, and let's be done with this. I do believe he's wet himself."

On a heavy exhale, Kaer Yin shrugged. "Robin?"

"Wait! Wait, I'll give ye anythin' ye want! I have fainne, a few gems from Scotia, wine from Cymru… women, boys, whatever ye want!"

Robin's nose twisted about ninety degrees the wrong way. He drew his favorite dagger from the inner pocket of his vest. "Ye shoulda thought that bribe through."

"Please, Robin! We was mates once!" Matt squished himself so far into the window that the pane cracked at the far edge. "Yer woman wants my recipes, don't she? They're hers! Anythin', *anythin'* ye want! Don't kill me, Robin. Ye don't have to."

Robin covered Matt's quivering mouth with his left hand, but before he could ram the point of his dagger through his eye, a familiar horn sounded in the distance. All the blood in Kaer Yin's veins ran cold. Robin's wide eyes met his when the horn came again, closer.

"Your Highness!" Eva called from the rear yard, "Steel Corps!"

Tam Lin's head whipped around. "What does that mean?"

Matt whimpered behind Robin's hand. His face purpled. Robin dropped his arm by a breath. "Friends o'yers?"

Matt swept his head side to side, apoplectic. "No! The Lord Marshal said he'd gut me if he ever saw me again. I don't know—" The horn blared beyond the southern wall. Matt looked like he would faint. Screams from the southern edge of town told Kaer Yin everything he needed to know.

"We have to get out of here, *now*."

Tam Lin wasn't convinced. "Why? My *Iolár Fola* can handle this rabble and—"

Kaer Yin jerked him close by the collar. "These are Bethany's shock troops — armored cavalry— and they're good, Tam Lin. Very, very good. It's not worth the risk." He released his cousin and slapped Robin's shoulder. "Make it quick or leave him. Dunno what Matt did to take the piss out of the Lord of Clare, but they can't be here for us. We have to go."

Matt blubbered, "Please! *Please*…"

Sneering at the fat glob of snot that slid down Matt's chin, Robin shook himself and stood, resheathing his dagger. "Not feckin' worth it, are ya? Snivelin' gobshite."

An eagle called from somewhere outside, and Kaer Yin cursed.

"What?" Robin bashed Matt's head against the wall with a crack. Matt sank like a soft-bellied stone into a stinking puddle of piss.

"Retreat," Tam Lin clarified, stepping over him. "My men know better than to let themselves be surrounded."

"That means *we're* bloody surrounded then, don't it?"

"Seems so." Tam Lin developed a dangerous tilt to his jaw. His brows knit together over a glare that should have boiled his cousin's guts to broth. "Yin, I swear to Danu, when this is all over, I will bash your worthless brains in."

"Duly noted." Kaer Yin peered through the window at the stream of horsemen in their flashy blue and silver armor. He was partially disappointed that the Lord of Clare himself was not apparent among them. "Not that many. Twenty or so."

"Twenty knights, Yer Arseness. Not twenty farmers' boys." Robin took up space beside him, his expression dour.

"Oh good," Tam Lin carped. "I was already having so much fun."

Matt's boys ran for the trees when the horsemen galloped through the gate. One of them, a squat fellow in a cobalt blue cloak trimmed with ermine, looked a bit familiar to Kaer Yin. The knight drew his sword. "Round them up."

His men rode down whoever had been slow or stupid enough to be caught. Quite a knot of old men, young boys, and lasses were corralled in the central courtyard beyond Matt's gate before Kaer Yin was forced to look away. "What are they doing?"

"Their job looks to me." Tam Lin pursed his lips over his head. "These are criminals, are they not? Good riddance."

"Be quiet."

"What more do you need to see?"

"I know that man," Kaer Yin said, indicating one of the officers.

The fellow, probably their commander, danced his horse around his easily won prisoners. "You stand accused of the brutal robbery and murder of the Lord Gaelin and his son—visitors to our shores and the good Duch's Court. How do you plea?"

A general outcry was met with several vicious kicks and horse lashings. One lad, who was perhaps no more than twelve, took the lash for a younger boy. "We didn't do nothin' o'the sort, sir! We was here, mindin' our harvest. Ye can ask anyone!" Yet more stragglers were shoved into the boy's ranks, and he stumbled.

"Is that so?" The officer was unimpressed. "Kerns?"

"Sergeant Douglas?" called a second, less decorated knight.

"Bring the archers up, and have the bodies loaded within the hour."

The second knight saluted with a fist to the chest. He waved an arm. A squad of longbowmen was brought up from the rear before a pair of emptied carts. The young boy who'd been brave enough to speak was the first to take an arrow through the throat. Two volleys and the deed was done. Fifteen men, women, and children crumpled to the dirt together, dead. Kaer Yin paled. Tam Lin recoiled.

"*Siora*," breathed Robin. "They was just bairns."

The commander turned toward Matt's house. "Bring Gilcannon to me, alive. He will answer to our lord for this."

"Time to go, lads," Robin urged, racing for the rear window.

"What about him?" Tam Lin motioned to Matt's unconscious body. "Thought you wanted to kill him?"

"I do." Robin kicked the bootlegger's pudgy form for good measure. "Looks like our fancy Lord of Clare intends to do it for me, in any case. C'mon, Ben. Let's shove off before we have to fight our way out, huh?"

Kaer Yin stared at Matt's piss-stained rump for several moments. Booted feet stomped through the house downstairs.

"Let's go!" Robin whisper-roared, waving his hands for emphasis.

"I agree," Tam Lin reminded him. "There's no point otherwise."

But Kaer Yin ignored them both, contemplating Gilcannon's fate. He couldn't leave Matt to the Southers when there was a chance the wily bastard would get away again. Decision reaffirmed. Kaer Yin hauled Matt's wide arse over his shoulder while Tam Lin made short of the two soldiers climbing the stairs.

"What in the Hells are you doin?" Robin looked like he swallowed a wasp whole.

"If Bishop isn't done with Matt here, then I'm not done with him either." Without further explanation, Kaer Yin shoved them both out of the window.

Reflections

The dead swirled past her eyes. Their flesh churned in the current, loose and torn, shredded and distended. Gnarled fingers caught in the tangle of her hair, caressing, reverent. Bulbous, waxy eyes stared up at her with gratitude and affection.

Thank you, their whispers comforted her.

Thank you, Lady.

Her foot caught in a bed of river moss, and she floated for a while in their embrace, timeless, ageless, *free.*

Thank you, Lady, they sang.

Come home to us now.

A child's lovely white skull drifted before her, its skeletal arms reaching to hold either side of her face. She sighed, releasing all the air left in her lungs. How she loved them, loved them *all.*

Una… crooned another voice, a deeper voice. It spoke of endless summer skies and the cool trickle of a starlit fountain. His eyes were green as the depths of the Lee.

Come home, Una, the voice sighed.

Content, she held the child close as any mother, rocking it against her convulsing ribcage. Then, a splash broke her reverie into a thousand, thousand pieces. She was ripped from the comfort of her frigid peace and into the searing light of day. Someone strong dragged her ashore, where she was lain against the reeking bank, and breathed into like a deflated waterskin.

Una's eyes snapped open.

She jerked upright in her mile-wide bed, clutching her throat.

"Una," said Damek, leaning over her. "I'm here. Tell me."

Her eyes welled with tears. "You wouldn't understand."

"Try me."

She drew her knees up. The moon was high in the sky outside her tall windowpanes. She had no idea how long she'd been asleep nor how long he'd been by her side. Did she care anymore? The harder she fought him, the less immediate her hatred of him felt. What did she imagine she had to hold over him any longer? He'd betrayed her, true, but so too had she betrayed him. They'd hurt each other many, many times. Yet, here he sat, despite every effort to be rid of him. Sighing, she leaned into the headboard. She could feel the unease seeping from him like a mottled breath.

He didn't believe she would answer, nor did she. *Yet…*

"You remember that night in the Greensward?"

"How could anyone who'd been there forget?"

She looked away from his shadow to the massive, iron-hinged door. "The Sluagh. There were so many of them, and I took his power. I took *them*, Damek."

"Took whose power?"

She whimpered, "The King of Tech Duinn. I didn't mean to. It just… happened."

Damek was quiet for a long time. His warm fingers threaded through hers in such a familiar, comforting way that she nearly wept anew. "Perchance, he had enough to share?"

She blinked into the dark where his face would be. "What?"

"The King of Tech Duinn is no vessel to be drained dry at the first sip."

Ice cold sweat broke over her brow. She attempted to unwind her fingers from his, but he held her fast. "I see, now." Damek's voice dropped to a new, impossible timbre that sent shivers down her spine. "A woman of conflicting desires. You don't know what you want at all, do you? Poor thing. Such power, and no idea what to do with it."

She fumbled backward, tugging him into the light. His hair was not black but purest silver. Eyes not violet, but a burning emerald so rich, there was no gem anywhere like it in the world of men. His smile was beautiful and cold, warm and cruel, all at once.

"We are bound, child. For good or ill, forever."

"No!"

The fingers holding hers became claws, black and dripping with malfeasance. His teeth elongated to obsidian fangs as he leered.

Such delights I will ssshow youuu…

Una woke screaming, the sharp chill of his claws had tunneled into the veins of her right hand. She snatched the wounded appendage to her, but there was nothing there save a slightly clammy palm. It was broad daylight outside. The sun shone from a cloudless sky. Her maids rushed to her side.

Damek got there first.

"Una, calm down!" She leaped from him, racing to the corner of her bedchamber, eyes wild. For once, Damek looked truly afraid. He set down the goblet he'd meant to hand her and held his hands palms up. The world spun a bit around him. "Una, you had a fever. It's passed now, but you need to eat and drink, then rest. Do you understand?"

She swiped at her streaming nose. "How long have I been asleep?"

"Two days. Your fever broke last night, finally."

"Where is he?"

Damek looked around slowly, spreading his hands. "Who? The Duch?"

"No, the King of Tech Duinn."

His mouth compressed into a thin line. "There hasn't been anyone here but me all this while. Come sit down. Drink something, for Reason's sake."

"I'm not mad, Damek! He was here. He wants revenge."

As if approaching a skittish pony, Damek moved to her side. She flinched. "There now. I'm not he, I swear it. Let's have some broth, shall we?"

Seeing her maids' panicked faces brought the truth crashing in. Una's ears burned at the sight. She *was* mad! She allowed herself to be led back to bed like a recalcitrant child. "A fever, you say?"

"Una, the Lee is barely above fifty degrees in the summertime. Now, it's damn near frozen. You're lucky to be alive."

She'd never had a fever before. In fact, had never been sick aside from the occasional Spark drag. Maybe her Spark had exhausted itself keeping her alive? If that fisherman and his wife hadn't pulled her from the river, she would have drowned. There were slight scratches on her wrists and ankles that she sucked in a breath to see. Rats had been testing her flesh, it seemed. She gagged as Damek sat her down.

"Drink your broth," he prodded gently.

"I can't."

"I'll have these girls hold you down if I must."

She made a face but took the cup he proffered, gulping down its greasy contents without pleasure. Setting her fingers to her mouth to stall herself from vomiting, she handed the cup back. "There were rats in the river, Damek."

He pulled up a chair and waved a girl with a shawl over. She draped the velveteen garment over Una's hollow shoulders. "Of course there were. Patrick's physician has already treated you for the scratches. Good thing the current was up that day, or it would be a damn sight worse." He pointed to her wrists.

She chose to stare at the lovely flat wall rather than imagine those disease-ridden beasts digging their teeth into… "*Siora.*"

He dismissed her maids, then regarded her in silence for a while. When he spoke, he did so with measured confidence. "I don't want you chasing this man again, Una. He could have killed you."

"He tried."

She heard his teeth grind together. "My point, exactly. You have no bloody business traipsing around the castle, anyway, let alone in pursuit of a man who's murdered two girls already. Enough. Let me handle it."

"Like you've *been* handling it?" She squeezed her quivering hands together. "I'm well aware that the Duch is mildly put-out about these crimes, being that he has so many esteemed guests arriving this week. I, however, can and will make this murderer stop."

"No, you won't. You'll be in bed for another day or two until the doctor says otherwise. Then, you'll be very busy with your… admirers. You won't have time to hunt criminals and get half-killed in the process."

"Admirers." She huffed, "Pretense is everything at Patrick's court. How banal."

He leaned forward, steepling his fingertips. "It is, and simple enough too. This is about fainne, Una. Give him what he wants this one last time, then you'll be free to do as you please. We both shall be."

That gave her pause. "What does that mean?"

"Play your part, as I must play mine."

She didn't like the sound of that at all. She studied him for a moment, nose twisted. "What have you done, Damek?"

"Why should I have done anything?"

"Because. I know you."

He opened his mouth to say more, but Shanley opened the door for Patrick, bowing as the Duch shuffled inside. Patrick's grey cheeks brightened at the sight of her sitting upright. "Ah! Wonderful news! Wonderful. You look much improved, my dear."

She repressed a groan. "I wish I felt that way too."

Patrick waved her comment away, patting her knee as he sat beside her on the bed. "In no time, child. No time at all. Food and rest, you'll see."

Nodding, she chewed at her chapped lower lip. "You're anxious. How many have arrived for your charade?"

His smile flickered. "Never mind that now. Despite what you think, I have a care for your well-being."

"Right," she said, drawing up and hugging her knees. "What's been done about Henry, father?"

"It isn't Henry. I've told you."

"I'm not sure," her voice trailed off as she tried to recall her assailant's features. He was stronger than she and taller— though this was not a remarkable feat. She couldn't remember if his chest was broad with youth or wider for shoulder span. He'd been clever, whoever he was, and nearly got the best of her overconfidence. "It could be someone else, but I doubt it. Who else has a reason to murder me?"

She ignored Damek's answering scoff. Patrick eyed her sidelong. "You're not going to let this go, are you?"

"No."

He smoothed his fur robe over a bony thigh. "Fine. You'll rest for two more days, then make yourself available for Court, beside me, twice daily."

"I don't see—"

"If your villain is a member of our number, you'll have the opportunity to observe the Court and its servitors daily, will you not?"

"Y-yes."

"Besides, there's trouble in the North."

"What trouble?"

Patrick stared at the wall ahead, a calculated gleam in his eye. "Word is, the Sidhe have been raiding in the Midlands. Four towns and two farmsteads have been attacked, Hells, even Tara."

Una's gut dropped out. "*What?*"

"Nema has applied to the High King for an investigation, but we all know he will never answer. The matter has been relayed to the Consulate in Ten Bells, though that will not dissuade her from further extreme measures."

"The Sidhe would not raid in Eire," said Una evenly.

Patrick looked long and hard at her. "Wouldn't they? They've done so in the past, many times. I imagine eternal life gets rather monotonous."

"I wouldn't put it past that ingratiating snake to have invented this crisis as a means to consolidate her power," Una replied matter-of-factly. "Nema has the same goal you do, Patrick— absolute rule. Why else would she work so hard to strip the nobility from Tairngare?" She caught Damek's swiftly concealed smirk and narrowed her eyes at him. He said nothing.

What was he up to?

"That may be. Whatever the cause, I smell opportunity." Patrick stood, using the bedpost as a crutch. Una noticed how white his knuckles went. "Strife in the North aids our cause. My Barons will gobble this tidbit right up."

"The Sidhe would not raid over the Boyne, Patrick," Una persisted. "This is a ploy. Nothing more."

"Oh? An expert, are we? Let's say you're right, and Nema has a plan. Her power base weakens by the day, and her revolution flounders. She may make allies of the unwashed and powerless, may even bind the masses to her through brutality and avarice, but she has no real army. Half the Tairnganeah have fled with their mothers. The other half lack the skills or education to lead. While she might point the finger at Aes Sidhe for a power boost, she's busy making sure enemies surround her. Do you want your mother's city set to rights, or not?"

She bit her tongue. There was a plot here. She could smell it. "Of course, I do."

"Then, take it back, *Duchess*. Learn from me and unify Eire."

Ah. "You mean to sack Tairngare soon."

"Your mother's people are being ground beneath the bootheel of a tyrant. Or do they mean nothing to you?"

Damek rocked back in his chair. She'd nearly forgotten he was there. "I told you, it's a matter of *fainne*, didn't I?" He didn't wait to hear her response. He got to his feet and adjusted his swordbelt. "She won't see sense right away, uncle, and anyway, I have other business. I'll tell her women to bring more broth and tea." He spared Una a last, meaningful glance. Her brow came together. "If you'll excuse me?"

Patrick's voice caught him at the door. "You and I are not finished, boy."

Damek winked at him on the way out. "Never are, uncle."

⚜

By morning, Una decided she'd had enough convalescence for a lifetime. If she never saw a bowl of porridge or a cup of broth again in her life, it would be too soon. When the sun's first rays threatened the heavy clouds outside, she slipped past her sleeping guards on bare feet, carrying her boots under one arm. Most of the castle was abed at this hour, and she highly doubted she'd run into much trouble on her way. The stone in the corridor was so cold that she might have been tiptoeing over ice. Partway down the stairs, she leaned against the fine glass window to shrug her winter cloak tight and step into her fur-lined boots. A few maids and washerwomen were getting an early start to their labors when she made it to the landing below the South Tower, but they scarcely glanced her way as she passed. Una hung a right at the bottom of the stairs, striding past the kitchens with its kindling twin hearths and bustling servitors.

The cook and her minions would inform Shanley of her whereabouts if she were seen. Thankfully, no one batted an eye at her. She remembered having her fingers swatted raw by that behemoth for a stolen oat cake as a child. After passing through several nondescript stone passages with very few doors, she emerged into the sweeping Grand Hall under its gabled timber ceiling and an army of smoldering braziers.

There were people asleep *everywhere*.

Soldiers entwined with castle girls on or beneath tables, in various stages of undress. Men and women snored away on benches at each long table, clutching their ale or mead. The husks of several boars and pheasants were left to spoil in the artificial heat—so many people. More than half must have been guests, yet, Patrick expected more. No wonder the Duch was desperate for funds. Imagine trying to feed and entertain half a thousand people for ten straight days, once a year. The cost must have been unfathomable. She wrinkled her nose. The absurdity and hubris of the feast probably annoyed her more than the subject, the lure of her bride price, as it were.

She picked her way over and around the room, careful not to step too close to any snoring inebriate. Martin O'Rearden snored away in the rear-left corner of the room nearest the dais, hugging a pitcher of mead and mumbling into his beard. If he cracked an eye, she'd be back in her room in a trice. Tugging her skirts up, she hurried past as quietly as she could. In moments, she pushed open a side door to the inner bailey and sucked in a hard breath for the bite in the air. Dor Cromna was already at full gallop in the South, it seemed. The Boyne mouth at Drogheda must have been four inches thick with ice by now. Una exhaled slowly.

There was no point dwelling on things she couldn't change.

She filed those feelings away for later with the rest.

Coming through the armory from the opposite side of the Hall, she skirted the door leading to the dungeons and the subterranean Moorings she'd nearly died in a few nights before. With a shudder, she straightened her spine and marched onward. No one seemed the least concerned about this person wandering the castle, with all the guests and bootlickers arriving for Cromnasa. Well, she bloody well did. As long as she drew breath, that bastard's days were numbered. She wasn't quite sure where the inspiration had come from. Perhaps, this feeling was inspired by the strength of his arms, the confident clap of his well-made boots against the stone floor, or maybe the clean, white flash of his gnashing teeth. She couldn't say for sure, but she had a distinct opinion that this person wasn't feeble or old enough to be her uncle. She winced to think that she'd been so very wrong all this while but couldn't deny the obvious, all the same. She'd gone over the incident in her mind, from the moment he struck in the dark to the clamor of his roar as she escaped.

The murderer was a robust, healthy *young* man. Too muscular to be a feeble old meddler like Henry of Bethany. Certainly, too fleet of foot. Indeed, her assailant had to be both well-fed and given to martial practice. Una would bet all of her fingernails that the murderer was a soldier or a noble. Likely, both. While castle servants might be healthy and strong, which dockworker or builder had she ever met, could afford peppermint toothpowder?

There'd been a moment when his hands clawed for her neck that she'd caught a dose of his surprisingly fresh breath and a flash of white teeth her uncle no longer possessed. The Duch was right. It wasn't his errant brother at all. As infuriating as that fact was, it led to a new string of possibilities. She had a wealth of information to work with once she sat down and thought about it hard enough. She knew his general weight, height, and strength. She knew he bathed in bergamot and used peppermint toothpowder. She knew he'd been free to explore the dungeons during the day, below the central keep, and that it wouldn't be odd to see him in the escort of castle maids. She also knew that the few men who fit these descriptions were officers or lower-level courtiers with community postings in the keep. It so happened, there was a list of every soldier and courtier in Bethany at the Guardhouse ahead, as well as definitive timestamps for their comings and goings.

Una entered the Guardhouse from the Armory Hall, pouring some speed into her gait so she wouldn't be stopped before reaching her destination. What few guardsmen she spied leaning upright in their posts, or stumbling bleary-eyed into the hall, seemed less interested in her than the prospect of meat and eggs beckoning from the Mess back the way she came. The clerk, however, was a fastidious fellow. At his post before the break of dawn, he was busy stacking vellum and arranging logs when Una strolled into his office. He started when he saw her, dropping a quill to straighten his robes.

"My Lady! What are you… what can I *do* for you at this hour?"

Una gave him her most disarming smile. "Good morning. I'm here to review your register for the past two months, sir. Specifically, those relating to male courtiers and officers among the Steel Corps."

The clerk paled from the flap of his overfull chin to the crown of his balding pate. "Ah, My Lady, we don't grant access to—"

She pushed back her hood so that he might see the fading bruise at her temple. "I am asking as a courtesy." She took off her gloves.

He licked his lips, eyes wild.

Sometimes, her reputation came in handy.

"The Duch, My Lady—"

"Is not going to live forever. Whom do you suppose *I* am?"

She could hear the cogs turn in his head. After a while, he cleared his throat and pushed a heavy volume forward. "Of course, *Your Grace*. These are the registers for this month, and," he gulped, reaching below his desk for another heavy tome, "this is Dor Oras' log. I'm afraid we do not maintain separate files for varied titles." He pointed to a symbol resembling a star, beside some Corpsman's name. "Though we do maintain a shorthand for rank and file. The Asterisk denotes the Corps, the circle, stewards and servitors, and this," he tapped the page at a cross-shaped squiggle, "the nobility. We also do not delineate by sex, though the names should be obvious."

She gave him a look.

His eyes darted sideways. "Ah, yes. Sometimes they do not, I suppose."

"This is a rather inefficient way to manage this Gate, you realize?"

"We are understaffed here, My Lady. It would be impossible to organize every visitor and servant as you expect."

"Do you imagine Bethany is larger or more complex than Tairngare?"

He flushed. "No, I erm… no."

She scooped the proffered registers into her arms. They were pretty heavy. "Nevertheless, I expect you'll staff appropriately from now on. Won't you?"

"… The Duch has expressly—"

"You realize women have been murdered beneath my father's roof?"

"Y- yes."

"Perhaps you'll have also heard that this same villain attacked me?"

"No, I had not—" his face belied a horror of realization that assured her *no one* in Bethany had the slightest idea, as she suspected.

Shanley had done his work well.

She kept her features neutral as if the confirmation weren't infuriating. "These logs, such as they are, contain the name and rank of a criminal. I might have arrested him this afternoon if they were sorted properly as they should have been. Do we understand each other, erm… what is your name?"

"Finney, My Lady."

"Right. I will take them with me and any other documents pertaining to the castle's residents before the remaining Cromnasa guests arrive. When I return them, I expect a much more efficient system will be in place. Have I made myself clear?"

Finney bowed so low his chin scraped his collarbone. "You have. I'm terribly sorry, Your Grace."

"No need for all that, but you'd best get busy."

"Yes, Your Grace."

Una slowly put her gloves back on, making sure he watched her do it. His shoulders sagged a bit as if in relief. She drew her hood back up and turned to leave. But there was a sudden commotion at the Gatehouse, outside. Several shouts filled the frigid air from both sides of the heavy iron edifice. Una craned her neck at the window to see a group of formerly sluggish guardsmen rushing toward the portcullis. Finney scrambled to retrieve an empty ledger from the shelf behind him and pocketed his keys.

"What is happening?" she demanded.

"Corpsmen returning, Your Grace." He dropped his keys twice.

"Returning from where?"

"Patrol." He almost tripped, rushing for the door. "They've brought prisoners, it seems." He hesitated in the open doorway, allowing a fresh gust of icy wind inside. "Forgive me, My Lady, but I must—"

She waved him ahead, tucking the logs under the crook of her arm. "No, by all means." He bustled out, and she followed at a sedate pace, curious. Several of Damek's men, whom she recognized from their journey south, galloped into the courtyard before a pair of covered wagons. Breaking dawn light flashed from their frost-ridden breastplates and illuminated the dark stains which dappled their cobalt cloaks and the soft kid of their breeches. Her teeth clenched, eyes darting to the wagons. These mud-spattered Corpsmen were led by Damek's foremost Sergeant, Cillian Douglas. He did not glance her way at first.

Douglas clapped the Gate clerk on the back hard. The poor fellow fumbled his ledgers to remain upright. "Wake the Duch's steward at once. The men responsible have been dealt with, as ordered."

Finney held a hand out at two lower guardsmen, who rushed for the inner bailey. Slapping his notes down on the guard dock, he hastily dipped his quill and began to scribble. "I'm sorry, milord, but I must have the name and rank of each man in your company."

Damek's newly minted Sergeant dismounted with a sour glance at Finney. "Are you mad, man? We're half-frozen and starved for sleep."

"All the same, milord," Finney gawked, tugging his chin at Una. "As My Lady requires, so must I answer."

Douglas' sharp eyes snapped to Una's with a snarl. She didn't flinch. As recognition dawned, he blinked a few times before the blood drained from his unshaven cheeks. His bow was clumsy. "I… forgive me, My Lady. I did not see you."

"Well, I certainly see *you*, Corpsman. What is going on here?"

He fidgeted like a much smaller man, glancing back at the wagons. His companions dismounted with wide eyes. "Prisoners. Nothing to concern yourself with."

"Is that so?"

He fumbled to catch up as she made for the wagons. He threw his arms wide. "Erm, this is not for a gentlewoman's eyes, My Lady!"

She moved around him. "Prisoners of whom?"

"The Duch and Lord Bishop."

"I don't see what—" but she did, all at once. Blood seeped from the rear of the front wagon in a steady stream. Piled atop one another in a sickening lump of tangled limbs and blue flesh were the bodies of a half-dozen men and boys. Looking on in horror, she saw the corpses of one or two girls in there, as well. A heavy knot formed in her throat. "I assume the second wagon is the same?"

Douglas moved to close the rear flap, blocking the macabre spectacle. "It is. I tried to warn you. This was not intended for—"

"What crime would urge you to slaughter old men and children, Corpsman?" She struggled to maintain the even timbre of her voice.

Shanley, in a state of half dress, stumbled into the courtyard. He exclaimed to see Una standing so near the Gatehouse. "Lady Donahugh! What are you—"

Una held out a hand to silence him. Nostrils flaring, she turned to Douglas. "Answer the bloody question."

He wouldn't meet her eyes. "They ambushed Lord Gaelin and his retinue on the road to Bethany. The lord and his eldest son were murdered."

Even if she didn't already suspect Damek's duplicity on that score, she would have heard the lie in Douglas' rasping voice. "Is that *so?*"

"My Lady!" shrieked Shanley, his vocal cords cracking, cheeks purpling. "The Duch has expressly ordered that you remain in your rooms until you're well. I really must insist that you return!"

"Where is Damek now, Corpsman?"

"Escorting minor Barons south from the Midlands."

Another lie. Douglas at least had the grace to flush with shame at the derision in her expression. Shanley caught up to them, huffing. He squeaked a bit at the sight of those in the wagon but knew where his first urgency lay. "My Lady, *please*! Folk will rise soon, and—"

Ignoring him, she spun on her heel and marched back through the inner Bailey, utterly unconcerned about who might be watching or why.

Subtle Diplomacy

The Cymrian Trade Ambassador ogled Gan like a particularly ripe species of pond scum. She gaped shamelessly; her pasty face pinched back in a sneer for the ages. Gan stared over her head. It wouldn't do any good to show offense. Not one of the people gathered would spare a tinker's fart for the Fawa Gans of the world. These were wealthy Merchers from all points of the Continent. They had wealth, position, and influence Gan could never have aspired to. Aside from this, many of them were veterans of the previous war and had seen worse than him in their time… much worse. Though, never in civilized Tairngare. Nonetheless, the novelty of his head-to-toe burns wore off after a few moments in his company. Once it had been established that he existed merely for the amusement of his mistress, the shock lost some of its luster.

Only Melba, the wan Cymrian bitch in question, could not look away. She was one of about a half-dozen dignitaries who'd arrived to attend Nema's open Trade Negotiations. Melba's province in Cymru was world-renowned for their carbon-rich peat and not much else. Though the soil in Tairngare's province of Meath was rife with the stuff, it proved much more complicated to harvest than in the wide boglands east of the mighty Danned Y Llew range.

Backwoods trash, Gan thought without a shred of irony.

No class whatsoever.

He caught Nema's disapproving frown from the corner of his eye and promptly looked down. The floor was a much safer place to devote his attention. Beside him, one of this Cymrian Tradesman's guards stepped a pace back. That was fine by Gan. Among the few senses the flames hadn't robbed him of was his sense of smell. This awkward Cymrian reeked of cheap uishge and sour fruit. Gan's haggard reflection winked up at him from the polished onyx floor.

He opted to close his eyes rather than share Melba's morbid fascination.

Breaking with hundreds of years of tradition, these dignitaries were invited to a feast in the Doma's ceremonial throne room on the Tenth Floor. Nema had promised an 'open government,' and thus far, she had been faithful to her word. The people, as usual, loved her the more for it. The pronouncement had been applauded in the Markets when announced, despite the ever-present soldiery which lurked around every corner. Of course, Gan had not been allowed to stray from the Citadel, but that didn't stop the chattering in every hall. The streets were heavily patrolled by the Cohort, day and night. Every gate, road, and warehouse leading to and from the Red City boasted cadres of watchful Corsairs. After the recent unrest in the wake of her coup, Nema would brook no further checks on her power.

Gan thought it excessive.

Anyone with influence or wealth enough to challenge her authority had been murdered or imprisoned weeks ago… and the commoners *adored* her for it. What additional security did she require? He braved the briefest glance at the dais. There she sat, on that great, glossy black throne. Her brilliant gold robes spilled around her like a lustrous golden river in flood. A surge of pure, unadulterated hatred pierced his heart.

Tamp it down, his subconscious warned.

She sees all.

He stood not six paces behind the throne. Close enough to be used but far enough to remain well outside her majestic tableau. Before the dais, where Nema reclined with a goblet of Lord Rhiannon's finest vintage, sat her many illustrious guests. She'd had their tables situated in a semicircle around the throne, clearly as a means to impress a feeling of 'conversational inclusion' upon their ranks. None sat higher than any other, as each was invited to worship her 'Holiness' on equal footing. Everyone seemed to be having a marvelous time in Nema's vaunted presence, and if Gan were a betting man, he'd assume the evening's purpose to be a success, save for one or two more speculative people in the bunch. Melba, for one. She simply wouldn't take her eyes from him. Nema noticed. She half-turned in her seat to raise an eyebrow at the ambassador.

"Mistress Melba, we are honored to list your delegation amongst our guests."

Melba affected a half-bow from her seat. "We are pleased to be included, Your Eminence." Her gaze flicked to Gan once more as if she couldn't stop herself.

"Did you find your quarters satisfactory?"

"Yes, quite comfortable, Eminence. We thank you."

Nema raised her goblet in a brief toast before summoning another round. The servitor, in this case, turned out to be Gan. He shuffled forward on his crutch, as gnarled and knock-kneed as a man thrice his age. With shaking, partially bandaged hands, he refilled Nema's cup and shambled back to his place by the wall. Having regained every ounce of attention he'd previously lost, he faced away from his audience, sucking at his cheeks for shame. If only Melba knew her bloody place, Nema might have forgotten he was there.

You must not weep, Gan old boy.

You'd make a further spectacle of yourself.

"Have we piqued your interest, then?" inquired Nema, with a cruel grin.

Melba tactfully cleared her throat. "You have, Eminence. Though, I'd be remiss in my duty to my shareholders if I didn't consider the matter for a while first. Haste and finance are not happy bedfellows."

"I find it intriguing you would say so, Mistress. I've been told your Guild elected you to office just this year," wheezed Lord Rhiannon. "What wisdom could you have possibly gained in your position since?"

Melba dried her mouth and returned Rhiannon's smirk. "Well, I'm a peat farmer. Own several thousand acres, as it happens. My father left me the family business, along with his Guild's dues. Way things work in the East, you see?"

The far wealthier, far more refined Lord Rhiannon of Swansea, Head of the Vintners' Guild and owner of *ten thousand acres* of the richest soil in Western Cymru, hummed, "Hm. Quite."

"Not everyone can buy a lordship selling fruit, Rhiannon."

Coloring, Rhiannon gave a slight cough. "I beg your pardon?"

"You heard me." Melba's expression hardened, and Gan could see why she led her particular territory. "Without my Guild, you fancy Southers would have frozen to death years ago, your grapes long withered. Be careful whom you insult, sir."

Lord Rhiannon muttered into his goblet but looked away.

Nema flashed her perfect white teeth. "Now, now. Let's all behave in a manner that reflects our stations."

Melba laughed wryly. "Funny you should expect such a thing in *this* court, Eminence."

Nema's mouth drew into a line. "Whatever do you mean, Ambassador?"

Melba gestured to Gan. "We can see the lengths you'll go to attain power."

A collective hush descended over those gathered, save for Lord Rhiannon's shrill gasp. He had expected his Northern colleague to share his fiscal interests with the new regime in Tairngare. Nema's guards shifted closer; Melba's mirrored the action.

"I believe you mistake us, Ambassador. What was meted here was a much-desired justice. The people are grateful to be free of Libellan yoke. I wonder that you, who represent such humble origins, would not be sympathetic to our cause?"

With a sneer for her fellow Ambassadors, Melba dipped her head. "No one who works for a living can argue that the rich get far above themselves, far too often. Though, it's not your argument I find fault with, rather, your methods."

"You think us harsh?" asked Nema softly.

Melba stood. She wasn't incredibly imposing but there managed to be something sizeable about her. "These fools may grovel at your feet because you now control the port at Drogheda, but Cymru has long since outgrown the need for Tairnganese tariffs."

Rhiannon shot to his feet. "Your Eminence! May I assure you that Melba *does not* speak for all Cymrian Merchers. The rest of us are well pleased by your terms."

Melba stared a hole in him. "You'll find that claim proves false. If you haven't noticed, you're missing the Kernian Trade Ambassador, the Bretagn Assemblage, the Alban Agricultural Chief, and the Sidhe Delegation from Scotia."

"Your point being?"

"All save the Sidhe are headed to Bethany to treat with Donahugh," Melba replied. "The Duch may be many things, but he does not burn his opponents and dissenters alive, nor display his disfigured victims as a subtle reminder of his power."

Gan shrank away. He knew he would likely suffer for this later on.

"Well," Nema spoke up after a thunderous silence. "Is that all you wish to say?"

One of Melba's lackeys helped her shrug into her traveling cloak. "It is. Cymru— that is, the Energy and Agricultural Guild— shall not accept your terms. We cannot support a tyrannical regime responsible for class warfare and nominal genocide. I would bid you farewell, Eminence, but what would the point be?" She turned to waddle off, but several of Nema's silent Fir Bolg guardians slunk in with their weapons drawn. Before anyone could flutter an eye, a brief skirmish ensued, pitting the far stronger Fir Bolg against Melba's unprepared guards. The surprised Albans were overcome with embarrassing swiftness. Who could have imagined that the Doma of Tairngare would have such creatures in her employ? In the midst, Melba attempted to intercede and took a shallow wound to the temple. She backpedaled into the arms of her nearest defender: eyes wide to the pearls. Her colleagues below the dais leapt to their feet to retreat. Holding their easily defeated opponents with little effort, the Bolg guardsmen waited for Nema's order. Staring at the blood on her hand as if it were a serpent coiled to bite, Melba shrieked, "You'd harm an Ambassador under a sacred treaty? Are you *mad*?"

"Clearly," Nema agreed from her monstrous black throne. "As you've implied, my ruthless dedication to power is tantamount to my purpose here." She lifted a single finger. Her Sidhe mercenaries answered, drawing long, bone-handled blades across their captives' quivering throats. Too quickly, Melba's retinue sank en masse to the floor, dead. The rest of the ambassadors quietly retreated to a far corner, holding their hands out to show they had no interest in dissent. Melba's furious scream didn't stop her from being snatched up in the guards' merciless grip. "Ambassador Melba," respired Nema. "We find your actions as grievous as they are slanderous. The people of Tairngare no longer recognize the Libellan Court nor its pandering policies toward foreign Merchers. You have lobbed a grave accusation at the Doma today. As such, the Union of Commons must investigate your claims. You shall be held in contempt until proceedings. Do you have any further comments before you are taken to your cell to await trial?"

Melba looked around frantically. "She commits murder before your eyes, and none of you will gainsay this?"

Her colleagues looked anywhere but at her, obviously terrified.

Nema's smile was warm and light as a summer sky. "We will speak again soon, Ambassador. May Siora's mercy shine upon you."

Melba's cries reached a terrible pitch as she was dragged from the room.

FADING EMBERS SIMMERED IN THE gaudy silver braziers of Nema's amber antechamber, casting eerie shadows over gleaming walls. The grand golden dragon chandelier roared at Gan from her place in the heart of the chamber; ivory claws and fangs dripped garish garnets and rubies, like heart's blood. If there'd ever been a testament to the excesses of the noble class in Tairngare, this ridiculous centerpiece was in desperate contention. As if the gems and precious metals decking each over appointed room on the Tenth Floor weren't extravagant enough, the half-ton monstrosity hanging from the ceiling tipped the scales to the floor. No bloody wonder the Mouras were so officious. It appeared the former Doma couldn't relax in her apartments unless her every glance was accosted by one obscene display of wealth or another. Gan side-eyed the lot. He might be a nerveless, scabrous villain, but at least he had some fucking taste. Nema didn't seem affronted by the absurd décor, but she wouldn't, would she?

Appropriation was also one of Nema's numerous vices.

Gan should know; he'd served the witch for nearly forty years.

Nema's chambermaid had shaken Gan awake at the third bell to order him to attend his lady in her antechambers at the fourth. Ever since, he'd been hugging the wall beside Nema's bedchamber door, waiting for Her Eminence to make an appearance, and watching this strange figure pretend he wasn't in the room. No matter how hard Gan stared, the visitor wouldn't spare him a single glance.

Beneath his notice, Gan surmised.

That's interesting.

This guest waited patiently by the windows, hooded and stoic as a statue. His entourage waited in the Obsidian Hall beyond, a gangly, surreptitious group, mercurial and solemn as their leader. They wore indigo cloaks of costly sealskin with deep cowls. So far, all Gan could discern was that the fellow wore his black hair long and loose over his collarbone and that his hands were long-fingered and well-manicured when he removed his gloves. Gan had never met a man so tall who wasn't feeble at the shoulders, like a poorly cinched taper. This person didn't seem to share the unhappy trait of so many. Gan wondered where he came from. The longer Nema's guest stared out over the city, the more curiosity nibbled at Gan. Who on earth would come to pay court to Vanna Nema in the wee hours of the morning without invitation? More puzzling, who would she accept into her apartments at such an hour, uninvited?

In his many years of playing her lap dog, Gan had yet to see *anyone* make such a bold presumption. Who was this man? He'd never seen Vanna take a lover or make assignations of any sort. Indeed, she had always been asexual, so far as he could tell. If anyone would have been apprised of a lover, surely Gan would have?

Finally, the door to Nema's bedchamber swung open, and the malicious witch herself swept into the room. Nema had taken care with her appearance. Her hair swept back into a wide opal clasp that left the grey-speckled mass to pool down her back. She wore a vibrant chartreuse robe that billowed when she moved and knocked off at least a dozen years for its waist-cinching daring. Her maids had even applied rouge to her lips and cheeks, which Gan might have raised a brow at, did he have eyebrows to raise. Striding past Gan, she held out both hands for her guest to clasp. The fellow took them, if with some hesitation.

"Darling Falan," she lilted. "So good of you to call."

Gan felt, rather than saw, his eyes flick toward him. "Do you think an audience is wise?"

Nema snapped her fingers at Gan, who knew what she wanted without a word more. He limped to her larder to fill two goblets with Bretagn sherry. He served Nema first, who smirked over the rim. "Gan is my creature, through and through. Aren't you, my love?"

"I am, Eminence," lied Gan, atonally.

He passed a glass to her guest, who sighed, "If you say so, Lady." Gan felt that cold gaze rake him once more. "What have you done to him?"

She sipped from her goblet. "What he deserved. Now, enough about my servants. What news have you for me?"

Nema's guest took the farthest seat he might without appearing rude. Gan empathized; no one wanted to sit too near a grinning she-wolf. The stranger removed his hood, and a great hole opened below Gan's feet. If ever there had been a man to match this Falan, Gan had never seen him: skin like burnished copper, hair like the blackest depths of a twilight sea, his eyes cut the light like polished amethysts glinting in the sun. Indeed, no one this beautiful had ever existed before— no one human? He was Sidhe. *Fir Bolg.* Gan pressed his hands together so neither individual would see them shake.

Falan, the Elder?

No, it couldn't be… the patriarch is ancient… and why would he travel to speak with the Doma of Tairngare in the middle of the night? This makes no sense.

Falan leaned back, stretching his long legs below the warmest brazier. "Perhaps your newfound power has clouded your reason? Do you take me for a servant?"

Nema made a face. "There's no need to take offense to a simple question."

"I require answers rather than questions."

Nema straightened, setting her goblet down. "Do try to recall to whom you are speaking, boy."

Watching the two of them stare each other down, Gan was riveted. *What in the nine Hells is happening here?*

Who in the Hells is this Falan?

"Liadan, what do you believe you're accomplishing here?"

Liadan? Who…? Gan's thoughts reeled. He had no idea where he'd heard that name before or why it should relate to Vanna Nema, whom he'd served most of his life.

"I'm remaking Eire for you, my love. As has ever been the goal."

Falan's smile was sharp. "Is that so? You burned a group of nobles and loyalist Merchers alive, I hear. Aoife too."

"A necessary measure."

"Was it?"

"A demonstration of strength was required. Pity is a weakness to be exploited in Eire. Don't presume to know these people, Falan. You've never lived amongst them. Like cattle, they must learn their place."

Falan's brow raised. "Tell me, by that logic, how shall I answer your overreach? You were not meant to rule here, *seanmáthair.*"

Gan's heart pounded against his ribs. He'd grown up in the Cloister. Education was an essential demand from each individual within its walls, servants or acolytes. Why would this Falan call Vanna Nema 'grandmother?' He forced his features to utter stillness rather than let on he was in the least surprised or interested in this conversation. The ideas swirling between his ears ran through a microcosm of infinite possibilities. How could this be? That Falan was Fir Bolg was plain as the nose missing from Gan's face. That Nema was not… was equally notable, and hadn't Gan known her for ages? Since when did she have children, Fir Bolg or otherwise? He felt Nema's attention slide his way and triple-enforced his 'no matter' mask. It had saved his life more times than he could count.

"You dare speak to me this way?"

Falan sat up, smiling. "I am no supplicant, and you are no queen. It's rather the opposite, or have you deluded yourself otherwise?"

The muscles in Nema's jaw flexed. "Any title you aspire to has been a gift of my blood. You forget yourself."

The room chilled by twenty degrees or more. Gan found himself shivering.

"I am heir to a seven-thousand-year legacy, and *I* rule Armagh now. That is my blood right, whether you will it or no. My grandfather was slain in prehistory, and your throne with him. You *will* obey me."

This… was…? But how? Falan the Elder was merely a client-king at best, and everything Gan had ever heard of him suggested he hadn't left the Sidhe Underworld in so long that he might immediately die if he set foot in Innisfail. A man some three thousand years old or more, by all accounts. Would he be so young, so *fresh* as this Falan seemed to be? Gan had little experience with the Sidhe. He had no idea. How Nema knew him was the greater mystery. His grandmother?

Surely not?

Nema drew a deep breath. Gan rushed to refill her goblet, then melted back into the wall. Falan frowned at him but made no further comment. "How good of you to visit. Perhaps you'd prefer to leave before another unkind word is spoken?"

"You do me no honor by persecuting and torturing my future subjects."

"How dare you pontificate to me? I *am* Armagh, you ungrateful, spoilt child. Without me—"

"Eochaid would have wed another, and his grandson would *still* be king. You overvalue yourself, as always."

Nema purpled. "I was Queen of Armagh when—"

"Ages ago. Now, you are a pampered dowager with more time on her hands than common sense. You seek vengeance for ills wrought in another life, another world, sowing chaos and misery wherever you are left unchecked. My father might subsist on dreams and fantasies in the Oiche Ar Fad, but you are the one living in the past."

Nema got up, tossing her goblet to the floor. "Leave. I will see you regret this."

"You'll do nothing," said Falan, flexing his beautiful fingers. Something electric and frigid swept through the room, dousing the braziers in a wisp of smoke and wrapping itself around Nema like a vice. She gasped, clutching at her neck and staggering to the floor. Falan rose slowly, hand shaking with an unknowable power. "These intrigues of yours have a limit, Liadan. Your purpose here was to prepare the Eireans for my arrival, not drive them beneath your boot. I am meant to appear before a grateful lot of Milesians who seek the justice and mercy of their *true* Ard Ri— not a whipped mob with no willingness to conform to Fir Bolg rule and nothing left to lose. In your vanity and greed, you attempt to supplant me. I will not allow it."

Choking, Nema threw up a hand. A gust of wind opened a gash on Falan's cheek. He gnashed his teeth, and she cried out. Gan shuffled out of the way as a window broke across the room, spraying shards in every direction. Falan was unphased. "You and Grainne may convince yourselves that you should be worshipped in Eire all you like; it will never happen. Do you know why the Dannans maintain their grip over Innisfail? Because their women have no power, no imaginary pedestals to place themselves upon. I have no queen and will take none… for obvious reasons, *grandmother*."

His fingers twitched, and Nema screamed, writhing on the floor. "Stop!" she pleaded breathlessly. "We are *clann*."

He knelt so she might get a good look at his passionless expression. "More's the pity. What of Damek, Liadan? Aoife? Hells, your own *son*? All forgotten or used in your pursuit of godhood." His expression spelled disgust. "Well, I'll tell you this— Damek is mine, as Grainne, Aoife, and *you* are mine. Each of you serves at my pleasure or not at all. Do I make myself clear?"

"Y-yes," she croaked. Gan was beside himself. He'd never seen anything like this, nor had he ever imagined anyone might get the better of the mighty Vanna Nema.

Liadan… where have I heard that name?

"Morcan?" Falan said.

One of his men came through the door. "*Mo ri?*"

"My gifts for the Dowager, if you please."

His lieutenant bowed and ducked out. A heartbeat later, he and two others returned bearing the grisly remains of two women. Gan couldn't help the moan that escaped his mouth. He crammed his scarred fingers between his teeth to prevent any further outbursts. Pors Yma had her head twisted all the way round, the whites of her eyes bulging from their sockets like a fish. Her tongue wagged loose from her broken teeth. Kalen Hamma had been split entirely in half, as if from the sharp edge of a giant axe. Each half was tossed casually at opposite ends of the room; organs and sinew that stubbornly clung to the severed halves dribbled gore onto Nema's precious carpets. Gan scrambled backward, drawing Falan's notice.

"Should I kill this one too, I wonder? Perhaps, in this case, it would be a kindness?" Falan's servants turned toward him, and Gan knew equal parts fear and the thrill of relief. Falan cocked his head at him. "Shall I free you from her menace, or would you endure more?"

Gan's partially missing lips flapped open and closed in soundless elation and terror.

Finally, the mysterious Sidhe pursed his lips. "I suppose I should leave her someone to vent her anger upon since she must cease torturing my subjects. Mustn't she?"

Nema whimpered, and Falan spread his fingers again, letting the spell go. She coughed into the plush layer of carpets beneath her, weeping. He knelt by her side to comb the hair away from her face. "Now, you will stick to your place, won't you? These Milesians will come to love me, through you, through our good works. Once Grainne has played her part, I shall be their savior. This is your purpose here, Liadan. If I learn otherwise again, it will be the end of you. Do you hear me?"

"I do." She shoved herself up to her elbow to glare back, huffing. "But I warn *you*, arrogant child, I am not so easily cowed."

Unaffected by her bravado, he gestured to the bodies splayed behind him. "If you say so." Then, he stood, sliding his hood back over his glistening hair. "Damek gets ahead of himself, but I'll allow it for now. His goal is also mine, as my son. You will not impede him again." He turned to leave but paused at the exit to smirk at Gan. "I should kill you for all you've heard tonight, Milesian. I can smell the hatred in your heart; it's blacker even than hers if such were possible."

Gan summoned all the courage he had left. "If that is your wish, *Your Majesty*."

Falan threw his head back on a laugh. "Clever too. What a shame."

His last comment drifted away on the frigid breeze screaming through the broken window. Snow swirled past the curtains, dusting both of Nema's fallen favorites white.

The Ferryman

Ten Bells was by far the loveliest place Rian had ever seen. Though she had spent some time here as a child, she'd never experienced it like this. Coming through the Eastern Gate from the Burren High Road, one couldn't help but gasp at the whimsical picture Ten Bells presented. The town sloped toward a deep cerulean harbor from the coastal hills dotting the Central Innish Plain. Two- and three-story houses and shops, built in the old style with latticed windows and gabled arches, rode that descending wave in tidy, colorful rows. From each of their brilliantly colored rooftops in varying midsummer hues, little tufts of green and white peat smoke puffed into apricot and lemon skies. Through each twisting lane, the sunset over the Sea of Aenghus warmed the elegant paving tiles a rich, dark red. Tall glass lanterns were lit throughout every visible street, enhancing this otherworldly glow. Recent snow had dappled each rooftop and lane with the barest hint of white, which sparkled like scattered diamonds in the blazing sunset above. Her eyes trailed through the center of town to the mighty Shannon. Glowing green and gold, the river undulated through the city on her way to the harbor. Rian held her breath. Maybe once all was said and done, she'd move here after all?

The view alone might be worth all the derision in the world.

Following her eye, Kaer Yin pointed. "There, near the harbor, is our destination, though tomorrow, first thing. Tonight, I need a bath, warm food, and all the ale in town."

"Too bloody right there," huffed Robin. "Me flask's been empty for two days now."

Rian was too enraptured by the panorama to scold them for their alcoholism. "Can't we take a moment to enjoy this?" She gestured to the burning sky above.

"Not unless you mean to drag this wagon to *The Ferryman*, all by yerself," grumbled Gerrod, whose turn it was at the wheel. His filthy face and hands were scabbed over, and the nasty bruise over his eye had long since ceased to swell, but his attitude had steadily soured. In the wagon sat his errant father, the infamous Matt Gilcannon. Everyone, save Kaer Yin, thought it would be wiser to kill the old swindler than cart him around like an invalid, Gerrod, especially. "I'm tired of the road and the company."

Rian twisted her chin at him. "Well, I'm tired of *you* and the awful snit you're in since we're being honest. You have no one but yourself to blame, you realize?"

Gerrod flinched. "Ouch, Rian."

Kaer Yin spared him a growl over his shoulder. "Talk to her like that again, and I'll blacken your other eye. You ungrateful git."

Gerrod ground his molars and started pulling again. "I said I was sorry. Besides, no one asked ye to come after me, did they?"

"Gerry, ye best shut that insolent trap o'yers, 'fore it talks ye out of a nice warm bed and a spot o'ale. Ye hear me?" said Robin, taking the other wheel. They had no pony with which to pull the cart, and as they couldn't exactly march their injured captive through such a charming town as Ten Bells without raising eyebrows, the wagon was their best option. Since they'd left Cairnream, wagon duty had been Gerrod's punishment. Rian couldn't say this was wholly fair, but she understood the logic. Rather hard for him to get into more trouble if he was dead tired every night.

His quest to murder his father had put everyone in jeopardy, costing them precious time and supplies and nearly getting several of their group killed. To Rian's mind, Kaer Yin might be a bit of a bastard, but he was always fair. Gerrod grumbled under his breath rather than argue. When Rian had finally thawed the boy out and treated the worst of his injuries, Robin had been the one to blacken Gerrod's eye.

Again, harsh, but perhaps well-deserved.

Robin poked the lad with the end of his bone pipe. "That's right, ye hot-headed ingrate. Pull the bloody wagon and keep yer grousin' to yerself." Everyone was exhausted, even Eva, who Rian was quite sure ran on clockwork and gears. Her companion, Mel Carra, looked worse for wear than she. Even the Sidhe in their company had taken on a bit of a sag at the jowls. Walking for so many days in freezing weather, up and down hills over rugged terrain and sleeping outside in the elements had taken its toll on them all. Rian's foremost fantasy involved a bowl of cockle stew and a tub overflowing with scalding hot water.

The sunset faded to a dusty violet as they wound through well-lit lanes toward the Harbor. If anything, it made the walk toward the massive *Ferryman*, with its huge glass windows and the rosy lanterns hanging from its well-maintained façade, all the more charming. Several black carriages waited on the side of the behemoth structure, each replete with a handsome pony and a waiting driver. Rian assumed they were to escort guests and visiting dignitaries about town. Ten Bells boasted a half-dozen theaters, two large opera houses, porterhouses for cards, dicing and gambling, restaurants and publicans by the score, and of course, houses of ill-repute to suit every taste. While Ten Bells lacked Tairngare's gleaming red Citadel and bustling markets, or Bethany's high stone walls and stoic edifices, it made up for all that in culture, class, and charm.

Approaching *The Ferryman*'s wide yellow veranda, Kaer Yin waved Gerrod and the majority of their band toward the stables. "Don't hand the reins over, nor speak to anyone until Robin comes to get you."

Shar took over for Robin at the wheel. "Will there be trouble, *Ard Tiarne*?"

"No," Kaer Yin assured him. "But there will be a fuss."

"Why? They should throw their doors wide for the two greatest lords in Aes Sidhe."

"Because I'm supposed to be dead, remember?"

Shar's smile flickered. "I hadn't thought of that."

Rian used Kaer Yin's extended arm to hobble up the icy stone steps. "If you think it might be a problem, maybe let your cousin handle it?"

"Like everything else." Tam Lin pretended to examine his nails.

Kaer Yin spared him an unfriendly smile. "No need. I outrank him, don't I?"

Tam Lin bristled. Rian groaned aloud, dragging Kaer Yin toward the entrance by the elbow. "Oh, for Siora's sake! I'm bloody sick of this posturing. Ben, I'm cold, hungry, and tired. Now get in there and use your da's name to get me somewhere warm, damn it." She half-flung him through the door. He stumbled a bit and opened his mouth to say something rude, but a thin fellow with an unassuming face met them in the foyer. He bowed from the waist. Rian thought his fuzzy grey eyebrows looked wolfish in the lantern light.

"Good evening, masters and mistresses. How might *The Ferryman* serve?" His voice held a soft but gruff quality that reminded Rian of her father.

Kaer Yin, chafing against his disguise, straightened to his full height. He reached into his tunic to produce his *ogham* charm.

"*Lorgaimid Coiriocht.*"[16]

"Ah. *Conas is féidir linn freastal ort?*"[17]

Kaer Yin held up a hand, fingers splayed. "*Cúig leaba laistigh, trí chliabhán i ngach seomra. Dosaen cruinneachán taobh amuigh sa bheairic, móide bia agus deoch do chách.*"[18]

The majordomo pressed his hands together in supplication. In the common tongue, he said, "We cannot accommodate so many at this time, sir. With Cromnasa on the horizon, we are nearly at capacity."

---

[16] "We seek accommodation."

[17] "How may we serve?"

[18] "Five beds inside, three cots to each room. A dozen cots outside in the barracks, plus food and drink for all."

Kaer Yin exhaled through his nostrils, raking a hand through his shaggy Ben-like hair. "You will make room for our party."

"Apologies, sir, but we cannot—"

Tam Lin strode forward, removing his *ogham* stone and shoving it in the man's wan face. His features shifted almost immediately, red hair glinting beneath the wall sconces. "Apparently, you didn't hear my cousin the first time. We need five rooms, three beds apiece, and all the bloody ale and food for twenty or more individuals."

The majordomo gawped at Tam Lin, then blinked again at Kaer Yin. "F- forgive me, milords, but we cannot shove paying customers out the door for you, gentry or no. Many of our guests are nobles. Our reputation—"

"Will mean exactly nothing if our needs are not met at once," articulated Kaer Yin, snapping the charm from his throat. "*Thiocfá mac an Ard-Rí ar shiúl?*"[19]

Rian felt for the majordomo as he backpedaled into the most awkward bow she'd ever seen. He stammered, "My lord, the Adair died long ago. Everyone knows that."

"Or the son of *Bov Dearg*, the King of Connaught, and his men? You mean to tell me you don't recognize *my* seal?" Tam Lin shook his bit of amber at the majordomo. "You have the honor of serving your Crown Prince this evening. Snap to your business, man."

Two assistants came around the corner with a pair of rods in either hand, ready to defend their boss, but they stopped dead in their tracks to see the two Sidhe males towering over the majordomo. As if in total shock, the hotelier squinted at Tam Lin's stone, hands shaking. "This... of— of course, *mo flaith.* If you say he is the Adair, who am I to gainsay you?"

"I am no liar, Milesian," cautioned Kaer Yin. "I don't need my cousin's word to press my point." He unraveled his sleeve, showing the mark at the base of his wrist. The poor man shriveled at the sight, gesticulating wildly for his inferiors to follow suit. "*Is mise Kaer Yin Adair, Prionsa coróin in Innisfail. Gach rud a theastaíonn uaibh, soláthróidh tú ... agus níos mó.*[20] Have I made myself clear?"

"Of course, *Ard Tiarne,*" the majordomo finally whimpered. "If you would please wait a short while, I will personally see to it that you have the finest rooms in *The Ferryman* and all the meals and ale you require. James? Please clear the private dining room for our most honored guests. Offer any within a free supper on any evening of their choice, once Cromnasa has passed."

"Excellent." Kaer Yin cleared his throat and smoothed his tunic. "Two issues more. In our company, we hold a prisoner of the Crown. We expect to detain him in your stables with our supplies and horses for the night; will this present a problem?"

Bushy eyebrows came together over a flaming brow. "No, *Ard Tiarne.*"

"Good. Furthermore, we are here to visit the Sidhe Consulate. Under pain of death, we advise you and your servants not to bandy my presence about. Do you understand?" His cold silver gaze flicked over each mortal face with hard-eyed sincerity. Rian heard an audible gulp. Kaer Yin replaced his charm, lest anyone else see his face prematurely.

"Yes, *Ard Tiarne.* No one shall breathe a word of this. I swear it."

Kaer Yin craned his neck so the majordomo couldn't escape his irritation. "I think we're all aware of my reputation for mercy, aren't we?"

Rian scowled over the majordomo's trembling back. Kaer Yin lifted a single shoulder in return.

"We are, Your Highness. I'm... that is, we are overjoyed that you have returned. Please avail yourself of every comfort."

"That's bloody grand news, that," chuckled Robin. "Now that's all sorted, point me to the bar, if ye'd be so kind?"

---

[19] "You'd turn the son of the High King away?"
[20] "I am Kaer Yin Adair, crown of Prince of Innisfail. Everything I require, you will provide ... and more."

After a night spent drinking far more ale than she'd ever consumed, Rian awoke in the same room as Eva, her head pounding like a hammered anvil. Making her way through their private floor to the cream and gold decorated parlor, she stumbled over half a dozen prone bodies to get to the larder, which bore a healthy portion of ice-cold tea and half-eaten biscuits. Gerrod, who somehow escaped his fate in the barracks next door or as guard-dog for Matt in the stables, lay upside-down in a plush green armchair before the fire, snoring against an empty bottle of Bretagn brandy. She stepped gingerly around Niall, Bru, and Dorcan, who seemed to have collapsed mid-scuffle, and were now facedown in the floorboards. Parched, Rian poured herself a healthy dollop of strong black tea, not minding its frigid temperature.

Eva, who never drank spirits, followed her in. "Have they returned yet?" she asked, wincing at her first sip.

"Who?"

"The princes and their most faithful guardians."

Ah, Rian thought, working the ice-cold tea down her parched throat. *They must have gone ahead to the Consulate.*

She exhaled into her teacup. "I've no idea how they can stand this morning, let alone make themselves presentable for the Ambassador."

Eva's mien told her it had likely been a near thing. Rian felt a bit better about her own state. "Since they've gone for the day, I wonder if you wouldn't accompany me for a few hours, Mistress Guinness?"

Rian set her cup down for a refill, cocking her head. "Where to, My Lady?"

Eva's long fingers tapped against her cup. "It wouldn't be fair for only the men in our company to leave here in finery, now would it?"

Rian exhaled a short laugh, "Well, I'd love that, but unfortunately, Ben has all my coin. I'm quite the pauper until he returns."

"Pish and posh, my dear," said Eva. "I told you, my family holds great wealth in Ten Bells. What are a few gowns and baubles to an Alvra? Besides, I see the questions nibbling between your ears. You'll want to share them with someone before they gobble you up, no?"

"I..." There was no point in attempting to bluff. Eva *would* see right through her. She wondered how Una had felt about her every thought being interpreted by her aunt.

Eva patted her hand. "She hated it, of course, but we can't change our stars so easily, can we?"

Of course, Lady Alvra had read that thought too.

Rian considered her for a moment. "No, I suppose not."

"Then, it's decided, yes?"

Rian looked around. It *would* be nice to get rid of this lot of fools for a while. She assumed that once Gerrod woke up, he'd be begging her for some remedy or another to ease his hangover. Once that was done, she'd be charged with Gilcannon's care. And when Ben and his idiot cousin returned, she had no doubt there'd be yet more chores for her to perform while they dove head-first into the nearest bottle. Why in the *Hells* would she say no to a day off?

"Lady Alvra, I would be honored to accompany you today."

⚹

By noon, Rian, Eva, Mel Carra, and two others in her retinue had nearly plundered the spice markets along the harbor, the haberdasheries and dressers in the Linen District, and finally, the apothecaries at the North End. Not only was Rian dressed in a lovely winter frock, with a thick wool underskirt and high collar, but she boasted a new trunk with additional cloaks, hats, boots, gloves, and underthings as well. While she'd been busy trying on second-hand but excellent quality dresses and shoes, Eva had taken it upon herself to furnish her with additional accouterment: a beautiful leather satchel to keep her medicinals in, a surgeon's set of sharps and tools, a box of needles in every shape and size with catgut thread and steel clasps, enough pungent herbs and salves to fill her new bag, and a new sealskin cloak, dyed a gorgeous indigo to flatter Rian's fair complexion. Rian protested vehemently, but Lady Alvra would not be swayed. Eva explained that, in Tairngare, 'twas the height of ill manners to reject a heartfelt gift. Immensely touched, Rian accepted them all as graciously as she could. When they stopped for tea, Eva paid a hansom to send the items ahead to their rooms at *The Ferryman*.

Feeling rich for the first time, Rian sipped her tea and tried hard not to cry. Aside from Una and her aunt, no one had ever treated her with such kindness.

Across their small round table, Eva reached over to pat her hands. Mel Carra took one look at Eva's thoughtful expression and excused himself. "Rian, my dear, it pains me that you should have such feelings. You are as deserving of love and respect as anyone, perhaps more than most."

Rian let out a long breath, blinking away tears. "That hasn't been my experience, My Lady. I'm sorry."

Eva's new kid gloves were soft against her knuckles. "It is easy to confuse outward perception with personal worth, but they are not the same thing. Perception is a lie we must counsel ourselves against at all cost."

"I don't understand."

Eva took Rian's hands and lay them flat against the table. They were scarred, rough at the joints, and quite small. Rian tried not to be ashamed of them. "You think these marks make you less lovely, less worthy, but scar tissue is strong. The flesh here," she tapped a healed gash Rian got from building the back paddock with her father, "is stronger than what surrounds it. It can't be cut as easily again. The same can be said for your foot, your poverty, and your parentage. None of these things make you *less* than anyone else, but they do make you twice as tough to wound."

"I appreciate what you're trying to say, My Lady. Truly." And she did. The call of gulls over the white-speckled harbor caught her attention for a moment. Though the sky today was a flat grey, the beauty of that cerulean expanse of water was undimmed. Indeed, it seemed bluer even than yesterday for the contrast. "I know I have worth, and I'm sorry to appear ungrateful and melancholy. Sometimes, I must remind myself that I'm here. Do you know what I mean?"

Eva's warmth was so like Una's; Rian felt a pang. "I do. I believe there is someone else who wishes to remind you of that fact, frequently, once it dawns on him."

"Ah, I don't... that is..." muttered Rian, flushing to the roots of her hair.

"You don't believe you're worthy of him?"

Rian squirmed in her seat. She wished with all her heart to be one of those gulls floating over the harbor: free and oblivious. "I... ah, well, he's so..."

"Wealthy? Imperious? Nonchalant?"

Rian's head popped up. That didn't sound like Shar at all. "Wait, Master Lianor isn't wealthy, as far as I know. Not to *our* standards of wealth, that is. I don't believe he can even attain a holdfast until he's served his lord for two hundred years."

Suddenly, Eva's smile faltered. She looked as if she had a great deal more to say, but just then, a rock burst through a nearby window. The lady seated there crashed to the floor with a scream, doused head-to-toe in shattered glass. Without thinking, Rian rushed to her side. Her right cheek suffered two deep lacerations and her ungloved hands dozens more. Thinking fast, Rian bound the woman's hands with two tea-stained napkins, then pressed her fingers against the seeping wound along her cheekbone. Someone handed her a third set of napkins, and she made swift use of them.

Outside, men shouted in the street. Several dark shapes swept past the windows, bearing signs, pamphlets, or things they could throw. Rocks and bricks struck windows on either side of the lane. "Imperialist scum!" they bellowed. Some took up a chant, "Purge the land. God's reckoning is at hand."

Rian looked at Eva askance. She shook her head. "Kneelers, or members of a new order. They seek... reformation."

"Reformation? Of what?" Rian cried.

"The church, as it had been in ancient times. Death to all heretics."

Rian had a pretty good idea to whom they referred. Eva straightened her spine as straight as an arrowhead. She opened the door. "No, Eva— don't!" screeched Rian, but Lady Alvra paid her no mind. Rian got up to chase her; even reached out to snatch at her sleeve, but Eva moved to stand alone in the middle of the street. She mumbled something unintelligible under her breath.

One brazen fellow in a black cloak and oiled boots sidled up to her with his hand raised. Eva's eyes met his, and he fell to his knees, clutching his throat. Another, after witnessing what had befallen his friend, made a dash for her arm. Eva glanced over her shoulder; he stopped mid-run, falling flat on his face and squealing like a cornered pig. She raised her right fist, and a third man mirrored the motion. Eyes wide with shock, the protester shoved that fist into a friend's head who stood beside him. Rian was utterly amazed. She had thought Una was incredible in a fight, but Eva was astonishing. The crowd mimicked every gesture and motion she made, one person at a time, or often all at once. No one made it near enough to stop her.

Sharp on these men's heels, the second round of protesters ran to catch up with the first. Rian made to run to her side, but Mel Carra beat her to it. He drew his weapon and raced headfirst into the knot of black-clothed miscreants. They went flying in every conceivable direction. His Tairnganeah followed suit, chasing the rioters downhill. Everyone on the street who wasn't a member of their number gave a little cheer. Rian, however, saw the sag in Eva's shoulders. She caught her in an awkward grip the moment she began to fall.

Breathing hard and sweating, Eva's lips twitched at her. "You're a sharp one. Let no one forget it."

"I'm friends with your niece, remember? I've seen Spark drag before. Let's get you inside for something hot to drink."

Eva allowed herself to be lifted like a child. Her expression wasn't one of pain or fatigue, however. Anger and fear burned bright in the amber of her irises. Mel Carra returned with a bloodied lip but otherwise no worse for wear. He knelt beside them, focused on Eva's stricken expression. He'd apparently seen this before. "Tell me."

"The Southernmost Star is fading," she said, gripping his arm.

"What does that mean, My Lady?"

"When Kevin's Heir dies, those men will rule the South. Reason fades as a Black Knight rides."

All the hair on Rian's neck stood on end. "What are you saying?"

Eva paled; her pupils dilated. "The South will bleed, and Innisfail will fracture. The Raven King marks the tide. All shall be consumed. All shall..." she drifted off into a stone faint. Gently as he was able, Mel Carra hefted her into his arms.

Rian didn't have the first clue what was happening. "Will she be all right?"

Using his free hand, he helped Rian hobble upright. People were staring but without hostility. Rian knew the difference. The shopkeeper from the teahouse bustled over, frantic. "Is the lady well?"

Mel Carra gave her a reassuring nod. "She will be. This happens when she wears herself out, you see?"

"Oh," she cooed, covering her mouth. "Please, bring her inside. I've hot tea and cakes aplenty, and after what she did for us, it's the least I can do. She's Siorai, isn't she?"

Mel Carra shrugged. "Yes."

The shopkeeper fanned her face. "My word. My sister won't believe a word of this!" She shuffled off, patting her frazzled hair.

Rian worried her nails as he sat Eva down in her abandoned chair. "That wasn't the Spark drag, was it?"

"No. It wasn't."

"Premonition is one of her gifts?"

He inhaled slowly. "Yes."

"Has she ever been wrong?"

His worried eyes met hers squarely. "Never."

A Dead Man's Name

In the wee hours of the morning, Kaer Yin, Tam Lin, Robin, and Shar had made their way down to the River District. The walk was a long, blustery one, punctuated by severe wind gusts and icy rain that fell in knife-slashing sheets. Each man drew his cloak tight, grumbling over the misfortunate decision to leave the coach behind at *The Ferryman*. The air dug into Kaer Yin's scalp like needlepoints, and his gloveless hands had gone numb less than five minutes into their stroll. Though the air was a good deal warmer here than in the wilds of Northern Eire, it was bloody cold enough to make his eyes and nose water at the slightest breeze.

None of their group had been to sleep the night before, and each was still stinking drunk. Kaer Yin had always preferred a late night to an early morning, especially when that morning's duties would include a healthy dollop of bureaucratic arse-kissing.

Having spent the majority of a lovely evening bootless before a roaring fire and tucked into a bottomless tankard of rich, dark ale, he almost wished they'd opted to spend the rest of Dor Cromna in similar vein. Yet, duty called, and they were out of fainne. Coin in the amount they needed wouldn't retrieve itself. Kaer Yin and Tam Lin's long-distant uncle Dian could supposedly rub two coppers together to make one solid royal, but neither of them had learned the trick. They were flat broke, and expeditions like this cost. Bellies cinched into their airways; they trudged on. A yard before the docks, the Sidhe Consulate emerged from the fog like a mountaintop from a curtain of clouds. This ungainly monstrosity squatted over a whole city block, pressing its imposing back to the rising sun. The massive, four-story stone edifice clashed with its surroundings. The charming, whitewashed plaster walls and elegantly tiled rooftops twisted up and down each lane.

The Consulate was situated near the docks at the far end of town, which certainly diminished the number of tourists and potential gawkers. Six dour-faced Sidhe guards standing at each entrance added to this ominous impression. In order to pass through the first of two enormous brass gates without being run through, Kaer Yin and the lads were obliged to remove their *ogham* charms entirely. The expressionless guardsman led them through the entrance with the barest salutation. The chains in their ears marked them as nobility, after all.

Inside was an even less-opulent stone hall, which wound up to a second-floor reception area with twenty-foot ceilings and no adornments whatsoever. Scratching his scarred chin with a dubious scowl, Robin looked around, unimpressed. "Figured ye lot would have fancier digs than these?"

Tam Lin jerked a thumb at Kaer Yin. "This boor's idea, actually. It used to be a fortress in the old Duch's time. He thought we'd have less trouble with the Southers if they felt a strong Sidhe presence here but weren't insulted by its grandeur."

Robin fathomed a guess, "I 'spose Ten Bells wasn't always so fancy."

"They were starved once," Kaer Yin confirmed. "This place used to be the seat of the Donahugh family, back before they declared themselves Gods of the South. Duch Kevin was no miser. The people of Ten Bells were taxed to the stars to provide funds for various rebellions and his new fortress at the mouth of the Lee." He squinted at torches lining the far walls, remembering. "I took this fortress from Kevin's brother in N.E. 397. Some would argue that was when the war truly started."

Shar, who hadn't been born when Kaer Yin marched through the South the first time, ogled the plain interior with something akin to awe. "I wish I'd been with you, *Ard Tiarne*."

"I was," complained Tam Lin. "A hot, fly-infested, shite-stinking mess, if you ask me. You'd much prefer the place now, trust me."

Robin shook his head with a wry snort. "Boggles me mind. Walkin' through history with ye lot. My mate, the hero in every tall tale."

Kaer Yin opened his mouth, but Tam Lin declared for him, "Far from a hero to these Southers. They hate him more than the pox. The way they get after him, you'd think he stomped down here and flattened their cities all by himself. Yin took this fortress, true… but it had been Falan the Younger who set the city ablaze and I who led the first sallies against Bethany. Won every battle too, I might add."

"But 'twas Ben who cut Duch Kevin in half, wasn't it?"

Tam Lin pursed his lips. "Yes."

"Well, there ye have it then. Ben's a hero to us *Northers* then, ain't he?"

Kaer Yin winked at his cousin, slapping Robin's shoulder. "Lin, you'll always be *my* hero. Never forget that."

Tam Lin rolled his eyes as they approached the chamber's far end. "Sod yourself."

The clerks behind the flat stone desk appeared less impressed by their motley group than the majordomo at *The Ferryman* had been. A lovely young Sidhe girl with hair the color of coal and eyes like the pre-dawn sky sighed at the group, "Your business, My Lords?"

Tam Lin sucked in a grin. "Withdrawal."

Not a single emotion crossed her brow. "From which account, lord?"

"Croghan."

She shuffled vellum around. Her pretty eyes flicked to Kaer Yin. "And you, Lord… erm?"

"Bri Leith."

She went very still. "I beg your pardon?"

Kaer Yin leaned over her desk so that she might get a better look at him. "Name's Adair. Should be right at the top of your list there." He tugged his brow at her chart.

"That is impossible." She looked around as if seeking the joke.

"Is it?" Kaer Yin tucked the hair behind his ears, displaying the nine gold chains in his right. After a long silence, the girl's face went white as milk. The clerks behind her cried out— one dropped an entire bottle of ink all over the dreary stone floor. "That's Kaer Yin Adair, mistress. Shall I spell it?"

She launched out of her chair, wringing her hands. "F-forgive me, *Ard Tiarne*!" She managed an awkward half-bow. "But you, you're…."

"Dead, I know. *Surprise*." He splayed his hands.

Tam Lin elbowed between them. "That would be Kaer Yin Adair *and* Tam Lin O'Ruiadh, mistress. We require access to our accounts if you would be so kind?"

Blubbering slightly, the girl looked around her in complete mystification. Her coworkers had little to offer but wide-eyed shrugs.

"I'm afraid," she gulped. "The ambassador herself must approve your requests, My Lords."

"Fine, fine," whinged Tam Lin. "Make it quick, though, I'm starving."

Fidgeting, she wilted under his gaze. "Ah, well. The ambassador is in residence, but she does not descend for some hours yet, My Lord. We are forbidden to disturb—"

"I believe she'll make the exception this time, don't you?" Kaer Yin's smile was hardly pleasant.

With another pained bow, the girl set off. He could hear her slippers slapping time against the polished stone floors as she bolted for the stairs. Tam Lin grinned at the two spare clerks.

"Got anything to drink back there while we wait?"

⚸

407

EVENTUALLY, THEY WERE ESCORTED INTO a windowless chamber at the rear of the mammoth building, well away from prying eyes. With tepid water to drink and nothing to eat, Kaer Yin braced himself for his oncoming hangover and seethed. How dare these sycophantic pissants refuse them the basic hospitality the Sidhe must show to a common Mercher? Two princes of the Tuatha De Dannan— one of them the son of the Ard Ri— hurried through the back door like a pair of criminals! Between the hammering in his skull and the fury rising in his chest, Kaer Yin was nearly ready to murder everyone in the Consulate when the door finally swung open for the ambassador. Robin snored from his corner chair, while Tam Lin and Shar dozed across the table with their heads cradled over their arms. A lone buoy in this dull, grey sea of stone: Kaer Yin stubbornly remained awake to scowl at the tiny, officious woman and her two silent attendants. With her greying black hair tied back in a complicated knot that was once popular in Armagh, Sioarse Cathal gave a slight start when she set her dark eyes on him.

"*Macha!*" she burst out but immediately cleared her throat to resume a dignified indifference. She snapped her fingers, and two additional chairs were brought in. Kaer Yin noted that absolutely none of the Sidhe he'd seen so far were Dannan. He wondered how that had come to pass. "Forgive me, *Ard Tiarne*, but this is quite momentous for us. We'd long believed you deceased." She sat in one of the proffered chairs, lifting a hand to invite Kaer Yin to do the same. He did not.

"Tell me, is it customary to show the Prince of Connaught to an interrogation chamber when he makes an appearance? ...Whether you knew I lived or not," he said coolly. "Tam Lin O'Ruiadh should command better respect."

He had the pleasure of watching her pinched face flex. "Ah, we apologize to Lord O'Ruaidh, but we must be sure he isn't escorting an imposter. Dead men do not often materialize out of thin air to demand an audience with the Consulate."

Kaer Yin crossed his arms. "My apologies for the inconvenience of my existence, Ambassador. I'm afraid I didn't consider your delicate sensibilities when I decided to call upon you for funds that belong to *me*."

Here, she returned his glare. "The collective wealth and privilege of Aes Sidhe is not now, nor will it ever be, *yours*, Highness. Furthermore, though I may now agree that you are alive and hale, many others must also agree to the validity of your claim before we may process any funds or aid. Kaer Yin Adair is dead, as far as Aes Sidhe and the cities of Eire are concerned. To prove otherwise, legally, should be your first step."

Inhaling deeply through his nose, he leaned against the wall rather than wobble on his feet. "You dare?"

The Ambassador plucked lint from her sleeve. "I wonder why you haven't returned to Bri Leith for your father's direct approval? Surely, if the Ard Ri is aware that you live and approves of your purpose, you wouldn't need to access the Consulate's funds in Southern Eire?"

He was quiet for a moment, feeling every last trace of the uishge leech from his bloodstream. Undaunted, the Ambassador glared back. Kaer Yin did not doubt that as soon as he exited this chamber, messengers would be sent in every direction boasting that he was alive and begging for coin from the Consulate. That he was *not* yet in favor in Bri Leith would be devoured by every Sidhe and ally in Innisfail by week's end. This visit was a mistake. Tam Lin had been right.

They should've found another way.

"My business is my own, Ambassador Cathal. When I return to Bri Leith, I will remember this slight."

"All the same, the Consulate rejects your claim. You may apply through the appropriate channels. Once the Court has formally acknowledged your identity, we will review your case again." She made a big show of getting to her feet. "While we are most pleased to discover our Crown Prince of Innisfail is alive and hale, we must bid you a good day, Highness." She curtsied and turned to leave.

Tam Lin's voice caught her at the door. "Not so fast, Ambassador. Does *my* good name not warrant access to Croghan's funds?"

She turned her mask of imperious disdain firmly in place. "Of course it does, Your Highness. But you must await the review period, like any applicant."

"Horseshite." Tam Lin slapped the table with the flat of his palm. "You will march your narrow arse back to the Exchequer and produce those funds, or I will have your badge, your lands, and possibly your neck."

She squirmed beneath his glare. "Your Highness, this is most irregular—"

"Shall I replace you as Ambassador now, or do I appear to be an imposter too?" He held out his *ogham* stone. "Shar. Return to our Inn and retrieve our men. I want the Ambassador and all of her Bolgish pets in this Consulate imprisoned within the hour. If any resist, you have my full and free permission to execute them."

"*Mo Flaith*," Shar answered, rising. He pressed his fist against his heart and pried the door open to pass the Ambassador. Her guards grabbed his elbow, but Shar's lark slipped out, splashing dull red blood in the hall. Cathal screamed, careening away from the two falling bodies. Kaer Yin caught her before she could call for more guards. Shar had already disappeared whence they came. She trembled against Kaer Yin's hand.

"Now, madam Ambassador, I believe you owe my cousin— your liege lord and Crown Prince of this realm— an apology. You will have plenty of time to reflect upon your error here whilst you await trial for treason and usury," Tam Lin said ominously. Robin, who'd woken up in the clamor of Shar's brief scuffle, swore under his breath.

"Lead us to your office, My Lady," growled Kaer Yin, jerking her into the hall. Robin darted after him while Tam Lin clasped his arms behind him to follow at a leisurely pace.

"No need to be rough, Yin. I think my men will arrive in no time, and our point will be made. Don't you?"

⚑⚑

In the end, Cathal's office was happy to greet and genuflect before both princes. Tam Lin's Blood Eagles and a smattering of Robin's Greenmakers waited on the Consulate steps, ready to slaughter everyone if need be. Cathal's officers glanced at Kaer Yin's face and instantly recognized him. There were few from Aes Sidhe who'd struggle to identify the infamous Crown Prince, even if he was supposed to be long dead. Not many Sidhe bore Kaer Yin's famous silver eyes, height, and build— save perhaps for the Ard Ri himself, of whom Kaer Yin was the spitting image. An hour into the exchange, Cathal was forced behind her desk to stamp the notes and documents her clerks hastily prepared with a sneer that should have peeled Kaer Yin's eyelids back.

He raised a haughty brow at her. "What? Should you be locked away until your Deputy can be sworn in as Ambassador, after all? Where is he, anyway?"

"Armagh," she sniffed, her hand poised over the official seal. "Then on to Bri Leith to remand taxes from Lord Bearn's Treasury. We are but servants of the Ard Ri, Your Highness. What you are doing here is illegal, and you know it. I cannot approve your claim, whether you wrongfully incarcerate me or not."

Tam Lin pinched the bridge of his nose. "You won your argument about the Crown Prince's revenue, madam Ambassador… though you are not approving *his* claim. You're granting legal access to *mine*. Now get on with it. I have many things I'd rather be doing now than arguing with a lowly diplomat over funds she has no power to withhold. Press the damned seal to that sheaf of vellum already, will you?"

Her gums pulled back over her white teeth. "I am hardly a personage for you to belittle, Dannan. My blood is as old and noble as yours."

"Perhaps." Kaer Yin's expression was leaden. "Although he's still your liege lord… and *I* am his. Now, do you wish to be replaced or not? That power, the Prince of Connaught *does* have, I'm afraid. See? We're all familiar with the law."

All the color drained from her burnished cheeks. She must have been in Eire for a very long time to have aged to this degree. While such was not common knowledge in Eire, the Sidhe could maintain their immortality so long as they regularly passed back and forth through the Oiche Ar Fad.

It would take decades to age as many years as Cathal had, far too many to be noticed by the Milesians in Ten Bells but plenty to mark her out as someone of little political clout. She might restore much of her youth and vigor by returning to the Otherworld, though after today's debacle, Kaer Yin doubted she'd ever be granted leave.

"I keep your father's laws here, *Ard Tiarne*. Not yours."

"One day, you may… or not." Kaer Yin's eyes went hard.

She failed to repress a shudder.

Tam Lin jabbed a thumb into his chest. "Forget him and this ridiculous display. My funds, madam. I have places to be, damn you."

She hesitated again. With a groan, he reached over to press her hand down. The first note stamped; he pried her hand up to poise over the second. She looked like someone who'd been ordered to swallow her tongue.

"Good. Now this one. Just three left."

She allowed him to use her hand to direct the seal, like a child learning to hold a quill. Her derision was plain. "You do your father and uncle a disservice this day, Your Highness. If you believe yourselves unanswerable to the Ard Ri's laws now, I shudder to imagine that either of you may ever inherit our kingdom."

Tam Lin met her frown with one of his own. "Who do you imagine you're speaking to, *seirbhíseach*? In Aes Sidhe, you know you'd lose a hand for that comment, not to mention the vitriol you've spewed at your future king."

Without another word of complaint, she stamped the remaining documents herself. Refusing to look at either of them again, she carefully gathered each sheaf in an elegant roll and passed them over.

"Your funds, as ordered, Your Highness. As is my duty, I shall write a full accounting of each coin to Bri Leith and Croghan."

…and Armagh, thought Kaer Yin with a tight jaw.

"Good day to you both, *mo thiarna*." Her bow was purely perfunctory.

Tam Lin gathered the documents, stashing them in a handsome leather valise a clerk handed up to him. "Make sure you tell my father what words you used to gainsay me in detail, madam. I'm sure he'll be impressed by your humility."

She sank into her chair to fold her quaking hands. The Red King did not take an insult lightly. Even one lobbed at his likely deserving heir. "I shall, Your Highness. Be sure you don't regret them yourself."

Kaer Yin's mouth pulled down at the corners. "What is that supposed to mean?"

"A fool is the man who believes his name a shield. You spoilt Dannans aren't the sole *Clann* in Innisfail, are you?"

⚳

Strolling through the markets of Ten Bells, leading a new team of lovely Eirean thoroughbreds packed down with half a hundred parcels swinging from their spanking new saddles… Kaer Yin fumed over their unpleasant encounter at the Consulate. They were corralled in the center of every street they moved through, wedged between the stalls on either side and their men's protective, watchful swords. The Dannans had resumed their disguises, leaving the perplexed populace who stumbled out of their way at a loss to explain why so many seemingly poor, bedraggled individuals could afford such mounts, let alone so many packages. If they had but an inkling of how much worse it would be when the tailors and haberdashers completed their orders by noon the following day. *The Ferryman* would be flooded with the best-dressed army Ten Bells never knew it had been hosting. The company of Tam Lin O'Ruaidh would exit the city in style.

The sun dipped low over the harbor by the time they rounded the hill toward their Inn. Robin stole a peak at Kaer Yin's sour expression. "What then? Should we turn back?"

"No."

"Then stop mewlin' over it. It's done. Ye'll have yer respect again soon enough, Yer Arseness. What're ye worried about?"

"She didn't seem all that surprised to see me, those mysterious parting words notwithstanding."

"Aye, well. She didn't strike me as the sort to be surprised about much."

"I think she knew I was alive before we arrived."

Robin lost a step to stare after him. Catching back up, he said, "How d'ye figure?"

"I don't know. It's just a feeling."

"D'ye suppose she knew ye'd come to Ten Bells for funds, then?"

Kaer Yin shrugged. "If a Sidhe is stranded in Eire for whatever reason, we have this one place to turn to for aid. If rumors about me are circling through Aes Sidhe already, it would stand to reason the Consulate would be a logical first stop."

"Hm," Robin hummed. "Maybe that's why she showed ye two through the back way? To control the tongue-waggin' before it got outta hand?"

"Possibly."

"Can't be every day two high lords come in, demandin' coin."

"We have a claim to our stipend at each Consulate in Innisfail. We don't truck with banks as you Eireans do, though each of the Great Clans may have access to their funds, permits, and power of warrant through the Consulate. It is also the single office in Innisfail with the power to veto any local laws that run contrary to the High King's commands and is responsible for collecting and distributing taxes. In other words, every Consulate is an extension of the High King's power," explained Tam Lin in a bored tone. "In this idiot's case, he flounced in there and expected to have his arse kissed by the most powerful Sidhe official in Eire."

"As did you." Kaer Yin's jaw flexed.

Tam Lin stopped, patting his skittish horse's neck. "Yet, I have an active stipend, a powerful father with whom I'm not out of favor, no *geis* to speak of, and the bloody right to anything I request. You, my dear cousin, cannot say the same."

Standing at the intersection between two less-busy lanes, Kaer Yin and Tam Lin squared off. Robin attempted to squeeze between them, knowing where this was headed but was promptly shoved aside. Shar called a halt to their group, who immediately began to pass coins around.

"I have every damned right," disagreed Kaer Yin.

"Maybe." Tam Lin conceded. "Though, not until you've made it up with your father and are officially reinstated in Bri Leith. Until then, you're just a grubby vagabond with a famous name."

"Midhir reinstated me. I'm in command unless you forgot?"

Tam Lin blew wet air through his lips. "Yeah, *in Rosweal*, to protect the North. Not down here in shite stinking Ten Bells, demanding coin and obeisance to chase a Godsdamned skirt to Bethany!"

Kaer Yin's face darkened. "Take it back, or I will take it out of you."

Dropping his reins, Tam Lin slammed his fist into Kaer Yin's nose. Kaer Yin staggered backward, smashing a hand over his streaming nostrils. Robin covered his eyes with a groan. Shar gathered up Tam Lin's abandoned reins and led his horse back to greet the others with a sigh. Shopkeepers ducked through their doorways to peer from open shutters. Citizens and fellow shoppers who hadn't already veered away from their group did so now, with a bit more urgency. Tam Lin dropped his swordbelt to the cobbles. Shar, again, waited for him to kick the item out of the way so he could pick it up.

"I'm done dipping my head for your arrogance, *mac soith!*"

Kaer Yin didn't bother to disarm. Roaring, he ran at Tam Lin full tilt, taking the redhead down by his midsection. Tam Lin hissed in pain as his back slammed against the cobbles, but Kaer Yin jammed a knee into his ribs to hold his cousin in place while he showered him with merciless blows. A woman screamed from an awning somewhere ahead, but neither noticed. Tam Lin twisted, dislodging Kaer Yin long enough to ram the crown of his head into his chin. Cursing, Kaer Yin scrabbled backward, hastily coming up to his knees. Tam Lin grasped him by the collar, throwing him bodily against a nearby lamppost. Kaer Yin's breath rushed out of him as his still-healing shoulder bore the impact. Face as bloodied as his cousin's, Tam Lin pummeled his waist with audible, organ-damaging blows. Hooking an arm around his shoulder, Kaer Yin jerked him upright to slam his forehead into his nose, taking them both to the ground.

More coins passed between their men while the two disguised princes bowled around in the mud and snow like a pair of snarling dogs. A great smear of bright blood trailed in their wake. Just when Kaer Yin had the upper hand, Tam Lin would wrench them both over and begin his thrashing anew.

Robin looked around them nervously. The Lamplighter, on his stilts, thunked down the cobbles in the opposite direction. People who weren't cowering in doorways began to duck around them to escape. "Eh, lads? We're drawin' a frightful mess of attention now. D'ye think ye'd better save this for later, maybe?"

Oblivious to Robin's voice, the two combatants were too busy making each other bleed. Kaer Yin held the high ground now, busily wrenching Tam Lin's arm aside so he could press his face into the gutter. "You petty, self-absorbed piece of shite!"

Tam Lin kicked out with his left boot, catching Kaer Yin in the ribs to dislodge him. Rolling him over again, he pressed his knee into Kaer Yin's back while he jabbed his fist into his liver.

"*I'm* self-absorbed? *I?* You commandeer *my* men, *my* title, *my* time, and *my* bloody fainne… and *I'm* self-absorbed? Remember we're all here because of some Gods-damned cunny you're mad for? *Not by choice!*" His knuckles came down with each word. "*This. Was. All. Your. Fucking. Idea.*"

As if the spell of competition had lost its appeal, Kaer Yin grabbed Tam Lin by the throat and flung him sideways. He followed close behind, skidding to a stop in the snow and mud, and delivered a blow to Tam Lin's solar plexus that had his cousin retching on all fours.

"That is the last time you speak of her that way, Tam Lin. By Brida, I swear it." Exhausted but determined, Kaer Yin pushed him over onto his back with the flat of his shin and dropped an elbow into his navel on the way down. They both lay in the filthy street, breathing hard up at the sky.

In the distance, faint whistles and raised voices flitted into the air. Wringing his hands, Robin prodded, "Yer makin' us popular."

Huffing, Tam Lin tuned over to spit blood. He narrowed a swollen eye on Kaer Yin, who was in similar straits. "Why are we here, Yin? Really?"

After a long silence, Kaer Yin's eyes met his. "You know."

Clutching his ribs with a pained laugh, Tam Lin sat up. "So, it isn't merely a skirt we're chasing to Bethany, then?"

"No."

"A *Milesian* woman." Tam Look shook his head. "I'll never understand it, no matter what you say. My apologies, I suppose."

"Accepted."

"Does she know how you feel?"

Kaer Yin looked away. "No."

Tam Lin and Robin shared a wince. "*Danu.* All this, and she may reject you?"

Kaer Yin didn't answer.

Tam Lin chuckled, "Well, let's hope she has equally terrible taste, then." With a grunt, he got up, extending a hand to help his cousin do the same. "Pray these scratches fade before we get there, cousin. You look like hammered shite."

⚔

Rɪᴀɴ ʙᴜʀsᴛ ᴛʜʀᴏᴜɢʜ Kᴀᴇʀ Yɪɴ's door with a slightly more harried expression than usual. She took in the tableau with a deep inhale. Amidst a room full of packets and brightly wrapped packaging, Robin stopped wiping Kaer Yin's nose mid-stroke. Her eye slid to Shar and Niall, who busied themselves with Tam Lin. He gave her a sloppy half-grin. Her mouth dropped open and reclosed. She shook her head and crossed her arms. "Right," she said. "I don't care enough to ask. I'll assume it went well enough, given the horses Gerry can't shut up about and the state of things here."

"Hello to you too," replied Tam Lin, without warmth.

As always, she ignored him. She raised her brows at Kaer Yin. "We have trouble."

"We heard. Mel told us what happened."

Mel smiled at her from his place beside the fireplace. "Is Lady Alvra resting?"

Rian waved his comment away. "Yes, and she's better now. But that isn't what I've come to—"

"Are you all right?" Kaer Yin interrupted.

Agitated, she took a deep breath. "Yes. I'm fine. But—"

"What in the Hells were these Kneelers after?" Robin wondered aloud while jabbing a scrap of linen up one of Kaer Yin's nostrils.

"Converts, obviously," ruminated Tam Lin. "Christers have always tried to force people into their faith. You should read about what they did to our people in the old days."

Rian opened her mouth, but Kaer Yin, again, interrupted her. "They're harmless in small groups, but once they gather, it can quickly become a problem. They call their gospel the 'good word.'" He scoffed. "Since when have violence and bigotry been 'good?'"

"Do you think it'll be a problem?" Tam Lin winced when Niall pressed too hard near his eye.

Kaer Yin lifted a shoulder. "Not that we have time to worry over the matter. We'll be gone before—"

"Siora *damn you*," shouted Rian, having gone a bright shade of red. "Will you bloody well listen to the words coming out of my mouth?"

Every male in the room flinched.

She crossed her arms. "Your prisoner is gone. While we were out, he escaped."

Kaer Yin launched upright. "*What?*"

"How?" seethed Robin, throwing his uishge into the fire.

Without waiting for an answer, Gerrod leaped to his feet with a curse. Before Rian knew what they were doing, everyone had followed him into the hall and through the massive building to the stables. Fergal waited outside in the courtyard with a smattering of Greenmakers and Blood Eagles and the majordomo, who wrung his hands.

"*Ard Tiarne*," the majordomo bowed so low his head could scrape the snow-blown cobbles. "Forgive us, but there has been a murder."

Rian watched Kaer Yin shove through to the well-lit stable. She drifted in after him. In the farthest, windowless stall, a young boy sprawled over the remnants of a modest meal of meat and turnips. His head was twisted about ninety degrees the wrong way. Already, the flesh of his face leeched grey and blue. Rian covered her mouth.

He couldn't have been more than nine or ten.

"Lionel." The majordomo came up behind them. "A good lad. Another stableboy found him like this nigh thirty minutes ago."

"He's been strangled," observed Rian, trying not to weep. Shar's fingers brushed her shoulder, and she accepted them without comment.

Kaer Yin shared a long look with Robin. "He can't have gone far."

"No," agreed Robin. "But if we don't leave tomorrow, we'll never make it in time."

Kaer Yin cursed as Rian covered the lad's staring corpse with her shawl. "Matt Gilcannon deserves to die."

"Ye'll get no argument there, but we came all this way, and it's now or never," Robin went on, with an eye on Gerrod. "Ye hear me, Gerry?"

The boy laughed wryly. The sound was lighter than the occasion demanded. "I've waited me entire bloody life to kill that bastard. What're a few more weeks?"

Tam Lin patted him on the back. "There's a lad."

Kaer Yin set a hand over his heart, holding Gerrod's gaze. "I vow, Matt Gilcannon lives on borrowed time. Whether by a blade or the hangman's knot, his guts will swing for this... and every offense. I, Kaer Yin Adair, *Ard Tiarne* of Innisfail, swear it."

After several tense breaths, with Gerrod's emotions tracing across his face, his head bobbed at last. "Aye. I suppose a man can't get more fucked than to cross a future king. Let's do what we came here to do. Ben, I'm with ye."

Robin pulled the lad into a bear hug and led him outside, uncorking his bone flask as he whispered encouragement in the boy's ear. Tam Lin helped Rian to her feet and handed her a handkerchief, which she accepted without question. The majordomo's sigh sounded ancient. "My lords, I must respectfully request—"

"Yes." Kaer Yin knew what he would say. "We're leaving at dawn. I'll see that the boy's family is cared for through the winter. Of course, we will pay double the rates, with my deepest apologies."

"*Ard Tiarne*, I hope you'll inform us when this man is brought to justice. It has been a pleasure to serve you," the majordomo said tactfully, bowing out of the stable.

Rian couldn't blame him. She doubted murders were widespread in Ten Bells, especially not at an establishment as fine as *The Ferryman*. Beside her, Tam Lin straightened.

"Well, Yin? What now?"

Staring at the covered shape of the dead child in the hay, Kaer Yin clenched his fists. "As Gerry said. What we came here to do."

FIDELITY

Cromnasa was but two days away, and Una was no closer to unmasking her villain than she had been the week before. Long hours spent in the library, in the Hall of Records, or trolling the Courtyard Market for details, all… fruitless. If not for the bodies continually cropping up around her father's Keep, the killer might have been a ghost. Two more girls were discovered in the old kirkyard west of the inner bailey. Both had been brutalized with a blade after having been bludgeoned and strangled. The dead girls lay tangled together in a snowbank, half-frozen and unseen for some time. Try as she might, Una had been unable to examine the remains directly. Instead, she'd taken a cue from her father and bribed the coroner for his report, the details of which kept her awake all that night, seething with fear and rage. That a mere mortal man was capable of such bestial acts was not in question to her mind. That she might know him, walk the same halls each day, and sup in his presence each night drove her to distraction. Having given up the Moorings as a dumping ground, the killer seemed to be searching for a suitable replacement. The kirkyard's victims might have lain there from the night Una herself was attacked, for he'd left behind no clues other than the very bodies themselves. She had yet to wrestle a full accounting from the coroner, and just yesterday, another body was found wedged into the sewer exit near the gatehouse.

Bethany's resident monster had claimed the lives of seven women.

So far.

Una resolved to investigate the newest find as soon as she could extricate herself from her father's ridiculous fête. All the major and minor lords and ladies of Innisfail seemed to have materialized within Bethany's walls overnight. The castle was stuffed to the brim with overdressed nobility, their myriad servitors, guardsmen, and soldiers garbed in a hundred different heraldic colors, and the Duch's household stewards racing up and down every hall to accommodate the lot. With so many strangers to house, feed, and entertain, who could afford the time to search for the killer now?

She made a face at herself in the mirror.

No one, she thought.

As soon as the feast was over, she would extricate the coroner's Godsdamned report if it meant following the fellow into his bedchamber, herself— hang propriety.

Until then… the charade.

She caught sight of a familiar blond head at the foot of her private staircase. He wore a handsome cobalt tunic and silver waistcoat. Micah startled when he glanced upward, face rifling through several shades of scarlet. She took his quivering arm with a rue smile.

"Into the breach, shall we?"

Getting where they were headed was adventure enough.

The corridors were choked with people coming and going, loitering, lollygagging, and ogling. She'd never seen so many bodies crammed into such close quarters before— the Cloister included. How in Siora's name Patrick had managed to accommodate so many, she might never grasp. Her guards led them into the bulk of the staring crowds, through tightly packed hallways, down two flights of occupied stairs, to the holly and mistletoe bedecked doors of the Great Hall. Painfully aware of the stares she received,

Una poured every ounce of Moura dignity into her bearing and glided toward the dais with the grace of an empress.

She felt eyes slide over her, some in envy, some in avarice.

So be it.

These dandies were nothing to her, and she would have them know it. She'd selected a gown of bright, gleaming gold cloth, a color only Tairnganese women owned the complexion to do any justice; backless so that gossips wouldn't mistake the coiling blue dragons riding high over her bare shoulders. Her hair had been arranged in Red City fashion. Long braids were roped together with golden beads and chiming bells, then tied into intricate knots at the nape of her long neck. She was a Moura noblewoman— Queen of Tairngare, or close enough as made no difference.

She would display no weakness.

The tableau was something to behold. The Hall sparkled like the interior of a forest hollow in winter. There were about thirty tables and long benches stacked in tidy rows. Between them ran several carpets lined with twisting arches of holly bracken and birch interwoven with silver streamers, flickering candles under glass, white-dipped vines, and snow-painted pinecones. The effort to construct these free-standing trellises must have been absurd. They ran the breadth and length of each junction, radiating with multifaceted candlelight and crisp-smelling herbs. The wooden timbers on the ceiling hadn't been spared either. Donahugh colors streamed nearly forty feet from the joists behind the dais. Huge red velvet tapestries, bearing the Southernmost Star in blue, swung twenty feet overhead, the largest of which spilled behind the Duch's throne like a crimson waterfall.

Below the dais, each long table was piled high with ridiculous mounds of food: braised duck with thyme, stuffed peacock with apple glazing, roast boar and venison, and in the center of each beckoned full hanks of smoked beef. There were also baked fish in cream sauce, freshly steamed vegetables, lovely fruits, cakes dusted in powdered sugar, and countless candies and biscuits generously sprinkled throughout.

Down a carpet littered with mulberry and cranberry leaves, Una and Micah strode toward the ungodly stone dais her father already occupied. Wearing an absurdly expensive white-bear fur cloak and a cobalt tunic belted with silver and gold, Patrick toasted the pair as they moved toward their seats beside him.

"Daughter!" he cried to the crowd at large. She suspected he concealed a charm about his person that allowed him to achieve that effortless boom. On his opposite side, Damek was resplendent but subdued, in plum velvet. He didn't look her way once. Instead, he sipped his wine and dipped his head to listen to what Martin said. Doubtless, Douglas had already filled his ears about what she'd witnessed the other day. Noting her blatant stare, Martin glanced up. Her narrowed eyes wiped the smirk from his face. She thought she caught the barest nervous tick in Damek's jaw.

They were going to have words soon enough.

Patrick took her hand to present her to the Hall. "Good people of Innisfail! I give you Una Alis Margaret Donahugh, Princess of Bethany, Countess of Kildare, and future Duchess of the House Donahugh." The Court, as one, bowed as low as they were able. Above the throng, Patrick and Damek remained motionless. When everyone rose, Una curtsied back as expected. She'd vowed to play her part, hadn't she? Pleased, Patrick lowered her into her seat before resuming his own. Micah, Damek, and anyone else on the dais followed suit. A servant brought over a delicious-smelling mead. She eagerly extended her cup. Patrick squinted at her. "Now then, you know the rules, girl. You're to smile, charm, and flutter your lashes at as many men as brave this dais to meet you. Are we in accord on that score?"

"I do love a good puppet show," she sang tonelessly.

Patrick grunted at her but lifted his goblet to the gathered. The golden fillet at his temple glinted in heady candlelight from the four iron chandeliers overhead. Dozens of blazing braziers near every floor-to-ceiling window added warmth to the festive atmosphere.

"Good families of Eire! What father could be more pleased to have his child home and safe with him at last?" A cheer traveled the length and breadth of the chamber. Una drank rather than allow her face to disagree. Patrick was a fine orator. His beaming, jovial expression seemed to leech the years from him. When he spoke, his voice rang clear as if he believed every word. His audience shared his fervor. "I bid you, come and greet your new lady. Show her your support. Let's give my precious child the homecoming of her dreams!" After the last round of cheers, Patrick sank into his seat once more, chuckling.

"Precious?" she quipped from over the rim of her cup.

Patrick shifted in his seat. "Wars are expensive, Una. All told, merely getting you here cost me more than I'd like to tally. So, *smile*. You're sitting in a place of honor at a feast, wearing a gown a woman from anywhere else would sell her tits to touch— and enjoying the adoration of hundreds of the richest men on the Continent. I daresay it could be a lot worse. You might enjoy yourself a little if you'd pull your head out of your arse."

Una took another sip. The mead was Cymrian, of course. Only the finest honey made it into the Swansea press. Hints of Bretagnic cinnamon and Alban pear went into each brew. Strong stuff, too, if she were any judge. She drained her cup and held it out for a refill. Her cheeks heated in appreciation. Damek frowned at her from Patrick's opposite side. She sat back, so she wouldn't have to look at him.

"I'll be a grand show horse, as promised, father *dear*."

Patrick made a sound with his nose. "You may be a tiresome nag like your mother, but you'll never hear me complain of your decorum. You're a Donahugh. That makes a thoroughbred of you, same as me." He cast a sharp sneer her way. "We are all on display, my love. Always. Artifice is everything from the lowest whore on the cobbles to the highest lord in any tower. We may be more or less in private, but to the world at large, the masks we choose set our place in the game."

"What game?"

"Life. Right now, you wish to wear a victim's mask and cloak yourself in its bitterness… oh, great Queen of Tairngare." He grinned sidelong at her. "You want to be a queen so badly? Take the crown I'm offering you and prove you deserve it."

Una said nothing; it would do no good to argue with him. Not here. Instead, she filled her mouth with teeth and bobbed her chin at anyone who meant to catch her eye. Silently seething, she pretended amazement at the first of three surprise courses (dueling swans stuffed with mint and blackberry confit). She picked at her food and made nice with Micah, those seated to her right, and any who dared present their sons to the dais.

⚔

AFTER THREE HOURS, UNA COULD admit to being slightly drunk. Her stone-walled liver had always been a source of pride, but Cymrian mead was no laughing matter. Her head swam. Her eyes glazed over in the hum of conversation, warm firelight, and incessant pageantry. Micah had moved on to speak to a pair of Kernian boys, whom she vaguely recalled as Lady Penwyth's sons. As far as Una could tell, they were having an animated debate about something inane. The Duch had taken himself down to the next table, reminiscing quite loudly with another portly man she couldn't remember. Lord Whoever was a Souther Baron and had a son who stared at Una like she might leap from her chair and eat him any second. Poor thing. The lad had to be at least six years her junior if he was a day. Feeling bad for him, she gave him a genuine smile.

He flushed red as a beacon and looked away.

Keeping her eye on him while she drank, she was amused to find him stealing glances at her whenever he thought she wasn't looking.

One conquest down, three hundred to go, she congratulated herself.

"I'll kill him, you know?" said Damek, sliding into his uncle's vacant chair. "And his fat papa. Would that please you?"

"Don't you have anything else to do?"

She felt his stare glide over her back, making her wish she'd worn the black shroud she'd initially planned to. "I can think of several things I'd rather be doing. Did you wear that dress just for me?"

"You're drunk." She wrinkled her nose.

He stuck out his lower lip. "I am, no lie. You're far from sober, yourself."

"True," she admitted, with a tilt of her goblet.

"Did you know your cheeks turn the loveliest shade of orchid when you're in your cups?"

"I'll knock one of your perfect teeth down your throat."

"You'd better get used to the flattery if you've agreed to play Patrick's game. I shouldn't be surprised if I have to sleep outside your door tonight myself— it's going so bloody well." He drained his goblet. "You should be happy I'm here, cousin. As long as I sit beside you, none will dare approach."

"No such threat. Most've avoided me like a bad smell. Half of these lads are barely out of swaddling, and the other half is far more interested in fighting Patrick's war. Only your new friend Castor had the bollocks to touch my hand."

Damek's mirth flickered. "Leave it be, Una."

"Considering where we are, I'll do so. For now."

"Thank you," he exhaled slowly as if he'd worried they would have this out in public. "Let's set unpleasant things aside for a while, shall we?"

"Fine." She handed him her goblet for a refill. "We'll drink rather than speak."

Sketching a seated bow, he tugged the wine flagon from the servant's arms and overfilled Una's cup. She couldn't say she minded a whit. Her cheeks burned under her eyelashes. "Now," said he, conspiratorially. "About this dress. Does it clasp somewhere in the front? Because it looks poured on. I find myself dying to know."

"Why don't you lean closer, and I'll whisper the truth in your ear." Her voice came out a lot harsher than she'd meant it to. A few sets of eyes drifted their way, momentarily. She winced and hid behind her cup.

"Next time, I'd wear something demure if you don't want men to flirt."

She choked a bit on her mead. "Flirt? You Bethonair dandies wouldn't know how to talk to a woman if she penned instructions. Anyway, if you're going to sit there and breathe booze and bullshite down my back, you could at least fill the time by marking out those I should take notice of."

He sat up. "Quite right. How thoughtless of me. Martin there at the end, you've met." The Commander at Arms and Damek's faithful dog winked from a pillar opposite. "His brother, Lord O'Rearden of Fennel, is the fellow in the orange doublet. His wife is the Lady Janet, beside him." He looked around. "Baron Chatwick and his prepubescent son are at the end of that table there. Squire Mayhew, you've met already, and his son, Jacob. They hail from 'Who gives a Fuck,' round Malahide. Ah, and Lady Dana Cooley— she's just there in the gauche red mantle. She has three sons and a massive fortune: those lugs at the end there, with the brass to stare straight at you."

She grimaced. "Wonderful. Is there anyone you don't think ill of?"

"That hopes to take my place? Not a one."

"If you're going to be like that for the rest of the night, I'll have my keepers take me back up to my rooms." Her neck grew hot; alcohol made conversation with those she despised less and less a chore.

He gave her an odd look as he filled her cup once more. "Dare I hope you're properly soused enough to find me a little less loathsome?"

She giggled, pulled a face, then laughed again. "I think I've had too much."

"I haven't seen you smile in a lifetime. Here, let's have some more."

"Wait," she protested atonally. "You've already refilled it!"

He pushed her cup toward her and laid his head against his elbow to watch her drink. His eyes roved everywhere at once, but she lacked the sober breath to stop him. A young man and his lady mother— had Damek pointed them out already?— approached.

"Greetings, princess. My name is Talia Mayhew. This is my son, Rory." The lad managed a shaky bow.

Una grinned back. "My lord, My Lady. It is a pleasure to make your acquaintance."

Damek waved them away with the back of his hand. "Get gone, little man, now." Flinching, Lady Mayhew grasped her son by the shoulders to lead him off the dais. Una apologized profusely with her eyes while her heel smashed into Damek's shin beneath the table. "Ouch!"

"Don't do that! You don't know what he'll do if he isn't happy about tonight."

"He's not going to kill your maids, Una."

"He's done it more than once."

"No, he hasn't. They were reassigned. You give him entirely too much credit as a villain."

Una sat with her mouth open, blinking at the vague shape a few tables away that might have been the Duch. "*What?*"

"It's mostly your fault for wishing to believe every ill of him in the first place. Besides, he couldn't be more pleased by the turnout tonight— never fear. My being here whets the stone of competition. Purses will empty to outshine me. So, as I said, relax."

She shot a glare at Patrick's back, where he sat drinking with his retainers. *Could it be true?* Had Patrick gone to so much trouble to make her believe the worst of him?

She mulled that over in silence for a while, pursing her lips.

Damek drained his cup and poured another. She removed her gloves and felt the tip of one raven-black curl brush her knuckle. It had worked itself free of his torc— a heavy silver piece featuring two hounds locked in a match. She couldn't repress a sigh. She'd given it to him when they were children. Before she could stop herself, her fingers stretched out to touch the cold metal. He drew in a deep breath, eyes growing more lavender by the moment. She used to think he had the most beautiful eyes she'd ever seen.

"I didn't think you'd still have this silly thing," she said.

"I have everything you've ever given me: a pair of the most hideous mittens ever knitted, that bundle of braid you gave me from your first haircut, the locket from Imbolg— do you remember?"

The clock seemed to speed through the evening the longer she sat beside him. After an indeterminable span, she realized she was enjoying herself. He moved closer. His hand curled around hers. Though his fingers were long and scarred, they managed to be elegant. That was who he was, after all: Damek of the Contradictions. Fascinated, she watched his pupils swallow his irises. "I love to see you like this, Una."

"Shut up." She took another drink to silence her fuzzy thoughts.

"I'd make faces at you for hours, trying to get you to smile as you are now."

Her mouth tugged up at the corners now for the memory.

"The sight of you tonight… it's almost… like I have you back."

That did it.

She jerked away, shocked into momentary sobriety. She stood so fast that her guard was forced to grasp her elbow for support. All conversation halted. Patrick's brow clouded over. "What's this?" A murmur circled the room.

"No, oh no. Una. I'm sorry, that's not—" Damek attempted.

"The mead, father. I fear it's quite got the better of me." She forced a blasé smile.

Patrick condescended. "Of course, child. You may go to your rest."

Her guards saluted and reached for her shoulders, but Damek got there first. "*I'll* escort her." Locking his arm around her waist, he swung her through the crowds before she could wrench herself free. Many unkind or curious glances followed them to the door.

⚜

"GET YOUR HANDS OFF ME!" Una shrieked as he dragged her up the stairs to her apartments. Unsure how they should respond, her guards trailed behind.

"No. You're going to listen to me, Godsdamnit. For once." Her main bodyguard, Belloch, set a hand against his pommel, but Damek paused to spare him a warning glare, and he thought better of it. The guards saluted, then backed off at least two flights downstairs. Una and Damek were alone on the third-floor landing. He pressed her into the wall, but she lashed out. Her right fist glanced the side of his cheek with a satisfying crunch. With a grunt, he caught and held her other arm against the flagstones. "Are you done?" he spat, leaving her stinging free hand to press into the meat of his chest as he inched closer. Baring her teeth, she dug her fingers into the exposed flesh at his collar. "Go ahead," he dared her. "Do it. I'm not going to stop."

Nostrils flaring, her nails carved half-moons into the skin below his Adam's apple. She could kill him now. She should. They stood there for some time, partially entangled, while she debated her next move. After several moments that beat like an eternity, her fingertips fell away. Pinpricks of blood welled from his throat.

Una swallowed hard. "I will kill you one day, I think."

"No, you won't. You love me."

"I do *not*."

"We are bonded, Una. Forever."

She cursed, low in her throat. "You're a delusional cudgel my father wields to keep his hands clean. You're a murderer and a liar." She tried to slap him again, but this time he squeezed the bulk of his body against hers, preventing room to draw back for another strike. His nose was centimeters away.

"I'll never forgive myself for hurting you."

"Right. You're so sorry, you'd force yourself on me to prove you can."

"Am I touching you in any way but to stop you from hitting me? Have I laid a hand on you that wasn't welcome *once* since you've been here?"

"Then take your hands off of me, right now."

"You'll hear this, whether you want to or not. Then, I'll let you go."

Her right hand was crushed between them, useless. He pinned her knees with his heavier thighs. Unless she wanted to fight for real, what choice did she have?

"We were too young, Una. At fifteen, the Duch had given me such a great responsibility. I didn't know how to behave." His voice wavered a fraction. "Here I was, this lowly, loveless boy. Related to this great, overbearing man… but never equal, never worthy. I wasn't raised like you. I grew up in Martin's holdfast, where I was taught to fear your father and heed his word as law. When he sent for me, I was so eager to prove myself that I would do anything he asked of me. Then, he gave me to *you*. This… this ethereal creature, both shy and sad. You were ten years old when he made me your personal guard. I never thought I'd be anything better than a guard and playmate at the time. Then one day, you were sent to Ten Bells, and I didn't see you again for three years."

"Schooling, my first. At the Libella."

"Yes."

"I was curious about my mother's people."

"Patrick didn't know what a fool choice he made when he let you study there, did he?" Damek laughed without mirth. "Your absence opened a hole inside me. You were my one friend, my sole family. The single person who didn't treat me as 'other.' I starved for need of you, and your father poured all his deceit, malice, and purpose into that chasm. By the time you returned, I was his tool, through and through. I was perhaps more changed than you, who left my heart a child and returned this glorious, otherworldly girl. By your fourteenth birthday, I was already so in love that I could barely look at you. When you finally reached for me at fifteen, I thought I would die of happiness." Feeling her warmth, he leaned closer.

She went still as the stone at her back. "Yet, you betrayed me."

Damek growled into her shoulder. "I had already been through three large battles, sacked two castles, put down one rebellion, and had been granted the title of 'Lord Marshal.' I was barely twenty years old but a man on the rise. When he gave you to me at last, I thought I'd earned my right to call myself a Donahugh. I was no longer a bastard-born half-breed, I was *Lord* Damek Bishop: a seasoned warrior, an accomplished statesman, and now I had the most beautiful wife in Innisfail. We had one perfect week before Patrick took you back. I was given seventy lashes for taking liberties, did you know?"

"No," she said, brows mixing. "I didn't."

"Our marriage was devised to alleviate pressure to wed you to one of his barons' sons. If you were married to one of his family members, he wasn't obligated to solidify allegiance with any of his lesser houses. Once it served his purpose— and Lord Gaelin's tawdry insurrection had been stamped out— I wasn't needed. He could hold your bride price open for further bait." His breath came hot against her skin. She felt herself relax slightly in his grip, despite her reticence. "He had no idea we were intimate until it was too late."

"Yet, you *betrayed* me," she repeated.

"What could I do? He's the most powerful lord in the South, Una. Everything I am or have originated with him. Where would we go? Where *could* we go? I told him the truth because I must. To save you."

"I lost a child because of your duplicity, Damek. I can never forgive—"

He gave a strangled sort of moan. "I didn't know!"

"You betrayed me, our future together— *everything*, to secure your position. Power is all you care about. All you've ever cared about."

"No. I never had the chance to crawl on my knees to you for your forgiveness. I never knew of our child until years later. I never knew what a fool I was until now. Forgive me, Una. Everything I did was for love of you. Misguided though I was."

"I left because you forced me to."

He fought tears. "If my life were enough to take it back, I'd gladly give it." She didn't need the Spark to sense his sincerity. It confused her. His eyes bored into hers, bleeding raw emotion that was very real. Somewhere deep down, something inside of her unlocked. She relaxed slightly in his arms, enough to slide her fingers up his swollen cheekbone. His skin was damp. He leaned into her palm until his lips caressed the pad of her thumb. "*Forgive me,*" he whispered. "I will love you forever, no matter how the world burns."

A small, helpless whimper escaped her lips. She wanted to believe him, or did she? She couldn't think anymore! Weeks of pent-up frustration, confusion, and mourning struck her all at once. Here was her most hated enemy, but also her oldest love. This man had wounded her far worse than any injury had ever done, yet… something within her *yearned* for him, all the same. Was it the same as her feelings for Kaer Yin? No. Never, but real, nonetheless. This was the part of herself that she'd buried so deeply that she'd almost forgotten it existed. She had loved him… once. Could she again? She didn't know.

As if sensing her internal dilemma, Damek's mouth moved over hers with a masculine sigh. Her heart racing, she felt suspended in disbelief and uncertainty. She raised a hand to shove him away but found it winding through his hair instead. He sucked in a breath at her caress and lifted her into his arms. So many doubts swirled through her mind, so many accusations— she shoved them aside. Her legs came to rest on either side of his thighs while he kissed her. Her hands slid over his shoulders and back, winding their bodies together. He whimpered something unintelligible into the soft skin of her nape, and she exhaled against his earlobe.

"Una… Una… Una…" he chanted along her skin, against her lips, like a mantra. She felt herself sink into the warmth of his embrace, but another voice entered her thoughts.

Someone else had called her name that way, hadn't he?

With a cry, she shoved against Damek's chest, dislodging him.

He broke off, breathing hard. "No, please, no."

Slipping down the wall, she covered her eyes in shame. "Leave, Damek. Now." Behind her eyelids, Kaer Yin's face was all she could see. "I'm begging you."

Damek knelt before her, prying her hands wide. "I love you. You love me. What complication can't we weather? I will wait for you, as long as it takes. I swear it."

Gingerly, he wound his fingers through hers. He was so near.

She need only lean into him.

Kaer Yin would be lost.

Her pain and grief would leech away like water from a sieve. "I…"

At that very moment, a single horn blew outside.

She blinked at Damek, who twisted his head toward the sound with a curse.

"I thought everyone had arrived?" she asked, alarmed by his expression.

The horn came again and was answered by the Gatehouse guard. Shouts rang through the courtyard. Una got up to peer through the North-facing windowpane. Damek came up beside her, clutching at her fingers.

"Don't look, Una. *Please.*"

She ignored him, pushing his shoulder aside to see what the commotion was. It took a moment for her eyes to adjust, but when they did, she gasped. A team of white and silver horses swirled into the courtyard below. Those who rode them were taller than the average man and unmistakably blond. Beneath their heavy cloaks, Una could discern the white cuirass of Aes Sidhe. Snapping in the stiff, southerly wind, the heraldic device on the flags was a blood-red eagle on a white field. *Croghan*, her studies reminded her. The blood eagle was the animus of House O'Ruaidh— the Ard Ri's brother, Bov Dearg.

Kaer Yin's uncle.

Una's heart crawled into her throat. Without a concern aside from discovering what in the Hells was going on, Una staggered down the stairs whence she came.

DECLARATIONS

Kaer Yin followed Tam Lin's train toward a raised dais overflowing with food and pomp. Behind the few staring people seated there swung two massive silver and cobalt banners with the Donahugh device: a shining blue star blazing through a scarlet field. Deeper into that cavernous nave behind the throne, he'd been told Duch Michael had commissioned a stained-glass relief of some renown. That he'd heard it bore his likeness in the act of slaying Kevin Donahugh intrigued him all the more. He hoped he'd get to see it himself before all was said and done.

The Sidhe, of course, entered in style. There were twenty in their group, each taller than the average Milesian by quite a bit and broader through the shoulder. Their fair hair and flashing green eyes gleamed by candlelight. A collective inhalation spread through the crowd, followed by excited whispers and nervous feminine laughter.

Tam Lin strutted forward with pure regal grace, head high, wrapped in his house's snow-white and blood-red colors. Around his head, he wore a crown of copper leaves. Down his back draped a cloak of white wolfskin. His red-gold hair hung loosely around his shoulders, save for the Dannan braids at either temple. Eight gold chains chimed from his right ear. Shar and Niall took up space at his right and left flanks, bearing leather chests with massive brass locks. Kaer Yin and Rian carried the O'Ruiadh pennants a ways back in their line. Rian looked lovely tonight in a white velvet gown and burgundy cloak. Even Robin and Gerrod were turned out—both clean-shaven and uncharacteristically groomed. They were each meant to look their very best, except Kaer Yin, who wore Ben Maeden's ogham charm and moderately clean façade.

When one sought to make an impression, veneer was everything.

Around their party, people struggled to their feet, mouths agape. Several wine vessels were upended. Dishes and crockery clattered to the floor. Musicians in the gallery above stopped playing. The murmur was deafening. Try as he might, Kaer Yin couldn't pinpoint which of them was Patrick. Several lords and ladies of greater Innisfail were gathered for this fête, each dressed in their best. Hard to identify one amongst the multitude. Then again, Kaer Yin had never actually met Patrick, had he? Tam Lin nodded to Shar, who stepped forward.

"Now comes the son of Bov Dearg: Tam Lin O'Ruaidh of Croghan, Second Prince of the Tuatha De Dannan, and future King of Connaught."

More flushed faces and wide-eyed stares. A portly man with a worn golden fillet half-stumbled to the center of the dais. His heavy fur mantle slipped awkwardly from one shoulder. Red-cheeked, he cleared his throat. "Ah, well met, Prince Tam Lin." His bow was half mockery, half drunken arrogance. "The Donahugh Clan welcomes you to Bethany."

Tam Lin slipped a grin over his shoulder at Kaer Yin.

The Duch.

Kaer Yin could admit to being underwhelmed. A man of Patrick Donahugh's reputation should be a giant. Instead, this short, relatively ugly, middle-aged Milesian ogled Tam Lin like *he* was the butt of some joke. Still smiling, Tam Lin swept forward, hands on either hip.

"I've come bearing gifts for the lady of the house, My Lord. To whom may I direct my admiration?"

With a belch, Patrick patted his gut. "Forgive me, Your Highness, but my daughter—"

"— is here!" cried a familiar voice from the rear of the Hall. All eyes turned to the sound with rapacious curiosity. Kaer Yin's skin prickled. His breath hitched when Una raced onto the dais from the opposite side. "I'm here," she panted, holding her side. Her cheeks bloomed scarlet, and her amber eyes sparked like gems in the light. For a moment, he couldn't see anything else. In her gold and black gown that clung to every curve, with silken curls pulled back into a complicated network of braids that accentuated the sharp incline of her perfect cheekbones, and wearing a full, eager smile— Una wasn't simply beautiful; she was like the dawn after a terrible storm. Raking their faces one by one till she came to his, Kaer Yin's heart burned at the inaudible sob that escaped her throat. So much that was unsaid passed between them in that moment; his mouth dried up. The moment did not last, however. Behind her, equally flushed and obviously furious, Damek Bishop strode onto the dais, fingers clutching for hers. As if jolted to reality, Una shook him free and quickly swiped at her cheeks.

"I am Una Moura Donahugh, Prince Tam Lin, delighted to make your acquaintance." Her elegant curtsy did nothing to detract from her regal bearing, but it did allow her another peek at Kaer Yin. He read the warning there, loud and clear. Meanwhile, Lord Bishop glared into Tam Lin's party with open hatred. When Una sidestepped him again, his hand went to his pommel. A larger fellow with a terrible scar reached out and clutched his arm in support, staying his sword hand.

Noting the exchange, but ever the statesman, Tam Lin gave Una his most flattering bow. "My Lady Donahugh, I am your servant." The genuine interest in Tam Lin's tone irked Kaer Yin moderately less than the hint of swelling around Una's lower lip and the general state of Lord Bishop's rumpled tunic. Nostrils flaring, Damek shrugged the larger man off to stomp around to the Duch's right hand. His violet eyes scanned each of the Sidhe's faces with unrestrained loathing. When they settled on Kaer Yin, they paused long enough to make Rian squeeze Kaer Yin's fingers.

"Steady," Rian whispered. He doesn't know it's you, for sure."

Kaer Yin pledged, "He will, soon enough."

Jaw set, Damek smoothed his tunic and readjusted his belt. Holding Kaer Yin's eyes with a sly grin, he wiped his mouth with exaggerated hesitation. Rian's nails dug into Kaer Yin's palm. "If you keep staring like that, he will know *now*."

Kaer Yin forced himself to glare at the back of Tam Lin's head and nowhere else, willing his blood to cool. "He forced himself on her."

"No one can force himself on Una, Ben."

That was *worse*. Kaer Yin cursed beneath his breath.

Tam Lin held out a hand. Shar and Niall moved forward to lay their trunks at Una's feet. Once opened, the crowd burst into excited titters and murmurs. They pressed forward to see the bounty. One chest overflowing with gold, silver, and myriad gems from Aes Sidhe. The other, bolts of brilliantly hued silks, satin, and gossamer. Bethany's ladies made appreciable, envious noises. As expected, Una gave another deep curtsy.

"I thank you, Your Highness. Never have I been so honored." Her eyes flicked to and held Rian's, welling with tears. She set a hand against her heart. Rian made a little sound that told Kaer Yin the sentiment was shared and squeezed his fingers anew.

"Steady on," Rian repeated. "There'll be time later."

Patrick seemed to rediscover his voice. Rubbing his hands together, he waved guards over to remove each trunk. "We are all honored to have you here, Your Highness. We accept these tokens and invite you to feast with us." Damek growled an inaudible rebuke, but Patrick shouldered him aside. "Please, avail yourselves of my Hall."

Tam Lin set his fingers to his temple in respect. "We thank you, Your Grace."

Patrick motioned for Tam Lin to follow him to the dais, offering the seat beside him. From the look on Damek's face as he watched them, he guessed that one had recently been his. Una took the next chair over, on Tam Lin's right. She poured a healthy dollop of mead into her cup and passed it to him— a sure indication of a lady's favor. Her other suitors would gnaw their tongues in envy. Lord Bishop certainly did.

Kaer Yin wanted to rip Damek's spine from his throat.

Tam Lin's entourage was shown to a table near the front of the Hall by the large, scarred man. Someone referred to him as 'Commander,' Tam Lin assumed the fellow to be Martin O'Rearden, Damek Bishop's first lieutenant. The fellow's crisscrossed brow spoke volumes. Rian relaxed a bit when she sank onto the bench beside Kaer Yin.

"Okay. The hard part's over. Keep your eyes down and look disinterested."

"I think ye've mucked that already, Ben," Robin coughed, glancing at the dais. "If looks could kill, ye'd melt on the spot." He indicated Damek, who hadn't stopped glaring Kaer Yin's way. "Not such a great fool as we'd like, I think."

"Doesn't matter," Rian said. "He can't prove it this second, can he? He won't risk making a scene in front of all the fine guests here tonight. The Duch needs their support. If all goes according to plan, we'll be long gone before he can make his move."

Robin twisted his lip at her. "Ye'd make a fine Greenmaker, girl. Ye know that?"

She grimaced. "Thanks, I guess."

"He means that as a compliment, Rian," grumbled Kaer Yin, trying not to look up into Damek's accusatory stare. Instead, he stole a furtive glance at Una and Tam Lin. Though she leaned close as if to listen to his conversation with the Duch, her eyes met his more than once. Relief and so much more radiated from her with each breath. He couldn't help but smile her way. *Soon*, his eyes told her.

With a snarl, Damek got up, knocking his chair backward. He held his goblet up. "My Lords and Ladies of Innisfail, may I propose a toast?"

Patrick's displeasure was plain. "You may not."

Damek ignored him. "To our grand overlords, in their fancy white armor… may you all rot." He drank deep, then threw the empty vessel at Kaer Yin's table.

"Martin," Patrick warned through his teeth. "Get him out of here."

Martin moved to haul him away, but Damek wrestled out of his bear-like grip. "You all might sit here in awe of the Adair's bloody kin, but I won't. Bootlickers, the lot of you."

Tam Lin threw back his head on a laugh and patted his chest. He got to his feet, Una's cup in hand. "Perhaps I've usurped someone's place at table? My apologies, *isasáeligh*." Damek sucked in a breath for the insult, which none but the Sidhe would grasp. "But I assumed we were welcome here?"

"You are," Patrick reaffirmed. "My nephew is merely drunk. My apologies."

"Good. I would hate to lose the favor of such a fine lady for such a paltry offense."

"You could never," flirted Una with gut-piercing sincerity.

Damek shrugged Martin off for a second time. He didn't linger any longer, save to point at Kaer Yin once. Kaer Yin's chin came up.

Anytime, his expression replied.

Without further ado, Damek Bishop stomped from the dais, trailing a horde of whispers in his wake.

⚜

HEAD AND HEART SPINNING, UNA climbed the stairs toward her chamber again, both weeping and laughing to herself. Belloch averted his eyes, no doubt believing she was either inebriated, or stark raving mad. Perhaps she was both? She cared less about what these people thought of her now than ever.

He's alive! screamed her heart, over and over.

Alive, all this time!

Her blood pounded the litany in her veins: *alive, alive, alive…* until she thought she might run wild. As usual, Damek had lied to her, and she foolishly believed him. Of course, he would tell her Kaer Yin died that horrible night. Knowing her as he did, Damek knew nothing would wound her more. She was too happy to waste one more thought on her cousin's duplicity. Absently, she scrubbed her mouth with the back of her hand.

NOT another bloody thought!

She heard Belloch apply the lock behind her when she slipped through her door. Patrick's orders. He'd say men are likely to be inspired by foolish notions. That was as well tonight— Kaer Yin was alive… nothing else mattered a whit to her, not even internment.

She leaned against the door, burying her smile in her hands.

The blow came out of nowhere.

She staggered forward, colliding with the nearest chair and taking it to the ground. Clutching her ringing ear, she struggled to push herself upright. Her assailant struck her again, spinning the world round her eyes.

"Whore!' accused a disembodied voice, buffeted by a strong hint of peppermint. Una gagged. Gloved hands tore her head back and down. She felt the press of a blade at her throat. "Disgusting, devil-fucking whore!" The edge bit down, but just enough to make her bleed. Belloch was a step outside the door. If she could suck in enough air, he would come crashing through with his sabre ready. A wet tear slid over her overheated cheek. It wasn't hers. "You choose *them* over your own kind?"

She knew that voice, that accent.

No, she wept inwardly.

It can't be.

"Micah?" she managed to squeeze out. Her attacker flinched; his knife hesitated. "Not you. Please, not you."

He snarled in her face, spittle dripping into her eyes. "Don't you dare attempt to beguile me now, you slut. I will make you pay for this."

His blade had yet to plunge through her flesh. His hands shook. Shoving her shock and revulsion aside, she slid her hand over his leather-encased fingers where they struggled with his blade. "Micah, this is not you. It can't be you."

He stifled a laugh, a dark, hideous sound. "Who else would it be? My deranged but feeble da? He can scarcely hobble through these halls, yet ye were so eager to accuse him. All he cares about is his Lord these days, or his grand mission to make me Duch. I don't care what that old fool does. He's nothin' to me."

"You… you tried to kill me, Micah. Why?"

His shadow shook its head. "No, not at first. Ye surprised me down there, s'all. Ye weren't 'sposed to be there, were ye?"

That was true. She struggled to swallow, drawing a trickle of blood down her throat. "Why do you want to hurt me now? We're friends, aren't we?"

"You want to fuck that unholy spirit, don't you," he gurgled through tears. The knife pressed deeper. "Battin' yer lashes for him like a bitch in heat. Ye was meant to be mine but thank god I'm stronger than me Da. Who would want a witch who fucks monsters, anyway?"

The knife began to separate the flesh at her throat. She had to keep him talking. "I am no whore, Micah. I have lain with one man, and he was my husband then. My father ordered me to entertain his guests. I had no choice but to smile."

He hesitated again, trembling. "Ye lie! I saw your face. Everyone in the Hall saw yer tears of joy. Watched as ye fawned over yer ex-husband first, then panted for the next comer with renewed vigor. Yer a vain, spoilt slattern!"

His blade slipped into her throat, just enough to tear a gasp from her chest. "Micah, no! I've asked my father for you! I want you too— don't you know that?"

He paused again. She reached for his damp cheek, but he jerked away. "Lying witch!" His knife bit into her soft flesh, slicing clean through to the floor. Not immediately fatal, perhaps, but immensely painful and likely bleed her like a sow in minutes. She cried out, drew one knee up, and jerked, forcing him to fumble sideways with a guttural shriek.

Her hand slammed over his brow before he could right himself. "*Burn*," she hissed, though he broke contact too quickly for her Spark to take hold. He knocked her backward, slashing his knife against her wrist. The gash would be four inches wide if she weren't mistaken— it, too, would bleed her dry if unstaunched.

Wiggling sideways, she fumbled in the dark for something she might use as a weapon. Once her fingers came into contact with the leg of the upended chair, she attempted to drag it over. Unfortunately, she couldn't push herself upright far enough for the slick puddle of blood beneath her. She hit the tiles with a thud that knocked the wind from her chest.

"My Lady?" called Belloch from the other side of the door.

She opened her mouth to cry out, but a gloved hand slammed over the lower half of her face. "It's locked from the inside, cousin. He'll never break that door down in time." The banging and shouts outside didn't assuage her rising panic. Bleeding profusely as she was, without her Spark, and without a weapon... Micah was stronger than her, and they both knew it. She felt his free hand fumble with her skirts, tearing the fabric. Summoning all the tactile strength she could, she slammed the crown of her head into his nose. With a mewling screech, he broke contact, knife clattering to the flagstones.

Her hand closed over it, blade first.

Roaring, he rushed at her, half-impaling himself on his own knife. With a grunt, he shoved her off, leaving the weapon's tip in the meat of his shoulder. His fist crashed into her chin, cracking her head against the wall. She slipped downward, and he followed, dragging the knife out of his skin... readying to plunge it into her heart.

The blow never came.

A white hand snapped out of the shadows, catching Micah's wrist mid-strike. A pair of ruthless silver eyes flashed in the sliver of moonlight from the open window. "Not so vicious now, are we?" A sharp twist and Micah's scream rattled the casings. His wrist bent back about 90 degrees the wrong way. Kaer Yin lifted him by the collar; the toes of Micah's boots barely dragged the floor. "Perhaps you should see your way out?"

Micah had a fleeting moment to gape at Una in surprise before Kaer Yin threw him through the open window one-handed. Her cousin's terrified shrieks could be heard for a long while, and then they abruptly stopped altogether.

Kaer Yin was at her side in a trice. One hand clamped over her throat while he tore off a piece of his tunic with the other. "Why are you *always* bleeding, Una? You're going to stop my heart one of these days." The banging at her door intensified. Shouts and screams flitted through her window with the cold ocean air. She held out her wrist while he wound shredded fabric around it. "You'll have to help me, quick. Press here. Good. Now, let's get you up." He set her gently against the wall, tearing and wrapping the second piece of cloth around her seeping throat. His face blurred a bit around the edges.

"Y-you're here," she croaked.

"You shouldn't talk."

"How?"

"Climbed through the window. Lucky too."

She winced when he pulled the fabric taught for a knot. "No, how are you... *here*?"

Through a haze of tears, she thought she saw him swallow. "I came for you, stupid. Who was that anyway?"

"My cousin."

He made a rude sound. "I just *love* your family, Una."

"He was going to kill me."

"Might have succeeded too, from the look of things."

She couldn't hear much over the pounding at the door. "You have to go. They can't find you here."

More guards clattered noisily up the stairs. The banging and clamor intensified.

Kaer Yin took a deep breath, moving closer. "I have to talk to you, ask you—"

"Yes," she responded without hesitation.

He blinked back. "I haven't even said—"

With more steam than she thought she had left, she pulled him to her by the hem of his tunic. Her mouth met his with a force she might be embarrassed by later. He had a heartbeat to sigh against her lips before she shoved him away.

"Whatever it is, my answer is yes. But you have to go, *right now*, before they kill you. You can't be seen with me… or anywhere." The door cracked and splintered while Kaer Yin's eyes devoured hers. Even bleeding and bruised, she'd never been happier in her life. He was alive, and he'd come for her. What more could she ask for? "Go."

"Una, I need to tell you—"

An axe blade burst through the center of the door. "My Lady!" roared Belloch.

"Tell me later… now get out of here, or you'll watch me puke."

He got to his feet, looking back at her from the open window. "Are you sure?"

She really *was* going to throw up. "Do you want me to say no?"

His answering smirk was infuriating as it was endearing. "I dare you to try now."

Prodigal Son

Henry watched them sew his firstborn into his shroud, boiling with a rage he could not quantify. There hadn't been enough fabric for the task at first, considering that Micah's body had been smashed and mangled so severely that his muscles and intestines had to be removed to make room. It took nearly three hours to gather Micah's remains from the crags below the South End. His son had been smashed against the rocks below the witch's tower as if he'd been a melon casually flung from the window— discarded like refuse.

Murdered, Henry wept internally.

Slain by a foreign whore on the eve of his ascension.

The coroner had yet to sew the heavy tarpaulin over Micah's remaining eye, which was still beautiful and clear as a spring sky. A knotted wad of formerly golden hair clung to the two inches of skull left above. The rest was a red and white waste: a mass of scrambled tissue, organ, and bone. The fall had removed Micah's head from his spine, along with an arm and leg. Both now presumably lay at the bottom of the sea, washed away by relentless waves before the body could be recovered. All that remained was a broken husk of fluid and gristle. The coroner drew the tarpaulin tight over Micah's sightless eye, blotting it from view forever. Henry's hands shook. His gums ached around their dentures from clenching his jaw. He longed to wrap his fingers around his niece's throat and press his thumbs into her eyes. He craved revenge, as a starving man craves bread. He watched the needle wind in and out of the flat, white fabric and vowed an end to his brother's bloodline.

"Henry," came Patrick's voice from the open door. Henry didn't turn, though the fresh fury that traced through his heart burned the brighter for his presence. "You shouldn't be here."

"My son is here, so must I be."

Patrick shuffled inside, breathing labored. He came to a stop at Henry's side.

Henry spared him a single glance. "You look like shite, Patrick."

Patrick's gnarled, sweating fingers seized Henry's forearm. "Leave the coroner to his task, brother. Come away."

"Take your hand from me, or I swear to God, you'll lose it," rumbled Henry, facing resolutely forward. He refused to sully his eyes with this lying, manipulative bastard. "My son is dead. Slain by your whorish daughter. I do not heed the demands of the damned."

The chamber rang with drawing steel, but not from Patrick's guards. Tonight, Henry had his own. Lords Harrington, Coltrap, and Murphy drew their weapons. The Duch's guardsmen responded, but Patrick raised his hands. "Stop. This is not necessary. My Lords, I respect the sentiments that urge you to defend my brother in this tragedy, but I implore you to reconsider before it kills you and your men and strips your families of their livelihood."

Each man hesitated, as Patrick surely knew they would. Henry perceived all of this humorlessly. "Even now, you'd haggle for power?"

"If they draw against their Duch, that is treason."

Henry held up a hand, and they sheathed their sabres. "Why have you come here?"

Patrick exhaled long and hard. "Micah was killed in an attempt on Una's life. Please don't make this worse in misunderstanding, Henry."

"You say *my son*, a boy who wouldn't harm an insect for biting, attempted to harm your worthless daughter? *Lies*. You're a bloody liar, Patrick, and you'll pay for it." Patrick's guards raised their weapons, though more of Henry's followers filtered into the gatehouse, bearing candles in one hand and the pommels of their daggers or sabres in the other. Henry was pleased to note Patrick's surprise. Did he take the smallest step backward? "How dare you come here, slinging accusations while my boy lays here in pieces. In *pieces*, Patrick!"

The examination chamber sat at the far edge of the gatehouse, near the inner portcullis, a much more public venue than Patrick would have preferred. Passersby from various clans and states paused in the courtyard outside or in the hall at the Keep's entrance. Patrick licked his dried, flaking lips. "If we may speak in private?"

"No. Our people saw what your precious daughter did to me in full view of everyone. She is a vicious bitch, unfit to bear my father's name. God will grant me justice."

"That son broke into my daughter's chamber and tried to cut her throat. He very nearly succeeded. She bears the wounds now. You're telling me she did that to herself?" he raised his voice. "Your sweet, golden-haired boy butchered seven girls beneath my roof, Henry. We've already been through his chamber. He kept mementos from each of his victims and made drawings I will see in my sleep. Everywhere in his room, the signs were there if we had thought to look. I would've strung him from the walls tomorrow if he hadn't fallen from an open window tonight. How do you feel *now*, brother? Knowing that you raised a monster?"

As if he'd been physically cut, Henry staggered forward. "Lying dog! You dare—"

"It is no lie," Patrick raised his voice so onlookers could not mistake his words. "Micah *Fitz* Donahugh was a rapist and murderer. The proof was recorded in his own hand, even if he hadn't perished in an attempt on my child. Your son, your shame, Henry."

The gatehouse tilted on its axis, and Henry felt himself tumble into its vortex.

Could it be true?

Snippets of memory flashed through his mind at once. Micah running through a field, chasing a pup. Micah in the barn, holding a dead hen. Did he smile? Micah giggling as his father hefted him high. Micah drawing the tip of a dagger across his finger, fascinated. Micah reading his bible— such a clear, calm voice. Micah kissing his mother's gaunt cheek. Micah whipping his pony with the blade of his father's rusted sword.

Henry choked.

Could it be true?

Patrick's sigh was less resigned than pained. "Take him into custody."

Henry fought, gripping the edge of Micah's slab to stall the inevitable. Micah's remaining shoulder was bared to all and sundry in the tussle. Significant scratches— fingernails, no doubt— appeared, half-healed over this exposed flesh. Henry wailed and tried to wrap his hands over the spot. Patrick tore his fingers away.

"There, you see. These have faded, Henry, but there are more yet unhealed below. Every one of the girls he killed had fought for her life and fought hard, it seems."

"No," blubbered Henry. "Not Micah. Not my son. My perfect son."

Patrick waved him away. "I will hear no more of this."

As he was hauled back into the Keep, Henry's shrieks reverberated through the courtyard. His followers backed away at Patrick's advance. "Arrest any who don't disperse immediately," he ordered his guards. Though they retreated, Henry's congregation did so with eyes full of hate and self-righteous judgment.

The last through the portcullis gave him a cold smile.

Despite the men at his back, Patrick was unsettled.

He looked around at the gathering onlookers and realized the impressions he elicited were far from sympathetic. The whispers came next.

Heretic, he caught more than once.

Kinslayer was loudest.

Ignoring them, Patrick turned to the coroner as he resumed his work. "When shall he be ready for burial?"

"This morning, My Lord."

"Excellent. See to it. No fuss or pomp. He's already done enough damage."

"Yes, milord," the coroner agreed.

Patrick turned and strode toward the Keep with Shanley and his guards trailing in his wake. Courtiers and visitors moved aside for the Duch, but many expressions bore silent reproach. Patrick's guts knotted. Holding his breath, he strode through the hall toward his private apartments, with his spine as straight as it could reasonably go. By the time they crossed the inner arch, he doubled over, huffing and groaning. The pain was unimaginable.

"Your Grace!" cried Shanley, rushing to his side.

Patrick leaned against the balustrade and retched into the dark hollow beneath the staircase. White stars clawed at his vision as he vomited, his throat molten hot. When it was over, he slouched against the railing, held upright by Shanley and a nameless guard. He couldn't help but notice that the pile of fluid that he had expelled was naught but blood and foam. Though the dragon in his guts had settled down, the ice in his veins soon took its place. He shook, feeling empty and heavy at once.

"Help me get him to his chambers!" Shanley demanded from his guards, but Patrick's hand squeezed his elbow hard.

"*No*," he struggled to say. "Take me to my daughter."

"But My Lord—"

"Shanley… remember when I asked you how martyrs were made?"

Realization crossed the haggard fellow's beady eyes. "Yes, Your Grace. I do."

"Unless you want to empower my brother, I suggest you do as I say."

As Shanley helped him up, the lightheadedness struck. Patrick took a deep breath and willed it down.

So soon?

He clamped down on his jaw rather than give in.

Not now, damn you.

Not bloody now!

⚓

"Sprout," came her father's voice from the dark.

Una opened her eyes. The room was poorly lit, but she could see him smiling ruefully down at her. He looked… "What's wrong?"

She tried to sit up, but he gently pushed her back against her pillow with a shaking palm. "You're the one who's nearly been murdered for a second time, and you'd worry about an old meddler like me? I'm touched, daughter."

He did look terrible. Was that blood around his mouth?

"What's happening?"

"Micah's dead."

"I know," she rasped. It hurt like the Hells to talk.

"Did you kill him?"

She gave him a long look. "No, though I wish I had."

"Me too." He pinched the bridge of his nose with quivering fingers. "He's here, isn't he?"

431

"Who?"

"Una, don't play with me now. You have to know what a terrible mess this will become. Henry is an influential man. His followers plot revenge as we speak. If I hadn't had my Corpsmen around me minutes ago, you might already be strapped to a pyre."

"Me?" she inhaled and did sit up, though it pained her to do so. "Micah was a murderer, father. He killed all those women… he… did *all* of that." Her voice cracked a bit.

She had liked her fair cousin a great deal.

Patrick's sigh sounded wet and tired. "I realize that I've outsmarted myself. I've made a terrible mistake that I will regret for this time that I have left."

She'd never heard him say such things. Never heard him admit to being wrong, either. "What do you mean?"

"I thought to leave a parting gift before I shed this mortal coil, something that would remind our overlords that even immortals may bleed."

Unsure exactly what he was talking about, she *did* have an inkling of what his 'parting gift' would be. "The Kneelers?"

"Sharp one, you are." He beamed; his cheeks were chalk white. "I'm dying. I won't last the week if my surgeons speak truly."

A bottomless well of contradictory emotions opened at her center, rushing into her eyes, mouth, and nose. Patrick made a face, patting her hand. "There now. We weren't always enemies, eh, Sprout? Somewhere in there is that little girl who used to weave my beard with flowers and charge *papier maché* knights with her old man. You were the one thing I ever loved in this world, Una."

She couldn't see anything anymore. She swiped at her eyes with her unbandaged hand. "Nonsense. You can't die. Everyone knows Souther physicians are little better than barbers. Get a second opinion."

The whimsical, earnest expression on his face burrowed into her ribs. *He's joking, right? Dying… it's a ruse of some sort.*

Yet, his cheeks were gaunt, and the flesh beneath his eyes was all but black. There was a rattle to his breath she couldn't recall hearing before. What would the world look like without Patrick Donahugh?

She began to cry.

Patrick took a seat beside her and wound an arm around her shoulders. "There now. I haven't been the best father, I admit freely."

Angrily, she scrubbed the tears from her face. "That's an understatement."

"I should never have given you to each other, so young. I had never been in love, you understand. I had no idea the damage it could do."

She absorbed that in silence for a while. She supposed that was as close to an apology as she might ever get. "Your granddaughter would have been about twelve now."

Patrick's chest shook a bit against her back.

"She would have been an empress, wouldn't she?"

Was he *weeping*?

So… Patrick Donahugh has a heart, after all?

She choked back a fountain of anguish. "She might have been."

"You were too young," he heaved a clumsy sob. "I did what I must to protect you."

"You poisoned me. You robbed me of my child. Who could forgive such a bestial act?"

He went quiet for a while, with his nose at her brow. To the touch, his skin felt like a thin scrap of parchment stretched over ice. "I've made many blunders in my time, Una. That wasn't even the worst, though it's the one I regret most."

She took her time to respond. The oily knot of grief at her core unwound itself ever so slightly. "We have all made mistakes, father. I am no exception."

Patrick wiped his face and gave a dry laugh. "Old rivers, ruined bridges."

"Something like that," she settled.

He squeezed her shoulder a bit. "He's come for you, hasn't he?"

She said nothing.

"Damek loves you, you know?"

"I know."

"He'll never stop fighting for you, no matter whom you choose."

"I know," her voice broke. "I can't... not after...."

"I understand, but... give it time. As they say, it heals all wounds."

"Not this wound."

He chortled. It was a frail sound. "Perhaps. I think we have more immediate fires to douse."

"Henry?"

He nodded.

"Where do you think Micah learned—"

"I know."

She studied his profile in silence. "You fear his following is too great? That he'll stage a coup?"

"I imagine it has already begun. I never expected to hand him such fuel as a dead son. If I'd known, I never—"

"How many men does he have?"

"Hundreds, maybe. Micah's death won many more to his side."

"Powerful men, too?"

"Some of them, very powerful."

Her heart pounded against her ribs. "He'll try to overthrow you because of me?"

"He planned to overthrow me from birth, girl. Now, he'll use the death of his worthless spawn as an excuse. You have little to do with it save to serve as his scapegoat."

Hadn't this been the story of her life?

Would she ever be free of the burdens she placed upon others?

Free yourself, Una, whispered a rich, beautiful voice in her memory.

She shivered.

"When will it happen?"

"Tomorrow, I expect. He'll strike while the iron is hot."

"Damek won't let it happen."

Patrick made a face. "Damek isn't here. I have men out searching, but there's no telling where he might have gone to drown his sorrows."

My fault, she knew.

What wasn't, anymore?

"I'll ask you again, is he here, now?" Patrick persisted.

Una met his eyes. "I don't know."

He scoffed at the lie. "For your sake, I hope he is." With a feeble hand, he slapped his knee. "How embarrassing I might lose my throne in front of such illustrious company." He rose, reaching for and buoying himself against Shanley's arm. "But we won't make it easy for them, will we? Shanley will see to it that your guards are doubled for the night. In the morning, may I ask you for one last farce, daughter?"

Her chest felt raked from the inside.

She remembered a time when she loved this ruin of a man.

"Of course."

"That's my girl," he said. Shanley got him partway to the door when he paused and turned back. In the candlelight, the grooves of his face seemed skeletal. "Do you choose him?"

Una weighed the urge for pretense and found it wanting. "Yes."

The coughing fit he entered into held laughter. "Good. Then you have my blessing, such as it is. If we survive tomorrow, maybe I'll get to meet him?" He tilted his head. "Kaer Yin Adair. Of all the men in the world, you choose the most infamous. I suppose it's fitting, isn't it?"

He limped through the door.

Her voice caught him in the hall.

"Did you kill my mother, Patrick?"

He stood there in Shanley's grip so long that she thought he might have fallen asleep. When he spoke again, his tone held genuine regret. "She plotted with Henry to overthrow me."

"Is that an answer?"

"I wish I knew," he replied sadly.

Martyrs

Gods, he felt like hammered shite. The new girl did her best to keep his bollocks dry as Alba, but no amount of fleeting pleasure could calm the rage, emptiness, and mourning that surged through his veins at each reprieve. Even now, with her wide hips swinging over his, he couldn't summon the least enthusiasm for anything. His body responded, sure; when had it ever failed him in that respect? *Never.*

His mind was the poison, armed with carnivorous thoughts that couldn't be satiated, no matter the device. The girl, her brown skin shining like polished ochre in the lantern light, her spine curving like a taut bowstring, was not enough. Her hair was the right texture, if not the right glorious shade. Her mouth was too large, breasts too full. If he closed his eyes just so and consumed enough uishge straight from the bottle— almost there. He'd been furious, bleary-eyed, sodding drunk for nearly twelve hours, and he could not catch his fill. For the dozenth time in as many hours, he ground her rump into his sex in a ruthless, near painful rhythm. When her lips met his with a contented purr, he tried and failed to imagine they were the ones he craved. She gripped him internally, throwing her head back on a series of raucous moans. When he could no longer contain himself, she dismounted, then leaned down and allowed him to grip her hair as he finished deep in her throat. After, he lay back against the headboard while she opened another bottle. He took a drink, then another, before wedging the bottle against the curve of her sinuous thigh.

She smiled against his chest, and he stirred anew. "You're insatiable, My Lord," she giggled, running her fingertips over his crown. The offending organ was quite sore after such rough use, but uishge had only ever seemed to make him want more. "Do I look a lot like her, your lady?"

His eyes drifted closed as her palms plied their trade. "Not really."

"Shame. She must be quite something to inspire such desire."

Her fingers closed into a fist over his length, and he grunted. "She is."

"What do you want to do to her, My Lord?" She moved his hand to her hip, dislodging the bottle, which spilled between her thighs. His fingers followed. "Do you want to fuck her, My Lord… or taste her?"

He made a low sound.

When Martin burst through the door a few moments later, Damek had to frown at him from between the lady's legs. "Martin? The fuck you doing—"

The girl, ever the professional, slipped from the bed with a ladylike sniff, taking the coverlet with her into the dressing room. Damek groaned, lying face-down on the mattress, his bare arse in the air. "You're not invited, damn you. Get out."

Shaking his head, Martin kicked the mattress once, hard. Damek spilled onto the carpet below, sputtering. "The *fuck* you do that for?"

"You are shite-stinking drunk, your lordship… and you've got business at the palace. Get up, or I'll drag you home like this." Martin was a large man. Much larger than most men. Sober, Damek might have had the better of him— in his present state, not in the least. Martin had his tunic over his head and was already jerking on his breeches before Damek could figure out which way his arse was even pointed. "Been here for most of a damned day, My Lord! Had half the palace guard out looking for you, your uncle in a lather even the Gods have not seen."

"So what? I want to stay here."

Martin snorted as he fumbled to buckle Damek's swordbelt. "Aye, I'll bet. Playing pretend like a little boy while your lady endures at home. Some noble gent, you are."

Damek pinched the bridge of his nose, willing the floor to stop rolling beneath his heels. He was developing quite a spectacular headache. Martin smacked him upright, then leaned down to help Damek into his boots. "She hates me, Martin. It's no use."

Martin glanced up. "If you fucking cry right now, I'll spare her the trouble and slit your throat myself! Now, push down here." He moved to the next boot. "Of course, she hates you. You're an ambitious, womanizing, manipulative little shit, Lord Bishop. You deserve every ounce of her ire."

"I know. I *do*."

"I mean it, boy, if you shed a tear in my presence, I'll rip off your jaw. Man up, damn you."

"Martin, remember who you're talkin' to." Damek shrugged away from the wall and toppled straight into Martin's barrel chest.

"That's the spirit, My Lord," sighed Martin, shaking his head.

🦌

BROAD DAYLIGHT GREETED THEM WHEN they emerged from the tunnel below the inner bailey and into the courtyard. Soldiers milled about in every direction, not all of them Bethonair Corpsmen. Servants darted to and fro like small missiles seeking various targets at once.

One nearly ran Damek down on his way past.

"The hell is happenin' here?" he slurred. Martin gave him an uncomfortable look but said nothing. Instead, he led him through the courtyard and Great Hall, all the way to the rear stairwell that wound toward the royal family's apartments. Una would be on the top floor. She was probably dressing for another day of flirtation with the bloody prince of Connaught. Damek's stomach churned.

"There was an incident here last night. I've been looking for you since midnight." They were up the stairs before Damek could properly absorb this statement.

Martin cursed to discover a flurry of activity on the second floor. Damek dangled from his arm like a loose sack of turnips, reeking of stale uishge, dried vomit, and sex. Shanley paced at the top of the stairs, wringing his already chapped hands. He nearly wept aloud when he caught sight of them. "Thank Reason, you found him!"

"My lord was… ah, dicing," lied Martin, badly.

Shanley seemed too preoccupied to notice. "His grace will be relieved."

"Where is he?" demanded Martin.

"In his quarters. He's due to hold Court in an hour. Were your men able to locate our quarry?"

Damek shook himself semi-straight, suddenly curious. "Who else are you searching for?" Watching the shadow cross Martin's face, Damek croaked, "What happened?"

"He doesn't know?" Shanley wheezed incredulously, clenching his hands together so tightly that his knuckles bleached white. He opened his mouth to speak again, but Martin dragged Damek aside, waving a dismissive hand.

"I'll explain. Inform His Grace that we'll be ready in fifteen minutes. My Corpsmen have already taken position by the Northern Gate."

Shanley bowed once and dashed off. His slip-shod gait echoed through the hall for some time. Meanwhile, Martin dragged Damek toward his chamber door.

"Martin, what's going on?"

"Henry's escaped. He and about three dozen of his more powerful converts, I might add. Those men have soldiers and resources. Not to mention the people outside in the city." He gave a rough laugh. "It's Cromnasa. The streets are packed with revelers, aren't they?"

Confused, Damek clapped a hand over Martin's shoulder once the door closed. Inside, the fires had already been lit by some dutiful servant. His waiting armor glinted from its stand, oiled and ready. Hisk stood beside it. Cortram, the squire, waited by the larder with a bowl full of water, black tea, and a clean tunic.

So, he'd missed quite a bit. "Tell me."

Martin inhaled slowly. "Micah's dead. He tried to murder Una last night, after the feast. He was waiting for her in her bedchamber. Damek, he cut her throat."

The hand Damek draped over Martin's shoulder became a fist. The world spun ruby-red at the edges. "*What?* Is she... you said, '*tried to?*'"

Martin backed into the door so Damek couldn't tear it from its hinges. "She's alive, fought him off, and somehow, Micah fell from her window."

Damek backed away, rubbing his face. "Where is she now?"

"She's fine. I vow it."

Godsdamnit... while he'd been fucking and drinking himself into a self-pitying stupor, Una had nearly been killed. There wasn't a hole deep or dark enough to crawl into from which he could hide from such guilt. Instead, he let fury take up the charge. It seeped through his blood with slow-simmering heat.

"Micah?"

The disgust on Martin's face was palpable. "Had the blood of a half-dozen women on his hands already. I hope the Gods see he's arse-raped every night in Tech Duinn," he spat. "It's Henry we must worry about now."

"Cortram, water," Damek demanded. While he availed himself of the cup that was passed over, his mind raced through half a dozen scenarios at once. "How many followers does Henry have?"

"Enough to be a problem. Worse, we have no idea where they are or how many are already within these walls. It's going to get ugly, Damek. There could be fighting in the halls."

"With so many guests, it'll be impossible to search everywhere." Damek removed his soiled tunic and scrubbed his face in the basin Cortram guarded. Once done, he dried himself and reached for a clean shirt. "Why is Patrick holding Court rather than dealing with this as he should be?"

"Appearances. As you said, many powerful people are here for your uncle's fête. The fewer that know his nephew was a murdering brute, the better. Yet, Henry will take it upon himself to martyr the boy anyway. Without a trial, it would appear Una is a kinslayer. This will bolster Henry's argument."

"We have the Corps. Henry has a few old men, women, and peasants. What can he do but make noise?" interjected Hisk, a clever man to be sure but not clever enough.

"If I were Henry, I would accuse her in open Court. Demand a trial. In front of so many of his barons, Patrick could never refuse. Where is his son? The other one?" responded Damek.

"Also missing, My Lord."

"Then we must find Isaac before Henry can make his move." Damek shrugged his breastplate on. He met Martin's eyes over Cortram's head. "Move Una somewhere else. Somewhere no one knows about and do it fast. The Prince of Croghan is a ruse; the bastard's come for her. You know whom I'm talking about." Martin shifted uncomfortably. Damek growled, "What?"

"Against my advice, the Duch wanted Una close... in case. She sits in Court with him today. To maintain appearances."

The room shrank around Damek's ears. "Nevermind searching. I know exactly where Henry will turn up. Get our infantry to every gate, our Corpsmen at every exit in the Keep, and our officers to the Great Hall. Hisk? Gather Castor and the Bretagn contingency. I would have them meet me in the throne room."

"My lord," Hisk saluted as he took his leave.

Damek strapped on his vambraces. Martin waited with his sword. "How many men do we have, Martin?"

"Inside the walls? Two hundred."

"That should be plenty if we're quick."

Taking and sliding his sabre into his scabbard, Damek looked up, eyes wild. "Where are the Sidhe?"

"One problem at a time, My Lord."

Una had felt better, that was sure. Wearing a high collar and long sleeves so no one would detect her wounds, she sat beside Patrick on the dais, trying not to sweat. Truth be told, she wasn't doing that great a job. Her Spark was a versatile tool, but even Siora's blessings took time to recharge. She hadn't slept, eaten, or taken anything for the pain, of which there was plenty. Micah had sliced through nearly two inches of flesh midway between her collarbone and jugular. Though she no longer bled like a gutted fish, the broken capillaries and lacerated tissues wouldn't heal so easily.

She *should* have been abed for a while yet, but Patrick had insisted.

The façade would make or break them now.

She stole a glance at him from the corner of her eye. At least she wasn't suffering alone. Her father looked grey round the edges, himself. Had he somehow managed to lose more weight in one night? The hollows under his eyes looked carved in, and his skin bore an unhealthy, limpid pallor. Indeed, she couldn't be sure which of them was in worse straits. Without disturbing the land dispute being argued before the Court, she leaned over to whisper, "Are you all right?"

Patrick gave her a tight smile. "Of course, I am."

"You don't seem to be."

He scanned the crowd to be sure no one overheard them. "We must keep order. The fewer people know what happened here last night, the better."

Una worried her nails, feeling weak and helpless. Across the room, Rian's blue eyes met hers in nervous fear. Tam Lin, behind her, chatted amiably with several women. His closest attendant stood beside him, with one or two others—no sign of Kaer Yin.

Though the Great Hall had been cleared of benches and tables, many of last night's Cromnasa decorations remained in advance of the anticipated final feast. Una certainly didn't feel up to more festivities, and from the looks of everyone else, her reticence was shared. Most of the courtiers gathered to either side of the large scarlet, and cobalt carpet that divided the room appeared as sober and fearful as she.

The day's grim reality was not lost on anyone.

"This is foolish. Micah was a murderer. He died trying to do the same to me for the second time. Declare it. Who cares about my reputation?"

"I couldn't toss a fig for your reputation right now, girl. This is bigger than you or I. Henry has support from among my barons, much more than I ever intended that he should. Until he and Isaac are found, he's a threat. It's better to maintain the appearance of order."

"How many men could he muster in so little time?"

"How many are here with us in this room now, child? Every one of my barons has soldiers within and without these walls. Given the opportune chaos Cromnasa affords, even one could be critical."

"What about *our* men? Aren't we armed and ready too?"

Patrick's head swiveled toward her. "Did you say, 'our men?'"

She flushed. "The Corps is in here with us, hundreds more than any of your barons could summon in time. Henry has no chance."

"He wouldn't have fled his cell if he didn't believe he had one. I know my brother, and I know his tactics. He'll be here soon."

"Here?" she asked, a little too loudly. She gave the crowd a nervous smile and settled back into her seat. "Why here?"

"To plead his case before those in power."

"*You're* in power, Patrick."

He shook his head. "Power like mine is an illusion. I need others to believe in my right to rule for it to hold. Accusing me publicly will earn the division he needs to cull my support. I expect he'll demand your life in return for his son's. I will refuse, and my barons will decide my fate."

A slow, creeping panic inched along her skin.

"Then we should leave, now!"

Suddenly sweating and shaking like a leaf, Patrick reached over and clasped her hand. "*We,*" he placed intense emphasis upon the word, "have something he doesn't. *You,* and Damek."

She absorbed this, brows knitting together. "Why did you set him free in the first place, father? He's brought nothing but trouble."

He coughed and clutched at his gut. "For the Sidhe, of course. If my plans should falter, if the worst should happen… they will pay for it. Faith will exact my vengeance if strength of arms should fail." His attention drifted in Tam Lin O'Ruiadh's direction, though his eyes glazed over. Alarmed, Una touched his shoulder. Even through his clothing, his skin was burning hot to the touch. She inhaled sharply.

"You're ill!"

He patted her hand. "I'll be fine. Wait for Damek, Una. He knows my mind." But his pallor grew worse by the moment, his breathing more labored. While the two farmers made their case before the Court clerks, Una looked around for help. She didn't see a single friendly face, save for Rian's. A wordless plea passed between them. One of the Sidhe Una had never met, a fellow with bright green eyes and six silver chains, helped her through the crowd toward the dais. They were right on cue. Suddenly, Patrick doubled over with a violent groan, vomiting blood down the steps. The Court fell silent, save for Patrick's uncontrollable retching. Una dropped to her knees beside her father while he writhed against the carpet.

A guard stepped forward to block Rian's ascent, but Una cried, "Let her through, damn you!" He stepped aside. Watching Patrick convulse, tears sprang to Una's eyes. "Do something!" she begged Rian.

The faerie took command immediately. "You there," she demanded of a guardsman. "Help me get him out of here!"

Una, Rian, and three guards had him halfway lifted when the door burst open upon the Court. Henry and a dozen armed men stalked inside. He wore a habit black as pitch and a scowl that could carve stone. He moved forward with purpose, his eyes blazing. None could miss Patrick and Una on the dais steps amid a growing pool of blood and bile. Henry's finger came up like a spear aiming for Una's heart.

"*Witch!*" he exclaimed.

Around him, the courtiers were taken aback. People moved out of his way, aghast and outnumbered. Una met the inferno of his gaze with a raised but trembling chin. "Guards. That man is not to take another step forward." The guards answered by drawing their sabres and taking defensive positions around their fallen lord and his daughter.

Henry raised his hands. His men fanned out behind him, weapons ready. "You murdered my son! I'll see you burn for this, whore of Babylon!"

Coughing, Patrick slapped his hand against the stair to push himself upward. Blood and other things stained his mouth and nose. His eyes were nearly black.

Surprised, Henry took a faltering step back.

"Y-you!" struggled Patrick. "Your son was the mu-murderer. He tried to slay my daughter in her bed. He was rightfully killed for his treachery."

Rian dug her nails into Una's arm. "I can't treat him here, Una. We have to move him. Now!"

At first, Henry gawped at his younger brother, bleeding all over his dais… but that didn't last. Una watched a slow, smug smile drag his wormy mouth wide. "She's attempting to slay her father too! *Poisoner!* Stop her!"

A courtier moved forward to grab her arm, but one of her guards slammed the butt of his pommel into his temple, and he crumpled to the floor. That seemed to inspire Henry. He turned, raising his empty hands to the gathered noblemen. "Quick! Someone stop her and her faerie accomplice before we lose the Duch!"

"Liar!" Una hissed. "Your precious son slaughtered seven girls under my father's roof. *You* made that happen. Your example."

Her guards shoved people backward. The situation plummeted from there. Something heavy grazed her chest, and she grunted in pain. Rian tried to raise her voice to be heard, but Henry's drowned her out. "Murderess! Stop her, STOP HER!"

For a brief moment, no longer than the span of a wingbeat, Patrick set his hand against her cheek. "Too late. I f-failed. *Go…* and *forgive* me."

She gritted her teeth. "Get him up! Help me!"

The Court had devolved into chaos. Her guards made an admirable show of strength, but the crowd was so busy tearing into one another what they were pitted against mattered very little in the end. Someone's booted foot nearly connected with Una's jaw, but a large shape grabbed the fellow mid-leap and threw him bodily over the dais: Tam Lin O'Ruiadh, prince of Connaught, no less. His Sidhe warriors spread out at the base of the infamous relief of Kaer Yin Adair, striking her ancestor down. He held out a hand for her.

"My Lady. It's time to leave, I think."

"Not without him!" She gripped Patrick's gore-painted tunic. But where his skin had been warm, now it was cold. She looked down. His empty grey eyes were fixed on the ceiling, clouded and sightless.

A long, low scream built in her throat.

Rian's fingers found her shaking shoulder. "Una. There's nothing we can do."

A bone-rattling sob escaped Una's lips. She shook her head. "No! No. He's fine. He'll be fine. We need to get him—"

Henry howled into the sea of writhing, angry people. A chair struck the wall above them and shattered the stained glass. Thousands of shards rained down upon them. Tam Lin held his cloak over the girls while another series of screams pierced the air.

"Rian!" he shouted. "Drag her if you have to! More are coming."

But it wasn't Rian's hands that pried her away from her father. Kicking and screaming, Una was carried up and away from the violence. She fought with everything she had left, but he was stronger.

He was always stronger.

"Hush now, love," Kaer Yin whispered into her hair. "It's over now. We're going home."

Black Knight Rising

Damek heard Henry's shrill, contemptuous voice long before he saw him. The halls bore signs of a sudden, violent skirmish. Large, gilded frames bearing important faces from Bethany's past lay torn or smashed in limp heaps at either stone wall. Sconces and candelabra had been upended or smashed, some leaving great smoke stains over the fine Bretagn carpets below. Bedraggled courtiers with stricken features and shredded clothing gripped each other in fear as they shuffled past Damek's men. The two mahogany doors Duch Kevin had carved for the Keep hung askew from their hinges like flags at half-mast. A stalemate of sorts had been brokered through the breach, though the shouting and general discord had not. Not yet. As Douglas and Hisk pushed through the doors, shoving people and debris aside like so much dross, Damek followed Martin into Patrick's courtroom, sword in hand. The room was a disaster. Broken glass was everywhere; blood coalesced beneath victims forgotten and trampled on the floor by dozens of feet that had now pulled into either corner to rail abuse at one another. Henry and his black-clothed followers had taken the dais and the door to Patrick's apartments, Damek noticed. The others, Patrick's loyal barons and friends, occupied a much smaller space near the exit. Damek scanned the room furiously, searching for the one sight that would condemn the man who stood before the throne. Finally, he found him.

Patrick lay on the steps in a bloodied heap.

He did not move, not even when Henry's booted foot trod over him.

Dead, Damek's blood sang with rage.

Dead and discarded, like a forgotten toy.

He felt a surge of pity commingled with loathing and disappointed hope.

Even a pillar must someday fall, lad, Patrick had said once. *Only our ideas live on.*

Nostrils flaring, Damek glanced at Martin, whose face was hardly dry.

"Kill any man that dares lay a hand, or foot, on your Duch."

"With pleasure," choked Martin.

Henry looked down, his mad red face full of unblinking black eyes. "*YOU!*" His followers— and there were many— turned to greet the newcomers with weapons high. Some filtered out of Patrick's private apartments, three here, four there, until the dais nearly swarmed with black-cloaked zealots. Henry's victorious smirk set fire to Damek's throat. "Come late, it seems! Your lord has been murdered, and your wife fled with Norther devils! Where were *you* when she mixed the brew that slew your uncle?"

Damek waved a hand, and his armored corpsmen took flanking positions around him. The light of whatever righteous horseshite they believed shone from Henry's supporters' eyes. Nevertheless, the gleam of all that steel surely began to sink in. Some visibly hesitated, and some backed away in cowardice. Others, well, their zeal burned bright as bloodlust. So be it. Damek vowed they would be first to feel his wrath.

"That's how you intend to spin this? Una is supposed to have murdered her father?" Damek gave a short, barking laugh. "For what possible reason?"

"Witches need no reason to do evil. They are Satan's playthings."

"So too, are old men chewed up by envy, greed, and ambition, like yourself."

Henry gave him a grin full of wooden teeth. "Have you come to plead her case before the Court, nephew? This slut who spurns you, even now?"

Damek glanced around. "*Whose* Court? The man who rules this land is dead. I would advise you to remove yourself and your grievances from this chamber while I am asking nicely."

Damek's great-uncle, Lord Bishop, cackled from the rear doorway. "Who do you imagine you are to speak to a son of Duch Michael that way, boy?"

From nine paces away, Martin drew his dagger and flung it into the scabrous old fool's throat. As the old traitor sagged to the floor, the crowd gasped as one. Martin swept his sabre in a wide arc, encompassing the room at large. His blue eyes were wild with grief and anger. "The next man that *dares* insult my Duch will die by my hand. Patrick Donahugh is dead... long live Duch Damek *Donahugh*!"

Damek's Corpsmen took up the chant.

Henry threw back his head and laughed until his eyes misted over. "Oh, that's rich! *You*, a faerie bastard, Duch? Never. Not one baron here will support you."

Martin took a threatening step forward, but Damek's hand caught his elbow. He looked behind him at Patrick's loyal retainers. Many visibly supported him. Some looked away. *No matter.* "I think you'll find, uncle dear, he who controls the army controls the nation. Una is the rightful ruler here, and until she is found, *I am* your liege lord."

"Una murdered her father in cold blood and fled this hall to escape justice. We stood here while she took his life! We saw her do it! None would see a murderous foreign whore take up Patrick's throne." Here, he sneered. "Neither would we seek to vaunt her faithful cuckold. There is a sole, trueborn choice to take the throne. Isaac Donahugh will be Duch!"

His supporters cheered so loud that Damek's ears popped. Were there more of them now, filing through Patrick's apartments and over Lord Bishop's corpse to drown the few loyalists in a sea of black? Martin shot a nervous glance over his shoulder. The courtiers began ducking out. Less than a handful stood to watch the proceedings.

"Damek," Martin warned. "We're outnumbered."

Damek shrugged him off and stalked forward until the vambraces at his shins brushed the bloodied furs at Patrick's collar. In death, he was so much smaller than he had been in life. "Do you think this rabble is a match for my men, Henry?"

"Your worthless wife murdered my firstborn before murdering my brother. None of us will *ever* bow to her."

"Murdered Micah, you say?" Damek cocked his head.

"*Yes*," Henry slavered, gone puce.

"That would be rather virtuous of her if she had. Considering your son was the creature responsible for the brutal deaths of several girls within this very Keep."

"You lie! Micah would never—"

"Oh, I'm sorry. Did you think I, like the simpletons behind you, would take your word on the matter? Douglas?" While Henry struggled for an appropriate insult, Douglas stepped forward to upend a box of items at the bottom stair. A journal flapped open with crude drawings of the female anatomy as it would appear if sawed into with a broad blade. Hanks of bloodied hair tied off with red ribbons fluttered to join several sexually explicit instruments and figurines. Henry lurched away like the pile had slithered forward to touch him. Damek stooped to pick up two separate bits of paper. One was a poorly rewritten verse from Callaghan's *Seasons of Transition*, bearing Micah's name and writing. The other was a journal page detailing the names of several women, Una's included. The text was hastily scribbled and repetitive in furious knife-slashing relief. "This is your son's handwriting, is it not?"

Henry said nothing.

Damek passed the pages to the battered loyalists in the room's rear. When he returned, Henry seemed to have collected himself. "This proves nothing. My son did not write any of this."

"No? Douglas, where were these found?"

"In Micah Fitz Donahugh's quarters, My Lord," rejoined Douglas.

"By whom?"

"The Duch's steward, Shanley, My Lord."

Damek beamed up at Henry. "Is he here?"

Shanley was led up to the dais, shivering in fear. When he saw the Duch crumpled up on the second-to-last stair, he wailed. Damek patted his back, turning him toward the loyal barons he was pleased to note seemed less inclined to leave by the moment.

Good.

"Shanley, please tell the Court where you found this rubbish?" Damek indicated the pile.

Shanley gulped. "In young Lord Fitz Donahugh's quarters, the night he attacked my mistress."

A collected gasp swept through the gathering.

"He did attack her then?" asked Damek, with a pointed glare for Henry.

"Yes, My Lord. He was found clutching the knife he used to slash her neck and arm. The coroner wrote a report detailing the type and make of the knife, concerning her ladyship's wounds."

"Do you have that report?"

"Y-yes." Shanley dug around in his valise until he produced the documents. Damek held them aloft for the whole room to see, his eye on his uncle, before passing those too to Patrick's barons. "Is the coroner present?"

"I am, milord," said an unassuming voice from the far corner. A balding fellow of middling years stepped forward.

"Do you attest to the validity of your report?"

"I do, milord. The girl was brutally attacked by a fellow matching your cousin's approximate height and weight. His hands and fingers bore sure signs of their struggle and the practiced use of a bladed weapon of the description listed in my report. The very same weapon was used on each victim. Furthermore, her ladyship was in a state of exsanguination and acute shock the night of the attack and therefore could not have 'thrown' or 'pushed' the Duch's nephew from her window. She would have been far too weak. The only explanations that make sense are that he either leapt from the window himself, was heaved through by an unknown third party, or fell by accident. Given his cruel proclivities, I believe suicide can be ruled out."

Henry went white as a shroud.

Damek pressed on. In the doorway and hall, some courtiers returned to see what was happening since the fighting had stopped. "So, he either fell or was thrown by someone not bleeding from several serious wounds?"

"Yes," said the balding fellow, shoving his spectacles up the bridge of his sweating nose. "More than this, the individual must have been quite strong to shove the window and latticing with Fitz Donahugh to the cliff below."

"And if Micah fell?"

"If he hit the window with some force, say after tripping over an unseen object— he might have struck the casing with the full force of his back, but really, I doubt this explanation. It's far-fetched."

Damek paused to gauge the shock and anger brewing around him. "Then you believe someone else was in the room with them?"

The coroner coughed. "Yes, milord. The window was already ajar when the young lord went through. He did not have shards of any size lodged in his back, which he would have, were the accidental death an explanation."

"Lies," Henry whispered, trembling.

"You're sure of this? Please answer the Court," Damek ordered.

The coroner turned. "Given the lady's state that night, there is no way she could have murdered Lord Fitz Donahugh's son. I examined her wounds myself. In my hearing, her father instructed her to conceal her wounds and put on a brave face for the fête, but by rights, she should have been abed for a week or more."

"She *did* look quite pale today," said someone.

"Aye, and what a high collar she wore," whispered another.

"I never liked that milksop lad. Had his father's temper."

Henry snarled at them all. "*Lies.* We're to believe my mild-mannered son was a vicious murderer *and* that he was thrown from the South Tower by a mysterious savior? You're reaching, the lot of you." At the coroner, he levelled a righteous finger. "This man is a known drunk and lickspittle. For enough coin, he'll swear to anything you wish to tell. If Una did not murder my boy…. *who am I to believe did?*"

Damek shrugged. "Me, obviously."

Henry's scoff spurred his supporters on. "Was that before or after she was seen fawning over that Sidhe devil at table?"

"After. Everyone saw *us* at the feast, didn't they? I entered her chamber about a quarter past midnight— I have a key, you see— and discovered Micah hunched over her with a knife. He'd bashed her skull against the floor and the door panel then opened several wounds in her arm, hands, and throat. I picked him up and tossed him through the window. I can't recall if the shutters were open or not, as I was far too enraged to notice. *I* killed your wretched spawn, uncle, and good riddance."

The murmur ran up and down the breadth of the chamber and did not end, even with Henry's rasp. "You're a bloody liar, boy. My men saw you leave for *The Butterfly* before midnight."

"A ruse cooked up by my uncle," he gestured to Patrick. "Who never intended that anyone should have Una but me. Shanley?"

"Ah, yes," the steward blanched. He pulled several more documents from his valise. These bore the Duch's infamous hand, as well as his seal.

Lord Wender read in silent fury for several moments before marching forward. "This stipulates that the Lady Una and Lord Bishop are the Duch's sole heirs."

Henry collected himself in the face of their indignation. "Whatever this charlatan sells you is false. Una Moura murdered my boy— and her father— for the throne. Once I appeared to accuse her directly, she fled with her Sidhe cohorts. We were *here*. We saw her with our own eyes. Where were *you*, Lord Bishop, hm? If you and she were together last night, why weren't you here to support her before the Court?" Henry's men caught their bearings from this impassioned display; weapons raised once more.

That was fine by Damek.

He'd been hoping there'd be a fight.

"I was detained, uncle. My cousin Isaac was loath to leave his games and toys behind, but in the end, the promise of a proper squireship was enough to tempt him from the Keep."

Henry stopped. Every muscle in his face froze.

"*What* was that?"

Martin answered for him. "Did you believe we'd allow you to usurp *My Lord's* rightful place without a proper accounting? You've no right to stand upon that dais, Henry Fitz Donahugh, and even less to slander My Lady's good name in favor of the murderous beast you spawned." Martin would not be restrained. "If you don't remove yourself, I will do the honors myself."

"Where have you taken my son, Damek?" asked Henry, ignoring Martin entirely.

"Where he'll cause little trouble, I assure you. The lad will not be victim to your ambition while I live, uncle. Now please, do as Martin has asked and desist. You may retire to whichever country estate you favor, with all due rights and tithes. Do it not, and I will have your head on a spike at the gate. Choose now."

Henry visibly counted the growing number of Courtiers at Damek's back. Many had returned with better weapons and more of their household guard. His was now the losing hand. "If I refuse, I suppose Isaac will suffer for it?"

"Not at all," disagreed Damek. "I am not a man who condones the senseless slaughter of innocents for power. That is *your* forte, uncle. Isaac will grow up to be whatever he wishes, far out of harm's way… whether I am forced to kill his rabid hypocrite of a father or no." Several minutes passed while Henry stared between Damek, his brother's cooling body, and the throne he'd been after his entire life. Damek watched the emotions trace across the old boar's face. He even empathized a bit. He knew all too well what it meant to want something you will likely never have. Douglas, Hisk, and Gordin advanced upon the dais. "I have places to be. Make your decision."

Henry held up his gnarled and fingerless left hand in the face of bloodshed that he could not direct. "I have your word that my son is unharmed."

"Yes," Damek vowed through his teeth.

"I will leave if you allow me to collect him."

Damek drew in a dramatic breath. "Not now, certainly, as you'd no doubt use him to further your agenda. No, I think I will hang on to him if you attempt to betray me in the near future. Perhaps one day, he will seek you out himself?"

Henry took a step back. He met the eyes of his staunchest supporters with as guilty a look as he could manage. "I'm sorry, brothers. God has called upon me to make this sacrifice for an innocent child. I have no recourse. Forgive me in your prayers." He limped down the steps toward a Corpsman with open manacles. Willingly, he placed his twig-thin wrists in the restraints. "Brothers, I now urge you to surrender your weapons and leave the scene with dignity."

Damek's laugh caught him short. "We made no agreement for your followers." He tugged his chin at the black-clothed throng. The result was a swift and bloody affair, over in mere moments. The Steel Corps moved through the zealots like scythes through wheat. Their sabres came away red, again and again.

As he was dragged from the room and down the hall, Henry's apoplectic screams echoed through the walls for quite a while. "This is not over!" he roared to no one and everyone at once.

Unperturbed, Damek knelt beside his uncle's body. Patrick had died with blood on his lips. Damek did his best to scrub the offal away. Martin's hand slid over his shoulder. "He was a good man."

Several courtiers took a knee, vowing fealty to their new Duch. Damek scarcely heard or saw them. His eyes were all for the man who'd raised him, taught him, loathed, and loved him. "No, he wasn't. Though, that hardly diminished him. Whatever one thought of him, he was a force to be reckoned with."

Martin wiped at his eyes with the back of his hand. "What's to be done with the boy?"

"Which boy?"

"Isaac. What will you do with him?"

Damek stood, hands on hips as he accepted the oaths of the shocked and bleeding nobles of Patrick's Court. "It's done."

Martin blinked several times. "In what way?"

"The only way, Martin." He gave his old friend a long, meaningful stare. "Who do you think raised me?" Martin didn't so much recoil as shrink into his own body. The deflation was subtle, but Damek noticed. O'Rearden nearly flinched when Damek patted his arm. "Now, how about we go and find my wife before she gets away, hm?"

⚔

As it happened, Henry was not incarcerated for long. Indeed, his captors had scarcely skirted the bottom stair in the Great Hall before his followers caught up with them. The Steel Corpsmen were fine fighters, it was true. Several men died in the fracas at the sharp end of both sabres, but two swords were not enough to quell the dozen men who poured down the stairs with clubs and knives held high. Henry was sharply shoved aside, whereupon he took a slight tumble that knocked the breath from his lungs. Lord Tendrick's son helped him to his feet after several bloody moments, bearing the key to his manacles. "My Lord, you are liberated."

Using Tendrick's hand to steady himself, Henry leaned against the wall to observe the carnage his men had wrought. Passerby had all but fled from the chamber, except for Lady Penwyth and one of her young sons. At any other time, he might have been impressed by her lack of fear. Now was not that time.

"Declare yourself, My Lady. Duch Isaac or the faerie pretender?"

Her nose twitched. "Surely you realize your son is dead, Lord Fitz-Donahugh?"

A dull ache in his gut attested to the truth of this statement. Though he longed to refute her claim, he'd known from the moment Damek had uttered his youngest child's name that there was very little likelihood he'd have been spared. Giving voice to that fear, however, was its own torture. Henry choked down the cauldron of rage and grief at his center. There'd be time enough for vengeance later. Now, he had a city to wrest from an idolater. He pulled his bony shoulder back. His followers fanned out behind him, wielding their clubs menacingly.

"We shall see. I'd loathe to learn you and your men have thrown support behind my brother's evil children?"

She noted the dangerous enthusiasm each of Henry's followers bore in their eyes. She half-smirked. "Not I. The pair of them snubbed my excellent sons for lesser creatures. I've no cause to align my house with theirs."

Henry dipped his head once, gesturing for his men to lower their weapons. "I have your support, then?"

"Depends." She crossed her fleshy arms. "Who shall follow you as Duch, now that your sons are both dead?"

He would see her scalp peeled away from her skull before a roaring crowd for such a flippant, calculating comment. He smiled. "I may yet make more sons, Lady Penwyth."

The dubious glint in her eyes sealed her future fate, as far as Henry was concerned. "I have a daughter, as it happens, My Lord. A worthless girl, to be sure. Far too old and ugly to be a prize, but wide of hip and meek as a mule. She'll make a grand broodmare, I'll wager."

Henry wiped the blood from his cheek. So that was to be the way of things, was it? His sons were scarcely cold in their shrouds, and this officious whore would peddle her daughter to him for a chance at power. Well. "How many men are at your disposal, My Lady?"

"Two hundred, My Lord. And you may rest assured, Lords Kendall and Pough share my table. I can add three hundred soldiers to your rabble. Enough, do you think?"

Henry did the sums in his head. Damek had many more men in his company, though they were even now in pursuit of Henry's slattern of a niece. The city guard could be bought with little action and coin, and the traitorous lords of Patrick's court could be dealt with… if he moved quickly. Now was the moment, he knew without much deliberation. Now or never. He muttered a silent prayer for strength of purpose; vengeance would be his, by God. "I would require assurances."

The lady's son gave a bark of surprise as she shoved him forward. "Take this one. He's quite stupid, but he's my firstborn, nonetheless."

"Mother," breathed the young man, wide-eyed.

"Shut your mouth, Kai. You'll serve as the Duch's squire, won't he, My Lord?"

"Indeed," Henry prevaricated. He waved a follower over with the manacles removed from his own wrist. "Though, I'm afraid one lad will not be sufficient."

"Take them both, then. Ned is out whoring, last I checked. Once you find him, do with him as you see fit."

"Agreed," assented Henry. "In exchange?"

"My daughter as Duchess, and Malahide for the Clan, of course."

"Done. Liam, will you?"

Tendrick's son led the Kernian lad away, protesting the while. Henry limped toward her. He held out his hand. She took it with the barest hint of hesitation. "We have an accord, Lady Penwyth. Now, let's go and greet your men, shall we?" As he led her away, he paused to ask, "Why me, and not Damek?"

Her shrug was ruthlessly casual. "One bastard Donahugh's as good as another."

From Below

They'd made it to the lowest point in the Keep without much incident. Patrols were primarily restricted to the walls and the lanes outside the palace. Any soldiers rushing to Patrick's Court beyond the Great Hall would never have spied them making their way down to the Moorings. The chill, damp air that greeted them from within the cavern made Una's flesh prickle. How many foul deeds had been performed in this place, she wondered? How many women dead, girls and boys taken, goods and wealth stolen, stealthy attacks mounted? She'd been nearly murdered here recently, hadn't she? Evil oozed from the walls, dripping into the filthy black water below like a drumbeat.

I have ssssuuuch delighhtsss to ssshow youuu… whispered her memory.

She shuddered.

Having been attached to each other's side since the throne room, Rian's arms tightened around her shoulders. "Are you all right?" They hadn't had much time to talk, but some things didn't need to be spoken aloud. Her friend's sure and steady presence was already more than Una could ask for.

Una patted her hand. "This place reminds me of Samhain, is all."

Her friend hadn't been conscious through much of that nightmare but had witnessed enough to empathize. She frowned. "You're right."

"Which way?" demanded the Prince of Connaught with an impatient growl.

Una pointed. "Down that set of second stairs, to the right there. I know that much, but then there are three forks. I've no idea where the other two lead."

"I do," promised Robin. "We veer left, then hook right. Leads us up under *The Butterfly* and into her cellars. That'll be the easy part, though. The second tunnel separated. We'll hafta access it from the first floor."

"Wonderful," Una sighed. She was so tired. Someone passed her a flask; she took it without glancing down. They hadn't spoken much, but Kaer Yin's quiet, steady presence at her back was her sole warmth. "This door bears a heavy lock. I have no key."

"No need," Robin grinned. "Ye have me, princess." He tugged a thin but sharp sliver of iron from his sleeve. It slid into the lock with a clang. Two twists of his wrist, and the bulky lock popped open and clattered to the wet stone floor. Opening the door sent a blast of dry, stale air into her face. "*Siora,*" sneezed Robin with a curled lip. "Somethin' died in there, sure."

"It'll be us if we don't get moving," said Kaer Yin, glancing behind him. He and his Sidhe companions could hear things she, Rian, and Robin would never hear. "They're gathering at the gates, and I hear boots in the halls above. They're looking for us now. Whatever happened after the attack in chambers must be over now."

"Then we should leave," Tam Lin urged, sparing Una a curious twist of his brow. "Unless you're having second thoughts?"

Una didn't care for his tone. She narrowed her eyes. "Charming, aren't you?"

Kaer Yin jerked the torch out of his cousin's hand while Tam Lin appraised Una in silent judgment. "Come on. We're wasting time here." Kaer Yin's voice was slightly gruffer than usual.

Ah, Una thought.

I suppose every *family is complicated, then?* "After you, Your Highness," she ground out. "Unless you'd prefer to wait here?"

Tam Lin shared a small laugh with Robin. "This makes more sense by the moment."

"I told you. A pair," agreed Robin.

"I told *you* to hurry up!" barked Kaer Yin from somewhere in the dark ahead.

RIAN DIDN'T MIND THE DARK as much as Una seemed to, but the smell… *Siora*. More than one thing had perished in here, surely? The high-pitched squeaks of various rodents chased them through the tunnel, and though she didn't want to think about it, she felt her boots smash several thousand similar skeletons along the way. She ran straight into every damned cobweb in their path, or maybe just the ones too low for the idiot Sidhe in their company to reach. Whatever the case, by the time they came to the fork in the passage Robin spoke of— she was thoroughly put out. Even wounded, Una fared better, though barely. Her delicate black gown was far worse for wear. Her amber eyes seemed hollow and dark in the torchlight. Every step she took amplified her silence. Rian gripped her fingers. "I'm here, Una."

Una gave the slightest squeeze back. "I'm grateful."

"Do you want to talk about it?"

Una shook her head. "Not now."

They rounded the right-hand corner. Kaer Yin, Rian noted, stared straight ahead with a fixed jaw. She didn't need to read his mind to know what he was feeling. Una's physical and emotional pain radiated from her, despite her visible efforts to choke it down. Her father was dead. No matter how she'd felt about the man in life, the finality of his demise was inescapable. No reconciliation, no reprieve. Rian understood this, perhaps better than anyone else; her own father had died suddenly, with much left unsaid between them.

In Una's case, the Duch had died in her arms.

Rian had no doubt the event would haunt her for a long time. She wanted to take a break and wrap her arms around her friend, whose shoulders shook ever so slightly from the effort to repress her emotions. However, the quiver in Una's shoulders convinced her to leave it be for now.

Tam Lin exhaled through his nose. "Thank Danu for that. We have more pressing matters to see to, don't we?"

Rian stopped short so that she might stare Tam Lin down. After bumping into her, Robin held his hands up and moved on, navigating by the bobbing glow of Kaer Yin's light. Though she struggled to see his face in the quickening dark, she could make out Tam Lin's haughtily raised brow.

"Yes, My Lady?" his tone was husky and flirtatious enough to be insulting. Shar ducked his head and took up Rian's place at Una's side. Once moderately alone, Rian's right hand lashed out so fast that Tam Lin's head snapped into the wall with a mild crack. His fingers flew to his offended cheek. "Ow! What in the *Hells* do you think—"

"Listen, you arrogant swine. For weeks and weeks, I've listened to you rant and rave, pout and instigate, prattle and prod— and kept my peace about it. Only when your outrageously overinflated self-love has attempted to harm someone else have I butted in. The stupid grudge between you and Ben, for one." Her chest heaved with the urge to smite this vainglorious creature on the spot. "But so help me, *Siora*, if you ever speak to or about Una that way again, I will kill you. Am I making myself clear? All that she has suffered for those of us in your presence, aside… she lost her father *today*. You will keep that insufferable narcissism in check, or I'll make you regret it."

She couldn't see his face anymore at all. "I'm—"

"I don't give a tenth of a shite who you bloody well are! You're a vain, spoilt, monstrous boil of a person, and I *despise* you." She wiped her mouth with the back of her hand. She could hear him breathing and hated that too. "Remember what I said."

"Come on then!" called Robin from the front. "We're about there."

Without another word, she spun on her good heel and limped toward her friends.

⚳ ⚳

At the terminus of the forked passage, a dusty wooden door perched above a set of nail-starved stairs. The lanterns on either side were equally encrusted and disused. Robin slipped past Kaer Yin to take a closer look for himself. His iron stiletto once more slipped from his sleeve. He caught the lock before it fell. When the door creaked inward, he stuck his head in and looked around. He whispered over his shoulder, "Empty as a Kneeler's church."

Kaer Yin clapped him on the back, taking point. He drew a single lark and climbed into the moldy cellar first. Heaps of boxes, dusty crates, and assorted oddments filled the dingy chamber to the rafters. The only light came from a handful of barred, arched windows set at intervals in the brick exterior wall. They could hear the street traffic from the cobbles outside. The day rolled on, unaware of the handful of warriors and thieves busily spiriting their Duch's heir away, far beneath their feet.

He selected one with the tip of his blade. "That door, I presume?"

"Yeah." Robin mopped his brow with a sopping sleeve. "And up into the parlor from here. Across the hall to the other side, then to the sewer grate in the opposite wine cellar. The one way out, unseen."

Kaer Yin reached the door first and stretched his fingers toward the handle, but Rian caught his wrist. "Wait! You heard what Barb said about this place?"

"Greenmakers have been here before." Robin boasted from over her shoulder.

"Right. If you were invited to smuggle in goods, then I'd presume they'd keep it clear of clients and guests."

He stuck out his lower lip. "Well, yeah."

"Any way they'd mistake you for a guest, now?"

He fidgeted under her scrutiny, muddy face and all. "Probably not."

She shared a long, unspoken glance with Una, who relented after some hesitation. The pair retreated to a darker corner, each doffing garments from the muffled sounds they made. When they emerged again a few moments later, each wore the other's garb. Rian's fine linen tunic, and now dusty brown leggings had to be rolled up at the cuffs and cinched in at the waist. In Rian's case, she was thin enough to wear Una's gown but far too tall. In the dim, mottled light, it became apparent that the dress hugged curves no one had ever noticed Rian had.

Tam Lin picked invisible lint from a nonexistent cuff.

Kaer Yin rolled his eyes. "Why?"

"Because none of you can pass for someone who should be here, can you?"

Robin scratched the scar on his chin. "No, I 'spose not."

Kaer Yin noted Una's pinched expression.

He groaned, "It wasn't my idea this time. I swear."

"Right," she said dubiously. "I think the lot of you know more about brothels than anyone ought to."

Rather than answer, he jerked a thumb at Robin. "His plan."

Robin held up his hands beneath her imperious stare. "Barb's plan, actually."

Her face fell. "That's *loads* better, isn't it?"

"We should go," interrupted Tam Lin with a petulant scowl.

With a faint whimper, Rian bit her finger to produce a tiny spot of blood, which she smeared over her moon-pale cheekbones and across her lips. Once Una managed to unbraid and shake out her smooth, cornsilk hair, Rian looked very much like someone who might be employed upstairs. Hands on hips, Una took a step back to admire her work. "It'll do."

"I'll say," chuckled Robin appreciatively.

449

"Still look like a sallow guttersnipe, you ask me," snuffled Tam Lin.

Rian fixed him with a piercing blue eye. "You want another smack?"

He did not, insofar as far as Kaer Yin could tell.

"Barb said this place caters to a specific clientele," she said, making awkward progress toward the stairs. "Men that prefer their women a bit… odd."

"Rian, I think it might be better if—"Una attempted.

"No, it won't. It's you they're looking for. Robin?"

"Hm?" He stared openly. She ignored him.

"How far down the hall is the next door?"

"Four or five yards, give or take."

Inhaling and exhaling, she stood up as straight as she could. "Okay. Leave the door cracked and follow me when I wave. Ready?"

"Rian!" Una tried and failed to grab her wrist before Rian tottered through the door and into the gilded hall. Here, the floor shone a brilliantly polished grey marble, so dark it was nearly black. Red glass sconces adorned fine sateen wallpaper trimmed in gold thread. There were many heavy doors, and each was painted a glossy obsidian. The sconces between rooms were either lit, or the door lay wide open, beckoning occupants with its sumptuous, velveteen décor. The rooms with lit sconces were very much occupied.

Kaer Yin caught Rian's deeply embarrassed blush. He often forgot she was barely seventeen years old and had lived most of her life in deep seclusion. She'd never set foot in a slum before they met and certainly never a brothel.

He felt a bit bad right about then if he were honest.

He would have to wait his turn to worry over her, in any case. Una dashed ahead of him into the hall behind her. He muffled a curse. She stopped a few paces from Rian, waiting for her to crane her neck around the first turn. Rian waved them forward, her cheeks burning beneath her rudimentary rouge. Having passed the first of two adjoining halls, she approached the next with an audible breath. A hair before the last puddle of protective darkness in the distant corner, a door slammed open on the opposite side— the parlor, or so the most cursory glance confirmed. A servitor bore a tray piled high with delicate confections and tiny glasses of sweetly scented wine.

Rian flattened herself against the wall. As he passed, the servitor spouted hushed abuse at someone in the doorway behind him. He didn't see her. He then turned down the first hall, mumbling something under his breath. Rian met Kaer Yin's eyes over Una's head. He waved her on. Before she reached the next threshold, a couple burst through the parlor door, hands and mouths all over each other. As swiftly as they appeared, the couple disappeared into one of the empty rooms; its sconce suddenly bloomed red, lit from behind the closed door.

Kaer Yin knew a servitor would come and blow out the candle after a quarter-hour, though the mark would have paid for the entire hour: a simple trick to squeeze the local gentry of more coin. The savvy knew to bring their own or would demand to leave a servant in the hall. This customer was new to the game.

Robin sucked his teeth.

He and Kaer Yin shared the briefest of grins.

Una bloody saw, of course.

She whispered, "Rian, get moving before I murder this pair of ingrates."

Rian took a deep breath and peeled herself from the wall. She crept forward as quickly as she might, without making noise. She was near to the far side of the hall when a figure emerged from the parlor. Bleary-eyed with a drink that Kaer Yin could smell from nine paces and partially dressed, the fellow turned to retch into a potted plant near Rian's left elbow. She recoiled so fast that she half-tripped over her own feet. Wiping his mouth with the back of a mealy hand, the patron set a hand against the wall to steady himself. A slow smile broke over his mouth when his eyes finally fixed on her flushed face.

"Well, hello there," he belched. "That's a lovely, lovely dress."

Rian said nothing. She took a step backward.

With a burst of agility one might not expect from a fat, drunken sot like this, he reached out to grasp her wrist. He caught Una's, instead. Kaer Yin glared at her over the clod's head, his lark poised and ready to hamstring the bastard on the spot, but the light from within the parlor cast long shadows in the hall. She shook her head at him. Several people stood shy of that door. If the patron cried out, they'd be discovered, and their escape critically hampered.

Dry as parchment, Una broke in, "My Lady has another appointment. If you'll excuse us, milord?"

His clumsy hand slid over Una's left breast and squeezed. Una didn't move a muscle. Kaer Yin took a step forward. Again, she shook her head at him. "Oh, you're a piece!" tutted the patron. "Where's Janet been hiding you, love?" He did something to her that Kaer Yin couldn't see but vowed the fool had mere seconds to live if he persisted. The patron wrestled her around with a laugh. "It's novitiate today then? My favorite! There's an empty room over there. Why don't we see which of your holes is supposed to be fresh, hm?"

Kaer Yin had trouble keeping himself still.

While he'd no doubt they'd escape *The Butterfly* without much blood, the attention they'd bring to themselves might pour dozens of soldiers into the tunnels after them. He couldn't afford to risk everyone so soon. Robin placed a restraining hand on his shoulder; thus, he didn't see them move toward an unlighted doorway. The drunk menacingly leaned over her. "How about it?"

"By all means, lead the way," she replied flatly.

"You like it a bit rough, do you? Or do you prefer to do the hurting?" He rubbed her captive hand against the front of his breeches.

Rian failed to smother a gag.

"You know something," purred Una, as she maneuvered the patron through the open door, slipping her uncovered hand over his bulbous chin. "I absolutely *do*." An unseen force gripped his throat from the inside. Suddenly, he staggered sideways, clutching at his collar as his throat visibly caved in. She kicked him through the open door and gently closed the door behind him as he fell. Taking Rian by the hand, she tugged her along behind her toward the exit. "I've had enough of this place already. Kaer Yin?"

"Coming," he called after her, trying not to smile.

"What in the Hells was that?" demanded Tam Lin, horrified.

"I told ye she was scary," Robin said with a shrug.

"Dagda," Tam Lin breathed as he passed the door she had closed on their way down the hall. The patron gurgled slightly, on the other side. "I don't think I care much for the women of Tairngare, Master Gramble."

"I don't think *they* much care," hissed Rian, from the end of the hall.

Once they descended the stairs into the dry cellar, then latched and barricaded the door at their backs, Robin and Shar made short work of the sewer grate on the far side. Una wrinkled her nose at the noxious odors that swept into her face from its gaping maw.

"*Siora.* One nearly forgets how much fun our little adventures can be."

"Aye." Robin whistled to himself. "Something *has* died in this one, sure."

"No help for it, I'm afraid. Once they discover the gift Una has left for the proprietor, they'll search the place top to bottom," advocated Kaer Yin.

On cue, a riot of screams trilled overhead.

Una lifted a shoulder. "Too late."

As a group, they clambered from a storm drain sometime later, which spilled directly into the Lee on the Northeast end of the city wall. Sputtering and freezing, they shuffled up the riverbank one by one, seeking the minimal shelter of a small copse of trees. Rian, now in Una's uselessly thin gown, suffered the worst of the Dor Cromna air. There were small chips of ice stuck to her eyelashes and woven throughout her long damp hair. Shar removed his own cloak and spoke a few words over it. It dried as he placed it over her quaking shoulders. He moved on to Una next, who mumbled indecipherable gratitude into her collar.

"Now w- what?" Her teeth chattered, looking out over the eastern plains. She saw nothing but rolling hills and farmland for leagues into the Midlands.

"Gerry and the others are a few miles west, waiting with our horses. They left the city last night. I wanted them well out of sight," Kaer Yin said, strapping his swordbelt around his waist.

Tam Lin scrubbed cobwebs and ice from his own scalp with a colorful Sidhe curse. "Yin, this has been a grand escapade thus far, one I'm sure we'll enjoy the telling of for many centuries to come... but we should take the Shadow Path."

Kaer Yin gave him a long look. "We've discussed this. It's no place for Milesians, cousin." He tossed Una a dagger, which she carefully slipped into the knot of hair she'd tied to the crown of her head. He raised his brows.

"What? I don't have a belt or a pack, idiot," she sniped.

"I'd thought they'd made an elegant lady of you, at court?"

"I'll make one of you, if you don't shut your mouth."

"Gods," moaned Tam Lin, clearly having the worst time of his life. "Which bloody way, then?"

Robin clapped him on the back. His answering curse was slightly less banal than before. "Through this thicket here, then we swing east afore the next village. 'Bout ten miles, as the crow flies."

After retrieving something from his pack, Tam Lin passed the overlarge satchel to Niall and marched up to Rian, whose lips had gone blue, with a dark scowl.

"Here," he grumbled, holding out a pair of thoroughly extravagant fur-lined gloves. She stared at him like he had two heads. "Well, take them already. Consider them a peace offering."

Several uncomfortable moments later, she slipped them on and tucked both hands within the folds of her now dry cloak. Rather than thank him, she strode over to Una, who tied the girl's gaping cowl together beneath her chin and fastened it with a small hairpin. Appropriately swaddled, the pair followed Kaer Yin and Robin through the trees. Tam Lin and Niall took up the back, each eying the city walls behind them with equal parts derision and wariness.

Two hours of intermittent freezing rain and six miles later, riders appeared on a far hill, silhouetted against the distant haze of the setting sun. Tam Lin exchanged a knowing look with his lieutenant, who sheathed his larks for the dash ahead. "Yin," he boomed, as Niall ran past. "We've company."

Kaer Yin stopped to squint behind them. There were hundreds of them, heavy cavalry from the glint of steel at their helms.

He spat. "He's early, damn it." With a distant snap of spurs, the mass of dark shapes began to descend in a flawless, lethal vanguard. He cursed long and low under his breath. "We have no choice. We'll never outrun them in this."

"I won't say I told you so," quipped Tam Lin, without mirth.

"Still, we ought to try."

"What are you talking about?" Una's eyes widened at the distant threat.

"If followed, we meant to lead them into a trap, My Lady," replied Shar. "But your kin is remarkably determined."

"A trap? Are you mad? Did you imagine we could outrun my father's destriers for four straight miles?"

Kaer Yin's brow darkened. "We weren't supposed to. Though, if you hadn't killed that fat pervert in *The Butterfly*, it would have taken them a great deal longer to figure out which way we'd gone."

"You're saying this is my fault?"

"He didn't need to die, did he?"

"Not now, you two!" screeched Rian.

Una opened and closed her mouth like a fish. "I didn't ask you to come, did I?"

Kaer Yin bared his teeth. "I'll forget you said that… damn you."

"I won't." She crossed her arms.

Gods above and below, help me not to murder the woman I…

"Yin? You know what choice we face. They gain. I'd rather not die in a muddy Souther field today," prodded Tam Lin, interrupting his train of thought.

A call went out among the riders. They turned sharply west, as a flock of birds might. Kaer Yin knew what they were doing before it played out. Rather than allow their quarry to dash ahead any further, Damek's cavalry would arch westward then turn again to hammer them from the North, a pincer move, which would block their exit and encircle them. With the bulk of Tam Lin's forces only four miles out, Kaer Yin had no choice.

"Herne, bloody damn your infuriating family, Una."

He reached deep within himself, willing the earth roll away beneath their feet; the sky opened up around them. The air, static and pregnant with purpose, halted the blood in his veins and sucked the sound from his ears. Time swept over and through him, then drifted away.

He spoke the words.

Served Cold

N.E. 508
21, Dor Cromna
Tairngare

Grainne was displeased to see her, Aoife knew, but the fear in her eyes outweighed her aversion. Carn helped her from her saddle, watching the Fir Bolg princess advance upon their party. Aoife was exhausted and equally disinterested in anything Falan's sister might have to say. She'd been out riding and murdering in the High King's name for the better part of a month, thus couldn't care less what this spoilt bitch had to complain about. Grainne paused five paces from her, twisting her nose at Aoife's grooms. With a put-upon sigh, Aoife waved them away. Whatever this Mac Nemed fool wanted to say, she might as well get it out of the way in private. Aoife was hungry and meant to fuck Creahal until sleep finally claimed her. She preferred him to his brother, whose body worked miracles, but he had taken some fool notion of love into his head.

She had no time for such drivel.

"What? If you've come to order me back out, I'll have you know the work is all but done. You're welcome, by the way."

Grainne wrung her hands. "Nevermind that now. We have problems."

Aoife guffawed while she unlaced her tack. "What else is new?"

"Your attitude is unwarranted, girl."

"And your urgency is uninteresting. Step aside, *Highness*."

Grainne did not. Sweat dotted her burnished brow. That gave Aoife pause. Had the great Grainne Mac Nemed ever labored a day in her long, long life? What on earth could have the daughter of mighty Falan the Elder in such a lather?

"What?" she repeated.

Grainne appeared to struggle over the words. "It's my grandmother. She's… deviating."

"Deviating, how?"

Grainne craned her head around like the walls themselves had ears. Aoife knew, well enough, that they probably did. She inched closer, whispering, "She's broken with our lord."

Aoife snorted. "You'll have to work much harder than that, if you mean to make a traitor of me, cousin. I wasn't born a fool."

Grainne, growing ever more nervous, pulled Aoife below an awning, out of sight of the walls. "It's no ruse. I vow it, on Emain Macha." She placed a thumb over her heart. Instinctually, Aoife mirrored her. "She's had her minions in the Cloister draft a new gospel."

"Yes, that's to plan, is it not?"

"She makes no mention of the Ancestor's divine son… only the Queen Mother."

That was *not* to plan.

Aoife was silent for a few moments, mind racing. "She wouldn't."

"She *has*. Any who have dared to question her have been immolated, as you were. Two days ago, she filed a motion to have Siora's name stricken from all Patent of Maternas. In this absurd pantomime, you can imagine whose name is meant to take the Ancestor's place?"

That was… well. "She would never break with our lord for such a paltry platitude."

Grainne exhaled through her nose. "Many things I believe she'd never do, she has already done, and swiftly, I might add. The Fir Bolg who accompanied me into the Cloister have already been pressed into service or incarcerated. They won't even receive the benefit of a sham trial, I'm afraid. She's gone insane, Aoife. Drunk with power."

"Liadan Mac Nemed has never lacked for power, Grainne."

"She means to make herself a god. How else would you describe such behavior, except as madness?"

"What difference does it make if it's her or Falan we are meant to adore? Like grandmother, like grandson. Neither will be satisfied with one city to crush, and now that she's succeeded here, why should she hand it over? I don't care which of them means to rule here. They're two sides of the same hideous coin."

Aoife turned to leave but Grainne grasped her arm and squeezed, her eyes bright amethysts in the starkness of her thin face. She looked nearly… ill, like she had barely slept or eaten in days. There was hopelessness, anger, and terror in the directness of her gaze.

"He was here, you see, some weeks ago. He came to remind her whom she was meant to herald. Something changed in her that night, as if a dam was bursting. She will never bow to him, or anyone else again. I can feel it."

"Can't say I blame her, Grainne. Falan's always been a bit of a cunt, hasn't he? The single play he's ever made was to convince the world of his untimely demise in hopes of raising Innisfail against the High King from the shadows. Why not come at the Dannans directly, hm? Challenge Kaer Yin Adair for the throne?" Aoife giggled, wrenching her arm out of Grainne's bruising grip. "Because he knew he'd *lose*, that's why. All of this, every plan, every subterfuge, every murder and action— all of it— is built upon a precipice of ultimate failure. The only way the Mac Nemed's will rule again in Eire is to cheat. If Falan meant to turn the most powerful woman in the world into his faithful lapdog, one who not only birthed his line but also gave him the means and will to see it through— then more fool, he. If I were Liadan, I might have done the same thing."

Grainne drew in a breath. "Loyal even now, cousin? After everything she's done to you?"

"Oh, I hate her more than you ever will, princess. I don't care which of them takes power. Innisfail is in for a treat, whichever megalomaniacal beast is on the throne. Don't pretend we're suddenly allies just because old granny isn't playing by your rules anymore."

They stared each other down for half a millennium in a minute's passing. Grainne broke first, looking away with a huff. "I'm leaving, tonight. This is the last time I will extend my hand to you, Aoife Ap Sionnavar. Reject it now at your peril."

"Why do *you* support your brother, Grainne? What possible benefit is in it for you?"

Grainne's answering smile was cold and empty as a cavern. "You could never understand the importance of placing one's family above oneself, Aoife. You have none. You're as bereft of worth now as you've always been, *isasáeligh*. They should have strangled you in your crib, traitor that you are."

"As you're always so eager to point out, cousin— I'm no Mac Nemed. I don't give a shite what imaginary line you believe I should be toeing."

Grainne tugged her heavy cowl over her ears, leaving the burning derision of her violet glare. "Farewell, ungrateful wretch. When next we meet, I will have your skull polished and placed upon my mantle."

"Ooh," Aoife exaggerated a shiver. "I've been murdered many, many times, little princess… and here I stand. I wonder how long you'll hold up when it's your turn?"

With one last hateful smirk, Grainne took her leave. Once she was gone, Aoife allowed her grin to fade to a tight, concerned line. Carn appeared at her elbow like a faithful shadow. "If what she says is true, My Lady, I would fain encourage you to linger here. Her Dark Majesty will accept nothing less than your total subservience."

Aoife turned to wrap herself in his arms. His heartbeat tapped beneath her earlobe, warm, loyal, and wholly *hers*. She had planned to take his brother tonight as a reward for so many days and nights bathed in blood. But perhaps not? As soon as they were well clear of the city, she'd take them both, one at a time, or perhaps together? She pulled his head down for a lengthy, promising kiss. She could taste his love for her on his tongue—bloody fool.

"You are right, my love." She pressed her face into his neck. "I think someone else might appreciate us more."

"Your kinsman," he frowned, jealously. Poor soul. "He'll betray you again."

"If he lives so long," she smiled, running her nose against the drum of his pulse. He sighed. Men were so… easy. "You will protect me."

"We shall," declared his brother as he came up beside her, voice husky with caution and desire. Aoife recalled her youth spent in the half-light of the Oiche Ar Fad with these two as her sworn keepers. Until Liadan summoned her to Court, they'd been her favorite toys. So they would be again. She was a great-granddaughter of Falan the Elder, great-great-grandchild of the mighty Eochaid Mac Nemed, who'd wed the fearsome daughter of Balor and united the Clans. No man on Macha's green earth could resist the song in her blood, once bonded.

Well, save for those who shared it.

"Good," she hummed, accepting Carn's hand into her saddle. "We should leave before we're announced. My cousin will need my help, if he's to usurp this abhorrent family."

⚔

Basa blinked at the flickering candles in her path, as if she stared directly into the sun. Inside, she cringed away from the merciless, soul-snatching light— reviled it as deeply as any shadow shrinks from illumination. Once her eyes cleared, she recoiled from the shape that emerged from that blinding, limitless brightness. Garbed in saffron, Vanna Nema spared her a garish, red grin. She stood at the edge of her newly constructed balcony, the very one she'd graced to pass sentence on the nobles of Tairngare. Beneath them, the Grand Arcade was silent and still as an etching: a ghost of its former use, and majesty.

Basa leaned heavily against her escort, who stared at an invisible point above their Doma's head. Now that her eyes had regained their ability to focus, she noted, not a single individual on that balcony had the gall to glance at her terrible Magnificence directly. Well, save for Basa, of course. What could this overdressed, self-important gash do to her now? Her family was gone. Her daughter's shriveled fingerbones rested against her breastbone. Basa's wealth and privilege were figments from a past life. She was a shade that could not die, a husk without solace. No, Vanna Nema had nothing to gain from her now. She couldn't even toss out the odd word of defiance. Nema had taken that from her too. Voiceless, humorless, careless— she raised her chin and radiated everything she lacked. Nema waved a grey-robed Secunda over to offer Basa a chair. She took it without a struggle. What point would there be?

Basa could glare death and defiance just as easily on her arse.

"You've lost a deal of weight, Basa, dear."

Tongueless, Basa could but sneer in return.

"I don't think I've ever seen you so thin, old friend."

We were hardly friends, you interloping bitch, her expression read.

"Lily, would you please remove that horrid decoration from her neck? It's quite pungent," Nema sniffed in disdain.

Basa closed her fingers over Ana's desiccated flesh, with a determined jut of her fragile chin. She'd sooner die than part with it now. The Secunda made a half-hearted attempt but backed away when Basa's three good teeth latched upon her reaching arm. "Ow!" she cried, leaping away.

"Now, now, Basa. Don't you wish to be rid of that thing?"

I wish you'd fuck yourself with a Bethonair sabre.

"Well, so be it. If you prefer to carry her with you, I shall have a craftsman make an appropriate housing for you. Would that please you?"

Basa cocked her head in confusion.

"Oh," Nema said. "Forgive me, I should have explained my summons. You're to be reinstated, my dear, with certain… stipulations, of course. Foremost among these would be your appearance. We cannot allow our Altas to wander these vaunted halls in such a state, can we?"

Reinstated?

Horseshite.

There was a game here, as sure as the moon would rise in the east. Nema did nothing by halves. Besides, Basa would never serve this power-hungry witch, no matter what boon she might dangle from her manicured claws.

Might as well kill me, old girl.

I'd sooner eat my daughter's mummified flesh.

Nema accepted a cup from a second lickspittle. She took a long sip. "You know, it isn't like you to be such a sore loser, Basa. In your youth, you'd have disassembled this palace stone by stone with your teeth, for such slights as I have shown you. That beaten dog in your eyes disappoints me. Where's your fire? Your rage? That clever, unrelenting shrew I know so well? She would never have sat quietly in a cell for so long, waiting to die. Do you accept defeat so easily?"

The heat this statement inspired, crept through Basa's veins— a thousand flames licking through the remnants of her heart.

I would smash your mind to pieces with one touch, did I have the strength, Your Eminence.

Nema gave her a mocking pout. "Look how far the mighty have fallen, Basa. Once queen of the Cloister in all but name." She shook her head. "What a shame. So, shall that be your legacy? A lifetime of fear and intimidation, ending in abject failure?"

Basa was ready to die.

This harpy had taken everything of value. Yet…

Nema sensed her hesitation. "Not you, Basa. Not the woman who famously defied her enemy on her appointed execution day, who refused to break, even as her daughter perished before her. Why pretend that I have cowed you, lessened you? You are more than a hobbled old woman without a name to cling to, aren't you?"

Basa narrowed her eyes to slivers.

I will never *serve you, Vanna.*

Kill me, imprison me, break me… never.

Nema's sigh was absolute. She brushed a stray feather from her sleeve. "As long as I've lived among mortals, some of you never cease to surprise me. You're all short-sighted and pigheaded without the proper motivation. That's always been true. Though," her voice took on a whimsical quality. "In the rare few, that pigheadedness speaks of something more. Something finer. I shudder to use the term 'courage,' but there it is, all the same."

Mortals?

"Yes," replied Nema, as if she'd understood Basa perfectly. "You Milesians are brute creatures, full of spite, need, and fury. It's very rare to find one who isn't the sum of its parts. I'm complimenting you, Basa, for your sense of self."

Milesians?

"Once, I thought to create a kingdom here for my kin. To remake Innisfail as it had been, long before the Dannan *curraghs* rocked ashore and destroyed the world. Return it to the paradise it had been ruled strictly by women, in Macha's name. There were no kings then, did you know? No word for them, either. Even when my father rose to power, he was no king, rather…" She searched the air for the equitable term. "A consort. My mother was queen, you see. She ruled the Fomor with a soft, but unyielding fist. Balor was brought to her at Beltane for her First Night. I was the result. A queen with no rivals: granddaughter to mighty Macha, daughter of Maeve, sister to Mabh. The Morrigan, they called me— *'the thrice death.'* I would have ruled all of Innisfail, had Eber Finn not plagued our shores."

Basa did not move, for fear this madwoman would launch from her place by the railing and flap about her head like a bat. What lunacy was this?! The Morrigan? What did a death goddess of the Tuatha De Dannan have to do with this tyrannical upstart? She would have the impudence to insist Basa believe she was the Dowager Queen of Armagh?

Basa tried to scoff but found it difficult to do without a tongue.

"Ah, but that is precisely what I intend you believe, Basa Alvra… as it is— and has always been— quite true."

It took a moment for the realization to sink in. Vanna *was* reading her thoughts! Shocked, Basa lumbered to her feet, breathing hard. Vanna's Manipulation exhibited through mind manipulation? No wonder! No bloody *wonder*. No amount of scheming had ever come close to diminishing Drem Moura's fiercest rival, not even Basa Alvra who once could crush an object with her will alone. Nema had known for *forty* years what she was working toward and how she would manage it. She'd used their own plans against them, the while.

Nema patted Basa's empty chair. "I suppose, in a crude way, you're correct. Although, I don't believe my grandmother would have denigrated our gifts with such a simplistic term. Your Siora never labeled her talents in this way. One of your Domas decided this distinction, if I recall. Many, many years before Tairngare ever incorporated. I believe I was mystified by the arrogance, whence first I heard it. As if you could boil such an art to its most fundamental element. Siora knew better. She was blood of my line, after all."

Basa sank into her chair like a brick. Her heart pounded against her ribs, like a captive sparrow.

You're telling me the truth… Vanna?

"I've never understood why none of you smart women ever put the core of my name together. 'Woman from nowhere' is fairly self-explanatory, I find. Especially for you, Basa. You studied Linguistics at the Libellum," she tsked. Had her teeth always been so white, so perfectly formed— did the green of her eyes always sparkle like a forest spring in sunlight? Basa clasped her hands together to keep them steady.

It cannot be.

"Can it not? Mortals used to say the same, before the Transition. You would have been appalled by the world at that time, Basa." She wrinkled her nose. "Great stinking machines rolled over every beautiful hill and dale, gorged themselves upon the earth and her minerals. Feasted upon our sacred trees and animals, spewed filth into the rivers and seas. It was a Hellscape of steel, rabid overpopulation, social decay, and decadence. Even from the confines of the Oiche Ar Fad, the bleakness of that world, the emptiness… I cannot accurately describe its horrors. Left unchecked, your kind will breed and breed, crave, demand, and plunder yourselves into extinction. You Milesians are a plague upon this realm, and always have been. That is not to say, however, that you do not have your uses— in strict moderation, of course."

She paused to observe Basa's thunderstruck features.

"Women, as it happens, bear your species' singular worth. Once you wrest control of your tribes away from greedy, selfish, warmongering males, there's promise for your race. That's why I chose you, chose Tairngare, the sole bright spot in Innish history, since the Fomor ruled this land. Through women, the natural order is restored. Men make much noise about being the more rational sex, yet in three millennia, I've never seen evidence to prove this. Rather, the opposite. They expend every effort to dominate and subjugate women as the 'lesser' creature, when it is quite the reverse. Siora's Acolytes prove this false, do they not? For only women may bear the power to rule the world."

Basa cleared her mind of all riotous thoughts, save one.

What do you want, Vanna?

Those swirling green eyes rested on her face for a long, breathless moment. "I want Tairngare to replace Bri Leith as capital of the civilized world, Basa. I mean to enslave all males on this Continent to our will, as it should always have been. I intend to break the cycle of war and conflict, of aggressive male dominance. The promise of Tairngare, which I've helped to foster these many decades, is peace, harmony, and women in their proper place. Help me. Help me build this world, this new Innisfail."

You murdered my daughter, my family, my friends, and servants.

Why you imagine you could enlist my aid now… you've gone mad, Vanna.

"Eva and Una are alive. Your line is not yet spent."

Basa unfurled her hands. Her eyes stung with tears she refused to shed. She knew her relief would be a tool Vanna would use to enlist her power and remaining influence with the Tairngare's disparate nobility.

"Of course I will," Vanna rejoined. "Why do you suppose you're still alive, after the trouble you and your family have caused me? A bent, broken old woman you may be, but your name means something to those who yet defy me. Your obeisance to the cause will bring a hundred thousand to the fold: an army of holy warriors, ready and willing to wipe the land clean of taint, and remake it anew."

With you on the sole throne: a living god.

Vanna gave a demure smile. "A vulgar misrepresentation of the greater good."

Greater good? Basa grunted.

You murdered the best Manipulators in the city, dismantled Parliament, scourged the Treasury, executed Judges, Merchers, Primas, and Altas who might ever challenge you. You say you did all this to vaunt Tairngare and her women? To make us the center of the world. What bollocks! You did this to elevate yourself, to make Vanna Nema the next High Queen. You hope to erase anything or anyone who stands in your way— and good luck! You've done your job so well, you're pandering your dreams of domination to an enemy, because you've run through all your allies. Isn't that right?

Vanna absorbed her unspoken speech with a faint tick in her upper right cheek. A gull called overhead, trilling like a scream.

Basa squinted at her. Beneath that ageless beauty were cracks in the veneer. Her lips were thin and dry as paper, nails dull and bloodless as glass. Faint lines hugged the curve of each eye, so fine, they were scarcely noticeable, but plentiful enough to suggest an ancient and endangered sort of porcelain. Her strength and power pulsed from her narrow frame, as a beacon on a far shore, yet, looking at her now— really looking— Basa knew her age, her fatigue, and fear.

You're dying, aren't you?

Nema didn't reply, which was answer enough.

Basa crossed her shaking arms.

How long have you got?

"Eons, years, weeks. Who knows?"

I didn't think your kind could die.

"A common misconception. It is the Oiche Ar Fad that sustains immortality. Without its benefit, our cells age and die, as yours do. The process is much slower… but ultimate, nonetheless."

Then, all of this— Basa waved a hand, encompassing all.

Was to cement your legacy? That must be a bad joke? You've murdered half of Tairngare and enslaved the other half to give yourself a last chance at immortality.

Why not return to the shadows, and leave us be?

"I cannot. I am no longer able to survive there, as you could not. It is not a place for… mortals."

Basa sat back, mystified.

Vanna went on, "With the time I've left, I mean to cure the world of the masculine plague. Return our tribes to their divine roots— in Macha's name. Help me do this, Basa. Together, we can bring a real, lasting peace to this continent, forever."

Tea, please.

Vanna glanced at her nearest servant. The girl launched herself at the larder so fast, Basa felt sure she would trip. With a trembling wrist, she handed her former Alta Prima a steaming cup of something rich and dark. It smelled faintly of Bretagn chocolate. Basa held it for a while, waiting for it to cool.

You knew I'd say no when I was brought here.

Tell me, what trick do you have in that sleeve, to force my hand?

"None. As you said, I have nothing left to barter with where you're concerned. I've taken from you and shall not beg forgiveness for that fact. Here, I hoped to appeal to you as a rational patriot, who loves Tairngare enough to help me save it."

Eva and Una?

"I see no reason why Eva ever need suffer her family's fate, if you join me. Una, on the other hand, must not be allowed to thrive. The girl will die."

Ah, we're getting to the point.

"How do you mean?"

When you say her name, I hear fear, Vanna.

She can stop you, can't she?

Vanna's lip curled. "She's an abomination, Basa. She should not exist. If Drem hadn't been so greedy for power, so eager to scar her mind and body to produce this 'prophesied child,' Una would never have been born to tip the balance. I might never have been forced to accelerate my plans to such an unfortunate degree."

So, she is Siora's heir? My young, bookish niece, who'd rather flee than rule this land as she was born to?

This girl is the reason you've lain waste to Tairngare?

"She too, is of my line, Basa. In case you haven't figured that out already. She was never meant to be born, never meant to carry such horrible power. If she rises to the throne of this land, many thousands will die. The ice will descend and bury us all. My grandson was meant to take the High King's throne, to lead us through the next Transition, but he has strayed from his path, as all men are wont to do. He fancies himself Midhir's equal, and my superior." She blew a long breath out of her nostrils. "Even he shall be lain low. If balance is not restored to this land, nothing shall survive— no one. The future of both our races is in question, my dear. I seek allies with the capacity to grasp an inconvenient truth, and the will to do what needs to be done to prevent calamity."

Una will destroy the world?

"If she takes power, Milesians will once again dominate Innisfail. You were not alive during the Transition, Basa. You did not see what these mortals did to each other, to the land, to *all* lands, in their desperation and stupidity. With my last breath, I will fight to prevent it happening all over again."

Basa sipped her tea, studying Vanna blankly. Her thoughts summoned and fixated on the sound of the bells dangling from her own balcony on the Ninth Floor, her home for four decades. She loved those bells and had always been soothed by them. Ana had grown laying beneath them reading, laughing, while she basked in the sun or stared out to sea. Basa ran her finger over her daughter's shriveled hand.

She set her cup down on the stone floor beside her chair. Inside her heart, she felt what was left of her Spark leap at her touch.

Perhaps she could help? Perhaps she *would*.

Vanna's narrow lips pulled back over a genuine smile. "I am pleased you are the reasonable woman I always thought you were."

Basa resumed her pleasant mien, filled with renewed vigor. Her gums vibrated with it. She didn't bother to stand; she'd have that much farther to fall, and if she were to do this, she'd do it with dignity. She clenched an arthritic fist, summoning every ounce of strength she had left. Vanna's eyes flew wide, a hair too late. From the core of each of Basa's cells, she unfurled her Spark. It flew from her as an arrow, lancing her enemy through the black chasm of her heart. Vanna's cup shattered against the tiles. She dropped to her knees, shrieking as her cheeks were torn open, divided from the inside by Basa's Spark. Next, her forehead, chest, and throat. A red line carved itself across Nema's neck.

Here is my answer, Vanna Nema, or whoever you truly are.

I curse you with failure at every turn.

You take from us today, steal from us tomorrow, and kill us at a whim— but that is all you will ever achieve.

Your descent is nigh, and it will be as swift and merciless as your rise… you villainous, lunatic cunt.

Basa had the extreme pleasure to watch Nema's pretty face open in widening gashes, hear her pitiful screams, before her Spark burned out. Empty of all but a lingering sense of joy at joining her beloved Ana in the Undying Lands, Basa grinned before she slumped from her chair and her head struck the ground.

Falling Star

Time and space stretched long and wide, popping his ears and stilling the blood in his veins. Beside him, Una lurched against him, unsteady as a reed. Rian gave a slight whimper as she, too, was nearly swept from her feet. Kaer Yin grasped Una's shoulders, pressing her heels into the earth. Suddenly, the group was alone in an ocean of gleaming grass beneath a sweet, summer wind. The air was ripe and fragrant as honey. A low-slung sun trailed over the whispering treetops ahead while the moon chased her from the twilit fields to the west. Bright stars glistened at either end of that rose and violet sky. Gone was the winter chewed Souther field. Their pursuers' whistles and spurs were snuffed out in a moment. Taking a deep breath, Una slid her hands over her knees.

"I can guess where we are, by how badly I want to puke."

Kaer Yin patted her back, feeling like the captain of a sinking ship. "More fun than the alternative, I'm afraid."

"Thank you, Yin," hooted Tam Lin, breathing a mite hard from all the running they'd been doing for the last few hours. "I was starting to get a stitch in my side."

"Have Shar find the others." Kaer Yin held his nose and blew out to clear his ears. It had been many, many years since he'd been in the Oiche Ar Fad. He'd all but forgotten how disorienting the shift could be.

Tam Lin waved his order away. "No bother. They'll find us. Fergal will have heard the bell. That was rather inelegantly done, cousin."

"I'm out of practice."

Shar held his ribs, sides heaving. He pawed at a tree for support. "I'll say."

Kaer Yin made a face at both of them. Robin spun around and retched into the grass. Ignoring him, Kaer Yin turned to check on Rian. She had color in her cheeks already. "We've been here before, Una and I."

"So, you have," he acknowledged. "Recently, too."

Una, also, perked up faster than everyone else. She wiped a hand over her nose and squared her shoulders. "Well, where to now?"

"Tir Falias," he sighed. "Not much choice."

"Where the hell is that?"

"Tech Duinn."

She paled. "Are you mad?"

"Do you want to go back?"

"No, I…" she searched Rian's face for affirmation.

The girl couldn't help.

Kaer Yin wasn't sure what exactly had occurred in that cabin on Samhain, but whatever had been, its recollection altered Una's entire demeanor. He watched as she seemed to deflate before his eyes.

"What did he do to you, Una?"

"He tried to— well, it isn't really what he did, rather what I…"

Her explanation trailed off, just as a flash of pealing light trailed across the sky like a falling star. The sound, like a balloon being filled and summarily popped by a large pin, made each person in their party flinch and cover their ears.

"Bloody Hells," grumbled Robin. "What was that?"

"A rider," Shar told him, green eyes on the horizon. He pointed. "There."

Indeed, a lathered warhorse perched against the terminally setting sun.

Kaer Yin clutched his pommel. "Son of a bitch."

"He's alone, at least," Tam Lin noted. "Even if I've no idea how he got here."

"I bloody well do."

"Well, grand. He's on his way over."

"Let him come."

Damek Bishop kicked his horse into a charge. As he neared, the hard determination in his eyes shone bright. Una made a move to shove to the front of the Greenmakers, but Kaer Yin elbowed her back. He drew his dagger and waited. If this arrogant, obsessive child wanted to play, by Herne, the Lord of the Wild Hunt was ready. Two months of unspeakable pain from wounds that had yet to fully heal, countless sleepless nights worrying over the fate of those he cared for, hours of discomfort and cold— low on uishge and ale— wondering what this poncey, overdressed fop was doing to Una... All of this broke over him like a fever.

"Ben, no!" cried Rian, but Kaer Yin couldn't care less.

He wanted this.

He'd wanted this since Samhain, the moment Bishop rode away with the woman he loved over his saddle, like a prized doe. Kaer Yin widened his stance. Nemain's pommel brushed his waiting fingertips.

Come on, you fool.

Come and die.

As Bishop neared, Una shouted, "Damek, no!" Ignoring her incredulous plea, he launched himself from his saddle mid-gallop, taking Kaer Yin to the ground with him. They rolled sideways, each pelting the other with bone-jarring blows. At first, Damek had the upper hand. He drove an elbow into Kaer Yin's jaw that set his ears ringing anew, but Kaer Yin grabbed the back of the young lord's head by the scruff and bashed his forehead into his nose. Damek skittered back onto his knees, coughing blood into his palms. Kaer Yin rocked to his feet, flicking the tip of his dagger toward his opponent's ear. Hissing in pain, Damek staggered to his feet, fumbling at his belt for the same weapon. Kaer Yin didn't give him too much time to recover. He drove him back toward his charger, which was much more unsettled by their surroundings than was his master. With a grunt, Damek dug his heels in, ducking under two of Kaer Yin's quick-stop thrusts. At the third, however, Damek managed to hook an arm around Kaer Yin's shoulders and slam his fist deep into the Crown Prince's right eye, before kicking him roundly in the chest.

Kaer Yin backed off, if only to breathe through the fresh fury that surged through his nerves with the pain. Glaring at Bethany's beloved Lord Bishop, he slid his fingers over Nemain's pommel. Four eager Sidhe took their places behind their prince, larks raised.

Damek choked out a dry laugh, drawing his sabre and using it to point at Tam Lin. "I knew, if that really is the Prince of Connaught, there was no way you'd have missed the chance to press your luck. Glad you could make it, Prince Adair. Truly. There's so much I didn't get to say, last time."

"Damek, please stop. Go back," pleaded Una, genuine sorrow in her voice.

Damek's facial muscles twitched at her voice; otherwise, he kept his full attention on the Prince of Innisfail. That was as well. Kaer Yin wanted things simple. He cracked his knuckles. "You heard her. Go home, boy."

"You know, I saw you once, at Dumnain—*from* a distance, of course. The way the old men whispered fear of you, you might have been some kind of god."

"I am no god," observed Kaer Yin, wiping blood from his own mouth.

"Obviously. Gods don't bleed, do they?" Damek flexed his fingers over his hilt, eyeing Kaer Yin carefully. "Give her back."

"I am not her keeper, and you are not her jailer."

Silence stretched between them.

"How did he get here, anyway?" Tam Lin asked, aside.

"His father," Una told him. "He was like you."

Tam Lin recoiled. "Ugh, *another* faerie?"

Rian shot O'Ruiadh a look that should have boiled his tongue from his skull. He quickly shut his mouth with an audible snap of his jaws.

"He looks a bit too human if you ask me," ruminated Shar.

Damek ignored them all, his focus on Kaer Yin. "Fight me for her, then."

Una groaned, "Damek, go home!"

Finally, he met her eyes. Watching them both carefully, what Kaer Yin saw in her returned gaze burned. Deep, complex feelings were not something he hoped to witness in her expression, but there they were, all the same.

"Not without you," Damek promised her. He unbuttoned his doublet very casually, as if fear were the furthest emotion from his mind.

Kaer Yin's smile was forced. "I won't mind killing you, Bishop, but I think someone here would rather not have your death on their conscience. Last chance."

Damek flung his doublet and cloak away, brandishing his sabre with a flourish. "I'll pass. Shall we?"

"Kaer Yin," Una said softly. "He's blood. Please, don't—"

"I'll try," he heaved a heavy sigh. Truthfully, he wished no one was in that meadow save for him and Bishop. Then, he'd have the pleasure of bleeding the arrogant little prick, drop by drop.

"He couldn't," boasted Damek. "No need to worry, Una. We've fought before, you see. I know his footwork by rote. Tell your men to stay out of it, Adair."

Tam Lin said, "Boy, if you manage to land a single blow, I'll congratulate you by taking each of your grubby hands off at the wrists.

"*Tam Lin, tóg na cailíní agus lean ort. Gabhfaidh mé suas?*"[21] asked Kaer Yin.

"*Ithe cac, col ceathrar,*"[22] Tam Lin declined.

"I'll catch up."

"I said no, you grimy blighter."

Kaer Yin wasn't granted freedom to argue. Damek rushed him, and it seemed he was everywhere at once. Kaer Yin dodged, parried, rolled, and leapt under, over, and around each thrust— but the attacks wouldn't stop coming and were much, much more skillful than they should have been. *Neithana.* Not only did the Lord Bishop know how to handle a longsword, he did so in pure Sidhe fashion. Someone had taught this young man to fight like one of Kaer Yin's own. Someone good. He'd sparred with this man a mere two months previously, and already, his skills had raced so far ahead.

How? Where in the *Hells* did Bishop learn to fight like this?

"Herne," avowed Tam Lin, mouth agape. "That's—"

"I know!" Kaer Yin broke out in a real sweat, busy putting every effort into defending his vitals for each eyeblink it took for Bishop to attack.

"Stop dancing around and fight back!" Damek jibed, leaning right to swat Nemain's tip away with the flat of his blade. A heartbeat later, his knuckles crashed into Kaer Yin's nose. Kaer Yin staggered a few paces, leaning against Nemain to catch a break. Through the red haze in eyes, he barely marked the meadow, the group, or the sword in his own hand. All he could see was the triumphant smirk on the Lord of Clare's petulant mouth.

"You've done it now, lad. I hope you feel good about your chances," called Tam Lin, knowing very well what that look meant.

"That's a dead fellow, or I'm buggered," whistled Robin.

"Good! Come on!" Damek roared.

Kaer Yin Adair answered.

⚚ ⚚

---

[21] "Tam Lin, take the girls and go ahead."
[22] "Eat shite, cousin."

HE CAME.

Damek, now on the defensive, was in awe of the speed, calculation, and brutal grace the Prince of Innisfail forced into every stroke. His footwork was intricately, inhumanly precise, and maddening. Damek considered himself a master of every sword form he could study. In fact, he'd always had such an affinity for steel, he could garner a fair understanding of each discipline after one or two bouts. His father had told him his talent was a gift of his blood, but Damek didn't care about the particulars. He knew he wasn't merely good: he was excellent and knowing it didn't encourage false humility. He had an intuition, an aptitude that most swordsmen could never hope to match.

Though, in the Prince of Innisfail's case, Damek could but marvel. For the second time, he realized there had never lived a man more skilled with a sword.

Neithana, as with all other styles Damek had studied, bore a specific formula. Once he mastered the complex foundation, from there it was only a matter of time before the art came to him as naturally as breathing. Neithana, all said, took lifetimes to properly conquer. Watching Kaer Yin move, feeling the power behind each stroke, he finally understood. Even after having fought the prince once before in the wilds of Northern Eire, he'd never seen such measured skill in his life. Not even Damek's father had it, and he had once been lauded as the greatest swordsman in Armagh.

It wasn't simply the fluidity, the practiced motion without thought that shocked him most, rather the complete dissolution of self that all sword masters speak of, and none have ever achieved. To become the blade itself, to merge with it as an extension of one's own will— *that* is what made Kaer Yin a peerless opponent.

In two minutes, Damek was already sweating heavily and taking hacking breaths that sounded terribly reminiscent of an old man attempting a sprint. With a grunt that cost him something deep in his gut, he lurched away, putting a fair distance between the prince and himself. The bastard didn't even appear winded. "Damn!" He couldn't help but laugh. Kaer Yin didn't seem to share his amusement. His silver eyes gleamed like ice chips in a storm. "They weren't kidding when they said you were the best Dannan swordsman alive." This was a genuine compliment.

Tam Lin snickered from the sideline.

Robin scratched at his scar. "Best leave it at that, yer lordship. I've seen him cut through scores o'fellas with that face on him. I'd get on, were I ye."

Damek shrugged. "Let's try a different tack." He slid his feet toward the opposite position: one foot slipping forward, the other behind.

He lifted his sabre into a high guard.

⚸⚸

"GODSDAMNIT," MUTTERED TAM LIN.

"Adrac," Shar concurred.

"What's that?" Una asked, lost.

"Armagh's private discipline," he replied. "Fir Bolg stuff, very complicated."

"That explains a great deal. Yin," bellowed Tam Lin. "You'd better quit messing about and kill that faerie cunt. He's a fucking Mac Nemed!"

"I knew that already," Kaer Yin snapped. "Stop distracting me."

Tam Lin threw up his hands.

⚸⚸

"YOU READY?"

Damek grinned. He was having the time of his life, regardless of the outcome. If he died fighting the greatest swordsman in the world, he couldn't think of a better ending. If, however, he won… He launched himself again, giving everything he had.

⚸⚸

465

Adrac lacked the sinuous beauty of Neithana, but made up for form with function, patience, and kinetic power. Neithana was clean, hard to follow with the eyes, and always presented a moving target. Adrac was the opposite. Using the inertia of an opponent against itself, it took lethal advantage of any gaps in one's endurance.

Damek Bishop was good. Again, far too damned good.

Even a faerie lad who'd embraced his Sidhe heritage would scarcely have the time and training to achieve such skill in this discipline— *let* alone, the permission to do so at the behest of the Mac Nemed Clan. Yet, Kaer Yin sensed no magic in his talents. They simply... were. It seemed the boy had a gift. He must be the first true prodigy Kaer Yin had ever encountered. He was too good to be just anyone's son. Once, many, many years ago… Kaer Yin fought a man who very nearly carved his heart out in a drunken duel. That man, as it happened, was to die on the battlefield at Dumnain, decades later. There wasn't a shred of doubt in Kaer Yin's mind who this boy's father might be. Again, Damek had him on the defensive, pressing his advantage of surprise. When Kaer Yin redoubled his efforts by attempting to make a steel wall, Damek took a low guard, sweeping up from the ground and leaping around Kaer Yin to jerk Nemain's tip backward. That opened up a vicious gash in Kaer Yin's right arm.

"There went your hands, Lord Bishop!" sang Tam Lin, with honest concern.

He'd never seen his cousin lose a bout before— *especially* to a faerie Souther who fought for the likes of Patrick Donahugh. Kaer Yin shot him a glare. Well, he wasn't about to see it happen now, either. The good Lord Bishop had a flaw in his footwork… and when he'd come in too close once before, Kaer Yin saw the ogham stone sticking out of Damek's damp tunic.

No wonder the lad had been able to chase them into the Oiche Ar Fad so effortlessly. He had a bloody key.

Oblivious, Damek glowed with martial fervor. He moved back into a high guard, as if winding a clock. "Are we done playing now, Highness?"

Kaer Yin flashed Una an apologetic glance.

"Yes." He moved, dogging every step Damek took, swallowing up every space he'd meant to slide into. Before he could fix his heels, Kaer Yin pushed him back. Again, and again Kaer Yin pressed him this way, until Damek faltered a bit on advance, temporarily stymied by the speed with which his adversary attacked. When Damek reared left to get under his elbow, Kaer Yin suddenly turned, leaning in to clutch Damek's sword arm from below. A single vicious jerk, and Bishop cried out, dropping his sword. Then for the second time, Kaer Yin's forehead smashed into Bishop's nose, then he hefted him by the collar and threw him bodily over his own shoulder. Damek struck the earth with a dry thud.

He howled in pain and, no doubt, rage.

A broken arm and nose will do that to a man.

Kaer Yin kicked Damek's sword away from his grasping fingers, and knelt beside him, leaning against Nemain for support.

"Don't," Una repeated, from somewhere behind him.

Kaer Yin exhaled long and hard. "Do you hear that, Lord Marshal? Una alone kept you alive today. Perhaps you'll remember that when next you decide to take a woman against her will." With that, he reached into Damek's tunic and ripped the *ogham* stone away, as if from a naughty child.

Only when Bishop disappeared from the meadow altogether did Kaer Yin meet Una's eyes. She knelt before him, tucking herself into his arms. She didn't speak a word— she didn't need to.

He understood.

Over Una's head, he looked up at Tam Lin, his arm burning like someone had stuffed his skin full of nettles. "That was a lot fucking harder than it should have been." He turned the *ogham* stone over in his free hand, as if spinning an entirely new threat in his mind.

LATER, WHEN THEY WERE PACKED and ready to meet the others some miles hence, Kaer Yin pulled Una aside. He knew what he had to do, though he had no desire to do it. If he didn't say it now, he never would.

"Una," he began, hesitating. "Where do you want to go? Truly?"

Her brow gathered. "I thought—"

"No. That's what *I* wanted, why I came here. I hoped… well, it doesn't matter now. I don't need to know what I want: I want to know what you do."

She stared off at the distant treetops waving in the mild summer wind. Her eyes were bright with tears, though they did not fall. "I want to make up my own mind. I want to live my own life, be my own woman. I want to be free."

His heart clenched. "That's what I thought. I can— I will take you anywhere you want to go, Una. Alba, Bretagne, Kernow, Hells, I'll even take you to Iberia, if you're feeling adventurous. Wherever you want to go, whoever you want to be, I'll give it to you. I want you to be happy. You deserve to be."

He let her fingers go; resolved, even if it killed him.

"You know," her voice broke. "My grandmother always says freedom is a choice you make every day. I never really understood that till right now."

"I don't follow."

"I *am* free, Kaer Yin. Finally, free to choose for myself."

He felt like drinking himself dead, right about then. "So, what do you choose?"

"You're really stupid, you know that?" Her hand slid over his cheek. She pulled him in so close, her nose brushed against his. He flinched— bloody hurt for the number of times he'd recently taken a punch— but didn't budge. "This is freedom, Kaer Yin. Freedom to follow my heart."

When her lips met his, this time, he didn't allow her to dart away.

Blood Magic

Melba was unceremoniously dragged through a garish room decorated in silver plate and ugly red gemstones. The room stank of incense and mold, and something sweeter— bolder, which left a sour taste at the back of her throat. She gagged. Before she could locate the source of the rot, she was thrown to the floor by a dark-haired man who was obviously Sidhe and seemed too large for the space. It took several seconds to gain her bearings, and a sharp boot to force her to her knees.

Her guard backed off after a last brutal kick for good measure.

After several sucking breaths, Melba could focus on her own filthy hands against the expensive silk carpet beneath her. She couldn't help but flinch. This was the first time she'd been outside of her cell in weeks. Had it been so long that her skin should look like the shrunken husk of a fish's belly? She imagined she must smell even worse, though with the pervading scent of decay so prominent a feature in this enclosed space, her hygiene might be of least concern. She pushed herself upright, eyes level with a broad, walnut desk. Flinching a bit in the invasive lanternlight from the far corner of its smooth surface, she didn't see the shriveled occupant of the room until she caught a haggard reflection in the polished wood.

Melba recoiled.

Nema? But how?

The figure cackled, drawing Melba's gaze to the real thing above.

The sight was startling, to say the least.

Though there was no discounting the identity of the individual seated behind that desk, her appearance was far removed from the face that haunted Melba's dreams. Where once Nema had been stately, regal, and quite handsome to look upon, now she was painfully thin and overly pale. Her eyes had shrunken into her skull and her once beautiful ochre skin sagged from her bones. Though, this was not the worst of it. A jagged gash had opened the tissues of her face from her right eyebrow to the line of her throat. Melba could plainly see through the torn skin, yellow fat, and shiny muscle, to Nema's browning teeth.

Melba felt her airways constrict.

How long have I been imprisoned?

"Not long," answered Nema, as if she had plucked the thought directly from Melba's mind. "Have you had time to rethink your hasty words, Melba my dear?"

Melba had read about a serpent once that would issue a rattle when it prepared to strike. The rasping quality of Nema's voice reminded her of this now. She cleared her dry, dusty throat. "Yes. I have, Eminence."

Nema's smile was a horror that turned Melba's empty stomach. "Excellent. Then you will sign and merge Alba's interests with our own?"

"I will," Melba replied, and hated herself. Truth be told, strong though she might have been, she had not prepared herself for internment. Confinement and darkness had done unspeakable things to her mind. She would readily admit that she would sign away her own children at that point, if to be spared that long, cold, dark a second time. "Gladly."

Nema waved a withered hand and Melba felt herself shoved into the desk. The guard laid a scrap of vellum before her, and a sharp quill was crammed into her shaking fist. She didn't even care to read it. With tears in her eyes, she clenched her teeth and signed her country away. Before she might recant her decision, the document jerked away, even as her ink was wet on the page.

Not everyone is a mountain, she told herself.

Siora will forgive me.

Nema's laugh felt like a lash against her skin. "Not likely. You see, Siora was a bit of a fanatic about these things. I should know. I made her."

Melba's embattled heart raced anew. "You can read my mind?"

Nema shrugged. "Most times. Some people broadcast more loudly than others. Your thoughts are like a shout underwater, but I can gather the gist."

Melba opted to remain silent and stifle her thoughts. They might betray her. Nema drew her heavy fur stole more tightly around her shoulders. The room was too small to accommodate braziers and was therefore quite cold. "Have you any requests for me, now that you've seen the proverbial light?"

Melba didn't hesitate. "I want to go home."

"Perhaps something less... demonstrative?"

Silence stretched between them, and Melba let out a breath. "I've done as ye asked. You have no further opposition from Alba, Eminence."

"Nor will I again, Mistress." The macabre grin alarmed Melba once more. "You see, I can't have you returning to power with that troublesome family of yours. You'd make a poor influence and would surely convince yourself and others that this concession was made under duress."

Some of Melba's old fire leapt in her belly. "It *has* been made under duress, Eminence. Ye killed my men and imprisoned me for daring to debate yer terms. To pretend otherwise would be disingenuous."

"Hm." Nema grinned again. "If only your hand bore the same courage as your mouth, no?"

Melba shrank into herself.

Equal parts rising panic and boiling fury commingled in her breast.

You're going to die.

Do something!

"Alba will rise against ye, with me or without me. If ye spare me now, I vow to plead yer case to my people and vote to uphold yer interests."

Nema ignored her comment and nodded to the tall guard behind Melba. "Bring her to me, Raes."

Melba was allowed a momentary breath of perfect fear before she was wrenched to her feet then forcibly prostrated before Nema. She struggled against her captor, to little effect. He delivered a blow to her left ear that made the room spin around her, Nema's glowing green eyes loomed at the edge of her spinning vision. A scream built deep in her chest.

"There now," Nema said, reaching out and digging her sharp nails into Melba's delicate collarbone. The bones beneath that hand trembled with some unknown current. Instantly, Melba felt the oxygen whisk from her lungs.

What is happening?

To her rising horror, Melba watched the flesh around Nema's damaged cheek begin to stitch itself together, and the hollows of her eye sockets fill with sudden vigor. Simultaneously, Melba felt her body crumple beneath Nema's hand. Her muscles collapsed while her veins drained of fluid. Her throat closed up when no blood or water was left to hold its passages open. She felt her eyes wither in their sockets, and she let out a pathetic gurgle that should have been a scream.

She's eating me!

"That's a crude way to put it, Melba dear," purred Nema in Melba's weakening ears. "I like to think of it as a 'repurposing' of useless organic material. Sounds much more elegant that way, don't you think?"

THE CHILDREN OF DANU

THE INNISFAIL CYCLE:
BOOK THREE

THE NIGHT PATH

n.e. ʃ08
ðor cromna
oiche ar faд

The light was the worst of it. A hazy sun spun aimlessly through a rose and violet sky, incandescent as backlit crystal and maddening in its course. Its warmth felt surreal as its path, at once warm and chill, neither waxing nor waning. As they walked, Una couldn't decide if she were over or underdressed. The cold sweat dappling the back of her neck made her shiver in the half-summer breeze. For that was the root of the Oiche Ar Fad, no? The contradiction. They strolled through late spring into early summer, billeted by winds, scents, and smells from the opposite horizon. She turned her head rather than stare into that dizzying kaleidoscope in the distance. Brilliant white stars swirled through a sliver of infinite dark as if the nighttime sky shied from the weak sunlight but inched forward anyway: a cold, persistent menace. The barest hint of a full moon crested a nearby hilltop, waiting its turn. In this Otherworld, dawn climbed the sky in the north before it crept south, while twilight traced east-west in equal measure. Thus, it was never whole light nor full dark but a commingling of the two, treading the border between misty morning and evening's chill. Una watched the moon's glacial progress with a wary eye.

She suspected it followed them with interest.

Kaer Yin smirked at her wariness.

"Think it can see you?"

She said nothing.

She knew it did…. and that was not all.

The air held alluring scents she could no more classify than the frightening array of colors that assaulted her eyes. Everywhere she looked were greens so lush and multifaceted, the leaves gleamed as emeralds, grasses in violent shades of red-gold, deepest midnight, and dewy sapphires that glowed at the barest touch of moonlight. Merely blinking could alter their façade forever. Each palette seemed to rearrange itself with every gust of wind or shift beneath the queer prismatic light of both celestial bodies.

When the sky couldn't choose between night and day, why should her senses decide upon one or the other?

With each step, her mind feasted upon these strange inconsistencies with wonder and dread. A tinge of honeysuckle and deep loam wafted to her, sunbaked lavender and frost— then the crisp scent of snow-damp pine, night-blooming jasmine… and death. Indeed, amidst so much staggering, confusing beauty lay the omnipresent sense of rot and decay. But there was also life. The fauna she glimpsed through the trees or saw leaping through glimmering meadows as they passed were perhaps even more startlingly lovely than their environs. Great white and gold deer flitted here and there, intransient as wisps of cloud. Slinking cats with haunting yellow eyes hissed from their tree boughs. All manner of birds soared overhead, flashing plumage brighter than any jewel. Sometimes she was so awed by these gorgeous beasts that she forgot that other, less benign things were watching them too. From the shadows of the moon's domain, there were also eyes filled with hunger and very little fear. The allure of sweet mortal flesh was an unspoken reality. She knew if any wandered into that nighttime world alone, they wouldn't return.

Again, she shivered in the almost heat of their morning world.

Kaer Yin's hand found the small of her back.

"What is it, *mo grá?*"

She pinched the bridge of her nose.

"I feel… things I can't explain."

"What do you mean?" His breath dusted her ear.

She stared into the night with a clenched jaw. A thing she thought she recognized stared back. "Familiar." In that deep dark, she could almost hear the shuffling of many feet. Human feet. "We aren't alone."

His fingers caught hers. "Are you afraid?" She tore her gaze away to find him smiling down at her, a teasing tilt to his brow.

She pursed her lips. "Not at all. I told you, I can't explain it."

He gave her an odd look but didn't reply. Instead, he squeezed her hand and led on, holding his harness with his free hand. Una walked beside him, still fascinated with the creatures winding through the dark on her right. She *should* have been afraid. Rian certainly seemed to be. If Robin felt the same, he didn't show it, nor did any other Greenmaker in their company. She imagined their reticence had more to do with bluster in the face of so many Sidhe warriors rather than any actual emotion. She wished she could mask her expressions so easily. No… she wasn't afraid. She felt something far more concerning, a tremor of elation.

A thrill she couldn't describe tapped its claws lightly up her spine.

They are there, she thought. *They see me too.*

Without meaning to, she shot Rian a glance over her shoulder. Her attention was fixed in the same direction. *Does she feel them, too, maybe?* But she wouldn't ask. Not here. How could she tell anyone that of all the wondrous, terrifying things to see in this place, the dead enthralled her most? The Sluagh were out there, waiting to greet her. This knowledge burrowed deep in her gut, raising goosebumps over her arms. Though, this feeling was not all. Her Spark flared within her blood and had yet to fall silent. Giddy with surgent power, she pressed her free hand to her mouth to halt any uncontrollable laughter.

What was *wrong* with her?

I have sssuch delightsss to ssshow you…

She jumped for the memory.

Kaer Yin stopped, tugging her chin up with his thumb. "Are you all right?"

"Yes," she lied.

He didn't believe her. She could tell. "Shar, why don't we take a break?"

Tam Lin's lieutenant squinted at the sky. "I don't know, *Mo Flaith.* The dawn won't hold for long."

"How long afore we reach yer uncle's digs," asked Robin, pretending he wasn't alarmed by those whispering leaves Una couldn't stop staring at. To his credit, he was a much better actor than she. "Seems we've been on the road a while, and the girls need a rest."

A snort from behind said Tam Lin O'Ruaidh knew better. "If that's fatigue on Lady Donahugh's face, I'll be buggered. She looks a tad inebriated, you ask me."

"No one did," remarked Rian sidelong. She moved forward to press her chin into Una's shoulder. "You don't have to tell me."

Una let out a long breath.

Kaer Yin backed off. "What do you know?" he asked Rian.

"We're close to Tech Duinn now, aren't we?"

He, too, glanced at the sky, concerned. "Yes. Why?"

"He did something to her that night."

Una turned, flushing. "Rian, please. I'm fine."

"What did he do?" His brow darkened.

Rian smoothed a lock of hair from Una's damp cheek. "I don't know, but whatever it was left a mark. Una, let's sit awhile. You should eat something."

Una shook herself, once more tearing her attention back to the road. She gave a sheepish smile. "That's probably a good idea."

"What do you see out there?" Kaer Yin asked.

"Nothing. Everything, maybe. I don't know." She let Rian lead her to her mare, rubbing her eyes. "Robin?"

"Milady?"

"You've any uishge left in that flask?"

Rather than answer, he proffered the vessel with mock fanfare. She took it without further comment.

Tam Lin edged close. "You and Diarmid have met, I take it?"

"For a moment."

His violet eyes cut suspiciously. "And…?"

She refused to look at Kaer Yin, who'd been asking this for quite a while. She took a sip of Robin's uishge and made a face. "He tried to take me… here, I presume. I think he thought he could absorb my erm, gift."

"Is that all?" Tam Lin's brows raised.

"You took his power, instead?" Kaer Yin answered for her, crossing his arms. "That's how you did it? The Sluagh?"

Without seeing her reflection, she knew the shock of white at her temple stood out like a blood-red hand. "I didn't know until it was too late."

"Are you implying she took his power?" Tam Lin prodded, disbelief evident in his expression. "A *Milesian* girl?"

"I'm marching you back in there, thoughtlessly too." Ignoring Tam Lin, Kaer Yin cursed under his breath. "Why didn't you tell me?"

She avoided the tender regret on his face. "I'll be all right."

Tam Lin made a rude sound. "You mean to tell me we're headed to Tir Falias with a woman who stole our uncle's powers, and you are just telling us now? He's going to keep her, surely you realize?"

"Would you *shut* your bloody mouth?" Rian nearly shrieked.

He threw up his hands in response. "What? Do you want me to lie to you?" He pointed at Una. "If she's been marked by *Fiachra Dubh*, she'll never see the mortal world again. You'll have to trade for her, Yin. No bones about it. Whatever he asks for will be dear, indeed."

"I know," Kaer Yin hissed. "That's twice I owe him. Thank you for the reminder."

Una swallowed hard. "I'm sorry. I didn't know how to tell you."

There was foreboding in his expression. "You should have."

He turned and strode into the trees.

She knew better than to follow.

🦌 🦌

HOURS, OR PERHAPS DAYS LATER— who could tell? — they came to a fork in the leaf-strewn road. The nighttime hemisphere seemed closer than usual, though distant enough that her skin didn't prickle every time the wind blew.

Kaer Yin wasn't speaking to her much, which pained her almost as severely as the look in his cousin's eye every time he glanced her way.

Monster, she read there and wanted to weep.

Rian kept close to her side, her presence the only reassurance Una had left. Despite this, she refused to be cowed by an element outside her control. She'd never asked Diarmid Adair to attempt to spirit her and Rian into the Otherworld, had she?

If her Spark hadn't interceded when it did, they might both be dead… or worse. What right did anyone have to judge her? She'd make the same choice again if she must. So, why did she feel so guilty?

Kaer Yin took a turn around the fork, scratching his chin at the various paths. Each trailed beneath grand stone arches etched with Ealig words she couldn't read. In the center of this convergence bubbled a large granite fountain full of sweet water, rimmed by stone maidens bearing deep pots bursting with mature fruit trees. This was a Waycross. Una instinctually understood its importance for the Sidhe magic radiating from its center. Nothing from that ravenous realm on their right could stand within this circle for long. She relaxed a bit in the shadow of the southernmost arch. Her Spark dwindled to a whisper.

Kaer Yin watched her from the opposite side.

"We'll camp here for the night."

"Bad idea. We should keep the night at our backs, Yin," argued Tam Lin, with a firm shake of his head. "Press on."

"We won't outpace the shadows. I'd rather we face them within this circle than out there in the wild."

Tam Lin quirked his mouth to say more but cursed at the sky instead. "You're right."

"What's that mean then?" Robin fidgeted, scowling around.

"Night descends," Shar answered, unloading his pack at the fountain's rim. "We must be ready."

"Ready for what?"

Shar shared a look with his lord. "For what comes after."

"My men, if it pleases the Gods," sighed Tam Lin, hopefully.

"They'll find us," said Kaer Yin. "I pray from the right side."

"What d'ye mean?" Robin heard something in the woods and stepped back into the light. "*Siora*, but I don't like this place, none at all."

"Gerrod and the Tairnganese are with them, so now would not be a grand time to arrive in our midst," replied Kaer Yin. Una looked away when he glanced over. She didn't miss his frown. "Mortal flesh is a powerful lure, Robin. Even our presence can't deter every evil lurking in the nightscape."

"Bloody wonderful."

"Why don't we just leave?" Rian interjected. "They can't hunt what isn't here."

"Not that simple," said Kaer Yin. "I wish it was."

"How so?"

Kaer Yin threw his hands wide to indicate the fountain and arches. "South to Bri Leith—the seat of the High King, then Tir Tairngare— Midhir's gift to your people." He pointed. "East to Croghan and the mountains of the West— to Tir Na Nog. North, to the harbor of Tir Gorias and West, to the halls of Manannan Mac Lir."

"So?"

He exhaled through his nose. "It doesn't matter what the signs read. From any direction, these roads lead only one place."

"Tech Duinn," whispered Una, disheartened.

"Yes," his answer was gentler than before. "We must pay homage to *Fiachra Dubh* for safe passage."

"Mortals must, anyway," said Tam Lin. "If we attempt to steal his due, our uncle will seek vengeance. Family or no, he is lord and master here, not we."

A slight wrinkle etched between Rian's brows. "Wait. This is a puzzle. West is east; North is south, and so on. We can figure that out."

Kaer Yin rubbed his chin. "The Oiche Ar Fad mirrors your world, but that is not all. The only way out is *through*. One must pay homage to the Raven King for that gift or wander here forever."

"Well," laughed Tam Lin. "Until something eats you."

⚔

AS IF THE PRINCE OF CONNAUGHT bore the burden of prophecy, they swiftly learned the truth of his jest. Una and Rian had scarcely laid down on their shared bedroll by the fire when Una felt that prickling along her skin once more. Her head swiveled round to face the dark. Long shapes slithered out of the trees from the night side, nearly upon them. The drunken, half-risen sun spun away toward the eastern horizon, and the patient moon turned into the center. Only traces of rose gold sky shone overhead.

Twilight loomed.

Kaer Yin wasn't far. He hadn't been since her father had died in Bethany. If possible, she might have loved him the more for the quiet subtlety of his support. That he was still unhappy with her was also readily apparent on his face. All the same, there he was. Kneeling to whisper at her nape, his fingertips brushed hers. "What's wrong?"

She turned back to the woods. "There's something out there."

"There will be until we quit this place for good. Dor Sidhe love mortals, remember? Lu Sidhe too. I expect we'll be stalked the whole way."

She couldn't stave a smile. "And Ban Sidhe?"

He made a face. "Gods, not at all. You'd start talking and ruin our appetite."

"Never heard that fable before."

"Wouldn't want you to guess our weaknesses."

She rolled her eyes. "Oh, that's easy enough."

"That so?"

"*Uishge.*"

Across the fire, Robin burst out laughing.

Exhaling through his nose, he threaded his fingers through hers again. "I was going to say something *far* more romantic, but we've an irritating audience, I'm afraid."

"No need to woo what you've already won, *Ard Tiarne,*" she said under her breath, and his pupils dilated. Cheeks filling with blood, she looked away. Rian groaned and pulled her blankets over her head. Embarrassed, Una bit her lip. They'd been here before, hadn't they? "Anyway, I'll stay up for a while. Help keep watch."

"Niall and Bearn have that honor. Sleep, Una. You need it."

The trees ahead shivered in the breeze, and she knew she wouldn't sleep, no matter what she promised. "I'll try." At least it wasn't a lie.

He set two fingers against his heart, then pressed them lightly against her temple. She gathered that he had more to say, but they *did* have an audience. It would have to wait. He stood as she lay down, dragging her blanket with her. "Sleep, *mo grá*. I'll wake you in a few hours."

"What does that mean?"

He tossed her a smirk and strode off without an answer.

She leaned over. "Rian, was that an insult?"

"No," she laughed for a long time.

Una snuggled into her blanket, cursing.

She'd learn the bloody language soon or die trying.

Despite her own opinion, Una did fall asleep after a while. She only knew because she was startled awake soon after. Her eyes snapped open. The disheveled moon hung directly overhead, leering at her like a mad beggar awaiting coin. Then, she heard it. The softest of sighs on her left. Almost afraid to see, she turned her head.

A pair of gleaming opalescent eyes flashed at her from the treeline. No, not one pair… *dozens*. A black shape carefully dragged something heavy toward the forest so as not to alert the Ban Sidhe in her midst. Una drew in a sharp breath. A bevy of eerie, milky orbs flashed her way. They'd heard her.

So had Niall.

"*Dúisigh*! Dor Sidhe!"

Una scrabbled to her feet, shaking Rian's shoulder on her way up. The other girl had barely blinked when Una's arm was seized from the other side.

"Una!" Rian cried.

All nine hells broke loose at once.

Kaer Yin was on his feet with Nemain before Niall finished calling his warning. He had a feeling they'd be attacked tonight. Some Dor Sidhe were bold enough to brave the Ban Sidhe's wrath for such an irresistible feast. As he'd told Una, mortal flesh was a reckless temptation. The first goblin struck him from the front, snapping at his eyes with razor-sharp teeth. Gripping the misshapen little beast by the throat with one hand, he sent Nemain across its middle with the other. Oozing, oily blood scattered over his boots as he flung the creature's hindquarters into the next incoming wraith. He backpedaled as a half-dozen of the snapping; snarling beasts clambered atop him in their attempt to stay his sword arm. This was undoubtedly their plan. While they were no match for Ban Sidhe at the Waycross, the goblins could delay them long enough to spirit their actual targets away. Upon this thought, Rian's shriek tore the clearing in half. "Una!" she screeched. Her screams amplified while Kaer Yin struggled to remain upright.

One of the little bastards took a bite out of his left thumb while he spun about to regain footing. With a roar, he whirled Nemain in a vicious semicircle— hacking many of the Dor Sidhe pests in half at once. Enraged, he stole a glance at the bedroll beside the fire. Una and Rian were surrounded. One goblin had Una by the arm. "Una!"

"Ben!" Rian howled, swinging her little dagger every which way.

"Siora, damn it!" Robin was in similar straits. "A little help, here."

Shar was the first to bound in the right direction. Swords were all but useless in a swarm. He went for his bow. Once the arrows started flying, the Dor Sidhe snarled a retreat. That didn't mean they weren't taking their prey with them. Kaer Yin ran toward the forest, leaping goblins and Sidhe on the way. Una crouched by herself in a sea of hissing goblins, inflicting grievous wounds upon any who dared touch her. In the process, she clung to Rian's hand while slashing wildly with her dagger. They both bled profusely, drawing more and more ravenous assailants every moment. Una lost her footing. She was towed into Rian with a furious cry, who struggled to keep her friend from being pulled into the woods as several Greenmakers had already been.

Horrible sounds rent the air.

Kaer Yin cut deep rivulets in the earth in his haste to dislodge so many grasping claws; Shar and Niall's arrows did the rest. Recovering from the surprise of the assault with their typical, inhuman speed, the Sidhe gathered and fired indiscriminately into any writhing shape. As swiftly as they'd invaded, the goblins departed in a roiling mass. Though a few of their number had perished in the attempt, most of the Greenmakers were alive, if missing hunks of flesh. Una and Rian clung to each other against the fountain rim. The water had gone a pale red. Without thinking, Kaer Yin threw his arms around both. "Are you two all right?"

Una bled from bites on her neck, hands, and fingers. Nothing serious, however. She nodded. Rian was the worse for wear, not having Una's ability to self-heal. She had so many wounds; he couldn't count them all. Her face, arms, and chest bore much of the damage. She, too, would live, as the cuts were shallow and haphazard. She sagged a bit in Una's arms. "I'm all right," she declared, though it sounded more like a question. "Will they come back?"

He swallowed. "Your blood is on the wind."

Rian sobbed. Kaer Yin couldn't blame her.

"We must wash your wounds as best we can and keep moving. Our swords and arrows will deter most."

Una rested her chin over Rian's trembling temple. Her eyes closed. "How long to Tir Falias?"

"Hours if we ride hard."

"Then, what in the hells are we waiting for?"

⚷ ⚸

Not even their burning torches, galloping haste, or steadfast determination to arrive safely in Tir Falias could prevent the next attack, the third, or the fourth. They'd quit the Waycross mere minutes after the horde had struck them at camp, riding at full gallop through the Western Arch. Rian was given to ride with Shar and Una with Kaer Yin, hoping that the Ban Sidhe would mask their scent. Tam Lin's Blood Eagles surrounded Robin and his Greenmakers, bows strung while they scanned the forest on either side. Una could not tell how long they'd been on the road before a giant beast came crashing out of the foliage ahead. Kaer Yin wheeled to a halt just as one of its massive forepaws slammed into the cobbles on their right. Una's heart caught in her throat. A thing like the ghast Kaer Yin had killed in Rian's yard those months before— yet not. This was a bear; if her eyes didn't deceive her… huge and pitch-black, its eyes glowing an unnatural red. She'd never seen a bear in Innisfail but had been told they roamed the wilds of Aes Sidhe by night.

However, she highly doubted *this* particular bear had a thing to do with the world she came from. Its bloodcurdling roar danced along the strands of her nerves, promising glorious pain, snapping bones and muscle hewn from the flesh.

Teeth like long knives, it charged.

Sssuch delightsss to sshow you… her memory taunted.

Kaer Yin wasted no time. Trusting her to hang on, he kicked his destrier into a canter, pulling Nemain in one hand and a lark in the other. The bear was twice as large as their mount, its vast maw wide and waiting. Kaer Yin slashed as the bear swiped at him from the left, guiding the horse with his knees. Then, he turned his mount to do the same to its other side. A furious, erratic snarl escaped the creature's mouth as it rolled head over hindquarters into an ungainly sprawl. Kaer Yin didn't stop or pause to complete the deed. Instead, Tam Lin severed the bear's head in a single slash while his horse leaped its falling bulk. Like a stone dividing a river's rush, the Sidhe sped past its corpse, sheathing their weapons to gain more speed.

Una buried her face in Kaer Yin's spine, squeezing her eyes shut. She knew the Oiche Ar Fad was a terrible place, but never in her imagination could she fathom the depths of its bloodlust. Every breath, every step a mortal took in this realm— spelled doom. In fables, when men and women were spirited away by the Sidhe, likely none lived happily ever after in the Land of the Undying. They died screaming as soon as the moon's pale light kissed the sky. She shivered to think of it. Still, just beneath the thrum of her pulse, she felt her Spark beat a steady tattoo.

Not you, it seemed to say.

You are no feast.

Hours later, perhaps, as the light shifted in the west and the nighttime world slunk into the east, they came to a lovely stone bridge. A stream trickled below, cascading down a rocky outcrop bedecked with hawthorn and sweet-smelling berries. Kaer Yin raised a hand to halt their party. While close, it was not yet dawn. He glanced at Tam Lin beside him. "The horses need water. There won't be another source for miles."

Tam Lin looked around, mouth tight. "Swiftly, I think. We shouldn't linger."

"Agreed." Kaer Yin pulled Una down with him. "The water is clear and clean, but don't go near any pools. All right?"

She nodded, feeling Rian limp to her side. Robin's rudimentary bandaging did little to conceal the damage. "I think we'll wait right here, thank you."

"I'll stay with them," Tam Lin assured him, gesturing for Kaer Yin to go on. "Refill my skin with theirs, won't you?"

Kaer Yin caught his skin while juggling the others, mirroring Una's wary expression. "We do this fast. Keep your sword ready, Lin."

Tam Lin saluted as his cousin strode off toward the river, pulling their nervous mounts along by the reins. Robin paused to pat Rian on the head on his way past. Una took a deep breath, watching the foliage glisten in the moonlight. "Don't worry, *ceann beag*. I will look after you." Tam Lin took off his cloak and draped it over Rian's shaking frame. She didn't protest, for once. "*Fiachra Dubh* will heal you both."

Una said, "Before or after he kills me?"

"He won't," he laughed. The sound was dry. "But he will keep you if he can."

"What does that mean?"

He blew air over his lower lip, eyes watchful, hand on his pommel— in case anything thought to spring at them from the leaves. "My uncle is as opportunistic as he is wise. Bit of a cunt, too, you ask me. That you *can* take anything from him means he can't afford to let you go. Not without a price, anyway."

She heard Kaer Yin barking orders down by the river's edge. The sound gave her equal parts comfort and fear. "I won't let him sacrifice anything for me. You have my word."

Tam Lin regarded her in silence for a long while. "If you keep that vow, you and I will square, My Lady."

"I swear it."

His stare turned cold. "We'll see."

A voice peeled from the riverbank in shock and sudden terror. Robin's, if she weren't mistaken. Muttering an oath, Tam Lin drew them both close, sword up. "Yin?" he called. When there was no answer save shouts and the occasional scream, he tilted his head at Shar. "Go." Shar drew his larks and bounded down the bank. The following sounds were unearthly shrieks and the ring of drawn steel. Tam Lin edged near the bridge, keeping the girls at his back, and pressed into the granite wall. A white shape emerged from the far bank, thin and supple as a reed. Its face was almost lovely, womanly. Long black hair poured over its nude body, dragging wet streaks over stone. Its long fingers terminated in claws. Black eyes wide, it crept close.

Hello, sweet ones, it cooed through Una's mind.

Your men are hurting us.

You wouldn't hurt us, would you?

Despite herself, Una felt a pang of concern. Rian covered her ears.

"Get back," Tam Lin warned. The sounds of slaughter reached a crescendo below the bridge. The thing got down on all fours, wailing. Such a voice, Una had never heard. It rent deep wounds in her already knotted guts. Before she knew what she was doing, her fingers gripped Tam Lin's sleeve.

"That's an ondine, isn't it?" Another macabre beast of legend Una had only read about and never knew she'd face. The ondine dwelled in forest pools and seaside coves, luring the unwary with the heartbreaking beauty of its voice. Once a victim fell under its spell, the ondine was sure to seize its prey.

"Yes," growled Tam Lin. "Don't be fooled. She'll suck the marrow from your bones while your heart still beats." He pressed them more firmly into the wall as another siren slunk onto the bridge from the opposite side.

Lies. Males always lie, sister.

You know they do.

Come with us, smiled the first with small, pointed fangs.

We will dance among the waves together, fierce and free.

Una might have been susceptible if her Spark weren't a burning candle at her center. Alas, she held lightning at her core and could not be swayed. "Kill it! Kill them both," she told Tam Lin.

Together, the ondines sprang.

Dark Horse

Castor eyed him quizzically from the mirror, his too-full lips pursed. "You know, *mon cher*, I think it makes you more dashing." He sipped from a silver goblet, watching Damek shave. The bruises and abrasions had all healed, save for a long gash from temple to chin, a gift from the Crown Prince. The wheal was an ugly, red mass of raised flesh and healing scabs. It ruined an otherwise perfect face, as far as Damek was concerned. The razor slipped over his chin with practiced ease. Usually, he'd have a groom to manage this task. They were far from home, the Steel Corps and regular troops of Bethany.

Henry fucking FitzDonahugh had seen to that.

Damek made the last pass, then set his razor down on the larder. Drying his face with a clean rag, he tossed the offensive garment at Castor and poured himself a drink. The lord and lady of Malahide had been loathe to leave their precious silver behind, but what use was finery in one's crypt? They and around three thousand villagers, workers, and farmers had met a rather nasty end—the price for ignoring Damek's generous ultimatum. No city in the South was prepared for the might of Bethany's forces with Lord Marshal Bishop at the helm. He'd warned them not to trifle with him.

Now they were dead, like so many others.

Pity.

"My looks are the least of my concern, or yours. Where are my ships, Castor?" he demanded, working hard not to snarl. When dealing with the Bretagne, he found a direct approach worked more swiftly than a veiled threat. With Castor, most of all. The skinny little shite had had Damek murder his father, after all. "I'm not accustomed to waiting, My Lord."

Castor made an effeminate gesture. "*Non*, I never give my word unless I intend to follow through. You shall have your fleet within the week."

Damek took a long sip of his wine, never breaking eye contact. "You said that nearly a week ago. My patience grows thinner by the hour."

"I've given you six ships already, Lord Bishop. My men tell me you've had them harbored in old Dubh Lin for so long; they'll struggle to navigate the Straits soon. Why ask for more if you're not using those you have already?"

"That is hardly your concern."

"Ah, is that so, *mon ami?* I delivered upon my promise, yet you've given very little explanation for their purpose. With Bethany in your uncle's grip, I'm not sure why you would imagine I'd protest an assault?"

Damek's answering grin was tight. "Shall I repeat myself? Where are the ships you promised me? Do take care to answer with actual dates. I'm weary of asking."

Castor muttered a Bretagn curse under his breath. "Two weeks, no more."

"Your word?"

The Marquis bit the inside of his cheek. "Yes. I swear it, Lord Bishop."

"Good. I'd hate for our relationship to end on the lowest possible note."

Castor bowed from the waist, duly chastened, allowing his long hair to obscure his expression. "As you wish. Still, I am here to advise and aid, *non?*" Damek noted he did not wait for the affirmative. "Were I you, I would not let that mad Kneeler sit your throne long. My spies tell me he assembles an army to march in his God's name. I know you've heard this too."

"I have."

Castor rose, throwing his hands wide. These Gauls were so expressive. "March on them, before 'tis too late! How many Barons have joined his side?"

"Eight."

Merde! That's half Duch Patrick's bannermen, yes?"

He was sure the Marquis had known the total before he asked.

"Yes," Damek crossed his arms. He was always amused by the effrontery of those who couldn't help but attempt to deceive him. Perhaps it was his bastardy that convinced so many of some intellectual shortcoming? Or maybe… Duch Patrick's death had opened a chasm of ambition among his uncle's inferiors.

Whatever the case, each lord in Damek's retinue, thought to assert influence over him before he became too powerful to control. "The only thing I require of you are ships, Marquis."

Shaking his head, Castor stuck his nose into his wine. "My father, brutal brigand though he was, did know a thing or two. A tower *sans* foundation will fall. You lose face." For a moment, Damek considered killing the anxious little fop today. Castor read the thought as it crossed his eyes. He flushed but did not flinch. Instead, he raised his head. "We are partners in this. If you lose your crown before it is won, I will have wasted millions of *francs* for nothing. If you are no lord of Eire, then I am weakened in Bretagne."

"Is that a threat?"

"Not at all. I am merely curious. What will you do if your uncle succeeds?"

"I'm going to be plain, son of Gaelin," remarked Damek dryly. "Attempting to hedge your bets will kill you, your men, what is left of your family, and wipe your pathetic little kingdom from the face of the earth. My Corpsmen have sacked Bonleith, Gibbons, and Malahide in a fortnight. I'd say they have a real knack for it."

"You threaten *me*, now?"

"No, I promise you."

Castor snorted. "With half the South rising for your uncle and his puny god, no ships to speak of, and the North unwon? I think not. You bluff."

"Ah, but I *do* have ships, my lord."

"In Dubh Lin, where they are useless."

"No, in Portmarnock, being fitted for cannons. Such weapons are hard to come by and even more difficult to conceal. Hence, the necessity for discretion. Lord Devereaux has been most accommodating."

The young Marquis paled by three shades.

"Furthermore," Damek went on. "We've come to terms over two or three vessels. Your lovely, swift clippers, for two massive barges, to break the ice through the Straits. Devereaux seems most eager to please me, Castor, as you might. Did you know whom you were attempting to fleece?"

"*Mon, ami…*"

"We are not friends, kinslayer. We had an arrangement. If you do not have those ships here within the fortnight— and not a day longer, mind— killing you will be the very last thing I do to you. Do you understand?"

The wind rattled the casings outside the chamber window, punctuating the uncomfortable silence. Damek, arms crossed, nodded to his Hisk, who waited just shy of the open door. "See that Lord Gaelin has everything he requires. Well, whatever he can manage from his quarters, that is. I think quill and vellum should be the highest priority."

Hisk, the large fellow that he was, towered over Castor. His gauntleted fist closed over a silk-clothed arm. The Bretagn lord spat, "*Tu! T'es un bâtard!* You betray your only ally?"

"Betray?" Damek shared a long look with Hisk, who guffawed. "I think you'll agree it's wise to protect one's investments. You'll be my honored guest here at Malahide, my lord. You'll want for nothing."

"Save freedom," Castor grumbled.

Damek walked over to clap him on the arm so the Gallic lordling couldn't miss the genuine threat in his eyes. "In future, remember that I have my own spies." He gave Castor's shoulder a squeeze that made the slighter man wince. "Take him," he said to Hisk. Castor sneered as he was led from the room but refrained from further comment.

Damek sank into a chair behind his desk with a groan when they were gone. Though he'd no doubt Castor would eventually attempt to betray him, he hadn't expected it to happen so soon. What he'd said about Henry's moves in Bethany weren't wrong. Damek *did* need to deal with the old bastard— and soon. However, to do so without destroying what he meant to rule, he must have coin… unlimited coin. Where to get it, but from the prosperous Siorai-dominated cities of the North? Malahide was a crucial steppingstone toward a greater goal; Tairngare and the Eirean crown.

His uncle threatened that outcome with every breath. With backing from Kernow, Henry had wed the insipid daughter of the Earl of Penwyth. The girl was no more than a child, barely fifteen years old. Yet, her dowry guaranteed Henry an additional four thousand Kernish troops, a bride price of one hundred thousand fainne, and a yearly stipend of eight thousand from a vineyard she'd inherited in Swansea. She was the granddaughter of the old Lord Rhiannon of Cymru, who had minted the art of cold-growth grapes. Without his genius, the land of Cymru would still be a dry, mountainous backwater. Henry's new wife brought him the money, means, and men required to make himself Duch. All it had cost him were two sons— which, Damek could attest, were no loss. His hoary uncle made much of his righteous zeal, but Damek knew a killer when he saw one. Henry mourned his sons for dashed hopes rather than genuine affection.

In that way, he and Patrick were alike. People held little value if they could not be used. Damek should know. He'd been Patrick's pawn all his life.

Una, too, though she pretended otherwise. At the thought of her, his fists balled of their own accord. *Let me go*, she had said, with tears in her eyes.

His fist came down hard on the table.

You will not think of her until you've accomplished what you must.

You've no time for self-pity.

Again, he swore himself to his task, and that alone. He would hear nothing, see nothing, nor feel anything until it was done.

Once you are King of Eire, she'll come back, one way or the other.

For now, you are a machine built for a single purpose.

Machines feel nothing.

A knock at the chamber door helped purge his mind of that Otherworld dawn and the ignominy of dual defeat. Her sweet face full of sorrow would at once enrage and enthrall him with endless pain if he allowed it to.

He must not.

He *would* not.

Clearing his throat, he waited for Martin's salt and pepper head to appear before he relaxed in his chair.

O'Rearden took one look at him and sighed, "Again?"

He coughed. "Report?"

Martin heaved himself into the opposite chair. Damek didn't like to notice how heavy the task seemed to be. Martin O'Rearden was not a young man any longer. All the riding, raiding, and battles had begun to show. He smirked at the concern on Damek's face. "Ah, 'tis nothing, this. Earned a few bumps on our way into the city. Nothing to worry yourself over, lad."

Damek didn't believe him but wouldn't argue. Martin, too, had his pride. "You were right about my ships. They're not coming."

"Of course they aren't. Gaelin is practically impoverished. Why would you ever believe he could produce more warships after taking over a bankrupt kingdom? The Marquis spends what little coin his father left him on silk and jewels. His people will tear Morlaix down around his ears soon enough. That is if you don't kill him first. Be happy we took six, boyo."

Damek's nostrils flared. He sat back. "Four warships are hardly an armada, Martin."

"More than your uncle had, Tairngare has, or Henry could dream of. Devereaux can build more, but it'll be a year or more before they're ready. In the meantime, we need—"

"*Fainne.*"

"Yes."

"I need Tairngare. All else is foreplay."

"Not yet," Martin said, scratching his beard. "I know of at least seven Baronies rife with coin we should turn our attention to first."

"We'll get to them. I'd rather cut Henry's purse strings after accumulating more land and wealth. Every county we march to must be strategic. Why lose men and arrows for lesser prizes?"

"Tairngare is a reach with so few men."

"We have twenty-thousand soldiers," Damek scoffed.

"And they have twice that number in the Cohort alone. The Corsairs make it fifty-five. Not to mention high walls, a self-contained port, and a water supply. They'll outlast anything we throw at them. We'd need an army sixty-thousand strong at least and hope they were fool enough to meet us on open ground."

Damek bit his tongue over the information he was privy to that he could not share— even with Martin. Instead, he cast his eyes to his map and tapped the Red City with a thumbnail. "Nema's new government is weak and fractious. She kills nobles and wealthy Marchers indiscriminately, making enemies of potential allies. You heard what she did to the Cymrian Trade Ambassador— Melba, was it? Nema won't last the year, or I'm buggered."

"I can't speak to her efficacy as a ruler, but the people are behind her. The army, too."

"What army? The Cohort is comprised of boys and beardless men, Martin. All the commanders and their officers fled with the nobles or were executed. The Corsairs haven't been anything but flashy dandies since Dumnain. The time is *now*, Martin. While I have the numbers and the ships."

"You'll still need coin. Malahide was a rich prize, but supplies alone will gobble all that up in a month. Tairngare will take much longer than that to tame."

"I disagree. My spies tell me the old woman is driving herself mad. Last month she even attempted to bend Basa Alvra to her side in hopes the Domina of the Alvra Clan would aid her in her quest to purge Eire of nobles and naysayers. Alvra nearly killed her, did you know that?"

"I did not," said Martin, eyes narrowing.

Damek missed the look. He exhaled a laugh. "She hasn't left the Tenth Floor since, merely issues decrees through her horde of Secundas and uses her honor guard to enforce them. Men, I might add."

"… Fir Bolg, you left out."

Damek had the grace to look away. "Ah, well. They are in the city, yes."

"Please inform your *spy* that I am fully aware of where you're gleaning your details, and I like it not. She, as ever, seeks only one thing, Damek."

Damek was tired of playing two hands close to the chest, but if his mentor knew what was going on in the North, he'd never consent to his plans. "The point is that her meteoric rise precludes a devastating fall. If I strike now, her house will crumble."

Martin sucked his teeth in silence for a while. When he spoke, his voice held a fatherly note. "Be mindful of your own words there, lad. I will do my utmost to propel your vision north if you command me, though I urge you to reconsider."

"Every day we waste in the South costs us men and fainne. Rather than founder them on meaningless trifles, I'd rather expend both to pursue the only goal that truly matters. You know that I'm right. Patrick dared once, but he did so against the full might of a powerful Cloister. In tatters, as it is now, the Citadel's gates will swing wide in no time."

"Or bring us all to ruin."

"… perhaps, but you don't believe so, any more than I do."

"Very well," said Martin, rising. His bones made music along the way. "I need an ale, a bath, a fuck, then a good night's sleep. I'll see to it the men begin drills in the morning."

"Thank you, Martin," Damek said and meant it. Without O'Rearden's support, every plan he'd ever had would have been dust.

Martin paused at the door. "Henry is not going to go away, my lord. He is an experienced soldier and ruthless tactician. He'll fatten like a tick in your absence."

"That is why I must do this now. Tairngare gives me a strength I might otherwise lose in pursuit of Bethany. No other prize compares."

"No matter how they tried, no Donahugh has ever managed to take the Red City. So few men, aside."

Damek felt his lips slide over his gums in a wide grin. "Thank Reason; I'm not a Donahugh."

⚚

He STALKED THROUGH THE COURTYARD sometime later, looking for Aoife. She'd been gone several days already with her bondsmen, doing Reason knew what. Thus far, she hadn't been forthcoming about her plans and tended to come and go like the winter wind. He only knew that she'd somehow managed to break her *geis* and spent most if not all her time on the road. Wreaking havoc, no doubt, and sowing discord in the Mac Nemed name… or, perhaps not? Aoife's motivations were changeable as the tides. Without Liadan's *geis*, there was no way to tell what she would do next. A wild mare without a tether tramples everything in her path. Still, she was his ally, for now.

Whatever designs she spun behind his back were irrelevant until he was in a position of power. At present, allies were a commodity in short supply.

He had no choice but to accept her help.

That didn't mean he had to like it.

He was in a foul mood by the time he arrived at the door she'd mentioned. Knowing he was walking into a trap, however seemingly sweet, did not improve his humor. The structure he equivocated before was a workmen's storehouse or some other facility built into the keep's inner wall. A single candle flickered behind a tattered scrap of burlap in the window. The interior was dark and bland.

He bit his lip. They probably should have brought a guard, at least. His fingers closed over his pommel as he raised a fist to knock. The door swung inward before his knuckles had even brushed the ancient wood. A rush of stale, moldy air blew into his face.

He coughed. "Hello?"

Nothing at first, then a shuffling from within. "Come," Aoife said. "We've been waiting."

He hesitated at the door. "Show yourself."

Aoife made an impatient sound and emerged into the weak candlelight from the hall. Her shorn hair and vibrant eyes made the hollows of her pale cheeks stand out. This was only their second meeting in a month, and he still wasn't prepared for the shock of her appearance. Gone was that burnished beauty he'd known all his life as if the spirit had been roasted out of her. She was thin to the point of waifish. Huge black pools collected beneath her eyes in a face that was more bone than flesh. Her collarbones stood pronounced at the crux of her neckline. There was a sag and bend to her spine that had never been there before, and what visible skin he could see was covered with pinkish, shiny scars. Damek's jaw tightened. The last time they'd been in each other's company, she'd been tending to him in the shadows of his sickbed, and he had been in such pain that he never really saw her.

"*Reason*, love. What happened to you?"

"Liadan, of course."

He stepped into the room, closing the door behind him and removing his hood. "What did she do to you?"

"What will never be done again," she sniffed, grabbing the candle from the sill and drawing the burlap tight against the window. The light traced strange planes and angles over her features, making her look like a Lu Sidhe sprite. "Were you followed?"

"No, though Martin knows you're here. He's no fool, Aoife."

Laughing, she said, "If he were, he'd be no use to you. Follow me. We should speak where there are no windows."

Inexplicably, Damek felt a chill of fear at the thought. He'd never had cause to be afraid of Aoife before, and she'd gone out of her way to heal him recently— but that didn't mean he trusted her or her two hulking henchmen. Carn and Creahal, he vaguely recalled. Former bodyguards to her father, Sionnavar. He had only seen them once, many summers past, at Beltane in Armagh. He'd been fourteen and meeting his family for the first time. The experience was well remembered. The court at Armagh made Nema's sham theocracy look dull. "I'd prefer to wait here if you don't mind?"

She stopped, framed in the black hall. "What? You don't trust *me* now?"

"I trust no one, Aoife. Say what you must, here."

"I saved your life, you ungrateful wretch."

"You saved my arm and leg."

"Same difference. What do you imagine might have happened if any of your enemies found you so defeated?"

"'Might have' and 'did' are not sisters. Besides, you've given me every reason to mistrust you. Don't pretend you aren't complicit in my response."

She chewed on that in silent condemnation for a while. When next she spoke, her voice held the faintest edge of regret. "If I'd succeeded, you'd have been spared humiliation, cousin. I did it for you."

That was the closest he'd get to an apology, he knew.

"Why am I summoned?" There would be no point in pressing further.

"She brought you here at my request," chimed a familiar voice from deeper within the hall. Aoife half-turned in the jamb, bowing. "I'd prefer to have this conversation where a casual eye might not spy us. Do you mind, Lord Bishop?"

Damek's heart leaped into his throat. Without thinking, he dropped to a knee. "F-forgive me, *Ard Tiarne*. I didn't expect you."

"Obviously," smiled the voice. "Else, what would have been the point? Will you follow me into the parlor?"

"Yes, Your Highness."

Damek rose and trailed behind Aoife as she limped through the hall. His host entered a well-lit room in the back, filled with a hodge-podge of mismatched chairs and dusty tables before a modest fireplace and mantle. There were no adornments or bric-a-brac to be found anywhere in this chamber. The room was peeling paint, bare wooden floors, and charmless furnishings. The prince sat near the fire, gesturing for Damek to sit opposite. His guards eyed Damek from far corners, emotionless and threatening. Damek sat, careful to leave his scabbard unlocked. Just in case. One never knew with the Bolg.

Falan the Younger's teeth were very white against his bronze skin. "It's been an age, hasn't it, My Lord."

Damek dipped his head. "It has, *Ard Tiarne*."

"Still refuse to call me 'father,' eh?"

Damek said nothing.

"Well, perhaps you're wiser than I surmised?"

Being the Prince of Armagh's bastard-born son was not something to bandy about, especially if the prince in question was supposed to be dead.

Damek did not return his smile. "Perhaps."

"Such mistrust I sense in you. You imagine I'd harm my only son?"

"… I have a vivid imagination, *Ard Tiarne*."

The prince's gaze flicked to Aoife for a moment. "As do we all. So," he leaned forward. "One uncle dead, and the lesser claims your throne. How'd this come to pass?"

"Many things happened, not the least of which was a visit from the Crown Prince and his cousin, Tam Lin of Croghan. Patrick collapsed in Court, and Henry had seized the moment. His followers clamor for the old ways, and they are numerous."

"The Adair came for the girl, didn't he?"

A muscle flexed in Damek's jaw. "Yes."

"Interesting," said Falan, rubbing his hands together. "This girl proves a thorn in our *seanmáthair's* side, it seems. Hard-won power can be easily lost when the right names are involved— as we, ourselves, hope to demonstrate." He leaned back. "I like it not that the Donahugh girl has sided with the Adair Clan. By rights, she should die."

Damek stilled. He knew better than to reveal his irritation. The Prince of Armagh had never been cruel to him, per se, but that hardly implied that he was kind, either. Damek had to be very, very careful here. "I believe the Dannan exile encourages her nonsensical passion for freedom. Una Moura Donahugh will be the queen of Eire if she lives. Escape from that burden is a fantasy and nothing more. She'll see reason. I vow it."

"I've no time for misguided romance, Damek. If she does not sit beside you, she must die. I cannot afford the added boon to Midhir's claim. If he marries her, Kaer Yin will reestablish Eire for the Tuatha De Dannan."

"He won't. The High King would never approve the match. At best, Una would become a concubine or hostage in Bri Leith. Once she sees the truth of this, she'll return home with me."

"Claim Eire by proof of blood and strength of arms, my son. You don't need her."

"If I want the Northers to embrace me as King, then I must have her by my side," Damek paused to clear his throat. He looked down. "No disrespect intended, My Prince, but the opposition to Vanna Nema is proof of my argument. While the peasants in the shade of the Citadel love and fear her, she's alienated most of the nobility in Innisfail with her barbarism. Nearly every Merchers Guild has united against her rule, and the colonies in Alba and Cymru have declared their independence from Tairngare's Charter. What's worse, I've had a report that a force of Dannan Sidhe marching south from Skye, with Drem Moura in their train."

Falan nodded. "I've heard the same, though my informants tell me she is carried in a litter behind the Queen's entourage. Drem is dying, or so I'm told. Surely, Eri Bres means to take the old woman to her father for council."

"With a host five hundred strong?" Damek's brows raised. "Sounds to me like the Dannans are banding together. The second force of nearly the same strength marches toward Rosweal under Fionn Shiel O'More, the High King's Champion. They may not know what we plan here, *Ard Tiarne*, but they muster all the same. Why?"

"Kaer Yin Adair is freed of his *geis*. They come to pay him obeisance."

"So, he gets a force of one thousand peerless Dannan warriors, and this doesn't concern you?"

"He's the Crown Prince of Innisfail, Damek. His return is significant to his people, as mine shall be to the Bolg."

Damek exhaled slowly. As long as he'd been aware that the Prince of Armagh was his father, he'd always believed him to be the canniest man alive. Patient, cunning, and cautious was Falan the Younger. Having fabricated his death, Falan had been free to weave a beautifully subtle plot that spelled ultimate doom for the Dannan High King in Bri Leith. Though… to get there, he must depend upon agents united by their loathing of Dannan rule and sworn to the utmost secrecy. Agents like the power-mad Dowager Queen of Armagh. Did he not see it, Damek wondered? That the fatal flaw in his plans was critical arrogance. "So, while they're gathering to consolidate power, we're— what? Wasting men and resources to spread hysteria in the Midlands and allowing Liadan to destabilize the wealthiest city in the North? Is that all?"

Falan's brow darkened. "I've no need to share my stratagems with you."

"No?" Damek laughed. "Seems I'm the one with an army behind him."

"You threaten me?" The room vibrated a bit at the edges.

Damek wasn't cowed. "Why are you here now?"

"Do I need an excuse to meet with my son?"

"Horseshite. What do you want from me, *Ard Tiarne*?"

Falan's features settled into a calm, observational disdain. For the Bolg, to get straight to the point was the height of ill manners. Damek couldn't give a shite less. In thirty-two years, he'd seen this man who claimed paternity only a handful of times. While it was true that Falan had sent him letters, gifts, and the odd servant (Damek's swordmasters, for example), any feeling or paternal warmth had been lacking.

Damek, as always, was meant to be a useful tool.

Between Patrick Donahugh and Falan the Younger: Damek was unsure which relative he loathed more.

"I wish you to march against the Dannans at the Confluence."

Damek nodded once. "I see. Put Bethany on the hook for Armagh?"

"To defeat the Crown Prince would be a spectacular victory."

"… and while I'm doing your dirty work, what will you be doing?"

"I do not need—"

"Let me stop you there. The answer is 'no.' I've plans of my own."

"You dare defy *me*?"

"I'm talking to a dead man with no army save a smattering of followers from an insignificant city in Aes Sidhe. Your men serve to harass and mystify groups who are far too busy fighting each other to notice."

"I am the rightful *Ard Ri* of Innisfail."

"Perhaps. Suppose I can give you the crown. Isn't that right?"

Falan fell silent. Dark energy radiated from his person like smoke.

Damek was unafraid. He stood. "Whatever you wish for, *I* am the rightful King of Eire, without your blood or blessing. If you wish my help stealing the Dannan crown, you had better start asking yourself what *I* want in exchange."

Falan's voice followed him into the hall. "I will kill the Siorai girl."

Damek shot back, "I dare you to try. Or didn't you ask Aoife what happened the last time she made an attempt?" Aoife's nostrils flared in shame as he passed, but he paid her no mind. Damek opened the door, allowing a blast of chill wind into the tiny house. He knew he'd be heard, even without raising his voice. "Tairngare is my price, *athair*."

"You will never keep it," said Falan, with a sigh.

"You have my terms."

He didn't bother to shut the door on his way outside.

Blood Ties

Grainne had so little experience with regret; even faced with it as she was now, she was at a loss to fully comprehend the feeling. Her family had made a terrible mistake. Sound traveled quite far in an open market. Once thriving shops were shuttered and bolted, many slathered with red paint that read '*look for us at Tara*' or '*permanently closed*' in the common tongue. In the shadow of the Citadel, nothing moved but the wind and whatever detritus it carried from one empty corner to another. Dirty snow melted from unpatched rooftops in the unseasonably warm sunlight. Avenues lacked cobbles for want of care. Carts and wagons full of broken crates and fraying baskets were scattered over every street as if the people who owned them had fled in extreme haste.

Indeed, Grainne spied only soldiers marching through cross lanes or lurking upon the walls. Despair clung to the city, a heady pall that cast a shadow of fear over the stoutest heart in her midst. Each step they took through the Drough Quarter trumpeted doom. If anyone saw her or her company, none bothered to call out. The Cohort, too, seemed listless and hollow as the streets they guarded. Once they came to the Citadel's high iron gate, Grainne looked up and gasped.

There, dangling from the walls, were the people she'd believed fled.

Dozens of men, women, and even children— rotted to rags and bones in high crow's cages or swung from frayed ropes creaking in the crisp winter breeze. The living wouldn't meet her eyes, as if the hope of rescue had long since faded to rot in their mouths. Their moans and cries sent chills up and down her arms.

The smell hit her next. She gagged, covering her mouth with a shaking hand. Human feces, vomit, and urine assailed her group in a miasmic cloud. The glass-eyed guards who met them didn't appear to notice.

Their captain held his hand out. "What business?"

Bracing herself, Grainne uncovered her face. "We're ambassadors from Armagh. I am Grainne Mac Nemed, daughter of Falan the Elder, King of the Fir Bolg."

The captain didn't blink. He held up a scrap of vellum. "Hm. Says here you were 'sposed to arrive two days ago."

"We were delayed."

"I see," he droned. He waved two more soldiers over. "Search them."

Her guards bristled, stepping in front of her. She spoke around a muscular shoulder. "You have no cause to lay hands upon a visiting dignitary."

Again, he waved his bit of vellum bearing Nema's seal. "Doma's orders."

Grainne stiffened. "Since when?"

"I don't make the rules, highness, just enforce them. Kada?" A lieutenant shuffled over, fingers spread, sporting a broad leer over his blemished face. "Submit or move on," scoffed the gatekeeper with a shrug.

Grainne's retainers drew swords. Her bodyguard, Leal, stepped forward, forcing the young Cohort officer back. "Try it and die, mortal."

Several guards rushed the gate on either side of the wall almost instantly, bowstrings drawing back tight. The Cohort Captain at the entrance dropped his vellum to reach for his shortsword. The Warhammers at Grainne's back drew and aimed their bows. All of this happened so fast that she scarcely had time to suck in a gasp. Just as the moment strained to the breaking point, a high-pitched voice sailed high over the

Citadel's wall. Beyond the portcullis, a disheveled, deformed figure slumped into view. The captain's hand halted over his pommel. He turned to see Vanna Nema's servant shamble forward. Hideously scarred cheeks having gone an odd shade of puce, Fawa Gan leaned into the bars, huffing. "Her highness is expected, Captain! Stay your men."

The gatekeeper spat; eyes narrowed. "Bit late. One of these faerie fucks just drew down on my man there. Next one moves will be full of holes."

"The Doma requests the lady Grainne's presence upon arrival, sir. You're ordered to stand down."

The captain snorted, peering around Gan's newly skeletal frame. "Yeah? Who's going to enforce that? I don't see anyone in there but you."

Gan fidgeted. "I ran ahead. Lady MacNemed's train was spied from the Cloister, Captain. Corsairs are on their way."

"Hm," said the captain. "Until I see a warrant, no one gets through this gate. Especially not this ragtag without the sense Siora gave a gnat."

"My men," said Grainne, having found her voice. "Apologize for their weapons. They do so in defense of me. We are not accustomed to such treatment. Men are disallowed from laying hands upon a member of the royal family, Captain."

The odious little man did not flutter an eyelid. "These are dangerous times, mistress. Submit to a search or leave. Many folks hang behind me who thought to argue the justice of our Doma's commands."

Sobered by the warning in his tone, Grainne unbuttoned her cloak and stepped past Leal. "Do as you must, but be quick about it," she said through her teeth. "If that young man approaches me again, many more of you will die at this gate than we."

The captain raised a brow but relinquished his pommel. He stalked over to perform the deed himself. Gan eyed her helplessly from behind the portcullis. She raised her chin while the officious Milesian soldier raked rough hands over her body, none too gently. At least he had the grace to keep his internal opinions from his expression. She might have been a wood block, for all the man appeared to mind. Once done, he waved her past. "Do you have anything to declare?"

"Many things, but none related to your inquiry," she sniffed, shrugging her cloak back on. It was cold in Tairngare now, and the sky promised another light snowfall. Soon, the heavy ice storms of Dor Imba would descend and halt travel altogether. "In the wagon, we've brought supplies for our journey and gifts for your Doma. Every saddlebag contains more of the same."

Having rifled through her belongings, he passed her white leather satchel back, oblivious to the necessary documents inside. He couldn't read Ealig, could he? "Your men will surrender their weapons at once."

Leal's dark brows wound together. "*Lig dom é a mharú.*"

"*Ní anois,*" she answered but nodded to the gatekeeper. "Of course. Most of my retinue will remain and await my return. Those who follow me into the Doma's chambers will do as you ask. Leal?" Leal cursed under his breath but lowered his blade. With the sourest possible expression, he passed it to a waiting Cohort guardsman who couldn't have looked more nervous if he tried. These men had grown reckless in the wake of Nema's ascension. With so many citizens hanging from the walls like discarded meat, Grainne had no doubt the guards would grow bolder by the day. She paused at the gate while the portcullis raised. Gan awaited her on the other side, wringing his hands to ribbons. The captain gave her a mock bow as she passed.

She'd see to it the brute supped on his tongue by nightfall. "Where are your Corsairs?" she asked Gan quietly.

With a glance over her shoulder at the remaining Warhammers and Bolgmen filing through the gate, he lowered his voice to a mere whisper. "What guards, My Lady?"

THE SURREAL SILENCE IN THE streets was nothing to the thunderous quiet inside the Citadel. Slack-faced girls in gray robes (Secundas, Grainne recalled) scrubbed already pristine floors and window casings or tiptoed through wide-open spaces usually overflowing with people. As her party passed, no single girl dared to meet her eyes. These nameless Secundas, leftovers from a formerly robust caste system, drifted through empty halls like disappointed ghosts. If Grainne were inclined to such nonsense, she might feel for them. All hope of advancement through the Cloister had faded since Nema had stripped the city of its Libellan and Mercher classes.

Who would foster them for the Fifth Ordeal now?

Bound as they were to Nema's edicts, Grainne did not doubt that each was beginning to realize they would likely serve in drudgery for the rest of their lives. Nema had no use for rivals. If a girl did not serve, she would be dispensed with. Grainne hadn't failed to notice that many of the sad creatures begging for death in the cages at the wall bore the infamous grey of the Secundas' robes. Who was there to speak for this faceless multitude of forgotten women? Everyone with any influence had died or fled in the first Cohort purge. Any that lingered soon found themselves in servile grey. Nema was the queen at the heart of an enslaved hive.

Grainne and Leal shared a long look. This was not to plan. None of it was. Whatever was happening here had *never* been on the agenda. Gan led her through several halls and short staircases toward the Grand Arcade and the formal entryway into the Cloister. Here, the cloying stench of burning incense was nearly worse than the sickly-sweet scent of death outside. Though the steps were polished to an impossible sheen, Grainne felt like she was plunging her feet through tainted oil. Another simpering maiden shrank from her advance, making her frown. What in the nine hells was her grandmother doing to these people? Leal clutched her elbow as they climbed the opulent Agate staircase toward Nema's Tenth Floor throne room.

Aside from soldiers and newly indentured servants, was *no one* else left in the Citadel? Had Nema destroyed every one of note within the city… so swiftly?

Macha, Grainne thought, looking around and hearing nothing but the wind tease at the cracks in the walls. *She truly has gone mad.* Nema, drunk with power, had imposed this thorough and terrifying decimation. Every time Grainne had visited this monstrous structure, it had been filled to the brim with stinking, screeching, arguing, laughing, loitering, and otherwise busy mortals. As her footsteps ricocheted from every wall and sparklingly clean surface, even she could not stall a pang for such loss. The cost of Nema's madness was more terrible than she imagined.

It's hush… even worse.

Breathing laboriously, Gan paused at the Ninth Floor landing. The two hunks of odd-shaped flesh where his eyebrows had been knotted together. "My Lady," he leaned in as close as he dared with Leal's burning violet gaze so near. Grainne drew back. If he noticed her revulsion, he didn't let it show.

Quick, this one is.

No wonder he lives where so many have died.

"I must warn you."

"No need. I have eyes."

"Not about this… tomb." He gestured to the massive, gilded doors at the next landing. "About *her*."

Grainne took a breath. "She's run mad. A blind woman would see it."

He fidgeted, his small, piggish eyes roving every crevice and corner. "Lower your voice. I'm trying to help you."

"Who do you believe you're speaking to, little man?" She whispered back mockingly. "I am an emissary from Armagh. She wouldn't dare—"

"You're mistaken, My Lady." His voice took an edge. "She *would*. She has."

Leal towered over Gan. "Speak plain."

"How many of your kind did you leave with her last time? Her guards?"

"Two dozen, no more. Why?"

"You'll find eleven or so in the dungeon beneath the Citadel; the rest seem to share her… malady. They do her bidding, whatever she asks. 'Twas they, who imprisoned the others. Well, those that lived through the exchange."

Grainne sucked in a breath, but Leal asked, "When? How?"

Gan snuck a glance over his shoulder, clearly wary the warriors in question would soon stomp down the stairs looking for them. "There's no time. Her Eminence doesn't like to be kept waiting." He pressed something cold and metallic into her hands. She didn't need to look down to know what it was. "That will open any door in the Cloister, and most in the Citadel, save the Treasury and Archives. Get your men free when you can."

"Why would you aid us? I can feel your hatred from here."

He gave her a dispassionate smile. "Someone has to stop her. Why else would you come to this hell she's crafted after the butchery you witnessed during your last visit? If you're not here to reason with her, why else would you bother?"

"*I* am not here for any such purpose. I've brought gifts from the King of Armagh."

Again, he glanced at the top of the stairs, licking his missing lips. "You're here to read terms from your brother, My Lady." He shook his head at the flash in her eyes. "Yes, we've met, Lord Falan and I. A shame he didn't kill her when he had the chance, for he may never get another one."

"You dare speak so of your mistress?" hissed Grainne. "I should have Leal hang you from the balustrade by your entrails for such disloyalty."

He laughed. "I no longer have much of a nose, but I know fear when I smell it. She's gone too far. She kills on a whim, sometimes a score at once. She won't be satisfied until the entire city is enslaved or dead, and if you believe she means to stop at the Drough Gate, you're sorely mistaken. Her followers, zealots all, speak of marching west and south to press her Reformations deep into Eire. Your 'king' does not factor into her plans at all, and believe me if anyone knows her mind, it's me. I've been her footstool for forty years."

Grainne fell silent for a while, considering his blunt sincerity. She'd told Falan what she'd seen when last she was here, but her brother vowed the old woman had been dealt with and would come to heel. Seeing the city's state and suffering, people only told her she'd been right all along. Liadan Mac Nemed had lost her mind at last. Too many decades spent in the Milesian world had eroded her sanity with her loyalty. "Why are you telling me this? What do you hope to gain?"

"An end, "Gan sighed, shivering. "Before it's too late. For everyone."

Another of Grainne's men scoffed, and Leal said, "You speak as if she were a monster in some tale. She's an old woman."

"I know who she is, sir, and how long she's waited for this chance," Gan said. "If you leave her to this, so many will die. The Transition will pale by comparison."

"You give her too much credit," argued Grainne.

"Do I? Has there ever been a sharper sword than belief? Listen, any moment now, one of her loyal followers— maybe one of your own— will head down here to retrieve us. If you think I'm lying or conflating the issue, share your misgivings about your reception here. I beg you, prove me wrong."

"She isn't all-powerful. She wouldn't dare—"

"Why do you keep saying that? Do you imagine you know her better than Aoife or myself? Do you have the faintest idea what she has done to either one of us or so many others? It goes beyond counting. No. If you march in there and deliver those terms, you'll never leave here, My Lady. I promise you that. She dispenses with those who aren't ready to die by her word in short order. I'm giving you your lives in hopes you'll escape to return in *force*." The jangle of metal and the ring of booted feet trilled down the stairs. Gan went white as death itself. "Decide for yourself when you see her. She's… much changed. I pray you make the right decision."

He made as if to resume his progress upward, but Grainne's fingers caught his sleeve. "If you want to die so badly, why not do the honors yourself?"

His eyes were like two chips of black glass. "Not until she does. Else, how would I ever rest?"

⚔

Vanna Nema did not look like a queen with the world at her feet. She appeared to have lost a great deal of weight she could ill afford to lose and sat the Doma's massive onyx throne like a rumpled, sullen child. Grainne covered her mouth lest her grandmother see the shock and horror on her face. Nema's hair was unbound and unwashed, trailing over her shoulders in a graying, frizzled rat's nest. Her cheeks were drawn with huge shadows tucked into their hollows. Deep black pools gathered below each of her bright green eyes, making them wider and ever more piercing than usual. Though she wore the Doma's heavy golden robes of state, the reams of fabric did little to hide the hollow bones at her collar, throat, and wrists. When she smiled at Grainne, her teeth were dull and brittle, as if they had not been tended to in months. The glaring evidence of rapid aging aside, the poorly healed scars over her face and neck were most alarming. As if a giant eagle had raked its talons from her scalp to her exposed collarbones, jagged, poorly healing rents tracked diagonally from her right temple to her left shoulder. These cuts may have run further, but Vanna's robes prevented further evidence.

Grainne nearly choked at the sight.

This was the mighty Vanna Nema— the dowager queen, Liadan Mac Nemed of Armagh? *This* was her grandmother, the one woman she had idolized and revered the whole of her long life. At some point, Leal pressed his hand against the small of her back to remind her to breathe. "Welcome, Lady of Armagh," wheezed Nema, her voice like a broken wind flute. "What news do you bring us of Aes Sidhe?"

It took a while, but Grainne found her tongue. She dug through her white leather satchel for the roll of vellum she sought. From his place behind Nema, she could swear Fawa Gan's eyes flashed in warning. What was she to do? If she came into Nema's presence empty-handed, wouldn't that have been the greater danger? Grainne must as always, keep her wits sharp. "I bring you terms from the King of the Fir Bolg, your Eminence. As requested upon our last meeting, Falan the Elder sends you these gifts," she declared, waving a hand at the chests her men set down. "And his best wishes for a fruitful Imbolg."

"Hm," Nema cackled, nodding to her Cohort guardsman to collect the items and remove them from the throne room. Grainne had never seen so many soldiers around her grandmother before. There had to be a score, at least. Several Secundas stood in tight lines in each corner and archway with their heads bowed, awaiting the slightest command. That chill Grainne felt earlier returned with a vengeance.

An army of dolls, she thought, her throat constricting.

Puppets have more life in them.

"No need to stand on ceremony, child. How does my son, your father?"

Grainne's head snapped up. "I— I don't... that is—"

Nema's laughter grated like sandpaper. "We keep no secrets in this city, My Lady. Only the loyal may enter the Ancestor's Hall." There was a note here that Grainne readily identified. She dared not look at Gan. "My name is revealed and my purpose clear. Tell me, what is yours, granddaughter?"

Her name 'is revealed'?

"I have said, Eminence. I bring tidings from the king."

"To swear fealty, I presume. The Ancestor rules in Tairngare, and soon, all Eire shall bend its knee. Isn't that why you've come?"

Nema's mad gaze burned.

The vellum in Grainne's hand shook. She closed her fist around it so that she wouldn't see. That is *not* what this vellum read. It was a veiled order for Liadan Mac Nemed to return to Armagh and leave the city to Grainne. This was meant to be shared in private, of course. Grainne hadn't expected to be dragged before the throne. "If we may speak in private," Grainne attempted, noting the many sets of eyes that slid her way, none of them friendly. For all he breathed, Gan might have been an ugly statue behind Nema. "There are many items I have been tasked to discuss with you."

The way Nema's thin lips pressed together told Grainne everything she needed to know. She had been right to leave the city when she did two months ago under cover of darkness. She should not have returned, no matter what her idealistic brother proposed. Liadan was insane. Mortality had come for the Dowager Queen, and with it, madness. How long had she dwelled among these Milesians? A hundred years, two? How long had she plotted and schemed to overtake them? Long before she stepped foot outside of the Oiche Ar Fad, that was sure. The mortal realm was lethal for one so old as Liadan, and seeing her now, Grainne knew she had to get word to her brother fast. First, she had to appease the most potent lunatic in the land.

Think, Grainne!

Once she reads this scroll, you're doomed.

What can you offer?

What does a madwoman want? "Fine," she said after several tense moments. "If they know you, *seanmáthair*, then I shall not fear to speak freely. My father, as you know, hasn't the wits the gods gave a toad. Instead, my brother seeks your removal from the Doma's office and a temporary replacement put in place until the Parliament is reinstated."

Those hostile stares grew murderous. A wave of whispers circled the chamber while the Cohort reached for their pommels. From some hidden door came seven fully armed Warhammers— Leal's men— with their black cuirasses shining in the light of Nema's multitude of braziers. Not one of them seemed to recognize Grainne or her party.

Ah.

This must be an enchantment.

There is no other explanation.

What did Liadan trade for the power to bend so many to her will? But then she thought about the people strung along the walls like hanks of beef and understood.

This is blood magic.

She trades lives for power—no wonder she is rotting from the inside out. Macha, save us all. "However," she was proud of her even tone. She threw the scroll to the shining black floor in disgust. "My brother does not speak for me. I, like you, am my own woman. It is my right to choose whom I serve."

Nema gave a slight smirk. "You would betray the Black Prince so easily? I think not. You've been his faithful dog from the day he was born, Grainne. Where he walks, your adoration follows. You'll have to try much harder to convince me you haven't come to supplant me."

Leal was wise enough not to draw his larks as Nema's guardsmen inched nearer. They might fight free of the throne room, but they'd never pass the city gates alive. There were too many of them.

Falan had miscalculated when he'd sent her here to negotiate on his behalf… or, *had* he? An unpleasant thought crossed Grainne's mind like a cloud flitting over the sun.

He sent you here for an excuse.

You're here to tempt her to violence.

A queasy certainty sank into her blood. Falan, her beloved brother, had sent her here to remove two further obstacles to his scheme. If Grainne lived, he could use her again; if she died— he'd take Tairngare with all of Armagh's blessing.

That… clever, cruel bastard, she thought.

I vow he'll perish by my hand if I live through this.

Who'll rule Aes Sidhe then, hm, brother dear?

Keeping her rage in check, Grainne raised her chin high. "Why should Falan rule Innisfail? Why should it always be a man? What has he ever done to deserve the honor? Nothing. He thinks he has the right to take whatever he wishes because he was a male born of an ancient line. I say, why should it be *him?*"

"I hear the truth in your voice, granddaughter. This pleases me. You are the elder child. In Tairngare, primogeniture does not hold sway. A male may only inherit when he is the eldest, and a powerless female is the only alternative. You are not powerless, are you? Armagh is as much your inheritance as his, but only through *my* grace. Do you understand?"

"I do. I will swear absolute fealty to you, *seanmáthair*. If you will have me?"

Nema sat back, weighing Grainne's words. Grainne bowed low, her heart hammering against her ribs. "I don't believe you, child. You're duplicitous as your brother but half as bright. Surely you've realized why he sent you here?" She sucked her teeth. "Must be frustrating to see oneself reduced to a commodity, hm? I know, firsthand."

Leal slipped a dagger into her pocket.

It wouldn't help.

Already, Nema's loyal Warhammers surrounded their small party.

"If you'd intended to offer your allegiance to me as you claim, you wouldn't have fled with Aoife and her lickspittles in the middle of the night. I have a long memory, you see, and forgive very few slights of the sort."

The lights in each approaching Bolg's eyes had long gone out. She wondered how she might have missed that dull, haunted shade. Were the Warhammers in the dungeons immune to influence somehow, or had Nema just not gotten to them yet? Had the Cohort at the Gate been enchanted as well? Likely not. The meanest among the Milesians leftover here worshipped Nema as the Ancestor's second coming. She empowered them: their rivalries, bitterness, and prejudices. Nema gave their hatreds and fears a focus.

The Bolg, however, were a different story.

"My Lady, when I say run, you do it," murmured Leal at her nape.

She opened her mouth to protest, but Nema answered for her. "No need for such theatrics, my young friend. I would not harm my grandchild. I merely wish to… correct her behavior." Nema's mouth was a red knife slash in the distance. "Take her. Kill the others if need be but spare them, if possible. We could use more capable hands around here, no?"

A fellow Grainne remembered as Earc came within a hair's breadth of clasping her wrist. She dropped her satchel and drew Leal's dagger from her pocket. "Leal, get out of here. You are the strongest among us. If anyone can slip through her guards, it's you."

Another reached for her wrist. Her blade nicked out, nearly taking a finger. The assailant recoiled with a grunt. A third guard took his place. She was obliged to slash at this one a few times before he backed away. Aware that she would make it difficult for them, Nema's converts went around her in a circle.

"I won't leave you." Leal insisted, drawing both hammers. His men fanned out before their lady, prepared to do their duty. Grainne retreated within their protective circle if only long enough to spare Leal a frown.

"Only one way to go. From the Seventh, on this side. Falan must hear of this."

Leal exhaled long and slow. He loved her, she knew, and leaving her was never something he'd do willingly. "If you don't, I'm dead anyway… or like them. Go. Now!" She wasted no more energy debating the issue. She dashed toward the closest guard with a small war cry taking a brutal swipe at his cheek with her blade. He staggered backward, giving her the opening she sought. The second set of hands reached out to grab her, but she slipped below them to her knees, gliding effortlessly over the glistening black floor. She'd barely come twelve inches past when she regained her footing. Dagger high, she raced toward Nema on her throne. As every head swiveled in her direction and the guards scrambled to catch her, Leal gutted his cover with one hand and dashed for the open doorway. He didn't get far before the Cohort filed down the stairs after him. Grainne didn't get to see anything else nor hear the distant crack of broken glass, which would signify his successful escape.

An unseen force caught her midleap, slamming her into a far wall.

Nema got up, clutching her side for want of air. The cost of such magic was likely more than one dying Sidhe could handle— and she was, Grainne had no doubt. Nema seemed to shrivel where she stood.

"Stupid girl. You *dare* move against me?"

Grainne cried aloud as she was dragged back to the throne by an invisible hand. She gagged. The force of Nema's power sought to choke the life from her.

"Did you imagine your little ruse would free your man, and he'd run off to tattle to your little brother? How noble, Grainne," Nema said. "I'm quite disappointed in you."

Grainne only had the air to send one last prayer to Macha for deliverance before she sank into that obsidian floor and saw no more.

Tech Duinn

At first, Tir Falias was nothing but a glimmer upon a distant hillside, a speck of light in the dark. If one stared too long, its shape would flicker then wink out altogether, like a half-remembered dream. Each step they gained seemed to chase it farther toward the horizon until its turrets crested the foothills of an unfamiliar mountain range. Nearer still, its spires beckoned from the shores of a distant sea. Up, over, under, the road wound— and never did its gates draw close in all the hours they walked, rode, or ran. They trudged through rain, sleet, snow, hail, and even the heat of a summer's day. Hours, days, perhaps weeks passed while they pushed on— ever forward, ever onward.

Still, the hall of the Raven King eluded them.

The wind blew hot and cold at once, and the sights and sounds deceived. When night receded toward the east, and the roseate sun baked the earth beneath their feet, Kaer Yin breathed a sigh of relief. Their worn, bloodied party rounded a rocky outcrop overhanging the path, and suddenly Tir Falias loomed ahead. Ultimately tucked into a high tor surrounded by lush green forest and sweet, rushing water, the hall of Diarmid *Fiachra Dubh* Adair was revealed at last. A sturdy stone castle erupted proudly between two great rivers, encircled by white-capped mountains that crashed into a vast turquoise sea. Hewn from the bedrock beneath the tor itself, the rolling hillside parted from the fortress' high walls like a lady doffing her cloak. A mammoth waterfall crashed from the tallest snowy peak like a gossamer veil, feeding both rivers that diverged around the hillside. A large stone bridge, easily a mile long, spanned the confluence from that bulbous green island.

Robin coughed. "*There's* a sight. Can't say it's what I expected, though."

Kaer Yin passed his old friend his waterskin. The Greenmaker looked like he'd been murdered and resurrected again in the same hour. Perhaps he had? Maybe they *all* had? He glanced at Rian, who glared back from Tam Lin's saddle. Without his cousin's arm supporting her, she would have fallen from her seat ages ago. With his cloak torn to ribbons over Rian's thin shoulders and his tunic in bloodied threads— so might Tam Lin, had he not been occupied with her care. Shar was missing hanks of hair from his nape and bore scratches up and down his arms. Kaer Yin didn't want to think about the cuts, scrapes, bruises, and other wounds he, himself, bore. Robin had lost a tooth and wore a nasty bite wound that would have torn his jugular out had Shar not acted quickly enough. "What?" mused Kaer Yin dryly. "Think it'd be a gloomy black tower in the middle of a swamp?"

"Aye," Robin agreed. "Given what we've seen, I don't think ye could blame me for that." He passed the skin back, his brow heavier than usual.

"No. I couldn't," admitted Kaer Yin, truthfully. Noticing the direction of Robin's stare, he resisted the urge to turn around. "She's fine."

"Is she?"

No, Kaer Yin's jaw clenched.

But I can't bloody well say why, and neither can you.

Robin nodded at the unspoken warning. "This place is no good for anyone, saving maybe ye lot, but it's doing something to her, Ben. Ye see it, plain as me."

"Keep your voice down."

"What are you two jabbering about?" demanded Una. She had the ears of a bat; Kaer Yin was quite sure. On foot, he led his overworked mount by the bit while Una sat high in the saddle, tucked into his cloak. She hadn't had time to prepare for the journey when they'd left Bethany properly, and the night had been cold as it was lethal. Sparing a scowl for Robin, his head swiveled round to face her. The sight of her whisked the air from his lungs all over again. Though she was equally as filthy and unkempt as the rest of their party, she alone did not share in everyone else's general state of shock, pain, and exhaustion. Aside from a few blood smears in places he'd seen her take wounds, she was the picture of glowing, perfect health. Point in fact, he couldn't recall ever seeing her look so lovely— which disturbed him more than the idea that she was healing herself much more swiftly than she ever had before. The question of 'how' lingered in the warming air over his head like a cloud. Her dusky gold cheeks pulled down sharply as she frowned at him. "What?"

Clearing his suddenly dry throat, he glanced away. "Are you all right?"

"Me? I'm bloody grand, thanks. Why?"

"You look… well, you look—"

"Spit it out."

"*Fine*, that's what. If I hadn't seen you take half a dozen wounds last night, I'd never believe it. You're scaring Robin if I'm honest."

Robin threw up his hands. "I didn't bloody say that!"

Una twisted her lip at him. "Right you are."

"— That aside," continued Kaer Yin. "The nearer we come to Tir Falias, the healthier you appear. What's happening?"

Chewing her cheek, she glanced back at Rian, whose lips came together in a tight line. Kaer Yin nearly bristled. What the hells did the girl infer that he didn't? "I don't know," Una answered. "But I can guess."

"Samhain?"

"Yes," she sighed.

"Tell me," he pleaded, leaning close. Even mounted as she was, Kaer Yin's face wasn't far from her eye level. "I don't judge you for something that saved hundreds of lives, Una."

"It's just," she hesitated, scanning the trees in the fading twilight opposite. "I feel… different somehow. Stronger. I don't know how to explain it."

"Maybe Diarmid can?"

She struggled not to flinch. "If he doesn't kill me, yeah."

His hand closed over hers through his mud-stained cloak. "He won't."

"You keep saying that, but we're at his mercy now, aren't we?"

"Some of us are, sure," grumbled Robin.

Kaer Yin pulled away from Una's side, tugging the reins tight around his hand. He led on. There was no telling what his uncle would do when they arrived, but he'd be damned if he allowed anything to happen to her. Diarmid might still be in a snit for the surprise he'd received at Samhain. So be it. Una was family now.

Besides, Kaer Yin knew him better than anyone. Diarmid would never harm a woman, especially one as beautiful and intriguing as Una Moura. His scowl deepened until it might have been carved into his face. That *was* what worried him. They were halfway across the causeway when the sun finally chased the memory of evening into the east. He stole another peek at Una over his shoulder. She had closed her eyes to absorb the sun's hazy rays, her long eyelashes sweeping her cheekbones. His heart squeezed against his ribs. He'd only half-won her and knew, down to his bones, he wasn't done fighting for her.

Diarmid would never harm so unique a prize.

No.

Instead, he would try to *keep* Una.

That was much, much worse.

By what amounted to mid-morning in this strange, hauntingly lovely place— they arrived at the gates of Tir Falias. With the rush of both rivers heavy in her ears, the scent of crisp ozone and fir blowing down the mountains, Una made a slight sound of surprise. Kaer Yin pointed to a more minor, hollowed-out hill about a mile away. It bore a stone edifice with a massive, blackened maw for an entrance.

"Bri Reis," said he. "The Hall of Slumbering Kings."

Huge braziers burned tirelessly from each side of the doorway. Nothing but mist traced the endless dark at its center, yet, she felt watched, all the same. Her skin prickled with gooseflesh. "Who lives there?"

"No one. That's the tomb of Crom Dagda." He and every Sidhe in their midst tapped their temples and bowed to the distant tor. "Bri Reis is the holiest place in the Oiche Ar Fad, where my people are taken when we die. It is a great honor to house one's bones in the Hall of the Dagda."

Una nodded but offered no commentary. She understood the veneration of ancestors more than most. As they filed into the courtyard beneath a wide-open portcullis devoid of soldiers or courtiers, her eye couldn't stray from the Dagda's beckoning monument. Something was *present* about it as if it had thoughts and feelings. Attuned to the undercurrent of energy, she couldn't describe the impression she felt as either warmth or welcome, though neither did it feel expressly hostile.

Curious, she thought.

It sees us too.

Her Spark flared in greeting.

"Crom Dagda?" Rian wondered aloud, her voice grainy and hoarse from screaming. "I thought he was interred at Tara before the Milesian Invasion?"

"He was," replied Tam Lin, still holding her upright in his saddle. His voice, as usual, held a note of bored disdain. "When Eber Finn was crowned at Tara, he returned Crom's bones to Midhir."

"To placate him?"

"No, 'twas a sign of great respect. By then, the Milesians had roundly defeated us. Their weapons were finer, their numbers too great. When Nuada fell, Crom Dagda gave his life to give us a better one."

"Cromnasa."

"Yes." Again, he saluted Bri Reis. "We were mortal once, or mostly so. The Dagda sacrificed himself to give us dominion over Death and its realm— the land we tread today— Tech Duinn. Its king must be eager for company, don't you think, Yin?"

Kaer Yin grunted as they passed through the portcullis into a second courtyard cloaked in shadows. Una didn't need to read his mind to know how worried he was.

She swallowed the lump in her throat.

"Come, ladies," Tam Lin chimed, dismounting in the courtyard. He reached up to help Rian down. She sagged against him just enough that he was obliged to keep one arm wrapped tightly around her waist. Despite the riot of conflicting fears and emotions raging through Una's heart, she raised a brow at the smug triumph in the Prince of Connaught's expression. Shar noticed too and glared at his boots, jaw clenched.

Una's eyes flashed at Kaer Yin as he helped her dismount.

His compressed lips said it all.

Yeah, I saw.

"Let's go greet our dreaded old uncle, shall we?" said Tam Lin cheerfully.

Rian allowed herself to be scooped high into his arms without ado.

Her acute exhaustion was plain.

Una opened her mouth to protest, but Kaer Yin's hand caught her elbow. "No, love. She can barely walk alone, and he means well, anyway, for Tam Lin. Let it be for now."

Shar Lianor followed the pair through the courtyard.

He seemed far from happy. Had the signs been there all the while?

"How long has this been going on?" she demanded.

"Since Rosweal. She's oblivious, of course." Una socked him lightly in the ribs. He winced. "Ow! What was that for?"

"You're a bloody idiot! That's why," she whisper-screeched. "If he tries *anything*, I will murder him."

Kaer Yin rubbed his offended bruises. "He's hardly a predator, you know?"

She narrowed her eyes. "Consider my warning lodged."

"Well," he cleared his throat, threading his arm through hers. "As threats go, that might do the trick but don't count on it. We have greater concerns, and their affairs are not our business."

"*Our*, nothing. I love that girl, Kaer Yin."

"As do I," he said, realizing he meant it. "No harm that doesn't naturally befall any young heart shall happen to Rian in my care. All right?" On a whim, she stood on her tiptoes to kiss the right side of his mouth. He made a low sound. "What was that for?"

"So you'll keep your promise, no matter what happens in there."

"You're afraid of him, aren't you?"

She looked up at the imposing central keep; rushing water echoed around the courtyard. "I think I'm afraid of myself."

His lips brushed her forehead as he led her up the steps toward the entrance. Robin and the rest of their road-worn band queued up behind them; none seemed overeager. "Let's hope my uncle shares your sentiments."

⚜

Inside the massive but silent fortress where the servants appeared no more than flitting shades, they walked single file along a grand gallery upheld by intricately carved granite columns. The way forward was lit by gleaming orbs of pearlescent witch light, placed strategically at each darkened corner. There wasn't a shred of gilding to be seen anywhere, nor tapestries or other decoration upon the walls— just stark stone and haunting, cold light. Kaer Yin seemed to know where he was going without glancing up. He worried Damek's Ogham stone between two fingers, frowning while he turned it over repeatedly. Without breaking stride, he hung a right and up a single curving stair, then through a series of stately (if spartan) rooms warmed by blazing hearth fires.

Una had yet to see a single soul, even if she heard their whispers and felt the ever-present tingling sensation between her shoulder blades that told her she was being watched.

"I thought he'd have at least aimed to impress the mortals in our midst by now," observed Tam Lin. Robin pretended to smirk at his jesting tone, but he and the other Greenmakers clutched their weapons, clearly terrified. Down another hall, a large archway led through to a broad chamber that was swallowed up by a floor-to-ceiling slate hearth one could likely roast a bull upon. Beside it stood a frail old man wrapped in a delicate white, woolen cloak. He shivered though he should have been ablaze.

The figure turned as they approached.

Una sucked in a breath. Faris— or Diarmid!

He smiled weakly back at them. Though one could never confuse him with someone else, he was significantly changed, diminished somehow. The light in his skin had faded, and his lustrous green eyes were dull and listless as glass. The ailing King of Tech Duinn coughed. "Welcome, nephews. So good of you to drop by for a visit." His voice, too, held a dusty, hollow quality it hadn't before. Without waiting for a response, he hobbled over to an oversized velvet chair and sank into its cushions with a haggard sigh.

"What in the *nine hells* happened to you, uncle?" Tam Lin whistled as he deposited Rian onto a nearby divan. She reached out, and Una's fingers found hers of their own accord. "You look *lovely*."

Diarmid Adair had not glanced Una's way, but she knew it wouldn't be long. Her heart thundered.

"Yin happened to me, princeling. Bloody Kaer *Yin*." He shot his oldest nephew a glare that should have turned his guts to water.

"I didn't ask you to do it, Diarmid." Kaer Yin dragged a chair away from the inferno in the hearth and flounced down with a petulant scowl. "Why you're being a prat about it now is beyond me."

"Do me a favor and shut your fool mouth," retorted Diarmid, shaking his head. "Given time to think it over first, I might have made a better decision."

Una noted the seeping bandages peeking from beneath his tunic. Their placement was mirrored on Kaer Yin's lanky frame. "You took half," she observed without thinking.

Naturally, Diarmid's head swiveled toward her. "There is much you have to learn, my dear."

She didn't realize the Sidhe had that ability— or could! This was High Manipulation for the Siorai. Only certain Alta Primas in the Cloister bore such skills. She didn't bother to ask him how he'd followed her train of thought. Fascinated, despite her fear, she didn't look away. "Can you heal too?"

"Surely you know I can't, Prima Moura."

"Right. The Sixth Law prevents one from—"

"That's the wrong question, and you've often proven it untrue enough, haven't you?"

She flushed. "No, there is *always* a cost."

His green eyes scanned her from her torn slippers to the crown of her matted hair. "Is that right?"

"I mean…" her tongue felt heavy and sour in her mouth.

"What are you talking about?" Kaer Yin scowled freely now.

"He's a Manipulator."

"Like you?"

"Yes."

"No," Diarmid interjected. "Apparently not."

Tam Lin blew air over his lower lip. "Are either of you capable of speaking the common bloody tongue? What does this have to do with anything?"

Diarmid exhaled long and hard. "You've come here for a purpose, I gather? Aside from safe passage for your mortal companions, that is?" he was addressing Kaer Yin, though he never took his eyes from Una's face. She repressed a quiver, her mind racing with a host of impossibilities. If he was a Manipulator, it stood to reason that he'd be beholden to the Inimitable Laws.

The Sixth Law would prevent him from exerting Spark without exchange— but if he couldn't do it… how could *she*? No trace of his thoughts touched the calm veneer of his face, but something told her he burned with curiosity.

He knows, she reasoned.

He knows what's happening to me.

"Let's get to it, shall we? Mistress Guinness needs attention, so far as I can tell."

Rian said nothing, merely squeezed Una's fingers until she lost feeling.

Kaer Yin got to his feet and handed his uncle Damek's *ogham* stone. "I took that from Una's kinsman after he chased us into the Oiche Ar Fad."

Diarmid squinted at it. "Hm, Armagh?"

"I think so."

"Interesting. Prima Moura?"

Una jumped a little. "Yes?"

"You are aware that your cousin is half Bolg?"

"Ah," she fidgeted. "Everyone in Bethany does. It's no secret."

"You'll have to fill me in; I'm unfamiliar with your family history."

She shrugged. "I don't know much, only that my aunt disappeared at Beltane during a High Council fete in Bri Leith. Months later, she stumbled out of Aes Sidhe alone, half-mad and heavy with child. She died not long after Damek was born. No one ever really talks about it."

"He's a Mac Nemed," added Tam Lin firmly. "I'll wager my best stallion on it. He's practiced in Neithana and Adrac, almost killed our idiot Crown Prince more than once, and pranced through the Veil as if it were merely a flimsy curtain. He's been instructed by someone. Someone with great power."

Kaer Yin twisted his nose at him for the insult but nodded assent. "Agreed. No one wastes so much effort on a bastard child of little import. Only the Mac Nemeds hold any real influence in Armagh. The question is, *which* Mac Nemed sired him?"

"My fainne's on Falan," Tam Lin guessed with conviction. "The old goat might be a useless dandy, but he's never lacked stamina. Half the city is rumored to have sprung from his overused stock." He made a rude sound. "He's as old as you, Diarmid. Gives one hope for the future, eh?"

Una rolled her eyes.

Rian sneered.

Bloody men.

Kaer Yin cleared his throat. "Ah, well, he could be. I've long heard the Bolg King has kept well behind his walls at Tir Macha on the Lough, and in all these years, I've never heard of any of his bastards enjoying the favor Damek must have done."

"Who else could it be, Yin? Aside from Sionnavar and Morcan, the Mac Nemeds are out of living males to extend their line."

"Falan's son was alive then, wasn't he?"

Tam Lin was startled. "Falan the *Younger*? I think not."

"Why? It's hardly a stretch."

"Because I knew him, that's why. He's a cousin on my mother's side. Falan was many things, but a lover of women, never. If you take my meaning?"

"While that may be true, I don't see how it staves my argument. Or do you imagine men who prefer men cannot sire offspring?"

"Oh, I remember the day you two met, well enough. Until that upstart faerie had a go, I've never seen another man put you on your back foot during a duel." He shook his head over a caustic laugh. "Utterly enamored of you, too. Fought hard for your attention that Imbolg. I'll never forget it."

Kaer Yin shrugged a shoulder. "He had good taste. Still, it doesn't negate my argument."

Una pinched the bridge of her nose. "Wait, you're saying Damek's father was the Prince of Armagh?"

"The late prince, yes."

"The one who died at Dumnain?"

Kaer Yin flushed, and Una immediately felt sorry for the reminder. "Yes."

Diarmid exasperated, "Why is any of this important?"

"Because," said Kaer Yin. "Bishop has claimed the Duchy of Bethany, uncle. What do you imagine is next if he is indeed the son of Falan Mac Nemed?"

"He may declare whatever he likes. Henry FitzDonahugh has also lain claim to Bethany. You might remember him, Yin, as the man who near singlehandedly conquered half the bloody Continent for his brother."

"Yeah, five decades ago, when he still had teeth. Bishop boasts twenty thousand men: superior cavalry, infantry, and bottomless archers. These are seasoned knights and yeomen, fully armed and able to wreak havoc in the Midlands. He'll accrue silver and men aplenty the further he's left to his own devices. If I believed that was his purpose. I suspect he'll march on the Red City before long."

Here was Robin's turn to snort. He'd worked his way to the larder, where many wine decanters had mysteriously appeared, and was busy pouring himself a large goblet. "Bollocks and nonsense, that. He's dreamin' if he thinks he can take the Citadel so easily."

With a sharp intake of breath, Una lashed out to knock the vessel from his hand before he could manage a single sip. "What in the bloody hells did ye do that for?" he grumbled petulantly.

"Don't you know where you are, *idiot*?" Rian hissed from behind her.

Diarmid chuckled. "No need for such theatrics, Mistress Guinness. They're hardly poisonous."

Her eyes cut deep. "Forgive me if I don't take your word for it, *Faris.*"

"Suit yourself," he said, though his lip bore a slight twitch that spoke volumes.

At the mention of poison, Una stared once more at her shoes, her heart pounding against her ribs like a war drum.

It won't be long now, she thought.

Conversation is foreplay to demand.

How would she answer him when the time came? She snuck a nervous glance at Kaer Yin, who, she knew, played for time. Though he seemed affable enough, she could feel the controlled menace rolling from Diarmid in waves.

He's good at hiding his emotions, but he's angry, perhaps more than that, even?

She felt a tremor of anticipation.

No doubt aware of her attention, Diarmid craned his neck toward her. "If I'd wanted to harm any of you, I daresay I wouldn't need to be clever about it. You are my guests. You may eat and drink without fear of reprisal or debt. I give you my word."

Robin sauntered back to the larder without ado, sparing Rian an exaggerated brow lift. She wiped her nose. "It's your funeral."

"Now, mistress," laughed Diarmid. "That's hardly fair. I've offered you no violence."

"Perhaps our opinions of abduction, forced starvation, and imprisonment differ, my lord?"

A cold draft crisscrossed the chamber. "Is that right?"

Well, here we go…

Una gritted her teeth and straightened her spine. She had beaten him once. If called to do so again, she'd trust her Spark to answer in kind. "You heard her."

Diarmid sat up a bit straighter, his expression bright as can be given his state. "We come straight to it, then?"

"Might as well."

Kaer Yin drew closer. "Una, *mo grá*. You know I won't allow—"

She held up a hand. "He'll cheat you if he can, and you know it. I'll handle this." She thought she caught the briefest flash of approval on Tam Lin's face but focused on Diarmid. "He's been waiting up here when he could have interceded days ago. Half of us have been cut to ribbons while he twiddled his thumbs. Whatever you ask him, he'll ask for something grand in return."

"Surely, you don't mean to give offense, Prima Moura?" grinned Diarmid.

"Take it however you like."

"Una," Kaer Yin began dubiously.

"No, love. I'm the only one here who's ever bested him. Isn't that right, my lord?"

"I think 'surprised' is a more accurate term," Diarmid pointed out.

"What do you want in exchange for your help?"

"You know what I want."

She crossed her arms. "I refuse."

"What's happening here, Yin?" Tam Lin's wine halted midway to his lip, brow quirking.

"How should I know?" he spat.

"Don't tell me you don't feel the rightness of this place, sighing along your skin, Una. You belong here," Diarmid went on.

Una gave a frustrated sigh. "Look, I can stand here all day and bandy words with you, or we can be done with this?"

"You'll stay with me, willingly."

"No. I'll give you something better than that. In exchange for granting us safe harbor and conduct through your lands, untainted food and drink, supplies, and anything else we might ask of you without hidden agenda or toll— I'll heal you right now."

His mouth opened and closed like a fish. After a while, he croaked, "This is something you can do?"

"I think you know I can. Do we have a deal, or do I challenge you directly?"

"Challenge… *me…?*" He gawped at her like she'd sprouted fangs.

Una clenched her fist, and the chamber seemed to darken around her. Diarmid didn't cringe so much as slam himself back into his chair. Kaer Yin snatched his hand from the small of her back like she'd burned him. Her Spark was a raging river in her blood, limitless and free. "What's it going to be, my lord?"

Diarmid stood with effort, closing the distance between them with exaggerated menace. He stopped a hand's breadth away. She stared up at him (and it was quite a hike) in unblinking confidence. "You," he smiled down at her. "Are a prize I cannot forego. I will heal in time, but you… you will be mine. *My* subject." He raised a hand as if to pat the thickening air around her. "My Lady," he crooned.

"*My Lady*, uncle." Kaer Yin's hand gripped his pommel.

"Does Midhir know whom you're bringing home, boy? He makes much noise about being a humanist, but you and I know he'll never accept a Milesian for your bride. She's better off with me."

Una took a step forward, and Diarmid recoiled. He recovered quickly enough but too late to conceal his reaction. He was afraid of her. Her lips pulled into a leer. "You will heal, sure. In a few weeks, maybe a few months. Yours is not an ordinary wound."

"You promised you'd give me *anything* I asked for in return. Remember? You begged me to save his life. You owe me."

"I refuse," she repeated, though she knew he had a just claim in the back of her mind. "I'd rather fight you and die now. You decide what works best for you."

"You would lose. In the Oiche Ar Fad, one does not simply circumvent fate. I hold your *geis*. Such a vow is forever."

She blew a lock of hair out of her eyes, her fists balling at her sides. "What compromise, then?"

"Una!" screeched Rian.

"Damn you, woman." Kaer Yin rounded on her rather than his uncle. "Have you lost your bloody mind?"

"Answer my question," she continued, ignoring everyone but Diarmid. "What will you take in exchange for all I have asked?"

Diarmid contemplated her in silence for a few moments. "I will set all your friends free, help my nephews with whatever they ask, and come to Kaer Yin's aid when he calls— if you remain here with me."

Kaer Yin drew Nemain. Tam Lin caught his arm. "Cousin, let her manage this, as you admonished me."

"Denied," she argued. "I vow to return all the power I stole from you right now."

"You stole nothing that was not already yours to take. Besides, my powers are not so easily diminished, child."

"What do you mean?"

"Did you steal from me or unlock something within yourself?"

Licking her lips, she shared a nervous glance with Kaer Yin. She hadn't expected such a question and had no idea how to respond. He shrugged off Tam Lin's staying arm. "Enough with this bait and catch. Una is not a mare I'd trade for road access. I am a son of Midhir Adair, and any claim you think to make is moot."

"I am a *king*, boy," laughed Diarmid. "And you are in my realm. You will—"

"No, I won't. I think you'll find this belongs to the High King, my father, and all other realms. I am your liege lord, uncle dear. I do not give you leave to make deals with my future wife."

"The mortals in your midst won't survive your arrogance, princeling."

"You will grant them safe passage because I command you to. You will aid us whenever I deem necessary because I *ask* you to. Are we clear?"

A goblet appeared in Diarmid's hand without fanfare. He took a long sip, and then it vanished again as quickly. He smoothed his tunic. "Only my brother can command me, Kaer Yin. You may outrank me at Court, but not here. In Tir Falias, you are subject to my whims. I prefer to deal with the girl, thank you."

"Should I kill you to prove my point?"

"Again," he smirked. "You're free to try."

Before Una could turn her eye from one to the other, Kaer Yin had shoved his cousin backward and lunged for Diarmid. Though it was hard to track the speed with which the two circled one another, Una saw Nemain score a shallow cut to Diarmid's shoulder, one against his thigh before he clenched his fingers, and Kaer Yin was lifted into the air. With a grunt, Diarmid held him aloft only long enough to slam him into the stone floor with dizzying force. Nemain skittered across the room.

Drink in hand; Robin hopped over it.

Undeterred, Kaer Yin was on his feet and at his uncle again with both larks in hand. Breathing heavily, Diarmid doffed his cloak, eyes fierce. He cracked the knuckles of both hands, a dark shimmer hovering over each digit. She next saw Kaer Yin sailing bodily over the Diarmid's abandoned chair and crashing into the wall. Laughing, Diarmid advanced on him. "Not so confident now, are we, boy?"

Kaer Yin got up, wiping blood from his nose with a filthy sleeve. He winked over his head at Una. "I don't know; it seems I have you right where I want you."

Too late, Diarmid turned to discover Una slipping up behind him. Her fingers dug into the skin at his torn collar. "*Down*," she sang, and down he went—to his knees only— this was the King of Tech Duinn, after all. "*Hold*," she ordered, panting with the effort required to keep him still. Like before, there was so, *so* much power beneath his skin. She struggled to contain her Spark's immense greed at the touch.

She sank with him, whimpering.

To her surprise, he covered her hand with his own. "I'll give you everything you want. Don't be shy."

She struggled with the effort to keep them both still. Her blood surged like molten lava in her veins. She heard the dead whisper from the corner of her conscience and felt their calm presence at the edge of her sanity.

Yes, sister.

We feel you too.

She opened her mouth to speak but choked on her words. Her Spark roared, *yes, yes, yes!* — through her cells.

"Una, let go!" cried Rian, one hundred miles away.

But she couldn't. They were locked together, she and the King of Tech Duinn. As she took from him, so did he steal bits from her, an exchange more intimate than anything she'd ever experienced. Her Spark, however, grew so enormous that Tir Falias rumbled beneath her knees. Diarmid moaned with pain and more— pleasure or triumph, she couldn't be sure which, "Enough! Stop, Una, before you destroy yourself."

She could drain him dry now.

She knew it.

He knew it.

Although, he was right. One cannot consume the cosmos and remain corporeal. The flesh could only bear so much. "Compromise, or we both die now."

His spine bowed a bit. His forehead touched hers. He gnashed his teeth. "Agreed. Una, let go."

It took every ounce of strength she'd ever had to pry herself away. They collapsed together on the cold floor, exhausted and breathing hard. Rian limped to her side, though she and Diarmid saw only each other. Kaer Yin caught Rian around the waist, backing her off. Diarmid sat up, once again whole. His hand pressed against his chest, and the wound was no longer there. He exhaled slowly. "I grant you your boon; ask it."

It took a while for her to find her tongue. "My freedom, our freedom, their safety, and Kaer Yin's aid. That is my price."

"For how long?" his tone hinted that he wouldn't wait indefinitely; his eyes gleamed with a desire of a nonsexual nature. He craved the power in her blood. The flesh was irrelevant.

Her nerves thrummed with renewed energy. Whatever had transpired between them, they were bound. She could never deny it. "However long I might live, I will always be mortal. You may have what you ask upon this life's *natural* conclusion."

"Una! Stop it!" Rian whimpered.

Diarmid glowed with health and vigor. "My Lady, we have an accord."

Avowed

"I've come to tell you, you were right. My sources have revealed a large, two-pronged force, moving north as we speak," commented Diarmid from Kaer Yin's doorway many hours later. Kaer Yin kept his back to the door, staring at the waxing moon from his balcony railing and taking long puffs from a witchroot pipe. Seemingly disinterested, he merely grunted in response. Tapping his bowl clear on the stone railing, Robin patted his shoulder on his way out. Diarmid took Robin's place with a heavy sigh. "I did what I must, Yin. You were never meant to keep that girl."

"That is not for you to say."

"Though she may be mortal, she is far from human. You know I'm telling the truth. You've seen her power. She's a Brehon, born and bred." He paused to note the ticking muscle in Kaer Yin's jaw. "In the old days, she'd have been given to me as a child. Unguided power like hers is dangerous."

"Who do you think you're talking to, old man? I know what you want her for, and it has little to do with anything *she* might gain from you."

"I will not deny that she stirs me— her gifts are unlike anything I have ever seen. These many eons, I've never been bested by a mortal. Not once."

"You will be again. I promise you."

Diarmid gave a soft laugh. "She is mortal, nephew. One day you will be parted, no matter how special she is."

Kaer Yin fixed him with an ice-cold glare. "I'll kill you long before then."

"You might be the best fighter among the Tuatha De Dannan, but you're not a god. You can no more defeat me than you could cut the moon in half."

He didn't lie.

Many believed the Oiche Ar Fad would wink out of existence without Diarmid's stewardship. Kaer Yin had no idea if that were true but was tempted to toss the old fool from this tower to test the theory anyway. Much good it would do him, Diarmid could fly. "Release her from this vow."

"No."

Kaer Yin took a long, deep breath. "What will you take in exchange for her promise?"

"I've already agreed to wait until her life has *naturally* expired. You will have lost her by that point anyway. I'm being exceptionally generous."

"Generous?" Kaer Yin cringed. "You mean to enslave the woman I love. Whether she is among the living at that point makes no difference."

"She would exist. Isn't that what you want?"

"Do you think I haven't seen the Sluagh here in Tech Duinn? If they've any memories before they were dragged here for one misdeed or other, they cannot share them. You would take her soul, damn her here to this horrible place, all because you're bored or lonely. I'll ask again. What will you take to release her from her vow?"

Diarmid smirked at him. "What if I ask for your throne, Yin? Would you be so willing, then?"

Kaer Yin's rebuttal caught in his throat. Was that even something he *could* give? He didn't think so. Kaer Yin might not have the power to rip Diarmid from Tech Duinn, but Midhir certainly did, and he'd never allow his son to bestow his birthright upon his duplicitous younger brother. "You jest."

"Crom was my father, you realize. The blood that makes you Dannan flows doubly strong within my breast. Midhir rules because his mother was queen while mine was merely a wandering Brehon." He mimicked Kaer Yin's posture at the railing. "I will make her immortal. Isn't that what you want?"

Kaer Yin stretched to his full height. "I care about what *she* wants, you meddling old fool. I will not allow her to bargain away her soul for meaningless platitudes. Name your price, Diarmid."

"Have you considered the damage she might do, the horrors she might sow one day if you forbid my help? You know many things, *Ard Tiarne*, but you are no Brehon. You cannot understand the weight of her burgeoning powers."

"Very well, then train her. Guide her. Be of assistance to her. If you care so much about her future, you can offer her this much without demanding payment in return."

Diarmid laughed through his nose. "You are no god, no Brehon, no king— and I am no Kneeler's saint."

Knowing the argument would further devolve, Kaer Yin tapped his bowl empty against his boot and tucked it back into this belt. "I'm done with this, for now, Diarmid. There will be further violence between us if you don't shut your mouth. You have my offer, and you *will* take it. That's all there is to this. You may believe this place can't exist without you, but I doubt it." Diarmid inhaled to rebut. Kaer Yin cut him off. "I would ask you not to insert yourself into my life and relationships in such a heavy-handed way, uncle. Set your price since you're a selfish turd who can't resist. The next time I broach this topic, you'd better be prepared. Una is not for sale."

"I don't—"

"Tell me more of Bishop's forces," Kaer Yin snarled, shortening his following exhortation. "If you speak her name to me, it had better be with a counteroffer. Now, what of the Southers?"

Diarmid recovered himself, but a deep fire burned behind his irises.

You have no right to take offense, you self-aggrandizing bastard, Kaer Yin thought.

This isn't the dark ages any longer.

He considered that there might be a real contest between them one day very soon. If Diarmid refused Una's freedom, Kaer Yin would have no choice. There was little doubt what Midhir would make of this. The Ard Ri would never support Diarmid's heavy-handed claim to Doma's granddaughter, less the Princess of Bethany. Diarmid was dreaming if he thought he would get away with this.

Unless… another thought tiptoed through Kaer Yin's mind.

She isn't really what he's after.

With no hint of intention, besides mild irritation visible in his uncle's expression, Kaer Yin cautioned himself.

You have only one thing, which Fiachra Dubh could want. His flippant comment from before rang red, despite its seeming sarcasm.

'What if I ask for your throne?'

What if, indeed?

Kaer Yin needed to discuss this with Tam Lin and his uncle Bov. If anyone could help unravel the labyrinth of Diarmid's ambitions, Bov Dearg could.

This is not the first time Diarmid has made a play for my father's crown, and he's one of two men with the power to be a real threat.

Be careful here…

"They're amassing on two fronts. I've learned that Bishop marches with a quarter of his cavalry from Tara, which he sacked in one night. They move along the Taran High Road at quite the clip."

"And the second?"

"Infantry, yeomen longbowmen, and short-range artillery, led by some three hundred cavalry. Nearly twenty-thousand men, as you surmised earlier."

"And?"

"Four Bretagn warships follow an ice-breaker through the Straits of Manannan, bearing an additional thousand men."

Kaer Yin swore under his breath. Sometimes, he hated being right. "Then it begins."

"The march to Rosweal must be a feint."

"It's not."

"Why do you say that?"

Kaer Yin shrugged. "He knows I'll be there."

Una and Rian's rooms were the least oppressive she'd seen in the Keep. Despite the impression of its gorgeous setting and backdrop upon arrival, Tir Falias was the coldest, starkest structure she'd ever set foot in. Perhaps Diarmid expelled so much energy managing the vagaries of this terrifying Otherworld realm that he had very little verve left over for himself? What did one do for an eternity locked within a world of death, anyway?

It seems, she thought, ruefully, *you will find out soon enough.*

She paused as she sifted through the clean but straightforward tunics, leggings, and other garments; one of Diarmid's unseen servants had laid out for her. Rian would tell her this was a riddle, wouldn't she? Well, she might, if she were speaking to her. Neither Rian nor Kaer Yin had spoken to her since the fight in Diarmid's parlor.

Una sighed. Perhaps that was for the best, considering she'd have no clue what to say to either. She'd done what only she could do, and rather than try to arm wrestle the most powerful wizard in Innisfail— she'd chosen to trade. Since she had only one thing of value, her friends' safety and a powerful Manipulator's aid were well worth the bargain. Besides, a lot could happen before her 'natural' death. She could be murdered any day now, her deal rendered moot.

There was always an upside, she supposed.

Having availed herself of the giant copper tub before the fireplace and tossed the frayed remnants of Rian's homespun into the flames— Una nearly groaned in ecstasy, pulling a dry, soft linen shirt over her head. One could easily forget such luxuries roaming the wild and dangerous places between realms. Since she'd spent many warm and well-fed weeks at her father's court, she'd nearly forgotten how hard the elements could be on the body. Tucking her tunic into her belt, she glanced at Rian's closed door. She had no doubt one of them suffered more for the latest misadventure. Without thinking, she padded over on bare feet, her fist poised to knock.

"Don't wake her," Kaer Yin said. Her head whipped around. She hadn't heard him come in. "Diarmid's seen to her. She'll be fine."

He leaned against the outer door, eyes glittering with fury, hurt, and more.

She swallowed, lowering her hand to her chest to keep it from shaking. His expression made her nervous. "How long have you been there?"

"Not long." He uncrossed his arms. He'd bathed too and donned the same simple yet elegant linen she now wore. His long silver-blond hair had been combed and plaited along the sides, exposing the nine gold chains in his right ear. He looked beautiful. With a hitch in her breath, she sent her gaze away. Unsure where to go to gain some distance, she went to the window and sat down. Unfortunately, he followed, sparks trailing in his wake. "Anything to say?"

She lifted her chin. "I did what I had to."

"I know you believe that, but you're wrong."

"The two of us together couldn't beat him, Kaer Yin. If I'd held on much longer, we would be dead. I know it." She shivered. "There was so much… *too* much. I'm not omnipotent."

"Neither is he."

"Coulda fooled me."

Exhaling, he sat beside her, moving her legs across his lap. She tried to squirm aside to give him room, but he held on— not tightly enough to be commanding, but enough to send a message. His hand felt very warm through the flimsy fabric of her leggings.

"What's done is done. I know why you did it, even if I know how bloody stupid it was."

She made a face at him. "Fine talk, for a man who has no idea what he's talking about. Diarmid's power is like a sky pregnant with lightning. If you imagine I could absorb all of that on my own, you're mad."

"You've done it before."

"Yeah, in our world. Not here. This place is different. My Spark feels bottomless." She paused, mulling it over. "There was a moment in the parlor where reality felt permeable, like a thread I could pull and unwind the universe. I can't… you wouldn't understand."

He laid his head against the shutters with a soft smile. "I'll never let this go, love. You know that. Your *geis* must be destroyed."

"No argument there." She distracted herself from his nearness by brushing a wrinkle from his sleeve, where it draped over her thigh. "If you've any brilliant ideas, I'm all ears. We must accept what few fortunes this trade has bought us. All right?"

He nodded.

"Good," she breathed a relieved sigh. "When are we leaving?"

"Tomorrow evening, as dawn breaks."

"Is he coming with us?"

"Yes."

She made a face. "He'd better. The bastard."

Kaer Yin's fingers ran back and forth over her knee. If he didn't stop doing that, she'd forget that they had much to discuss. His eyes were mirrors, reflecting the vivid flush of her cheeks. Clearing a small mountain from her throat, she tried to squirm away. He held her legs fast. "That tickles."

"Does it?"

His hand moved higher.

She drew an audible breath. "Yes. Leave off, you. What about Bethany and Tairngare? Shar told me Diarmid had news of the Midlands. What did he say?"

Kaer Yin's pupils darkened.

"I don't want to talk about them right now." Tucking an arm under both knees, he pulled her closer. The fingers exploring her thigh slid up her side to assert the faintest pressure against her breast, summoning a small gasp from her throat. She couldn't recall them ever being so close before. There was always someone nearby, watching. There was no one now but the two of them. Her heart went feral against her ribs, like a trapped hare. "Come here, Una."

"I don't—" she began, but his fingernail brushed her nipple, and she gasped. "What are you doing? We need to—"

"It can wait."

His overlarge hand closed over her breast, soft but demanding. Una's flesh yielded readily, molding to his probing palm like unmolded clay. "I, for one, have waited long enough."

A soft sigh escaped her lips.

Kaer Yin's fingers wound through the hair at the base of her skull, crushing her mouth to his. The next thing she knew, she was entirely astride his lap with his face buried in the 'V' of her tunic. Through the gauze of their linen bottoms, she felt him pressing upward. Her eyes fluttered shut with his tongue tracing a wet line between her breasts and the heat of his length resting against her navel. She moaned despite her nerves. Very lightly, he rocked her hips over his.

When his mouth claimed hers for the second time, she forgot what she meant to say to him. Thoughts leaked from her mind like water from a broken sieve. He unlaced her tunic to her ribs with one hand while the other pressed her bottom against him, establishing a slow but insistent rhythm. After several gasping breaths, Una reached down and unclasped her belt.

Kaer Yin tossed the offensive accessory away with a growl. Her braes and brassiere revealed themselves through the gap in her tunic. She watched his pale hand roam the expanse of the tattooed bronze flesh at her collarbone, gently over each breast through her filmy undergarment… then lower still. She couldn't recall if his eyes had ever been another color besides black.

"May I?"

"You're asking now?" she huffed, working her own hands into his shirt. His skin felt cool at first touch, then heated below her wandering fingers. His upper chest and shoulders muscles were enough to make a sculptor weep. Forcing him back against the shutters, she tore the garment over his head just as his right hand cupped her mound of venus. She cried out into the flesh of his solar plexus, teeth grazing his nipple. He muttered something nonsensical in Ealig, and she sighed, "Don't you dare stop."

Her tunic vanished entirely.

Kaer Yin's fingers pushed below the hem of her braes, working lightly, maddeningly against her sex. Her ears drowned in her heartbeat and the soft but masculine sounds he made as her nails dragged along his shoulders.

She kissed him so hard that his breath puffed into her mouth. A delicious fire built in her low belly, stoked by the unrelenting heat of his hands. As his fingers worked against her, his free hand squeezed and molded her posterior. For several minutes, she lost herself to the ruthless cadence he set.

Una's back bowed.

Her hips moved of their own accord.

At last, when she could take no more, a long slow whimper escaped her throat. Stars swam through her vision, flashing white and red at once. "Kaer Yin!" she cried, feeling herself hefted into his arms.

Though she couldn't begin to tell how it happened, the mattress yielded to her form, now fully nude. Breathing hard, she cracked an eye, finding him leaning over her, his face shining. She doubted she'd ever seen a more lovely sight in her life.

He was winter and summer together, glorious as a moonlit glen and powerful as a sun-soaked mountain. The words to describe him failed her. He leaned over her, all corded sinew and grace. His hair brushed against her naked shoulder. "Are you ready, *mo grá*?"

Her legs wrapped around his waist, drawing him down. "I thought we were done talking?"

KAER YIN GRINNED THROUGH THE following day (or evening, as all was opposite in the Oiche Ar Fad*)*, unconcerned by the glares and grumbles his comrades sent his way. Tam Lin whistled upon first sight of him. "Someone's awful chipper, considering how buggered we all are."

Kaer Yin poured himself a tankard of mead from the larder, smirking as if it were carved in. "Perhaps a proper bed and a warm meal were just the thing."

"A warm somethin', all right," said Robin with a squint. "Thought ye were peeved enough to boil her yesterday?"

"Looks to me like someone boiled his brains, instead," commented Tam Lin, absently chewing on an apple while Shar loaded his horse. He turned out rather smart, considering the long ride they were about to undertake. The distance might be covered much more swiftly here than in the corporeal world above, but it would be an arduous journey. All that fine white linen would be smattered in mud— or worse— in no time.

Still, Tam Lin managed to appear resolute. He wore his long red-gold curls in a complex braid clipped with a silver club. If Kaer Yin cared enough to ask, he might wonder aloud why his cousin had made such an effort. Then, he saw the girls come down the outer stairs, each clean and dressed in crisp white linen and fur. Rian's hair was unbound and silver-white in the queer Otherworld light. Diarmid's magic had done its work well. She appeared healthier than he'd ever seen her.

Sparing Tam Lin a long side-eye, Kaer Yin quipped, "Whose brains are boilt?"

"Nonsense. Lacking cuisine, one must make do with *hors d'oeuvres*, no?"

"Hey now," Robin spat from around his pipe stem. "Say that again, and it'll be me that ruins yer fancy duds. That girl's a good'un, she is. Mind yer manners."

Tam Lin raised his hands. "No harm. Just a mild fascination with a pretty face. Ask Yin; he'll tell you all about it."

Kaer Yin's fist cracked out faster than Tam Lin could account. He staggered backward, clasping his hand over his streaming nose. "Ow! Why'd you do that?"

Stubbornly smiling, Kaer Yin shrugged. "If I didn't know she'll tell you to go to the hells herself, I'd warn you to watch your mouth."

Shar tossed a handkerchief at his lord but otherwise made no further move to help him. Tam Lin scowled. "You too, Lianor?"

Shar didn't answer. Instead, he beamed at both girls as they arrived on the scene, confused at Tam Lin's bloodied nose and Kaer Yin's stupid grin. He bowed. "May I help you with your bags, ladies?"

Rian accepted, but Una waved them off. She sidled around Kaer Yin and Rian to her mare. "Made a disparaging comment, I take it?"

Kaer Yin held her bridle while she looped her bag around her saddle horn. She flushed a gorgeous shade of dusky rose at his nearness. That he could affect her so powerfully, so quickly… made him smile the wider. Her skin against his, fists balled in her hair, the cradle of her hips rocking above him, tracked through his thoughts nonstop. He was the luckiest man in Innisfail. "Nothing of import, I swear."

"Humph," she said, turning toward him. "You're as bad a liar as ever." Standing on her tiptoes, she kissed the center of his chin before swinging herself into the saddle. Once seated, Kaer Yin handed up her reins. His pulse pounded in his neck. "Stop looking at me like that. We have places to be."

"I think Rosweal can rot."

"Now, now," chided Robin from his saddle. "That's not very nice, is it?"

"Later," she promised, with a wink that turned his guts to jelly.

"For Maeve's sake," groaned Diarmid from the stairway. "Can we *please* proceed without the ridiculous mating rituals?" He didn't look overly happy to be leaving the comfort of his home, either. He was the only one appropriately dressed for the occasion, head to toe in black. The depth of his scowl only deepened the singularity of his appearance. He leaped onto his destrier's back in a single motion— a move so graceful that Kaer Yin was reminded his people were once horse lords of a distant tundra. "It's not even spring, is it?"

"No," remarked Kaer Yin dryly. "It's not. Though Beltane will be here soon enough."

"Don't hold your breath, princeling. I know your father better than you."

Kaer Yin knew something too. His epiphany at Samhain sang through his blood. "I don't think you do, old man. Anyway," he sighed, swinging himself (far less elegantly, mind) into his saddle. "How long before we reach Gerry and the others? All of them had better be hale, or you and I will revisit yesterday's conversation."

"They're fine," Diarmid enunciated through his teeth. Well, wasn't his uncle in a black humor today? Kaer Yin grinned wider. He couldn't help himself. "They never made it to Tech Duinn. We'll find them sheltering at the Crossroads."

Tam Lin had managed to clean his face up enough to look sullen. "Lucky for them. You let us be hacked halfway to the Kneeler's Hell. Why's that, by the by?"

Diarmid rolled a shoulder. "I wasn't feeling well."

Una twitched beside him. "All better now, aren't you?"

"Immeasurably." He bowed.

"Excellent. Renege, and you forfeit. Remember that."

"As My Lady commands."

Kaer Yin thought he'd be bloodying another nose in moments, but Robin broke the spell. "Ah, for fuck's sake! Can we get to the bloody war already? This is boring the shite outta me."

"Indeed," smirked Kaer Yin. "I hope Barb's brought all the uishge up from the river by now. I think we deserve a few drams."

Interlude

Barb was, for once, at a total loss. She crumpled the third message in as many days and tossed it over the balustrade. This newest message had been brought by post rider from Pormark— the very same village Damek's expeditionary force had marched from the *last* time they'd attacked Rosweal. At least the little bastard was consistent. Dumnain, then Vale would be next; she didn't need to be told. Though, on this occasion, it seemed that his cousin wasn't Bishop's primary objective.

'Bend the knee, or suffer my wroth,' it read.

'Any resistance to the one true lord of Eire will be met with swift, lethal force. She'd just bet. *'Divest yourselves from Tairngare's corrupt influence. Submit, and be rewarded.* At swordpoint, no doubt. *'You have one week to comply,'* it went on, then finished with a bit of bollocks. Barb laughed out loud to recall. *'I await your favorable reply. Signed, Damek Bishop Mac Nemed, son of Falan the Younger of Armagh— the true Crown Prince of Innisfail'.*

Well.

One could never accuse Lord Bishop of cowardice, could one? His balls swung lower than any man she'd yet encountered. In Barb's case, that was quite a number. Pormark had surrendered without a fuss. Dumnain knew better than to try, given their history of defying Souther lords on the march. When his army reached Vale, Rosweal would receive no such warning. She'd already made friends with the Lord of Clare once before, hadn't she? A sound somewhere between a snort and a growl issued from her throat. Beside her, Dabs slunk away. "Don't fash yerself, Dabs. I haven't killed anyone yet for bad news. I don't aim to start with ye."

Dabney, all three hundred pounds of him, visibly relaxed. Sighing, she crossed her arms over the railing, looking down on her rebuilt taproom. It had only been a few weeks since the last assault, and she had no desire to repeat the process a third time. Alas, she knew life wouldn't trade a tinker's fart for her wishes. No stranger to adversity was Barb Dormer. Unlike many wealthy cousins, she hadn't spent her life in the Red City. She'd started there, but life in the Cloister hadn't been in her cards.

Watching the workers dart around, she thought about all she had lost and gained. *The Hart* had never quite been the soul of comfort or refinement, though it bore a certain rustic charm as most things in Rosweal tended to.

There were no fine oil lamps, plush carpeting, or velveteen curtains to add that touch of class. Instead, the walls and floors were simply grooved pine. Large timber beams raced along the ceiling to meet at the crux of the primary support, which had once been the keel of her father's last merchant vessel. From this, a vast chandelier crafted from iron and antlers squatted over the tap's center, a macabre centerpiece, she reckoned. Still, with two massive stone hearths, clean tables and chairs, and a brand-new oak bar— what need did she have for finery?

The Hart was handsome enough, her girls were clean and attractive enough, and her pride of ownership was more than bloody enough. *The Hart* was hers.

It was *hers.*

Her father had left her a windowless, dirt-floored taproom stuffed with dive barrels, broken stools, and semi-conscious inebriates. In just fifteen years, she'd built this place into an institution, carved its stellar reputation from literal muck and gloom. Barb's mother's family had been something in Tairngare long ago. They'd been right sorts, with plenty of wealth and position. But fortune, as ever, had been a cruel bitch of a mistress. After her mother's death, her father made many bad investments, eventually costing Barb her place in the Cloister. She lacked the Spark to attain a rank higher than Nova and was summarily dismissed for non-payment. Without her mother's family's support, she and her father were left to scratch a living out of this most inhospitable corner of Innisfail. Her father drank himself to death in this very room.

And she… well, she'd ventured to Ten Bells for a span, then to *The Butterfly* in Bethany. She soon made a name for herself among the lower Bethonair nobility for a time. When her beauty began to fade— as often happens in this, the oldest of professions— she came home.

Now here she stood, fifty years old, owner of the best if the least presumptuous establishment in the Borderlands. Barb Dormer was the undisputed queen of the Greenmakers' Guild, the most influential gang of ruffians, thieves, courtesans, and smugglers this side of the Straits of Mannanan. She'd be Siora-damned if she were going to hand any of that over to the Duch's calculating prick of a nephew.

Dabney, sloe-eyed and quiet, waited while she struck a match. Her eyes met his as she took a long pull from the fancy brass pipe Robin had brought her from Ten Bells. "How many barrels of oil did we find in Matt's cellar, Dabs?"

He shook his meaty head. "Dunno, missus. Lots."

She sucked her teeth at him, poor lamb. It wasn't his fault Siora had neglected his brains for his girth. "Do they fill at least half the cellar?"

He thought it over for a while. "'Spose so."

She took another drag, mind racing. Georgie, Pad, and Mac stared up at her, afraid. They'd worked night and day to fortify the town walls for weeks. Most houses on the Hilltop had already donated garden fences, carriage houses, and even rear walls in their quest for more stone. She could almost hear a collective groan from their overworked minds. "An' how much of that black powder did we find in Solomon's warehouse? Someone other than Dabney, if ye please?"

Mac cleared his pimply throat. "'Round fifty crates, missus. However, half was soaked through after the attack. All that rain and no roof left."

She nodded. "That should be plenty. Mac, I want ye to take Dabs down the docks to Brewer's Quarter and bring me every brewer, tanner, and doper left in Rosweal."

"What for?"

She gave them all an earnest grin. "We're gonna show this faerie bastard why no one in all of Innisfail has the bollocks to fuck with Rosweal twice."

FIVE DAYS LATER, BARB GOT the news she'd been expecting. Dumnain had thrown the gates wide for the Lord of Clare's advance army. Though this was far from a surprise, there were two other tidbits her messenger included, which she hadn't expected to hear. Damek Bishop wasn't with his men; he encircled Tairngare with the bulk of his forces, including his vanguard. Twenty-thousand men, or so her messenger told her with wide, bloodshot eyes.

The two thousand camped at Dumnain were an expeditionary force meant to accrue coin and secure the roads between each small town and hamlet, while Bishop and his allies went for the grand prize. It didn't make Rosweal any less fucked; it just gave them a bit more time to prepare for the most epic suicide one could muster. Cursing, she made her way over the planks her boys had lain over one of her fancy new moats to ogle their progress on the inner wall. Mac Looked up, sweaty and half-starved. He was a shit digger, being all knees and bony elbows, but his side of the trench between his and the outer wall fared better than those across the field.

With naught but women and skinny lads between the ages of thirteen and sixty, Barb couldn't afford to be particular.

"Mac, make sure they're savin' that dirt. We'll need it for mortar." Without waiting for a response, she took a turn around the eight-foot by a four-foot-wide chasm that she'd ordered dug through the center of what had been the Slums three days prior. As was the case before Robin had left with Ben on his fool's errand, anyone inexperienced with masonry or woodcutting, or too young or too small for stone-cutting or hauling— had been sent outside to dig.

All the massive conifers to the south had been cleared, revealing a killing field some one-hundred and fifty yards deep along the Taran High Road. The timber had been used to erect her two beautiful guard towers at either end. With nearly three hundred and sixty degrees range, standing fifteen feet high, and constructed of sturdy oak and ash, her Greenmakers could pick off Damek's cavalry from hundreds of paces away. Two more were being erected on the east and west ends, respectively.

She stepped back to admire her new trench.

It was one of three.

She'd gotten the idea from a book her father had given her many years ago, some yarn about a city defended on three sides by six concentric rings of a deep, complex moat. She couldn't manage all six with her limited resources, but she *could* and *would* make sure these three were done right. When finished, their newest defense mechanism would boast hundreds of sharp, merciless skewers below the waterline.

Instant impalement would deter any fool that dreamed of attempting to leap in, and with an eight-foot-wide mouth— impossible to wheel siege towers up to any of Rosweal's lovely new walls. Her towers stood sentinel above a settlement of some might; thanks to her fainne, quick thinking, and ornery nature, she didn't mind boasting. Their little backwater had been the sad, crumbling relic of a bygone era a few months before.

Now, it was a fortress.

She hoped they lasted long enough for Robin to see it. Tugging her furs high around her thinning throat, she paced the edge of her soon-to-be moat. "I want another row here," she shouted to Kira Boma, another Tairnganese reject of former middling importance. He was at least twelve years her senior but had studied law and engineering at the Libellum in his youth. If it could be built or argued, Kira knew his way around it. "They should jut out— like so." She gestured.

"At a seventy-five-degree angle, you mean?" he sounded bored, though he had worked as many hours each day as the rest.

Barb made a face at him. "Whatever the bloody hell ye need to do, Kira. I want whole and half trees sticking out here, ready to unhorse or impale any man brave enough to get this close. Am I clear?"

"As glass."

"How many days we have left, missus?" Mac had crept up behind her. She scowled down the Taran Road. Instead, they might have marched along the Navan High Road, but the terrain was much less agreeable for large machines and far too marrow to avoid raids from the trees. The Taran High Road was a much broader and more meandering affair, with far less cover for Greenmakers and other bandits to get ambitious about. "It takes a long while to march that many men and horses up a hilly road, miles, and miles from where they started. I expect they'll take longer than last time, lad. Soldiers need to eat, fuck, and pillage, ye know? I should think, as long as his lordship keeps busy at Tairngare, we have a few weeks yet."

Mac's face went a ghastly shade of grey. "Will we be ready?"

She didn't have an answer that would appease the boy reasonably, so she spun him about by the shoulders to get back to the dig. Kira followed her at a sedate pace.

He knew better than to ask.

On the twenty-ninth day of Dor Enair, a pale sun climbed into a snow-bright sky. The southern wall had grown by another six feet, and her spike-filled ditches were ready to take on water. The wall was rudimentary, lacking functional elegance of formative appeal. Large stones were haphazardly stacked on top of the other, mortared with black clay, stone dust, and sap. Kira's invention, as it turned out, and while perhaps not impregnable, it certainly was sturdy. No attempts to dislodge the stones housed in the center proved fruitful. This was hardly proof positive of its intrinsic value, but Barb would take what she could get.

Many timbers were cut into wide planks atop this wall section, piled in soaring rows some ten feet high. Plenty of height to deflect the average arrow and spear, but low enough for her towers to peer over the side at the killing field. Kira's woodworkers had done a beautiful job fitting and forming these planks into rows so tight she couldn't slip a finger between them. Beside herself with pride, she strutted across Rosweal's fresh ramparts with a sloppy smile. Though she was fully aware, with an army over two-thousand strong marching up the Taran High Road— their efforts might not be much more than window-dressing. Still, the Southers would take it as an ominous message of the ingenuity of Rosweal's stalwart residents.

Lord Bishop would get no free meal here, by Siora.

Her jaws aching from all the smiling, she caught a strange sound on the wind to the north. Her head whipped around. The mists of Aes Sidhe, as ever, occluded the distant shore. It sounded again, and her watchmen at the north wall answered belatedly. They would have to work on that bit, wouldn't they? She hefted her skirts high and bolted along the ramparts toward the horns. She'd never been much of a runner, but she dashed off as if Siora's flames licked at her ankles. It took a great deal longer than was flattering, but soon she made it to the ancient northern wall facing the river. Huffing, she saw some of her boys skip into the street. Dabs and two of Lily's brats had been busy loading barrels of gunpowder onto a wagon. They froze when they saw her, red-faced and wheezing, atop the wall. "Which way did that horn come from?"

Dabs scratched at his balding pate— the nonce.

One of the other lads pointed behind her at the river.

What? She thought.

It can't be?

Before she could crane her neck toward the border, the horn came again.

That horn *was* from Aes Sidhe!

Faster than she imagined, she skidded down two ladders to the muddy ground and out the rickety iron gate (which would also need fixing). At the docks, she stopped cold, heaving and clutching her side. The others had followed her, each wide-eyed and whispering.

From the misty shore opposite, there came the gleam of white and silver armor, the flash of pure, sylvan steel by the hundreds. They materialized from the trees— fair hair shining in the weak sunlight, brilliant eyes flashing, white stag banners snapping overhead— the Sidhe walked their mounts into the Boyne. Barb's heart flew straight into her nose.

An Fiach Fian...

The Wild Hunt.

The personal guard of the High King himself had come to Rosweal.

In the Oiche Ar Fad, the realm above was reflected in every body of water they passed. The stench of smoke and blood drifted toward them on a gentle morning breeze. Kaer Yin watched Una's face fall when she glimpsed the distant spires of the fortress at Tara in flames as they moved west through Tech Duinn, so the world above spun east. They would head south for two days, then swing east to reach Rosweal. Kaer Yin remained silent beside her but knew what she was thinking, regardless.

He opened his mouth to speak, but Diarmid beat him to it. "It's not your fault, Prima Moura."

"Whose fault is it, then?" she scoffed, her amber eyes full of flames. "Is this happening now?"

"No. This was some weeks past. Your cousin took Tara and Malahide by surprise, but this wasn't the first time they were attacked."

"What do you mean?"

"Groups of Sidhe raiders dressed in the High King's colors ransacked towns and villages for almost two moons before Bishop chased you from Bethany."

"One of Gilcannon's boys said something about that," Kaer Yin added. "I wouldn't put it past Bishop to attempt to turn the poor against the Ard Ri in such a low way."

"It wasn't Bishop," Diarmid argued. "A girl named Aoife Sona led the raids at the behest of her grandmother, the new Doma."

"*NO!*" Una hissed. "That *cannot* be!"

Diarmid shrugged. "I assure you it is. Liadan Mac Nemed is your Nema's true name. I always wondered how a name like 'Nema,' as in 'no one,' managed to escape the learned women in Tairngare for so long?"

Una tugged her horse to a halt. She'd gone a milky sort of green. "You know this for sure?"

"I know many things you don't, Una. You have but to ask."

Kaer Yin wanted to knock his uncle's teeth out daily.

"Yin," Tam Lin cut in. "That solves your conundrum. He is a Mac Nemed."

"I knew that already."

"Liadan Mac Nemed is the matriarch of the whole Clan, which includes him if we're right. They took Tairngare for him."

Kaer Yin shook his head. "No, they wouldn't. However highborn he is, he's still illegitimate at best. Why would Armagh plot to put a faerie by-blow on the Eirean throne? It doesn't make sense."

"He's not just *any* bastard, is he? He's Patrick Donahugh's nephew. I assume they engineered this from the beginning," Tam Lin reasoned. "Alis Donahugh disappeared from a feast at your father's table, Yin. The Duch declared war on Aes Sidhe for the slight when she returned. Wouldn't it have been convenient if the Crown Prince *had* died after Dumnain instead of Falan the Younger?"

All the warmth leeched from Kaer Yin's head at once. He struggled to hear anything but the rush of blood in his ears for a moment.

"All this time," breathed Una. "Nema was my grandmother's nemesis for forty years. That's quite an interlude to plan a rebellion."

"The subtle knife plunges deep," agreed Tam Lin.

"Took her time, didn't she?" asked Robin.

"I'm a bloody *fool*," Kaer Yin whispered. His hands shook.

"What was that?" inquired Tam Lin.

"I said, I'm a bloody fool!"

"How so?"

"'Wouldn't it have been convenient if the Crown Prince had died instead of Falan the Younger?'"

Tam Lin laughed, "I said it two seconds ago—"

"I was *supposed* to die, Lin! Only the Sidhe knew I hadn't. Falan… it was Falan all along!"

"Slow down, love," Una said, laying her hand on his. "Falan did what, exactly?"

Kaer Yin sucked in a deep breath to cool his ringing ears. "Falan was in my vanguard that day before Dumnain. He was my *aide-de-camp*. After the first day's skirmishes, he came upon me in the tent as I was preparing to break camp. Patrick was planning to withdraw and march east. I meant to follow and stamp his bones into the earth, once and for all." He winced. "Forgive me, Una."

She waved his comment away. "Go on."

"Anyway, our plans were laid and agreed upon by every officer. Falan had been the sole dissenter. He posited that the citizens of Dumnain had plotted to betray the High King from day one, which is why they eagerly joined Donahugh's rebellion. He argued in Council that we should raze the city as a lesson for the next town that would foolishly throw their coin to Patrick's banners. I remember he and Fionn arguing over the matter for nearly an hour before my uncle Bov silenced them. I might never have thought of it had you not said anything, Tam Lin."

"I still don't have the first bloody clue what you're on—" Tam Lin started.

"Don't you see? Falan Mac Nemed tried to lure me into a pointless conflict, which would have placed me in a precarious position in Eire. If I'd accepted his advice and chosen to attack, I'd have broken Dannan law at the very least. Otherwise, he could have had me killed somewhere in those narrow, twisting lanes."

"Yeah, but he got himself killed in an early morning raid on Donahugh's baggage train, and you… well, you know."

Kaer Yin stared up at the sky, laughing coldly to himself. "Who do you think ordered him to raid that train after I was informed of the execution of our prisoners in the town square? He seemed so eager to chase the perpetrators down."

"Are you saying that the townspeople didn't murder your men?" Una's voice was very soft.

"Not at all. A dozen or so *were* guilty. Many more fled when they heard Patrick had abandoned them. That was why I sent Falan to round them up, but then I saw what had been done to our men— and I— anyway, Falan and Sionnavar's agents were responsible for bringing the information to me. Patrick had given orders upon his exit, and the townsfolk had gotten carried away. The horror on Falan's face when he told me."

He pinched the bridge of his nose. "We'd cut our men down, punished the few guilty parties, and were about to leave, when the situation changed. The townsfolk grew aggressive. Someone tried to shoot me from my horse twice. The next time I looked up, I'd… everyone was gone."

Una's fingers melded with his.

"So, you're saying Falan led you into a trap? Bollocks. He took a spear to the throat an hour later," sneered Tam Lin. "If he was a criminal mastermind, he died an idiot."

"Unless," Diarmid broke in. "He didn't die."

Kaer Yin's eyes darted toward him. "You know, don't you?"

"I am not omniscient, Yin. Recognizing a face and voice from my past is hardly mysticism."

"How long have you known about Nema?"

He pursed his lips. "Years. It doesn't matter."

Una squeezed Kaer Yin's fingers so hard he thought he might lose one. "Ah, leave the skin, if you please?"

She ignored him. "If you knew who she was, why didn't you ask yourself why she was there in the first place?"

"Why would I? Do you know how many human lives *I* have chosen to live, My Lady? Eternity is quite a long time. Many of us choose to live among mortals for a span. Break up the monotony. Liadan is older than I."

Una struggled to absorb that statement. Instead, Rian asked, "So you thought a Fir Bolg queen in a position of contentious power within the greatest city in mortal Eire wasn't nefarious in the least?"

"I assumed she sought to live for a time among mortals. After all, what are seventy years in five thousand?"

"Still—"

"Nothing!" he snapped. "I might have investigated beforehand if I thought there was the cause. Until her coup, I never had reason to bother. Have we all been duped? Yes. Am I evil for failing to see it? No. Try focusing on things you *can* change rather than things you failed to."

"That comment means nothing if Falan is alive." Kaer Yin wound his reins around his right fist. "If he is, he'll take Eire through his bastard, and Bri Leith is undoubtedly next."

Tam Lin scrubbed a hand over his face. "Diarmid. If Yin is right, Tairngare will surrender without much fuss. What possible purpose would her reformation have served if not to help her family to power? On that note— how fast can you get to my father?"

"Quick enough," he answered, his pupils shifting with unnatural light like a nighttime predator.

"Do it," Kaer Yin urged. "Once we meet up with the rest of our party. Go ahead of us. Please, Diarmid. This isn't about Una and me anymore."

Diarmid's expression held sarcasm, sadness, and malice. "I doubt it ever has been or will be, princeling."

⚔ ⚔

ANOTHER ODD, HALF-FORMED DAY passed in the Otherworld before they came across their lost party members. Having spied them first, Gerrod flew out of the Waycross on bare feet. His hair had grown long and shaggy, and his chin bore a fair bit of stubble. Beaming, Rian dismounted and threw herself into his arms. Robin grabbed them around the waist to crush them against his chest in a great bear-hug. Eva poked her head out the door next, squealing for joy when she set eyes upon her niece. Una was crying openly when her arms encircled her. Kaer Yin couldn't help the grin that split his face from ear to ear at the sight. In tears, Eva whispered something into Una's ear that had the girl nodding into her shoulder.

Robin tousled Gerrod's hair. "Ye've grown a bloody mile since last I saw ye."

"Well, it's been almost four months, hasn't it?"

"Wait, what?" laughed Rian. "It's been a few days, silly."

"Not for them, it hasn't," said Diarmid, brushing a stray snowflake from his nose. "This close to the Veil, time runs nearly parallel with Innisfail."

Rian gaped at him like he's just told her the sea was full of jelly. *Four months?*

"At least."

Gerrod gave her a bashful smile that looked odd on his new adult-like face. "I'm older than ye now, I gather?"

"Are you daft, other than this codger," Tam Lin jerked a thumb at his uncle. "Rian's the oldest thing here."

Gerrod and Rian ignored him simultaneously. Instead, they made room so Rian could hug Mel Carra, Small Dan, Finster, then Tall Dan. A few others made the rounds. She'd half-killed herself, once upon a time, to tend to every one of them, and was well-loved by all. Even Carra's tiny cadre of Tairnganeah took their turns. The only person who seemed more enthusiastic to great everyone was Una. The pair couldn't have been happier to see so many friendly faces if they'd tried.

Tam Lin crossed his arms. "Bloody women."

Kaer Yin dismounted in one leap without comment and caught Gerrod in a bear hug that almost cracked the lad in two.

Diarmid examined his nails next. "Indeed."

"Right," said Robin, wiping a stray tear from the corner of his eye. "Let's go home, shall we?"

Small Mercies

Dor Imba descended upon the hills at Drogheda with snow flurries and famine. A fortnight later, an army of Southers followed. By the dawn of the fifteenth day, they'd surrounded the massive outer wall in neat rows, dozens deep. By mid-morning of the sixteenth day, bare-chested men by their hundreds painstakingly hacked shallow trenches into the frozen ground. By noon of the next, they'd already begun constructing a timber wall on the opposite side of their growing ditch. Back-breaking work, to be sure, but they neither stopped nor slowed. The Southers' speed and strength of arms were astounding to witness.

Gan observed all from the Citadel's topmost tower. Nema had tasked him to keep watch and send regular reports to the Tenth Floor. One of her newest guardsmen had kicked him from bed two hours before first light, dragged him up to the roof by his collar, and left him with two Secundas to stammer messages to the Cloister. By mid-afternoon, Gan had watched Damek Bishop's army gather for about twelve hours in the frigid cold. Gan had had enough by evening, knowing that Nema did not need him on the watch to understand what was happening. When the tents started popping up in the distance, Gan handed a milk-faced Secunda his spyglass and took his leave without ado.

It wouldn't be long now, anyway.

He might as well greet death warm and well-fed. Heading downstairs, he encountered the same Fir Bolgman who'd forced him upward. The fellow's dark violet eyes narrowed as Gan attempted to squirm past him. He must have come up to see the encampment for himself.

Gan wished him the joy of his discovery. "Let me pass," he sighed.

The Bolgman's dark hair spilled over his collar when he leaned down to sneer back. "You've been ordered to remain aloft."

"I decline," giggled Gan. "If you'd prefer to beat me rather than feed me, I should warn you; I no longer have the nerve endings required to register physical blows. My lungs and eyes, however, do feel the cold. I need food and a warm drink. Unless you'd like to kill me now and save Bishop's men the trouble?"

The Bolgman glanced out the latticed window where thousands of fires flickered to life outside the city. "They'll never breach the Gates."

"Oh, I doubt they'll need to. You see, Bishop has studied his Classics. In ancient times, Caesar had perfected this strategy at the battle of Alesia. A mighty king named Vercingetorix thought his superior numbers and high walls would save him, too. He was wrong, and so will you be."

"You're barking, old fool. We have twenty thousand Cohort and Tairnganeah behind these walls."

"… and half a million mouths to feed. Half a million disease vectors. Half a million corpses to clog the streets and cloud the air with flies."

The Bolgman cringed a bit.

Perhaps whatever Nema had done to him might wear off in the face of bald logic? Gan certainly was no expert. Nema's powers grew more horrifying the madder she became… and she was now mad as a rabid mare. Whatever malady which leeched the color from her skin and eyes, added that sag to her once sharp cheeks, and thinned her glorious hair— had set to work in her mind. The last time Gan had snuck into the dungeons to visit Grainne (who looked as well as one should expect while starving in prison), she'd said Nema was finally afflicted with true mortality.

She'd grow madder still before the end. It seemed the Sidhe were only immortal so long as they never strayed far from their Otherworld home. Nema had been plaguing the city of Tairngare for half a decade. For one as old as Nema, the mortal realm was a slow poison.

Grainne had posited the only way Nema could maintain herself now was through blood magic, but the more she used, the worse the rot became. Finally, understanding that their chosen hero was a beast in disguise, the people had turned from her en masse. They kept to their homes; doors locked, and windows shuttered. The silence in the streets was a deafening harbinger of impending doom. While Bolg goons kicked down doors to drag unwitting citizens from their hearths to supply their mistress with fodder for her dark sorcery, many escaped to the townships, bringing news of Nema's misdeeds to greater Eire, at last. In the Midlands, Gan had learned, a petition to reinstate the Libella and reelect a new Doma made rounds. So far, it bore twelve-thousand signatures, or so he'd been told. The Reformation's brutality was no longer a secret. The Union of Commons was disbanded. Several of its ranking officers had already committed suicide or fled.

Vanna Nema existed on borrowed time.

Elated at the prospect of imminent freedom, Gan couldn't care less which happened first. Nothing would deflate his mood now, not even the threat of violence or death. It would happen whether he feared it or not, so why worry? "Now, if you don't mind, I'd like to eat before we're starving."

The Bolgman stepped aside with an elegant gesture. "To your demise then, stooge."

"And yours, barbarian." Gan bowed as he passed.

The Bolgman snorted but made no further effort to stall him.

⚓ ⚓

Inside the Citadel, chaos reigned. Secundas raced hither and thither, carrying grain sacks or other perishable items from the kitchens to the cellars or moving already sparse furnishings against the windows as rudimentary blinds. As for the Cohort, officers and archers crowded the windows and rooftops, fumbling for position. Most of these soldiers were newly minted, children of suddenly elevated commoners or impoverished recruits with family members imprisoned or swinging from the outside walls. These Secundas were the first orphans of the Reformation. They had no idea which threat they should fear most, and their confusion was palpable.

Gan sympathized. He strolled through the halls toward the Grand Arcade, munching on a moldy piece of bread and humming to himself. A veritable concert of noise, frenetic activity, and dread enveloped him.

He couldn't help but smile.

How many times a day did he shuffle up and down the Grand Stair, praying for a falling star or another cosmic catastrophe to crash through the ceiling? Hundreds. Now that calamity had finally arrived, Gan couldn't be more at ease. Soon, Nema would meet her end; her ruthless, absurdist regime would topple. Her bootlickers and apologists were fodder for the flames. The stain of her rule would be scrubbed away like so much muck.

Gan was finally free to die.

He was ready.

He'd *been* ready for so long; he couldn't contain his joy. No more suffering, waking each morning with the blinding pain in his joints, his head— worst, his soul. While his outer flesh might be numb, he writhed in torment internally. Every step he took was agony. For the incessant tremors plaguing his damaged nervous system or the insufferable spasms that intermittently ripped through his muscles, he hadn't achieved a whole night's sleep in ages.

522

To make matters worse, with his tear ducts now only moderately functional, he'd been forced to carry a tincture of saline on his person. Now the apothecary who procured it for him was dead, having become a member of Nema's Wall of Fame. Gan's headaches had become unbearable in the weeks since, and both eyes were puffy and inflamed. He carried boiled water to help mitigate the struggle, but to little avail. If the infection persisted, he would very likely go blind. Well, he need no longer fear fumbling through these stairwells on swollen feet, blind, and insensate with pain.

It would all be over soon, thank Siora.

If he had the ability, he might skip up the stairs to Nema's throne room and dance a jig for her bemusement.

In the end, he did not.

When he stumbled into the Obsidian Hall, a contingent of Southers had taken up residence before the dais, in full armor and mail. What bright uniforms they had! All done up in cobalt and silver, with splashes of crimson. Beside them, the youngish Tairnganeah crowding Her Eminence's throne looked drab, under formed, and untested. The second tallest man in the group stepped from the center of that handsome mass of knights. He had long, raven black hair curling over each shoulder, bright hazel eyes with flecks of green and violet around the iris, and wide, broad shoulders. If Gan weren't mistaken, the lad bore an uncanny resemblance to someone he'd seen recently. He glanced at Nema, swaddled upon her throne in her garish yellow robes.

He looks a lot like her Falan, doesn't he?

The height, the eyes, and the hair... even Grainne bore these similarities. Neither looked much like Nema, save for the size and hair, maybe?

They're related, surely?

Has this always been her plan? He wondered.

Though he second-guessed himself at her reaction, Nema was furious. He knew her well enough to know when she wore her mask and when she didn't bother. "Lord Bishop," her voice slithered from the throne without welcome. "We're quite amazed to see you here today, in such company."

The Duch's nephew smiled. Even Gan's heart fluttered.

Definitely related.

"Not at all, your Eminence. I think you'll find that I am answering a summons."

"From whom?" She raised an imperious brow. "To what purpose have you marched an army of invaders onto our lands and encircled our city?"

"Liberation," he smirked, accepting a stack of rolled vellum from his superbly tall and scarred attendant. A colonel, or somewhat more, perhaps? Bishop held one roll up. "Each of these begs the Duch for aid. A tyrant has taken over the Red City and systematically executes its citizens without crime or trial." He tossed the messages onto the polished floor. They rolled to a stop at the dais stair.

She coughed disdainfully. "Who are *you* to accuse us, Lordling? The Duch is dead, or so I hear, and his brother has taken his place. Another son is on the way already. You? You're no one, boy. A bastard whose lands have been seized, backed by an army of brigands and lawless thieves. I ask again... *who do you think you are?*"

"The bastard son of a king, madam. That's who I am." He turned to give the audience the full effect of his posture. "I am the son of Falan Mac Nemed and the rightful Duch of Bethany. My father—"

"You *lie*—" Nema attempted to shriek.

"— the true Crown Prince of Innisfail has ordained me the rightful Lord of Eire. Though I am eager to grind my murderous uncle to dust in Bethany, I am here at Falan of Armagh's request. Anyone who seeks to flee the city now will be granted safe passage through our ranks. No harm will come to a single man, woman, or child who braves the gates until dawn tomorrow. If you do not or cannot flee, we urge you to take cover and surrender to my commanders once the walls have been breached. Any that take up arms in this viper's defense will be granted no quarter."

"Are you mad?" screeched Nema, rising. "*My grandson* would never acknowledge—"

"Ah." Damek waved her comment off. "But he has, grandmother. Martin?"

The tall oak tree beside the Duch's nephew stepped forward, drawing a warrant from within his tunic. "'*I,*" he boomed. "*Falan the Younger Mac Nemed of the noble Fir Bolg, Lord Marshal of Armagh, and rightful Crown Prince of all Innisfail— do decree—*"

Nema covered her ears with shaking, liver-spotted hands. "Stop him, stop him, STOP HIM!" She screamed, though no one made a move to do any such thing, including her loyal Fir Bolg honor guard. They watched Damek Bishop pace the room like men possessed. The Cohort, however, clutched their weapons, indignant but wary.

"*— that my son and sole heir, Damek Bishop Mac Nemed, is tasked to remove the heretical threat from the Tairnganese throne and set the city to rights. To the usurper who now occupies the Doma's robes, I admonish you to surrender your miter and crown, along with the prisoners you've detained in your dungeons. My commander Leal, who escaped your clutches only weeks past, will join Armagh's elite forces with Lord Mac Nemed's, their every intention to remove you from your unlawful occupation of Tairngare. My sister Grainne is to be released, unharmed, into Lord Mac Nemed's keeping. Defiance demands death, seanmáthair. Signed, Falan Mac Falan Mac Nemed, of Armagh.*'"

When finished orating, the large fellow dropped the page and used his boot to slide it across with the others. The wink he spared Nema gave Gan's pulse a pinch.

Apoplectic with rage, Nema struggled down the first step. She pointed. "We do not recognize Falan's authority here, *bastard!* A man who falsified his death has no moral authority over the Red City. We abjure his demands, claims, and anything else you would have of us. *Get you gone* from our halls!"

At the intensity of her tone, the Cohort found a bit of their brass. Around twenty drew swords to surround Nema's dais. Damek was undeterred. He moved closer, tucking his hand into his belt, and bowed deeply. Through a range of leveled spears, his eyes met hers squarely. "If your people survive tomorrow's bombardment, and perhaps the next— they will starve within weeks. No supplies will reach you here in your high tower, *seanmáthair*. How loyal will these boys be when they are dead or wasting away?"

She made a snide sound. "What fear have I of a ground assault, boy? In three hundred years, no one has ever breached these walls. The Citadel is impenetrable."

He cocked his head and stood up. From his cloak, he retrieved a spyglass. "You, there?" He nodded at a nearby Cohort officer. "Tell your Doma what waits outside in the harbor." The boy gaped at him for an uncomfortable amount of time. "Hurry up now. We don't have all day."

The boy took the glass and rushed to the rear, eastern window past the golden doors and above the Grand Stair. Everyone in the room heard his gasp before he raced back, huffing. "Ships, your Eminence!"

"How many?"

"Four, but…"

"Out with it!"

He cleared his throat, his puny adam's apple bobbing. "Our fleet, m'lady. It's already burning."

With a furious squeal that should have cracked the onyx beneath the lad's feet, Nema reached out with one gnarled hand and clenched her fist. The boy convulsed, went purple, then collapsed on the spot. While a collective gasp spread through her audience, Nema staggered to her knees, wheezing. Damek looked on in horror. After a silence so deep one could hear an eyelash fall, he glanced up to find her clawing herself back atop her throne. "You *have* gone mad, haven't you? Look at yourself, Liadan. It's not too late to see what you've become."

At last, after regaining a bit of her composure, she glared down her long nose at him. "We will hear no more. You shall have your answer at first light tomorrow, Lord Bishop. You will vacate our city within the hour."

Knowing that was as good as he would likely get, Damek relented. His beautiful eyes rested a moment on Gan, who flushed with shame at the revulsion writ there, but there was more too— sympathy, if he weren't mistaken. That was enough for Gan. Not many powerful men possessed such emotions to display them. He would help the young lord before the end if he were able. "My offer for clemency stands. Any brave souls who dare shall fear no reprisal. We have hot bread and ale for the hungry and warm tents prepared for families. I bid you all Godspeed."

When he turned on his heel to stalk through the doors, it was as if the light had been sucked from the hall.

🦌

Tis no simple matter, to abandon one's *geis*. As he made his way from the kirkyard along the western wall toward the Southers' timber and shield wall, Gan thought he finally understood why it had taken Aoife so long. His lungs, one of the few organs he had left that didn't pain him as much, felt like they might burst the further away he went from the city. A few stragglers crept beside him, hoping the darkness would protect them. That soon proved false when the Cohort lit the night sky with flaming arrows. Many temporarily bathed in their light were immediately impaled from above, their twitching bodies illuminated in the fog. Gan rushed as fast as anyone would, despite his malady.

When he'd made it a good fifty yards, halfway to the enemy line, his heart was seized as if by a cold hand. He collapsed just as a flare went off overhead. An arrow whizzed out of the dark, but someone had rolled him over. "Watch yourself, Master Gan," whispered a boy with a familiar voice. The sparse light available through the haze of smoke and torchlight afforded him a glimpse of cherubic cheeks and lovely copper skin.

"Lon?" Gan asked, mystified. Once upon a time, he'd been one of Gan's 'boys.' Through the pain and discomfort, Gan burned with shame. He remembered Lon had had a beautiful voice. His clients paid top fainne to hear him sing… before.

Gan swallowed hard, though his throat was as dry as his eyes.

Lon gave him a cautious smile. "The same." His voice was deeper. "Can you make it over the ditch on your own?"

A white flash of pain tore through Gan's mind at the thought. "I… I don't know."

Lon was quiet for a moment as if weighing his options. The flares above them resulted in further cries from those attempting to escape. The next thing Gan knew, Lon had a grip on his collar, dragging him along.

"What—why are you helping *me*?" Gan asked the night sky since Lon was engaged out of eyesight.

"You were less cruel to me than my parents. I won't forget that."

Gan wept without tears. "I sold you. You should leave me to die."

"I didn't say I forgive you, old man, only that I won't leave anyone to die out here like a dog. Besides," Lon's shadow sniffed. "I'd say you've been punished plenty."

The fourth round of flares went up, and a screaming woman was summarily silenced.

Lon recovered quickly, his teeth glowing white in the dark. Gan was dragged through bramble and thorn. He knew he had to be bleeding though he couldn't feel it. Aside from this small blessing, the claws piercing his heart relaxed the further away he was led.

He took a tremulous breath. Lon ducked over him as a fifth flare exploded over their heads. This time, the arrows came down in a torrent. Several voices cried out at once as the missiles fell. Lon slumped over his knees with a grunt, then teetered sideways; an arrow had taken him through the throat. Straining with every ounce of energy he could muster, Gan crawled over to him on his elbows. Dead. A boy with every cause to hate him had traded his life for his. Making dry hacking sounds, Gan shoved himself up to his knees.

The ditch was just ahead. Lon had dragged him almost fifty yards and a thousand miles through his *geis*.

Gan must not waste this chance.

Nema had to be stopped.

An officer stared down at him from their shield wall, ten yards away. "Better hurry," he said, tugging his chin at the sky. A sixth flare went up. The men and women in Gan's company scrambled for the trench. Gan threw himself forward on all fours with a guttural scream and fumbled like a wounded dog for the ditch. He had only one thing left to live for.

Gan would be damned if he'd forget his purpose now. When the arrows thudded into the earth beside and behind him, he tumbled arse over heels to the bottom. With a stranger's foot in his face and a tangle of limbs around his torso, Gan looked up to note the Souther winking at him.

"Welcome to Bethany, folks. It looks like you're just in time."

⚜

At dawn, Damek strode up the rampart with Martin and his officers. Two shieldmen stepped aside so that he could view the killing field below. The sun had yet to rise, but the city was backlit against the horizon by her glow. In the quickening light, last night's degradation was revealed. The plain was littered with bodies, many of them children. So many that even Damek's stomach turned. The crows had been at work for hours already. For a moment, he turned away to collect himself. "How many?"

"Around four hundred, my lord. Give or take," answered Hisk.

Damek cursed under his breath. "That bloody woman is a demon."

"No argument there."

"Any chance she'll surrender, you think?" Martin's frown was leaden as he handed Damek his spyglass. "She didn't strike me as the surrendering sort."

Damek held the glass to his eye and shrugged. "Who knows, Martin. You ask me; she's no fool. She must know they're doomed without the harbor or their fleet."

So far, he could spy no activity at either visible gate nor along the ramparts save for Cohort and archers. The bodies swinging along the walls made his stomach oily. He removed the eyepiece for a moment to scrub his face with the back of his hand. Damned if he wasn't tired. He'd been marching for weeks, sacking one town after another. Now that he was here and his goal was within reach, he wanted it over with as soon as possible. All those people… Damek had never seen so many casually discarded humans. The hardened soldier that he was found it unsettling. "She's gone insane. Leal, forgive me for doubting you."

Down the line of officers, Leal pressed a fist to his chest. "No offense taken, *Mo Flaith*. Who could believe a woman would incarcerate and starve her people to such a degree?"

"I've never seen so many corpses outside of a battlefield. Those are simple townsfolk dangling from those ropes. Here, the same." Martin covered his mouth. Despite the cold and the wind, the dead still reeked of rotting flesh and shit. "Forgive me, but she deserves to die for this."

Damek made a face. "I agree, but that wasn't part of the bargain with Falan." Martin flinched a bit at the name. He didn't care for the reminder that Damek had been keeping secrets for thirty years. He'd always had his suspicions; of course, O'Reardan was a wise man. But Damek had never actually told him who his father was until now. Martin had learned when the men had, which was most unfair of Damek, given their relationship. Damek vowed to remedy the rift as soon as possible, but he was starved for time with the long marches, changing tactics, and preparations.

"We're meant to take the city, liberate whoever's left alive down there, and hold her until he comes to claim her. Apparently, there's a punishment reserved only for those of her advanced age. I don't much care, as long as that old bitch is gone by week's end."

"That's a trifle ambitious, lad," chuckled Martin. "It takes a city that size, with those high walls, *months* to give in. Hells, this could drag on for a year if we're not careful."

Damek shook his head. "No. She doesn't have a year. You saw her, Martin. What do you think all those people are doing on the wall?"

"I don't take your meaning."

"Blood magic," Leal answered for Damek, his violet eyes very bright in the rising light. "Forbidden to our kind. She sustains herself with death. Whoever can't be bent to her will, she kills." He gestured to the south wall. "If she stops, she dies. She'll grow madder and madder the more lives she claims."

"Wonderful," Martin grumbled. "After this, we have the bloody Northers to look forward to. Again."

"Which Northers," Leal asked.

Martin cut an exasperated glare at Damek. "I imagine you'll find out if we survive this siege."

Finally, lights flickered on the Citadel's southern parapet. Torchlight. A line of men and women followed the lead torch. Brows drawn, Damek set the glass to his eye once more. There walked Nema, with her bright vermillion robes, tiny and frail against the might of those red granite walls. She held the lead torch. In her wake trailed dozens of Tairnganese citizens— women and children all. Each had their hands bound behind their backs and nooses tied around their throats. Screaming, they wept into the void.

"*Reason*, Martin!"

Hisk handed his Commander a glass.

Martin stiffened beside him. "She wouldn't."

Damek jerked back when the prisoners were shoved over the wall, one by one. The youngest of these was barely out of swaddling. The toddler's tiny legs kicked out for nothing when she went over. "Oh, gods!"

"What, what's happening?" Leal demanded.

Rather than answer, Martin handed him his glass.

The Bolgman made harsh choking sounds at the back of his throat for the barbarism he spied there. Damek himself felt like throwing the offensive item into the mud and spilling his guts over a nearby fern. He did not, however. He counted the lives being snuffed out for his benefit. Fifty, by the end; most, just bairns.

They died to defy him.

He owed them his full attention.

Despite the distance, Damek caught a flash of Nema's coy grin like a knife in the dark. Wait, or was the knife in her hand? A final prisoner was dragged up the line by a rope at her throat. This one was tall and lovely, with long dark hair, wearing the dregs of formerly delicate garments. He'd never met his aunt Grainne, but she looked so much like Falan that it would've been difficult to mistake her for anyone else. A guard wrestled Grainne to her knees. Even with the rope, she put up a good fight.

Leal ground his teeth together so hard that everyone heard it. His shoulders shook. "Grainne!" he shouted, though she'd never have heard him.

"Reason damn it!" barked Damek. Don't we have a ballista with the range?"

"Not that won't hit the lady too. I'm sorry, my lord." Douglas answered.

Leal whimpered like a wounded animal. Damek distantly realized that he probably loved her. He wondered how he would feel if it were Una up there, waiting to die.

His chest seized with the thought.

Grainne's head was jerked back by the soldier with the rope. Another held a silver bowl just beneath her collarbone. Nema drew the blade across her granddaughter's slender throat with a vicious leer.

Leal's anguish was nothing to the pounding in Damek's ears.

The rearguard held Grainne's body upright while the second milked her open throat over the bowl. One final convulsion, and the pair kicked her twitching body over the wall. Throat cut from ear to ear and dangling at an awkward angle, Grainne lived but a few moments more.

Nema lifted the bowl to her lips when she went still and drank deep.

Damek couldn't be sure, but he might swear he watched the years fade from the Doma of Tairngare like an unwound clock. Victorious, she raised both hands to the sky. *Tairngare is mine*; her smirk seemed to say.

Not for long, you old bitch, Damek thought.

"Martin," he said.

"My lord?"

"I changed my mind."

"How so?"

"We will not march within the hour."

"What order, then?"

"Fire their markets, docks, fields, and granaries outside the city, and I want every rooftop within range aflame by mid-morning."

"Aye, and what else?"

Damek let out a long breath. He gripped the spyglass so hard that his palm bled. "Bring up the trebuchets. This ends now."

THE WHITE QUEEN

Drem woke to discover the Queen of Scotia staring down at her. Long white-blonde hair coiled over her shoulders in a complex braid that brushed Drem's knuckles when she moved. The wind howled outside their carriage, attacking the shutters with a vengeance. Eri Ap Midhir Bres' beautiful cheeks were tinted pink from the frosty Innish air.

"Good morning, Eminence. Did you sleep well?"

Her famous silver eyes tilted upward at the corners when she smiled.

Drem understood the look as kindness, though it also held a note of condescension. She tolerated it as she'd learned to tolerate so much of late. "Well enough," Drem lied. Her bones felt hollow as a reed flute and brittle as aged vellum. It had been quite some time since she could recall a day without extreme discomfort or pain. She struggled up to her elbows, wiping her eyes. "How long did I sleep?"

The High King's daughter pursed her lips. "A half-day, no more."

Drem winced.

That was far too long. The sudden illness that had kept her abed in Bres for weeks might have abated enough for travel to Dale, but she knew every mile cost her more than time. Just then, a deep, rasping cough overtook her. When she'd finished, and her ribs felt shredded from the inside by unseen talons, Eri Bres passed her a clean handkerchief. "I beg you; please allow me to arrange rooms for you at the *Windbreaker*. We'll be there in less than two days. I'd prefer to carry your tidings to my father without further risk to your health, Eminence," she pleaded.

They'd been having this debate for many weeks now.

As usual, Drem shook her head, folding the handkerchief into her fist so the blood might escape the queen's notice. A certain tilt to her chin told Drem their argument would soon reach a climax, and there was minimal guarantee that Drem would win. Each day that passed, she grew weaker, her lungs more volatile. *Pneumonia*, her studies whispered at the back of her mind—a product of her weakened immune system.

Too far gone.

Without the Spark to purge her lungs of bacteria and viruses, she was fully aware that she didn't have long. Something worse crept through her body like a sneak thief, robbing her Spark of fortitude and cellular renewal. This rapacious entity had a name.

Cancer, her Practicum of fifty years before, assured her.

To ascend to the Fifth and Sixth Floors in the Cloister, one must achieve merits in natural law. Cellular Disease was just one of the many subjects she had excelled in.

Ironic, she thought, *that I should perish of the very same sickness that had intrigued me so much in my youth.*

She might have laughed if she could spare the breath. "No," she replied firmly. "I must speak to your father personally. Even if it is the last thing I do."

"It shall be," Eri sighed without malice. Cold she was, but never cruel. She simply refused to mince words. Drem liked that about her most. "You're dying, Eminence. I see the black thing nibbling at your lungs quite clearly. If you were to rest and remain well out of the cold, you might live a few months more. At this rate…" she trailed off, shaking her head. "I doubt you'll make it to Bri Leith, Doma Moura."

"Perhaps if we took ship from—"

"We've been over this. The roads are impassable whence we came, and the marshes are treacherous in the best weather. It would take weeks to sail around Dingle and negotiate sleds and barges for the Straits, which are nearly frozen solid. You'll be dead long before then, I'm afraid."

Drem swallowed a fresh surge of despair at that. She didn't feel her years as many her age might and longed for life as a drowning man pines for shore. There were many things she had yet to see and do, so many plans gone awry that she could set to rights if only she had time. Though, in her heart, the queen's words rang true. Drem had just enough Spark left in her to be certain.

"What would you have me do? My city is overrun with lunatics in service of a tyrant. My people are scourged or swinging from the Citadel's high walls. My granddaughter has been kidnapped twice, chased through Eire by a power-mad warlord, and has only just lost her father *and* her inheritance to a zealous uncle. I do not have the luxury to fade into the wilderness while Eire burns. I must speak with your father, garner assurances—" she meant to elaborate, but another coughing fit took over. This one left her breathless and trembling for a long span afterward. She lay back against her cushions with the queen's hand wiping the sweat and blood from her mouth. Moments like these almost convinced Drem that perhaps death would be a relief after all. Deep in her marrow, she knew she couldn't go on this way.

The pain had become a relentless, daily trial.

The indignity of such an end was infinitely more taxing.

"You don't have a choice, Drem," said Eri, meeting her eyes. "I refuse to let you die in the back of a wagon for an uncertain outcome. I'm afraid Dale will have to do."

Drem bit her quivering lower lip, feeling hot and cold at once. From what she had gleaned of the High King's daughter over these many weeks, she recognized regal finality when she heard it. She would simply have to seek alternative methods when they reached the famed Scotian trading hub and keep her own counsel till then. Though Drem was fully aware the queen had her best interests at heart— Drem Moura was not one to be told when she was done with anything. She would get her way, whatever the cost.

In her Spine, she chanted to herself.

Siora would see her through. She must.

"Tell me, what news of Bethany?"

Eri reclined against her cushions with a scowl. "Henry FitzDonahugh has a new child on the way, I'm told. He's wed some Kernian woman's girl and declares the South independent from my father's rule. My source tells me that citizens must attend mass at Court nearly three times daily. Those who don't are fed to the stocks, their lands confiscated by the crown."

Drem made a noise. "He and Nema are two sides of the same coin."

"Yes. Though one at least believes the drivel he espouses. Liadan Mac Nemed has only ever solicited for one deity; herself."

Over the decades, Drem might have suspected that the mysterious Vanna Nema was more than she claimed to be but never in her life would she have imagined the viper to be the ancient dowager of Armagh. In hindsight, she supposed there had been legions of hints and warnings she should have examined. At this late stage, torturing herself with the past seemed redundant. Nema had eons to enact her fatal plans. Drem only had weeks, at best, to reverse them. "Perhaps, I should linger at Dale for a while?"

The queen laughed softly. "My brother is the gullible one, Eminence. You'd make other arrangements as soon as my back turned."

Drem thought about lying, but what would be the point? The hourglass ran thin. "I am not your subject, Highness. You have no right to dictate the terms of my death to me. This is a thing that must be done for my granddaughter's sake."

Eri Bres was silent for a time, mulling over the sincerity of Drem's proclamation. If the woman had any sense of justice, she could not refute her logic. Death was a highly personal issue, of the sort the queen of Scotia might never experience. Who was *she* to order the ruler (albeit former) of a sovereign city-state to meet hers in any other way aside from that she chose? "Drem, what good do you think you'll do?"

Drem was too tired and sore to bristle. "I have allies. If I won't live long enough to reach your father, there are others to whom I might apply."

"There are not. Your allies are defeated or fled. Tairngare is at Liadan's mercy until my father intervenes, which he will, but in his own good time. Your desperation to achieve nothing is admirable but misguided. I remain your best and most logical course."

Siora damn her eyes, thought Drem.

She is right, as usual.

She swallowed her retort.

"Una," Eri went on. "Is safest with my brother. I suppose he will look after her since he refuses to be parted from her."

The last made Drem quirk a brow. "Their alliance bothers you?"

"Mystifies me, more like. You only met my brother once, I recall."

Drem bobbed her chin. "At the High Council meeting. My daughter was there. That was the first time Patrick spied her."

Cursed be his name.

"Intriguing that so many chance occurrences during one occasion would affect us these many years later."

"If you prefer to look at it that way. I view that Gathering as a curse."

"Yes, I understand why you might. However, you've a legacy *because* of these events, however distasteful. Is that not right?"

Drem mused over the past once more, as one was wont to do when their future bore a certain finality. At the High King's fête, Alis Donahugh had been kidnapped by an unnamed Sidhe lord, an event that instigated a vicious civil war and ripped Drem's daughter away from her.

She still remembered the moderately handsome young Duch in his smart blue cloak and scarlet tunic, kneeling to request her Arrin's hand. The look on his face when Drem summarily dismissed him. She might have known he was not the sort to accept the rebuff of a mere woman— however powerful she might be. When his sister was taken, he and his men disappeared overnight from Bri Leith's keep. Drem would always rue the day she allowed Arrin to travel to Ten Bells for her Law Practicum. Ahead of his declaration of war against the High King, Patrick had snatched Arrin from the High Road in bald daylight.

The rest, as they say, was history.

She'd never seen her beautiful, brilliant daughter again. "Loving my exceptional granddaughter is no chore, Highness. Nevertheless, the circumstances of her birth still wound me deeply."

"I understand. I've lost children too."

Drem winced. She realized; she was a very selfish creature.

The Queen of Scotia had lost two sons in that same war. One to a Souther arrow and one to a festering wound some months later. Even the Sidhe, however long-lived, could be slain.

"I'm sorry," Drem said. "I forget myself in my grief."

Eri Bres peeked through the shutters at the white, whirling sky. "I have a daughter still. She is young yet, but I wish to keep her safe. I empathize with you, Eminence."

To be a mother and a ruler requires a strength few men could dream of.

"Then you understand why I must carry on?"

"Your courage is admirable. What is that phrase you Siorai use?"

"*In her blood, in her heart, in her spine*," answered Drem.

"That's the one. Well," Eri exhaled long and hard. "If you choose to live out your final days on a snowy road within a dispassionate Sidhe entourage, then you have my permission, if not my approval. If this is what you wish, I will honor your choice."

"It is." Drem's eyes welled with tears. She blinked them back. Mourning or acceptance, she couldn't be sure which, untied the knot of tension at her core. "I remember your father fondly, Highness. He will not turn me away, and my plea will be best served personally."

"I am sure he's already been apprised of the situations in Tairngare and Bethany. Though I do agree, he will respect and honor your efforts."

"Thank you, Highness."

"You are most welcome, Doma Moura." She pressed three fingers to her temple, then broke into a smile. "I must admit, I am anxious to see my father again. It's been—" she broke off, head jerking toward some sound outside that Drem could not hear.

Their carriage ground to a halt.

"What is it?" she asked, alarmed.

Eri leaned forward. "Men… *many* men, ahead."

Before Drem could reply, Eri leaned over and grabbed a beautiful black longbow from the center wall. Its shaft was inlaid with carvings of trouping nightmare beasts Drem had no names for. *Dorchadas*, the famed bow, was named; literally, 'Darkness.' Eri paused at the wide oak partition long enough to grab her quiver and sling it over her fur-cloaked shoulders. "I think you should stay here," said she before throwing the door open and allowing a blast of winter air inside.

Beyond the Queen of Scotia's elegant frame, Drem spied riders in black whipping their mounts directly into the Scotian line, their long, dark hair billowing behind them. Their eyes blazed violet or green, furious and bloodthirsty.

Fir Bolg?

Drem had but a moment to marvel before the first arrows were loosed.

⚜

Two shafts pierced the door, inches from Eri's right cheek. Without thought, she ducked and returned fire. The Bolg horseman tumbled from his horse into a snowbank, dead. Her *garda* whipped themselves into a frenzy in retaliation. Hers was an advance party. The bulk of her forces yet negotiated the Dalriadan Pass, some ten miles behind them. Others lay ahead, stationed at the Skenian Outpost, before Dale. Only twenty Dannan warriors stood between the Queen of Skye and this incoming troupe of Bolg lunatics. She leaped from the wagon, kicking the door shut as far as possible.

Drem Moura's blanched face stared back at her from the remaining crack. "What's happening?"

"An attack, apparently."

She heard Drem heave a rattling sigh. "I am ready."

"No," argued Eri. "Stay where you are. We'll handle this."

Another arrow whizzed past Eri's flank, and she hissed as it grazed flesh. Again, she drew and returned fire, and again, her assailant slid into the snow. Indiscriminate shouts and the ring of steel on steel accompanied by the sweet tang of Sidhe blood filled the air.

Thankfully, Skenian warriors were the finest in Innisfail, or so they proved. Their white and amber cuirasses winked like gems against the leaden sky.

Eri drew and slew two more before a sudden crash on her right alerted her of a new presence. He came at her fast, silver hammer poised to bash her brains into the snow. Eri spun on her heel, bringing *Dorchadas* up by her butt to smash her shaft into the fellow's windpipe. The force of the blow painfully reverberated through her elbow. Hands stinging, she couldn't regain her grip in time to halt the next

Bolgman from slamming her back into the wagon. She had not thought to wear larks and daggers in her lands, thus had nothing left to fight him with but claws and fists.

He raised her to his eye level by her throat, teeth clenched. Choking, Eri kicked out with everything she had, and he merely grunted when the toe of her boot glanced at his testicles. He smiled down at her as if he might enjoy watching her eyes dim. Just as her eyelashes began to flutter closed, his nose and mouth erupted in a steaming geyser of blood. Twitching, he fell backward. She slipped into the snow to retch and claw at her bruised flesh.

Another fellow attempted to take his place, but Drem stepped between them, wielding only a shaking bare hand.

The Warhammer leered. "What's this? Milesian bravery?"

"Milesian *sorcery*, you gobshite."

Brandishing his hammer, he rushed her.

Without a shred of fear, Drem closed her fist and whispered, "*Break*."

The Bolgman crumpled like a wet cloak.

Blood welled from his mouth as his eyes took one last glimpse of the sky. Two of his comrades raced toward Drem with their weapons high. With her spine as straight as it could go, her iron-gray braids blowing in the breeze, she looked like a vengeful deity, risen to exact retribution. Eri's heart clenched, for she was educated enough to understand what it cost her.

Unmoved by the Warhammers' theatrics, Drem swiftly twisted her fist once to the right, then to the left. Both men fell in a tangle of limbs, their necks bent at unnatural angles. Drem dropped to her knees, coughing.

Eri saw the blood dripping from her chin.

The skirmish was nearly over, with Eri's Skenian forces emerging victorious. Though, a few stragglers remained to cover their general retreat. Having as yet failed at their goal— the assassination of the Queen of Skye— a trio of braves made a last-ditch rush to get the job done. Eri managed to drag *Dorchadas* and her quiver over by the straps, but she didn't have time to nock before a hammer glanced the wagon door over her head. She drew a short dirk from the bodice of her gown and slammed it to the hilt into the Bolgman's boot. He'd barely had time to cry out when she withdrew the blade again, only to ram it into his kidney. Climbing his falling body, she nocked. Her next arrow caught another assailant in the back of the neck as he fled the scene.

Amriel, one of her stoutest *garda*, made it to her side with both larks drawn. He was splashed head to toe in blood. "*Mo Bhanríon*," he huffed. "*Bhulaileamar ar ais iad.*"

"Not yet," she rasped, pointing.

The last pair dashed toward them. Amriel whirled into the first, sylvan steel flashing. The second ducked one of Eri's arrows, smacking it into the reddened snow at his feet. She had two arrows left in her quiver aside from her dirk, but she'd never have time to nock before he was upon her. They stared each other down. While Amriel was engaged, the rest of her *garda* chased the bulk of the Bolgish raiders from the road.

"Who sent you?" she demanded.

"The Ard Ri," the Warhammer laughed proudly.

She must have blinked. "Are you daft?"

"Not at all, *isasaeligh*."

Without further ado, he ran for her. Eri braced herself to accept his impact, confident that if she could displace his weight far enough, she could ram her dirk into him before he could strike. However, he anticipated the move, cracking his hammer into the ball of her right knee instead. Brilliant stars burst behind her eyes. Brutal fingers gripped her hair. He prepared to run his dagger over her throat. She backed into him, bringing her undamaged heel into his groin. He grunted and let go long enough for her to drag herself partially away. She held her dagger up. "Come on then. Whatever happens, you'll leave full of holes."

"Don't you know when you're bested, Dannan bitch?"

"She might," said Drem from behind him. "But I sure as hells don't."

Then, a horrifying sight that would haunt Eri for the rest of her days greeted her wide-open eyes. Drem Moura displayed a feat of power no Sidhe could ever hope to match. Lips trailing blood, she held out her palm, fingers up. The Warhammer was lifted into the air by an unseen source. He made a strange mewling sound as if he guessed the fight was over already. Drem gave him a cruel, dry smile. "*One, two*," she sang, tucking her pinky and thumb down. His right arm and left leg snapped 90 degrees the wrong way. His frantic cries were drowned out by the power throbbing from Drem's rich, singsong voice.

"*Buckle his shoe. Three, four*", she chanted, and he inverted in the air. "*Lock the door. Five, six, pick up sticks.*" His left arm and right leg snapped forward until he resembled a half-broken scarecrow.

Eri didn't know how she got to her feet, unable to look away. She could only hope to face her death with such courage and pride.

"*Seven, eight,*" Drem grunted, balling her fingers into a fist. The Bolg Warhammer's spine cracked in the center, folding the fellow neatly in half, the wrong way. "*Lay them straight.*"

When his body struck the ground, he might have been a pallet of stained clothes; he lay in such a tidy stack. He gurgled a bit as he died.

Drem shot Eri a triumphant grin before tumbling face-first into the snow. With a cry, Eri skittered to her side, rolling her over. "No, no! Why would you do that, you silly mortal? Why?"

Drem smiled despite the blood bubbling freely from her mouth. The Doma of Tairngare had proven herself mighty, indeed. "You will speak for my Una."

"Yes," agreed Eri, as her battered *garda* gathered around, mystified.

"She is… the rightful Queen of Eire. Swear to me."

"You have saved my life today, Drem Moura. *Twice.*"

Bloodied fingers clasped the ruin of Eri's bodice. "Every… thing I have… all of Tairngare… all hers. Take nothing… from her. She is better than me."

Eri set a hand over her heart. "I will see Una Moura Donahugh claims her birthright. I vow it."

Seemingly satisfied, Drem let out a long sigh that rattled in her hollow chest. Her mission was accomplished to the best of her abilities.

She died smiling.

⚰ ⚰

EVA'S EYES SNAPPED OPEN FROM deep within the curling folds of steam licking their way along her face and shoulders. Instantly, her heart clenched. A jagged, guttural cry escaped her lips, and she jerked forward in her bath, splashing piping water over the floor tiles. In a flash, Mel was by her side, nude but armed, nonetheless. He took his paths seriously, no matter the occasion. Between rasping gasps and wails, she stammered a disjointed explanation.

Drem Moura was dead.

Not one for tears, Mel Carra, could not help but respond as any human beloved of another might. Great salty tears poured down his cheeks to mingle with the dampness of Eva's hair. She shuddered against him, teeth grazing his collarbone in her wide-mouthed anguish.

"Gone, all *gone*," she moaned.

His guts twisted to knots. "I am sorry, love."

After a while, her wracking sobs calmed, though she remained pressed against him, small and trembling. He would have done anything to take the pain for her, as that was the duty of the Bonded. Though, some pains could never be assumed… only observed. He slipped into the bath beside her, tucking her into his lap. She shrank into him, frail and childlike, as she would never appear to anyone else. Not Eva Alvra, the most feared of Drem's enforcers.

She shuddered, and he knew without asking what came next. Her prescience tended to follow emotional triggers. A shock such as this was bound to summon at least one. Her spine jerked backward, and he instinctively clasped the base of her skull to keep her head above water. She convulsed a few times, eyes going glassy and dark at once. Her breath stilled while she stared through the ceiling to the universe beyond. The sight always made the hair on his neck stand at end.

"*The black knight,*" spoke the cosmos through her. "*Burns, high and low.*"

Yes. He recalled that bit. They were to face the man himself soon enough, were they not?

"*Child of dark, child of light… the price of peace.*"

He hadn't heard that bit yet.

Cocking his head at her, he asked, "What child?"

"*Siora's chosen.*"

He closed his eyes. "Will Una survive?"

The glassy black of her pupils seemed fathomless. "*All that is born must perish. Look to the tide.*"

His throat squeezed at that, but before he could ask her to elaborate, she sat bolt upright, eyes clearing gold. She blinked up at him.

"What did I say?"

"Una."

She swallowed. "No."

"Do you feel the truth?"

Her face fell, and he mourned for her anew.

"How soon?"

"I can't see, but not long now," she whispered.

They sat in mutual grief, clutching at one another for strength.

"Can it be averted?" he asked, hopefully.

"I don't know."

He sighed heavily into the crown of her head. "The last Moura."

"Yes," she wept.

"Regardless, we will try, won't we?"

She gripped his hand hard. "We will."

Duch FitzDonahugh

Henry shoved his fat little piglet of a wife to the opposite end of their marital bed. She was heavy with his child. That thought alone should have made him hard as the crags at Dingle, as there was something quite stirring about the visible evidence of one's potency. On that score, Henry had never failed to congratulate himself. Even well into his fifties, as he was now, he could still fill a woman's belly with legacy. Despite this, he had never cared for round girls like this, never mind her plump rump, and swollen teats.

When he took her, he had to work very hard to achieve the threat of a broken bone or a bleeding vulva. Henry preferred his girls bony and fragile. What could be more pleasing than seeing one's handprint over a tiny white backside or the spine-tingling crunch one could elicit by pounding a less sturdy cavity?

His member throbbed at the thought. God did say a woman's purpose was to be put to 'use,' did he not? Upon second glance at his young wife and her mash of bruised flesh, he went limp again.

Useless witch.

He'd find better fare elsewhere tonight, as usual.

Henry tugged on his robe while the Kernian girl wept into her pillow. He didn't see what she had to cry about. She would soon be a queen, wouldn't she? All she must do was spread her meaty thighs and bear a few grunts and blows to manage it. The ungrateful sow. "Stop your grousing, or I'll fuck your skull. You didn't like that much last time, did you?"

Immediately, the girl shoved a fist into her mouth to still her sobs. Disgusted, Henry shrugged his robe over his head. This one was much finer than the rags he'd be relegated to while his criminal brother had yet lived. Now, he wore black Bretagn silk rather than coarse wool, and his body no longer ached from pretending to hobble for Patrick's benefit. He stood, finding himself in the mirror beside their bed. The Duchy had done wonders for Henry FitzDonahugh. Languishing for a decade in the blackness of a damp cell had robbed him of his hair and most of his teeth. The wooden dentures his brother had crafted for him had been replaced by good porcelain, and the muscle mass he'd lost shivering in the dark was mostly regained. He would never be the handsome rogue he'd been in his youth; years of deprivation and malnutrition would do that, but he *did* cut a fairer figure than the last Duch.

He smirked at himself in the glass.

Yes, God cared for his faithful servants, didn't he?

Almost sad to abandon his reflection, he turned to tug on his breeches and boots. "You may keep to your quarters this eve, my dear." He sighed into his collar while he fastened his belt. "I've had enough of your sniveling at supper."

"…but My Lady mother will—"

"Never utter a word about you if she's wise, and I believe she is."

She sat up, her face purple and ugly. "I hope I bear you a daughter, you filthy old beast."

Henry paused to shrug at the door. "A former maid bore me a son this past week. God will forgive you if you prove worthless, but I will not. Be a shame to elevate a common woman's child over my own duchess' get, but needs be, I suppose."

"You wouldn't dare!"

"Wouldn't I?"

He didn't bother to bandy further insults with her. She had a brain as soft as her face and the mettle of a pile of feathers. Her mother was no fool. Lady Penwyth had engaged the runt of her brood for a reason. The girl was expendable. If she proved fertile and obedient, she would live to serve as a forgettable queen. If not, she'd merely be forgotten—her fault for stuffing herself with pie rather than improving her feeble mind with scripture and sense.

Whichever way God laid her fate, Henry couldn't care less. There could be no replacement for the truly excellent sons he'd lost to his brother's perfidious slut of a daughter, but he'd be damned if he'd allow another woman to stand in the way of his God-given destiny. Soon as he found his vicious Tairnganese witch of a niece, he'd finally have everything he could hope for to avenge himself upon her and his brother's failed line.

Henry FitzDonahugh had a calling, after all: a sacred undertaking. He would be the first Christian king of Eire in nearly two thousand years.

With his head high, he strode into the hall, where two of his vassals waited. Taylor and Corrick bowed, then dogged his heels as he stalked toward the Great Hall. Upon entry, his courtiers silently ducked their heads. The women dipped curtsies from the gallery above, where they belonged. He never understood why his brother thought God's lesser creatures deserved a place among the men at Court. Feeling jaunty, he threw himself into his throne, tossing a leather-clad leg over one arm. Above him, a half-finished stained-glass relief celebrated Saint Brendan the Navigator, whom Henry had taken for the patron of his house. As Henry was tasked with leading the people back to God, he felt Brendan a kindred spirit. Besides, determined as he was to erase all evidence of the Sidhe from this land, if the previous relief of Kaer Yin Adair slaying his grandfather hadn't been shattered in the revolt— he'd have had it removed, regardless. Already, the pagan symbols etched into his grandfather's chapel were being scratched away, as were all semblances of Sidhe influence from the city and townships beyond.

Henry would stamp them out in every possible way.

Sparing a newly charming grin for his Court, he waved Shanley forward with his scrolls. "What news of the North?"

Patrick's former toady bowed low, unraveling his first vellum. "The new Doma of the Cloister of the Eternal Flame has been revealed for a Sidhe convert from the House Mac Nemed."

"Yes, yes," Henry groaned. "That was last week's news."

"Forgive me, Your Grace." The steward bowed double but didn't relinquish the floor. "She has also taken her grandchild captive, Grainne Mac Nemed."

"That's interesting. Why?"

"Our sources say the girl decried the old woman's tyranny in Court and attempted to maim or kill the Doma when such failed."

Henry chuckled. "A shame she failed. And Shanley? Grainne Mac Nemed is nearly one thousand years old, last I checked. Nothing 'young' about her. Well, what happened?"

The steward flushed. He wasn't a brave man. Henry despised him on principle, but there was no man better suited to the job at hand for now. "Our source does not say, though another assures us she was executed before the Traitor's army a week ago. To what purpose, we do not know."

"That's easy enough," growled Henry. "They're related, my mutant nephew and this atrocious Sidhe witch. What might she do to one such as him if she'd be happy to slay a favored grandchild? Very good. Mayhew? Have you anything more?"

The black-cloaked baron stepped forward to bow. "Yes, Your Grace. The rebel Southers have been encamped now for a fortnight. I feel certain the siege will break before the month is out."

"Sooner than that. It's winter, and Nema has not prepared the city for a protracted engagement. Their defenses will fade with the food, and if I know my nephew as I had my brother— Damek will figure a way to shorten it further by trickery or whatever else he can manage. The boy is a bit of a martial genius, I must admit. If sources are to be believed, he seeks to march on the Western settlements against the Sidhe. One can only pray he is so arrogant."

"Yes, Your Grace."

"Excellent. Let them hack each other to bits before we march. Either victor is our weakened enemy. Lord Pough, what news of our proposal to Ten Bells?"

Pough shuffled forward with a nervous cough. "Rejected, Your Grace."

That wiped the smirk from Henry's mouth. "What reason do they give?"

Pough trembled a bit at his tone. Another coward. Unfortunately, Henry's court was full of such men. How Patrick stomached them all, he'd never know. "Well, Your Grace, they, ah… do not recognize the ascendancy of your house."

The Court went so quiet; Henry could hear the clock ticking on the wall in the next room. "Is that right?"

"It is, I'm afraid. My source was quite appalled."

As they fucking should be, thought Henry.

"To whom do they grant their recognition?"

Pough looked eager to tunnel through the floor. "Lord Bishop, Your Grace, in consort to Lady Donahugh."

"*Lady* Donahugh rests upstairs, heavy with my babe."

"So my source argued. The Libellan Council confiscated his house and tavern, Your Grace. He was turned from the gates as a rabble-rouser."

Henry sat up straight, grinding his teeth. "They would dare denounce *me* in favor of my brother's murderer?"

"The Alderman claimed they have no right to reject the ancient claim of House Donahugh, on scant evidence from a…" he swallowed. "From a…"

"Spit it out!"

"'From a debauched zealot, likely guilty of fratricide.'"

Henry went silent for quite a while, willing the blood to course through his veins unabated by ice.

Those heretical cunts have tried you before.

Why shouldn't they now?

He took a few deep breaths before he spoke. "And our funds, what of them?"

Pough went very pale. "The same, Your Grace. They refuse you in the most colorful language."

Again, Henry kept silent for several moments. At last, he said, "Lady Penwyth?"

"Your Grace?" she answered from the gallery.

"Will you stake a hundred-thousand fainne to make your daughter Queen of Eire?"

She snorted, "Of course."

"And you, Lord Mayhew, will you match her to wed your first grandchild to a child of mine?"

"Gladly, Your Grace." Answered he.

"Well then," said Henry. "Seems we're off to reclaim Bethany's inheritance and eliminate the idolaters who preside over the city. All in favor, say '*aye*.'"

Only a few voices went unheard.

Thus, it was decided.

Henry would have his holy war.

⚜

LATER THAT WEEK, WHILE THE munitions, horses, arrows, and swords were accounted for, a messenger was dragged into Henry's study, sopping wet from head to toe. He'd been caught in a snowstorm in the Midlands and suffered frostbite at the end of his bulbous nose and swollen left hand. Henry knew the fellow would lose both when he was done delivering his message. He poured the brave Christian soldier a drink with his own hand. The messenger needed help to hold it to his mouth but bowed deeply in awed gratitude. "Your Grace, I bring the direst news from the North."

"He's broken through?"

"Yes, milord. Bretagn ships blocked the harbor at Drogheda from the start and have been bombarding the city daily. Five days ago, an agent fouled the city's wells and the river mouth. The Citadel surrendered at dawn yesterday. Only the Cloister resists now. Lord Bishop's men have taken the Red City."

"I suppose his men will loot and burn to their wicked content?"

"Lord Bishop has expressly forbidden it. Instead, he brings aid— food, medicine, oil, and peat, to the people. Most have already sworn fealty."

In less than one month, his nephew had managed to do what neither Henry nor his brilliant brother ever could. The lad undisputed King of Eire... for now. Henry would just see about that, wouldn't he?

"How many men does that give him if the Cohort kneels?"

Shanley replied, "Another twenty thousand, Your Grace, give or take."

Twenty thousand? "Giving him *seventy* thousand, in total." Henry cursed. "We stand no chance if we do not make an example of Ten Bells, my lords."

"Your Grace," Mayhew interrupted. "Perhaps we should start with Patrick's Barons? Many have opted to sit on the sidelines rather than choose a banner in this contest. They have two thousand men or more who can be pressed into service or face the gallows."

"You're right," muttered Henry, looking at a map. "Lords Wender, Morley, Dorr will give us an additional 6 thousand troops and piles of fainne. I like the way you think, old boy. Where else might we improve our average?"

Mayhew pointed at a dot on the map.

Henry smiled. "That would be rather crass, don't you think, as they've only just been sacked by the traitor's army?"

Alistair Mayhew rolled a shoulder. His family had scores aplenty to settle in the South. Henry was as amused by the man's many hatreds as he was impressed by his devious mind. "They make up his supply train, do they not? Hamstring him there and purge the heathens while we're at it. Besides, our men could use the practice before Ten Bells; I'll wager."

"We'll send the Cyrmians to deal with old Wender, then march through Malahide on our way to Ten Bells."

"Perfect, Your Grace."

Henry said to the poor, frostbitten messenger, "And you, my loyal friend, will receive a Corpsman's salary for such timely news at such personal loss."

"T-thank you, Your Grace." The messenger looked like he might topple over any moment.

Smiling, Henry rubbed his hands together over their modified map. "The Christian Kingdom of Eire. I rather like the sound of that, Alistair. I think Our Lord does too."

A King of Eire

The sack of Tairngare took far longer than Damek had hoped in the end. After the trenches had been dug out and the Tairnganese fleet had been fired, all the Southers had to do was wait. Thirty or so days might seem a miracle to any other commander (not the least of whom had been his deceased uncle, who'd spent years in the failed attempt)— but Damek had three times the men, Bretagn ships loaded with newly minted cannons, and a lifetime's example to learn from. He had won the greatest city in Eire in a handful of weeks… and it still felt too long. Despite his momentous victory, he itched to move on.

Damek would be crowned today.

That did not mean he felt he deserved the honor.

Not yet.

He might walk through the Citadel to accept the obeisance of twenty thousand Tairngaenah and reams of half-starved, grateful citizens, but the crown would feel weightless upon his head, his achievement hollow. He crumbled the hastily scribbled note in his left hand and tossed it through the open window to the icy street below. In the frame, the Cloister rose like a red phoenix from the ashes of its surrounding structures, impervious and aloof. In her high tower, his ruthless, bloodthirsty great-grandmother ignored her defeat.

Having lost the Citadel, which Damek and his men now occupied, Nema and her remaining zealots had locked themselves inside the Cloister and barricaded every entrance. Since the enormous inner fortress was comprised of one seemingly smooth piece of red granite, it was impervious to cannon fire. While her city smoldered around her, the best Liadan could manage was to hide in plain sight.

His sigh cut bone-deep.

Men and women were tossed daily from a high window to the cobbles beneath the Cloister.

Blood magic, Leal had once said, and Damek had no reason to doubt him. It seemed Liadan could go on indefinitely, so long as she had willing victims to tap for life.

Coming up behind him, Martin matched his sigh. "Staring at it won't help, lad."

"There are innocents in there with her. Dying for her."

"Some have chosen to. Some are beyond our aid. Torturing yourself over it won't change their fate."

"I helped put her there, Martin."

"Well," said he, failing to mask a sharp note of disappointment. "I daresay neither you nor your noble father expected she would change course mid-plan. You cannot account for everything, in any case. These events were in motion long before your birth."

Damek flinched. "I'm sorry I did not tell you, old friend."

"I'm merely a soldier, highness. You owe me nothing."

"That is far from true."

Martin disarmed him with a warm grin. "The river rolls on, lad. We swim, or we drown, no?"

"Yes," answered Damek, though he was not mollified. He let the subject drop. Martin wouldn't appreciate further meaningless apologies.

"What does he say?" asked Martin, jerking a thumb at the window.

"'*Tairngare is yours, make Eire mine.*'"

"To Rosweal, again?"

"Of course," Damek laughed dryly. "The High King's army gathers as we speak."

"How many?"

"Two-thousand, maybe three."

Martin coughed. "That's a rather large number for an insignificant hamlet full of thieves and beggars."

"The Dannans place importance upon it for the same reason Falan does. That is where Kaer Yin Adair will take my cousin on his way to Bri Leith. The Prince of Armagh would fain see his rival reinstated as Crown Prince."

"Yes, and you bear a rather strong grudge there yourself, Highness."

Damek discovered he didn't care for the title as much as he thought. Although he might have won Tairngare's people, soldiers, and fainne, Nema defied him. His success was far from total. Then, there was Rosweal and the coming clash with the Sidhe to think of too. Could he genuinely call himself a king when both outcomes remained undecided?

Sensing Damek's train of thought, Martin clapped a hand over his shoulder. "You aren't claiming the crown for yourself alone, lad. You're doing it for all of us. A king of Eire, even one afflicted with enemies, has more power than a simple warlord. You've won the grandest city in the North and bear the support of most of the Souther lords, merchers, and townships. Your uncle may twist this way and that, but you managed to do what neither he nor his brother ever could. Even the Sidhe would fail to see the merit of your claim, and in the end, 'tis better to bargain from a seat of power."

"Unless we lose, Martin." Damek looked away. "Kaer Yin Adair is a general of no mean skill. We have set two thousand men down the Taran High Road, who might be swamped by the Sidhe any day. Once he arrives, if he hasn't already, it will begin in earnest."

"You'll be there."

"Will I?" Damek doubted aloud. "Nema must be seen to. She cannot linger in that tower unchecked. There is also the matter of my uncle marching toward Malahide with his Kneeler's army and the prisoner I can't bear to lose."

"Castor will cut his deal. What of it? Even together, neither can hope to match the combined might of Tairngare and the majority of the South."

"Even if we lose at Rosweal?"

"Aye, highness," replied Martin. "Even if. Supposing one hand is slapped away from Rosweal, the other bears a force fifty thousand strong. The Northers are behind you, as Nema has done her job well. The High King may have superior forces, but they are not all gathered, and Rosweal is a terrible place to defend a kingdom. Whatever happens in this contest, you will remain the undisputed King of Eire."

Damek heaved a heavy breath and squared his shoulders. A king who suffered no doubts was a fool or madman. Damek was neither. "So be it. Let's get this farce out of the way, shall we?"

Taking the golden fillet that had belonged to his uncle in one hand and clutching his sabre hilt in the other, Damek sighed. Martin dipped a curt bow and kicked the door open. The Grand Arcade, which had previously housed the courts of Parliament before Nema's ascendancy, erupted into cheers. A thousand people, soldiers, and citizens alike, leaped to their feet in roaring approval. Despite himself, Damek smiled.

See uncle? he thought.

This is what it's like to be loved by those you mean to rule.

From Nema's obsidian terrace, he held the fillet above his head; arms stretched taut. The crowd in the Arcade below hushed. "You have suffered," he said, his voice clean and clear. "You have waited." He turned, holding the fillet to the light that filtered through the massive holes in the once beautifully arched ceiling. "You have longed for justice."

He turned to bask a bit under his foster father's misty eyes. He set the crown upon his head. "Your king hears you."

⚜

Later, at the feast, Aoife came to him with the Warhammers that filtered into the West Hall, the sole room of any size in the Citadel that still bore a roof. Damek sat in the center of the room upon a hastily constructed dais in a simple wooden chair. He drank but, so far, had yet to feel any joy. He had yet to earn the crown he wore, and it chafed at him—the itch to leave and prove his worth burned beneath his skin.

Aoife saw it soon as she saw him. Her knowing grin irked him. "Majesty," she mocked a bow and took a seat without waiting for permission. "The warriors of Armagh have come to swear fealty to their Crown Prince."

Leal led them before the dais, decked out in the red and black cuirass and greaves of House Mac Nemed, and wearing the kohl stripe over the eyes, which signified mourning. All two hundred of them bore the same black line. An homage to the slain Princess of Armagh, whose body Leal himself had washed and burned. Leal's mighty left fist struck the metal over his heart: the black bull of Ulster. "Armagh comes to swear allegiance to their mighty Prince and serve him as King of all Eire. Will you accept us, *Ard Tiarne*?"

"I do," said Damek, hand over his heart. "I choose you as my honor guard, Leal MacDenron, you and twenty of your chosen warriors. Do you grant me leave to claim you?"

Leal beamed. "I am honored, Your Grace."

"Excellent." Damek snapped his fingers. Ridley and twenty Corpsmen rushed over with new benches. "Be seated among my officers and hold yourselves high in my regard."

Though leery of their newfound Fir Bolg comrades, the Steel Corps cheered them as they took their place beneath Damek's eye. Aoife snorted from beside him. He spared her a dry glare. "No one invited you here, Aoife."

She snatched a bite from his plate. "Here I am all the same. So, how does it feel to have what you've always wanted?"

He resumed his seat while the feast reached a raucous volume. "Aren't there two mindless servants somewhere you should be fucking?"

Her hair was finally growing in. It gave her sharp cheekbones a pixyish set when she laughed. "What's the matter, dear cousin? Bed grown a bit cold, has it?"

"Is there a reason you've come?"

"I longed to see my handsome cousin take his place among the kings of old, of course." She sat back, popping a dried grape into her mouth. "Most impressive feat, my love. I congratulate you."

"Thank you," he minced. "Now, what do you want?"

She took a deep sip from his wine. Damek waved Hisk away, whose hand had already pulled two inches of steel from his scabbard. Seemingly oblivious to the threat, Aoife smacked her full red lips. "I'm not here for you."

"Good, because you'd be bound to be disappointed. I leave by week's end."

That did wipe a bit of the smirk from her face. "She will be the death of you, you know?"

"I go for Falan, not Una."

She laughed with just her throat, still possessing his wine. "Do I look like a fool?"

"Think what you like." He shrugged, wrenching his wine away. "I want her back, of course, but this isn't my primary focus. Not at the moment."

"If she falls into your hands, you can pretend it was an accident. Do you think you have the stones to rape her, I wonder? I don't imagine your men will support you for long without a string of heirs to solidify your House."

Damek's molars ground together, though he didn't let the urge to throttle her show on his face. "I've no need. Once the Dannan prince is dead, she'll choose me. She chose me before he came for her." He willed his heart still. "But if she does not, no matter. I am king, in my own right."

Aoife, for once, did not cut her eyes at him sideways. She gave him a long look full of something he'd never seen on her face before: *pity*. "She never deserved you, my love, whatever happens."

Damek opened his mouth to retort, but that horridly burned creature limped into his line of vision, escorted by none other than Martin himself. Aoife stiffened at the sight of him. The disfigured fellow shook against Martin's staying arm. "Your Grace," Martin asserted. "This is Fawa Gan. He has something to say to you, privately."

Aoife got to her feet, staring at the shrinking mass of ruined flesh.

"Gan," she whispered, half-menace, half-promise.

"You're here for him?" Damek asked her aside.

She shook her head. "For Nema. Though, I owe him too."

Then, Damek saw it— the trembling was anticipatory, not fearful.

He wants to die. Damek frowned to himself.

So might you, if you'd suffered what he has.

The King of Eire got to his feet. "Follow me."

Some hours later, Damek, Martin, Leal, Douglas, Hisk, and a dozen more of his men and honor guard crept through a tunnel toward a hidden door. Gan and Aoife followed at a sedate pace. One breathed so hard Damek feared they'd pull the Cloister down around their ears. In a small, dank room, the large black door loomed in the light of Martin's torch. Damek nodded to Hisk, who pulled a chisel from his belt and applied himself to the door. With so many of them crowded into that musty chamber, Damek was surprised to catch the faintest glint of white in the deepest corner. He trained his torch toward the object.

A small bundle of bones dressed in the remnants of a Nova's brown rags lay crumpled in a dried puddle of effluence. Damek covered his mouth and nose. The burned man squeaked, then fell to his knees before it. Aoife stood behind him. "Another of your victims, Gan?"

He turned away, nodding.

The child couldn't have been much older than five or six.

The Tairnganese call us *barbarians*, thought Damek.

"Shall I do it here?" she asked softly, squeezing his shoulder.

Gan seemed to gather himself. "I would see her brought low, first."

"As would I," she said, helping him to his feet.

Damek wasn't sure what they meant but heard the lock spring free under Hisk's clever fingers. When the door swung open, a blast of chill, fetid air rushed into their faces, sputtering the torches. He turned to Gan. "After you."

Gan wiped his nose and stepped into the dark.

Gan led them through halls and stairs once bustling with people: servants, students, and craftsmen of all stripes and stations. Now, the halls were frigid, hollow, and empty. Their footprints left shallow impressions upon dusty floors, their tremulous breath the only sound. Gan seemed to stand taller the farther they delved into the interior.

Huge tapestries bearing the Golden Dragon ascending over an ink-black field hung tattered or partially torn in the Grand Arcade. An open roof spilled fresh snow into the courtyard, and ice dangled from Nema's newly constructed balcony. They didn't spy a single soul on their way up the granite stairs.

Damek felt like a fly in a web. "Where is everyone?"

Aoife didn't appear to share his trepidation. "Dead, I expect."

"*Blood magic.*" Leal covered his nose, looking around. "I can smell its foul taint from here."

Aoife nodded. "She'll be waiting for us."

"Wonderful," said Martin, gripping his sabre.

Gan paused at the top of the stair. He reached for Aoife's arm. She didn't pull away. Damek couldn't help but be surprised. She even patted his hand. "I know. I vow you'll live long enough to see."

The relief in his eyes commingled with something else; courage, Damek would swear, though he had little experience of the man. Fawa Gan didn't seem the sort, whatever his truth was. Aoife trailed the fellow up the stairs, her mouth a firm line. Damek had no idea what was between them but suspected a lifetime of shared indenture to a madwoman formed certain bonds.

At the mouth of the Grand Stair, Aoife took the lead, drawing her dagger. The look on her face was almost giddy with anticipation.

"Martin," Damek whispered. "Whatever happens, see she doesn't kill the old woman."

"Why *not?*"

"What do you think is a worse fate for someone like Liadan Mac Nemed? A swift death or long internment?"

"Neither sounds ideal."

"She'll fight us if only to encourage the first outcome."

By the Fifth-Floor landing, the truth of Damek's statement rang clear. There was no railing in the Grand Stair. Nothing but a long, twisting column of vivid roseate stone curled upward, with intervals at each level. Without torches to light their way, the first few screams seemed to come from nowhere.

A body barreled into Aoife first, knocking her into Gan, who yelped. The next caught Martin with a grunt. When a fetid-smelling missile caught him around the legs, Damek barely had time to draw his sabre. Instinctively, he slashed at his attacker, who slumped forward at his feet, dead. He scarcely realized the assailant was a child before three more were upon him, snarling like dogs. One went over the stair face first, taking a while to strike the bottom with a sickening crunch.

Another tried to sink stinking teeth into his throat while its companion struggled to jerk the sabre from his hand. "Martin!" Damek shouted though it would do no good. Bethany's Commander at Arms found himself similarly inundated. Cursing, Damek grabbed the tallest of the group and flung them bodily into the stairwell. He bashed the smaller ones together like bookends, and they crumpled, alive but unconscious. "Stun them if you can. They're insensate."

"Witchcraft," agreed Leal, tossing two down the steps to the next landing. Damek thought he heard one neck break, but the other might live.

Aoife didn't share Damek's optimism. Beneath her breath, she spoke, and the stairway filled with an uncomfortable electric pulse. All the hair on Damek's neck stood on end as a bright violet light whipped through each tiny chest, felling five children in one go. The smell of burnt hair and scorched flesh assailed his nostrils. The remaining children stopped their ravening assault to watch the others tumble into the void. A whimper or two was all they managed before skittering down the stairs while hugging the walls. Whatever she had done, Aoife had stripped Nema's spell from them. Undeterred, she lifted her chin and continued upward.

"Warm one, isn't she?" quipped Douglas.

Martin, who loathed her, said nothing— but Gan replied, "It costs her more than you will ever know, soldier."

"Gan," she said over her shoulder. "That's enough."

He obeyed, resuming his place behind her.

Damek had some idea of what he meant. The cost of such magic would grind a lesser practitioner to nothing. Even Una, whose power was fearsome indeed, had her limits. He could only guess how hard Aoife struggled to conceal the effects.

When they arrived at the Ninth Floor landing, it wasn't feral children they encountered but armed Warhammers. Gan pressed himself into the wall to avoid a crushing blow to his temple that would have killed him on the spot while Aoife rammed her dagger into a Bolgman's neck. As for Damek and Martin, they were too busy defending themselves against the vicious hammer falls and short-sword thrusts to be much help. Leal dispatched one of his countrymen, then was quickly engaged by another.

"*A bhráithre, nach bhfuil aithne agat ormsa?*" he pleaded.

They did not seem to hear him.

Worse, they did not slow.

Damek was sweating two minutes into this skirmish and knew if he didn't take every opportunity he could muster, one of Nema's Bolgmen would cut him in half. "Aoife, if you've got more of that in you, now would be the right moment!"

But Aoife was too busy fighting for hers and Gan's lives to heed him. A Warhammer thrice her size had them both pinioned against the wall. Aoife's teeth flashed as she fended him off. Redoubling his efforts, Damek managed to slay one of his two attackers and then hurl himself her way.

His sabre slammed into the back of the fellow's head, nearly skewering her through the eye. She gave a little gasp but scrabbled from beneath the falling body with a hiss. Already back to business with his third dangerous opponent, Damek only had the air to bellow, "Aoife, now!"

He couldn't tell what motion she made, only caught the barest suggestion that her hands had come up. She huffed something he could not hear.

His opponent dropped his blade, blinking.

Unfortunately, Damek had already thrust forward before Aoife's counter-spell could do its work, and his sabre plunged through the fellow's guts into the wall. With an apologetic glance, Damek withdrew his blade. The Bolgman slipped to the floor, burbling. The rest, blinking at their raised weapons, backed away, mystified. Leal said something to them. Damek couldn't hear over his racing heartbeat. He knelt beside Aoife.

Gan had taken a severe gash to his ribs. He grew paler if that were possible. Aoife's nostrils streamed blood. "Are you all right?"

She ignored Damek's outstretched hand, instead helping Gan to his feet as if he were the most important person in the world to her. The ugly lump leaned against her. "I'll make it."

"Yes, you will."

They brushed past Damek and resumed the path upward.

Damek understood then, seeing their shapes huddled together in the shadows.

They *both* meant to die.

Something sharp gripped Damek's heart. "Aoife?"

She didn't turn, but her voice carried down to him without effort. "Leave it alone, my love."

THE GREAT VANNA NEMA, OR LADY Liadan Mac Nemed, appeared neither great nor a lady as she wheezed at the base of her onyx throne. Instead, some slithering, boneless monster with sagging brown jowls and huge hollow eyes quivered upon the steps in a heap of yellow and saffron fabric. Her miter was smashed to an unrecognizable mess near the windows. The throne room reeked of stale breath, unwashed flesh, heady magic, and rot. There was no one in the chamber save Nema… and a dozen or more corpses, abandoned where they had fallen. The floor was stained with blood, a hard reddish crust that marred the perfection of that glossy midnight floor.

"Aoife." The thing tried to smile.

"Yes, *seanmáthair*. I have come for you. Look, Gan's with me."

Nema gurgled at him as if cooing to an infant. She reached out with one desiccated hand. Gan sank to his knees before her.

"Don't touch her," Aoife warned. "She'll do the same to you just to cheat us."

"Aoife let us—" Damek began.

"Stay out of this," she snapped. "This has nothing to do with you."

"I think you'll find," he said as Martin and Leal approached her, bleeding and deadly serious. "That it does. Come away, Aoife. There's been enough death on her account."

Aoife's skin bleached a pale gold. "What did you say?"

"You heard me. Let Falan choose what to do with her. Leave her, both of you."

Martin got closer than Leal, but his usual loathing did not reach his eyes this time. There was, however, a noticeable dose of sympathy there. Aoife lashed out. Martin backed off, only slightly. "You wouldn't *dare* do this to me, Damek. Not me. Not now."

"Self-sacrifice is not your style, Aoife."

"How would you know, you arrogant, self-absorbed fool? Do you know how long I've waited for this day? Slaved for this day? Bled for this day? Do you have the faintest idea how old I am, how many decades this horrid beast commanded my every waking thought? You see Gan here and shake with pity and contempt. She did the very same to me, Damek. Only my blood has the power to reverse the external wounds. Inside, Gan and I are the same!" She reached out and clasped Gan's hand in her own. "How *dare* you attempt to interfere."

Gan leaned close to Nema's twitching face. Her eyes were wild though her throat could not form the words she sought. "We're ready to go, all three of us together. That sounds nice, doesn't it?"

He made as if to smooth her hair. Aoife drew in a sharp breath too late. Nema's hand closed over Gan's, where it lightly connected with her brow.

"*Fuil san, Fhuil amach*," she croaked.

Aoife shrieked a warning, but Gan shriveled where he knelt. His body hit the stone floor with a sigh, bloodless and shucked of all vitality.

Nema pushed herself upright like a wounded boar.

"Gan!" Aoife wailed, kicking against Martin's shins.

Swelling now with the life she stole, Liadan Mac Nemed's eyes found hers. She opened her cracked lips to speak, but Leal jammed his sword straight down her gullet. With a growl, he drove the point in until the tip struck sparked against stone. "No more spells for you, *cailleach*."

When he withdrew the blade again, Nema was long gone.

Aoife's shrieks rent the stone above. "No, no, NO!"

"Martin, let go of her!" warned Damek.

The speed by which O'Rearden obeyed suggested he'd done so seconds before Damek said anything. Aoife slipped to her knees and then scrambled forward. The air around her crackled with energy. Over Gan's husk, she wept the first real tears Damek had ever seen from her. When she turned to him, her eyes flashed with unholy light. "You *betrayed* me!"

"Damek, get back!" bellowed Martin.

Hisk threw himself before his king, but he needn't have bothered. Leal got there first. He struck Aoife once, hard, in the temple. She slumped forward over Gan's corpse, whose fingers lay scant inches from his former mistress'.

Damek couldn't tell for sure, but the strange little fellow seemed to be smiling.

⚘

546

By the first of Ban Apesa, Damek MacNemed, King of Eire, boasted an army nearly seventy thousand strong. He controlled most of the North, the Midlands, Bretagne, the Reaches of Bethany, and much of Kernow. He was the undisputed master of the wealthiest city in Innisfail. He boasted of a fleet of twelve ships. Those who survived the Bretagn assault now bore his colors above every mast. Come spring, he expected to have twice that number.

Damek had the support of the Merchanta Charter in Tairngare, who were now returning to the battered and bruised city with their families. The citizens who'd fled during Nema's brief but tyrannical regime came home to discover Damek's soldiers already working to repair their roofs, clear their streets of debris, and rebuild houses smashed in the onslaught. His men did not rape, pillage, or otherwise maim his subjects, taking his cue from the Sidhe they would soon meet on the field. Instead, they were rewarded with fine housing in the city or the countryside and funds to set aside for their families and future businesses.

There wasn't a single soul in Tairngare who did not love their new king… save one.

With the bulk of his army preparing to march west, Damek climbed the Grand Stair to the Tenth Floor. Nema's devices had been ripped from the walls. The filth and taint of death had been scrubbed from the floors. People began to return to Cloister for work and duty. Secundas poured through the halls, paving the way for the arriving Primas and a return to their devotions.

The Citadel's renovations were already underway, as Damek claimed the fortress for himself. The Southern Wing had become his royal residence, with its gorgeous floor-to-ceiling windows, high iron doors, gold wainscoting, and gleaming mahogany floors. The Siorai were welcome to maintain their religious pursuits in the Citadel, but he vowed to return the city to secular rule. The renovations he'd ordered would ensure the Citadel would become the hub of law and order while encircling and protecting the pastoral pursuits of the Siorai faith. Tairngare was to be his northern stronghold and his seat of power in greater Innisfail.

It would never again rise a theocratic empire.

The days of absolute religious autonomy were over.

Whether Damek died on the battlefield in a month or a year… the Siorai would fail to reclaim power in Eire. It may have taken a thousand years for Tairngare to build such fabulous wealth, learning, and prestige— but it had taken less than a year to produce a tyrant responsible for the deaths of thousands of innocents.

Damek's first promise to the people was, 'never again.'

He appointed Seamus Wender— the Lord of Kerry's heir apparent and a shrewd commander— First Minister of Eire. Wender's purpose would be to entrench the new, secular, Eirean government and reinstate Parliament under the crown. A return to law and order being his sole task. In Damek's absence, he would manage the city coffers and Parliamentary proceedings as well as the stewardship of the Eirean war machine. Thirty thousand troops would remain at Tairngare to defend the city. Another five thousand marched to Tara with its new Governor and workers.

Five thousand were sent to Damek's holdings at Clare to guard the West against Henry's advance… and five thousand to Killarney with Lord Bellin to defend the Coast and make his uncle nervous. Damek was marching west with his loyal Steel Corps and nearly twenty thousand men in the vanguard. The Sidhe might have three times that number in the north, but he gambled that the High King was unaware of the danger Damek posed.

He would, soon enough.

For now, Damek looked up at the ornate golden doors ahead, wishing this task might fall to someone else. He would rather be anywhere else in the world but here. His guards shoved the doors open for him. The Doma's throne room was empty, but he felt he knew where Aoife had hidden herself. With a narrow eye, he strode past the onyx throne. Before he left today, he'd be sure to leave orders to have this monstrous misapplication of wealth stripped-down, panel by panel and stone by stone. He'd never seen such hubris in his life. Actual gemstones greeted his eyes from each chamber. Soaring walls in every variety of precious metal, chandeliers dripping diamonds and rubies or worse, accosted his sensibilities.

No bloody wonder Drem Moura believed herself divine.

Just look at all this rubbish.

In a room decked with silver and garnets, he found her. In a plain white shift, Aoife hugged her knees to herself on the windowsill, staring down at the forces that gathered in the streets, cheering their new king. She didn't look up. "They're hailing you as the Star King," she said.

He leaned against the doorframe. "For Reason, of course. The Southernmost Star. Lord Wender made a lovely speech about the importance of secularism and Reason in the newly formed Parliament. It charmed some, as it was meant to."

She made a rude sound. "Secularism? Wait till they see what their new High King has planned for them."

"He can plan as he likes. I will fulfill my vow to engage his enemies, but the people here answer to only one king."

Her head finally swiveled his way. "You can't be serious? He'll destroy you."

He pursed his lips and crossed his arms. "The soldiers here will never bow to him, and he doesn't boast a tenth of the men to hold them all. Whether he takes Bri Leith or not, I am King of Eire. If I am killed, Tairngare will be run by Parliament and Ministers, as it should be."

She watched him in silence for a moment. "You expect to be killed?"

"I accept that it's possible."

"Perhaps you *would* make a great king, my love." Then, he felt it, that tiny crackle of malice. "You cannot hold me here forever, you know?"

Such was life, was it not?

One long series of accounts marked 'to be paid.'

According to Aoife, this is one debt he could never clear.

"Forgive me," was all he said.

"Never," she vowed in return.

Allegiances

"Obviously, Mistress Dormer," sneered Fionn Shiel O'More, the High King's Champion, from Barb's favorite chair. "We are in command of this outpost. Consider yourselves fortunate that the High King has seen fit to honor your rabble with his advance guard. I fail to see how a brothel-keeper should hold delegatory powers in a martial matter?" The Marshal of Bri Leith's Wild Hunt and Commander of the Dannan Legion stared down his long, patrician nose at Barb. This man was Midhir's right hand, closer to the Ard Ri than his brothers. Aside from Ben, Fionn O'More was the most decorated soldier in all Innisfail. Such ego demanded utmost respect.

Well, Barb was used to arrogant males attempting to diminish her.

Calmly and with all the pride she could muster, she leaned over her pilfered desk (the Lord Marshal had ruthlessly appropriated her *entire* office). Wordlessly, she poured a handful of black powder onto the outdated and frankly useless map he and his fellows had been examining. It took her nearly two damned months to get this far, and the fury of being in limbo for so long rankled.

This was her bloody joint! Her office, her desk, and *her* Siora-damned chair! She might be glad to have a thousand extra archers on the walls— but that didn't give these big, blond bastards leave to order her about in her own home.

The two guards beside him reached for their sword hilts. Fionn halted them with a gesture.

Barb resisted the urge to leer at them.

One wore his long hair in a complicated series of braids doffed at the ends with silver clubs in the shape of maple leaves. Like most Dannan Sidhe, he had the cornsilk and cream coloring only found in the Ban Sidhe of Nuada's kin. Almost all were taller and broader through the shoulder than your average mortal man: their features were sharper, finer, their eyes brighter, keener.

As for Fionn himself, he wore his hair short, trimmed neatly around his chin. Dangling from his right lobe, six gold chains caught the light from her open shutters. His pale jade green eyes narrowed at her in disapproval. His white cuirass, decorated with a silver stag crowned by three stars, creaked when he steepled his long fingers. His armor must not have seen much action of late—too much wax.

"What is this?" he asked, more tired than annoyed. He had the mien of a man who'd rather be reading at his hearth than marching off to war.

"I think yer lordship knows very well what this is," answered Barb, crossing her arms over her shrinking bosom. Her dress, which once hugged every curve like a stretched canvas, now had to be pinned beneath her arms to keep it in place. She tried not to dwell on it.

Fionn's lip curled. "Gunpowder is illegal in Innisfail, Mistress. I'm sure you're aware?"

Dragging a free chair under her rump, she waved at a glass of amber liquid near his elbow. "So is uishge, now ye mention it, Lord. Does that mean I should stop havin' it hauled up the stairs for ye and yer men?" She gave him her best, gap-toothed grin.

She watched his pretty eyes slide from the glass to his braided comrade, then to Barb with an accompanying frown. "Fair point, Mistress Dormer."

"It's just 'Barb' if ye please?"

"Fine," he relented. "I'm listening."

She pointed. "I have fifteen casks to work with and over sixty barrels of unfiltered lamp oil. I'd like your leave to use them as *I* see fit. Your men have commandeered the oil. I'm telling you, that's a mistake."

He regarded her carefully, his expression dubious. "Jan Fir?"

"*Mo Flaith?*" answered the tallest Sidhe on his right. This one had sea-green eyes, purest emerald at the iris, ringed in a startling storm-blue. He wore his hair long and loose, save for two strands tied back at the temples with a silver pin. His cuirass was as white as the others, but the device was a roaring bear in copper. Barb found him slightly more inviting than his companions. There was something nearly human about the sardonic tilt of his chin.

"Do we have sixty barrels of lamp oil at our disposal?"

"*Stolen* barrels," added Barb.

Jan Fir's lip twitched at the corner. Yes, she decided she liked this one much better than his friends. "We might."

Fionn exhaled through his nose as her grandfather used to when he was vexed. How *old* was the Lord Marshal? She could only guess. Most Sidhe were obscenely long-lived, true, but only the Daoine Sidhe, like the High King and his kin, were genuinely immortal. "If— and I use that term very loosely," his tone was dry as sawdust. "I allow you to take these items, what purpose do you intend for them?"

"The bloody defense o'this town, of course," she hissed. "I'll remind ye that yer even now, sitting in me own Da's chair, in me own establishment, in me own fecking city!" She leaned forward again, so he couldn't miss her point. "I'll thank ye for yer help mannin' these walls we've just built— but don't ye get on makin' yerself free to take whatever ye like! That oil is mine. I'll have that and me feckin' tavern back, *right bleedin' now!*"

The only perturbation her speech seemed to inspire in Fionn O'More, was the barest elevation of a single golden brow. "I beg your pardon, madam, or you'll do *what*, exactly?"

Sure, that took a fair bit of wind out of her lungs, but her temper burned on. "Why go out o'yer way to make enemies of allies? By necessity or otherwise, our end goal is the same, is it not?"

"No," he answered without pause. "I think you'll find we are *not* here to help you, Mistress, any more than your many poachers and brigands have attempted to aid us. You raid our lands, take our sacred creatures, rob the unwary, and break the Ard Ri's laws with every breath we've allowed you to take for the last hundred years. Our presence here is tactical. To halt an assault upon our border and return Innisfail to lawful rule. Perhaps in your short-sighted arrogance, you assume we intend to allow you and your ilk to retain your autonomy? If so, I assure you, you're mistaken."

He stood, taking a pinch of powder between his fingers and dropping it onto his open palm. "What I find most disconcerting about you is the pride you exhibit by barging in here with something many have been sentenced to death for possessing and then demanding I return these ill-gotten gains to you." He shook his head at her. "Yours is a most perplexing species."

Barb swallowed her fear. She was an old woman now, no getting around it. An old whore, thief, and criminal profiteer. She'd neither deny it nor bother to explain herself. Her ilk was nothing to these grand Sidhe lords, never had been, never would be, but she had something they didn't: *knowledge*. "That's all very well, yer lordship, but I ask ye, how many men do'ye imagine gather down the Taran High Road? How many spears would that be against yer handful of capable warriors?"

"My scouts tell me some two thousand. A rabble, largely comprised of foot soldiers."

"'Fraid not. They've some two thousand in this expeditionary force, yes. Twenty thousand are on their way from Tairngare as we speak. Yer not just outnumbered ten-to-one, yer outfoxed too."

At last, he flushed. "Damek Bishop is entrenched at Tairngare. If he leaves the city, he loses his advantage in the Midlands. His zealous uncle will receive the brunt of his next assault, or the man is a fool."

She'd been trying to tell him for *weeks*.

"Not true. He's comin' here, first."

"Madam, the Ard Ri has sent us to guard the border and hold for reinforcements. It is not our duty to march on Tairngare... yet."

"Yer not gonna have to. He'll come here first, as I've said many times."

He shared a long look with his braided lieutenant. "Rosweal serves no tactical purpose. The Ard Ri agrees that there is a need for a strong Sidhe presence here, but aside from this, has given no orders to prepare for the assault."

She raked a hand through her thinning hair. "Look. Ben hisself knew that Lord Bishop would be back. Even now, his men are marchin' this way, and ye still won't listen."

Fionn gave her a tight smile. "You've a fertile imagination, Mistress Dormer."

"Do I?" She reached into her cloak and brought out a wad of crumpled missives, which she tossed onto her desk for him to gape at. "That's the thing about us 'criminal' types, milord. We're well connected and informed. You'll find the latest news there if ye sort through to the bottom. Not only has Damek Bishop begun his march west, but he's also been hailed the King of feckin' Eire! How is it the grand lot o'ye lack the spies to tell ye where yer arses are?"

Furiously, Fionn rifled through the various scraps until he came to the one she'd indicated. He growled down at the crumpled vellum like it had bitten him. Disgusted, he passed the message to Jan Fir. Jan Fir tossed it back onto the desk with a snort. The braided fellow, she hadn't caught his name, asked, "Bretagn ships broke the siege? But why? Aes Sidhe has many bonds of fellowship with Bretagne."

"Ain't it funny how that works?" she asked. "When was the last time any o'yer folk sat down with the Colonials in Council? People tend to change with the times they live in, ye know? Life may be grand yer high towers in Aes Sidhe, but here, where real folk live, die, and scrabble in the muck to survive — *autonomy*, I think he said? — sounds pretty feckin' good to men and women who've never seen their lofty masters from some faraway land they're forbidden to enter."

"Madam," attempted Fionn evenly. "While I will admit the most recent news is surprising and concerning to us, the Ard Ri's orders stand. We are to—"

"Sit here with yer cocks in yer hand with an army headed yer way? Don't ye get it? He can't *be* King of Eire if towns like Rosweal are loyal to Ben. He'll stamp us into the dirt to solidify that claim and outnumbered as ye are, yer just askin' for what's comin'!"

While the trio of Commanders mulled over her words, a slight commotion kicked up in the hall. Barb refused to be distracted from her purpose here. It was probably just another scuffle about rations again. She'd sort that once these fancy fools gave her bloody gunpowder back. "Now, I know yer all smart enough to see that this were no accident. I'll bet the late Duch and Nema had something worked out between 'em. The boy finished it. Either way, yer about to have yer bollocks handed to ye by a King of Eire, and I, for one, would rather die than kneel to him."

Fionn opened his mouth to respond, but the commotion outside escalated to an intrusive level. Suddenly the door blew inward on its hinges, slamming into the plastered wall with a clacking bang. In walked a ragged but no less proud Dannan retinue, with one particularly tall silver-haired male in the lead. The newcomer sported a white yew longbow over one shoulder, a frown that could cut through steel, and nine gold chains chiming from his right ear.

Barb had never been so relieved to see anyone in her bloody life! "Ben!"

Ben Maeden... rather Kaer Yin Adair spared her a wink that nearly melted her heart in her chest. Behind him stood the arrogant redheaded prince of Connaught, eight chains chiming in his left ear. Barb watched him tuck his hair behind that ear, so none could mistake which two men bore the most adornment. That slight motion hammered home the stark reality of the company she had been keeping all these years.

Ben Maeden *was* the Crown Prince of Innisfail.

She swallowed.

As if on cue, the two lieutenants at Fionn's side, with only ten gold chains between them (Jan Fir bearing six), sank to their knees. "*Ard Tiarne*," they breathed in surprise. Fionn, however, did not deign to show homage.

He stilled.

The little Tairnganese noblewoman that had started this whole mess in the first place slipped into the room behind Ben. Barb knew none of the events were her fault but couldn't halt the curl Una's presence added to her upper lip. If the girl noticed, she didn't respond.

"Fionn Shiel O'More," said Ben dryly. "Nice haircut."

Ah, Barb thought.

Ben don't care for this prig neither, I see.

"Kaer Yin Adair," Fionn saluted as he might to a subordinate.

A third tall Dannan behind the redhead growled, his blade halfway drawn. The Prince of Connaught caught his elbow, shaking his head. "What's this, Lord O'More? Since you mean to disrespect the son of your Ard Ri, do you intend to give insult to Connaught as well?"

"If you stand behind this vagabond… this traitor, you have your answer."

This time, three more Dannans stepped forward, weapons already bare. The two on the floor made no further movements. Just then, Barb felt the room was suddenly overcrowded with aggressive Sidhe in a pique.

Her chair made quite a racket as she scooted out of the way.

Ben burst into laughter for quite a while. When he stopped, he swiped a tear from the corner of his eye. "Ah, Fionn. It's good to see that at least some things haven't changed. I won't force the issue if you don't care to genuflect. Shar, Niall, Conor? Put your blades away. We didn't come here for this."

"What *did* you come for?" asked Fionn, noting the speed at which the two Blood Eagles obeyed. Barb saw it too. "I see you've taken command of your cousin's warband? How sad for you, Prince Tam Lin, to blindly relinquish your blood guard to this—" he snarled "— relic of failed ambition."

Tam Lin's smile held all the warmth of a cairn. "Jan Fir Brés?"

Jan Fir stood, looking mightily uncomfortable. "*Mo Flaith?*"

Tam Lin jerked a thumb at Ben. "You're his sister's consort, are you not? That makes you the Crown Prince's bannerman."

Jan Fir bowed. "Yes, my prince." He turned to Fionn with apologetic candor. "My LordO'More, please relinquish your weapons."

Barb let her hand slide over her heart.

That's the King of Scotia? she thought, then remembered her studies. There were only three kings in the Dannan lineage, with the High King at their center. All else were lords or consorts to queens. Ben's sister was the Queen of Scotia in her own right. Therefore, this Jan Fir was a great lord indeed to be wed to the High King's daughter.

"That won't be necessary, Jan." Ben smiled. "We came here to help, not pick a fight."

Barb released the breath she'd been holding. "Where's me man, then?"

"He's in the tap, drinking a gallon of uishge and telling the tale," Ben chuckled. "He said he'd come up when he was sure none of us were about to kill each other."

"Ah well, that remains to be seen."

Ben shrugged. "What else is new?"

"Help?" Fionn repeated. "What possible need have I for *your* help, traitor?"

Una bristled. "I would watch your mouth were I you, My Lord."

"Una, must you?" Tam Lin glared.

She held up her hands, then crossed her arms.

"Yes, Fionn, *help*. You have an army twenty thousand strong marching this way. Damek Bishop means to hammer you into the Eirean border and any Sidhe that might imagine themselves his overlords. My uncle tells me he's been crowned king."

"The Red King is not here."

"Not him," Tam Lin interrupted. "The other one."

Despite his bravado, Fionn paled. "*Fiachra Dubh* is here?"

"Was," corrected Ben. "He will return with reinforcements, gods willing."

"From Connaught?"

Ben nodded. "And Bri Leith."

"Then," sighed Fionn. "I don't see where we should worry overmuch."

"Even traversing the Shadow Path, it will take two weeks to muster their forces and arrive here, at the fastest," argued Tam Lin. "We don't have two weeks. We have half that, if not less. We saw the echoes of Bishop's handiwork in the Oiche Ar Fad. We may need to evacuate the city."

"Oh no!" Barb broke in. "Not a-bloody-gain! I'm ready for that fancy fecker. You best believe that. He won't take nothin' more from us."

"We saw the palisades and towers on the way in," Una broke in. "I believe you might be brilliant, Mistress Dormer."

Barb tried and failed to conceal her blush.

"Anyway, whatever happens, we have one week to get ready and a prayer to stall them for another." Ben paused to allow Fionn a long look at his face. "Fionn Shiel O'More, I am taking command of my father's forces here at Rosweal. I ask you to relinquish your men as the Ard Ri's bannerman and, therefore, mine. Will you do so willingly?"

Fionn's perfectly composed features immediately lost their luster. He sputtered. "Over my corpse, you arrogant—"

"Your objection is noted," Ben cut him off. "Mordu?" He turned to the braided fellow, who leaped to his feet in salute.

"*Ard Tiarne?*"

"Tell the troops to assemble at the docks in a quarter-hour. I would address them directly. I come to them, Kaer Yin Adair, Crown Prince of Innisfail and Lord Marshal of the Wild Hunt."

Mordu grinned from ear to ear. His fist slammed against his heart with such force that Barb felt sure he'd broken a rib. "It is my honor, *Ard Tiarne!*"

"As for you, Fionn, I'd have you at my right hand if you'll take it."

Fionn sputtered, he went for his scabbard, but Jan Fir gripped his arm. "I will NOT! You cannot do this! You've no right!"

"I think you'll find," ice wouldn't melt in Ben's mouth. "I bear the *only* right, by birth and blood. Shar? See, Lord O'More has a good long time in private chambers to clear his head."

Shar saluted. Between Jan Fir and Niall, they managed to lead him from the room without much fuss. Ben sat on Barb's desk and heaved a heavy sigh. "Well then, Barb, love?"

"Yes, Yer Arseness?"

"What were you trying to tell the most stubborn fool in Aes Sidhe before wiser fools arrived?"

⚜

"He's challenged you to single combat, Yin," japed Tam Lin. "As if we'd time for theatrics just now. Bethany's scouts were spotted down the road only this morning."

Kaer Yin, shirtless and covered in mud and filth, set his spade down to glare at his cousin, who was spotlessly clean and impeccably dressed from head to toe. "What else is new?" He went back to digging. Despite the rudimentary ramparts and hastily hacked trenchwork, Kaer Yin was impressed by what Barb had managed in their absence. With all hands bent on last-minute tasks preparing for the oncoming assault, Barb's bloody moats were the most important thing to finish now.

At dawn, Kaer Yin, Mel Carra, Shar, Niall, and any available men not assigned to various labors, had volunteered to see the thing done.

They'd received further news from Tairngare in the night.

Vanna Nema was dead.

The North had bent the knee to Damek Bishop.

The Duch of Bethany's nephew, who was also Falan Mac Nemed's bastard son, had claimed the crown of Eire. That his crazed uncle now sat on Patrick's former throne and marched against cities that had declared for Bishop and that he now must contend with the Sidhe to prove himself worthy of the claim— seemed to make no never mind to the people. After months of Nema's insane rule, the people of Eire were desperate for the stability he might provide. Already, he'd taken pains to reinstate Parliament and set up a secular Court.

This was a wise move that Kaer Yin couldn't help but be surprised by. The fellow hadn't appeared so clever when they'd met, but he supposed a man in love might be forgiven the odd act of hubris. Bishop's standing order that his troops refrain from raping and pillaging was even more interesting. Any man caught disobeying that edict found himself twisting from the end of a rope in short order.

Again, this showed tactical brilliance.

The Lord of Clare came to the people a savior, which meant, even when the Sidhe eventually put him and his audacious rebellion down… they wouldn't be loved for it. The longer Kaer Yin was subjected to the man, the more he was obliged to appreciate his intellect. Bishop might be a rash, headstrong bastard, but a fool he was not. The self-styled King of Eire now marched toward them with nearly twenty thousand men out of a standing force of almost triple that number. Damek would not send the entire force to Rosweal. No, that would be overkill, Kaer Yin reckoned. Instead, he'd split his forces and send half south and west to secure a safe route to Ten Bells. Regardless, Rosweal faced an incoming force boasting ten-to-one odds.

Kaer Yin was immensely proud of the martial skill, endurance, and cunning each of his warriors possessed— the Greenmakers included— but such would not save them.

He knew it.

Bishop surely counted on it.

The only hope they had to halt a force of such size was to delay for as long as it might take for Bov Dearg to march from Connaught. Once the fighting began, even if the new walls and ramparts managed to keep Bishop's army out, Rosweal would last days, a week at best. If they couldn't hold the walls long enough for reinforcements to arrive, they'd have no choice but to concede the border. If Bov did not arrive in time, Kaer Yin's father would have lost his grip on Eire. Something that had not happened in a thousand years.

These events foretold a crisis and no mistake. That tiny, insignificant Rosweal should bear the brunt was a failing on the Sidhe's part that Kaer Yin would be hard-pressed to repair. Thankfully, Barb had an uncanny sixth sense about the ambitions of ruthless men. She'd prepared as well as anyone could have hoped. Now it fell to him to ensure none of her work was wasted.

He sighed, leaning against his spade.

About six feet ahead of him, Niall dug at a furious pace that should have made all present men quake with shame. Beyond his immediate band, Kaer Yin caught a glimpse of a golden head bobbing along the walls. He hadn't seen much of her outside of the occasional midnight visit when no one was meant to notice him creeping to and from her chamber in his old tenement. He'd been busy with the men and fortifications, and she'd been… well, he had no idea. As always, she was a mystery to him. He wondered what it might be like to wake with her hair spilling over his chest in the light of the morning sun, to watch her golden eyes flash from beneath her dark lashes as he pressed himself into her. It would be wonderful not to have to sneak around.

Not that they fooled anyone, of course.

Shar had the dubious honor of guarding his chambers on the second floor every night, keeping his eyes trained tactfully on the ceiling whenever Kaer Yin crept past. Though he knew he was the luckiest man in

Innisfail to have that warm, infuriating, sinuous creature to himself, Kaer Yin starved for the sight of her during his waking hours. At the thought, someone hoisted her up onto the rampart. Dangling there, she ran her hands over the wood, chanting with closed eyes.

When he could tame the absurd rush of his pulse, he asked, "What's she doing up there now?"

Two of Barb's burlies held her steady while she was lowered to the masonry layer by rope. Her aunt Eva leaned over the wall to grab one of her arms. She kept her eyes closed. Kaer Yin guessed she was either lending her niece strength or praying she didn't fall and crack her head open. Maybe a bit of both? He caught that sound of rushing insect wings, which usually hinted that Una used her powers.

He shivered at the sound.

Tam Lin made a rude noise. "Something more or less useless, I suppose."

Kaer Yin speared him with a level glance. "You would prove the expert in that quarter, wouldn't you? Have you lifted a finger to do anything but gossip all day?"

Tam Lin raised his chin. "That's for peasants and people with hope, *Ard Tiarne*. I am neither."

Before Kaer Yin could give him the earful he was itching for, another round of horns went off at the docks. Fionn's *garda*— well, Kaer Yin's *garda*, now reclaimed— announcing newcomers. Without waiting for a second blast, Kaer Yin clambered up the trench to shove his cousin aside and stomp toward the river. When he got to the docks, a wide grin split his face. Without fanfare, a host of riders swept over the river from Aes Sidhe. This one was easily five-hundred strong, most bearing the Ard Ri's device upon their breasts. Some, he marveled, wore the red eagle of the *Eiloar Bas*. Hundreds of cavalrymen, pikemen, and bowmen bearing the leaping silver stag arrayed before them. At their front rode Diarmid, wearing his plain black cuirass, his midnight cloak billowing behind him.

Fiachra Dubh needed no sigil to mark him out.

As he dismounted, his nephews pushed toward him. Kaer Yin's smile flickered when he saw the look on his uncle's face. "Herne. What now?"

Diarmid pulled them both close by the shoulder. "We need to talk."

Devotions

This far north, the air chilled dramatically as night approached. Though Sidhe did not feel the cold as powerfully as a Milesian might, tonight, Kaer Yin couldn't seem to get warm, even squatting before a roaring fireplace. Perhaps he owed his thinned blood to the relatively balmy temperatures of the Oiche Ar Fad or the long hours he'd spent outside helping bolster the city's defenses. Now wearing only a thin tunic over mud-soaked woolen trousers, he realized how weary he was. His limbs were leaden, and his back was sore in several places. He half wished Damek's army would show up already and put him out of his misery. Una took the seat beside him and tucked a tankard of spiced ale into his frozen palm.

If possible, he fell in love with her all over again.

Kneeler's bloody angel, this one.

He thanked her profusely with a glance, his free hand around hers.

They were in the tap at *The Hart*, one of the few solidly built structures left in Rosweal. Some months ago, most homes and buildings had been razed in the last Bethonair attack, including Kaer Yin's Hilltop abode. Whatever remained of that neighborhood housed the bulk of Rosweal's citizens or had been deconstructed to build Barb's impressive triple wall. As for the complex moat she'd imagined, they would open the floodgates tomorrow and see if her mad plan held merit. Kaer Yin thought it might, although even that wouldn't halt such a large force of hardened pikemen and cavalry. Besides, he knew Damek and his men had cannons and trebuchets. If that weren't dire enough, he had a feeling his uncle Diarmid was about to deliver worse news. Or would, whenever the Greenmakers finished fumbling around to make the old bastard comfortable, of course.

Having so many Sidhe strutting up and down their streets, bartering freely in the enfeebled markets, and drinking in their jukes and taverns was one thing… hosting the Lord of Tech Duinn was quite another.

Fiachra Dubh was afforded the finest seat in the house, upstaging Kaer Yin as if he were merely an errand boy. Diarmid was a king. Kaer Yin supposed he needn't begrudge his arsehole of an uncle a better chair.

Everyone seemed to be gathered according to their political importance, which was Barb's doing, no doubt. He and Una sat together at the banquette near the fire, with Tam Lin and Eva opposite. Barb and the others gathered at tables surrounding the bar. Diarmid shifted awkwardly in his seat. If not for the stares the gathered townsfolk gave him, perhaps for Eva's, because the Siorai unnerved him, Kaer Yin was pleased to note. Diarmid ogled the ale in his hand and leaned closer to Kaer Yin. "Is this… palatable?"

"Try it and find out," Kaer Yin said, tapping his tankard against it and draining his pint in one go. With a small cheer, Robin and the others toasted and tipped back their own, even Gerrod, who let out a rather large belch which made him flush red to the roots of his dark hair.

Rian didn't seem to notice, so he needn't have bothered. She was far away, at the opposite end of the tap with Shar Lianor.

"Uh oh," said Una, sipping her cider. "There's another broken heart, I fear."

Kaer Yin winced, trying not to see how Rian smiled at Shar. "Might have to bloody well wall her up at this point." Tam Lin, who was not meant to hear that exchange, followed Kaer Yin's darting eyes. His scowl cut deep lines into his otherwise effeminate face.

"See?" Kaer Yin added to Una, aside.

"Shar is merely being friendly to the girl. He wouldn't pursue such a lowly quarry," Tam Lin sniffed, pretending boredom. Kaer Yin saw the tick in his jaw, regardless.

Una set her mug down to glare over at the Prince of Connaught. "Listen here, you. If I even *dream* you attempt anything with that girl, I'll melt the hair from your head. Do you hear me?"

"Una, love. Be nice." Kaer Yin warned half-heartedly.

Tam Lin pressed a hand to his chest. "I do not starve for partners, thank you."

Una's smile rattled. "Consider yourself duly warned."

"If she chooses to come to me of her own accord, what business would it be of yours, *My Lady*?" Tam Lin grinned back. "The girl is an adult, by all accounts."

Well, fuck.

Kaer Yin leaned back in his seat, crossing his arms. Diarmid seemed too intrigued by his ale to notice this tiny pre-meeting storm. Across from them at another table, Eva sat up a bit straighter, ready to defend her niece at the first provocation. That would be terrible news for Tam Lin. Kaer Yin opened his mouth to interrupt, but Una beat him to the punch.

"I'm adopting her. I will never give you consent, and that, my dear princeling, is that." Una retorted.

"You can't adopt a fully-grown person."

"Males get such ideas," quipped Eva dryly from the rear.

"I'm technically the Duchess of Bethany and the Domina of the Moura Clan. I'm quite a wealthy woman, and I vowed to give that girl every advantage she might have. While you two have been digging, drinking, or playing cards, I've been busy. By the time my signature reaches Ten Bells next week, Rian will be the Countess of Ardgillan— a property of no mean size. Balbriggan and the fishing port at Skerries will make her an heiress of spectacular means. So, from now on, you may call her 'Lady Ardgillan' rather than 'unworthy quarry'… you abominable twat." She took another long sip, then sliced her eyes away from him with a dismissive sniff.

Tam Lin blinked rapidly for several moments. "I didn't mean to give the impression—"

"Too late," she snapped.

Speechless for a moment, Tam Lin spared Kaer Yin a confused shrug, then buggered off to glare at Una and Rian from a far corner. Kaer Yin could see his cousin couldn't decide which woman was more vexing by the look on his face.

"I didn't know you'd been making wills, love," Kaer Yin said, trying and failing to catch her eye.

"It's not a will. The properties and monthly rents are hers as soon as she wants them. I presume my signature will hit the Libellan Bank sometime in the next few days. It's done. Furthermore, I've granted her an additional two-hundred thousand fainne and set aside funds for Gerrod and his sisters. The people of Rosweal have also been granted enough funds to purchase their charter from Tairngare. Provided we win, I've seen to it all."

Kaer Yin was dumbfounded. "You don't think we're going to live through this?"

She rolled a shoulder. "Whether we do or not, we will have left something behind for those who didn't deserve what we brought upon them. That's the very least I could do."

His fingers threaded through hers, overwhelmed by a feeling he couldn't explain or quantify. "Does she know?"

"Not yet. She'd argue, and I can't bear it."

"Una… I love you."

She gave him a sideways smirk. "You'd better."

Diarmid was close enough that Kaer Yin caught his raised brow. "What?"

His uncle shrugged. "Just musing over the charms of youth."

Kaer Yin opened his mouth to retort, but Barb got up on the nearby table to bang a wooden spoon against a pot. "Shut yer gobs now! The fancy folk have things to say!"

A swift hush swept the gathered, and Diarmid took his cue. He set his empty tankard beside Kaer Yin's and stood. The room instantly felt smaller for the command of his presence. Kaer Yin couldn't help a smirk. He hoped to bear one-tenth of his uncle's gravity one day. "I am come to tell you, good people of Rosweal, that Bov Dearg is delayed in the west." His green eyes were soft as a collective gasp and murmur followed. "It seems Lord Bishop sent a contingent of Armagh's Warhammers over the border some weeks before he sacked Tairngare. These Bolg fighters belong to his honor guard, I'm told, special forces. As a result, the bulk of Croghan's forces are engaged in the hills of Sligo, thus will never make it here in time to halt Bishop's advance." Here his attention shifted to Una, who reddened under his scrutiny.

"The Ard Ri has been made aware of the peril here and has sent what soldiers could be mustered in so short a timeframe."

Leaning against the bar, Barb pinched the bridge of her nose. "Ye mean to tell me, the High King sent the pittance what came with ye?"

Diarmid spread his hands in answer.

"*Feckin hells,*" she spat and drained her tankard, wiping her mouth with her sleeve. For the first time, Kaer Yin thought her very small indeed. "Well, that's that then, innit? By the time Ben's da manages to rouse the whole of Aes Sidhe's forces, or the Red Boar can rout Lord Bishop's advance forces… we'll be properly buggered already."

Diarmid spared her a sad smile. "I'm sorry, Mistress. None in Aes Sidhe could know the depth of Patrick Donahugh's conspiracies. A plan this audacious and far-reaching can have no other author. That man was cunning as a badger."

Una shifted beside Kaer Yin. In his heart, he burned with rage for the injustice of her blood. Barb, however, felt no such loyalty. Her nose twisted deep. "Ye there, missy. I believe I told ye once, Rosweal will not bear the brunt for ye, didn't I?"

"Yes," said Una. "You did."

"Here we are anyway, huh?"

"Seems so."

Kaer Yin bristled. "Now, just wait a minute—"

"Shut up," they both hissed at once.

He did.

Una stood, glaring back at Barb. "I am committed to stopping my cousin cold."

"Is that right?"

"Yes."

"How?"

Una squeezed Ben's fingers, which was all the warning she gave him. "I have offered myself and my titles in exchange for Rosweal's neutrality. If Damek accepts, I will reside in Bethany as Duchess once it is liberated from my uncle."

Kaer Yin shot to his feet, blood rising, but Barb held up a hand to halt his comments. She bustled over to press her knuckles against the tabletop between her and Una. They stared at one another in silence for several heartbeats. "Aye," said Barb, finally. "I know ye did."

Una crossed her arms. "It's rude to read others' mail, you know."

"Do I look like I care?"

"I damned well do!" hissed Kaer Yin through his teeth.

They ignored him. Una crossed her arms. "Well, then you know I'm telling the truth. My terms should arrive any day now."

Barb laughed. "Ye've some bollocks on ye girl. I'll give ye that. Who gave ye the right to barter for Rosweal, anyway?"

"What bothers you more, Barb? That I'm the reason you got caught up in this mess or that I'm the solution to the problem?"

"If either were true, I might." Barb sucked her teeth. "Too bad ye don't get to make those decisions, Princess."

Una opened and closed her mouth, looking to the crowd as if they held an answer for Barb's cryptic comment. "What is that supposed to mean? I'm trying to—"

"I bloody know what yer trying to do, but I'm tellin' *ye*, it's not yer place to do it. Yer comin' got lots of Greenmakers killed." Una flushed, but Barb went on. "That means ye owe us. Ye think ye'd be buyin' our freedom by surrenderin' yerself to that kin o'yers, but we're not foolish enough to believe any o'that's why he's makin' his way here. Did ye not hear that he's the son of Armagh's heir yer own self? A man that wants to be king doesn't march on a foreign prince for a bloody woman. He's comin' for Ben, not ye… and don't ye fool yerself none about that."

"I agree with Mistress Dormer," offered Diarmid, though no one asked.

Internally, Kaer Yin seethed. Bloody women and their stubborn, foolhardy, arrogant, devious minds! "Una, I think you and I need to discuss this privately."

Again, she ignored him. "Perhaps you're right, Barb, but I am within my rights to try, nonetheless."

"Nah, yer not. Ben's made some claims that many a loyal ear has heard. Ye mean to marry him or not?"

Now it was Kaer Yin's turn to flush to the roots of his hair. Tam Lin ogled him sidelong.

Una cleared her throat. "Well, I mean, if I had the luxury to—"

"Oh, fer feck's sake, girl! Yes or no will do."

Una wouldn't meet his thunderous expression, which was as well because he might throttle her before the whole of Rosweal. "If I were free to choose for myself, I would never choose another."

Now, with that spear tip to the heart, he couldn't decide if he'd kiss her before throttling her or not.

Barb stood up and returned to the bar where a fresh pint waited. "That settles that, then. Whether I like it or not, if yer the Crown Princess o'Innisfail, yer *not* free to barter yerself for anyone. As our lady, ye'll do no such thing."

"But I've already sent—" but Barb pointed to a thin face sitting at the opposite end of the bar. Colm, whom Dabney's bulk had partially obscured, shrugged back. Una flashed her teeth at him, and he shrank into his tankard, looking guilty. "Bloody Greenmakers."

"Now that's settled, yer majesty, please tell us how buggered we are."

Una resumed her seat with a sulk. It took a moment of staring daggers into the top of her head before she snarled up at him, "He never took my message, obviously," and said no more.

Mollified, Kaer Yin tried not to gloat.

He decided Barb should have her patent of nobility soon.

Diarmid cleared his throat. "Yes, well, you gather the gist, I'm sure. With no further reinforcements and a force of Bishop's size on the way, my advice is to evacuate all civilians from Rosweal, posthaste."

"Appreciated, but denied," disagreed Barb, sipping her pint.

Diarmid started. "Madam, many thousands of men will be here within the week. More to arrive. The only hope we have to retain the Ard Ri's grip on Eire rests with the time we might delay Bishop's army long enough to be reinforced."

"Ah, but we have somethin' better than men, yer majesty."

Diarmid quirked a brow at Kaer Yin. "Bravado is not a boon in warfare, Madam."

Barb held up a finger while Robin handed her a little pouch. She took a tiny pinch of the black powder and tossed it into her emptied tankard, which she then set on the floor a foot away. Every Greenmaker scrambled to get clear. A long, slow smile spread over Kaer Yin's face as Barb struck a match and threw it into the pewter tankard. A loud BOOM sent the mug upward, pinging from the ceiling to the bar, where it ended its trajectory after bouncing off Dabney's broad forehead. The big lug could only blink and mumble, "Ow, Barb!"

Fully grinning now, Una said, "That's bloody brilliant."

Diarmid scratched his chin with interest. "And how much of this do you have?"

Barb's gold tooth winked at him in the firelight. "*Loads.*"

Three hours later, Kaer Yin, Barb, and Diarmid stood on the docks while Robin, Dabney, and four Greenmakers hefted the winch on Barb's floodgate. Stripped to the waist in the cold current, each man gave a grand cheer when the gate slammed upward, diverting the second river of tea-colored water into their meticulously hewn trench. In moments, Rosweal suddenly boasted a fully serviceable moat, eight feet wide and easily as deep. Robin roared in victory and allowed himself to be tugged from the river before his lips turned a dangerous shade of violet. He pulled Barb into a playful waltz at the far end of the dock while Gerrod and Dabney shared a pint of warmed cider.

Diarmid was the only one who seemed unaffected by the general mood. He kept his attention trained on the western gate. Kaer Yin followed his eye to witness Tam Lin and Shar escorting Fionn to the water's edge. Fionn's mood didn't seem to have improved during his brief internment. Kaer Yin met them at the end of the dock. "What's this then?"

Fionn wouldn't look at him.

Diarmid grasped Kaer Yin by the collar without ado, shoving him to a knee. "*Ack,*" Kaer Yin managed to get out before Tam Lin nodded to Fionn.

With all the dignity he could summon, Fionn sank to his knees. His face could carve wood. Diarmid retrieved a small vellum scroll from within the folds of his cloak. "Fionn Sheal O'More."

"*Fiachra Dubh,*" he droned tonelessly.

Diarmid unraveled the scroll.

Kaer Yin's heart thundered to life at the seal he spied at the bottom.

A stag crowned by three stars.

His father's seal.

"'I, Midhir Mac Nuada Adair, Ard Ri of all Innisfail and lord of the Tuatha De Dannan, declare the *geis* of my son and heir Kaer Yin Mac Midhir Adair, satisfied. To wit, all titles, real and honorary alike, are remitted to their former owner once more. Kaer Yin Adair is reinvested as Crown Prince of Innisfail. The combined forces of Bri Leith, Croghan, and Scotia are his to command as Grand Marshal of the Wild Hunt and Commander of Aes Sidhe. All those who bear the blessings of the Oiche Ar Fad owe him fealty as the future Ard Ri. In Crom Dagda's name, and with our love and blessing, we beseech our son to defend the Continent in this time of need','" read Diarmid aloud in the Common Tongue for the human audience gathered around. "It lists Kaer Yin's necessary titles and those who owe him allegiance." He handed the scroll to Fionn, who regarded it as if it were a pot of piss. "Your name is at the top there, O'More. He expects your signature, next to mine and Tam Lin's."

He pointed.

Tam Lin held out a quill while Shar passed him a pot of ink before presenting his back as a makeshift writing desk.

It took several moments of audible molar grinding, but Fionn eventually dipped his nib and signed away his leadership. His loathing and derision couldn't be plainer, but none could or would refute the word of *Fiachra Dubh* nor the signature of the Ard Ri. In moments, Kaer Yin Adair went from vagabond usurper to lord and master once again.

Fionn bowed his head, though curtly. "My prince, I am yours to command."

The Sidhe as one, knelt.

Diarmid jerked Kaer Yin upward and jabbed a thumb stained with ash and blood between his eyes. Mystified by the speed of Diarmid's hands, Kaer Yin hadn't seen his uncle cut open his hand. The next thing he knew, Diarmid drew his dagger across Kaer Yin's palm. He winced as Nemain's pommel was then thrust into that bleeding hand. "*Ard Tiarne*, will you defend the people of Innisfail with your last drop of blood?"

"I will," Kaer Yin coughed.

"Will you honor the Gods of your homeland and revere the memory of your ancestors till the day you are carried to Bri Reis in Tech Duinn."

"I will."

"Speak your oath to the Undying and take your place in the Innisfail Cycle."

Kaer Yin took the dagger from Diarmid's outstretched fingers, then drew two thin lines down either cheek. Warm blood dribbled over his jaw and neck, staining his recently cleaned tunic red. "I am the sword at the fountainhead. I am the stone that cleaves the waters of the world. I am the storm that hides the evening star. I am Kaer Yin Mac Nuada Adair, and I swear blood, bone, and spirit to the house of *Dagda Ri*."

The Sidhe chanted in return, but Kaer Yin could not hear them. Marked by ash and blood, he sheathed his sword. Turning from Diarmid, he looked over the gathered.

Diarmid called out in a voice that shook the treetops, "Let those who would be counted come and swear fealty to their future King!"

Robin, of course, elbowed his way to the front of the line. He took a knee. With a snort, Kaer Yin dabbed a dot of blood in the same place Diarmid had him. "Blood binds, and spirit cleaves. I take thee, Robin Gramble as my captain. Do you accept?"

"Course I do, arseness."

Kaer Yin gave him a sideways smile. "Rise a member of my household guard and a knight in the Ard Ri's service. Robin Gramble, Lord of Navan."

Robin paled to a dull ochre and stumbled to his feet. "What's that?"

Kaer Yin gently pushed him aside for the next man in line but winked at his old friend. "Well, I promised Barb I'd make a lady of her, didn't I? I suppose you'd better make an honest woman of her before she has you murdered and takes the title anyway."

By nightfall, every man, woman, and child in Rosweal had sworn fealty to the Crown Prince… and only the night air seemed to fear the coming dawn.

Whence Comes the Knife

The nightly raids began to take their toll on his men. Superior numbers or no, a large army was a fat snake swallowing roads and villages on its slow course to destruction. Were it not fed; it would starve. Were it to gorge itself; it would implode … and were it to pause too long; it would wither. Their progress was glacial, racing toward Rosweal at a spectacular clip of nearly three miles a day. Moving troops, artillery, beasts, and supplies required more space than a single road could accommodate and more food, drink, women, and blood than the sparsely populated north could provide.

Already this week, Damek had ordered three dozen men hung for desertion or rape and an additional thirty or so branded and scourged for theft and dereliction of duty. Whether to the cold, disease, or mischief, his army dwindled. But this was not all. Every night, the raiders came. Each morning, Damek ordered the corpses of a score or more men burned. His second march through the North cost him a hundred men a day.

Since leaving Tairngare, he'd lost nearly three thousand soldiers. At this rate, they'd lose another fifteen hundred before they made it to Vale, where he intended to set camp for his campaign against Aes Sidhe. Marching at the tail of winter was never a simple prospect. Still, with so many men in such cramped quarters, in such hostile territory— they might have been sending out invitations to every thief, criminal, and rebel for a hundred miles in every direction. Yet, what choice did he have? Falan the Elder had set this *geis* upon Damek in exchange for his crown… besides which Damek knew he'd never truly be king so long as Kaer Yin Adair drew breath.

So, they pressed on.

Thoughtlessly, relentlessly, ruthlessly.

He burned the weak and punished the treasonous, gritting his teeth against the cold, the death, the tedium, and the raids. By the time they neared Navan, Damek was immune to all but his purpose. He saw nothing but the road ahead, swirling with snow, ice, and inevitability. He heard nothing but the thrum of his heartbeat and the steady trudging of many thousands of feet. Nothing would stop him now, not even the Gods, however much he expected they cared.

Even Martin's jaw set in a determined line. His steel-grey eyes had taken a hard cast, unwaveringly resolute. When Damek commanded men to be slain or punished, Martin attacked each task with an emotionless efficiency that might have shocked Damek once. With so much riding on the outcome of this endeavor, even stolid O'Rearden had pinned his every hope upon this march.

The die, as great Caesar had once boasted, was cast.

After another grueling day amidst the frozen waste of trees, sleeting snows, and frigid mud… the raiders came again. No matter how prepared they were by sundown each night, the attacks could never be halted. Desperate men believed they had nothing left to lose and would risk anything for the mountain of supplies Damek's army dragged behind them. Others might imagine themselves as freedom fighters and wish to exact their vengeance upon the new King of Eire. Whichever the case, Damek's men took the brunt of these attacks every night, trailing a gory line of human waste back to the gates of Tairngare.

Damek's officers carried on.

The men greeted nightfall with the same tired, irascible sense of purpose. They were all of them, working toward a single goal— *glory*. Then, the raids grew more vicious. The attacks costlier. Damek no longer faced a rabble of ragged bandits or displaced villagers. They were in Greenmaker territory now, and these men knew their business.

In a single night, Damek had lost four wagons loaded with costly arrows and spears, two sleds full of dried rations and tea, and four dozen horses. Damek's vision doubled over the report, leaning over the desk in his tent by midafternoon's accounting. Opposite, Ridley and Douglas fidgeted. None wanted to be the bearer of bad news, especially when their new king was in the mood he'd been in since the Tairngare. Damek leaned forward on his knuckles, his expression flat. "How long before we're ready to march again?"

Douglas blanched. His damp hair hung in greasy tendrils over a breastplate stained with days-old blood. He, nor any of Damek's officers, had been afforded much time to bathe or rest. "Two days at the earliest, My King. The men are—"

"Unacceptable," snapped Damek. "I want to be back on the road within the hour."

"But My King, there's simply no way we can manage that with our supplies in such disarray! We've men to burn, supplies to replenish or recover, and must somehow account for the horses our cavalry has lost."

"I don't want to hear excuses, Sergeant. By week's end, I want to be twenty miles down the road."

Douglas looked to Ridley as if he could answer for the absurdity of Damek's request, but he merely averted his gaze. "It's not possible, My King. Forgive me, but—"

Damek brought his fist into the tabletop, turning over his tankard, which spilled sweet-smelling ale all over his report. "Do you know how many men we will have lost by the time we make it a score of miles down that road? Nearly *five thousand*, Douglas. Can your small mind grasp what a blow that is for any commander, least of all a newly consecrated king?"

Douglas swallowed. "We marched North with much fewer and succeeded."

"In autumn, yes, when the roads were passable and a night without a fire wouldn't cost a man his legs. When every cutpurse and rogue for a hundred miles didn't know exactly where we were.

"When a thousand men weren't burning up with fever or shitting themselves bloody in their bedrolls. When a horde of practiced bandits and a few hundred extremely lethal Sidhe weren't picking us off from the sidelines. No, Douglas. A winter march with this many men is a far different animal altogether."

Douglas chewed his cheek. Once, before his lord had become a king, he might have had the bollocks to laugh in Damek's face… but not now. If Damek wished to, he could have him hung or burned alongside the rest of the traitors. He cleared his throat. "Forgive my insolence, My King, but perhaps we should split our forces or return to Tairngare until spring?"

Damek inhaled slowly, his mouth cracking into a dangerous smirk. "With twenty miles to go, you'd have me make it easier for the Roswellians to pick our bones dry?"

"My men can close that gap in less than a day, my king. Give me the men, and I'll serve Rosweal to you on a platter."

"And give Kaer Yin and his crony Robin Gramble— a man that has made a career out of forest ambush, I might add— the means to crush my Steel Corps before I even arrive? Absolutely bloody not."

Frustrated, Douglas sent Martin a pleading glare. With a heavy sigh, O'Rearden stepped out of the corner he'd been standing in. The light from Damek's boiling braziers cast heavy shadows over his grizzled features. "A word, My King. In private."

Damek's nostrils flared. He stood his flagon back up and poured himself another. "So you can plead the same case with a fatherly tone? Save yourself the trouble."

Martin coughed. "Fine. I agree that we should pause the march until the thaw. This Reason-damned weather, the raids, and the bloody flux are costing us more men than you account for, my king. Five thousand men are more than the standing army of a reasonably large city."

Damek knew.

Oh, he knew.

Yet…

"I've no choice, Martin."

Martin pulled a face. "My king, I beg to speak about this privately."

"I said I have no choice, Martin!" Damek's voice nearly cracked. He threw a hand at the open tent flap as if it encompassed the whole of his camp. "Either way we march, we lose men. If we hunker down in Navan, the Sidhe will harry us every night before you suggest that. If we retreat, we lose yet more… only to attempt this when the Sidhe have gathered their full strength. That is a battle we likely lose, Martin, twenty-thousand men against thrice that number under the most celebrated commander in Innish history. We must strike them *now* and strike hard, or we'll lose the whole of the Greensward to the Sidhe by Beltane, then Tairngare and Ten Bells by Samhain. Let's not forget, my uncle gathers his Kneelers in the south whilst we're up here wanking off in the trees. The only move I have is forward, Martin. You are wise enough to know this."

Several long minutes passed while Martin processed Damek's point. After a while, he turned to Douglas and Ridley. "Leave us."

They looked to Damek askance.

He waved them away. "You heard your Commander."

Martin poured himself a flagon and took a long draught. When he was finished, Damek was surprised to discover his old mentor was angrier than he'd ever seen him. Without realizing it, Damek took a step back. "Look here, boyo. I warned you not to meddle with the bloody Sidhe, and make no mistake— I give no shites who your bloody father might be. I bleedin' *begged* you not to swear any oaths to those duplicitous whores in Armagh.

"When you stood upon the dais at Tairngare, that was the proudest day of my life. My foster son, my squire, become King of Eire on his own. He was under no obligation to anyone that day, save the people he'd come to free." He took another drink, then sneered, "Now look at you! Had the whole bloody Continent quivering in their boots, replete with a *justifiable* claim upon the greatest cities in Eire, for which you might have negotiated fairly with the High King. Now? You're not a liberator or a king.

"You're a warlord in open defiance of the High King's throne. You're the puppet of a lesser prince and a traitor to boot. You're no hero now, boy. You've made yourself a villain…. *and I helped you do it!*"

Damek flinched as if he'd been struck.

Martin threw his cup onto the carpeted floor. "All this potential, so bright, so shiny and new. Just look at us. You've gone and made us the black hats, Damek. I hope you're pleased with yourself?"

"I— Martin, how can you say this to me? I am no villain. Every action, every decision I've made, has been to give us the opportunity for liberty. To free the South, to give our people autonomy, power, and purpose."

Martin snorted. "No, every action and decision has been orchestrated to get you what you wanted and nothing more. You wanted to be king. I presume if you win this fight for your dear ole Da, you'll be out to cross him next to climb higher still… and I wonder if you even recognize these facts, or if you're so far gone that you're even lying to yourself now."

Damek went quiet. His hands shook. In all his life, no one had ever held power to wound him more than Martin, not even Una.

"Martin, be careful—"

"Or what?" Martin laughed. "You'll string me up with the rapists and deserters? The ashes of thousands follow us down the road to Rosweal, Damek! You lost *five thousand bloody men* in less than a month, and still, you would spend more to chase your obsession to Tech Duinn! Why can't you see it? What happened to that bright, beautiful lad I raised?"

Damek's guards rustled shy of the door, and Martin, unfortunately, watched the possibility of violence cross Damek's eyes. "Oh, fuck you, boy. You might be a king, but there's one order I dare you to make."

Seething, hurt, and confused, Damek shook his head at his guards, and they let the flap fall back over the exit. "Stop calling me 'boy,' damn you. I am your king."

Martin made a rude sound. "Then bloody well act like one. Your men, your good loyal men who love you and saw you crowned with tears in their eyes, are out there dying for your ambition. I hope you make the right decision." He spun on a heel and made to stalk out of the tent, but Damek's voice caught him shy.

"Where are you going?"

Martin half-turned to ask over his shoulder, "Do we press on or no?"

Damek gulped air like a goldfish. What did he expect him to say? He had come this far. They had *all* come this far. Tucking tail now would finish him faster than the Sidhe ever could. Who would follow a half-legitimate king who couldn't even take a little town at the edge of nowhere, defended by a smattering of criminals and browbeaten Sidhe? No one! He couldn't turn back now... he *would not*. "You knew the answer before you asked, Martin. We're committed. We must be."

"Then I'll be with the men, My Lord, where I belong. Inform Douglas of any strategy you might think will cost us least after the next massacre."

He didn't wait for Damek's rebuttal.

The tent flap swung into place behind him.

⚜

THAT NIGHT'S RAID WAS SOMETHING special. They came out of the setting sun; faces painted white and black with ash and soot, silent as the spirit of winter itself. Long white hair streamed behind this set, short swords with white-boned handles dealing death in every direction. Naked to the waist save for whorls of white and black paint over their chest and shoulders, they attacked in a swath, a single, swift wave.

The men weren't prepared for the Sidhe, not *these* Sidhe.

Damek emerged from his tent when the first shouts went up to spy several tall men racing through his forward line, targeting officers, specifically. With deadly accurate archers providing cover from the seemingly barren Greensward, these elite warriors— and it would be pointless to argue otherwise— cut through men and beast like a knife through hot cream. They dashed through their line like the wind, never pausing, never wavering.

An Fiach Fian, Damek recognized them immediately.

The Wild Hunt.

For a few moments, all Damek could do was stare at the speed and precision of these inhuman beasts. No mortal man could move so quickly nor kill with such accuracy that they need not stop to guarantee their blows were true. Knowing that his sword would be useless in such a shock attack, he grabbed his bow and quiver from their place near the entrance of his tent. He'd never been the finest archer, as he preferred the sword, but at least two of his arrows found their mark. Two blond creatures sank to the frozen earth between the ranks thanks to his meager efforts. When he drew back for a third shot, a flash of red dragged his eye to the right. Roaring with fury, Hisk threw himself at a Sidhe nearly twice his size, with flaming red-blond hair and a rudimentary eagle painted on his chest in dark woad. The redhead sidestepped Hisk's clumsy thrust, grasped his face with one massive hand, and snapped his neck like kindling. As he tossed Hisk's body away, he must have heard Damek's growl.

He turned with an unperturbed grin.

The Prince of Connaught, Damek thought, fumbling to draw.

I will kill you, you jolly bastard.

But his arrow went wide, pinging from a tree and harmlessly into the snow. The redhead smiled the wider, waggled his fingers at Damek, then took off after his fellows. By the time Damek had a moment to drop his bow, the Sidhe were gone. In their wake, a blanket of bodies littered the ground surrounding his tent. All the officers in steel armor wore cobalt and scarlet tunics bearing the Southernmost Star.

A painted target might have been more subtle.

Cursing, Damek rolled Hisk over just as Martin and Douglas jogged up with their swords out. Damek noted that neither blade bore a drop of Sidhe blood. The darkening sky overhead reflected from Hisk's glassy brown eyes. A creeping rage kindled in Damek's gut, then tracked upward into his throat. Douglas, who'd been Hisk's mate from swaddling, wept openly. Damek looked up into Martin's deepening scowl. "Thirty men. Officers, all."

"I know."

Martin spat. A thin trickle of blood raced down his chin. "They'll be back."

"I'm sure we can expect them daily between here and Rosweal."

Martin's expression bordered outright mutiny. "Your orders, *My King*?"

Damek stood. He clapped Douglas on the back and sighed. "We must move faster. That is our only option now. The longer we delay, the more it will cost us."

A single angry nod was all Martin could give him. "If that is your decision."

"It is," hissed Damek. "Order an inventory of all nonessential supplies and personnel. These can be redirected to Navan, which will be simpler to garrison than this icy hellscape. I want them stripping timber for walls by midday tomorrow."

"Very good, my king," his tone implied this was a forced concession. "And the rest?"

Damek's head swiveled to glare westward along the road. "We ride for Vale, posthaste. I want a speeding train of steel and horseflesh barreling into town at dawn."

Here was Martin's turn to sigh. "We'll kill our horses in the process."

"Would you rather we lose another thirty officers in the night? Thirty more the following, and the next? We're a juicy pie waiting for the knife out here. I'd rather cram this steel engine down their gullets, thank you."

"Point taken, My King. Some wagons have been damaged beyond repair, and loading the others will slow us down."

"Leave them."

Martin scoffed, "These are essential supplies."

"They'll likely burn or be stolen while we dawdle here with our cocks in our hands. The moment The Wild Hunt entered the fray, this became a matter of speed. We're too slow, and that is to their advantage."

Douglas wiped his face with the back of a gloved hand. "I'm tired of waiting for them to pick us off. My sword is thirsty."

"Go, prepare the Corps. We leave within the hour. Ranks tight, steel ready, and eyes sharp… do you hear?"

Douglas slammed a fist against his breastplate. "As you command, my king."

When he took his leave, Martin sent Damek a wordless warning. Damek exhaled and shook his head. "I can count, Martin. I know what you would say, and I hear you… but to retreat now would finish us faster than defeat."

Martin went silent for a time, staring down at Hisk's mangled body. "You're going to lose, Damek. Whether you win or not makes no difference."

Damek tried not to flinch. "I know."

"I hope it was worth it." He stalked off for the second time that day without waiting to hear his king's reply.

Henry supposed he had his nephew to thank for the ease of Malahide's capitulation. His scouts had barely made it a quarter-mile past the gates when their new mayor and several of the city's Merchers rode out to welcome him. Not a single drop of blood was shed, more's the pity, and the entire town seemed eager and happy to fête and feast him. Indeed, he'd spent two pleasant days in the mayor's house, enjoying his ale and fucking his boniest servants.

On the third day, and thoroughly bored with the events of the previous two, Henry decided to line the townsfolk up to determine their level of heresy. He couldn't, after all, be a genuinely Christian king if he suffered idolaters the run of his kingdom, could he?

At first, the mayor and his councilors balked at his 'regressionist' policy. In response, Henry had each man nailed to a cross just outside the city walls, lining either side of the old Innish road to Tairngare. Their Bretagn silk robes flapped in the frigid, early spring breeze, ill protection against the elements. Most died in a matter of hours, frozen stiff. One or two lingered a bit, their moans useless, ignored. Afterward, the next mayor had fewer qualms about converting to the true religion. Similarly, the townsfolk suddenly discovered a newfound zeal for Henry and his faith.

Pleased with himself, Henry watched the townsfolk gather to toss their Siorai trinkets onto the bonfire his men had erected from the guts of the previous mayor's home. One by one, the people ushered past, dumping books, pendants, artwork, or other sacrilegious materials into the roaring flames. If any felt the situation amiss, none dared to voice those concerns. Instead, they filed past, glassy eyes reflecting only the fire and the armed men standing by.

Henry had received word that the other half of his forces had already visited similar judgments on the towns of Killing and Morn, round Kerry, Mayhew's territory. Served the fool right for backing Henry's mutant nephew over God's chosen in Innisfail. Still, the people must be shown. They must learn that Innisfail was God's territory, and no man-hating she-cults or star-worshippers would be tolerated.

When the flames died down and the people retreated to their homes, Henry, delighted with himself, winked at his Lord Tendrick. "Ten Bells next, d'you think?"

Tendrick shared Henry's faith, though he was the more cautious man by far. "Should we not consider smaller fare first? Perhaps Tara, or—"

"Why waste resources? Ten Bells is the prize we need to upend my nephew's claim to the North. Without the banks, he's buggered, and he knows that."

Tendrick appeared uncertain. "My Lord, while I agree that we should make ingresses into Ten Bells, perhaps we might take a lesson from your grandfather and avoid stalling commerce in the city?"

Henry exhaled through his nostrils. "I aim to stop all currency exchanges, Tendrick, until ours is the only standard on the field."

The young lord bit his lip lest he say more.

Henry liked that about him. He knew his place.

Clapping the fellow on the shoulder, Henry strolled back indoors, gnawing on a tea cake. His mood lightened by the hour. "Let's be ready to leave by mid-morning tomorrow. I think it's time for a real test, don't you agree?"

In Love or Vanity

"Invitation accepted," sang Tam Lin jovially as he stalked into Kaer Yin's war room. Barb, whose office it had once been, was not around to frown at its misuse. When Tam Lin made his entrance, Kaer Yin himself had been in conversation with Colm and couldn't help but smile at his cousin's bravado. "You're sure?"

Tam Lin blew air over his lower lip while he helped himself to a dollop of Kaer Yin's uishge. Nearly the first thing Kaer Yin did when he assumed his title and honors once more was to claim a hefty share of the uishge in Barb's cellars. She couldn't say 'no' to the future king… though she did try. "We watched from a distance. He split his forces as you said he would, cutting his supplies into thirds and dividing the bulk of his cavalry from his infantry. The latter was on its way to Navan when we left, and our friend is even now riding hells for leather to Vale with his Corpsmen."

Kaer Yin clapped his hands together. "Bloody well done, Lin!"

Tam Lin shrugged and took a seat on Kaer Yin's desk. He was filthy and covered in blood, running with ash and woad. He smelled fantastic too. On his opposite side, Mordu covered his nose. Tam Lin ignored him. "I thought this fellow was meant to be a military genius or some such?"

"He managed to sack Tairngare in a handful of weeks. At the very least, he's not stupid."

Robin looked up from the map he'd been studying. "I'd say he knew very well that he might be forced to split his forces. Don't mean he wanted to, just that he knew it might happen. Why else would he bring such a large number o'lads with him? Marchin' in winter would mean an obvious loss to a goat."

"He's in a hurry," agreed Kaer Yin. "I gather Falan didn't grant his support without a price. Thank the gods, because he has twenty-thousand men headed here, let's not forget."

"Fourteen now," interjected Robin. "Or at least by week's end."

"Which means we're still outnumbered five to one."

"I'm likin' the odds better every day, meself."

"Me too, but that won't stop them from razing this town." Kaer Yin shoved Tam Lin's leg from his desk so he could have a look at Barb's map. He traced the distance between Navan and Rosweal first. "He wants us to attack Navan for the supplies he's setting out as bait."

"Which we need," remarked Robin.

"Which he *knows* we need. Meanwhile, he'll dig into Vale like a mole while we split our defenses to attack his leavings. No. We stick to the plan," argued Kaer Yin, moving his finger to Vale. "If this drags on, Navan will be there, waiting."

"Aye, all defenses up and waitin' for us. We won't get a better shot at 'em."

"No plan is perfect until it succeeds."

"Ben, I love ye, but ye know that's puttin' us in the middle of two large armies. We'll be bloody surrounded, and no one and nothin' will be able to get supplies in or out if it comes to a long siege."

"If he lacks officers to carry out his orders and manage the rabble, he won't last more than a week. I assume he knows *that* too," said Tam Lin dryly. "Tonight, we took at least twenty. If we take the same tomorrow, he'll be forced to throw everything he has at us before hunger, desertion, and disease do the rest. His men are already suffering the flux, piles, and trench foot. Hells, half the men marching on Navan are similarly plagued."

Kaer Yin scratched his eyebrow while staring down at his map like it would answer a riddle. "We share that opinion, Lin. We have one shot at this."

"Do we want him to throw all he's got at us?" asked Robin. "Not for nothin' he's draggin' bloody cannons behind them warhorses. My girl did a grand job shorin' us up, but them walls won't stand cannon shot."

"They will," said Una from the doorway. Rian, as usual, took up space behind her. Her amber eyes slid to Kaer Yin's. "At least for a while."

"So that's what you were doing up there?"

She nodded. "They can never be solid as the Cloister, but they'll stand up like stone. Buys us time, anyway."

"That's brilliant, love."

Una flushed. "Well, Rian and I came to say the bathhouse is ready and set up for patients if anyone needs stitching."

Tam Lin raised his brows. "None of my men were injured, ladies, but I appreciate it."

Rian folded her hands in front of her. "I assume that will change soon enough." She didn't wait for his following comment. She pivoted and bowed to Kaer Yin, which sent his hackles up. She only deferred to him when she was about to bust his bollocks in front of everyone. His chin sagged in a scowl. "My Prince, I intend to make that my ward for the duration. Do I have your blessing?"

He blinked back at her like a cow.

Una chewed her lower lip.

No help there.

"Ah, I intended you'd take up residence in the tunnels below the north wall with the others."

Rian straightened. Her lovely face seemed a bit drawn at the edges. "I'm the only physician we have, Ben. People are going to need me."

Kaer Yin waited for Una to say something, but she crossed her arms in unhappy solidarity.

They've already hashed this out, and Una lost.

Fuck.

Robin, too, looked away. The blasted girl had come here to ambush him in full view of his council.

Fine. "No."

Rian took a deep breath. Her eyes were cold. "Respectfully, Your Highness, you can't deny me the right to save lives… lives that will surely be lost for my absence."

"Actually, I can. Una Moura Donahugh is my prospective bride."

Una tensed, realizing too late the card he was about to play.

Don't blame me.

You should have handled this, he told her with his eyes.

"What does that have to do with me running a clinic?" demanded Rian.

The glow of murder settled around Una like a halo, but Kaer Yin ignored her.

"You're Una's heir." He rummaged through a bundle of vellum until he came to the one with the bright blue seal, the official seal of the Libellan Bank. "Lady Rian Guinness of Ardgillan, to be precise. You're, therefore, a member of my extended family."

Rian's head rolled toward Una as if tugged by strings. "*What?*"

Una was the most petite woman he'd ever met, but her ire seemed to gain her ten feet in stature. "You bastard."

Kaer Yin made a face. "Don't make me the villain, love."

"*What?*" Rian repeated, louder.

"Would everyone excuse us for a bit, please?"

"Not on your life," said Tam Lin, slapping his knee. Robin and the rest of Kaer Yin's council quietly exited, shutting the door behind them.

Rian's face blazed red. "When were you planning to tell me?"

Feeling cornered, Una raised her chin. "This is the first I'm hearing their answer. I didn't take you for the sort to read through one's mail."

"Jan Fir is in charge of all communication coming in and out of Rosweal. It got tossed onto this mess," Kaer Yin gestured to the mountain of papers wadded at one side of his desk. "Obviously, you should assume Barb read it first."

Una rolled her eyes and sniffed. "Crooks, the lot of you."

"I don't give a shite about any of that," cried Rian. "What gives you the right to decide my future for me, Una?"

The look on Una's face spelled danger for Kaer Yin later. So be it. He'd been itching to hash this out with her, himself. He might as well take care of both issues in one go. "You should answer, love," he prodded gently.

"Because I can, and bloody well should." Una stood her ground. "Whether I want to or not, I technically own half of Eire, Rian. I owe you my life. Kaer Yin owes you his life. At least a hundred people in Rosweal owe you their lives. What I have done is guarantee you'll live well; however this plays out. I love you and want you to be happy."

Though her face could set a brushfire, Rian burst into tears. Both males in attendance flinched away, unsure where to stand. Una wrapped her arms around Rian, who attempted to swat her off. "Why are you writing wills, Una? I don't want anything if you're not here."

"Hush," Una said into her hair. "This is not a will. From this point, the title and income are yours whenever you want them. I cannot go on without assuring you're cared for. All right?"

"I don't want it."

"It's done, Rian. You can pick it up or lay it down, as you please."

Rian backed up, wiping her eyes.

Kaer Yin took the opportunity to press his case. "Now, as a seventeen-year-old girl of my household, I can't in good conscience allow you to—"

"You shut your stupid mouth, Ben," sniffled Rian. "First of all, I'm eighteen as of last Friday and legally an adult."

"Wait, what? Why didn't you tell me?" gasped Una.

Rian tugged a shoulder at her. "It wasn't important with all this happening."

Kaer Yin exhaled. "Doesn't matter. I still have—"

"No, you don't. I'm an adult, apparently of means, and have skills the people in this town desperately need. You may order me not to, but you won't win the love of the people that way."

Now it was Kaer Yin's turn to sweat. Una quirked a lip at his discomfiture. "Rian, it's too dangerous. When the Southers breach the walls, they'll look for anyone they can find to sate themselves upon— women first. I can't allow you to do this."

She clasped her shaking hands together. "We all know what happens during a siege. I'm just as scared as everyone else. *I* don't have a choice. Don't you understand?"

"You do not know what happens during a siege, girl." This was from Tam Lin, who hadn't been invited to remain. Kaer Yin shot him a dark look. "If caught, the old men and young boys will be slain on sight. The women, whether whores, old women, or young girls… might escape with a rape or two. But you—" here, he let his eyes roam every inch of her to make her squirm. "A sweetmeat like yourself will be passed around for a long while. The Southers aren't like the Sidhe. Many sign up for the promise of a treat like you."

"Bishop ordered his men not to rape in Tairngare."

"If you think that'll work here in this backwater no one gives a shite about, you're mistaken."

Rian swallowed though she put a brave face on it. "Then give us guards."

"Can't spare the men," Kaer Yin said.

"So what? You'll leave the bloodied and cleaved to their own devices?"

"Rian," sighed Kaer Yin. "There won't be time to evacuate you when the horns blow. You know that. You might save one or two, but surely you realize those that can't walk will be left behind? We are not omnipotent, and we're vastly outnumbered."

"I know that!" she snapped. "I'm not asking, gods, damn you! 'One or two lives' are no meager thing to me. Nor should they be to the prince they're dying for!"

Kaer Yin leaned over his desk to snarl, "I said *no*. That is final."

"You can't do that!"

"For Siora's sake, you two," attempted Una.

"What are you going to do about it? Tie me to a uishge barrel in the tunnels?"

"Keep giving me ideas."

"I am not a child, nor are you my brother, husband, or bloody father!"

"I'm the Crown Prince of Innisfail, and my word is law."

"Ha! We'll just see what Barb says about that."

In a moment, he would leap over his desk and choke her to death; he was pretty sure. As he opened his mouth to issue the threat, Tam Lin raised his hand with a self-satisfied smirk. "I will give you the guards."

Kaer Yin growled, "Stay out of this."

Tam Lin pursed his lips. "The girl isn't wrong, Yin. She's proven herself before, hasn't she? Who else could manage the task better?"

Una's eyes lowered to slits.

Undeterred, Tam Lin's teeth were very white. "What say you, Mistress Guinness… or should I say, Lady Ardgillan?"

"I need your men on the walls, Tam Lin," warned Kaer Yin. "I don't know what you're playing at, but—"

"What do you want in exchange for your help?" Rian interrupted, her mouth drawn in a dubious line.

"Nothing," he answered. "You are right to ask for them, and I can offer them. Yin may be my liege lord, but my father is a king in his own right. I don't owe my position to the Ard Ri. The men are yours because I will it so."

The tilt of his cousin's jaw began to give Kaer Yin indigestion. "Tam Lin…"

"You know," his cousin cleared his throat. "I can ensure that you never have to ask this ingrate's permission for anything, should that be your wish?"

"*Tú mac soith*," hissed Kaer Yin.

Una's fingers closed over her belt knife. Kaer Yin caught her arm before she could launch herself at his cousin.

Rian asked, "How do you mean?"

Tam Lin affected nonchalance. "You could become a member of my household, instead."

Una ground her heel over Kaer Yin's big toe. The next thing he knew, Una's right fist glanced almost comically from Tam Lin's bemused face. It took Rian and Kaer Yin pulling at full strength to pry her from him. Inverted and huffing, she pointed a finger at him. "Next time, you won't be laughing."

Tam Lin patted his swelling cheek. "You would threaten to murder one of the peers of the realm? Rude."

"I *warned* you. How dare you insult her like this."

"Insult her? I'm offering my hand, woman, not a life of shame."

Everyone stopped at once. A single whistle could have dropped Kaer Yin on the spot. "What?"

Una, too, said, "What?"

Abashed, Rian said nothing.

Tam Lin went on, "My father won't love her heritage, but my mother was hardly a princess when he claimed her either, so he won't have much room to gainsay me. *You* made her a wealthy countess, which makes this appropriate." He rubbed his chin. "We will have to do something about her apparel, though."

Kaer Yin paled. "*Nach bhfuil sé seo greannmhar.*"

Tam Lin's smile widened. "*An bhfuil mé ag gáire?*"

Rian rubbed her face with both hands, then stared down at her own feet like they might explain this to her. "Since when?"

"I believe my interest has been marked, girl."

"Don't call me 'girl.' I mean, since when did you decide this?"

"My father's been pestering me to choose a bride for eons. Why shouldn't it be a girl I respect, my cousin the Crown Prince, and my own men respect?"

She pondered that in silence for a moment. Kaer Yin thought that might have been the first compliment Tam Lin had given her. "Without any conversation with me, any idea what I might want, any clue if I would even consider such an offer?"

"We've had several conversations. I am second in line to the throne. Any woman would consider such an offer seriously unless she were mad."

Rian closed her eyes and mumbled beneath her breath as if she were praying. "Ben?"

"Yes?" his voice came out a squeak.

"Will you give me the men now?"

Una glared up at him with a genuine threat burning from her irises.

He cursed under his breath. "Those I can spare."

Tam Lin's brow creased, but Rian gave him no further chance to wax moronic. She gave him a serviceable curtsy. "I decline, your highness."

Before he could say anything else, she stalked out of Barb's office with her back straight as an arrow. Una was not far behind.

Kaer Yin held out the remnants of his flask.

Tam Lin took it with a curled upper lip. "Traitor."

"What in the hells did you mean by that? You've spent months complaining of her in every possible way, decrying any interest in her above the illicit and generally being a prat."

"Seemed like a good idea a moment ago."

Flabbergasted, Kaer Yin could only stare at him.

"Shar asked me for her hand."

"Is that what prompted this? Competition?"

Tam Lin was quiet for a time. He drained the dregs and tossed the flask onto Kaer Yin's desk. "Who knows?"

He was gone before Kaer Yin could gather an appropriate response.

⚹ ⚹

LATER, AFTER RIAN HAD GONE to sleep, Una snuck out of their quarters and into Kaer Yin's. Shar was nowhere near the door, which was unusual. It wasn't like the men to leave their *Ard Tiarne* unguarded. But she found Kaer Yin huddled over his maps and sipping uishge from a tankard beside a dying fire. He scarcely looked up when her arms came around him. "Can't sleep, love?"

He grunted into her hair. "I managed an hour, maybe."

She pulled away to rifle through his maps. The fire cast her hair in molten gold—"Same. Rian finally drifted off. It took some doing, I can tell you."

He chuckled. "There's no way she hasn't gleaned that Barb's been dosing her."

"I think they've agreed to a détente on that score. One can pretend they're doing a good deed, and the other can accept a good night's sleep without guile."

"You bloody women."

Her lip quirked at him. "Still, she did have much on her mind tonight."

"Yes," he said, shifting uncomfortably in his seat. "Una, what's worse is I think he means it."

"I don't care if he does."

He pulled her into his lap and toyed with her fingertips. "That is not for us to say. She's rejected him as he deserved, but her choices are hers from here on. He wasn't overstating his worth. She might change her mind."

"He's a womanizer at the very best."

"To be fair, I haven't seen him with any women since we've been back. I think he means this, and no one is more shocked than me, save maybe Tam Lin."

She chewed at her cheek. "She said 'no.' That's that."

"Maybe." He clasped her hand to his chest so she couldn't miss the sincerity in his eyes. "I don't think it's fully one-sided."

Una snorted. "Bollocks. She's rejected every advance he's ever made. Has rebuked him in front of everyone, slapped his arrogant face, and— oh." Her brow crinkled. "*Oh no.*"

"Right. I don't think she's aware of it either."

She stared off into the distance. "What a mess! Did you know even poor Gerry has been asking Barb for a better position in order to earn enough to marry?"

"Yes," he said. "And Shar Lianor himself asked Tam Lin for her hand only yesterday. The girl is a headache."

"She's beautiful, brave, intelligent, and kind, Kaer Yin. Of course, this would happen."

"Annoying, pinched of face, rude, lanky, and bossy."

"Well then. I must seem a beast by comparison?"

"Oh, the very worst. I don't know how I can bear to look at you sometimes."

She gave him a long kiss that turned his brains to jam. When she finally laid her head against his shoulder, he said, "I suppose Tam Lin and I might have similar tastes."

"Rian's not ready to marry anyone. I don't know that she's even aware of men for their own sake. She was quite sheltered, as you recall. What if she prefers women, like my aunt Eva?"

"She doesn't."

"You don't know that."

"Yes, I do. I've seen how Rian looks at Shar, and so have you."

Una paused for a moment. "Well, I guess so."

"… and Tam Lin."

She wrinkled her nose.

"Nothing to be done about it. We'll just have to wait and see."

"Tam Lin will be bored of this by tomorrow."

"I doubt it. I've never seen Tam Lin behave this way. He's got the time, as he sees it."

"And Shar?"

"Even then."

Una sat up to stare down at him incredulously. "You can't be serious? He's his liege lord."

"Shar could ask to enter my household, and I would be obliged to accept. Tam Lin will never approve of the match, but if Rian wants it, he can't stop his lieutenant from taking his bride to a new court. Even so, Tam Lin may issue a challenge for her. It will get bloody complicated if Tam Lin wants it to be."

"I'll talk some sense into him."

"You?" Kaer Yin coughed. "You just punched the Prince of Connaught in the face, love. You're the last person I expect he means to be scolded by."

"Fine. I'll talk some sense into her."

"How's that worked out for you so far?"

The sour look on her face was his answer.

"Thankfully, Rian is a smart girl with more stones than my best fighters. I doubt she'll choose any of them. At least, not for a long while."

"If Siora is kind," prayed Una. "But I worry."

"Why's that?"

"Young men don't hold a monopoly on callous behavior."

"You think she'll do something stupid?"

Una shrugged and settled against him. "She is wise beyond her years. More than I ever was. I hope you're right."

⚜

The following morning when Una reentered their apartment, Rian was gone. Her bedside had been neatly made, and her homespun hung from the mantle to dry. The remnants of her breakfast were perched on the larder, covered with a handkerchief. Rian must have gotten up long before the sun broke, as its light only dusted the horizon a dull pink when Una entered their chamber. Una bathed and dressed without much concern to seek her out in the bathhouse. When she arrived, the girl was again nowhere in sight. Cots and carts they'd cobbled together and scrubbed for use lined each dry wall in tidy rows of eight. Many more were stacked in the hall outside. The floors and walls were spotlessly clean, and the baths themselves had been covered with wooden planks to keep them free of effluence. Una spied Violet and Zania coming to prep the workstations they'd been assigned to, yawning and carting piping hot cups of tea— but still, no Rian. Perplexed, Una tugged on the rabbit fur cloak Mel Carra had brought for her and went in search of her friend.

After nearly an hour of strolling the length and breadth of the Quarter, she returned to *The Hart* nonplussed. Barb hadn't seen her, Colm, Dabney, or Kaer Yin's lieutenants Mordu and Jan Fir. It wasn't until she returned to the tenements to wake Kaer Yin did she spy the girl in the causeway, wound tightly in Shar Lianor's arms. Eyes wide, Una stopped dead in her tracks. Visibly embarrassed, Rian broke from their embrace, her cheeks livid. A lovely smile stretched her bruised lips wide. "Ah, good morning, Una."

"My Lady." Shar bowed, not removing his fingers from Rian's, Una noted.

"Oh no," Una muttered.

Fidgeting, Rian held out her left hand. "Ah, well, we wanted to wait to tell everyone, but," she wiggled her ring finger, which bore a silver band it never had before. "I'm glad you were the first."

Una needed a stiff drink… maybe five.

She stared at a scrap of metal like it were a snake that might bite her friend at any moment. Rian didn't seem to notice her discomfiture. Her face was rosy with youth and infatuation. Shar, however, was not so naïve. He gave Una a sheepish smile. "I apologize, *Ard Bhean*. We meant no offense."

"Whether you meant it or not, you have to know you're giving some," said Una. Rian bit her lip and shifted her eyes away. "You have a liege lord, which complicates things for the Crown Prince. Rian? I need to speak with you *now*."

But Shar dropped to a knee before her. "I am at liberty to choose whom I serve as a free member of my tribe. My father is *Tuaithe* of his rath, and my mother was descended from Bov Dearg's line. It is my right to choose a bride and offer my services to you, *Ard Bhean*, should you deem me worthy."

Ah, thought Una.

He's clever, this one.

Damn.

He pressed a hand against his heart. "I will serve you faithfully unto death if you allow me."

Kaer Yin, always with impeccable timing, rounded the opposite end of the causeway just then. His silver eyes were wide as saucers. "Oh, Fuck," was all he said.

Unsure what to say or do, Una tried to look anywhere but at Lianor. Rian caught her eye instead. Her expression was earnest, frightened, and the least of which, a bit desperate. "Please, Una."

What could she say?

Rian is no fool, however innocent she may be.

If this is her choice, you owe her your support.

"Is this what you want?" she asked Shar, though her eyes never left Rian's face. "Once you make this decision, I think it'll be fairly final."

"Shar…" Kaer Yin said softly. "If you do this, he'll never forgive you. Enter my service, and I'll let you two marry when an appropriate amount of time has passed."

"Una, *please,*" begged Rian.

"I am sure, *Ard Bhean,*" said Shar. "I would not be the stone that parts the waters."

"You'd ask it of me, instead." Una tapped her foot.

He dipped his head. "Forgive me, but you are an outsider, not a party to our politics. This is the most elegant solution we could devise."

Una supposed it *was* elegant, even if it put her at odds with the Prince of Connaught. She let out a long breath, appropriately hoodwinked. She splayed both hands at Kaer Yin, who shook his head vehemently. "Rian, I would advise you not to ask this of me. Let us get through this siege first, if we even make it. Don't put me in this position."

"This is my choice," said Rian, and only when her cheeks flamed a brilliant scarlet did Una realize Tam Lin, Robin, and Barb were behind her. Una heard Tam Lin's gasp. Rian squared her shoulders, regardless. "We are already handfasted and only require your blessing, Una. Will you give it?"

"Are you giving me a choice?"

Rian fidgeted. "I'm sorry."

Fully aware of the anger boiling over her shoulder, Una accepted Shar's dagger and jabbed it into her waistband. "Shar Lianor, I accept your service. Go now and celebrate with your bride."

Tam Lin's hiss of fury was barely audible over Kaer Yin's cursing and Rian's girlish squeal. Shar clasped Rian's hand and stood without fear or shame, leading her past Una and a growing collection of surprised onlookers along the way. Shar gave Tam Lin only the briefest salute.

After they'd gone, Barb fanned her face. "Bloody me. Who needs a dram?"

Una raised her hand, but Tam Lin caught it and swung her around to face him. "How could you?"

The emotions in that voice dented even Una's less than warm heart. "I'm sorry, your highness. I daresay this was a brilliant trap."

"You took them both."

"Neither was yours to barter." He squeezed her hand so tight she heard her bones grind together. Still, she did not flinch. "If I had my way, Rian would remain free of connubial strings her whole life. It seems I am overruled."

"I won't forgive you for this, *Ard Bhean.*" He made the last sound as derisive and mocking as possible.

"Tam Lin," growled Kaer Yin. "This is not her fault. Go and drink it off somewhere."

"It's done," Una sighed. "I'm sorry for you."

Tam Lin let her go and stalked away, nearly flattening Barb in his haste.

Robin held her upright.

Kaer Yin glared at Una for several pregnant moments before he followed his cousin out.

"Siora," cooed Barb. "Our girlie seems to have stirred it up this morn. Who knew she even thought o'the boys that way?"

"That's what I said," agreed Una darkly. "Not the first time I've been wrong."

"Nor the last, I suspect," laughed Barb. "Well, no point to long facin' it through the day. Might as well get good and soused afore the Southers come to kill us all for our brass."

Una nodded eagerly. "For once, Mistress Dormer, we are in perfect agreement."

Surrogates

By noon, Una was fully inebriated. With her head resting on Colm's bar, and her hand woven through her aunt's, she sat groaning into the small puddle of ale accumulating beneath her tankard. Beside them, Barb, who didn't seem drunk despite the dozen ales she'd already downed, winked at Eva.

"Lost in the woods, this one," she said, patting Una's shoulder.

Eva sighed. "It's been a trying day."

Una made a rude sound. Colm tossed a folded cloth at her, which she ignored. Instead, she sagged into her seat and sighed at the ceiling like it might hold the answers she sought. "I'm a terrible mother."

Barb choked out a laugh. "Well, yer not her mother, ye know."

"I know."

"But I agree, ye'd do a shite job."

"Thanks so much, Barb."

Barb saluted her with her tankard. "Anytime, love."

Ignoring that comment, Eva tucked a lock of Una's hair behind her ear, as she had when she was still a girl. "You were a brilliant mother, Una. Rian is not Zeah, and the circumstances are not the same."

Barb's elbow froze mid-sip. Her eyebrows shot up. "So that rumor was true then?"

"Yes," answered Una, atonally.

Barb set her ale down, sharing a long uncomfortable look with Colm, who threw up his hands and sauntered off. "Ah… well, fuck me then. What happened to the lass?"

Una teared up and buried her face in her hands.

"Ah hell, girl. Pay me no mind."

Eva rubbed small circles into Una's back until she was sensate enough to hiccup into her tankard. "Zeah died young. A fever."

"I thought ye Mouras were illness-proof?"

Eva looked down. "So did we."

"I'm sorry."

Una nodded blithely, staring at nothing. "I don't confuse her and Rian, so you know."

"Of course not," Eva swiftly assured her.

"I just want a better life for her… than *this*."

"Well, ye don't get to decide that fer anyone, bairns included."

Eva sent a sharp eye over Una's head. "What were their names?"

Barb laughed mirthlessly, "Ye'd have to ask Robin. I couldn't bear to give 'em any."

Una stopped and looked up. "You?"

"Oh, aye. Four or five o'me own. Only two drew breath more'n a week, poor mites."

"*Siora*, Barb. Forgive me…"

She waved her comment away. "Oh, hush. We're three decades on now. Done me grievin'." She paused to make sure no one was paying too close attention. "Does Ben know?"

"Yes."

"That why yer cousin can't let ye go?"

"Partly, I believe. For the other half, Damek's been obsessive since I was young enough to understand what that meant. When he fixates, it's forever. I'm certain that's why he's such a good swordsman and soldier. He threw himself into that part of his life with a razor focus."

"And ye?"

"I think I represent a normal life. He always wanted to be my father's son and the people to respect and love him. I think he believes I'm the way he can have all that and more."

"Love is a strange mistress, I'd say."

"To Damek, there is 'useful,' 'significant,' and 'detrimental.' I oscillate between the latter two."

"You don't believe that's love?"

Una grimaced. "Do *you*?"

She pursed her thinning lips. "As I see it, that's one way to, yeah. Men ain't like us, ye know. They don't burn with emotion the way women can. Rather it's boilt down; ye know what I mean? Cut away the introspective parts, the keen eye for detail, and yer left with the core thing. That's love to men. That thing they can't describe or quantify."

"That's rather apt," added Eva. "I believe I agree."

Una scratched her nose. "Kaer Yin can quantify. That's what I like about him. He isn't afraid to feel things."

Barb threw her head back and laughed until Una's face was red as a winter beet. "Oh love, ye have no bloody idea how *dull* that lad is, do ye?"

"Well," Una sniffed. "My experience with him might differ from yours… or anyone else's."

"That's as may be, but I promise ye, he's as lost as the rest of 'em. They know they want. They know they need. Maybe even know they'd die for ye. Just don't ask 'em to explain why. Bloody lost, the whole lot."

"And Shar Lianor," asked Eva pointedly. "What do you think he feels?"

"Lust. Bit o'competition. Maybe an ideal or two to scratch?"

"He loves her," said Eva confidently. "As men do. It's the girl I fear hasn't the same notion."

"I bloody *knew* that." Una cracked her fist against the bar, splashing herself with dark red ale. "I said as much to Yin."

"A young girl's head is filled with wax and her gut with fire. She's acting out, though she hardly realizes it."

"I should talk some sense into her. Who gets married to prove a bloody point?"

"I'll talk to her," vowed Eva, turning to her pint. "You finesse matters between the menfolk if you can."

"Ach," Barb winced. "'Fraid that'll make it worse. No offense intended, Princess, but yer the worst diplomat I've ever met. *I'll* talk to the men."

"You'd do that?" Una hiccupped.

"Who better? I, unlike ye, speak 'male.'"

That was a fair point.

Una nodded. "All right then. What should I be doing in the meantime?"

"I 'spect ye'll be asleep fer the better part o'the morrow."

"Nonsense," hiccupped Una again. "Liver of a god."

"Robin'll be tickled ye stole his line."

"It's a good one," she giggled before laying her head back on the bar. "I hope I don't fall through this time."

"Believe ye me," Barb inhaled. "So do I."

Aᴛ ᴛʜᴇ ᴏᴘᴘᴏsɪᴛᴇ ᴇɴᴅ ᴏꜰ town, Kaer Yin and Robin were busy shoring up the defenses along the Navan Gate and working very hard to stop themselves from throwing Tam Lin over. He was, for once, avidly ignoring everyone who spoke to him, including Kaer Yin. Miffed that he should be caught up in such a meaningless debacle, Kaer Yin grew more irascible as the day progressed. Robin, too, was at a loss about how to proceed.

He pulled Kaer Yin aside for the second time that afternoon. "Ye sure ye can't just brain him like ye did last time?"

"It wouldn't solve anything," frowned Kaer Yin. "Besides, it isn't me he wants to fight."

Robin squinted over at Tam Lin and spat. "This is a bad business all the way 'round."

"I won't argue."

"Lovelorn fools fight like piss."

Kaer Yin scowled. Is that what this was? He had no idea. Tam Lin never gave a half-hearted fart for any woman before; he couldn't be sure he did, even now. Was this for show? Grandstanding for the sport of it? Tam Lin caught his eye, sneered, and turned his back. That did it.

"Hey! I bleedin' saw that ye blighter," huffed Robin. "Why doncha get over here and explain yerself before we each take a turn bashin' yer bloody brains in."

Tam Lin drew himself to his full height, nearly a head and a half taller than the wiry Greenmaker. "Try it, Milesian. I won't go easy on you just because my cousin enjoys the shape of your arse."

Robin turned to Kaer Yin, bemused. "That true?"

"'Tis a fine arse, Robin, all told."

Robin pursed his lips and shrugged. "Well, when yer right, yer right."

"Why do either of *you* care about my business?" demanded Tam Lin over his shoulder, crossing his arms. "I don't see how it's of concern to anyone, and we're busy, aren't we? Find something else to titter about with the rest of the women."

Kaer Yin threw his trowel at Tam Lin, where it pinged from his chest, eliciting a dull grunt. "You're being a twat. Again."

Tam Lin faced him, fist clenched. "Say that once more."

"Of fer feck's sake," muttered Barb on her way up the stairs. She smelled more strongly of uishge than she had in years, though it did little to stall her gait. "Don't ye wee bairns have any other way to manage yer troubles?"

"None as fun," answered Kaer Yin dryly.

She rolled her eyes at his jest and wagged a finger at Tam Lin. "Now ye know ye've stuck yer foot in, so I won't waste me time tellin' ye what a prat *I* think ye are, but I got one gal down there drinkin' herself twirly for guilt and another determined to wed the first prick that passed fancy at her to avoid ye. Mind tellin' me why yer makin' me climb these stairs to ask what in the hells is yer problem?"

Tam Lin blinked slowly. He still wasn't used to the sheer volume of insults lobbed his way since he took up residence with the citizens of Rosweal. "I beg your pardon?"

She made a rude sound. "I don't give a tinker's shite for your title, so save yer indignance. Ye need to get down there and make it right with yer man and apologize to that sweet girl before I lose my temper."

Tam Lin coughed, "I was *trying* to marry the bloody girl, thank you. I still fail to see why this is such a godsdamned insult to everyone within fifty miles of Rosweal."

"Yeah, right," argued Barb. "Ye might be tellin' yerself that now because it makes ye feel better about challengin' yer man for a prize, but ye must realize I've known yer sort me whole life, and not one o'ye *ever* means it when they make a promise. None o'this is about her. It's about ye bein' bored. It's about yer man darin' to leave yer service to claim somethin' ye don't value. It's about winnin'. 'Marry' the girl my bleedin' foot."

Tam Lin said nothing.

Kaer Yin cleared his throat. "If she's wrong, Lin, say so now."

He still didn't answer.

Robin scratched at his scar. "Mate, if ye did that to me when I was a younger man, I'd have yer ears by nightfall. Shar's a bleedin' Kneeler's saint, ye ask me."

"Tam Lin?" Kaer Yin repeated.

Cursing, Tam Lin threw his tools down and stomped down the rampart in the opposite direction. Men and Sidhe scrambled out of his way, lest the look on his face was meant for any of them.

Barb threw up her hands. "Ye shoulda beat him senseless, love."

Kaer Yin wasn't sure how to respond to that. "I don't think it would help," he repeated for her benefit.

"Think it's gonna be a long week," Robin sighed.

⚑ ⚑

NIALL CAME TO TELL RIAN that Kaer Yin had agreed to give her three men, so long as she decided to move her patients beneath *The Hart*. While she was less than pleased by the prospect, she figured it was best not to add to the trouble she'd caused the night before.

Everyone was furious with her.

Niall was curt as ever, but before he took his leave, the look in his river-green eyes told her what he thought of her at that moment. When she came up to the tap to ask the girls for help setting up the cellar, Gerrod cut his jaw so hard that she felt like her stomach had been sliced clean open.

He took his leave with nary a word to spare for her.

Indeed, even Rose winced at her coming up the stairs. "Ach, love," she said. "Yer in for a shite day, ain't ye?"

Rian would have loved to argue, but Rose's words proved prophetic. Most of the Greenmakers in the Quarter found a reason to visit *The Hart* that day, and every one of them seemed excited to ogle her over their tankards whenever she came into the tap... which she had to do rather often since she was busy preparing the rude, ungrateful clods a clinic, the while.

At first, she was angry, but then she empathized.

Rian was also mad at Rian, so there was that.

She was busy cramming clean linens into an abandoned dresser drawer in the cellar and cursing at the fresh splinter she'd given herself when Eva swept downstairs with a small dagger already to hand. Rian cursed anew when she clasped her hand and dragged the offensive finger beneath her blade. "I'm not sure I like your abilities, Eva."

With a smirk, she deftly swept the half-inch splinter from Rian's finger, who immediately wrapped the stinging appendage in a rag soaked with witch hazel. "So the Crown Prince has repeatedly remarked."

At the word 'prince,' Rian gave the barest flinch.

Of course, Eva noticed. Her smile deepened.

"That's irritating too," grumbled Rian.

Eva crossed her arms to lean against the stone doorjamb. She wore a simple red dress that, on any other woman, would manage to look gauche. On Eva, it might have been spun from the finest silk, such a figure she cut. She wore her long black braids loose this evening, and the bells woven into the tips chimed slightly where they brushed her hips. Her impressive golden eyes, Una's very own, stared down at Rian with a warm, motherly sort of humor. "Got yourself into it today, haven't you?"

Rian huffed, her cheeks burning. She scooted away to pretend to work on something else across the room. "I don't know why everyone is making a big deal about this."

"Yes, you do."

"It's not anyone's bloody business, is it?"

"It's Una's business now, isn't it?"

579

Rian felt a deep pang of guilt. She set down the scissors she wasn't going to use anyway and swallowed hard. "I didn't mean to take advantage of her adopting me."

"But you were angry with her for her presumption."

"I mean…"

"And knew she would defend you."

"That's true, but—"

"And also knew the Crown Prince would not gainsay her in front of his men."

Now, Rian fidgeted. "I don't… I mean, I didn't want to…".

"You understand that the Sidhe marry forever, right? Shar, even if you grow apart or die before he does, he'll never take another wife. If you take him this way, you'd be doing him and yourself a disservice."

Rian went quiet for a moment, her thoughts racing. She had to wipe tears from her face when she spoke again, but Eva didn't move to comfort her. Her eyes were hard as amber. "I didn't mean to. I was angry, and I thought it would make everyone happy."

"Rian Guinness," Eva sucked her teeth. "Do you suppose I can't hear that bald lie?"

Rian threw up her hands in defeat. "How do I fix it?"

Eva sighed and shrugged. She entered the cellar, lingering over the humble collection of medicinals she had bought for Rian in Ten Bells. "You're a smart girl. Probably smarter than I am, and I have been an Alta Prima, Domina of a great Tairnganese Clan, sometime spy, and counselor to a Doma of the Cloister. You know what you have done and must do, though neither sits well on your conscience."

"I don't want to hurt him."

"Which one do you mean?"

Rian's head snapped around at that. "You *know* it wouldn't be him!"

"Hmm," hummed Eva. "Not yet, you mean."

Rian quickly cleared her throat. "If you came down here to judge me…."

"Oh stop, silly girl. You'd hardly be the first foolish woman of some relation I've ever had to council against an unwise match."

"Which relation?"

Eva smiled. "You instantly recalled a name that your lips did not utter. See? Smart, as I said."

Rian scrunched up her brows. "With *Patrick?*"

"He was quite dashing in his youth. I recall that he made Arrin laugh something awful during the High King's Council. Such affairs last weeks, and they got to know one another quite well. Drove Auntie Drem completely mad."

"Oh, *Siora*," Rian's hand went to her mouth. "But everyone said he kidnapped her on the High Road in broad daylight."

"Well," Eva sniffed. "Your brain conjured her name because you already had doubts about the whole sordid tale. Are you shocked to hear confirmation?"

"They… *eloped?*"

"They did. Against my urging and Drem's command, of course."

Rian's head raced through a thousand conversations at once. "Does Una know?"

"I intended to tell her when the grief and anger over her father's death subsided, but perhaps I should do so sooner, given our approaching doom."

Rian took a seat. Well, *that* certainly changed things. "Una told me she suspected her father had her mother killed."

"My aunt commanded me never to speak of Arrin to her daughter upon pain of disinheritance, and I, too, blamed Patrick for my cousin's death. So, I obeyed, and that silence has complicated Una's life." She folded her hands tight. "I often wonder if all of this might have been avoided if only Una knew how much her parents loved her and each other."

Stunned to total silence, all Rian could do was blink back at her.

Eva toyed with a stray braid. "What are *you* going to do, little bird?"

Sucked back to her reality, Rian immediately shut her mouth with a snap. "I have no idea. Everyone hates me now."

"Everyone does not hate you, but you did overplay your only hand. Honestly, I would ask you what you were thinking, but I believe it's fairly obvious."

"I thought marrying Shar would make me powerful enough to tell them all to go to the hells. I thought I liked him a lot and enjoyed his company… and erm, the things we do together." She flushed. "I thought I would make Ben treat me as an equal and not a burden, and I thought it would twist that redhaired bastard's nose to no end."

"Well, some of that turned out to be true, at least."

"I hurt Una, instead."

"Yes, but yourself, first."

Rian chewed her lower lip hard enough to make it bleed. "What do I do, Eva?"

"You tell Shar the truth."

"It'll hurt him."

"The fiction will hurt him more."

She squirmed under that imperious gaze. "Tam Lin, won't he try to take revenge, somehow?"

"Do you believe Una would ever allow that?"

"After what I have done, maybe she'd consider it."

Eva let out a long, patient breath. "Do you love Shar Lianor?"

"I have no idea," Rian answered truthfully. "I know I love Una and Ben, but it's different."

"They're surrogate family."

"Yes."

"Do you want to marry Shar Lianor?"

"No… I don't know."

"And Tam Lin O'Ruiadh?"

Rian colored as she ground her molars. "*Never.*"

"Hmm," Eva repeated. "Then, after this battle is over, you need to tell him."

"Which one?"

"You decide."

Under the White Flag

n.e. 509
23 ban apesa
Rosweal

Damek strode through the oppressive canopy of trees, old snow crunching underfoot. A limpid sun hung from a light blue sky, and the air was so dry it whisked the moisture from his lungs. Leaving the warmth of the headwoman's bed before dawn and up the Taran High Road, over hills, through dales, and past several frozen villages on his way, he set about the day's parlance. From this elevated vantage, he could see down the crested hillside where the two rivers wedded in the crux of the flatlands— and following the thinner of the snaking brown lines, he saw the little walled town he expected to see.

Only, all was not as he remembered it.

A newly fortified hillfort sat beneath a thick white cloak upon a corrugated plain, bisected into two broad sections between an eight-foot moat and an earthen bulwark another ten feet from vastly heightened walls. Massive chunks of masonry topped with upended timber rose almost a dozen feet from the ground. The walls ran in a uniform semicircle around the southern approach, marred only by rectangular arrow slits and the occasional murder hole. Behind the wall on either side of the reinforced gate stood two siege towers built into the framework, each featuring half a dozen archers and flying the silver and white standard of House Adair.

Damek smiled mirthlessly.

Rosweal had been busy.

He passed his spyglass to Martin with a laugh he didn't feel. "They've divested me of my trebuchets."

"*Reason*," Martin breathed, pressing the glass to his eye. "How in the hells did they accomplish all that in less than six months?"

Damek shrugged, settling his chin into his ermine collar. "Desperation is a master motivator."

This was disappointing. He had been expecting more challenge from the ruffians in Rosweal— but he wasn't expecting *this*. With the night raids and the snows deepening around them, this siege could become quite troublesome for him in no time. Men would continue to desert, and the colder it got, the less he'd be able to mitigate his losses.

"They're waving the High King's standard," observed Martin.

"I saw."

"And that moat must be what— nine feet wide, give or take? That negates cavalry too." Martin jerked the spyglass down, gnashing his teeth. "Ripped down over five hundred trees to build up that wall."

"More."

Martin turned to him, incredulous. "Noticed maybe a handful of rooftops still visible in town. Tore their own houses down too." He exhaled through his nose. "In this weather? There's a message in there for you."

"Of course. Some blather about freedom meaning more than comfort, but we'll see how long that bravado lasts when they're starving, and the late winter snows are piling around their ears."

"That'll be a fine kettle of rotted fish for us all, I expect." Martin's temper had yet to cool from their argument a few days before. These were the most words they'd exchanged in several days. "I bet they're better supplied than we are."

"But not better armed. Wooden walls are still made of wood, no matter how high."

"They're forcing a protracted siege."

"I can see that, Martin."

"Puts a damper on many of your plans."

"So it does."

"That's all you have to say?"

Damek passed the spyglass to Ridley. "My cannons have range."

"True," acknowledged Martin. "But if I'm not mistaken, those are oak trees lining the walls. Oak doesn't burn easily. What's worse, from the look of things, they've managed to move all habitable dwellings closer to the river and far from the walls. Whoever planned this… I'd like to shake his hand before I gut him because he's bloody brilliant."

Ridley winced as the glass came away from his eye. "When it snows again, there'll be nothing to catch fire at the southern gate, and with soaking wet thousand-pound tree trunks lining a reinforced rampart— we're gonna be here a while."

Damek refused to be cowed. "We'll have to draw them out, bring them in reach of our cavalry. How many mounts do the Wild Hunt hold within their vanguard?"

Ridley took another look in the glass; his face scrunched up. "Can't tell, but with less than three thousand soldiers and civilians, it can't be more than two hundred."

"Not enough to challenge us in an open field," mused Damek. "But enough to give us a headache or two if they catch us from the sides— which I expect they're aiming to. Notice the trees on the east and western flanks? They mean to funnel us right up to the walls."

"No," disagreed Martin. They'll use footsoldiers and archers on either flank. They'll save the cavalry for anyone we get over the walls. I've seen Sidhe lords use this tactic at Dumnain. When Fionn O'More and his four hundred horse evaporated from the field, Patrick's men found them again once they'd breached the walls. Numbers count for nothing in narrow streets and alleys, doubly so when mounted combatants are barreling down every one."

"Wonderful," grumbled Ridley. "We'll have to starve or draw them out, no matter what. This could mean weeks of fucking around in the freezing mud with the flux, the pox, and all with nearly sixteen thousand mouths to feed. Bloody Tairngare is proving less a challenge." He drew his cloak tight and stamped his feet. Ridley was a brave bear of a man, but the cold was one of his least favorite things, and it would only worsen.

The mercury in Damek's brass barometer had already swept well below zero. The longer they mired here playing the waiting game, it would dip lower still.

"No," he said. "Impressive as these new defenses are and irritating as they were meant to be— I am not going to waste men and time on them."

"What orders then, My King?"

Damek eyed the slow, ice-infested Boinne as she made her way east to the Sea of Mannanan. The trees had been stripped naked by months of merciless, frigid wind. The air itself felt static and charged. It hadn't snowed in several days. The season's usual blanket of thick, iron-gray clouds had given way to a weak low-slung sun and nights illuminated by starlight. He felt himself smile. "Take two hundred of our best yeomen and send them five miles upstream toward the confluence. Send a second, ten miles west. I want them gone before the sun sinks over the mountains."

"They will have expected us to foul the river."

Damek continued, "Each man must carry ten liters of pitch and lamp oil in his travel pack."

Martin couldn't help but laugh. "It *is* dry as Siora's cunny out here."

"Ridley said it himself, when the snows come back, we'll be at their mercy. I'd rather not wait to give the Sidhe that advantage."

"You sure it'll work?"

Damek took off his glove and spat into his palm. In seconds, the little wad iced up, then crumbled. "Yes. In these conditions, a forest fire can quickly get out of hand. Let's hope so. Ridley, you have my orders."

Ridley saluted. "Yes, My King."

Damek considered the little hamlet in silence for a moment. "They mean to funnel us into one approach and let the weather do the rest. Well, I must refuse their invitation. Once the forest is aflame, I'll have that eastern gate down. Keep our men back, and don't risk anyone unnecessarily. I want them too busy putting out internal fires to stop the Greensward burning on either side of the river."

He'd be damned if he'd be foolish enough to march his men into such an obvious trap. His eyes drifted north over the Boinne.

He knew exactly where he would strike next.

"At dawn, I expect to see the valley scorched black. In the meantime, let's go down and say hello." He couldn't wait to show these people how ruthless he was prepared to be.

⚚

AFTER THE HORNS, KAER YIN flew up the watchtower to glimpse the approaching horde for himself. A cadre of mounted men waving Bethany's cobalt and scarlet colors stood in the killing field below the southern wall. Damek Bishop at the center, waiting patiently, stared straight at Una, whom Kaer Yin hadn't even realized was standing just at his elbow. Her conflicted frown irked him a great deal. "I didn't mean for him to see you," he said, incensed by the self-assured smirk on the bastard's face at the sight of her.

"It doesn't matter. Even if I weren't here, he'd treat you no differently. It's the premise that got him this far. The reality is merely a footnote."

Kaer Yin studied her. She was so small. The crown of her head barely crested his ribcage, yet she swallowed so much space in his mind's eye that he could scarcely breathe. He felt a little overwhelmed by the thought. "It will galvanize his troops, regardless. For a while anyway. When the cold gets to work, maybe that will change." While he spoke, Damek raised a hand to wave at them. It would be a simple task to put an arrow right between his eyes. The distance might be too great for most, some five hundred yards or more, but not for Kaer Yin's. Sinnair was the most famous bow on the continent. Kaer Yin gripped her topmost pinnacle, leaning into her impressive height, and watched the mirth drain from Bishop's face.

Sinnair meant 'king killer' in the old tongue.

Sometimes, irony had its perks.

"I will go down with you," Una stated, chewing her lower lip earnestly. She was afraid, he knew. Not for herself. She feared for the others, Rian, and the people of Rosweal. She blamed herself for all of this and would doubtless take matters into her own tiny hands if he let her. He'd never met a woman more endearingly reckless in his life.

"No."

"Are you telling me what to do?"

"I'm not telling you— I'm asking you to stay up here where I won't be goaded into a scuffle in the first three seconds of this parley."

"Fine, but he's only doing this to pick your ribs. He wants to draw you out."

"He'll try."

Una threw up her hands. "Well, what do I know? I just grew up with him. Why are you looking at me like that?"

"Like what?"

"Like that." She squinted up at him. "Don't."

"I'm not doing anything."

But he lied. Before she could stop him, he pulled Una in for a brief but very public kiss that was sure to pick the fight Kaer Yin was after far more efficiently than words would ever manage. On the stairs below, Robin groaned.

"Ben, can ye knock that off afore it comes to battle *today*? The lads ain't ready yet."

Kaer Yin broke away as noisily as possible.

"You might be overplaying that leer, my love," remarked Una coolly, though her cheeks were red as an apple. "Now, get out of here before you get in your own way."

"Later?" he asked, lowering his voice for her ears only.

"Not until you stop embarrassing me in front of all of Rosweal."

With a grin that said he knew better, he took the stairs two at a time on his way to threaten the newly minted King of Eire.

🦌 🦌

Damek's jaw ached from grinding his teeth together. That lecherous inhuman dog! How *dare* he treat the Duchess of Bethany like some common dockside trollop? Damek would see the man's guts served to his hounds in tidbits. He would drink ale from a goblet shaped from Adair's skull. He would nail the man's teeth to his spurs.

The insolence!

The sheer, bloody arrogance.

Sitting beside Damek, Martin moved his brindle destrier closer. "Easy now. Surely you know that was for your benefit?"

"I will eat that creature's heart, I swear it."

"And that's what he wants you to feel. Angry men are not prudent men."

Damek took several stilling breaths as he watched his enemy and two other riders approach from the southern gate.

"Smile, My King. Give them no advantage of you."

Damek couldn't smile, but he managed to smooth his face into the pleasant mask he'd perfected in his uncle's tutelage. The riders neared. The leader's silver hair gleamed nearly white in the weak winter sunlight. Beside him, the Prince of Connaught and another Sidhe noble in a plain black cuirass and obsidian cloak took Damek's measure. Damek had never seen the fellow before and had trouble placing him. Meanwhile, Una watched from the rampart. It took every ounce of effort not to look up.

"There's a lamb," Martin coughed into his fist. "Don't give 'em the satisfaction."

Without answer, Damek kicked his roan into a canter to meet the prince's entourage. Each group halted five paces from the other.

"Well met, friends," called the rider in black. His silver-blond hair was very similar in cast and color to the Crown Prince's. Though where there was a solid, almost brutish angle to Kaer Yin Adair's bones— by Sidhe standards anyway— this one's held a nearly feminine beauty and grace. The figure's sheer, unfair elegance tugged a sneer from Damek's mouth.

On the newcomer's opposite side, the Prince of Connaught had a go at him. "I don't think he cares for your face, old man."

Martin cleared his throat before the mysterious fellow could respond. "If it please you gentlemen, we are come to discuss terms with the townsfolk of Rosweal," he said. "We've had the pleasure of meeting the Prince of Connaught and briefly encountered his highness, the Crown Prince. You, sir, we do not recognize."

The man in black gave the ghost of a nod. "Mortals rarely do, Martin."

Something in his tone made Martin stiffen.

585

Damek crooked a brow. The dark rider's green eyes burned into him, and he could admit to the slight tinge of unease his attention inspired. "I'll have your name."

"You have the very *great* honor," interrupted O'Ruaidh dryly. "Of meeting *Fiachra Dubh*. Diarmid Mac Nuada Adair, Lord of Tech Duinn, and of the Oiche Ar Fad, king."

Damek's men twitched and whispered amongst themselves; several backed away. Damek himself raised a dark brow.

This was the infamous Raven King? This too pretty, effeminate creature was the Lord of the Sluagh? *Bollocks.*

Why would the High King's brother bother to meddle in Milesian Eire?

"That's easy enough to answer, My LordBishop, if you'd repeat that question aloud?"

Martin shifted in his saddle. Damek willed his nerves still. It would take more than parlor tricks to intimidate the blood of Patrick Donahugh and Eochaid Mac Nemed. "Very well. What business have you here, My LordAdair? This is a regional matter and none of your affair."

The Raven King smiled enigmatically, but he did not answer right away. The wind turned colder, slithering into the crevices between Damek's armor and flesh. He repressed a shiver. "You lay claims to lands that don't belong to you, Lord Bishop. In this, I am my brother's right hand."

Damek knew better than to quibble over the title. One did not rebuke the king of the underworld lightly. Damek chose his following words carefully. "We are not here to quarrel with the High King, nor you, Your Grace."

"Your presence here, in such force, begs to differ."

"Forgive me, but while I do not seek to insult you or the High King, the land of Eire has unified under my banner. We are here for our queen, which your nephew has stolen. Should we come to terms today, you and all your people may leave in peace with our blessing."

Diarmid Adair's mouth quirked at that. "Is that all?"

After a few tense moments, Kaer Yin found his voice. "What I wish to know is why you make war upon innocent, loyal citizens of Eire. You burn their villages, rape their women, and plunder their resources. You realize, the Ard Ri has not given you license to claim land and titles that are his— and only his— to grant or take?"

"Forgive me, My LordPrince," interrupted Martin. "But we do not condone rape and slaughter. Either is punishable by death."

"Hm," beamed Tam Lin. "How noble we've become, all of a sudden."

Damek finally met Kaer Yin's eyes, inwardly seething. "You've stolen my wife, the Princess of Bethany, Domina of the Moura Clan, and Queen of Eire." He paused to make sure she was watching. "I want her back."

"No," Kaer Yin denied him. "Una will not be your excuse. She does not subscribe to Bethonair laws, whichever way they are twisted to suit your cause. You're here for me. Well, on that score, I won't disappoint you. I promise."

Damek absorbed this statement and shared a look with Martin. "Nevertheless, here are my terms. One, you will surrender the Queen of Eire to my company, alive and unharmed. Two, you will immediately march your occupying force back into your cursed lands. Once there, you are free to rule your people and decide the fates of your women as you see fit. Three, you will renounce your claim to Eire and divest yourself permanently from matters here. Four— and this is non-negotiable— you will cross that border and never return. Those are the terms I offer you as a courtesy. Accept them or die."

To Damek's eternal irritation, Kaer Yin laughed through an open mouth. "And here are *my* terms, boy. One, your union with Una Moura Donahugh was annulled in your youth, making your presence here is illegal as it is laughable. Two, she rejects your claim… I reject your claim, and the whole of the Tuatha De Dannan rejects your claim to the crown of Eire. Three, if you linger here, you will never leave the

Greensward alive, and all the men who followed you on this foolish quest will be hunted down and slain for this insult to the Ard Ri's family name."

Tam Lin tugged his chin at the men behind Damek. "I wonder how many men will fight for you when they're starving. Through the wet and cold, hounded and terrorized by ruthless cutthroats, poachers, and bloodthirsty creatures of the Otherworld— all so you can steal another man's bride?"

Something bright flared behind Damek's eyelids. "We'll see how many of you live to make good those threats. Presently, you are alone. None of your allies have made it in time to save you. How many women and children are you holding hostage in there? You talk a good game, Adair— but I have the numbers, and you will feel them soon enough. Tomorrow it begins." He jerked his reins to turn his horse around, but Kaer Yin's voice caught him short.

"Do you know how I met her, Lord Bishop? The mercenaries you hired to kidnap her from Tairngare spirited her away in burlap and kept her bound and starved for three days. It was I who freed her. When I saw her next, she was hunted down and nearly beaten to death right in front of me. Ever since, she's been chased from one end of Eire to the other, captured and held prisoner, then nearly raped and murdered by her own kin. All this, and the only thing you can whine about, is yourself. *Your* right to her. *Your* claim to her father's lands and titles. Everything, *yours*."

Kaer Yin paused, the derision on his face plain.

"I could have killed you once, remember, but Una stayed my hand. Despite all, she thought your worthless life held value. You think about that the next time we meet. I will."

Damek thought about the bloodied linens he'd found in that ramshackle farmstead in autumn. The rage, knowing whom they belonged to. The fear and uncertainty of searching for her for weeks on end. The relief he experienced when he found her at last… and the burning jealousy he felt now, knowing this man had been there for every moment he'd lost. "I'll look for you on the field, Highness," promised Damek with every ounce of loathing he could summon from the deepest recesses of his gut. Spine rigid, he kicked his mount away without another word.

Only when Rosweal shrank in the distance did the fear settle in. It wasn't the presence of the Raven King that unnerved him, the bitter justice he read in Kaer Yin Adair's frank expression, nor the unspoken but genuine threat either represented. This was something else. Something deeper, darker.

For the whole of his life, he'd never felt such an inexplicable, insidious emotion— and it ate at him, even as he slumped in his command tent, surrounded by thousands of capable Bethonair troops who believed in him.

The feeling was doubt.

Martin was right.

He didn't like it one bit.

Scorched Earth

Dawn had just begun to creep over the tops of the tallest trees in the east when the first noxious clouds of smoke descended upon Rosweal. The air had been dry enough to irritate the end of every nose in town during the night, which was just the sort of feast that a forest fire would require to consume an entire region. Kaer Yin, who got up well before sunrise to install the windlass on the southern rampart and oversee the return of last night's raiding party, had been one of the first to spy the orange haze on the horizon. His throat seized at the sight long before he smelt smoke.

They'd been expecting Bishop to burn the trees to the west of the city— counting on it, actually— but the scale… the way the sky also lit up red in the west said they had been far from prepared.

Kaer Yin raced along the rampart to the Ward Gate without wasting a moment in shocked silence. Already, the heat was staggering. Flames raged over the western hills, nearly twenty feet high. When he skidded to a stop facing the north wall, eyes watering, he covered his mouth with the back of his hand. Tam Lin and Robin were already there, pouring buckets of melting snow over the wooden walls. Barb, who was never up at such an ungodly hour, directed more up the stone steps at the north end. A raucous shout went around the city from the Quarter to the vacant hilltop. People poured out of homes and rundown buildings, hauling whatever vessels they could carry to keep the walls from catching. With a nod to Tam Lin, who busied himself with managing the traffic along the ramparts, Kaer Yin leaped to work, shouting commands to heave water from the river and moats to keep the supply steady.

Oak and ash did not burn quickly, but under such blazing temperatures— even ten yards away, the walls would get so dry that the slightest spark could catch. No matter how strong the wood, it would still burn. Barb's brilliant moat system might keep that risk at bay for a while. He could only pray that whatever Una had done would help.

"Keep these walls as wet as possible!" He heard Tam Lin roar against the quickening blaze. "Set up lines here and there," he pointed to Robin and Dabs, who'd just dashed up the steps as fast as his bulky frame could carry him. "I want a constant chain of water streaming over these walls until that fire molders out."

Una, too, raced up the steps at the far end. She came around Tam Lin, her face already smudged with soot. Dark ash fell from the sky like snow. "What can I do?"

Tam Lin turned. "Can you put out a forest fire?"

She blinked back. "I don't think so."

"Then nothing." He wiped his nose and spat, eyes shifting to the Navan Gate on the east side of town. Muttering a colorful curse in Ealig, he noted, "On second thought, I want every available yeoman and pikeman along that wall and double the men on the southern rampart." He gesticulated so Robin and Barb would hear him. Robin nodded and dashed off, hollering for more men.

Una followed his gaze. "You think he'll attack from the east?"

The rising sun gave them a better glimpse of the distant inferno. Though the fire raged right beside them in the west and east, the worst of it was yet miles off; encroaching but slowly. Tam Lin gave Kaer Yin a stern look. "He won't come from the south. Too many traps. He'll want to pull his trebuchets in as close as possible, and the Navan Gate is weakest."

He was right. Kaer Yin could glean the logic as clearly as his cousin. He snatched Jan Fir by the collar as he passed with an empty bucket. "No one is to drink the water they take from the river, nor use it to treat any burns."

"You think they fouled it?" he asked, hair black with ash and eyes smudged.

"Count on it." Kaer Yin nodded to Una. "Make sure Barb and Rian know and spread the word, fast." She took off at a run.

Robin, huffing, and coughing, came past her. "What now?"

"It's time," Kaer Yin replied. "The Navan Gate."

Despite the severity of the situation, Robin's teeth flashed whitely in the haze. Kaer Yin grabbed him by the sleeve before he sped off to do his duty. "Make it hurt, Rob."

"Oh, Ben," said he. "It'll be my pleasure."

Kaer Tin looked around when he'd gone, searching for the one figure he needed to see most. "Where's Diarmid, Tam Lin?"

Tam Lin threw up his hands, then accepted another bucket. "Fuck if I know! I'm a bit busy here."

Niall jerked a thumb behind him. "I've seen him, *Ard Tiarne*."

Kaer Yin gestured for him to lead the way. "Good, Niall and Conor, with me!"

⚹ ⚹

AFTER NEARLY AN HOUR OF searching, barking orders, and lending a spare pair of hands wherever needed, the fire had mostly burned itself out at the western approach. Far afield, however, the hills were red with roaring, furious flames that sent massive billows of smoke downwind into Rosweal. The ash came down in deep drifts that were often deep enough to sink into.

Untold thousands of acres burned. The Great Greensward was swiftly reduced to a smoking scar upon the Riverlands. In the west, the devastation appeared total. Charred sticks and blackened earth buffeted by cinders and grey ash swallowed the eye for as far as one could see. To the east, there was no telling how far the fires reached. Possibly even to the walls of Navan or beyond.

Bishop hadn't merely intended to remove any additional cover the Roswellian forces meant to preserve— he intended to utterly destroy the land itself: the forest, river, and valley that could revive the city, should they manage to survive the assault. Through the rage and despair that clenched his heart at the knowledge, Kaer Yin resolved to focus on the task at hand. Bishop had studied his classics, it seemed. Scorched earth served to crush an enemy's resolve and, in this case, make clear there was no escaping Bishop's wrath.

Well, Kaer Yin thought.

Let's see how you enjoy my *strategy, young lordling.*

Finally, he spotted Diarmid at the Northern rampart, leaning into the wind. Diarmid's cloak and hair were entirely coated in soot, but he didn't appear to notice.

"Uncle!" Kaer Yin asked, breathless. "Have you been here the whole time?"

Diarmid absorbed his question without reply, nor did he turn to acknowledge him. Instead, he stared intently over the river and into the mists shrouding Aes Sidhe, a heavy furrow between his brows.

Kaer Yin drew up short. "What is it?"

He knew the look on his couldn't be good news.

"A threat. One I cannot do much about and remain here."

"What do you mean?"

Diarmid met his eyes, his expression solemn. "Your father has charged me with your support, Yin. The outcome of this battle will decide much."

"I don't know what you mean." Kaer Yin tried to crane his neck around Diarmid to see what he was staring at when his uncle's arm snaked out and brought their heads together.

"Don't look, Yin."

Kaer Yin broke the uncharacteristic fatherly embrace with a nervous laugh. "Diarmid, I don't know what you're on about...." But then Diarmid moved, and he saw for himself. A glimmer of light— a glowing made unearthly and soft by the near-impenetrable mists over the border. Just a hint, but every moment he stood there gaping, it grew broader.

Aes Sidhe.

The fire had spread over the river into sacred lands—their home, their gods... burning. Rooted to the spot in horror, Kaer Yin watched the glowing snake further northward through the mist, like some mythic wyrm writhing beneath a cloud. Within his dawning shock and outrage coiled a kernel of fury so bright that it threatened to shove his bones through his skin.

"Yin, stay the course," Diarmid warned, though, for the blood pounding in his ears, Kaer Yin scarcely heard him. "If you give him the satisfaction, you will forfeit every advantage we've gained. Use your head now, not your heart," he went on, trying to set himself between Kaer Yin and the view.

It didn't work.

Whatever Diarmid said, Kaer Yin could no longer hear him. All he could see were the flames rolling casually north, hear the cries and bleats of beasts and birds attempting to flee the blaze, and taste the char at the back of his throat. The Greensward north of the Boinne was virgin forest.

Sacrosanct.

Many of those trees were well over a thousand years old, some *far* older. Their roots reached far underground, while their towering limbs soared to heights sometimes exceeding a hundred or more feet.

This was a heresy akin to genocide.

His uncle was right. Damek Bishop had no intention of suing for peace, ever. He was declaring war on *all* of Kaer Yin's people.

You're going to get what you're asking for, isasaeligh.

Kaer Yin slid Nemain from his back, his hand shaking on her pommel.

Diarmid's hand shot out to stall him. "It's what he wants you to do."

"I don't care. That boy dies today, I vow it."

"If you go out there now, everything you planned will fail. The people here will be slaughtered or enslaved, and Una will become his pawn. Is that what you want?"

He didn't answer. A general outcry circled the walls. The Dannans, having finally seen what was happening across the river, rushed to gape and moan at the north wall. Their horror and grief were palpable. This fire, easily double the height and twice the ferocity, choked the air with so much ash and smoke that the sun was entirely blotted. Everyone and everything in Rosweal stopped as if time itself held no meaning. Many hardened Sidhe warriors wept openly, Kaer Yin included. He heard a woman wail somewhere below him and knew true despair.

He made to brush past his uncle, but Diarmid pushed back, physically placing himself between Kaer Yin and the ladder he aimed for. The keening grew to a terrible pitch. "I am as angry as you are, but don't hand this usurper the advantage."

"Get out of my way!" Kaer Yin attempted to shove him aside again, but the old Brehon might have been made of iron.

"Listen to *Fiachra Dubh, Ard Tiarne*," said Fionn, who materialized from the smoke behind him. His long face was grave, though Kaer Yin could see the flames reflected in his eyes. "We must hold our defenses."

Fionn's mouth pulled into a knife-slash line. He had never used Kaer Yin's title before, which gave him pause enough for Diarmid to turn him around. "Swallow it down. Save it for the appropriate moment," he urged.

Kaer Yin's blood ran cold as the ice in Donn Bay. "The appropriate moment?"

He watched Diramid's jaw clench and unclench. There wasn't a Dannan among them who didn't feel this sacrilege to their marrow. "Can you stop the fire, Uncle?"

Diarmid shook his head. "The cost would be tremendous, and you need me now, Yin. More than ever. I promised my brother."

Kaer Yin closed his eyes, counting to ten, twenty, a hundred. When he opened them again, his hands had stopped shaking. "Fionn. You'll take the South Wall?"

"*Mo Flaith*," he saluted, fist to his chest— for the first time since Kaer Yin had been placed in his service as an adolescent so many eons ago.

Fionn disappeared through the smoke whence he came, and Una was suddenly there, brushing his fingers with hers. "I can help." Only the whites of her eyes and teeth were visible.

"Can you?"

She sent Diarmid a pointed glance. "You said before what happens here echoes in the Otherworld, right? Like a reflection?"

He shifted. "Yes, but time is not always relative."

"You can change that, though, can't you?"

"The cost, Una, as you know, would be—"

"Let *me* worry about that. Is it possible or not?"

Something calculative slid behind Diarmid's façade, and were Kaer Yin paying more attention, he would have been furious to have spied it. Just then, he was having a hard time keeping himself from launching over the wall with naught but Nemain in one hand and a song in his heart. "It is, Princess."

"Then, let's go." She pulled Kaer Yin's face down for a brief kiss. "Stick to your strategy, love."

Kaer Yin held her tight for a moment, then clung to her shoulders so she couldn't miss his nod. "I will. Una, are you sure?"

"I am. I'm useless here, and Eva says Damek's men will attack next. Let me try."

"All right. Please… just don't—"

"I won't." She squeezed him again, then stepped away to take Diarmid's outstretched hand. Without further commentary, the two snapped out of existence with that horrible ear-popping sound that all Sidhe understood as the key to the Oiche Ar Fad.

Kaer Yin stared into the space they'd vacated, feeling a surge of anxiety that he didn't have the luxury to fret over.

Be safe, my love, he thought but knew he had his own trials cut out for him today. He turned to find Gerrod and Shar Lianor waiting by the steps.

Kaer Yin's sigh was bone-deep. "Boys, let's get to work."

⚲ ⚲

As the fire raged over the Boinne, dark shapes flitted through the wasteland that was now the eastern approach to the city. They waited for the sun to sink over the smoldering hills in the west to strike. First, two catapults were wheeled up the Navan High Road, guarded by a host of some four hundred pikemen and troopers with long iron shields. They moved in a phalanx that would prove troublesome for any ground defenders. Behind them, yeomen with longbows prepared to fire volley after volley over the wall. The defenders braced themselves for assault. Sidhe archers returned introductory fire from the ramparts with far less efficacy given their vastly inferior numbers. Many men that had been busy fighting fires on the western edge of town were late arriving at the eastern wall. All was as Damek had planned. From the rear of the attacking horde, he raised a mailed fist.

Issuing a guttural cry, five hundred uniformed infantry raced through the forward line toward the wall— axes, cudgels, and swords held high. Every tenth man dragged yards of rope from vicious grappling hooks that dangled over their armored shoulders. Many didn't make it past the smoking treeline before they were shot down, but dozens did. Soon, these howling soldiers were pouring up the wall by the hundreds. Meanwhile, the phalanx of pikes and shieldmen directed their attention to the gate. In under twenty minutes, an overwhelming number of screaming, bloodthirsty Southers, who'd been told the only way home to their warm hearths was through Rosweal, ran for the walls as if they intended to chew through them. They had more to gain than lose, given the confidence in their numbers.

Damek watched his men scramble over the wall, largely unchecked.

Hand still high; he closed his fist.

The catapults and their protective phalanx of shields moved into position.

He brought his fist down.

Douglas shouted a command. Seven-foot balls of hawthorn and bramble dipped in pitch and oil were set ablaze.

Damek swept his arm forward.

"At will!" Boomed Douglas.

A trio of steaming, white-hot missiles streaked toward the Navan Gate, swiftly followed by another round and another— until they were launched regularly at five-minute intervals. Cries of alarm rang throughout Rosweal as the newly built wall bore the assault. The defenders hasted to solidify their positions upon the ramparts. Damek waited another twenty minutes, surprised but undaunted by how long it took the Gate to fall.

He had more yet to throw at them and plenty of time to wait.

"My King, the walls!" Second Lieutenant Ridley gestured from his right. "They've been shored up somehow, and I'm not sure we have the ammunition to—"

"No matter," said Damek, knowing only one person who could manage witchery of that kind. He refused to pay it any mind. "Bring up the battering ram."

The Navan Gate was the only part of the newly heightened wall that was not surrounded by the defenders' hastily constructed trio of moats. The water system curved around the outer walls in a crescent, bisected by large, sharpened stakes and wooden arrow blinds. The lack of its continuance wasn't a failure of ingenuity but rather a nod to basic geography, which Damek had no doubt the Sidhe intended to exploit. The old stone road here snaked along a high escarpment, shored up by loose earth and soft sand. They didn't need to extend their moat around this side to keep his larger siege toys at bay. The road was too narrow and uneven here for his twenty-foot, top-heavy siege towers to be wheeled up to the walls or for the massive and cumbersome wagons required to haul up bulky cannon or trebuchets. The south end would have once been the ideal place to use his trebuchets, but that moat and all its new decorations completely prevented that. He might not be able to drag heavy ballistics up to the walls, but he could hammer the hells out of them with his lighter, ten-foot slings and a focused assault on the weakest spot they bore.

Today was not about showing off.

Today was about speed and efficiency.

Damek gambled that they'd spend so much time putting out fires on the west end that the east wall would be distracted long enough for his men to get that gate down. However, he was no fool. He understood that Kaer Yin had always planned to draw them to the east gate, but with the Sidhe busy putting out fires and their nerve unsettled by the blaze over the river— Damek hoped to be in the city well before the Dannans could marshal the defense they'd prepared for. No matter what surprises Rosweal had in store, the Navan Gate was still their greatest weakness. A fatal flaw, he hoped.

Just in case, he had plans aplenty.

"Ridley," he said. "Redirect one sling at the southern approach. I want every arrow blind and bit of moat furniture in ashes by midday, whether this gate is down or not."

"Yes, My King."

Ridley barked his orders, and the sling was reloaded and aimed at the wooden defenses along the southern wall. Many were aflame in minutes.

A killing field worked both ways; he was sure to remind Rosweal if the siege stretched on. If the Dannans could hold those walls for one more day, Damek didn't want a single obstacle to mar the perfect scorched ring of earth around the city. He held the bulk of his forces in reserve for today's adventure. Still, by the following day, those same men would encircle the town from the opposite end and erect their blockade— trapping the Roswellians in a circle of death and barren land without food or untainted water. But that plan would only be necessary if he failed to knock the wall down today… and on that score, he had a seventy-percent chance of success.

He would take those odds.

Rosweal could tuck in and ration out supplies for a week or so, but without fresh water, they wouldn't last more than ten days. Given the sad state of his own supplies, he needed to make this quick as possible. Knowing the averages, however, did not negate the need for caution.

Kaer Yin Adair, Fionn O'More, and Diarmid Mac Nuada Adair all together at once… Damek knew speed was his sole ally. There was a trap here; he was well aware. These Dannans were all celebrated commanders. Not one would leave an open door for him. His eyes roamed the wall from the south end to the river.

Where is it?

"Douglas. I want at least five guards per every officer in our midst. Double that on each of our slings."

"Already done, My King," Douglas assured him from the Corpsmen's line. "I've ten more pikemen in check for your guard as well."

"Good." His officers were on the same page, as always. They could smell a snare as well as he. "When it begins, you know what to do next."

"Yes, My King." Douglas pounded his heart.

Damek inclined his head at Ridley again while watching the gate shudder under a succession of blows. One section of the timber wall had finally caught flame. Whatever wards Una and that Dannan devil had set upon them worked far better than he liked. "Send in another hundred infantry. Archers to the forward line."

Ridley called the order, but Kinney, his foremost legionnaire, stuck his neck out. "Won't we hit our troops?"

Damek shot him a blank, dispassionate glare. "Are you insinuating that our men lack aim, Captain?"

"No, Milord," Kinney paled. "Just figure it stands to reason they'd take some friendly fire."

"It's possible, Captain. But, which man here would rather starve than fight?"

Damek watched his adam's apple bob. "None, My King."

"Then do as I command."

Kinney bowed and gave his men the signal to advance. With hair-raising war cries, the foot soldiers threw themselves at the walls. On the way, many trod over fallen members of the first wave, who'd taken arrows or had been cut in half by a Dannan blade. If they minded, the legionaries didn't show it. They leaped onto the ropes and hauled themselves upward, dodging arrows and stones the whole way. Some did not make it, but a handful did. For several minutes, Damek watched them square off with the defenders on the ramparts, blade to blade. At least half of those who made it up were thrown back down in a trice. In the meantime, the gate groaned beneath its bombardment but did not topple.

"Doubles," he ordered next.

Douglas repeated his command, and the slings were refitted with their backup loads of heavier shot. When the catapults were fired, the iron ball at the center of each burning knot of oil and bracken struck the gate with a resounding thud. The earth beneath their feet shook for each strike. By the third round, the stone lintel cracked under strain. Damek didn't allow himself to smile, though that was his first instinct. The Roswellians had obviously been preparing for that gate to come down for months. Thus he wouldn't write them off to failure just yet.

"Proceed to phase two," he said.

Kinney jerked forward to advance with his men, his squire following with a raised flag depicting a black longbow on a red field. "Yeomen!" he bellowed, his voice louder than a man of his short stature should expect to own. "Forward march!"

❧ ❦

From the river's edge, just east of Damek's middle flank, Robin, Gerrod, Skinny Colm, and a smattering of capable Greenmakers watched the Bethonair mass wind up the Navan Road toward the gate. Behind them, over the river, much of Aes Sidhe burned or smoldered beneath the enchanted mist that had ever obscured its details from Eirean eyes. But that was not their concern now. The Sidhe soldiers Fionn O'More had led further east had more reason to care than the Greenmakers did— and they went about their duty, as had been carefully laid out by their Crown Prince. As for Robin and his lot, their livelihood had already been consumed beyond recognition. The lives of their families, of every man, woman, and child in Rosweal, were on the line.

"We should go now," Gerrod whispered, eager to wet his shiny new axe with Souther blood.

"Not yet." Robin spat a wad of witchroot into the duff, his scarred jaw hard against the flickering backlight. "We wait for the Champion's signal, as agreed."

Gerrod pulled a face. "I don't like it, boss. That Bishop cunt is a lot cannier than we thought. He's got to be expectin' us to make a move. He'd know we left the road clear for a reason."

"So we did, Gerry," griped Robin. We're here to give him what he expects, remember?"

"I know, but—"

"Are you questionin' my orders, boyo?"

Gerrod paled. "No."

"Then shut yer gob and get ready."

Without another word, Gerrod shuffled back into position.

They waited for an eternity, watching the gate take a third critical hit that bent the top planks inward. Then, they heard an unmistakable horn blowing from the southeast, where the bulk of Bishop's forces waited in reserve.

Robin's smile was gruesome in the half-light. "Let's go, lads!"

Like phantoms, they slid up the riverbank and into the trees.

❧ ❦

Damek heard the horn, same as every one of his men, but he barely had time to register surprise at its direction before a screeching mass of soot-blackened men came streaking into his lines from the river. Men with axes, cudgels, daggers, and pikes scattered through his right, rear flank— hacking down light-armored infantry with haphazard ferocity. In the vanguard, the Corpsmens' chargers shied as the road filled with wet, sickly sounds: shouts and the occasional scream.

Murphy, another captain from the Dingle Peninsula, darted forward to place himself between the raiders and his lord, but Damek's hand shot out to halt him.

"Be still. We must give them something to aim at." His composed smile was a flash of white against the firelit sky. He turned back to Ridley, who sat his mount with practiced ease. He returned his lord's lazy, unconcerned grin. "Ridley, you're up."

"My king," Ridley saluted and dismounted with a flourish. He drew his sword, not the typically thin, folded sabres Southers were known to favor. This was a proper two-handed broadsword, a brutal weapon meant to cleave bone and sinew. He stalked to the curve in the road, the southern edge of the remaining forest at his back. When he was about ten paces away from Command, the Roswellians came straight at him with hellish determination for Damek's standard— Ridley cupped a hand over his bearded cheek. "All right, you lazy cunts! Time to quit lyin' down on the job. Second battalion, to *me!*"

From the tangle of remaining trees over his shoulder, well over fifty men emerged from the ground as if they'd sprung from the earth itself.

Damek spared a laugh at the expense of the raiders who'd sped straight into the jaws of a well-laid trap. Experienced, well-blooded swordsmen had been lying under cover for hours, waiting for this moment. He watched as a half-dozen Greenmakers died in the first rush, eyes round with shock. Amused, he turned to nod at the standard-bearer on his left. The lad hoisted a red flag emblazoned with three swords. The call went up, and a path opened for Damek and his cavalry officers. Ridley and his unit closed ranks behind Damek and his chosen knights as they cut sharply south along the treeline. They headed for the horn they hadn't expected to hear so soon.

Damek's honor guard raised their shields high, protecting their king from sharpshooters along the walls. The gate that protected them wouldn't long survive the iron-tipped battering ram his infantry were dragging up the road. But just as Damek and his guards rounded the south-eastern curve of the city wall, an ear-splitting boom shook the ground they'd vacated. The blast bore such strength that it nearly unhorsed him. Correcting course as quickly as they could, his officers locked shields around him again, leading him back to cover at the far end of the southern line. They had almost made it when yet *another* explosion followed the first.

For several moments, all was chaos.

Damek couldn't tell where the sky started nor the earth ended. He tasted blood and soil. His ears throbbed with heat and pain. When the dust cleared, and his equilibrium returned, he could hear the defenders cheering atop the wall… over the screams. Damek rolled upright. He'd barely missed being crushed by his bisected horse.

Holding himself aloft in the blood-soaked mud, he took stock of the situation. Huge, smoking pits had opened a chasm between the damaged but still intact gate and the bulk of his forces racing away from his fallen standard. Those who bore all of their limbs, anyway. His battering ram, catapults, and at least two hundred infantry and their captains lay scattered around the Navan approach in various pieces.

He felt the blood drain from his face.

The raiders had been a feint!

They were meant to discharge explosives buried well before his troops had surrounded the city.

That was why they had left the gate wide open.

He'd been sucked into his own godsdamned strategy!

Arrows struck the ground near his broken mount, and he scrabbled for cover. Not having a bloody clue who was left alive among his officers, he cried, "Sound the retreat!"

Someone dragged him to his feet, only to take an arrow through the throat and topple forward into the mud. Damek lost his footing again. Another lethal missile sailed past his cheek, taking half his left ear. A junior Corpsman, Forsey, flung a shield over Damek's head and half-ran, half-slithered with him to cover, taking arrows the whole way. They trod over the pieces of so many men and horses that Damek couldn't begin to guess how many of his Corps and infantry had just been blown to bits in the killing field.

"Orders, milord?" Mouthed Kinney as if from a great distance.

Damek was glad to see him alive.

"To O'Reardan! To the rear!" he rasped, waiting only to hear his command being reissued before he let himself be shoved into a waiting saddle.

HAVING MADE IT TO THE safety of his rear lines— the majority of which straddled either side of the Taran High Road for ten miles— he was just in time to watch another explosion rip through his reserve infantry: some three hundred men-at-arms, two of his trebuchets, and several of his supply weapons. Men and material launched into the air only to return to the earth in misshapen pieces. Another line of archers on standby and the lead cavalry in Martin's rearguard took the brunt of the falling debris. The soldiers who weren't flattened by flaming hunks of metal or showered with human gore scattered. Those few infantrymen who weren't blasted to the Hells with their comrades wandered about bloodied and dazed or fled for cover in the southern treeline. The scene was utter chaos. With an angry, frustrated growl, Damek spurred his mount for the remnants of Martin's center.

Be alive, godsdammit!

About ten paces from the smashed phalanx of officers at the center, Damek caught sight of a flurry of silver and white cuirasses, dealing death in every direction. He didn't need to issue an order; someone in his surviving honor guard had blown the cavalry horn, drawing every knight left in his vanguard to heel. Groaning in pain, Damek kicked his charger harder this time, drawing his sabre.

The Dannans were nothing if not efficient, disciplined, and calm in the face of his advancing cavalry. He was so intent on getting to Martin's side that he didn't see the next danger until it was too late. Several pale shapes gathered at the edges of his vision. Too slowly, he turned to watch in useless alarm as these newcomers queued up, knelt, and drew their arms back over their massive longbows.

Oh, fuck!

A volley of arrows sailed directly into his flanks.

In the lead and moving fastest, Damek was the first to come down.

The Skysinger

Una's Spark surged the moment she stepped through the Veil. Its violence sucked the air from her lungs, dropping her to her knees. This was something new. Her first breath in the Otherworld drew white-hot lightning to her core. The blood in her veins seemed to freeze, thaw, then reorder its flow. Her ears popped, and her eyes cleared. Even in the unending rose-hued gloaming, her vision came into sharpest focus, as if she'd been wandering blind and hampered through the fog for her entire life. She felt a current track through her cells, overwhelming and so painful it was almost pleasurable. For a moment that spanned an eternity, she trembled in the soft, blue-bladed grass, trying to will her lungs back to working order. Goose flesh tracked up her arms. A cold sweat trickled down her spine.

… come home, Lady, the Sluagh whispered in her mind. She shivered so hard that her teeth clacked together. She rolled over onto her back, huffing at the dizzy sky.

What is happening to me?

"Una?" Diarmid asked from somewhere nearby. The world spun around the edges. The next thing she knew, she was on all fours, retching into the soft loam. When her stomach was finally empty of all but bile, she bit her lip and turned her face away in shame.

Will you piss yourself next?

Diarmid's hair spilled over her collarbone as he leaned over her, cool fingers tracing her brow. "Tell me."

She opened her mouth but had to wait for her tongue and throat to recall how to form words. His nearness made her bones quake with queasy fear. Confused and terrified, she reached for him. Without a word, he pulled her to him, stroking giant circles into her back like a patient grandfather. Her helpless tears soaked his collar. "What haven't you told me?" he asked.

"I feel… different," her voice sounded alien to her ears.

"Your Siorai markings are gone."

"What?" She struggled upright to stare at her naked palms. But for the barest hint of an intangible sheen, her skin was as bare as a newborn. Mystified, she tore at the lacings of her tunic, searching for the blue dragons winding over her breastbone. They, too, were conspicuously absent, as were the wards etched over her shoulders, forearms, and legs. When she finished her fruitless examination, her frantic sobs rent the peace of their small clearing like a series of alarm bells. Diarmid folded her against him once more, as one might a startled pet. She had never been more frightened in her life.

… sssucch sights to show you…

"Hush now," he crooned. "You're all right."

The molten current at her core leaped at his voice.

Jumping, she buried her face in her hands. "I d-don't know."

"Every time you come here, it gets stronger, doesn't it? The pull."

Elation and fear braided through her taut nerves. She bit her lip until it bled and bobbed a response.

He pulled away to smooth the tears from her cheeks.

"I can feel it," he said softly. "The Oiche Ar Fad quakes within you."

"Feel what?"

He smiled that sad, enigmatic smile. "Whatever you took from me on Samhain… it is growing inside you like a seed. When it fully blooms, I wonder what you will be?"

"What is that supposed to mean?"

"You're changing, Una. *Becoming*."

A frigid spear of dread caught her in the throat. "Becoming what?"

The wind teased at the curls at her nape and then over her cheeks like a kiss. She brushed a stray lock away, only to realize that her hand hadn't moved an inch until after she'd done it. Shock replaced fear, and she stumbled to her feet, bombarded by surging vitality and quickening perception. A riot of color and sound accosted her senses, imparting jubilation, comfort, and terror. Her heart hammered against ribs that warmed from the inside, like stones around a hearth. Her scalp tingled, and her teeth ached. She again examined her glowing, unmarked skin, feeling a pang for the loss.

Her tattoos had been earned, as her aunt Eva's had been. They *meant* something. For every floor she had climbed in the Cloister, for every Ordeal, her skin had kept the record. Now they were gone. The Siorai, too, were all but gone. Her life as it had once been. All of it… *gone*. Tairngare was irreparably changed. Her family shattered. Her father was dead.

She was being erased.

"Remade," Diarmid corrected.

"Stay out of my head."

"Apologies."

Wrapping her arms around herself, she shot him a look. "That almost sounded sincere."

A flicker of a smile. "That is how it shall be between us."

"There is nothing between us."

He gave a subtle shrug. "There is." He gestured at the swirling clouds above.

Swallowing, she looked away. "I don't know what's happening, but I feel…" the words eluded her.

"Take your time."

Every moment she stood in that clearing, gathering her thoughts, she felt more and more at one with everything around her. The rush of the river beside them, pure and impossibly clear as it could never be in her realm— glittered in the half-light, making music she could never describe. The air tasted sweet but smelt of wet slate, blooming wildflowers, and damp pine— and many more sensations far outside her experience. Even the grass beneath her booted feet thrummed with charge.

That rhythm seemed to say *home, home, home*.

Her eyes drifted closed, and she reached out with her Spark. The answering current nearly doubled her over again. There was so much, too much, to take in… yet flood through her every fiber, it did. Could she hear her pulse echo from the trees and her breath on the wind? The power building inside her was too massive for one body to contain, yet hers did.

"It feels like… I can do anything."

Diarmid walked in a slow circle around her while she stood there, hugging herself in rapturous fear. "Show me."

Of a sudden, they knelt at the river's edge together. Una took one of her hands in his and pushed it below the crisp, bubbling surface. The water was deliciously cool. "What do you see?"

She opened her eyes, expecting to find her reflection staring back at her. Instead, an afterimage of the world above flickered beneath her gaze, as the cities had when they passed them on their way to Rosweal. In the reflection, the Greensward behind her burned— a blaze so bright and fierce that it hurt to look. She could feel the flares, smell the smoke, hear the snapping limbs and cracking timber. Tears welling, she glanced over at him. "I don't know what to do."

"Can you feel the heat?"

Her cheek felt like it might blister sitting so near that reflection. "Yes."

"Smell the charred wood, taste the ashes?"

"Yes. Can't you?"

"Of course, but you shouldn't." He leaned his chin against his knuckles, a shrewd calculation behind his impassive features. "When you called me, what was it? A 'manipulator' at Tech Duinn— that was no insult, was it?"

She flinched inwardly. "Ah, no. It's how we describe our gifts in the Cloister. A girl born with the Spark, or the ability to 'manipulate' particles at will. Not every girl is born with Spark enough to change the basic composition of an object. Still, some, usually girls from the oldest families, can rearrange those particles to alter that object entirely. We call these girls 'Manipulators'. Only..." she wasn't sure if she should share so much of this with an outsider, especially the King of the Underworld.

"'Only' what? You may speak to me about anything, Una."

"Males are never born with that much Spark, and none I have ever heard of achieved the status of a true Manipulator."

"Ah," he said, reclining away from her. "'Never' is an odd word that rarely holds any meaning. For instance, my instinct tells me you— a female of Milesian heritage and a mortal to boot— hold gifts only Skysingers like myself should possess. Isn't that funny?"

Her brows drew close. "I don't know what you mean... what's a Skysinger? Is that also a sort of Manipulator?"

He laughed. "Well, if I'm forced to answer in simplistic terms, yes. In a way. A Skysinger is a born Brehon— a person who can channel the gods' power or command elemental spirits. In the Old World, Brehons would commune with whichever spirits they were attuned to. Some held an affinity for earth and wood spirits, some water, some the flames that kindle or consume all life. A select few held sway over the spirits of the air, rain, wind, ice, and more. Skysingers are stormbringers." He paused, his lip quirking sardonically. "I was born a Skysinger, was venerated by my tribe long before the birth of the Oiche Ar Fad, many thousands of years before the Transition."

She knew the Sidhe were very long-lived, but this man... Kaer Yin's vindictive, flirtatious, mendacious uncle was *ancient*. Before she knew her mouth had opened, she asked, "How do you stand it?"

The briefest flash of a bottomless sadness crossed his face, and she felt something akin to empathy for him for the first time. How could anyone stand to live so long? She would never know, thank Siora. As swiftly as the emotion crossed his expression, it was gone. "All boring tales are best told over mead, my dear. As we have none, I think it prudent for you to tell me how you knew you could help me quench the Greensward."

She considered him in silence for a time. She had volunteered, and if they didn't try something soon, Aes Sidhe would burn to cinders while everyone she cared for risked their lives. They didn't have time for mistrust and prevarication. Rosweal needed them— him, more than anyone.

"The cost."

He stilled. "What's that?"

"All magic— Manipulation— bears a cost. We've briefly discussed this before in your keep. For Siorai, it's the Spark-drag; that's our First Law. Once massive energy has been expunged, it must be replenished."

"And?"

"And I don't know how or why I know— but I can feel it. There's this void... perhaps that's the wrong word? This *well* of energy at my core. Like my Spark is replenishing itself from the air around me in this place. The farther I reach inside myself, the deeper that pool gets."

He stared at her as if what she was telling him was as absurd as it was to her. "You mean to say that's how you healed me before by giving me some of this Spark?"

"Exactly. That's the Ninth Law and forbidden... but I knew I could do it."

"How?"

She shrugged. "Because I've done it many times, in reverse, in Eire. If I can take energy when my Spark is limited, I could surely give some back when it's boundless."

"*Boundless.*" He made a sort of half snort, half-strangled whimper. He scrubbed his face with the fingers of his right hand. "Una, do you know who I am?"

"The King of Tech Duinn."

"No. I *am* Tech Duinn. My father's blood was the price paid to create this realm for his kin, and that same blood ensures its stability. Do you understand?"

"No."

He gestured at the clearing around them. "I am what remains of his blood, my brothers and I. We keep the realms together but separate; without us, both would either fade to nothing or be ripped apart by eternity. Innisfail is kept warm and hale despite the ice threatening to swallow her whole. Even now, the blood in our veins heats the currents surrounding this continent, fills the earth with black, rich soil, and blankets her reaches with game and vegetation. If even one of us were somehow eliminated from this precarious equation, the entire system would collapse. This magic, the Dagda's sacrifice, is the engine that powers the world as you know it. Without the Tuatha De Dannan, Innisfail would be a barren tundra choked with ghosts and human scars."

"Why are you telling me this?" In her mind's eye, she could almost see the white hellscape he spoke of. Nothing alive for hundreds and hundreds of miles in any direction— just sparkling white death blown about by a merciless northern wind.

Ice age, her education whispered.

The earth as it was before man took over—an empire of ice and death.

"Yes," Diarmid said. "As it will be again if the Sidhe should leave these shores."

She struggled to piece that together. "That can't be true."

"It *is* true. Your ancestors destroyed what they stole from us those many eons ago at Magh Tuiradh— raped every corner of this world too, from the deepest ocean floors to the highest peaks, until there was nothing left in the soil to sustain them. Rivers ran dry. Every creature, great and small, save those kept for livestock, dead or dying. Seas near to boiling in the southern reaches and clogged with refuse. Cities choked with toxic fumes and pestilence, born aloft by teeming hordes of mortals without function or purpose, all clamoring to subsist on chemicals and technology— none aware that they had died long before the Transition. They didn't understand that men can't multiply in a poisoned mire, though try they did. For hundreds of years, your people existed this way, taking, scraping, consuming everything in sight.

"Eventually, their world collapsed as it was always going to. Millions perished in the first few seasons. The seas slowed, became toxic, and rose so high they gulped your cities down like sweet succor. Men used to believe their world would end in fire, the whip-crack tongue of some celestial serpent. Instead, it ended slowly, painfully with the unceasing wash of stinking, venomous water." He shook his head. "My brother couldn't ignore the suffering, though I wish he had. When Midhir returned to Innisfail, the land bloomed anew. Trees sprouted in long-barren lands. Rivers were purged of their foulness, and animals returned to these shores. He took the Milesians in… all who came to beg sanctuary. All of them. How was he repaid for his blessed kindness?"

Una dipped her head, ashamed of a culture she had no control over. "They tried to take it from him."

"Yes," he smiled. "Again. They tried to take what they did not understand, nor deserve, once more. Worthless creatures, mortals. Present company excluded, of course."

She didn't take offense. She was educated enough to understand human failing but compassionate enough to realize that most didn't know any better. "Why have you told me this?"

"So you will know the truth, Una. The Sidhe are what keeps this land, and you all, alive. If we leave, you die. If we retreat into the Oiche Ar Fad once again, you die. If mortals retake the Continent for themselves, they will multiply out of control, consume and destroy until nothing is left. The Sidhe are tied to this land. If we go, you go."

"I don't understand—"

"I've shared this truth to prepare you for the next." He dug his fingers into the iridescent earth beneath his hand. Black soil blossomed in his palm, the color of a beetle's back. "I am the heartbeat of the Otherworld, but even my strength is not limitless as you claim yours to be. If what you say— and what I can feel from you, that 'otherness' I can't explain— is true, you are perhaps more Sidhe than I."

A thousand thoughts and questions tangled in her head. She took a deep breath to clear them, chewing on her tongue. His words wove an invisible question around her kneeling frame, a shimmer of purpose that was alien and familiar as her skin.

Yes, it said, and she turned to catch a glimpse of a small dark girl darting through the trees beyond. Her thick braid caught the wind as she leaped and bounded through the bracken, giggling. Una's heart thudded at the vision.

Siora, she thought.

Yes, the wind repeated.

Una's eyes snapped back to Diarmid, but if he'd seen the girl, he hid it very well.

The trembling along her spine subsided. She closed her fist tight. "I don't know what this means or why it should happen to me, but I know what I feel."

"And what's that?"

I am the spine of the world.

In my blood, you are reborn.

In my heart, you rise.

"Strong," she answered without fear.

"Good," he said, standing. "Show me."

⚜

A MASSIVE BLACK BRUISE GATHERED in the sky to the north, bearing such wind that torrents of smoke and heat were blown into the frigid Boinne valley, extinguishing all but the most stubborn flames over the border. Lightning struck from snow-heavy clouds, the slow, cold grey haze at the mass' center. Thunder rolled over the hills, rattling every stone to its foundation, nearly striking men from their feet. The storm had appeared from nowhere— simultaneously darkening and lightening the sky within its strange, unearthly power. Sheets of thick, wet snow began to fall in heavy white torrents over Aes Sidhe until all that remained for the raging inferno that had raged for hours and stretched miles and miles to the far horizon sizzled out beneath a cloak of cool, clean precipitation.

Rosweal's defenders cheered from the walls, blackened by soot and caked with ash and blood. The storm spun south by southwest, choking the life from the blaze on both sides of the river, and coating semi-scorched rooftops and walls with snow.

In the cellars below *The Hart and Hare*, which Barb set aside for a makeshift hospital— Rian looked up from dressing yet another wound at the gleeful outbursts above. Rose struggled down the stairs with a fresh basket of linens, still wet and stained red, but would have to do.

She was smiling.

"What's that all about?" asked Rian blithely. She was impervious to alarm at this point. Almost fifty men were stacked head-to-toe on makeshift cots, filthy mattresses, and hastily assembled gurneys inside her close, musty little clinic. Still more men, perhaps a hundred give or take, waited in long queues upstairs and up and down the alley outside. Rian only had two hands and one mind to occupy with priorities. She'd been stitching, binding, severing, cauterizing, and sometimes euthanizing those who were beyond hope since the fires began last morning. Nearly two days of nonstop work with no time to rest or eat would eventually exact their toll if she didn't keep moving.

The man Rose came back down with new bandages for was going to lose his leg. There was no saving it. His calf had been partially severed; if he didn't bleed to death within the hour, he would undoubtedly sicken with sepsis and die anyway. There was only one cure Rian knew for such a wound, and it was likely to kill him anyway.

Another lad, no more than twelve, had been designated her assistant by Barb yesterday afternoon— a kitchen lad, by all accounts. Barb's girls called him Strong Tim, though Rian had seen twigs with better musculature. The boy had proved to be worth more than she'd given him credit for. He was serious, stoic, and seemed to own a constitution belonging to a grown man twice his size and experience. He'd already assisted in two amputations and had administered belladonna to those who couldn't be saved. Just then, Strong Tim raised his eyes to hers, expectant. It seemed he knew what was coming without asking. But Rian's attention was on Rose, who set her bundle down with a delighted squeal. "Isn't it wonderful, Rian? Them fires is out!"

Rain blinked. "Inside?"

"That's the best part! *All* the fires, mistress. Both sides o'the river."

Rose's cheeky, beatific grin made Rian scowl. "All? How?"

The Hart's favorite splayed her hands as if to say, 'who knows.' Her once lustrous dark curls were singed and coated with sticky grey ash. Her heart-shaped face was streaked and smudged with sweat and soot. Even wearing a leather smock that had once belonged to the town butcher and had been dipped in countless vats of blood and gore— Rian was easily the cleanest person in the room. "Not that ye'd hear it with all this dirt above our heads, but a loud, ugly, mad beast o'a squall just blew down from the north. Never seen anythin' like it neither. Fair fills the sky, it does."

Rian set one tool down and wiped her brow with a damp elbow. She had no idea what Rose was on about. "A storm? It's raining?"

"Snowing, silly! And already past me knees in places too! Look, my legs are right blue—"

Rian bent back over her patient, who'd thankfully passed out. To Tim, she nodded. "Go get Dabney. I'll need him to help me hold this one down." The boy darted off, but her voice caught him at the landing. "And tell him not to bother whingeing about it this time! I've enough to deal with as it is." While he disappeared, she dipped her finger in charcoal, drew a circle on the man's forehead with her index finger, checked to ensure his tourniquet was as tight as it could be, and then moved on to the next patient. Yet another lad barely twenty. In truth, she wasn't much older, but the fear in the young man's expression made her feel a thousand years his senior. She gently tugged him forward to inspect the seeping hole just beneath his shoulder bone. He yelped, but she ignored him. "Who pulled the arrow out?"

"My mate. Dunno if he did it right."

"He did fair enough, considering you're talking and not bleeding to death on that stack of crates." She prodded the muscles along his back. No tearing, she could spy. "Can you move it?"

"I… I think?"

"Good," Rian said, tearing two stained but clean strips out of the linen sheet Rose handed her and went to work winding it round and round his arm and shoulder.

He looked away, his doughy cheeks a bit grassy.

She finished, tugging his torn tunic back over the wound. "I expect they'll need you on the wall again. You wouldn't want to leave your mates up there pulling your weight, would you?"

He swallowed, knowing his next wound might not be so lucky. "No, mistress."

"Then off with you," she said, turning to the next patient without waiting for him to leave. Triage in wartime was not a pretty nor poetic profession. She didn't have the resources to be merciful, and for every wounded man she could send back up top, two more seemed to take his place. The following three patients served as an example. One had taken a morbid gash to his neck and shoulder and wouldn't last. She drew a black 'X' on his forehead. He was carried away to the rear of the cellar to die. The girls would talk to him and hold his hand long enough, but when he passed, they'd drag him upstairs and line him up with the others.

Rian refused to think about how many were building up out there.

The following patient died before she got to him, and the third just as she reached for him. This was the way it was. They dealt death without thought outside, but she was the one that had to pull it close and hold its black hands. She backed away from the dead man, pressing a shaking hand to her temple.

"Ye should lie down for a bit, Rian," urged Rose gently, shoving a cup of something warm but bland into her palm. "You'll fall face-first into one of these boys, and then where will they be?"

"I can't, Rose. You know that." Rian took a long, grateful sip only to realize the cup held more than a dollop of uishge. She was so tired that she couldn't even taste anything anymore. The sights and smells of her makeshift ward were too monotonous. "Tell me more about that storm, please."

She downed the rest of her cup and followed Rose to the other side of the room, where most of Robin Gramble's raiders lay propped against the far wall. Only a third of the sixty men that had volunteered for the honor had returned. Most were either hacked to death by Lord Bishop's knights as they fled or blown to bits in the explosion— which, thankfully, had dealt a disastrous blow to the Southers' foreword infantry, artillery, and cavalry. The Greenmakers, however, had been caught between the blast and its intended targets and paid dearly for the mistake. They'd been tasked to raid, set the charges, and vanish— but Bishop's men had been waiting for them. They couldn't escape fast enough, so most did not leave the Navan Gate alive.

… those that did…

She found Robin where she'd left him, with his back to the wall, legs stretched out before him. He cradled Gerrod's upper body against his shaking chest. The lad's legs were missing. Rian had applied tourniquets and managed to cauterize much of what remained, but nothing would save him. He'd lost far too much blood. His color and weakened breathing told all. When Robin finally turned, Rian could barely blink off the tears that burned her eyes. He nodded.

"Aye," he choked. "Figured as much." Robin himself had taken a fairly severe slash to his midsection, but he'd refused her every attempt to treat him.

"Oh no, no. Gerry, love," wept Rose, slipping to her knees beside him. She clasped the lad's fingers in hers and sobbed when he tried to give her one of his winks. His weak smile was for Rian, who sank beside them, filling his vision.

He opened his mouth to speak, his expression telling her everything he wished to say. She knew he would never have the chance. She smoothed his cheeks and gave him the best smile she could manage. "That's all right, Gerrod. I know, and I'm here."

This seemed to please him. He settled back against his foster father and stared at her as if he'd burn every curve of her face into his memory. She took one of his hands from Rose and lay beside him, pressing her lips against his cheek. "Tell him about the storm Rose."

As Rose began her tale, Rian whispered in Gerrod's good ear. "You are loved, Gerry. I'll never forget you."

He gave a last sigh and was gone before Rose spoke her first word, but Rian didn't stop her. She tucked herself against Gerrod's body and cried openly. Robin held them both the while.

"Ah, ye should see it, Gerry. The snows are so thick, ye can't catch a glimpse o'yer own nose ahead o'ye, and the fire's all blowed out. Can ye imagine? And what ye boys done— wiped half that bastard's army clean out of mercy, ye have." Her voice caught when Robin closed the lad's eyes. He'd been smiling. "Ye did good, Gerry. Yer ma'am, yer sisters, everyone… we're so proud o'ye."

With an unhealable tear in her soul, Rian pushed herself up to her feet, wiping her streaming eyes. Dabney was suddenly behind her, his arm steady. She didn't see his face but only had to hear his snuffling to know he understood what had happened here.

She took a heaving breath, tucking lovely, bright-eyed, gorgeously good Gerrod Twomey deep within her heart.

That is where he would live now, same as her parents.

She went back to work, moving dutifully from tragedy to another.

❦

Later, though she couldn't be sure when exactly, Rian found Eva upstairs in the alleyway, watching the sky swirl with smoke and dwindling cinders. She leaned against the cold brick wall, smoking rolled witchroot. Without a word, Eva lit and handed Rian one of her own. She had never smoked a day in her life, but she'd try just about anything at this point.

"It'll give you a boost," Eva said, not looking at her.

Rian took it, attempted a small puff, and coughed. After a minute, her lungs warmed from the inside and her head cleared. She tried another.

Eva eyed her sidelong. "Better?"

"I guess so." She scrubbed her eyes with her free hand. "Why aren't you with Ben or Una?"

"I'm more useful here, for now. Your girls mean well, but they are hardly fighters."

Rian empathized. Neither was she. "That's not a good thing, is it?"

Eva didn't answer immediately, but after a beat, she said, "I'm not all-knowing. I can't see everything and certainly can't summon that part of my Spark at will, so you know."

"I gathered… but you know more than you're saying."

Eva gave a humorless laugh. "Too sharp by half, you are."

"So you keep telling me."

"I can't tell you anything you haven't already deduced was a possibility and prepared for."

"Great, thanks so much," sighed Rian. She stubbed the smelly roll of gold tobacco out in the snow. Witchroot was a costly, very odorous habit. Grown in Aes Sidhe by mysterious methods and only traded through the Dalriadan reaches, the golden leaf was scarce and hard to come by. Thus, it was the particularly nasty habit of very wealthy persons… and Barb Dormer, who had her sources. "That is a disgusting habit." She didn't bother to admit that it had made her feel better.

"And so delicious."

"Humph," said Rian.

Rose's voice drifted upstairs, and Rian let out a long breath. She smoothed her apron and flexed her aching fingers. "All right then."

Eva's arm caught her elbow as she prepared to sweep back downstairs, gently spinning her around. Rian couldn't see her face, it was so dark, but she could see the solemn cast to her amber eyes. She passed a small tincture of blue glass with a silver stopper, and Rian took a startled step backward. "That's—"

"You'll know when to use it."

Rian's eyes filled with tears. "How soon?"

Eva gave her fingers an encouraging squeeze. "All is not lost… but it will be a trial unlike any you have known."

"Eva, *when?*"

She looked at the sky again as if lost to things Rian couldn't see. "Be ready."

Nowhere to Run

Kaer Yin met Fionn at the Western tunnel mouth, Tam Lin just behind him. Jan Fir, Niall, Mordu, and Shar trickled through the dank opening— bloodied but breathing. Kaer Yin did a cursory headcount as the Dannans came up into the snow-bright, ash-leaden evening air. He stopped at twenty and frowned. Twenty Sidhe left out of nearly double that number. His throat ran dry. They might be satisfied to have spent that many good men for the decimation they'd just handed the new King of Eire, but the cost was high, regardless. Kaer Yin could only pray Robin and his Greenmakers had fared better.

Fionn, leaning against Shar for support, shoved the taller man away. His chin jerked high at the sight of his crown prince. "We were successful, *Mo Flaith*," he declared proudly, despite the wheeze in his lungs. He looked like he'd been toiling at the bottom of a cauldron all day with his singed hair and blackened face, neck, and hands. Every man, woman, and child in Rosweal was positively caked with ash and soot, and not a single defender along the wall had come away from the battle without their share of burns, cuts, scrapes, or debilitating wounds.

However, these twenty returning Sidhe bore evidence of toil and slaughter that no others could match. Fionn's cloak dripped runnels of blood into the freshly fallen snow.

"*Danu*," exclaimed Tam Lin, whose teeth and eyes were the only humanizing features in his obsidian face. "You look like Donn himself chewed you to bloody bits."

Tam Lin had been fighting fires first over the Ward Gate facing the Quarter with Mel Carra and several others for nearly thirteen hours. Thanks to their resolve and the backbreaking labor of Rosweal's citizens, he'd managed to keep the wall intact and protect the majority of the buildings inside. If it hadn't been for them, there might not have been anything left to defend.

As for Kaer Yin, he'd taken command of the Eastern Wall— as he would again tomorrow when the Southers came in force at the critically damaged Navan Gate. Whatever they had managed to exact from Damek today, he hoped it was enough to make the Southers move on. Failing that minor miracle, having deprived Bishop of so many men and supplies, they'd at least be dealing with a drastically reduced threat. It would be hours before they could sort out the numbers. Lack of sleep, exposure, casualties, and cold took their toll on the city.

They could not keep this up much longer.

"What happened?" he asked Fionn, nodding for Tam Lin to grab his arm before he toppled into the snow face-first. Fionn put up an admirable front, but in the end, Tam Lin's weight won out. To Shar, he said, "Take the others to *The Hart*. Rian's got a half-decent clinic running down in the cellars."

Tam Lin swore under his breath.

With exaggerated slowness, Shar saluted Kaer Yin with a bloodied arm. He was no longer Tam Lin's man, and being sworn to Una meant his next liege lord was Kaer Yin himself. Kaer Yin scowled at both of them. "Today, if you please. None of us has time for this grandstanding."

"*Ard Tiarne*." Shar dipped his head, gathered the wounded Sidhe, and led them away without another word.

Tam Lin watched him go, a hard tick in his jaw. "I hope someone has the sense to see to their own cuts and bruises so that girl can take a rest. She'll work herself blind if someone doesn't stop her."

"I know, but she's right; there's no one else."

Tam Lin looked like he had more to say but patted Fionn's shoulder instead. "You had a time of it, I reckon?"

"We came from the southwest," Fionn answered, spitting out a wad of reddened ash. "As planned, we took them completely unawares. At first, anyway."

"The siege weapons?" asked Tam Lin.

"Destroyed. All but one catapult set too far back in their lines."

Tam Lin clapped his hands together over a ghoulish, macabre grin. "Yes! You bloody beautiful, brilliant bastard. I'd kiss you if it wouldn't knock you over." Fionn's lip quirked at the praise, but his expression was far less enthusiastic.

Kaer Yin scratched his grimy chin. "How many supply trains?"

"Fifteen or more, *Mo Flaith*. But we ran out of powder halfway through and were forced to call our secondary unit from cover to get us out." He paused on a sigh. "We cut through their reserve infantry who awaited orders at the Taran approach. Our archers marched out of the trees to give cover. That was when Bishop and a large cavalry contingent returned from the vanguard."

"Damn it to the seven hells," grumbled Tam Lin. Like everyone, he hoped Bishop would have met his end in the first or second explosions at the Navan Gate, but Kaer Yin had known it wouldn't be so simple. Things rarely work out as one might wish. He'd been on the Eastern Wall and had watched Bishop survive each blast and ride for his rear. Kaer Yin was disappointed, but he couldn't say he was surprised.

"Diel, my lieutenant, directed his bowman to fire at their mounts. That bought us a little time, but that man—" he bit back a slur. "I believe he must have been born under Balor's star, the luck that creature has. It began snowing heavily before Diel's archers emerged to give cover. Maybe four or five minutes of near blinding snow— and Bishop dodged every arrow, driving his horse into a snowbank. His officers rallied around their lord and dragged him to cover under locked shields."

"I don't suppose his horse happened to roll over him in the process, maybe crush his legs or his blasted skull?" Tam Lin groused, annoyed that luck had not been a factor today.

Fionn shook his head. "Once they were out range, he got back up, urging his cavalry to give chase. That large, scarred fellow he keeps at his side gave me this personally." He pried his hand away from his right side, revealing a vicious wound that might have ended a mortal man. "I beg your pardon for not killing him on the spot, *Ard Tiarne*, but I will correct the error tomorrow… I vow it."

"No." Kaer Yin squinted at the whitewashed horizon, thinking about the next stage of his plan. They'd weakened Bishop today, sure, but he would regroup and refocus in the morning. They'd lost so many men in this attempt that Rosweal might not have enough defenders left to man the walls come another day like this. One day, maybe… two, definitely not. He needed another plan. "I'll need you handling the Navan Gate first thing tomorrow, Fionn."

His jade green eyes flashed. "I owe that bastard now, Kaer Yin. Those are my men out there in the snow."

"Yes, and there are many more of your men in *here*. I think I'll visit our Lord Souther myself this evening, and I can trust no one else to defend our people as you can, Fionn. Do you accept this responsibility?"

Fionn mulled that over in silence for a while. "You would raid his camp?"

"I would murder that blight in his bed if the Gods are kind."

"*Yes*," hissed Tam Lin with an eager grin. "By Herne, I volunteer."

Fionn nodded. He knew well what another twenty-four hours of siege would cost them. Fionn O'More was the greatest commander in the Ard Ri's legion for a reason. "I will do as you ask, *Ard Tiarne*."

"Thank you, My Lord. If we fail, we proceed to stage three, as planned."

"Understood." Fionn saluted.

"Jan Fir?" Kaer Yin craned his neck to acknowledge the Scotian regent. "Will you escort Lord O'More to mistress Rian and get yourself seen to while you're at it?"

Jan Fir sported a few nasty cuts that would take a while to heal, even for a Sidhe of his age and pedigree. Kaer Yin's brother-in-law offered Fionn a shoulder but paused to give him a serious look. "Mordu and I go with you."

"My sister won't like it."

Jan smirked. "Who's going to tell her?"

"Not me; I like my fingers, thank you," muttered Tam Lin.

"Meet us here at dusk," Kaer Yin told him and crossed his arms while he and Fionn took their leave. "Let's get to it?"

Tam Lin followed him through the Southern yard, with its rows of burned-out ramshackles and free-standing walls that had once belonged to buildings that had been excavated for stones. Up the ladder to the wall, then another toward the south-facing rampart. The snow still fell in heavy, wet sheets, covering the valley with an increasingly grey coating. Charred trees in every direction, but their immediate east popped and cracked beneath its weight, releasing little puffs of steam. All around the walls, the devastation was plain. Men and horses lay in haphazard puddles of gore, now slick and sparkling with frost. Successive blasts had opened several pits along the eastern ridge, punctuated by corpses and splintered trees. The arrow blinds Barb had worked so hard to install between the city and the killing field were toppled or reduced to piles of smoldering ash. There was nothing between Damek's advance forces and Rosweal now, save uneven ground and ghosts.

"How many do you think we cost him today, Yin?"

Kaer Yin exhaled slowly. "Not enough. A thousand?"

"Mostly officers and heavy cavalry, though."

"Yes, and good for us, but if he keeps his head, we've already lost."

Tam Lin absorbed that with a stiff lip. "We have to take him tonight or evacuate the city tomorrow."

"Agreed."

His cousin sighed, leaning over the railing. "He'll take the gate by midmorning tomorrow at the latest and overrun the city by the afternoon."

"Yes."

"Unless we kill him first."

Kaer Yin narrowed his eyes at the blast pits. "Even if we don't."

"What do you mean?"

He reached into his ruined tunic for his bone-flask, which he passed to Tam Lin first, then took a long-deep pull, smacked his chapped lips, and slipped it back into his pocket. "I say we give him what he wants."

Tam Lin didn't need further explanation. They knew each other very well. "Thought that was the last resort?"

"Your Da isn't going to make it in time, Lin."

He considered that with a wince. "The headwoman is going to scratch your eyes out."

Kaer Yin made a face. "Someone else gets to tell her."

"Fuck, not me. I don't know why you surround yourself with so many harpies."

"Yes, you do," laughed Kaer Yin. "Go get some food and ale into you. I'll need you at your sharpest tonight, Prince O'Ruiadh."

"Who drinks ale anymore?" Tam Lin toasted him with his flask of rotgut uishge. He glanced at the storm above. "She did this, you think?"

"Yes. I have no idea how."

"Diarmid will fight for her."

Kaer Yin snorted. "I was worried, but now I'm not."

"Why's that?"

Kaer Yin pointed at the blinding center of the maelstrom. "Diarmid might have been able to do this alone, but I doubt it. She's something else… something he fears."

"Even more reason to be wary, Yin."

"I'll cross that river when it's time. For now, we have a red carpet to roll out."

Tam Lin's answering smirk was knife-slash against the ghoulish streaks crisscrossing his face. "Should we set our wagers now or later?"

Kaer Yin's expression burned cold. "If Donn loves me, I alone will bear the honor."

Una awoke on the riverbank, lying in a warm bed of heather and clover. The clearing smelled of fresh snow, even if the air was warm and sweet as a summer's evening. Blinking up at the rosy half-light, she knew she was still in the Oiche Ar Fad but had no idea what had happened when Diarmid grasped her hands. Had they done it? Was Rosweal safe from the flames? Yawning, she sat up and looked around. There was no sign of him. Groggily, she rubbed at her eyes with the heel of her palms. She hadn't slept so well in ages! A languid, fulfilled sense of peace pervaded her thoughts. Slowly, lazily, she looked around for Diarmid, a pleasant smile on her face. "Diarmid?" she called out but heard no response but the breeze rustling through the leaves overhead and the lapping of water against the shore.

Una stopped, blinking away the cobwebs.

Where was she?

The copse beside the river was long gone. Instead, she stood beside a mist-shrouded lake surrounded by low hills, tall, elegant rowans, and birch trees. Now aware if unfazed by the change in scenery, she strolled along the water's edge, hoping she might find Diarmid somewhere nearby. Perhaps he, too, had fallen into a blissful repose? What was it they'd been doing?

She struggled to recall.

Birds chirped from their boughs, beautiful, jeweled plumage flashing colors she couldn't name. Delighted, she watched them launch into the violet-tinted gloaming, singing merry tunes she found herself humming. Before she realized it, she'd walked a fair distance. The sand behind her bore her meandering, rhythmless footsteps. Feeling a little drunk, she giggled.

How silly! She'd been turning herself round and round.

"Diarmid?" she laughed into the forest.

Where was he? Did he leave her to enjoy herself while he went to do whatever he had to do? What was it again?

She couldn't recall.

A silver and sable doe drank from the lake around the nearest bend. The water's mirror-like surface cast a haunting glow around her reflection, making Una gasp. Had she ever seen such a magnificent creature before? The doe's dappled white ear tilted toward her, but she did not rise, as if a woman in torn tunic and muddied trousers, with wild hair and a dazed look, was the least exciting thing around her.

Una had no idea how long she stood and stared at the graceful creature before it finally bounded away from the lake, but before she realized it, the darker evening slid in from the west— stretching long, cool shadows between the trees.

They reached for her like fingertips.

I have ssssuch ssssights to ssshow...

She started.

Suddenly, a frigid blast of wind blew over the lake, striking her full in the face. Everywhere the wind disturbed, heavy, blinding snow followed. Reams of blue ice raced over the lake toward her, and her hair blew back, dripping with frost. She threw up her arms to protect her eyes but staggered backward in the surge. The trees behind her groaned under the white assault, bending under the weight of winter's sudden wrath. Half-stumbling, half crawling, she dragged herself out of the wind to hide behind a copse of sturdy rowans. Breathing hard, she wiped at her eyes, her head clearing.

What in Siora's name are you doing here?

She cast her gaze around the forest, noting the swiftly darkening sky peeking through the tree boughs above. Whispers danced through the snow and ice, echoing from tree to tree. Menace as cold as starlight crept over the tiny, damp hairs at her nape. Full awareness of her situation dawned over the next few breaths. She was on the wrong side of the sun in the Oiche Ar Fad. Panic gripped her heart like a talon. Not even the blistering change in temperature could penetrate this veil of fear.

What do I do?

What do I do?

The first pair of glowing yellow eyes appeared twenty paces ahead of her. Frantically, she clawed at her collar to locate the quartz stone around her neck. Finding nothing, she froze.

The *ogham* stone Diarmid had given her was gone.

A low, rumbling growl rattled the bone-white leaves opposite. Una had no time. She got up and ran through freezing bracken, bramble, and fern toward the east, where the sun still shone.

Something silent but swift followed.

⚕

"YER BLOODY MAD!" BARB SHOOK her finger at Kaer Yin, spilling uishge over his boots. He grunted and shoved her hand away, but that didn't staunch her tirade. "Why'm I workin' so damned hard to defend the place if yer just gonna blow it to the hells anyway?"

They stood together on the western rampart facing the north wall. The snow still poured from the sky in a steady cadence, concealing much of the day's atrocities, save for the black husks of mighty trees from one horizon to the other. Thankfully, no such flame would stand such a chance again, as the valley was pregnant with damp and spin-cracking cold. Barb's heavy sealskin cloak was coated white, but her deep, fur-lined cowl did little to conceal her angry scowl. Kaer Yin, having taken the time to change into something warmer, wore a gray cloak and tunic of a similar fashion, only lighter and better suited to the sword strapped once more to his side. For a raid like this, he needed every blade available and thus was forced to eschew Nemain's back-mounting sheath. Instead, his lark handles protruded from a hidden fold behind his cowl, which would allow him to draw without uncovering his face.

Beneath this, a plain white cuirass fitted over a pale grey tunic and leggings, bound tightly together with wool and greaves of white leather. The vambraces at his shins and forearms were pure sylvan steel. Every Sidhe in his entourage would be dressed the same.

In the dark, they would appear as wraiths to the untrained eye—vapors in a snowdrift. "Barb," he said. "We could wait until they do it for us or take the initiative. I think I prefer the latter."

She sneered up at him, stomping down the rampart in a huff. "Feck's sake, Ben! We've lost more n'enough as it is, damn ye. Ye want more still?"

He crossed his arms. "I'm not asking, so you know."

She opened and closed her mouth like a fish.

He sniffed, ignoring her discomfiture. "Besides, you stand to lose yet more the longer we delay. What's left but boys too young to fight, women who can't fight, and old men who might die climbing the stairs? I mean, what choice do we have? Tomorrow will be worse."

"Yer Sidhe mates—"

"Have *died* defending you and yours. They will do so as long as I command them to, but their loss won't save you, and you know it."

She stopped, cursing. "We can hold out a few more days."

"To what end? He's got the numbers. He's going to win."

"Ye don't believe that."

"Knowing when to retreat is a commander's duty. I'm more concerned about saving as many of your lives as possible than Bishop claiming this territory temporarily. You know we'll never let him keep it. He knows that too."

Her jaw softened. She set a mittened hand on his elbow as a mother might do. "I've never heard ye give up like this, Ben. Rosweal's yer home too."

"Yes, and it can be rebuilt. The lives it houses cannot."

Sensing she had no other cards to play, she dug through her cloak to find her bone-handled pipe. Dabney struck a match for her. She took several silent puffs before she nodded at Kaer Yin. "Yer right."

Kaer Yin slapped a hand against his heart. "Why, Barb Dormer, did I hear that right?"

"Ach, stop. It's not the first time I've admitted ye had the right o'things."

Yes, it bloody well was, but he wouldn't press the point.

"Rosweal is done, and may it be his tomb."

She picked a stray speck of witchroot from her tongue and bobbed her head. "What do ye want me to do?"

"You know."

"*All* of it? Can't we just—"

"All of it, Barb. Every last barrel."

Grumbling to herself, she scanned the horizon and sucked at her pipe. Finally, as if accepting a loss she couldn't quantify, she wiped a tear away with her sleeve and squared her shoulders. "Get to it then." She turned to leave but paused at the top of the ladder. "I'd better have me own palace when this is all over, Ben, with a pond and fountain full o'the finest uishge."

He laughed; the sound bore more irony than mirth. "If we pull this off, I'll erect a statue to you right here and toast your deeds every Imbolg."

"Bloody right ye will."

⚊

WELL PAST MIDNIGHT, WHEN ALL the preparations in the Eastern End were finished, Kaer Yin, Robin, Tam Lin, Skinny Colm, Shar Lianor, Jan Fir, and about twelve other Dannans gathered at the Western tunnel mouth. Another twenty Sidhe bowmen approached from the alleyway behind. Kaer Yin nodded at Robin, who he'd been glad to learn had come through the raid earlier that morning with only a few scratches. He looked around. "Where's Gerry?" he asked, expecting to see the scrawny lad sharpening his knives. "This is just his sort of game."

Robin didn't smile back.

He glanced away, a tick in his jaw.

Kaer Yin's grin flickered. "Robin?"

Robin shook himself, tugging a half-hearted shrug out of his shoulders. "Restin', he is. I expect he's doin' better than we are now, freezin' our bollocks off out here."

A jolt of concern speared through Kaer Yin's middle. "Is he… is it serious?"

"Nah." Robin waved him off. "Don't worry. Mistress Rian gave him one o'her drams, and he drifted right off. He's sleepin' soundly now."

Kaer Yin let out a long breath, reassured. "Thank Danu for that. Are your men ready then?"

"Eager, ye might say," Robin growled.

"Excellent." Kaer Yin turned to Tam Lin, who passed around a bowl full of ash for the men to douse themselves. He'd scrubbed his face clean of soot and donned a clean grey tunic like Kaer Yin. They'd be tough to spot in the snow without anything dark to distinguish them. "All right, bows forward. We split up at the fork, where you'll head east. Stay out of sight no matter what happens to us— no exceptions!"

"*Ard Tiarne*," the archers chimed, saluting.

610

"Their officers aren't roughing it in the cold with the men. From Fionn's scouts, we know Bishop and his top brass have taken over a farmstead halfway between Rosweal and Vale, approximately two and a half miles from his front line. They'll be expecting a raid on their remaining supply trains and will have doubled the guards standing at ready."

Kaer Yin sent his silver gaze around to every ashen face.

"Bishop is in the house with his two top captains— O'Rearden and that bastard Ridley."

Robin bared his teeth at the name.

Kaer Yin shot him a pointed look. "Not yet, Robin. If he's the first out, he's yours. If he lingers to guard his Lord Marshal, you'll leave him. Understood?"

Robin spat. "Don't like it, but I hear ye."

"We're out for the barn, where the other officers spend a nice, warm night by the fire. They won't expect a raid on the brass, so we'll have the element of surprise— but not for long. We have minutes to get in and get out. Make them count."

Tam Lin stepped forward, sweeping a lark pommel around. "Here's the most important part. We're in, and we're out, no dallying. I'll personally hamstring any fool who thinks to make a hero of himself. Am I understood?"

A bevy of 'ayes' went round.

"Good, because I haven't had much fun in the past two days. Spoil it for me now at your peril."

The raiders snickered back.

"One last thing, and this is crucial," Kaer Yin added, noticing a familiar face materialize from the shadows ahead. "We're in as a unit and out as one. From the west to the east and back up the Navan High Road— make sure you're seen heading in that direction. We don't want Bishop to miss the opportunity to chase, do we?"

"Hells no!" Roared Robin with the others as they pounded their cuirasses in unison.

"We are ghosts—"

Thump.

"We are blades in the dark—"

Thump.

"We feel no pain, no cold, no fear—"

"*Is muid an ghaoth*[23]—"

Thump.

"*Rianta báis inár ndiaidh*[24]!"

As one, the raiders bellowed their enthusiasm, then followed Tam Lin into the ancient, stinking sewer mouth. Kaer Yin lingered, allowing Diarmid to emerge into the unnaturally bright night. He didn't look happy.

"Where's Una?"

Diarmid cursed, "She's not returned?"

Kaer Yin felt the blood drain from his throat. "What do you mean?"

Diarmid gathered himself and set a hand on Kaer Yin's shoulder. "I will find her, I vow it."

"What happened, Diarmid?" Kaer Yin lunged, dragging his uncle's head down to snarl in his ear. "Where did you leave her?"

"I didn't leave her anywhere. One moment she was there with me— such power, Yin— I have never felt." His expression went almost slack with shock. "I didn't call this storm. Somehow she tapped into my power and ripped it out of me like a thread she could unwind. I can't... in all my years..." his voice trailed off, awestruck and horrified.

Kaer Yin wrapped his long fingers around Diarmid's throat, showing him against the iron grate behind him. He didn't struggle. "What have you done with her, gods damn you?"

---

[23] 'We are the wind.'
[24] 'Death trails in our wake.'

"As soon as the sky darkened and the clouds descended, she simply wasn't there beside me any longer. I don't know what magic could have managed such a thing." His jaw set. "I will find her, Kaer Yin."

Kaer Yin backed away from a sudden thought. "Una's in the Oiche Ar Fad? Alone?"

"That's what I'm trying to tell you. I don't think it matters if she's alone or not. The girl is… she's a Skysinger… I don't know how. Even *I* don't hold the power she doesn't realize she has."

Kaer Yin had no clue what Diarmid was on about. He only understood that the woman he loved was in the most dangerous place in all the realms, alone, and likely hunted for the mortal blood in her veins. She would die there, he knew. "I'm going. Catch up to Tam Lin and tell him to stay the course."

Diarmid caught his arm. "No! I'm telling you, she's strong there— impossibly so! Never mind the details. I doubt any harm *could* come to her. You don't understand Yin."

Kaer Yin shoved his arm away. "Your doubts are no comfort to me, Diarmid. If anything happens to her—"

"It won't. I swear it by Nuada's Star, I will find her."

Heart racing, Kaer Yin considered him for several breaths. There were too many lives depending upon his plans tonight for him to leave and too many emotions tugging him in the opposite direction.

"Go. I only came to you to rule out the possibility that Una would return alone. There is nowhere in my realm that I can't find her. I'll bring her back."

"Damn you, Diarmid," Kaer Yin's voice had gone dangerously low. "If you don't, I'll nail your head over the mouth of Bri Reis with my own two hands."

❧ ❧

AS MUCH AS IT PAINED him, he didn't have time to worry about Una. His instinct was to let Robin and Tam Lin take the lead and dash off into the Otherworld to find her himself, but he couldn't, and he knew it. There were hundreds of lives, mostly women, children, and old people, depending on him tonight. If he faltered now— no matter how just the cause— many, if not all, could die tomorrow. He had to trust Diarmid to keep his word. More than that, he had to have faith in Una to save herself.

There was no other way.

He didn't even have the introspective luxury to ponder the meaning of Diarmid's cryptic claims about her.

A Skysinger? Una? That was impossible. No mortal ever born could boast of such. Although, if any Milesian woman were capable of it… she *would* be the exception. Kaer Yin must trust her. He *did* trust her. Una was the strongest woman he'd ever met. If anyone could do it, she could. Kaer Yin sent every prayer he could think of to Danu, in her wisdom, to make it so.

Tam Lin was the first to mark the determined white line Kaer Yin's teeth made as he emerged from the dank, narrow tunnel mouth into the frigid wastes of the western Greensward. "What is it? He steal your girl after all?"

"Worse. He lost her."

Tam Lin's eyes flared. "You can't be serious? In the—"

"Yes."

"Ah, Yin. I'm sorry." Tam Lin had the grace to own his careless words. He scratched at his ash-coated cheek. "The old man can spot a flea on a mare's arse from a thousand leagues in the Oiche Ar Fad. Try not to worry."

Kaer Yin felt Robin's hand clasp his shoulder. "Frankly, Ben, that woman scares the shite outta me. I say that with all the respect I have in my black heart. She'll be fine. Believe it."

He did.

He *must*.

He cleared his throat. "Now then. Who's ready to pay these Souther cunts back for the past twenty-four hours?"

In the snowlit, pre-dawn darkness, several more pairs of white teeth sparked ghostly white in answer.

THE BETTER MAN

In the wee hours of the morning, the farm was as still as a pond. The officers quartered in the oversized barn were quiet at last— worn out from a frenzied night of mourning and drink. Damek couldn't sleep, not that he slept much these days. He was marshaling the conquest of the North— a feat that required every ounce of energy, strategy, and endurance he could muster.

He'd lost over seven hundred men today.

Good men.

Solid, earnest Southers— *his* men.

For someone who rarely made such mistakes, he was highly disappointed in himself for the only one that mattered. He'd ignored his own advice and underestimated the Roswellians for the second bloody time. It had cost him, dear. Four catapults, three trebuchets, an entire supply train (that must now be replenished in winter, a feat about as likely as finding gold buried in the snow) consisting of nearly a dozen wagons full of food, tack and rigging, weapons, and necessary oddments. At least a hundred and fifty men who'd clambered over the wall would never return, and another three hundred blasted to bits in the explosion beneath the Eastern Wall. He lost fifty more on the Navan Road to raiders and a hundred or more in the raid on his supplies. Not to mention the two dozen warhorses he's sacrificed in his charge at the raiding party and the inconvenient hitch he'd acquired in his stride from his charger spilling into a frozen gulley beside the road. If it hadn't been for the deep, unnatural snow that had yet to cease squalling, he'd have broken his godsdamned neck. The loss of his second favorite horse, notwithstanding.

He had expected raids and guerilla attacks. This was Rosweal in the borderlands, after all, and entirely outside the typical Innish social collective. In Bethany and even to a degree in Tairngare, the usual martial tactics tended to apply. Surround a walled city of any considerable size with a moderate to swelling population. You'd either find cause for negotiation, engage in civil siege, or simply wait out the city's dwindling supplies. In Rosweal, the concept of honorable warfare was a foregone conclusion. He found it somewhat ironic that he'd managed to take Tairngare— the greatest and most populous city in Innisfail— with fewer losses than tiny, insignificant Rosweal had cost him in a single day. While his valet saw to his wounds, he poured over the area's maps for hours on end to puzzle out Rosweal's next surprise.

By the ninth bell, he'd thrown his cold meal against the far wall and sought out something living to vent his frustrations upon. The farmer's young daughter seemed as good a place as any to pour his malice into. The farmer himself hadn't been pleased to surrender his farm and his life, and now his dripping head graced a wooden pole at the gate, along with his fat wife and their three snot-nosed sons. His daughter, however, had round teats that would serve her well in her next profession, and Damek was filled with enough spite to break her in himself. He would be sorry for his actions later, but his misery needed a home. Why not the broken entrance to this girl's blooming womanhood? Why should the women be spared?

The servants were in the barn with his officers. After a day like today, his men deserved the distraction. The girl had stopped weeping a few hours before, but as he sat at the window, naked and smeared with her blood, her occasional whimpers irked him. He turned, flagon in hand, to spear her with a warning glare. "Shut your mouth."

She complied by cramming a fist between her teeth.

He hated the satisfaction it gave him.

You're every bit what she said you were.

He drank rather than see Una's brows cinch in disgust. If only that Dannan bastard had killed him today, this girl's family would still draw breath, and her virginity would be hers to bestow on some lucky fool one happy eve. So, he drank, turning his thoughts to strategy rather than carnivorous self-loathing.

The Sidhe posed the only real threat here. Even outnumbered, they were still a considerable force to be reckoned with. On the field, hand-to-hand, or from a distance unseen— the Dannans earned their martial reputation with every minute this conflict pressed on. That bastard earlier, for example. Damek ground his molars, feeling very stitch Hisk had sewn into his abdomen at the memory. The Dannan had short, silver blond hair and a smattering of gold chains in his right ear. That made him a lord or someone of import in Aes Sidhe.

That son of a bitch had almost cut his heart out. If Damek's honor guard hadn't been nearby, he'd have died face-down in the snow with so many of his officers.

His fingers tightened around his flagon, threatening to break the glass to shards. If he'd known how bloody taxing Rosweal would be, he'd have heeded O'Rearden's plea from the first and told Falan the Younger to fuck himself raw.

I lost five hundred men today.

For what?

For a woman who didn't want him. For an overlord he didn't want to serve. For himself… for pride?

You're here to surrender the crown you earned with your own sword to a father who couldn't have given a shite less if you died to bring it to him. You're here for nothing. You are committing treason against a benevolent high king for nothing.

Your men are dying for nothing.

Damek sneered at his reflection in the glass.

Some king you are.

He only had so much time left to linger in this backwater. His uncle spread his venom throughout the south, burning and murdering in his God's name. How long before the south fell entirely into Henry's greedy, vindictive hands? What then? It would be a pointless goal to rule a unified Eire that is far from unified. The longer he wasted at this border picking a fight with the Sidhe on his 'father's orders,' the greater the chances he would lose everything he'd earned on his own. Damek heard the girl whimper and knew he shouldn't even be here.

He should have listened to Martin.

A true King of Eire did not need the Sidhe to rule.

As if summoned by Damek's toxic thoughts, Martin shoved the door open so hard that it bounced from the wooden wall, rattling the windows. His grizzled features purpled with a barely restrained fury at the sight of the weeping girl in Damek's bed. Her black eye and bleeding nose might have borne Damek's blazing red hand. Martin sputtered, collected himself, and waved the girl toward him. "Come on now, sweeting. There's a bath and food for you in my quarters, and I swear to Reason no hand shall touch you there."

Terrified, she glanced at Damek, who shrugged on his dressing cloak as if she didn't exist. He didn't turn to Martin when the girl leaped from the bed and darted for the hall.

Martin slammed the door shut behind her with the heel of his boot.

"Long night, My Lord?"

Damek pretended to examine the map on his desk, unable to meet Martin's accusatory stare. "What's it to you, Commander?"

"That girl's face was far fairer this afternoon, as I recall."

"You were all for this last season, so don't pretend you care about any of the women here."

"It was you who put a stop to it, remember? That asides, those girls volunteered and were *paid* for their time. None were beaten within an inch of their lives, either."

"That's a rather fine hair you're splitting."

"Is it?" Martin laughed. "There are two dead women in the barn this time, Damek. What was done to them was unspeakable. You encouraged your men to behave that way… and came up here to make a mess of your own."

"So?"

"What the hells do you mean, '*so*'? You should be ashamed of yourself!"

"Are you my mother?"

"I bloody well wonder if that's not what you need."

Damek's shoulders shook. He couldn't look up.

"Was it not bad enough to kill her entire family and leave them for the crows, but then shame and beat her for transgressions that aren't hers too?" Martin stalked over until he towered over Damek's bent head. He leaned forward on his knuckles so the judgment he wielded could not be misinterpreted. "Tell me, My *King*, have you and your cunt uncle somehow merged beneath the flesh? Because the boy I raised is not a base rapist and murderer, or have I been laboring under a misapprehension all this while?"

Damek snapped up, filling his face with every ounce of loathing he had. "You watch your tone, Commander. I am your liege lord and—"

"*Fuck your title*, you sniveling gobshite!" Martin roared. He dragged the map out of Damek's reach and shredded it. "I'm speaking to a lad I taught to sit a horse, eat like a gentleman, draw the bow, and tilt like a fine Souther knight. Is he in there under this entitled snit, or not?"

Damek turned away, pouring himself a tankard from the glass flagon that shook with shaking hands. He left it on the table and moved to the mantle. "Martin, I—"

"Again, I ask you, what would your lady think of this, hm? This girl you claim to love above gods and men. What would she say to you now if she saw what you've wrought here?"

Damek said nothing.

She hated him… and she was *right* to.

At this moment, he realized he was the villain of this sad tale. His motives had always been impure. His actions were high-handed and self-serving. His beliefs… everything, were irrelevant to his ego. Damek was every inch the monster Una knew him to be, Falan wanted him to be, that Patrick had tried to mold, and Martin feared he'd become. He was a patchwork of evils, woven together by lofty ambitions. "Maybe this is who I am, Martin."

Martin made a sound like a half-strangled bear. He swatted the flagon to the floor, where it shattered, leaving a bright red puddle on the pine floorboards. "I will not hear that! I've been with you from the start, young lord. I loved you, raised, and supported you from your first breath because I believed in my bones that you were best for the South— for Innisfail. Reason knows you have your flaws, lad, we all do, but rape and unjustified slaughter are *beneath you*." He drew himself up to his full height. "Until now, I've never doubted my loyalty and love of you was right. Tell me, will you do the same to Una when she's in your keeping at last?"

Damek choked. "No, I would never. I…"

"You what? You love her? Isn't that why you started this campaign in the first place? Why half a thousand men are rotting in the snow tonight. Because you were going to save her, save us all from tyrants and unworthy rulers. Isn't that what we're all bloody here to do?"

Damek's gaze flicked upward. He hadn't seen such a look of disgust and disappointment on Martin since that night those many years ago when Una had fled the comfort of her father's hall. That night, Damek had driven away the only thing he'd ever really wanted for himself by behaving much the same as he had tonight. Then, as now, the same emotion shone from his foster father's steady gaze.

Shame.

That was it.

Shame not for Damek, but *because* of him. That look spoke of a deep disgust caused by raising a creature of no worth to heights he could never have aspired to otherwise.

Mistake.

Grief.

Damek couldn't bear it. He shrank under that derision.

Martin was the only father he'd ever had.

"If you mean to conquer just for its sake, do what you will. I cannot gainsay you. You're a brilliant commander and a fine leader of men, but I will never serve you again. You lost me tonight, boy. You may accept this as my formal resignation."

Damek stumbled forward, pleading. "Martin, no. I'm sorry. I am a terrible man… I need you to make me better."

Martin blew a stream of air from his nose. "It is not our victories that make us men, Damek. Our worth is proven by how we handle defeat and loss, how we get on with things, and how we treat those who depend upon our mercy. That makes a man, Damek. A *king* would know better."

Damek felt like he'd been lanced straight through his heart.

You are no king. First Una, now Martin.

A man should be judged by the quality of those who spurn him. He struggled to find a word, anything that might make his adopted father look at him with less disappointment. The well of excuses from which he usually drew was bone dry. He had none. He couldn't breathe another lie into life. He just stood there, quivering like a leaf in a gale, staring at his own feet below the hem of his purple robe.

Martin mocked a salute. "Now, we shall finish this farce of your father's if for no reason other than that I swore you my sword for its execution. When it's over, whichever way, we are done, boy. Do you hear me?"

Damek could but nod. Hot tears stung the pits of his eyes and burned his throat like acid.

"Good. In that case, do you have any orders for me, Lord?"

After a while, Damek managed a weak response. "Have we doubled the watch on our supply trains?"

"We have," Martin replied dryly. "Though it's quiet as a tomb out there and cold enough to freeze the air in a man's lungs. I expect they're licking their wounds tonight, same as we are."

"Don't count on it. They'll raid tonight. It's what I would do in their place. They know I have more men than I can feed, and with our stalemate this afternoon— their only shot at getting out of this on one piece is to encourage desertion in our ranks."

"We'll be at them again at dawn, regardless. Southers don't care much for these Norther snows, but we're made of harder stuff than they expect."

Damek winced. None of them deserved such faith from this most excellent of men. "If the Crown Prince claims her, I might as well sign my death warrant."

"I'm aware, My Lord."

"Martin, I… I don't know what to do."

Martin heaved a heavy sigh. "Sleep on it. It'll come to you, as it always does."

"What if it doesn't?"

Martin visibly wrestled with the words he wanted to utter and those more prudent. In the end, he shrugged. "You lost the moment you marched here. Falan sent you to ruin yourself, and you, like the arrogant, headstrong fool you are— committed to it to save face. If the greatest warrior in the history of Innisfail doesn't kill you tomorrow or the next day, your rule will certainly finish here… and miserably, I might add."

Damek's chest bled all over again. "I know."

Martin chuckled. "If you know, why bother to ask? We're here to die at your word, My LordKing. I'm so happy to spend mine for so vaunted a cause as your wounded pride. Will that be all?"

The great chasm between them was hundreds of miles wide and deep as the blackest fathom. "If I could go back, Martin—"

"I don't care to hear. If there are no more orders, I'll be off to discipline your officers for behaving like their worthless king. I expect to hang four men tonight and will brook no refusals. Are we clear?"

He cut away, prying the door open with quaking fingers.

Just then, a chorus of screams rent the night outside.

His hand paused on the knob.

Damek rushed back to the window seeing nothing at first but swirling snow, until there, in the storm-bright darkness, he caught the glint of steel in from the treeline. Damek felt the blood drain from his face. He *had* said they'd raid tonight; he just hadn't imagined they'd penetrate so deeply into his rear lines nor come for the one commodity he couldn't replenish— his well-trained, fiercely loyal officers. "Gods damn those Dananan cunts!" he spat, rushing over to tug his discarded clothing on.

Martin was out the door well before him, and it wouldn't be until much later that Damek would realize he'd never thanked the old bear for raising him nor for the wisdom and justice of his council. The shame he felt at Martin's disapproval had always been the guiding star of his life. Martin's faith in him, his steady, stable nobility, was the only reason Damek had *any* redeemable characteristics to speak of. When this affair was handled to whatever end, Damek swore he'd see Martin rewarded for his unwavering loyalty and prayed he might still be worthy of it.

⚸ ⚸

THEY WERE IN THE BARN before a single sentry caught the slightest sound. There were roughly twenty men inside, slumbering in stalls heated by iron biers loaded with slow-burning peat logs. Those not afforded the privacy of a heated stall gathered together in the center aisle on cots piled high with furs around a hastily dug firepit that had burned to cinders. Rough accommodations, to be sure, but much better than the infantry forced to brave the elements outside. In places, the snow had piled so high that tents became igloos. Half of the farmhouse had been swallowed nearly to the chimney.

The time was much closer to dawn than Kaer Yin would have liked for the effort required to wade through such a thick coating of snow over the forest floor. Now that they had finally made their mark, he wasted no more. Miming a silent signal, the Sidhe moved through that barn like the shadow of death itself. The affair was over in moments.

Kaer Yin's party slinked past the sentry, who took his last piss at the end of Colm's blade. The first knight closest to the door he sent to Tech Duinn with a quick dagger jab to the clavicle, then held the lad's mouth shut while he choked to death on his own blood. The second startled awake in the next stall. Kaer Yin leaped over the short wall and onto the fellow's chest before he could stand up to alert his comrades.

That one, Kaer Yin, took through the eye.

Robin and Tam Lin wrestled and slashed their way forward outside the stalls in a gruesome ballet— step, pivot, cut, turn, slash. Jan Fir caught up with a large man who tumbled from his cot, still tangled in his furs. His lark came through the back of the fellow's throat before he could gather his voice to call an alarm.

Although they slew most everyone in that barn before they could get away, Kaer Yin had anticipated that they wouldn't get to everyone without a sound. Two men escaped their clutches and spilled out into the snow outside, screaming bloody murder. Shar made short work of both, but not before the men gathered in half-buried tents nearby, and indeed, the whole of the farm was roused to the danger. Kaer Yin finished off one man after another until a red-bearded captain in a stained tunic leaped to his feet with a sabre in one hand and a short-handled axe in the other. This one swiped at Kaer Yin with his axe, which Kaer Yin ducked without effort.

"Kinney, kill that blond fuck!" One of his comrades screamed as Tam Lin's lark lashed out, taking his head from his shoulders. To his credit, Kinney tried. It did him no good, but the effort was admirable.

Kaer Yin cut him in half with one stroke from Nemain's broad blade.

His top half blasted through one of the closed wooden shutters. The shouting outside increased in frequency and nearness.

Well, so much for our surprise.

"Men comin'," warned Colm, wiping his knives against his dirty wet trousers.

"How many?" Kaer Yin asked, drawing Nemain's point from another man's corpse.

Tam Lin dashed for the open door. "Shite. All of them, looks like."

Robin shuffled over. "What now?"

Kaer Yin answered by kicking the wooden slats out of the back wall and spilling into the night outside, his sword high. So many men poured out of the farmhouse and grounds toward their raised position; they might have been ants streaming from a hillock. "Kill anything that comes at you, and don't stop until we're over the far ridge."

⚶

THE SIDHE COURSED FORWARD, DEALING elegant death without a break in stride. Each comer was met with equal and swift ferocity, slipping into the snow, missing heads, limbs, or sporting holes and gashes from which there could be no recovery. As the Southers' numbers increased, so too did the dead. The Sidhe could not be stopped even in such a small number. Shar had grabbed a torch from a fallen sentry and busied himself with setting fire to anything that might catch— wagons stacked near the farmhouse, outbuildings, and even the smattering of tents gathered close to the barn. Colm had freed what few scrawny animals were left to die in the pen, thus bleating sheep and cattle charged ahead of the Sidhe, trampling many defenders well before they could greet the edge of the sylvan weapons headed their way.

The farmhouse door tore open, spilling light and soldiers from its interior. A large man Kaer Yin recalled seeing in Bethany at Bishop's side like a faithful shadow, emerged sporting a fairly wicked crossbow. "Sound the horns!" he bellowed, his voice cracking like thunder. He pointed his crossbow directly at Kaer Yin. "Let none leave alive."

The quarrel he fired whistled through the air and would have taken Kaer Yin through the throat if he had not moved away quickly enough. He lost several strands of silver hair in the process. Another whizzed by, forcing him to twist his body into knots to avoid being struck somewhere dear. Before he had time to move out of range, two men came at him from the sides. The snow was up to his thighs, impeding his ability to wiled Nemain with ease. He sheathed his longsword, drawing his larks from their holster behind his quiver. Some Dannans wore their larks high to use gravity as a natural aid in close combat by eliminating the time it took to attack from a draw.

Kaer Yin wore his upside-down, preferring to draw from the sides and strike low in the opponent's guard. Most swordsmen fought with a high guard, like Neithana but with far less finesse. The purpose is to halt one's opponent by using his inertia against himself. For Kaer Yin, who moved in a complex series of loops when engaged— the lark served best at the unguarded torso, ribs, the pit of the arm, the hip joint, and kidneys. Stringing his holster upside down saved him the precious time he would have lost on a downstroke.

The two soldiers went down just as fast as they had come on. Three more followed suit, one slightly faster and more skilled than his fellows. That one, Kaer Yin was forced to take seriously. The Corpsman's sabre sliced forward, rending a gash on Kaer Yin's bicep before he backed up and scored a second line at his shoulder. Kaer Yin gnashed his teeth and spun right, sweeping his left hand horizontally across the Corpsman's ribcage. He then pivoted, wobbling forward just a hair. Kaer Yin's knee connected with his forehead just as his right lark bit into his neck joint. As the dying soldier crumpled into the driving snow, Kaer Yin used his falling body as a platform to launch himself out of the drift and back in line with his comrades.

"Yin, behind you!" shouted Tam Lin from several lengths ahead.

Barely fast enough, he whirled, catching the big man's stroke from behind with both lark blades—shoving it back and away. He grunted with the effort. This Souther was made of stronger stuff than the others. Damek's man grinned and lunged forward with a dagger, inches from Kaer Yin's eyes. He jerked back, tipping the point away with his left blade and ducking beneath a second slash. The burly was good, *very* good for a man his size. Even in this sucking snow, he wielded a longsword as easily as his fellows used their lighter sabres. Despite the sword's weight, he made each stroke look as effortless as a reed in the wind.

Kaer Yin scrabbled backward, using his larks to maintain his footing. Before long, he realized he was sweating. Still, the grizzled old soldier grinned down at him from the high ground. Larks were no good against longswords. The blades were too thin, even if they were made of folded, refined steel that was much harder than the average Milesian make. The difference came down to fundamental physics. A heavy object propelled by a heavier force exerts more power— superior craftsmanship aside.

Cursing, Kaer Yin tucked his larks back into their sheaths and reached for Nemain again. He would have to maintain a high guard due to the snow, vastly decreasing his mobility and speed. The Souther knew it too. His smirking face complimented his height, which was close to if not higher than Kaer Yin's own. Having the high ground meant he didn't need to exert half as much energy to swing his bloody sword. "That's right, you pretty, prancing prick," he laughed, a grey-bearded bear with a crooked chin. "Let's see whose arm is stronger."

"Gods damn it, Yin," snapped Tam Lin from somewhere close. He must have circled back. More men poured from the farmhouse nearby. "You weren't supposed to stop."

Jan Fir and Shar came hurtling through any men who approached the two combatants on the hill, but Kaer Yin barely noticed. "*A fháil chun clúdach*[25]!" he barked while absorbing each of the larger man's sword strokes with molar-rattling impact. He tried to inch back toward the trees, which would strip the Souther of his height advantage. Displeased by Kaer Yin's seeming lack of interest, the Souther growled and redoubled his efforts. Kaer Yin saw dozens of men shuffling uphill from the farmstead below, many held torches or crossbows.

He was out of time.

Kaer Yin spun away as neatly as possible in the heavy, boot-sucking snow, switching Nemain's pommel to his left hand. The big man's eyes widened at the reveal. Many Milesians could never understand that to practice Neithana, one must be as effective with either hand. His right might have taken a beating warding off his blows, but he had another that was just as strong and somewhat rested. Moving his left foot forward, Kaer Yin whirled right, dodging a startled thrust. When he turned, he faced the Souther's broad back: Nemain's blade dripped gore from a point above his tailbone. Spitting blood, the Souther gripped Kaer Yin's arm as his sword dropped from his fingers. His eyes were surprised but almost amused. Kaer Yin didn't remove his arm as he slid Nemain from the Souther's body.

Though he shuddered against him, he gave a small smile. Someone screamed "Martin!" in the distance.

Despite the fatal blow, the Souther's hand snaked out and grasped Kaer Yin's by the back of the neck, smashing his hard forehead into Kaer Yin's nose. A thousand stars burst behind his eyes, and Kaer Yin stumbled, feeling sure he heard something crack. The big Souther chuckled, resting his girth on one fist while the other uselessly attempted to stall his guts from working free. His eventual death would be slow and painful if Kaer Yin left him this way. He was clearly a brave man and a capable soldier and deserved better.

The truth of his situation must have shown on Kaer Yin's face. He nodded. "An honor, *Ard Tiarne*."

Kaer Yin exhaled long and hard. "The honor is mine, Commander."

The Souther pulled himself up as far as he could, spread his arms, and shut his eyes. He was still smiling. Kaer Yin sent Nemain through the man's heart to the hilt. He doubled forward again as Kaer

---

[25] 'Get to cover!'

Yin withdrew, then slipped sideways into the snow. Men and arrows came charging uphill at him, but he spared the time to salute the old soldier as he deserved.

He had been a worthy foe.

Amidst a swirl of white and grey, Damek saw red. His piercing fury was a glowing stain in the night. Martin's grinning corpse lay cocooned in swiftly darkening snow. Half-burned trees tore at the sky in a deafening keen. Men screamed. Dark shapes struggled uphill with blazing torches. White-tipped arrows streamed from the shadows. His guards dragged him back from the arrows covering the raider's retreat. Several bolts hissed into the snow on either side. He couldn't see them and didn't care. The only thing he cared about lay in a blooming pool of white and red.

Martin was dead. His foster father, his body still steaming, lay curled up in a darkening snowbank. Dead. Martin was… *dead*.

Memories flashed before Damek's eyes: Martin tucking his fingers around a spoon, wrapping a cut with a thick white bandage. Martin laughing as Damek foundered in his first suit of armor, beaming down at him from the dais at Damek's wedding. Damek sucked in a breath, rooted to the spot by feet that could no longer obey him. He relived his whole life in the space of a few heartbeats, and for nearly every moment, Martin had been there. His dearest friend. *No*, he thought with deepening rage and pain—my *father*.

The only father he had ever needed.

Martin O'Rearden was dead.

"Milord," prodded Ridley, his hand finding Damek's right shoulder. "Should we pursue?"

He didn't look up. He couldn't. Not even when the unnatural snowfall ceased and the light from a weak, mottled sun peaked over the trees.

His men filed around him, waiting, unsure.

All Damek could see was Martin, staring blankly at nothing. The big, callused hands that held him atop his first saddle placed a wooden stave in his hand, drew his fingers back over his bowstring, dusted his kneecaps after a fall— those hands that seemed to carry him through every stage of his life, now clenched with rigor over still seeping wounds. It was *so* like Martin to die with a smile. He always did admire an opponent who knew his business. Damek had watched him fall from a useless distance, too far away to stop the Prince of Innisfail from cutting Martin's heart out right in front of him.

"Milord!" Ridley cried, face gone purple with emotion. There wasn't a dry eye among his men. Martin O'Rearden was a legend in his own time. Better men simply did not exist. Some of Martin's favorites had given chase without Damek's consent. "Do we pursue?" asked Ridley again.

Damek collected himself, hearing Martin's voice come out of his mouth. "Take your best trackers up that hill. Bring down anything you can catch, alive if possible. If not, I want to know how they renter that cesspit of a town… in detail."

Some of the last words Martin would ever speak burned in Damek's gut like red-hot coal.

Their worthless king.

"What if they've laid more traps, My King?" Ridley had lost dozens of men the day before. For a soldier of his ilk, it was a blow from which he'd be slow to recover.

"They haven't. The trap is inside the walls."

"How do you know?"

"This was an invitation to follow. They came here to make sure we do it sloppily, dash headlong at the Navan Gate." Damek knelt, allowing himself only the barest touch of Martin's cold hand.

"So, we're not going to attack?"

"Did I say that?"

"But the men? Without their captains, how will we direct the siege?"

Damek shrugged off his cloak and laid it gently over Martin's still form. "We're going to give them exactly what they want, Ridley. Only we will show them what a grave mistake they've just made— tossing kindling at a brushfire."

He trained his eyes north, watching a menacing fog settle over the hills. "I want every man we have ready to march in three hours. Every last one."

Ridley's face took on a murderous sheen. "It will be done, My King."

"And Ridley," Damek said over his shoulder as he signaled to have Martin's body lifted from the snow. He took Martin's sword and laid it over his chest. "Tell the men I will personally award a thousand fainne to the first hundred men over that wall and another ten thousand to the man that brings me that silver-haired cunt's heart on a platter."

Siora's Chosen

Una ran around the lake as fast as her legs would carry her. Something large, with snapping teeth and a snarling maw, dogged her every step. She leaped over an overhanging tree limb up a slight rise just in time. The air whistled over her neck as the thing's claws swept past her head. She re-doubled her efforts, dumping Spark into both legs at a rate she could never survive in her realm. A dip in the terrain ahead heralded an overgrown but mostly dry ravine that terminated at the lake's rim. With a cry, she ducked under the creature's next strike, rolling into the ditch by inches.

Una scrambled up the far embankment before the thing could turn— snapping tree boughs and rending great rivulets in the earth with its massive foreclaws. It keened in frustration, displaying rows of fetid, razor-sharp teeth.

"Siora!" she squeaked, finally catching a full glimpse of her hunter. This was the same creature Kaer Yin had slain at Rian's farmstead. *Ghast*, he'd called it. Una had no weapons, nothing to protect herself with, save the swiftness of her own two feet.

The ghast lunged for her, upending a few ancient trees on the way. Wasting nothing, she slid straight onto a game trail about ten paces abreast of the ravine and darted forward with all the speed she could summon. There was quite a bit more than usual, she couldn't fail to notice, and a good thing too. One swipe from the ghast's claws could cleave her in two. Regardless of how fast she was in the Otherworld, so was the ghast. She felt its breath on her skin, torpid and sour. It gained. From one breath to another, a stinging gash opened over her upper spine. She bit her lip against the pain.

If she stumbled or faltered now, she was dead.

Instead, she raced onward, branches and thorns tearing at her hair and clothing. She poured all the Spark she could safely manage into her core, feeling it burn like bottled starlight— and ran. She ran until the woods around her were blurred until the ghast howled in fury. She'd outpaced it, thank every one of her ancestors. Being chewed to bits by such a monster was not a death she craved. With inhuman amounts of Spark and a bit of luck, she rounded a bend atop the next hill, completely removing herself from the ghast's sight. Its grating, knife-sharp keening trilled not far behind, but she forced herself to stop and turn west into denser foliage. Her hands shot out to two enormous elms, standing side-by-side over a creek.

"*Braid*," she huffed, her Spark flooding from her fingertips like water from a spring. As swiftly as possible, she touched all of the trees in her immediate vicinity with the same command, then pulled deep at her Spark to summon speed all over again. The trees she'd touched knotted together behind her, roots tugging out of the earth and winding together like interwoven threads. She'd made a wall of wood nearly thirty feet high, which moved toward the ghast as it sniffed the ground after her. She didn't wait around to watch what happened.

Howling snarls and the sound of splitting wood rent the air. Her wall wouldn't last long.

She stopped again, chest heaving, and held her palms out. "*Catch*," she gasped. The air shimmered with sparks and cinders. She dug into something behind her belly button and pulled hard. "*Multiply*." The shimmers of heat divided and divided again. She held her breath. "*More*." Soon her cheeks started to sweat from the heat. She waited until the ghast burst through her impressive but useless wall of trees, its rows of shark-like teeth clicking with glee.

Through the eyes, through the mouth, she meant to say aloud, but the flames flared without her verbal command. They zipped into it like tiny, glittering missiles. The creature's shrill screams made her clap her hands over her ears. She would hardly be surprised to discover they were bleeding after such an unearthly trill. The ghast struggled onto its hind legs, clawing its eye socket out in desperation to stall her flames. When it opened its jaws to roar, she caught the glow of an internal fire raging down its throat. It choked and thrashed, sending up huge chunks of earth and bisected trees.

Still, it did not die.

Una had no idea she could actualize thoughts on this scale.

Brushing a stray lock of hair from one's eye was not the same as burning a Dor Sidhe beast from the inside without uttering a sound. If this was her new reality…

What else can I do?

She backed up further from the thrashing creature, reaching into that tingling inferno at her navel. It responded like an eager animal.

Break, she thought.

The ghast's bones snapped. Its jaw unhinged from its skull. It sank to the forest floor, dying. Its one good eye trained on her in total fear. *Fold*, she thought. As if in a cosmically powerful vacuum, its body twisted in on itself, bones and sinew crushed together by some unseen hand— like a fist crumpling parchment. The whine emitted as it died almost made her feel pity for it.

Obliterate, she thought next.

All of its parts compounded in upon themselves until the ball of mass suddenly winked out of existence with an ear-splitting pop.

When it was gone, Una sank to her knees. She stared at her hands as if they had been screwed onto her forearms by some mad god. What had she just done? She trembled.

She *shouldn't* have been able to do anything like that… no matter where she was.

It was impossible.

Unthinkable.

Una had no idea how long she sat there pondering what sort of monster *she* might be before that same little girl she'd spied before appeared among the trees ahead. She had dark braids, lovely nut-dark skin, and bright, amber eyes. She opened her mouth to call out to her, but there was something in the child's enigmatic expression that clapped her mouth shut— a warning.

She understood too late.

A faint giggle from behind her spun her around. A woman stepped from the night, wearing the white robes of a Siorai Prima beneath a simple grey cloak. Her short, black hair curled around slightly curved ears marked black at the lobes. *Fir Bolg*, Una's studies informed her, though she'd never met one aside from Damek before, and he was only half Bolg. The newcomer's eyes gleamed a brilliant violet in the Otherworld twilight. "Now that was something, I must admit," she laughed.

Una thought her voice sounded familiar though she couldn't place her. "Who are you?"

The woman merely smiled and stepped forward. Una could tell she was unwell. Beautiful she might have been once, her shorn hair revealed several patches of scalp that seemed to reject any further growth. There were deep bruises around the cavities of her eyes, and her cheeks bore skeletal hollows and faint, pinkish scars. She seemed naught but scar and bone, this strange Fir Bolg visitor.

"What happened to you?" Una asked without thinking.

A brief flash of fury tracked through the women's features, then faded. A wry smirk graced her too-thin lips. "I am *so* glad you accepted my invitation, Una Moura. I so rarely have the pleasure of meeting my prey face-to-face."

Una's hands were still splayed before her, crackling with an unending supply of cosmic wrath. Her brows drew close. "I know you. Your voice."

The woman curtsied. "Left my bell at home, I'm afraid."

Come and feast… all the warmth you require is just ahead, Una's memory sang. She lifted her chin. "Thought I killed you."

"I'm very hard to kill, My Lady."

Una sniffed, cracking her knuckles. She got to her feet, which didn't help her advantage. She was at least a foot shorter than this skinny tower of a woman. No matter. She was stronger… and she had no doubt. "You wear the robes of a Prima, whoever you are, but you are not Siorai. I would know."

The woman pursed her tiny, malformed lips with a slight shrug. She moved into the light of the menacing moon. "Remember every Siorai in the Cloister, do you?"

"I… well…"

She snorted, "Of course, you wouldn't, sweet pet that you are. You and I moved in different circles, I'm afraid."

Una gasped. "*Aoife?*"

In her mind's eye, she recalled the tall form that stood beside Nema without a single exception; midnight curls, curves to make any woman mad with jealousy, and bottomless malice that saw many Siorai skittering away from her in fear. *This* was Aoife Sona? It couldn't be? "What happened to you?" she repeated.

"You and your thrice-cursed cousin happened to me, girl. You and Damek did this together." She held her arms out. "See your mighty works and despair."

Una felt a quick jab of pity but quickly swallowed it. "You murdered innocents on Samhain. You'll get no sympathy from me."

"Oh," chuckled Aoife. "I've murdered *many* more than that, Una dear. I could argue some were outside of my control, but there'd be no point in lying, would there? It's rare for people to love what they're good at, but I've been blessed that way."

Una glared back. "So, you interrupted Diarmid's power? How?"

"Irrelevant. Here we are now, and that's all that matters."

"Let me guess. This is about Damek."

"The same."

"Take him," Una scoffed. "He and I have nothing to do with one another."

"A bald lie, but that's neither here nor there. I owe him, you see. He took something from me. Now I'm taking something back."

"I have no quarrel with you."

Aoife slowly lifted her own hands. Dark buzzing energy trickled through her fingers. "Oh, Una, I don't care."

ᛉ ᛣ

Diarmid could move through the Otherworld more swiftly than any Sidhe alive. As the Dannan Skysinger who had assumed the Dagda's place in their tribe those many eons past: he'd developed the ability to mold time in the Otherworld to his will. Here, such flashy, depletive magic would cost him practically nothing. Time did not move in the Oiche Ar Fad as it did in Innisfail. It was less predictable, less structured. He would liken it to spilling water down the face of a large, cracked stone. The water would find its way down the edifice, seeking the swiftest path possible. Even if droplets separate from the main bulk, eventually, they must converge again at the bottom. Just as the water sought the lowest point possible, time also sought its eventual confluence. If one was not careful and clung to a fragment too long or strayed too far from the main course, one could lose the path and be forced to wander those fragments forever.

Diarmid had many thousands of years to ponder and perfect his use of time in the Otherworld. As a result, he could travel forward, back, and around as he saw fit— provided he didn't linger in any fragment

624

too long and never attempted to dare such volatile magic in the corporeal realm. Time was only fluid in the Oiche Ar Fad, a domain just below, between, and besides living reality. Its environment, features, and landmarks were nearly identical, the dark twin of the realm above.

In Innisfail, time marched only forward without pause, but in the Otherworld, time was softer and more malleable. There was no rule he knew of, but often, a week or so here would comprise a month or more in Innisfail. Sometimes more, sometimes less. For Diarmid and only Diarmid, as far as he knew, this allowed Diarmid to travel the length and breadth of the Shadow Path at a clip nearly in pace with the progression of time in Innisfail. Searching high, low, in valleys, dells, and dales— he passed through the sky like an intransient vapor, constantly moving but indefinable as a whisp of cloud.

So, imagine Diarmid's profound surprise when he felt himself torn into a fragment, not of his own making or management. Ripped from the air, as a falcon dives for prey, he came down hard, crashing into a hillside with enough force to rattle large tracts of granite free. The resulting avalanche swept half of the mound away.

Disoriented, confused, and infuriated, he struggled upright. Careful not to lose footing in the loosened scree and snow, he looked around. The wind screamed around his ears, blowing his cloak back over the mark he'd made on the face. Frowning, he brushed dirt and dust from his sleeves, only to discover a trickle of blood running from one nostril. Immensely displeased, he stared at the stain on his fingers with rising fury.

Who would dare?

A faint impact behind him, followed by a familiar laugh, sent his pulse into the atmosphere. He turned. A craggy, unkempt Bolg with milky, light-deprived eyes and stringy black hair waved at him from the summit. "Son of Nuada! How lovely to see you again!" cried the ugly figure with genuine glee.

"Ruidraghe?" Diarmid made a face. "Who let you out?"

The Bolg Firesinger sneered back. "I prefer the solitude of my hall, but no help for it. I come when called."

"A stinking pit in the earth's bowels can hardly be called a 'hall' Ruidraghe, but that's beside the point. What are you trying to do— be careful. I'm not overfond of being interrupted."

"Nor of bleeding, I shouldn't wonder." Ruidraghe gave over to a rasping fit of laughter, clearly enjoying himself.

Diarmid didn't have time for this. "Get to it, old man. What do you want?"

"Your death, *Fiachra Dubh*. Failing that, I'll settle for marking up that lovely face. Maybe I'll scorch the skin from your bones or boil your eyes from their sockets? Who knows?"

That was Diarmid's cue to laugh. "Had some time to think things over, I see. But we've been here before, Ruidraghe, and you and I both know you can't beat me. I wonder who permitted you to try, hm? An attack upon me is an attack upon the Ard Ri, after all."

Ruidraghe made an obscene gesture with a gnarled right hand. "Fuck your *Ri*, you Danna twat. I couldn't spare a tinker's fart for your tribe's absurd hierarchy. I came for *you*."

"I suppose I'm flattered. Still, if you're brave enough to try now after all these years, you must have been granted permission by someone from Armagh. Your lord, perhaps?"

The hermit's toothless leer made Diarmid's lip curl. Of all the Brehons in Innisfail, and there weren't many to be sure, this Bolg dog hated him most. He wouldn't be here, acting with such definite confidence, if he hadn't been sent to do so by the Bolg Ri— Falan the Elder himself— and if this was true, the fire in Aes Sidhe had served another purpose than a siege against Rosweal. Una's absence might not have been by her design.

Suspicions tugging at Diarmid's subconscious for many days seemed to bear more weight than previously assumed.

"I'm not here to talk," Ruidraghe assured him. "Which do you choose? Skin or soft tissues? I rather like the idea of you going around eyeless, myself. What an absurd pantomime you'll make."

Diarmid shook his head, reaching into the sky for his power, feeling it whirl around him in eager, electrical readiness. Whatever Una had given him in Tech Duinn was a great deal more than mere replenishment of his own 'Spark,' as she would call it. This surge of strength felt like she'd pumped a hundred years of stored power into him with a single touch of her hand.

The girl was a prize like nothing in all nine realms.

"Well," he said. "You'll have to forgive me for making this quick, but I have business elsewhere. I wish you'd tell me which MacNemed I have to thank for our reunion… however brief it will be."

"Does it matter? Come on then, great *Fiachra Dubh*. Come and die."

With speed no mortal eye could track, Diarmid accepted his invitation with relish.

⚐ ⚑

Bracing herself for impact, Una was tossed bodily against the trunk of a large oak. The tree seemed to groan beneath her weight, its multifaceted leaves shivering in a bevy of sighs. All of the breath in her lungs rushed out of her at once. Galaxies swirled behind her eyes. "*Corrupt*," chanted her attacker, with a grin Una could *hear* in her voice.

Una cried out as the oak began to blacken beneath her, stinging any exposed skin like acid. She turned away, throwing out a hand to protect her face from the oncoming miasma from Aoife's raised fingers.

"*Suspend!*" Una exclaimed, throwing a hand out. The black wall of corruption froze mid-reach, like ink trapped in ice. Breathing hard, she got to her knees, each palm bleeding profusely. She turned back to the Bolg Prima. "*Return.*"

The miasma expanded in a stinking cloud, shooting up over the treetops like a pillar of smoke, then rushed back into Aoife's startled face. She backed up with a grunt and closed a fist. "*Dissipate*," she said through gritted teeth, clearly exerting more Spark than she thought she must. The miasma blew away, scattered into the forest like fog before a gale. She clutched at her ribs, panting.

"That was very good, Una. Quick thinking."

Una didn't care for her praise. She got to her feet, her skin healing with every breath.

Aoife, who shriveled where she stood, saw. "How are you doing this?"

"I'd tell you if I knew."

Aoife made a sound. "I'd be disappointed if it were easy to kill you, anyway."

"What have I ever done to you, Aoife? My grandmother was a corrupt ruler, and my family was heavy-handed in their reach for power— I can admit to and accept that— but what have I done to you, personally? Your mistress has tried to kill me at least three times that I know of, and you have tried and failed once already yourself. What's the point?"

"I told you," Aoife growled. "I owe Damek. It's nothing personal aside from the fact that you irritate me by breathing. A sad, spoiled little princess ever waiting to be used by the next hand that would hold her. Pathetic thing. Your lack of purpose offends me."

Una scowled back. "You steered me on this path from the very beginning, Aoife. You and Gan made sure I was at the docks that morning in Drogheda and that Rawly and his men would find me.

Aoife shrugged, leaning against a tree to catch her breath. "I'll admit it. I, like you, am a tool wielded by others." She laughed to herself. "What irritates me most about you is that you're too self-entitled to see the many opportunities you had to make your life mean something in the process. Me, I've never been more than my *seanmáthair's* slave. You could have been so much *more*. What a waste you are."

Una chafed under the derision in her violet gaze, more or less because her conscience had echoed the same sentiments many times. "I… know."

Aoife perked up, tucking a finger behind one black-bottomed ear. "What's that?"

"I can admit when I have been wrong, Aoife. Can you?"

626

"Oh, no one cares what I think of anything, little Princess. I'm *no one*. You were supposed to be *someone*. Not some simpering female cowering behind various male protectors. You are Siorai! You were meant to rule. Alone, and mighty as the sea." She waved a dismissive hand. "How pathetic you turned out to be."

Una failed to respond for several moments. When next she spoke, she measured her words with care. "You're truly Siorai, aren't you?"

"Of course I am. While I hated Nema more than anyone, Tairngare was a miracle. An idyllic society governed by rational, empathetic females. Men's baser urges were put to use in the places they served best but eliminated from rule. Tairngare never declared war for gain. Never starved, raped, or tortured their citizens. The people were largely educated, successful, and enamored of justice. Although my grandmother went mad and destroyed what she'd created, Tairngare had been her great vision all along. I shared that dream, I must admit, and am more disappointed than I can say at the overall outcome."

Una swallowed. Her fault, essentially. "What could I have done to stop Nema, Damek, or anyone, Aoife? Truly? Who am I but the product of people who want it all?"

"You could have taken up the mantel you were meant to, for one, instead of whingeing your way to escape like the vain, selfish child you are. How many women might you have saved, educated, or improved? How many evil men might you have punished? How many just and fair laws might you have implemented? Instead, you're off to marry a bloody prince." She snorted, slapping a fist against her chest in mock shock. "Color me impressed."

She had omitted many essential things from this diatribe, but she was right. Aoife's loathing of men and oversimplifying Innish politics aside, Una *was* meant for more than this. The feeling she'd had in Bethany when she'd discovered the slain girls in her father's keep swept over her once more. How many lives might she have improved if she had accepted the crown? How many women could she have lifted out of insignificance? How might she have righted the ills of Eire if she'd taken the role she was born to play?

Her heart squeezed to think of Kaer Yin, whom she loved without question. She would happily die for him… but was that selfish? When was a woman in such a position of power with the potential to uplift so many of her sex?

None was her answer.

Not since the Ancestor walked Innish shores.

She stood for a while, staring at her own feet, her cheeks inflamed.

"Struck a nerve, have I? Good."

Una drew herself up to her full height.

Enough, a voice called from somewhere deep. It was a voice she'd never heard before— and suddenly realized it was her own, assured, resigned, and confident.

I've had enough.

"Aoife," she said aloud. "I am sorry for your many misfortunes. Truly. Please, let's end this here. I don't want your life."

Aoife twisted her chin. "Oh? Feeling magnanimous, My Queen? I'm not."

Una met her eyes without a shred of mirth. She understood this creature, even if she did not know her well. Maybe they shared a misfortunate star? Each of their families meant to wield them to achieve more than their due. Aoife let it rot her from the inside.

Una would not.

Today is the day I choose.

"Thank you for teaching me this lesson. You are right. I must do more."

"Ugh. What gave you the idea that I wanted you to do anything? Just answering your questions as honestly as I may. I'll never let you leave here alive."

"Killing me won't change anything."

"It'll make me feel a teeny bit better. That's worthwhile, you ask me."

It was Una's turn to snort. "For Damek? Seriously?"

"No, no, my sweet," Aoife opened her hand, and that same dark energy burned above her palm. "*Because* of Damek, which is entirely different. This is an act of vengeance against him for depriving me of an honorable death. Your death will destroy him… and maybe finish Armagh's bid for the High King's throne at a stroke. The fact that it will also be a pleasure is my own business."

"Fine," said Una. She was done apologizing and done being a victim. Done pretending power didn't suit her like a second skin. The universe wanted her to choose… so she did.

I will choose for myself… as Siora did.

The small clearing filled with a deep current, making the hair on her arms and nape stand on end. Aoife scrubbed at her arms in confusion. Still, Una pulled power from nothing until the space between them felt like a balloon about to burst. "I'll give you what you want in my cousin's place."

Aoife hesitated, confused. "How are you doing this?"

Una had no reason to lie. "I am stronger here."

"That's not possible."

Una closed her eyes and raised her chin to the sky. The air rushed beneath her feet, lifting her high. She heard Aoife's gasp. When Una cast her gaze upon her opponent again, she looked down on her from ten feet above, held aloft by winds rife with limitless power. Aoife had no idea that Una held the King of Tech Duinn's power in thrall. She had no idea that Una's Spark was far from drained nor that it grew more potent by the moment. Aoife had led her to this place in hopes that the creature she'd summoned would have killed her, and if not, her Spark would be so depleted that she'd stand no chance.

Una smiled. "You look tired, Aoife. You sure you want to do this?"

"But, the cost… you should be drained. You should be…."

Una crooked a finger, and several trees ripped themselves from their roots. She would get the hang of this in no time. "Guess you were wrong, huh?"

She fired every missile Aoife's way at once.

Unbearable

Kaer Yin emerged from the tunnel mouth last, sending Jan Fir ahead to his next task. He then continued in the other direction with Robin and Tam Lin, past the remnants of the south slum.

"*Ard Tiarne!*" called Aoedhan Mol, another of Fionn's lieutenants, from the southern parapet. "They're gathering in the Navan woods!"

"How far?"

"A mile, Highness. Maybe less." Aoedhan hid it well, but like all Sidhe, he loved a fight as well as the next man. Many who hadn't been on the raid seemed eager to meet the Southers face to face rather than hide behind the shoddy walls or be picked off on the ramparts. Kaer Yin might agree if not for the people who called Roweal home— people who depended on him and these men to save them. Kaer Yin hit the ladder to the southeastern rampart without slowing. Robin and Tam Lin followed, but Aoedhan was already there, having raced over from the other side. Everyone else returning through the tunnel dashed off to make final preparations below.

"They beat us here," said Tam Lin, at least having the grace not to smile. "You were right, Yin. They're gagging for it now."

"They still outnumber us. Let's not forget, more is yet *more.*"

"Aye, a starving, angry, desperate lot they are too."

Kaer Yin sent him a long look over his bow shaft. "Tam Lin, you are closer to me than any brother." He clamped a hand over his shoulder so he couldn't miss the sincerity of his statement. "But you're insufferable. You know that?"

Tam Lin laughed, but Kaer Yin was already shouting orders down to the men moving into position along the wall. Robin wheezed a bit at the indifferent Sidhe all around him, he'd run the same distance they had, but none of them seemed to feel it half so much as he did. "Couldn't ye at least pretend to be as knackered as we poor mortals?" he grumbled, coming up beside Kaer Yin. "Anyway, the lads below said they're all set. How long did it take us to get back?"

"Too long," Tam Lin complained. "The bloody snow saw to that. Whatever Una did, worked too well, you ask me."

"Better than being on fire, I think," frowned Kaer Yin.

Tam Lin cleared his throat. "Anyway, what of the women and children?"

"All save Barb, Mistress Rian, that Siorai woman, and a few lookin' after the boys under *The Hart*— safe as they'll get for now," Robin answered.

Tam Lin shot Shar an unkind look as he'd taken up real estate near Kaer Yin's back instead of his own. "Can't you make her see sense?"

Shar didn't rise to the bait. He kept his eyes forward. "She knows her mind, *Mo Flaith.*"

"Yes, but she risks much. That bloody girl—"

Kaer Yin's hand pressed into his chest, stopping his advance. "That bloody *brave* girl, I think you mean? And invaluable. She's doing what she must, like all of us. Respect her choice."

"I don't like it."

"I don't either, but I won't devalue her by forcing the issue, and neither will you."

Shar looked away, something moving in his jaw.

"She could die down there, Yin," argued Tam Lin softly.

"I know that; believe me, she knows it better than any of us." Kaer Yin let go of his cousin's lapels and faced the incoming threat. "Now, they're going to come from every angle they can—no orders, nor direction. Bishop will give them their head— he must. Leaderless men are impossible to direct without captains." A ruthless sort of chuckle circled the returned raiders gathered around him. "They'll be mad dogs. Their only purpose is to get over or under this wall. When they do, their blood lust will make them sloppy. That's good news for us."

"*Ard Tiarne!*" everyone shouted but Tam Lin, whose thoughts were elsewhere.

"A sloppy soldier is a dead soldier." He snatched up an arrow from the pile beside his murder hole. He'd had them placed there before they'd gone on their raid. Hopefully, they had enough to make a convincing display. "When that gate comes down, I don't want to see any of you trying to be a hero. You move to Phase Two. Am I understood?" His command was relayed to every parapet along the wall, then down to the men below. "All right."

He turned back to the killing field, bow ready. "Let's give these Southers what they came for. "*Boghdóirí*[26], nock!"

"*An dara cór*[27]," Tam Lin shouted down to the yeomen on the ground. "Hold!"

They waited.

⚹

Ridley and his last remaining captains managed to assemble every available troop into something resembling an organized line. Every unit, minus the highly disciplined cavalry that Damek himself led, the archers that Earl Murphy and Sir Angus Simmons held in neat rows, and the remains of the Steel Corps and other heavy infantry that Ridley held in check at the front— were a teeming, screaming, chaotic mess. Nearly a thousand men, mostly infantry at the front, waved axes, sabres, clubs, and spears at the defenders lined up on the wall. It had only taken two hours to get them all here and less than two more to get them ordered, but here they were. Every man was ready to end their short-lived but brutal sojourn in the northern snows.

Damek had promised the first hundred over the wall a thousand fainne each. That few, if any, of those men would live to claim that boon wasn't the point. The din was all-encompassing.

"All is ready, My King," said Ridley, nodding to the catapult that was already loaded. Damek kicked his mount forward and waited until his remaining officers shouted the bulk of his forces to silence.

Wearing black from head to toe, the device on Damek's breastplate was Macha's golden bull, crowned by the Southernmost Star. Today, he wanted none to doubt who he was and what he sought to claim. When it was quiet enough, he lifted himself in his saddle, rising above his Bolg *garda's* long shields. His aunt Grainne's paramour Leal was first among them. Eyes blacked out with kohl, hair tipped with ash— the Warhammers were a dark smudge against the landscape, save for the golden bull on each shield. He hoped Kaer Yin was watching.

You're not the only Crown Prince on the field today.

"Who wants to go home?" Damek asked. He waited for his question to be repeated around. There was a nervous murmur at the front. "I said, *who wants to go home?*"

The crowd howled in commingled rage and bloodlust.

Damek drew the longsword at his side; Martin's longsword. He had vowed to bury his father with it, dripping with Kaer Yin Adair's blood. "Which way is south, boys?"

The answering roar shook the ground beneath his mount's hooves.

---

[26] 'Archers'
[27] Second corps.'

"Bethany is *that way*!" He pointed the longsword at the charred and battered hamlet. "A lordship to the man who brings me Kaer Yin Adair's head… and *ten thousand crowns* to the man who takes the most Dannan scalps!"

His men surged past him without ado, a sea of bellowing, red-faced bulls. They swarmed the wall from the southeast as one mob, dragging ladders, anchors, and ropes over their shoulders. Dozens fell before reaching the center of the killing field, but many more did not.

Damek rode back to Earl Murphy. "Loose." Hundreds of arrows launched into the sky, arched, and came down over the wall. Then another volley, and another. The defenders were too occupied with the horde scaling up the wall to do much about volleys sent from the ground at two-minute intervals. "Ridley!" Damek turned again to nod at his newly appointed Corps Commander. "I want that fucking Gate down now!"

Ridley saluted and marched down the line to the Navan Road, barking orders.

Simmons approached Damek from the left. "Permission for pitch?"

"Granted."

Simmons moved to the rear line of yeomen— longbows loaded with flaming shot. Many of their infantry would die— but Damek was beyond caring about the details. He expected to be within Rosweal's smoking corpse within the hour.

"Corps two, nock!" screeched Simmons in his high-pitched voice. The longbowmen dug their yew bow shafts into the earth at their feet and drew back, nearly pressing their backs into the dirt for heft. The shot gathered at every arrow point was heavy with iron and flaming pitch. Even from a distance, Damek could feel the heat on his face.

"Fire at will!'

Damek smirked at the glowing arc of fire as it sailed straight up into the sky, stopped at an angle, then plummeted over the wall like a bright red scythe. He didn't listen to the men die on either side nor witness several of his foot soldiers plummet to the snow with flaming bolts in their backs or chests. He kicked his horse toward the road, where his last two catapults were already hurling vast chunks of masonry, pitch, and fire at the buckled gate. After a dozen strikes, the gate groaned inwardly, a large crack splitting its face in two. Damek raised his sword high at the cavalry gathering behind him. The final load was piled into the catapult while the top half of the gate toppled inward. The last shot would do it. "Hold until the dust clears!" he shouted to his men.

Another well-aimed shot— a direct hit at the busted center of the gate. The resulting rumble was ear-splitting. The gate pitched backward into the city, taking half of the eastern wall with it.

Smiling, Damek's teeth filled with dust.

He kicked his charger forward, his faithful *garda* at either side.

⚹ ⚹

KAER YIN SPUN, USING A LARK with his left hand and Sinnair's silver-capped butt in his right. There was already a pile of dead Southers beneath his feet; even more had fallen over the parapet into the mud behind him. Still, they came. A mass of hacking, breaking, screeching beasts that barely held the frame of men. Thankfully, in his haste to get inside the walls, Damek's archers had done half the work for Rosweal's defenders. The Southern dead outnumbered the defender's arrows by a tidy sum. They littered the uneven ground of the killing field, strewn over ladders, tangled in piles along the battlements. The black fletching of every arrow that had speared one or more of these men was a testament to Bishop's lack of control. He craved only vengeance. By Herne, Kaer Yin would see that he got what he came for.

Kaer Yin ducked under another volley, using the corpse of a dead infantryman as a shield. Without time to recover, another opponent came howling at him from the right. He tossed the corpse directly at him and then turned to engage the next comer without waiting to watch the first tumble from the wall.

631

He took the one combatant through the kidney and spun away to meet the next with Sinnair's shaft, cracking his skull like a gourd.

"Yin!" Tam Lin called over the steaming mass of wriggling, slashing, burning bodies. "Time!"

Kaer Yin stopped, kicking the man he'd slain down the ladder. He flung the blood from his lark before returning it to its sheath. "To the North Wall!" he bellowed, slinging Sinnair around his shoulder so he'd be free to nock and draw. He'd purposefully loaded triple the regular number of arrows into his quiver, saving them for this moment. While running, he took four men that stood in his path through the eyes and throats in less time than he'd spent on a single breath.

He raced over the bodies littering the rampart, dodging every hand or blade that reached out to stall him, to the crux of the mortally wounded eastern wall and the gaping hole where the gate had been—and aimed. Even from this height and distance, he could make out the men shouting orders to Damek's archers. He exhaled, loosing one shot and another, then drew again. One arrow struck the nearest Souther commander in the center of his forehead, sending his armored body backward into the mud *sans* his brains. The second was challenging to see because the yeomen commander was much further back in their line. Longbows were always placed in the rear because they had range and carried the burden of greater weight and bulk. That is, for Milesian archers. Dannan archers practiced firing longbows from trees, on horseback, and even in close quarters. His second shot found its target from a pace of nearly two hundred and fifty yards. The redhaired Souther's head split open like a melon, coating the men beside him with gore.

Kaer Yin hadn't realized Shar and Niall were right behind him until he heard one of them whistle. Grinning, he slung Sinnair over his shoulder to free his hands for the climb down. He took a moment's satisfaction to witness the terrified, awed stares of the Southers who'd made it up the wall. The shot would have been impossible for any mortal man, and indeed, for most Sidhe. The remaining commander below stared up at him white-faced. He was the only infantry captain Damek had left that wasn't currently riding into a trap with him.

Kaer Yin spared the man a grin.

"Shall we, gentlemen?"

The defenders on the wall took up a cheer as he and his chosen men descended into the city, beginning phase two.

⚑ ⚑

Ridley raced to catch up to Damek's mount through the hot smoke and dust that blew down on them from the collapsing gate. "Murphy and Kinney, My King," he huffed, out of breath and near purple with rage.

"What?" Damek shouted back. He could hardly hear a word.

"Our infantry commanders. Kinney and Murphy, they're both dead. I don't even know the fellow who's left, but he can't hold that many men in check on his own. Troops are deserting."

"*What?* How, for fuck's sake?"

Ridley pointed to a familiar silver head as it ascended the ladders to the northern stone wall. The way that figure moved, with such sure-footed grace, there could be no mistaking him for anyone else. Damek cursed under his breath. He knew what had happened before Ridley could finish getting the words out. "I've never seen anything like it. Took 'em both through their crowns from almost *three hundred yards!*" He shook his head, open-mouthed and pale. "Who would have believed such a thing was possible?"

"Who gives a shite?" Damek snarled back. "When this dust clears, I want *you* to show *them* why the whole bloody Continent fears *us!*"

Ridley's jaw clenched tight. "Aye, My King."

632

"It doesn't fucking matter what these cunts cook up or how the least among us might shirk their duty. The Steel Corps can dismantle this hovel on their own."

"Yes." Ridley's face colored with fury. "You're right."

"Now, get your men ready. Send word for our remaining archers to follow our cavalry inside. I'll assume command. After that, I want your men over that debris and your ass up that hill. Lead us inside, Captain."

Ridley saluted; murderous grin restored. The Steel Corps moved into position, sabres rattling against their steel breastplates in a deafening roar. Their two-foot-tall steel-coated shields slammed into the debris beneath their horses' hooves in a thunderous rhythm.

"Cavalry!" Damek bellowed, swiping Martin's sword forward. "Advance!"

INSIDE, AS EXPECTED, THE SIDHE had picked off or ridden down any soldier too foolish to avoid the narrow alleys and twisting lanes that crisscrossed a toppled neighborhood in the south end. Near the northeast, just before the massive hole in the wall where the gate once stood— Fionn Shiel O'More, the High King's Champion and the most accomplished cavalry commander Aes Sidhe had ever known, sat a giant, cloud white destrier at the center of the Navan High Road, in the heart of town. The Dannan cavalry held the high ground and the network of lanes that spiderwebbed from that point outward. At the reinforced Southern Gate from the Taran approach, merely twenty Sidhe horsemen and archers had all but eliminated Damek's straggling infantry inside the walls. Those who were wise regrouped behind Damek's Corpsmen or fled back through the eastern wall. Now, the factions inside the city stared at each other from the east and center.

The Sidhe, it should be obvious, didn't appear the least bit alarmed by Damek's superior numbers. They were serene as house cats, smirking back at Damek's rattled Corpsmen as if it were a sweet summer's day at a fair.

Ridley called a curt command, and his flank marched forward over the debris, shields snapped together in neat rows to craft an impenetrable wall around his men; a mounted phalanx, rendering arrows and spears useless from shoulder to shin, and also protected their mounts' soft underbellies from harm. His unit advanced through a hail of arrows fired from atop the wall, each missile pinging from their steel-dipped shields. They made fantastic progress until they came within a hundred yards of Fionn's waiting equestrians.

The Southers halted. Ridley barked, "Break away!" and the shields separated. Foot soldiers raced up from the rear to stack their shields until the wall was twice as tall as the vanguard, and pikes were inserted at each joint. "Advance!" Ridley shouted from somewhere inside the armored knot of men and horses.

As he watched Ridley move up the road to Fionn's waiting *garda*, Damek considered the ramshackle rooftops laden with sharpshooters. He'd ordered his archers to the front before his cavalry, tucked neatly behind their wall of shields, and divided into two filing rows. For every arrow that scored one of his men's shields or somehow made it through a chink in their armor, four more were fired into the city in answer. It wasn't long before the defenders' arrows thinned to the merest trickle. Despite the genuine concern that he was doing exactly what he was expected to, Damek nodded for more of his archers to root out defensive positions along the alleyways ahead. He was likely sending men to their deaths, but he had to trust his men to get the job done. Meanwhile, Ridley's phalanx continued up the road. Fionn didn't move a muscle.

Damek didn't like it. He glanced around the rooftops, alert for the next surprise. Ridley's men neared Fionn's line, and Damek's wait was over.

The Dannan cavalry split ranks, dividing at the center. A screaming tangle of blue-faced warriors— over seventy strong— came crashing into and over Ridley's shields from the high ground. Shieldmen were knocked down or cut from their feet, banging into each other as they tried to maintain their footing. They bayed in alarm and reared up, dislodging several riders in the process.

It couldn't hold; the phalanx broke apart, forced back downhill from three sides. Foot soldiers were forced to abandon their shields and engage while the equestrians hacked down at men who harried them in teams, dragging heavily armored Corpsmen out of their saddles. In exactly ten minutes, the unit was mired in a common street brawl with a mob who had rendered their shields and horses useless. Behind this, Fionn called an order Damek couldn't hear but could guess its gist. "Gods damn it!" he hissed. "He's going to divide his forces and get behind us. Pull Ridley back!"

But Ridley and his flank were too far up the road to back down. Ridley's only chance now was to spread out and hope to penetrate deeper into the city while preventing Fionn's men from bottlenecking them in the streets. Ridley was on his own.

When O'More's horses backed off, turned flanks, and split into five directions, Damek cursed anew. "Six men abreast. Get down those lanes now!" he ordered, kicking his mount into a canter and steering sharply right with his Bolg *garda*. He headed for the North Wall, shields at the front. Whatever nasty presents Fionn intended for his men, Damek had no intention of being there to greet them. However, it seemed Fionn had anticipated this decision. He saw Fionn's riders keeping pace with them between neighboring lanes. About twenty lengths ahead, two of his riders darted east along the alley ahead. They were trying to hem him in! "After them! Break the Sidhe line!" Damek belted, and a handful of his men prepared to do just that when something he didn't expect came hurtling down his north-facing lane. A flaming barrel raced downhill from the stone wall. Thinking quickly, Damek jumped an abandoned pushcart and leaped into the next alley, but two of his honor guard were not so lucky. Men and horses went down, dragged over the cobbles toward the eastern dip in the main road.

Another and another barrel followed suit.

Damek watched in horror as the barrels careened into buildings at the base of the hill, exploding on impact. The main of his cavalry were caught in the open, unprepared. In the resulting explosions, a hundred men were knocked from their saddles, went down in a mess of broken limbs and steel, or were blasted apart wholesale. That quickly, his cavalry was fractured at its center. The vanguard he'd led to cut off Fionn's double envelopment was scattered or unhorsed. He kicked his mount into a second canter and crashed through a wooden doorway. Without stopping, he burst through a low-slung window, maintaining his seat by sheer will alone. He heard the fifth explosion downhill and the screams of men who hadn't had time to escape.

He heard a shout on his right and saw one of Fionn's knights galloping straight for him. Damek drew his sword and spurred his horse broadside. The Dannan didn't have a chance to turn, so he tried to rein in. His horse's hooves skidded over the snow-slick cobbles, causing a collision with Damek's larger mount.

This was why Bethonair cavalry decked their horses out in padded steel. His horse grunted but was otherwise unmoved by the impact.

The Dannan's eyes flew wide as his horse buckled beneath him and went down screaming. He was jolted upright, where Damek's vambraced arm shot out to drag him the rest of the way. He slit the Sidhe's throat, hefted him over the opposite side, and trampled the remnants. Turning north again, two blue-faced Roswellians slammed into his horse from below, splitting its unprotected guts onto the cobbles.

Damek tucked and rolled away as he went down and came back up with his sword drawn. He decapitated one villager with a single slash and spent maybe two minutes with the second, simply for lack of space to swing. The lanes were tight here, and his arms were long. The Greenmaker was slightly better with a sword than he'd hoped, but it wasn't enough to save his life. He split the man's skull in two, then kicked his wilting corpse into the next group that meant to rush up at him.

Four of Ridley's shieldmen made short work of the rest.

Everywhere Damek looked, his men were fighting and dying. Knowing he needed to regroup, he moved toward his brawling forces at the foot of the hill— but a flash of pale hair drew his attention like a bloody red hand to the base of the north wall. In the middle of a cross-alley, the unmistakable gleam of gold winked in the figure's ears as he danced left and right, cutting through foot soldiers, archers, and Ridley's surviving Corps like cheese. Damek killed the next few comers without blinking. His blood roared to flame in his chest. Suddenly the battle, the South, hells, even Una— faded from Damek's mind like dry leaves blown away in the wind. He could only see Martin's cold, grinning face staring at nothing.

Kaer Yin Adair saw Damek too. He held his arms wide, bloody blades dripping as if to say, 'Here I am.'

Far be it for Damek to keep him waiting.

With a cry he didn't know he was capable of making, Damek threw himself up the lane toward the only foe that mattered.

Belladonna

Perhaps the wisest move Lord Bishop had made that morning before the gate came down was to send a ragtag of men around the wall to the west. On that trek, there would be nothing but scorched trees and deep gray snow rolling into a smog-laden horizon for miles and miles around. Rosweal's defenders, knowing the wall was strongest at that end, had left it primarily unguarded to prepare the city for Phase Three. The bulk of the defenders collected along the eastern wall and tracked north to give the Dannans cover. Robin himself spent most of these last furious hours prepping the quarter for the next challenge. A cold needle of dread tapped along his spine when the horns blew atop the western wall.

Most of the people in Rosweal huddled in cellars and sewers, waiting for the Greenmakers to get them out. So far, Robin wasn't anywhere near ready. Ben had held men in reserve for such a risk, but given the intensity of the fighting on the other side of the city, they were shorthanded. The horns called again. Robin looked at Colm and felt himself pale. They held a large cask of gunpowder between them destined to line Taverners' Lane. They had only just begun to deposit its contents when the first screams filled the air. "Oh feck," Colm said.

Robin blanched, "Knew that retreat was too bloody good to be true."

Colm dropped his end of the cask, which was bound for the lanes around Solomon Trant's brewery. "They're early."

"We don't have near enough fellas up there."

Colm sucked in a breath as a gang of fully armored marauders swung down the wall on ropes, making a beeline for the structures below. "Not infantry."

"No," Robin agreed, eyes narrowing. He lost count after watching at least forty men make it over and then dash into the streets. "Siora's tits!"

These bastards meant business. Armed to the bloody teeth, it was no mean feat to cross Barb's muddy moats, up a slick embankment with at least fifty pounds of added weight, then up and over a wall defended by men who were crack shots, despite arrows not being plentiful. The Southers were elite Corpsmen, Robin could tell at a glance, and there could be only one reason they would split from the main force.

"Vick! Get yer scrawny arse down to *The Hart* and get them folks to the river, *now*!"

"Now?" Vick parroted, wiping his filthy hair from his eyes with a sooty hand. "But we ain't finished—"

"I said now, Siora damn ye!" Robin purpled.

Vick must have recognized the horror in his boss' voice. He finally looked up at what he and Colm were ogling. "Oh shite. We can't get all o'em out in time. There's too many!"

Robin's hand snaked out, slapping Vick's ear into the cask he'd dropped. The lad cried out, a tear sliding over his grimy cheek. "If ye don't get there afore they do, everyone down there will die. Ye hear me?"

"I'll get there first. I swear it," Vick answered soberly.

"Ye'd better. Go!"

He let go and Vick, quick as an adder, zipped into the brewery on legs hastened by desperation. Robin could only pray he was fast as he claimed to be. His mother was down there with the rest of Rosweal's women and children.

The horns sounded for the third time, now from the North Wall.

Robin turned to Colm, who nodded back, knives drawn. The Greenmakers behind them followed suit. Robin hefted his own stolen sabre. "These lads came here for a brawl. Let's show 'em they came to the right town."

❧ ❧

Tᴀᴍ Lɪɴ ʀᴀɪsᴇᴅ ʜɪs ʜᴇᴀᴅ at the third horn blast. He was back on the eastern rampart in the north corner, just shy of the debris gap. He and twenty Dannan bowmen, primarily his own Blood Eagles, lurked at crux to pick off Southers on both sides of the wall. Any of Bishop's cavalry that attempted to retreat through the gap never made it past the rubble. Their horses thundered away as their riders piled up at the gate, riddled with arrows. Fionn's mounted knights had done an excellent job of scattering Bishop's forces so far, and the remaining few had no idea what awaited them in the narrow lanes and alleys ahead. It had been Tam Lin's job to make sure Souther corpses blocked their sole means of escape while Fionn's men rode in seemingly every direction at once, either running down knots of straggling infantry, chasing the remnants of their cavalry, or throwing torches through the windows of buildings designated for Kaer Yin's Phase Three.

A fourth horn called, this time, closer.

Southers were in the Quarter.

"*Mo Flaithe*!" called Niall, tossing a bloodied figure over the rampart by his head. "That's the West Wall!"

Tam Lin was aware. He loosed three more arrows he didn't need to watch fall before drawing his lark to slay one opponent, then turned to open a gash in the throat of a second, who he then shoved off the wall. Covered in blood and every type of dirt imaginable, Tam Lin paused to look around. Nearly every one of his men was low on arrows and the fight though decidedly tipped in their favor now, was far from over. He looked west and saw the glint of steel clambering down the wall on ropes.

Where were the bloody Greenmakers?

There were people in the buildings below. No help for it. He muttered a foul oath in Ealig. "Niall! You have the wall. Jan Fir, with me!"

He barked orders on his long way around to the old stone battlements on the north side of town. Funny that Rosweal's ancient defenses were built to keep the Sidhe out, and now they were busy trying to help the modern citizens save the city. The irony, as always, was not lost on Tam Lin O'Ruiadh.

Despite several attempts to stall their progress, they made excellent time racing around the wall to the west. Kaer Yin's tangle of defenders occupied themselves with the barrels and casks of gunpowder and pitch they heaved over the wall into Bishop's men. Tam Lin didn't slow to help. Kaer Yin knew what he was doing.

As for Bishop and his men, he might have overestimated the wisdom of a full-frontal assault on such a small but lethally tight city like Rosweal. He and his cavalry were having all the fun Kaer Yin expected them to, thanks to Fionn O'More. Still, he *did* have more men, and they'd expected him to throw some at the Quarter eventually. Just, not so soon.... and certainly, not his best. Bishop was cannier than Tam Lin would like.

He threw Kaer Yin's strategy back in his face.

You took my best from me; Bishop seemed to be saying.

It appeared he was returning the favor.

What purpose did Kaer Yin have to defend this insignificant, unenlightened, and frankly unimportant collection of ramshackles at the rim of a wilderness but its people? The new 'King of Eire' might be after a crown and might even win it here today... but he intended to pay for it with innocent blood.

Pumping everything he had to spare into his legs, Tam Lin ran, shouting for all available men on the wall to follow him to *The Hart*— where most of Rosweal's people waited beneath the grandest, most obvious target in town.

❧ ❧

On the street, Robin and his Greenmakers clashed with the first wave of Souther Corpsmen headed for a dense tumble of mostly intact buildings gathered near the northwest end of the city. These Southers were no madcap, lawless foot soldiers sent to choke the streets with fallen bodies, like so many pawns. These were professional soldiers. Greenmakers were hardly blushing girls, but they weren't decked out in thirty pounds of armor either. Speed would be their best chance. They came running at the Southers from the alleys and dropped down from the rooftops, hacking away with whatever devices they could get their hands on. Often, with the Souther sabres, lifted from the bodies of fallen men that littered the snowy lanes like scattered breadcrumbs.

Any hope that the invaders had worn themselves out hauling themselves over the wall in such heavy armor was a thin one. Robin directed his men to focus attacks on their heads, the back of the knee, and the unprotected spots under the arms. If their target didn't fall immediately, Robin warned his men to get away and come back for a second shot rather than attempt to cross swords with better-armed, better-trained men. Swiftly seeing Robin's strategy, the Greenmakers clustered together to watch each other's backs.

At least ten Corpsmen went down in the first blitz.

Unfortunately, the element of surprise couldn't last. The Southers rallied together in a lock-joint knot of sharp steel and practiced arms. Any Greenmaker who got too close wouldn't live long. Nonetheless, Robin was committed. He dashed through the center of a southbound lane, two streets west of *The Hart*, skidding down an icy slope on the cobbles toward a man brandishing two sabres.

The big Corpsmen hacked at anything that came too close; landing bone-crushing blows on either side of whoever was unlucky enough to sway into his orbit. Three of Robin's men went down before he slid to a halt at the Corpsmen's knees, jabbing his dagger deep into the Souther's booted foot. The Souther howled in pain, staggering off balance long enough for Robin to roll up to his knees and jerk a sabre point into the fellow's exposed underarm. With his heart and lungs critically damaged, the Souther tipped backward into the snow, coughing blood.

Robin relieved him of his sabres and passed them along to men who needed better fare. "Thank ye, sir," one said, then trudged down the lane toward the Ward Gate, where a handful of Greenmakers gathered to push the newcomers into the wall against Robin's orders. The Southers knew their business. Speed was only effective so long as everyone kept moving. "Siora damn ye, get outta there!" he spat, pulling as many men back up the lane with him as he could. Those he could not pry away died in moments. Traipsing over the fallen, the Southers moved uphill after Robin and his group as a unit. Robin paused a moment, thinking. The lanes would converge in Hilltop square about five blocks ahead. He didn't want to give them that much room.

"Into the narrows, lads!" They backtracked, intending to wedge these over-armed bastards into a space too tight to wriggle from, but another cadre of Corpsmen came jogging up the hill from the east. It seemed they had heard the horns and had their orders.

Robin saw Bishop's grizzled infantry commander— Ridley— he'd heard him called, emerge from the knot of newcomers. He was smattered with mud, and blood dripped from his beard and seeped from a cut above his swollen right eye, but he was otherwise live and hale. Their numbers were drastically reduced, but with these fresh reinforcements from the west, it wouldn't make a lick of difference to the Greenmakers.

"*Back*!" Robin raged at his men. "Get yer arses back to Wanderer's Alley, *now!*" He turned to run uphill toward the North Wall, reaching into his tunic to find the silver whistle he'd been hoping he wouldn't need all day.

⚥

Rian heard the horns before Barb did, her hands freezing over the half-smashed skull of a fourteen-year-old boy who'd been thrown from the east wall when the gate had come down. She watched the boy's pupils dilate with fear. A second and third blast echoed through the tap, then down the stairs to Rian's infirmary in the cellar. She stood up. That one was close.

Too close.

Barb waddled down the steps, her thinning face white as a pearl. She did not look well at all. Rian had a bad feeling that there was more to her weight loss than simple hunger. "Those are behind us," Barb said, clutching at her sagging bodice. She had lost nearly sixty pounds if Rian were any judge.

Barb Dormer was ill.

Rian cursed under her breath.

Why hadn't she seen it until now?

Barb cocked her head at her. "Did ye not hear?"

Rian opened her mouth, but the boy she'd been tending responded. "From the Ward Gate. Me Da said they wouldn't come from that direction."

Another horn trumpeted so near that it might have been over her head— and likely was— with men stationed on the roof. Everyone in the cellar had heard all manner of blasts, shouts, mumbles, and screams filtering into their hiding place, but none had been so close nor so late in the fighting. This could only mean that Lord Bishop had kept reserves for insurance. Of course, he would. Ben had said he might. That didn't make it any less a lethal blow. "Apparently," Rian sighed. "Your Da was wrong." The boy whimpered. Rian and Barb stared at each other over his head. "We have to get out of here!"

Barb moved faster than a woman her age should be expected to, Dabney's quiet bulk dogging her heels. "Get them up! Hurry!"

Frantically Rian moved from corner to corner, dragging those who could walk toward the cots and crates loaded with those who could not. "On your feet! If you're strong enough to walk, by Siora, I pray you're strong enough to carry! Show us the way, Barb." Rian got two people up beneath either of her arms, but she was hardly strong, and the going was tough.

"Be quick about it, Dabs!" Barb shoved Dabney at a grate on the floor. One-handed, the hulking figure hoisted the heavy iron grate out of the floor, revealing a foul-smelling passage downward. "Come on, come on. No! Not them that can't walk, girl."

"I'm not leaving them!" Rian snapped back.

Before Barb could argue, Vincent flew down the cellar stairs, two at a time. He was redder in the face than usual and wheezing. He must have run a long way. "Th-they're comin'! I dunno how many."

Rian leaped at him. "You! Good. Help me move these people—"

"Ye can't save everyone, Rian. They'll slow those who have a chance."

"I'm not bloody leaving them!" She fisted Vick's collar. "Help me."

Swallowing, he bent to take up the patients she had trouble balancing on her own. He wasn't much bigger or stronger than Rian, but between them, they managed to get about six people who could at least limp through the opening in the floor. Her new shadow, Strong Tim, held the ladder for them.

"Think you can hold it still while me and Vick pass some of the people who can't move down?" she asked him.

"Oh, fer feck's sake!" growled Barb in frustration, throwing her hands up. Dabs, ye grab that lot there, young Tim, help me with these here."

Between the five, they managed to move about twelve individuals from their sickbeds and hand them down to the walking wounded waiting in the passage. "Careful there, Dabs. That one there don't have much blood left in 'em, from the look o'things." Rian was busy dragging a man over by his shoulders, leaving a red stain in the dirt. Barb grabbed her wrist and spun her around. "That one's dead, girl."

"But he's still breathing! They all are."

They were all men sporting the ash 'X' she'd drawn on their foreheads. The 'critical' wing of her musty, highly unsanitary triage.

"No, they're bloody dead, girl. Ye said yerself if we move any o'em, they'll die. Well, *we* must move now— right bloody *now*— or *we'll* all die."

"But—" It was not in Rian's nature to abandon people that needed her.

Barb's hands came alongside her face, forcing her to look straight into her eyes. "Rian, yer a good girl, and I'm sore sorry I played a mean trick on ye once. Truly. Yer a brave, sweet soul, ye are, but listen to me now and listen well. Those poor devils in that corner may be spared just for posin' no threat and no profit, but ye, little lass— and all the other young things down that tunnel— will suffer a fate even an old professional like me has never even seen. Do ye hear me?"

Rian's eyes welled with tears, but she nodded.

"Good girl." Barb tugged her into an awkward embrace. "Now come away, quick! We still have two more cellars to empty before we can get outside the walls."

IT STARTED SNOWING AGAIN AS several dozen townsfolk gathered in a vacant building just shy of the stone North Gate— which was the official 'end of the line' for the Taran High Road. The North Wall had been constructed by actual stonemasons when Rosweal was incorporated after the Transition. It had been built to protect the docks from marauding river clans and, as always, dissuade attacks from Aes Sidhe just across the river. In the hundreds of years since, the North Gate had scarcely been used and hadn't been opened for as long as anyone could remember. No one was even sure if its mechanism— a complicated set of pulleys and weights—*could* be used anymore.

Rosweal's citizens took the long way around to get to the docks, which had been moved further west for its deeper channel. Since the gate was firmly shut, they had no choice but to escape below the wall. However, there were many buildings between them and the exit— at least four alleys and two broad cross lanes before the underground passage they sought. The sewer didn't connect the total distance from *The Hart* to the wall. It stopped two buildings closer, that portion having collapsed sometime in Barb's grandsire's youth. She'd been meaning to have it properly restored for years. Chamber pots dumped from upstairs windows were hardly a hygienic practice, after all, and Barb had always dreamed of better for her people.

Yet, the cost to refurbish a pre-Transition subterranean waterway was a mite rich for the hardscrabble outlaws and miscreants of Rosweal. Besides, Barb had spent nearly every copper she had to spare building their new and bloody useless wall, hadn't she? She frowned. The townsfolk emerged into the old goal, which served little purpose save as a storing house for nefarious goods or the odd Greenmaker who'd neglected to fork over his dues to the Guild. From a filthy, soot-streaked window, they had a decent view of the North Wall, where it connected with the charred timbers of the lower western. It wasn't snowing as hard as she hoped it would be. Against all that flat white, they'd stick out like a bleeding thumb. She grumbled something unintelligible.

"What?" asked Rian, from her elbow.

"I said, 'Siora's cunny.' Barb turned to spit onto the dusty floor.

Rian looked for herself. There were hordes of men racing up and down alleys directly between them and their escape. Men fought hand to hand on the stone wall above. Men dashed along the western wall, or through the lanes, with weapons raised. Men slashed and hacked at each other from every conceivable direction. Too many men *everywhere*. They'd never make it. They couldn't even cross this street to the next without being seen. Barb watched the realization dawn on Rian's wan face and turned away to rub at her own eyes with her thumb and forefinger. "It appears we're stuck here," she said.

"Nonsense," argued a Dannan fighter that didn't bother to introduce himself. Rian had stitched a chunk of his scalp together, leaving a wicked line that snaked from the dome of his shorn pate to the edge of his eyebrow. His eyes, bloodshot and blackened, narrowed at the scene outside the glass. He, too, cursed at the sight.

"There now, ye see? Do I look like a silly girl to ye? If I say we're trapped, we're feckin' trapped."

The Sidhe officer blinked at her brass but backed off, appropriately chastened.

"We'll have to fight our way out," added Rian, her voice small.

Barb could practically see the cogs spinning in that fair head of hers. She snorted, "And what? Choke armored men to death with our bandages? Maybe club 'em to death with our crutches?"

Rian scowled over at her. "You have a better idea?"

"None. I need a bloody drink."

"We can't stay here and wait, Barb. They'll find that grate eventually, and even if they don't, you heard what Ben said, same as me."

That left a sour taste on Barb's tongue, sure. She had vehemently opposed this hair-brained scheme from the outset, and look! Now she didn't even have any uishge left to make it sting less! "Aye, I did. Them sewers aren't stable in the least. More cave in every year and with what His Arseness means to do— I doubt any will be there in the morning."

"So what are we supposed to do? We can't stay here."

"We could lead 'em off," said Strong Tim, visibly hoping no one would hear.

"What's that, boy?" Barb pressed.

He swallowed audibly. "We could split up. Half make a run for it, half stay behind to draw 'em into the narrows. We know our way 'round. They don't."

Barb fiddled with her chin while she considered the lad's comments. His arms were sticks dangling from ill-fitting shirt sleeves that swung from him like parliamentary robes. His brown, slightly hazel eyes were huge in their sunken sockets.

"No, Tim," Rian hissed and made to paw at him, but Barb threw out a hand.

"Let him be. It was yer idea to fight through— he just had a better one."

"He's just a boy!"

Barb nodded, her jaw tight. "Aye, and a good deal older than twenty more behind him.

Rian glanced around at the gathered citizens and wounded of Rosweal, who'd either been hiding in the tunnels or laid up in her infirmary and looked back down. She was quiet for a while. Her conversation with Eva began to make perfect, brutal sense. She couldn't help but wonder where Eva was now and what fate she saw for everyone else. She must have known this would happen and what Rian would decide. She finally shook her head. "Fine. But he's not going alone."

Barb reached out to grasp at her shoulder. "Oh, no, no, lass—"

Rian shrugged her hand off. "No, you were right. Rose knows what to do now if someone needs help. Don't you, Rose?"

Rose moved up the hall toward the window. "Rian, it should be me. Not you. You don't know—"

"No," Rian cut her off. "You're a comfort to those kids. They need you."

A bevy of protests sprang up at her decision, but she waved them all away.

"There's a lot of our men out there too— the Prince's men—" She pointed at the Dannan who'd spoken up. He wore the same device as the Prince of Connaught. "They know me. If they see me running around out there, I might have a chance to lead them back to help. I'm going. That's all there is to say."

"It would be my honor to escort you, Mistress," said the Sidhe, with a handsome bow.

"And me," added Violet, another girl who worked for Barb, one of her best.

"No," Barb said again, fighting tears she felt shamed to shed.

Violet patted her on the arm. "Got littles of my own in here. I wanna give 'em what chance I can. Me mam will look after 'em."

There was a murmur of outcry, but Violet shushed them all with a playful smirk. "Ye all know what a fast runner I am."

"And me," said Eva, who had been stone silent until now. She stepped forward, her robes a white smudge against the smoky interior.

Rian shook her head. "No. Rose will need you more than we do."

Eva's stare was unnerving. "Rian… you will need me."

Rian swallowed. The little phial she'd been given suddenly felt heavy in her pocket. "I'll be fine. Won't be alone." She gave her a weak smile.

Eva nodded. "May Siora walk with you."

When she walked away, there were tears in her eyes.

Rian pretended not to see them.

Three more lads, two older men, and a smattering of women stepped forward to volunteer. It took a while for the crowd to calm down. When it had, Tim moved to the window. "We should wait till it gets dark."

"We can't. If that whistle goes off—" she broke off. "We must get these people to safety while we have a choice." Rian smoothed her skirt and wiped her nose. She looked more ready to get on with it than afraid of what would probably happen to her.

"Well, logic says me and Dabs are the most expendable here," Barb laughed. "Besides, waitin' around with no uishge and my thumb in my arse is borin' me to tears. Think we'll be joinin' ye's, after all."

Rian's head snapped around. "You can't be serious?"

"I'm not lettin' ye go out there alone, girlie. Dabs neither. Would fair break his heart to leave ye. Wouldn't it?"

Dabney nodded, eyes misty. He didn't say much, but he had a heart; he did. Rian took his meaty hand in hers. "We'd better get going then."

Barb grabbed the girl's elbow, stopping her just shy of the exit. "I want ye to know, yer as fine a lady as yer friend, lass. Finer, ye ask me."

Rian sniffed, then patted Barb's thin fingers. "I appreciate what you're trying to say, but you don't understand her."

"We'll just have to agree to disagree there. Let's hope we run faster than I think we do."

⚔

Ultimately, they did not make it through the following two alleys unscathed. They stuck together in one large group until they came to a stable overlooking the wider east-west cross lane, about twenty yards from the gaol. As the townsfolk snuck uphill toward the stable— a long line of sickly and wounded women and children— shouts sounded from the alley behind. Torches lit up the evening sky, and the sound of steel and stomping boots muffled by snow soon followed.

Barb watched Rian pale.

The girl didn't have the first clue what her sacrifice would mean.

"All right folks, get yer arses to that gatehouse! Go, go, *go!*"

People raced by as Barb half dragged, half shoved Rian at the stable.

"Fer fuck's sake!"

The nameless Sidhe in their company stepped between them and the incoming soldiers, drawing two thin shortswords from behind his empty quiver. He bowed to Rian and Barb, then jogged back toward the gaol, screeching like a hawk. Barb didn't wait to watch him clash with the Southers. Instead, she dragged Rian away as two more groups came howling at them from opposite directions.

"Run the other way!" Barb shrieked. Dabney kicked down a door on the far end of the darkened stable, and she, Rian, Violet, and young Tim threw themselves into that exit. Steel dogged their heels. Barb felt the air rush by her ear as a sabre swept past. They pushed and pulled each other through the narrow bottleneck in a tangle to get to the gatehouse ahead. They could see its dark maw, just there.

If only they could get there.

Rian ran as fast as her useless left leg would carry her. Twice she slipped in the snow, only to be hauled to her feet by Tim, who was much stronger than he looked. Laughing and whooping like dogs on a hunt, the Southers snapped at their heels, outnumbering them three to one.

642

A huge fellow snatched a hank of Rian's long hair. Crying out, she lost her footing again, but Violet launched herself at her attacker, gouging his eye with the cheese knife she kept in her bodice. The Souther howled and went down on his back, blood pouring through the fingers he crammed into the empty socket. His companions surged forward, but Tim ducked into an open doorway to the house next door, urging the others to follow, then slammed it shut behind them. Rian and Violet put all their combined weight into sliding a bureau against the wood, shoving it against the pounding door. The glass window blasted inward, and axes hacked at the soft, fire-damaged door.

"Go on!" Tim's voice broke as he gestured to the back of the house. The group burst through the burnt-out kitchen to the rear door, then again into the snow outside. "This way!" he cried, leading them through another alley. They could see the gatehouse now, ever closer, yet still so far. Barb had the intense satisfaction of watching several haggard shapes make it through that tiny black hole. At least the majority of their folks would make it. That was the point, wasn't it? That four Souther soldiers chased them inside; Barb would leave to Siora. She had her own problems at the moment.

At the end of the alley, their luck ran out.

Two fully-armored men ran at them from the street, weapons raised.

Without thinking, Violet ran straight for them, brandishing her tiny blade like a longsword and screaming at the top of her lungs. "Get out of here!" she hissed at Barb, who didn't have time to think as Dabney already had his hand on the back of her neck, shoving her through another door.

"No!" Rian sobbed, but Tim would not let her stop.

They made for the next exit, then the next, now facing south and further away from the gatehouse. Tim seemed to realize his mistake and tried to course-correct, tugging Rian along by the hand. One of Fionn's knights rode west down the neighboring cross lane, trampling men like so much rotted fruit. Another, then another, galloped by. Rian tried to call out to them, but they were moving too fast to hear her.

Tim turned to yank her through a nearby door by the wrist, but when he nudged the door open, Souther Corpsmen waited on the other side. They must have heard Violet's screams through the houses on either side. With a chuckle, the soldier rammed his sabre through Tim's throat to the hilt. Rian screamed as he fell. His murderer withdrew the blade, only to rear back and slam his mailed fist into the side of Rian's head.

Dabney roared and threw himself into the pair of onlookers, but two against one— when two are coated in expensive armor, and one was not— was hardly a fair contest. Barb could do nothing but stand in the shadows and watch. Time seemed irrelevant, and everything moved in slow motion. She drew her dagger, weighing her options. She might kill one of them, but they would surely kill her and rape the girl anyway.

Feck me, thought Barb.

What do I do?

While she debated which one to sacrifice both of their lives to kill, the soldier ripped the front of Rian's dress to the navel, exposing her small, pale breasts to the biting cold. She fell backward into the snow. He covered her with his body, fumbling with her hem and the stays at his crotch. Barb didn't have time to mull it over any longer. She lurched forward to slit the nearest man's throat. He caught her arm and threw her bodily into the wall.

Something cracked in her chest, making it nearly impossible to breathe. Dabney bayed like an enraged bear but took a sword slash to his side that would have split a smaller man in two. He staggered forward, huffing, while the men behind him gathered up his massive arms and pulled. The Souther who came for Barb didn't even bother to finish her off. He chuckled and turned back to the entertainment on the ground.

Barb heard glass break.

"What's this then?" asked the one atop her, lurching away.

Another who stood above them scratched his chin. "Whatever it is is, it smells like shite."

The first sniffed and spat. "Ugh! Fucking whore tried to poison me."

He pummeled the girl beneath him with a meaty fist. Barb could only whimper. Hot tears spilled over her cheekbone.

"Mouth's no good now."

"She drank some?"

"All, seems like."

"She get some on you?"

"No, but close enough."

The second said, "What a waste. That was a pretty enough lass."

The first shrugged, removing his sex from his trousers, working it back to rigidity. "Still warm, though."

"Warm is good," agreed the second. "Hurry up."

"Can you be poisoned if it gets on your cock?" asked a third.

"Why?"

"Knock out her teeth, and I'll show you." The soldier leered.

Barb gagged.

Siora, please… not this way.

Strong Tim's murderer jerked himself toward Rian. Barb heard him moan and wished for the sky to explode with Siora's vengeance. She must have squeezed her eyes shut, for several loud noises snapped them back open. Two tall figures leaped into the gaggle of soldiers from their rear. Jan Fir made concise work of the three Southers at the entrance while the Prince of Connaught snapped two necks on his way to Rian. The Souther made a sort of strangled whimper when Tam Lin's blade slid into his guts from the groin, and slowly, very slowly, up and up and up. Lip curled, Tam Lim kicked the Souther's split halves into the muck.

Freed, though dramatically slowed, Dabs made it to Barb's side as quickly as he could, scooping her up as he might an injured bird. She struggled to breathe. "Not me. Get her off the ground." But Tam Lin had already done so and was tucking her into his cloak.

"Please," croaked Barb. "Belladonna. She's had it all."

His violet eyes flashed her way. "How long?"

"Minutes."

He looked over at his companion. "We're in time then. Are you sure that's what it was?"

Barb couldn't bear to look at the lass's poor, bloodied fingers as they dangled from his now blood-stained white cloak. "I'm sorry, milord, but a woman in my line o'work never forgets that smell."

His gaze was steady. "That means we'd better hurry. Can you walk?"

"I'll carry her," gruffed Dabney.

"Good. Let's be gone before that whistle blows."

The Tenth Law

Una took a hard blow to her side as the uprooted elm nicked her on its way past. Aoife grunted, and the massive bulk of wood smashed into a granite cliff face on the trail ahead. Una rolled away with a cry. One of her ribs was broken, and although she knew she could heal in minutes given the mysterious strength she'd discovered in the Oiche Ar Fad, she didn't have time to wait. Aoife was powerful. She seemed able to move objects four times her size without contact— something Una had never seen before or had even imagined possible. Soon as she got to her feet, Una was obliged to dodge a heavy rain of stones by jumping down a dry creek bed to avoid them. They pounded into the earth near her feet with a ground-shaking impact.

"Stop moving around so much, little Princess," Aoife huffed from the debris field she'd formed around herself. At least it *sounded* like she was finally tiring, though Una had to admit she'd seen little evidence of that so far. She was bleeding from about a dozen places, and the woods around them looked like a giant claw had cleaved through the forest from the heavens.

"Hold still, and I'll make it painless."

Una had no idea how Aoife was Manipulating using only her thoughts. She had done so only briefly herself and by accident. To do so on this scale was… was that another secret the Otherworld held for her? Could she do the same? As if in answer, she felt a warm vibration at her center. Her fingertips, skin, and even the roots of her hair tingled in response. She climbed out of the creek bed and faced Aoife from the opposite side.

Nema's pet's breathing told the tale of her fatigue— the oncoming spark drag that Una was waiting for— but the sheer confidence she bore, the power shimmering in the air around her, gave Una pause. Aoife might be accruing cost, but it wasn't happening fast enough. There was no telling how long she could maintain her Spark. Una was suddenly unsure that her strategy was working in the least. She had to stall as long as possible.

She dug her fingers into her screaming ribs, breath coming hard. "Surely that can't be all?"

Aoife cocked her head. "What was that?"

"Pissing on Damek isn't worth someone's life. Why are you doing this?"

She pursed her chapped lips. "Fun, I suppose. I won't lie and say I ever liked you much, sweet girl. Watching you haunt the halls of the Cloister, burying your prim nose in whatever tome you fancied while the rest of us worked ourselves to the bone to please our mistresses. That's one." She examined a torn nail. "Two, my cousin's infatuation with you aside, must you *always* be passed from man to man, dear? Do you not have a spine of your own?"

Una stood up a bit straighter at that. "I'm flattered by your concern."

Aoife made a rude sound. "Jealousy's a collection of feelings, you know. You were free when I was enslaved, cossetted while I punished, loved where I was reviled … and you waste all."

Una coughed. "I haven't had a moment's peace since that day at Drogheda. Don't pretend you could have done better in my position."

"Oh, but I would have. I'd have taken the crown ages ago if I were you." She shook her head. "Do you know what your uncle wreaks in the south? How people suffer under his resurgent faith? I would never have surrendered my agency or birthright for a *male*. I would have claimed the throne of Eire from my first bleed and crushed *anyone* who stood in my way."

"I don't crave power, Aoife, and pity those who do."

Aoife laughed; brows pinched together in mockery. "You're radiating it now, and you'd bother to lie to me?"

Una swallowed. Target struck. The heat boiling in her blood was better than any feeling she'd ever had. She *did* love it. The shame she felt at the thought didn't sting as much as it might once have. Aoife was right. Una had to admit that on some subconscious level, she had always craved this power… this, *everything*.

She could feel the river racing toward the lake, the wind in the trees, the spinning sun and moon above. If she crooked her finger now, might they bow to her whims?

Who was *she* now?

"These men are nothing to you, you realize. Only women are born with the Spark, Una, and only those of Macha's bloodline could ever dream of the power you and I share."

"What do you mean?"

"We're kin, obviously. However distant the relation. Who do you think founded the Moura bloodline?"

Una's heart skipped. "Liadan."

"The same. You might say Tairngare had always been her goal. She came from a time when no man could be a king if he were not consort to a powerful queen, and there were never queens as powerful as the Daughters of Emain Macha. Liadan dreamed of a return to the old ways. You wouldn't exist if not for her hand in your making."

Aoife spoke true. Una could feel it in her bones.

She doesn't hate you, her Spark whispered.

She wants to be you.

From nowhere, a flash of Aoife's life tracked across Una's vision, a lifetime of pain and servitude in an instant. The violence of it, the sadness, insecurity, and fear. It staggered her. She wobbled, dropping to one knee.

She wants you to kill her.

Una looked up at Aoife's confused face. "I'm sorry."

"For what?"

"All they've done to you."

The hiss of air between Aoife's teeth narrowed her eyes to slivers. "Keep your pity, little cousin. I'm here to murder you." Sliding off the slab of smoky granite she straddled, she moved back about five paces and shrugged off her cloak. The bones of her chest strained against the parchment of her skin, like a bird stripped of feathers. She took a deep breath and cracked her knuckles. "Right then. I'm curious which of us is the better breed."

Una said nothing.

She saw the beads of sweat gathering on Aoife's forehead.

She is tiring.

The granite slab Aoife had been perched upon moved a few inches.

Good, Una thought. Another demonstration of power would be her last. Aoife put a good face on it, but like any other Manipulator, she would wear out. That's what Una hoped for, anyway.

But not you said the other voice in her ear.

You're different.

She bit her tongue rather than retort.

Una knew she was stronger, could hear the wild, frantic pulse beneath the veneer of her reality, taste its charge on her tongue. As if the particles around her were a slumbering leviathan in the bedrock of her bones. Una was the mightier, but she'd come to this realization late. Aoife was more *skilled*, and the difference might prove fatal.

Throw the fucking rock, damn you.

As if she knew the direction of Una's thoughts, Aoife paused. "I'll have that crown, I think. When I've finished with you, our sweet cousin is next. His arrogance begs an answer. His father won't mind much, as Damek has ever been a means to end and nothing more."

"This Falan pretender? The High King will make short work of him."

"Pretender? Well, I shan't argue that. His sense of entitlement came directly from his beloved grandmama, as all things do. You can't imagine a more deluded, twisted individual. Still, he'll make a good ally on my way to High Queendom."

"You forget the Dannans. Midhir will never—"

"Love, you know next to nothing about Aes Sidhe. Just because you take one of their cocks to roost does not make you an authority on the Sidhe. Midhir is dying. Hasn't been seen in decades. Armagh has its spies, you know. Falan, for all of his scheming, does have good timing."

She's stalling now.

The beast inside Una shifted in its sleep.

Not yet, she told it. She worried that to unleash it would be like trying to hit a gnat with a sledgehammer. However, if Aoife didn't make her move soon, Una might implode.

"What's the matter, Aoife? Are you tired?"

She smirked back, and a four-inch gash opened on Una's cheek. "Hardly."

Una swiped at the blood with the back of her hand. "Then let's get to it. Kill me if you can."

Aoife threw out a hand, and Una was tossed backward into a tree trunk. The impact rattled her teeth and cracked her spine. White sparks glittered behind her eyes.

Almost there…

Una struggled to her knees. The rock shifted another few inches, and she heard Aoife grunt with the effort.

That's it.

"Goodbye, Princess," grinned Aoife one last time. With a wrenching, guttural cry, Aoife hurled the two-ton stone at Una with everything she had.

Even if Una attempted to dodge the mass, it was too wide and heavy to be avoided. It hurtled toward her, blotting out the sky overhead. She was unconcerned. The leviathan reared its head, claws unfurling.

Stop, she thought, and the stone froze in midair, hanging as if from an invisible chord. She felt its weight in her mind— heavy as half a city wall— but it might have been a pebble for all the difference it made to her overwhelming Spark. She discovered that she didn't even have to focus on the object to hold it in place. The slow, satisfying smirk she sent Aoife made the other woman pale by nine shades.

"How?" Aoife gasped, incredulous and visibly exhausted.

"Who cares?" laughed Una dryly and thought *Rebound.*

The stone flew backward so quickly that the ground rumbled for a full minute when it struck. Aoife had managed to use her Spark to scramble away, but Una saw her gulping air like a drowning man. A long red trickle of blood dribbled from her right nostril. Her eyes were black pits of fear. Fresh out of sympathy, Una chuckled and looked up at the trees around her. *Up*, she thought. At least fifteen massive trees groaned their way out of the earth, leaves shuddering as their roots snapped from their trunks. Into the air, they rose, held in place by Una's will alone. *Down*, Una thought, and they shot themselves at Aoife like a bevy of spears.

Aoife, the silent menace, the knife in the dark— covered her face and shrieked, "*Within!*" a heartbeat before Una's missiles landed. When the dust settled, Una saw the mound Aoife had erected to protect herself from the impact, but it hadn't been enough. Aoife clawed herself free from a half-excavated crater at the top, below a pile of lance-sized splinters. Bloodied and covered in dirt and splintered wood, she drew in a noisy, grasping breath. Her one remaining eye found Una standing a short distance away. "Wh-at a-re…" she tried to ask, but her jaw was smashed inward and twisted awkwardly to one side.

"I have no clue," answered Una, truthfully. "But I'll say this much; I'm not going to complain." She inhaled long and slow, allowing the current to sweep through every particle of her being. "Give my regards to the Sluagh, cousin. I think you'll find their embrace warmer than you deserve."

Open, she thought, and the dirt below Aoife dropped away, sucking her and all the tree trunks Una had torn from their roots into its gaping pit.

Fold.

Aoife of Armagh gave one last pitiful scream as the earth clapped over her head, sending a spray of splinters, blood, and other tissues into the air in a geyser of gore.

Una stood there for a moment in silence, cataloging what had transpired. She wasn't human any more than Aoife had ever been. Had circumstances differed, perhaps she might have been as polluted a creature, and their situations reversed. Fate, as ever, made japes of everyone.

In the darker reaches of the trees, several pairs of glittering eyes watched her fearfully. In her mind's eye, she knew their terrible shapes and felt nothing. They could not harm her now. Not here.

In the Oiche Ar Fad, she might be a god.

Not one to gloat, Una turned toward the Otherworld dawn.

The universe quaked in her steps.

Diarmid could still hear Ruidraghe screaming into the wind behind him. Their skirmish, as expected, took all of five minutes. Whoever had sent him— and Diarmid felt confident he knew which MacNemed would dare— knew very well that a Firesinger, even one as powerful as Ruidraghe, didn't stand a chance against a Skysinger with the great Dagda's blood flowing through his veins. They didn't call Diarmid the Raven King for nothing. No, whoever had sent Ruidraghe had come for Una, not him, and hoped to stall him long enough to get at her. Diarmid hadn't wasted time with the Bolg Brehon, realizing immediately what was afoot. He'd left him on the mountaintop, partly fused to the rocks at the summit. Unfortunately for him, he'd be up there for ages, as long as it would take him to burn through the igneous particles that held the dark, carbon-infused rocks together. Being that igneous rock was harder than granite— it would take decades. That is unless another Skysinger with the ability to tamper with time and air particles happened by. That Diarmid was the only Sidhe Brehon born with this power made him very much doubt that possibility. He frowned at the thought.

Una was no Sidhe.

Yet…

The girl was something new. The sheer impossibility of what he suspected about her could only mean that for all his years and all the fairies he had met— some he'd even sired— none had been born with power approaching the Brehonic, not even a modest Earthsinger. For Una to possess the abilities of a Skysinger, she *should* have been born to a noble, ancient Sidhe lineage of immense power. But such was not so. Her parents and grandparents had been human. Though he did have to admit, whatever went on in the Cloister often produced women with uncanny abilities. He had always been impressed with them and their practical, scientific approach to magic. Regardless, some things should be beyond any mortal, no matter how gifted.

The fact that someone had gone to so much trouble to get to her told him that he was not the only one who knew how horribly powerful Una was. Even he could not summon magic in the Otherworld without incurring a cost. His tiff with Ruidraghe had slowed him, despite the added strength Una had given him so blithely as if she held a personal tap into the internal mechanism of the Oiche Ar Fad itself.

Hells, maybe she *did*.

How was the bloody question.

He could sense no Sidhe blood in her essence, and he could always tell. Faerie genes were hardly a boon to the host, even if one was born powerful or gifted. It would corrupt them, haunt them, and often dominate every aspect of their lives. In Mistress Rian's case, he believed the girl funneled the obsessive genetic predilection into her studies, which would explain why she excelled at them and what kept her from the madness that was so common among her kind. In others, like Damek Bishop, who bore no outward deformity, the madness took a darker and more insidious turn. He appeared sane, attractive, clever, even maybe brilliant— but inside, he carried that genetic imbalance in force: the obsession, inhuman ambition, and perversion. Megalomania had ever been a hallmark of the powerful and bored, but in Damek's case, his was exacerbated by his most ancient Sidhe bloodline. If he survived this conflict he had started to glorify himself; he would be afflicted by self-loathing and depression on a scale humans had no metric for. He would either slay himself or become something worse than he was already.

As for Una, he sensed no such thing from her. She was odd, indeed. A bit self-absorbed as most wealthy young women tended to be. Hot-headed at times and a bit authoritarian in her opinions of the world, she was also unfailingly kind, mentally strong, cautious, and ethical. He found that he rather liked her and was more than a little jealous of his errant nephew for his luck. Yet, through all this, she was still mortal. She couldn't be carrying a latent Sidhe gene, but what else could explain her gifts? These were unmistakably Sidhe-born powers.

He swore under his breath for the dozenth time that day. This was a puzzle he had no idea how to solve. It ate at him, now more than ever, and someone wanted her dead badly enough to risk the wrath of *Fiachra Dubh*.

Ahead of him, through the swirling fog he traveled through, he felt a sudden shiver of power that nearly stopped his heart. It was too strong… *too much* to be misconstrued. He had found her!

He stepped from his fragment and into a warzone. Not war as it was in Innisfail, with men rushing at each other with blades or other grisly weapons, but old war, the sort that harkened to the Innisfail before the Transition. What he was looking at now reminded him of the battlefields he'd walked over a thousand years ago. "*Herne*," he breathed, marveling at the utter devastation around him.

Whole trees, some a hundred feet high, had been ripped from their roots as if by a giant's hand and tossed about like so much kindling. He found a dead ghast not a mile from the lakeshore and beyond that, yet more horrors. Here, not just the trees had been uprooted. The ground had been blasted apart to expose gaping pits filled with shredded bracken and splinters. Shorn tree trunks jutted from each like stickpins from a sewing kit.

On top of the dust and the pervading scent of split lumber, the reek of death and blood greeted his nose. He covered his mouth as he approached one curiously constructed mound. A trail of blood and guts spilled from a hole in an unnatural hill just ahead as if a gory spring had burst from its middle. Already, piskies and other Lu Sidhe beasties gathered to lap at the feast. They scattered at his approach but wouldn't go far— this was Ban Sidhe blood, after all. *Old* Sidhe blood, at that.

Fir Bolg blood.

Interesting.

He backed away to appreciate the enormity of the scene fully. What Una had wrought here— for it was surely she who had done this— was a vulgar but Herculean display of power. He looked around, trying to glean any indication of where she had gone. Opalescent eyes gleamed at him by threes on the dark side of the clearing. *Goblins.* Drawn, no doubt, by the overpowering stench of rare, High Sidhe blood. He could hear the repellant creatures' jagged jaws clenching in excitement. They would surely dig up whoever had died in this hole and gorge themselves insensate. They waited a respectful distance away. No Dor Sidhe would dare cross *Fiachra Dubh*.

"You may as well come out," he said.

Shyly, three haggard, misshapen figures moved into the morning moonlight.

"Did you see who did this?"

The largest of the goblins, a fellow with teeth too large and sharp for his mouth, stepped forward, head bowed low. "Smelt her, not saw," it hesitated. "Not your kind, but for them who dwell under the lake."

"Not this one, the other… the victor."

The goblin shuddered. Goblins were famous liars and deceivers and could not help but prevaricate and embellish. It was in their nature. Though, not even the bravest of them would dare lie to the King of Tech Duinn… much. "This one smelt of Sionnovar, *Fiachra Dubh*. We would not try for her clan, be she not dead already."

Diarmid snorted. The first lie.

He raised a hand, and the creature fell to its knobby knees, gasping for breath.

"The next lie will be your last."

"This one be Sionnnovar's girl-child! We think to catch her, but the great lady appear, so we wait. Hope for the best." The other goblins snickered. "But the lady, she do… this." It gestured to the mound of gore. "We scared. She terrible, like you, milord."

The Great Lady, indeed.

"Which way did she go?"

The goblin pointed, its razor-sharp teeth grinding in fear and hunger.

Diarmid stilled himself to feel the pull of her power once more.

Of course, this was in the opposite direction the lying little beast had indicated. He turned away, and the goblin screamed behind him as its intestines burst from its deceitful gut. Its fellows wasted no time launching themselves at their fallen brethren, then on to the mound full of the precious nectar that remained of Aoife Ap Sionnovar's mighty Fir Bolg blood.

⚜

UNA WALKED FOR SO LONG, her feet bled. The power she felt coursing through her might have kept her Spark unbelievably plentiful, but it did little to assuage the fatigue she felt in her bones. She had liberally applied Spark to every wound, causing all but the deepest to close. But as she did so, she realized there were *some* limits to this newfound ability, after all. Her Spark might be boundless, capable of performing any Manipulation she set her mind to with abandon, but the flesh had trouble holding and processing this impossible strength. She could feel the vitality of her human cells wither before this new external energy as if it were sapping her dry from the outside in. This was the opposite of the usual Spark drag and much worse. The more she expended, the more she invited this overwhelming force to shove her human cells aside or away altogether. She felt like she was evaporating, breaking apart in this vacuum; her cells altered and replaced. With every step, she grew stronger and weaker at the same time. The vessel of her body was no longer sufficient to contain her external presence.

Beside a lovely, trickling stream, she finally collapsed. Allowing herself to be bathed in the warm but weak sunlight in the day side of the forest, she shivered in the sweet-smelling grass. Strange, curious creatures flitted overhead. Her eyes drifted closed, and she slept. An unknowable span later, a humming over the thin trickle of water woke her. The little girl she thought she'd seen before smiled back at her. Her large, dark eyes were still and wide as a mirror. Had she been following her? Una felt a dash of fear. Things were never what they seemed in the Oiche Ar Fad.

Could she fight if she needed to in this state?

At this rate, your Spark might consume you, she warned herself.

"Poor child," the girl said, her voice at once high and endearing as a child's but earthly and robust as a woman grown. Una was in too much pain and feared to marvel at the sound. With nothing to do but watch her death approach, Una could only gurgle upward at her when the girl came to her side and laid a warm hand against her temple. "You must learn control, or your gifts will devour you."

Where her fingertips brushed the hair back from Una's forehead, she felt a steady calm spread inward, clearing her mind. The sensation radiated downward, uncoiling her muscles and soothing raw nerve endings. Tears of relief spilled from Una's eyes. Whatever the girl had done eased the pain and fatigue to such a degree that it felt like she'd doused a fire in her blood. If she ate her now, at least Una wouldn't die in knots.

But the child did not display any fangs nor appear interested in her mortal flesh.

Instead, she smiled down at Una and sang,

"I knew a place

Far Away

In a dell

Upon the lay…."

She stroked Una's hair.

"A maiden waits near

What does she there?

With the rain in her hair

We may only fear…."

Una thought she'd heard the song before but couldn't recall where. The song was a balm, warming the cold cockles of her heart. She wandered in the clouds above.

"Will she dance

Or will she sing

Who, oh who knows these things?"

It was a nursery rhyme. That was it.

Someone used to sing it to her when she was a bairn.

"He comes now, Una. All will be well. I will have his vow."

Una believed her but was too exhausted to ask how or why.

She sank into a lovely dream, with the girl's fingers combing through her curls.

⚜ ⚜

DIARMID FELT A STRANGE PRESENCE he could not place, something ancient and nearly familiar. He braced for another surprise, but as he emerged from the fragment, he found a small girl staring up at him with huge, liquid black eyes. His brow furrowed. The girl seemed and smelled like nothing but another human. He could sense neither the undeniable magnetism of Sidhe blood in her nor the taint of the Lu Sidhe, who were native to the Otherworld. Yet, she was *not* human. If anything, he could feel the oppression of mind-boggling age— non-threatening but overpowering nonetheless.

Una lay just beyond her, beside a bubbling stream, sleeping peacefully.

The girl had woven flowers into a garland for Una's tangled, bloodied hair. Humming while she worked, her eyes never left Diarmid's face. "So, you've come for her now?"

Diarmid moved slowly into the pleasant wildflower scented dell. "Who are you?"

The tune she hummed sounded so familiar. She wove another ring of violets around Una's temple, unconcerned by his authoritative tone. "You know who I am, Diarmid, son of Crom Dagda— even if you think you do not."

He had no clue how to interpret that. "I assure you; I would remember."

"Perhaps it'll come to you when it must?"

He frowned. "It is ill manners indeed to insult a king, child."

She laughed. The sound raised the hairs all over his body. He suddenly felt very small, young, and out of sorts. Diarmid had never felt so… even while his father lived. He took the slightest step backward. "You are not in any position to make demands of me, boy."

In his mind's eye, he had a sudden impression of a shape, a behemoth afterimage that blotted out the sky, the earth below, and the stars beyond. Its mass obscured all. It snatched the air from his lungs and nearly stole the ground beneath his feet. He blinked, and the image dissipated. She was just a girl again, innocent and unafraid.

"*What* are you?" he gasped.

"More than you will ever be, Brehon, and I am disinclined to submit to your fumbling interrogations. Be still and hear me while I deign your presence."

Diarmid sputtered. He was King of Tech Duinn! Whatever this thing was, it had no right to insult him in his domain. He opened his mouth, but she cut him off.

"It is hardly your realm, Mac Crom," she sneered. "Though I sometimes find your people's arrogance amusing, I find it taxing just now."

"My father wrought this realm from his blood, carved my people's future from his bones. The Oiche Ar Fad is mine! I don't know what or who you are, but you will give her to me now or—"

"As I said, pure arrogance," she giggled. "But, I will let you take her for now."

Suddenly, she was behind him. Her eyes glowed amber, pupils mere slits against her irises, like some mythic beast of old. Her small hand shot out, clapping over his forearm with a strength that dried his throat. He could feel her power, the staggering, shocking, near cosmic *vastness* of her. He sank to his knees under her limitless gaze.

"Be warned, ambitious thing that you are. I give her to your ilk for a time only. You may not keep her. None of your line should dare to try. She is my child, my gift. Try to harness that at your peril."

"I... I don't understand."

She looked away as if seeing a horror above his head. "It comes. You cannot stop it; this time, all shall be consumed. The girl is the sole hope you have. She is the bridge, the gift I leave you. You will return her to me, in the end, or perish."

Diarmid's heart spun under the obliterating weight of her fingers. "What comes?"

"Death."

Just as swiftly as she'd touched him, she disappeared. The pressure that ground him into the earth vanished with her presence. His head cleared, and the blood pumped once more through his veins. He fell forward onto his hands, a most undignified position for a Sidhe king of his age and station. What *was* that thing? And what in the nine hells had she meant by 'death'? Of course, it was *his* realm! The implication that Crom Dagda hadn't created it was absurd. Diarmid had been there! He remembered every detail as if it had happened yesterday. Yet... He was a Brehon, the highest in the land. He could taste a mistruth, could smell one, as easily as breathing. He could discern no falsehoods from his strange visitor. She had told no lies. Whomever she was— *whatever* she was, every word she said rang true. Shaken to his core, Diarmid swallowed his confusion down deep. Now was not the time. He would ponder these strange events as soon as he returned his nephew to Aes Sidhe, and the latest Milesian threat to the Daoine Sidhe was laid to rest.

Gently, he lifted Una into his arms. She was such a small, slight woman for all her mystifying strength. How could anything so fragile, so mortal, carry what she did inside and not be broken apart?

He didn't know.

Perhaps as the creature vowed, he wasn't meant to? Troubled, he moved into the fragment, his thoughts torn between death and a pair of dragon-colored eyes.

Sacrifice

Kaer Yin slashed through a Souther Steel Corps line toward the battlements' northwest corner. He leaped from the higher stone rampart to the lower, hastily assembled western wall, which bore the charcoal-tinted remnants of yesterday's catastrophic blaze. These Corpsmen were fresher and more skilled than the infantryman who littered the streets and ramparts in various stages of death. They hit back a lot harder too. Though far from beat, Kaer Yin had to admit that his arms weren't what they were at the start. He hadn't slept in days, and his legs burned, worn from pumping pure, unfiltered adrenaline for almost fifty straight hours. His hands felt like two heavy stones.

But the Southers didn't stop coming.

Left, right, over, under, and aside; he moved through men with every breath. He killed with a sword, fists, feet, fingers, and bow. Every way he turned, another combatant came at him, thus, another man's blood stained his skin, clothes, hair, and steel. Everyplace he stepped, a pile of misspent bodies sprang up, and there seemed no end to the mind-numbing monotony of battle.

One fellow ran straight at him, his gauntleted fist swinging forward to ram Kaer Yin's skull onto his sabre, but Kaer Yin spun away, jerking another Corpsman forward instead. The two men died in shock, having killed each other instead. Another he took through the eye. Yet another, through the skull below the jaw. On and on it went this gruesome symphony of death.

Below, in the cross-lane behind Wanderer's Alley, he saw what he had both been hoping and dreading to see ever since the horns blew over the Western Gate, what felt like many hours gone by. A limping, skulking line of Rosweal's citizens running as fast they could manage in knee-deep snow. They were pursued by many fully armored soldiers and some wild-eyed, undisciplined infantrymen who had managed to survive everything the defenders had thrown at them until now. Kaer Yin dodged a wildly thrown dagger and rolled back up with Nemain's heft, delivering a backhanded slash that severed the Souther's neck almost to the shoulder. He jumped over the next man on his way to the ladder, which was clogged with men fighting up and down its rungs. He didn't have the time to spar with them.

"Shar!" he called ahead to Una's new (and only) liegeman. Shar was elbow-deep in a Souther's ribcage. His head snapped up— a grisly sight indeed. "*Ullmhaigh clúdach a thabhairt!*[28]"

Shar nodded, then bellowed orders to the Sidhe beyond him. They stepped away from the wall in twos, every second and third bow on the rampart turning from hand-to-hand combat to aim at the rear of the fleeing citizens on the ground.

"*Tine ag toil!*[29]" Kaer Yin ordered, leaping onto the ladder from a distance of at least five feet, raining death on any Southers barring his way down its rungs. By the time his boots crunched into the snow, ten more men lay dead at its base. From ground level, the fighting was thinner and less intense, which was owed almost entirely to Fionn. The barrels had played their part by relieving Bishop of his Bolg *garda*, but Fionn and his brilliant cavalrymen had done the hard work. They'd ridden down scores of men faster than Kaer Yin could light pitch. Standing soldiers were no match for mounted knights, less so when clogged into narrow lanes and alleys only a few handspans wide. Everywhere Kaer Yin looked, dead Southers lay

---

[28] 'Get ready to give cover!'
[29] "Fire at will!"

trampled, cleaved, or smashed into the snow-ridden cobbles. He couldn't help but smile at that. Bishop had thrown in his last little surprise, costing them, but the number of upright defenders was beginning to outpace the pockets of fighting Southers.

They were winning!

He shoved that surge of relief way down deep.

They still had nearly two hundred fresh Corpsmen to deal with, and at least thirty of those were now chasing Rosweal's women and children toward their sole exit. He saw Robin racing toward those Corpsmen from the southeast with a small but lethal host of hardened Greenmakers at his back. The whistle he'd blown like mad swung at his neck and glinted in the fading light.

Time was almost up.

As he ran downhill to help cover the people's exit, Kaer Yin looked around for the figure he was sure he'd seen running toward him earlier. How long ago now? An hour, less?

So many groups fought in close quarters here that he could hardly distinguish any individuals among them.

Where are you, Damek?

He scanned the whole north end of town, from Taverner's Alley to the Hilltop Dells.

I don't want you to miss what happens next.

Kaer Yin figured Una's cousin must have been caught in another skirmish or had already run back to the rear of his scattered force to regroup. Either that or he was dead… Herne willing. That angry, tortured look he'd given him went far beyond the calculated, level-headedness Kaer Yin had come to expect from the self-appointed 'King of Eire.' Even the filthy, murderous glare he'd shot him at parlay did not come close.

If Kaer Yin had to guess, that large, brave man he'd been forced to kill upon their escape from the farmstead sprang to mind. He hadn't wanted to kill him more than any man, but he'd seen the two of them together and understood him as Damek's right hand. Martin O'Rearden had been his name, Kaer Yin vaguely recalled from the parley. When they'd caught sight of each other earlier, the fury in Damek's eyes had burned with profound grief. But Kaer Yin didn't have much time to mull any of that over now.

He caught sight of Eva, huffing and clutching a screaming child under each arm, as she trudged uphill toward the gatehouse. At least fifty people in varying stages of health limped along after her. She saw him and nodded as if he were right on time. Rose sidled up behind her, trailing a gaggle of filthy children. "Ben!" He darted to them, catching Eva before she stumbled into the blackened snow. The children wriggled, red-faced and terrified. She had a wide gash over one leg, dying her once-white skirts a sopping, red-brown.

"What happened? Mel was up on the wall, last I saw."

He didn't like the look of that wound at all. If it went untreated—

Eva clutched at his hopelessly filthy tunic. "They're getting between us," she exclaimed, putting everything she had left into getting the kids up the slippery hill and through the cracked gate as fast as she could.

Soldiers harried those who followed their group from the sides, and a knot at the rear seemed to grow in number and ferocity, like wolves scenting prey. Kaer Yin shoved the women toward the gate, tossing his exquisite, priceless bow into the bushes beneath the shadow of the stone wall, along with his empty quiver.

Eva paused long enough to grip his arm hard. Her eyes were flat sheets of golden glass. "It isn't over. Remember."

"I don't understand."

Rose grasped her hand. "She's been this way for a while, but we wouldn't have made it this far without her. The things she made them soldiers do, Ben." She shivered. "Dunno who'm more afraid of, her, or yer Lady."

Eva's sightless eyes stared straight ahead at Kaer Yin, seeing things he couldn't see. Una had told him about this. They didn't have time to discuss her vision, but Una had said her prophecies were rarely wrong. He felt the blood drain from his face. "You need to go, now!"

Eva dug her nails into his arm. "It isn't *over*."

"Rose, take her and go!" With Nemain in his right hand, he drew a lark with his left. "Shar!" he roared upward. Many accurately aimed Sidhe arrows answered, mowing down leering, redfaced soldiers like they'd simply been standing still, waiting to die. Another volley and another until Kaer Yin counted three dozen Roswellians making it safely through the gate. Robin neared from the far side, interrupting another pursuing force with gusto. Kaer Yin decided where he was most needed and ran downhill to give the Greenmakers a much-needed hand. He shoved more people at the gate on his way past them until he lost count.

Suddenly, Jan Fir's bloody face emerged from the cross at Wanderer's Alley with Barb and big Dabney wheezing behind him. She sobbed when she caught sight of him, and he couldn't help but notice that Dabney was carrying her clumsily in one shredded arm. He opened his mouth to ask what happened when he saw Tam Lin and what— *who* it was he carried— and the state she was in.

Kaer Yin's heart stopped altogether. "*No.* Is she—"

"Alive," replied his cousin. "But not for long if I don't get her out of here."

Kaer Yin's eyes burned with tears he could not shed. He reached out to touch her face. Her right cheek was swollen black and cold as ice. Her clothes were torn from what he could spy beneath Tam Lin's gore-stained cloak. "Was she—"

"Near enough. She drank something. I don't have long."

Men were spilling from the alleys and coalescing nearby.

"Barb?"

"Yeah, love?" she answered. Her voice was small.

"Still with me?"

She gave a hacking cough that said otherwise. "Always."

He patted Dabney's back and gave Rian's frozen fingers a squeeze, but his attention was on Tam Lin. "Get them over. Do what you must."

"I will."

"Jan Fir, Niall, with me. The rest of you follow Tam Lin out. We'll cover you."

He stepped in front of Tam Lin, putting all worry and sadness from his mind. There were still fifteen stragglers being harried uphill on the way out. He met Robin's eyes over the mass of Corpsmen racing up at him. He thought he caught Robin's nod.

Nearly time now.

Jan Fir growled, slinging blood from his larks. Kaer Yin knew he could count on him to help thin the Souther herd.

They went to work.

Making his fourth circuit around the inner walls, Fionn reined in at the remnants of the Eastern Gate. His first shield commander drew up beside him, spattered red from his forehead to his horse's pale forelegs. The underbellies of each beast were a grim sight from the carnage they had wreaked in their passage. There was not much left to do at that end of the city now, save tread over the corpses of fallen Southers or watch them flee through the rubble like beaten dogs. Fionn couldn't hold back an ear-splitting grin. They'd done their work well. His Wild Hunt were the finest horsemen in Innisfail, and let none forget it.

He had never been prouder of his men than he was at that moment. For a force less than two hundred strong, to defeat an army over five times their number— with so little loss of life— was nothing short of a triumph.

He whispered prayers to Brida for watching over them.

"Shall I sound the horns, My Lord?" asked Diel, also beaming with pride.

"Aye, let us return to the Western Gate once more to drive the remaining rats into the nice warren we've made for them."

Fionn couldn't wait to see the look on Midhir's son's face. Indeed, the Prince of Innisfail was alive and hale. As much as he was hesitant to admit it, the man *was* a gifted commander, and in combat, well, he had yet to see his equal. Fionn would never tell him this, of course. He preferred the stony, tight-lipped respect they'd developed over the last few days. He doubted he would ever call the Ard Ri's heir a 'friend,' but in his heart, he realized he would be pleased to call him '*Tiarne.*'

He was still smiling when he and his four nearest turned about to ride back west through the alleyways. Diel blew his horn loudly and proudly for all to hear. The enemy was in retreat! Lord Bishop's cavalry had long since given up the ghost, and now, only the most determined, bloodthirsty infantry and stubborn Corpsmen were left in various pockets throughout the city. The alley narrowed, forcing Diel in front, his mount dancing gingerly over fallen bodies in the snow and slimly avoiding overhanging awnings, eaves, and shutters. A third blast— the horns on the North Wall then sounded in answer. It wouldn't be long now. Fionn and his knights crept down the twisting alleyway for their last circuit around the wall when something heavy struck Fionn full in the chest. He went flying backward several feet. Knocked clear of his horse, he landed flat on his back. If it hadn't been for the snow, the fall alone would have cracked his spine like an egg. His horse screamed— Winter, his name was— Fionn heard him go down with a last pitiful whinny. Fionn tried to get up, but he couldn't move. He felt something warm and wet under him but could see nothing but the snow falling through a crack in the twilight sky. He thought he heard Ciaran shout his name… but from far away, like the wind through a glen.

A dark smudge appeared above him, and he knew.

The shape reared back.

He closed his eyes before it came down.

⚕

KAER YIN HEARD FIONN'S HORNS as he pried Nemain's edge from a Corpsman's skull. Robin was at his elbow, dealing death in every direction with a fallen Souther's sabre. Jan Fir stood at his back, guarding the iron grate that led into the gatehouse and the tunnel that wormed its way below the north wall. He had one hand tucked into his cuirass; his tunic dripped blood down his bare arm to the torn sleeve at his elbow. Still, even one-handed, Jan Fir Bres was no easy victim. He'd slain more than his fair share of Southers with only a single lark. There were only a few dozen enemies left in their immediate vicinity, and from their uphill vantage, perhaps four hundred Southers left to fight in the streets, much less on the walls. Their numbers were far better matched now!

With Fionn's horns, Kaer Yin knew the Southers had already begun to retreat. Bishop's cavalry was either dead or fled, and only foot soldiers and clusters of Corpsmen were left. The Dannans had outshot their archers hours ago, and those who remained were well outside the wall. All told, Damek's force had dropped to a mere tenth of its original number. Most seemed to have fled after so many of their infantry had been swallowed up in the streets, and the rest had either been cut down or had never bothered to clamber over the walls in the first place. It was nearly over now! There was only one move Kaer Yin had left to make… one surprise left in store for Bethany's thieving, pillaging, raping throng of overconfident thugs.

He rushed for the ladder again, about fifty paces from the gatehouse, and nodded to Jan Fir, who kicked the portal closed so hard it dented inward. Robin slid the iron lock in place, smashing the knob inward with the butt of his sabre. No chance anyone would get that door open in time to retrieve any of the people who'd fled that way. Both soon followed close at Kaer Yin's heels. "Right. Get into position," he barked over his shoulder, killing two Corpsmen who blocked their path to the ladder and their last stand. "Now, Robin!" he added, meeting another sword thrust crosswise, which sent the sabre's tip glancing from Nemain's wider blade. With his right hand, he reached down to hamstring his attacker, then drove his lark to the hilt through the man's screaming mouth.

Robin reached for the whistle around his neck but froze before he could set it to his lips. He stared straight ahead, showing teeth. Kaer Yin followed his gaze, seeing a familiar shorn head making its way up the wide cross lane toward them. The Corps Commander Ridley did not know Robin, who glared bloody murder at him over the smattering of bodies struggling between them. Ridley's eyes were all for Kaer Yin, who recognized him from the wall on sight. Robin yanked the whistle from his neck and threw it to Kaer Yin, who was forced to dodge a blow to catch it. "I want this one, Ben," Robin said, spitting a wad of blood from his mouth, then placing himself between them. "I'll be right behind ye."

Kaer Yin didn't bother to argue. Robin was the most dangerous Milesian he'd ever met. Still. He paused at the ladder. "Don't you dare die, damn you. You still owe me fifty fainne for porter and uishge!"

Robin spared him a look that said exactly where he could shove that remark.

Kaer Yin was already up to the rampart before he blew the whistle in earnest.

Damek heard the whistle just as he and ten of his remaining Corps made it back to the North Wall. That he'd all but lost this fight in Rosweal's twisting lanes was not lost on him or any of his men. It had been a long hour since he realized he'd been beaten. His cavalry broken, his archers dead or deserted, and at least a thousand infantry and yeomen lay dead within the clever trap that the Prince had made of Rosweal. Many of Damek's commanders outside the walls had blown the retreat already, despite his fervent orders to send in more men to deal with this rabble. Disloyal traitors, the lot. He had ordered no withdrawal. Would not. While he drew breath, he would not allow that grinning silver-haired cunt to see his backside.

Kaer Yin Adair might yet have won the day, but that didn't mean he'd live to crow about it. Damek would have his head if it were the last thing he ever did.

His Corpsmen seemed to share his sentiments. With grim, determined murder glowing in their eyes, they trekked to the wall with weapons stained red with blood. Some Southers might be soft-bellied cowards when faced with a serious challenge, but not Bethany's Steel Corps. They would march to their death before they'd turn tail and run. Damek still had the numbers, if not by much. If he could dismantle the Sidhe leadership by killing their commanders, his Corpsmen alone could yet tame this fracas. But this was less about winning at this point, less still about saving face.

Whatever happened, he had one goal in mind.

As they neared the North Wall, elbow to elbow, shield to shield, Damek scanned the smoky ramparts for his foe. The rage in his heart was a propeller, driving him forward. He couldn't look away now if he tried. His men gnashed their teeth in a similar vein. None seemed cowed by all the losses they'd taken this day.

Vengeance was all.

At last, his eyes found what he sought. A hundred paces down the stone rampart whirled the bright-haired Dannan he longed most to behold. The hatred in his mouth burned. "Draw them back!" he said with a calm he did not feel. "We march in unison."

He watched Kaer Yin move down the wall toward him and saw him blowing that absurd, irritating whistle. The retreat, Damek presumed with a tight smile.

About fucking time!

That still wouldn't save him.

"Single cover!" Damek ordered, drawing the stragglers back into their ranks and behind the protection of their long shields. They gathered another thirty soldiers west along the wall, with more queuing up every moment. Now a shielded phalanx, they cut down everything in their path on their way uphill. Damek barely blinked. He watched Kaer Yin swing his two-hander around him like a dancer twirling a ribbon and smiled. He would fucking have him now, by Reason. Nothing in the way that he couldn't trample or climb.

I've got you, you bastard.

I've got you.

Kaer Yin blew the whistle a third time, and defenders who'd been fighting for all they were worth suddenly backed away— abandoning each fight, some midstroke. Without ado, they tucked tail and ran for the western rampart in a tangle, heedless of any chase. Many died in the attempt; many did not. Not bogged down by heavy shields or armor, the Dannans were light enough to get up and down their ladders at a fair clip.

Damek's heart stilled in his chest. He glanced around, eyes darting between lanes, noting abandoned houses, darkened windows, and empty streets. No light save the stubborn smolder of trees miles distant. Where was O'More's cavalry? Had they pursued his fleeing infantry outside the walls? Everywhere he looked, Rosweal was deserted. Nothing was left alive in any lane, alley, or structure save his men. On a sharp breath, he glanced upward to witness a host of Sidhe archers line the western ramparts along the wall. A snap and hiss, and each arrow flared to life. The smell of pitch coated the air as two dozen arrows caught flame.

Damek's eyes bulged.

He threw out a hand as if that would help.

Fuck!

"Break ranks!" he bellowed. "Retreat, retreat!"

Too late.

The arrows whizzed overhead, bursting through open windows and overhanging gutter. Why hadn't he thought about the fucking windows?

"Gods damn you all! *Run!*" His shout drowned in the terrible pops he heard go off in the remaining neighborhood behind him. The second floors of several buildings burst into loud, spitting flames. Structures shuddered, and he backpedaled, throwing himself behind a wagon beneath the stone wall and covering his head with his hands. His men either followed suit or stood dumbfounded as half the buildings in Rosweal blasted apart from the inside out or top-down. The chorus of explosions buckled the street beneath their feet, sending them flying upward, tossed into a more extraordinary succession of blasts that ripped them to burning shreds in a matter of heartbeats. Stones catapulted into the snow-laden sky, at least twenty feet overhead, along with substantial wooden pylons, joists, and floorboards scattered to dangerous, flaming wreckage.

Damek howled in fury and pain as the wagon rolled over him, burying him beneath a mountain of piping hot debris.

Crown of Ashes

Tam Lin waited for the explosions to quiet before deciding it was safe enough for his charges on the riverbank. He nodded to his Blood Eagles to climb back up the wall. There was still work to be done in the city, he knew very well. Not satisfied with a straightforward victory, The Tuatha De Dannan would crush this upstart king and all hope of another like him, here, this night. Kaer Yin was slow to anger despite his general air of perturbation but woe to any fool that thought him weak. This was the same man who had smashed every rebellion the Southers had mustered for nearly a thousand years.

Tam Lin hoped his cousin had the bastard's head in burlap by now. With a deep breath, he let go of Rian's hand to examine her wounds. She'd taken several blows to her face that bore broken bones, a seeping gash to her side, and the back of her head was swollen and black from where her would-be rapist had smashed her head into the cobbles. This was also work that needed doing, and since Diarmid had seemed to bugger off on holiday with Kaer Yin's girl, there was no one here with the blood to do it but him. Una's aunt was no use. She'd taken a spear to the thigh and was in grave danger of bleeding out before they made it across the river. The girl Rose was doing her best to treat her, but she hadn't moved save for the occasional moan. As for Rian, her external wounds were serious, but these weren't what was killing her. Barb had said she'd downed a bottle of poison. He'd waited to act in case she might live unaided, but she grew colder by the minute. He took a second breath and nodded.

No one else here with the blood.

Decision made, he knelt and scooped Rian up from the clammy riverbank. She weighed less than she had an hour ago if that were possible. He carried her to a small curragh moored nearby. Barb came at him like a furious gnat, for all that she could barely walk herself. "What are ye *doin*!" she spat, clawing at him. "Ye shouldn't move her. She's bleedin' inside her skull!"

He shoved Barb gently against Dabney, who hooked a meaty arm around her lest she collapse. "Get in the boat with as many kids as you can manage." Tam Lin's tone brooked no refusal. Dabney hefted Barb beside Rian before helping several frail women and children into the far end. Each stared up at the red and black stained prince with owlish eyes. He could guess what he looked like to them. Barb curled herself around Rian protectively. There weren't enough boats for everyone, meaning many healthy adults would have to risk the icy current or wait ashore for any Souther stragglers that may attempt to drag them off for sport or ransom. No help for that either, as no plan was perfect.

Sighing, he pushed the little boat into the water, just shy of the current. The river's chill seeped into his trousers above the knees, but he scarcely felt it.

You can't let her die.

If he allowed himself to feel anything right about then, the fact would singe his nerves with rage. Why should it be him? He was the least talented of his entire cursed bloodline. She deserved better.

Yet… he thought.

You're the only one here.

He stared at her like a broken bird he wasn't sure wouldn't be better off under a rock. Barb saw the expression on his face and frowned. "I don't like the look o'ye just now."

"I've never done this before."

"Forgive me. She's gonna die slow if the belladonna doesn't do her first," she choked back a sob. "You're right. Sweet lamb deserves a rest."

Whatever she'd just said sent hordes of flies buzzing in his ears. His thoughts clouded. This furious little thing had a twisted foot, an angry brow, wits as sharp as any blade, and a tongue to match. Infuriating. Loyal. Rude. True. Ugly. Lovely. Errant. Wise.

He realized then he wanted her to live.

More than that, though, he did not have the words.

Tam Lin O'Ruiadh did not speak such a language.

Kaer Yin, you bastard.

With a groan, he reached down and dug his fingers into the mud just below the waterline, whispering ancient odes he'd heard only once when they were spoken over his mother's sickbed. She'd taken an arrow wound on a raid into the midlands, and were it not for his uncle Midhir, she would have died then. In the end, she sailed away to Tir Na Nog with her sisters and away from his father forever.

The Dagda blessed our family with this burden, Midhir had said.

I use it now not for your mother, nor your father, but for you, my boy. May it teach you balance. The Ard Ri had clapped him on the shoulder, looking deep into his eyes. *There is no life without sacrifice.*

Tam Lin withdrew the mud, smearing it between his palms. He drew his dagger along his wrist, letting the blood and soil mingle in his hands.

Barb drew Rian close as if to croon to her, but Tam Lin ignored her.

Over Rian's side, he packed the mixture, then the ballooning wound at the base of her skull, and the myriad cuts along her collarbone, face, and finally the ruin of her brow. These, he knew, were only the visible hurts. What lurked inside was far worse and final an agent than mere cuts and bruises. Gently he pried her lips open to drag a bit of the mixture over her teeth, satisfied that some had worked itself into her mouth. He closed his eyes, drawing the words inside himself, then imagined them flowing down his arm and into her heart, from his flesh to hers.

Blood is first, said the Midhir in his memory.

And Crom's is sacred.

When the last line had been uttered, Tam Lin didn't have to wait long.

His knees buckled, and he sagged against the boat, boots trailing sideways in the current. Dabney's massive hand caught him before his head could dip beneath the surface. A good thing, too, for Tam Lin would surely have drowned. He had *never* felt anything like this. The bones in his face creaked under new pressure. A bright flash of stars swirled in his vision as if his head had been cracked against a stone wall. He gasped for air as the rush of black belladonna sped through his blood toward his heart. Dabney held him aloft while he flapped around like a dying fish.

"What in the *hells* did ye just do?" Barb demanded, agog.

Tam Lin couldn't answer for several minutes because of his impending death, but then as suddenly as it accosted him, it lessened until it stopped, leaving aches and pain behind— if no immediate threat of doom. He breathed a bit easier and let himself dangle from the side of the boat for a few minutes, exhausted and feeling worse than he ever had… but better than he should. He wiped a trickle of fresh blood from his nose.

"What did you do?" Barb repeated.

Get up, he silently commanded himself. After a moment, he managed to push himself upright without vomiting. Gods, he felt like hammered shite. "What needed doing. Take care of her," he told Barb, turning away. He would ignore the pain. He had other business.

A cold, clammy hand snaked out of the boat to clutch at his fingers.

Rian's pale, bruised (but no longer broken) face stared up at him. "T-the cost!"

He smiled at her with genuine relief. "Was worth it. It'll take more than that to kill the mighty Prince of Connaught." He winked with an eye half swollen shut, then shook himself and shuffled onshore with renewed purpose.

"Wait!" she cried. "Where are you going in that state?"

"To watch my fool cousin's back, where else?"

❦

With the north end of Rosweal in flames, all that was left for Kaer Yin and his archers to do was to pick off any stragglers that tried to climb the wall to escape the blaze. The Southers had come here dealing fire, and now they were trapped in a hell of their own design. Kaer Yin has always been a great fan of irony. Any Southers who made it through the gap in the Navan Gate hours before could count themselves lucky. Dannan archers made short work of any Corpsmen who managed to stumble out of the inferno unscathed, and at this stage, the act was mercy for most. Those who hadn't been blown apart in the recent explosion wandered the streets in such a state of deformity and shock that the arrows must have been a relief. None of the Sidhe were feeling very sympathetic to the Southers' plight after nearly three straight days of violence… but neither did they revel in misery. Screams did not make pleasant music.

The day was a red, unequivocal rout!

Every goad, every trap Rosweal's defenders had lain, had achieved the impossible— the obliteration of Damek Bishop's incredibly numerous vanguard. They had not only survived this vicious assault, but they had bloody well won! So much for Bishop's advanced artillery, superior weaponry, and numbers.

He'd suffered as ignominious a defeat as one could at the hands of a ragtag group of poachers and thieves led by a smattering of Sidhe warriors. They had done it! Nothing short of a miracle, considering Roswell had been outmanned nearly five to one. Kaer Yin was almost too relieved to bother killing any more Southers. As it was, only the very determined had the bollocks to climb the wall in search of vengeance, and the rest were either grievously wounded or fleeing for their lives. Besides, he was bloody tired. Nemain felt like a two-stone weight in his hands, and the air in his lungs tasted of blood and charcoal. He needed a nice warm place to lie down and sleep a week or more away. Frankly, he was beginning to feel a *wee* bit sorry for the Southers. They had been led to this backwater at the edge of their world by a lie—the promise of a great glory that was not to be— not today— not for them.

Not at Rosweal!

He turned, remembering that half the town was burning and most of the other half was already burnt black or in pieces. These were people's homes, their livelihoods, their very lives. He had to remind himself that a victory at such cost was not so cheap that it bore something as crude as levity. Even a well-earned moment of gloating glee had to be tempered by the lives lost to achieve it.

Jan Fir strode toward him through the haze. The look on his face mirrored Kaer Yin's sentiments. They'd been fighting back-to-back through most of the day, and Kaer Yin thanked Herne his brother-in-law had had the grace to come to Eire with Fionn. It was not every day that a King should bleed for a group of miscreant mortals, but bleed he had. His arms trailed a bit at his side, blackened and swollen. Still, he flashed white teeth at Kaer Yin, who returned the gesture. But alarm flickered in the depth of Jan Fir's green eyes, and he frowned. Kaer Yin's head swiveled around to see what he was looking at.

A booted foot connected with the back of his left leg, making a crunch. Kaer Yin cried out and threw himself forward into a rolling dive, just in time to narrowly miss the sword thrust that came from behind him. The air whistled in his ear as the blade swept past. Grimacing in pain, he watched as Damek emerged from the smoke beneath a light but a steady dusting of fresh, clean snow.

Damek was wounded— badly, clutching the dented, singed remains of his formerly shiny breastplate. His hands and one side of his face were pocked with severe burns, and his bare right arm that held his sabre wasn't much more than charred meat; what remained of his cloak dangled from his back in strips. Most of his hair had been singed off.

Kaer Yin had never been so glad to see someone in his life. "Good! I would hate for you to have missed any of this!" He held his hand out to the puttering flames below. The snow would again save Rosweal from further damage— as he'd hoped it would.

Damek made a rude sound. "It doesn't matter to me how many you killed today or yesterday, you Dannan cunt." His voice shook with a rage Kaer Yin knew all too well. With grief. He had been right. That big man *had* been the Lord of Clare's weak point.

And all that fury had cost him thousands of men and, likely, a crown.

"These men are replaceable," he went on. "As long as *you* die— as long as I can carry *your* head out of here tonight— I'll count this a worthwhile endeavor." He slid his right foot forward, leaving a black streak against the snow, a high guard. "I think I'll fuck *my bride* on a bed carved from your lovely bones. What do you say? Maybe we'll drink a toast out of your skull at her coronation?"

"I wonder if you can smell the shit as it spills from your mouth, boy?" Kaer Yin laughed.

Damek smiled back mirthlessly. "Did she tell you that she bore me a child, Your Highness?"

Kaer Yin stopped. His grin faltered.

"That's right. Our marriage was consummated, making it a legal arrangement in *whatever bloody court* you hope to contest it in. All of this," he waved his hand. "Is for naught. You jumped in the middle of a family squabble for a woman you could never hope to understand." He stared straight ahead, eyes dark as pitch. "Did she tell you my daughter was four years old when she died? Una doesn't know I know. Her name was Zeah. She had black hair, like me."

It took a while for Kaer Yin to find his voice. "Una is a free woman, Damek. You did not own her then and don't own her now. You had many chances to respect her and spat on all of them. *That* is the only law I know."

"Everything I've done has been for her, for Zeah... for all the children we may yet bring into this world. No Patricks to twist the law to suit his whims, no High King to flatter, no Aes Sidhe to lord over Eire's good, honest people. *We* were born to rule here, to found a new dynasty, to lead our people out of the bloody dark age your kind have built for them."

"You'd have me believe you betray her for her own good?"

"Giving her a crown is hardly a betrayal."

"Tell that to the women of Tairngare, all of whom your grandmother destroyed— with your help. You knew what you were doing when you allied with Armagh. How many of Una's people, her family, have died for your greed?"

Damek shifted where he stood, hesitating.

Kaer Yin continued, "I can see you struggle with the concept of selflessness, Damek. For someone who claims to have committed every sin for the benefit of someone else, that someone seems to have suffered most for each of them."

"I don't—"

"None of this is love. Using someone to gain power is not love. Hurting someone for hurting you is not love. Refusing to respect someone's decisions is not love. *Murdering thousands is not love.* You have done absolutely *nothing* for Una, save take from her, exploit her name, and destroy what she cares for. How can you honestly tell me you have aggrandized yourself... *for her?*"

Damek was silent for a moment, teetering between emotions Kaer Yin could not discern. After a few breaths, he finally laughed a dry sound. "You're just like *him*. You're using her too, same as he did, as her grandmother did, her aunts— everyone who has ever met her. Deny it. I dare you."

It was Kaer Yin's turn to stew in culpability for a spanse. While he chewed on his retort, one of Damek's Corpsmen ran up to Damek and placed a hand on his shoulder. He opened his mouth to shout something in his ear, but Damek shrugged his hand off, drew a dagger from his belt, and shoved it into the soldier's throat without a backward glance. As he withdrew the blade from his dumbfounded subordinate, he didn't watch him fall. His hateful glare was all for Kaer Yin.

"*Ard Tiarne!*" Jan Fir shouted, clutching his lark in his good hand.

Kaer Yin threw a hand out. "Don't interfere!"

"Well? Tell me a lie, son of Midhir. Tell me all of this," he wagged his dagger back and forth. "Didn't start with that little *geis* you earned yourself at Dumnain. Tell me that you never meant to use her to better *your* position. Tell me that you, the most famous butcher Eire has ever known— that you fight for her out of the kindness of your heart."

"What's between us is not your business."

"Fucking hypocrite. Now *that* is living up to my expectations of you." He snorted and adjusted his guard, expression hard. "Are you ready? Talking to you is boring the shite out of me."

Kaer Yin nodded, swinging Nemain up over his shoulder. "I thought you'd never ask." He shot forward so fast that he might have been an arrow.

⚲ ⚲

ROBIN WAS EXHAUSTED. HE HAD never gone so long, or so hard, without sleep. He'd never know how High Elves did this shite— making it look so bloody easy. Well, most of 'em, anyway. He fought off two burned Corpsmen trying to drag him and the Dannan he carried from the ladder. Thankfully, the two Southers were so wounded they didn't stand a chance, even one-handed. They'd come for the ladder as he had, looking to escape the smoke in the city below. His eyes and tongue stung something awful; even with the torn scrap of tunic he'd tied over his nose and mouth, he had trouble breathing without coughing. The Sidhe on his back— Shar, if Robin recalled correctly— was nearly beyond that now. He'd almost dropped him in the last tussle, and it took a few precious minutes of hacking and coughing to right him again.

He'd dragged the elf a good twenty yards along the wall already, and the big bastard wasn't getting any lighter. Shar had saved his life from the sneaky dagger thrust Ridley had tried to plunge into his guts by shooting the red-bearded fucker in the face from a dozen yards. Winded and disoriented by the smoke and chaos, Robin hadn't had a moment to salute him before watching a fleeing infantryman jab a short sabre through his back and out of his chest. Shar fell face-first from the wall and was half-burnt to a crisp by the time Robin made it over to drag him away. When Robin rolled him over, he'd smiled weakly, more in surprise and humor than anything else. He sputtered a few times, blood bubbling from his lips, then the sputtering stopped altogether. Shar still breathed, but barely. With all the flames, smoke, and roaming soldiery— Robin decided he would not leave a man who's saved his worthless life to die alone on a pyre. He hadn't known the fellow long, they'd barely spoken four words between them, but he was a Greenmaker too.

Greenmakers didn't leave men behind.

Robin might have made a different decision if he'd known how bloody heavy he'd be. Mercifully, by the time he got to the second from top rung, a hand came down to pull them up the rest of the way. This one was the other Dannan noble, the one Ben called Jan. Robin lay back, gasping against his makeshift facemask, while Jan Fir examined Shar.

"Is he—" Robin huffed.

There was such a sincere expression of mournfulness that Robin felt himself tearing up despite not knowing him long or well. They'd all lost people here today. All of them, even the Sidhe. Jan Fir slid his palm from his temple to his chest— several of his nearby companions did the same. He glanced over at Robin, green eyes tearful. "You carried him."

"He saved my life. Couldn't let him burn. Not like that."

Jan Fir nodded. "For this, we thank you." The respect Robin saw blooming in his eyes put him at a loss for words. Usually, Daoine Sidhe, like Jan Fir hunted Greenmakers for plying their trade. It was quite odd to feel how swiftly a perception could change. His included.

"Where's Ben then?" he asked, uncomfortable.

Jan Fir hefted Shar's body over his much taller, much wider shoulder, tugging his chin toward the bend in the wall. Ben was engaged in a serious swordfight, moving like water through a canyon. It took a minute with all the smoke, but Robin's eyes flared when he realized whom he fought. "*Siora*! That's bloody Lord Bishop, hisself. Somebody shoot that prick!"

"We can't," sighed Jan Fir. "*Mo Flaith* has ordered us to go. In any case, he is peerless."

Robin blew air over his lower lip. "Never played Porter with his Arseness then, I take it?"

Jan Fir gave him an odd look. "No. Why?"

"Because Ben always lays the best strategies," said Robin watching Kaer Yin with genuine concern. They were all dead tired, and he might put a good face on it, but the Prince of Innisfail was slowing. "But he never considers that his opponent is *always* trying to cheat."

⚒

DAMEK CAME BACK AT HIM— switching between Adrac and Neithana with smooth, practiced ease. He pressed forward, his footwork much like the inner workings of a clock: a step, one-second pause, rotate, then step. Every inch he moved, his sabre came down from his high guard, then around his body for a slice at Kaer Yin's midsection, then back up for another high thrust. It was predictable but methodical and difficult to counter without leaving his side or head exposed. With the slippery, snow-dusted battlement being both narrow and coated in scattered debris and ash, every back step Kaer Yin took to defend himself became more and more precarious. Not to mention, he was beyond exhausted. He might have been born with the immortal, seemingly boundless constitution of his forebears, but after nearly three days without sleep, two battles, two raids, and the endless killing he'd been forced to do— his bones felt like jelly beneath his skin. If he allowed this to go on too long, he might make a mistake that could cost him his life.

Damek also had to be tired, but he was fueled by desperation and hatred Kaer Yin had never seen glowing from a man's eyes so brightly before. The Lord of Clare knew very well that if he failed to kill the Crown Prince now, he would never get the chance again. He also must have realized that today's loss would sorely dent his reputation as a newly minted King of Eire, and the head of the Ard Ri's son would be a consolation any of his backers would respect. Perhaps even the zealot who had usurped his seat in Bethany.

Well, if he survived.

Kaer Yin Adair had never lost a duel.

On the advance, Damek switched to his left foot, sliding forward on the balls of his feet to resume his clockwork cadence. His purpose was clearly to hammer away at Kaer Yin's worn-down dominant arm. A clever stratagem, as every stroke reverberated through Kaer Yin's bones with excruciating regularity. He braced himself against the pain. Damek grunted with each thrust, putting everything he had into each jab.

Kaer Yin knew his right arm couldn't stave off this merciless rhythm much longer, so he flipped Nemain broadside, glancing Damek's sabre and breaking the concentrated pattern in his footwork. He staggered back a half-step, forced to block Kaer Yin's next stroke on vertiginous heels. Swinging Nemain over his opposite shoulder, Kaer Yin brought her back down in an elegant slash that terminated in a down-striking spin.

Damek caught himself and leaned against his sabre for support. "That's a fancy guard for an arm as weak as yours."

"Come try it and see."

Shrugging, Damek slid his right foot to the side, thinning the line of his body and taking a low guard. He would twist his blade crosswise as Nemain came down from above, then turn, taking advantage of his vulnerable side. Kaer Yin realized the danger in a flash. He didn't have the strength to play chess with Bishop.

He must end this now.

Kaer Yin slipped his left foot forward as if he would begin the terminus of his slashing guard. Damek, as expected, committed to moving in from his undefended side and under Nemain's descending stroke. But Kaer Yin slid back onto his right foot at the last moment, pushing himself out of the way and causing Damek's sabre to dash uselessly to the left. Kaer Yin flipped Nemain broadside, smacking his opponent's chest with the flat of the blade— drawing his exposed back onto Kaer Yin's lark. The thinner, more rigid blade slammed into Damek's kidney with ease. The Lord of Clare whimpered in pain, dropping his sabre. He clawed wildly at Kaer Yin, trying anything to dislodge him. Instead, Kaer Yin rolled his left soldier, slowly forcing him onto his knees while withdrawing his lark. As he stepped back, he swept Nemain across Damek's chest, biting through the gap in his breastplate, leaving a vast chasm that spilled dark blood.

Damek gasped a sick, wet sound.

His expression marked disbelief.

Kaer Yin resheathed his weapons, breathing hard.

"All hail the King of Eire," he sneered and turned his back.

He didn't wait to watch Bishop fall. It was only a matter of time now, and he didn't care to watch him die. Kaer Yin had people to look after, a woman to find, a city to rebuild, and a family to return to. He'd expended all the energy he intended to on Damek fucking Bishop.

As he walked west along the battlements, he nodded at his men helping each other down the ropes toward the river, their faces blurred in the haze. He was pleased to note how deserted the city felt just then, as everyone who hadn't died in the streets was long gone or leaving.

Flames still raged in the Greenmakers' Quarter along the western wall. Even *The Hart* was a torch against the night sky. He stood and watched it burn for a moment. The sight was soon eclipsed by a cloud of smoke and cinders that sent him backward, hacking.

Right, he thought.

Best get to it then.

He made his way to the ropes his men had already descended, even though he could scarcely see his fingers four inches from his face. Now that the Quarter was finally in flames, the smoke had become a maelstrom. He clasped the top of a rope ladder and hauled himself nearly over the wall, save for his left leg, which he used for balance as he adjusted his scabbard to climb. Something sharp suddenly bit through his calf, pinning his leg in place. He cried out in surprise. Damek's blistered hands snatched out and wrenched him back over the stone rampart.

He struck Kaer Yin with fists, elbows, and skull— anything he could. Disoriented, Kaer Yin felt himself being dragged back toward the fire. Damek hit him full in the face with his forehead, filling his vision with white lights. He reached up in time to catch Damek's right fist as it plummeted toward his heart with a bloodied dagger point. The angle was not to Kaer Yin's advantage, and Damek laughed manically, spurting blood into Kaer Yin's eyes and mouth.

He gagged.

The dagger's tip plunged through his cuirass and into the skin above Kaer Yin's ribs, tearing a hiss from between his clenched teeth. Further still it came, inch by inch, until he felt it scrape across his breastbone, threatening the organs beneath.

"That's Ard Ri Mac Nemed to you, you Dannan Piece of shite." Damek laughed as Kaer Yin's weakened right hand began to give.

Kaer Yin wrestled as much as he could, but every motion brought the blade further into his flesh. He felt bone give way and knew it would tear through his heart at any moment. He was about to die at Damek fucking Bishop's hand.

Maybe he *was not* such an admirer of irony, after all.

A rush of hot air swept over his head from the west, and suddenly, Damek was knocked backward. A jagged gash split his face open from ear to nose. He screamed, scrambling away to regain footing, but Tam

Lin launched himself forward, larks spinning through the air between them. One entered the hollow of his gut, and the other took his right hand off at the wrist. Damek had time for one last wide-eyed shriek before Tam Lin withdrew the lark and placed his foot over the wound— shoving him from the wall to the licking flames below.

"I bloody well warned you, didn't I?" Tam Lin asked as he fell, howling into the smoke rising from the street. Tam Lin spat, resheathed his larks, and turned back to his cousin, who was trying to stand up. He threw out a hand to help him. Kaer Yin sagged a bit against him. "Some men just don't know when to stay dead."

"Indeed," agreed Kaer Yin, as they limped to the ropes and escape.

The Dawn Tide

For a few hours, the survivors watched the snow pile up over the walls from the safety of their boats or sheltered behind fully armored defenders gathered on the docks. Some blessedly brilliant individual had at least thought to stock the area with enough tents and tarpaulins to spread over the shabby, partially burnt-out rooftop over the main pier. Thankfully, they did not lack for dried-out timber to build fires; stone pits were thrown together on either side of the snow-dusted bank, around which dozens of people milled for warmth, simply happy to be alive.

Under the last tent, Rian's patients were laid out side by side for body warmth and shelter from the elements. Despite the harsh, barking command Tam Lin had tried to give her— she moved among them, tying bandages with torn tunics, petticoats, whatever she could get her hands on. Though Tam Lin had taken half her wounds upon himself, she was still fairly covered in bruises, minor cuts, and several scabbing scratches. Thankful or not, she ignored everything that came out of Tam Lin's mouth and treated him first, bearing a stony-eyed determination that snapped his mouth shut tight.

In the end, he had learned it was wiser to concede defeat.

When she'd finished wrapping him up like an invalid, she ordered him into the line of wounded waiting for broth along the wall. Grumbling, he sat next to Kaer Yin, who watched him sidelong.

"What?" he gruffed.

Kaer Yin pursed his lips. "Not a thing."

Tam Lin muttered something unintelligible.

"Glad to see she is feeling better."

"Her evil is strong," nodded Tam Lin.

"Hm," said Kaer Yin.

"Must be Dian Cecht's blessings."

"Interesting that you both bear the same marks."

Tam Lin shrugged.

"You going to tell me about it?"

"No."

Kaer Yin let the matter drop. He declined a lukewarm bowl of broth and a scrap of moldy bread from one of Tansy's girls (others needed it more, as far as he was concerned), then slapped his knee. "Right then. We have work to do anyway." The dead needed counting, and though Kaer Yin would rather not bear the terrible knowledge he was about to tally, the responsibility was his. Tam Lin's grim expression mirrored his own. He merely nodded once.

A job no one wanted was a leader's burden.

Kaer Yin had no idea how many familiar faces he would discover lying face up in the snow upriver, but he did know there were hundreds. Among them were Damek Bishop and a score of his officers. Kaer Yin had ordered that they be left for Una to choose their method of burial, less Bishop's armor and rings of state. These would be sent to Tairngare, Armagh, and Bethany, respectively, along with the Crown Prince's sentiments.

Innisfail has but one ruler.

He had many things to see to and many additional fires to put out across the Continent, but first, he must make it through the day. He and Tam Lin walked through the still-smoldering remains of a once healthy forest toward the one duty neither wished to see through. The dead had been stretched out by the townsfolk as honorably as they could be. More people were carried from the city every hour and lain out beside their fellows: friend and foe alike. Say what one would about the North; they understood dignity, even for those who did not deserve it. Kaer Yin spotted Damek and his men first, for their cobalt and scarlet cloaks. Damek's face had been covered with a scrap of his banner, his blackened arms folded over the gaping chest wound Kaer Yin had given him, his right hand missing.

Find peace in Tech Duinn, brother, Kaer Yin thought and steadied himself for the sea of forms ahead.

"Ben!" called a familiar voice from down the shore. "Is that ye 'neath all that blood and grime?" Robin hobbled up the causeway to stand beside him.

Kaer Yin clasped his forearm. "Glad to see your ugly face."

Robin threw his arms around his friend, slapping his wounded back hard. Neither had dry eyes. He cleared his throat as he broke away. "Well, I woke up on the bank a while back. My sweet woman nearly beat me half to death for glee."

"Is she all right?" Kaer Yin's expression clouded. She hadn't looked very good when last he saw her.

Robin waved his comment away. "Mistress Rian is the boss, Barb has learned. Got her laid up under a pile of furs taller'n me an' sippin' broth like a good lass. She'll be fine, I 'spect."

Tam Lin shook Robin's hand. "Pleased you aren't dead as you look, mortal."

"An' I'm happy to see ye Sidhe bastards bruise like the best o'us. Look like oversqueezed shite, highness, if ye don't mind me sayin' so."

"Not at all," laughed Tam Lin. "I'm hoping it makes me more dashing."

Kaer Yin rolled his eyes and pulled Robin away by his shoulder. "The Greenmakers?"

"Putting out what's left of the fires. Ye won't believe it, but *The Hart's* still in one piece, if a bit charred. Stone foundations."

Kaer Yin smiled. "The luckiest woman in Innisfail."

"Ain't she just?" Robin jerked a flask out of his bloodied vest. "To Barb Dormer, more lives than a barnyard cat!"

He took a long pull and passed the flask.

Kaer Yin's eyes misted at the smell of raw *uishge* inside. "Oh, you bloody beautiful bastard." He tipped it back with a groan of pure pleasure. The fire it lit warmed him clear to his arse. He took a second sip and passed it to Tam Lin.

"A bed in my future," Tam Lin toasted, smacking his lips after a long gulp.

Robin reclaimed the vessel and glanced around to ensure no one saw him. All the uishge was meant to be at the bottom of the river in barrels, but Robin couldn't help but keep a stash. If Barb found out, she'd have his guts for lacings. "Any sign o'yer girl yet, Ben?"

Kaer Yin frowned. "Not as yet." He was trying not to think about it. The least he could be sure of was that she did not await him amongst the pile of defenders he was about to tour. He'd given orders to report any sightings of her or Diarmid. Una's aunt and uncle were both wounded but relatively in one piece. During their flight through the streets, Eva had taken a serious wound that Rian had spent the better part of ten hours stitching.

The Siorai Alta would live, though she would likely never walk again. Barb had already told him what happened in the cellar and what they had been forced to do to escape. If not for Eva, all of the children might not have arrived at the gatehouse in time.

Knowing what happened to Rian and Barb only streets away, told Kaer Yin everything he needed to know about the gravity of Eva's choice, for surely she had known what would happen to both groups. He sighed. He still had no idea if she'd been talking about Damek when she warned him it wasn't 'over.' He'd be sure to ask her next time she was conscious.

"Well, she'll turn up. No doubt there," said Robin, like a man who said far less than he needed to.

"What is it, Robin?"

"Well, I dunno if it's the time to… I dunno."

"Just say it, man," Tam Lin cut in. "What's one more tragedy?"

Robin shot him a sharp look but seeing the fatigue and resigned preparedness in his expression, he immediately softened. "No help for it then, milords. Follow me."

Kaer Yin didn't need to be told where they were headed. He was already aware that two clearings had been prepared. He tucked his head down and followed without bothering to glance up once.

🦌 🦌

THE GREENMAKERS HAD BEEN MOST respectful. Shar, Fionn, Mordu, and over a hundred and fifty of Aes Sidhe's finest were stretched out, side by side, below the blackened western wall. Their faces were uncovered one at a time for identification, then recovered gently by Robin's shaking fingers. "We know ye don't bury yer fallen as we do, and we wanted 'em to have the honors they damn well earned."

Choking, Tam Lin fell to his knees in the snow, weeping openly at Shar's feet. They had been friends for decades, no matter how the affections of one woman might have divided them. He wept like a child, blubbering apologies Shar would never hear. This was a regret Tam Lin would bear for the rest of his life, and it was painful to watch.

Kaer Yin swallowed hard, throat dry and cracking. "Thank you, Robin."

Jan Fir was already there, huddled a few paces away, whispering prayers over Fionn's nearly cleaved body while his fingers wound through Mordu's. They had been lovers all their lives, and it broke Kaer Yin's heart to see his wracking sobs. Eri would be devastated. They had made a family, despite their marriage of convenience, and Eri loved Mordu perhaps as much as she loved Kaer Yin.

After several minutes, Kaer Yin let out a long, haggard breath and turned around to wipe his burning eyes. "They sail to Bri Reis, where they'll feast with the Gods on their way to Tir Na Nog."

"*Bíodh sé amhlaidhsaid,*" said Tam Lin, tracing the line from his forehead to his heart. He dug his palms into his eye sockets. "Does Rian know?"

"Not yet," answered Robin soberly. "Haven't had the heart to tell her, 'specially with all she's been through."

"Gods, Yin, how do I begin—" Tam Lin's voice broke.

"I'll do it. You must prepare his boat," Kaer Yin said firmly.

Tam Lin nodded.

Robin was shaking when next he spoke. "Not to dig the blade deeper, but we're burying our own now, Ben. The lads, well, it would mean the world to them if ye'd come say a few words."

Robin was perhaps more stoic than any man Kaer Yin knew, and to see his jaw trembling that way could only mean one thing. Barb was accounted for.

"Robin, where's Gerry?"

Robin covered his face with both hands, and Kaer Yin clutched his shoulder. "Follow me," he managed to say again.

🦌 🦌

AT DAWN THE FOLLOWING DAY, the sun shone over a white and black landscape that was startlingly beautiful, despite its many woes. When the boats had been hewn, and the Sidhe were laid out in their biers, when the townsfolk had finished patting earth over their loved ones' graves, Kaer Yin lined up with his fellows, facing the rising sun. He wore white from head to toe, as was the custom among the Tuatha De Dannan— as white was the color of death and rebirth. His hair had been braided by Tansy's children, Robin's new wards as the Lord of Navan.

669

Tansy, Violet, and even Gerry were all tucked beneath the forest floor, waiting for spring rains to bless their graves with the flowers each deserved.

"Great Bel," he said in the common tongue, so all might hear. "We give you these souls to carry with you that they might sup in the halls of your kin, forever and a day." The gathering repeated his words, saluting the rising sun with their heads bowed low.

Kaer Yin waded out to the curraghs held just shy of the gentle current between the city's scarred stone wall and the misty, blackened trees on the opposite bank. He waded among each, pushing their footings downriver as he passed. The last two were Shar and Fionn's. Both were decked out in every scrap of fine fabric the women could find. Their hair glittered with shining beads spread out around their seemingly sleeping faces. Fionn's hands had been wrapped around the hilt of his greatsword, while Shar Lianor's pale fingers clasped the bow his father had made for him the day Bov Dearg had chosen him to serve the Prince of Connaught. In repose, he seemed to be smiling.

"Only the glorious dead live forever."

Kaer Yin severed a lock of his hair and gifted it to his father's champion. A gift for Donn, who would know the price Fionn had paid to protect Crom's Clan. To Shar, he gave two of his daggers so that he might boast of his deeds in the Dagda's Hall. After pushing both boats into the current, he waded back to shore, where Tam Lin, Jan Fir, Robin, and a score of others waited with flaming arrows. Kaer Yin took Sinnair from a boy he did not recognize. The bow was blackened at the ends but was otherwise unharmed. He dipped his arrow into the bonfire and drew, waiting for the boats to huddle together at the nearest bend where it widened into a deep, churning pool, then onward toward the sun.

Rian's white skirt swirled in the shallows as she and the other women tossed flowers after their dead. He heard her sobbing, and it wrought fresh sadness—poor girl. To have found and lost love so swiftly was a terrible fate for a heart as worthy as hers. He felt for her, and worse, for the stolid suffering it gave Tam Lin to realize the truth of his feelings amidst so much grief.

Kaer Yin mourned for all three.

What else could he do?

Jan Fir's damaged right arm quivered against his bow, but he did not complain. Mordu's passage was his responsibility. Kaer Yin also mourned for his sister, whose heart would break anew.

As the sun crested the hills to the east, they let their arrows fly: once, twice, three times, until every bier roared to light, sailing into the rising sun and, eventually, the sea.

℣ ℣

After the funeral, Kaer Yin walked through the western woods toward the graves of so many Milesians he'd come to care for, stopping finally at Gerrod's. He couldn't help but admire the odd twist of fate that had placed him here among those he swore to loathe all of his life— and in the end, had been willing to die for. Silently, he thanked his father again for the *geis* he'd been given. It had saved him, sure as the sun would set in the west. In his wisdom, the Ard Ri had blessed his son with compassion, humility, kindness, and the understanding of true courage. To be brave, one didn't need to be the finest warrior or hold the highest titles. Bravery was the willingness to lay one's life down for those *weaker* than oneself, to stand up for people the powerful deemed valueless.

That was what it truly meant to be brave.

After a thousand years in Innisfail, Kaer Yin had learned this last and hardest lesson. It took three decades among those he never had a thought for to drive the point home. He felt a surge of gratitude for his father's incredible mercy, tolerance, and patience. For the lives that he'd been honored to be a part of. For the sacrifices they had made for his decisions. For the purpose they had given him. He stared down at the large rock that served as Gerrod's headstone, the cairn marked by the dagger Robin had made for his fifteenth birthday. Its brass scabbard had been polished to a high sheen.

Kaer Yin felt Gerrod's loss acutely as if he'd been a brother… and perhaps he had been.

"Never again," he said, unsheathing his dagger and sweeping it across his palm before snapping the blade back into its sheath. He buried it beneath several of the smaller stones and closed his eyes. "Innisfail shall be one land, one people, and no more boys should die for the whims of rich men. I vow it as *Ard Tiarne* of the Tuatha De Dannan— your sacrifice shall not be in vain."

A stray tear wound its way down his cheek as he stood. "Farewell, my friend."

He was silent on his walk back to town, mulling over all the mistakes he had made in his attempt to shirk his destiny. No more. This land would not fall prey to power-hungry madmen as long as he drew Innish air into his lungs.

A twig snapped in the bracken, bringing his head up sharply. He set a hand on his pommel. There hadn't been any Bethonair stragglers in days, but that didn't mean they weren't out there, waiting for their chance to raid or attack unwitting villagers for coins or food. Scanning the wasteland for his unseen visitor, he waited. Then, Una stepped out of the barest beam of sunlight. The air shimmered with Otherworld power for a heartbeat. She didn't see him at first, wide eyes taking in the crippled Greensward with a gasp, her hands flying to her mouth.

He must have made some sound, and she turned, her face the most beautiful thing he'd ever seen. With a cry, she launched herself into his eager, open arms.

⚯

IN THE GLOAMING, FOG-SHROUDED, and bitterly cold evening air, several large gray flags bearing the white stag of House Adair snapped to and fro in the wind that chewed its way over the frigid Boinne. Overnight, the winter had returned with a vengeance, forcing the people of Rosweal back inside the city to reside in Sol Trant's undamaged brewery. It would house everyone inside its high stone walls and mostly intact roof until the Quarter could be rebuilt. Kaer Yin had no doubt the Greenmakers would set it to rights in no time. With the funds he, Una, and Tam Lin had given them— they could build two Rosweals with proper walls.

Kaer Yin admired the city from his saddle with a small smile. Maybe the Quarter would be the wealthiest district in the North when he returned?

Robin and Barb stood together on the wall, waving like lunatics. The former shouted something about *uishge* and a woman's fat thighs.

Kaer Yin laughed and turned toward the far shore, its omnipresent mists swirling just ahead. Tam Lin, Rian, and Jan Fir road ahead, breaching that smoky white curtain before him. As his mount neared the bank, the land beyond revealed itself in hints: a hill and a knot of dark trees. Una waited patiently behind him, knowing what this moment meant to him. Grinning, he closed his eyes and drew that mist into his lungs, his heart.

It had been so long, so *very, very* long.

At last, he was going home.

"For Herne's bloody sake, pull yourself together, you sentimental girl!" Tam Lin admonished from somewhere beyond the mists.

Laughing, Kaer Yin kicked his horse up over the bank, eager to race his cousin over the hills of Aes Sidhe.

—FIN—

The Waning Moon

"*Mo Flaith*?" a polite voice issued from the interior hall behind him. Falan didn't turn, for only bad news would prompt intrusion. Instead, he set his card down and picked up his wineglass. "Speak," he sighed.

Sionnavar took a deep breath before he replied. He wasn't as brave or cunning as his father, but he was a useful servant, nonetheless. "I have news."

Falan swirled his glass, emotionless eyes forward. "He's dead, isn't he?"

"Yes, My Lord. My deepest apologies."

Falan didn't move a muscle. "How?"

"We cannot be sure, but Leal, your sister's champion, vows he died fighting Midhir's son."

"A good death, at least. Where is his body?"

He felt Sionnovar's flinch. "The Moura girl insisted he be taken to Tairngare for internment. Many of his men have sworn her loyalty, as it happens."

"As well they should if their sole alternative is that murderous boil in the south. Where was he, last we checked?"

"Ten Bells, *Mo Flaith*. Riding back to Bethany, as far as my sources can glean."

"A stunning victory."

"A slaughter."

Falan pursed his lips, staring into the flickering flames ahead. "Ther can be no victory without it."

"He murdered the town's nobles, the Libellan charter, the Mercher's Guild, everyone." Falan heard the anger in his voice. "His men razed the Sidhe Consulate to the ground and crucified its inhabitants. Their gruesome corpses decorate either side of the High Road a mile in either direction."

"How devout he is," Falan smirked into his cup. "How many men did he leave in the city?"

"Not enough. If we aim to reclaim it."

Falan laughed through his nose. "Not at all. Let Midhir's son deal with Henry FitzDonahugh. The longer they busy themselves with yet another Souther distraction, the closer we shall come to our true goal."

"Yes, *Mo Flaith*," answered Sionnovar, without hiding his displeasure.

Falan did turn then. "We aim higher than Bethany, do we not?"

"Yes." Sionnovar flushed and nervously looked away.

"I take it the Bretagn's ships are now in his possession as well?"

Sionnovar nodded.

"Excellent. Promised him his newborn daughter or some such?"

"Yes. Had the girl formally betrothed to him after the battle. Gaelin's son had many ships to lend to the effort, each bedecked with cannons. Blasted away half the Merchanta Quarter."

"Too bad Castor won't live long enough to claim his prize. Henry will use the boy to take Tairngare, then dispose of him in short order." He chuckled to himself. The cards he'd laid out in front of him bore ominous sigils. He set his glass down and reached out to reshuffle the deck. "In any case, we've lost the element of surprise. Midhir's son won't take kindly to our intervention."

"He will take that information to his father."

"Is that where he's headed now?"

"Should have arrived by now."

Falan's hands paused over his cards. A slow smile then broke over his face. "Well, I suppose that places all of our prey in one place."

Sionnovar shared his laugh, if without the same humor.

Falan was still smiling to himself when he set down the next card.

Death and the Waning Moon.

"Be seeing you, Kaer Yin," he whispered to himself. "Soon."

Bonds

Castor, son of Gaelin, Lord of Bretagne: patricide, plotter, hostage, and meat for the Eirean grindstone: sat his mare without the slightest hint of the internal war raging within him. A single head among thousands in the Grand Duch FitzDonahugh's procession, Castor's shorn and scabbed scalp and faded silk doublet marked him out like a bloody thumb. Amidst so many men in full-black and blue armor, Castor looked every inch the hostage he was despite his efforts to pretend his breeding made the slightest difference. The men around him couldn't care less about his pedigree nor the vaunted heights he imagined he'd fallen from so recently.

In the lead, nearly a half mile ahead, sat Henry himself. Castor noted his position beneath Bethany's bright blue and scarlet pennants that snapped in the wind beneath Henry's flat black standard. As usual, Henry was decked out in glossy black gauntlet and greaves, hoping to further the legend of the famous Black Knight of Bethany.

From Castor's middling position down the line, he could barely make out the flash of white beside the old man. Lady Penwyth, even now, attempted to fatten her coffers from Henry's leavings. Since her daughter had displeased Henry by birthing him a worthless girl and then dashing off to a nunnery somewhere in Cymru, Penwyth was desperate to maintain the alliance with the soon-to-be King of Eire by offering him another virgin daughter to abuse. Unless the old bastard were a fool, he'd accept, as the Sidhe outnumbered him by the thousands and were undoubtedly going to take exception to every ill his family had visited upon Innisfail in the last months, sooner or later.

Castor should know. He was now betrothed to the worthless girl-child Henry had forced upon his fifteen-year-old child bride. Not that Castor had a choice, but was death not the alternative, he would have far preferred a bride whose father proposed better prospects than the ensuing genocide Henry had invited upon them all.

For the thousandth time that day alone, Castor made a face.

They were all going to die.

He and his countrymen included… unless…

If he could escape, he might make *different* allies. Better allies. Ones that did not get themselves killed tangling with the Sidhe.

But who?

He had hoped to ensnare Lady Penwyth at the previous evening's feast in Damek Bishop's former hall at Clare. Not one to forgo an opportunity to capitalize on another man's successes, Henry, of course, had taken the manse and town for himself. There wasn't much left of Ten Bells to amuse an army of this size, so Henry had proposed one last venture as a lark for his men. And what a lark it was. The Christianized Bethonair troops marched into Clare like locusts, consumed everything in their wake, and left nothing but the white stone manse overlooking the harbor amidst a barren wasteland.

It had been much the same in Ten Bells.

Once, when Castor had been young, his père had taken he and Vexos to Ten Bells for the festival at Imbolg. Until he'd seen that glittering city with his own eyes, he'd never imagined such beauty was possible. Every street and cobbled lane was scrubbed and gleaming. Charming houses of every color trekked downhill to the Bay, their polished roof tiles catching the sun. Stone bridges replete with fine glass streetlamps dotted every river crossing, and the smell of fresh bread and cinnamon-dusted scones wound through each lane. The apparel… *lá*… Castor had been so enraptured by the fashions on display in the city of Ten Bells that he'd been having his clothing imported ever since. It was a place of learning, commerce, and culture that had no equal.

Ten Bells had been the wealthiest, cleanest, most lovely place he'd ever set eyes on until Henry FitzDonahugh passed through. Now, it was a coal-black scar against a white hillside: a pyre spilling billowing trails of smoke and ashes over a cerulean and turquoise sea. Its once beautiful schools, libraries, and markets were toppled and plundered. Its lanes were choked with corpses or the human scarecrows left behind. Ten Bell's coffers were emptied: its wealth a memory. Its people were either enslaved, left to starve, or had been nailed to crosses for a mile in every direction. Castor had never heard of such atrocities as Henry committed at Ten Bells… all because he imagined he had been slighted.

The hate that burned in his heart for such a brutish, disgusting reprobate, Castor could scarcely qualify. He had hated his own family, it was true. Despite taboos, he hated men who sneered at him for loving whom he pleased. He hated oafs and braggarts of every size and stripe imaginable.

Still, he hated Henry FitzDonahugh more.

A great pity that the dashing Damek Bishop had met his end in the North, for indeed, he would have marched south next to shove Henry's aging arse onto the point of his own cross. Alas, it was not to be. Soon enough, they would all pay the forfeit when the Sidhe roused themselves for revenge.

He shook his head. So many plans wasted.

Bishop had not been a fool, whatever Castor had thought of him. Once, before he had been summarily disabused of the notion, he had hoped to cheat the handsome young lord and had paid a hefty price for this hubris. Having spent the better part of a year in a moldy cell in Malahide had taught Castor the error of his ways. He'd had many months to consider another more mutually beneficial course that might have propelled Castor where he'd always wanted to be: of consequence in Innisfail. Then, that star had fallen, slain by his mortal enemy in a northern backwater by the High King's reborn heir, taking Castor's hopes with him. He had nothing now but a name. A name Henry would use to press his claims into greater Francia on his quest for timber and gems to make war against the Sidhe. Bishop's own plan meted out with far less finesse and concern for human life. Thinking of his losses once more only made the blood rush straight to the top of Castor's head, kindling shame and rage.

Ahead of him about four paces, a soldier turned to give Castor a small, embarrassed smile. Daniel, his newest paramour. The fellow had his uses but had as yet been too cowardly to help Castor flee Henry's entourage. Castor returned the gesture if his heart held nothing but the blandest disdain. He needed someone, someone with the *power* to do something about Henry. These little distractions were amusing, but none would save his life.

Who?

He asked himself for the thousandth time that day.

Who can help me?

The wind did not answer.

Bethany loomed in the distance, and he was no closer to his goal.

But then, he saw something very interesting at the front.

Henry's mailed fist lashed out and clipped Lady Penwyth on the crown. With a shriek, she nearly toppled from her horse until one of her grooms managed to catch her reins and right her teetering form. With very little interest in her fate, Henry and his vanguard rode past her, shouting abuse. Penwyth got her mount under control but was forced to the side of the column, glaring after the Duch with a venom Castor could certainly empathize with.

Perhaps all was *not* lost?

Immediately, Castor began to cough and wheeze as dramatically as he could. Rather than halt the column to give him any aid, he was pushed to the far right edge of the line. Soon enough, he found himself apace with the powerful Kernish noblewoman Henry had so publicly scorned… and Castor had been seeking all this while. She covered the lower half of her face so as not to display the blood streaming down her chin, but it was obvious to absolutely everyone, Castor included.

Recognizing his one chance, Castor tore a shred from his now threadbare silk tunic and kicked his horse free of the column. His guards would follow, but that would only improve his chances. When he arrived at Lady Penwyth's side, he shoved his revulsion toward her down deep.

Remember, this woman barters her children for power.

He would not forget this, any more than she might ignore the well-circulated rumor that he'd had his father and brother killed to take the Bretagn throne.

Allies are born of necessity, he told himself.

Castor pulled his mare up short, reached out to the dumbfounded Lady Penwyth, and passed her the fabric as if it were the finest lace. He caught her eye moments before his guards caught up to him. "We have made many mistakes, you and I, but perhaps we might fix them together," he managed to eke out as he was dragged from his saddle and flogged for all to see.

A Light in the Dark

Una stared into the flames, a woman possessed by turbulent emotions. They were less than a day's march from Bri Leith, but she grew more tense as they drew near. Though the company she kept was jolly indeed to be returning home after so much blood and toil, she could not feel that same jubilation. She smiled when appropriate, answered when spoken to, and otherwise made light of the urgent mood that had taken hold of her once they crossed into Aes Sidhe. Kaer Yin, so absorbed in the terror and joy of meeting his father again after three decades apart, was unaware of the turmoil boiling within her. This wasn't his fault, as it was him she avoided most. He could hardly suspect that his love struggled with emotions she could scarcely quantify if she smiled and laughed rather than broach the topic with him.

Rian, awash with grief for Shar, Gerry, Tansy, and Violet, spent most of her time forcing a silent but brave face during the day and weeping in her bedroll at night. For the thousandth time, Una felt a pang for her many losses. That she hadn't been there when Rian needed her most kept her awake at night.

But come to think of it, *everything* kept her awake at night or tortured her waking hours each day. She saw it all, over and over in her mind: Aoife's hand attempting to stall her doom from above, the ghast's teeth as they reached for her throat, swirling flames without end, and the cold, dark stars burning behind her eyes.

My child, a voice whispered in her memory.

She shivered.

In the distance, the Sidhe played a particularly dangerous game that had them howling in pain and laughter. Apparently, the Dannans found it incredibly entertaining to beat the hells out of anyone who couldn't split another's arrows. Braying like donkeys, they pummeled each other with such relish, one would think they were mad, drunk, or both.

Well, perhaps both were true.

As for Una, she'd developed a small tremor in her hands that she had no idea how to stall. She tucked them around herself, where no one would see.

No one, that is, but Diarmid.

He watched her from across the fire, eyes burning with curiosity, judgment, and greed.

She frowned back.

"What?"

He leaned toward the fire, his eyes glowing emerald. "When do you plan to tell him?"

"Tell him what?"

Diarmid shot her a half smile. "I can see it on your face, Una."

"What is that?"

"That you're going back."

A hundred curses, rants, and arguments raced through her mind at once, but she refrained from using any. After staring back at him for a long while, she answered, "Yes. I am."

"He believes you will be wed. Have you decided otherwise?"

"Must I choose?"

He sighed. "That's a complicated question, you realize. My nephew is hot-headed and may feel you're breaking your arrangement."

She rolled her eyes. "You know, you're fairly thick for a man who's lived a thousand-thousand lifetimes."

He ignored the insult. "Una, you've sworn your troth to a future king. It's unlikely he'll allow his wife to march off to war."

"Nonsense, Sidhe women do it all the time. I've read about Kaer Yin's sister, Eri."

"That's different—"

"Is it?" she snapped. "I think you'll find he's marrying a *queen*, not the other way around. If I consent to marriage, it'll be on my terms… *Eire*'s terms, Diarmid."

He observed her in silence for a moment. "You don't have the men to stake that claim."

"She does, actually," said Rian from the opposite side of the fire. Her hair spilled from her bedroll onto the wayhouse's stone floor; her eyes sunken into her too-thin face. "Before we left, many of Damek's men swore her fealty. Besides them, all of Rosweal and anyone who wishes to see Henry deposed will follow suit."

Una's heart clenched. "I'm sorry, Rian, I didn't mean to wake you."

"I don't sleep much now," she sniffed. "Anyway, why do you listen to him, Una? He's just stirring up trouble, as usual."

"Young lady," Diarmid said. "You are being rude."

She sat up and shrugged. "Doesn't make me wrong." She turned to Una. "But he has a point. When are you going to tell him?"

Una stole a glance at a familiar blond head through the trees. He was slightly shorter than his fellows, but at nearly 7 feet in height, that hardly mattered. He was laughing, one arm around Jan Fir, one grasping a flask full of uishge. She let out a long breath. "My aunt Eva said we must retake Tiarngare before autumn, or Henry will seize it for himself."

"So? Ben will help. Remember, he still has to deal with the Bolg who were raiding the Midlands dressed in Dannan colors. Ask him, Una."

"You're right, but, he's fought so hard to come home. It would be cruel to ask so much of him now."

"He won't let you go alone."

It was Una's turn to shrug. "It's autumn or nothing. I'll ask him soon, but I must go whether he does or not. Henry won't stop until the whole Continent is in flames."

"Una, he'll go."

She hoped so, truly.

But it wouldn't stop her, either way.

She recalled Aoife's admonishments in the Oiche Ar Fad. She would never forget them.

Queens do not answer to princes.

Even those one loves.

"No matter how much I wish it were otherwise, Eva is right; Tairngare comes first. I must go home."

Rian nodded. "I'm going too."

Una didn't bother to naysay her.

Rian was a woman grown and had experienced war as Una never had. She was the smartest, bravest woman she'd ever met. "Thank you, Lady Ardgillan."

"Well," interrupted Diarmid once more. "Though I am loathe to make promises I may not have the fortune to keep, you may depend on me to help where I can."

This time, Una *was* surprised. "Why would you?"

He pointed. "You carry the next prince of Innisfail beneath your heart. I can't in good conscience allow either of you to come to harm."

Rian's sharp gasp made Una's ears burn, but she did not turn. "How did you know?"

He made a face. "Don't you know who I am, child? I am *Fiachra Ri*."

"Eva told him," said Kaer Yin from behind them. Una jumped half a mile. "Or he eavesdropped when she told me. Probably, the latter."

"*Siora's tits*," Una squeaked. "Don't bloody *do* that!" Flushing, she shrank away from him. "When did she tell you?"

Kaer Yin pursed his lips in thought. "When was it? Well, it doesn't matter, does it?"

Rian went red as coal. "Well, *I* didn't bloody know! Why didn't either of you tell me?"

Una shot to her feet. "I wasn't ready for *any* of you to know... I mean, I..." She flushed purple.

"Too late, love," said Kaer Yin with a sloppy grin, folding her into his oversized arms. "Now, what's this about 'autumn.'"

Kaer Yin &
Una Will Return
In
Another Cycle

AUTHOR'S NOTE

2022
sunny florida

This series was the culmination of 24 years of hard work, self-doubt, disbelief, giddy anticipation, relationship strife, stolid determination, depression, sidetracks, renewed hope, disappointment, stubbornness, imposter syndrome, begrudging self-respect, supportive peers, toxic peers, success, failure, and love.

In 24 years, Kaer Yin and I have stormed many castles, lost many battles, and found that inner peace we thought would forever lay just beyond our grasp. We weathered every negative thought and comment, each self-fulfilling prophecy, and every 'yeah, but what do you *really* do' question.

Kaer Yin and I have been together a long, long time. You might say we grew up together. Thank you for joining us on this journey.

We'll be back.

L.M. Riviere

www.lmriviere.com

Social: @LMRiviereAuthor

About the Text

This series leans heavily on Irish Gaelic. As a student of the language, I have done my level best to include the appropriate usage of every term and phrase, from syntax to punctuation. That said, I am not entirely fluent, and there are bound to be mistakes in the text.

Additionally, most of the terms I use were derived from the most archaic forms, as the characters and place names are meant to reflect a time period and etymology that precedes written alphabet by at least a thousand years. In that order, there are bound to be minor variations in spelling and pronunciation. Some terms I changed to suit myself and the rolling language I hear in my head when my characters speak… and I daresay, that is my prerogative in a fantasy novel.

For example, there a few obvious 'me-isms', like the use of '*Tuatha Dé Dannan*', which is historically spelled '*Danaan*', or '*Danann*'. I elected to place a hard focus on the interior 'n' to aid its pronunciation for non-Gaelic speakers.

If there are any mistakes or unbearable abuses of the language that distract from the text, please keep in mind that this story exists in a (semi) fictional continent a thousand years from now. A few liberties were taken.

GLOSSARY

A

- *Aenghus Mac Og-* (Aynn-guss-mack-Oh-ge) Dannan god of the Western Sea, love and poetry. Comparable to the Greek god Dionysus.
- *Aes Sidhe-* (Ayess-Shee) "Land of the ever-living', or 'Land of the Sidhe'. Northernmost region of Innisfail, home of the Immortal High King, and his people. Comprised of two major tribes; the Tuatha De Dannan, in Bri Leith and the Fir Bolg in Armagh.
- *Agrea-* (Ah-gray-ah) The Agriculturists Guild in Tairngare, run directly by the House of Commons in Tairnganese Parliament.
- *Alta-* (All-tah) A priestess second in rank to the Doma, in the Cloister of the Eternal Flame, in Tairngare.
- *Amer Gin Gluingel-* (Ahmer-genn-glonn-gall) "Amer the White kneed". A son of Mil Espanga, bard, druid and magician. Helped his brother Eber Finn, conquer Innisfail, and defeat the Tuatha De Dannan.
- *Aoife-* (Eee-Fah) "Radiant one".
- *Ard Ri-* (Ardh- Ree) "Highest King".
- *Ard Tuaithe-* (Ardh-too-ah-hee) "Highest Landsman". A common way to address a Sidhe noble. "Tuaithe", simply means 'countryside'.
- *Ard Tiarne-* (Ardh-tee-arh-nah) "Highest Lord, or Prince". A title reserved for the Crown Prince of Innisfail.
- *Armagh-* (Arr-mah) Capital of the Kingdom of Ulster, and seat of the ancient Kings of the Fir Bolg. As the Fir Bolg's power has waned over the centuries, the Kingdom of Ulster is less than one-third its size in ancient times. Ruled by the Mac Nemed Clan (House of the Black Bull).

B

- *Badh-* (Bae-ve) Sidhe goddess of discord, disharmony and dread. Pestilence and famine are also her domain. One of three divine sisters. SEE MORRIGAN AND MACHA. Her herald is the crow.
- *Ban-* (Bahn) "White", "Light" or "Bright". As in "Ban Lug"— or the Month of Midsummer (formerly August).
- *Ban Sidhe-* (Bahn-shee) "White Spirit" or "Good Folk". A term reserved for the higher classification of Sidhe (or Immortal Ones). The Tuatha De Dannan and Fir Bolg, belong to this class, on whole. See *DAOINE SIDHE*, for nobility.
- *Bel-* (Ball) The Sidhe sun god. Considered a male figure, but otherwise one of the few non-personified deities in the Sidhe pantheon, save for Samn, his mate.
- *Beltane-* (Ball-tinna) A festival celebrated on the first of the Month "Ban-Bela" (Bahn-balla), formerly 'May'. A celebration for seeding crops, full spring, and fertility.
- *Bethany-* (Beth-ahn-nee) The Southernmost Kingdom in Innisfail, and second-most powerful city in Eire. Ruled by the Donahugh Clan, under their line of ancestral Duchs. Seat of Duch Patrick Donahugh, fervent enemy of Aes Sidhe. Sometimes called the 'Machine City', for their use of cannons and other siege devices in warfare.
- *Bodhran-* (Bode-ran) A circular frame drum made from animal hide and polished wood. The Sidhe carry bodhrans into battle.
- *Bov Mac Nuada Dearg-* (Bove- mack- new-ah-dah-derrck) King of Connaught, and former High King of the Tuatha De Dannan, in pre-Celtic times. Known as 'Bov the Red', for his famous temper, and rash behavior. Rules from his capital at Croghan. Brother to the High King, Midhir.
- *Breccan-* (Breck-ahn) "Freckled one".
- *Brehon-* (Breh-honn) "Teacher" or "Knowing One". Brehons are the highest ranking magic users in Innisfail. They are considered 'holy men', for the ability to commune with both spirits and nature itself. Their advice is sought by Sidhe leaders before any major commitment, such as war, marriage, treaties, or policy making. They are as feared as they are respected, for to incur a Brehon's wroth is to endure all manner of travesties. It is illegal to harm a Brehon, and they are immune to Common Law. A Brehon may gainsay even the High King, without fear of repercussion.
- *Bretagne-* (Breh-tan-ee) A peninsula jutting into the Southern sea, from the old kingdom of Francia. A major sea power in its own right, and one of the few remaining kingdoms free of Innish over-rule.
- *Brida-* (Bree-dah) The Sidhe goddess of the dawn. The Dagda named one of his own daughters for her, who died in ancient times. The horse, is her herald— speed and strength, are her creed.
- *Bri Leith-* (Bree-leyth) "Highest Realm", or "Foremost Hall". Capital of Aes Sidhe, and home of the High King, Midhir. Ruled by the Adair Clan (House of the White Stag).

- *Bru Na Boinne*- (Broo-nah-boyne) A valley of ancient hillforts at the Northern border of Eire, along the river Boyne (*Boinne*, in old Innish). The passage tombs of Newgrange, Dowth, and Knowth— gird the river from the North, in Aes Sidhe. The passage tombs are older even than the Sidhe, having been built many thousands of years before the Invasion Cycles of Innish history. The Sidhe call these first peoples 'Fomorian', or sometimes 'Stone People'; for the complex network of standing stones, passage tombs, dolmens, and hillforts they left behind. Considered the holiest site in Innisfail, by the Sidhe.

C

- *Clare*- (Clayre) A sea province along the South-Western Coast of Eire. Ruled by Lord Damek Bishop.
- *Connaught*- (Cuhn-aught) Westernmost kingdom in Aes Sidhe. Ruled by King Bov, 'The Red'.
- *Croghan*- (Crew-Hahn) Capital of the Kingdom of Connaught, and seat of Bov Dearg, and the Marshal of the West. Ruled by the Dearg Clan (The House of the Red Eagle).
- *Cu Chulainn*- (Cu-hoo-linn) An ancient Innish hero, and champion of a Milesian King of Eire.
- *Crom Dagda*- (Cruhm- dagh-dah) The 'good father'. First King of the Tuatha De Dannan, and also a Skysinger of unimaginable power. Sacrificed his own eye to save Nuada's life after the battle at Magh Tuiredh, against the formidable Fomorian King, Balor. And years later, sacrificed his own life to save his people from the onslaught of the Milesians, after Nuada's death. He is honored at Cromnasa, each midwinter. Opened a path into the Otherworld with his own sacrifice, which granted all Sidhe tribes everlasting life.
- *Cromnasa*- (Cruhm-nah-sa) "Festival of Crom" or "Crom's Feast". Celebration of the Dagda's sacrifice for the Immortality of the Sidhe. Midwinter festival, celebrated on the Longest Night of the year.
- *Cymru*- (Kim-ree) An ancient Kingdom at the Easternmost reaches of Innisfail, having once been called 'Wales', before The Transition. A mineral rich country, for its mountains and hills are filled with precious ores. In the West of the Kingdom, their major export is wine, which is grown largely in the South, toward the capital at Swansea. Cymru is a Tairnganese colony but pays homage and tithes to Aes Sidhe. Over the Cyrmian mountains in the far east of the Kingdom, lies a region known as the 'Wastes', for its inhospitable, uninhabitable, and arid landscape.
- *Cymrian*- (Kim-ree-ahn) One who dwells in Cymru.

D

- *Dagda*- SEE CROM DAGDA, under 'C'.
- *Danu*- (Day-new) The goddess of the earth, in pre-Innish Europe. The patron goddess of the Tuatha de Dannan, who claim to be descended from her and her mate Donn, the god of death.
- *Daoine Sidhe*- (Doone-Shee) A term reserved for the upper echelons of Ban Sidhe society. The nobles and royalty of Aes Sidhe.
- *Dearg*- (Derckk) "The Red".
- *Damek Bishop, Lord of Clare*- (Dahm-eck) Alis Donahugh's illegitimate son, fathered by an unknown Sidhe lord. Adopted by Duch Patrick Donahugh after his mother's death. An accomplished soldier and statesman. Commander of Bethany's armed forces.
- *Dian Cecht*- (Diahn-caysht) Sidhe ancestor god, son of the Dagda. Forged Nuada's Golden Hand, after the battle at Maigh Turiedh. The Sidhe consider him the father of healing.
- *Diarmid Mac Nuada Dubh*- (Derr-mett-mack-nu-ah-dah-duvv) King of Tech Duinn, and Lord of the *Oiche Ard Fad*. Called *Fiachra Ri*, by the Sidhe- or Raven King, in Eire. A Skysinger, like his father Crom Dagda; and Brehon of the Tuatha De Dannan. He is the only member of his house, as he rules a kingdom of the dead. All lesser Sidhe call him 'King', including the Lu Sidhe, and Dor Sidhe- which would unleash themselves upon mortal kind, did he not guard the gates of the Otherworld with a firm hand. Brother to Midhir, the High King. An ambitious, mercurial man, whose loyalty can never truly be counted upon. Also known as "Diarmid, The Black". Servant of Donn- the god of the dead; and Donn's daughter, Morrigan.
- *Doma*- The title of the High Priestess of the Cloister of the Eternal Flame, in Tairngare. The theocratic and secular ruler of Tairngare. Holds a seat on the High King's Council, and the highest-ranking official in Eire. Currently held by Drem Moura.
- *Donn*- "Dark One", the Sidhe god of the dead. Mate of Danu, goddess of the earth. Donn is the only god the Sidhe and Milesians shared before the Invasions. Donn, was also the name of one of Mil Espagna's seven sons. He died after cursing his brother Ir. Diarmid as a Skysinger and Brehon, is his servant.
- *Dor*- (Door) "Black" or "Darkest", see also 'dorchas'. As in "Dor Samna" (Door-Sawa), or the Month of Winter's Birth (formerly, October).
- *Dor Sidhe*- (Door-shee) "Darkest Spirits", or "Evil Folk". A term to describe the darker denizens of the Otherworld. Unnatural beasts and spirits that harm and hunt mortals for food or sport. They only exist within the Otherworld, or sometimes on the fringes of the border with Aes Sidhe- where the veil between worlds is thinnest. Often roam wild in Eire on Samhain, when the veil vanishes altogether, once a year. Goblins, selkies, pookas, trolls, ghasts, giants, and gnomes- all belong to this classification.
- *Drem Moura*- (Drehm-More-Ah) The High Priestess of Siora, the Ancestor; in the Cloister of the Eternal Flame at Tairngare. Head of the wealthiest and most influential family in Eire, and most powerful woman on the continent. Not well-loved by

the common people, for her frequent attempts to crown members of her own family Queen of the Commons; in order to shore up absolute power for the Moura Clan. Mother of Arrin Moura, and grandmother to Una.

- *Donahugh-* (Donnah-hew) The ruling clan of Bethany, and the greater South of Innisfail.
- *Dubh-* (Duvv) "Black".
- *Duch-* (Duke) A lord second only to a king in rank— but far removed from a High King, who rules over all lesser kings and lords equally.
- *Dumnain-* A village in the lower Midlands of Eire, which was destroyed by the Crown Prince Kaer Yin Adair, during the war with Bethany in '84. The site of one of the bloodiest battles in Innish history, and the very place Duch Donahugh lost his right to a seat on the High King's Council, in exchange for his life. Due to this battle, the Kingdom of Bethany pays the highest tithes and taxes in Innisfail, in reparation for the horrors inflicted on the Eirean people for Bethany's warmongering. Also, the site where the High King's son was exiled from Aes Sidhe for war crimes, after the extreme measures he took to safeguard his own troops.

<h1 style="text-align:center">E</h1>

- *Eber Finn-* (Everr-Feen) A Milesian King, son of the King Mil Espagna. The first 'celtic' king of Innisfail.
- *Eire-* (Ay-err) The Milesian (mortal) region of Innisfail. It borders Aes Sidhe at the Boyne in the Midlands and ends at the Bretagn Straits in the far South. Straddles the Straits of Mannanan in the East. Cities like Tairngare and Ten Bells have colonies in Cymru and Kernow (formerly Wales, and Cornwall).
- *Emain Macha-* (Aavvinn-mash-ah) A holy hillfort, in the Kingdom of Ulster.
- *Eochaid Mac Nemed-* (Yoh-hee- mack- nehm-ehd) Ancient King of the Fir Bolg. Slain by Nuada, king of the Tuatha De Dannan for his throne and the right to rule in Innisfail. Married to his cousin Liadan, by their Fomorian Grandfather, Balor. Was a just ruler, and fearsome warrior.
- *Eri Mac Midhir Bres-* (Ayre-ee-mack-med-heer-bray) Daughter of Midhir and Etain, Princess of Innisfail, and Queen of Scotia. Married to Jan Fir Bres, King of Scotia; and Lord of Skye.
- *Eriu-* (Ayr-yoo) One of the Dagda's daughters, for which Eire was named. Died in ancient times.

<h1 style="text-align:center">F</h1>

- *Faerie-* (Fare-ee) "Doomed One", or "Touched by Doom". A racial slur for those of half-Sidhe blood. Also used to denigrate people born with deformities, mental disorders, or those whom suffer from depression or madness. It is believed that the blood of the Sidhe is a curse for mortal kind, and often leaves its progeny unnaturally lovely, but usually deficient in every other area. Faeries (whether real or slandered) are largely reviled in Eire.
- *Fainne-* (Feene) The literal gold standard, upon which all Innish currency is based. Also called "Crowns", or "Royals".
- *Falan-* (Fahl-ahn) The given name of two members of the Armagh royal family, Falan the Elder, and Falan the Younger, respectively. An ancient Bolgish name.
- *Fiachra Ri-* (Fee-ah-cruh-ree) "Raven King". Refers to Diarmid Mac Nuada Dubh, the King of *Tech Duinn*— or the Land of the Dead.
- *Fir Bolg-* (Feer-Bolck) A tribe of Sidhe warriors, descended from the ancient warrior Nemed. They fought with the Fomorians for several generations, and were expelled for a time to Southern Europe, where they were enslaved by the Greek tribes in Macedon. Forced to carry bags of stone up and down ladders into mines, before their escape back to Innisfail, they became known as the "Bag Men". Close cousins of the Tuatha De Dannan from their mutual ancestor, Nemed- but dark complected, where the Dannans are fair. Sometimes called, "dark elves" for this trait. Their last stronghold in Innisfail is the city of Armagh, ruled by the Mac Nemed Clan.
- *Fodla-* (Fole-ah) One of Crom Dagda's wives.
- *Fomorians-* (Fov-or-ee-ahns) Ancient people whom lived in Innisfail before the first invasions. Worshipped dark gods of earth and stone, harvest and reaping, until a Comet known as Lug of the Long Arm came sailing out of the west, bringing calamity, and famine. They began to build stone circles and passage tombs to mark the heavens after this, to honor their new god. Defeated by the Fir Bolg in ancient times. The Tuatha De Dannan revere them as wise ancestors and keep their holy places sacred. They also adopted several of the Fomorian gods, like Lug of the Long Arm, Bel the sun god, and Samn the moon goddess. Also known as the "Stone People".

<h1 style="text-align:center">G</h1>

- *Geis-* (Gay-ehss) "Unbreakable Vow". A curse, taboo, or restriction placed upon an individual of power, to restrict their actions. In a Dannan warrior's case, it is an obligation one cannot break, without great personal sacrifice.

<h1 style="text-align:center">H</h1>

- *Hamish-* (Hay-mesh) A soldier from Bethany.
- *Herne-* (Hurrn) The White Stag, or God of the Forest. The patron god of House Adair.

689

I

- *Imbolg-* (Em-bolk) A festival in high winter, to summon spring. Celebrated on the first day of the Month of Blinding White, "Dor Imba" (Formerly February).
- *Innisfail-* (Enn-ess-fay-ehl) "Land of Destiny". A small continent at the rim of the Northern Ice Flows, comprising much of what was once Ireland, Scotland, Wales, and Cornwall. Much of what was England has largely become tundra, or inhospitable wastes; due to catastrophic climate change, and trace human corruptions of the land. In many places, the soil is either frozen under two feet of ice, or simply too toxic from long-forgotten nuclear reactors that have leached radiation into the soil. Innisfail is the last bastion of relative habitable land in what was Europe. Parts of Northern France, Spain and Portugal, are similarly liveable- but not as biodiverse. This biodiversity and ecological prosperity are due in large part, to the Sidhe, whom have reclaimed dominance over the land.

J

- *Jan Fir Bres-* (Yahn-feer-bray) King of Scotia, and Lord of Skye. Descended from the Half-Fomorian king Bres, whom married one of the Dagda's daughters, and emigrated to Skye. Second cousin to the High King and married to his daughter Eri.

K

- *Kaer Yin Mac Midhir Adair-* (Kayer-eeann-mack-med-eehr-ah-dare) The *Ard Tuiathe* of the *Tuatha De Dannan*, and Crown Prince of Innisfail. Son of Midhir and Etain, he was the first Dannan to be born in Innisfail after The Transition. Grand Marshal of the Wild Hunt, and Commander of Aes Sidhe's standing armies. Slayed Kevin Donahugh in single combat, during the first Bethonair War, and ended the war of '84, at Dumnain with another victory over the Donahugh Clan. Prince of Eire, and Cymru. A cold, unfeeling character, who values martial might over all other virtues.

L

- *Libella-* Tairngare's elite class of nobles. To be a member of the Libella, and its House in Parliament, one must hold a Patent of Maternas, which must be traced back at least three generations, in the Cloister of the Eternal Flame. Also, refers to the House of Nobles in Parliament.
- *Libellum-* (Ly-bell-uhm) Founded by the Tairnganese aristocractic class. The Educator's Guild in Tairngare, also a collection of schools, in which all Tairnganese citizens (even those whom live in the Colonies) may study free, although to earn a degree in any field, one must pass a series of aptitude tests before and after each school term, to assure the student is devoted to his or her craft. The schooling might be free, but each school requires a sizeable donation from the family to ensure employment afterward. Most students who are not from Aristocratic families, often take secondary education in the Agrea for agriculture, or buy into the Merchanta to apprentice for a trade. The Libellum educates all children not accepted in the Cloister, until the age of 16, when the more expensive secondary education begins. Usually specializing in Law, Engineering, Rhetoric, or Medicine.
- *Liadan Mac Nemed* (formerly, Mac Balor) (Lee-ah-dann-mack-neh-mehd) Queen of the Fir Bolg in ancient times, and Dowager Queen of Armagh, after The Transition.
- *Lir* (Leer) A Sidhe ancestor god. His children were changed into swans by his second wife and were forced to languish in these forms for hundreds of years.
- *Lug-* (Lew) Lug of the Long Arm, was a Fomorian sky deity that the Dannans appropriated when they conquered Innisfail in ancient times. He is represented as a traveling god, who comes only once every eighty years or so— sometimes bringing fortune, and others, calamity. The Sidhe pray to him for luck and guidance. Often considered the God of Law, and Chance.
- *Lugnasa-* (Lew-nah-sah) Festival of the sky god Lug; to curry Lug's blessings upon the Harvest, and to guard the living from the coming starving season. Lugnasa is the time of year in which the Sidhe's major policies, treaties or major martial and agricultural matters are decided. Trials are held during Lugnasa, children are named, and funerals are held. Property may change hands or be gifted at Lugnasa. Celebrated at the start of Ban Lug, or 'The Month of The Bright Sky' (formerly, August 1).
- *Lu Sidhe-* (Lew-shee) Less powerful, wise, or long-lived denizens of the Otherworld. Some share blood with the Ban Sidhe, but many are simply spirits or other mischievous creatures who assume a human-like shape. Often, faeries and other half-bloods are classified as Lu Sidhe. Such as: Slyphs, satyrs, Pixies, Niskies, Dryads, Nymphs and Brownies.

M

- *Mac-* (Mack) "Son of", or "Daughter of".
- *Macha-* (Mah-sha) Sidhe goddess of strategy, ambition, and courage. She is associated with sovereignty. One of three divine sisters. See also: Badh and Morrigan. Her herald is the eagle.
- *Maeve-* (Mae-ve) Sidhe goddess of wisdom, magic, and mystery. Her herald is the Owl. SEE BABH, the goddess of discord, strife, and pestilence.

- *Magh Tuiredh-* (Moy-teer-ah) Site of two ancient battles, the first of which was waged on the Fir Bolg by the Tuatha De Dannan. The Dannans took control of Innisfail at the end but granted the Fir Bolg their own corner of the land to rule— Ulster. The second battle was fought between the resurgent Fomorians, where Nuada of the Golden Arm was killed.
- *Manipulation-* A form of magic studied by the *Siorai* acolytes of the Cloister of the Eternal Flame, in Tairngare. Using one's own body energy (or Spark*)*, one can force particles to join or separate, and even build unnatural chains which change an objects trajectory, composition, or shape.
- *Mannanan Mac Lir-* Sidhe god of the Eastern Sea. Son of the god Lir.
- *Merchanta-* (Merr-cant-ah) The Merchant's Guild of Tairngare, run directly by the House of Commons in Parliament.
- *Midhir Mac Nuada-* (Mehd-eer-mack-nu-ah-dah) *Ard Ri* of the Tuatha De Dannan, and High King of Innisfail. Brought his people out of the Otherworld at the end of the Third Age of Man- also known as The Transition. Conquered the surviving mortals and brought them firmly under unified Sidhe overrule. A kind and compassionate ruler, if distracted and detached.
- *Mil Espagna-* An ancient 'celtic' king, hailing from the Iberian plateau. Forced to search for a new home when climate, war, and famine struck his people; they came to Innisfail— a lush, green, fertile land— in such numbers and with far superior weapons than anything the Sidhe could muster. His victories forced the Sidhe into the Otherworld and began the long period of Gallic rule. To the present, all Sidhe refer to mortal men and women as 'Milesians'
- *Morrigan-* (More-ah-gahn) Sidhe goddess of war, bloodlust, fury and pride. One of three divine sisters. (Equivalent to the Greek Fates). Her herald is the raven.

N

- *Navan-* (Nah-vahn) A small town on the river Boyne, at the border with Aes Sidhe.
- *Nemain-* (Neh-mayne) Sidhe goddess of the waterways and springs. It was said that her beauty drove men to madness for desire of her, but her kiss was poison and tortuous death. Kaer Yin's longsword is named for her. Her sister Niamh is the goddess of purity and love.
- *Nemed-* King of the first Innish invaders, in ancient times. Mortal grandson of the earth goddess Danu, and her mate, Donn— the god of death. Their daughter Brida took a mortal lover, from the tribe of Abraham. An accomplished sailor and adventurer, Nemed led his sea-faring tribe around the Mediterranean before a storm swept them out into the ocean, to Innisfail. Nemed fought the Fomorians for almost thirty years, before his death. His people divided and fled in separate directions. One half went South and were enslaved in Macedon; the Fir Bolg. The others took their ships far into the north and west, battling gods and monsters, until they returned with 300 ships, to oust their cousins from Innisfail- The Tuatha De Dannan.
- *Niall-* (Nay-all) A Dannan warrior, in Tam Lin's retinue.
- *Niamh-* (Neh-ve) Sidhe goddess of purity and love. Dwells in the waterways and springs, with her corrupted sister, Nemain.
- *Norther-* One whom dwells in Northern Eire.
- *Nova-* An initiate of the Cloister of the Eternal Flame, in Tairngare.

O

- *Oiche Ar Fad-* (Eesha-arh-fah) The Otherworld. A realm that exists just below the mortal. The Sidhe retreated to this realm for thousands of years, until the Milesians nearly purged themselves from the world. Only the Sidhe may come and go from this realm unmolested. To humankind, it holds mainly horror, forgetfulness, or death.

P

- *Porter-* A game of cards and two-sided dice.
- *Prima-* (Preema) A tertiate acolyte of the Cloister of the Eternal Flame, in Tairngare.

R

- *Ri-* (Ree) A king, or high lord.
- *Ruiadh-* (Roo-ah) "Red".

S

- *Samn-* (Sow) Sidhe goddess of the moon. Bel, god of the sun, is her mate.
- *Samhain-* (Sow-ahn) Festival of the moon, and the onset of winter. Celebrated (or mourned, considering perspective) at the end of the Month of Oncoming Night or Winter, or "Dor Samna". Samhain is the passage of life into death, and of autumn to winter. It is the one night of the year, in which the dead and all manner of Otherworld creatures may wander free of its borders— to trouble, torment, or comfort the living.

- *Scota-* (Skoh-tah) "Fierce One". The Queen of the Milesians in ancient times. Wife of Mil Espagna. Died fighting on the beach during the first Milesian invasion. Her son Amer Gin, who led his own men across the sea of Mannanan, named the land east of Skye after her (formerly Scotland).
- *Secunda-* (Seh-koon-dah) An intermediate in the Cloister of the Eternal Flame, in Tairngare.
- *Shannon-* The longest, widest river in Innisfail.
- *Sidhe-* (Shee) "Ever-Living", Describes the Immortals who dwell or dwealt in the Otherworld. Some are powerful and human-like, the Ban Sidhe; and some merely aspire to take human form— or never wish to.
- *Siora-* Patron goddess of Tairngare, also known as the 'Ancestor'. A goddess of unity, knowledge, and feminine power.
- *Siorai-* Acolytes of the Cloister of the Eternal Flame. Considered witches, by most of the peoples of Innisfail.
- *Souther-* One who dwells in Southern Eire.
- *Spark-* The life-force, or energy within one's body, that can be harnessed to manipulate the actions and properties of an object's compositional particles.

T

- *Tara-* (Tare-ah) A midling-sized town in Eire, south of the Boyne. In ancient times, it was a hillfort, fortress and castle— belonging to the High Kings of old Eire. Site of the *Lia Fail*, or "Stone of Destiny", before which all Kings of Eire were crowned. Now, it is a hub of the Merchanta— or Merchant's Guild, in Tairngare.
- *Tairngare-* (Tare-ehn-gare) A matriarchal city in the Northeast of Eire, at the mouth of the Boyne (formerly Drogheda). A city run by a religious order of women, and a Parliament elected from noble families and commoners. Founded by a woman named Siora, a former prostitute who had magical abilities she shared only with the women who swore their supreme loyalty to the nameless earth goddess she claimed to have been born of. She vanished after the women took over the city. They call her the 'Ancestor'.
- *Tech Duinn-* (Teck-Doon) "House of Donn", or "Realm of Donn". The god of death in pre-Innish Europe, also the mate of Danu, goddess of the earth. His realm is the land of the dead, and all whom share his blood (Such as the Tuath De Dannan, Fir Bolg, and Milesians alike), must come to his realm after death. In the Otherworld, Diarmid is the king of Tech Duinn, and Donn's servant. All whom are given the god of death's name, are said to be cursed, or bring misfortune to their families. Such as the son of Mil, whom was angered by his brother Ir's rowing abilities, and cursed him, causing the oar to snap and both boys to die. The realm of Tech Duinn is a peaceful but solemn one within the otherworld, and only once a year on Samhain, are the dead given reprieve to wander outside its confines.
- *Tir Na Nog-* (Teer-nah-noge) "Land of the Undying Ones". The realm of the Sidhe gods. Only great heroes or those with divine blood, may enter when they die. All else must go to Tech Duinn
- *Tir Falias-* A Sidhe city in the Otherworld.
- *Transition-* SEE TUATHA DE DANNAN.
- *Tuatha De Dannan (or Tuatha De Danaan, or De Danann)-* (Too-ah-ha-day-dahn-ahn) "Children of Danu". A half-divine tribe of warriors descended from the demi-god and adventurer Nemed. Unlike their Fir Bolg cousins, the Tuatha De fled Innisfail in ships, toward the north and west. They traveled from Isle to Isle, fighting monsters, hostile tribes, and brushing elbows with the gods. When they returned to Innisfail in ancient times, they defeated the Fir Bolg for supremacy over the land; then defeated the Fomorians, the old Fir Bolg enemy. They ruled in peace for many seasons, until they were defeated by the crafty Milesians from the Iberian Peninsula. Their greatest Brehon, Crom Dagda, sacrificed his life to the god of death— Donn, to give all those whom shared the Dagda's blood immortality, and a piece of the Otherworld to rule. They remained there for thousands of years, vowing to return when the rule of Mil's spawn failed. In N.E. 1, when the Milesians were fast becoming extinct, the Dannans came back to reconquer what was stolen from them in ancient times. This is known as the 'Transition'.

U

- *Uishge-* (Whisk-ey) "Water of Life". An ancient, amber colored spirit.
- *Ulster-* (Ull-Sterr) Kingdom in the north of Aes Sidhe, its capital is Armagh. Ruled by the remaining Fir Bolg nobility, the Mac Nemed Clan. Has been one of the chief Innish kingdoms since ancient times.
- *Una Moura Donahugh-* (Ooh-nah-more-ah-donnah-hew) "Bright One". Prima of the Cloister of the Eternal Flame. Reigning Domina of House Moura, and proposed Queen of the Commons, in Parliament. Studying to ascend to Alta Prima, and being groomed to succeed Drem as Doma. Daughter of Arrin Moura and Patrick Donahugh.

V

- *Vanna Nema-* (Vah-nah-Nee-mah) Alta Prima, Mistress of the House of Commons in Parliament, and second-in-command to the Doma.

Dramatis Personae

Eire-

Tairngare

- *Drem Moura*- Doma, high priestess of the Cloister of the Eternal Flame. Highest ranking noble in Tairngare. Represents all of Eire in the High King's Council.
- *Vanna Nema*- Alta Prima, Mistress of the House of Commons in Parliament, and second-in-command to the Doma.
- *Arrin Moura*- (Deceased) Former Alta Prima of the Cloister of the Eternal Flame. Former Queen of the Commons, appointed by the Doma, her mother. Taken from a market by Duch Patrick and made Duchess of Bethany, against her will. Committed suicide in *N.E. 487*, when her daughter was but two years old.
- *Una Moura Donahugh*- Prima of the Cloister of the Eternal Flame. Reigning Domina of House Moura, and proposed Queen of the Commons, in Parliament. Studying to ascend to Alta Prima, and being groomed to succeed Drem as Doma. Daughter of Arrin Moura and Patrick Donahugh.
- *Aoife Sona*- Prima of the Cloister of the Eternal Flame. Servant of Vanna Nema. Rumored to hold Fir Bolg blood.
- *Eva Alvra*- Member of the Libella, and Domina of House Alvra. Servant of the Doma, and former Prima of the Cloister of the Eternal Flame.
- *Pors Yma*- High ranking member of the Libella. A staunch opponent of the House of Commons.
- *Mel Carra*- Member of the Mercher's Guild, and highest-ranking member of the House of Commons. Ardent supporter of Vanna Nema.
- *Fawa Gan*- Steward, to Vanna Nema

Bethany

- *Duch Patrick Donahugh*- Ruler of the South. Ardent opponent of the High King in Aes Sidhe. Instigator of two wars, which cost him many men and most of his fortune— as well as his seat on the High King's Council. Chafes under Sidhe rule, and plots to take the throne for himself. Kidnapped Una's mother from a market in broad daylight and forced her into a loveless marriage of convenience. Una's father; he means to conquer all of Eire, and rule in her name.
- *AlisDonahugh*- (Deceased) Kidnapped by an unknown Sidhe lord in *N.E. 474*, returned home several months later, heavy with child and mad. After the child was born, she threw herself from the north parapet. Some say, her death prompted the battle at Dumnain, ten years later.
- *Henry Fitz Donahugh*- Patrick's illegitimate half-brother. Attempted to overthrow Patrick after his failure at Dumnain. Banished to the wastes of Cmyru, for nearly twenty years. A fervent Kneeler.
- *Damek Bishop, Lord of Clare*- Alis' illegitimate son, fathered by an unknown Sidhe lord. Adopted by Patrick after his mother's death. Accomplished soldier and statesman. Views himself as Patrick's rightful heir, and plots to conquer the whole of Eire to force his uncle to legitimize his claim to the throne. Commander of Bethany's armed forces.
- *Martin O'Reardan*- Lord Marshal at Arms, of Bethany. Damek's self-appointed right-hand man, and protector. Damek reveres him as a father figure and close confidant.
- *Wallace Cunningham*- Major of Bethany's Steel Corps (formerly, Captain, (Heavy Cavalry). An accomplished tracker, and talented swordsman.
- *Killian*- A lieutenant
- *Hamish*- A corporal
- *Douglas*- A sergeant
- *Dawes*- A corporal
- *Blane*- A ranger

Rosweal

- *Barb Dormer*- Madam of the tavern and pleasure house, *The Hart and Hare*. A former Nova in the Cloister of the Eternal Flame. Mistress of the Greenmakers' Guild. Aims to be the Town Headwoman, and dreams of modernizing their backwater town.
- *Robin Gramble*- A poacher, and town crime boss. Master of the Greenmakers' Guild, answers only to Barb, his undeclared mistress. Well-respected by his men, and greatly feared by his enemies.

- *Ben Maeden*- A drifter, and sometime poacher. Mysterious origins, and curious loyalties. Fond of drink, dicing, and women.
- *Matt Gilcannon*- A bootlegger, distiller of illegal spirits, and whoremaster. Owner of the *Black Corset*. A bordello of ill-repute. Fond of using the sons of his whores to do his dirty work. Desirous of destroying the Greenmakers' monopoly on trade, and opening new revenue streams outside of the North.
- *Solomon Trant*- A brewer and tavernkeeper, in the Greenmakers' Quarter. Member of the Greenmakers' Guild.
- *Samuel Trant*- A butcher, tanner and crime underboss. Brother to Solomon Trant, but not a member of the Greenmakers' Guild.
- *Gerrod Twomey*- A competent woodsman, and member of the Greenmakers' Guild, despite his youth and optimism.
- *Colm*- Tavernkeeper at the *Hart and Hare*, member of the Greenmakers' Guild. Barb's right-hand man.
- *Seamus*- A tracker and woodsman. A member of the Greenmakers' Guild.
- *Dabney*- Barb's dimwitted bodyguard.
- *Dean*- A bouncer at the *Hart and Hare*, and sometime hired thug.
- *Paul*- A hired thug, sometime member of the Greenmakers' Guild.
- *Rose*- A prostitute at the *Hart and Hare*, from a disgraced Tairnganese noble family. Soft-spoken and loyal.
- *Violet*- A prostitute from the Midlands.
- *Tansy*- A prostitute.
- *Vick*- One of Matt Gilcannon's street toughs.

FERNDALE

- *Arthur Guinness*- (Deceased) Physician. Once a triage doctor for the Tairnganese forces in the war of '84.
- *Aednat Guinness*- (Deceased) His wife. Sidhe half-blood.
- *Rian Guinness*- Took over her father's practice after his death. Reviled by all whom seek her out for her faerie blood. Methodical, practical and intelligent- if not overly friendly.

aes sidhe-

BRI LEITH

(House of the White Stag)

- *Nuada of the Golden Arm, Nuada Mac Crom*- (Deceased) Ancient ancestor of the House Adair (White Stag). Son of the Dagda, and King of the *Tuatha De Dannan*. Defeated the armies of Balor the One-Eyed, King of the Fomorians. Defeated the Fir Bolg King, Eochaid Mac Nemed in single combat for the title of *Ard Ri*. Slain by Eber Finn, son of Mil Espagna- a mortal man.
- *Crom Dagda*- The 'good father'. First King of the *Tuatha De Dannan*, and also a Skysinger of unimaginable power. Sacrificed his own eye to save Nuada's life after the battle at Magh Tuiredh, against the formidable Fomorian King, Balor. Years later, sacrificed his own life to save his people from the onslaught of the Milesians, after Nuada's death. He is honored at Cromnasa, each midwinter.
- *Midhir Mac Crom*- *Ard Ri* of the *Tuatha De Dannan*, and High King of Innisfail. Brought his people out of the Otherworld at the end of the Third Age of Man- also known as The Transition. Conquered the surviving mortals, then brought them firmly under unified Sidhe overrule. A kind and compassionate ruler, if distracted and detached.
- *Etain*- (Deceased) Midhir's Queen. Died in childbirth, or some say, retreated to *Tir Na Nog* on the other side of *Tech Duinn*; to await her beloved in peace. Long believed to be the daughter of the sun god Bel, and Danu, the earth goddess. Midhir's winning of her hand, is its own tale.
- *Kaer Yin Mac Midhir Adair*- The *Ard Tiarne* of the *Tuatha De Dannan*, and Crown Prince of Innisfail. Son of Midhir and Etain, he was the first Dannan to be born in Innisfail after The Transition. Grand Marshal of the Wild Hunt, and Commander of Aes Sidhe's standing armies. Killed Kevin Donahugh in single combat, during the first Bethonair War, in (408), and ended the war of '84, at Dumnain with another victory over the Donahugh Clan. Prince of Eire, and Cymru. A cold, unfeeling character, who values martial might over all other virtues.
- *Eri Mac Midhir Bres*- Daughter of Midhir and Etain, Princess of Innisfail, and Queen of Scotia. Married to Jan Fir Bres, King of Scotia; and Lord of Skye.
- *Fionn*- Lord Protector of Aes Sidhe, and Midhir's sworn Sword.
- *Ysirdra*- High Priestess of Danu, and trusted advisor to the High King.

Croghan

(House of the Red Eagle)

- *Bov Mac Crom Dearg-* Son of Nuada of the Golden Arm, and King of Connaught. Called Bov 'The Red', by his people, for his fiery hair and disposition. Some call him the 'Red Boar of Connaught', behind his back- for his stubborn pride, short temper, and devotion to the hunt. A peerless warrior in battle, but too hotheaded to make much of a commander. Brother of Midhir, the High King.
- *Grainne Mac Eochaid-* Bov's Queen. A Former Fir Bolg Princess, daughter of Eochaid Mac Nemed, and his wife, Liadan Mac Nemed- also, his first cousin. She was married into the *Tuatha De Dannan* as part of a peace treaty with Armagh, after Nuada slew Ecohaid, and took his throne. She and Bov have a stormy relationship.
- *Tam Lin Mac Bov Dearg-* Prince of Connaught, and Marshal of the West. Son of Bov and Grainne, making him the only living Dannan prince who is also half Fir-Bolg. Beloved nephew of the *Ard Ri,* Midhi— and Commander of Croghan's Blood Eagles; an elite fighting force, second only to Bri Leith's Wild Hunt (*An Fiach Fian*). Favorite cousin and trusted friend of Kaer Yin Adair.
- *Shar Lianor-* Tam Lin's First Lieutenant, and right-hand man.
- *Niall-* A Blood Eagle
- *Oisin-* A Blood Eagle

Tech Duinn

(House of the Raven)

- *Diarmid Mac Crom Adair-* King of Tech Duinn, and Lord of the *Oiche Ard Fad.* Called *Fiachra Ri,* by the Sidhe- or Raven King, in Eire. A Skysinger, like his grandfather Crom Dagda; and a Brehon of the Tuatha De Dannan. He is the only member of his house, as he rules a kingdom of the dead. All lesser Sidhe call him 'King', including the Lu Sidhe, and Dor Sidhe- which would unleash themselves upon mortal kind, did he not guard the gates of the Otherworld with a firm hand. Brother to Midhir, the High King. An ambitious, mercurial man, whose loyalty can never truly be counted upon.

Armagh

(House of the Black Bull)

- *Eochaid Mac Nemed-* (Deceased) Ancient King of the Fir Bolg. Slain by Nuada, king of the *Tuatha De Dannan* for his throne, and the right to rule in Innisfail. Married to his cousin Liadan, by their Fomorian Grandfather, Balor. Was a just ruler, and fearsome warrior.
- *Liadan Mac Nemed-* Queen of the Fir Bolg in ancient times, and Dowager Queen of Armagh, after The Transition.
- *Falan (the elder) Mac Eochaid-* King of the Fir Bolg, and lord of the ancient city of Armagh. A notorious philanderer and by all accounts, a terribly irresponsible ruler. Often wanders the *raths* of his Sworn Shields, to seduce their wives and avail themselves of their forced hospitality.
- *Falan (the younger) Mac Nemed-* (Deceased) Prince of Armagh, and former Marshal of the North. Despised his father so much, he took his grandfather's surname. Believed to have been the mightiest warrior in Armagh, and the greatest swordsmen in Innisfail— until he was defeated by Kaer Yin Adair at a tourney, years before his death. Slain at Dumnain, by a nameless Milesian soldier from Bethany.
- *Grainne Mac Nemed-* Princess of Armagh, and daughter of Falan the Elder and his third wife, Taliu. Half-sister to Falan the Younger, and an astute pupil of the Dowager Queen. Named for her aunt Grainne, whom married Bove Dearg in ancient times.

Innisfail Lore

What is the significance of the white stag in *The Sons of Mil*?

As one might have gleaned from the series covers, the white stag that is slaughtered at the beginning of Book One serves as an omen for the events that follow.

In Celtic and Pre-Christian lore, the white stag is often associated with the forest god Herne (or Cernunnos) and is a physical manifestation of purity, innocence, and good faith. The white stag was often considered a messenger of the Otherworld and an indication of sudden change, or violent upheaval.

To slay a white stag, is to encourage the gods' wrath, sacrosanct to Celtic cultures. All those who have a hand in such a travesty are bound to either die or have their lives upended by the gods.

The Sons of Mil focuses heavily on Irish myths, holidays, and legends. What is the significance of Samhain?

Samhain, or Halloween to modern audiences, was born in ancient Ireland during the stone age.

During Samhain, the ephemeral veil between the realms of the living and the dead were believed to be at their thinnest. As such, many spooky things were allowed to pass between both realms, such as the dead or other frightening personages.

In order to understand the importance of Samhain to the ancient Irish, one must first understand that the Irish believed each year could be boiled down to a light half (6 *ban* months) and a dark half (*dor* months). Samhain marked the beginning of the dark months, or starving season.

To ward off evil spirits on Samhain, the ancient Irish would place a candle or lantern on their windowsill or doorstop, with a bowl of cream or a loaf of bread. If this sounds slightly familiar, it should. Instead of cream and lanterns, we place candles in jack o'lanterns, and pass out candy. Instead of goblins and ghouls, treats are handed to children in masks and costumes.

Who are 'The Sons of Mil'?

According to the ancient Irish annals (see mythology: *The Invasion Cycle*), an Iberian Celtic tribal leader or king named Mil decided to invade the islands to the north-east that were rumored to be rich in game, timber, and rich, dark soil.

Some discussion about the historical viability of this fable indicate that Mil's tribe was suffering from climate-related famine and similar conflicts. The competition for resources during years of drought, for example, are cited as reasons why such a tribe might seek better fare elsewhere.

When they arrived, however, the island was already inhabited by a god-like race known as *The Sidhe* (or 'greater spirits'), who could be broken down into two tribes: The Fir Bolg and The Tuatha De Danann (Danaan, or Dannan). These tribes were constantly at war and during the time of Mil's invasion, the Tuatha De Danaan had recently won total control over the island from their cousins, The Fir Bolg.

Therefore, 'the Sons of Mil' in this story represents mortal men descended from Mil's tribe. They, by magic and might of arms, eventually took over the entire island in a few years, banishing the Tuatha De Danaan to an 'Otherworld' to wait for a time in which they might rule again.

All Irish, British, and Scottish faerie tales have roots in this story.

In *The Innisfail Cycle*, the Milesians have been subjugated by the Tuatha De Danaan once more.

If Ireland is an island, in the story, how is Innisfail a continent?

Innisfail actually encompasses all of the British Isles from Ireland to England, Scotland, Wales, and Cornwall.

Despite it being flooded with water today, around 8,000-16,000 years ago, it was one large landmass called 'Doggerland'. At that point, the Irish Sea and the English Channel did not exist.

In fact, recent archeological expeditions in the English Channel have discovered evidence of villages and other habitations between England and France under hundreds of feet of water.

In *The Innisfail Cycle*, the events of the story take place during an ice age some 1000 years after our civilization ceases to exist. A severe ice age would likely reveal Doggerland once more… or at least, that's the author's intention.

A frequent theme that runs throughout the whole series is the role of women through various city/ states in Innisfail. Where does that come from?

Historically, a majority of societies have been patriarchal (male-dominated), including medieval Western European societies. The city/state of Bethany in Eire harkens back to this era.

In pre-Christian Celtic cultures, on the other hand, were almost strictly matriarchal (female-dominated). That is to say that ancient Celtic cultures generally revered the women of their respective tribes or clans. Chieftains tended to be elected as a king only if the candidate descended from a powerful mother.

Furthermore, women were expected to fight alongside their men during conflicts and war, were well-respected councilors, and often believed to bear magic powers of foresight.

In the *Innisfail Cycle*, the city/state of Tairngare takes this premise to the next level, with only women bearing any political power at all.

Although there is some debate about whether the peoples of ancient Ireland *were* Celtic or not, I would argue their cultures were at the least very similar and have taken some liberties with this chronology.

The word 'faerie' is used as an ethnic slur by several villains in the story. What is the reason for this?

The word 'faerie' (or fairy) has its origins in Irish and Scotch and Slavic folklore. The oldest versions depict very unhappy interactions between the 'otherworld spirits' and their mortal counterparts. Thus, in ancient Irish and Scottish Gaelic, the term means something like 'fey touched', which is generally considered 'unlucky'.

In *The Innisfail Cycle* 'faeries' represent people who are part human and sidhe. They are usually considered unfortunate or damaged in one way or another.

Another running theme that factors heavily in the plot is the ideas of 'light' and 'darkness'. Many characters seem to struggle with their alignment to either abstract. Why is this?

Although both the ancient Irish and the continental Celts were very fascinated with life and death, light and dark; in this story, those lines are purposefully blurred to mark the duality of human nature.

No one is all good, or all bad. I see people in various shades of gray, including our favorite characters.

What unfolds between Damek and Una, for instance, is the burgeoning of one's sense of self and purpose… and the other's descent into self-aggrandizement and eventual destruction.

These characters, like living people, are the ultimate product of the decisions they make.

Lastly, if you say 'Kaer Yin and Una will return' but *The Innisfail Cycle* is complete, what does that mean?

All the ancient Irish annals come in three's (trilogies)… you can expect another set in the near future.

What questions do you have about *The Innisfail Cycle* lore?

Visit www.lightsoutink.com to start a conversation now!